Twin
Griffin
Books
PRESENTS

Published by Twin Griffin Books
www.TwinGriffinBooks.com
www.AuthorJustinThomas.com

's PATH TO NOW

Book III of The Fable Avenue Saga

BY JUSTIN THOMAS

<u>**To the Royal Court 7**</u>:

The King

The Prince

The Princess

The Advisor

The Jester

The Rogue

& The Giant

1

The celestial bodies fading behind the rising sun's daylight were not the only ones spying on the events below, partly clouded as their vision was. The story too had eyes, self-reflective by peering through the point-of-view of all its players. And everyone saw something. Even the unheard was anticipated. One such sound was a light rapping on a brownstone door on this day, the seventh of June, at eight-thirty in the morning.

The sun drew back a curtain of thin clouds and watched with bright anticipation. All the way down, it spied below a shimmering visitor dressed to the nines in a 1950s-style three-piece suit, brown in color, with a matching fedora. The ghostly figure stood outside the parlor-floor entrance to the Barnes' family brownstone on Fable Avenue in the Bedford-Stuyvesant area of Brooklyn, New York.

The sun and all the heavenly bodies were not the only spectators to the incandescent phenomenon standing at the door. Up the street, alone in her garden-floor sanctuary, but with the entirety of the universe at her fingertips, sat Fable Avenue's third matriarch, Lena Franklin, titled Lady Arachne. The slender, dark-skinned woman was dressed in a blue and white, floral-print gown that clung tight to her body. Her long flowing locks were cloaked in a lavender and white head wrap, the pattern of which matched her gown.

The quaint room was furnished with her most essential, occult devices. An altar burned a sweet and spicy aromatic incense with sage. The room's centerpiece was a decorated divination table where she did her tarot readings. Four candles were lodged inside empty rum bottles at the table's corners. Their wax ran along the sides of the bottles like lumpy snakes. The candles were of varying heights, and the small amount of heat produced from the candles' brilliant, white flames was far from equal to the intense light they gave off. 'Blind' Willie Johnson's song *Soul of a Man* crooned on an old phonograph that was incanted to play whatever song Lady Arachne desired to hear. This particular song repeated when finished.

Lady Arachne sat at her table's bench. A black runner, lined with gold print, lay across the seating. In front of the conjure woman was an ancient and powerful deck of Tarot cards, long sought by the Fable Avenue matriarch. They were procured in November of the previous year by cunning graft played out by a crew of mystical hoodlums at her command. The deck was incomplete, missing The Lovers card, but still potent enough. These cards were a periscope of sorts. They were a window into all that existed, and Lady Arachne had since created a morning ritual to peer into the lives of the conjure community and their hub on Fable Avenue. Her ritual, however, originated as a command from Fable Avenue's First Matriarch, Maman Anansi. Lady Arachne didn't mind. It kept her busy as she waited for other matters to unfold, ones pertaining to her incomplete Tarot deck. The same Tarot deck she had just recently shuffled. Reaching out her hand, Lady Arachne began her sight into the goings-on and things in her community. She drew a single card from the deck. The Page of Wands.

The colorful picture was of a young, African man taking pause on his journey through the desert, pyramids in the background. He admired his sturdy, wooden staff, a smile on his face. The aged and slightly faded image dissolved as Lady Arachne used her arcane knowledge to pry deeper into the card's meaning. First came a swirl of gray clouds. Only there for a moment, they hastened away, parting like an opening curtain. And suddenly there it was. Outside. Up the street. Lady Arachne could see. Her eyebrows went up, and her gaze softened as a tender expression came over her. She saw the handsome, ghostly man knocking on the door. Then came an image from inside the brownstone. The specter's knocking stirred only one of the two occupying residents. The spirit's son, who was now in his late forties.

Wilson Barnes rose from the couch, onto his feet, and pleaded with his mother to answer the door. He knew the knocking. The otherworldly reverberation of its sound coupled with the rhythm, the timing. Wilson knew his father's spirit stood on the other side of the door. A shimmering legend of a man. Stories preserved him, kept him alive. Only one album was recorded that played back his skills as an unmatched piano player. Jonathon Richard Concheroot was attempting his yearly visit. But Miss Nadia Barnes, Wilson's mother, wanted nothing to do with the spirit of the overly lecherous Johnny Concheroot. She loved him as much as she could in life. Now past, she'd forsaken him.

Nadia, with a scowl on her face, wasn't paying his knocking, or her son's pleas to answer the door, any mind. She was patient, and it wasn't too long before both noises yielded to her stone demeanor. Her son's verbal petitions quieted, and he left the room to tend to the store located on the parlor floor. He didn't stop at the door to open it for his father, or even look through. The ritual wasn't for him.

With the knocking also in pause, quiet resumed.

But Nadia Barnes didn't feel alone. She had instinct to know better. Even within a blanket of quiet, her peace was disturbed. She looked out into the hall, peering through her spectacles with a hard stare. She saw the door and rolled her eyes. She thought for a moment, tightening her teeth to suppress a smile. She breathed in, holding her breath for a time. Then she exhaled and made the decision to stand. She fixed herself and walked over to the door. Each step melted years off her until she was fixed at the age of thirty-four. She opened the first door, eyebrow raised as Jonathon Richard Concheroot winked at her. She stepped out into the foyer, and stopped to look at him through the window.

Miss Barnes managed a smile, but she didn't open the door. Before they danced, Mister Concheroot had some explaining to do. All those other women. Wasn't she woman enough? She grit her teeth, huffed, and opened the door to the outside. She told him to come in, sounding like a wife chiding her husband for being late to dinner. And for the first time in the many years since he'd passed, and since he'd been coming around year after year, Jonathan Richard Concheroot walked inside his former home.

Respectful of Miss Barnes and Mister Concheroot's privacy, Lady Arachne loosened her mystical gaze. The clouds rolled back onto the face of the card, and the scene of the African journeyman faded up into place. Lady Arachne moved the card aside, faced it down, and drew another. The Six of Cups. After placing it in front of her, Lady Arachne was compelled to draw again. The Ten of Wands. She placed the card partially over the first. The card depicted an African man weighed down by cargo, carrying a bundle of ten hefty wooden staves.

After a concentrated stare from the seer, it was the Six of Cups that changed first. Its picture of two African children planting flowers into six chalices yielded to swirling clouds. Parting, the card's face revealed a jovial, and peculiar, scene in Queens, New York. The setting was a graveyard, and children of all colors and varying ages darted mirthfully through the cemetery. The children glowed with a soft shimmer around them, playing tag and floating up trees. Their parents watched them from afar, eyes wet, but with delighted expressions on their faces.

Fable Avenue's first matriarch, Carolyn-Theresa Dumas, called Maman Anansi, presided over the visitant daycare session. Her wide, grayed Afro clung to her like a personal cloud. A bright smile and eyes lit up the features on her dark, round face. A lilac blouse and a long, frilled, cobalt-blue gypsy skirt paid homage with their colors to spirits conjured not too long ago. Maman Anansi welcomed the praise from parents who'd lost a child, spirits now playing in the graveyard.

To the regular folk passing by the sacred, gated grounds, all that was noticed were people paying their respects. The energetic spirits of children passed were invisible to their eyes. Parents kneeling down to speak to their departed child looked normal within a cemetery's setting, though it did seem peculiar to passersby that the atmosphere was far more joyous than imagined within a cemetery. Living siblings were there too, some not too much older than their ghostly brothers or sisters.

It was early in the morning, and there were few people rushing by as of yet. The children mingled with one another, but most of them were entertained by the conjure displayed from a man they believed was a clown. He didn't wear bright colors, though. Quite the opposite. He was in all black. Black slacks. Black shoes. Black longcoat with tails. He even wore a black top hat with his long dreadlocks spiraling down from underneath. His socks were white, and his shirt was purple. Both articles of clothing breaking the black monotony. His dark face, with broad features, was done up as a white skull. The kids were not frightened by this look. He played with them by displaying wild conjure, summoning animals made of spirit and exploding small, firecracker-like bursts from his hands. The adults called him *Nibo-Chile*.

The card focused on another figure, mingling with the children on God's acre. It was an elderly woman, aged and just as slender as Lady Arachne. Her name was Savannah Forrester, and she was the woman who campaigned for the idea of a *timoun ẹmí gadri*, a daycare for transitioned children. This was nothing new to Savannah. She delved into the practice while being a part of the Fable Avenue community, and even after she became estranged from the Brooklyn-based conjure culture. She was back among her folk, returning with all her talents.

Savannah tended to a young, black single mother named Aniyah who was kneeling down and engaging the spirit of her departed daughter, Charlotte. Savannah met the child at eye-level and spoke instructions to the young girl on how to maintain a physical presence on the earthly realm. Charlotte was still having trouble, though she'd been at practice for months now since her violent passing at the hands of her mother's ex-boyfriend. The laws and court handled the perpetrator. Aniyah's tears had been shed for her daughter's extinguished life, but the spirit visits, something she hadn't expected, were more than therapeutic. Charlotte wouldn't age, though Aniyah would. It was enough for mom and daughter, for now.

Little girl Charlotte inquired about Savannah's granddaughter. She recalled her name, Fey. Most of all, Charlotte remembered the young woman's ability to conjure four sprites that were referred to in the Senegalese language as 'yumboes'. Savannah answered the little girl that her granddaughter was away for the moment, and unfortunately her yumboes were with her. Savannah did promise to bring the yumboes next time, if she could recall the words to pull them into existence. Charlotte smiled and attempted another embrace around her mother. She ghosted through and grimaced. Aniyah found it adorable. She didn't care. Her daughter was here and determined to touch her sooner or later.

Savannah stood and watched mother and daughter play as best they could. Aniyah did encourage Charlotte to play with the other children running about the sacred grounds, but the little girl insisted on practicing to keep a physical presence. Savannah looked on, staring at mother and child and seeing her and her own daughter, Emma, now coming up on fourteen years lost to her. She reflected on her granddaughter, Fey, and her final, terrible moments where she'd reenacted, with similar outcome, her mother's suicide. Both events driven by a powerful hex cast by the Fable Avenue community's shadowy antagonists.

Lady Arachne inspected Savannah's demeanor. A smile hung on the woman's countenance, but the prying matriarch could feel the ripple of pain and loss underneath the mask. A flicker of movement from the Ten of Wands tugged at Lady Arachne for attention. The card's picture dissolved, followed by a billow of clouds on its face. Parting, the scene opened. Still within the graveyard in Queens, the sagacious card focused on Stephanie Dumas, Maman Anansi's daughter. The thirty-two-year-old lawyer's demeanor was similar to Savannah Forrester's. A smile was worn only as a mask, camouflaging a deep, choking regret as she overlooked the joy painted on the faces of parents who were reunited with their lost children.

Everyone saw something. But Stephanie's gaze stretched a thousand miles away, up close to something personal. A burden gestated in her, the memory of her commitment and enactment to a terrible deed. Unbeknownst to Lady Arachne, Stephanie had taken a life. A young life. A boy stunted in his growth to become a man by tumultuous circumstances and the seduction of gang life. Stephanie halted the progress indefinitely. She was reminded of her odious actions as her eyes caught sight of the joy surrounding her. Parents and departed children. Stephanie's thoughts tiptoed away from the backdrop, and she concluded that somewhere someone wept for the life she took.

Somewhere a mother and father had no child.

Stephanie could feel their grief like a fluttering wind. Stephanie's actions had continued the circle of pain in a gang-ridden community. A young man found dead in a jail cell due to a hex she'd given him. She convinced herself that he was prison bound, like his father before him. Stephanie upped his life's wager. The price for the attempted murder of a young boy in the Fable Avenue community. Guilt made sure this no longer held weight to excuse her deed. The boy's mother grieved at home. His father grieved in prison. Both were prepared for their son's early-age death, but this was no excuse.

An instinct scratched at Lady Arachne, the prick of which pierced deeper and throbbed more as her gaze locked onto Stephanie. But not even the matriarch's clairvoyance could discern what was troubling the woman. Too much of her power was focused on keeping an eye on the activity. She considered doing a private reading, something less stressful to draw out what ailed Maman Anansi's daughter.

Lady Arachne's instinct jumped again. She deciphered the otherworldly reflex and relaxed. The understanding came to her that Stephanie had confided in her mother, and in time, Maman Anansi would bring the subject to both her and Madame Jeliya, Fable Avenue's second matriarch. This revelation settled Lady Arachne. She figured there was no more to see at the *timoun ẹmí gadri*. She extended a hand to take up the cards, and it was then she noticed something stir near the trees in the distance. Both she and Stephanie reacted to it. It was a ghostly shade, and out of the dark, shadowy specter came the physical form of a teenage boy. He was no older than sixteen, dressed in sagging pants, an oversized short-sleeve t-shirt that was decorated with the colors and logo of a basketball team, a cap from a different team and sport, and sneakers on his feet.

His presence startled Stephanie. She flinched, and then the young man was gone. Stephanie backed away from her mother's view, and the view of the family around her. The mask she wore had fallen. A look of concern was exposed, but only the prying Lady Arachne could see it. Stephanie covered her gaping mouth with her hands, but her widened eyes broadcasted her genuine chord.

Lady Arachne's concern filled up again. She leaned closer to the card, watching Stephanie as she fixed her face and lowered her hand. She cleared her throat and whispered to her mother, requesting permission to leave. Maman Anansi nodded approval, noting her daughter trying to fix her expression. The head matriarch didn't call her daughter out. Instead, she expressed it would be best for her daughter to scurry off to work.

Stephanie thanked her mom, a sincere smile brightening her face. She kissed her mother on the cheek, said her goodbyes to the families around her, and then walked away. She took a quick look back to the tree in the distance where she'd seen the teenage boy. He was gone, and Stephanie looked grateful as she made her way back to her car.

Lady Arachne saw the teenage boy appear again. The card's face crept closer to him. She watched him as he watched Stephanie. He possessed a sharp stare, eyes bent. Then his countenance shifted. His anger evaporated despite his will to hold onto it. Lady Arachne could feel his struggle. The teenage boy was a spirit, and she knew he was connected to Stephanie. Her concentration allowed her to understand that he was connected to the Fable Avenue community. He'd made an offense against it.

A revelation was plucked from her unconscious. *Sean Commons. That was his name,* Lady Arachne thought to herself. He was the teenage boy that shot and hospitalized Dajon Brickhouse, a young boy who'd just turned thirteen in May. The shooting was due to a hex, a scar left upon the teenager by a man the conjure community dubbed *Willie the Lich*.

Sean and the scene faded from the card's face. Both cards' ancient sketches reappeared. An instinct buzzed against her forehead, and Lady Arachne was compelled to draw again from the deck. She first put aside the Six of Cups and the Ten of Wands, flipping them face down. Then she obeyed her preternatural instinct and took up another card. She laid the Two of Cups in front of her. A warm and soft expression crawled across her features.

The ancient tarot deck that Lady Arachne now used was incomplete, absent one card. The Lovers card. But the Two of Cups, with its colorful etching of an African man and African woman standing opposite one another, chalices touching, and the sun, with fiery wings, glowing bright above them, sent a tremor of sentimentality through the sylphlike woman. Its potency was by no means equal in conjure to The Lovers card, but what it signified was just the same.

Union.

Lady Arachne used her mastery to pull into focus the new scene called up to substitute for the ancient sketching. The familiar fade and swirl of clouds repeated. They parted, leaving a blank card. Out of the blanched face there came the silk sound of a violin. Lady Arachne required no instinct to discern the person responsible for the slow, sweet melody. It was thirteen-year-old Dajon Brickhouse. His image appeared. He was in the bedroom of Melinda Clarke, a friend from school. Lady Arachne was intrigued by their surroundings, being the girl's bedroom in Harlem and not in school as they should've been at this hour, or at least heading that way. She had to admit, their behavior was innocent enough, even with the house only consisting of the two of them.

Melinda sat cross-legged on the floor, back against her bed. She beamed up at Dajon as he serenaded her with his music. But Dajon's artistry didn't halt at weaving melodic sounds from his violin, and Lady Arachne scowled as the adolescent boy put flashy conjure on display for the girl. Strands of golden light rose from the violin strings, undulating in rhythm with Dajon's playing. Melinda cupped her hands as the light poured onto her palms, weaving together to create a shimmering ball two and a half inches in diameter.

Everyone saw something, and some stares were in awe at self-discovery. Melinda's face lit up, already bright with her large, curious light-brown eyes and her beige skin swirling with hints of a dark, blood-orange color. All of this a fusion of her African-American father and Dutch-Irish mother. Melinda was not a part of the conjure community, whether Fable Avenue or otherwise. And here Dajon was, considered Lady Arachne, showing off for an outsider. She would have a talk with him, as well as her fellow community Elders.

Lady Arachne observed Melinda's smile. The gesture brightened both from its stretch and the light swirling in her cupped hands. The young girl folded her fingers over the balled light, smothering it. She opened her hands, and the bright ball of light was now a caliginous, purple sphere. Streaks of lightning churned at its core. Melinda's smile transposed into something sly and confident. The expression in her eyes articulated the same cunning. She turned to the window and extended her arms, holding out the dark ball of mystical energy as an offering. Tendrils of spirit emanated from the sphere and dismissed the sun's light. The sun's rays respectfully retracted from the room, and the conjured, lightless strands filled the window's glass, keeping the sunlight from returning.

Lady Arachne's instinct brought her to the conclusion that the light's transmutation in color was not the effect of an incant supplied by Dajon. She at first believed the boy was showing off to impress his female friend. It was Melinda's use of a personal conjure, and Dajon had been guiding her on its use.

The young boy continued playing. His music summoned a fresh harvest of braided light that kept the room illuminated. Melinda tossed the dark sphere into the air where it floated, bobbing up and down as if in water. Lady Arachne put a finger over her lips and watched with a curious eye as Melinda made steps toward Dajon. The young boy ceased playing his enchanted melody and opened his arms as Melinda embraced him. She asked of him to recount the story of the Orisha Oshun, and her sadness pertaining to her children, the children of Africa, being taken from their homeland and enslaved in the New World.

Dajon obliged. His usual young and tough-laden voice gave way to a soft sincere tone. He spoke first of the pangs tormenting the Orisha of Love's broken heart. He recounted how Oshun confided her feelings to her sister, Yemaya, who told her this was how things were meant to be. "A change had come," he told her, quoting the Orisha. "And worst of all, it would be for the better. Alchemy was taking place in the children of Africa. But Oshun was afraid, believing that the many terrible deeds done to her people were changing their alchemy, and the brutality of the slave master against all things African was causing the children of Africa to lose the understanding of their grand heritage. Oshun was a goddess, though, and her intelligence was divine in nature. So, she hatched a divine plan, borrowing from aspects of the trickster Elegba. She spirited away to the New World, all the places her children were scattered. But first, she asked of her sister Yemaya to grant her the ability to present herself in the appearance of all the scattered children of Africa. All sixteen shades and styles of hair. She wanted to appear to them as they had been so that they would not forget the magic and beauty of Africa that still resided within them."

Melinda hugged Dajon tighter, burying her face into his shoulder.

Lady Arachne exhaled. Delight beamed on her face. Her eyes returned to expressing sincerity. But she now considered the difficulty of initiating Melinda into Fable Avenue's conjure community. She would do a reading later concerning Melinda's parents, gauging their frame of mind.

The card filled with fog, and its original sketch reappeared.

Another instinct tugged at Lady Arachne. Before she acted on it, she flipped the Two of Cups onto its face and moved it aside. The Knight of Swords was her next pull, placed face up and in front of her. Clouds swallowed the picture of an African warrior waving his sword atop a white steed, charging forward into battle. Fade up to the interior of a moving subway train. The 8-Train, referred to by locals as *The 8-Ball Ride*, materialized into the physical world at the same moment Fable Avenue appeared within the Bedford-Stuyvesant area of Brooklyn, a little under sixty years ago.

The card's face moved through the half-crowded train until it centered on two Fable Avenue community members. The young man and young woman were sweethearts. Benjamin 'Benny-Jah' Brickhouse and Neyeli Kimball. They sat in one of the train's middle cars, heading into Brooklyn from Harlem. Both were distracted at the moment, great concern on their faces. Their attention was locked onto a disheveled, dark-skinned black woman rambling aloud. She made the passengers visibly uncomfortable as she carried on, loud, possessed of drugs and a foul spirit.

The passengers kept their heads down as the woman cursed them and the rest of society. She mostly cut herself down with her words. She called herself ugly, and, to what Neyeli and Benny found more disturbing, she blamed the sable pitch of her flesh. She spat venomous words on how no man would find her attractive because of her dark skin. It was a biblical curse, according to this woman. Her lot in life was to drag the foul-colored flesh around *"Like chains on a damned ghost!"* she spat.

'Blind' Willie Johnson's song replayed on Lady Arachne's phonograph. His deep, guttural howl accented the distressed woman's loud ramblings.

Lady Arachne observed Neyeli's reaction to the woman's drug-induced tirade. A visual effect stirred in the young conjure woman's hair. Her draping, shoulder-length locks shifted in and out of color vibrancy. This was an effect brought on by her conjure's potency. It was a gauge, of sorts, registering her emotions and the emotions of the people around her, a side effect she was still training herself to control. Initially, Benny teased her, calling her *Mood Ring*. But she eventually adopted the moniker, and her ability to tap into emotions caused a change to her college focus from business to psychology.

Neyeli sensed her hair's revision, feeling the colors. Her hair fluxed between lime green and a shade of brown unnatural to hair color. Neyeli was grateful that the passengers kept their heads low, ducked eyes fixed on the ranting woman while keeping her proximity noted. Neyeli mouthed an incant, absorbing the emotion for the use of preternatural abilities. Her locks momentarily shimmered gold. The texture of her coiled hair became scales, and the ends sprouted with the heads of snakes. Their tongues slithered, then retracted, and her hair returned to normal. She gave thanks for living in New York City. No one noticed her phenomenon. Another note, Neyeli was now in control of the emotions possessing her hair.

It appeared that Benny's firm gaze stayed centered on the dark-skinned woman as she made her way toward them, yelling and cursing herself and her skin color. But his eyes saw something else directly behind the woman. It was a tall, gangly shadow. Its humanoid, smoky frame followed the woman's every move, towering over her. No one but Benny, Neyeli, and the spying Lady Arachne could see and hear it. The waving shadow yelled unintelligible noise into the woman's ear, and she translated its screams as her philippic discourse shouted at the passengers.

Benny took his eyes off the woman and her haunt. He looked at Neyeli, asking with his eyes if she could see the specter too. She nodded, eyes holding all the empathetic weight for the woman's dysfunction. Benny turned back to the smoky haunt.

The shadowy thing was called an *inawo* in most conjure communities. The word was Yoruba in origin, roughly translating to *expense*, or *that which you pay all tribute to*. Another Yoruba word used to describe the shade was *erù*. This word carried a heavier weight to define the creature, as its translation was *baggage* or *burden*.

Neyeli concentrated and redirected the emotion she'd taken in. She closed her eyes and channeled a thought. *Leave the car, sweet lady. Leave the train station.* Still vomiting her tirade, the woman took post at the exit adjacent to Neyeli and Benny-Jah. The foggy creature turned to Neyeli and screamed at her. The sharp sound stabbed at Neyeli's and Benny-Jah's ears. It was a ghastly, unearthly din, but Neyeli and Benny-Jah were used to such sounds and prepared for the outburst. Benny used his conjure and manipulated the air around them into an unseen aegis.

The covert matriarch knew all-to-well this was not Benny-Jah and Neyeli's first encounter with *inawo*. The pair had been exorcising people of the shadowy burdens for several months. The two didn't haunt city blocks with a purpose to find those encumbered by hexed shades and specters. They battled the nightmares they found shackling people on a *'come what may'* basis. But in a city of eight million people, that was too often enough.

The train slowed and stopped at the next station. The woman continued ranting. The doors opened, and she was the first to exit, yelling while flailing her arms at the people waiting on the outside. Benny and Neyeli followed her.

Instinct tugged at Lady Arachne's right eyebrow, arching it above her eye. Intrigued, she watched, patient and pensive as the young conjure-warriors stalked the haunted woman.

Neyeli channeled another silent suggestion to the woman. The projected thought steered her against the inawo's wishes, keeping her from re-boarding the train on a different car. The woman continued straight, making her way to the exit. Losing control of the woman's faculties, the inawo turned and screamed another loud curse. Benny-Jah's invisible buckler deflected the ear-scratching noise.

Disembarking passengers drained from the station while awaiting commuters wormed their way into the train's cars. The 8-Train's doors shut with a smooth slide, and then the steel beast dragged slow and sluggish until it rushed away through the tunnel, rattling and roaring. The train station echoed with the ferocious noise until the sound funneled away. The station was now bare of sound and empty of all souls, save a burdened, disheveled woman possessed of a weighty specter and two, young pursuers fit with conjure or incant to exorcise such phantoms.

Benny-Jah and Neyeli inched closer. The inawo turned and hissed and screeched. Benny's conjure deflected the piercing, unearthly sound, as Neyeli's hair shifted through colors, reacting not to the specter's shrill, but at the pedestrians repopulating the empty station. A new flow in the tide of masses. None of them heard the grinding squalls squealed from the inawo, but there was still an effect. The pedestrians appeared patient as they waited for the next train to scoop them up, but Neyeli could feel their frustration rising, the threshold of their patience cracking. The inawo yelled again, and Neyeli's instinct alerted her to the people combining their growing impatience with personal, past agitation.

Neyeli's hands trembled. Her ears were flooded with everyone's heads mentally projecting screams, cries of agony, and regret. They stood perfectly still, waiting for the train, agitated but noiseless. They were mannequins made of flesh and blood. Still. Hushed. But Neyeli heard them, and her hair reacted, colors fading in and out. Wading through the people felt like hearing the inawo's icy shrill. Their bodies closed in on her like walls. Her perfect vision blurred, and the scene around her throbbed, shrinking and expanding, never reverting back to reality's correct size and shape. Benny noticed his beautiful Mood Ring fighting against an attack he couldn't shield her from.

But he could do something.

Neyeli felt Benny-Jah's tender hand on her shoulder. Her hair shifted from pitch black to a calm, sky blue. She mouthed another incant, a prayer she'd scripted and empowered. The suffocating emotions seeped inside her. Her limbs, impregnated by the gathered attitudes, shuddered for only a moment. Neyeli balled her fists, holding the energy of the people's dissonant chords within the lines on the palm of her hand. The people calmed, and she calmed too.

The inawo shrieked! The woman it possessed cursed herself.

Neyeli and Benny pushed their way through the crowded train station, keeping their eye on the inawo and woman. One of Neyeli's coiled locks reshaped with scales and a snake's head. She pulled at it, detaching the straightened snake from her head without removing the lock that birthed it. Its tail was a sharp point, giving it the appearance of a thick, scaly needle with the head of a venomous copperhead. She handed the instrument to Benny, and the two of them quickened their pace. She spoke a plan of attack, keeping her eye on the inawo-burdened woman. Benny nodded.

They waded through the people, moving closer. The inawo screamed another attack at them, again deflected by Benny's conjure. Neyeli opened her palms. The lines were aglow with all the people's emotions, something the inawo was hoping Neyeli couldn't handle. Other adversaries had second guessed her too. The outcome for them was never good.

Neyeli took three long strides, passed the inawo and wrapped her arms around the disheveled woman's shoulders. She, the woman, Benny, and the inawo disappeared from the scene, unnoticed by the commuters.

Lady Arachne flinched at the moment Neyeli and Benny vanished. She watched the scene thereafter of the people waiting for the train, unsuspecting that conjure and otherworldly acts were at play in front of them. The matriarch was wild eyed, but she controlled her breathing. Ahead of her instinct, Lady Arachne pulled another card. The Three of Hearts, upright. The time-worn picture of a floating heart, stabbed by three ancient swords, whooshed away, and brought up the same scene. The difference, Neyeli and Benny were there, and a dreamy haze hung like a fog.

They were outside of time, invisible to the physical world, but still on its plane of existence. This was *the reverie*. Throughout the conjure diaspora it was also known as *the mirak, miujiza,* or *ajaba.* It had many purposes. Sometimes it was to shadow high-level conjure rituals from normal folk. The distinction here was to tap into a person's mind, assisting them on a spirit walk for the purpose of coming to revelations or to battle their burdens. Here they were. Outside of time. Inside the mind of the disheveled woman. Hallowed space to battle her burden.

The bedraggled woman sat with her back against the tiled wall. Her head dangled, chin against her right shoulder. Neyeli knelt in front of her, holding her upright, and whispering into her ear that her blackness was the beginning of time, the beautiful, dark matter of the cosmos that birthed the planets and stars, and bound the galaxies together. Its true name was *Gira*, Neyeli told her.

Benny, making himself as light as air, tussled with the inawo. He dodged the specter's arms, ducked its strikes, looking for a moment to counter with the snake needle in his hand. Their brawl ghosted through commuters, but a small, clear area became their fighting ring. Benny jumped in the air and twisted around, floating effortlessly behind the inawo. He landed and stabbed the shadowy thing. The inawo attempted to holler, but its voice was muted by the incanted sting and Neyeli's words spoken into the woman's ear. The creature evaporated, taking the snake-like needle with it.

Lady Arachne wanted to applaud the young conjure-warriors, but she stayed her hands and remained a proper lady. A smile would do, as she watched the Three of Hearts retrogress to its ancient drawing. Lady Arachne's eyes moved back to the Knight of Swords. Neyeli and Benny-Jah reappeared inside time. They were unnoticed, until Neyeli yelled for assistance. She held the woman up, gentle hands on her shoulders. Benny stood at her side until others surrounded them. He rushed through the crowd, jumped the turnstile, and alerted the man behind the booth about the fallen, unconscious woman. The man picked up an emergency phone and called for assistance. All would be well.

Fog filled the card and faded up to its original sketch.

Lady Arachne flipped the card over and moved it aside. Her instinct buzzed, but before drawing again, she took a moment to reflect on what she'd witnessed. Her focus was on the two sweethearts, working together and blossomed with conjure. She believed there was never a more beautiful sight.

But her instinct buzzed like a persistent phone call, and Lady Arachne answered irritated that she couldn't take a moment for pause. She plucked the next card and placed it face up in front of her. The Ten of Cups. An African family stood below a bright, blue sky. A vibrant rainbow arched across the firmament. Ten gold chalices hovered against nature's colorful structure. The wife and husband embraced one another with one arm, and they lifted their free hand to the heavenly body. Their two children, a young girl and a young boy, danced and played next to them.

Lady Arachne concentrated. The picture faded away, and clouds swirled in its absence. A soft melody from a piano played behind the smoky, gossamer shroud. It seemed as if 'Blind' Willie Johnson's repeating tune muted a bit out of respect for the piano's music. Up came the scene of a Harlem brownstone's front room. There, playing on his new, black grand piano was Maximillian Goodspeed, a prince of sorts in Fable Avenue's conjure court. He was definitely a descendant of what could be considered Fable Avenue royalty. He, and his siblings, were the great-great grandchildren of the late Madison Goodspeed, the British-Jamaican man who'd come to the United States in the early 1920s and assisted the spirits in creating Fable Avenue, working its construction with ritual from a place outside of time.

The tall and handsome, brown-skin Maximillian glided his fingers across eighty-eight keys with professional precision, flushing out a tune. He wore black slacks and dress shoes, a white dress shirt with the cuffs unbuttoned, and a black, buttoned up vest.

Everyone saw something, indeed. And Maximillian Goodspeed fashioned a sly grin as his eyes locked onto his wife's shape. He didn't need to see the keys to play them. No key was missed or improperly struck while Althea Goodspeed danced a simple routine next to the piano he played. She passed away many years ago, poisoned by a hex injected into her. But here her spirit glimmered as an apparition so strong she could maintain a physical presence and hold her husband and two, grown sons should she so desire. She didn't return to her husband for quite some time. There were trials and rituals her spirit endured. And when she finally could gather strength to return to the physical plane as spirit, she observed from ethereal perch her husband's indulgence in other women. It was not out of any spite of her, or some newfound freedom from the 'shackles' of marriage. It was for the purpose of dulling the pain of her death. Knowledge of that didn't lessen Althea's heartache from watching her husband engage with other women.

It wasn't until last year that she decided to emerge from the ethereal blue and present herself to her family. She felt compelled. Her youngest son, Gordon, had completed a ritual designed for Goodspeed children, and it was successful. The ritual was on his nineteenth birthday when it was performed by Fable Avenue's sole patriarch, Vencil Peters, called Papa Solomon, and his sister, Maman Anansi. Later that evening, at the nineteenth hour, her son received what no other Goodspeed had received before him while undergoing the ritual of the second gateway rites. The cosmic, lilac spirit possessed him, putting Fable Avenue on a course to do greater things through conjure.

Naturally, a mother had to appear and congratulate her son.

But the reunion was far from jubilant. Althea's spirit recalled all her heartache, hearing past women's giggling scurrying through the halls of their second residence located in Brooklyn. But she also remembered the sounds her husband could make on the piano, and she danced to smother the anger that possessed her. Her son watched her dance, and he consoled her, young man with spirit as he was. She revealed herself to her husband weeks later, and their reunion was much the same. They were silent and embraced for a long moment, and then she spoke on what ailed her. It was an infirmity far more debilitating than the hex put on her. But it wasn't long before the two of them felt like no time passed at all. They were laughing, sharing stories, and as in love as the first day they'd met. Maximillian commissioned Papa Solomon's son, Oliver, to etch a tattoo on his left arm. A perfect rendering of Althea was drawn and blessed with incant. It wasn't just a tattoo. It was a doorway for Althea's spirit to pass through with ease, blossom into the physical world, and visit her family.

At this moment, she danced to her husband's music, matching every chord struck. Husband and wife were in unison through music and movement. Whether he slowed the melody or spiced it with quick, quirky flashy pings, Althea's motion never faltered to keep up. She commented without delay in her dance, "We should take this act on the road." Maximillian burst into laughter, then he gave a freestyle attempt at song. A whimsical, jazzy falsetto came from him. Not perfect, but not cracking. He improvised, *"If you don't mind, I'd like to love you some more. I think eternity defines how much I to you adore. Your cosmic skin, your starry, bright eyes…that big ol' behind…everything just swingin' like a door."*

Althea laughed, but didn't lose her dance.

Lady Arachne let loose a chortle.

Husband watched wife while his hands had a life of their own across the piano keys. His stare held happy memories recalled by spirit, dance and music. She could see him too, just as clear, though she twirled around and around and around.

As if her elegant moves were a ritual, clouds were conjured on the face of the card, opening to a new scene. The piano music could still be heard, sounding distant. 'Blind' Willie Johnson's volume returned, his deep, bluesy cry inquiring about the soul of a man. It was revealed to Lady Arachne that some stares were hard to dissolve, such as it was with Althea and Maximillian's eldest son, Cedron Goodspeed. The cornrowed, muscular behemoth, dressed in a high school basketball jersey and jeans, stood in the doorway of his garden-level bedroom watching contradictions collide.

Writhing seductively in a wheelchair was his girlfriend, Leah-Kimberly Peters. The wheelchair was once his throne. It earned him the nickname 'King'. He was put there by bullet and a misunderstanding. His anger seethed for years while seated on his throne. He expressed that irritation through authoritative command of a misfit crew that took orders from Fable Avenue elders to procure ancient, cultural items.

Lady Arachne was thankful for Cedron's misfits.

The blossom of his conjure restored his legs, but the revelation on how the bullet came to rest in his spine drenched his eyes with anger and blinded him. His younger brother calmed him. Of course, this was only after fisticuffs so intense between them that it conjured windstorms and snow, shattering windows up and down the Harlem block. When he awoke from his brother's calming strike, he retained his conjure to lace his flesh with black, cosmic fabric and circuitry. When he wore his skin as pitch as night, movement was restored to his legs. Even now, the cosmic apparel covered his legs underneath his jeans, the rest of his flesh bare of conjure for the time being. This was his morning ritual, watching his queen dance for him in his former throne, his father's music often coming from upstairs.

Fog faded the scene. The family, open sky, and chalice-covered rainbow returned to the card's face. Instinct chipped at Lady Arachne. She turned the card over and placed it atop the others, taking another from the deck.

It was The Emperor, written in Swahili on the card as *mfalme*. The picture presented a strong and seated African man. His beard and coiled locks were white like wool, and he was dressed in robes made of lion skin. A crown as heavy as his authority rested atop his head. He held a gold scepter, the shape of the Kemetic ankh atop it. His throne was made of bronze with silver ram heads protruding out at the end of the armrests and at the right and left corners of the chair's tall back. Mighty mountains rested in the background.

The card's grand detail was washed away by clouds and substituted with a scene occurring just across the street at the Peters' residence. The image of Vencil "Papa Solomon" Peters was put on display. Tall, bald, black and imposing, the fifty-seven-year-old man, sporting a bushy, white goatee, was the perfect substitute for the emperor previously featured on the card. Papa Solomon too was seated at his desk, in his study, surrounded by shelved literature. His workspace in front of him was decorated with all manner of ritualistic baubles. None was more important than the musical instrument situated in the center of his desk. A trumpet mounted on a wooden stand. The horn's mystical harmonies, that only a male Peters could play, helped bring Fable Avenue into physical existence almost sixty years ago.

The magical horn had a long history. An African enslaved in the eighteenth century forged the horn from a sacred tree, and used its power to lead a rebellion on a plantation. Reshaped in the heavens, it fell to Earth centuries later, appearing as a modern-day jazz trumpet, and landing in the hands of a jazz musician, who just happened to be the enslaved African resurrected in a new life. Papa Solomon's grandfather and father were masters of the horn. And though Papa Solomon was no musician, instinct guided him to play a few mystical notations so that he could manipulate the horn's magic. It was always a struggle. He wasn't his grandfather or father, but he didn't mind. He had gift enough to wield the mystical notations.

Papa Solomon had a visitor. A black man in his early forties. The conjure man listened attentively. Lady Arachne's instinct lifted the man's name from the ethers. Daniel Harbor. He wasn't a community member, and though Mister Harbor was an avid churchgoer, in private, he and his family practiced a form of *Las Reglas de Congo*, an African spiritual system developed among enslaved Africans in South America and Cuba. Through these ancient rites, he knew of Fable Avenue's lore, and on this day, he was seeking assistance with a personal problem.

Mister Harbor explained his situation. "My wife and I just settled outside the city with our two children," he stated. "We live in Greendale on the Metro North. It's a lovely place, but we've been greeted with prejudice." Papa Solomon urged Mister Harbor to proceed. "Staged robberies have been carried out, and my family have been accused as the culprits. We're not being blamed directly, but I've stumbled upon whispers suggesting that our 'kind' have brought undesirables into the neighborhood." He leaned forward and appealed to the good nature of Fable Avenue's patriarch to assist him in proving the wrong done against his family.

Papa Solomon didn't ponder long. He stood from his chair, rising like a strong, onyx tower. He came from behind his desk and motioned for Mister Harbor to stand, which the gentleman did. Papa Solomon assured Mister Harbor, "A blessing will be given to you and your family. Protection." He put his hand against his chest and an arm around Mister Harbor, "I, myself, will create a mojo bag for you. It will be filled with enchanted trinkets to ward off these false accusations, and draw out all offenders to your family." Mister Harbor thanked Papa Solomon repeatedly. The conjure man assured, "Let us go see my wife. She will cast a blessing that will see justice done in your family's favor." As they exited the room, Papa Solomon told Mister Harbor that no tribute would be necessary, and no favor needed to be done in return. Papa Solomon was showered with more enthusiastic gratitude. Despite assurance of no tribute, gratitude would become gifts a few days later when injustice was exposed and made the news.

Clouds closed the scene, and reemerged the emperor's mighty presence.

Lady Arachne took another card, flipped it over and saw the soft, feminine form of the African Empress, or as the card referred to her, the *malkia*, laying out on her lounge. Lady Arachne placed the card over The Emperor's card. Clouds swallowed the picture, and up came the sanctum sanctorum of Thelema Heathwicke-Peters, called Madame Jeliya. Much like the empress, she rested on a chaise lounge. Hers was of a Victorian style. She laid her plump, voluptuous figure against its arm. Her legs were crossed, and she nursed a glass of wine while waiting for her husband to deliver to her their current client in need of a blessing.

A record played. It was the only jazz album Papa Solomon's father, Horatio Peters, recorded with his band. The recording was laced with an enchantment that only those of the African conjure diaspora could hear. This was more than a jazz album. It was conjure and soul; and its music sent out a call that helped populate Fable Avenue.

Madame Jeliya followed the footsteps of her husband and Mister Harbor as they descended into her sanctuary. She observed Mister Harbor's eyes as he panned the ancient decorations, paintings, and bewitched items placed with purpose around the room. Mister Harbor's expression turned apprehensive as he noticed the presence of her two conjured familiars cuddled up warmly against one another just left of her lounge. They were blanketed by shadow, but a cool, blue glow outlined the figures of the lion and the lioness.

Mister Harbor paused in his forward motion, eyes locked on the massive creatures. Madame Jeliya assured, "My kittens will do you no harm, Mister Harbor." She put her eyes on her husband and inquired, "What trouble agitates this client?" Papa Solomon informed his wife on Mister Harbor's troubles, and Madame Jeliya rose when the details of his complaint were completely disclosed. Papa Solomon added, as his wife stood, that he was preparing a mojo bag for the circumstances. Taking one last sip of her glass and laying it on a pedestal already occupied with the essential oils and slips of paper with proper prayers to be recited, Madame Jeliya approached Mister Harbor. She dismissed her husband with a smile and a wink.

The Fable Avenue patriarch bowed at the neck to his wife and stepped away, returning upstairs to his study to prepare and bless the precise ingredients for Mister Harbor's mojo bag. Madame Jeliya brought Mister Harbor to the lounge and instructed him to lay flat across it. Mister Harbor did as tasked while keeping his eyes on the big cats snuggled up to one another. Madame Jeliya again assured him the 'kittens' would do him no harm. She coaxed Mister Harbor onto his back, leaned over, and swiped an open palm over his eyes. She mouthed a Yoruba prayer, and Mister Harbor fell fast to sleep. She stood upright, moved to the pedestal holding her oils and prayers and stated it was time to go to work.

Clouds dropped onto the scene like a curtain closing an act. When they lifted, the Empress' soft, feminine portrait returned and Lady Arachne lifted the card, turned it over, and placed it atop the other cards she'd pulled.

The card reader let her instinct ring and ring. This time she ignored it well. A smile curled on her face as she thought about Madame Jeliya, specifically recalling the matriarch's image resting against her lounge, glass of wine in her hand; and the smile and wink she gave to Papa Solomon. She'd never witnessed Madame Jeliya resonate so much sensual energy. Madame Jeliya was always so cold around her, mostly because of the false impression that Lady Arachne pursued Papa Solomon, as they had been an item several years before Madame Jeliya came to Fable Avenue. They were all in their early to mid-twenties. Madame Jeliya and Papa Solomon beheld one another, an instinct two people shared when they'd found the other half of their spirit. Their soulmate. Lady Arachne respected that, but not without consequence.

The two matriarchs had been cold to one another ever since. But seeing Madame Jeliya in her natural habitat was a remarkable sight. Lady Arachne was more than intrigued. She was aroused. Her smile curled even more.

Her instinct buzzed again. Its twang was peculiar. Lady Arachne listened closer. Her instinct didn't only instruct her to draw another card, it requested for her to create a spread consisting of four cards. She moved the pile of pulled cards farther away, and then drew the first card. She placed the card in front of her, picked three more from the deck, and placed them to the left, right, and above the first card.

She turned over the middle card first, revealing the night-themed picture of a hoodwinked, African woman bound while standing and surrounded by eight, hulking swords. She flipped the card above it and uncovered The Hierophant. Her instinct chimed again, and Lady Arachne moved the two turned cards down in position on the table, making the four-card spread a plus sign. Before she could touch the remaining two cards, the Eight of Swords was drowned in clouds. Up came a scene just as foggy.

The day was hazy and gray. Rain drizzled. Black men and black women trudged along. Lady Arachne guessed they had a destination, but their walk appeared aimless, traipsing like the undead. Even the cars appeared slow as they trekked through the cracked and muddied streets. Lady Arachne deduced she was observing the citizens of Water Bug Hollow, Louisiana. So much history was there. Once a plantation, one of its slaves led a bloody rebellion toward the end of the Civil War and emancipated the grounds, turning it into a safe-haven for freed blacks. It became a small, wealthy community bustling with activity and its own celebratory rituals. Its magic flourished as jazz that rivaled New Orleans, which lay twenty minutes east. But wars waged by occult procedures toppled the community's wealth and culture. Conjure and incant seemed stifled, and the area was now a part of a greater parish called Jakobiville, segregated by *de facto* rather than by law.

It was upon this thought where Lady Arachne's attention moved to The Hierophant card. It swirled with clouds, erasing the ancient sketch of an East African holy man, rearranging inanimate color into photorealism until motion was brought to life. Lady Arachne beheld the interior of the only church in Water Bug Hollow. The inside was elegant, as the church had been remodeled over the years. The matriarch wondered if all the money Water Bug Hollow possessed was funneled into keeping the church up-to-date. Its pews were empty, producing a haunting atmosphere. The card tracked the aisle until it spied for Lady Arachne's eyes the reverend kneeling at the front pew. A hard, pensive stare stabbed his open hands. His dark-brown eyes moved along the lines in his palms, as if searching for answers.

Lady Arachne's senses informed her that this was Reverend Mathieu Pouvwa. He had brown skin, was of average height and build; and he wore thin, round-lensed glasses on his oblong-shaped face. His black hair lay flat, shaped with natural waves. A light dusting of hair surrounded his chin and upper lip.

Lady Arachne found him to be very handsome, but a strange feeling possessed her as she watched him. She believed she could feel his emotion. Through the card came the reverend's sense of fear and curiosity, blended together in a sea of paradox and confusion.

I don't know how, Lady Arachne heard Mathieu's thought in her head. *But, I just know what to say*. It was at this moment that he spoke softly, uttering what Lady Arachne could only perceive as an incant. A quiet, reddish glow congealed as a small sphere in Mathieu's left hand and confirmed her suspicions. The red light rippled to a bright brilliance, expanding and taking a specific shape. Brown and green mixed atop the red, heart-shaped cast of light. Mathieu' eyes never flinched or squinted, instead they widened as if defying the light's red glow that lasted for a few moments more, bursting from existence with a pop, and leaving behind a solid apple in the reverend's palm.

Mathieu's eyes hinted at the combined emotions of disappointment and concern writhing within him. He put the apple on the pew, turned around, and lay his back against the bench, seated on the floor. He exhaled and wiped his brow. A melancholy expression fully matured on his face. His eyes went to a painting of Jesus. The Christian savior looked up, pointing toward heaven. A brilliant, yellow light shined behind his head. The reverend's sight drifted toward another painting. This was of Eve being tempted with an apple by the serpent.

Lady Arachne chuckled at the reverend's ironic journey. He found himself at Elegba's crossroads. She could feel the conflict within him, but she knew he'd be okay. Perhaps she would visit him when the time was right, and she would escort him through the crossroads to Fable Avenue.

Lady Arachne let the reverend have time alone. She wiped her hand over his card and the clouds engulfed the scene. The Hierophant's ancient sketch reappeared. Instinct moved the matriarch's vision toward the card on the right. She turned over the Seven of Wands. A young, African man, wearing a turban and warrior attire had the advantage against six unseen foes as he stood above them on a solid, stone precipice. Their staves reached up to him, but he fended them of with ease as he had the high ground.

But the ancient drawing melted into a scene that was less noble and more grim. A fight occurred. Two, young black men were a part of the scuffle. One young man was sprawled unconscious on the sidewalk. His limbs, stretched out, were bent like waves of water. His face had been beaten to an unrecognizable state, a lumpy plight of purple, brown, and dark reds. His mouth, agape because of a loosened, lower jaw, previewed missing teeth and gushed with blood that spilled like a waterfall. On his feet were bright, neon yellow sneakers, and he was dressed in baggy, dark-blue jeans that, when he once stood upright, hung below his buttocks, exposing his underwear. On his torso was a tight, white tank-top.

A short, wild haired woman, dressed in a loose and long t-shirt and gray sweatpants fled screaming from the scrimmage, hands in the air.

The young man standing over the first had no relation to him, but he could've passed as his brother. At the shared age of twenty-five, they could've been mistaken for twin brothers. They were of the same height, reddish-brown copper tone to their flesh. Their body type was slim like a snake but muscular. Their facial features were also similar, though not much could be examined of the swelled and bloody attributes of the fallen young man. Both had small, almond-shaped, brown eyes, high cheekbones, and a sharp, pointed chin. A few differences were hairstyle, as the unconscious young man wore his hair straightened and in a ponytail. The second man had a freshly cut low fade.

His fists were still clenched and dripping with the thick, red blood of his vanquished opponent. He stood over him wearing a business suit and a leather traveler's bag slung over his shoulder. Lady Arachne deduced that before the young man engaged in fisticuffs he'd been ready for another frustrating and exhaustive day of interviews and job searching. Somewhere between his door and this moment, he'd exercised his frustrations on the man he stood over. Lady Arachne's instinct rustled. She deciphered its low hum, retrieving more insight on the suited, young man. She pulled a name. *Armand Gideon*, grandson to Savannah Forrester, born from her oldest daughter. She also decrypted that the surrounding neighborhood was not located in Jakobiville's Water Bug Hollow.

This was Atlanta, Georgia.

Armand panted. His teeth were clenched, and his bloodied fists trembled. Then the frame froze. It didn't fill with fog or revert back to its original picture. Instead, Lady Arachne was urged to turn the remaining card. Instead of physically lifting it, she made a gentle wave of her hand and let an unseen power provide the move. Revealed was the Nine of Wands featuring the same African warrior displayed on the Seven of Wands. He stood firm and at the ready, holding strong to a mighty, wooden quarterstaff. His eyes observed eight other staves standing upright behind him. The picture was erased by clouds, and into frame came a quick sequence of events summarizing Armand's day-to-day routine of looking feverishly for a job and encountering nothing but pushback. He perceived it all as prejudice. It was no different than his experiences searching for employment back home in California.

Then the day's opening events happened, and the picture slowed down the movement to a normal pace. The beaten man was whole now, walking swiftly with his older, short, female companion beside him. They were talking wildly, eyes bulging and giggling. Armand was ahead of them, in their path. Lady Arachne heard them speak of scoring a drug, calling the substance by a street name she wasn't familiar with. Their giggly chatter alerted Armand. He looked over his shoulder and saw the two of them approaching in haste. He assessed they were no harm, and out of courtesy he moved aside to let them pass. They scooted by him, but still came close. Armand kept his eyes on them, making sure there was no collision.

The yet beaten man cackled, commenting to his friend how scared Armand looked as they passed him. Anger boiled in Armand's stomach. It crawled with a rapid pace up his throat, contorted into words, which he spat to the addict. *"It's called* 'courtesy'!" That wasn't all he said. He added the word 'jackass' not so much as a curse, but as if it could be found on the addict's driver's license as his honest, parent-given name.

The addict turned. The woman tugged at him, telling him not to be bothered, scoring a hit was more important. The addict ripped his arm from her and demanded Armand repeat what he'd said. His stance was firm, arms out, muscles flexed, fists tightened, and face screwed by a scowl.

Armand obliged the addict. But before he reiterated his words, Armand made the promise to speak slowly so that the addict would understand him. And once he finished repeating what he'd said, he added the definition of the word 'courtesy,' for safe measure and further insult. The addict stormed up to him! Armand didn't flinch. He told the addict to keep walking and go and get his fix. His companion agreed, again tugging on the addict's arm. The addict cursed her, pushing her away, and then he swung at Armand. His punch connected with nothing as Armand dodged away. The addict lost balance. Armand balled his right hand and retaliated with a powerful hit to the addict's cheek.

The picture froze.

The Seven of Wands regained motion. Armand panted, clenching his teeth behind a closed mouth. He stared long at the bloody, bruised, and broken consequences of his deed, the pulverizing of another human being. Flesh mangled by his bunched fists. Everyone saw something, and Armand's stares couldn't be closed even when he blinked. The image of the decimated addict was just too wide open to look away.

Armand recouped his composure. He brushed his suit off, fixed his shirt and tie, turned around, and walked back to his apartment to wash his hands, and reattempt going to his interviews.

He would have to apologize for being late, of course.

Even looking into the bathroom mirror, Armand's stare remained on a moment past, rewinding time and playing the bloody dustup he had just left. Seeing it all again, he let out a breath. Lady Arachne's instinct caused her to tremble. She heard Armand confess a conclusion for his actions. A whispered thought he believed was kept safe and secret as it was cached deep within his cerebral belfry.

He whispered that he wouldn't change a thing.

That was not the day's events. The image cracked into tiny shards that rearranged into letters and words that swirled onto loose notepaper, rearranging the scene into Armand sitting at his kitchen table composing a letter to his grandmother, Savannah Forrester, pleading for her help in the matter that stained his hands and conscience.

Lady Arachne didn't realize, until both the Seven and Nine of Wands reverted to their maiden forms, that her mouth hung open, dragged down by shock. She covered her mouth with both hands as she gasped deep. She breathed out into her palms, feeling the warmth of her exhalation against her skin.

A different word appeared on the face of each card. The Nine of Wands read: *Ogun*, the name of the Yoruba warrior-Orisha and spiritual metalworker. The simple letter *'a'* materialized on The Hierophant card. The word *'mage'* ran across the face of the Eight of Swords. And lastly, dawning on the Nine of Swords was a word foreign to Lady Arachne. *Doni*.

She knew not what to make of them, or how all of this connected to the Fable Avenue's conjure community. She decided it was best to counsel with her sister matriarchs, Madame Jeliya and Maman Anansi. The words faded. It was these moments in her reading, cards pulled that didn't show any immediate members of Fable Avenue, that she was tasked to note and bring to her fellow Elders.

Her instinct purred, and she recognized its purposeful timbre. Her morning monitoring had come to an end. Even without pulling what would be the final card of the day, she knew what card it was, and who it would display when transformed to motion.

She moved the other cards to the used pile, and then she carefully slipped the top card from the deck and laid it in front of her. It was The Star, upright. Fade to clouds, and up came the moving image of goings-on not too far down the road. It was in the backyard of the Forrester residence. Stirring there was a young man of nineteen years. Gordon Goodspeed. Dressed in black shoes and slacks, and a white dress shirt with the first few buttons undone. His shirt's sleeves peeked through his jacket, cuffs unbuttoned, covering the back of his hand.

Gordon looked tired, though the fire-like twists of his hair burst with life. Lady Arachne guessed he might have been up the whole night haunting the streets, protecting the neighborhood in his *Dooley* form, perchance still in pursuit of children who had been abducted from the Fable Avenue community. Or perhaps he'd spent the night in his bright and fiery lilac configuration traveling to the stars to be among the cosmic spirits, possibly seeking their guidance.

Tucked under his arm was an ancient device called the *Nigrum Nigrius*

Nigro that functioned much like a modern-day laptop. A spirit of long ago possessed the device. Gordon named it *Spook*, and it spoke by lighting up the device's black screen with characters from a forgotten language. Gordon, with his lilac-colored eyes, was able to read the symbols. With concentration, the Elders of Fable Avenue could also translate the ancient letters. Another who could interact with the device was Fey Forrester, Savannah's granddaughter and Gordon's sweetheart.

At the moment, Spook was folded much like a portable, personal computer with its black mirror closed against its bejeweled console. Slipped in between the shut device was one of Lady Arachne's tarot cards. Judgment. Gordon was once again attempting a meditative read, using Spook's potential to draw out the history of an object and send a person, in dream, through yesteryear. Gordon was under task by Lady Arachne to find her tarot deck's missing card. The Lovers.

Gordon hadn't seen much of history, save the card's creation by a sect of African priests and priestesses who'd fled Egypt during Ptolemaic rule. This revelation surprised Lady Arachne, as she'd believed the cards to be a recent rendering, around the tenth or eleventh century. Her heart fluttered to know she wielded a more potent deck. A later reading revealed that the cards' colorful inks were only mixed with the ashes from the first deck of Tarot cards, also known as the *Mkuu Set*.

There still was nothing concerning the whereabouts of the missing Lovers card. Gordon did mention being taken on a journey to the past, observing a young warrior-priest named Tedros sneaking into occupied Egypt, burrowing into a closed temple, and retrieving a set of scrolls that would be translated into the symbolism represented on a single card. Gordon recounted the story with so much life, an essence that had been sapped from him when his sweetheart, Fey Forrester, had been taken by a hex.

Gordon sat on a green, steel bench. He never opened Spook. He looked up at the silver, life-sized statue of Fey Forrester. It was a memorial of sorts, appearing the moment Fey's life was taken. The shimmering sculpture captured Fey Forrester in her dazzling, spirit form, face toward the heavens, arms at her side with balled fists. Her lower half was an amalgam of her thighs and a blaze of the power of her spirit expressed as a comet's tail that began at her knees. A translucent chamber, once filled with Fey Forrester's faint, ghostly image rested beside the silver likeness. It was now empty of that spectacle. That didn't matter to Gordon.

Everyone saw something.

Gordon Goodspeed still saw her.

His love.

She was the cobalt-blue spirit possessed with all the feminine blackness of the grand cosmos. Fey Forrester. A power the malefactors of

Fable Avenue had been determined to silence. And to the eye of normal folk, it appeared they'd succeeded. Card reading and instinct guided Lady Arachne to stumble upon Fey Forrester's resurrection coinciding with the eventual discovery of The Lovers card's concealed location. When Gordon returned from his self-imposed exile into the heavens, Lady Arachne informed him of her research.

She watched Gordon speak a silent prayer. It was a saying he and Fey shared. Then he laid his back against the bench, placed the ancient device against his chest, and folded his arms over it.

Gordon shut his eyes to see history bloom in dream.

A soft glow came from between the *Nigrum Nigrius Nigro*.

All stress was soothed, and Gordon fell fast to sleep.

The *Nigrum Nigrius Nigro* scanned the aged item lying between it. A time period was determined. Spook connected its spirit with Gordon's sleep, channeling his dreams through time.

The star reappeared on the card's surface.

Lady Arachne placed it face down with the others earlier pulled. She gathered them together, gave them a quick shuffle, and then returned them to the deck. She shuffled all the cards. She cut the deck into three piles, reversed one of the piles, switched tops around, and shuffled again. She let the cards be, as the matriarch was tired.

She stood from her bench, spoke an incant as she twiddled two fingers outward, and removed the light and sound from the room. The door unlocked and opened just a crack, letting in a long and thin rectangular spread of light.

Lady Arachne stood and left her sanctuary.

The Before Animosity

"I will be the hero of El-Nord whether history
and all the people she births remembers me or not."

A lilac fog gave way to history long, long, long ago. The haze split into patches, turning white and slowly burgeoning into a majestic exterior. The thin, ghostly fog descended and swirled through a lush rainforest. Vibrant greenery and strong, dark browns blossomed in all directions. They extended up toward the blue sky, which held in its presence a solid black moon with a golden halo shimmering anemic at its circumference. The moon's siblings were on either side, faded into the blue like half-sunken ships submerged in water. Their colors were red and green, and the morning sun washed out their waxen halos. The heavens peered down at nature's metropolis constructed of mighty trees. And as flush as the flora was at its canopy, it did not keep out the sun's extended brilliance.

There were large areas where the foliage drew back like royal subjects and allowed the sun's bright, yellow tendrils entrance to the earthy green and brown kingdom. Billowy rushes of water cascaded off the side of hard, grey stone mountainsides, continuing a stream's journey from high above to the valley below. Faint rainbows passed through puffs of mist, shimmering in and out of existence with the mix between cloudy, white moisture and sunlight.

Bright feathered birds gawked, blending with the roaring breaths of rushing waterfalls. Four- and two-legged animals shuffled through forest brush, a prance and frolic here and there, a dance of nature and animal that snapped twigs and rustled loose flora. Other creatures swung from branch to branch, communicating with low growls and grunts. Buzzing and humming insects landed on twigs, grappled with one another, or were sucked up by the slurp of long-tongued creatures.

There was an anomaly to the forest's structure. A misshaped feature. There were areas that appeared bent and broken with its trees. The deformity was symmetrical. The trees' unnatural concinnity outlined walled settlements scattered below, miles apart from one another. The colonies were pristine in nature, and of nature they were made. Houses ranged from simple huts concocted from straw and sticks to complex, mortared limestone buildings. Nothing but guard towers extended above the height of the walls, not even the buildings designed for government.

Each of the settlements possessed the same uneasy quiet.

A peek over the walled communities revealed barren streets, doors swinging in a light breeze that welcomed nothing but the feline push of air that played with the doors, back and forth. Every building was empty.

Population, zero. In theory.

A northernmost settlement was the village of El-Nord. In the uneasy silence bonding the walled communities, it was one exception. Flinches and twitches would perhaps accompany a neophyte dreamer experiencing the historical scene materialized from lilac haze. El-Nord wasn't so much bustling with daily routine and life as it was brimming with its population, aimless and changed as they were in the streets. Fires occupied homes instead of citizens, and black and grey smoke swiveled like ghosts trying to escape the flames.

Blunt and sharp weaponry littered the area, dripping with a black, tarry substance that mixed with bloodstains. Some of the weapons dangled loose in the soft grip of fallen town guards. Other weapons had been taken up by desperate citizens who lay dead alongside the lifeless bodies of those sworn to protect them. Women and children were counted among the dead, not spared from the carnage. Large, jagged incisions and deep, wide holes dressed the fallen citizens better than their half-hanging, lacerated clothing.

At the town's center was a one-story, domed temple. Its windows were covered from the inside by black cloth, allowing no light to penetrate. The temple's interior could've been mistaken as a blend of a gothic-styled church and a small round theater. Built-in seating surrounded a circular stage. Candles lined the back rows and were grouped together at a small area near the stage. Sconces were mounted on the walls near the entrance. The flames' glow was peculiar. No smoke emanated from them. No wick kept them in place, nor oil helped sustain them. The credit for their kindling was from something otherworldly, manipulated by the twenty-five-year-old man standing at the intricately designed rock-carved lectern emplaced at center stage.

This wasn't just history being viewed. This was a legend witnessed as it truly was.

The brown-skinned gentleman was positioned at the beginning of a story. His story. A story that would be recounted by conjure-folk for millennia upon millennia. His name was Ziko Yswil, and he was from a long line of alchemists on his father's side and grand storytellers, hunters, and teachers from his mother's lineage.

El-Nord's culture thrived on pride in vocation and the crowing of exploits, and they had an affinity for the number thirty-one. An explanation for this fixation had been lost to time. Because of El-Nord's nature for recounting life exploits, it was often called by other settlements as *Brag Town* or *Boastville*. This was all in good-natured jest.

Until two weeks ago, Ziko had only few life stories, and they were mundane at best. He was twenty-five, not too far from the monumental year of thirty-one, and in the middle of the years designated for gaining experience and independence. But the years drifted by with Ziko showing little interest in any adult craft or trade that would define the rest of his life. To the El-Nordites, thirty-one was the start of work, marriage, and the beginning of sharing life tales and learned lessons. Ziko had nothing to talk about. But his lack of experience had no correlation to a lack of initiative.

Here now, Ziko stared with his golden-brown eyes at a lectern filled not with a scholarly scroll or book, but with a miner's tool. He looked up, out into the empty audience and imagined an auditorium filled with spectators. He did not know if he was playing the part of statesman or professor, though he wore the latter's robes. No matter, however, as he was the bearer of dire news.

"It is a time of war," he said. His voice was low, but it carried through the lecture hall by way of the room's design. "It's been a continuance of politics," he added. He spoke each word as a sentence, deliberate. He never moved, eyes resting on the miner's tool set upon the lectern. "These politics have escalated into bloodshed over the interpretation of prophecy and fate." He paused, eyes flickering like his voice. He wiped his mouth and took a breath. "We of the El-Nord settlement, we shied away from worldly, diplomatic affairs as an attempt to maintain peace within our walls, no different from the rest of El-Ham." He broke into a smile, remembering the innocent ways of his community. "We were never a place to produce statesmen or ambassadors for anything more than simple representation of our existence in the greater El-Ham Republic." He tapped a finger to his temple. "The mind, according to we of El-Nord—no different than El-Ham—was best at use calculating alchemical equations, not diplomatic strategy." His solemn manner returned, wiping away his boyish grin. "But let's be honest, my people. A culture so focused on trade and the mastery of craft is not so easily overlooked in wartimes."

Ziko placed both his hands on the lectern. His head dropped. No one watched him, but he was conscious of how his distress played out. He stood straight and cleared his throat, looking around at his invisible audience. He hoped that even imagined eyes didn't look upon him with pity.

"Our Regional Governor, Pajon Ohn, and his wife, Chieftess Ishel Nofre vowed that war would never breach the individual, walled townships and villages making up El-Ham." He stepped away from the lectern, waving his hands for dramatic effect as he paced the stage. He kept his voice elevated for his imagined audience. "Part of their pledge insisted that a support of war efforts should be made." He stopped and looked around at his audience. "Naturally, this created a schism among our many settlements. El-Nord was called upon to lend its best metalworkers, healers, and even alchemists." Ziko pointed out into the audience as if he was singling out men and women who fit the professions he listed.

Ziko slapped his hands together, rubbed them, and then returned to his place behind the lectern. "Many of us were grateful for the volunteers. They kept tensions low. No one felt we needed to toss our glove into greater, worldly politics." He paused again, thinking of the complexities of it all. "But once in a while there were people chosen by lot. And while many protested the random pull of fate for being sent to the war, I confess, I was curious. I often hoped that my name would be drafted for random choosing." He tried to suppress a smile, but imagining friends and family in the audience made him chuckle, trying to hide it through a cough. "I know," he said, eyes and smile on the floor. Looking up he noted, "Those of you who know me understand that I've been struggling to find my place and story in life. Yet, here I was thinking that these events could lead me to them." He walked to the edge of the stage and sat down comfortably, legs dangling. He spoke in a casual tone to his empty auditorium. "No one was being selected as a soldier. Not even the men and women trained as guards. So, I figured, how dangerous could it be?"

Ziko leaned back on his arms, swinging his legs. "As a man, it had the potential to be my first steps in growing muscles pregnant with experience and script. Perhaps even my belly would too expand with might and ink—*earn my guts*, as some with bellies say in our El-Nord culture." He slapped his abdomen. The stories told and experienced by some men of El-Nord might've given them a bloated stomach, but it was packed with muscle and magic that strengthened their physicality. A gut scrawled with scripture was no cause for shame. As anywhere experience swelled on the body, it also scripted an indelible design of words from a language lost aeons ago. That was experience. And the women of El-Nord were quite attracted to the visual record that reshaped their men, even those with inflated bellies. And the men were very much attracted to the somatic influence of the women's experiences. Exploits expanded their hips, thickened their thighs, and protruded their buttocks. There was magic and muscle in those fleshy, full-figured curves—pregnant with mysticism.

Slender and lithe or stocky with script, words, words, words assisted in the shaping of the men and women of El-Nord.

With Ziko, his brown skin was still blanched of ink, and his corporeal frame lacked concrete definition. He was a scraggy, rawboned lot. Then, a few days ago happened, and muscle with clarity swelled, if just faint. Blotches of ink appeared on his arms and legs. Like a tadpole growing limbs, there appeared branches as the patches thinned. Ancient lettering burgeoned, and separate paths of script began its scribble on Ziko to fill him full with importance. But he'd give it all back if he could.

His eyes swept the empty lecture hall.

He would proudly wear deflated and undefined limbs in exchange for the resurrection of the people of his settlement, and most definitely his family. Experience would dictate otherwise.

Ziko laid down on the stage, looking up at the domed ceiling, feet still dangling over the side. He spoke, "I never thought myself a soldier." He was an El-Nordite, after all. The men were far from cowards, but might was best served plowing fields, or smashing a hammer onto a nail, or shaping orange-hot metal.

Ziko lifted up quickly, telling his fantasized audience, "You have to admit, war always makes for a good tale." He shrugged, but maintained a smile, acquiescing to what he believed his imagined audience would say. "Yes, I know. We're raised under the belief that blood-and-guts conflict is a great hindrance to stories. And, I admit, war tends to smother the continuance of tales, taking away life and future yarn to spin." He shook a finger toward the empty seats, one eye open. "But, you must also agree that war gives rise to as many stories as it snuffs out. Just look at the news we receive daily about the war front." Keeping his finger straight, he rotated his arm, and demanded, "Think of the legends and heroes who have been born of war." He jumped up, feet on the stage. "Think of how those stories always excited us as children, and equally frightened us."

Ziko began remembering those stories. He fast-forwarded through their telling, slowing down imagery at the more exciting points. He turned, head down, hand over mouth as he considered the possibility of being the first soldier of El-Nord had his name been pulled for the draft. There were many hunters, but no soldiers. Hands on his hips, Ziko then wondered, should he perish on the battlefield, who would recount his stories—should he have any at all to tell. What if Death had summoned him before a narrative of his exploits could be fully fleshed out? It didn't matter, and not just under current conditions. Ziko truly wanted nothing to do with the participation of conflict. He admitted, only to himself, and not his envisioned audience, that he was more enlivened by the stories themselves, the placing and time, the understanding that a battle was an actual event, something going on in real time or that had transpired long ago.

War itself started off humble. It wasn't always loud. The noisiest of wars often began with quiet disputes, mostly on taxes and land ownership. Those politics also intrigued Ziko. Perhaps that was his calling. He used to contemplate if he could be a statesman beyond simple representation. He never shared these thoughts among friends, and definitely not family, as that would've been a declaration to commit to something. He didn't even share it aloud among his private gathering of no one. But something might've been there within that thought. A true politician with a voice strong enough to silence all wars, bring peace to the world's many lands. A grand story to tell, reworking politics like puzzle pieces or totems on a game board. Ziko was able to rationalize this desire because the war was so far away. It was easier to negotiate the conflicts of war in a chamber rather than on a loud battlefield.

War was difficult to bargain with. That's why Ziko hid in various places with family and friends when conflict presented itself in El-Nord. When war crept into the corners he and others had taken cover in, uprooting and killing the people around him, Ziko found new places to hide with new survivors. This repeated until no one but Ziko was left, and he barricaded himself inside this lecture hall, covering the windows, securing the doors. He ventured out for food, gathered what he could, and stowed back inside before a lingering unit of war ensnared him.

Ziko stored his victuals in the lecture hall's basement. There he came across a small library. History was the predominant subject. He indulged himself in the origins of the world's war. He carefully perused the writings, noting any passage concerning the longwinded fight. He found the sage's robe he currently dressed himself in. He slipped it on, taking various reading material to the lecture hall's theater, placing a book upon the lectern and speaking to an invisible audience. This act led Ziko to believe that his calling could've extended beyond politics. Perhaps he was suited to be an historian, perhaps a lawyer, a journalist, or a professor.

When not too lost in would-be professions, and actually concentrating more on the writing, Ziko discovered great details on the machinations surrounding these wars. He'd deduced their history was recorded not just for keepsake, but they were intended to be warnings for future generations.

A lilac cloud filled the lecture hall. Ziko appeared unfazed by its presence. He didn't seem to notice it at all. Thicker and thicker it became until the glittering, lilac mist lifted. Ziko was again at the podium. He had on a different set of professor's robes, this one being the colors blue and gold instead of purple and red. Time had changed within the historical dream setting. It was weeks earlier now. Ziko was reading aloud the history of the current war, and all the conflict that it descended from. But he came to a pause, stopping his lecture when his eyes were drawn to an engrossing point about the war.

It seemed there were small sects that used the recorded history as strategy, studying the nuances of the turbulent times collectively known as the *Pious Wars*. They observed the mistakes of the wars' antagonists and aggressors, and vowed to not, "*...recreate the same follies,*" Ziko found himself reading aloud, face close to the page, and eyes squinted in observation. He ignored his invisible students and participants, reading further, keeping his words to himself. "*These individuals wrapped themselves up as peacemakers,*" he read, finger gliding underneath every written word. "*Prophets promising the coming of a hero or heroine with the power to rearrange the stars and keep our three-moon world of*

Pambunjila from falling victim to a bodement etched on a wall long ago." Looking away from the page, Ziko spoke, *"When were such lessons to be given to us as students?"* Upon this reading, Ziko considered that the walls of El-Nord influenced too much of its culture.

He continued his read:

The first Eke Woli, or rather false prophet, was named Huls Kuni. He was a wealthy man who ordained himself a seer, declaring to be addressed as Dimbwi.

Ziko was familiar with this part of the war's telling, pieces of its origins.

Huls Kuni used family monies to create an extravagant palace designed as a replica of a star configuration worshipped by his culture. Though there was beauty to his palace, inside and out, many remarked that it looked much like a scorpion, an oddly curved tower acting as a tail. But once these quiet ramblings made their way back to Dimbwi Kuni, he declared it was not purposeful, laughing it off as only his charm could do.

At age thirty-six, six years after his palace was constructed, Dimbwi claimed to have had a vision that sent him on a pilgrimage. He returned with an apprentice, a man just as charismatic, in his late twenties, and named Abub Tetif. Dimbwi Kuni titled him the Xiddig-Akoni, or Star Hero. The world's leaders saw them as nothing more than a high-class cult, even when they took in many followers. The House of Dimbwi could not be ignored when the prominent kingdom Xamarku embraced them and their philosophy to change the stars, and with it, the fate of our three-moon world of Pambunjila.

With the world leaders already at odds on the interpretation of a prophecy, war was inevitable. The first conflict was only six years long. The fighting was contained, but woe unto the village, town, or city that its tornado passed through. Kingdoms burned in its wake. In the final year of that first war, Huls Kuni was branded a heretic. Eke Woli the people called him, a false prophet. Spies uncovered terrible acts of debauchery within the walls of his palace. Acts of human sacrifice were committed, leading to the extraction of people's incants and conjures. All the power he plucked from his fervent followers was stitched into Abub Tetif, who in the last year of conflict was seen more as a false messiah than hero. The majority branded him Eke Almas, and as kingdoms fell, the people of Pambunjila focused the war on him and his master. Many continued to embrace the pair. Their army was called 'arjai'.

Six years long, many believed the war was the prophecy fulfilled. But its foreboding etch did not fade from the prophetic wall. Fear lingered, though dim. But its light, soft presence was enough for new Eke Wolis and Eke Almas to take advantage of and manipulate. Each new diabolical duo rose to power with keener ways of seduction, and the battles became bloodier, louder. Some pairs were strictly male or strictly female. A few were mixed-gendered, married under a self-perceived divine right.

Twenty and seven generations lived through the tumultuous Pious Wars, though the wars were not in succession. Pauses filled with peace and prosperity were well received. Hundreds of years passed with no signs of a zealot pair bent on ushering in destruction through the promise of rearranging the fates. And like the fifteen pairs that came before them, the contemporary, silk-tongued despots have clouded the world in a fog so blinding and thick with sanguinary war, all are now declaring the end is near. Once again, zealotry has become the order of the day. But how has this all repeated? With all our understanding, how does this continue to come about? Within these pages I will document a close look at all fifteen killer pairs of the world and present a profound history of evil.

The book was self-published and authored by a woman named Khalfuray. Ziko knew of her. She was a middle-aged seamstress, always dressed in her craft and the finest jewelry cut and fashioned by her younger brother. He defended his sister against accusations of being a zealot in her own right. People considered that Khalfuray was too focused on the war and its history, something the walled settlements often avoided. Mentions of the war were small when it came to delivered news. And the news was mostly received as to make sure the war had not inched its way toward El-Ham. Very little of the war was taught in schools.

Ziko absorbed the information he read like a meal, his eyes devouring every syllabic morsel. His physique didn't fill with experience or ink, as all this was a vicarious journey through history. But Ziko was well aware that the knowledge of the past would aid him in the present and the future. He often said a prayer to Khalfuray, honoring the knowledge she'd left behind. He was grateful. Now he had a better understanding, knowing precisely why that despite their opposition against aiding the war, his home of El-Nord, like all the other walled settlements of El-Ham, felt a sense of pride when support in the war helped turn the tides, and even led to a brief pause in battle.

Until the day a long and scaly, black cloud moved across the sky, and the devoured reanimated bodies of men and women fell from its maw.

Ziko remembered, and his memory produced a shimmering, lilac mist. Time turned backwards. The scene changed. Ziko played dice in an alley, assisting his younger brother in dodging school. He heard rumbling from above. He searched the sky for rain clouds but saw none. His brother commented that it was unusual for thunder to be heard on such a clear day. But it wasn't thunder at all. It was a creature's roar that reverberated from above. The sky beast's holler rolled through the air in a low growl. The unassuming citizens of the El-Ham settlements paid the soft rumble no mind, passing it off as distant thunder as they continued their daily routines. Ziko and the company he and his brother kept were much the same.

Then its shadow appeared. It was unlike the shadows cast by the intertwined foliage or a moving cloud. It encroached, stretching long and wide like a black, ethereal blanket. A rough wind was its harbinger, and when the long stretch of cloud didn't give, a curious sentry standing guard in a tower investigated the oddity. He placed a violet crystal to his eye, increasing his vision's depth and bringing what was far away close.

The massive, black cloud disappeared in a swift motion.

The citizens noticed, and then it became more than just a probing sentry holding a crystal-covered eye to the sky above. A crowd gathered to focus their vision to spy the enormous creature. And as if it didn't want to disappoint its viewing audience, the black cloud returned.

The creature's reprise was more concrete in appearance. It had a long serpentine body, scales crisscrossing one another like organic platemail. The creature possessed a round head and angled, red slits for eyes. Its nostrils were much the same, fire and smoke leaking from them. Thin strands of soft, braided flesh ran along its head like a beard and mustache. Pointed ears flapped like the wings of a bat. An ever menacing thin, red smile blistered against its pitch-colored flesh.

It dipped its large body beneath the foliage, crushing branches and scattering leaves and loose vines. The black creature swooped close to the walls of one settlement. Its massive frame slammed into a tower, sending debris in all directions, and killing two sentries posted inside. It rose back into the air, dived down again, coming from the opposite direction. Thick, forest trees bent or broke as the colossal serpent's elevated slither bore through the woods. It hammered through the walls of the El-Roy settlement and opened its mouth. Its lower jaw dug into the El-Roy streets, ingesting earth and swallowing a crowd of citizens as they attempted to seek hiding. Mouth closed, the serpent returned to the sky.

The giant, black snake descended again, distance muddling the observation of its speed. It appeared slow and sluggish. But when it dug into the woods again, it was loud and fast. It crashed through another settlement's walls, scooping up another heavy meal of screaming, scattering citizens.

Up into the sky it went, leaving behind debris, fire and empty streets.

Settlements alerted to the tumult provided a new dish for the black serpent. Citizens filled the streets, hearing the cries and chaos from the neighboring walled towns. Guards took their stance, spears and bows at the ready. Sword and dagger strapped to their sides. The captains of the guardsmen ordered citizens inside. Some listened to the orders. Others fed their curiosity and stayed. They were gobbled up along with the captains and guards.

El-Nord had time to prepare, little as it was. They wasted no minute. Citizens locked themselves indoors, staying low. Ziko was already home with his brother and some friends. His father and mother were stranded at their jobs.

The El-Nord guards waited in formation, weapons at the ready. Two of six catapults were in position and prepared to fire when the shadow returned. But darkness swept over the day, and no one was able to move. Even the trees leaning on a threatening bend paused before a final snap sent them crashing to the forest floor.

Herald as the serpent's shadow was, his physical form was not too far behind. He climbed into the sky, and then turned for a violent descent. The enormous creature opened its mouth, seemingly to devour the guards volleying arrows and spears in its directions, or the few citizens remaining on the street arrested by fear and awe. Most expected a deluge of fire to spill from the serpent, and they said a prayer before their lives were extinguished by flame. The beast instead vomited the citizens it earlier devoured.

They were not dead, nor were they alive. They were in between, and they were this creature's army. Tightly wound, ash-colored chains sculpted from the ink of the serpent's stomach enzymes squeezed their foreheads, spiraled down their neck, and ran along their arms. Fresh tattoos of chain and submission concealed words and experience. The chains gobbled up the ink, became solid, and were so compressed against the flesh that a grotesque, gray and green color bubbled up beneath the surface of the victim's dark skin and washed away their natural colors. A metal implement, forged from the stomach ink, was fastened in their hands, arrow-like in design with a triangular tail at both its front and back ends. Sitting atop the tail end was the complex design of a man with his arms crossed. The triangular, wing-like pattern resting at the front end had, at the tip of its shape, a long, sharp stretch of metal.

Extending from the victims' heads, lodged deep through their skulls, was the same tool acting as an antenna. There was a subtle vibration to the slender, arrow-like device as it received orders to kill or alchemize through the tips of their needles forged from their serpentine leader's blood and stomach ink.

Family and friends, neighbor and fellow citizen no longer existed. The beast was now their kin and nation. Statesmen no longer advocated for the people. Guards became turncoats through digestive means. This was the *mzigo*, the burdened. Local mythology referred to creatures such as these as *dubwana*. Alchemy weighed heavy like the chains that ensnared them. The refined shape of men and the curvaceous thickness of the women showed they were full with experience, and burden was a part of it. Now, they were fat with grief and on command to transmute the weight of troubles into the refrain of the living. Even their teeth were sharp, laced with metal from the giant, black serpent's blood and enzymes.

Some mzigo landed inside El-Nord's walls, crashing against the street but remaining intact. Their rise to their feet was slow after impact, casting an aura of intimidation as their eyes locked onto their living victims. They waited for the serpent's inaudible command to shiver their needles and murmur into their punctured brains orders to stir into violent action. The beast also let it be known through a jarring holler, *"I am Chilombo-Wroch!"* His enormous voice reverberated waves of heat and pressure, causing many to tumble to the ground with his announcement. *"I am the Sky Demon of Lies summoned for war! I devour your living and set them upon you to join my ranks or die!"*

Chilombo-Wroch soared over the other settlements. He brought violent winds with his movement and holler, knocking guards and townspeople to the streets. His mouth opened, and he again regurgitated more citizens he'd earlier consumed, their bodies chained and twisted from being digested, and their minds empty of all independent thought, save a set of silently transmitted commands: feast upon the living, stab them, and strengthen the mzigo army.

The people of the El-Ham settlements were not the only occupants stored inside the beast. Chilombo-Wroch had traveled far. He'd already devoured so much in his path, consumed many for an army. Here he vomited them to join the battle, ingested men and women who had succumb to the wretched turn the serpent's cursed belly bestowed.

Ziko recalled the decaying, chain-laced bodies creeping by or smacking on the window, scraping or stabbing the doors with their needles. He shushed his younger brother and his friends, making them duck low. The younger kids' nerves got the better of them, though. Their bodies trembled, their teeth rattled, adding to the quiver in their voices. Adding to the children's nervous clatter, the regurgitated men and women demanded entrance through unintelligible, guttural groans. Their lamenting requests came in all directions. From every house to outside the settlement gates. Nothing as civil or pedestrian as words were heard coming from the other side of the town's enforced, wooden gate. What seeped through the air, snarling and mocking the citizens and the warriors whose duty it was to guard them, was a disturbing, crinkled cluster of sounds. They scraped and clawed at the wood, gargling and hissing like sick animals. The sounds were clumped like a beehive as thousands gathered to moan unintelligible wails.

A crash through the gate with his giant, serpentine frame permitted the mzigo entrance. Town guards and citizens were overwhelmed, and not just in the settlement of El-Nord. What Chilombo-Wroch's army could not gouge or bite into and transmute, the Sky Demon of Lies did so himself. It was nothing for him to consume human flesh, screams and all. Alchemy took place in his belly, transmuting life into the chained and obedient, discolored soldier. Then his human meals traveled back up his throat, spat back into the world, undead, but with no less a purpose.

Ziko's memory of the following events was blurred and fractured, but they were relived through puffs of lilac smoke transitions that were accompanied by headaches. The start was solid enough to recall. He remembered glass breaking from a window; his brother's friend surrounded by green- and gray-skinned, decaying hands that stabbed his flesh with long, metal needles. Ragged mzigo heads pushed through, almost fighting one another to pull the sixteen-year-old into their ranks. The teenage boy, named Leck, cried a high-pitched howl, sounding as if his soul was making a hurried exit to escape the pain hacking into him. Ziko and the remaining teenage boys were taken aback, staring, listening to the screams that sounded like the electrical hiss of a lightning strike. Leck's shriek quieted into a muffled crackle as blood flooded his airway and gurgled up from his lungs to his throat. His eyes rolled back into his head, and then as quick as the mzigo had gathered around him, stabbing and groping, they let go.

Leck's eyes opened, their color shifted from brown to pale. Life hadn't been extinguished from them, but they were empty just the same. His eyes bent as he looked aimlessly at his friends. His skin rippled as if his flesh cooked in a fire. He bled, but it wasn't blood that seeped through. It was a dark-green, foul-smelling substance that twisted into chains, wrapped around his arms and forehead. The shackles tightened around his appendages, shifting his dark brown to a mix of gray and green patches. Ink bled from his palms and turned solid for him to grip the needle that was fashioned from possession. The transformation was fast. Leck limped toward Ziko and the others, hissing and hacking up unintelligible sounds, stabbing the air with wild swings.

The sight fragmented Ziko's vision, and his memory of following events echoed in a rupture as a headache crept in. He remembered suggesting to his brother, *"To our pa-tah's laboratory! Now! He'll have something to fight them. We'll find ma-mat next. We'll fight our way to her!"* He tugged at his brother who was like stone. His gaze captured by the sight of his friend's transformed figure limping toward them, drooling the blood that had flooded his throat, and determined to transmute his peers just the same.

"Rallah!" yelled Ziko to wake his brother.

Nothing happened.

Ziko's memory jumped. He and Rallah were running through the streets. Screams filled the air. No dust or dirt was kicked up to add to the confusion. The atrocity of mzigo stabbing and transmuting the living was clear for the eyes to view without pollution. A few houses bathed in fire, but the flame and smoke swirled upward, never contaminating the grotesque visuals. Chilombo-Wroch's long, black shadow swooped over the area like a pall, delivering armadas of mzigo with every pass.

Ziko recollected on a moment that occurred before running from the house. Leck had converted a friend attempting an incant on him. The youth was new to conjure, and the cast had no effect. Rallah woke from his catatonic stare, following several tugs from Ziko.

Outside.

More of Rallah's friends would succumb to the mzigo creatures, first consumed by the scenes of horror surrounding them.

Inside pa-tah's lab.

They found their father dead among a pile of men and women. A hole punctured his temple. His body reclaimed its natural, dark shade, bleeding over the rotten, green patches that once possessed him and transmuted him to a mzigo for a short few moments. A foul-smelling, dark-green fluid pooled under him. Gone were his chains.

Ziko covered his brother's eyes. He could feel Rallah trembling, his younger brother rattled by anger and sorrow.

Their father's fellow alchemist, Lurahn, confessed to the killing. *"Strike their heads!"* she asserted. *"No special powders. No incants or conjures needed. Strike their heads! Knock their needles further into their brains!"* Ziko swiped a book filled with alchemical recipes, despite being instructed on the simplicity of slaying the mzigo.

Another alchemist was found, and a blacksmith named Gillow.

Ziko and Rallah spied their mother in the streets, alchemized to mzigo. Rallah's eyes watered. His lip quivered as he watched his mother limp and snarl among a pack of turned citizens. Her skin's ebony luster was now choked by chain to a rotten and crinkled, absinthe green.

Time jumped, broken by mere seconds, separated by a lilac flash and a crack in vision. Rallah was no longer at Ziko's side. He was by their mother's, trying to embrace her, and pleading for her to wake up. She embraced him, bending low, digging her teeth into his neck and dragging him toward her pack for them to make a stab to his body, sacrificing life to initiate into the transmuted.

Ziko wanted to scream, but instead turned away, inhaling deep to hold back tears, and choke down his choler. His vision switched between the chaos in front of him and at his sides to the frightening images of his transmuted mother and her newfound family feeding on and stabbing his brother.

Fractured memories whipped him. Events went missing, but still moved to where he stood now, in the lecture hall, staring at the lectern and the gleaming object placed upon it. Ziko recalled being hit by a mountain of muscle. It was Gillow the blacksmith, crashing into him, doubling back in pain. Gillow's leg had been harpooned by a mzigo woman's needle. Gillow's weight knocked Ziko off balance, but saved him from an attacking mzigo. The creature's grasp encircled Gillow instead, stabbing him in the chest for sure transformation. Ziko recovered, skipping on one foot and catching his balance.

The blacksmith's large, hefty arm reached out for Ziko as he passed. His thick fingers clutched Ziko's shoulders and dragged him back. Gillow screamed, bites and stabs already beginning to hex his person. Ziko faced Gillow, his feet skittering forward, bringing him closer to the alchemizing blacksmith and the monsters. The blacksmith's skin dissolved of its natural, dark gloss. The mzigo curse coursed through him. Chains compressed around his forehead and arms. Natural color siphoned from his flesh and eyes.

Gillow's grip dug into Ziko's shoulder. A needle filled his hand, allowing Ziko space. Gillow lost his grip, making an unintended swipe at Ziko. The weapon didn't puncture skin, but the tip scraped his leather tunic. Gillow reached up and caught Ziko with his other hand. Ziko looked down and glimpsed the thick flesh of Gillow's broad fingers shriveling. The mzigo swarming and stabbing the blacksmith backed away as his transformation was complete. They waited, snarling and impatient, for mzigo-Gillow to drag Ziko to them. But Ziko kept his ground, digging his feet in. Gillow's might dampened with his transformation, withered as his flesh.

The transformed blacksmith opened his mouth, ready to take a first bite. He cocked his arm back to make a fatal stab. Other mzigo crowded around Ziko. Then it started raining. Not condensation falling from oversaturated clouds. It was arrows tossed from remaining guards and citizens who took up arms. The tips found their marks, knocking into the creatures' heads. Their human forms returned, resting in peace.

Ziko reached for the large hammer clipped to Gillow's belt. His hands scrapped against the heavy, metal head, causing the instrument to swing back and forth. A mzigo snapped at his right. Its bite only took air, teeth cracking together. Ziko grabbed under the monster's chin and brought it forward, using it as a shield. Gillow stabbed the mzigo in the back, breaking through spine and stomach, barely missing Ziko. Another was on the left. He moved Gillow's ragged arm toward the mzigo's mouth, and the creature broke its teeth biting into the blacksmith's forearm, hitting metal chain wrapped around it. Dark green ooze gushed from the putrid appendage. Mzigo-Gillow howled. He bent forward, grip loosened on Ziko's shoulder. The blacksmith's hammer swung toward Ziko, and he caught the mighty tool and ripped it from Gillow's belt. He raised the hammer, holding the hilt with two hands, and smacked it against the end of the needle burrowed in Gillow's head. The blacksmith stiffened, but life still existed in him. Ziko swung the hammer again, knocking the heavy head against Gillow's temple.

The memory of that incident was very clear for Ziko. He wore the recollection like a piece of clothing. Almost everything else came as a feeling or a fleeting picture with cracks in it, accompanied by flashes of a single moment leading not to the next but somewhere further down the timeline of this terrible experience, barely there to contemplate.

But, Ziko remembered killing Gillow. He felt and heard the crack of the man's skull. The head of the hammer, with Ziko's force, drove the fragments of skull deeper into the blacksmith's brain. The inaugural hard crack gave way to mush, and the jolt of the strike softened to a push, as if Ziko had taken a swing at a pile of mud.

It was the immediate limpness of Gillow's body that Ziko remembered the most. He felt the man's strength disappear. It had already been sapped when he succumbed to the mzigo hex. Life's sudden departure, the spark flickering from existence was so quick to blow out. Ziko's forearms rattled like his nerves. Not even the reemergence of Gillow's natural features, his body free from the curse, could reassure Ziko that something right had been committed.

Ziko was far from naïve. He didn't stay put to ponder the life he'd snuffed out. Lingering meant he would eventually be meandering aimless with a violent purpose to commit crimes under unnatural alchemy. He snapped out of his sudden shock, and he began the fight for flight. He swung the procured hammer left and right, dropping mzigo after mzigo, cracking their skulls open and felling them. One strike sapped the wind from Ziko. The crafting tool's heaviness challenged his vigor. He huffed with each swing. The hammer's bulk appeared to gain weight. A mzigo stumbled toward Ziko, mouth open, hissing and readying itself to tear into Ziko's arm. Ziko shoved the hammer's hilt into the mzigo's mouth, let go of the heavy weapon, and kicked the creature away from him. The mzigo tumbled into a swarm of its own, causing the lot to topple over one another. Ziko took the moment to duck down, crawl through another flock of mzigo, and rise in open space. He was standing on a main street. People joined him.

Fractures in memory occurred again, and his recollection found him hiding in a house. It was night, and he barely knew the people surrounding him. There were no more than twelve among them. They were exhausted, terrified and sad. They would've been hungry too, but the dizzying mesh of emotions muted their stomachs' stirs for notice.

The mzigo found them an hour before dawn. They ran and found another hiding place at an inn. There were now eight of them. After barricading themselves, believing they were secure, they found food and attended to their crying bellies.

Rest was minimal. They were found again and again.

A jump in memory, and only Ziko remained. He lived in what used to be a miner's house. He was alone, but he had a bed to sleep on and a sack filled with food to keep his hunger at bay. Rest was short lived again. The winds of Chilombo-Wroch shook the walls and shattered the windows half a day into Ziko's stay. The noise steered a mzigo horde toward the miner's dwelling. He smelled to them, as they smelled to him. Their rotted limbs, fit with needles in their grip, reached through the broken windows. Their direful wails flooded the house, a chorus of horror.

Ziko had no weapon. He never could seem to keep one. He'd lost the hammer, swords, and spiked maces. He'd even used an arrow without the bow. It snapped in two after he'd stabbed a mzigo in the head. Now that weapon was gone too.

The door rattled. Mzigo gathered on the other side, their huddled horde pushing against the already damaged hinges. Ziko watched the door give way, its desperate hold to its hinges creaking. Its wooden frame bent, beginning to splinter.

Ziko remembered the strangeness of it all. Mzigo were at the windows and the door. Their snarls and wails reached out toward him no different than their horde of arms stretched through the windows, making empty stabs at him with their needles. But it wasn't the monsters. It was not being the lone survivor of the people he hid with, his family, and perhaps the settlement of El-Nord as a whole.

No.

Ziko remembered the sense of calm. Mzigo at the door. Mzigo at the windows. The danger was unimaginable and inescapable. But fear could find no place to rest in Ziko's person. It wasn't an acceptance to a possible fate, but a profound knowing this was not the end.

But how? he asked himself, looking around.

The door separated from its hinges and crashed to the floor. Ziko flinched. Mzigo dammed the entrance with their bodies, wriggling against one another mindless and caught in a struggle to enter. Ziko moved a heavy table in their direction, flipping it on its side and creating another obstacle for the monsters. Ziko knew he had little time. The mzigo's self-made dam would eventually break, and the house would be overtaken. The ones at the window he considered no matter.

Ziko spied the chimney as an escape. It could at least be a place to crawl up into. The mzigo were aimless if should there be no smell of the living to follow. He considered the ash and cooled cinder of the fireplace would cast a shadow over his alluring aroma. They didn't duck down in search of prey, search up nooks, or open doors with the use of a knob. Even if they'd made it into the house, with Ziko gone, and no body to join their ranks, they would tire and resume an aimless walk out the door, into open ground. He needed first to clear the fireplace of wood, make it easier for him to scurry up the chimney. The action would also kick up more dust and ash to cover his scent.

But how long could he wait? How long before they wandered away from the house?

Ziko took a step toward the fireplace.

The pulse of mzigo squirming through their doorway clog increased. The monsters at the outer rim of the blockade slipped further inside, their decomposed flesh loosening against the entrance's sides. Their chains ripped into the wood, splintering the doorframe.

And then the dam broke.

Ziko remembered falling back, startled by the deluge. The rush of mzigo made it appear as if their wails increased, filled more with a deep, guttural bass in their haunting cries. The mzigo at the window joined the chorus. Ziko was terrified, but he didn't rush any quicker to empty the stacked wood from the fireplace. Instead he backed away from the hearth, appendages scrambling along the ground like spider legs. He reached for a poker, but his right hand snatched another object. It was a hammer-pick, blunt on one side, sharp on the reverse. Four mzigo stood over Ziko. He rolled to his left as they bent down to stab or bite him. Standing, hammer-pick gripped hard in his hands. His stance, ready to strike his would-be transmuters. Ziko smirked as he remembered what he'd said under his breath a moment before felling the monsters. *"I have alchemy for you as well."* And then he removed the curse from them, boring the sharp end of his hammer-pick into their skulls. He didn't discriminate. Man. Woman. Child. He felt as if he was a priest performing an exorcism as he relieved them of their haunts.

He liked the feel of the hammer-pick. The tool was light, easy to handle and keep in his grip. Ziko felt a rush when swinging it. This hammer-pick was like any warrior's weapon. His final strike put strategy in his head. Ziko looked over his shoulder in time to duck away from a mzigo swiping at him with a needle. He swerved around the creature and struck it in the back of the skull. He rolled to his right near a wooden seat where his sack lay. Ziko snatched his sack while jumping up from his roll. He flung the straps around his shoulders in the same swift motion, and then came face-to-face with a swarm of mzigo. He stepped back as one charged to strike. Pivoting right, he smacked the creature with the blunt side of his hammer-pick. Ziko jumped over the body, onto a wooden bench. The other mzigo followed him, gurgling hisses at him, reaching out with putrid, chained palms or swiping at air hoping to scratch his flesh.

Ziko jumped down from the bench and kicked it forward. Two mzigo tripped over the barrier, and Ziko broke their skulls while they were down. He was tempted to pull free a mzigo's needle, but he thought better of the action and stayed his hand. He instead grabbed a mzigo woman's chained, green forearm. His hold slipped on a greenish liquid coating the chains and loose flesh. Ziko still managed to drag the mzigo nearer to him, the creature almost looking pleased that she was closer to her prey. But Ziko stabbed her forehead with the pick side of his weapon. Her eyes rolled up into her head. Ziko let go of her, and her body, while changing back to its natural hue, slumped over the bench. He saw her as she was, and the sight of her killed body was more gripping than any mzigo reaching out for him.

It was easy to recall this particular fight and all its emotions. The memory wasn't as fractured as the others concerning Chilombo-Wroch's wrath. But it wasn't entirely clear either. The most concrete aspect of the memory was the weightless feeling that overcame him. He tossed his slender frame around, twirling through acrobatic routines, dodging mzigo in the tight quarters. Nothing in Ziko's movements flared theatrical, such as a high backflip, or a tuck forward into a roll. It was simply the ease in which he dodged and pirouetted around the monsters, and the heavy strength he felt when he struck them with his hammer-pick.

Ziko thinned the mzigo herd inside the miner's house. The greatest difficulty was that none of them would back away. They just kept coming, mindless and with the intent to infect him with their hex. But he carved his way to victory, dodging their advances, hacking and cracking skulls. Surrounded by the life he'd taken and souls he'd spared from burden, Ziko took a moment to look around. The mzigo at the window didn't retract their bodies and parade around the house to confront him. He rushed to lather himself with ash and soot from the chimney, erasing his living odor.

Ziko crept outside. The streets were far from empty. Mzigo wandered, grunting while gripping their needles to find a victim to strike and recruit. Ziko avoided them, sneaking from one turned over carriage to another, hiding at the corner of houses, even jumping into a tree to avoid a mzigo procession marching his way. None of the creatures noticed him by sight or scent.

Ziko searched the sky while in the tree. It was cloudy, with no sign of Chilombo-Wroch. No wind or shadow previewing the serpent's presence. Ziko didn't want to stay too long in the tree. He understood that if the mzigo sensed him, they would gather around and trap him up in the branches. Ziko panned the mzigo-infested streets. He deduced a pattern to their cluster. He climbed higher, stopped after scaling a few more branches above, and then looked out. His suspicions were confirmed. The mzigo kept at the edges of the domed lecture hall, never approaching closer than a ten-meter perimeter of the building. Ziko perceived the pattern as so deliberate that he concluded that an unknown force must've been at play. *Someone casts an incant to keep the monsters at a distance,* he remembered thinking to himself while up in that tree. *The cluster is thick, but that hall is my sanctuary. And there will be more El-Nordites huddled there.*

Lambent flashes mixed with bursts of lilac dust. Ziko was down from the tree, his feet shuffling quick and light to maintain silence. He ducked around corners, dived into alleys. Each turn brought Ziko in confrontation with a small pack of mzigo. Ziko bested the creatures with his hammer-pick, carving his way to the domed lecture hall at the center of town.

His memory cracked. A lilac spark of light erupted into glittering cloud. Ziko stood within the lecture hall's safe perimeter. He watched the mzigo swarm around the outskirts. The monsters strolled by him, paying him no mention. He walked around the lecture hall, keeping within the safe area. He noticed orange crystals the girth of an adult's fist placed at the safe area's edge. There were four in total, glowing softly. Ziko didn't touch the crystals, correctly crediting them with keeping the mzigo at a distance.

Ziko's memory from this point was more pristine and streamlined. He was surprised to find no one inside the lecture hall. He searched every room, hammer-pick gripped tight, weapon at the ready to strike any wandering mzigo that found its way into the lecture hall. Nothing living or transformed was inside. Ziko discovered foodstuffs, books on history, abandoned professor robes, a working kitchen and running water for a bath. All that, but not a single soul that could be found. No one. Not even a stray mzigo.

Ziko climbed up a ladder, opening a hatch at the top and popping through the domed roof to see out into El-Nord's ruination. He observed the aimless mzigo and concluded that among them must be the person who'd laid down the crystals and made this his or her home. Perhaps they wandered out to find more supplies or others, and then tragically joined the ranks of the alchemized.

"Thank you," Ziko remembered saying to the wandering transmuted. Then he climbed back down, closing the hatch. The next thing he recalled was finding a room with a cot. He lay down, but as tired as he was, a restless sensation kept him from sleep. He placed his hand on his right bicep, exhaling the past days' events in a single huff.

He felt the swell and hardened reshape of experience in his muscle.

A mystical curvature that was far different from being shaped only by physical activity.

Ziko couldn't sleep after that. The person who'd occupied the lecture hall before him made a sacrifice, even if unintentional. From the refinement of his physique, to the thought of the mysterious domed lecture hall, it all petitioned Ziko to remain awake. Ziko jumped up and slapped his belly. *"I'm about to earn my guts!"* he declared. He grinned as he recollected the bold announcement. *"The foodstuff can't last forever,"* he continued. *"There's a good month's worth,"* he said pacing. *"But then what? And what happens to my sanity when all that's here is me? Lucidity and food will run out. I can't live here forever. And the outside world must know the story of El-Nord and the surrounding settlements."* He spun around, hand cupping his scruffy chin. *"What of the capital? Our Regional Governor? Our Chieftess? What is their fate?"* Ziko rummaged through his sack and pulled out the alchemy book he swiped from his father's laboratory. He snatched up his hammer-pick and left the room. He traveled through various, winding corridors with the book tucked under his arm and the hammer-pick firmly in his grip. His journey stopped at the door to the main lecture hall.

Ziko opened the door and stepped into the unlit room. He waved his hand, exercising one of the few incants he could perform. The wicks on the candles positioned around the room brightened with flame. He walked down to the stage, and then up the stairs leading onto it. He set the hammer-pick on the lectern and opened the book in his hands. *"I will build a weapon,"* he said aloud. *"I will enhance this hammer-pick."* Then he patted his slightly swelled muscle and declared, *""I will be the hero of El-Nord whether history and all the people she births remembers me or not."*

Ziko skimmed possibilities on what incants he could lace the hammer with. It was within that moment where his story became inked into history and on his flesh. He would discover experience's faint signature when taking a wash later. He didn't care should history forget him, however. That would be an added spice to his story, though his exploits would prove unforgettable by heirs to the larger narrative. Ziko's part would be remembered the only way a legend could be: through exaggeration. It would not be his triumphant accomplishments or wondrous skills that would be aggrandized as his story passed from generation to generation. Those would be lost to time, purposefully substituted with entirely different folktales. The reason? All desired to add their creative yarn to the weapon forged by the young man that time would remember only as *The Alchemist with a Hammer.*

And here was the weapon of focus.

This was what philosophers called 'the sublime moment'. This was the border where history blurred into legend, and the tradition of storytellers became alchemists in their own right. For it was not a hammer wielded by Ziko Yswil. It was truthfully a hammer-pick. Not a significant detail, just the truthful one.

Ziko recalled his story on how he blessed his hammer-pick, following instructions from the book on alchemy. He ventured out, fighting his way outside the settlement, scavenging for ingredients. He killed a large fire beetle out in the rainforest, extracting its fire sacks from its pincers, which he kept to add a bleeding effect. That was day one of the hunt, and with mzigo dawdling through the woods, Ziko stayed no longer than needed. He claimed the next two elements of his design on his second hunt: the white feather of a gray wind-bird and a crushed ice stone, which was always cold no matter what temperature it was placed in. He almost met his end on his return, but he fought his way back to the lecture hall, slipping into the enchanted perimeter exhausted from skirmishes. He sought a fourth ingredient, an additive for a poisonous effect. But, after his tiring ordeal fighting his way through mzigo, he let it go.

Ziko ate and slept first. When he rose, he went to work, calling upon his father's spirit to guide his hands. He mashed and blended together the elements he'd hunted down, boiling the contents under the proper heat. He used the flame incant he had knowledge of to strengthen the fire to cook the elements. Finished, he anointed the head of the hammer-pick with the incanted oil. The fire beetle's liquefied pincers and fire sacks imbued the tool with a burning strike. The gray wind-bird's feather component blessed the hammer-pick to project a strong wave and current of air. The final constituent, the crushed ice stone, enchanted the hammer-pick with a chilling ice attack.

Ziko tested his new, alchemized weapon. It now functioned like a magic wand as well as an instrument designed for close-ranged melee.

Alchemy touched him too. Nimble, but with muscle, his body sculpted into graceful definition. It was a subtle change, but Ziko felt his growth spurt, accompanied by some emotional growing pains. Experience notarized his composition with a conjure of ancient ink on his person. The words were not quite spelled out, but Ziko wouldn't have been able to read them, anyway. The pathways to form ancient script had been plotted and marked, but not fully constructed.

When Ziko wasn't practicing the hammer-pick's newfound powers, he was studying the *Pious Wars* history. Both the reading and the use of his weapon drained him. Ziko's headaches became more frequent after wielding the newly forged hammer-pick, channeling magic. It was something his body wasn't accustomed to, and the maturing, magic shift of his anatomy was not expanded enough to balance the conjure of magic conducted through him. His story was still in its first chapters.

So, this was his current standing. Rations were low. The presence of mzigo were thick. His incanted weapon had slain many, but more seem to fill in their ranks. Weighing on him as well was the increased use of his incant-induced hammer-pick, which made his head throb more for the effort. Ziko pondered his weapon's use on the mzigo. The hammer-pick's mystical properties no longer renewed the bodies of the transmuted victims. Now their corporeal forms turned to dust, and their spirits were set free, climbing to the sky as ghostly light cast upon the deformed, demonic-alchemized bodies. The release of spirit might be proving too much for Ziko. He was neither alchemist nor true conjurer, and he knew too little of incants to call himself an incanter.

Ziko retired from the auditorium, taking with him his magical hammer-pick, clipped to his belt. Remaining robed, Ziko made his way to the ladder leading to the roof. Through the hatch, he let the afternoon sun catch his face, bathing in its natural light for a moment. He climbed onto the roof, careful of his balance. He left the hatch open, stooped down next to the opening, and observed the roaming mzigo. His eyes moved from the undead monsters to the sky, looking for any hint of the foul serpent responsible for the wandering dead. He saw nothing. Perhaps Chilombo-Wroch moved on. Ziko's expression fell. There was nothing left for the sky demon to conquer, and therefore no giant monster for Ziko to slay and carve his name into history.

This is my story, he determined. *I am the last of El-Ham.*

Ziko continued thinking on everything. His eyes welled with tears, and he considered his body's reaction peculiar. He wasn't sad, at least not moved-to-tears, or so he believed. No, he was certain. That was a bit extreme for his state of mind. But, nonetheless, here were salty streams moving down his cheek. He wiped them away, and as he touched his cheeks he felt his head pulsing at the temples. He rubbed the side of his forehead, but the stirring drumbeat palpitating in his head didn't withdraw. It grew, and Ziko grit his teeth.

He decided to return inside, get rest on a bed. The rhythmic thud curbed while climbing down, but a tightening impression wrapped around his head. Ziko became dizzy, his footing slipped as he positioned himself on the ladder. He remained steady enough to keep his balance and not fall to his death below. Ziko took his time on the ladder. One foot down, and then the next. He repeated from rung to rung. It occurred to him the difficulties of simple actions once under duress. Ziko's fingers trembled and perspired. He feared his grip would loosen, sending him tumbling down to the hard floor beneath him. He gave thanks when he neared the ladder's end. He hopped off and fell against the wall, trying to hold himself up. His head fell forward, as though a heavy weight was tied to his forehead. He tried straightening his posture, pushing himself off the wall, but the invisible monster called gravity squeezed his head and tugged him backward. He slammed against the wall. His knees trembled, buckled, and he dropped to one of them. He palmed the wall and floor, trying to resist the force that weighed him down and compressed the top and sides of his head.

There then came a brief pause in Ziko's suffering. It was preceded by a hollow, icy noise that sounded like someone gasping for air. Ziko's headache broke, leaving behind small remnants of discomfort. The icy gasp popped too, and a feminine voice echoed, *"Hear me, Conjurer!"* Ziko flinched, his senses wobbled with his body being unsteady. He managed to stand, using the wall as a crutch. He struggled to lift his head, and then he looked in either direction. At first his eyes were wide, and then he squinted to peer into the dark hallway. His headache reemerged, slamming into him like Chilombo-Wroch crashing through the settlement walls. The pain dispersed again, combined with the icy wheeze that popped. The feminine voice echoed, words mashed together, *"Isenseyourmagic!"*

Ziko buckled again. He felt warm blood funnel from his nose, snake down his upper lip, and dribble onto the back of his hand. Ziko wheezed. Exhaling allowed him to relax. He sat on the floor, back against the wall. He wanted to hear her voice again, but he knew at what cost that would bring. Headaches. Body trembling. Nosebleed. He'd rather fight an army of mzigo-dubwana or their master Chilombo-Wroch.

He waited, bracing himself to receive another preternatural broadcast from the woman no matter the consequences. He decided to talk back. He considered it a waiting message for the woman reaching out to him. He started thinking, *You're hurting me. Relax your sending.* He repeated this until a headache and icy snap penetrated his brain. She replied, *"I'm outside your settlement. I am an inspector-medium from Praidol. I've been trying to contact you since I picked up your conjure use some days ago."*

Ziko wiped the sleeve of his robe across his face, mopping up the streak of blood running from his nose. *I'm no Conjurer. Just surviving,* he repeated in his mind, hoping this message would be picked up by the woman calling herself an inspector-medium. His message was received, and she replied, *"You're alive. Be grateful, even if you're all that represents your settlement."*

Ziko thought, *I don't know where my determination to live came from. I've had no purpose, no story to continue. I fought back, but it had nothing to do with the fear of dying. It wasn't the need to live either. I just simply fought.* The reflection was private, but it was still intercepted by the inspector-medium, who was somewhere not too far away. The woman didn't respond out of respect. But Ziko had a message for her. He relaxed his mind and body and thought, hoping she would reply, even at the cost of his comfort. *The building I rest in is a safe place. Charmed crystals keep its perimeter safe from the mzigo-dubwana. I can help carve a path for you.*

"Thank you," she answered. *"I can sense you're weary—and my sending might have something to do with that. My apologies. Rest,"* she advised, voice filtering through Ziko's head like a cool breeze. *"My conjure assists me as we speak. I will make my way to you."*

I'll be in the perimeter, thought Ziko. She didn't reply. Ziko stood, surprised to find more strength than he'd expected. His nose stopped bleeding. He gave it another wipe and then unhooked his hammer-pick from his belt. The moment Ziko gripped the instrument, the metal head bubbled with a vibrant, yellow gel of energy that gave off thin swirls of white smoke. The hammer-pick's brilliance bathed the dark corridor with light. Ziko held up his hammer-pick as if it were a torch, making his way to the lecture hall's entrance. Unlocking and pushing his way through the heavy, wooden front door, Ziko stepped outside.

Mzigo roamed the perimeter. Their feet scraped the roads. The sound mixed with their low, guttural hissing. These were the only sounds populating an otherwise quiet day. Ziko moved forward, stopping only a few strides into his walk. He stood several feet away from the mzigo. The creatures paid him no mind, looking for a victim to stab or feast on. They continued sauntering and dragging their weight around the invisible wall surrounding the domed lecture hall. Ziko looked beyond the mob of cursed ramblers as they sloshed through the dusty roads. He listened but heard nothing other than the sounds of mzigo feet scraping the road coupled with their collective moans and hisses. He stood on his toes in an attempt to elevate his sight range.

Where was she? Ziko questioned.

A sound like thunder ripped through the calm. Ziko flinched. His eyes blinked as he almost lost his balance. He bent into a warrior's stance, hammer-pick at the ready, glowing with a gelatinous, bubbling yellow glow and white smoke. An electric hiss followed the globulous resonance. Even the mzigo reacted, turning their heads in the direction of the explosive rumble. But instead of looking out, Ziko lifted his gaze upward, peering at the sky. He stepped back, waiting for the day's light to be smothered by Chilombo-Wroch's massive shadow.

The heavy sound thundered again. Ziko took his eyes away from the sky, looking straight ahead. From the horizon of mzigo rose three, lion-headed serpents beset with golden eyes. Their forms were ghostly with translucent scales. Each resembled a color of the three moons. One was red and with the head of a lioness. Another was black, male, and with a thick mane around its head. The third, also a lioness, was green. All three possessed the tails of a lion that had a snake's rattle at the end.

The amalgamated creatures slithered toward the mzigo, tongues of lightning flickering, cackling hisses that followed their collective, high-pitched roars. The lion-headed serpents were as tall as any building within the walled settlements, but nowhere near the mass of Chilombo-Wroch. They would be like children to the black demon.

Ziko watched the serpents attacked the mzigo. He observed a single bite from the diaphanous creatures bled the entrapped souls jailed inside the cursed bodies. The souls swiveled free as glowing, black smoke. The serpents' feline jaws snatched groups of mzigo and thrashed them about, tossing the monsters aside when they became deflated of soul and putrid-green, lifeless color. The bodies slapped the dusty road with a violent tumble. The ashes of previously slain mzigo, defeated by Ziko, kicked up and created a dirty fog.

Ziko kept his stance. He tightened his grip on his hammer-pick. He took a step forward, cocking his arm back to swing the power of his weapon at the mzigo from a distance and assist the conjured serpents. *Stay your hand,* he heard the inspector-medium send to him. *Let my conjures part the way for me.* Ziko stepped back toward the door, keeping a close eye on the lion-headed serpents' ferocity. The black serpent-lion retreated from his attacks while the red and green serpent-lionesses kept the mzigo at bay on the left and right. Ziko noticed a woman walking within the black and ghostly serpent-lion's body, using the conjured creature's luminous mass as an aegis. A female mzigo, clothed in rags, managed to creep by the green serpent-lioness. She darted up to the black-serpent lion, screaming and swiping with her needle, desperately attempting to pierce the luminous creature's frame. The mzigo's needle only clinked and clanked against the candescent beast's scales as if it was comprised of a hard, precious stone rather than the ghostly light that defined it. The woman centered within her conjure paid the attacking fiend no mind, keeping her eye on the safe area surrounding the lecture hall. It wasn't long before the black serpent-lion reached down and snatched up the mzigo attempting to needle him. It shook the mzigo around, jaw clamped down on its body, then flung the creature behind him just as the dark, smoky soul was exhaled through the undead's mouth and nostrils.

Ziko backed away as the black serpent-lion slithered its way into the protected perimeter. The red and green serpent-lionesses faded. Wandering mzigo overran the space their large frames occupied. Ziko tilted his head up, his eyes meeting the black serpent-lion's as the conjured specimen peered down at him. Ziko clipped his hammer-pick to his belt and raised his hands. The serpent-lion huffed and looked to be nodding its head in approval. Then the creature's lighted body dimmed. Ziko looked forward at the woman standing within its ward. From bottom to top the serpent-lion's ghostly figure dissolved, lifting like a curtain to reveal the woman using its frame as a safeguard.

She was brown skinned with a golden tinge peeking through her flesh. She wore a fitted, purple gown that belled out into a multi-tendril star shape at the hem. Her long braids flowed neatly over her shoulders. Loose fabric draped under the arms and attached to the sides of the gown. A gold, embroidered heart stretched across her chest with embroidered circles linked at the bottom. Filling the circles were theurgic symbols. The gold heart expanded wide around her chest, and the voluminous heart shape mimicked perfectly the shape of her hips. She stared at Ziko, happy to see another who was left non-transfigured. She took her eyes off him for a moment, looking behind her to see if the mzigo were indeed at bay. With her body partially turned, Ziko noticed a leather knapsack strapped to her.

Ziko wanted to hug her. He wanted to pull her close for no other purpose than to feel another body. He smiled at his thought, but he didn't act on it, knowing it was inappropriate. "Forgive my smiling…" he stuttered.

The woman turned her back to him. Ziko felt as if someone had removed a warm blanket from him on a cold day. He wanted to see her eyes again. They had the sparkle of the cosmos within them. They had life in them. She was someone. Else.

"Dammit!" she cursed. Ziko flinched with the physical sound of her voice, nothing resonating in his head. He took a step toward her. The woman watched the mzigo refill the streets, covering what she so closely observed. Her eyes scanned the dead her conjures had mauled. Their bodies were maltreated, bleeding and torn. She turned back to Ziko. The cosmic shimmer Ziko had seen in her eyes now bubbled with frustration. "My conjures," she said, the physical presence of her voice again taking Ziko by surprise. "They're untamed," she stated through a sigh. "They've freed the souls of these men and women, but they have decimated the bodies."

"Oh…" was Ziko's only response.

The woman stood straight. "Where are my manners, gentle-man?" she questioned. "All these thoughts exchanged, and we don't even know each other's names." She politely bowed her head and extended a hand. "I am Oris Del, Private Inspector-Medium."

Ziko was again taken aback, almost missing his cue to accept Oris' hand. But he received her hand in his and bowed as a gentleman. "Ziko," he presented his name. "Ziko Yswil." He spoke as if out of breath. Standing upright and letting go of Oris' hand, he managed to calm himself. There was a long silence that neither of them considered awkward. The mzigo dragged their feet against the road as they wandered. Chilombo-Wroch hollered in the distance.

Ziko and Oris continued looking at one another, smiling.

Ziko broke the silence, confessing, "So much time alone. Now, there's another…"

"But you seemed hesitant to take my hand, Conjurer," Oris replied with an interrogative tone. "Does my presence trouble as well as intrigue you? I assure you, Ziko Yswil, you can trust me."

Ziko shook his head. "No, good woman," he told her. "I have no choice but to help you. If you wish me ill intentions, I will be your mark." He took a moment. His smile trembled a bit. He believed his words were running into one another. "I'm not attempting to be poetic."

"I would hope not," Oris replied matter-of-factly. She waved her comment away, shaking her head. "I'm sorry. I don't mean…I was just hoping that you weren't taking light the possibility of someone trying to take advantage of you."

Ziko inhaled deep. He exhaled, hand on chest. "My hesitation came with your title. You're a *Private* Inspector-Medium."

"Yes."

Chilombo-Wroch hollered again. Oris and Ziko looked up. They scanned the sky for the black demon's presence.

Ziko said to Oris, "Inside. Come." He ushered her toward the door and relayed, "This way, Inspector-Medium." Oris walked inside as Chilombo-Wroch roared again. Ziko followed, shutting and locking the heavy door once they were secure within the lecture hall. Oris conjured a ball of light in her hand to see inside the dark hallway. Ziko took up his hammer-pick and ignited its gelatinous energy. "Preserve your strength, Inspector-Medium," he told her. Oris dimmed her light out of existence. Ziko led her to the lyceum's auditorium. He allowed her to enter first, and Oris took his cue. She then stepped aside to permit Ziko admission after her. Ziko waved his hammer-pick carefully. He coupled the action with an incant, and the swirling gel of energy lighting the head of his hammer-pick separated and whooshed around the room. Its parts settled atop every candle housed in a sconce or candelabra, providing flame and light. Ziko clipped his hammer-pick back to his belt and led Oris to the stage. Oris removed her knapsack when they arrived, she dropped it and then sat down next to it on the stage.

"There's food and a gourd-canteen of fresh water in my pack," Oris informed. "Dried meats, crackers, and some fruit," she listed. "An incant has kept them fresh. If we holed up here long—or rather, longer for you—then my conjures will hunt and forage for us."

Ziko was hungry, but his mind remained on her title. "*Private* Inspector-Medium," Ziko repeated Oris' occupation. "So, you're not connected to any state or region's army or police-guard?"

"No," Oris confessed in a soft voice. She looked at the stage for a moment, running her hand across it. "I'm a caterer and planner by trade. I love it. It's my calling to present food in all its glory, being the accent on a special occasion." Her smile was as faint as the moons in the sky. "My call to create an ambience that reflects the manner of a people's celebrated event." She exhaled. A sorrowed expression pulled at her features. "Lately, I've catered a grotesque meal to my conjured creatures, exorcising people restrained with burden and at the command of a deceitful sky demon. Their transmuted Path minds and controlled bodies are a feast for my conjure, and unfortunately food has become plentiful."

Ziko sat opposite Oris, legs crossed. "Is your home place overrun with the burden-plague too?" inquired Ziko. "You said you were from Praidol. That's a small city in Vashion, correct?"

"Yes," Oris replied. "And, to answer your question, it all still stands."

Oris' smiled was strained. "It's lively, bustling with activity." The smile didn't keep. Oris sighed, looking down as she confessed, "Spared for its support of Dimbwi Toliv Angoj Wofiira and his so-called hero Xiddig-Akoni Keb-Biyarli Lorish." Oris let it be known, adding quickly while looking at Ziko, "And Praidol's support is genuine. They believe in Eke Woli Lorish and Eke Almas Wofiira."

"But they *are* false in *your* eyes…?" Ziko noted, unsure, and looking for confirmation.

"My eyes and my father's and mother's and my brother's," included Oris. "My sister is far too young to understand. She's only eleven. My brother is the most vocal of us. He was jailed and taken away for the volume at which he spoke, and what he spoke about. My mother and father, they're teachers who dabble in conjure work, keeping their greater abilities private so as not to be forced into military service. I work for them. My catering business grants me entry to parties hosted by the Dimbwi."

"I've read those events are filled with great debauchery," expressed Ziko.

"Not any I've attended. They are polite and beautiful affairs. Elegant," Oris admitted. "But human sacrifice is still a part of the agenda. Those are private affairs disguised as public wars." She pointed up, eyes to the ceiling. "Chilombo-Wroch's gluttonous appetite, turning the unsuspecting into what we call *xidachane*."

The word meant 'lost wanderers.' Ziko disagreed, telling his newly arrived guest what he and others of the El-Ham region labeled the alchemized army. "We call them *dubwana*."

Oris took offense to the stigmatic title. It was attached to old mythology, creatures that were referred to as 'hideous monsters' described by the simple word 'dubwana'. She told Ziko, as she shook her head in opposition to his claim, "There is still light in them. There is still soul. They just wander, lost. When the alchemy's hex is lifted, their bodies become as they once were, spirits freed."

Ziko didn't argue, though he felt the urge to do so. He'd seen these creatures paint the most horrific scenes and sprout others to do their bidding from bite or gouge. It was all too gruesome to let his choice description go. "Let's meet in the middle, Inspector-Medium. I've read that creatures of hex and needle are called *mzigo*, transformed and made monsters by their personal burdens."

Oris thought for a moment. It seemed appropriate. "Burdened…" she said in a low voice. "That is what they've become." She shook her head. "I agree. Mzigo."

Ziko nodded back. He took a moment to think on the titles he'd heard Oris Del speak on. "So, this *is* a result of the Pious Wars?" he inquired.

"What terrible mind would conjure a creature such as that black sky demon?"

Oris answered, "Like all of the most powerful conjures, Chilombo-Wroch comes from the depths of a great imagination. Terrifying, isn't it?" Her face fixed into a solemn expression. "I met the corresponding, terrifying Conjurer. I hosted his parties that helped seduce many people to his cause. A friend of my father feigns interest. His spying uncovered the beast's attack along the countryside. I was dispatched to investigate. Much has been decimated. I tempered my conjure to fight against the mzigo it regurgitates. But my conjure is wild. They need more training. They need to be calmed. They continue to maltreat the bodies. The bodies must be preserved."

"Why?" asked Ziko in an innocent voice.

Oris curled her knees up to her chin and embraced them. "I don't know why," she said. "I just think the mauling of the body is wrong, even if the souls are being freed. There is an alchemy we must all go through, but Chilombo-Wroch's hex is not part of Fate's plan." She rocked back and forth. Oris declared, "My mother has a sense of duty too. I take after her. She wishes to gather all the weapons of the world's armies and destroy them." Oris nodded an approval, looking out into the vacant seating. "Chilombo-Wroch's transmissions to his army have dampened the crystal I use to communicate with my parents. I've not spoken to them for a long time." Then she repeated in a low voice, "A long time…" Her voice perked up as she proudly trumpeted, "My mother is from central Alkebulan. Her land has been burned, scorched into a beige beauty. Tanned crystals create a beautiful graveyard where lays the buried strength of all of Alkebulan." She started rocking again as she announced, "I will make the armies of the world surrender their arms, and they will remember their covenant to my mother. My father will judge them."

Ziko stared at Oris, pondering as the woman rocked back and forth. Again, he kept his sentiments to himself, though his eyes betrayed him. "You ask a lot of yourself and this world," Ziko said, his words accompanied by a grin to lighten the mood. His voice darkened a little when he warned, "Be careful to not become a zealot yourself."

"I'm always careful," Oris remarked. "And, I make no apologies for my sense of duty—even if it's not my calling. As a child of my parents, my footsteps travel where they direct, especially in these uncertain times. Culture takes precedence."

Ziko took advantage of the moment and noted, "Absolutely. The mzigo are not the only ones with burden. They're just expressing it wild and raw." He was silent for a moment before stating, "Perhaps you're right, in a way, Inspector-Medium. *We're* the lost wanderers, the xidachane."

Oris stopped rocking. She raised her eyebrow at Ziko and asked him, "Will you help me find and kill the false prophet and false messiah that plague the world?"

Ziko nodded. It didn't matter to him whether it was possible or not, he just wanted a story to tell; or a story for others to tell about him should he fall. But Ziko brushed the possibility of death aside. This was now, and he was here to push his muscle out and shape his frame. He slapped his left bicep and declared, "If for nothing more than to have it told how the accidental alchemist and his hammer-pick brought an end to the *Pious Wars*. I will fill my body with the ink of every chapter future generations will speak on."

Ori observed the organic ink flourishing on his arms as he removed his robe. "Limber like a feather," she commented. "Deft to battle."

"Indeed, Inspector-Medium," Ziko said smacking his muscling belly. "This here is experience." He said it again, slapping his abdomen harder, "It's experience!" He added, "There's magic and brawn brewed in these slender muscles. It gives all El-Nord men the upper hand in the regional sports—even the national competitions. Hell, the internationals. Our experience—*our stories*—dictates our shape!" He looked at her frame and remarked, "You have lovely, fleshy thighs. You must be a very experienced woman."

Oris' face skewed with offense. She snapped, "Excuse me?"

Ziko explained, aloof to Oris' being offended by his statement, "The women of El-Nord, their thighs and hips become voluminous. They are shaped by experience of all sorts. It's never grotesque, always beautiful. Like you," he noted in a matter-of-fact tone. "An adventure here, a devouring of knowledge there," he pointed to the left and right as he spoke his final sentence. "An ancient language tattooed on our person to express the tale of our lives!"

"Oh… I see…" Oris replied comprehending Ziko's cultural pride. "Well, all Pambunjila women have shape, if we're being honest," she remarked.

Ziko replied, "Ah, yes. Beautiful are you all. But there are still those beautiful and slender, expressing the destiny of their biology. There are very few women who don't know the world or have knowledge here." He thought about the current standing of all of El-Ham. He said, a little wind removed of his spirit, "…Very few…"

Oris reached out to the ink brewing on his arm and asked, "May I?" Ziko allowed permission, and Oris lightly traced the ancient chirography. Ziko's arms were slender but Oris felt a solid piece of flesh, more muscle, almost as if made of iron. She also sensed a warm presence of vibrant incant. Oris retracted her hand and disclosed, "Good fortune is your personal conjure."

"Is it?" Ziko responded, pushing up a single eyebrow up. "How lucky am I to survive in the nightmare land, huh?" He thought for a moment about his words and tone. Nothing was said between them for some time, and then Ziko spoke, "I'm glad someone's here."

Oris didn't allow his earlier sentiments to pass unnoticed. She said to Ziko, "There's a lot of anxiety in you, naturally, with all you've been through." Oris surveyed the lecture hall. She inquired, "Do you meditate in this hall, Ziko Yswil?"

"Too restless here by myself," Ziko admitted, quickly seeing the irony in his statement.

Oris understood. She too hadn't indulged in meditation since her travels away from home began, at least not for prolonged measures. She engaged in active cogitation only enough to regain strength for her conjured serpent-lions.

"Let us engage now," Oris suggested. "Is that okay?"

"Yes," Ziko yielded.

Oris inched closer to Ziko, legs folded and crossed. Ziko was surprised that the fabric of her dress expanded with her position rather than tore. She said nothing to Ziko. There were no guiding words to assist in lulling him to trance. She put her hands on her knees, closed her eyes, and spirited within herself.

It took a few moments for Ziko to do the same. Eyes closed, he wondered what he should ponder on, or if he should ponder on anything at all. But he did find a 'something' for his focus. He reached out, noting the proximity of another human being to him. The closeness was not aggressive. It was not something he had to fight. It was comforting, and he wore it like a blanket. The black behind his eyes became a calm embrace in that moment. The tragedy outside the lecture dome, and within his person, dwindled away.

Ziko was at peace, and he was lost to the world and the stage he was on.

Absorbed in the dark calm, with his eyes closed, Ziko missed the shimmering, cobalt-blue light that covered Oris Del's body. The brilliant cocoon burst out of her person, strands of electricity swirling within it.

Then it lifted, leaving Oris Del a changed woman.

Gone were her long braids and stature. Her hair was now a short, Afro bush of twists. Her body was shorter, but still retained its shape. Her skin was darker, and her eyes were like the wings of a butterfly when she opened them.

She saw Ziko and scurried away. Her breath was rapid and her eyes were widened by fright. Ziko didn't stir, not even when her feet kicked at him as she hurried backwards. She stumbled over the knapsack, and her hastened, backwards crawl came to a clumsy end. She recovered from her stumble and stared at Ziko, waiting for the young man to break from his meditative pose.

He did not move.

She observed him, his bald head adorned with a single, long and thick lock draping down his back. She saw the hammer-pick clipped at his side, a weapon that left her transfixed for a moment. She pulled her gaze away from Ziko, looking up and around. Her wide, curious eyes swallowed the lighted auditorium's majestic scenery. Incant manufactured the candles' flames, and she could feel the presence of their magic as a tickling vibration.

She stood and inspected her dress, running her finger along its masterful embroidery. She felt the fabric hugging her, as if it was alive. The embrace was warm and loving, and it reminded her of wearing a similar piece stitched in the heavens by cosmic spirits. The memory shook the woman into a realization that she didn't belong here. Not in this time.

This was no longer Oris Del.

A spirit lost to time and place had taken the inspector-medium's body.

This new woman's name was Fey. *Yes!* She was Fey Forrester, and she could feel that someone, in a time she was more familiar with, was watching her in a dream.

Fey turned, eyes aimed up. She hesitated, unsure of what answer she would receive. She was as still as the man meditating and lost in trance. It took time, but the young woman eventually put forth a question by stating a single name.

"Gordon…?" Nothing answered back. She repeated, "Gordon…" And then she extended her query to say, "Are you watching me?"

The world shook as something beyond time screamed.

2

The world rumbled, but Fey Forrester stood unmoved on the ancient lecture hall's stage. Not unaffected. Shapes rattled. Images elongated and retracted while thunder rolled over itself. Fey closed her eyes and knelt down. She put the palms of her hands on the floor and then opened her eyes. She glimpsed the trembling image of the young, single-dreaded man in his meditative pose, eyes closed with legs crossed. He too was unfazed by the tremors.

Fey moved her eyes to either side. She observed that no candles or candelabras tipped. Everything was still despite the frantic rumble. Then the affect set in. Fey's vision whirled and her sense of balance lifted from her. She closed her eyes and a blurry vision developed out of the darkness. It was void of the chaotic motion she experienced with her eyes open, but far from a stable portrait. A sphere of cobalt-blue light assembled at her forehead and the image behind her eyes came into focus.

There was Gordon Goodspeed dressed in black shoes and slacks and a white dress shirt. He lay on a green, steel bench in the backyard of her family's brownstone on Fable Avenue in Brooklyn, New York. It was morning, and the sun shone bright in a clearing sky. Fey wanted to savor Gordon's sight, but the life-sized, silver statue that resembled her cosmic-spirit form distracted her. It was a polished effigy expressing her divinity. Recall occurred, and Fey remembered all of the poetry she and Gordon forged together into mythology. She remembered the nights that as spirits they haunted the streets, and the love they made in the cosmos surrounded by the stars. She remembered the moments that occurred before she journeyed into the continuous fall. Landing here was no solace, save for glimpsing her beloved Gordon.

Fey opened her eyes for a split moment only for vertigo to infect her. She closed them again, hoping to calm the sensation. Fey believed the image she viewed with her eyes closed should've calmed her, Gordon resting on the bench in her backyard. But she was disturbed by his body's feral seizure. His back arched while his head shook, legs possessed with violent tremors. His crossed arms, however, held tight to the ancient computer-like device. Fey clenched her teeth. Her stomach tightened, but there was nothing physical about the pangs echoing through her. It was the sight of Gordon's spasm and the icy, helpless feeling she experienced that provoked the twinge resonating within her. Gordon's cyclonic attacks mirrored the rumble and resonance of the world around her.

Fey had a thought. Or, more appropriate, she had an instinct.

She took a moment to open her eyes. Gordon's image remained within the spherical, cobalt-blue energy that floated against her forehead. Fey's physical's eyes tried to adjust to the shaking images of the time period she now occupied. She inspected the world's vibration. Her glowing, spherical eye continued perceiving Gordon's tumultuous spasms. It was in perfect synch with the tremors of her present environment.

This was where history and dreams collided.

Fey concentrated. Eyes opened. She propelled a thought through time and space. **Gordon!** She used the cobalt-blue sphere as a gateway to thrust her mental voice from ancient history to the modern era. **Gordon, just relax.** It became easier for Fey to speak as she focused her thoughts. The scenery's shakiness simmered as did Gordon's tremors. Fey felt a faint, cool breeze swirl around her, and she believed it was Gordon reaching back through time to her. **That's it, Gordon-baby. It's not just a dream you see. It's history. And I'm here, Gordon. Your Fey-baby is here.** She looked down and examined her appearance. Fey felt her face and hair. It was indeed her, but she felt different. She felt as if she wore more than clothes.

An instinct tickled the base of her neck. Gordon's image dimmed as her instinct tugged and turned her neck, forcing her to focus on the young man in deep meditation. She put a hand on her chest as the world and Gordon's spasms lightened further. She concentrated on Gordon again, image coming back to clarity.

Gordon-baby, let me remind you that you are a spirit, Fey articulated. Her mental voice broadcasted with an urgent tone. **And what I need you to do right now—** she turned her attention to the meditating man and concluded, **—is concentrate on that young man. He's open, in deep meditation, and ready to receive a spirit. Use him as a vessel, Gordon-baby.** She repeated like a mantra, instructing Gordon, **Concentrate. Concentrate. You are Lwa and spirit. He is your horse and mount.**

She repeated the words aloud. Her gaze bent in focus, aimed at Ziko Yswil's still and meditating body. The world ceased its vibrations, and all was once again clear to Fey's eyes. She was grateful for only a moment. Her third eye, drained of light and shape, popped from existence. The image of Gordon and home were lost to Fey, dashing away her once hopeful expression. She stared at Ziko for a moment. Nothing happened, and Fey began choking on tears. A sense more jarring than the dizziness that earlier bound her tightened around her neck. She cupped her hands to hide her face, but before she could feel her palms against her visage, Ziko Yswil's body burst into a lilac brilliance.

Fey's head snapped up, and her posture froze. Her eyes swelled, widening as the lilac aura brightened. The cobalt-blue energy sphere returned to her forehead just as the lilac aura lifted to reveal Gordon Goodspeed.

Fey waited as Gordon opened his eyes. She took a step closer to him.

The environment pirouetted in his vision, and Gordon toppled over.

Fey hurried to his side, lifting his back and sliding her legs underneath for support. She cupped his head in her arms. "Gordon," she said to him. "Gordon-baby, you okay?"

Gordon's eyes remained fastened shut. He rubbed them in an attempt to smother the vertiginous sensation that followed him behind his closed lids. He heard Fey call his name again, and he smiled. With his eyes remaining closed, Gordon reached up and felt Fey's cheek. His lilac-colored, third eye swirled into existence just as his fingertips touched her smooth and dark flesh. He could see her now without the use of his physical eyes. "Hey, Fey-baby," he exhaled. "There you are…"

His voice stuttered. Fey perceived his fatigue. She felt his face in return, making a quick swipe of his cheek with her fingers. She embraced the hand he used to caress her features, giving it a gentle kiss. "Here we are," Fey spoke with a flare of happy laughter breaking through her words. "Here are we so long ago," she expounded. Then she titled the two of them, "Spirits lost to time."

Gordon took quick breaths as if trying to remain conscious. "I'm still tethered to the present…" he panted.

Fey nodded her head, never losing her smile as she looked at Gordon and outlined the contours of his face. "Yes, of course," she said to him. She then asked, "What time is it there? All of it," she specified. "The season? The month?"

"It's late spring," Gordon answered. "June seventh. Morning." He cupped Fey's wrist with a hard grip and informed her, "Children were kidnapped from Fable Avenue."

"*Ohmigoodness!*" blurted Fey.

"Stanley Fallows sent needlemen, night doctors…" Gordon continued, swallowing large pockets of air between words. He coughed, and then he relaxed his breathing and settled again. "He took blood and essence from some. He took other kids entirely."

"Was this recent?"

Gordon shook his head. "No," he stated. "It happened months ago. The same night you…died."

Fey looked away, her expression drenched in perplexity. "I died?" she questioned, not remembering her death at all. There was absence in her memory after all. She again examined her surroundings, returning her eyes to Gordon. "No…" she denied. "No, I've been falling, endless," she explained. "It's a banishing. I close my eyes for comfort. The void echoes like rushing water. There's hollow screaming that sounds distant."

"I saw you, Fey-baby," Gordon interrupted. "You took your own life. You mimicked your mother's suicide. I tried to stop you…"

Still bathed in puzzlement, Fey loosened her cradling arms from around Gordon's limp body. She never let go, nor did Gordon lose balance and slip from her embrace. She closed her physical eyes and concentrated on recalling recent memories, using the aid of her blazing, cobalt-blue, third eye. Images first appeared as small, Enochian symbols. They drizzled in strands across blackness, piling atop one another until a memory was formed, animating as its picture developed. One memory atop another, the filled images leafed like a flip book. Gordon called out to Fey, but she didn't answer. He took the moment to relax and keep his spirit concentrated on possessing Ziko Yswil's body, anchored in the ancient time.

Fey scanned years in moments, encountering memories that were once only feelings and black gaps. She slowed her recollection to relive her mother's suicide, seeing it not from the point of view of a little, six-year-old girl, as when the event occurred, but as the young woman she was now, observing the scene in its entirety. Her mother drank and smoked at a table, speaking incoherent phrases. Little-girl Fey watched from across that table. Her mother stood and paced and sat and drank and smoked. Her speech was a disjointed rant. She cursed at the open sketchbook, yelling at the rendered, Senegalese fairy called a yumbo. Fey hated that her mother cursed her art. She cursed her absent father, and Fey hated that too. She said things like, *"Don't ever marry no codebreaker…"* A warning she would not understand until much later in life, and not by her own accord.

Fey's mother smoked a little more. She drank a little more. Then she rose from the table one last time, kissed her daughter on the forehead and walked away.

Little-girl Fey followed her mother. She stopped at the bottom of the stairs, losing sight of her mother's tipsy, drunken frame at the landing. The six-year-old girl continued calling up to her mother, but she received no response. Then there came thunder, a loud clap that echoed through time and space. Little-girl Fey climbed the stairs in a hurry, lifting her knees high to get a foot to the next step. A silver streak zipped by her, shifting into a physical shape at the top of the stairs. She saw that it was the drawn yumbo from her mother's sketchbook, conjured to life by the little girl's tears.

Light obstructed Fey's view of the memory, occurring at the moment her six-year-old self's eyes were flooded with brilliance emanating from the palms of the conjured yumbo. The dazzling strike was meant to spare the little girl from seeing her mother's lifeless body sprawled out in the master bedroom, bloodied from a self-inflicted gunshot to the head.

The light's swirl came to a stop, its tendrils grinding to a halt like gears in a failing machine. The blaze's stillness was momentary, and when movement resumed, the light faded away. She saw her mother's master bedroom, but her mother's self-slain body was nowhere to be found. A mirror rested atop a dresser, and Fey saw herself standing in front of it. Her expression was blank as she stared at her reflection. She watched as she lifted her hand, contorting her fingers into the shape of a gun. She placed her extended fingers near her temple and dropped her thumb. A green flash filled her view, and Fey was drawn away from her memory to her present location, seeing the world through her physical eyes.

Fey looked at Gordon, fright painted wide on her face. "I killed myself…"A faint memory curled up into Fey's third eye. The sun was fading outside. It was autumn, and Fey could almost feel the crisp breeze as her third eye recalled the exterior scenery. Water rushed onto the shores. Little-girl Fey was there. She was six years old and crying. Violence and remnants of violence encircled her six-year-old self. Her father's body lay lifeless on the cold and hard earth. Her mother was next to him, bent over and on her knees. Her sweater had been removed, and her bare back exposed. A man with a Dutch-style beard, and dressed in eighteenth century attire, whipped her mother's exposed back. Faint as the memory was, its intensity lingered.

Fey's physical eyes returned to Gordon. She held him close and said in a low voice, "I don't know what happened. My memory is in blots. I just had my memory…and now it feels punctured…" Then she repeated, "I killed myself!" She shook her head, frustrated. "Where was I during this fight between the Fable Avenue conjure folk and the needlemen?"

Gordon squirmed, inhaling, focusing to keep his spirit anchored within the body and time period it possessed. "You were at an art showcase, Fey-baby. Your professor invited you to her house in Long Island where it was being held. I spoke with them several months ago. I was looking for answers on what happened to you after the showcase."

"Wait," Fey protested. "Who? Invited? Showcase?" Her frustration rose when she questioned, "During something like this?"

"Professor Brede—Jacquelyn Brede," Gordon answered the 'who' of Fey's barrage of inquiries first. "Your art was on display at a showcase at her house in Long Island—Baiting Hollow, to be more specific."

Fey's memories attacked her again; all rolled together in one schizophrenic recall. Fragmented and minimal as the pieces were, Fey treated the memories as clues. "Something happened, Gordon. But I can't remember…"

"I think that's my fault," Gordon confessed, back arching and heels grinding into the stage. "I tried to pull the memory from you in the last moments of your life. You were hexed. I wanted to see how that happened. But you drifted away while the memories were between your mind and my own." Gordon grit his teeth, feeling something tug at him in an attempt to drag him back to his time.

Fey shook her head, piecing together what fragments of memory remained. She witnessed the memory of her six-year-old self and the memory of her contemporary self walking the path of her mother's suicide. "Gordon, you're correct," she said. "I was hexed." Another nebulous memory focused just enough inside her third eye. The same man who whipped her mother also scarred her back with lashes. The same scenery painted around Fey. An Eastern European woman with raven-colored hair stood next to the man as he beat Fey with his whip. The memory lingered long enough for Fey to understand. "They took me through everything they did to my mother. They scarred me with a hex."

Gordon put a name to her attacker. "Willie the Lich," he declared.

"Yes," Fey remembered. "He hexed you too, Gordon-baby. I searched through historical dreaming to find the missing elements of your chamber to put you back together again."

"Yes, Fey," Gordon wheezed. "I'm better now because of it. But we have to figure out the attack on you." Despite the power in his lilac-glowing third eye, giving him a heightened awareness of time and place, Gordon wanted to open his physical eyes and see through them. It would serve as extra movement he could use to balance himself within the physical body he possessed. But he knew vertigo would set in, twisting his consciousness about like a ship in stormy weather. He would lose his hold on time and reality and be thrust back to the contemporary age where he belonged. "Were you ambushed after the gala?"

Fey shook her head, eyes away from Gordon. Frustrated, she refuted his earlier claims. "*No!* I should still have my memories. There shouldn't be a fading of my experiences."

"No offense, Fey-baby, but can you remember?"

Gordon's third eye attempted to back away from the austere and irritated expression Fey aimed at him. "Your timing for sarcasm, Mister Goodspeed, has never been your strongest trait." Then something occurred to her. "Maybe I don't have to remember." She asked, "Is it okay if I lay you down so that I can pace?"

"I'll be fine," Gordon assured.

Fey lifted Gordon's limp frame. She slid her legs from under him, laying him down. He felt better being against a flat surface. He exhaled, feeling himself gaining a better grip on possessing Ziko Yswil. Fey paced, closing her eyes and concentrating through the vibrant, cobalt-blue sphere that swirled against her forehead.

"They whipped me like they did my mother," she summarized, walking to and fro on the stage. "I see the imagery of angry waters invading a shore. In one time, it's autumn, and there's my mother. The other, it's winter, and there I am."

"Where are you, Fey-baby?" Gordon inquired. "Concentrate," he instructed.

Fey stopped pacing. She attempted to focus on the faint and violent memories, to lift them from her swampy consciousness up to the surface for her to scrutinize. A new memory manifested alternatively, a brief spark of reminiscence that illuminated her third eye. "A dark room?" questioned Fey as she realized the picture wasn't coming into focus because of her inability to recall the events, but because it took place in a room with little light.

Fey saw herself crouched like a cat. Her face was covered by a black, African mask that had been attached to the frame-hugging bodysuit that clothed her. The suit's fabric had been stitched from dark, cosmic elements making up the heavenly firmament. Also occupying the memory was the man with the Dutch-styled beard and eighteenth-century attire. He readied his whip for Fey as she charged him as a suited spirit. Her conjured yumboes kept needlemen at bay. She dodged attacks made upon her by the whip-wielding man. Her intentions were not to engage the man but to scoop up an unattended wooden box. Snatched up and cuddled under her arm, Fey called her pixies to her. Each yumbo transfigured into a beam of smoky light and seeped into Fey's cosmic suit, boring through the skin-tight outfit and filtering into enchanted tattoos lining her back. She hesitated to pop from existence, curling up and bracing herself. Her brief pause of action allowed the whip-wielder to strike her with a vicious lash.

Fey opened her physical eyes, and she remembered something. "This was my own doing, Gordon!" she said, words laced with a disconsolate guilt. She walked back to him and knelt down. "I am so sorry. My hubris got the better of me."

"Your own doing?" questioned Gordon. He took in another barrel of air, clenching his teeth as he exhaled. He reached up and gripped Fey's wrist again.

"I had a plan, Gordon-baby," she told him. "I was going to find Stanley Fallows and kill him." Gordon's body jerked as if lightning had struck it. The world rumbled with his movement. Fey rubbed his cheek, and Gordon crawled up into her embrace. The world's tremors ceased. "I allowed Willie the Lich to land a lash against me. I felt I could control the hex. Your lashes connected you to one of Fable Avenue's villains. I thought I would take that knowledge and use my hexed lash as an antenna. I could find its source and then slay Stanley and all his henchmen."

Gordon writhed, anger rippling inside him. Small tremors agitated the world. "Why didn't you consult me? The elders? Someone?"

"Would you have agreed to my methods?"

"Me?" Gordon responded. "Yes. Absolutely. I could've assisted you." He banged a fist against the stage, light temblors an effect.

"Goddamnit, Fey! You got yourself killed! The grief you caused your grandmother. For her to relive—"

Fey choked back tears as she interrupted Gordon with an apology. "I am so sorry, Gordon." A memory struck her. It came in flashes like lightning. Fey saw a close-up of her arm. A needle pierced her skin. When the plunger was drawn back, it wasn't blood the vampiric instrument appropriated from her, but a thick, illuminated, cobalt-blue essence. The image burst into confetti. Fey told Gordon, "Stanley took from me too…"

"I know!" Gordon hissed. "I was able to tap into your memories before you faded. I saw that much."

Fey spoke as if she hadn't heard Gordon's confirming words, "He had a needleman take from me…" Gordon didn't say anything. Fey could sense his disappointment in her. "The showcase was the ambush," she revealed as the notion came to her. "The Bredes are either needlemen or perhaps they were dolled in some way—*kontwòl'd*." Fey advised, "Don't interrogate them again. If they were dolled, you could be putting them in danger."

Gordon concluded Fey's sentiment, noting, "And if they're night-doctors, then I'm putting myself in danger." A third option came to him, however, and he expressed, "But the two of them are pieces to this puzzle. I can get inside their mind. I can go visit Mister Brede. It would look less suspicious. I could be catching up on old times with him while probing his mind for memories. I'll be ready for my find's consequences, whatever they might be."

"I aimed to be careful too, Gordon," Fey continued her warning.

Gordon asserted, "I'll speak to James Brede in public, on campus."

"He could have a needle on him," Fey warned.

Gordon insisted, "My defenses will be at the ready. I've talked to them before and got nothing. They said you showed up and left shortly before sundown." Gordon paused to think. He considered Fey correct, and expressed to her, "I spoke with them months ago. If I go asking questions again, I'd be running the risk of making them suspicious as to your whereabouts. People have been asking about you. Your grandmother says you're studying art abroad."

Fey didn't respond. She nodded her head and said a prayer to herself that Gordon would be protected, powerful as his spirit was. But she did inquire, "Gordon-baby, why are you dreaming of history?"

Gordon took several breaths before answering, "I'm searching for Lady Arachne's missing Lovers card from the tarot deck my brother procured for her. I don't know why I dreamed so far back in history. Maybe it was to see you."

"Perhaps," Fey beamed. Her smile fractured the tense mood, and she kissed Gordon on the lips. His body's shiver ceased, and he smiled in return. "Who are we?"

"You ever heard the stories of Alchemham and his magical hammer? Hammer-pick, in truth."

Fey's features brightened. She scanned Gordon's attire, eyes zooming in on the hammer-pick latched at his side. She caressed the head of the lethal and enchanted instrument. "Yes!" she exclaimed. "My mother and grandmother would tuck me in at night with stories of him and his wife's adventures. The stories are all over the place. You mean to tell me they're true? Have I possessed his wife?"

"Future wife, I suppose," said Gordon. "These two just met. Your possession's name is Oris Del. What was her name in the stories told to you?" Before Fey could answer, Gordon added, "I've never heard of a married Alchemham. There was a story about him and a princess he loved and lost. Oh! It turns out his real name is Ziko Yswil."

"Well, '*Alchemham*' was not a real name," Fey explained. "It's simply the words *alchemy* and *hammer* put together."

"No! Really?" protested Gordon.

"Yes, Gordon. No one told you that growing up?" Fey reacted. Gordon said nothing more on the matter, considering what he'd just heard ridiculous. Fey answered Gordon's question concerning the alchemist's wife. "In the stories I heard as a little girl, his wife was named Essie. She could conjure dragons the colors of the original moons: red, black, and green."

Gordon exhaled, smiling. "Well, historically her name is Oris Del," he reiterated. "She speaks in a peculiar way. She talks about her mother, building a throne in the desert, and having the warring armies of the world surrender their arms to her." He aimed his lilac-glowing eye at Fey and asked, "Doesn't that remind you of anything?"

It took a moment before Fey answered, "The opening scene of our poetic mythology—with Mother Covenant. *In Thirteen Pieces*, correct?"

Gordon nodded. "I always felt the beginning had an historical context to it, symbolic, mostly."

"What object are you making your inquiry with?"

"The Judgment card," answered Gordon, before informing, "Hasn't been the first history I've seen, either. The other time period was longer ago than the supposed age of the cards too. It wasn't this far back, but it was before the cards' inception."

"That can't be," Fey challenged. "Either the age of the deck is in error, or somehow, someone from these ages you've dreamed of, have come in contact with the cards."

"I'm still investigating, Fey-baby," Gordon insisted, impatience trembling his voice. He caressed Fey's cheek to relax himself. "I will find a way to bring your spirit home too." Gordon then proclaimed, "Believe me, and remember."

Fey looked at Gordon with an endearing expression, focused more on his latter statement. Then a thought occurred to them at the same moment. Gordon lifted his head closer to Fey. She lowered her head to him. Their foreheads touched, and their third eyes synthesized. Lilac and cobalt-blue swirled into jet black, and a once lost memory was recalled. The empty space between Gordon and Fey, where her memories faded, was now bridged. The memory glowed bright in the black center of their shared third eye.

Gordon and Fey witnessed the entirety of Fey's capture. Closely noted was Professors James and Jacquelyn Brede's melting and remolding flesh. Names and faces worn as veils were now discarded, and the truth emerged. There stood Stanley Fallows and his wife Lucretia. Fey's voice cut into the scene. *The villains that surround us in shadow wear masks made of flesh and blood!* Her sentiment was lost to Gordon, as while the scene progressed, Stanley Fallows alleged that the global conjure community was born of evil. He declared their destiny was to destroy the world while his was to preserve it.

Gordon opened his physical eyes with the revelation's impact. His mouth hung open, inhaling massive breaths of air. The world resumed its dizzying dance and rumble, echoing the spastic gyrations that shook Gordon's body. Gordon fell back. His movement was peculiar, like video footage in reverse. He resumed Ziko Yswil's meditative pose as the sphere against his forehead resumed its lilac hue.

Fey reached out to him, shouting his name.

Gordon closed his eyes. A lilac gleam encased his body. The fulgent fluorescence forced Fey to shade her eyes with her hands. When nothing but shadow remained, Fey moved her hand aside. Ziko Yswil meditated peacefully in front of her. She sighed and cursed, "Shit!" She crawled up to Ziko and assumed a meditative posture. Closing her eyes, Fey felt her spirit be dragged away. A cobalt-blue beam surrounded her body. It lifted, and Fey Forrester was gone. The flesh of another woman no longer draped her spirit. Darkness clothed her, and she fell through an infinite void.

Oris Del opened her eyes in time with Ziko. "What did your calm show you?" she inquired.

Ziko beamed. He commented in a whisper, "There is a future."

"Indeed, there is, Alchemist with the Hammer," Oris replied. "And those who know our story will pave its road with conjure and incant."

3

Althea Goodspeed was mesmerized by the lucent, lilac glow cocooning her son's body as he lay atop the green, metal bench. Its brilliance would've blinded her had she been living flesh and blood and not a spirit. Instead, her eyes' phantom constitution managed to endure the blistering radiance.

She had been standing over her son's illuminated encasement for an hour, having been called by presage as she enjoyed time with her husband in Harlem. The premonition rumbled loud like thunder and flashed like lightning. Althea's spectral form whisked away from Harlem, giving no warning to her husband. It took only a moment to travel the distance, manifesting within the exterior environment she now occupied, the walled-in backyard of the Forrester brownstone on Fable Avenue in Brooklyn. Her son's body was already immured in the lilac brilliance. The glow made his body shimmer as if he was in his spirit form. From the depths of the incandescence escaped the faint sound of Gordon's voice echoing the Swahili phrase, *"Wakati hatua..."* Although there were many ways of expression within the conjure community, Althea understood the East African idiom translated as *time stepping. Wakati hatua* was a performed incant that forced a person's spirit through time to possess the body of another, or their younger self.

Althea was aware of the task set upon her son by Matriarch Lady Arachne. She knew that at this moment he was recalling history within a dream, aided by the ancient tech he named *Spook*. Althea considered what her son was experiencing at present was too much for him, but she didn't want to disturb his sleep, fearing it would cause mental and physical damage to his person. Althea found solace in hearing his voice echo the Swahili expression, but each time the phrase was spoken, and the light's encasement grew brighter and wider, Gordon's voice became fainter. A few moments ago, the voice drowned in the light, and Althea just watched the great glimmer that swallowed her son's body and voice.

She fashioned a plan. Should her son remain corralled within his glow for another five minutes, Althea would project her conscience into the light and see if she could retrieve her son. Her biggest hope was to do no damage to her spirit or her son's, should fate pull her to such a desperate act.

Althea counted every second. A minute passed, and halfway through her count for the second minute, to her great relief, the glow surrounding Gordon retracted in size and effulgence. Althea backed away, clasping her hands together and placing them against her lips. She heard Gordon's voice again, repeating *"Wakati hatua..."*

The glow dimmed further. Gordon's voice turned into gasps for air, and Althea bent down. She reached out with her hand, penetrating the light, which had a frothy, cool texture. She sensed her son's physical presence as her ghostly hand hovered over his chest. He was breathing, and Althea was further relieved. The light ebbed, retreating back into Gordon's body. Althea made her hand physical, and with her son's lightless appearance, cupped his arms holding tight to Spook.

Gordon opened his eyes wide, and he scarfed fistfuls of air. He choked as his throat tightened. He sat up and breathed out, an easier feat. He clutched his throat with both hands, and Spook left his grip. The ancient device tumbled into Gordon's lap. His mother's spirit focused her spectral form solid and took up the mystical gadget. All the while, Althea told her son, "Gordon, relax. Breathe." She placed Spook gently on the ground.

Gordon flinched, taking notice of his mother's presence. The shock of her appearance dropped him back into a frantic spell.

"Gordon, honey, you have to relax. Your spirit's riding you wild like you a horse in ritual." Gordon listened to his mother. He breathed in, taking in the morning air. He breathed out, pacing himself as his mother coached him in a delicate tone. Gordon moved his legs off the bench, ghosting through his mother just as she reverted back to her spirit form. Althea stood and said to her son, "You okay, Gordon?"

He nodded yes and reclined his posture, hand on his chest. He continued breathing, not always at ease, gulping heavy breaths through his nose. Gordon blinked his eyes wildly. Althea let her son have his moment to balance himself from the dreamed, historical incident from where he'd awoken. "What did you see?" she asked him after several minutes.

"It was long ago…" Gordon stuttered. "It was far back…" he mumbled. He looked directly up at his mother. He realized he was shaking, speaking erratically. His mother's expression wasn't worried, but she didn't look comfortable either. Gordon considered his state the cause and took another moment to decompress. He rubbed his hands together and then placed them on his knees. He tipped his head back and closed his eyes. His third eye appeared, congealing as a golf ball-sized swirl of lilac energy resting against his forehead. He opened his physical eyes and looked at his mother. He grinned and shook his head. His sly smile put Althea at ease. Her son was truly relaxed.

"Ziko Yswil," he uttered through his smile.

Althea inquired, "Who is that, Gordon, dear?"

Gordon wiped his palms on his knees. He didn't answer his mother. Instead, he inquired, "Ma…why're you here?"

Althea's motherly instinct raised her eyebrow as Gordon questioned her presence rather than answer her inquiry. But she calmed. Perhaps a reminder of who was the parent and who was the child wasn't exactly what

Gordon needed after his ordeal. Althea lowered her eyebrow like a gunslinger placing a gun's hammer back to a safe position. "I was in Harlem with your father," Althea explained. "I heard your cry from there. I materialized here and your body was all aglow with that lilac spirit of yours. I was worried." She paused before asking, "You need some incanted lemon water or tea?"

"No, thank you, Ma," Gordon answered. He ruffled the twists in his hair. "I was glowing?" he asked his mother.

"Bright, and as wild as your hair," she answered. Althea looked at her son, head cocked to the side. "You sure you don't need anything—your chamber for healing, perhaps?"

"Yes, Ma…" Gordon assured.

Althea stated her initial query. "Okay, then, who is Ziko Yswil?"

Again, Gordon didn't directly answer his mother's inquiry. Instead he blurted in a soft voice, "I saw a world with three moons. It was our world—this world," he emphasized. "It was long ago as our conjure legends tell it. Pambunjila."

Althea's lips curled into a gentle smile. "Beautiful and interesting. Our world's three moons. Red, black, and green," she said in a tone that matched her son's. "Golden halos surrounding them," she added. "You've seen them before, though, Gordon. Haven't you? In the living story you composed with your darling, Fey Forrester."

Gordon blushed and shrugged at hearing his mother address he and Fey's relationship. He replied to his mother, but was mainly speaking to himself, pondering. "I considered the events the Pious Wars, and now I know them as true," he said. He looked at his mother and continued, "It was wrapped up in mythology—symbolism pimp walkin' as a story and such, y'know. Like the rest of the story."

"*Pimp walking?*" commented Althea, eyebrow raised at her son. Her smile changed its definition. "Our myths are *pimp walking* now, are they, Gordon?"

Gordon chuckled. "Yeah…you know what I mean, Ma," he defended through his boyish smile and reddening color. He lifted his shoulders and continued, "I mean, something felt real about the ambience of the introduction of it—armies and Mother Covenant, but the rest was—"

"Forecasting," Althea interrupted. "You and Fey's role in procuring the Grand Conjure and Wish."

Gordon agreed. "Yeah. Just figuring ourselves out, I guess. Our spirits."

"Yes, your *spirits*." Althea cleared her throat, throwing a curious eye at how the activities of her son and Miss Forrester were 'figuring themselves out'. "Now, dear boy, clear the mystery up for your mother on who this Ziko Yswil is, or rather, was."

Gordon's face lit up. He informed his mother with a child's excitement, "The mythic alchemist-warrior from those stories you and Pop told Cedron and me growing up," he clarified. "His name is Ziko Yswil not Alchemham."

Althea informed her son. "Well, Gordon, dear, *Alchemham* was not a real name. It's simply the words *alchemy* and *hammer* put together." She asked, "I never told you that?" She saw her son's expression freeze. She thought that maybe he was taken aback by her minor revelation. But she observed her son pat the air, just above his knees. His eyes were possessed with an intense, inquisitive stare and he started snapping his fingers.

"I was there..." Gordon said in a low, reflective voice.

"There? Where, Gordon?"

"There!" he expressed, looking up at his mother. "My spirit possessed Ziko Yswil. I was him." Gordon scanned his mother, waiting to see skepticism own her expression, but incredulity never appeared.

"I heard your voice coming from the glow," Althea spoke. "You were saying the Swahili phrase for time stepping. You repeated it over and over like a chant." Concern blossomed on Althea's face. "Do you feel overwhelmed, Gordon?" his mother asked. "Conjuring history through dream can tire even the powerful, cosmic lilac spirit that you possess. Did you see something that pulled your spirit to the past?" Althea let her son know, "I would hate for you to be trapped in history. Your spirit in another's body," she shook her head at the thought. "I've heard tales—rumors mostly. All centered on the fear of changing history." Althea rambled, "Time stepping is called many things in many cultures. I don't believe anyone has truly achieved it. Even the great horn blowers Pete Peters and his son Horatio just composed history into a visual song and rhyme."

"I was there, Mom," Gordon repeated.

"I believe you, Gordon," Althea assured her son. "But I ask again, what pulled your spirit into the ancient past? Can you remember? For the sake of caution when you dream of history again."

Gordon did, and his emotions stirred. He dropped his head, eyes closed. He leaned so far forward his head was almost on his lap. Althea's specter shifted solid, and she sat next to her son on the bench. She rubbed his back, which helped stifle the storm brewing inside him. The lilac color swirling in his two physical eyes brightened to match the third. "Fey was there..." he spoke.

Althea flinched at the sound of Gordon's voice. Her spirit picked up the faint timbre of obsessive determination. "A past life?" questioned Althea.

Gordon shook his head, straightening up and looking at his mother. A bright smirk decorated his face. "No," he said. "Her spirit was pulled there. She possessed the body of a woman named Oris Del who was assisting Ziko

Yswil in meditation. They were fighting monsters, *dubwana*, Ziko called them. I've heard our composition make mention of them. They're true name is *mzigo*."

"Mzigo," Althea repeated, recalling. "Dubwana. Yes, I've heard of such creatures," she noted with a nod.

"While Ziko and Oris meditated, their bodies were open for possession," Gordon continued, smile growing wider. He was now looking at the ground, remembering almost everything. There was an overview, but not the finer details. "Fey possessed the woman first. I saw her, and she could feel I was watching her through the dreaming. She called to me. She instructed me to possess the alchemist, and I did." Gordon's smile dissolved as his memory started failing. Perplexity remained on his face. Gordon struggled to remember the moments between he and Fey. "We spoke," he stated. "I *know* rather than *remember* it. Like a feeling. I can recall having a hard time keeping my balance."

"Being another person is not easy," Gordon's mother disclosed. "I've counseled with other spirits in my realm who've done so. It's no journeyman's task, and definitely nothing for a novice to take on. I've never tried it myself. There's no need since I can make myself flesh long enough for your father and me to…" her voice trailed away. She and Gordon looked at one another, exchanging awkward expressions. "…*enjoy* one another's company." A nervous laugh only added to the uncomfortable direction the conversation between mother and son had steered into, and Althea proved that spirits could indeed blush. "My point, Gordon, is to make note that the task of possession is not easy. You added time stepping to it. And your travel didn't hurry you several decades past but millennia before, before, and before that. You saw things only considered myth in the Conjure world. You saw a time when our sky was bejeweled with three moons."

Gordon nodded at his mother. He turned all three eyes to Fey Forrester's silver monument. Frustration continued swirling on his face. "I could probably quote specific lines of dialogue from the alchemist's story, but I can't think of one word Fey and I said to one another." Gordon's knee bounced with nervous energy. He looked at Spook. He looked up at the sun for a brief moment, calculating the time. It was 10:54. He was scheduled to meet with Lady Arachne in six minutes. Gordon didn't want to be late, as he'd been putting off this reading for months. But he had matters to discuss with his mother. "Ma," he called. Althea looked at him. The tremble in Gordon's voice was ever so slight when he inquired, "Do you have an instinct on time stepping?"

"I did try," Althea admitted. "More truthfully, I considered it. This was when I died and rose as a spirit. I wanted to possess my former self with the intent on changing history, preventing my death. But I let the sentiment go when I believed your father had moved on…in his way…" She cleared her throat and masked her distress with a smile. "I only had other spirits reiterate to me the dangers of such conjuration." Althea's heartache broke through. "And after your father began seeing other women…well, as you know, I didn't even present my yearly visits." Gordon bobbed his head, trying to keep at bay a somber expression. Althea noticed the change in her son's mood.

"Yeah…" Gordon reacted. He changed the subject. "Achieving the time step isn't the problem. It's keeping stable while I'm…" Gordon's words dropped away. His eyes spied the ancient device, Spook. He bent down and lifted the *Nigrum Nigrius Nigro*, setting it on his lap. He opened the laptop-like mechanism to its black mirror face. He set The Judgment card aside and then inquired, "Spook, can you pull up a list of rituals or curios used to aid a conjurer with wa-wa-wakati…ha-hatua." Three ancient symbols appeared on the black mirror's face. Their spacing was flush, suggesting the three symbols created a single word. Another set of distinct symbols, four in total, materialized beside the first. Their spacing, as flush as the first set of symbols, also hinted at a single word. Gordon, assisted by his third eye, translated the ancient script. "Ma," Gordon called, eyes still on the two words lighting up the black mirror in front of him. "You know anyone with a…" He squinted at the words, making sure of their translation before speaking, "Magic clock…?" Gordon looked up at his mother. He missed the words on the screen shift into English script, spelling out the phonetic pronunciation of the Swahili, *uchawi saa*.

Althea understood the Swahili. She pondered a moment before she spoke. Her eyes remained locked on the black mirror's face. "We have plenty of bokor tinkerers on hand. The question is: can they build that?" Althea addressed a second inquiry, speaking to the black mirror. "Spook, would you happen to have stored in that ancient memory of yours some schematics on how to put together such a device, and a list of parts one would need to create such a thing?" Spook's black-mirrored face lit up with ancient text scrolling across it. Althea looked close, but her spectral eyes couldn't translate the language. She looked at her son. "Gordon, what's all that say there?"

"It's a list of parts," Gordon translated to his mother. "They're everyday items: crystals and particular metals. But they require specific incants and rituals to activate 'em." The ancient script dissolved, and in its place faded up a purple-line graphic of a schematic resembling a pocket watch. "I guess I would clip it to my belt when I went into the dreaming. That would keep me locked in time."

Althea rubbed her son's arm. She warned in a low voice, "Now, look, you be careful with all this information."

Gordon bobbled his head, affirming, "Sure, sure, Ma. Of course, I will."

Althea reminded her son, "We are at war, Gordon." Mamma Goodspeed's voice was a whisper but stern enough to get through to her youngest child. "Stanley Fallows still has conjure children in his keep, and sadly enough we can't up and go to the police with our affairs. We have eyes in uniform, but they haven't been able to pull any information—most likely because Stanley too has eyes in uniform. Above all, I can only imagine what the parents are going through, this long with uncertainty."

"I know, Ma," Gordon said.

Althea took her hand from her son's arm and lifted a single finger close to his face. "Reveal this information to the Elders only," she stressed. "Maman Anansi can assist in finding a bokor tinkerer." She penetrated Gordon's temple with her ghostly finger. Gordon flinched, but settled moments after. "There's information in there, young man. I'm sure you and Miss Forrester didn't just stare at one another with goofy grins. You all had to've talked about something. When and where she received her hexed scars, I'm sure." Althea retracted her finger and lowered her hand. "Perhaps we can find Stanley Fallows' whereabouts and locate our lost children." She added, "And put an end to their parents' worries, and perhaps, this destructive conflict."

"Right, Ma," said Gordon. He gave his mother's spirit a kiss on the cheek. She leaned into her son's affectionate gesture, concentrating to make her form solid to accept his light kiss. "I have to get to Lady Arachne's sanctum," Gordon stated. "Madame Jeliya will be there. Not sure of Maman Anansi. You can go back to Pop in Harlem." He put The Judgment card into his jacket pocket and then closed Spook, black mirror folded against the bejeweled console. He stood and joked, "You go *enjoy* one another's company."

Althea looked at Gordon with a side-eyed expression. "Watch your freshness, young man."

"Absolutely, Ma," he replied in a playful voice, bending down and giving Althea a final kiss on the cheek.

She accepted, focused solid.

Gordon popped away.

Althea stayed behind, staring up at Fey Forrester's silver monument. A smile appeared on the spirit's face. Her ghostly presence dimmed, becoming translucent. Althea's specter faded away, returning to her husband in Harlem.

4

Gordon materialized at the front door to Lady Arachne's brownstone accompanied by a snap and burst of lilac smoke. Spook was tucked under his arm, and before he could knock, the slender and alluring oracle answered the door. Gordon extinguished the blaze of his spherical, lilac-glowing third eye and took a step back. He bowed at the neck toward Fable Avenue's third matriarch.

Lady Arachne's presence forged a red-hot, magnetic signature that pulled all masculine bodies to her center. Gordon was once no different, but his lilac spirit was beholden to the cobalt-blue flame now, though she was lost to time. His beloved Fey Forrester. There was still gravity to Lady Arachne, however. It possessed her smile, the resonance of her voice, and her breathtaking, cool-dark skin that gave her slender frame a shadowy wave, like a flickering flame when she walked.

Gordon shared an awkward moment with Lady Arachne. It occurred in late May during an intense tarot reading. Fable Avenue's third matriarch was able to draw out animated scenes from the past using her ancient tarot deck, coupled with a heavy concentration using Gordon's cosmic spirit and her own magnificent conjure. Together they witnessed the first fortune told concerning Fey Forrester's inherited cobalt-blue flame. It came from a woman who led a small conjure community in an African-American town in Kansas. It was the late 1930s. The woman's name was Patricia George, who loved nothing more than frolicking naked and drunk with her husband, Robert George. This was where Gordon and Lady Arachne's spying eyes peeped in. Their focus was so strong they couldn't look away as the moving picture was broadcast between the Two of Cups, the Three of Cups, and the Six of Pentacles.

It was an awkward moment to watch while seated across the matriarch's divination table, peering into the drawn cards and holding hands. Drunken dancing between the community conjure queen and conjure king became a wild, sexual scene that played out inside the frame of Lady Arachne's mystical cards. At the height of passion, the conjure queen straddled her husband, holding him close and whispering prophesy into his ear. *"Over the crossroads and below the single moon, the cobalt-blue flame blossoms and blooms!"* she exhaled in a fiery whisper. Her hips gyrated faster on her husband, and her words became louder when she expressed, *"Fiery, intertwined with him—like The First Two!"* Then her body raised, and she bounced with a spastic enthusiasm on her husband's manhood. Gordon remembered being drawn into the conjure king's emotions, and at the same moment, Lady Arachne was pulled into the heightened state of the conjure queen.

Gordon remembered the seer squeezing his wrists as the conjure queen hollered, "*Up, up, she soars to nurse the sickly, pale Selene—*" Then, lifting her face to the heavens, the woman shouted with icy-blue smoke emanating from both her mouth and eyes, "*Oṣupa, split into three—the cobalt-blue flame returns our colors, red, black, and green!*"

The image snapped from existence, returning the cards to their original, sketched state. Lady Arachne let go of Gordon's wrists and composed herself. Gordon checked in a casual manner if he'd reached climax. He hadn't. Lady Arachne tilted her head back and bellowed a loud guffaw. Gordon managed a smile that sputtered into uncontrollable laughter. The moment would be their secret, though he would tell Fey in time. Until then, peering into the past would remain a solo outing, using Spook. It took far less focus anyway. Perhaps, he considered the moment, a brief, emotional encounter with time stepping. A precursor to today.

"Hello, Lady Arachne," greeted Gordon.

The grand conjure dame replied, "Good morning, Gordon. Come in." She peeked over his shoulder and witnessed Madame Jeliya crossing the street and traipsing up to her house. Gordon noticed Lady Arachne's gaze and made a turn of his head and upper body to see Madame Jeliya slipping through the brownstone's front gates.

Fable Avenue's second matriarch beamed bright at Gordon as she ascended the stairs. She said to him, "Now, Lilac Spirit, I have seen many things being a part of our community—things strange to common folk but normal to us." She stood next to Gordon when her ascent ceased at the top of the stairs. "But that bursting pop-in, pop-out you do through your remarkable lilac conjure…?" she aimed a finger at Gordon and remarked in a deep, craggily voice, "Now, that's the jazz that brought this street into existence."

Gordon grinned in return, chuckling a bit out of sincere modesty. He dipped his face away from the words Madame Jeliya anointed him with, but then recovered. It was catching a glimpse of Lady Arachne that brought him out of his bashful dodge of Madame Jeliya's compliment. Peculiar, her look. Eyes filled with want, aimed at Madame Jeliya. Gordon's instinct pricked at him, but he ignored whatever code it tapped up his neck and against the back of his head, resisting the urge to interpret. Gordon wondered what Papa Solomon would make of the exchange, the older man who was once caught between the two women in his younger days. Their muted rivalry was often stocked with subtle jabs at one another. Now, here was a subtle amorous gaze grinning from the tarot reader, swallowing Madame Jeliya whole. Gordon noticed that Madame Jeliya too held an odd, lingering stare at her matriarchal sister. Her gaze ran up Lady Arachne's slender frame and attached itself to the tarot reader's eyes.

"How are you, sister?" Madame Jeliya greeted her fellow Matriarch.

Perhaps Madame Jeliya's gaze was not as friendly. Gordon spied her expression. She held tight to her smile, though her eyes betrayed a tightness of another sort.

Lady Arachne straightened her posture and answered, "I am very well, Thelema. How has your day been?"

Madame Jeliya's clenched posture melted, and she sighed, "I've performed two rituals this morning for clients, and I'm a little winded." She paused to make a face showing frustration. She huffed, "And I still have the dead to attend to at the funeral home."

Lady Arachne's eyes filled with concern, and she remarked, "My apologies, Thelema. You and Maman Anansi were present for Gordon's reading last February. I wanted you to be here to take up where we'd left off." She sighed and proposed, "Maman Anansi can't be present, and you're not feeling well. Perhaps I can handle the proceedings alone."

"That's no bother, Lena," Madame Jeliya declined in a polite voice. "Thank you, really. It will be your energy at play here. I will assist where I can."

The concern didn't leave Lady Arachne's eyes. She suggested to Madame Jeliya, "I just worry about your strength, Thelema." Lady Arachne made a face, feeling uncomfortable for bringing up the subject as she stated, "That needleman, taking a bit of your essence."

Gordon braced himself for Madame Jeliya's curt defense, but was surprised when the matriarch conceded. "Yes, I'm sure that has something to do with it," she said. Then she stated, "Maman Anansi hasn't been able to find a residual hex. It's taken my strength, but I'm okay." Madame Jeliya turned to Gordon and offered an apology. "I'm sorry, Gordon. I'm not sure if this talk of hexes is bothering you, considering what happened to your mother and what she encountered with a night doctor."

Eyes were now on Gordon. The subject matter didn't bother him at all, and he expressed, "No bother, Madame Jeliya. My mother's physical body was taken from my family, but as you know, her spirit is around and doing well."

Madame Jeliya managed a smile and a nod, feeling better for having not offended Gordon. Lady Arachne put forward, "Either way, Thelema, I would like to offer sessions. You give so many to people. I'd like to offer one for you in return. I'd do a ritual using my tarot deck, focusing on the Strength card, help you regain yours."

Madame Jeliya accepted Lady Arachne's offer without hesitation. Her quick acceptance came rather as a surprise to Gordon. But before he could dwell on the matter, Madame Jeliya cited that she would need her strength to assist in an upcoming ritual being performed at the crossroads.

Gordon perked up. "Is that for the Old Goon's daughter?" he inquired. "Lillian?"

"Yes," Madame Jeliya answered him. "They were going to wait until July for the Rising Festival, but Satchel is already making an impromptu appearance overseeing the Eledas crossroads property, taking control of the Fable brother's houses. We'll have Eledas representation on the street. Old blood," she added. Madame Jeliya noticed Lady Arachne roll her eyes. She ignored her conjure sister's gesture and stated, "He and Lillian's mother will arrive at the crossroads in a few days. Lillian will be with them."

Lady Arachne brightened. "Simaetha will be there!" she exclaimed. "Wonderful. That will offset that old fool's presence."

Madame Jeliya chuckled at Lady Arachne's sentiment, exhaling a bit, showing a renewed sense of strength. It was then that Lady Arachne progressed the proceedings. She turned, and from over her shoulder, directed Madame Jeliya and Gordon to enter her home. Gordon displayed his manners as a gentleman and allowed Madame Jeliya to proceed first.

Lady Arachne instructed her guests to follow her to her sanctuary's depths. Once her guests were all the way inside the hallway entrance, the tarot reader mouthed an incant to close and lock the doors. On the garden floor, Lady Arachne turned to Gordon and snatched Spook from his hands. It was a playful gesture, and Gordon was surprised by the matriarch's swift grab. He wondered if she'd used an incant to buff her agility. Madame Jeliya lost her manners, face becoming bent, scowling at her fellow Matriarch's actions.

Lady Arachne remarked as she lifted the *Nigrum Nigrius Nigro* above her head, examining underneath Spook, "I've wondered what dreams this device has shown you, Gordon." She turned to him and stressed, "And I mean concerning my personal inquiries." She opened Spook and presented a query to the *Nigrum Nigrius Nigro*. "What dreams have you revealed to Mister Goodspeed?" Spook's black-mirror monitor scrolled ancient text. Lady Arachne understood none of it. "Gordon, can you translate?" she asked. Lady Arachne passed the occult mechanism to Gordon.

Madame Jeliya swooped in before Gordon could extend his hands, seizing the device from Lady Arachne's loose grip. The sultry matriarch gasped with a bit of a jump as Madame Jeliya passed her, Spook in her hands. "I believe this language is saying not to hog the spirit's time," she scolded in a playful tone.

Lady Arachne raised an eyebrow and snapped back through a smirk, "I've seen you drink, Thelema, and know all too well that hogging all the spirits is a job only *you* are highly qualified for."

This was the manner Gordon was more use to from the two matriarchs.

Madame Jeliya gave riposted with her own grin at Lady Arachne, but stayed her tongue from rejoinder. Instead, she set the ancient technology on the long wooden dining table in the middle of the room. She stood straight and thought for a moment. She started her reply just as an instinct came to Gordon. The phone rang and interrupted the retort she'd crafted from her wit. While she and Lady Arachne scoffed at the phone's sudden intrusion, both women fixed their faces when their buzzing instincts felt the presence of Maman Anansi on the other end of the unceasing, ringing phone. Lady Arachne stepped to the side table positioned next to her sofa, maneuvered around a stylized lamp, and picked up her cordless phone.

She stood straight and greeted through a polite smile, "*Hujambo*, Maman Anansi. Have your duties at daycare ended?"

"Yes," the other greeted back. "Has Gordon resumed his reading? I can still attend through spirit. He has his black-mirror device?"

Lady Arachne spotted Spook from the corner of her eyes. "Yes, Maman Anansi. Gordon brought his device."

"I'll project from my mirror to his," Maman Anansi proclaimed. "You know my spirit, sister. Attune Gordon's mirror to mine, and I will come through."

"As you wish, Grand Mother," Lady Arachne saluted with her syntax. "We will see you shortly." They gave parting words, and then Lady Arachne returned the phone to its base. "Well, this is delightful. Maman Anansi will attend after all. She will project from her black mirror to your device's black mirror, Gordon." A sigh escaped her, and her eyes changed to sympathy as they focused on Madame Jeliya. "Would you be strong enough to assist, not in the projection, but in the conjure of a strong *aabo*? I don't want to offend our Grand Mother, but we need all the protection from prying eyes that we can get."

"I can assist, sister," Madame Jeliya assured. "We will not be outside of time, but I will add to the protective *aabo* conjured by Maman Anansi."

Lady Arachne presented a gracious bow at the neck. A smile defining her relief accompanied the gesture. Then she looked at Gordon, ordered him to take up the *Nigrum Nigrius Nigro*, and follow her and Madame Jeliya into the reading sanctuary. Gordon was swallowed by the ambience of Lady Arachne's divination room. It was a small room that appeared to give off a feeling of expansion when the door closed. Lady Arachne added to the otherworldly environment by using an incant to create a vibrant, mystical lighting from the candles in the room.

Gordon took a seat at the candle- and cloth-decorated divination table. Its intricately carved, long-running sides were not covered by the runner, exposing the well-crafted designs at its edges. Gordon set Spook down in front of him. He didn't interact with the magitech's console or black-mirror screen until directed by Madame Jeliya. Gordon spoke to the ancient device, giving it commands, as his fingers sailed across the jeweled console, typing on the gems making up the keyboard.

Maman Anansi's image lit up the black mirror's face, pale from her actual color, resonating with a flickering shimmer of indigo. She was dressed in her cultural wear and sitting on a throne-like ebony chair. The mirror then projected the image from its flat surface onto the jeweled console. And there she was: a miniature, holographic casting of Fable Avenue's First Lady of Conjure.

"Gordon," the matriarch smiled at him while speaking his name. "How are you, young man?"

"I'm well, Maman Anansi," Gordon answered. He turned Spook ninety-degrees, and pushed the antediluvian mechanism to the left-end of the table, stretching his arm to position it at the table's edge. Fable Avenue's head matriarch was now seated at the head of the table, granted a full view to the proceedings. Madame Jeliya sat at the end opposite Maman Anansi's projected form, and Lady Arachne sat across from Gordon.

"Hello, sister," Maman Anansi's projected form said to her sister-in-law. Madame Jeliya extended a hello in return. "I can feel your concentration strengthening my casted *aabo*. Thank you. We will be safe from prying eyes belonging to those unalike to our nature." Maman Anansi spied Lady Arachne's deck of cards on the table. An incomplete spread was already laid out in front of Gordon.

The alignment was familiar to him. This session saw it completed. Originally, the reading was interrupted by a series of events that would steer Fable Avenue to this moment defined by kidnapped children and his beloved Fey Forrester hexed and taken from him. The drawing, with its color faint, was of an African couple standing opposite one another, touching chalices. From Gordon's perspective, this card was upside down, in the reversed position. Over the Two of Cups was The Devil. Covering both cards was The Tower card. But despite the view of the Two of Cups obscured by an overlay of cards, Gordon saw its full appearance. To his eyes only, the African couple shifted to resemble him and Fey.

The events that interrupted the initial reading were not the only reason there had been such a long pause. Overwhelmed, Gordon committed what he can now admit was a selfish act. He flew to the heavens in cosmic form, isolated himself from the world below, and lived among black cosmic spirits. That was February. He returned in April, but Lady Arachne gave him his time and space. Now it's June, seventh day of. No more delays. There had been other readings conducted, but this particular read had not recommenced.

Gordon leaned forward, locking his hands together with the palms of his thumbs touching. After a moment, focusing, he rested his hands on the edge of the divination table. His right leg shook, and his eyes scanned the cards configured in front of him. Gordon's demeanor didn't escape detection from the three matriarchs. Even Maman Anansi could feel Gordon's anxiety through her projected form.

"What do you feel, Gordon?" Lady Arachne inquired.

Gordon's leg ceased its tremble when he answered, "The weight of the world on my shoulders."

Lady Arachne nodded. "I see. Draw two cards," she tasked of him.

Gordon pulled a card from the deck. He flipped it over and placed it on the table. It was the Eight of Wands. Drawn on its face was an African man walking a path, burdened with the weight of carrying eight, mighty, wooden staves. Gordon drew another card. It was The World, and he smirked when he turned it face up. He placed the card atop the Eight of Wands and chuckled, "That's a neat trick. Eight of Wands—burden—and The World card over it. Cute."

The Fable Avenue seer was not offended by Gordon's mordant wit, and truthfully, she meant no harm with her jape. Lady Arachne grinned back at him. "It's what I do, Gordon," she relayed in a proud voice. Then her smile faded from her countenance, replaced by an austere expression. "Or rather, it's what I show," she corrected. "Your current state," she told him. She reached forward and took The World card, placing it with the initial configuration. She asked Gordon if he had The Judgment card with him. Gordon removed it from his jacket pocket, handing it over to the third matriarch. Lady Arachne then situated the cards into the completeness of the formation's familiarity: The World and The Judgment cards laid over one another, slipping them underneath the Death card. "And here we are again," commented Lady Arachne.

Looking at fate's carefully positioned cards, Gordon's heart skipped in its pulse. His teeth tightened behind his lips, and his leg trembled again. His eyes darted between the drawings on the cards laid out before him. The weight he felt evaporated his courage and shifted into a baleful fog. He believed a truth was to be revealed. It made him feel as if he was a guilty man who'd convinced himself that he had to commit an atrocious act, but the truth was coming into light, and all that could remain was the fact that he was a monster. His instinct didn't tingle against the back of his neck. It burned.

"Gordon," Maman Anansi called him. He turned and faced her diminutive projection. "It's time for us Matriarchs to reveal to you what we've already come to know. The insight granted by the cards." She turned to Lady Arachne and called, "Lena? Would you please, dare I say, do the honor?"

Lady Arachne nodded at the Grand Matriarch's miniscule projection, and then she faced Gordon's wide-eyed expression that was breaking down into an aggrieved articulation. The seer knew that things wouldn't get better when she revealed the pregnant significance of the cards.

She unveiled, "The Lilac Spirit and the Cobalt-Blue Flame are the Grand Conjure summoned to bring about the Grand Wish." That didn't sound too bad to Gordon. But his supernatural instinct slithered up his neck and fabricated a façade of disquiet separating him from relief. And indeed, the seer had more to say. "That Grand Wish is your path and purpose—you and Miss Forrester's." Lady Arachne presented the cards' total interpretation, "You are here to destroy our world." Before Gordon could react, the matriarch had more to say. "You and Miss Forrester are the final storm," she announced. "You are the all-consuming fire for this world. The two of you hold the Rada in you. But you are also the Petwo; you are the drum that beats with the anger of endless generations of African conjurers enslaved and stripped of power. You are the final tide to wash away the grim, terrible conditions that we endured, and continue to endure, at the hands of a once openly brutal system, now sly with its oppressive behavior."

Her words were finished. A beat of silence struck with little movement. Madame Jeliya and Maman Anansi met eyes. They then looked at Lady Arachne who continued watching Gordon. The young man's face was stone. His body was fixed in place, but all three Matriarchs could sense the flash flood of emotions storming inside him.

It took a moment, and then, a feeling.

Potential-turned-kinetic reaction dripped down his face.

Gordon's lilac eyes bent and squinted as perplexity burst through them like light. There was no accretion in the pale-purple brightness of his eyes. However, his cheeks flushed with anger boiling through them. His lips curled in disgust, and then parted for him to question audibly, *"Destroy the world?"*

"Will anyone miss it, Gordon?" queried Maman Anansi.

Cold seeped into Gordon's person. It funneled through him, traveling through physical canals and leaving him feeling like a pit, where ice breathed its frosty breath up and out of his lungs. His body felt as if it donned a coat carved from the arctic ice, with no incant to warm him.

"No!" he rejected. "We're here to make a change, yes, but this is too extreme." He looked at each of the matriarchs, a look of annoyance scrawled on his face. His eyes, though, pleaded for them to agree with his words. "Destroy the world!" he repeated. "We're heroes, right? Saviors of some kind…?" He kept the action at bay to conjure his cosmic, shadowy suit and take to the stars as the lilac flame. But the thought remained. He debated the echo effect of leaving Fey to her fate and again indulging in self-displacement among the spirits above. He could accomplish this action after the children were secured and Stanley Fallows and his horde defeated. Then he would banish himself far from the reach of any earthly conjure that could summon him to engage in such a fatalistic act.

It would hurt him to allow Fey to remain drifting aimless through time or whatever realm she spun through. Perhaps the spirits that possessed them would eventually dissolve away, passing to another generation. Their bodies would then evaporate from existence should physical flesh not be attunable to their environment. They would no longer be responsible for the vast lives lost in whatever destruction their conjuring would produce.

That was Gordon's plan.

Lady Arachne moved her eyes toward Maman Anansi's projected image, but then she shifted her sight to Madame Jeliya. The matriarchs noticed Gordon's eyes intensifying in their glow, matching his visibly distressed expression.

"We're given stories at such early ages that define what makes heroes and heroines," said Madame Jeliya in a serene tone. Her warm, incant-laced voice eased Gordon's emotions and dimmed the strengthening glow in his lilac eyes. "Your cartoons, your comic books, even. The lessons are there. Age appropriate. They teach you that heroes make challenging decisions, especially ones where the narrative shows more difficult paths taken. Some heroes destroy instead of build or restore."

Gordon interjected in a polite, but correcting tone, "I read *The Moops*. They're unorganized thieves belonging to an ancient order. I read *Iboju Boy And Nkisi Girl*—they help expose assuming heroes as the real villains. I read *Shadow Tales: Rose Tail and Old Black*; they're two dimension-hopping, talking squirrels."

Madame Jeliya chuckled. "I think of those *akọni* specifically as I speak—those heroes created by conjure folk from the community. There are moral lessons in those funny books. They're encoded with our culture. We get them. You've grown up with them. Your emotion clouds you now, but you know a lot has been staring you in the face since childhood. Our spiritualism—our *conjure*—reaches back to the beginning. To the Grand Two, *Ixu* and *Gira*. The black bodies that intertwined, loved, and created light and life. Within those small morsels of knowledge, we retain their All, our Beginning. We know it's not so easy with the decisions we make. There comes a time where all that is created must be uncreated; and all that is done must be undone. You and Fey represent those spirits, that beginning. You two are the Omega to the long, long, long ago Alpha."

Gordon relaxed, withdrawing to the thought of this revelation. His instinct buzzed, and then anamnesis of sorts occurred. A tap into the past using Spook and a pair of goggles with black lenses carved from the crystalized eyes of an angel named Sekhet. She was cobalt-blue in spirit, similar to his beloved Fey Forrester. She fell to Earth in the late eighteen-hundreds. More specifically, Tanzania, Africa, eighteen-eighty. Her fall was witnessed by an African man named Tembo. Her body was a bright, streaking comet in the clear, noon-day sky as it dived toward the sandy floor.

Gordon recalled her impact. A vivid image. The desert sand attempted to climb up and touch the sky when she slammed into the grainy, flaxen surface. It was as if the ground wished to trade places with the magnificent ball of cobalt-blue fire fallen from the heavens.

The thick, sandy pillar attained a great height, but was far from the reach of the stars. It billowed out, rolling at its apex. Then came a succession of noise—like cannon fire that deafened even the thunderous magnitude of the impact. Springing up from the ground were tall, lively trees with thick bodies and branches. Their foliage intertwined and formed a dome.

Gordon was lost in this thought, and the matriarchs allowed him this time. He replayed what he saw. Explosive impact to explosive life springing up from the barren ground. Something other than a glow was in his eyes. He peered at the divination table, eyes going back and forth as if scanning a monitor scrolling with information. A conclusion was ascertained, and Gordon looked up at Lady Arachne.

"No!" he said. "Life came from her. She brought life to a barren area."

"Who, Gordon?" asked Maman Anansi.

He turned his head and answered the Grand Matriarch, "Her name was Sekhet. Named after the goddess, I suppose. Sekhet Nefer. Professor Khepri's family kept a trinket carved from her eyes. They were crystalized into a black substance. She was a cobalt-blue flame, and she came to Earth."

"You saw her through your black mirror?" inquired Lady Arachne.

"Yes," Gordon revealed. "I don't know what happened to her lilac-flame counterpart. I don't even know who might have been responsible for her conjure to Earth to perform the Grand Conjure and Wish. I'm also not certain as to why a woman possessed with the cosmic flame, clearly from the time of ancient Kemet, didn't come through until the late eighteen-hundreds. I do remember her saying that Earth's despair pulled her into its orbit." Gordon thought to himself that perhaps she and her counterpart wished to exile themselves from the responsibility of destroying the world. But he also remembered her saying that her impact was not strong enough, especially without her other half. Gordon recounted for the matriarchs, "She hit the desert after coming through the atmosphere. There was a mushroom cloud made of sand and soot. Then these big trees sprang up from the ground." Gordon became animated as he narrated the historical account, throwing his arms up as he described the trees sprouting from the earth. He widened his reach horizontally and explained, "The trees covered a wide area, and they domed and intertwined. She created life, though I remember her saying the impact was not enough to destroy the world." Another thought came to him.

Maman Anansi called him on it. "You have an instinct, Gordon. Express it."

Gordon relaxed. He made a face as he was unsure of his thought. "It's from a lesson I remember. It was recited by W. Eric Reinwahl—the conjure lecturer who lives out in Queens." Maman Anansi's image was Lilliputian in its projection, but even out of the corner of his eye, Gordon's instinct caught the subtle smile brighten her countenance. He looked at her, and his vision narrowed on the subtle, diminutive motion. He rolled his eyes at all three of the powerful conjure women surrounding him. "And how long were the three of you waiting for me to come to a conclusion you're already aware of?"

Lady Arachne eyed her watch. "I believe Madame Jeliya wins the bet on how long it would take." Her eyes moved to her sister-in-matriarch who was gloating through a wide, beaming grin. "Those little set of words you gave were very eloquent, and they were well placed and timed to extend the wager in your favor, Thelema."

Madame Jeliya continued grinning. Her sly smile was the only form of confession she gave. But she did have words on the matter. "And to beat a seer, though you say your cards were not used."

"They were not," Lady Arachne assured, voice springing up into a harmonious, and teasing, falsetto. She added a gesture of raising a single finger and waving it back and forth. Then she turned to the Grand Matriarch's projected form and noted, "Maman Anansi, I'm sorry to say that since your time was the most off, you'll be buying drinks when next we indulge in Matriarch's Night Out."

"I accept my fate in this gamble," Maman Anansi yielded to her loss' demands.

The banter was entertaining, but Gordon interjected to let the matriarchs know, "You three are aware that I was willing to exile myself back to the stars—and leave Fey to her fate—so that we would not have to be responsible for the deaths of the Earth's population?"

"We apologize, Gordon," Maman Anansi comforted. "It is a burden. I felt the charge in you that conjures *inawo*—and I can only imagine how great a monster that would be for you to confront. But we matriarchs, playful as we might have been, were confident that you would reach the conclusion you did. The world and the Earth are two different things—as you remember from Mister Reinwahl's lesson. The world is simply our surroundings, our environment. What once was a paradise has become a poisoned, prison planet. *That* is what you and Miss Forrester are here to destroy. And new life will come from the two of you when you carry out the will of the Grand Conjure and Grand Wish."

Gordon nodded his head. He jokingly straightened his attire and commented in the same style of manner, "That's more like it." Then he relaxed. A moment passed. A more serious thought surfaced, and he divulged, "I saw the Pious Wars, a bit of their history." He looked at Lady Arachne and expounded, "In the dreaming."

"Oh…" Maman Anansi reacted, expressing aloud the interest piqued within all three of the matriarchs.

Gordon continued, facing the Grand Matriarch, "I saw the Alchemist with a Hammer. He's real, but he was stripped down as a hero. He was human, a person. He was brave for different reasons than what we've been nurtured on as young boys and girls thrilled by his exploits. Where he lived was ultimately caught up in the war's politics." He couldn't help but smile when he said, "There's so much to our conjure history, our culture. There's so much lost to time." Gordon caught himself before his words trailed to other matters. "Ziko Yswil—the Alchemist's true name—he took refuge in a lecture hall and found books that told the history of the Pious Wars. Like most paths to hell, the war has its origins in people with good intentions. Principles at war, and now we're here. It's a history so long ago, so lost to time, but we don't understand we're still so affected."

As powerful as the surrounding matriarchs were, none could imagine the things Gordon had been made privy to through his historical dreaming. Gordon's thoughts melted into a confession that his tongue and lips held tight. He'd seen Fey Forrester, and he wanted to tell the gathered party this information. He looked to his Elders, the people his mother said he could trust. But he hesitated to reveal the information. Instead, he told the matriarchs, "I have information. Sensitive," he defined.

Maman Anansi understood. "I declare without arrogance, that I am a black woman powerful in conjure; and the *aabo* I cast is made stronger by my sister-in-law. But, more powerful than any conjure I can put forth, is my paranoia. I trust none of these devils, lesser with their tricks and hexes as they may be. Gordon, I bid you farewell. You visit me and tell me this information in person. Impart it, for now, to the other matriarchs."

"Yes, Maman Anansi."

Before her image faded, Maman Anansi articulated to Gordon, "Remain wary, young Goodspeed. Our theory in your duties for the Grand Conjure and Wish is not law until otherwise proven and conducted. We urge you to take breath and not flight, or exile yourself from your responsibilities."

"Yes, Maman Anansi," Gordon repeated.

The first matriarch spotted the other two and said, "My sisters, carry on." Madame Jeliya and Lady Arachne offered parting words to the Grand Matriarch, and then Maman Anansi's projection faded from Spook's console. Madame Jeliya relaxed, no longer having to concentrate her otherworldly efforts to strengthen the cast of the invisible *aabo*, or shield, surrounding them. Gordon closed the ancient device for safe measure, and then he revealed, "I saw her. I saw Fey," he added increasing his tone, desperate to prove his experience. "Her spirit is lost in time, trailing. I saw her," he repeated.

Lady Arachne was stone. Madame Jeliya had a tremor of movement that she turned into words. "Hold your tongue, Gordon," she said. "I think Papa Solomon should be here for this." She turned to Lady Arachne, looking for agreement from her sister-in-matriarch. The seer nodded, and Madame Jeliya stood from her chair. "May I use your phone, sister? I'd send a mental thought, but I don't want it being picked up."

"Yes, yes. Of course," Lady Arachne permitted.

Madame Jeliya was up and through the door, giving it a soft close. Silence and preternatural candle light possessed the divination room. Lady Arachne didn't speak; too afraid her curiosity would pry more information from Gordon while Madame Jeliya made her call. The matriarch's voice was heard on the other side of the door. As, Gordon peered at the cards configured in front of him, his ears picked up Madame Jeliya's urgency to her husband. His instinct confirmed the other side of the conversation. Papa Solomon was on his way. Private Investigator for the conjure community, Martin Kimball, would be with him.

The conversation became a ghost, and it seemed that just as Madame Jeliya returned the phone to the receiver, the doorbell rang. Madame Jeliya's feet were heard scurrying up the stairs. Lady Arachne mouthed an incant, and the front doors on the parlor floor unlocked. Their unlatching infiltrated the silent divination room. Then came a muffle of polite greetings, which included a soft scolding from Madame Jeliya to her husband to have come through the garden-door entrance. Papa Solomon could be heard huffing his wife's words away in a tone more playful than serious. Then the doors closed. Lady Arachne spoke another incant. Her front doors locked. A march of feet down the stairs, and into the divination room returned Madame Jeliya with her husband Papa Solomon and Private Investigator Martin Kimball at her sides.

"Leave the door open," instructed Lady Arachne through a smile aimed at Papa Solomon. Martin entered behind the patriarch and locked the door. "Have a seat," she persisted to eye the Fable Avenue patriarch in all his tall and ebony glory. Her eyes were fixed like a solid tree holding steady to its roots. Madame Jeliya too beamed a sly smile at her husband, eyes in a sensual nature. Lady Arachne peeked at her, spying Madame Jeliya's subtle, epicurean glimpse.

Madame Jeliya gave Papa Solomon a light kiss on the cheek and then took a seat, motioning for Gordon to move down and give room to her husband. Papa Solomon thanked both Gordon and his wife as he sat down.

Martin took a seat at the end, opposite Madame Jeliya.

Lady Arachne's sly eyes and grin floated from Papa Solomon to Madame Jeliya. "The bottle of a good drink ain't all you hog and keep to yourself, little mamma," she teased.

A laugh broke through Madame Jeliya, which she tried to suppress. She covered her mouth, surprised by her reaction to Lady Arachne's comment. Her eyes shifted, spying her matriarch-sister. Madame Jeliya cleaned up her smile and said through a grimace that trembled with a little laughter, "I apparently didn't slap you hard enough out there for that fresh mouth of yours."

Lady Arachne purred, "Oh, sister, you'll definitely have to slap me harder to put this sweet and black, South Carolina woman in her place. And you might want to aim for the ass next time if that's your intention."

Gordon and Martin's faces widened with surprise.

Madame Jeliya's mouth dropped, and she gasped, *"Lena!"* But her laughter could not be kept down. She sputtered in an attempt to suppress it.

Lady Arachne sat up straight, smile still curved on her face, bubbling with a giggle that never penetrated her closed lips. Madame Jeliya let out another breath and shook her head, as she wondered why the often-antagonistic Lady Arachne was acting so jovial and inaptly lewd toward her this day, and with all the earnest aspects of the matters at hand. She was ready to make another statement, focused on commanding her conjured lions to pounce on Lady Arachne. But Madame Jeliya thought better of it, considering other words that referred to 'cats' that Lady Arachne could choose to twist around and make another lascivious remark.

Papa Solomon kept a stern eye on the two conjure matriarchs. The tension in his face exposed how tight his jaw had been clenched. It loosened for him to say, "I thought we were being brought to matters a little less light." His eyes remained thick with tension.

Both women put their humor aside.

Madame Jeliya rubbed her husband's arm and said, "There are urgent matters, Papa." She looked at Gordon. "You had news…" Her arm retracted. She focused on Gordon, as did everyone else.

Again, he hesitated to reveal the information. He specifically noted Martin. The private investigator was a strong conjure man, but far from the community Elders. *Should he be kidnapped in this war, would he break?* The haunting question floated through Gordon's head. He volleyed the arguments for and against relaying information in Martin's presence. Gordon felt dismissing him would be rude, and so he considered Martin's strengths. The detective focused his incants on heightening insight and skills as an investigator. But it was one of his personal conjures that was the deciding factor for Gordon. The detective possessed an ability to shield his mind from intrusion and strengthen his will's threshold. He was hard to break. But even as Gordon thought of the destructive power of Willie the Lich's hexed whip and the cursed point of a needleman's syringe, he blurted, "I saw Fey!"

Papa Solomon went to speak, but stopped mid-word. Martin had the same reaction. The revelation's jolt still managed to have impact on Lady Arachne and Madame Jeliya.

"I saw her," Gordon continued. "She's sailing through time. Her spirit," he clarified. He looked at Lady Arachne when he explained, "I saw her in the dreaming as I searched history for your lost card. I saw her in a very ancient time." He looked at Papa Solomon and Martin when next he revealed, "The history focused on Ziko the alchemist, the one who wields the hammer in old tales."

"From the children's stories?" asked Papa Solomon. A soft grin came through him. 'So that's his real name…" he pondered.

Gordon nodded, yes. "His settlement was overrun by mzigo—zombie-like monsters, but different." The Elders and Martin nodded, acknowledging their familiarity with the folklore. "It was an attack by zealots—leaders of a violent, spiritual movement."

"The Pious Wars," voiced Martin before Gordon could speak the title to the sanguinary battles. Gordon confirmed with a nod. The private detective lifted his eyebrows and whistled. "I'll admit, I was in the camp of conjure folk that believe those events as mythological. Symbolic, not historical."

"World conjure community is divided on that," addressed Papa Solomon. "Looks like we've all lost a couple bets," he concluded, looking at his wife.

Madame Jeliya beamed a triumphant smile at her husband and told him, "I'll accept my payment in a nice, cooked meal."

Papa Solomon chuckled. Remembering some of their earlier conversations surrounding the topic, he said to his wife, "You've been waiting twenty-plus years to say that, haven't you?"

"You bet your incant," Madame Jeliya replied, smile glued to her face.

"Good thing I didn't…" the patriarch commented.

She looked at Lady Arachne but still addressed her husband when she stated, "I've been cleaning up on wagers today."

Lady Arachne observed Papa Solomon and Madame Jeliya's banter. She liked looking at it, but Gordon's revelation stirred a curiosity that averted her attention back to the subject at hand. She inquired aloud, but to no one in particular, "My cards have touched the hands of someone from that ancient, ancient past?"

"They're connected somehow," answered Gordon. Then he

continued his tale. "Fey possessed someone in the past. It was a woman named Oris Del. She was meditating, and it made her body open to accept Fey's spirit. Once in control, Fey called to me…and I time stepped." Gordon observed the quiet awe brewing on everyone's faces. "My spirit took control of the alchemist Ziko as he meditated alongside the woman. Fey and I talked, but I can't remember anything. It's hazy, but I know it all happened."

"Your mind and spirit are adjusting to the time step, Gordon," Madame Jeliya stated. Her eyes, now scanning Gordon, bent by way of her inquisitiveness. She removed her expression when she noticed his gaze on her. The matriarch told him, "It could be months before the memory is recalled."

"I could barely remain stable while possessing Ziko," Gordon responded, looking away from everyone's stare at him. His gaze returned to the cards in front of him, centered mostly on the Two of Cups. "Fey and I spoke. She knows where Stanley Fallows lives. The children might be there." He looked up and asked Madame Jeliya, "Could you help me recall the memory?"

"Absolutely," Madame Jeliya assured.

"I could get Neyeli to assist," suggested Gordon. "My mother said to keep this information between a few of us in the community. She also said Maman Anansi would know someone who could put together a device to keep my spirit stable should I encounter that again." Gordon sounded impatient when he expressed, "I wish she'd stayed to hear this, but I'll visit her in Queens."

Martin raised a question, "Did Fey and you discuss where she was headed when she was ambushed by, what I can only guess were, needlemen?"

Gordon closed his eyes and rubbed his forehead. "I know she had a showing hosted by her art professor. Professor Brede." The image of a needle flashed in his head, accompanied by a bright, red light. Gordon opened his eyes by reflex. "The Bredes…" he uttered. "The Bredes could be needlemen. Husband and wife," he emphasized and then named, "Jacquelyn Brede and James Brede. I think that's something Fey and I discussed. They're both professors at Timothy Drew University. I had her husband for an English course." Then Gordon added, "I questioned them both about that night. I spoke to Fey's art professor. She said Fey left their place a little before sundown."

Papa Solomon contemplated. "Needlemen, night doctors. They're a long-standing network of lawyers, doctors, and politicians. We also got school teachers, administrators, and businessmen that wear the mask and carry the needle. Some have badges and guns too. We know that. And gender-wise, they don't discriminate among their ranks. That means we can't discriminate against any possibility on who carries a hexed syringe." Papa

Solomon thought for a moment and then expressed, "But, to keep all things fair, the conjure community operates in the same manner."

"We're not looking to hex people and end lives and divert destinies," Madame Jeliya said, countering her husband's comment in defense of their conjure-folk's hidden numbers in the workforce.

Papa Solomon considered his wife's word, gesturing his head in her direction and saying, "Point taken."

Martin suggested to Papa Solomon, urgency in his tone, "I can buff up my incants together and investigate them. Macario and I will see what we can dig up."

Papa Solomon waved the suggestion down. "Hold on, now, Martin. Let's take the safer route on this." He pointed at Gordon. "Let's first have the boy remember what he can—my wife and your niece leading that ritual. If those professors turn out to be night doctors—and damn good ones—it might alert Stanley Fallows and his wife. Let's move forward with the investigation we have going." He looked at his wife and Lady Arachne. "We've made some progress there." Back to Martin he addressed, "Stay your eyes on those matters. Let's not move up the food chain just yet."

"Yes, Papa Solomon," Martin acknowledged.

"Okay, then, that's settled," said Papa Solomon. To Gordon he asked, "You okay, Gordon?"

The question from Papa Solomon had the strength to lift the emotions weighing Gordon down. "I'll be fine." Though his voice sounded anything other than convincing. But he beamed a bright gesture, and it assisted in lifting his spirits, influencing his voice as he stated, "Having seen Fey…I'm at ease. Though, I don't remember much. She's alive. That's real, and I know it. It's not just a possibility or theory anymore."

Madame Jeliya assured, "Not only will Miss Kimball and I see to it that you reconnect to your memories, but also with Fey's wandering spirit."

"Thank you, Madame Jeliya," said Gordon to the nurturing matriarch. He scooped Spook up and tucked the device under his arm and ducked away from the Elders.

Madame Jeliya paid close attention to Gordon's movement. She asked him, "You in a rush, young Goodspeed? We old folks keeping you from something?" she joked. Papa Solomon chuckled at his wife's playful suggestion.

A guilty look ran across Gordon's face. "I'm sorry." He addressed her, but then extended his apology. "Everyone," Gordon said. He faced Madame Jeliya and Papa Solomon again. "I've been moping around here for months. I've been escaping into dream—history—to get my mind off Fey. Now she's here. Like I said, it's real now, not a theory that she'll return. I got a little spark in me."

"So, what's your next move?" asked Papa Solomon.

Gordon sighed. "Look, uh, I think the information about Fey should stay in a small group," he stated. "We extend that to Maman Anansi—as she's requested—and Neyeli. But I think there's someone else who should know." Gordon then iterated in a corrective voice, "Someone who deserves to know."

Fey's grandmother came to everyone's mind.

Lady Arachne gave the permission. "Yes, Gordon, dear," she said. "Please also inform Savannah that I'll be giving her a call later."

"Will do," Gordon assured. Then he asked, "Oh, Lady Arachne, do you need your Judgment card?"

"No," the matriarch answered. "I've been using The Judgment card I fabricated and blessed. It works well with the ancient deck." The card was hidden in a shadow at the corner of the table on Lady Arachne's right.

Gordon bowed at the neck, and then he scooped up the authentic Judgment card from the spread in front of him. "I'll continue my historical search for the missing Lovers card," he assured as he pocketed the card.

But Lady Arachne understood that Gordon had other motives behind completing her assigned task. "Excellent, Mister Goodspeed. Conduct your search for your sweetheart's spirit, and bring any information concerning the missing Lovers card to me." She added, "Be careful, lilac spirit. Time stepping can be dangerous."

"I will," Gordon promised. He looked at everyone as he asked, "Anybody mind if I make a quick exit?"

Everyone's voices overlapped permitting Gordon's departure.

Gordon popped from existence, forming solid out of lilac dust in his family's Fable Avenue brownstone. He was in the basement, an area of the house once drab but now recreated by spirits from another realm to be his resting quarters. Blessed, organic vines channeled natural energy into a meditation and healing capsule that was forged from stone and fused through incant and conjure to create a fiberglass substance. The end product was dubbed the alchemical chamber. Much like the *Nigrum Nigrius Nigro*, the capsule was a device originating from very ancient times.

The basement was now a luxurious space fit for a spirit trying to escape the outside world. The floor was lined with a plush, golden-yellow carpet a and large recliner. It all could've been seen as gaudy, something out of the 1970s. But it worked. Gordon felt like he was standing on the sun, especially when he was barefoot and the carpet's soft, golden-yellow twists snuggled up in between his toes and rubbed the soles of his feet. The chair was big and cozy enough for two. He and Fey often found themselves embraced while being reclined and snug in the chair, a blanket cocooned around them. They'd made a small space a home. Even with Fey's absence, the room brought a sense of comfort to Gordon; and he felt as if her spirit was still in his presence.

Gordon fastened the *Nigrum Nigrius Nigro* to a metal extension attached to the alchemical chamber. "Spook," he called to the device. "Hold it down, kid. I've got an agenda. I'll be back, and with some friends for you."

Spook's mirror lifted. Words appeared, written in ancient text. *Company? That's a change.*

Gordon rolled his eyes. "Yeah," he responded. "Perhaps they'll babysit while I'm out tonight at the Hours club. My spirit's in a good place, now, but I ain't crazy enough to leave you alone." He laughed harder. Ancient text flashed across Spook's screen, and Gordon considered it was a quick-witted retort from the incased spirit. His fleeting glance at the black mirror's face turned into an anchored gaze. Gordon's laughter bubbled away when his instincts took notice of the newly written words being presented on the screen. He cleared his throat and looked closer at the text.

There's something familiar about it all, read the new set of ancient characters. *The Pious Wars*, the ancient text continued streaming. *Was I there? I think I was…*

Gordon made a face. "Get. Out! Well, thanks for springing this on me before I leave. C'mon, Spook! You know I'd have questions." Gordon bent down, eye-level with Spook's mirror. "You fought in the Pious Wars? Which side were you on?"

It's just a feeling, really. Sorry. Not recalling much.

Gordon stood and shook his head. "I understand that feeling." He sighed. "Perhaps we can both sleep on it. Tonight, we go back into the dreaming with The Judgment card." He removed the ancient, enchanted etching from his jacket pocket and placed it on Spook's console. "I can't wait for a mystical watch or some ritual to spark my memory. I need to see Fey again. If it's possible and even if I don't remember it." He put his hands on his hips as a pensive look hardened his features. "Spook, could you put all your power into recording the dream?"

Pulling history from the card, connecting to your inquiry, fusing conjured history to your sleep, and keeping images stable, the device's screen read.

Gordon rubbed his eyes. "I get it, I get it!" he remarked. "You're working at capacity." He exhaled. "Okay, then, I'll return soon. Rest up, or, whatever it is you do."

The magitech device closed, mirror folded against the console.

Gordon disappeared in a snap, leaving behind a glittering puff of lilac dust cloud. The same phenomenon preceded his arrival by seconds before bursting into existence in his upstairs room. Gordon removed his clothes, tossing his garments onto the bed. Once stripped down to his boxer briefs, black smoke swirled from his flesh and formed into a shadow that reached for Gordon's limbs. The sable fog formed solid, wrapping skintight around Gordon's physique. The same pitch colored murk seeped from his neck and wound up the rest of his person. His face enshrouded, the black and airy cosmic substance formed into something resembling an African Chokwe mask. Gordon's natural hair burst wild from the top. A lighted, lilac sphere, swirling with mystical energy, materialized against his forehead.

He smiled and rubbed his fingers against his arms. Being embraced by the cosmic fibers calmed him. Gordon could've remained dressed and still conjured the dark matter apparel around him, but he would've continued feeling the fabrics of his earthly clothes. Stripped down, he could feel the heavens against him. He wore galaxies around him now, and a closer inspection revealed a cosmic scene swirling on the suit. This was his 'Dooley' form, and it was a great escape.

He tilted his head to the ceiling and then jumped up. His body configured into an electron formation and swirled away from existence. A snap, and a cloud of black matter, accompanied his disappearance.

Dooley stretched out of the electron formation on the brownstone's roof followed by a second snap and burst of black dust. He landed on his feet and stood, looking around at Fable Avenue and the neighboring streets. He spoke an incant and became invisible to the world, save for those with any magical sight. Dooley levitated high above the rooftop. He spotted the block's protective aegis, a large, intangible conjure in the shape of an African dragon. Her name was Nyami, and she too was unseen to the non-conjure world. She traipsed through backyards on the even-numbered side of the street, ghosting through full-bloomed foliage. Her long neck extended over the brownstones, sniffing for hexes or ne'er-do-well agents looking to do harm on Fable Avenue's conjure culture.

Dooley floated higher. His body burst into a lilac flame, giving him the appearance of an astral djinn. He increased his speed and arced across the sky, blazing a trail north toward Mount Vernon.

5

Dooley retracted his lilac incandescence just as his swift flight came to an abrupt halt outside Savannah Forrester's Mount Vernon residence. He hovered outside Fey's bedroom window still invisible to the world. He examined the room, bobbing up and down in the air. He inspected each piece of untouched furniture. His instinct deciphered that Fey's grandmother was still anticipating her granddaughter's return. They were, after all, from a culture steeped in magic, and such a notion was not out of the realm of possibility.

Dooley writhed from existence and reemerged inside Fey's undisturbed room. Dooley's African mask retracted into his flesh as shadow and smoke. The glowing, lilac sphere remained against his forehead. Gordon inhaled, eyes closed. He took in the lingering imprint of Fey's presence. There were traces of her everywhere, almost overwhelming. He always indulged in this ritual when he visited. She was alive in the room. Her energy was in all her possessions.

Gordon's instinct reached out, leaping from his glowing third eye and zipping through the rest of the house. It returned within seconds with information that no one was home. He would wait, but Savannah Forester wasn't the only person Gordon was here to deliver the news that he'd seen Fey. His head turned toward his sweetheart's dresser drawer, eyes narrowing on the closed sketchbook surrounded by occult baubles that made up Fey's altar. Gordon walked over to the intricately staged shrine and carefully lifted the sketchbook from its place. He flipped through the pages, taking only quick glances at the passing illustrations. He stopped on one.

The image was a splendid recreation of Fey's likeness dressed in jeans and a t-shirt. On her back were the wings of a yumbo, tattered and torn. Sorrow was etched on her face. It was a beautiful, haunting melody etched on paper. Gordon ran his fingers over it and felt more than paper through his cosmic garment. All of Fey's emotional chords embedded into the drawing burrowed through the tip of Gordon's finger, gamboling up from the page. Happiness and grief mixed, and neither held a quantitative edge to suffocate the other. Fey titled the drawing *The Broken-Winged Faerie.*

Gordon soaked up Fey's resonance imprinted in her artwork, taking it in like a breath of air. He then flipped through several more pages until he came to a lively and colorful drawing of four, female Senegalese fairies, called yumboes, dancing around with open smiles on their faces and mugs of liquor in their hands. Gordon flipped the book around to keep the page, and then he returned it to the altar. Taking a step back, he recited an incant Fey taught him.

Bright lights outlined the finished artwork and extended from the page as four pillars of light. The drawings animated, reaching up from the page. The mugs disappeared as the sprites came to life, summoned from their world to Earth. The tallest was the leader, named after the color of her lighted flesh, Silver. She fluttered her cobalt-blue wings, but didn't rise off the page in flight. Silver relaxed her wings' rapid movement, making them come together. She looked up at Gordon and smiled wide. The pillars of light dropped away as the other yumboes came into existence. There was Zee, a purple fleshed yumbo with lavender wings. She was considered the second-in-command, a little more serious and motherly than even Silver, but she kept the others in line. Next to her was the clever Em, blue colored all over. And last was the feisty Jade who, much like Silver, was named after the color of her lighted flesh. Her wings were yellow, and though they were together, she used her magic to hover above the page from where they sprung.

They greeted Gordon with a wave and in their sing-song language, saying, *"Hello!"* in unison.

"Hello," Gordon responded. Em inspected Gordon and deciphered he had news, commenting on his facial expression. "I do, and I can't hide my excitement." Silver stared at him, pensive and curious. The others were in wonder. "But how's everything been in your realm?" he teased.

Jade put on a scowl and fluttered up to Gordon's face. She balled her fist and gathered around it a bubbling storm of magical energy. She shook it at Gordon, and he didn't know whether she was being playful or serious. "Okay, okay, Jade, I'm just playing," he told the yumbo. Silver called her to the sketchbook, and Jade responded, floating back without the use of her wings. "Take a seat," Gordon directed the yumboes, his voice urgent but polite. He decided to have a seat as well, sitting on the corner of the bed. He waited for the yumboes to do the same. Silver and the others sat on the edge of the sketchbook, legs dangling over the front of the dresser drawer. Settled and still, Gordon looked at the sprites and told them, "I saw Fey, alive and…well…somewhere else…"

Surprise burst on the yumboes' faces, and they lifted into the air.

"That stillness didn't last long," Gordon commented, rolling his eyes.

Silver made a face and crossed her arms at Gordon. The information was electrifying, and the winged, diminutive creatures couldn't remain at rest on hearing such spectacular news. But Silver settled her celebratory behavior, turned to her sisters and batted her hands down, signaling for them to repose. Once simmered, all four gently fluttered their wings and returned to sitting on Fey's sketchbook.

Gordon hesitated on his next words, as his own Fey-inspired happiness faltered. He informed the colorful sprites, "Fey's spirit is tumbling through time, and I was able to time step and meet her. We possessed the bodies of a man and woman who were meditating. I don't remember much of our meeting, but I know it happened."

Silver's eyebrows angled as her eyes widened with sympathy. She flapped her wings and floated over to Gordon, taking a seat on his shoulder. She leaned her head against Gordon's cheek. He smiled. "Fey is alive and well," he said. "We'll get her back here. Mind, body, and spirit whole," he promised.

Silver sprang off Gordon's shoulder. He flinched, dodging the quick flutter of her wingspan. The yumbo met her small coven, the other yumboes themselves now in the air. They danced, feet against nothing, heads tilted back with smiles. Gordon regained his happiness looking at the yumboes merrily dance a jig. Gordon said nothing to the pixies, letting them continue their mirthful mambo.

He lay back on the bed and closed his eyes. A spark occurred from the lilac sphere swirling at his forehead. His instinct leapt from the orb, soared out of the room and traveled down the hall to the front door. A picture was beamed back to him. The door opened, and Savannah Forrester entered her house, mail in her hands and purse dangling from her forearm.

Gordon's instinct snapped back to him. His eyes opened, and he stood up on the bed. "Gordon!" he heard Fey's grandmother call from downstairs. She was part of the community, and she had instincts too. He heard the door close. Savannah called up to him, "Stay where you are, boy. I'm coming up."

Gordon leaned over, hands massaging his knees. He heard Savannah's footsteps ascending the stairs. In the hall, Savannah's steps were softened by the carpet, but to Gordon's spirit, they echoed a path of thunder. He used his cosmic suit's power to stabilize his temperature, to keep from sweating. The bedroom door opened and Savannah appeared, leaning against the side of the entrance. She smiled at Gordon, but the floating and dancing yumboes pulled her attention away. Savannah's face contorted. She raised an eyebrow and aimed her gaze back at Gordon.

"You was able to pull them flying rats out that sketchbook?" Savannah commented, waving her finger at the sprites. Silver and the other yumboes paused in their dance to fold their arms and cast crumpled expressions toward Fey's grandmother. Savannah only returned a teasing grin. "You oversized glow bugs loosen up," she scoffed. "You all know I'm happy to see you." She pointed a stern finger while flipping her wrist. "And I know a little girl who'd be happy to see you, too?"

The yumboes sang the little girl Charlotte's name in a delightful harmony. Silver zipped toward Savannah, bringing her flight to an abrupt stop inches from the woman's face. She inquired on the next time she would see the child's spirit. Savannah answered, "I speak with her every morning. You all can come with me."

Silver scuttled back to her sisters and they revived their merry dance.

Savannah smiled as she watched the sprites. She thought of her daughter and granddaughter.

"I can teach you how to conjure them," Gordon's voice trickled into her moment. He sounded apologetic, knowing Savannah was embraced by a warm and happy memory.

She waved the suggestion away. "No need, boy. I can never get them words right."

"Well, I'll make sure to appear here and conjure them from the page every morning," Gordon assured.

"Thank you, Gordon."

"I would like to borrow them for the night, though," he added. "Keep Spook company while I'm out."

"Keep 'em," Savannah insisted. "Just make sure they at the *gadri* every morning."

Gordon thanked Savannah, and he assured her he would. Then he asked the yumboes if it was okay to return and stay with him on Fable Avenue. Silver accepted the invitation. She then exclaimed in her sing-songy language, *"The news!"* and then zoomed toward Gordon. She hovered in front of his face, palmed his left cheek, and flapped her wings with an urgent swiftness, trying to gain momentum to turn Gordon's head to face Savannah.

"I'll tell her, Silver! I'll tell her!" Gordon pleaded as he tried ducking away from Silver's push. The sprite followed his head's every move. "I…I can't say anything while you all up on a brutha."

"Silver!" scolded Savannah. "Move aside so Gordon can tell me this what-ever-it-is-news." Silver paused. Her head snapped in Savannah's direction, face caked in wide-eyed astonishment. Silver released her pressure against Gordon's face and fluttered backwards. Savannah watched the diminutive pixie glide up toward her circle of yumbo sisters. She then put her eyes back on Gordon. "Whatchu got to tell me, boy?"

Gordon didn't hesitate. "I saw Fey," he informed Savannah.

Savannah's tough, grandmotherly countenance dwindled. Her usual stern mien fluxed between perplexity and awe. Her eyes sparkled with the faint dew of tears. They shifted within their sockets, up and down, looking at Gordon. "What…do you mean, Gordon?" she asked. "You 'saw' Fey…"

Gordon repeated his story, "I time stepped when I was meditating on Lady Arachne's Judgment card." He also added as an aside, "She's tasked me with finding the location of her missing—"

"I know, Gordon, I know," Savannah interrupted. She stepped into the room, inching closer to Gordon.

"Yes," he said. "Well, on my last dream, I saw Fey's spirit possess the body of a meditating woman, and she knew I was watching."

Savannah gasped, "What...?" She dropped the mail in her hands, and her body went limp. Gordon shifted to catch her, but Savannah planted her hand on the bed, pivoted, and sat down next to him. Her body leaned toward him, as she was unable to hold herself up, winded by the news. Gordon embraced her, head on his shoulder. "You saw my little Fey," Savannah began crying.

"Yes. She's okay—for the most part," Gordon assured. Silver and the yumboes flew close to one another. Soft smiles and sad eyes clung to their faces as they watched Gordon explain to Savannah, "I remember little. So much happened all at once: the time step, focusing on history, leaving my body—it's left holes in my memory. Fey's spirit drifts through a void, but we'll get her back."

Savannah composed herself. She stood up, Gordon opening his arms to let her free. "Of course, we will," she said, sniffing back tears. She took a breath before asking, "You think you'll see her again?"

"I hope so, Miss Forrester," Gordon answered. "I intend to, but I need some kind of incanted watch to hold me steady in time. Perhaps I could then recall the conversation we had."

Savannah took a deep breath. She felt the need to do something. Anything. She went to retrieve the scattered letters on the floor, but Silver and the other yumboes swooped down and snatched up the letters and brought them to her. She thanked them. "Maman Anansi could help you with that," Savannah suggested. "More specifically, her husband."

"My mother told me," stated Gordon. Then he notified Savannah, "I'm on my way there, now. I've informed Madame Jeliya and Lady Arachne while I had a reading. Maman Anansi projected her form through the *Nigrum Nigrius Nigro*'s black mirror, but she didn't want to risk invisible eyes or ears picking up on the information I had to give. She dissolved her projection. I'm making rounds to give the news. Your stop was first. The circle is getting wider on who knows this. You, Papa Solomon, Martin Kimball, and the yumboes know now—my mother too. I have one other to inform. Martin's niece. Neyeli Kimball."

"I understand," Savannah affirmed.

Gordon stood. "I'll take the yumboes with me." He turned to the winged sprites and asked, "How do you wish to travel? We gon' blink away? Y'all want to jump back onto the page? Or y'all wanna follow a brutha through the sky?"

The sky! Their jubilant voices answered in unison.

Gordon looked at Savannah, then he said to the winged troupe, "All right, then. Make yourselves invisible to the world. We're leaving now," he insisted. Then he lifted his shoulders and stated, "I don't know when I'll see Fey again. To be honest, I'm not sure if it was because I was near her shrine or what, but I am intent on seeing her again—and this time remembering the conversation between us. I have an instinct that we spoke on where Stanley Fallows is located and the possibility of her art professor being a needlewoman. Her husband, too."

"Yes," Savannah agreed. "It all makes me anxious. I'll need a ritual stronger than a cigarette to keep me down. Visit Maman Anansi. Speak with Mister Dumas." Savannah's mood shifted when she added, "He'll know someone…" Then she repeated with a slight word change, "He…*knows* someone."

Gordon didn't pry, keeping his instinct from burrowing into Savannah's thoughts and pulling free the reason for her subtle mood change. "I'll visit," was his only reply.

"Yes," Savannah repeated in a modest tone. "We will bring my granddaughter home, and perhaps solve the mystery of where her mother and father's spirits reside."

Gordon thought of his mother. She completed his family, though she no longer lived on the physical realm. Fey could have a complete family too, but in a more 'conjure culture' type of way.

"Absolutely!" Gordon said perking up with the thought. Then he remembered something. "Oh, Lady Arachne said she'd give you a call later. Not sure when, specifically, but I believe sometime today," Gordon iterated.

"Thank you. I'll be here the rest of the day. Fly on, little spirit."

Gordon's Chokwe-like mask coalesced around his face. He stepped to Fey's altar and lifted the sketchbook, tucking it under his arm. "You little women ready?" he asked the yumboes. They responded with a 'yes'. "Incant shielded?" he questioned. Again, the yumboes responded 'yes'. Dooley said to Savannah, "Text me the address where you meet the little girl, Charlotte, Miss Forrester. I'll send these glow bugs over in the morning." He and Savannah laughed. The yumboes didn't find being called 'glow bugs' as humorous, and their expressions projected their disdain. "I'm just kidding, you guys. You are yumbo, magical spirits through and through." The yumboes' faces relaxed, and they each raised a single eyebrow at the same time. "I'll talk to you soon, Miss Forrester." Then Dooley instructed in an exaggerated manner, "Yumboes, to the roof!"

Finger in the air, he and the yumboes disappeared. Through the window, Savannah witnessed a lilac stream arcing across the sky with separate silver and blue trails on one side and purple and jade trails on the other. Savannah exhaled. She surveyed her granddaughter's room, turned, and exited. From the hallway, she made an immediate left and walked into her bedroom, a large space with vintage furnishings, a wide closet, and a Queen-sized bed.

Grandmother taught her granddaughter well. Savannah too had her altar mounted atop a dressing table. Specifically, Savannah's altar was the entirety of her vanity, decorated in African medallions dangling from leather-braided necklaces, and small Orisha pots sculpted from stone, iron, and clay. Each pot had intricate veve designs carved into them. Inside were talismans and tools made from bronze or copper. Glass figurines in the shape of West African spirit dolls, filled with perfumes, arced around the vanity, leaving an open space for actual primping. Old photos of family members passed on lay in between or underneath the baubles. Absent from the photos were any pictures of her late husband or her slain daughter and granddaughter.

On a pull-out shelf were two, fist-sized candle holders in the shape of skulls. One was laced with gold, the other laced with silver. One had an Erzulie veve etched into the forehead. The other had a veve of Papa Legba. A lilac candle was planted in the Legba skull. A cobalt-blue candle extended from the Erzulie skull.

Savannah sat down in front of her vanity and placed her mail in the open space. She closed her eyes and exhaled, focusing her thoughts on her scattered family. Eventually, she opened one of the front drawers and removed two photos. The first was a picture of her daughter, Emma. A wide, toothy smile brightened her face as she embraced a five-year-old Fey on a mid-summer day. Savannah studied the photo, realizing she was unable to place it or any other photo of her daughter on the altar with the family members who'd passed. She noted aloud, "Because y'all two comin' back to Big Mamma O-jewel, hear?" she sniffed back her tears and cursed through a sly grin, "Shit!"

Savannah's eyes dropped back to the open drawer. She spotted a second photo, another she had trouble putting on the altar. The setting was the same. Her daughter, Emma, holding her granddaughter, Fey. Added to the scene was Emma's husband and Fey's father. Lewis Banneker. Savannah cherished the photo. It was a forty ounce of good liquor compared to the sobering reality of the way things became.

She didn't blame Lewis, though she expressed, "Damn your good heart, boy." She ran a soft fingertip across the photo's surface, and then she returned the photo in her hand to the drawer before thumbing through the others. Emma's college graduation photo, a photo of Fey with friends from junior high school, and a photo of her high school senior prom. Savannah considered it strange not to see Gordon on her granddaughter's arm. But those were estranged times between Savannah and the Fable Avenue Conjure community. Savannah looked away from the drawer in an attempt to ease the aqueous melancholy throbbing against her eyes.

She wiped her face and blew her nose into a handkerchief. She meant to fix herself up using the mirror, but instead her eyes wandered to the drawer of photos again. Staring up at her was a picture of her late husband, a photo she never added to her altar in honor of his Christian beliefs. Instinct moved her arm like a carefully operated, mechanical crane. Down her hand dipped, into the drawer. Her fingers clamped together, taking her husband's photo and lifting it to her face. Before she could admire her husband's strong presence in the photo, making it seem as if he was still among the living, instinct had Savannah place the photo next to the pile of mail.

She examined the photo with a close scrutiny, her instinct ablaze.

Her husband's arm extended long, pointing at something off view. From Savannah's vantage, it appeared her husband was signaling to the pile of mail she lay on the vanity. She made a curious face, reached for the mail without looking, and thumbed through it. She let her instinct guide her fingers, flipping through bills and junk mail until she'd stopped at one envelope. She pulled it from the pile and saw that it was a letter from her grandson, Armand. She flipped it around, ripped the side, and pressed the bottom and top of the envelope with finger and thumb. She blew into the opening, her breath widening it. Then she removed the folded paper inside.

Her instinct burned at the back of her skull, quickening her heartrate as she unraveled the handwritten letter. The words were small. Armand had a lot to say. Savannah read quickly, though her eyes bent and ingested each word with a stern focus. The letter was a magnet. She couldn't look away or even gasp at the horror she'd read. Armand's carefully chosen words described a sense of choking. The atmosphere of job rejection based on deep-seeded racial idiosyncrasies asphyxiated him. Her grandson described sleep as rare, writing how he'd often hung between transitional states of wakefulness and sleep. *Sinister sorcery stirred hallucinations*, read the letter. *I often find myself surrounded by a harem of horrors, and these ghosts wrapped their hands around my neck, held me down. Cool currents cascaded through me.*

Armand recalled the rejection. Job after job. He said the sinister smiles followed him home and manifested into supernatural creatures that crept into his room and kept him from sleep.

Anger coursed through the circuitry in my palms. They connected, and Nana, believe me when I say making a fist felt like a release. But not release enough. Fists are hungry monsters that need to eat. I swallowed pills of pride and alcoholic cocktails of anger every day.

Armand's letter detailed his panic attacks before job interviews, a sense of his throat closing, rushing to the bathroom to splash water on his face, slipping into stalls to find privacy in an attempt to calm his erratic breathing.

Calmed, I only had minutes before I'd regurgitate my anxiety again.

Savannah's interest piqued, and for a moment her worry subsided when Armand articulated on having an instinct concerning how he was being judged in interviews. *Something spoke to me, poking at me first, and then I could hear the inner voice of whoever was interviewing me—what was really on his or her mind. It was like the pin of a grenade being pulled, and anger exploded in my throat, tightening it. I clenched my fists, Nana.*

Savannah's agita returned with what she read next.

These words have been in past tense for a reason, Nana. And it's not because I've calmed any fires in me, but because I've allowed them to burn. I've exploded, Nana, and the release was like kissing creation.

The letter depicted Armand's explosion. The average day was the wick enrooted into his volatile emotions. A run-in with a drug addict was the lighting of the braided, bundle of intangible cord. An exchange of words was the flames crackling crawl toward Armand's unstable ardency.

His words drizzled with a sense of relief. He'd made a fist, and he'd fed the hungry monster. *Flesh mangled by bunched fists,* he wrote. *Broken bone crunched by my balled, hungry monsters. The image of his decimated countenance stays with me. I went to an interview that day, and I got the job. I felt like I'd made a blood sacrifice. I glowed different, I guess, Nana, and the interviewer could see that. She was both enticed and afraid, but she couldn't look away or ignore me. I have a job now, and I don't want it. I feel as if I've gained acceptance on a plantation by showing I could put another slave in his place.*

Savannah couldn't recall at what point her mouth fell open while she read her grandson's letter, but it was hanging agape now. Wide like her eyes, which now sailed over the remaining words. Armand illustrated the young addict he'd battered was in a hospital, unconscious, clinging desperately to life. He read about the older woman accompanying the young addict. She had been listed, in what first appeared to be an unrelated news report, as shot and killed. Her incident was suspected as a drug deal gone wrong. Two days later, the young addict, James Swann, was connected with the older woman. His beating was classified by police as related to the woman's slaying. Two drug addicts looking to score, short of money from their previous hit. The police were waiting for James to recover to gain more insight to who their dealers were.

Nana, Armand's letter pleaded. *I need your help. I don't want to be here anymore, and I can't return to California a failure.* She read the number where he could be reached. Then he signed off with his signature.

Savannah's home phone rang. The trembling chime was startling, but her body was too gripped by her grandson's words to rattle. The phone's clang took effect after a third ring. Savannah's lower jaw quivered. A fourth ring sounded, and she put the letter down on the altar. A fifth ring sent the jolt through her that should've been caused by the first. She shook her head and stood, walking with hastened steps toward the end table. She sat down and picked up her phone from the receiver. Lady Arachne was on the other end. "Savannah," she said in a cool voice. "You know about your grandson."

"Yes," Savannah answered. "How do you know?"

"I'm watching you now through my cards."

"Is this what you wanted to talk to me about, Lena? Did you gain sight into his trouble on an earlier read?"

"Yes," Lady Arachne answered, voice still calm and cool. "I wasn't keeping any information from you. I only found out this morning," she clarified.

"Oh…" Her eyes drifted back to her vanity, centering on her grandson's letter. Her voice stuttered as she expressed to the Fable Avenue matriarch, "He's gone and done something…oh, how can I put this? Rather rash… He needs my help, Lena. He's talking about instincts and hearing the thoughts from the people he deals with. My daughter, his mother, she dismisses such things, resentful of the conjure culture. But her son, Armand, he's angry and blooming with a possible conjure he doesn't understand, and with his mother, never will."

"We'll help him, Savannah," Lady Arachne assured. "Would he have a problem coming to the crossroads?"

"He left a number," Savannah responded. "I'll make arrangements."

"Satchel Eledas is on his way. He can pick him up."

Savannah objected politely, "No, Lena! That would be too much, too fast for this boy. I should be the one to bring him into the fold, talk to him. This should all come from me."

"I do no protest, Savannah."

"Until then, Lena, let me rest on all this."

"Certainly, sister. I'll leave you to your peace."

"Thank you, and good day."

"Good day, sister."

Savannah placed the phone back to its base. She dropped her head and exhaled. *"Hooo, chile!"* she expressed. Her grandson was the easiest to deal with. Her daughter would be something else. "Lawd, these ch'ren! I swear, I swear!" She lifted her head and declared, "I need a drink, and then another one, again and again."

6

Unmasked. Seated. Gordon stared at the yumboes' lighted flesh as they danced in the air above his alchemical chamber. He'd been transfixed for minutes with his two physical eyes on the partying pixies. His lilac eye, swirling at the center of his forehead, scrolled through memories of he and Fey occupying the basement as their *sanctum sanctorum.*

Bright, unintelligible symbols flashed and popped across Spook's black mirror. Gordon noticed them. His memories dwindled into fog, the present reality becoming solid from the murk. The symbols on Spook reconfigured to something comprehensible. Gordon read the ancient characters. *You okay?*

Gordon blinked the remaining fog away from his eyes and head. "Yeah," he responded to the spirit haunting the ancient device. "Just remembering." He leaned forward, elbows resting on his knees. He put his hands together, pairing fingertips with fingertips, palms apart. "I'm trying to cover my frustration. I got a feeling, Spook, but no memory to bring it together." Silver ceased her dance and zoomed down toward Gordon, floating near his shoulder. The other yumboes flew into position around him, faces askew. They created a choir of singsong complaints lofted at Gordon. He hid his face in his palms, then spread two fingers, able to see Spook's screen light up with new characters expressing a laugh and saying, *They're right, y'know.*

Gordon leaned back, taking his face away from his palms. "All right!" he protested over the yumboes high-pitch hollering. The yumboes stopped chattering. "I'll look at the bright side," Gordon assured in a calmer, though sarcastic, tone. "There's been progress." He lifted his legs onto the recliner, folding them into a Buddha pose. Silver and the yumboes backed away from Gordon, giving him space. He smiled at the pixies and said to Silver, "I'm just fiending to get Fey back. Ain't you?" The yumboes agreed. Gordon uncrossed his legs and stood. "Okay," he said. "You all can take care of yourselves? I'm going to visit Maman Anansi." The yumboes and Spook gave signals that they would be okay in his absence. Gordon stepped toward Spook. He spoke to all the spirits in earshot. "I just know I was next to her again. There's this hope, but it's as faint as my memory." Silver flew up to him again, hovering at his left. Her lighted presence made him smile. She had a sarcastic scowl on her face. "I know. I know," Gordon chuckled. "The bright side," he stated. "I'll be upstairs putting on some clothes. I'll signal before I leave. You know where food and drinks are." The yumboes nodded, and Gordon popped away to his bedroom. He dissolved the tight, cosmic suit hugging his frame and redressed in his earlier clothes. He didn't know if

Maman Anansi would have guests outside of the conjure community. And if so, they certainly wouldn't be prepared to see Gordon's tight, spandex-like, cosmic attire.

Fully dressed, Gordon summoned his cosmic suit. His earthly clothes faded from his person, substituted by his spirit outfit. His mask covered him, and he popped away to the roof. Atop the brownstone, his spherical, lilac eye glowed bright. He signaled the yumboes and Spook through instinct that he was leaving, and then he took to the skies, arching toward the borough of Queens.

He landed safely at the side of Maman Anansi's two-story, corner house. Feet against the ground, his earthly clothes shifted over his person, and the incant cloaking him from the world dissolved along with his spherical, lilac eye. Gordon made his way to the front door, walking coolly with hands in his pockets.

Coming around to the front yard, he spied Maman Anansi stepping out onto her porch. She was dressed in denim overalls and a straw, wide-brimmed hat, ready for gardening. One of her gloved hands carried a metal toolbox filled with different types of yard tools. "Ah, Gordon," she said, undisturbed by his presence. "I felt your spirit approach before I walked through the door."

Gordon was clearly excited, and Maman Anansi's could tell it was connected to the news he desperately needed to share. Gordon fixed his demeanor. "Forgive me, Maman Anansi," he said in a polite tone. "I feel alive again. Hopeful. I mean, with all I can do with the Lilac Spirit inside me, it's sometimes frustrating to come across the impossible or understand the humility in defeat."

Maman Anansi consoled, "We had a setback, Gordon. It's okay to be upset."

Gordon acknowledged the Grand Matriarch's sentiment with a nod of his head. "I just came from speaking with Savannah Forrester," he informed her. "Pardon me, please, for imparting this news to her before coming to see you. She too deserved to know."

Maman Anansi lifted her head, moving the brim of her hat out of the way to ensure Gordon saw her smile. "Savannah called ahead," she confessed. "She said you had some wonderful news to share with me." She stepped down from the porch and rested her toolbox near bushes that had been newly mulched.

Gordon moved in close to whisper, "I saw Fey Forrester, Matriarch Anansi. That's why I sought an audience with her grandmother first."

Maman Anansi bloomed with hope on her visage, though she was filled with questions. She inquired, "How did you come by seeing young Miss Forrester, Gordon? Was it an echo of her spirit or a conjure dream?"

"No, Maman Anansi," Gordon answered. Then he affirmed, "I *was* in a dream state, however." He looked over his shoulder before continuing.

Maman Anansi assured him, "You can speak freely, Gordon. I have our voices outside of time and protected with an *aabo* incant. I ain't taking the risk of talkin' community business all out in the open here—not in these times."

"Yes, Maman Anansi…"

"Tell me your story, young Goodspeed."

Gordon nodded again. He said, while more at ease, "I continued my research for Lady Arachne this morning, using my device to aid in the inquiry. I went into dream, viewing history. It was long ago. I saw monsters and heard people speak of the times as being a part of the *Pious Wars*. There were three moons in the sky: red, black, and green."

Maman Anansi's stern, curious manner returned. "Ah, that old, ancient world of conjure. It had balance even when there was war," she remarked. Maman Anansi inquired, "Did you see Miss Forrester living in a past life?"

Gordon shook his head. "No," he replied, voice again a low hush. He spoke up when he explained, "I saw a powerful conjure woman named Oris Del lead a desperate man into meditation. He was anxious. He'd been thrown into a terrible time. His settlement was decimated, overrun with a type of undead called *mzigo*." As those before her, Maman Anansi nodded, acknowledging her understanding of the mythological creatures. "She too needed rest," continued Gordon. "While they were huddled in a safe haven, deep in meditation, Fey's spirit possessed the woman's body." Maman Anansi couldn't hold back her gasp. Gordon concluded, "She—Fey—felt my eyes, my presence observing history in dream. She called to me. I concentrated, and my spirit leapt from my body in this time to—"

"*Child!*" Maman Anansi exhaled. She caressed Gordon's cheek with a gentle touch. "You time stepped."

Gordon confirmed with a motion of his head.

Maman Anansi moved her hand from his face and asked, "You and Miss Forrester spoke, I presume." Gordon answered, yes. He mentioned he couldn't keep himself stable, nor could he remember their conversation when his spirit returned to his present-day body. Maman Anansi patted Gordon's chest while noting, "You powerful with spirit, boy, but what you performed took you by surprise. It's a wonder you ain't stark-ravin' mad right now." She called over her shoulder, "*Alec!*" Her voice was loud, but was sent by incant to go straight to her husband's ear. When he didn't answer for a time, Maman Anansi called again, voice laced with incant, "*Alec!*"

"He knows a bokor tinkerer that can build and bless a device to keep me stable?" Gordon asked, his words hurried.

Maman Anansi answered in a quick breath, "Yes." She turned to shout for her husband again but stopped. Her head shifted back to Gordon, and she notified him with an austere expression, "A blessed device will keep you stable, but there are other dangers, Gordon. You could be trapped between time, anchored in two bodies and unable to control either. You would be split in two and lost to oblivion."

"Well, that sounds inoperable…" he replied with a worried look.

The door creaked open and Andre Alec Dumas stepped out onto the porch, questioning his wife, "Whatchu hollerin' for, Cal-T? Voice all in my ear," he said jiggling a finger in his left ear. "I'm old, and I take pride in my hearing. Done lost most my hair, 'cept what thin and gray hair on my face. You puttin' what little o' my faculties I got left at risk." The slim light-skinned man of average height halted both his talk and stride when he noticed Gordon standing near his wife. "Well, I thought I had an instinct about a spirit out here." He came closer and greeted, "How you doin', boy?" He looked at his wife and said, "I thought it was Enock out here on visit. He been concerned with Stephanie; and she been actin' all strange for the past few months. Cal, will you tell me what's goin' on with our daughter?"

"All these goings-on has her up with emotion, Alec," Maman Anansi brushed aside. Then she chided her husband for his earlier remarks. "And fool, you as healthy as a newborn!" she scolded, adding a playful slap to the back of his slender, oval-shaped head.

Alec chuckled at his wife's antics. "Man only as healthy as the hair on his head," he remarked. "My health done thinned down and dropped off." Though Gordon smiled at Mister Dumas' mannerisms and sayings, Alec shifted his demeanor. He put his hands in his pockets and continued, "But if you here, I'm thinkin' my health need to be at peak. Stanley send more of them needle boys to the Avenue?" Before Gordon could answer, Alec asked his wife, "We cloaked?"

"Voices outside of time, Alec-baby," she assured.

Alec turned back to Gordon, saying, "Can't just be whisperin' nowadays."

"Why don't we just take this inside?" suggested Maman Anansi.

Gordon and Alec agreed. Maman Anansi led the procession through the front door, into the hallway, and into the kitchen. Gordon took a seat. Maman Anansi offered him a drink and Gordon politely replied with a request for lemon water. The first matriarch posed the question to her husband, and he jested as he took a seat at the table, "No, thank you, Cal-baby. What I'd like to sip on would get me swimmin' in the head. And you want my assistance out there in the yard." He chuckled at his words, and so did Gordon. "Now what's your presence all about, boy? Papa Solomon and his love triangle finally got news on our children or a plan on some retaliation?" He looked at his wife and pointed, "Whichu gon' give the okay on when your brother got somethin' concrete."

"In time, Alec-baby," Maman Anansi replied, impatience crowding her tone. She procured lemons, a glass, and a pitcher of water. "Gordon needs some assistance with creating a talisman. A watch," she emphasized.

Alec inquired, "For true? What's all that about now?"

"I time stepped, Uncle Andre," said Gordon. "It happened against my will when I was dreaming of history, doing research for Lady Arachne. There's a chance I'll do it again. I need something to keep me stable."

"Somethin' conjurin' that spirit of yours?" he inquired. "That's odd. Somebody in the past connectin' to you by ritual? How far back did you go?"

"Our world had three moons in its sky," Gordon enlightened.

Alec beamed. "Goddamn, boy! That lilac spirit, I do say! I'm sure your sweetheart could probably much do the same. Y'all cosmic twins like that." He put a hand on Gordon's shoulder. "We gon' call her back, you know. Got to!" He bobbed his head. "Cuz I done some figurin', and I—"

Maman Anansi told her husband, "Alec, that's the point of Gordon's visit. He met Fey." Alec retracted his arm from Gordon's shoulder. His face melted into bafflement. Maman Anansi proceeded, "Her spirit sails through a void, and she found her way into the history Gordon dreamed. Miss Forrester possessed a woman in meditation. Gordon's spirit possessed a man in meditation and—"

Alec interrupted his wife. "The other matriarchs should be informed."

Maman Anansi raised a hand. "I know, Alec-baby. This proves your point." Gordon's instinct buzzed with the remark. His eyes narrowed on Maman Anansi. She noticed his stare and felt his instinct's breeze. "I'm going to call a gathering after Satchel and his daughter arrives," she declared.

"I'ma call a gathering too," said Mister Dumas. "Ol' Goon owe me a rematch in chess. We was in the middle of a game, and that fool—"

Gordon inched his way into the conversation, asking, "I'm sorry to interrupt, Uncle Andre. But what point was proven?"

Maman Anansi looked at her husband. Alec looked at her. He waved a hand in Gordon's direction and said, "You go on an' tell the boy, Cal-baby."

Maman Anansi faced Gordon and told him, "You were gone, Gordon. Alec had his instinct about Fey's death. He said it wasn't a death at all. She was banished as a spirit."

"Oh…" Gordon responded by reflex. Something clicked in his memory, and he believed he recalled Fey saying the same to him back in time. He made it known. "I think…I recall Fey saying something to that effect when we were back in time together."

"Musta been a powerful hex on her," Alec took up. "The spirits you two possess don't just bow to any ol' hex."

Gordon nodded his head. "They're…Old World, the spirits inside Fey and I. Like, three moons Old World." He let that sink for both the Elders and him. "I wish I could do more with it, believe it or not. Simple things like understand the language of the cosmic spirits Fey and I visit. I almost got it."

"Oh, there's more to unlock, now," said Alec. "You right. But, I'm sayin', it takes a powerful hex like what was in that Willie fellow's whip."

"We figure Stanley is stalling," Maman Anansi voiced, cutting into the lemon. "He knows we're closer to bringing about the Grand Wish, the Great Conjure. All his soulless matter, and those of his negative un-nature, will burn after that. But if he can put pause on our progress, he can make gain on his. As we discussed today, Gordon: You and Fey are here to destroy the world. Stanley has a grand conjure to perform for his benefit."

"He tryin' to make himself us," Alec broadcasted with the force of fact in his voice. "He gon' twist about our purpose through his own grand conjure. You watch." He jabbed a finger and a set of stern eyes at Gordon. "That's what this all about, banishin' your sweetheart. His kind of folk be like that, y'know. He can't kill the sprit, but he can set it back. B'lie'e that shit."

Gordon nodded his head.

Mister Dumas swatted the air with tight fists. "I found my conjure not too long after you took in that spirit." An aura of golden energy whipped and crackled like lightning around Alec's fists. "Wish I'd been dropped into that block fight back in February. I might not've stopped them needle boys from snatchin' them children, but they woulda known me." He opened his fists. The bright aura retracted into his palms. He rested his arms on the table.

"Let's not dwell on that, Alec-baby," said Maman Anansi as she placed a glass for Gordon on the table. "Here you go, Gordon." She sat down, a glass for herself in front of her.

Alec considered his wife's comment. "You right, Cal," he agreed.

Gordon thanked Maman Anansi for the lemon water and took a deep sip. Fresh water with a hint of lemon tickled his tongue and rushed down his throat as he swallowed. The cold coated his senses, and his anxiousness dissolved. He put the glass down and took a breath. He steered the conversation back toward the objective of his visit when he asked, "You know a boker-tinkerer, Mister Dumas?"

Alec flinched, as the question jogged his memory to the purpose of Gordon's visit. "Oh, yeah! That's right, boy. You need to stable yourself in the long-ago." He shifted in his chair, caught in a thousand-mile stare over Maman Anansi's shoulder. He bobbed his head as he thought of the best of the boker tinkerers that could build and bless the device Gordon required. "Yeah, I know someone who can help. He down in Baltimore." Then Alec's eyes shifted from aimless stare to Gordon. "He's your sweetheart's great uncle," he revealed. "*Paternal*," he expounded. Then he asked his wife, "Albert still strong on Lena?"

Maman Anansi's face contorted in annoyance. "I don't know about that shit," she remarked.

Alex continued, "He sure did have a *thiiiiiing* for Lena. Always did. Even when he was married." Alec put his eyes on Gordon and said, "That ain't what caused the divorce. He tried to bring his wife into conjure. That was the devil's work, according to her religious background. He thought her being Caribbean, it'd be different. The spoiler alert on that story is that it wasn't. She ran as if he had horns and a tail."

"Oh…" Gordon exhaled in a low voice. He asked, "How is that side of Fey's family? They aware of what's been going on?"

"More or less," answered Maman Anansi. "Most of Lewis' family got sight. They practice through some ol' African spiritual system. A lot of their fashion involves Judeo-Christian syncretism. Not many of them can negotiate incant, and fewer have a personal conjure. But when there's power among them, it's great." She paused to sip her lemon water. "Who knows what their power extends to now, since the arrival of the cobalt-blue and lilac spirits," she added after a swallow.

"Yeah…" Gordon stated. "Fey did say her father was considered very special among his family."

"Some looked at Lewis as either a martyr or a traitor," Maman Anansi continued.

The comment caught Gordon by surprise. "Really?" he reacted.

"Oh, yeah," she drawled. "Yes, indeed, they did. He was helping Stanley Fallows." Another sip, and then the matriarch continued, "I don't know the extent of his family's knowledge 'bout all the goings-on in the conjure world, but they know the name Fallows is a bit of a curse word; they knew Sarinda was bad. They know somethin' happened to Luis and his wife. That's enough."

Gordon turned to Mister Dumas and asked, "Is Fey's great uncle someone who'll help?"

"Yep," he answered quickly. "He like the politics like he like Lena. Make him feel like he part of myth. The Great Story." There was a beat. Alec added, "Nigga owe me a favor anyway." He rapped a finger against the table. "I'll put that order in now. It'll take some time to put it together, but he'll have it running right."

Gordon remarked, "I'd like to see more of Fey's family."

"They good folk," Alec stated. "I mean, they niggas like everybody else, y'know. They got they politics too. He'll drive the device up personally to see Lena. I can bet on that."

Gordon chuckled. He finished his drink and sat back. "Thank you,

Maman Anansi, Uncle Andre," he said rubbing his thighs. Another one of his doubts dwindled and disappeared. "Today's been an emotional storm."

Maman Anansi reached for Gordon's hand. She embraced it and squeezed tight. Her instinct surveyed Gordon's demeanor. "There are answers locked in you, Gordon. Not even I can see them. They're shadows of your time with Fey. They're silent and in silhouette." She opened her grip and patted the back of Gordon's hand. "Stanley and our abducted children's whereabouts are there. We'll procure them and conjure your Fey back to life."

"Yes, Maman Anansi," Gordon replied. "Thank you both, again."

"You have other places to be…" said Maman Anansi, reacting to her instinct's buzz.

"Yes."

"Well, go on, boy," waved the Grand Matriarch, playful tone in her voice.

"Papa Solomon does have some things to discuss," added Gordon. "Plots, y'know. Him and Martin are working them out. Don't know much of the details. I'm sure he'll let us all in on it soon."

"Of course, Gordon," Maman Anansi said patting Gordon's hand again.

Gordon nodded to both Maman Anansi and Mister Dumas.

Then he popped away.

7

It was night, and the most fun of fools were out in Harlem, up on 136th Street. All type of folk hung at a club called *The Hours*, nicknamed, *The Obeah Palace*. Many non-conjure folk swore hand-to-God that it was the most bumping place in the city. Colors could be seen without wine or weed, and patrons believed a strange feeling of weightlessness occurred while entranced by the music's reverberation. Strong drinks were heavier than in most places, and they were always referred to as spirits. Even the brand names had an extra kick to their flavor.

Conjure men and women mingled with the regular folk at the entrance. This night was like every other night. Practitioners kept their voices outside of time while trading verses for incants and formula for alchemical equations. Talking to one another, they each bragged about how much bite their incant or conjure possessed. It was grain-of-salt bravado. There were also conversations on the bullshit of the mundane world and day-to-day life. Ghosts and spirits haunted the inside. Some glowed and glided around, others appeared solid and blended in with the living. The illuminated, air-drifting spirits were only visible to those with extrasensory sight. A haunt named Cabin Jack drank at the bar, telling jokes and having a good time with the patrons able to see him. He was a runaway slave caught and hanged in North Carolina in the year 1856. His opening line to newcomers was always, *"I finally made it North. Hot damn!"*

Cabin Jack had a wife named Dolly Faithful who also socialized with the patrons. She too met an unfortunate end at the hands of the plantation master and the overseer. Her death was what inspired Cabin Jack to attempt escape. Because of things she'd seen and experienced firsthand while enslaved on a Southern plantation, Dolly would use her spirit to monitor women who would make their way home from the club. Her spirit would accord protection if a foul hood crept from the night to do a woman harm, and she was a ubiquitous phantom with a wraith dagger at the ready for the toughest ruffian.

Live music from a band played psychedelic conjure and soul. A long, extended jam reverberated as Gordon walked into the 'Obeah Palace'. A bald, dark-skinned man with a bushy go-t, recited lyrics heightened by incants. He was dressed in white slacks and a long, white buttoned shirt with gold-colored fabric laced in an intricate pattern around the buttons. His name was Burton, and he blared blessings in song that were beamed to all in attendance. His band was called the Descendants of a Higher Tribe. Like Sly and the Family Stone before them, they could take a person higher with their funk.

The audience, bathed in consecrated ballads, wasn't suddenly going to find themselves drenched in good fortune. It was just enough to let them shine a little brighter for the moment, loosen themselves from troubles. Sanctified songs were sung, and doubt dissolved. It was only a Wednesday. Something a little extra was needed for Hump Day, and The Hours club provided.

There was always spirit in the place even when there were no conjure folk pitching tent in its interiors. It was established in the early twenties. Burned and revitalized sometime in the thirties. Abandoned sometime after that, but reconstructed by the Fable Avenue conjure community in the late sixties, early seventies. History as well as ghosts possessed the happening spot.

Gordon took in the music and washed himself with the blessing. He greeted people with polite and simple acknowledgement, but kept his concentration on Burton's resonance. He pushed through the crowd, making his way to the backroom, slowing only when Burton's wife joined the song. Thunder was added to lightning and the musical blessing increased. Gordon's lilac spirit refreshed. He considered coming more often. But away from the stress releasing pounds of Conjure 'n' Soul music, duty possessed him. It made Gordon anxious, but it was a propellant to secure the tools absent from Fable Avenue: missing cards, his beloved Fey's banished spirit, and abducted children. Securing one had the potential to secure all. Where to begin first was the dilemma.

Gordon let the music swallow his unease. He was standing straight and as tall as he could by the time he'd sifted through the crowd and approached the backroom. Gordon was met by security. Both men recognized Gordon and allowed him entrance into the hall leading to the back. Gordon saluted them with two fingers, brushed the velvet, purple curtain aside and entered the hallway. He was underage, but he was conjure royalty.

There were seven rooms, three on either side of the hall and one at the end. Gordon was interested in the room located at the end of the corridor. His instinct jumped from him and ghosted through the door as he approached. His brother Cedron was inside seated at a table and playing a Tarot card game with the members of his crew named The Court of Gypsy Moon Misfits. Stacks of chips were in front of the seated men, as well as half-full whiskey glasses. Jugs of the alcoholic drink named *dragon spit* sat on a bar cart behind Cedron. Cigar smoke filled the room. Gordon took roll call around the table. On Cedron's right was Gordon's best friend, Benny Jah Brickhouse. Also in attendance was Oliver Peters, having the night off from his job as a paramedic. He wasn't a legitimate Court member, but he loved to hang and play cards when it was 'Misfit Night' at the club. The Shaw brothers were on opposite sides of the table. They were two, Filipino conjurers. The oldest, in his early thirties, was named Edmundo "Edmond" Yiao-tian Shaw. His brother, Raymundo "Raymond" Ma Chao Shaw, was Cedron's age. The two were the best of friends. Another non-member engaged in cards was Wilson Barnes. He had a cigar in his mouth, mirroring Cedron and Oliver, and he was talking the most trash to the other players. Wilson was the only one not dressed in black slacks, white collar shirt, and black suit jacket. He was dressed down in jeans and a t-shirt. Being an 'elder' among the people, Wilson was allowed to wear what he wanted. But Cedron enforced a strict dress code on the Gypsy Misfits he commanded. Oliver obeyed the rules of dress as he was seeking membership into Cedron's outfit.

Gordon was surprised that Jamie 'Tap' Ryan was not among his fellow Misfits, but Gordon sensed his presence somewhere outside the club. Gordon stood at the door. He knocked on it a few times and heard his brother jump up with excitement. The door opened, and Gordon smiled up at his brother's massive frame. Cedron wrapped a muscular arm around Gordon's shoulders and swept him into the room. Gordon's neck snapped back, feet dragging, but he managed to keep up with Cedron's pull.

"There's my little brother! He's even dressed right!" Cedron hollered, cigar clamped between his teeth. He snatched the bulky tobacco stick between two fingers and pointed at the table. "We're in the middle of a round. It's Royal Tarot. Buy in is only fifty bucks. Small time, but big payout if you play right. Right?"

"I got in on the next round," Gordon remarked, his voice barely audible while compressed in his brother's tight squeeze. Cedron let him go, and Gordon exhaled a hard breath. Then he coughed on the smoke crowding the room. He used an incant to clear the air, and everyone hollered at him.

"C'mon, bruh!" cried Cedron as he took his seat. "You killin' the atmosphere."

"Y' killin' my lungs," Gordon replied as a matter-of-fact.

Cedron huffed and rolled his eyes. "Just watch the game until it's y' time to punch in," he growled. He remarked, "Kid can fly into the cosmos as a spirit, but he can't deal with a little smoke."

"I won't clear the next stuffiness," Gordon promised as he grabbed a loose chair and propped it next to Benny. He sat down and nudged his friend in the side. Gordon asked him, "How you holdin' up, man?" He noticed Benny looked tired.

"I'm okay," Benny responded concentrating on the game. He made a gesture to swap cards. He placed two cards on the table, face down, and he took two from the deck. He tossed in some chips after he saw his two new cards.

Gordon opened his mouth to ask a follow up question pertaining to hunting *inawo*, but Cedron cut into Gordon's attempt. "Let him concentrate,

Gordon," Cedron scolded. "Ain't in the round, don't open y' mouth."

Wilson grinned. "Translation: don't distract *me*.'"

Cedron removed his cigar, blew some smoke and said to Wilson, "I want my wins legit. I take his money this round and suddenly Benny gonna be hollerin' about he was distracted by Gordon."

"Oh! Legit?" said Wilson, eyes on his cards, and eyebrows arched high in curiosity. "Like this game? All this cleared with the New York State Gaming Commission? How 'bout the youngins sippin' on the alcohol?" he pointed out.

Cedron chuckled. "Shit," he drawled, swapping cards on his turn, and then throwing chips into the pile at the center of the table. "Benny the only underage drinker we got here—that is until my brother walked in. But beside that point, I don't follow *all* the rules. I admit that. Sometimes, I make my own. Hence, Misfits, right?" He took a puff of his cigar and exhaled.

"Yeah, that'll hold up in a court of law," Wilson remarked.

Cedron chuckled, "Court of Gypsy Moon all I care about."

"Damn fool!" Wilson barked, shaking his head. "I knew yo' ass was gonna say that shit. I walked into that one."

Cedron took it further, needling Wilson, "Nigga got a higher instinct, still walkin' into shit. Eyes open." Everyone broke out into laughter. Cedron removed the cigar from his lips and tapped the table with his fingers. "But I follow the rules of the game, established *and* unwritten." He looked at Gordon and reiterated, "No distractions!"

Gordon put up his hands, relenting to engaging in any talk during the round. He jumped up from his seat and made himself a glass of dragon spit, pouring more than a sample for sipping. He returned to his seat. Cedron's eyes went from his cards to the amount of dragon spit in Gordon's glass. "Whoa, little spirit! That's kinda topped up. Pops come in here, he'd have my ass! There's a lot of kick in that particular brew."

Gordon lifted his shoulders and tossed Cedron's words back at him. "What? I can fly into space, but I can't enjoy a simple drink?"

"Yer gonna be flyin' into airliners if you drink all that, little brother. Not even an incant gonna erase the haunt in that drink."

"I'll nurse it," Gordon assured. He took a sip. It was strong. He stayed focus to watch the remainder of the round.

Oliver took the pot with a cosmic hand consisting of the Moon, the Sun, the Star, and the World. Cedron joked, "I was distracted." The table burst into laughter. Gordon took some more sips. He removed fifty dollars from his wallet and handed it to Cedron in exchange for the chip amount. Cedron placed the cash in an envelope, and then he shuffled the cards and dealt them out. "It goes without saying," he said to Gordon, "but just as a reminder: no incants, no instincts, no conjures."

"Got it," Gordon acknowledged. "Hey, where's Tap?"

Raymond grinned while stating, "He outside flirtin'."

"Oh…" said Gordon, inspecting his cards. He almost had the royal suit of Pentacles complete. He had the king, the queen, and the page. He'd hoped to score the knight. He took a chance with his incomplete hand and put in a bet. Perhaps he'd find it among the deck. He stayed his instinct as imposed.

"Yeah," continued Raymond, keeping his grin. "It's quirky?"

Gordon inquired, "Quirky how?"

"She's one of his shadows," Raymond spilled.

"Whoa!" Gordon responded.

Wilson took a drag of his cigar. He exhaled and rested the cigar in an ashtray. "It's cool, though, y'know," he voiced. "He conjured her a couple days ago. I teased him that he'd been hidin' her from us."

Cedron added, "She got shape and dimension. She not like his other shades. He brought her here tonight, introduced her."

Edmond noted, "Tap can hear her voice. We can't."

Wilson finished by saying, "She cloaked too, so, the regular folk can't see her. He out back with her. In an alley." A childish grin wormed its way onto his face. "I wonder how they gettin' down with that."

Cedron shook his head. "Man, throw in the money I'mo take from you or fold!"

Wilson folded. His childish grin remained, and he remarked, "I just wanna know what a shadow chick feels like."

The other card players joined Cedron in the head shaking, chuckling as if still in middle school. Gordon didn't really know what to make of his friend Tap's 'dating' situation. It was as quirky as Raymond described. But he wouldn't be the first person to cuddle up to a shade or haunt of some kind.

Gordon lost the round, but took the pot on the next two. His fourth round came down to him, Cedron, Wilson, and Benny Jah. Cedron smirked looking at his cards. He didn't care if it was a tell. He licked his lips and looked around the table at the people still functioning in the hand. He shook his head in short beats, saying, "Oh, no! My hand giving me the Sabby Duck Disease," he announced, keeping his rhythmic head spasm going.

Wilson rolled his eyes. "Oh, here we go with these two dummies." He peered over at Gordon, and sure enough, the younger Goodspeed was mimicking his brother's short, spastic head movements.

"Gordon," Cedron called. *I wanna play – I wanna play,*" he said in a metronomic voice.

Gordon also parroted Cedron's cadence when he spoke, *"Whatchu wanna play, kid?"*

Then the two of them said together, *"Sabby Duck! What? Sabby Duck!"*

Everyone shook and bubbled with laughter. Snorts came from their noses, and gurgling noises pierced their once tightly shut lips. Wilson and Benny Jah made the best attempts at suppressing laughter, trying to remain concentrated on the hand. They covered their face with their cards in their hands, shaking their heads. Oliver Peters just burst. Everyone followed in succession as the brothers repeated their silly song for a few more bets and card swaps.

"Yo!" Wilson bellowed, finally allowing his laughter to escape. "You Goodspeed negroes stupid, I swear."

Cedron and Gordon continued their song. The reference was to a two-year-old Gordon Goodspeed's inability to properly pronounce the name of an anthropomorphic duck character in an old video game. Skyler Sky Duck. It was even worse when the toddler Gordon mistook the character for a more famous anthropomorphic duck cartoon. It didn't help that he mispronounced the more famous animated character's name. And it stuck. But it was never a teasing point from older brother Cedron to younger brother Gordon. It was something that morphed into absurd and silly, as put on display.

Gordon's voice cracked. His rhythm splintered, turning into laughter. Cedron continued his silly head jerks, repeating as he swapped cards and put in another bet, *"Sabby Duck! What? Sabby Duck!"* The remaining participants placed their wagers. Cedron ceased his antics to call for the others to reveal their cards. No hand could challenge his. Cedron took the round, and the table's occupants roared. Wilson declared, while coming down from excitement, that the silly anthem Cedron and Gordon blurted was an incant. His accusation was merely play, however. He gathered the cards and asked whose turn it was to shuffle and cut. Edmond took the deck from him.

Wilson nudged Gordon and said, "Guess who showed up this morning?" The others already knew the answer. Gordon asked, *"Who?"* and Wilson answered while beaming, "My Pop's spirit, and my moms let him in."

Gordon exclaimed, "Get. *Out!*" He pushed Wilson on the arm.

"For real, kid," Wilson let out. "I spoke to him too! The legendary Johnny Concheroot. My dad!" Then he admitted, "I gave him and my moms the privacy they needed. I left the house. My instinct let me know when to return. We talked on the porch." Wilson took a sip of his drink. "I'm gonna close the club. My moms is coming later. My pops is jumpin' on the piano. I'ma stay for a bit, but let my moms have the moment. I'll wait outside or back here. I'll drive her home."

"That's wassup, man," Gordon said lifting his glass and clanking it against Wilson's. "Glad your moms opened the door for his spirit. I like that they talked."

"Shit," Wilson exhaled. "That nigga had some talking to do. Some 'splainin!" he jested. "They workin' it out."

Gordon considered it was a day of rare appearances. He wanted to tell the people at the table about his encounter with Fey, but he had to keep that a secret. He enjoyed the positivity in the air, and he decided to drink to that, and so he took another swig of his drink. The gulp was sizable, and the spirit owning the brew spread into his head. He figured he would have to 'pop' home. Cedron advised him again to take it easy, perhaps sensing Gordon's faculties being touched by the drink's kick. Gordon assured his older brother he was fine. Cedron gave him a look.

"I ain't drowning sorrows, if that's what y' face is about," Gordon grimaced. Cedron's demeanor was killing his buzz.

Voice filled with sincerity, Cedron asked, "You okay, then?"

Emotions escorted the drink's influence, but Gordon was able to keep them at bay. "As can be…" he told Cedron.

Edmond finished his shuffle. Cedron held up a hand, keeping the Shaw brother from tossing out the first card. "Hold up," he said rising from his chair. He stepped over to the bar cart and knelt down. He reached through a curtain beneath the cart's surface and pulled out an object. Gordon and the attendance were curious. Cedron rose and turned. In his hand was an object wrapped in a white, silk cloth. He unveiled the article, a piece of medieval armor. A right-handed gauntlet, the single component for a far more complex set of armor forged in the 1200s, carved with the number nine just below the wrist, and blessed by a blackamoor conjure man. The piece shined bright as if newly forged.

Fable Avenue antagonist, Brice Cadogan, an old British gentleman blessed with youthful vigor and the healthy, strapping body of a man in his mid-thirties, wielded the enchanted metal glove for decades. The blessed gauntlet conferred on him otherworldly strength and agility. He was a lieutenant in the attack on Fable Avenue that took place outside of time earlier in the year. It was the same attack that secured for Fable Avenue's enemies several of the conjure community's children. Cedron and Benny tussled with Brice that night. The two ultimately relieved the British hexman of his power source, the gauntlet. Gordon, in his Dooley-spirit form, swooped down and snatched Brice, taking him up and beyond Earth's atmosphere, surrounding him with lilac energy to preserve his life while journeying to the stars. He and Brice had a connection. The aftermath of a fight where Gordon had psychically merged his hex-laced battle scars with Brice. In dreams, he and Cadogan would battle one another at the crossroads. Psychological and physical, both Gordon and Brice would wake exhausted, comforted by someone from their respective conjure and hex factions.

In the end, on the physical plane, Gordon showed him what true conjure spirit was. The hexman at first marveled at the cosmos, transfixed by all the stars and planets his eyes could see in the heavenly realm. A gate swirled open in the heavens, and cosmic spirits detained Brice, pulling him back through the black portal from whence they came. He begged for release, hollered a plea for his life. But the cosmic spirits had a trial ready for him. Judgment was waiting. All the hexes he used to maintain his body, and the crimes he committed against the true black conjure man and black conjure woman, would be submitted as evidence. The trial wasn't long. Brice was sentenced. The spirits determined he would burn by black, cosmic fire. Not even ashes remained. The fire's hunger consumed everything. Brice was dead before Gordon returned to the stars for his self-imposed exile. The cosmic spirits informed him of Brice's demise. Gordon didn't like thinking on it too long. He might've been able to pull information on Stanley Fallows whereabouts. Or discover where the children were taken. But cosmic law was served first.

Cedron placed the armor piece at the center of the card table, standing the metal gauntlet on its opened-end at the forearm. The fingers curled almost making a fist. Cedron slipped back into his seat. He picked up his cigar, took a puff, and filled the room with exhaled smoke.

Cedron proclaimed, "Before us, gentlemen, is a lethal weapon."

Edmond spoke, "Hey, Cedron, ain't this supposed to be upstate with the other artifacts?"

Cedron shifted his eyes at Edmond, a stern look on his face as thick cigar smoke seeped through his parted lips.

Oliver answered, "My Pops gave that as tribute for a job well done on the block." He shrugged and added, "Kids was taken and all, but we held it down."

"Papa Solomon got it cleared by Maman Anansi?" asked Raymond, eyes fixed on the shiny, metal prize.

Benny too was mesmerized by the gauntlet's shine. Its invisible aura and enchantment tugged at the young, Jamaica-born man.

"Yeah," Oliver rejoined. "It's all cleared. Any foolishness," he added, "and it's snatched away."

Edmond dealt the cards. Wilson picked his up, and without looking, tossed them into the center of the table. "I wasn't there. Ain't mine to earn. I fold." He put his eyes on Oliver, signaling with a head nod.

Oliver did the same. "I'm out too," he announced.

Wilson and Oliver sat back and observed the game.

No bets. Everything was already on the table.

The Shaw brothers folded. Then Gordon tapped out.

Benny and Cedron faced off.

Cedron swapped cards and made a face. Benny challenged him to reveal his hand. Cedron had nothing. Benny grinned and let drop to the table a hand consisting of the royal suit of swords. The room rattled with the collective roar from the card players. Gordon shook his friend Benny by the shoulders. Cedron got up and made a humble bow toward Benny Jah. Then he announced, hands aimed at the gauntlet-centerpiece, "This blessed object, Benjamin Brickhouse, is bestowed on you. Explore any spirit that possesses it. Merge with its blessing, and haunt the block with its power." He cast his cigar between his teeth and joined in the clapping. Benny remained seated. Cedron removed his cigar and placed it in the ashtray near him, smoke swirling thick from his lips. He said to Benny as the clapping subsided, "I know you've been a loyal soldier, Benny Jah. By now, all the knuckleheads in here know the whole story. A gun sold, and its consequences on me."

Half of Benny's smile faded.

"I'm walking now, though. My personal conjure got me back on two feet."

Gordon interjected a joke. "I remember knocking you off those two feet," he boasted.

It could've been awkward, Cedron being emotional at the referenced time. The joke could've been tasteless, and perhaps might've been. But Cedron made a face, a half smile accepting defeat as he pushed his cheek out with his tongue. The others snickered. Wilson remarked behind a balled fist, "That's cold, sun."

Benny turned his eyes toward Gordon. Then he rolled them while expressing, "Goddamn, man!"

Cedron shook his head. He wagged a finger at Gordon and noted, "I'ma letchu have that one, little brother." He raised the finger he shook and proclaimed, "But, I would like to have on record that I was under a hex. I hadn't been on my feet for years, and I still got some good licks in."

Wilson interposed, "Noted."

Gordon lifted his hands and signaled that he conceded to his brother's declaration. Cedron nodded in Wilson's direction. "Thank you. I can't remember much of the dogs I threw—I know I knocked Benny unconscious." He looked at Gordon with one eye while shaking his fist at him. "And I know I caught your lilac spirit in my grip—by the neck."

Gordon sat back in his seat and admitted, "That cut my ego a lot."

"Don't let it eat you up too much," remarked Cedron. "We've had some good team ups since then. Brothers got each other's back haunting the block out there." Then Cedron steered his remarks back to Benny. "You've been in my debt because of a mistake you made, but you wear this gauntlet— *that you've earned*—and the debt is washed away."

Benny agreed with a reluctant nod of the head. "I'm still a Misfit!" he declared.

The behemoth picked up his cigar. "Of course," he stated. Then he waved his hand at the other players in the room. "Okay, let's take pause. My girl's outside. I wanna groove a bit. We'll be back in here later for some more cards. I know some of y'all got work or intermission sessions for college. Gordon, you'll be here?"

"No. I got my own studying."

Everyone filed out, save Cedron, Benny, and Gordon. Benny admired his prize as the two brothers conversed. Cedron gestured for Gordon to stand and come to him. Gordon did. Cedron gave him a hug. Then he held his shoulders at arm's length and asked Gordon again, "You okay, little brother?"

"I'm good, man. I'm good. Seriously," he assured.

"I know the Elders got you doing some heavy lifting," the older Goodspeed brother remarked.

Gordon let it be known, "I'm sure when the kids are tracked down we'll all be pulling weight. Papa Solomon hinted at plans already coming together. On some things, I gotta stay silent. Even with you guys…"

"Oh, I know. The Misfits are on standby for any call."

"And there will be one," Gordon told him. "Bet," he emphasized.

Benny remained seated. He told Cedron, "Hey, if you see Neyeli, can you have her come back here?"

"Yeah. I gotchu, kid."

"Neyeli's here?" Gordon queried. "I'ma stay behind. I gotta talk to her." He looked at Benny. "Do you mind? I don't wanna break into anything private."

"You good, man."

One more parting hug with his brother, and then Gordon returned to his seat. Cedron left the room and closed the door. Gordon and Benny admired the gauntlet for a moment. Benny then broke the silence. "Dajon's in trouble again," he informed. "At least I think he is."

"What's it this time?" inquired Gordon.

Benny shook his head. "Don't know," he uttered with disappointment in his voice. "Lady Arachne called my house and asked to speak with my parents. I put my Pops on the line. She wants to talk to my Mom and my Pops about him in person."

"Your brother'll be okay," Gordon assured, tapping Benny on the shoulder. "He always is, right." Then Gordon inquired, "But, how you holdin' up, man? You look tired."

Benny's answer surprised Gordon. He started with, "I love Neyeli, I really do."

Worry bewitched Gordon's voice when he asked, "Everything okay?"

Benny assured immediately, "Everything's fine, man. It is. I don't know if we've beheld one another officially, but that spirit is there with us." He shook his head. "No. It's the burdens we've come across. The *inawo*." He took a breath. "Neyeli can handle it all, but it exhausts me," Benny confessed. "The raw emotions that haunt a person," he continued. "It's potent, and I've felt it before. When I went to Water Bug Hollow," Benny revealed. "When she and I…get busy…she can get a release, but if I'm not careful, I might take in the emotion that she has no problem controlling. That's her, y'know."

"She's strong," Gordon said to his friend. "Willie's whip had no effect on her. That's saying something."

"I know, right?"

That's when the woman of their discussion walked in. Neyeli Campbell. Her getup was like that of a flapper from the 1920s, wearing a short and shimmering black gown that popped against her sunset-colored skin. She greeted the two men waiting for her. All smiles with her dreadlocked hair tied back, fanning out behind her head like a flower's petals in full bloom. Her hair was shifted into a bright pink color. She was cool and happy, having fun. A small purse hung from her shoulder, and gold earrings dangled from her ears. Both young men smiled in her direction as she entered. Gordon saw Neyeli as a sister. Benny saw her as the woman he was falling in love with, and always had feelings for.

Her eyes immediately moved toward the gauntlet planted at the table's center. She inquired, face lighting up like a lightbulb, "Who won the prize, or has it not been fought over yet?" Benny acknowledged the win. "Benny-baby, you got the piece!" she cried out. She moved closer to the table, the palm of her hand stretched out toward the gauntlet. "Oh, there is much to explore with this treasure. I can feel a spirit's emotion inside. There's more than a blessing, there's a possession." Gordon noticed a maturity in Neyeli's voice. She spoke like an Elder. Gordon believed she was approaching a moment in her conjure life that suggested an aged and refined acumen. Neyeli's conjure to manipulate and commune already had people in the community seeking her out to receive guidance through a journey into the *reverie*, also called the *mirak*, where they would confront their burdens as *inawo*. She studied with the matriarchs to hone her conjure. A titling ceremony would be next for Neyeli, on a path to become a matriarch herself one day.

Despite her conjure woman maturity, there still was a child-like innocence as Neyeli ogled the gauntlet. Benny also marveled at the medieval, metal glove. "When we got the time, Neyeli-baby, let's study this relic and see how it can benefit us on our haunts."

"Indeed!" Neyeli agreed, bending closer to the armor piece. "There is a history here." Her eyes popped up, spotting Gordon. "Cedron said you needed to speak with me."

Gordon nodded. "Yes…" he said. He made a face, uncertainty

mangling his features. Neyeli took a seat. Benny leaned away from Gordon, giving his friend space. Gordon fixed his face. "I need your help, Neyeli."

"Anything, Gordon," she replied in a tender tone.

Gordon's eyes went from Neyeli to Benny and back again. He looked at the door and used an incant to close and lock it. He faced his friends and relayed, "The Elders know what I'm about to tell you. Your uncle knows too, Neyeli. My mother, Fey's grandmother as well. You two are the last to know—I swear…" He rolled his eyes. "Keep this information tightly wrapped twice in a shadow. *Please!*" Gordon begged them.

"Yes, Gordon," assured Neyeli.

Benny leaned forward.

Gordon revealed, "I saw Fey's spirit." His two friends froze. Neyeli's hair turned maroon in shade. Gordon explained the circumstance as he'd been doing all day. Frustration hung his head. His eyes were fixed on the floor as he recounted how he and Fey came together in a time long ago. "Neyeli," he said, head now lifted and beholding the look of disbelief saturating her face. "The conversation between Fey and I is locked in my head. I can't recall it. It's not even fuzzy. It's just a feeling. Not now, but sometime soon, I need you to take me into the mirak and guide me to that conversation. All the answers are there."

Neyeli blinked and shook the incredulous look from her face. Her hair shifted into a mustard tint. "You might not find your memory, Gordon. Not intact. It could still be a puzzle."

"I can work with a puzzle," Gordon told her. "I can bring that back and piece things together, and then remember. I'm good with that. I need something. Stanley's location is in there. The kids…"

"Do you think you'll see her again?" asked Benny.

"I'll be prepared for that," responded Gordon. "I'll have a device that'll keep me stable. Maman Anansi's husband knows a guy. Fey's great uncle. Tinkerer."

Neyeli sensed something in Gordon. She deciphered the emotion emanating from him and questioned, "You're going into the dream tonight, aren't you? You're going to explore history again?"

Gordon raised his hand and protested, "It's not just to see if I meet Fey again. I'm so far back in time—"

"You're inside what people believe are just mythology, legends," Benny threw in.

"Right," Gordon reacted, wondering if Benny used instinct to pry his final words from him. He didn't. It was just obvious. "The things I'm dreamin' of ain't in any history books. And the cards you lifted for Lady Arachne were supposed to have been created around medieval times like this gauntlet here, but they're colors are made from the ashes of the most ancient of decks. Lady Arachne also said the original spirits possess her cards. What I know for certain is what I've seen. And if I'm tappin' into what-can-now-be verified history—once debated as myth—then the cards have something to do with it." Gordon stated further, "Fey's not dead. She was banished. That puts me at ease. She's close. She and I are close." A sheepish grin molded on his face. "I know it sounds corny, but…" he hesitated, and then stated, "Our love for one another hasn't been stopped only delayed."

Neyeli protested, "Gordon, that's not corny."

Benny held his thumb and pointer finger an inch apart. "It's a little corny," he remarked.

"*Benny!*" Neyeli scolded, her hair forming a new shade.

But Gordon laughed along with his friend. It was all in fun. He felt good. He continued, "Look, in all seriousness, Stanley Fallows is building his grand wish and conjure. He needs time for that; and he's bought himself a good amount of it."

"Negating us is part of his grand hex," Benny snarled. "Bet!" he added. "He probably gonna send some more goons our way, too. We'll give him a fight again." Then he reiterated, "Bet!"

Gordon's smile widened, and Neyeli liked seeing the sun break through the cloud of despair that veiled her friend as of late. He pointed to the table and asked Benny, "You wanna put that bet on the table?"

Neyeli raised an eyebrow. She inquired, "Can I get in on it? Or is it still a 'boys only' club?" Gordon and Benny shied away, guilty expressions on their faces. Benny insisted that it was all Cedron's rules. She replied, "That's fine. Leah and I have something planned for the womenfolk."

Gordon and Benny paused for a moment. They looked at one another, and Benny commented, "That sounds sexy."

Neyeli radiated a seductive twinkle. "You'll just have to dream about it, Mister Brickhouse, what we womenfolk do when we get together." She winked and added, "That should keep you guessing."

Gordon stood. "*Damn!*" he remarked. "Y'all work that out. I gots to get home," he announced. He turned to Benny, bent down and engaged in an old, farewell handshake they invented that consisted of multiple moves. "Keep your emotions right, kid. Don't let nobody else's burdens get you down." Benny assured he wouldn't. Gordon turned to Neyeli and gave his friend a soft kiss on the cheek. "Keep an eye on this one, sister." Neyeli said she would. "I'll get back to you on the dream walk."

Neyeli returned the friendly kiss. "Be careful tonight, Gordon. There are many consequences to time stepping."

"I've heard," he told her. "I'll be cautious." He reached for his drink and gulped the remainder of the dragon spit. The flavor burned his chest. Gordon made a face, squeezed his eyes shut and shook his head. "I said, *got-*

damn!" he hollered.

Benny scoffed, "Watch y'self with that too, sun. You've downed a good deal of dragon spit tonight. How you gettin' home? You stayin' in Harlem or you headin' to Brooklyn?"

"Brooklyn," Gordon answered after exhaling the hard taste of the alcohol. "I'm just gonna pop back."

"Make sure you don't solidify inside a wall," Benny warned.

Gordon chuckled, "I'll be fine." Then he repeated to Neyeli, "The mirak. It's a date."

"Yes," Neyeli confirmed.

Benny's face burst with surprise, recalling Gordon's story. "You were the alchemist-warrior, huh?" he exclaimed, words laced with wonder. Gordon certified with a quick nod. He was readying himself to snap away from existence, but Benny had questions. "Did you get to wield the hammer?"

Gordon chuckled. He curled his fingers to his thumb and made a tugging motion. "Did I play with his hammer? Is that what you're asking?"

Neyeli put her face in her hand and started laughing while shaking her head.

Benny's expression distorted. "Man, c'mon. You know what I mean!"

Gordon assured, "I'm. Just. Playin'." Then he answered Benny, "No. You think I'm tipsy now, I couldn't remain stable, on my feet," he explained. "But I saw him fight. He was newly inducted into his role as warrior, not the hardened man-of-war we've been told about."

Benny remarked, "That's crazy. It's all real. Pious Wars and stuff!" His voice faded to being reflective. "It's hard to wrap my head around, y'know. Like someone saying my favorite cartoon about giant robots was actually real. I'm used to conjure and incant, secrecy and stories on Mafia-type hits against us by outside hexers, and vice-versa. But it's all just intense when it comes to this fantastic past." Then he shrugged and added, "I'm more partial to the stories of Dabo Barawo anyway. But we know that's all tall tales and myth. He ain't real."

Neyeli rolled her eyes and scoffed at Benny, "You would like those perverted tales of that thief. That New Orleans conjure man, Papa Iwah Jack. He made all that up? Or did he just collect the tales?" Then she huffed, "Nasty, old man."

Benny lifted his shoulders. "He collected the tales. I grew up on 'em," he defended. "Not the raunchy ones, just the thieving exploits. I came across the lewd stuff in eighth or ninth grade. I had no idea." He recounted through a grin, remembering the events as he described them, "I would swipe the books from under my parents' bed where a couple two, t'ree volumes were hidden. There's like ten, right? I've read three of 'em. Hey, couldn't resist. I was curious. Plus, I always considered myself like Dabo, minus the harem of conjure women he had. I liked his thieving antics. He was an antihero I looked up to. Our conjure culture's antihero. Like the Alchemist and His Hammer, and so many others."

"I'm sure," Neyeli remarked, eyebrow arching, hair color transforming to a soft, but warning, red. "I liked Granny Heirloom growing up."

Gordon made a face and shook his head, "She got raunchy tales too! That was that whole family, especially Dabo."

"And the witches who loved him," Benny adjoined to Gordon's comment.

"Yeah, some *witches* alright," Neyeli commented, features askew.

Gordon divulged, "I still got a passage memorized from one of Granny Heirloom's stories. I came across it when I was ten or eleven, actually." Then he recited, "*She possessed a man's masculine mass in every openness on her feminine frame. In both hands she held tight to thick, swollen—*"

"I get it!" Neyeli interrupted. "It reads obvious." She grinned as she confessed, "I've…I've read a few of them naughty tales…" Her eyebrows playfully rose and set in a quick moment. "She had her share of men. Sometimes all at once."

"Something *I* discovered when I read that passage," Gordon noted with an intense look of disbelief, reflecting on what he'd read when too young. He addressed Benny, telling his friend, "I'm like you. I couldn't resist the titles. *NiggErotica Magica* and *The Black Cosmic Human Exotic*. Written by anonymous men and women."

"Interesting title indeed," Benny remarked.

"*'Nigger'*-rotica!" Neyeli chuckled, hiding her laughter behind the palm of her hand. Her hair's color shifted teal. She straightened her face and posture. "I was told the stories were written for the purpose of reconnecting black people to sexuality. Conjure is about creation, and black conjure folk took to the writings. They were outlawed in some countries, still a secret in others. I like how each book breaks down the word fetish and its African and conjure connection, the problematic areas of we as a people thinking our slave owners fetishized us. We were raped of our sexuality for hundreds of years, and the stories—as graphic as they can be—were intended to restore our sexuality. Like my mother tells me, actually quoting the books: *There was never a desire to lay with us, to have us, or even to fuck us. There was only a desire by our oppressors to conquer us. A lot of us have fallen for that belief in the desire for black in all its shades. They do not want us; they just want to conquer us. No more! We own us! We own our bodies!*" She grinned and said in the Yoruba, "*Ibalopo Iyika!*" And Benny footnoted how the phrase translated into *sexual revolution,* and all three friends giggled like school children.

Gordon stated, "It's all a bit of a 'fuck you'—"

"No pun intended," Benny interjected.

Then Neyeli said in a posh accent, "It's black! It's sex! It's black love—the ultimate taboo!" She looked up and exhaled dramatically, "The Five Chambers of Sexuality: Naughty! Dirty! Nasty! Filthy! Forbidden!"

Benny quipped, "We gon' get Nasty tonight, baby!"

Neyeli slapped him on the shoulder, and all three friends tipped back in their chairs with laughter. They had more drinks, and Gordon remarked, "Supposedly the various authors left their imprints behind in the titles of the chapters or stories. Not enough to identify," he concluded. "Not sure why. Some have found the benevolent haunt of an Afro-Cuban woman from the late twenties, early thirties. Supposedly, Papa Iwah Jack was trying to emulate the authors' stories of a young Granny Heirloom when he scratched them lewd tales of her grandson Dabo. Lady Arachne says she's related to one of the authors. No surprise." He lifted his shoulders and expressed, "Oh, well, I have my own mystery to solve concerning a woman out of my reach."

"Shit!" cursed Benny. "She out of your league, man. Let's talk some truth with our words. We got a responsibility, incants and such."

"Negro, please!" Gordon snapped back. "On that note…" he said before beaming a parting smile, saluting his friends, and popping from existence.

Differences of child heroes aside, Benny and Neyeli moved their seats closer to one another. They kissed as if they hadn't seen each other in ages. Neyeli's hair turned a passionate purple. Benny told her as he backed away from their kiss, "You look beautiful, Mood Ring."

"I'm having a ball out there with the girls," Neyeli stated. "But I miss you, Benny-baby." They held one another's hands. Neyeli turned her eyes to the gauntlet. "Such a splendid piece," she commented. "There's emotion there. Its aura is talking, but it'll take a ritual to release the voice so we can commune with it." She asked her boyfriend, "You boys coming back here for more cards?"

Benny nodded. "Just for a few more rounds," he told her. "We both got two finals tomorrow, but that's in the afternoon. We can do some work on the gauntlet when we get home."

Neyeli disagreed. Her hair shifted to a light green of mixed emotions. "At least Friday," she suggested. "Classes will be done by then. We'll see what's bound to this object at the end of the week."

"It's a date," Benny smirked.

"More than that, Benny-baby, it's an adventure." Neyeli's hair returned to its purple color. She leaned toward Benny, eyes closed. "That was a nice steal, *Dabo*," she teased. Benny moved in. He noted to her that only one witch was needed for his harem. "You better…" Neyeli warned. The two kissed deep, mouths open, tongues sliding into one another.

In Brooklyn. Gordon popped into the middle of a basement pixie party. His arms were folded, a single eyebrow arched high. Conjure music blared, streaming from the ethers. Zee and Em grooved in midair. Silver and Jade whirled atop Gordon's sealed alchemical chamber. Cups were in their hands, spilling a bit as they boogied. The snap of his sudden presence put all of them on pause, however. Their mouths hung open, eyes just as wide with surprise. Silver twiddled her fingers and the music playing through way of pixie sorcery lowered in volume.

Gordon glared at the yumboes with a suspicious eye. "Sorry," he told them. "I gotta be the parent. It's time for bed." He pointed to the sketchbook and reminded, "Besides, you four got an appointment tomorrow morning with some kids."

The yumboes conceded, faces a sad frown. Silver wiggled her fingers again. The music stopped. They each guzzled the last of their drinks. Zee used an incant to clean up the messy spills. Each of them tossed their cups into the air where the objects burst into cloud and dissipated. Gordon spoke the incant Fey taught him. The sketchbook opened to the proper page. The yumboes said their goodnights to Gordon, flew over to the page, and dived down to become etches on the paper's surface, truthfully returning to their realm.

"You rested, Spook?" he asked his ancient device.

Spook retorted in script, *With that racket?*

Gordon eyed the words. "Well, we got work to do. We're going back into history. You good?" he posed. Spook answered with a 'yes'. Gordon closed the device, Judgment card still on the console. He snapped from existence, forming solid in his bedroom. He turned on the lights using an incant, the air conditioner too. He then set the *Nigrum Nigrius Nigro* on the dresser and undressed with a toss of his clothes into a pile on the floor. Stripped down to his underwear, Gordon picked up the archaic machine. "I had a much-needed good time, Spook, even if it wasn't an all-nighter. I got a little alcohol in me. I'm swimmin' in the head good enough to be relaxed. There's more than an instinct buzzing in me."

Lights turned off. Gordon got into bed. He put the *Nigrum Nigrius Nigro* against his chest, folding his arms over the device. He closed his eyes and had a simple thought. Being among his brother and their friends was more powerful than any healing incant. Hope's warm emotion, which blossomed from his night out, cocooned him tighter than the magic that all at once washed over him. His last thought before a mystical sleep pulled him under was that he'd hoped to see his sweetheart, Fey Forrester.

Them Fall

Nature was a drunken mess, tripping over Herself and staggering without focus. Such was revealed when raised the glitter of lilac fog across the dreaming. Here again was long ago, a time whose ink had been faded from history books. Autumn was early—months early, to be exact. Leaves were polychromatic fire, clinging with their last ounce of life with stem to branch. Sprawled out in single file, or in piles beneath the trees, were the drained-to-dry, crinkled brown leaves that had fallen victim to Nature's schizophrenia. The ground blistered with summer's heat, shriveling the verdant grass and syphoning the polish from its color. The air snapped with a tearing bite of the winds that produced a wintry mix of precipitation. The icy atmosphere bit like sharp teeth, cutting into the nerves of those with even the thickest of skin, save the burden-possessed, transmuted mzigo populating the area. A few, gathered hordes of these monsters were on their knees, stabbing the soil with their needles, injecting hex into the earth.

El-Ham's desecrated settlements no longer exhaled angry plumes of black smoke, nor were they garbed in furious flames that flapped from the ruins of its diverse architecture. El-Ham was quiet and caught between the heat and cold. There were areas tucked in by a thick coating of an advanced winter's snowy cloak, while other parts drowned in humid waves that rose from the heat cast up from the ardent soil.

It would've all been peaceful and serene had it not been for the chained, ragged-fleshed creatures trudging aimless through the blended fields of snow, piles of leaves, and scorched earth. They had been birthed by a tenebrous sky-demon named Chilombo-Wroch who now roamed the upper atmosphere. The grand, black snake ducked in and out of the billowy clouds. Only months ago, the desultory mzigo had no organization, striking living men or women with both needle and bite, bleeding vitality and injecting the contagion of burden to strengthen their ranks. The greater population of El-Ham walked among them possessed with lifelessness and insatiable hunger. The massive serpent was an organic factory. He had within him an assembly line of organs passing the humans he devoured through a series of stations. He implanted needles into his victims' heads that intercepted his orders of bloodlust, controlling their thoughts. Another station bled ink onto them that turned to metal chains that wrapped around their arms and forehead. People were digested, and the consumed individual was vomited as a soldier for Chilombo-Wroch's personal army.

While haphazard in their movements, the mzigo fell under the mystical command of two dangerous hexers. Rretch and Wrage, the appointed names for the captains in the notorious arjai formed by zealots Toliv Angoj Wofiira, and the man he presented to the world as the messiah, Keb-Biyarli Lorish. The captains' wicked magic permitted them to walk among the mzigo. The same magic shielded them from nature's extreme, kaleidoscopic mesh of seasons. The captains allowed the creatures to roam wild for the moment while they kept watch on a settlement that still vibrated with movement.

The settlement's heart kept a faint beat all because of an unassuming hero that emerged from its historical horizon. El-Nord was the community's name. Ziko Yswil was the hero. At first, a champion unto himself. Up until his current age of twenty-five years, he was considered a layabout in a community of doers and boasters. The cultural crowing shaped the men, even expanded their bellies if that's the way their shape formed, giving them a gut packed with experience, muscle and magic. It thickened the thighs and hips of the women all the same.

Nothing defined Ziko in the days before Chilombo-Wroch's gluttonous wrath. He was flat in muscle and stomach. He had no stories to tell, and he had no personal history tattooed into his flesh. His ambitions were the same. Then one day the sky cast a gargantuan shadow that was decorated with scales, had orange slits for eyes, ears that looked like a bat's wings, and a slender, ominous smile. Like some of the men of El-Nord, it too had magic in its belly. A hex, to be particular, and the beast heaved up its digested meals, transmuted and savage. Mzigo they were called. With one bite or swipe of a metal needle, these consumed and alchemically changed men and women would infect a living person, and into mzigo their victims would change.

El-Nord's living population died, and it became burdened. Ziko's family transitioned into mzigo, friends too. Ziko lived. A hammer-pick came into his possession. It was a weapon, an offense so effective that it was a shield as well. Ziko's nimble frame gave him an advantage. His light muscles hardened with magic and experience. His shape and story arced, and he endowed his hammer-pick with otherworldly properties. It was a furious weapon, and wield of its magic was a marvel to behold. It was a legend, and so would also become the young man who employed and configured its power, though the facts of his story would be lost to time.

Ziko was the last life in El-Ham, so he believed. The terrible wave of transfigured citizens evicted him from the home where he was raised. Ziko took residence at a lecture hall, which had been protected by enchanted crystals that kept the mzigo at bay. His days were filled with repetition. Hunt. Read. Self-educate on a war that began long ago and beyond his settlement's borders but now ravaged the countryside. Chilombo-Wroch, the Sky Demon of Lies, was much like his hammer-pick. The monster was only a weapon in this war. Ziko wondered what other territories of the world had been wrecked the same as his home. Ziko declared to an invisible audience that he would bring an end to the sanguinary Pious Wars. However, he was not the only pioneer roaming the frontier of history to stake such a claim.

Private Inspector-Medium Oris Del possessed such an extreme declaration too. She followed the traces of conjure left by Ziko Yswil's blessed weapon, roaming the desolate settlements of El-Ham, protected by her own conjure: three giant serpents with the heads of lions. Red. Black. Green. Their colors mimicked the moons in the sky. She fought her way to Ziko's sanctuary, communicating with him telepathically. Safe inside, recounting her involvement as a spy to help turn the tides against the zealots spilling blood in the name of their belief, both Oris Del and Ziko Yswil were grateful for one another's company. They enjoyed conversation and a relaxing meditation on first encounter. Dinner never had so much flavor, and sleep was never so peaceful than on that night.

In the morning, Oris and Ziko moved forward in their story. They made war with the mzigo and carved a path to other settlements finding survivors, bringing them back to their sanctuary. Months passed. Their sanctuary became a new kingdom. They named it *Laarin-Ndoto*, which translated to *'Within the Nightmare'*. They even managed to find El-Ham's Honorable Governor Pajon Ohn and his wife, Chieftess Ishel Nofre, and their family, including a newborn son named Babak. A few remaining guards and a conjure man were in their company.

Pajon Ohn declared that he received a final communication by crystal that El-Ham would be spared if they surrendered and vowed allegiance to the reigning zealots Wofiira and Lorish. El-Nord was populated with few living citizens, but Pajon Ohn considered sparing the remaining gathered inside the lecture hall of the El-Nord settlement. Provisions were low, even with the brave conjure men and conjure women and guards that went out to hunt.

"You cannot surrender, Honorable Governor," remarked Oris Del. *"El-Ham is obliterated and no more. This is Laarin-Ndoto. This is* my *kingdom. I am Queen, called Madame Bhlud. Ziko Yswil is King, called Papa Ghut. We will not agree to these zealots' terms."* The refugees tucked away in the Nightmare Kingdom concurred, and power shifted to the self-appointed royal couple. Tensions tightened. Word of no surrender traveled to the infernal zealots. Retaliation came through Chilombo-Wroch's hex. It was the sky demon's sorcery that was the culprit for Nature's manic behavior, hissing a glacial chill while also exhaling the searing humidity of summer's heat. The foul enchantment was

cast not only as a retaliatory measure for not surrendering, but for keeping the survivors of his ferocious mzigo attack from escaping while he fulfilled orders to attack other territories of the world. And so, with the harsh mix of seasons, hunts produced little food, and eatables for Laarin-Ndoto's population were few. The nightmare kingdom's king and queen mounted an offense, and it was here that dreaming and history collided.

Chilombo-Wroch had returned.

A hatch at the top of the domed lecture hall opened with a cumbersome push, fighting against the weight of packed snow. Hatch opened, the snow plunged from the roof and melted immediately upon hitting the scorched ground. Ziko Yswil emerged, shoulders and chest above, the rest of him submerged. His face was masked with a skull dressed with the feathers of a large bird running down the center from brow to base like a rooster's coxcomb. The lower jaw of the skull had been removed, substituted by dangling gold chains. Whether the skull belonged to human or some other creature, it was unknown, and no one asked. It was clear, however, that Ziko Yswil's veil of bone was once a living entity before it was his second face. His countenance could not be seen behind it. It was black. The eyes were a shadow that puffed short, black strands of conjure energy.

Ziko scanned the grounds. Not all of the slain bodies were covered by patches of snow or dead leaves. The cold in the air preserved them, and Ziko recognized a few faces and bodies. Chilombo-Wroch's weighty yowl rumbled the earth below. Remnants of nature's precipitated madness separated and revealed more of the dead. Ziko braced himself. He held tight as the building rattled, his hands gripping the ladder's rung where he stood. The snow slid off the roof as the building shook, dissolving on contact with the parched soil. Frigid and warm air swirled around Ziko as he clung tight.

Chilombo-Wroch's holler dwindled, and the quake in the land settled. Ziko scanned the area again. His sight narrowed in on the burdened settlement. Mzigo plagued the streets. Ziko wondered if they were all El-Ham citizens. He asked the question in his head, *Where do your stories begin?*

Per the usual, mzigo hovered around the perimeter, a safe distance away from the entrance. The mystical frequency humming from four, orange crystals kept the mzigo back away from the lecture hall-turned-sanctuary.

The domed tower's heavy, wooden door swung open. Oris Del stepped outside. The atmosphere's fractured temperatures rushed at her, its winds screaming like a mad spirit. An incant shielded her from the blistering heat and scraping cold. Her shoes kept her protected from the simmering ground below her. She waved a hand, and into existence came her enormous, translucent serpent-lions. Red and green wore the heads of lionesses. Black was a male lion with a thick mane. They were as tall as the tower and their bodies were as thick as four men standing together. Their great size was still comparable to a caterpillar against a cobra when likened to Chilombo-Wroch's magnitude. The crystals' frequency had no effect on Oris Del's conjuration. Red and green slithered forward but remained inside the safe zone. Black didn't move.

Oris Del turned. She signaled two men at the door. Their names were Yre and Dual. Before Chilombo-Wroch's animosity swooped through the settlements Dual and Yre were wily law offenders, a pair of smugglers and hucksters whose marks consisted of dangerous gangsters and ruthless pirates. Despite their victims being malicious men and women, Yre and Dual's activities were still considered criminal, and the pair were wanted men with bounties across many lands, including El-Ham. Chilombo-Wroch's activities shifted their focus when the prison they occupied while awaiting trial was pulverized by the black serpent's attack. Now, they were soldiers of sorts, assisting a self-proclaimed king and queen in a nightmare kingdom.

The two men shut and bolted the door on Oris' signal. They returned to the lecture area where a little less than two hundred men, women, and children were packed inside. Yre and Dual maneuvered through the close-packed refugees. They jumped to the stage where the Honorable Governor Pajon Ohn, his wife Chieftess Nofre, and their guards were gathered. Chieftess Nofre nursed her eight-month old child, Babak. Loyal guards surrounded the Honorable couple. A tall and burly man with broad shoulders and a muscular frame stepped in front of Yre and Dual. His name was Annand, titled The Lawful. He was dressed in a fur cloak. His skin was dark with a forest-green hue resonating from it, so was expected from someone with *nlawọ* ethnicity. Also expected were the sharp, lower canines that protruded slightly from his lips when tightly shut. He had a wide, square-shaped head, aquiline features with thick twisted dreadlocks that dangled low enough to tickle his shoulders. His eyes burned with authority. A large crossbow was strapped to his back. There were two daggers sheathed at his hip. He crossed his arms as he blocked the smugglers' approach.

Yre and Dual backed away at the same moment, looking up. "Sniff, boy. It's us. Allies," the bald-headed and brown skin Yre quipped through a trembling voice.

Annand's lip curled up into a snarl. "Report," he demanded in a low grumble.

"Madame Bhlud is on the move," the lock-haired Dual answered. "Papa Ghut is ready to sail up and confront the serpent."

The guard captain ordered the smugglers to sit. Annand's sister, Kymsaan, stepped to his side. She was younger by a few years, dressed the same as her brother with a sword on her back instead of a crossbow. Her locks were longer, tied into a ponytail. She was as tall as her brother, muscular in her fit, feminine frame. "So, we wait?" she asked Annand.

Annand turned his head. "On Madame Bhlud's orders," he grumbled with a nod.

Oris Del was, at the moment, observing her serpent-lionesses' charge and break through the thick, mzigo wall. The conjured creatures snatched several of the monsters in their jaws and snuffed the unlife from their bodies. The red and green serpent-lionesses were unfazed by the attempted needle pricks or bites from the mzigo that attacked them.

Oris, Ziko's voice echoed inside her head. *My sight has spotted the faint sense of two men. Incant cloaks them from Nature's distress. Insight provides me their names. Rretch and Wrage. Any intel on who these two men are? They walk freely among the mzigo.*

Wanted men, by my standards, Oris transmitted. *Captains sent by our two zealots. Conjure men specialized in hexes. They're probably here to negotiate terms of surrender. They're an addition to our plans, but all the same. We'll take them and the sky demon today. We'll return their heads to Eke Almas Wofiira and Eke Woli Lorish. Those will be our terms for the zealots' surrender.*

As you wish, my Queen, Ziko replied to the conjure woman below.

Come then, Papa Ghut. Take flight, Oris commanded.

Ziko rose from the hatch, skin coated with incant to withstand the mixed cold and heat. He wore billowing, black and purple pants. Bare of shirt, a black vest covered his torso. His flesh was filled with scripted magic that had tales to tell. Black slippers, curled at the toes, were on his feet. Clipped to his belt was his hammer-pick weapon. Ziko made a path through the snow on the roof. He lunged into the air as he reached the edge of the slanted rooftop, arms out wide.

"Nwa-ǫdum," Oris addressed her black serpent-lion by name. "Up!" she commanded.

The serpent-lion roared and hissed as it soared into the air. It curled its body into an S-formation. Ziko landed within its coil, legs straddled across the body. He put a hand through the serpent-lion's ghostly frame and something locked solid at Ziko's wrist, gripping and according him stability while sailing atop the serpent-lion's back. He unhooked the hammer-pick that dangled from his belt. The weapon's head swirled with a glowing yellow gel of energy. "Up and up and forward!" he shouted to his ride, pointing with his hammer-pick.

Oris Del kept eye on her two serpent-lionesses. They chewed and lashed mzigo with tongues made of lightning. The conjure woman flinched when a buzzing sound snapped inside her head. A breath of white noise followed, and then Oris heard a voice relaying a communication to her.

It would be wise to surrender, Captain Rretch spoke to her, mind-to-mind.

And since you understand this, perhaps you should do so, Oris retorted.

Wrage tunneled his voice into Oris' head. *My lady, we have more than mzigo at our command. We have creatures unfazed by the crystals that keep you safe from the burdened.*

Oris didn't care. She was as determined to rid the world of the zealots as they were to subdue it. *I'm impressed, gentlemen. You did your schoolwork on our sanctuary. As for any other creatures at your command, well then, my serpentine felines will feast upon them as well. The two of you little scats are worth less than a fine meal for them, but you'll do.*

Sparks of magical light snapped in and out of existence beyond the path carved by her serpent-lionesses. Oris lifted her right hand and held it out. She closed her eyes and concentrated. The lines in her palm glowed a bright white. A vision came to her. The picture of Rretch and Wrage's conjuring developed. There summoned by the captains were two armies made of barbaric creatures. One was called *weynee*. The other was referred to as *pangomutu*, or the 'unfinished man' in some cultures.

The weynee were tall, broad, and muscular with beige skin, and armed with swords and crossbows. They were fat headed, bald and with round and flat noses that rested against their faces. Should they lose their weapons, and their muscles somehow failed them, their sharpened teeth came into play against an adversary. Their hunger was like mzigo, but a vicious consciousness motivated their actions. No alchemy would take place save death, spilled blood from bitten flesh. Only fifteen numbered their ranks, but it was enough for creatures conjured and built for war.

Summoned in greater mass were the man-like pangomutu. They were hunched over and had round heads and angular features, draped with stringy light-brown hair, walking with one hand assisting their move forward and another armed with a dense club. Gray eyes were inset deep into their heads, resting beneath a protruding brow. Their skin's reddish color was stained with dirt. Their speech was less language and more unintelligible grunts, but commands were given by their captains, and the legions came forth.

Oris opened her eyes and cursed. *"Dammit!"* She clapped her hands together and spoke a prayer, "Mother and father, cosmic in nature. Siblings of the Earth, guide my conjure. Give me a drop more of spirit to fulfill this summoning." She then rubbed her hands, separating them after a time. She twiddled her fingers, and up from the ground rose four additional serpent lions. There was lilac, a male lion with a mane the color of its form. There was cobalt-blue, a lioness. Silver and gold, both females, were also a part of the pride of newly summoned feline serpents. "Sick 'em!" Oris instructed her silver and gold conjures.

The serpent-lionesses slithered into action. Electric lightning spewed from their mouths, and the conjured creatures widened the path first cleared by red and green. Oris directed the lilac and cobalt-blue serpent-lions, "Hold for now." She and the creatures guarding her watched on as silver and gold wriggled up next to red and green, doubling the damage to the mindless mzigo.

Ziko assisted from above, riding the black serpent-lion as the creature strafed the mzigo horde. He swung his hammer-pick at the unliving legion, striking with a wide cast of yellow energy that knocked back the advancing creatures.

I appreciate your assistance, King Ghut, Oris sent to Ziko. *But please ascend to your mission. Slay the sky demon with your hammer.*

Ziko pulled back on his submerged hand as if tugging on a horse's reins. The black serpent-lion roared and changed directions, shooting up into the sky toward Chilombo-Wroch.

A rumble occurred in the distance, a combined battle cry from the summoned weynee and pangomutu. Their legion scrambled forward, and even more problematic was the path carved by the serpent-lions was now filling in with a new mzigo militia. Oris directed her lilac serpent-lion to whip the flooding mzigo with its electric hiss. She walked toward the cobalt-blue serpent-lioness, watching the lightning storm lather the incoming mzigo. The strikes were fierce but not enough as more of the unliving inundated the area.

Full marks for bravery, little girl, Rretch taunted her.

Wrage concluded, *Surrender is still your best option. We are everywhere, and we have conquered far larger kingdoms than yours.*

Oris sent a retaliatory promise, *Our kingdom will be your worst nightmare.* "The perimeter!" shouted Oris to the cobalt-blue serpent-lioness.

Oris' conjure slithered around the lecture dome's safe area. Three weynee sprang from over the grouped mzigo. They landed against the cobalt-blue serpent-lioness, clutching at her body and using their weight to bring her down. The serpent-lioness fluttered while coughing up lightning streams. Several strands hit two of the serpent-lioness' attackers, incinerating them. Oris ducked away as her cobalt-blue conjure bucked and tossed the third over her head.

Pangomutu leapt into the fray. A unit of five smacked their clubs against the cobalt-blue serpent-lioness. They did little damage to the crystal-like serpent, clubs splintering when pounded against the hardened, translucent scales. The serpent-lioness reached down and scooped up one in its jaws, biting and puncturing, crunching through bone and bursting the tote of flesh, squeezing all manner of liquid life out of the unfinished man. It dropped the life-drained pangomutu from its maw and sprayed the others with an electric hiss.

The attack on the serpent-lioness served as a distraction, removing focus from the four crystals shimmering loud with their orange aura. The diversion was fleeting, as additional pangomutu entered the safe zone and commenced clubbing the crystals. Oris hurried to one of the pangomutu and put the tips of her fingers against the back of its head. She flooded the creature with heat that cooked its brain, and the pangomutu fell dead. Another slammed its body against Oris Del, knocking the conjure woman to the ground. Oris rolled with the attack against her, palmed the ground and pushed herself up on her feet. But it was already too late. Doing little with their weapons, the pangomutu then picked up the crystals and tossed them to a group of weynee who'd joined the entanglement. The mighty creatures gripped the crystals and crushed them to powder within their tightened palms.

The mystical aura was strangled, and the mzigo turned toward the tower. Rretch and Wrage broadcasted an order to the needle-wielding creatures. Their command echoed in what little mind the mzigo had. The mental order was like strings on a puppet, it pulled them, controlled their movement, vibrating the needle protruding from their heads. The lecture tower and all inside were their destination. Oris Del cursed, *"Scat!"* But she was far from defeated. She hurried toward the door, dodging sword swings and club strikes from weynee and pangomutu, being careful not to trip on her long-flowing pink and yellow gown. Lilac and cobalt-blue serpent-lions attacked the creatures that converged on her. They snatched them up in their jaws or burned them with electrical stream.

Oris palmed the door, placing into it an incant for protection. It wouldn't last long, but it would be long enough. She called, *"Koluboti-bulu!"* Her cobalt-blue serpent-lioness turned with the mention of her name, and then slithered to Oris' side. The conjure woman jumped on its back and put her hands through one of its scales until she felt the lock at her wrist. "Up!" she commanded, and the serpent dived into the air. She sent a silent command to her remaining serpents-lions to hold a front at the tower. The four out in the midst of battle pivoted and returned to the lecture dome, fighting their way back.

Kaapa! Oris sent to a conjure man huddled next to Chieftess Nofre as she held her sleeping child. Kaapa sported a thick mop of locked hair atop his head that hung far enough to cast a curtain over his ears. A black and bushy goa-t not only covered his face but also his age, making him appear older. He was from an ancient order of conjure-warrior men and women known as Farasin. They were the unseen, at first a secret. The emergence of zealots over the centuries was to the Farasin like water to growing flowers. So, did bloom from shade and silhouette these unseen conjure-warriors to battle them.

Kaapa flinched in reaction to Oris' voice. He returned the sending. *My Queen, what have you to report?* His voice merged both gentleman and rogue into one, eloquent in words, rough in sound.

The safe zone has been breached. The crystals have been destroyed, Oris reported.

"My goodness!" the Farasin expressed aloud.

His voice caught the ears of Annand and his sister Kymsaan. Annand, arms still crossed, turned to the conjure man. Kymsaan, standing next to him, did the same. The Farasin met their eyes. A concerned look poured over him. He put up a single finger in an attempt to halt their curiosity. Brother and sister looked at one another with surprised expressions.

My serpent-lions are holding the perimeter. Wofiira and Lorish sent two captains. They summoned units of weynee and pangomutu. Crystals were destroyed. Tell Annand to set up a welcoming committee should anything come through. Change of plans. I'm joining King Ziko in the sky against Chilombo-Wroch. We'll take him. Your power and blessing be with us.

Oris was gone. Kaapo didn't send back an argument, but he scowled so hard he believed the conjure woman might've felt his disdain. He stood and stepped to Annand. "There's trouble outside," he addressed, a hint of frustration coming through his gentlemanly tone and manner. Before Annand or Kymsaan could express a question beyond the look in their eyes, Kaapo stated, "The crystals have been destroyed." Annand snarled and swiped the crossbow from his back. He locked in three arrows. "Oris' conjures are holding the front. She's joined Ziko in his pursuit against the sky demon."

Annand turned away, expressing only a frustrated grunt at the news. He called for Yre and Dual. The two smugglers jumped on command. "We're in terrible danger," he told them.

"As opposed to *delightful* danger?" Dual joked.

Annand didn't have time for it. He ordered, "Usher the people away from the doors and walls. Is that clear, pirates? Get them closer to the stage. As close as possible. It will be uncomfortable, but they have to do it." Yre and Dual looked to one another and then back at Annand. They shook their heads in the same reluctant manner. "Is there a problem?" asked Annand, the cup of his words filled to the brim with annoyance.

Yre lifted his shoulders. "Well, I hate to bring it up at this time—

death at our front door and all. But it's the whole addressing us as 'pirates' thing."

Dual made an uneasy face and added, "We've pleaded a hundred times that we're not pirates."

Yre snapped his fingers. "Correct! Right on, my man!" he congratulated, slapping Dual on the back. To Annand he suggested an acceptable alternative. "We're businessmen," he proposed.

Annand rolled his eyes and bent down, getting into Yre's face to tell him, "You took things that don't belong to you. The items you transported were illegal. We had several warrants for your arrest in our kingdom alone; and you were awaiting trial for your crimes in a local prison. You're lucky we got to you first, because your marks weren't as protocol oriented as the law, should they have gotten their hands on you. They would've gone straight to execution without jury or judge. It also suits your luck that were it not for the sky-demon as a far more pertinent antagonist, I would again place you under arrest by will of the law governed by our Honor. However, we have circumstances to attend to. Make yourselves useful and heroic and perhaps when this is over, should we all be standing, we can discuss a pardon."

Yre and Dual considered the points. Yre spoke first. "Absolutely, officer!" he saluted. "Much respect! And I mean that with complete sincerity." Then he made a face, waving his hands around in a ridiculous manner. "I still don't understand the whole 'pirate' thing."

"I concur!" expressed Dual. "I reiterate my friend's definition of being businessmen in our own right. Especially since our so-called victims *are* pirates. We're doing civic duty at the very least."

"*Were*," Annand corrected, rolling his eyes again. "And if that's how you want to play it, then attend to your civic duties now or join the ranks of the mzigo outside."

Yre and Dual scrambled to complete their order. They headed to the top of an aisle and said politely to the nearest refugees, "Away from the doors. Move as close to the stage as possible."

Annand watched. He yelled to the people huddled inside the lecture hall, waving one hand while holding the underside of his crossbow with another. *"Urgent! Up! Move! Come on! Now! Quickly! Quickly!"*

Kaapo addressed the nlawọ again, "Wofiira and Lorish sent two captains. Units of weynee and pangomutu are at their command. Chilombo-Wroch has relinquished control of the mzigo to them."

Annand huffed. He gripped his crossbow with both hands. "Damned bitch's brood!" he cursed. He then yelled, "Ren! Your service, mercenary, is required!"

Kymsaan yelled an order to six guards to hold a tight formation around Governor Pajon Ohn and Chieftess Nofre. To a tall and slender man with a short haircut she called, "Danso, with me and my brother." The man named Danso jumped to call with a crossbow in his hands, three arrows locked.

The man named Ren joined he party, and he too sprang at command from Annand. He wore a dark-brown cape and cowl that mimicked his skin color. A green tunic with black pants were also worn on his person. Brown boots clothed his feet. Throwing knives lined his belt. Two daggers were in his grip. He was short and slender, but lithesome in movement. He was of *kurujuati* extraction, explaining his short stature, and most of all his ears that dangled just above his shoulders in one direction and curved and came to a point in the other. He was handsome, with boyish features, and clean-shaven as it was hard for most with kurujuati ethnicity to grow facial hair. That feat was a blessing in their culture, and mostly reserved by nature for kings and statesmen of their kind. As it were, he was a hired assassin, and it was necessary to be unassuming.

Annand walked through the guards surrounding the Honorable Family. He bent down and said to Pajon Ohn, "Our defenses are broken, Your Honor. We have the Nightmare Queen's—"

"Must you call her that, Annand?" the governor pleaded.

"My apologies, Your Honor," the guard-captain relayed. "We have her serpent-lions putting up a defense. But what's out there is in large and determined numbers. We know what we must do, and it's difficult. We just have to hope we can bring down the sky demon. Then all will be set right." He looked at the Governor and Chieftess.

Nofre held her child close. She looked at her husband. "We have a newborn, and for the sake of our son and daughter locked in the basement, we have no choice and no other plan."

Pajon Ohn sighed, "Do as you must, Annand. Hold fort, secure victory, and help us regain our power when this is all over."

Annand nodded and saluted. "Yes, Governor!" he said. He saluted Nofre and addressed, "Chieftess!" He stood, shuffled through the wall of guards and then pointed to his sister, Ren, Danso, and Kaapo. He thumbed in the direction of the closest door and waded through the people flowing opposite him on their way to reach the stage. His sister, and the others he called upon, followed.

At the door, Annand stepped through. Ren and Danso were close to him. Annand had his crossbow up as he journeyed into the dark hallway. Ren sheathed his daggers, taking up two throwing knives per hand. Danso, like Annand, held his crossbow up and at the ready.

The fray polluting the outside resonated hollow in the empty hall.

Hisses, roars and growls rattled the stone walls. Pounds thundered against the structure and echoed through the corridor. Oris Del's serpent-lions screeched. Electrical hisses cackled. The holler of creatures played like a choir. Annand and crew approached another door. Annand jumped to one side. Ren put his hand on the knob. Danso stood tall at the opposite side of the door, ready for action.

Ren opened the door.

The hallway was dark.

A ghostly air sailed through. The cry of creatures was less muffled in the passageway. Danso moved Ren aside and stepped through.

From down the new passage came the swift whistling sound of cut air. Two lethal arrows raced. One penetrated Danso's leg. The other punctured his jugular. Danso's eyes rolled up. His jaw dropped. A gush of blood salivated off his dangling tongue. Danso's grip opened, and his crossbow rattled against the wooden floor. He grabbed his neck and fell back. Another set of arrows were flung. One hit the lower-right of his abdomen, spinning him into a violent twist. Annand grabbed the guard and pulled him away from the assailment of arrows. Ren jumped aside, taking post where Danso stood prior to the attack.

Annand cursed. He cradled Danso with one arm as he got to his knees. He dragged Danso farther away from the door. "Kaapo!" he yelled. "Kaapo, can you heal him?"

Danso gasped as blood filled his lungs and throat. More blood seeped down the sides of his mouth. Kaapo inspected the convulsing Danso. He believed all he could really do was bless the body after its final breath. Danso salvaged a bit of strength to reach up and dislodge the arrow from his neck. Blood slithered from the deep puncture like a dark-red snake fleeing through grass and weeds. Danso shivered one last respiration and passed away.

Annand closed the brave guard's eyes.

More arrows were hurled through the door. They thwacked against the wall opposite the opening, bouncing off the stone or lodging into the grooves. Ren's eyes brightened to a shimmering yellow. He took a peek down the dark hallway. He moved away as two more arrows came through. His eyes lost their glow. "There's five of 'em. Elite weynee," he noted. "They're armed! Weapon class: crossbows," he reported. He grabbed the sides of his cape, knives still between his fingers. "Let's see if I can subtract from their numbers." The assassin wrapped himself up into his cloak and disappeared. He only had a few moments to remain hidden from the world. He tossed four projectiles down the hall and ducked away. He spun into sight on the other side of the door, back flat against the wall.

One of his shots went wild and dug into the wood panel on the wall. The second landed in a weynee's kneecap, dropping the beast. The knife sunk into the weynee's knee deeper as the beast buckled and the projectile's hilt pressed against the floor. Another hit the same weynee's shoulder, causing him to drop his weapon. Blood spilled and stained the floor, rushing into the niches and cracks. The fourth tossed knife stuck into a weynee's groin. The muscular brute hollered, and the sound filled the hall as he fell faced-forward against the floor, the knife lodging farther inside him with the impact.

Annand laid Danso's body on the ground. In the same motion, he kicked Danso's crossbow toward his sister. She rolled, scooping up the weapon. While on her knees, Kymsaan came from around the door and fired all three arrows down the corridor.

The remaining weynee were killed.

Annand snatched Danso's quiver and passed it to his sister. Kymsaan caught the case of arrows and hooked it to her belt. She looked at her brother and made signals with her fingers. *Should we go in?* was her communication. Annand lifted a hand to halt any action. They waited a moment, and then came a terrible sounding crash! High pitched screams filled the corridors. Annand turned around, crossbow up and ready. An arrow punched through his forearm, but excited by the fight around him, he felt nothing. He fired his arrows into the darkness. Ren's eyes glowed, and he filled his hands with throwing knives. He saw incoming weynee and pangomutu coming toward them. Two pangomutu were slumped on the floor dead, Annand's arrows in their necks, pools of blood under them. Their long and lifeless tongues spread out from their mouths. A weynee was against the wall, Kymsaan's arrow centered in its head. Her other kills lined the floors. More armed weynee marched into the hall through the open door.

High-pitched giggling echoed from either passage.

"We're. Coming. I-i-i-i-i-in," they taunted as one voice. "And we're going to lay with your women and slit your children's throats!" Their song echoed and the summoned creatures repeated the demented chant, becoming louder and louder as they came nearer and nearer. *We're going to lay with your women and slit your children's throats! We're going to lay with your women and slit your children's throats! We're going to lay with your women and slit your children's throats!*

The door leading to the lecture hall opened down the passage they'd traveled. Yre announced, "We have a mzigo breach!"

Annand locked in three more arrows. He got up and backed away, firing all three arrows down the corridor as he passed. *Welcome to the lecture dome!* he hollered as he pulled the trigger. Creatures were wounded, killed. "First lesson: We don't go down that easy! Scrape you abominations! My word!"

Ren pitched knives into the darkness in front of him. A knife landed in a pangomutu's eye, a second hit a weynee's throat. His last throwing knife hit a weynee's abdomen. The creature grunted. Annand shot him up with arrows killing the beast. Ren folded himself up in his cape and disappeared.

Launched arrows soared past the mercenary and hit Annand in the back just as he made a turn to focus his attention on the other invading creatures. The bulky guard-captain clenched his teeth, pain biting at him. He turned and fired a single arrow that caught the offending weynee's throat. Kymsaan locked and fired arrows down the hall, side-by-side with her brother.

Ren appeared visible near Yre. Kaapo had already returned to the lecture hall, priestly robes removed, revealing tan, baggy pants and brown boots. He wore a sleeveless, black tunic and pumped his fists like a pugilist as his robe slipped away. His arms radiated, bursting into cool, blue beams of incant. He dived toward the stage from the upper deck of seats, landing atop a party of mzigo readying to needle a family of five. Kaapo jumped up, striking the unliving with arms and fists aglow.

Annand and his small party backed into the lecture hall, continuing to assail the combined armies of pangomutu and remaining weynee. He took a peek over his shoulder. It was chaos, but there were a few good things his strategic mind counted. The mzigo weren't so overwhelming, and the mindless needle wielders were wracked with trouble maneuvering around the tight area, tripping over themselves. Some crawled, which made the panicking people have to dodge the creatures reaching for them at the ankles with needle or jaw.

"The Honorable Family has been moved to a backroom!" hollered Yre.

Ren tossed the smuggler one of his daggers. "Less words, pirate. Where's your first mate?"

Yre said nothing. His eyes moved between a row of seats and spotted his friend Dual, trapped and transformed as a mzigo, reaching up and moaning the song of the burden. Kymsaan spotted Dual's transfigured form. Her eyes went to Yre who was holding Ren's dagger, eyes frozen on his friend and partner-in-crime. She shouted to the smuggler, "Stay your hand, pirate! That damned Farasin has his theory!"

Annand fired off more arrows into the passage they'd just backed out of. Weynee and pangomutu died from his assault. He reloaded. "Slay these conjured creatures!" he yelled to all that could hear him. "Then start cold-cocking the burdened!"

The domed tower rumbled. A serpent-lion's body crashed through the structure, screaming as pangomutu crawled over its frame. A serpent-lioness roared and hissed, snatching the pangomutu assailing her male counterpart. Cold and hot air from Nature's dystopian atmosphere penetrated the sanctuary, clawing or smothering the refugees scrambling or being made victim by the mzigo and other monsters.

Lilac and green were the two serpent-lions remaining in defense of the sanctuary. Silver, gold and red had taken to the skies, assisting Ziko and Oris Del's strike on the massive, black sky demon.

Up there. The attack on Chilombo-Wroch was an exercise in focus for the skull-masked Ziko. His first strategy was simply to soar around the black dragon, zig-zagging as he swiped his hammer-pick's magic against the sky demon. The extended lashes were effective. The alchemized conjure springing from Ziko's weapon stung the flying beast. The serpent hollered, and the monster's breath moved the clouds. Despite Ziko's nuisance, Chilombo-Wroch rose higher, weaving through the sky. Ziko moved closer. His black serpent-lion struggled to keep its speed against the massive serpent-dragon. Ziko maneuvered to keep side-by-side, coasting along Chilombo-Wroch's long, colossal frame. He tugged left, a command for the serpent-lion to track closer along Chilombo-Wroch. When he was near the beast's scales, Ziko leapt from his mount. He turned his blessed weapon around to its sharpest point and dug the tip of the alchemized instrument into Wroch's hard scales.

The pick end cracked through the beast's tough, epidermal plates. The hammer-pick's head brimmed with a magical, yellow gel. Ziko held tight to the handle with both hands. *Now what?* he asked himself as he clung to the beast's side. He looked up. It was a long, long, long way to reach Chilombo-Wroch's back. He was barely halfway up the creature's vast right side.

He felt the sky-demon's flight speed slowing down, and Ziko found leverage enough to lift up using the hammer-pick's handle. He reached for a groove in the beast's scales, gripped, and raised up. He removed his hammer-pick and dug above him. He repeated the action.

Pick. Grab. Lift.

Pick. Grab. Lift.

Fatigue set in, and Ziko paused to regain his breath. He chanted incants and recovered his stamina. His strength funneled back into him with enough time to brace himself against Chilombo-Wroch's twisting and curling body as the sky-demon soared higher into the air, roaring. The creature had a plan, and it dived toward the earth to shake the nuisance off itself. Ziko held tight, and Chilombo-Wroch leveled out after its swift dive. Taking time, Ziko furthered his ascent, able to find footing and not rely simply on his upper body strength to hold him in place. When fatigue next set in, Ziko didn't use an incant. Instead, he employed his wits and performed a clever gambit. If he couldn't scale the mountain, he'd make its peak come to him.

His hammer-pick cracked back through the hardened scale. Ziko focused, using spirit and incant to send a shockwave through the black serpent. The channeled conjure energy nearly knocked Ziko unconscious, but he remained aware, nose bleeding and eyes watering. The attack's sharpness cut through Chilombo-Wroch with the effectiveness of a searing bee's sting against a person's arm, and the mighty creature's reaction was just what Ziko required.

Chilombo-Wroch hollered and rolled right. Ziko pulled his hammer-pick free, taking chips of the scale he'd burrowed into. Chilombo-Wroch's large physique twisted fast, his back now facing Ziko as he hovered in the air, using the alchemical wind of his hammer, and the buff and incant, to keep afloat. He plunged the point of his hammer-pick into another set of Chilombo-Wroch's squama and held tight as the massive beast straightened, Ziko now atop the sky demon's back. He managed to stand. Through the magic of his hammer-pick, he cast an aura around him. The aegis enabled him to keep balance, though he found it still an ordeal to trek across the black dragon. The sky-demon was like a floating landmass, and Ziko had to step carefully so as not to sink between scales and twist his ankle or fall and be a meteor cast to the earth below. Time was also like a childhood crush out of reach, and Ziko knew the battle below depended on the outcome of his battle in the sky.

Small as Ziko was to Chilombo-Wroch's frame, the sky demon could sense the flea scratching its bulk. Undulating did nothing. Ziko's incant aligned with his hammer-pick's alchemy and bestowed upon him perfect poise. But Chilombo-Wroch too had cunning ploys ready for use. He lifted his head and vomited up a battalion of mzigo that rained around Ziko. "Keep him from my eyes!" The serpent-liar's deep voice rumbled like an ominous roll of thunder.

"Scat!" cursed Ziko, as he found himself swarmed by Chilombo-Wroch's regurgitated and transmuted soldiers. He swung his hammer-pick at them, a long beam of conjure-spirit hummed from off the head and whipped unconscious several of the encroaching mzigo. They toppled and slid off the dragon, taking with them others of the needle-wielding mob.

While the mzigo were not the best of soldiers dispatched against Ziko, they were number enough to halt his advance. The sky demon soared slow and without curve or banking, allowing the mzigo a better footing to encircle and creep closer to Ziko. The alchemist swung wildly, knocking them back with lashes of conjure. Some turned to ash; others fell unconscious. Whether blackened ember dust or insensible, the fallen blew away in the wind. But the victories were small for Ziko. More moved in on him, and

Chilombo-Wroch teased him with laughter.

"And where is the rest of your band?" the sky demon growled.

In your eye! replied Oris Del with a strong thought into the black dragon's mind. She swooped in on her cobalt-blue serpent-lioness, and her mount spewed electric streams from its mouth. The static torrent flogged Chilombo-Wroch's right eye. The beast flinched, and the mzigo surrounding Ziko fell over, but Ziko held his ground. He looked up and spied his black serpent-lion joining the attack. The sky demon cried out in pain from the additional onslaught. His body zigged and zagged, and his flailing face almost collided with Oris Del, but the inspector-medium-turned-queen flew over the black demon's head and streaked toward the middle of the serpent's long form.

Chilombo-Wroch recovered and snaked around for retaliation, causing more mzigo to trip and fall on his frame. Some continued reaching or stabbing at Ziko while others were blown away with the sudden move made by the gargantuan sky demon. Ziko remained fixed, the alchemy of his hammer-pick buffing his balance.

Chilombo-Wroch opened his mouth. He snapped to swallow Oris Del and her pretty, cobalt-blue serpent-lioness too. Oris dodged the attack, but the black dragon still claimed a victim in his massive maw. Nwa-ọdum was swallowed and ingested. The black-serpent lion soared into the beast's belly, dodging the inner-working, organic gears that shuffled Chilombo-Wroch's victims into a biological conveyor belt. Being caught by the biotic mechanisms would not have affected the jet-black serpent-lion, as the summoned creature had no burden in its body.

Nwa-ọdum opened its mouth and sprayed electric fire at Chilombo-Wroch's internal factory, setting ablaze organs that produced the foul ink that transmuted its victims. The bio-structures exploded and burned, spraying thick, ghastly goops of ink in all directions. The murky matter spattered against Nwa-ọdum's translucent scales, burning the serpent-lion and causing it to buck wildly.

The dripping and tossed ink collected together in the air, sprouting into a gray and green-scaled serpent-lion, a copy of what it had touched. Nwa-ọdum turned to attack, its body radiating with smoke.

A pumping organ belched balls of ink at the black serpent-lion and incased the crystal-scaled creature in its muck. Nwa-ọdum's body slammed against Chilombo-Wroch's swampy, stomach innards. Pinned. Another malevolent serpent-lion was birthed out of the grime that covered the ensnared serpent-lion.

The sky demon felt the burn in his stomach, but he managed a grin as he spit up the two, baleful, gray and green-scaled counterfeit serpent-lions through his thin, red lips. Oris Del was in awe believing that Chilombo-Wroch's power infected her conjure, and the serpent-lion was no longer under her control. She attempted to banish the conjure back to the spirit realm from which it was summoned, but there was no effect. Chains wrapped around them, and as they flew faster she noticed it was two serpent-lions and not one. She sent a telepathic shout to Nwa-ǫdum, her conjure. She felt his presence, suffering inside Chilombo-Wroch's belly as it was submerged in ink and replicated. An army of devil serpent-lions were being mass produced, needles protruded from their heads. Their teeth sharpened to an infected point. The sky demon's offspring were ready to take flight.

Oris Del dived. The two serpent-lion copies attacked, spraying electrical strands from their tongue. Oris dodged the assault. The cobalt-blue serpent lion cried, feeling the burden of her brother trapped inside the belly of the beast, forced into submission and used to create false things. Oris turned her mount and commanded it to redress. The malefic serpent-lions dodged and hissed. Oris Del's mount slammed into one, and she held on tight. The vile serpent-lion sank its needle-like teeth into Koluboti-bulu's neck. The second did the same, and the cobalt-blue lioness shook with violent spasms.

Oris pulled her hand free and slipped off the serpent-lioness' body as the conjured creature's eyelids flapped wild. Chains sprouted around it, first bubbling up as liquid ink and then becoming a terrible, greenish-rust. Gray and green surfaced in its translucent scales as the chain tightened around it. But she was not transmuted. She was only subdued. Chilombo-Wroch's children dragged her back through his maw to assist in more malicious manufacturing.

Oris cried out as she descended at a rapid pace toward the world below.

Silver, gold, and red serpent-lionesses converged on the mzigo enclosing Ziko. They bombarded the transmuted soldiers with electric wallops sprayed from their opened mouths. Gold received a telepathic cry from Oris Del and dived to retrieve the conjure woman. The serpent-lioness scooped her up, and Oris locked her hands within its scales. She regained her composure and then reined her conjure to ascend. Chilombo-Wroch hollered, trying to use the might of his breath to stagger Oris' climb toward him. Her gold serpent-lioness spat electric strands at the hulking, black dragon. Chilombo-Wroch snarled and snarled at the attempt to injure him. He was only antagonized further.

"My children will eat you all!" he shouted. "*Our* children, conjure woman!" he taunted Oris Del.

Ziko sculpted a path through the mzigo, keeping clear of needle strike and bite. Ziko leapt into the air, putting his hand through the red serpent-lioness' frame and being spirited away. Silver made a hard dodge right and eluded an attack from Chilombo-Wroch's replicated children who returned to battle.

Ziko kept his legs up and at a distance from the marching mzigo. The red serpent-lioness soared over them toward the top of Chilombo-Wroch's head. Ziko detached from the ruddy scales and landed perfect atop the sky demon's head. The conjure carrying him joined its silver sibling in battle against their demonic counterparts. They swirled and swerved, dodging and attempting attack with bite or lightning. Chilombo-Wroch swallowed the melee in hopes that his created creatures would bring him more to corrupt and replicate.

Red and Silver were too vigilant. They coiled in the air and lashed at Chilombo-Wroch's innards with electric hisses. They swooped down and freed Nwa-ọdum and Koluboti-bulu with electricity streamed from their mouths. Their combined attacks burned the ink that covered their brother and sister. Black and cobalt-blue serpent-lions hollered, a battle cry that celebrated their freedom. They joined the other two in the air and the four serpent-felines colored the walls in electric hiss. Nwa-ọdum concentrated his electric stream onto the final ink-pumping organ, exploding it into chunks of burned, cindered meat.

A fleet of sixteen, spurious serpent-lions had already been assembled, resting in the sky demon of lies' belly. Now they were stirred to flight. Oris Del's four summons slammed into the armada, biting some, wrapping their bodies around others, and then crashing purposefully into Chilombo-Wroch's stomach lining while spraying everywhere with electric hisses. The attacking, benevolent serpent-lion would uncoil and recover from the crash, leaving its adversary downed. It would soar up into the air and chase down another.

The task proved too much for the four serpent-lions. Their fallen foes recovered quickly and continued their journey through Chilombo-Wroch's opened maw and out into the world with three moons. The people below now had Chilombo-Wroch's children to contend with.

Topside, inching his way to the middle area at the top of the sky demon's head, Ziko focused. He'd glimpsed the new armada of corrupted serpent-lions spewing from Chilombo-Wroch's mouth with Oris Del's four serpent-lions in hastened pursuit. He paid it no mind. Concentrated, Ziko had a task at hand—and in that very hand he gripped his alchemized hammer-pick. A bright bubbling gel of magic surrounded the head, and Ziko thrust the pick-end into Chilombo-Wroch's crown. The weapon was small but effective. Its alchemized magic had been enhanced, blessed by a rare gem suggested by Kaapo the Farasin to retrieve. The Farasin and Oris Del provided a further blessing, increasing the gem's power. Ziko had saved the use of the gem's might for this very purpose.

The strike of conjure coiled through the massive black serpent's brain, smothering its attempted roar and locking its eyelids open. Chilombo-Wroch's body went limp, and he fell back, appearing like a giant, black arrow shot from the heavens to the earth below. The remaining mzigo tumbled from the sky demon's black, serpentine body and plunged to the multi-seasoned world beneath the clouds. Ziko fell too, but he snared the sharp end of his hammer-pick into Chilombo-Wroch. He was on the climb again, with only a short time before the beast regained consciousness and mobility. He gripped a scale plate and planted his feet against the jet dragon. A demonic serpent-lion descended on him. Nwa-ǫdum slammed into the child of Chilombo-Wroch, knocking it away from Ziko. Another swooped in, mouth open and ready to strike. Red coiled her body around it and dragged the beast away.

Seeing that all was clear, Ziko used his hammer-pick and continued his climb, but he struggled, even as his incants shielded him from the ferocious winds and bestowed upon him balance. He was fatigued. *Madame Bhlud,* he sent. *Your assistance, please.* The conjure woman replied she was on her way. Ziko looked up and saw her approach. Four demon serpent-lions chased her. Ziko grimaced behind his mask and swore, "Scat!" He conjured another bubble of yellow energy around his hammer-pick and smacked it into another of Chilombo-Wroch's scales. He climbed and waited, taking a peek over his shoulder. Silver's body was wrapped around a corrupted serpent-lion, squeezing tight. The two hurtled toward Chilombo-Wroch's hovering body, slamming hard against its back, rolling, tumbling. Silver uncoiled, soared upward and then dived down casting an electric strand against the corrupted serpent-lion.

Ziko spied Oris Del as she zoomed in closer. Ziko loosened the hammer-pick from Chilombo-Wroch's scale, and when Oris passed close, Ziko lunged, bringing the hammer-pick with him.

He stretched his arms and legs, body sailing through the air. Ziko slapped against the conjured creature, almost sliding off and soaring down to a smattering death. But Ziko locked his wrist into a gold scale, let his body hang loose and be carried by the gold mount. Oris banked left. Ziko rolled up the serpent-lioness' body and straddled it proper. *Thank you, my Queen,* he sent. He peeked at the corrupted serpent-lions attempting to gain speed behind them. *Slow it down, Madame Bhlud.* He gripped the handle of his hammer-pick. *Swing around. I'll slow these false-forged creatures down with some alchemy of my own.*

Oris eased the speed on her translucent beast. Chilombo-Wroch's forgeries made a gain on her. Oris turned hard. Ziko slapped a magical beam across all four demonic serpent-lions as he swung his blessed hammer. His attack silenced and ceased the pursuing beasts. Their translucent bodies nose-dived, appearing like comets with their heads aimed at the ground far below.

Oris pulled up to Chilombo-Wroch's large, round head. She ascended higher, her gold mount maintaining a speed slower in descent with the unconscious, black dragon as it hovered above its face. Ziko held his hammer. He saw Chilombo-Wroch's eye twitch as awareness dissipated the fog in his mind. The paralysis clutching the sky-demon's body was melting away. Ziko jumped down, landing between Chilombo-Wroch's eyes. Buffed balance kept him stable, but he reached down and grabbed a scale to remain on the beast.

The sky-demon's lower jaw quivered, life trembling through it. Magic coursed through its body, and its descent slowed as flight gradually came back to its control.

Ziko fastened a thought, channeling it through his arm and up into his hammer-pick. The instrument's head brightened with bubbling, magic gel. Ziko pivoted to the left eye and swung the pick-end of his weapon down into it, producing a sound like shattering glass. Ziko concentrated harder, conducting more thought and conjure through him and into the head of his hammer-pick. The light from Chilombo-Wroch's eye drained, releasing a sigh of red smoke that swiveled free and surrounded Ziko.

He pulled his hammer-pick free and crawled to the right eye. An awakening groan rippled from Chilombo-Wroch, but Ziko remained coolheaded. Hammer-pick ablaze, Ziko jammed its pointed end through the tough, red sclera. A cackle of electricity and a burst of conjure energy exploded from the slender, red eye. There again came the sound of shattering glass. Ziko administered additional charges of conjure, and like the left eye before it, Chilombo-Wroch's right eye drained of light. Ziko dislodged his hammer-pick, and up from the crack in the eye spouted thick, red strands of smoke.

The conjure burrowing through the sky-demon seeped into its belly and turned its alchemical bile against him. It bubbled and brightened into a smoldering vat of heat, exploding the black dragon's stomach, and rising through its structure. The magical fire reached out from Chilombo-Wroch's slightly agape mouth and incinerated six of its corrupted, serpent-lion children. The creature was dead, and it never regained complete consciousness to understand its defeat. The beast tumbled back in the air. Ziko separated from the sky-demon, and the alchemist with the hammer sailed above the black dragon upon letting him go.

Oris Del swooped down and caught Ziko. She slowed her serpent-lioness' ascent and hovered in the air. She and Ziko watched as the sky demon raced toward the earth. Worry choked them both. Should the black serpent's giant frame crash against the ground, the force would wipe out all of the settlements of El-Ham, and its effect would be felt far and wide. Oris-Del wondered if she had enough strength to slow the beast's rapid descent. Ziko thought the same as he gripped his hammer-pick and scanned the magical object for its full potential.

But as Oris Del aimed an open palm to test her mettle, the serpent's large body shimmered with small points of light across its body. It dwindled into ember and ash that rushed away in the wind. Oris and Ziko sighed relief. Chilombo-Wroch was defeated, and in synch with the sky demon's disintegration, the heavy mounds of snow receded, the air shifted to a moderate temperature, and the areas of boiling soil cooled.

The dragon's alchemy lapsed. Its remaining squadron of corrupted serpent-lions and serpent-lionesses turned to ash. Kaapo's theory was correct. The Farasin's study and knowledge paid off. Oris Del's serpent-lions returned to her. Lilac reported through a telepathic, visual message that the captains Rretch and Wrage had been arrested. The two serpent-lions assisted Annand and the mercenary Ren in the captains' capture. No harm had come to the Honorable couple, and the governor ordered Retch and Wrage be executed.

Command given, Annand put an arrow in the back of their heads.

In the lecture dome-turned-sanctuary, Yre stood over the body of his sleeping friend Dual. It was a state of being echoed by other alchemized and burdened people, once mzigo. The puncture of their brains by needle filled in as if no injury or offense occurred. They were now slumped on the ground from hall to earth, fallen to a deep sleep.

The pirate felt a large and strong hand on his shoulder. It was the warrior-guard Kymsaan. "He'll be fine," she assured him, putting the crossbow in her hand down. She wasn't too certain, but she knew Yre needed to hear comforting words for the time being.

"He has a bit of a crush on you," Yre admitted. Kymsaan smiled. "He likes women with long legs." The female warrior chuckled. Yre confessed to her, "I'm in love with his sister. I've been keeping that from him. I hope he's okay with that because…I plan to marry her. She's safe. Far way." He cupped his friend's hand. "Then we will be brothers-by-law, as we have always been in crime and spirit." He grinned and thought aloud, "Brothers-by-law; and it will be the one law we don't break." He looked up at Kymsaan and remarked, "Pirates, huh?"

"That sounds sweet," grumbled Annand. He walked into the

poignant moment unfazed by the arrows still in his forearm and back. His voice was sincere, but he held a sly grin on his face. "Shall we talk about a pardon, *'businessman'*?" Yre looked up at the nlawǫ warrior-guard and smiled at him a 'thank you'. "Perhaps you two will do well in the service of our El-Ham kingdom as spies."

"Perhaps…" concluded Yre.

A deluge of lilac fog drowned the scene. It became dense and shimmering. Time shifted behind it, but only by an hour. Voices belonging to an older man and a young woman could be heard through it. Pajon Ohn and Oris Del owned the speech. The fog glistened from existence. Many of the refugees had been permitted leave. People were eager for the search of loved ones among the slumbering retrogressed. The governor and chieftess' son and daughter had been taken from a backroom, unchained and laid out on the stage deep in sleep. The palms of their hands were stained with ash from the needles they once held. Kaapo affirmed their sleep would last for no longer than three days. Newly transmuted would be less time than that. Yre expected Dual to awaken at any given moment.

That was the best of news. Everything else was up for debate, such as the state of the world. Pajon Ohn and Oris Del had differing views. Annand and Kymsaan along with other guards and Chieftess Nofre encircled Pajon Ohn. Kaapo and Ren stood with Oris Del and Ziko, who now had both his hammer and skull mask clipped to his belt. Unfinished chapters scripted on his arms and legs now concluded his recent experiences. There was even a noticeable bloat in his belly. He rubbed it and wondered if he would be that type of man of El-Nord. He enjoyed the muscle of his abdomen rather than its swollen bulge.

The pirate Yre sat on the edge of the stage, the debate at his back.

"El-Ham needs the attention of its governor and chieftess," said Pajon Ohn. "My wife, at sixty-three, is a mother again. I need as many warriors here." He turned in frustration and scoffed, "I have no idea why I'm even arguing with you!" He sucked his teeth and mocked, *"A self-appointed queen! Ha!"*

Pajon Ohn's back to her, Oris Del addressed him, "I agree with you, Your Honor. This—" she twirled and panned the broken lecture dome. "All of this—all of this here is no longer Laarin-Ndoto." She pointed to Ziko with an open hand. "Papa Ghut was born here when it was still a dream. You ruled over that dream until it was transformed by a serpent's wretched alchemy. Papa Ghut and I fought back, and together—with forces from your Honorable guard—we conquered this tormented land as sovereigns. We are now awake; and I relinquish the Nightmare Kingdom, dissolved as it is."

Pajon Ohn turned and faced Oris Del. "You *relinquish*…? I should have you arrested!"

Close to Pajon Ohn was his archivist turned advisor, Saluk Yoruh. He was a plump, bearded and very dark-skinned man with a thick dome of hair atop his head. His robe was black with purple and gold along the cuffs, collar, and at the ends near his feet. He was humble and sincere, and he understood the good of Oris Del's actions and words even when the man he served did not. "I wouldn't advise that, Your Honor," he whispered.

Pajon Ohn placed his balled fists against his hips and huffed, "And would you advise sending our finest off with this woman—a zealot in her own right—to try and put an end to this war? We'd no sooner see her rise in their place, and where would we be then?"

"Pajon!" hissed Nofre at her husband.

"What? Am I wrong?" He turned to his advisor to hear an agreement. Saluk said nothing for the moment. Ziko's eyes shifted to Oris. Her face was stone, but there was a subtle movement inspired by a disturbance, a stinging pain scratching her. Her lip trembled when she went to speak. She was given more time to simmer when Saluk spoke in her place.

"I am with you, Your Honor," the advisor assured. "I am. Believe me. But we have been safe here. There were few incidents under Madame Bhlud's rule in the Nightmare Kingdom."

Pajon Ohn aimed a finger at Oris Del and addressed, "Her false rule had little to do with our safety!"

"That's true, Your Honor," Kaapo interjected. "That's entirely true. My knowledge contributed. My theories and suggestions to find materials to aid in our attack on the sky demon—all of that assisted," he recounted. "Kymsaan, Annand," he listed. "All of your guards," he included. "The alchemist with the hammer, Papa Ghut, the mercenary, Ren, and—" he peeked over at Yre. The confidence man had his eyes over his shoulder. "The businessmen," acknowledged Kaapo. Yre raised his arm and signaled with thumb up. "We've all provided. We now wish to contribute to ending this war." Pajon Ohn groaned and scowled at the notion. Kaapo continued to reason. "Your Honor, let us at least discover if there is a possibility to cease the strife caused by these zealots."

Pajon Ohn argued, "These false ones are strong. With the hex of that sky demon they ravaged other lands. The world could be in their hands."

Oris spoke up, debating, "They sent two captains to command the mzigo. At their command were also conjured armies of weynee and pangomutu. If the armies of the world had fallen to Eke Woli Lorish and Eke Almas Wofiira, then we would've seen the march of more than monsters and summoned disfigurations. The armies of man would've been among their ranks. They had nothing but hexes and tricks." It was a good point. Oris dropped her head and put her hands together. "I am humble, Governor Pajon Ohn, Chieftess Nofre—Honorable Family of El-Ham. I ask for guards in your service to assist in bringing down the zealots that have brought our world to its knees and dulled the color of its three moons. The ones behind the wretched alchemy," she proposed.

Breaths were held. Eyes were on the governor.

He answered, "We need our guards here."

Breaths were released. Oris Del walked away. Ziko was still. He let linger a vexed expression aimed at the governor for the decision made. Then he pivoted and followed Oris out of the chamber. Saluk put his eyes on Chieftess Nofre as she held her child close. She looked up at the advisor, and the two nodded in unison.

Down a hall populated with the bodies of slain pangomutu and weynee, Ziko entered into a quaint bedroom where Oris Del sat at a vanity. Ziko said to her, "You were right, Queen Oris." Her head raised and she turned to him. Ziko smiled. "They were not dubwana after all. They were indeed xidachane, lost wanderers."

Oris nodded with little expression. Heavy, melancholy eyes weighed her head down. "Is he correct?" she asked. "Am I as much a zealot as the two I wish to extinguish? Would that make you the hero and star I wish to present to the world? Am I a false speaker?"

Ziko shook his head and answered, "No. You want to end wars without recognition or a bow to spiritual doctrines. You want nothing in return except peace."

Oris brightened a bit, turning in her chair. "I do have a strange sense of self," she admitted. "A strange sense of family—*my* family," she clarified.

Ziko folded his arms and leaned against the wall. "Indulge me," he asked of her. He'd known Oris Del for quite some time, developed some feelings for her. She was a woman, and beautiful at that. Most important of all, they shared so much growing together in a short time. But he was not prepared for her statement.

"My mother is the Great Matriarch," she began. "My father is the Grand Patriarch. In truth, they are judges of the cosmos." She stood and stepped toward Ziko, telling him as she moved closer, "My younger sister's liquefied body drained into the soil to keep at bay the coming hex of mankind." Her eyes moistened with the formation of tears. "We haven't seen the worst of it. There might come a time when we long for the days of zealots. They are not even a shadow of the terrible things to come." She put out her hands. Ziko embraced them. "Not even my brother's story, told in the stars, can hold back this tide. It's all told in his cosmic body as he remains jailed in twelve prisons. I hold the story on my cosmic frame as well. But I still have trouble deciphering the language of my stars." She managed a smile at Ziko while he concentrated to remain as stone with his expression. His features quivered. Oris asked again, "Am I a zealot?"

Ziko exhaled a nervous chuckle. "Perhaps you're strange," he commented. He was to say more when Advisor Saluk and Chieftess Nofre, without her child, walked through the entrance. Oris took a few steps back from Ziko. He stepped away from the wall, turning and taking Oris' side. Both he and Oris bowed at the neck.

"My husband has simmered," Chieftess Nofre reported. She pleaded to Oris Del, "Please forgive his outburst. He's very grateful—to the both of you. But there's so much for him to consider. He still sees our settlement, regency. It's not saved. We've only ceased the assault and damage to it. There is so much more he and I are responsible for."

"I understand, Chieftess," said Oris.

"Do you, child?" she asked in a sharp, authoritative tone. "We speak of events in beginnings, middles, and ends. But little is spoken of aftermaths. People slumber, but what will they awake to? What will their minds remember? They will see life changed. Love ones that did not survive. Will they remember their terrible selves? If they were responsible for death as mzigo, will they remember their actions?" Ziko and Oris considered the points. "They will discover their world to have gone through its own alchemy. And my husband and I have the stresses of overseeing all of that."

Oris agreed. She told the chieftess, "Those burdens weigh down our world. While our honorable and royal men and women deal with their countrysides, we must act against the zealots who've caused this. Should a country or state's army join the arjais of Eke Woli Lorish and Eke Almas Wofiira, perhaps the freeing of people from the terrible alchemy will inspire dissention and rebellion. The armies of the world might be marching against them as we speak."

Ziko pointed out, "We have no crystal to commune through to know this, but perhaps we can scour the settlements for a working one. Get word from another state or country," he suggested. "The hex used by Chilombo-Wroch is gone. We should be able to send a transmission without interference."

Chieftess Nofre and Advisor Saluk turned to one another. They nodded. Saluk looked at Oris and Ziko and said, "We'll agree to that. The two of you and Kaapo," he assigned. "Take the pirates too."

Chieftess Nofre assured, "If you can get some kind of word from a neighboring state, my husband will support you." Then she asserted with authority, "I will see to that."

All was agreed upon.

The chieftess and advisor bowed. Ziko and Oris returned the gesture, and the two politicians took leave. "It's all we need," Oris commented.

"Not all," said Ziko taking her hand. "Perhaps some rest before we journey out. A lesson I learned courtesy of you," he reminded.

Oris nodded, agreeing to Ziko's subtle suggestion. They embraced hands and sat on the ground, legs folded. They placed their heads against one another, eyes closed. It wasn't long before they were gone into a calm blackness. Observing eyes viewed history with anxious desire to be a part of the environment, possessing Ziko while a void-tumbling spirit took hold of Oris Del.

But a dense, lilac cloud permeated the room. It pierced the walls and seeped into the floor and filtered down through the ceiling. The wandering soul reached for Oris Del's body. The observing eyes extended a ghostly appendage toward Ziko. But the scene disappeared behind lilac fog, pushing back both entities wishing to possess the meditating pair.

A soul continued tumbling through time.

Observing eyes continued watching history in dream.

The shimmering, pale-purple brume parted. There revealed was a fortress named Sudozion resting atop a jagged landscape named the Orgama Cadaab Mountains. A natural path through the range led straight to the alabaster palace's iron gates. The craggy terrain at the base of the mountains bled into a blend of fine crystals of sand that spread farther south. The land rose to massive mounds like dry waves in the geography that smoothed to a body of shimmering sands. Hot gusts of wind swirled across the desert, and from the horizon came an army's marching feet. The Bari armada. The robed soldiers, on mount and by foot, had journeyed up from the south and the interior of Alkebulan, the Parent-land. They were led by a lean and muscular dark-skinned man in his late fifties titled and named General Jacius Land-Irland. His gray locks were covered by a wrap, and like the soldiers that followed him, his face was cloaked with black cloth. He wore a metal chest plate that was possessed with an incant that kept his body at a moderate temperature, regardless of the surrounding climate. In his hand was a finely carved wooden scepter. On its head, bound with conjure-conductive alloys, was a violet crystal.

Jacius rode atop a strange-looking mount called a hytack. It resembled a seahorse, with small, useless wings on either side. Its legs were furry but were shaped like that of a bird. The entire mounted cavalry rode atop these beasts. Jacius' eyes shifted to the left. On the other horizon, where the craggy land also stopped abruptly, there sprang up green grass and a large mesh of trees creating vibrant foliage. From the forest appeared a second army. It hailed from the kingdom-state of Wadri. Their cavalry was fitted with powerful steeds and dressed much the same as the Bari army that arrived on the flanking desert, save the colors and flag of their nation embroidered on their capes or robes. Their faces were not covered by wraps, but marked with white makeup. The male and female soldiers had markings unique to the individual wearer. All of the markings were like skulls, with differing patterns.

The Wadri army was led by a brawny, stout man of *kibete* descent. His name was Gbora. A heavy axe was on his back, and at his side, mounted on steed, was his wife Mtindo. She was short and shapely with brown skin. Mtindo was mixed with kibete and kurujuati blood. Like her husband, she was strapped with a large axe. But the steel of her weapon had been peppered with crushed, blessed crystals. The effect was a spark of flame with its scratch against all manner of physical contact. Their two sons, Hubi-in and Haaa served as lieutenants in their army.

Both armed forces carried with them an assortment of stray warriors, criminals and mercenaries picked up in their journey across the many lands traveled. But there was nothing more motley in its crew than the crew that poured from the direction opposite the forest.

From the fading plains, inundating with desert sands filling its radiant, emerald region, there advanced a ragtag wild bunch lead by the guard captain Annand 'The Lawful' Durkusa and his sister Kymsaan. Ziko Yswil, the alchemist with the hammer, Inspector-Medium Oris Del, Kaapo the Farasin, Ren the mercenary, and the pirate-smugglers Dual and Yre. They were two weeks from the El-Ham settlements. The mzigo, revived and awoken, were dealing with the trauma of having been alchemized and trapped in a nightmare that amplified their burdens. Full recovery was expected, but it was going to be a long and arduous road. Dual, who had shifted to mzigo for a short time, suffered nothing more than occasional migraines. He was fortunate. Kaapo believed many would not make it. He predicted that madness and anxiety would drive some to take their own lives or the lives of others. It would be a fight and a unifier among kingdoms at war on the support of the zealots' ideologies. Here Annand and the others were in attendance to make history—to end the Pious Wars, though their heroics would be forgotten to time. Accompanying them were the scraps of warriors, guards, and conjure men and women from other states and kingdoms. They were forty-four in number mounted either on hytack, camel, or mighty steed.

More armies surrounded Sudozion's mountain range, encircling the area like a gathering of ominous clouds ready to strike with hail and lightning. The climate was right. Everything was set for an all-destroying battle. The players, as elements for a clashing tempest, had arrived upon the stage.

General Jacius Land-Irland made the first move. He called for his daughter, a young archer whose beauty was hidden behind the black, leather fabric enwreathed around the lower half of her face. He gave order for his army to remain. Gbora and his wife Mtindo did the same, leaving their sons behind as acting authority of the Wadri army.

The four met on mounts at the blackened, rocky field close to the path snaking up the mountain range. General Jacius and his daughter Idalis removed the wraps from their faces. The general bowed his neck with respect to Gbora and Mtindo. The gesture was returned. All four gazed up at the path, and then they returned their attention to one another. It was an uneasy meeting. Jacius and Gbora commanded armies against one another, and between the two battle-hardened commanders, many soldiers had been killed. The Bari people once supported Toliv Angoj Wofiira and his star-hero Keb-Biyarli Lorish. Wadri's government stood against the two zealots.

Jacius clipped his scepter to his belt and extended a hand to the Wadri general. "I not only extend my hand, General Gbora, but I extend my deepest apologies and sorrows for the bloodshed we of the Bari kingdom helped facilitate in the name of these two bastards and all their false promises. It will not resurrect the soldiers slain, nor will it undo the damage to the land, but it is the first step for unification."

Gbora accepted Jacius' hand and nodded. He held his mount's reins as the firm greeting ended. "I admired you, General Jacius. My wife can attest to that. I plotted with great intensity on killing you only to kill everyone around you and have many in my company die at my volatile command. Now we fight together. The great sky beast was not the only thing that can cause alchemy. War is a modifier. It made us enemies. It now transmutes us into allies."

"*Politics* made enemies of us," Jacius corrected in a careful tone. "War was but an extension of that. My son warned me, but I had my duties to my kingdom. He defected to the Ambrah state. He became a senator there, and led the proposal to ally with your kingdom. He and I are, at the moment, repairing our relationship."

"I wish you well on that," Gbora pronounced. His eyes looked away from Jacius. With a squint, his vision locked onto Annand's approaching crew. "Who're them?" he asked.

Jacius turned. He moved his mount around, allowing the creature to stretch its limbs. He halted the beast once he got to Gbora's other side, taking note of the incoming group. *"They,"* the erudite general corrected Gbora. "Who're 'they'?" he put together the entire inquiry. He nodded his head in Annand's direction, though his gesture was more on Ziko and Oris' presence. "They are the true heroes to the stars. That is the alchemist with the hammer. And next to him, Inspector-Medium Oris Del. I recognize the slayers of

Chilombo-Wroch by way of a visual projected through crystal. Those in service to the zealots were deputized to hunt them down."

Gbora's face brightened with surprise. His eyes spotted the alchemized hammer dangling from Ziko Yswil's belt. Atop Ziko's head, he wore his skull mask as a hat, the gold chains dangling from the jaw partially covering his face. Gbora's sight then moved to Oris Del. The brave conjure woman journeyed far when the most massive of armies kept still. She took steps in the direction to slay the sky demon of lies. Months it might've taken, but her objective was accomplished. Nature's inconsistency that spread across the world receded; and the transmuted reverted back to their former selves. Not all were healed, however. When the former undead awoke, they had spoken about being under constant attack from the burdens in their life. They half-remembered the terror they caused. Many went insane, unable to remain stable. But progress was being made.

"We know you," Jacius told Annand's party as they reached them.

"And we are grateful," Idalis added to her father's statement.

Annand and Kymsaan slowed their mounts. Ziko and Oris took lead. Oris went to speak when a loud, grating sound rumbled from down the path. Sudozion's gates opened. Rusted iron scraped against rusted iron. The heavy sound came like a wild and ferocious roar. The storm was here. Its eye was watching. A weighty crash echoed, a weighty clank indicating Sudozion's iron gates were latched in place. It then went quiet, save for a whistle of wind across the landscape. Then there was a shuffling heard. The iron mouth of the alabaster castle dripped with soldiers, robed and armored, supporters of the zealots resting in the bowels of the palace. The armada was not entirely human. Created and conjured creatures paced down the winding path to meet the armies of the world below.

Annand checked his crossbow. Kymsaan removed her sword. The mercenary Ren did the same with his daggers. Oris dismounted and brought all the colors of her magnificent serpent-lions from the air with a wave of her hands. She jumped onto the golden serpent-lioness and fastened her hands into its scales. The creature curled and locked into S-position. Oris' former mount ran away into the desert as the conjure woman took to the sky. Her other serpent-lions sprang into action with her. Ziko traded his mount for the black serpent-lion and joined Oris above. He flipped his mask over his face and readied his nerves for battle.

The palace's towers discharged spherical, elephantine masses of fiery conjure. The massive projectiles were tossed in all directions, and leaders of armies called for their battalions to scatter. Infantry and cavalry dispersed into smaller formations. Soldiers were not spared even with the quick scramble. The large spheres of fiery conjure landed and scorched soldier and mount from the various approaching fleets. Ziko glided up to Oris and suggested telepathically, *Let's see if we can't disable those towers.*

Oris agreed, though she modified Ziko's plans. She ordered her lilac and gold colored serpent-lions to keep on pace with them against the towers. Red, green, and silver serpent-lionesses were instructed to assist the armies of the world against the zealots' arjai.

The colorful serpent-felines dived on command. Their mouths opened, and they hissed electric lashes extending from their tongues down onto the incoming, armored arjai. Conjured and human creatures were burned, but the colossal-sized army continued fanning out, merging with units from the scattered armies of the world, and overrunning the collective fleets.

The towers expelled more firepower. Oris and Ziko, along with the other serpent-lionesses, separated from formation as a volley of fiery spheres launched in their direction. Both Ziko and Oris shielded themselves with an incant that steadied their balance, diving and spinning on their mounts to maneuver through the conjured projectiles. Oris' lilac and gold conjured serpent-lions did the same. Upright, Ziko and Oris commanded their mounts to attack the castle's towers with their electric hisses. Lightning spewed from their mouths, barely scratching the alabaster castle coated with a powerful aegis incant.

Ziko cursed the minimal damage inflicted. He reached for his hammer-pick and rode his mount around, moving away from a launched, fiery projectile. He turned around and sped toward the tower, observing and counting. The entirety of the tower's wide floor glowed twenty seconds after launch. Ten seconds from that, another projectile was thrown into the sky. Ziko dodged the conjured sphere of fire and then moved in close over the tower. He counted and pulled his hand loose from his mount. Before jumping, Ziko thought to himself, *I'll have a brave story to tell should I survive this.* He pulled his leg from over his mount, and then slid from the conjured creature's body onto the tower's floor below. He grinned. *It's time to get earn my muscle with stories.*

It took only a moment to steady, and then Ziko plunged the sharp end of his hammer-pick into the ground. It bubbled with a yellow gel of conjure upon its break into the tower's floor. Its magic connected with the hexes projected from the deck. It scanned the entirety of the castle and found its origin deep within its walls. Ziko was given a vision. His extrasensory sight conjured the scene of a well-decorated room known as the Star Sanctuary. Ziko saw the so-called star hero himself. Keb-Biyarli Lorish floated inches above the floor. Behind him was a round bed with purple sheets.

The false messiah was dressed in a silk, white burnoose with gold stripes running down from his shoulders to the end of the robe. He wore leather sandals on his feet, and black gloves on his hands. He was old, but with few wrinkles lining his dark-skinned face. The wrinkles he did possess were distinguishing marks and only added experience to his appearance. He sported a small, triangular, silver-white beard, blues eyes, and no hair atop his head. Instead, he was tattooed on his crown with the mark of a gold-colored cross that shined against his dark skin. Every time he balled his fists and pumped them, the towers expelled their massive, fiery spheres. He had an endless supply of power, but winning the battle was not Lorish's intention.

Urged by his master, Toliv Angoj Wofiira, Lorish was firing his conjure in an erratic pattern. It was about death not winning. Killing was the agenda. Killing for the sake of bloodshed. A blood sacrifice as he channeled his power through his body, to the towers, launching large, conjure projectiles at the armies below, even if it meant killing their own.

Ziko retracted his hammer-pick. The ground shimmered. A green aura swallowed the cobblestone floor, burning Ziko's feet. He stood and ran to the tower's edge, jumping over it. He turned and smacked his hammer-pick into the side of the tower. A dazzling ball of conjure projected up and arced out toward the armies on the ground.

Ziko called the black serpent-lion with his mind. The conjured creature slithered through the air and ceased flight next to him. Ziko dislodged his hammer-pick and jumped onto the crystalline creature. He locked a wrist through one of the creature's scales and then piloted toward the castle's courtyard. Oris was already there, commanding her serpent-lionesses to spray and damage anything in their sights. The place was aflame, weakening the protective aegis lacing the castle's exterior.

Ziko spotted a man who could only have been the false prophet himself. Toliv Wofiira. He was old too, but he appeared youthful, with a turquoise glow to his dark skin. A blood-red robe covered the full length of his mighty frame. He looked more warrior than priest, standing at two and a half meters and muscular. His graying locks were thin, running past his shoulders. Small and beady black eyes were like scrying mirrors beset within his countenance, offering him a power of misguided sight. An aquiline nose protruded from his triangular head. He snarled at the damage Oris and her serpent-lionesses caused, ultimately throwing him from concentration on lacing the palace with a protective incant.

He stepped into the courtyard without fear, aiming a glowing palm at the damaging fires. His conjure extinguished the flames and reversed the damage. He yelled to Oris, "Do you think us afraid of death? Martyr us, woman! There will be others!" He aimed both of his palms at her lilac serpent-lion. He took hold of the beast with his powers and ran the massive creature into the ground. Dirt and decorations splintered as the beastly conjure crashed inches away from where Toliv stood. He increased his power and the beast hollered until it disintegrated, banished from the physical realm. Toliv yelled as he took hold of the gold serpent-lioness and did the same, banishing the creature from existence. Oris toppled to the ground, the wind knocked from her.

Ziko jumped from his mount, hit the disheveled grass, and rolled until back on his feet. "There's a bounty for you, old man!" he scowled, hammer-pick aimed at the false prophet.

Toliv shrugged. "So, would you take my head and the money it's worth? I admire you, alchemist with the hammer—and not just for assisting in the kill of my precious Chilombo-Wroch."

Ziko confessed, "To be honest, I don't care for the money. I just want the story."

Toliv rolled his eyes at Ziko's sentiment.

Oris recovered and took a place next to Ziko. She limped as she walked, holding her side. She projected a swift, telepathic command to her remaining serpent-lions to take to battle alongside the armies of the world. They obeyed and retreated, out of reach from Toliv's banishing might. The zealot said to her, "And then there's you and your family, Second Lady Del. *Hypocrites!* Just as fanatical as what myself and the star hero are said to be." He surprised Ziko and Oris with a forceful, telekinetic push against them. They lifted into the air and rolled across the ground on impact. "We plan to die today, Second Lady Del, and her alchemist with the hammer. Martyrdom awaits." He pointed to the sky. "Look as the moons grow pale and fade into one another. Our conjure to change the stars has not gone in vain, even on this day of defeat. A new epoch is upon us, and out there, in battle, blood is spilled and lives are sacrificed for our final ritual." Then he commanded, eyes looking behind Ziko and Oris as they lay on the ground, "Iron, Claw—have at these two." Toliv then dematerialized.

Ziko and Oris rose and turned. The zealots' final two captains crept into the courtyard, a unit of weynee and pangomutu behind them. Oris cast a fleet of small, dart-like serpentine missiles at the oncoming enemies. Her conjure appeared wild, corkscrewing toward separate targets. Ziko engaged with his hammer-pick, shouting at Iron and Claw, "There's a bounty for you two, and a story to tell of it!"

Oris called her serpent-lions back to her. Nwa-ọdum and Koluboti-bulu returned, lashing the hordes that flooded the courtyard in opposition to Oris and Ziko.

Iron and Claw proved to be more thugs than strategic captains. Their incants were used for the purpose of giving them strength, and their frames were as twins, bulky and packed with muscle. Ziko's hammer-pick clanked and sparked against their armor. Their size didn't dictate their movement. They were limber, quick, charging and grappling like gorillas. Their art was martial. Oris kept her distance, continuing to fire her magic missiles at the two captains. Her attacks only bounced against them, throwing them off balance for only a moment before they recovered. Her serpent-lions' electric attack only stunned the feral captains for mere seconds before they were charging again.

Ziko and Oris concentrated on the weynee and pangomutu instead, felling the beasts. Even with the weynees' brute size, there was no incant to increase the creatures' strength. Oris' magic projectiles were effective against them. Ziko's alchemized hammer-pick swings cut them down in almost one swipe. The serpent-lions' attacks incinerated them.

Down to the thug-captains.

Iron was the first target. Oris sent a silent command to her serpent-lions to keep Claw at bay. She then launched a volley of magic projectiles at Iron, striking his armored head, dropping him to his knees. Ziko charged the zealot captain and jammed his hammer-pick into the captain's metal helmet. The armor piece shattered, exposing his head. Ziko didn't hesitate. He lifted his hammer-pick and broke through the captain's bald head, killing him instantly.

Ziko turned to the final captain. Oris sent a command for her serpent-lions to back away, and then she and Ziko reenacted on Claw their maneuver that fell Iron. The final captain was defeated, hammer-pick cracked through the bush of hair atop his head and into his skull.

Oris exhaled and felt accomplished, though Toliv and Lorish's ritual had to be stopped. Her black and cobalt-blue serpent-lions landed in the courtyard, awaiting her command. She told them, "Rejoin the battle. Carve a path into the castle. We must stop this last ritual." Koluboti-bulu hollered and whined. Oris consoled her, petting the serpent-lioness as the creature lowered its head into Oris' face. "I'll be able to summon your brother and sister from banishment. Don't worry. It will take time, but they will reappear through my command. Concentrate on the battle now." Nwa-ǫdum rubbed his head against his sister's body. Koluboti-bulu raised her head, tilted its face to the sky and let out a roar as she and Nwa-ǫdum zoomed upward like arrows cast from a bow. Oris commanded Ziko, "Come, alchemist king." Oris made a swift turn and hurried down the passage Toliv journeyed into. Ziko followed where the story continued.

Arjai and the armies of earth mingled on the battlefield.

An armored weynee cocked back his fist and shoved his balled fingers straight toward Kaapo. "*I will slam my fist through your ribs and eat your corpse!"* it hollered. Kaapo didn't understand the creature's language, nor did he attempt to decipher the words. Instead, the agile Farasin tucked his stomach, launched himself into the air and executed a flip, escaping the brutish creature's deadly blow. He landed in a cat-like crouch, arms ablaze with conjure. The weynee turned, unsheathed its sword, and swung the sharp weapon at Kaapo. The Farasin threw himself into the air again, flipping, and missing his scheduled date with the blade.

Ren landed on the weynee's back and jammed two daggers into its neck.

Kaapo thanked the mercenary, and then he turned and engaged more of the oncoming soldiers with graceful, martial arts. His incanted arms shocked and burned his adversaries to death whenever his blows made contact.

Closer to the palace's gate, General Jacius and General Gbora battled with the armored arjai. Their numbers dwindled. Jacius was wracked with arrows. One was in his right shoulder. A second was in his thigh. A third was lodged in his side. But he kept fighting along with his once-adversary, General Gbora. He'd lost sight of his daughter, Idalis. She remained on the open field, leading a mix of soldiers comprised of Dual and Yre and other soldiers from the armies of the world. Jacius continued launching blasts of conjure at incoming foes from his weaponized scepter, knocking them back, and giving time for a close soldier to cut the creature down.

Gbora was no better. The hardened warrior tossed his axe in every direction, chopping down zealot soldier after zealot soldier. But he too was riddled with arrows and losing strength. His wife Mtindo had been surrounded, and he cut a path to her. Jacius followed. The small, worldly battalion dwindled as they backed up toward the palace's open gates.

"Looks to be the end, good General Jacius," Gbora grumbled as he slayed an arjai soldier attempting an attack at his wife.

Jacius shouted in return, "Should we die here, it's been a pleasure battling alongside you, good General Gbora!" He aimed his scepter and discharged a fatal blast into two arjai soldiers.

Then arrows came, sharpened with incants and knocking through the armor fastened to the zealot warriors. Kymsaan leapt into the arjai circle that surrounded Mtindo and the others. She swung her mighty sword as her brother Annand rained arrows down on the arjai, killing the incoming, armored masses. Mtindo and the soldiers by her side joined in.

The two led a brigade up the mountain path and to the palace's entrance. Their presence acted as reinforcements, cutting down the arjai moving in on Jacius and Gbora. "Stop the nonsense talk, you fatalistic idiots!" Annand grumbled, grimace on his face. His bulky frame was laced with arrows and cuts from enemy soldiers. He pointed toward the open entrance and yelled, "Move in! The men we've come for are in there." He turned, aimed his crossbow and shot down incoming soldiers. He locked more arrows into his weapon, and a conjure man blessed the tips.

The same conjure man looked at the arrows that struck Annand, Jacius, and Gbora. "Do you three require healing?"

"We'll feel it when this is over!" Annand snarled. "Let's keep moving!"

Above, the serpent-lions assaulted the castle's towers. The palace's protective incant dropped. The façade was weak against the serpent-lions' electric hiss, and the towers rippled with explosions and burst into debris.

The palace shook!

Toliv and Lorish didn't lose balance as Sudozion shivered with war made against it. The high ceilings cracked, raining debris on the floor of the elaborate dining hall. Lorish wiped his head of the loose dust as he sat at the long dining table. Toliv joined him, a flagon of wine and two, bejeweled chalices in his hands. He placed flagon and goblets on the table. Toliv reached into his pocket and pulled out two, thick caplets. He dropped one into each chalice, and then filled the cups with wine. The caplets dissolved in liquid, seething poison. Toliv reached for his cup, which rested next to a hammer-pick. Lorish took the one meant for him.

The two zealots knocked their chalices together.

"There will be more when we go," Toliv declared. "And should they fail, the final blood ritual will insure more until the tyrannous stars are rearranged."

"And The Wall crumbles," Lorish finished. He turned and spied Oris Del and Ziko Yswil bound by magic against the wall. They'd surprised him and Toliv, but the fight they put up was expeditiously put down. Toliv and Lorish's combined strength subdued them with little effort. It was a spectacular moment filled with bright colors of conjure and alchemy. The winds of battle echoed through the room as they fought, knocked over furniture, and split the walls on contact.

But it was over. Now it was time to drink and be merry and die.

Lorish asked his master, "Who dies with whom?"

Toliv boasted, "The woman dies with me. It rhymes—the action of it all. It's poetic." He gestured with his cup toward Ziko and then to Lorish. "Her hero dies with you." He lifted his glass and hollered, "A grand sacrifice for the two of them. Let us drink to that and die, my star hero."

Lorish put the cup to his mouth.

An arrow pierced his neck. Blood clogged his throat, and a little trickled from his mouth. His eyes bent in a curious manner. He almost raised an eyebrow, perplexity close to the final emotion captured on his face. Disappointment, though, was the last look that flashed across Keb-Biyarli Lorish's face. Eke Woli or Xiddig-Akoni, however history wanted to remember him, if it did at all. He was dead.

The chalice dropped from his hand. Its contents spilled moments before it clanged against the floor. The zealot's body followed, slumped and lifeless.

Toliv Angoj Wofiira's hand trembled, and his eyes followed his dead star hero's body as it fell to the floor. His vision saw the killing in slow motion. His mouth was agape. The rest of him was still. Another body thumped against the ground, shaking Toliv from his paused demeanor. He looked in the direction of the noise. Ziko Yswil was sprawled out on the floor unbound from the magic securing him to the wall.

Then the zealot's vision cracked. His sight blurred and then faded. The first arrow was in his cheek. Two more arrows hit his chest, one piercing his heart and killed him. Toliv's body left its chair and hit the floor, crumpled up next to his appointed star hero. His chalice of wine never left his grip. The contents spilled.

Oris Del fell from the wall, landing next to Ziko Yswil. Movement resumed in them, and they stretched their limbs as their strength returned. They rose, using one another as leverage to stand.

Annand and Kymsaan, along with Jacius and Gbora and other soldiers were at the entrance of the dining hall. Annand limped to the table. He dropped down in the seat once occupied by Toliv Wofiira. The arrows lining his body snapped as his bulk leaned back in the chair. He kicked the false prophet's body, checking for signs of life. He let his crossbow fall loose from his grip, and he exhaled. He reached for the flagon of wine and downed a huge gulp. "We should check on the armies outside," he suggested. "And conjure man!" he hollered. "I think it's time for that healing you've been offering." He spotted Gbora and Jacius. "I don't know about the two of you, but I'm starting to feel it all."

Gbora agreed, and then the stout warrior collapsed. His axe dropped, and his wife ran to his side. He would be okay, but he was exhausted.

Shimmering, lilac fog trickled down onto the scene. The act was closed. The Pious Wars were at an end, a spectacular event lost to history. But there was more to view. The dense, glittering fog whooshed away, substituted by Alkebulan's glittering sands.

Seated on a sable throne was a woman who resembled Oris Del. She was older, slender, less voluptuous when compared to the conjure woman, but more aged in her countenance. Oris Del stood at the woman's right.

Mother and daughter reunited decades after the aftermath of the Pious Wars, and in the midst of continuing wars waged on a much smaller scale. On the woman's left was Ziko Yswil, now called son-by-law. Surrounding them were twelve chairs, and marching in the distance were world representatives. There were still consequences to the sanguinary wars, and the stars would not be so forgiving.

The twelve representatives took their seats. The seated woman raised and waved her hand. A great conjure took place from her gesture. Walls formed around them. A domed lecture hall materialized out of the vapor of her magic, and in seconds the representatives found themselves in a council room lit by flames on sconces. "Zealots," stated Oris Del's mother, "wished to control the stars and rearrange the fates told within them. My husband and I are the stars, or rather, their true interpreters and representatives. I am Iya Majẹmu. I am the embodiment of half a covenant you worldly creatures have abandoned out of ego. Today, my daughter and her husband, and I, see fit to lay fate in the stars and bring about the destiny chiseled in stone into fruition. All that you feared, all that could have been avoided, is now set upon you. I bring a message from my husband: You will learn, and the lesson will be hard." She paused, keeping her anger at bay from turning her words into shouts and curses. That would happen in this meeting, but she wasn't quite there yet. She continued, "One day, we shall see our three moons returned to us. Until then, the Epoch of Edict rules the times."

A lilac murk filled the scene, fading Iya Majẹmu's foreboding words.

8

Four twenty-one. That's what the clock read when Gordon woke, lilac fog dispersing from his eyes as they opened. Murky sleep drained from his head. He loosened his arms and rested Spook beside him. He took a breath and rolled out of bed, walking to the chair resting in the corner. He exhaled, trying to relieve himself of the remnants of sleep too stubborn to leave his person. He looked outside and observed the very faint light of day. The firmament hummed dark blue, and staring at it calmed Gordon. He reflected on the history he'd dreamed, and the words of a crazy-eyed but erudite community lecturer came to him.

"It's our shit, goddammit!" Gordon could hear him hollering. *"All of it! Them movies they make, it's there. Our story, I tell you! That's them dressin' themselves up as us to be a part of history and mythology. That's all ritual to get them closer to being a part of our magic, to being the conjure people that work that magic! The original conjure people of the world, the original magic!"*

Gordon thought, *Papa Holiday might've sounded like a nut, but after what I just saw, I think I should have a sit down with him.* But Gordon knew such a thing would expose his private work for the Elders. The history he'd witnessed was for him alone to marvel. Perhaps he'd tell Benny and Cedron. Dajon too.

A second moment occurred concerning the history he'd dreamed. It happened moments before the transition into the last battle of the final Pious Wars. Ziko Yswil and Oris Del were attempting to meditate. It was in that moment where Gordon felt history's tug, calling his spirit to that particular time. Ziko Yswil's body was open for possession. Oris Del was the same, and a feminine spirit reached down to capture the historical woman's physical frame. The dream had other plans, and it shifted forward in time. Gordon Goodspeed and Fey Forrester's second encounter was deferred. While this frustrated Gordon, he held onto the incident. He could feel Fey's presence like a cool wind. He was as aware of her as any lover would be aware of their partner as the two slept side-by-side in bed, even as they both dreamed of separate things.

She was there.

He and she were almost together again in time long ago.

But Gordon didn't mind that his meeting with Fey was only a near encounter. Had they spoken, he wouldn't have remembered their conversation, anyway. He was frustrated, but the potential of it all excited him. And he used his circumstances of lacking a device that would stabilize his spirit in time to cast himself in the role of the fox seeking the high-grown grapes in Aesop's fable. He wasn't as bitter, though. Gordon was only recognizing reality. Not being properly equipped would be a waste when dealing with a brush with Fey.

The sky brightened, sun hiking farther above the horizon.

Gordon rose from the seat, scooped Spook under his arm, and zapped away to the basement. He came from the ethers solid in his magically renovated basement. The lights turned on with his presence. He attached Spook to his alchemical chamber and lifted from behind the constructed capsule an ancient tome. Scribed inside was a poetic mythology composed by both he and Fey Forrester. It was titled *In Thirteen Pieces*, and it was a tale spun around a young, feeble man striving for warriorhood and a young, broken woman in search of vengeance and the lost pieces of her spirit.

Gordon tossed the book in the air. It didn't fall. It floated, opening to the first page of the animated, heroic verse. He was interested in the prefatory scene to the bardic tale. It stood so far apart from the rest of the narrative. Gordon and Fey always considered it to be symbolic of actual events occurring long, long ago. Time had faded the ink on this history into breath, which only whispered its stories as nothing more than mythology or spectacular legends to entertain children. And even that had sadly gone quiet. The grand narrative composed by he and Fey Forrester treated the history the same. Gordon took a seat on the recliner and indulged in the tome. His eyes flashed a bright lilac color. Strands of lilac energy snaked from his eyes and landed on the first page.

The world around him dissolved, and history-turned-legend animated around him. A voice narrated the scene, sounding much like his. It spoke in poetry, describing the dunes of the sandy sea and the march of three armies across it. Their destination was a black woman seated on a throne. She was angry at the war they made with one another, and she had a judgment to bestow. Gordon heard her angry words as narrated by the poetic storyteller. The scene faded when the judgment was given, and reality reshaped around Gordon. The tendrils of lilac retracted from the page and to his eyes. The bright glow was extinguished, and his eyes returned to the soft, lilac color swirling in his irises.

Now, he understood. A subtle smile appeared, and then he thought of it no more. Gordon stood and walked over to Fey's sketchbook resting atop the alchemical chamber. He opened it to a specific page with a specific sketch of four yumbo creatures. He spoke a magical phrase that released the sprites from the page. Four lines of distinct colors jumped from the paper and then shaped into the fairies. They floated in the air, wings aflutter. Gordon instructed them to return to Fey's grandmother's house to volunteer with the spirits of children passed and their living parents. Silver nodded her head, and then led her all-female, yumbo troupe up into the air, through the ceiling, and out into the world. They used an incant to shield their sight from normal folk.

Gordon called his cosmic suit around his frame. Shadows seeped from his flesh and then formed into a tight, black fabric around him. His African, Chokwe-like mask sheathed his face. He bent his head back, eyes on the ceiling. He jumped, rippled from existence, and popped back into reality on the roof. Then he launched into the brightening sky. His body blazed into a lilac streak. An incant kept his shimmering, djinn-like frame from the eyes of normal folk, and into the cosmos he journeyed at accelerated speeds.

The world dropped away. The brightening sky reversed its stance on the growing morning, and the stars once again revealed themselves, far in the distance as they were. Dooley continued his climb above the galaxy until Earth's solar system was no longer a visible birthmark in space. His ascent slowed as he entered a new galaxy far, far away from his own. There was life on various planets, but he wasn't here to interact with them.

A black portal spun into existence in front of Dooley. An eyeless, dark spirit with a single, gold sphere at the center of its forehead seeped from the whirling opening. It was masculine in its shape and physical gender, and it greeted Dooley in a language he was only just getting to comprehend. The cosmic spirit was extending an invitation through the opening. Dooley accepted, and followed the black spirit into the portal. An unlit hallway in a magnificent, cosmic castle was on the other side. Dooley's lilac blaze vanished, stripped down to his black, cosmic suit. His mask and shimmering third eye remained. Two more masculine spirits joined them, forming behind Dooley. One bowed at the neck toward him, a formal greeting. The other slapped him on the shoulder and pulled him close. Then they made small talk in their cosmic, mathematic language. Dooley was able to comprehend most of the speech. One asked him about the cobalt-blue spirit named Fey.

She's not dead. She's just been banished by a powerful hex, but we're in the process of bringing her back to our physical realm.*

She will be okay, Lwa Dooley. Your wife is fine.

Dooley smiled behind his mask on hearing Fey referred to as his wife. *She might as well be,* he thought to himself.

They entered a magnificent theater hall. It was a round, and on the stage danced male and female black spirits of the cosmos. Their movements were snake-like and erotic. Dooley had witnessed the *Dance of Black* before. It was also known as *When Ixu Dances with Gira, The Great Cosmic Coupling.* He'd seen the dance many times, especially on his self-exile from the Fable Avenue community. He and Fey used to enjoy the performances when they would sneak away to the stars above.

The music to the ritualistic movements was never the same. It was sometimes symphonic. Other times, Parliament Funkadelic would be proud and envious. All styles in between as well, and some unearthly musical

harmonies composed only by magical instruments.
           Dooley observed the performance.
           Fey wasn't here, but he wasn't sad.
           She was somewhere, and she would return.

9

Hours ago. While Gordon slept and dreamed of a history barely remembered by even time itself, Lady Arachne was early to rise. She bathed and primped for the new morning, dark as it was. She appeared ready for a night with someone special. She was clothed in a black dress with gold embroidery around the top area, and a shimmering pattern on the full-length of the skirt. On her feet, and wrapped up to her ankles, she wore black, gladiator sandals. Her locks dangled past her shoulders, flowing from a navy-blue, star-patterned scarf surrounding her head. Gold veve symbols, representing the loa Erzulie, were pinned into her ears. A dark red shawl draped her shoulders and covered her arms.

She was seated in her reading sanctuary, incomplete Tarot deck in front of her. Candles lit by incant provided bright lighting. This moment was not motivated by the orders of Maman Anansi. Lady Arachne was inspired by her own curiosity. She reached for her deck and lifted the first card, knowing without dependence on instinct the exact card she was pulling.

She turned the Hierophant face up and placed it in front of her. Then she raised a hand, twiddled her fingers and spoke an incant. A small flame burned on the end of an incense stick at the matriarch's command. It brightened for a moment and then settled to a soft glow. Its sweet, candy-like fragrance swiveled as smoke into the air, wafting throughout the room. Lady Arachne inhaled the scent, and she was put at ease.

The Tarot reader returned her attention to the Hierophant card. She watched as the ancient, colorful drawing dissolved. The card then became a window into current matters in a small area down south called Water Bug Hollow in the state of Louisiana. There again, as was witnessed in her previous read when pulling the Hierophant card, was a church's quaint interior.

Candles provided light. Smoke and the waving shadows delivered ambience. Lady Arachne wasn't too curious as to why affairs had reached beyond the conjure folk of Fable Avenue. Water Bug Hollow appeared many times before in her reading, as did other conjure communities, especially the older families, *nasyons*, that held greater political might in conjure affairs. Lady Arachne was interested in the church's pious caretaker, Reverend Mathieu Pouvwa. Her eyes traced him like the artists she was. Most curious to her was his countenance. His face was a kaleidoscope of emotions, twirling and shifting through a melancholic frustration with a pinch of trepidation and wonder.

He stared at his glowing palms, holding them out and looking between both of them. He mouthed unintelligible words while adding disbelief to his repertoire of expressions. Then Reverend Pouvwa balled his fists and snuffed out the white-yellowish glow cupped in his palms. His face fell, and he smacked his forehead a few times. He sat back and tightened his teeth together. His head fell back and he let out a heavy sigh.

Compassion welled in Lady Arachne's gaze, which she was distracted from by a buzzing instinct that climbed her neck and kissed her brain. The tingle from her higher sense moved her to pull, face up from her deck, the Ten of Cups and Six of Pentacles. She set the cards next to the now-animated Hierophant card, and her eyes fixed on the newly drawn cards until she was able to bring out their significance in relation to the good Reverend Pouvwa. The denotation came to her like the pop of a balloon. Lady Arachne then took her deck in hand and shuffled through it, finding The Star. She returned the deck to her table and stood, The Star card in hand.

"Good Reverend Pouvwa," Lady Arachne spoke. "It seems like all good, strong men in times of high tides, you need a woman's voice to be your pillar. You will stand upright, my good man." The Star card clutched firm in her hand, Lady Arachne made an exit from her reading quarters and left her residence through the garden floor. She locked the door behind her using an incant. Brooklyn was quiet, save for the LIRR train she could hear in the distance. No soul stirred on Fable Avenue. Her eyes swept the street, left to right. She heard and saw the ghosts of a battle many months passed. She reflected on her part and its tragedies, and how it all led to this moment and the moments to come.

She opened the iron gate and stepped through. Closing it, Lady Arachne journeyed down the street to the brownstone of the late Gaston Fable. There she ascended the steps and placed The Star card before the door. A shimmering black light glowed around the ancient, sketched sheet. Its luminescence extended from the top of the card to the door, outlining the parlor entrance. There came a 'click', and the door unlocked. Lady Arachne bent down and retrieved the card. Its glow retracted from the door and snapped away on her touch. Card in hand, she entered Gaston Fable's abode, walked through the downstairs area that looked nothing like the interior of a brownstone. She exited out the backdoor where she was transported to Water Bug Hollow.

It had its noises. Shouting. Gunshots. Sirens.

Behind Lady Arachne, through Gaston Fable's house, back to Fable Avenue, and all the way to the sanctity of the conjuress' Tarot reading quarters, The Hierophant card remained animated with the goings on concerning Reverend Mathieu Pouvwa. He'd set down, at the foot of the pulpit, a small bowl filled with pulled, blue daisy chicory stems and heads. The reverend reached inside his jacket and removed from an interior pocket a photograph of his hands. The camera captured the glow of his personal conjure peeking through the lines on his palms.

Reverend Pouvwa took a quick glance over his shoulder.

No one was there.

He continued with his ritual, laying the photograph next to the bowl. He dug into his pocket, frantic. He wiped his nose with his free hand. With his other hand, Reverend Pouvwa removed his wallet, opened it, and plucked a piece of folded paper tucked between several dollar bills. After unfolding the paper, his eyes scanned a set of instructions scrawled there. He sniffed. His forehead perspired, and he wiped his brow. He cursed, asking for forgiveness afterward, looking up at the sculpted Jesus on the cross. Then his eyes returned to the piece of paper. Mathieu had forgotten something. The ritual he was conducting needed a picture of him. He'd had one in his wallet. He searched in the compartment and found behind his driver's license a two-year-old photograph with him and an ex-sweetheart. Her name was Bonnie, and he still thought about her, especially her smile. She didn't want to accompany him to Water Bug Hollow, but that's where he believed his calling was after leaving his job as a detective.

Perhaps that was why he was cursed last October with the Devil's power.

Mathieu tore the photo in half, sliding the half with his ex-sweetheart back into his wallet. He placed his half on the other side of the chicory-filled bowl. He tucked his wallet back into his pocket and stood straight after taking a few steps back. He closed his eyes and gathered his intent.

Remove ill health, he thought to himself. *Remove negative energy.*

Reverend Pouvwa repeated the two phrases in his head for precisely forty-seven seconds, and then he opened his eyes. He thought about what came next, and he remembered without having to scramble into his pocket for the instructions. *Draw backwards, in the air, and with your pointer finger, the sign of your faith,* he recounted the instructions in his head. He aimed his pointer finger straight. The sign of the cross was his subject. The air was his pallet. He drew the sign of the cross in the air backwards.

He closed his eyes and resumed his two mantras for removing ill health and negative energy. Another forty-seven seconds passed. Reverend Pouvwa opened his eyes again. He went into the exterior pocket on his jacket and pulled out a small book of matches. He opened it, took a single match, and struck it on the side of the small box. The flame was instant. Reverend Pouvwa paced toward the bowl filled with blue daisies. He bent down, ready to set the shrubbery aflame. He moved the lit match to the bowl, hesitating for a moment. "Now, might I do it…" he whispered so low that not even the grand acoustics of the small and empty church could lift and stretch his voice to an audible tone. He moved the burning match closer. The palm of his hands glowed, and the flame brightened and grew. His arm lowered, and his hand turned to drop the burning match onto the chicory. But just before he set the plant life ablaze, a strong gust of wind swirled around his hand and strangled the fire from existence.

Reverend Pouvwa's head snapped up. His eyes spotted Jesus on the cross.

Then he scrambled for another match, but a sultry, feminine voice expressed to him, "You'll hurt yourself, Reverend—" Mathieu jumped to his feet, turned toward the entrance where the voice was coming. "A person unfamiliar with ritual might get himself further into trouble."

The reverend peered at the woman shrouded in shadow. Her frame was slender, and when she moved closer, her walk created a seductive wave in her body like that of a flickering flame. The reverend observed closer, and he concluded the walk was more like a snake's slither. Either way, it was filled with a libidinous rhythm that he'd have to ask forgiveness for later, unable to take his eyes away.

Lady Arachne emerged out of the shadow, single Tarot card in hand. She used an incant to brighten the few flickers of candlelight, shooing away the shadows that coated the church's interior under their previous dim gleam. Her light assisted the moon's beam through the windows. Reverend Pouvwa adjusted his wire-frame glasses, noting the change in brightness. His eyes moved to the candles, and he had an instinct that the root of the volume in light was from the woman who'd interrupted his ritual. His wonder-filled gaze shifted to her, and he asked, "Are you here to seduce me and bring me to the Devil himself?"

Lady Arachne mustered all her strength to not break into a loud laugh. She kept her expression to a grin, and answered the reverend, "No, *chile*. My name is Lena Franklin. I'm a conjure woman, a Tarot reader, to be precise. I'm a part of a culture based in Brooklyn, New York, and I've had my eye on you."

Reverend Pouvwa remained cautious, attempting to suppress an instinct discerning trust in the woman in front of him. He understood that the Devil knew such tricks. Reverend Pouvwa pivoted, making a partial turn away from the admitted conjure woman, facing more toward the ritual he was engaged in. "That could be true," he said looking at the bowl and photographs at the foot of the pulpit. "If you are of the Devil, you can return to him and confirm that I'm straying from his path. This is a ritual that will cleanse me of the cursed power he's bestowed on me."

Lady Arachne raised an eyebrow. The reverend's melodramatic speech caused her to chuckle. She was able to keep it low so as not to offend. She stepped closer and took a seat at one of the pews located on her left. "I have a question for you," she announced. He turned to her. "More of an observation, really," she corrected. Then she noted, "A reverend using hoodoo rituals, not Christian ceremony, to rid himself of his *blessing*." All melodrama melted away from Reverend Pouvwa. He grinned at the irony. His smile merged with the brightness in the room, and Lady Arachne was drawn to it. It only widened when Lady Arachne commented, "Now, Reverend, with that smile I have to ask if the supposed roles have changed. Are *you* aiming to seduce *me*?"

Reverend Pouvwa sat next to the Tarot reader, appearing more relaxed. His hands were locked together, and he was bent forward. His eyes were fixed on the ritual she'd interrupted. The reverend looked at the Fable Avenue matriarch and stated, "My grandmother, on my father's side." His grin faded. He sat back and folded his arms, making a face. "I did this out of respect for her, and a lack of knowledge on what to do on the Christian end. This was my father's family's traditions, especially after his father passed. My grandmother, she believed in things like this. This was something she did to ward off negative energy and ill health. She would say 'bad spirit' instead of negative energy." He shook his head and rolled his eyes. "Magic rocks," he said to himself, quoting a movie from his childhood. He repeated, "She believed in things like this…"

"And you don't?" Lady Arachne inquired.

"My original trade? I'm a detective," he revealed turning his head toward her. "I believe in facts." He put a single finger on his glasses and pushed them firm against his face.

"And the fact is…?"

The reverend opened his hand and held it out. The lines in his palm glowed, and small points of light lifted from the snaking shimmer. They swirled together in the air, a multitude of them. They took shape, condensed into material, and then the light swirled away leaving behind a luscious, red apple.

"The fact is, I'm marked by the Devil," the reverend declared, now returned to his mournful mood.

Lady Arachne took the apple and bit into it. The fruit was flush with flavor, and its juices gushed into her mouth, around her teeth, and tickled her tongue with a tart sensation. She swallowed, recovered from her bite, and stated, "I don't think you're marked, not even from an Abrahamic religious point-of-view. I'd say you satisfied the hunger of a wanting woman."

The reverend's head flinched. A perplexed expression popped on his face and he asked, "Did you say *wanton* woman?"

Lady Arachne grinned. "Knowing me, *chile*, I just might have made that slip," she replied. "But, no, I didn't." Then she clarified, "*Wanting*. Famished," she emphasized. She crossed her legs and told the reverend, "Satiating a person in need doesn't sound devilish to me. May I ask if you want something in return for satisfying my hunger?"

"Return…?"

"My soul?" she questioned, listing a motive. "More money than I can afford? What do you want in exchange for this apple? The Devil and his cohorts always want something in return." She took another bite of the succulent, conjured fruit.

"No, ma'am," the reverend said. "I don't."

Lady Arachne pressed, "Nothing? Nothing at all? Your supposed boss wouldn't approve of that."

The reverend answered Lady Arachne by stating again, "No." Then he chuckled a bit, "No, I guess he wouldn't."

The conjure woman pointed her finger at Reverend Pouvwa and shook it. "Well, *chile*, the Devil always wants something, and a servant marked by him always presents his or her master's ultimatum." She turned her body to him, grinning wide and alluring. "And since you have none to give, Good Reverend Mathieu Pouvwa, I'd say the Devil ain't left a mark on you." She saw him thinking, pondering her sentiment. "You say you're a detective. Sounds like a television show, a reverend solving crimes," she commented.

"*Former* detective, Miss Franklin," the reverend elucidated. "There was a lot going on in New Orleans. The streets I could handle. The corruption that happened on my side of the law…?" He sighed. "Well, I walked away, and my feet led me here."

"Like I said," began the matriarch, "not a single mark of the Devil on you, my deliciously pious friend." She adjusted herself in the pew. "My point, Mister detective-now-reverend, is that you said you go by facts. The fact is, good man, you have a power. You should put that to use. The other fact is that if you're not practiced in ritual, you might do great harm to yourself." She looked at the ceremonial tools he'd gathered for his ritual. "You wouldn't have negated your powers, if that's what you were looking to do. There's a chance you might've turned them against you. Things like that can happen, if you ignore your blessing. Your incant or conjure," the matriarch added.

The reverend viewed Lady Arachne through squinted, observing eyes. "How did you keep your eye on me?" he asked her.

"Through my card readings," Lady Arachne answered, shaking The Star card in her hand. "My community in Brooklyn—all of New York and the Northeast, to be true—we're keeping our eye on affairs that concern us, because there are affairs that have eyes on us. We're not the only conjure community. There're so many outfits around the world." Lady Arachne took a breath and informed Mathieu, "There's a war, reverend, and we've taken hits. There are real devils out there, evil men and women of this world, more diabolical than any devil in any religion. And we are at war with them. I do readings every morning. The cards showed you. I've been curious, always seeing you mope around this church, rattled by your power. But tonight, I saw something interesting, Reverend."

"What's that, ma'am?"

The Tarot reader mentioned, "I drew the Ten of Cups and Six of Pentacles when making a query about you. Do you know what those cards symbolize?"

Interested to know, Reverend Pouvwa answered in a curious tone and expression, "No, ma'am. Please tell."

"Prosperity," she revealed. "Giving. Receiving," she continued. "Give your fruit, Reverend Pouvwa. Receive your blessing, and take in the knowledge of conjure. You are a good man. I promise you." Reverend Pouvwa considered the sentiment. Lady Arachne added, "I have seen the Ten of Cups—prosperity—pop up many times in my readings about Water Bug Hollow."

"This place?" the reverend questioned. "Prosperous?"

"Yes. Do you know its history?"

"I'm aware of some facts," he answered. "The emancipation, the old culture centered on jazz."

"The magic," Lady Arachne interjected.

"The corruption," the reverend countered.

Lady Arachne grinned as if luring a chess opponent into making a fatal move had paid off. "Magic is at the center of that plot, too, Reverend. The sect of conjure folk I represent and help lead, we have an adversary. This malefactor of ours is quite literally a son-of-a-bitch. He's a wicked and cruel antagonist, and he tricked us all, as devils tend to do. He had a charming smile and a humble plea for help to rid his mother's haunt from his head. Butchu see, Reverend Pouvwa, his mother's unintelligible holler, that was just a-scratching at his brain, was a code of sorts. He used us to help him break it." She paused to reflect. Then she informed, "Not even his iniquitous-hearted wife had the hex-with-all to unscramble or exorcise his mother's scathing screech from his head. He came to us—in peace, and even I have to say, very sincere. So, we tuned his dial, and he picked up his mother's ghostly transmission. It was an imprint, a plan. His legacy was given to him, his heritage. And when he heard his mamma's command, this devil of a man accepted the broken diadem his mother passed to him, and he turned against us as many feared he would. He has soldiers around the world, associates at his command. Men and women cursed with hex. Old lines of conjure killers." Lady Arachne pulled a spiced, clove cigarette from the air. "Do you mind?" she asked the reverend.

"No…" he answered Lady Arachne. Mathieu's eyes stared at the conjure woman's hand, clove cigarette claimed in its grasp. He was impressed at her carefree use of conjure, and his eyes followed her movement as she placed the clove cigarette between her lips. She touched the end of the spiced, smoke stick with her finger. An incant sparked a flame, prepping the cigarette for smoke. Lady Arachne took a drag. She exhaled away from the reverend.

She handed him the bitten apple, and Reverend Pouvwa accepted. "Our malefactor has a name," she continued. "Stanley Fallows. His mother steered Water Bug Hollow away from its magic. Sarinda Fallows," the matriarch named. "You search this area's history, and you'll no doubt come across her name. Trouble is they'll speak about her with favor and praise." She nodded at Reverend Pouvwa and continued, "See, it was she who suggested the building of this church."

"For true…?"

"Oh, yes, Reverend," Lady Arachne responded to his verbal incredulity. "It was built on the burial spot of the old slave owners. The village folk celebrated every year on August twelfth with a bright bonfire that stretched to the starry sky." A grin slithered onto Lady Arachne's visage, and she looked up to the ceiling, eyes filled with reminiscence as if she'd been there on those long-ago nights. She took a hit of her spiced cigarette, and then she exhaled a thin, ghostly stream of smoke through a small opening of her pursed lips. "Town folk practiced hoodoo. They pulled their conjures from Bible verses. They weren't a full-blown conjure culture, but they had their beliefs. Settin' this church on this spot disrupted their yearly festivities. Sarinda knew it would. That was her intention when she pranced in here with a smile—that's where her devil-child learned it from, his devil mamma." A pause for smoke, inhale and exhale. Then she commented, puff filtering from her mouth, "She came with a fabricated warning. She said white folk were calling Water Bug Hollow the Devil's Den—and they were. They hated Curtis Hollow, of course."

"I'm sure," Reverend Pouvwa commented. "A black slave-turned-revolutionary soldier who emancipated this place by way of a physical war?"

"*Chile, please!*" Lady Arachne hollered. She took another hit followed by a slender exhalation of smoke. "War is good for white folk to make," Lady Arachne commented. "Bring freedom and democracy all 'round the world at the heels of a bloody war." She shook her clove cigarette at Reverend Pouvwa while saying, "But damn the nigger fighting to free themselves from the hell white folk bring." She sat back. Another drag. Exhale. "So, Curtis was an unruly nigger that killed good white folks in their eyes. Sarinda fanned that flame. Said because of the people's yearly celebration to Curtis Hollow, white folks were ready to take up arms if it persisted. She had a devil-forked tongue and a *cha-riz-ma-tic* charm—I tell you! She passed that on down to her Stanley. And she had trinkets. She wore a bauble. It was a stone, or rather, a piece of a stone. It was something the women of her culture worshipped."

"This stone, though, it had magical or…hexing properties," guessed Reverend Pouvwa.

Lady Arachne nodded, yes, impressed with the reverend's proper use of conjure jive. "We call it the Skeptic Stone. That there curiosity-knickknack amplified her charm, her seduction. Didn't hurt that she had a body on her. Curves that could make an hourglass jealous. I say, shit and a Goddamn!"

And she did. Right there inside the church. But Reverend Pouvwa was not disturbed by Lady Arachne's profanity. He was too intrigued by her tale of Water Bug Hollow's history. "So, people fought over the change?"

"Oh, yes, shit they did," Lady Arachne answered, admiring Sarinda's cunning. "But that was just Sarinda having fun. Her real purpose of slithering into Water Bug Hollow was to procure an ancient veil left in the hands of a woman named Theresa Amat, whom Sarinda befriended."

"Now, her I know!" the reverend spoke, voice perked up. "A marvelous jazz woman and songstress," he stated. "And I'm aware of her under the title of Mamma Indigo, where she assisted with village politics."

Flirtatious, Lady Arachne let it be known, "Oh, my sweet Reverend Pouvwa, you'll be aware of so much more, all of this history." An incanted toke and a breath of mystical smoke exhaled. The spiced, clove-scented ghosts puffed in Reverend Pouvwa's direction possessed the pious man. The incanted-laced smoke streamed into his nose and mouth, and the reverend suffered no cough or loss of breath as he inhaled. *"Kite sot pase a pale pou tèt li,"* Lady Arachne purred, her words an enchantment in Haitian Creole, stimulating the sorcery intertwisted within the smoke. "Dream, Reverend," spoke Lady Arachne in her hypnotic voice that was filled with an alluring smokiness of its own. "Close your eyes and catch up on history. Dream in your own way, Pouvwa, and reveal the haunts of this church." Reverend Pouvwa swallowed the smoke without exhalation. He blinked after his eyes remained shut for a moment. It was Lady Arachne's power that commanded his eyes to open. "You ain't got to sleep now, Reverend."

He breathed in. He breathed out. He never felt more relaxed since the day his power manifested. Reverend Pouvwa was calm. "Miss Franklin, how did you come here?"

"A mystical passage that connects there with here," answered Lady Arachne in a whimsical, matter-of-fact tone. She fanned herself with The Star card. "Would you like to step through time and space and return to Brooklyn with me? You can stay at my place."

"I don't know if I'm ready for that, ma'am." Then the reverend asked, "Can we talk again, though?"

"Oh, absolutely," Lady Arachne answered, smoking. "I plan on it. I have work for you."

"Such as…?"

Lady Arachne answered with haste in her voice, "A friend of mine. Her grandson is in need of a little refuge. May I bring him here? He's in a type of trouble that calls for our spiritual work."

"I'll take him in, ma'am. It will be the start I've been looking for…for the last couple years I've worn this collar."

Lady Arachne thanked the reverend, nodding her head at him.

"If I need you in the meantime…?" asked the reverend. "This has been curative," he stated, breathing deep. "I too need spiritual work. Don't let the outfit fool you."

Lady Arachne and the reverend chuckled. She told him, "We all need the work of the spirit; whichever path we take to conjure and commune with it, tap into it."

"Amen…"

"So, to reach me, Reverend, simply draw a crossroads on a piece of paper. Write my name at the center of the crossroads and the number nine in the upper left-hand quadrant of the intersection. Then recite these words from the verses of Psalms 136: *To him alone does great wonders, who by his understanding made the heavens, who spread out the earth upon the waters, who made the great lights, the sun to govern the day, the moon and stars to govern the night. Love endures forever.* Hold the paper in your hand and let glow your palm—it's better than a phone call. To you, I will come when you call, Reverend." She smoked. "Just give me twenty minutes to freshen up and make my walk. I'll be here." She continued smoking, looking the handsome reverend up and down. She asked, "Are you Catholic, Reverend?" Lady Arachne exhaled another fleet of ghosts from her lips, swirling and smelling of clove spice.

Reverend Pouvwa shrugged his shoulders. "I don't know what I am." He pointed at his collar. "This is official…" A momentary pause. A roll of his eyes. "…through online courses," he confessed. "There's a denomination attached to it, but I don't think that was my focus. I should check the certificate. It's valid, though." The reverend sounded frustrated. Lady Arachne beamed with eyes on the reverend, taking in his handsome frame and all that he was in his youth and newfound powers. She inhaled a final drag. Exhale. She held the clove cigarette straight up. She opened her fingers, and instead of the smoke stick dropping to the floor, the remaining matter dematerialized into cinder and ash that sparked from existence. Reverend Pouvwa stared in amazement. He believed watching the sight of mystical means in use would never get old, especially by someone so at ease with executing the feat.

"I would like for you to see a ritual, Reverend," Lady Arachne suggested. "Would that be okay with you?"

"That would be fine, ma'am."

A loud pop came from outside. Reverend Pouvwa and Lady Arachne didn't jump at the sound, but they reacted, heads turned toward one of the stained-glass windows. "Could be an old car backfiring. Could be a gunshot," Reverend Pouvwa sighed. "Who knows?"

Lady Arachne used her instinct and reached out beyond the church walls, into the night, and out onto the streets of Water Bug Hollow. "It's a car," she assured. "But I understand your concern, Reverend. I do. It's far too easy for a place like Water Bug Hollow to have the other as a more common experience." She stood, straightening her attire. "I must be going, and to that I say, good night, Reverend. Contact me when your dreams have shown you the history of Water Bug Hollow. You know the ritual to use."

Reverend Pouvwa got to his feet. "Ma'am…"

"I too have a title, Reverend," insisted Lady Arachne. "Please, address me as Lady Arachne."

The reverend apologized. "Yes, Miss…" he paused and corrected, "*Lady* Arachne." He bowed at the neck, and then he hurried past the conjure woman. "Let me show you out." Lady Arachne followed Reverend Pouvwa down the aisle. They exited the church from the side entrance. Another pop polluted the night air. "I can walk you…" suggested the reverend.

"Thank you, good man," Lady Arachne said, a decline to Reverend Pouvwa's proposal in her tone. "No harm will come to me. Besides, you have history to dream of." She caressed the side of his face and told him, "I will see you again, handsome reverend." She peered into his eyes. She saw into him, and she grinned. "Who are you, Reverend Mathieu Pouvwa? You just might be the beginning of Water Bug Hollow's much-needed salvation."

Reverend Pouvwa said nothing. Lady Arachne smiled at him, turned, and walked away. The reverend watched her until the shadows consumed her. He walked back to the pews and took a seat. He removed his glasses and hung his head, sighing relief. The Hierophant card continued watching him. He didn't move for a while. Lady Arachne stepped back into Gaston Fable's house. She walked through it, journeying to the Fable Avenue side of the well-decorated abode and mystical gateway. The conjure woman, once outside, turned and used The Star card's power to lock the brownstone doors. She returned to her reading quarters, witnessing, just as she reached her doorstep, Gordon Goodspeed launch into the sky in his lilac, Dooley-spirit form. Lady Arachne beamed at the marvelous sight, and to the surface rushed a feeling of pity for black folk who refused to partake in witnessing their ancient magic.

Inside. Downstairs. In her reading quarters.

The Hierophant card remained animated with the church's interior. Reverend Pouvwa remained in the pew, head hung and wire-frame glasses in his hands. Lady Arachne sat down and whispered into the picture, "Sleep, handsome reverend. You've earned it."

The reverend lifted, sighing as he stood up. He stretched and placed his glasses back on his face, and then he moved into the back of the church where the living quarters resided. He bit into his conjured fruit and felt renewed by its juices. Even still, he set it down and slipped into bed as suggested by Lady Arachne. He closed his eyes, and the half-eaten apple disappeared.

Smoke filled the ancient card. The living scene was erased, and the thick, murky cloud filtered away, leaving behind the ancient and static sketch of the African priest. Lady Arachne yawned. "Let me take my own advice," she spoke. Then the conjure woman took herself to bed after removing her clothes and slipping into her nightwear. She too had a dream to dream. Lust from a youthful man new to his conjure. The things she would teach him in dream-wide-awake.

It would be purposeful, though. The power in her peak while indulging in the Reverend's image. It was to connect with him for a deeper cause.

When that fancy came to climax, she would only have a few hours before having to rise and do life all over again, peeking in on the goings-on in her Fable Avenue conjure community.

10

Reverend Pouvwa did dream. He dreamt of violence, gunshots and shouting that was supported by a cast of characters standing in awe under a partially-cloudy night sky. The fatal turbulence didn't make its appearance right at the beginning of his dream. The first character to appear on the dreamy stage was Reverend Pouvwa himself. He was in a field. The era was set on the stage of many decades past, a few years preceding the 1920s. Fog snaked and curved. Its haunt crooked across the face of the field in a slither so slow, it might as well have been still. Then there faded up a circle of dancing black bodies with their hands in the air, heads back, and legs bent to execute rhythm.

Though the bodies hinted at dance, they did not move. A ghostly wind spun them in a circle like a carousel. They even rose and set to music only heard by them. A large bonfire roared from the center of their celebratory, freeze-framed human merry-go-round. Reverend Pouvwa stepped closer to the festive people, and their physical bodies flattened two dimensional, thin as paper. They became silhouetted and cell-shaded against the massive, whipping fire. But still they rose, up and down, circling around and around.

Reverend Pouvwa was not the only one to approach, and when he spotted the new character to the dream, he paused his steps. A hunched over, red-haired woman wearing rags, hobbled toward the flattened merrymakers. By the light of the fire, Reverend Pouvwa could see her loose, shriveled skin. She belched and hacked up a frothy and chunky green substance that burned the field when its clumps landed on the ground. She wheezed and screamed, *"This is my soulless matter!"* Then she stood upright, and her body shifted into the physical manifestation of temptation. Her figure curved with wide hips, and voluptuous, ample breasts. Her dress mended from its rips, worn tight like her skin that smoothed, renewed bright and youthful. Her large, green eyes marveled at the fire and the flattened images that rose and set in motion around it.

The woman rubbed a stone pendant that dangled from a necklace, and then she opened her mouth wide and inhaled. The bonfire burst and struck the dancers around it, burning them to ash. Reverend Pouvwa jumped as he watched their embers turn into a thick, black cloud that mixed with the fire, turning the flames as black as the night. He watched as the carnal witch then exhaled a hex-laced breath that swirled the fiery, black cloud into shape. She continued expelling her curse until out of the chaos formed the quaint church the reverend presided over.

The woman released the last of her breath. She stood tall with a smile, balled hands on her hips, admiring her craft. *"Water Bug Hollow,"* she said. *"This is your new rhythm!"* she declared. *"No more shall you dance your devil culture!"* She turned to Reverend Pouvwa and cast at him a seductive grin. *"Look what my magic has brought for me to eat,"* she said walking up to him. Mathieu only stared at her as she circled him. *"Or maybe, you could eat me, Reverend,"* she chuckled and dipped her face away from him in a shy manner. Her coy behavior lasted for only a moment. *"You know my name, boy?"*

He nodded, yes. *"Sarinda Fallows,"* he answered. *"I was warned of you."*

"I'm sure," she replied with a sultry eye. *"But, isn't it such a pleasure to meet me?"* she asked. Mathieu didn't answer. *"In dream; and in all of my flesh?"* she flirted. Mathieu rotated as she continued her pace around his person. *"We are gonna have so much fun, Reverend,"* Sarinda promised. *"Dance with me, handsome nigger boy. I'm gonna ride your back while you sleep."* Then she noted, nodding in the church's direction, *"Mister Ladon wore the robes well, but* you, *Reverend Nigger Boy—"* She took a moment, a beat. *"You are* truly *a man of God."* She swung back around to face the church. *"This church was never meant to lead you nigger-folk anywhere but astray. My deviltry made sure of that."* She twiddled her fingers, and out of the air materialized a cigarette between her fingers. It lit without a match or lighter's flame. Sarinda puffed and blew smoke and continued talking. She relayed her side of the story, *"The niggers of Water Bug Hollow built this church in my honor, on my command. They were so proud of themselves, their history, and their ways. Yes. History, Reverend Nigger Boy,"* she said stomping her foot. *"Old folks remembered. New folks walked 'round like they was there with Curtis fighting for so-called freedom. But they were still scared that the tides of pale righteousness would come to collect and wipe them out. Stories of nigger towns being burned to the ground were commonplace."* She spun to face the church. Her arms lifted and spread wide. Her abrupt movement made Reverend Pouvwa flinch. *"And then* up *went this church! Under spell went the niggers of Water Bug Hollow, and down came their history— cradle of civilization and all!"* Back to Reverend Pouvwa she spun. She held her arms close as if embracing a very slender man or woman. *"Oh, so much chaos from the building of this house, and the removal of a sacred dance on a sacred day,"* she said in a proud manner, eyes closed. She opened them to spy Reverend Pouvwa. *"This is how it looked for a long time. Field and no church,"* she stated. *"Then church with no roads leading to it, cars stuck in the mud, rusted and lingering."* He followed her finger as she pointed to the church. *"Look, look,"* she directed.

He did. The haunting ambiance reemerged with a new set of flattened, cell-shaded bodies. These new pedestrians were assembled with the same fixed, eerie stillness. Light washed up onto their faces, exposing horror and disbelief across their countenances. Through the crowd, Reverend Pouvwa observed two men sitting on the steps of the church's front entrance. These men had volume, three dimensional, unlike the gawking church goers.

One man was well-dressed and groomed. He was the reverend of that time. He had broad shoulders, which gave him a very powerful, authoritative presence. He was brown-skinned, handsome, and had a thick mustache. The other was a man with swagger. He was a rugged musician—a jazz pianist to be more specific. He lived by music. They talked to one another in a friendly tone, though their exchange was morbid.

"You ready to die and haunt the cross?" the jazz man asked the preacher.

"I'm righteous in title only," the preacher said in return, a bright smile on his face. *"If you don't kill me, I'll keep pretending to do the Lord's work while taking the soul of young girls. My flock!"* he declared.

"Maaaan, I'm gunna shoot you dead!" the jazz man barked back.

The preacher stood. He fixed his suit and looked down at the pianist. *"They gon' take you as well. You ready to do this?"*

"Yep!" the piano man assured. *"I got my gun cocked, and I'm ready to receive my punishment for puttin' you down."* Ready as they were, the scene blacked out, and they did not move. There was no human movement. No walking to their marks to recreate the gruesome historical event of August 12, 1933. Instead, an otherworldly wind stood the piano player up on his feet and forwarded him to a spot on the lawn where the killing deed took place in history. The reverend turned around and was positioned by the same current. His foot was propped up on the first stair leading to the front door of the church. It all looked to Reverend Pouvwa as if someone sped up the play on a video.

In the time before the historical act played out, Sarinda Fallows commented, *"Now, I was up at my apartment when all this was happening."* She turned and pointed toward town. *"I was comforting little, Miss Philomena Amat."* She lowered her hand and smiled at Reverend Pouvwa. *"You see, she'd just been made a woman by Reverend Ladon over there. It was a little forceful, and she was so distraught. She was so young, if I can remember. Fifteen, I believe."*

Immovable shock exploded on the reverend's face. He attempted to shape his features into complete disgust, but nothing moved. He couldn't even shape his mouth to form words to describe the reality of what had taken place between the church's former reverend and the fifteen-year-old girl named Philomena Amat. Reverend Pouvwa wasn't even an idea in time's thought when the terrible accosting of the teenage girl occurred, and he understood what happened, even with this being the first time he'd ever encountered it all. Here in dream.

A voice woke him up, but not into reality. Reverend Pouvwa remained fixed in dream, but no longer was his focus on Sarinda Fallows, and his features were now movable. His surprise dampened. His attention pivoted in the direction where he'd heard the jazz pianist call out, *"Lionel!"*

Reverend Pouvwa's eyes, in unison with the eyes of the flattened onlookers, shifted to Reverend Lionel Ladon. The man turned around. The piano man cocked back the gun's hammer. Reverend Pouvwa wanted to intervene, especially when armed police were moved into position like chess pieces. Their bodies, too, were flat, but their guns were three dimensional. Reverend Pouvwa moved to make protest, but the dream kept him in place. All he could do was watch in horror as history played out in the dreaming.

Sarinda looked on with whetted anticipation.

"Put that gun down, Quincy!" a policeman ordered.

"Quincy, what's all this about, now?" an elderly man pleaded, barely balanced on his cane. When he spoke, the dream popped his flattened frame into a full, fleshed out man.

Reverend Ladon lifted his arms in surrender. The dream made the motion quick and unreal, the movement like a toy figure puppeteered by a child.

"He forced Philomena to bed!" the pianist expressed, teeth clenched and grinding anger. *"My little girl that I swore to protect!"* he declared.

The elderly man's expression drenched with shock, drying into sorrowful disbelief. His expression settled on stern and he asked Reverend Ladon, *"Is this true...?"*

Reverend Ladon confessed, *"Yes. I did lay with that young girl. I forced myself upon her, God help me. But, I swear there is deviltry at work..."*

Sarinda cackled. No one reacted to her laugh. Her icy laughter was drowned out by the pianist firing six rounds into Reverend Ladon. Reverend Pouvwa flinched. He watched as the reverend's body flattened and burned into ash and swiveled into a dance of dimly lit wisps that seeped through the church door, filling the large cross that overlooked the pulpit.

It was the pianist's turn to die. The armed officers shot him with quick, successive blasts of gunfire. The pianist's body bled for a moment, and then it flattened. Like the reverend before him, he burned to ash that swirled into lighted wisps. His translucence was brighter, swimming with yellow hues. It spun into a helix formation, and then rushed through the church door, following Reverend Ladon's dull light into the cross. The church's front doors opened by way of a cold, violent force exhaled from the building. The gale surrounded Reverend Pouvwa and injected a feeling of emptiness inside him. His stomach dropped as if experiencing the rush of a sudden descent. Everyone faded around him, save Miss Sarinda Fallows. Water Bug Hollow's lights faded, and its presence was consumed by a thick fog.

The pneumatic, red-haired and green-eyed seductress shook her head. An out-of-place, innocent smile crawled onto her face as she watched the scene play out, death and shock. *"Such an electrifying night!"* she gasped, voice excited as if remembering the thrill of a carnival ride. *"It wasn't the beginning of Water Bug Hollow's rebirthing pangs. It was one of many thrilling points in its rebirth—at least the events where my fair and delicate hands did the guiding. When my time passed, Reverend Pouvwa,"* said the sanguine-haired woman, *"oh, that's when the biggest hauntings took place. Water Bug Hollow is littered with so many haunts. Curses,"* she clarified. *"Hexes,"* she finalized with her word preference. *"So many* inawo,*"* she continued.

Instinct burrowed into Reverend Pouvwa, finding for him Sarinda's word use as uncharacteristic. He himself was befogged by the word, but there was something more perplexing to Sarinda Fallows that occupied the reverend's thoughts more than the foreign word's definition. The woman's voice was not her own. The reverend expressed his puzzlement with narrowed eyes aimed at Sarinda Fallows. His ears processed the voice, inhaling sound from ear to mind where he placed the voice to its proper owner.

Quantifying the voice's timbre prompted the genuine possessor to reveal herself. Out of the image of Sarinda Fallows emerged the conjure woman he'd spoken with earlier. Lady Arachne stood next to him. Wriggling, small strands of light bore into her as if she was a vortex they were attempting to penetrate. *"I don't know how much longer I could wear that harpy as a mask,"* she divulged with a scowl. She fixed her face and turned to Reverend Pouvwa. *"But, we have learned much, haven't we?"*

"Yes, Lady Arachne," he replied to her, voice wavering as he made a nod of his head.

"It will be your duty to remember what we've learned, Reverend Pouvwa," Lady Arachne expressed to him. *"This is your dream. I won't remember when I eventually wake. Is that understood?"*

He assured her, *"Yes, Madame…"*

"Lady," she corrected.

She faded before Reverend Pouvwa could offer his apology and address her with her accurate title. Everything was gone now. Church and town were absent, and even the fog that covered them. The dream shifted. The sun brightened the sky with its presence, and now Reverend Pouvwa stood in the middle of a dusty road that belonged to a boomtown in the Old West.

"There's five hundred dollars on that nigger boy's head," a voice said behind him. The reverend attempted to turn his head, but the dream kept him in place. The gruffy voice continued, *"But I'll kill the kid for free for all the shootin' he been doin' from Fort Negro to here."*

"They say that nigger's made of magic," another man informed. *"They call him* Armageddon. *They say he can't be killed."*

"We'll see on that!" said the other. *"Let him and his gang ride up in here."* A gun's muzzle was placed against the back of Reverend Pouvwa's head. *"Ain't you the reverend that's been assisting this gang out of Water Bug Hollow? You in a lot of mighty trouble, Reverend. You got trouble with us and God for the jungle, nigger-*

magic you practicin'. Boys like you go to hell."

The trigger wasn't pulled. Reverend Pouvwa blinked and the field returned. It was still morning. An old cabin rested where the church had sprung up earlier in his dream. The voice of his grandmother called him, and he approached the door, turned the knob, and walked inside. She was in the kitchen at a table with his grandfather. Both ate from plates filled with a hearty meal. A third plate was prepared at the table. Reverend Pouvwa took a seat and indulged in the food.

His grandmother told him, *"Don't you fret what them boys told you. You serve your heritage. You serve your conjure. That's God. That's your Ixu spirit. And that, my child, is a gift."*

His grandfather looked at him and commented, *"You a detective. Use your senses. Pay them boys no-never-mind."*

"Yessir!" he responded.

He ate in abundance for the remainder of his dream while slurs were hurled at him from outside the cabin.

11

He had seen days pass in moments—seven days in seconds. He'd heard conjure community members voice skepticism of his return and disappointment with his second departure, abandonment, as they called it. Dooley understood. He couldn't continue to be away, and the mass assault of voices from his community expressing doubt and disenchantment—also coming from friends and family—were like a ritual tugging at him, conjuring him back to Earth.

Residing within another realm through an unseen door in the cosmos afforded no sanctuary. No cosmic article shielded him from the collective voices crying out to him. More so, disappearing from the Avenue gave him no resolve. The woman he loved was not here. The missing children of the street could not be tracked and located to a hidden corner within this realm of black spirits.

But he was proud to hear one scruffy voice of dissention among the people's whispers and gossip. It came from his older brother Cedron. *"Yo, let my brother find some rest, some solitude. He got a lot going on inside. Give him his space and time. Besides, this ain't our only current event affecting all of us; and we still got the Gypsy Moon Misfits itchin' to act on the Elders' call."*

That was comforting when he'd heard his brother's words defending him. Though it did nothing to soothe their mother's worries, or erase the tension in his father's face when he heard the concern in their mother's voice or observed the sentiment sketched on her countenance.

Dooley peered down at the world.

The Earth was so small from here. If it wasn't for his instinct, Dooley wouldn't have known he was staring at its miniscule speck withn the black, cosmic fabric. Even the sun, stationed at the center of his solar system, was barely visible from Dooley's height and distance. But there below on that solid, blue-green dust particle lay an immense responsibility as vast as the cosmos itself.

Under the mask and lilac flame, he was Gordon Goodspeed. And he'd been truant for long enough, though not nearly for the length of time he'd been absent when he first displaced himself among the stars and the cosmic, black spirits. It was time to return to kin and culture, and ultimately, responsibility and duty. He considered there was too much influence from the heroes in comic books he'd read growing up.

He justified his self-imposed exile as a ceremonial right for brooding heroes, such as he'd become.

Even now, he bobbed in the cosmic atmosphere with his body

ablaze with lilac spirit, legs together, feet aimed down at a ballerina's elegant point, arms at his sides, hands balled into fists. There was something heroically stylish about his stance.

He looked down and spied Earth from a distant galaxy. Then he became a beam of lilac light, cutting through the blackness of space and leaving a trail of smokeless fire, legs shifting into a glistering, pale-purple, luminous tail. His flight was instant, and Earth appeared more to come to him than he to the planet. Waves of conjure spread through the dark, morning sky as he pierced the atmosphere, signaling his return to Fable Avenue. The instincts of the slumbering members in the New York City conjure community were wide awake, and Dooley's return was announced in dream. Recent tensions defined as uncertainty and cynicism, directed at him, would be dissolved by morning. His return couldn't remove the disappointment connected to his long stretches of absence, but Dooley considered the sentiments were deserved.

His comet trail arced across the city, barreling down on the Brooklyn borough.

He landed atop his family's Fable Avenue residence, and the instant his feet touched the brownstone's roof, the lilac spirit-glow and flame evaporated. His African Chokwe-like mask shifted into gossamer strands of shadow and dissolved into his neck. Gordon inhaled deep. His return to Fable Avenue was close to the time he'd left. He wanted to believe perhaps no time had passed at all; but respect for the emotions his absence stirred kept him from accommodating the thought.

Four bright lights popped around him like miniature fireworks. A silvery light discharged followed by purple, blue, and green bursts. Fey Forrester's yumboes configured from out of the radiant, sparkling snaps. The winged pixies hovered around Gordon, scolding him for his truancy, chattering in their sing-song language.

Gordon put his hands up, trying to wave them off.

"I know… I know!" he responded as they jabbered up a cloud of high-pitched curses and reprimands. "Hey!" Gordon snapped back. "*Language!* Watch the mouth!" He clenched his teeth and huffed with a single, stiff finger aimed up, "Stop!" The yumboes ceased their chatter and hovered in place. "Thank you…" he exhaled, frustration carried away in a sigh. Then in a sincere voice, he told the hovering, winged sprites, "I'm sorry…"

The vexed expressions coloring their faces melted to wide-eyed sorrow, absorbing Gordon's sincere emotion. Both Gordon and the yumboes took a breath. Silver said something about Gordon's presence being necessary to officiate Fey Forrester's return. Gordon nodded his head, agreeing. He went to speak, but Silver had more to say, or rather, confess.

She spoke.

Gordon made a face, contorted through disbelief and irritation.

Silver and the other yumboes wore guilty expressions. Then Silver made one last revelation.

Gordon rolled his eyes. "Cedron's here!" he huffed and smacked his forehead. He tilted his head back, face to the heavens, hand still in place. He popped from existence, going from rooftop to the brownstone's front room on the parlor floor.

Cedron was on the couch, which was dressed in a blanket and sleeping pillow. Gordon's older brother wore sweatpants and a football jersey. He was sitting in the dark, and he chuckled at Gordon's entrance.

"You know," Cedron started, "I like my conjure get up. All-black everything, circuit-like tattoo layered over my body." He jabbed a finger at Gordon and concluded, "But that poppin' into existence shit? That's wassup."

No sooner was that said by Cedron did the yumboes emerge next to Gordon from out of colorful bursts and sparks. They hovered and glowed behind him, two on his left and two on his right. Their bodies provided enough light to fill the room with a radiant, multi-colored glow.

"These glowbugs can't keep a secret, can they?" Gordon said through clenched teeth. He tossed a look at them. All four pursed their lips and threw a look right back at him.

Cedron sat back. "No, but my question is: Why you keepin' your time-travel meet-cute with Fey a secret? I found out you told Benny. I put him under the lights, got him to confess he knew, too."

Gordon relaxed. He explained to his brother, "He was in the room. I needed to talk to Neyeli. It was that night I came through for the card game." He tapped a finger against his head as he took a seat next to his brother. "I don't remember my conversation with Fey," he informed. "But I know we talked and met in time—time long ago."

"Yeah," Cedron acknowledged. "The glowbugs told me. Benny had his things to say."

Silver zoomed up to Cedron, stopping inches before his face. Her bright, silvery glow stung his eyes. Cedron shifted into his black and circuit-tattooed form. A glow covered his eyes to shield him from Silver's immense glow. "My apologies," he told Silver. "But back up, please!" His voice reverberated with a riveting bass that Silver took seriously. She dimmed the glow that flushed her flesh and zipped back into formation with her sisters. Cedron's form returned to normal, save his legs and back, to retain full motion.

"I asked for Neyeli's help," Gordon told his brother. "The Matriarchs will lend a hand. I got some other things going should I bump into her again in time."

"Keep all them details to you," Cedron said to him while patting Gordon on the back. "I don't need to know any of that. The Gypsy Moon Misfits got something bein' brewed for us. We workin' with Papa Solomon and Martin. Details to come," he added.

"Yeah…"

Cedron ruffled his brother's wild hair and then said to Gordon, "Go get some earthly sleep. You been up with them cosmic spirits too long."

Gordon smiled. "Yeah…" he repeated. He looked at the yumboes and asked, "You overdue to get back to your realm." The sprites danced in the air, wings wild in flutter. "All right," said Gordon. "Let's get you back in." He turned to his brother and gave him an embrace of the hand and a one-arm hug. "Appreciate you keepin' look out for me, and for stickin' up for me while I was gone. I was able to hear that."

"You got it, little brother. Now get some sleep." Then Cedron warned, "And I promised Mom and Pop—and the Elders—if you try some cosmic-sneak-away shit again, I'll put a dome over you."

The ritual Cedron alluded to consisted of snatching a charged object from an altar, putting a glass bowl over it, and reciting an incant that would keep a person in place. For a spirit like Gordon, he would most likely be banished outside of time until the dome was lifted.

"Yessir," said Gordon, gesturing a salute at Cedron. Then he popped from existence. The yumboes followed him, taking their lights with them. And so, it was dark again, and Cedron was relieved. He lay back down, curled up inside his blanket, and went to sleep.

Gordon was in the basement. The mystical lighting brightened the area, sensing his arrival. The ancient technological device, called Spook, opened, revealing its black-mirror face to Gordon. On the screen, in ancient characters, scrolled the words: *Welcome home, Mister Goodspeed.*

Gordon's lilac, incanted eyes translated the words.

"Hey, Spook. How you been?"

Resting, the machine answered. *With the exception of babysitting these four,* it joked.

Gordon chuckled at what he'd read. He fully expected the yumboes to fly at the sentient mechanism with scowls and high-pitched ramblings of curses and scolding in their language. Instead, Gordon's expression burst with surprise when he beheld Silver make a hurried approach above Spook's bejeweled console and then gently rest her feet against it. Her movement continued, descending until she was relaxed in a cross-legged pose, resting in between gems. Her large, ovate eyes peered longingly at the black mirror and the glowing characters on its face.

Gordon's features formed into perplexity. He looked at the other yumboes. They huddled close in the air, watching Silver stare at the black mirror. A hopeful, longing expression spread across their faces. An instinct tickled Gordon's senses and he understood that the other yumboes were charmed by the sight in front of them.

Gordon's eyes caught movement from Spook. His black mirror tipped toward Silver. Her neck bent back to keep her eyes on the black screen. The words dissolved away, replaced with the question: *How has your day been, wonderful, winged woman?* Spook's screen straightened. Silver stood and fanned her wings out into a full spread. The other yumboes giggled like schoolgirls, still huddled and hovering.

Gordon remained confused.

Silver answered Spook in her language, *"I am quite well, my dark-faced seer."* Gordon noticed her voice was a little more mature. Her tone was less squeaky, smokier. *"Our presence has brought such joy to those dear children who were fated to pass before their purpose. We bring great smiles to them, but we need to return home for a day or two. We know they'll miss on, but I told them we'd be back."*

Their conversation continued. Gordon became distracted by Zee when she flew close to him and whispered into his ear. *"They get along like you and Fey,"* Zee informed with a giggle.

Gordon remained still. His eyes, however, drifted toward Zee. Comprehending her words melted his inflexible disposition, and Gordon cocked his head, making a face. "I don't think Silver and Spook have been getting along like Fey and I," he told the purple-fleshed Zee.

The yumbo only responded by saying, *"Leave these two alone for a moment, if not the remainder of the night,"* she suggested. *"Speak us back into the page, to our world."*

"Sure," Gordon complied. He turned his head away from Silver and Spook's interaction, keeping his ear on Silver's half of the conversation. He stepped up to the alchemical chamber's capsule where Fey Forrester's sketchbook rested. He opened to the page hosting the four yumboes' drawings. He spoke an incant in an ancient language, leaving out Silver's name.

Zee's, Em's, and Jade's bodies swirled into dust and cloud, and then seeped back into their drawings, bringing color to the black and white etchings. Gordon was ready to pop himself away, upstairs to his bedroom where he'd finally get, as his brother suggested, 'earthly sleep'.

"Oh!" Gordon heard Silver say. He looked at the yumbo who was looking all around for her sisters. She turned to Spook's screen and told him, *"I can't leave my sisters. And it's been so long since I've been home."*

I understand, read Spook's black mirror in ancient text. *Good night, and good day, chrome-fleshed flier.*

"Good night, and good day, opaque dream-guider," she bowed her head and torso. Spook's screen tilted forward and straightened, returning the same gesture.

Gordon beamed while watching the two depart from one another's presence. Silver's wings fluttered and she lifted from Spook's gem-ornamented keyboard. She zipped next to Gordon's shoulders. Her wings fanned a cool breeze against his cheek. He told the yumbo goodnight, and then he spoke again the incant, stating her name.

Silver dissolved into dust and cloud that swirled in midair and traced its essence back to the drawing from which she was conjured. Gordon closed the book and then sat down in the plush chair facing the capsuled chamber. He asked his magitech companion, "Spook…were you a yumbo before your spirit possessed this device?"

I remember wings, the ancient script read along the face of the black mirror. *Bat-like wings,* the words continued. *Far less butterfly-like. But my memory is mostly set aside to make way for historical recall.*

"And the Pious Wars feel familiar too, huh?" Gordon reminded in question.

We all have our mysteries, Mister Goodspeed.

"I suppose we do," said Gordon, lifting his brow in contemplation.

Besides, with you gone and these yumboes zipping about, I had to 'talk' to someone.

"Point taken," replied Gordon. "I won't do that again, Spook. I'm here, and I'm all in."

Welcome back…for good this time.

Gordon burst into a chuckle. "Goodnight, Spook." Then he corrected, "Or morning. However you want to play with it." His eyes faintly made out Spook's identical response to him before the glyphs faded from existence. He materialized on his bed, sitting. His full-body, cosmic apparel stirred into shadow and seeped into his skin.

Gordon hosted a quick ritual at his altar, and then he slipped under the covers and went to sleep.

12

Satchel "Old Goon" Eledas bellowed along with Robert Leroy Johnson as the old blues singer's voice filled the 1960s camper interior. The song serenading the final leg of the drive toward the legendary Mississippi intersection was the classic tune *Cross Roads Blues*, more commonly known as *Crossroads*. But Satchel "Old Goon" had anything but the blues as he drove up to the famed, four-way crisscross.

Robert Johnson's complete catalog possessed the camper's Moorish, Gypsy-wagon interior for the entirety of the journey, save nights when the Old Goon's passengers needed sleep. On the drive's last leg, however, the artist's classic *Cross Roads Blues* was blaring and on repeat.

Satchel "Old Goon" drove and sang, observing the landscape with a prospector's eye. The road was dusty but pristine, worn and beautiful like a sepia-colored photograph, and Satchel "Old Goon" celebrated his arrival as if catching the Holy Ghost in a Baptist church. He bobbed his head and shoulders to and fro as the slide guitar from the song was plucked and licked, and Robert Johnson's canorous hound dog-like howl accompanied in tone. Satchel "Old Goon" harmonized with Robert Johnson, wailing just under the legendary blues man's singing voice.

Lillian Eledas-Ghedemere didn't mind the ruckus, and neither did her mother, Simaetha Ghedemere. Lillian was happy to see her father so excited. More than that, she loved seeing her mother by his side. They weren't a traditional family. There was so little time spent together, but nothing due to animosity. In fact, Satchel "Old Goon" and Simaetha together was a sight for true amorous affection and respect between a man and a woman. But Satchel "Old Goon" was always on the move, involved in conjure folk politics across the country and sometimes abroad.

When she was growing up, Lillian was often split between her parents, living long distances from one or the other. She mostly grew up with her mother, however. Lillian melted like a child when she saw her parents side-by-side, and she was expecting things to be closer between the three of them now. According to her father, a little more youth would be restored to him. But Lillian didn't know if her old, old, old man meant that figuratively or literally.

Satchel "Old Goon" was well over a hundred years old. He boasted one-hundred and twenty-five years of age, claiming, *"Black don't crack, but a li'l conjure and soul keep it all intact."*

He looked no older than his sixties—early sixties at that. He stood at five feet exactly—no more or less of an inch, and he had dark brown skin.

His face knew no wrinkle, but his bushy and white mustache and eyebrows betrayed his age. His hair was the color of smoke, resembling a brush fire and swiveling to a tight coil in the same erratic manner. His style of dress never changed. From the time of him being fourteen to now, Satchel "Old Goon" could be seen in a buttoned-up shirt, dark brown slacks with dress shoes to match, and a black driver's cap. People weren't quite sure if he changed into similar clothes or wore the same threads day in and day out. A small, burlap pouch dangled on his belt, the contents of which were two very miniscule bottles. One had a dab of rum in it. The other had Florida water, which had the mixed scents of sweet orange, a few drops of spice, and lavender and clove. An incant cast a faint aura of the aroma around Satchel "Old Goon" as long as he had his pouch strapped to his side. That didn't stop him from bathing, but he was always guaranteed to smell nice. The pouch also contained a single cigarette and an equilateral wood carving that resembled the crossroads.

Satchel "Old Goon" asserted his birthday as February 6, 1892. His lineage had been freeborn since 1770s. Beginning with his grandparents, they were conjure folk who channeled their mystical arts through a practice called *Ojulowo Atijo Oluwa*, and it was the standard study among conjure folk in the African diaspora, especially America. The spiritual system didn't have a name until 1877, and it was freeform until a pair named Lapen Jack and Elisheba Bloomscale put it all together, sewing up its numerous parts with a title to its sacred denomination. Their work brought them to the crossroads, where they accessed the guardians of the time, and were quested with uniting the conjure factions spread around the world under the *Ojulowo* spiritual banner.

At the time, it was simple incants and rituals. *Ojulowo* wasn't filled with the flare of magic from more ancient times and practices or conjure's rebirth in the modern area, though there was the rare occasion. The Middle Passage, and the breaking of Africa, was a ruinous ritual that dampened the original peoples' abilities to tap into the mystical, cosmic energies called conjure.

Driving up. The Old Goon's eyes inhaled the sight. Not too far ahead was the magnificent intersection, the plot of mystical real estate belonging to his family. The crossroads. Satchel's voice broke from the blues singer who immortalized the grand intersection in song. He mouthed an incant, and a crystal glowing with a soft, blue color, dulled in intensity. The music coming from the speakers lowered to a whisper.

Lillian moved closer to the front, sliding off the plush, half-moon-shaped couch in the back. She used the medium-length countertop as balance, tipping her head away from the wooden cabinet situated above the counter. Passing the cabinet, she put her hand on its knob, using the oval-shaped African mask handle as another source of stability until she was able to plop down on a small, square-shaped seat positioned behind her father. She leaned forward. Hands on the passenger seat headrest. She watched the road come up on the van as they sped up toward the mystical Clarksdale, Mississippi intersection.

Lillian's eyes widened, filling up with the grand and majestic sight in front of her. The fabled crossroads. It wasn't the first time she visited and beheld the magic of the cross section, but this was the first time entering the invisible grounds of the former homes of Jackson and Gaston Fable. It would also be the final time the hidden estates would wear their current facades. Their interiors would also be remodeled from their current design and layout. The Fable brothers had no heirs. The family conjure line died out with Jackson and Gaston Fable's fading. Ownership of the crossroads would return to the Eledas family, the direct descendants to the ones who blessed the area with incant and old, African magic. No close cousin families would preside over the mystical domain, as were Jackson and Gaston Fable.

Satchel "Old Goon" slowed the van. He crossed the intersection and parked to the right of the lot where Jackson Fable's house would appear when called through powerful conjure. Lillian remarked with a wide grin, "So this is it, huh, Papa?" Her words were not directed at their arrival, and they certainly didn't pertain to any notion of this being the first time she'd visited the blessed junction. This moment for the Eledas-Ghedemere family was a prelude, especially for Lillian. She would be blessed in ceremony as the crossroads' primary protector and reigning resident.

Satchel "Old Goon" put the van in park, cut the engine, and beamed at the sight. "Yes, my daughter," he told her in his stock-craggily, blues-singer, old-man voice. "This here, sho' is it." He gave his head a little shake, opened the van's door, and hopped out. Simaetha followed. Lillian opened the sliding side door, and stood at her mother's side. The two women joined Satchel "Old Goon" in the middle of the road. Lillian saw her father struggling to hang onto his smile. She followed his gaze and eyed a rundown gas station resting on the adjacent lot from where the invisible home of Jackson Fable waited in the ethers.

A scrawny and scraggily-bearded man in overalls named Jabo Judson observed the family with a squint to his small, round eyes. A snarl undulated across his lips, exposing missing and dirty teeth. Hands in his pockets, he leaned against one of the gas pumps.

Old Man Satchel's smile faded completely when he saw the yokel gnash at him with what few and brown teeth he had. "Now I didn't notice that boy and pump shop when we was drivin' up," Satchel "Old Goon" commented, face now compressed in contemplation. He had a thought, which he'd express when he met with Fable Avenue's Elders.

Simaetha stepped closer to the old, old man, the front of her left arm pressed against the back of his right shoulder. She noted as a matter-of-fact, "That's because it wasn't." She started twiddling her fingers. "This Fallows-Mister got our road on watch."

Satchel "Old Goon" made a quick glance at Simaetha's left hand, fingers swirling. The act produced worm-thin threads of glowing purple and black conjure that writhed between her fingers and thumb. The snaking strands murmured with a sound that sizzled like a snake's hiss.

Satchel "Old Goon" grinned. Simaetha sure was a beautiful conjure woman. No ritual or bauble required. Just a shake of her fingers and spirit was culled from the other side for attack or defense, as well as to heal. He looked her up and down. Her long and thick, silver braids dangled to her knees like plaited cumulus clouds spilling from the firmament. He admired her stern face aged by wisdom and affixed with beauty, now focused on confrontation against the yokel that observed them. Her heightened instinct divined that the hayseed gripped a needle in his pocket. Satchel "Old Goon" picked up on that as well, telling the conjure woman, "Ease your conjure, pretty *spithre*. I smell a fight brewin' that's closer than six months away. We ain't got to concern ourselves with that now. Let that grinning fool keep his place right there. But if he move, you move."

Simaetha considered Old Man Satchel's point, and she relaxed her conjure.

"I sense a fight has already taken place on this road," she spoke as her intuition pulled the happening from the past. "The lilac flame and the cobalt-blue spirit were involved. Needlemen and a man with a whip were their antagonists. All of them under the command of this Fallows-Mister, his wicked hexers."

Satchel "Old Goon" smiled up at Simaetha as her average height towered over his diminutive stature. He admired her skin color. It glowed like the African desert sands at full, high moon, a resonating beige beauty. He couldn't help but think that sometimes the darkest, cosmic concentration of the original spirit reflected the aura of the moon. She was bi-cultural, with two distinct, ancient bloodlines coursing through her. She was as much clothed in the indigenous blood of America as she was the magic of Africa.

Lillian was not aware of her parents' exchange. She was mesmerized by an otherworldly phenomenon, simple in its presentation. The white letters expressing *Gaston Avenue* faded from the old street sign. *Jackson Avenue* did the same. New names appeared almost instantly. A brief pause separated the moments in time when the crossroads were unnamed, and then old magic and conjure chiseled a new inscription.

Ida Avenue.

Penny Street.

"Papa…" Lillian vocalized in awe at the wonder she beheld. Despite her low utterance, Satchel "Old Goon" heard his daughter, and he turned his attention to her. "Papa!" she repeated. "Look!"

She didn't point, and she didn't need to. An instinct pulled at Satchel "Old Goon" that turned his attention to the newly inscribed names on the streets signs. He read the new names aloud and hollered with joy. He simmered his emotions and said to the new inscriptions, "Ida, Penny! Welcome back!" He spun around and told Lillian and Simaetha, "April eighteenth, seventeen seventy-five, just as the opening battles of the Revolutionary War were beginning, this roadway was being blessed by two runaway slaves. African women—conjure women. Ida and Penny. Now, some say they were sisters with a good deal of age difference between them. Penny was the younger. She was supposedly in her late teens, early twenties. Ida was older. She was around her early to mid-thirties. Some say they was niece and aunt. Either way, they was of the same blood." Simaetha and Lillian were well versed in the story, but like the music in the van, they didn't deny Satchel "Old Goon" his moment of joy.

"They were from Virginia," Satchel "Old Goon" continued. "But they fled farther south because of the fighting, y'see. They was chased too. Rumor has it, their pursuers was needlemen hired by their cruel, superstitious slave master." Satchel "Old Goon" took a moment to ponder. "That's a possibility, them pursued by the needle. The first lodge was set up in the early seventeen-hundreds, up there in Connecticut, thereabouts." He grunted, "Could be a reason they headed south, too. But a'cordin' to what we got on record, there was a lodge in the south, 'round about Virginia, I think." Satchel "Old Goon" scoffed and said, "They got so many secret quarters up 'round here, an' e'ryone of them claim to be the first—the ones on the east coast." He shook his finger at the ground and continued with the roads' story. "Them women found this intersection, something compelling them to this point." He explained, "A crossroads always got spiritual significance, and they never forgot that. They knew it was a doorway. And Ida and Penny, they did themselves a ritual that had to be conducted at high noon *and* high moon. Then, *poof!* Outside of time they went. Gone into the ethers. They became invisibles, and they chose the last name *Eledas* to honor Papa Legba for granting them entry into this here crossroads." He put his hands in his pockets before continuing the story. "A couple whiles later, in the middle of the hometown team goin' up against them British boys—that's the Revolutionary War I'm speakin' on," he took time to elucidate. "But, good into that time, two more slaves came wanderin' this way. Two men. Young men," he emphasized. "One named Xodus. The other man was named Merin. They weren't brothers, but they was close, good friends. Both were in their twenties, but Xodus was the older—near thirty." He took pause to note,

"Now, them two had some boys on their trail from both the British and American armies. Yep! That's for true! Them fightin' and warrin' folk could shake hands and find peace when it came to a hunt of some escaped Africans." Satchel "Old Goon" took another pause. This one lasted a little longer as he put his hands in his pockets and looked around, making a turn on the hallowed intersection. "They came here. Luck of the mojo, instinct, or a carefully calculated, written fate! Who knows?" he contemplated. He looked at Simaetha and Lillian. "The army had come upon them, and both those young men sang an African incant, an old prayer they was taught. That opened an invisible door. Ida and Penny appeared, popped out of the ether. The women took 'em in. There was a house on either side of the street." Satchel "Old Goon" pointed. "There and there," he said. "In time, they married, made a family and studied old-time magic from Africa—what they could remember. Ida and Xodus became man and wife; and Penny and Merin made their vows to one another, too. Xodus and Merin didn't have last names, so they took the name their wives had. That's the beginnin' of my folk. Just a little conjure went a long way. Went further when that conjure woman Elisheba showed up with that gunslinger Lapen Jack. They had all the *Ojulowo* knowledge, even if it led to the schism that put the place into them Fable boys' hands."

Simaetha told her daughter, "While the white man of America was involved in a war for his independence to establish a country here, there was also a war against conjure, invisible as the other side of this corporeal real estate."

"We still in that war, it seems," Lillian commented. "A war to get back on our feet and know our magic, our ancient selves, huh Mamma, Papa?"

Satchel "Old Goon" put a proud arm around his daughter and put her in a spotlight with a bright smile. "Absolutely, my daughter!" he said to her. "Absolutely!" he repeated.

Behind the hazy, barely visible clouds, and the veil of the blue sky, the grand celestial bodies looked on. The hosts of the hidden heavens were not the only entities peering from above, however. Up, up, up, and out, there examining the emotive moment between Satchel "Old Goon", Simaetha Ghedemere and their daughter, were the watchful eyes of Lady Arachne. She peeped in through the use of her ancient deck of Tarot cards. The exultant family's joyous return to their rightful inheritance resonated in motion. A chorus of magic was repeated through the single card. Fog faded the scene, and the ancient pictorial brightened out of the mist. An African couple danced beneath a welcome wreath, tied between four wooden wands.

A smile appeared on the seer's countenance as she stood. She shuffled through her enchanted cards and plucked free both The Star and

The Moon cards. A whispered incant opened the door. Light from her garden-floor room inundated and brightened the space. Lady Arachne moved around her long divination table and to the outside of her divining room. She waved her hand and spoke another incant in the same low and hushed manner. The bright candles in the room were extinguished, transmuting from flame to ghostly, swiveling plumes of smoke that followed her from the room like a brumous snake. The thin, slithering cloud constricted, and in a burst of light the smoke formed solid into the purple-fleshed and lavender-winged yumbo named Zee. She landed on the wise woman's shoulder, perched and waiting for instructions.

Lady Arachne smiled at the glowing sprite, greeting her. "Ah, Zee! Thank you for your provided light in my sanctum—and, of course, your time away from your sisters-in-wings," she said. "Would you be so kind as to inform Madame Jeliya and Papa Solomon that Satchel "Old Goon" and his family have arrived at the crossroads?" Happy to spring to task, Zee leapt from her perched position. Wings a-flutter, she zipped away toward the garden-floor door. Lady Arachne cocked her head, and in the same motion, raised and fanned out the two Tarot cards in her hands. "Oh, Zee," she called.

Zee paused in midair, bringing her speedy departure to a standstill. The yumbo floated by way of magic rather than the use of her wings, which were as still as she. Zee rotated with her arms and legs spread out wide, fingers the same on her tiny hands, and eyes in mimicked manner. The comical nature was self-aware and amused Lady Arachne.

The conjure woman presented The Moon card. "They'll need this," Lady Arachne advised.

Zee snapped out of her risible pose and floated back to Lady Arachne who handed her the card. Zee took the card with both hands. Keeping balance, she was able to tuck the almost identical-sized, magical item under her arm.

Lady Arachne thanked her, and she also notified, "Tell Papa Solomon and Madame Jeliya that I'll be at the crossroads shortly—if I'm not there by the time they arrive."

Zee took note, and then the yumbo was off again to fulfill her mission, dashing away to the door and ghosting through it.

Lady Arachne followed. By the time she was outside, Zee was already across the street and entering the Peters' residence. The Tarot reader continued down the street, pacing in the direction of Gaston Fable's brownstone. At her destination, she set The Star card at the base of the magically locked doors, initiating the ritual to unfasten the magic sealing the entrance. Up burst the light from the card, bright and strong even in the daytime. It outlined the doors, and Lady Arachne heard the 'click' confirming the locks had been unlatched. She took up the card and walked inside just as the light surrounding the doors dissipated. Through the house, and out the back, Fable Avenue's third matriarch journeyed to Water Bug Hollow to retrieve her new friend, Reverend Mathieu Pouvwa.

At the crossroads, Satchel "Old Goon" continued serenading his daughter Lillian and her mother Simaetha with tales of the magical, Mississippi intersection. Again, it was nothing they hadn't heard before, learned growing up, but the stories had the Old Goon in such an excited mood. More so than usual.

"There's a crossroads in Tennessee too, now," he told them, removing his hands from his pocket. He looked at the consecrated road. He held his hands out, palms down. "But this is ours!" He raised his head and put his eyes back on Simaetha and their daughter Lillian. "This is where our math is done, where people come to access their unknown. We hid it under superstition—talk on sellin' y' soul to the Devil, and what not. Talk like that keep folk with a bad or unprepared heart away." His expression turned solemn. "We forgot white folk on this world. They blew that shit up like a balloon. Now black folk too scared to seek their math, the unknown path." But it didn't take long for his expression to brighten again, and Simaetha and Lillian smiled with him. "This here is math," he declared. "That's what folk don't understand. The word 'algebra' come from al-Jabar. That's the title of the first book, and the name of the African moor who penned the subject, to some degree. And that subject, algebra, is derived from Elegbara, Papa Legba. He help you at the crossroads, that 'x', that unknown. He help you find yourself, your hidden path. It's all mathematics—a balance of thought. In them old, old, old, *old* times they called it Ma'at-Hermetics." He chuckled to himself. "We sho' know how to come full circle, I tell you."

"Mathe-magics, Papa," said Lillian, sly grin on her face.

If she was throwing her facial expression, Satchel "Old Goon" caught it, as the same sly grin bounced on his countenance. A little laughter escaped when he replied to his daughter, "Yes, indeed, my Voodoo Lily! Yes, *indeed!*" He peered at the street signs, taking a moment for remembrance for the names etched there minutes earlier. "I did like the Fable brothers. Hell, I loved them two, despite my feelings of a distant family having control of the Eledas crossroads. Them and they wives knew how to make war. They knew how to fight back against that hidden hand." He took a moment before saying, "And they were excellent teachers of craft and conjure."

Satchel "Old Goon" peered over at the lot where Jackson Fable's house would often manifest to any who knew the proper incant to call it into being. It was at that moment the late, musical mystic's home materialized out of writhing strands of conjure. The front door opened, and onto the front porch stepped Papa Solomon and Madame Jeliya. Satchel "Old Goon" sprung to life. He slapped his hands and hollered, "Watch out, now! Here they come! I knew you was 'bout to premier, yes I did. I was talkin' 'bout yo' side of things."

The two groups met on the lawn. Papa Solomon headed to Satchel "Old Goon". Then he pretended to ignore the short, old man. He pivoted toward Simaetha and put his arms around her, planting a graceful kiss on her cheek. He did the same to Lillian. Then he flinched as if startled. "Oh, Satchel! I didn't notice you there."

Satchel "Old Goon" waved him away. He made his way toward Madame Jeliya and gave her a hug. "Man, forget you!" he said with a scowl shot over his shoulder at Papa Solomon. "I'd rather greet the prettier of you two." He addressed Madame Jeliya, "How you doin', good woman?"

"I'm doin' just fine, good old man," Madame Jeliya responded in a playful tone.

They separated from their embrace, and Satchel "Old Goon" noted, "We missed your pretty self while your husband and sister-in-law came to visit at the gathering earlier in the spring." While he spoke, he and Papa Solomon gave one another a firm handshake and brotherly hug.

"Well, I and Lady Arachne had to oversee the street," she explained. "Besides, that was all business, I'm sure. And I needed a rest from the business side of things." She pivoted and stepped toward Simaetha. "Miss Ghedemere! How have you been, sister?" The two women folded their arms around one another, smiles as bright as the day on their faces. "You look good, mamma!"

Simaetha returned the compliment, first saying, "Thank you, Madame Jeliya. You look well and beautiful yourself. I heard so much had occurred. Fable Avenue had a scuffle! I can also feel a struggle happened on these sacred, intersecting roads."

"Yes," Madame Jeliya exhaled. "I'm sure you were informed of our share of trouble with them needle-holders. They came right on Fable Avenue, took us outside of time. A needleman even got to me, and…" her words trailed away. She looked around, eyes watering. "Here too," she steered her words to the sacred grounds. "There was a tussle here as well, yes. But we pushed them back, in both circumstances."

Simaetha blurted, "Not without some setback, I've heard." Her words and tone were not meant to be rude, and neither were they taken as such. There was too much emotion behind Madame Jeliya's next set of words to be concerned with any backhanded intentions from her sister-in-conjure.

"Yes," Madame Jeliya sighed. The brightness from their greeting dimmed further. Her voice was low when she clarified, "There are still outstanding matters of missing children. Abducted."

Simaetha frowned at the news. She turned her head, aiming her sharp glare at the gas station. Her eyes narrowed on Jabo Judson who continued observing the gathered party, still leaning against one of the pumps, as his left hand fumbled with the syringe in his pocketed.

Jabo grinned, a little spittle bubbling on his lower lip.

Satchel "Old Goon" snarled, "That grinnin' fool gon' watch us the whole time? We got rituals to do."

Madame Jeliya raised her arm, and from her side sprang two large lionesses that shimmered with a sky-blue aura around them. Their presence stirred Jabo to stand straight, even before they made their way toward him in light skips that gathered into long strides. The hex-laced syringe meant nothing to Jabo as instinct kicked in. He pivoted and scurried into the gas station. The lionesses growled as they approached, forcing Jabo Judson into his establishment. He slipped near the door, but regained his balance, avoiding a fall. Inside, he turned and locked the glass doors just as the two, glowing, big cats charged up to the glass entrance where Jabo believed he was safe.

He kept his quivering eyes on the beasts, lower jaw dangling and trembling with a shot of fear injected by the big cats' majestic and intimidating presence. With his heart trembling, he went against instinct and remained close to the locked doors, even as the lionesses hovered close around the outside. Thunder shook the establishment as one lioness roared and the second slammed her head into the door, cracking the glass.

The cats were merely playing with Jabo, scratching nothing more into him than fright. The lovely lionesses were amused as Jabo backed away. The yokel mouthed a perverse prayer that layered the doors with a hexed aegis. The lionesses sensed the invisible safeguard and backed away, but remained circling.

"That was beautiful, Madame Jeliya," commented Lillian, keeping her eyes on the shimmering lionesses.

The Fable Avenue matriarch turned. Her arms were outstretched, and she stepped in Lillian's direction. "Dear woman!" she exclaimed. Embracing her, she let out an enthusiastic, "My, my, my! It was wonderful to have you with us last October, Miss Voodoo Lily. How have you been since then?" Madame Jeliya didn't wait for an answer. She moved back, but kept Lillian embraced. Her eyes inspected the round tuffs of hair atop the young woman's head. "I see your Bantu knots are getting wider."

"Yes, ma'am," Lillian answered. "I've been preparing for this day, mostly," she answered Madame Jeliya's initial question. "The ritual," she accented. The two women removed their arms from one another, and Lillian continued, "Papa was so happy to learn of the crossroads being opened up. He wanted his last-born child to take control of the property."

Madame Jeliya expressed to Lillian in a kind voice, "Well, let me congratulate you on your new title and property, Miss Voodoo Lily." Her eyes spotted Satchel "Old Goon". "And bless your kind heart for giving up the deed. We all were sure you'd take control yourself, no offense."

"Now, Madame Jeliya, this old goon of ours ain't that generous," Simaetha chuckled. "It will still be under Eledas control," she announced. "Satchel will be overseeing matters—"

Satchel "Old Goon" butted into Simaetha's speech, first apologizing to her, and then relaying, "I have my eyes on other property." He clarified, "Other property lost to conjure folk before it could reach its full potential."

Papa Solomon narrowed his eyes on Satchel "Old Goon".

Old Man Satchel concluded, "Water Bug Hollow."

Papa Solomon peered over at the gas station. Madame Jeliya assured, "That yokel can't hear us, Papa. We're good."

The Fable Avenue patriarch turned and said to the old conjure man, "That explains your hesitancy in reclaiming this place."

Satchel "Old Goon" adjusted his hat and said, "Oh, I'mo reclaim my family's spot, now, understand. Yes, I will." He chuckled, and it was infectious, causing Papa Solomon to do the same. Old Man Satchel's demeanor shifted to a graver thought, and that too was contagious. Papa Solomon wondered what was on the old man's mind, but he didn't wonder long as Satchel "Old Goon" disclosed, "That plot down south, I got my eye on. Give that place the redemption it deserves." Then he perked up and said, "Hell, I'd be a patriarch of the place. I'll have Simaetha here be matriarch by my side."

Papa Solomon exhaled and grinned. "Shit," he said with a huff. "I was hopin' you'd help me with the duties of being patriarch over on the Avenue. It ain't easy bein' the lone gunman."

"I could do double duty," Satchel "Old Goon" suggested, a sincere tone rolling in his words. "But we'll see. I know what the cards hold for redeeming Water Bug Hollow. I've cleared that with the Gwuinee folk out in the mid-country. They're a just people, and they see this as justice." Then Satchel "Old Goon" made a face and said, "Speaking of 'all-in-the-cards', where is that always hot and bothered thang, Lady Arachne? Where is Lena?"

But like all things on their way, Satchel "Old Goon" could sense the nearby aroma of the woman-in-question's beauty and sorcery. It was then that Gaston Fable's house materialized out of conjure and into existence across the street from Jackson's abode. Satchel "Old Goon", as well as the rest of the gathered party, turned in the direction of the summoned residence.

The screen door opened first by way of a mystical operation. Then the main door was pulled inward, and Lady Arachne, clothed in a red and orange, floral patterned dress stepped onto the porch. Behind her, forming out of the darkness, was a handsome, brown-skin man of average height and build wearing glasses and a priest's attire. Papa Solomon and Madame Jeliya scanned the man close. They both guessed it was the Reverend Mathieu Pouvwa. Lady Arachne spoke highly of him, a former detective and a man who'd come into his own conjure. She wanted him present for the crossroads ritual being performed on Lillian Eledas-Ghedemere.

"Here I am!" she announced, as if she'd heard the Old Goon's query concerning her absence. She hiked up her dress as she made careful steps down the stairs. Reverend Pouvwa walked up beside her and offered his hand. Lady Arachne accepted, still keeping a watchful eye on her pace down each step. "Thank you, Mathieu," she said to the reverend.

Off the porch, the pair joined the others. Lady Arachne bent down to receive a warm and welcomed hug from Satchel "Old Goon". Standing straight, she was face-to-face with Simaetha. She leaned close to the woman, and the two kissed one another on the lips. Reverend Pouvwa considered the affectionate gesture more than just a friendly peck between acquaintances. The kiss was something familiar and intimate, but with less passion in its enactment than that of two lovers. It was his detective instincts that deduced this had more to do with the company around the women, more so him, as everyone else appeared as if their caress of lips was nothing more than a casual greeting.

A gleam shimmered in Lady Arachne's eyes as she moved away from Simaetha and said, "Hello, my sister-in-web!"

Simaetha greeted her with the same words, and she spoke a Creole greeting. *"Le web cosmic mare nou!"* She scoped Lady Arachne's hair and brightened as she asked, "Are you putting an incant in that hair of yours?" Her eyes inspected Lady Arachne's dreadlocks. She said, observing, "Brown and black, and not a hint of gray—and you older than me!"

Lady Arachne laughed and replied, "This is all natural, sister. Sometimes magic is having good genes," she continued. "But I do long for the days of smoke and haze in my locks." Then she turned and greeted Lillian with a small peck on the cheek and a hug. Like Madame Jeliya before her, Lady Arachne commented on seeing her last October, and she remarked on the growth of her hair. Then she introduced Mathieu Pouvwa to everyone. He shook Papa Solomon and the Old Goon's hands with a firm grip. For the women, his embrace was gentle and endearing. Lady Arachne informed, "The good Reverend here used his instinct to decipher how to come to the crossroads through Gaston's front door. They usually lead back to Fable Avenue." Then she explained, "Well, he made the assumption—said there was something buzzin' in his head. Somethin' 'bout a shortcut. I did a quick ritual, and I was told by spirit: close and lock the door, turn the lock four times and write an 'x' on the door with your fingers. And there you have it."

Satchel "Old Goon" observed Reverend Pouvwa. "You new to this, aintchu, Reverend?"

"Yes," Mathieu answered.

Lady Arachne interjected, "I'm showin' this young man that the magic he holds in his hands caresses the face of the Divine." She tapped the reverend on the arm. "He's comin' 'round to understanding there's no deviltry about it." To Satchel "Old Goon" and the others she teased, "You know how our people can be." She tossed her teasing expression back at Reverend Pouvwa with the added spice of her signature flirtation in her eyes. She told Simaetha, "He's from New Orleans, originally."

"Oh!" the conjure woman replied, perking up with the news. "Homeboy! I live there now, originally from Saint Louis."

"He lives in Water Bug Hollow, now," Lady Arachne continued speaking, her eyes back on Reverend Pouvwa. "He presides over the church built there so long ago." Addressing everyone, she disclosed, "There's a haunt at the church, possessing the main crucifix within the sanctuary. It's powerful, and it's angry. It's connected to the killings that went on there between that old lecherous reverend and the pianist named Quincy."

Bewilderment whirled on old man Satchel's countenance, crinkling his expression. "You from Water Bug Hollow, now?" he questioned. "That correct, young man?" But before Reverend Pouvwa could move his head to affirm with a nod, or speak a concurrence, Satchel "Old Goon" barraged Lady Arachne with a set of inquiries, "There a haunt in the church commissioned by that red-haired harpy? Gaston's place lead to Water Bug Hollow?"

Lady Arachne put her hands together and an inquisitive eye on Satchel "Old Goon". "You have interest in that hallowed territory, Satchel? Is that correct? There's no need to stay tight about it. I've seen your presence crossed with the Hollow in a suit drawn up from my cards. Came to me last April," she revealed.

His eyes bent on Lady Arachne, not liking what it appeared she was accusing him of. "...I was *just* tellin' Vencil and Thelema here," he admitted.

"Oh, I mean nothing by it, Satchel," Lady Arachne explained herself. "What my cards say is important; and I take their telling seriously."

"Then we should talk," Satchel "Old Goon" advised, swallowing the rising indignation burning from stomach to throat. Exhaled and cooled, he advocated. "Taking down that old haunt might be key to reclaiming that hallowed lot."

"*Might be?*" Lady Arachne exclaimed. "Oh, you ol' goon, that haunt *is* key—much as the Good Reverend and I have studied up on it these past few days." Satchel "Old Goon" looked from Lady Arachne to Reverend Pouvwa. His eyes swayed back to the conjure woman when she took up to say, "The haunt was a sort of time bomb, you could say, to keep the Hollow's magic stagnant after Miss Sarinda Fallows completed her task of seizing Mamma Indigo's veil."

Nothing moved on Papa Solomon, save his eyes, aimed straight in Old Man Satchel's direction. The diminutive conjure man stared at Lady Arachne with an inquisitive expression. "Look," said Papa Solomon, "we got a lot of heartache on the Avenue. Mothers and fathers are hurt. Let's discuss things elsewhere. Come on. We'll be back here at sundown to begin Lillian's ritual." Satchel "Old Goon" remained still, eyes fixed on Lady Arachne with an inquisitive gaze. Papa Solomon redirected his focus when he instructed, "Satchel, pull your vehicle up on the lawn. Let it disappear out of time with the houses." To Madame Jeliya he instructed, "Call your pets on back, Thelema-baby. Let's take this to the Avenue."

A mental command made Madame Jeliya's big cats scurry back to her. Jabo Judson snarled as the wild and large felines strode away to the intersection. They dematerialized into blue dust that swirled through the air and seeped into Madame Jeliya's flesh. Reverend Pouvwa observed the mystical occurrence with a locked, attentive stare and a mouth barely open to express awe. He blinked a few times and then came to, the paralysis of being mesmerized lifted. Everyone else considered the sorcery natural in its happening.

Satchel "Old Goon" sauntered to his van, the reclamation and acquisition of Water Bug Hollow on his mind. Papa Solomon walked beside him. Lady Arachne suggested her brownstone for Madame Jeliya, Simaetha, and Lillian to gather in. "Let the men talk in your residence," she recommended. "We'll use my sanctuary for catch up."

"I find that to be a good idea," Madame Jeliya agreed. Looking at Lillian she stated, "But I think a trip to my *laboratwa mystica* would fit best for Miss Lillian's preparation for her sunset ritual."

"For true," Lady Arachne concurred.

Simaetha remarked, "Your facility is very soothing, Madame Jeliya. It will serve Lillian well to settle her unease."

Lillian blushed at her mother's revelation. She said in a soft tone, but in her defense, "This is all such a great responsibility. Being guardian and Iya of the Crossroads."

Simaetha placed her palms on her daughter's shoulders. Through a proud smile she spoke, "You will govern just fine, Lillian."

Lady Arachne poked Reverend Pouvwa's arm with a single finger and teased, "You think you can hang with them old men over there, learn some things? You can get to understandin' that ancestral power and spirit of yours from a man's perspective."

Reverend Pouvwa saw Papa Solomon climb into the passenger's seat and shut the door, waiting for Satchel "Old Goon" to round the camper and hop up into the driver's side. He looked at Lady Arachne and answered, "Yes, Lady Arachne." There was a slight, courteous bow to his posture. "It'll be like hangin' with some of them old folks back home. I do indeed miss my family," he stated. He smiled as he reminisced, but his tone held a hint of sadness within it.

Lady Arachne took his arm and led him back to Gaston's house. "Well, Reverend Handsome, we will teach you to commune with the ones who have transitioned." She looked over her shoulder at the women she was leaving behind as they stepped away. "We'll meet you there. The Reverend and I will go back through Old Man Gaston's place. *Jouk lè sa a*," she said as she departed with the reverend in her arm. Up the stairs. On the porch. Through the doors. The two were gone, off to return to Fable Avenue through a different route. The house faded away.

Madame Jeliya gathered Simaetha and Lillian and led mother and daughter into Jackson Fable's house, not waiting for Satchel "Old Goon" and Papa Solomon to park the camper on the lawn. Up the stairs. On the porch. Through the doors. The women were gone, off to return to Fable Avenue through the common route.

Van parked. Out of the vehicle. Papa Solomon and Satchel "Old Goon" followed the women's path.

The house dissolved outside of time.

Jabo Judson's gas station faded too.

13

It was sunset. A conjure party was gathered outside of time at the crossroads. Jabo Judson watched them, standing a few paces behind the locked, glass doors of his gas station. He was still, not daring to step foot outside and disturb the ceremony. Madame Jeliya's large, feminine felines sat upright, tall and still as statues on the other side, keeping the needleman yokel in his place.

Lillian Eledas-Ghedemere lay flat on the road. Her head was aimed in the direction of sun-goes-down, feet pointing where sun-will-rise. Over her face was an African mask carved by her mother's gifted, artistic hands. There were no slits whittled within the mask's eyes. There was no peering out for Lillian. She may as well have been in a ritualistic, Egyptian sarcophagus. All was dark to the initiating young woman. On the mask's forehead was a 'plus' sign, or more appropriately, a crossroad.

In Lillian's left hand was a small bottle filled with dirt from a graveyard located in Missouri. The sacred acre was owned by, and accompanied the eternal rest of, conjure folk. The dirt was gathered from a section of the cemetery where strong conjure queens from the community had been buried, some of which were related to Lillian on both sides of her family. In her right hand, Lillian held a bouquet of rooster feathers, interspersed with palm tree leaves. The tips of the feathers were dyed yellow, gold, and white.

"See nothing, my daughter," Lillian's mother told her. "See everything—all at the same time. We thank spirit for family and home. We say thank you Loa. We say thank you Orisha. We say thank you to the Old Blacks—the old Gods and Goddesses of the far ancient world. We thank the Neteru of the East, and all the spirits of Nubia, Cush and Punt. Abyssinia is so strong." What Simaetha spoke next, Lillian imagined behind her closed eyelids. "See your home daughter. It is made of Heaven. It is made of Earth. Walk across its threshold. Enter. Move with bare feet from room to room. Speak prayer in each chamber of the house. Sprinkle holy water there. Your blessing and prayers will be an aegis. But should evil penetrate your protection, we pray the Hosts of Heaven have mercy on any evil that enters your home. It will be your wrath, powerful daughter, that will strike them down. These moments rare, if at all," Simaetha added. She continued, "May travelers with the correct keys unlock your doors and seek your wisdom and guidance at these crossroads. Their kindness will be an offering. Your respect will be their gift in return. Keep them safe from storm and troubles. Bless the bath that washes off the mud of peril and distress. May their meals be seasoned with love and nothing bitter. May your walls bubble with happiness;

and may beds be blessed for the travelers' rest. And may he or she unlock the talent inside them through ritual."

Satchel "Old Goon" hummed with his eyes closed. His lips parted, and from them came a harmonious flow, an incant that blessed the scene like holy water over a christened child. Next to him, holding out her hand, was Maman Anansi's shimmering presence. She was projecting through conjure. Her physical body lying on her bed in Queens with her right hand held by her husband who assisted her projection as she presided over the blessing and initiation. The triumvirate of Elders, coupled with their prayer and blessings, allowed Lillian to travel through the corridors of her psyche. It was there where she did as her mother asked, walking through the rooms of a new house situated at the crossroads. She aged as she went through the house, returning to the front room as an elderly woman. Lillian found that she was not alone. She had guests. Two women. It was Ida and Penny. They had youthful faces and bubbled with laughter as Lillian entered the front room. They drank hard liquor from mugs. Lillian knew them without verbal introduction, and she was so happy to see them.

"She is so beautiful!" declared Penny.

"With half of her favoring day, and the other half favoring night," Ida finished.

Lillian gasped when she looked into a mirror, *"I'm old!"* Her face sunk into a sorrowful look.

"No," Ida disagreed.

And Penny corrected, *"You're wise!"*

Lillian bloomed with joy. She grinned slyly and expressed, *"I am! Indeed!"*

"Yes," said the sisters. *"And in your age,"* Penny continued.

Ida concluded, *"Your flesh still glows with half the day and half the night."*

The door behind Ida and Penny opened. Lillian stepped forward, and the two women parted from her way. She exchanged places with the dawning sun. Its rays entered the house as she exited the abode. She took a seat in a rocking chair on the porch. Ida and Penny followed her outside. Lillian's eyes swept the crossroads at sunrise. A black cat traipsed up to her, seemingly formed from air and dust. It hopped up on her lap and curled into a comfortable resting position. She stroked it lovingly, and as she did so, a quiet breeze produced a small disturbance to the hallowed district, curving the tall blades of natural golden grass, as if an invisible hand were petting the spiritual estate.

A craggy noise from an old engine sputtered over the horizon. Lillian focused her eyes on the clamor's origin. The cat in her lap raised its head and straightened its body, eyes on alert. The car never appeared, though its noise increased. Like the cat before it, the vehicle materialized out of air, as if from its own scratchy cacophony. A reddish-brown Coupé with shaded windows pulled up on the lawn across the street, and the engines cut immediately when it stopped.

"*It is tradition,*" started Penny.

And Ida finished, "*For your first arrival to be your significant other.*"

Lillian made a face. Then her eyes bent, focusing on the car as the driver's door opened. His leg appeared first. There was movement. Lillian heard the trunk pop before the man revealed anymore of himself. Then out he hopped, an old and black man dressed in his mailman blues. He walked to the car's rear and lifted the trunk. Reaching in, he pulled out a moderate-sized package, holding it in both hands. Lillian turned her perplexed countenance toward Ida and Penny. "*Is that him?*" she asked. "*Am I seeing him as…wise…like me?*"

Ida smiled at her and waved a hand. "*Look closer, child,*" she instructed.

Penny continued, "*He's there. Just listen.*"

The old mailman asked, yelling from across the street, "*I have this package from Meghill to a Lillian Eledas-Ghedemere.*"

"*I'm Miss Ghedemere,*" Lillian answered, her voice as sweet as sweet iced tea.

The mailman walked to the front of the car, side-stepping and keeping his body faced toward the porch and Lillian. "*Then I guess this package belongs to you.*"

"*Well… I don't know a Meg Hill,*" Lillian confessed.

"*Sorry, Miss Ghedemere,*" the mailman apologized. "*Not Meg Hill, as in a person. That's one word: Meghill. It's a place overseas. Package here just lists that name, not a specific place like the country. I've heard of it, though.*"

Lillian interrupted the tall, old mailman and inquired, "*Oh! Who's it from, the package?*"

The mailman looked at the box. "*Soldier,*" he answered. "*Soldier Great Warrior,*" he read in full. He looked up and peered through squinted eyes. "*Don't seem like much of a name, now does it. Maybe one of them indigenous folk, uh, Indians—Native Americans,*" he guessed. "*Sound like how their names be.*"

Lillian contemplated. While she rummaged through thoughts, the second house at the crossroads materialized across the street. Its door opened when it appeared. The mailman looked over his shoulder and then returned his eyes to Lillian. "*Ma'am, I know this package is for you, but it needs to go there first. It has a blessing to receive. It's why I parked over there on this side of the property.*"

"*Go on,*" Lillian permitted. She knew such oddities happened here outside of time, in the *reverie-mirak*. Events played out in encoded ways. It was the job of the participant to play along and observe the things that were revealed to them through mysterious methods.

The mailman bowed and then turned. He made his way up the steps, and set the package inside the house while standing on the porch. He stood up straight and the door closed. He turned with a kick in his step and a smile on his face as he descended the porch stairs. He tipped his cap at Lillian, and she wondered if he could see Ida and Penny. She found it curious that even in the *reverie-mirak* their spirits could go undetected. She continued smiling at the mailman as he got into his car, started the vehicle, and drove away. It faded as it moved onto the road, and the sputtering sound of its engine dissolved a few moments after.

Though sweet to hear, Ida's voice disturbed the stillness. *"We know that father of yours is just a-jumpin' up and down."*

Penny concluded, *"Now that our family has claim here again."*

Ida agreed, nodding her head. *"But them other old men,"* she restarted.

"Them Fable brothers," Penny clarified.

Ida continued speaking as if the sisters were of one voice. *"They sure did know how to put up a fight-back."*

Penny shook her head, agreeing with her sister. *"Them and they wives were some heavy hitters."* Her eyes looked off into the distance. Over the horizon was a memory, and she could see Jackson and Gaston Fable, along with their wives, making war and progress against men and women of hex, needle, and burning cross.

Ida spoke in place of her sister, finishing their shared sentiment. *"Them Fable brothers lost a few wars, but they didn't hesitate to pull a trigger—"*

Coming out of her reminiscence, Penny stated, *"Or an incant to take away the air."* Penny chuckled. *"Their wives could be so vicious."* She took a sip of her drink, swallowed, and then looked at her sister. *"We didn't even mind when they was blasphemin',"* she started.

"Callin' our incants and conjures 'tricks' and what not!" Ida concluded.

Penny's eyes clouded with sadness. She stated, *"So much language was lost when we was crossed over here in chains."*

"So much found," Ida countered. *"Ojulowo Atijo Oluwa! But we've come together in these days,"* Ida declared.

"And that's not why we're here right now," Penny stated.

Ida revealed, *"This place was blessed by the Fable brothers and their wives."*

Perplexity coiled Lillian's face, and she questioned, *"Blessed?"*

"With war," the sisters answered simultaneously. *"War is not always a curse,"* Penny informed. Ida expounded on her sister's point, *"It can be a cleansing."* Both nodded their heads. Penny expressed to Lillian, *"You will carry that torch."* The two sisters smiled, and Ida was next to speak. She asked, *"Why else would your delivery be a 'Soldier Great Warrior'?"* Penny and Ida bubbled up a chorus of laughter. Lillian joined in. Together the sister's spoke, *"Bloom, Voodoo Lily! Bloom!"* They raised their glasses and drank to her. Lillian Eledas-Ghedemere, the new crossroads guardian and queen.

Lillian opened her eyes. The mask still covered her, but its material appeared gossamer. Thin enough to peer through. She saw the ghostly silhouette of her mother's shape reaching down toward her. It was as if she was gazing through a curtain's delicate fabric. The mask lifted off her face, and the world was revealed to her eyes. Her mother and father smiled down at her, and her body floated up to them, became upright, and propped her up on her feet. She stretched her arms, and Simaetha placed her hands on her daughter's shoulder and back to keep her balanced.

"I'm fine, Mamma," Lillian insisted.

Simaetha returned a proud smile to her daughter. Maman Anansi's glimmering presence said, "A few more times through the gambit of ritual, Miss Lillian, and this will be all yours." Her hand was outstretched, holding the levitating African mask in place. Lady Arachne took the mask from Maman Anansi's magical grip and tucked it under her arm.

"Thank you, again, Maman Anansi, for overseeing this," Simaetha expressed.

"My duty is my pleasure, Miss Simaetha. We'll meet in person soon enough. For now, I bid you all well. I'll return at midnight for the ritual's second part." Everyone said their goodbyes to Maman Anansi, and then Fable Avenue's first matriarch faded from the scene.

"I spoke with Ida and Penny!" Lillian shared. "I saw their spirits!" She handed the rooster feathers and bottle of soil to her mother and father. "Or something of that nature," she added. She did find herself off balance when she took a step. Her mother and Madame Jeliya had to assist her in the group's return to Jackson Fable's house.

Despite her unsteady gait, Lillian was lively. Simaetha instructed her daughter as they made their progress off the road, "Easy, now, Lillian. We'll get you to Lady Arachne's house, and believe it or not, a good shot of some drink will do you good. Wine, perhaps." Lillian chuckled at her mother's suggestion, losing her footing as she laughed. Madame Jeliya and Simaetha caught her. Satchel "Old Goon" hurried to his daughter's side. Simaetha gave him an eye, and he backed away with a nod. "Our daughter's fine, Satchel," she assured. "She's going through her process. The womenfolk have it from here."

Satchel "Old Goon" nodded again, hands up and yielding. Papa Solomon walked up beside him with Reverend Pouvwa. Papa Solomon looked at the two men and commented, "A good drink will do us all some good." He asked the reverend directly, "How you comin' with all this?"

Mathieu's expression curled into contemplation. He answered in a stern, honest tone, "I'm amazed at how much it's all growing on me, becoming less strange. It's like questions I never knew I had are suddenly presented with answers. Things make sense."

Satchel "Old Goon" grinned. "Well, I like hearing that." Both he and Papa Solomon slapped the reverend on the back, knocking him forward a bit. His thin, round-lensed glasses loosened from his face, hanging by a desperate piece of itself at the end of his nose. Mathieu chuckled at the old men's gesture while straightening his glasses. "You got any Christian rules against drinking?" Satchel "Old Goon" asked him.

"No, sir," Mathieu answered him. "I'm sure a good gulp is what I could use now."

Satchel "Old Goon" paraphrased his earlier comment, "What I like to hear."

They traveled through Jackson Fable's house, which was now starting to fade and reshape its interior to the preference of its new tenant, Lillian Eledas-Ghedemere. The conjure party separated by gender. The men convened at Papa Solomon and Madame Jeliya's residence. The women journeyed to Lady Arachne's brownstone where they assembled in her master bedroom. A bottle was already set for the evening. Finger food prepared by both she and Madame Jeliya accompanied the drinks. It was Simaetha that poured the wine, filling a glass for her daughter first and handing it to her. Lillian thanked her mother and took a sip. There was an oddity about having a glass of wine straighten and balance reality. Lillian remarked that the sensation was outré, but she was grateful to have the spin in her vision settled.

No one took offense when Lillian exposed only little of her journey to the *mirak*. There were private moments she wanted to think deeply about while bathing in the spiritual bath Madame Jeliya and Lady Arachne prepared for her. She did acknowledge surprise not in the presence of Ida and Penny, but in their voices. "Their accents were sweet and Southern," Lillian revealed. "I was surprised they weren't more African in sound."

Simaetha explained it to her daughter as the evolution of spirits, how they grow. "They shift according to who, or what, they are bound to," she elucidated.

Lillian whisked away to her pre-drawn bath. The water was mixed with a variety of materials. There were magical oils and herbs, blessed perfumes, and even a cap of liquor from a drink brewed in Brazil named *Gira's Dance*. The more expensive bottles were ported to Africa where the women of secret conjure societies made blessings over the drink, adding a stirred ingredient of flavor or two. Those bottles were highly sought, and they were very expensive. A good barter or a lot of cash was the only way a purchase could be made.

Lillian stripped and dipped inside the tub. Her mother, along with Lady Arachne and Madame Jeliya, said a blessing over her. The water felt like a warm blanket, a silky cocoon tightly wrapped around her. She felt all of the water's ingredients. At first, when she exhaled, her body tingled because of them. She was the galaxy. Her heightened, prickling nerves acted as the twinkling stars against her heavenly body. Then calm manifested, and the weight of her ritual transmuted, the added elements blessing the water blended and enhanced the bath's tranquil, warm nature. Lillian was at peace, even as she heard her mother conversing and laughing with the Fable Avenue matriarchs in the bedroom. She didn't drown them out. She listened. Stories were being shared. History was being relived.

Madame Jeliya and Lady Arachne squared off in an intense game of Royal Tarot. Cards were dealt, and then came the fiery stares as the two women aimed eyebrows at one another as if they were thumbing back the hammers on six-shooters. Cards were folded faced down, drawn from the deck, and then mulled over. Turns were forfeited, and rules were in motion, played against one another as if the women sat on opposite sides of a chessboard. Simaetha observed the two matriarchs, seated on Lady Arachne's bed, taking sips of wine and biting into a delicious chocolate treat. She gave no comments, just good observation.

Lady Arachne, however, broke the silence. Her eye outlined Simaetha's figure as she sat on the edge of her bed. It was a quick glance, but that's all the concupiscent matriarch needed. "You look like a well-served meal on that bed, Simaetha. You usin' an incant to keep that shape of yours?"

Simaetha rolled her eyes, taking in a bite of her chocolate delicacy. *"Nigress, please!* All the weight my age has put on me…"

"You wear it well," Lady Arachne complimented.

Madame Jeliya shook her head, eyes opened wide, as was her mouth. She made a noise that evolved into the single, repeated word. "No, no, no, no," she said, eventually lifting a finger and waving it back and forth. She put her eyes on Simaetha. "Don't you be sweet talked by this silk-tongued lecher. She's only tryin' to cause a distraction." Her eye went to Lady Arachne and she leaned forward, "I know how this one works when playing cards."

Lady Arachne put her hands to her chest. She dipped back in her chair. "Now, Thelema, are you trying to eye my cards?"

"I would think of no such deception," Madame Jeliya scoffed back in a playful tone. She mimed a glance at the cards tipped to Lady Arachne's chest. "Whatchu got there?" she asked. The two women chuckled. Simaetha grinned at the women and drank. When the chuckles sputtered away, and the women caught their breath, Madame Jeliya declared while looking at Simaetha, "'Nuther reason you pay her compliments no mind. Her needle is aimed at men for the moment." She turned her gaze toward Lady Arachne and commented, "You know you lookin' to devour that young man over across the street. You can't wait to turn that righteous reverend into a sinner. My husband and Satchel initiating him with story, but you, *Miss Pomba Gira,* you got other plans and ways to bring him into the conjure fold."

Lady Arachne's dark cheeks flushed with a billowing cloud of maroon against them. Madame Jeliya jumped at the gesture. Her mouth and eyes hung open, swallowing the sight of her sister-in-conjure and fellow matriarch, whose face was reddened in a self-conscious manner. Lady Arachne fixed her face, but Madame Jeliya wouldn't let the moment pass. She blurted, "I saw that!"

"What?" Lady Arachne questioned, returning to her natural demeanor.

Simaetha's eyes moved back and forth between the matriarchs.

"You know what I just saw!" Madame Jeliya gushed. She put her cards down, faces up. Her hand was insignificant with no semblance of a proper build to a win. She didn't care. "Well, I'll be hexed!" she declared. "Miss Lena Franklin, I just saw you blush?"

Lady Arachne answered by laying her cards over Madame Jeliya's. Her hand was a decimating win. She raised her eyebrow and replied, "Not even the first man that disrobed in front of me, and took me to his bed, could make my dark cheeks flush red." She sat back in her chair and concluded, "And that conjure man was well, well, *well*-endowed to do so."

Simaetha lifted her glass and hollered, "*Sander King!* Hex. Be. *Damned!*" She took another sip. After swallowing she revealed, "I tell you! Lena you've talked about that conjure nigga so much I feel like he took me to bed, too."

The women burst with laughter. Madame Jeliya pushed the played cards away from her. Through her laughter she remarked, "Shuffle them cards, Lena. Let's see if you can't beat me again." Lady Arachne took to Madame Jeliya's suggestion, gathering the cards and reordering them with a quick, sly rearrangement with her manipulative fingers. As she did so, Madame Jeliya commented while pointing, "And you were caught blushing."

"Perhaps," the third matriarch replied without missing an arrangement on the twists, turns, and flaps of her shuffling. "But it just might not be for the reason you believe. Definitely not that boy across the street." She cut the deck, restacked it, but left it on the table without dealing. Both she and Madame Jeliya took up their glasses and sipped their wine. Lady Arachne cocked a grin and eye at Simaetha and told her, "Seeing you sure does bring back some things. Those late seventies, early eighties years and so," she clarified. "Were you brought into the Asase Ya Afua covenant through Sister Rouge?"

Simaetha chewed and swallowed the last of her chocolate delight before answering, "Not the way you were. I had her as a mentor. You...*had* her *and* her man, Rime Luc."

Lady Arachne beamed a smile inspired by the accusation's truth. She asked Madame Jeliya, "Did you ever meet Sister Rouge?"

"Yes…" Madame Jeliya responded with unease in her voice. "But, she was standoffish to people outside the Asase Ya school. I got the feeling she thought I blocked Fable Avenue from having a trinity of *weebu* sisters."

"That does sound her way," Lady Arachne affirmed. She rested her glass down and sat back in her chair. Memories sprang up behind her eyes and summoned a smile on her face. "Sister Rose 'Rouge' Ambrose, called Maman Goolu Eruku—*gold dust*. She was born in Rochester but raised in the Boston conjure community. Maman Goolu brought me into more than just the cosmic web. Yes, she did!" Lady Arachne shouted as a praise while nodding her head. "She brought me into the art of erotic *ifẹ*—the control of it." Then she chanted, "*Imọ-Akọ-Tabi-Abo!*" She tilted her head back and hollered to the ceiling, "Yes!" Looking back and forth between Madame Jeliya and Simaetha, Lady Arachne described her *weebu*-initiator. "Maman Goolu's Afro was out to here, I tell you. That wild hair was a child of the sun—blazing, light-brown waves of electricity. She had that height to her, that thickness! And Lord Ixu, she was brushed to perfection with honey-brown skin. She and her man were both in their mid-forties. Rime might've been closer to fifty. Lord knows that man was stuck in the fifties, with his manner of dress and all. He had that cool vibe. He looked like he belonged on Fable Avenue, born out of jazz, y'know."

"That was one thing I did like about her," Madame Jeliya chimed in, making her words focus on the talked up Maman Goolu. "She felt the conjure community should have nothing to do with the outside world, and she cared nothing much for destinies and duties. I admired that, even if I didn't believe in it. I felt it was too easy, too much of a cop-out. I apologize, Lena."

"Oh, no!" Lady Arachne waved her hand. "I agree with you. She and I didn't see eye-to-eye on that issue. I mean she used her incants to toy with everyday affairs. She enjoyed the subtle fight. The ritual and incants that brought judgment against the open and seen world, especially white folk. That's what attracted her to Rime Luc."

The man whose name was attached to the modern legend of Maman Goolu, Rime Luc, was also called Penny Man or simply Luc. His conjure consisted of dropping pennies infused with luck. Whoever discovered them and picked them up would have luck for a day. He himself was also blessed with luck, which was why Maman Goolu kept him around as a lover.

Lady Arachne elucidated, "With Luc, his conjure could stop any bad bounce back from happening to Maman Goolu when she judged and hexed people at random with her rituals."

"Luc sure did have a dangerous conjure," Simaetha commented.

Lady Arachne concurred, "Yes, indeed. He put himself in danger every time he placed down a penny."

"What? How?" inquired Madame Jeliya, completely attentive for the answer.

"You don't know?"

Madame Jeliya reminded, "Lena, I told you that woman often gave me the cold shoulder. All I know are names—and barely those when it comes to anyone connected to her."

Lady Arachne revealed, "Anyone who picked up a luck-infused penny could take Rime's power if aware of the ritual to do so."

"And what was that?"

"What it was is what eventually got that man killed," Lady Arachne recounted. "Now, I don't know the specifics of the ritual itself, but his older brother Simon did."

Madame Jeliya bounced a bit in her chair. "Well, damn…" she said.

"Yes, ma'am," Lady Arachne stated. "Sometimes it all comes down to family." She took another sip before taking up the end of Rime Luc's story. "Simon took his brother's luck, and then he shot him dead."

"Well that's sad," Madame Jeliya responded, sympathy in her tone.

Lady Arachne finished her wine. She started feeling the effects, and only craved more. So, more is what she poured in her glass. "Wasn't worth it either," she voiced. "The luck worked for Simon for about a month or so." She lifted her glass and aimed it at both women. "There were rules to having luck: you get luck by giving luck; and Simon was a miser with his good light. He wasn't givin' out no pennies, so his luck was on borrowed time. And that was time enough for Maman Goolu to track him down, carefully concealed under a blessing, and she killed him. Hexed him good." Then the Tarot-seer sat back and sighed. Another sip was taken before she concluded, "With Rime's luck no longer protecting her, she died shortly after. That was in eighty-five, eighty-six or so."

It was silent for a moment. Madame Jeliya observed Lady Arachne, watching the matriarch drink, swallow, and think. Her voice pierced the quiet when she asked, "Lena, why the walk down this memory?" She was cautious not to be too loud, perhaps offensive with her words or volume.

Lady Arachne returned her glass to the table. She crossed her arms, tucked her body into the chair, but still managed a smile. Her eyes looked around the room, and then she uttered, "I just feel like I'm back in that moment, where things were so new. I've had this feeling ever since Gordon and Fey were blessed by the cosmic spirits. That's the personal thing I liked about destiny and duty. It's not routine. Maman Goolu preferred routine. Far as she was concerned, the bad things of the world can go ahead and happen. She did support the search for ways to bring about the Grand Conjure and Wish, end it all in one fell swoop, but in the end, it wasn't much for her. She liked routine, and it's hard to have routine when dealing with the outside and seen world, regular folk." She looked at Simaetha and remarked, "Your daughter is a new thing in all this. She's the presiding conjure queen of the crossroads. The unlocking of the doors was a new thing. My cards are a new thing—as old as they are. This conjure war, silent and dangerous as it is. It's a new thing, or rather, brought to another level." Then she put her eyes on Madame Jeliya. "That young reverend is a new thing." All three women giggled in a soft manner. "The feminine half of the cosmos, the Gira, she has me open to all the aspects of her that resides in me. She's excited, and not just to eat up that young reverend. She's dancing in me for all the new things. We will have the children of Fable Avenue returned to us. We will begin a new thing when they are returned. We will have our old world back. We will have our three moons. I believe so. It will be a new, ancient thing," she described in a clever manner.

"And you'll celebrate by making Reverend Pouvwa a new thing in all this," Simaetha teased before drawing her glass back to her lips for a final gulp.

Lady Arachne asked her, "Would you like to share him, Simaetha? He could entertain the both of us, I'm sure. That new thing could conjure up happenings between us." She grinned and lifted both eyebrows in a quick manner as she declared, "Old times in new things, yes, sister-in-web?"

"You are too bad, Miss Franklin!" Simaetha chuckled. "I could go for a cigar right now."

Lady Arachne continued teasing when she announced, "I'm sure you could go for something brown and thick between your lips. I know how that feels." She turned away from the conversation and grabbed a box of imported cigars. She presented the box to Simaetha and opened it. Her sister-in-web spoke a soft incant and lifted one of the cigars out of the box and into her free hand. "You need a refill on that wine?" Lady Arachne inquired.

Simaetha was glad she asked. "Yes, please," she answered, tilting her wine glass in Lady Arachne's direction.

The seer placed her box of cigars down on the table. She kept the lid lifted and asked Madame Jeliya if she desired one. Madame Jeliya declined. Lady Arachne snapped the lid shut. She lifted the bottle of wine and tipped it in Simaetha's direction. Again, Lady Arachne's fellow *weebu* sister uttered an incant, and the fermented contents of the bottle drifted up through the narrow neck, across the room, and filled her glass. Not a drop was spilled in the transfer.

Simaetha wasn't finished showing off. She kissed the tip of her cigar and lit it.

Not to be outdone, Lady Arachne licked around the tip with the same results.

Madame Jeliya rolled her eyes at the both of them.

"Are we gonna play another round of cards?" she asked.

Lady Arachne smoked her cigar, blowing its excess up toward the ceiling. "Yes, my sister-matriarch. Yes, we will," she assured. She stood and continued smoking. "But first," she said between puffs, walking toward the bathroom door. "How you doin' in here, Miss Voodoo Lily? You having a time listening to us old women talk all X-rated?"

Lillian soaked it all in from the water to the voices, eyes closed. "I can barely hear you old birds chirping in that room," she proclaimed in a teasing voice. "I. Am. *Completely* surrounded by blackness and calm."

Lady Arachne turned toward Simaetha and informed, "You know your daughter was swarmed last year when she came to visit? All the boys were lined up to hold a conversation with her. One in particular by the name of Cliff Johnson," Lady Arachne specified. "Now, if that name sounds familiar, he's one of the best damn Tarot players in the *global* conjure community. He from over that Connecticut way," she described.

"He was handsome," admitted Lillian. "But he was weird. His mind worked in puzzles. He couldn't keep his words straight, speaking in riddles like a comic book villain. It was like he was always testing you with a brainteaser, I felt uneasy, like he was working incants while holding a conversation."

Lady Arachne took puffs from her cigar, blowing the smoke into the bedroom so as not to disturb Lillian's bath. "Riddles or not, you did keep that boy close."

"I found him interesting, yes," she confessed with a guilty smile on her face, eyes still closed to the world.

"I'm just saying all this to build a proposition," Lady Arachne declared. She turned to face Simaetha to say, "If it doesn't overstep any bounds with your mother." Then she turned back to Lillian and proposed, "Since you closer to that reverend's age than I am, I'll let you slide in. Just stake the claim, Miss Voodoo Lily, and he's yours."

"Lena!" hollered Simaetha. "That boy is at least ten years older than my daughter, well into his thirties. I'm sure halfway to forty. I'd bet my conjure on it."

Lady Arachne raised an eyebrow and replied, "That's still closer in age than me." Then she reminded Simaetha, "If I'm overstepping any bounds, Simaetha, please."

Before Simaetha could answer, Lillian declined. "I didn't get much of a feeling from him when we met. He's cute though," she acknowledged. "I'm looking for more of a warrior. Your reverend is clearly of the house of Dii Mauri. I'm looking for a Ka Mauri boy—a warrior," she said as if growling. "A soldier at *my* command," she divulged further.

Lady Arachne hollered and clapped. "Someone's Gira seems to be waking up!" she commented. "Did you see something during your ritual, eyes all blocked from the world?"

Lillian couldn't help but smile. "Perhaps…"

Lady Arachne bowed her head in respect. "I'll leave you to that," she told Lillian.

"In all, Auntie Arachne," Lillian took up, "I'm focused more on fulfilling my duties as Crossroads Queen. I'm here to lead our people who've lost the knowledge of their conjure, and are wracked with burden, down a better path And I'll need a *warrior*-herald for that."

Lady Arachne liked what she heard, and so did Lillian's mother. Lady Arachne then turned back to face Simaetha. "The offer still stands. I won't part completely with that young reverend, but I will share. Or, are your legs all wrapped about that old, goonish fool exclusively?" Over her shoulder she relayed to Lillian, "No offense when it comes to your father." Back to Simaetha she concluded, "Do you want to join me in sharing this young man? Together or separate. I don't mind. Separate, I get first bite of him."

Simaetha's gasp broke into a chuckle. "You. Are. Insatiable, Lena," she expressed.

Lady Arachne bounced off the door and stepped toward her, cigar held tight in her fingertips. She bent down, face-to-face with her sister-in-web. "With all our adventures together, I shouldn't have to tell you. This old woman loves repeating the old adage: There is nothing like a new man coming into a recognition of his conjure and masculine Ixu." She stood straight and puffed her cigar. "And I got every intention of guiding his Ixu spirit down my Gira's path—all the way down into my bush."

Both Simaetha and Madame Jeliya burst with wide-eyed and opened-mouth expressions. Lillian volleyed up a guffaw from the tub, though her eyes remained closed. Simaetha explained aloud, "You. Are. Too. Much!"

Lady Arachne waved her hand and rolled her eyes. She said while pointing with her cigar, "Please! There is a new fetish just 'cross the street. Yes, there is." She then fixed her composure, blooming into a mock stance of a refined lady. Her eyelashes fluttered in an exaggerated manner, and she placed a hand over her chest. "Yes, I like him," she revealed the obvious. To Madame Jeliya she stated, "And no, that young man ain't have me blushin'. Save the cheek flush for later," she cooed.

Madame Jeliya raised a single eyebrow and quipped, "Well, then. Can I drop the *aabo* I got conjured around my husband?"

Lady Arachne hiccupped on potential laughter. Her bodily reflex rolled it into a cough that then managed to morph it back into a laugh. She raised her face to the sky and hollered. Her demeanor calmed, and she placed her cigar in her mouth, curious eye on Madame Jeliya. She sucked on her cigar, lips tight around the smoke. She puffed, and then she blew out a thick stream. "Well, ain't we all full of surprises today," she commented. "Thelema. Sihiri. Heathwicke. Peters," she said the second matriarch's full name. "I never thought I'd see the day when our lighthearted conflict would leave your lips as a joke." She stepped over to Madame Jeliya, and as she did with Simaetha before her, she bent down. Her face close to Madame Jeliya's. "Are you trying to make up—or make out—with me?" She moved closer and cocked her head to the right. "Be careful, Miss Story Time," she warned in a playful, seductive tone. A sensual grin slithered on her face. "I've had more fantasies about you and I than I have your husband. I been with that nigger before. I know what I'm missing with him, but you are a land yet be explored." Her lips parted, a chuckle escaped, sounding more like the low cackle from a witch. Madame Jeliya tilted her head away from Lady Arachne's advance. The Tarot reader revealed, "As of recent, my fantasies been about putting those lions of yours into submission. That's what has me blushing." Lady Arachne rose, standing tall and looking down at her fellow matriarch.

Madame Jeliya surprised her again when she answered, "I'm sure."

Lady Arachne made a face. "Oh, well, if you're so sure, sister, let's put it to a game." Her eyes went to the cards. Madame Jeliya's too. Lady Arachne, cigar between her fingers, caressed the top of the Tarot deck. "I win, I get to taste the power of your lions off your lips." Her eyes drifted back to Madame Jeliya. Then she finished the terms of the prize and purse of the win. "And when I do, I want to see them submit. If you win, Thelema…"

Madame Jeliya interrupted, saying, "You get my husband for a night?"

Lady Arachne kept her grin. "Under those terms, sister, it seems I win either way." The challenging tone in her words brought back the women's more scathing feelings toward one another. But then Lady Arachne made a comment that took Madame Jeliya off guard, and it changed both women's demeanor, if only slight. "No, he's done enough damage to me." To Lady Arachne, her words were ephemeral. She kept her sly grin and teasing laughter, but the skip, skip, skip of her heart's new beat, and heaviness that proceeded after she'd spoken, was lasting.

Simaetha's instincts picked up on the effects of Lady Arachne's words, even seeing physical evidence on Madame Jeliya herself. The Fable Avenue matriarch's eyes shifted, becoming full with sorrow. It was all in an instant. Madame Jeliya made a quick glance, surveying up and down the entirety of Lady Arachne's physical frame, but looking beyond the corporeal and wondering what pain Lady Arachne tried desperately to cover. She too worried about her husband, his actions, and whether she knew him as a whole.

The sound of water splashing echoed from the bathroom as Lillian adjusted herself in the bath. The swish of flopping water broke the moment's unease. Lady Arachne followed the noise's cue by saying, "I'll tell everything about my intentions toward your husband—my true intentions. It's never been what you think sister."

This too stunned Madame Jeliya. Simaetha remained drinking and smoking on the bed, keeping her instinct and eyes cemented on the two matriarchs. Madame Jeliya slipped out of her startled expression, replacing it with a sly grin. "Well, sister," she said with a teasing tone, "deal those cards." Then she warned, "And you play with your heart and skill. I want to best you honestly for my reward."

Lady Arachne slid into her seat like a snake curling into comfort and rest. After a puff from her cigar she set it into the groove of a wood-carved ashtray and commented, "I will put all the forces of nature into my game. I so do want to taste the potency of your kittens." She turned to Simaetha and directed, "Simaetha, would you do the honor of dealing the cards?"

Simaetha rose while taking a large swallow of her wine. She attempted to shake off the murkiness in her head as the alcohol set in. Stepping up to the table, she placed her wine glass down and lifted the deck.

Lady Arachne had one more thing to say before the playing started. "We do this, play this game, Miss Thelema—*I* do this—to make peace. And we need peace."

"Yes, indeed, Lena," Madame Jeliya agreed. "Fable Avenue has war on its hands. Being at each other's throats does us no good." Then she cleared her throat and added, "Now let me beat yo' behind in this game here." The women chuckled. Lady Arachne retorted for Madame Jeliya to do her best.

The cards were dealt, and the game began.

The men held counsel of their own across the street at the Peters' residence. Papa Solomon, Satchel "Old Goon", and Reverend Mathieu Pouvwa convened their small assembly in the kitchen. They shared a bottle of Madagascar rum called *Sweet Broth*, poured in separated glasses. Each man was nursing a second glass. Reverend Pouvwa listened to the conjure Elders with both ears wide-open, attentive and respectful. Satchel "Old Goon" monopolized the conversation, and Papa Solomon didn't mind.

"You in good hands with these folks," Satchel "Old Goon" remarked after clearing his throat. He knocked back a little more of his drink. "I got my criticisms of this huddle called Fable Avenue, but it's got some damn-fine-good people in it." Another swig was in order. Then Satchel "Old Goon" asked the reverend, "You know what makes Fable Avenue so special?" As it was rhetorical, Satchel "Old Goon" didn't expect an answer. The reverend, however, shook his head 'no' as a courtesy cue. Satchel "Old Goon" answered, "This whole street was built entirely outside of time. A brother by the name of James Weeks built around the Bedford-Stuyvesant area in the early eighteen-hundreds. His spirit built Fable Avenue with the help of a man named Madison Goodspeed. That was 'round the nineteen-twenties." Reverend Pouvwa nodded his head at the information, taking it all in. "The crossroads are special. That one in Mississippi ain't the only one. There's one in Tennessee. They all over this United States. The Moors created a few in Europe. African crossroads have been lost to time, sand and jungle. War, most of all," Satchel "Old Goon" expounded. "But all the ancient landmarks, pyramids and temples and such, they all been able to channel outside time and commune with that other world." He tapped his finger on the table. "But Fable Avenue is *from* the other world. It was built there, and conjure magic brought it here." He took a swig of his rum. "So, you in good hands with the folk 'round here, 'specially that Lady Arachne." Satchel "Old Goon" chuckled. "I know that look she gives you. She gon' have you spun up in her sweet, sticky web soon enough."

Reverend Pouvwa paid little attention to the comment, though he had to admit to himself the strong allure Lady Arachne held. He did assert, "Lady Arachne is very helpful. I'm grateful for her. I was very scared at what I'd come across—what I was able to do."

"She gunna open up his Ixu," Satchel "Old Goon" noted, lifting his glass and giving Papa Solomon a sly grin.

Reverend Pouvwa made a face, reacting to the word used by Satchel "Old Goon". *Ixu.* He wanted to inquire but decided he would take his inquiry to Lady Arachne. After all, Satchel "Old Goon" indicated she would be the one to open the attribute in him.

So much of what Reverend Pouvwa experienced and discerned from conversation existed as both familiar and foreign within the same time and space. *Heavy*, Reverend Pouvwa considered to himself. He joined the two Elders in taking a swig of rum. A contemplative silence fell over the three men as if they'd all fixated on the reverend's impression. Mathieu chuckled. He rubbed his collar and stated, "Perhaps I made a mistake in what I studied. I wear the wrong collar."

"No, no, no," Papa Solomon disagreed, shaking his head as he repeated the single word. "You might've spoken something within the Christian Bible that opened up your power. That's what this conjure community has the faculty to accomplish. We can decipher the magic of all spiritual words, regardless of corruption. Africa is at the forefront. It is the foundation, and all words spiral back to it. Those who do rootwork, hoodoo folk, they use The Bible as their guide, particular verses. We got some strong rootworkers in our conjure community." He listed, "Healers, ritual makers, apothecaries."

Satchel "Old Goon" insisted, "You got to stop listening to white folk. Stop gettin' yo religious talk from them. This is Old World magic. Ain't nuthin' stronger."

The reverend retorted, "People call it 'black magic'."

Satchel "Old Goon" didn't duck the remark. He instead embraced it. "Sho' is black magic!" he exclaimed. "That's what I tell them folk-who-all-scared. This is *black* magic because my black hand performs it. Damn straight!" All three men knocked back their drinks. No one reached for a follow-up glass. They let the alcohol settle in. It buzzed their brains and relaxed personal tensions. Satchel "Old Goon" resumed the talk. He put a curious eye on the reverend and said, "I got instinct in me that recognizes a little reserve in you, though, Reverend—not about Fable Avenue taking care of you, but your all in all this here." He observed the reverend, eyes looking to peer deep into the former detective. "Or, all of it in general. There's doubt in you. This is still the Devil's work to you."

Papa Solomon groaned. His face twisted. "C'mon, Satchel," he said adjusting himself in his seat. "The man's just witnessed some things."

Satchel "Old Goon" didn't move his gaze away from Reverend Pouvwa, though he directed his words at Papa Solomon. He shook his hand and said, "No, no, no, Vencil. I'm lifting the curtain because this concerns other matters. I have to know the reverend is centered." His fixed stare on Mathieu softened, and he looked away, putting his eyes on Papa Solomon. "I have to speak freely. I have to speak now on matters. This man gon' hear some things—how I intend to solve problems in his neck of the woods." Eyes back on Reverend Pouvwa, Satchel "Old Goon" resolved his words. "Water Bug Hollow is in need of a serious cleansing, and not every cleansing is handled with prayer, some candles or other burnings, and a bowl of fruit laid out for an aspect-spirit to receive." He leaned back in his chair and made it known, "You're a cop."

"*Former* detective," the reverend highlighted with a subtle bass put into his voice.

Satchel "Old Goon" was aware of Reverend Pouvwa's aggressive undertone. "Thing I'm trying to put on the table is that—"

"—People are going to die and you're wondering would I report the activity."

Papa Solomon grinned. Satchel "Old Goon" shared the same facial expression. He didn't hesitate or show any signs of offense that Reverend Pouvwa, a man many years his younger, interrupted his words. Instead, he parted his grin and hollered a short, guffaw toward the ceiling. He slapped his hand on the table and aimed a finger at the reverend. "Now, that's what I'm talkin' 'bout! That right there. Go 'head on, boy! You got my words rollin' off your tongue." He slapped his hands together. "Watch out, now!" he said.

Reverend Pouvwa presented a boyish smile. He exhaled through his nose, and then he held out his hand, palm up. The lines drawn biologically on his palm filled with light. Strands of bright conjure seeped up and configured into a solid piece of fruit. The reverend set the orange on the table. Both Elders marveled at the sight. Mathieu palmed the top of the orange, and like a chess piece, moved it in front of Satchel "Old Goon".

"I'm on your side, Mister Eledas, sir. I am," the reverend assured in a tone absent of humility but filled with determination.

Satchel "Old Goon" rose up in his chair, reached for the orange, and started peeling the fruit. He sat back, plucked out a wedge beneath the skin and put it in his mouth. The juice was sweet, seasoned by conjure. He chewed and swallowed. He felt revitalized by the conjured fruit. He said to Papa Solomon, "You gon' have them missin' children back. It'll be a quick fight. My instinct don't have a buzz. I don't smell a big war in that direction, but you should make a retaliation after the skirmish. Let them needle-hexin' bastards know: Fable Avenue got muscle. However, Stanley Fallows got something going. B'l'e'e that shit. That boy ain't nuthin' but war." He adjusted himself in his seat. He offered some fruit to Papa Solomon, and the Fable Avenue patriarch politely declined. "Some good fruit, now," Satchel "Old Goon" remarked. Then he went back to the subject of war. "I have my interests in Water Bug Hollow. Forgive me if my focus sounds biased because of it. There are properties out west that conjure folk want to make a move on. I got my eye on those politics but not a hand in them. I want Water Bug Hollow."

"And you're sure the Gwuinee are onboard, making war?" asked Papa Solomon.

Satchel "Old Goon" shoved another wedge of fruit into his mouth. He chewed as he said, "Indeed, brother, if you can believe it. Gwuinee going all *petwo* on us," he remarked with a laugh. He shook his head, swallowed, and then continued. "It was a unanimous decision among their High Elders in favor of this move, my proposal. Being an Eledas helped." He bragged with a smile, "Oldest *nasyon* and *fanmi*."

Then Papa Solomon inquired, "How your people feel on all this?"

Satchel played up offense and barked, *"Please, Vencil!"* Papa Solomon and Reverend Pouvwa chuckled at Satchel's antics. "Eledas family *revel* in taking real estate. Shit! That's how we started our family."

Papa Solomon's laughter cooled to a soft smile. He raised his hands and yielded, "I stand educated."

Satchel "Old Goon" adjusted himself in his chair. "Our intermarriage with the Gwuinee has slowed down our more *petwo frè ak sè*. They've cooled heads. But, now's the time, and I'm here to move you to charge. Two representatives will be on the way to oversee how this is handled." He plucked more wedges from the orange and ate them. "Now, I don't want to cause tensions, which is why I didn't say much 'round that mid-spring gathering down in Georgia. The bigger families want Water Bug Hollow cleaned up and back in our hands," Satchel "Old Goon" said more as an outright command than a matter-of-fact. "The Gwuinee feel you all here on Fable Avenue have the conjure to get that done. You at least have the proximity by way of the crossroads connecting you from here to there."

"So, we do the work, you govern it?" Papa Solomon summarized.

Satchel's eyes slimmed, his lip curled, and he bobbed his head as if ducking a thrown object. Papa Solomon's analysis of his proposal was what he wanted to avoid, but he'd played hearing it in his head enough to have an adequate response, despite the face he'd made. "I ask for help, if that's not too much," he replied in a curt manner. "*I* will lead the charge," he assured. Satchel "Old Goon" took a breath and then confided, "I won't be old for long, Vencil. When my time finally comes, I want a legacy more than just my last name. If something happens to Lillian—God forbid—the Eledas will hold lot on who manages the crossroads, even if she has children. I hold Water Bug Hollow, it's mine. It's my children's. I've already argued my case, working with you to tie it together." He set the orange down and added, "So *if*—on your blessing—I hold Water Bug Hollow, because of the legacy *you* hold there, I answer to Fable Avenue. That strengthens *your* real estate."

Papa Solomon reached for the orange. He paused, looked up at Satchel "Old Goon" and asked, "May I?" Satchel "Old Goon" answered in the affirmative by nodding his head. Papa Solomon took up the fruit and peeled, pulling out a wedge. "So, you want to borrow the Lilac Flame and all his abilities, the Cobalt-Blue flame when we reclaim her spirit. Help you clean up the place?" he postulated.

Satchel "Old Goon" didn't answer. He wished he'd not given up the fruit. Its juices were good and calming. He turned to Reverend Pouvwa and said to him, "Conjure folk lost a war we didn't even know was in progress. Old, red-haired slave mistress planted a hex there."

Reverend Pouvwa stated, "I'm aware. Sarinda Fallows," he named.

"That's right. Hex she planted there manifested over time," Satchel "Old Goon" continued. "Black folk took that land, rebelling against their slave masters, the Jakobis. Them folk became free. Surviving Jakobis used a political hand to build Jakobiville around Water Bug Hollow in the mid-fifties. Something else was moving their hand. Night Doctors, needlemen. Lady Arachne told you 'bout them?"

"Yessir," Reverend Pouvwa answered.

"A sister named Patricia Gale Freda moved into political position to stop Water Bug Hollow from being absorbed into Jakobiville. Law was in her blood. She was a descendant of one of the prominent families of Water Bug

Hollow. She appeared in the early nineties. She lost her political fight, and then she disappeared from public view. Water Bug Hollow been drained of spirit ever since Jakobiville absorbed it. It retains its name, but it's just a ghetto of Jakobiville now."

"Oh, I'm well aware, Mister Eledas," Reverend Pouvwa said. "There are gangs and poverty. No relief," he emphasized. "There's cops, though, policing the whole place. They bring tension, and I admit it has me torn. I like to believe my presence—in *reverend's* clothing—coupled with cop knowledge, helps relieve tension on both sides: the people, the police. It doesn't, really. Now I find out there's a haunt in my church—angry haunts. *Inawo*, Lady Arachne called them. Burdens. Also, police got needles. Not sure why that's a surprise."

Satchel "Old Goon" moved his eyes from Reverend Pouvwa to Papa Solomon. "I can handle Water Bug Hollow," he announced. "I'mo curb them gangs, and we'll be okay. A lot lies in exorcising them haunts. Free that church of burden, we have our first victory. Lena already got that in play."

"We'll see what other work needs doing after that," Papa Solomon decreed. He reached into his pocket and removed a round, black scrying mirror. He set it on the table and tapped it a few times. Four images popped up, flashing one after the other. There were three males and one female. All four persons were white. One male was a judge, middle-aged, framed in a lean build under his black robe, but still carrying a look of authority. The second was outfitted in an expensive gray suit, briefcase in hand, and clearly a lawyer. He was in his late thirties, dark haired, and with an olive glow to his skin. The third man was in his early thirties with shoulder-length, dirty-blonde hair. He sported circular shades, dressed in plain clothes: jeans, sneakers, t-shirt, and black denim jacket. He was in mid motion of placing a cigarette back into his mouth, mouth cocked to the side, opened as if just releasing a stream of smoke. The fourth person was a brunette woman in her early forties. She wore a royal-blue business suit. She carried a large, leather handbag, making her way up the stairs, into an office building.

Papa Solomon tapped when the judge's image reappeared. The image remained fixed in the scrying mirror. Satchel "Old Goon" was impressed. He remarked, "The Lilac Flame and Cobalt-Blue Flame show up and all the old, old, *old* ancient magic-tech pop up again for real use." He chuckled. "We still need deep seers to peer into them thangs."

Papa Solomon straightened and cleared his throat. He addressed Satchel "Old Goon" when he spoke. "The people popping up in this mirror are all a part of the Koningswinter family. All four of them work on the courtroom side of politics and law enforcement." He put down the last of the orange. Satchel "Old Goon" took it, finishing the fruit's final wedges. "Our in-house detective, Martin Kimball, along with a resident soldier named

Wilson Barnes, and my niece Stephanie Dumas, have gathered intel on our fine family of interest." He pointed to the present image cast of the middle-aged judge and said, "This is the Honorable Thomas Regan Koningswinter. He's everything you can imagine when it comes to being a judge. He's tough, and he's good at his job. Some say he uses a sledgehammer instead of a gavel. He's stood up against corrupt judges, mob bosses, and questionable political institutions—in and outside of his political affiliation." He tapped the face of the mirror and the judge's image faded into the next man. "This is Judge Koningswinter's son, Carsten Koningswinter. Lawyer. He's just as good at his job as his father is at his; and he's just as noble. Put that together with Carsten's older sister—" Papa Solomon skipped over the image of the youngest looking man, and brought up the picture of the woman, "Councilwoman Elisabeth Koningswinter. You got a trifecta of justice the likes of which people want to frame as the American judicial system." Papa Solomon rested his words. He tapped back to the youngest, plain-clothes dressed family member. Satchel "Old Goon" expected him to single out the younger Koningswinter, but instead, Papa Solomon followed up by saying, "Their work is airtight. Not a crumb of corruption."

"On the surface," Satchel "Old Goon" said more as a guess to where all of Papa Solomon's talk was going.

"Or beneath it," Papa Solomon added, neutralizing the old man's comment. "And even if that were so, we wouldn't be too interested in their corruption. You see now, the Koningswinters family goes far back in New York's history. It even crisscrosses with our missing Cobalt Flame's family, 'round about the early eighteen-hundreds."

Satchel "Old Goon" understood that Papa Solomon was referring to the young woman named Fey Forrester. It was her maternal side whose relationship with the Koningswinters began with Talbert Koningswinter, a resident of North Tarrytown. He had dealings with slave owners from the South. They used the spirit of the woods to keep people docile, mainly black slaves and indigenous folk. Fey's ancestors were able to free the spirit from bondage. A spirit Gordon Goodspeed was introduced to last October. Supposedly, Washington Irving created the Sleepy Hollow legend after the spirit, calling it *The Headless Horseman*. But the author's imaginative version, and others based from it, was terribly incorrect.

Papa Solomon continued, "Somewhere during that time, the Koningswinter family was inducted into the needlemen order. Not all of them served as soldiers. Some were businessmen, such as Talbert Koningswinter. He never officially made it into a lodge, but members of his extended family did. They existed solely for money and societal position for the needlemen and whomever they served. But a good many of the Koningswinter initiates were alchemists." Papa Solomon tapped into position four smaller versions of the images into view on the black mirror. He pointed to the three Koningswinter photos and stated. "Thomas, Carsten, and Elisabeth are alchemists among the needlemen ranks. They forge and imbue needles with their hexes." Finally, he pointed to the youngest Koningswinter and named him. "This is Michael Koningswinter. He's the judge's nephew from a younger brother who's a needleman soldier. Michael is a liaison. He carries information and tactical maneuvers on strikes against the conjure community. He also delivers packages of hexed syringes." His eyes looked from Satchel "Old Goon" to Reverend Pouvwa, making sure both were paying close attention. "There's a particular soldier in the needlemen ranks that we're concerned with." And then he named, "Wyatt Jakobi." He noticed both men sit back and straighten up. Satchel "Old Goon" took particular interest in the name. There was no other reaction beside this. Papa Solomon addressed Satchel "Old Goon" when he said, "This Wyatt Jakobi fellow is the youngest brother to the Jakobi political dynasty that runs Jakobiville."

The mirror faded the Koningswinter images and then reflected a photo of Wyatt Jakobi. He was in his forties, had an athlete's frame, and no signs of grey in his brown hair. His face was square in shape, and it held an awkward, eerie smile made prominent by an equally disturbing stare. Satchel "Old Goon" and Reverend Pouvwa leaned close to get a look at the photo on the black mirror's face. Reverend Pouvwa believed Wyatt Jakobi seemed like a truly happy man, and maybe, perhaps, a little too happy, in the way of someone in need of being institutionalized. So, it felt suiting to the reverend when he heard Papa Solomon inform, "He works at Howard Phillips Psychiatric Institution down in Hammonton, New Jersey."

"He looks like he should be a patient there," the reverend remarked.

Papa Solomon chuckled, throwing him off reporting more. Satchel "Old Goon" also had a comment. "So after all my mumblings and goings-on, Vencil, our interests *do* overlap. Water Bug Hollow."

The Fable Avenue patriarch nodded. Instead of addressing Satchel "Old Goon" directly, he continued his briefing, informing, "Wyatt Jakobi's placement at the institution is strategic. A lot of the institutionalized people are taken advantage of for occult, experimental purposes. Wyatt leads a team of needlemen to conduct those experiments." Then he let them know, "We believe the children were housed at the facility for a while, but we're certain they've been moved." Papa Solomon nodded toward Wyatt Jakobi's picture. "Wyatt's importance is that he's a go between for his brother Mayor Sampson Jakobi and Stanley Fallows. Our resident detective was able to uncover them good ol' boys out west. Call themselves The Kolonist Kings. They're tied to all this."

"Oh, them good ol' *bastards*," Satchel "Old Goon" interjected. He informed the reverend, "They're a conglomerate of businessmen that connect to a group of folk that call themselves The Line. They trade and bid on occult goods. They evil as hell, too. Them boys like a plague. They are cancer. Their blood connect to slave owners, slave traders, overseers and plantation runners, and they proud of it." He thought and then he figured something out. "That what your phone call to me a few weeks back was for?" he asked Papa Solomon. "You wanted to pry some information about them? I didn't return the call 'cause I knew I'd be here in a couple days. Hardest thing about them bastards is they got strong political and economic power. They also got some strong needles. Conjure folk ain't the only people they hex. They get their way with anyone they deal with. All folk who see the prick of a needle come under their influence, do their bidding," he concluded.

Papa Solomon took the information in. He wished Martin and his niece were present to hear it all. The particulars would be shared with them eventually. Papa Solomon was just feeling impatient. "It all comes together like this," he finally spoke. "While Stanley and Sampson play nice with one another, both are vying for control of The Kolonist Kings. Stanley has a bit of a one-up on Sampson in that regards because it was Stanley's mother, Sarinda Fallows, who helped the Jakobis regain their power in the mid-forties, though they didn't show themselves until the fifties. Lena did a reading on it all. Her cards spoke as if it was all done like a selling of the soul, if you will. Perhaps Sarinda gave them access to control the hex. Gave them rituals to perform. Stanley solidified their political powerbase while residing here on Fable Avenue. That was the late eighties to mid-nineties—and under our noses. So, any Jakobi accomplishments are attributed to Stanley's assistance, and The Kolonist Kings take note of that. Stanley also has great lineage through his mother. His biggest setback for a place among The Kolonist Kings is us. Sampson's been bogged down in a scandal concerning his son and the murder of a woman and her child, but the mayor's used his political power to get his son acquitted."

Reverend Pouvwa listened close. The territory his life had come to should've seemed new and strange, but he reveled in the familiarity he couldn't ignore. It wasn't a sense of déjà vu. It was as if the lights had come on in a pitch-black room he'd gotten to know by way of his hands feeling in the dark. The blanks in the definition of things he'd witnessed and done, passed off as unexplainable, were now filled in. Sense was made. His thoughts muffled as Papa Solomon and the Old Goon's voices articulated plots and gambits, ordering hits on the Koningswinters and their alchemical supply lines, but not before kidnapping Wyatt Jakobi for interrogation and finding missing children.

Reverend Pouvwa said a silent prayer.

14

The hour was eleven. Night was bright with stars and moon on Fable Avenue, even with the loud, man-made brilliance of the city fighting for supremacy. The stars had more presence at the crossroads, dancing lively against the calm and black wonder of the cosmos. Lillian and Simaetha were no longer in Lady Arachne's brownstone. They'd left for the crossroads to set up the second part of Lillian's initiation rites.

Madame Jeliya and Lady Arachne stayed behind, waiting for the midnight hour to make their journey to the crossroads for the next integrant to Lillian's initiation ritual. The two community matriarchs sat on the floor, shoulders huddled up against the foot of Lady Arachne's bed. Their legs were angled under them, no shoes on their feet. They shared laughter and a head full of spiced and incanted wine. Madame Jeliya reveled in her card victory. Three hands in a row. She was nervous when Lady Arachne pulled together a flawless win for the first game, but she used her head and natural instinct to take the next three. Lady Arachne's frustration was genuine. She'd overthought her hands, faltered at the gain of reward for victory, and ultimately staggered in the face of frustration with each successive loss. Madame Jeliya's win was genuine, and her teasing was aggravating, though the alcohol in Lady Arachne's system let her laugh along with the jibes. The last winning hand remained face up on the table.

Madame Jeliya insisted it be so.

Lady Arachne used an incant to sober her mind. The drink wasn't entirely washed away. She allowed the alcoholic waves in her head to settle enough to keep her words and vision straight. "Vencil was a good man," she stated. Her voice was light with the air of remembrance in her tone and in the gaze in her eyes. Her words simmered Madame Jeliya's laughter, as effective as an incant. The matriarch leaned close to listen. She too whispered an incant that cleared her head. "Your husband *is* a good man," Lady Arachne corrected herself. "He's strong. He has to be. He's the sole patriarch of this community. Rare in all of Fable Avenue's years," she commented, shifting her body against the bed. She smiled and noted through light laughter, "But he had his early years. Naïve," she listed first. "Irresponsible with this *konjure* of ours," she noted second. "He was in his early twenties. He wanted a wife, and so he performed a ritual that would bring love to him, brighten his aura like a male peacock's feathers. Enter me into this community, and I was smitten. He was a tall and sturdy, black mahogany tree." Her eyes closed. Her lips remained curled in a smile, and she shook her head remembering. She opened her eyes and continued, "There was a greater strength to his physical presence, tempered by the incant that crowned him. I couldn't help but step to him," she admitted in an uncommon, shy voice. She took a breath before saying to Madame Jeliya directly, "We had a good time."

Madame Jeliya made a preemptive strike. Her voice was playful, but there was a serious undertone when she spoke her words. "And then I showed up."

Lady Arachne nodded, but Madame Jeliya's presence in the story wasn't the problem, and she let her know that. Her voice remained light and reflective when she replied, "You and Vencil were meant to be together, Thelema. My instinct knew it. I saw his eyes. More so, I saw something I never saw in him. I saw his Ixu; and it was staring at your Gira. I wasn't hurt. My relationship with Vencil was always whimsical. I never saw myself with him for a long term, and even with him there were other men. That's just who I am. He knew, and he respected my *Oshun d'Hathor*." Her words rolled into a sigh. She stared at the rug for a moment, and Madame Jeliya stared at her. Lady Arachne lifted her head. Her eyes looked to the right, away from Madame Jeliya as she stated, "I guess I should be furious at your sister-in-law too. She helped Vencil."

"Helped him do what?"

Lady Arachne moved her eyes to meet Madame Jeliya's. She removed the alcohol's effect entirely from her head. "She did warn him," she explained in a manner that only came off as vague to Madame Jeliya. "She told him not to go through with the ritual. It was dangerous. Things could happen. But he was young, impatient. Vencil was already stepping into the role of a community leader—and you know our culture. We're not like regular folk. We hold the ability to peer at a person and see the other half of creation in them, to behold them, and taste the beginning of time off their lips. He wanted a good conjure woman at his side. A bit selfish, but understood," she added. "We not like regular folk, but we feel like regular folk."

"We feel more so," Madame Jeliya amended Lady Arachne's statement. "We understand emotions. It can devastate us more."

"I guess that's the problem," Lady Arachne conceded. "Vencil went ahead with it, the ritual. Then came the complication: you and I. He could've come to me. I would've assisted. Instead, he and Maman Anansi cleansed Vencil of his strong aura. The reversal of the ritual didn't come without ol' Carolyn-Theresa gettin' into her brother's *bee-hind*." Both women chuckled knowingly. The laughter subsided, and Lady Arachne said, "It was done, and then came the repercussions. I was still connected to that aura. My Gira was intertwined in its brightness. With it dissipated, a happening occurred to my inner spirit."

"Oh, Lena!" blurted Madame Jeliya.

Lady Arachne made a face. She shook her head and declared, "I don't want to say I was scarred or twisted. Cracked, maybe. Perhaps fragmented a bit. A piece of me was taken with it, that's true. I wasn't too changed. I've always been a very—" she chose her words carefully when she stated, "—*free*' kind of woman. I liked being with Vencil as an anchor, but it was so routine. With this splinter, however, my Gira spirit became restless. Sometimes I'm up all night. I prowl Fable Avenue, taking a walk on a nice summer night. It's four in the morning." She then assured her fellow matriarch, "There's a tired period. Not long, but it's there. I sleep. It's calm. Black. Very peaceful. Few dreams. The peace is good. All senses are heightened in me. I do revel in it. You know I have my ways." She grinned in a seductive manner. Returned to a more reserved state, she said to Madame Jeliya, "Everything sexual and spiritual is so damn bright. I'm on ten. It takes a lot to bring myself to a seven. And what we do to one another's nerves, Thelema." She put her hand on Madame Jeliya's arm. "The Lovers card, there's another half of a ritual I have to perform with it. Bring myself down from this height. To sleep," she adjoined.

"Perchance to dream?" quoted Madame Jeliya.

"Perchance to wake up," Lady Arachne answered.

Madame Jeliya understood.

Lady Arachne still felt the need to tell her, "Vencil is a good man. He's a *great* man. I'm not trying to turn you against him with this story. That would be irresponsible of me to allow that to happen, and for that to be my motive. I'm not blind to the subtext this can stir, make one believe, and get lost in. That's not there. Though it doesn't make Vencil innocent, he's unaware of all this. Maman Anansi brought it to me a good time after you two were married, the whole story." Madame Jeliya simply nodded her head, absent of expression. "I saw you in my cards days ago. Your image came through." She set the scene. "You were in your laboratory, resting on your lounge. You had a wine glass in your hand. Your conjured cats glowed, huddled in the corner. Vencil came to you with a client in need of a blessing. You took the client in, prepared him. You gave this eye to your husband. A wink, if I correctly recall. I'd never seen you in such a way. I get the winter of you, but there I got to see your summer. Your kittenish warmth in heat."

"I don't care what season I come at you with," Madame Jeliya told Lady Arachne. "You are my sister-in-conjure. You have *always* been my sister." Madame Jeliya lay her hand on the Tarot-seer's arm. "Speaking of seasons, I'm still glad I got to slap the mess out you last winter."

Lady Arachne pushed her hand away. *Thelema!*" she snapped. "We havin' a moment!"

"That was a moment too, now! I got you good," she teased, tongue out and features squished on her face.

Lady Arachne rolled her eyes. "Yo' old ass don't even remember it happenin', all hexed and void of spirit."

"I got a sense of something. Nice little clap across that face. Just like them cards I pulled on that last hand."

Lady Arachne stood. "I let you win!" she spat at her.

"That's some good actin' then," Madame Jeliya noted. "Girl, you was maaaaaad. All in yo' face upset." She started laughing. Lady Arachne had her in view from the side of her eyes. She huffed through a growing smile. Then a thought came to her. "It's close to midnight. If I may so change the subject, I say we need to be makin' our way to the crossroads. See this young woman get sworn in. We got to do this two more times after this."

"Is your restless spirit tired, Lena?"

Lady Arachne thought for a moment. "You know something? It is!" She contemplated again. "Huh! The things speaking the truth will do. Give you better rest than a ritual. At least I can hope."

The door buzzed downstairs. Both women's instincts shivered before the bell's timbre resonated through the house. Lady Arachne saw behind her eyes, within its blink, the handsome image of Reverend Mathieu Pouvwa. She exhaled, turned her head to face Madame Jeliya and directed with insistence, "Go to your man, sister. Hold him and make love to him."

"While you, Spider Queen, look to web up and devour that young man outside your door."

Lady Arachne displayed a half-hearted grin. To Madame Jeliya's surprise, the sensual seer replied, "I'm at peace with my truth revealed to you, Thelema. Tonight, I think I'll get some sleep instead."

The conjure matriarchs straightened their attire and then made their way downstairs to the brownstone's narrow foyer. Lady Arachne spied Reverend Pouvwa through the glass of the wooden doors. More than her heart trembled and seeped when she saw his handsome figure. An eyebrow lifted, and she used incants to unlock and open the doors. Madame Jeliya commented that she was showing off.

"I have so much more to show off," Lady Arachne murmured. She walked ahead of Madame Jeliya, her words trailing over her shoulder, "I guess my restless spirit emerges from its light slumber. It's good to know that even when I find peace, I will always be me and free." She added for good measure, "As my good Gira spirit intended." She stepped up to Reverend Pouvwa, who waited patiently for the women to emerge from the brownstone. She greeted, taking his hand, "Hello, Reverend."

"Lady Arachne," he bowed his head at her. He looked at Madame Jeliya and did the same while speaking her conjure title and name. "Papa Solomon and Mister Eledas are on their way to the crossroads. I came through to have far, better looking company."

Lady Arachne made a face over her shoulder at Madame Jeliya who was bright and bubbled with Reverend Pouvwa's sly compliment. She faced the reverend and replied, "Looks like you've loosened that collar, Reverend."

He put his hands in his pockets and opened the loop of his right arm. "Lady Arachne?" he said. She put her arms through and allowed Reverend Pouvwa to take lead, escorting her down the stairs and through the gate.

Madame Jeliya used an incant to close and lock the doors. She followed behind, saying nothing. She watched Reverend Pouvwa and Lady Arachne journey down the road arm-in-arm. She thought of herself and Papa Solomon doing the same.

She exhaled and all was well.

15

It was noon, and it was outside of time. Lillian "Voodoo Lily" Eledas-Ghedemere's ritual was at its end, and so did begin the rest of her magical life. Four times was Lillian Eledas-Ghedemere blessed with her back against the road, head aimed toward one of the four cardinal directions. At sunset, she began. At midnight, her blessing continued in a new direction. At dawn, Lillian's story had one chapter left to it. And at noon, she was Guardian of the Four Directions, the new Crossroads Queen.

Each ceremony had its similarities with the last. An African mask with no eyes covered Lillian's visage. The Fable Avenue Elders, her parents, Simaetha Ghedemere and Satchel "Old Goon" Eledas, stood over her body and blessed her with prayer and hymn. A newcomer to the ceremony attended. Savannah Forrester, who it had been said was at the crossroads to meet a family member.

For Lillian, there were dreams of redecorating the houses that rested outside of time, interior and exterior. There was a meeting with previous owners and guardians. She had a wonderful talk with Jackson and Gaston Fable and their wives. The old men made her laugh; and their wives spoke of a wondrous tales of a conjure war that spanned ten years between they and Sheriff Cornelius "Curly" Burneside and his needlemen deputies. She had tea during the talk. It tasted of brambleberries and was spiked with dragon spit liquor. Then she was awake. An action prompted by a final blessing in the *mirak* from the previous owners.

Lillian's eyes opened. The sun was directly above her. She could feel it, but her sight was blocked by the eyeless African mask covering her face. Also felt was the presence of the gathered Elders around her. As before, her body lifted off the ground. She became upright, and when her feet floated inches above the road, the mystical field keeping her in the air, gently set Lillian on her feet. Her body was again in her control. She took a step back to maintain balance, though coming from the ritual was not as disorienting the fourth and final time.

Lillian's mother took the bouquet of rooster feathers from her, and the bottle holding the sacred soil. Lillian removed the mask from her face and opened her eyes. The world glowed with aura. Everything appeared interconnected by a gossamer web that only she could see. Her mother asked her what she saw, as Lillian's face was bright with curiosity, peering at her surroundings as if new to her.

"I see possibilities, paths and endless streams of time." She opened her right hand by means other than her own will, and appearing before her eyes were a set of dice made from cowrie shells, carved with intricate symbols. Her left hand also opened by an action that seemed not in Lillian's control. A round, black mirror appeared in her left hand, four inches in diameter. "Cowrie dice and a black mirror!" Lillian exclaimed. "I can see my divining tools." And as soon as she uttered their presence, the images faded away.

"We will have our best craftsmen prepare and bless you with the tools you need," Maman Anansi's glowing presence declared. "When you receive them, Crossroads Queen, you can conduct a personal ritual to further strengthen them." Then she addressed Simaetha, inquiring, "Will you assist in the first blessing? You and Mister Eledas?" she clarified.

"Yes," Simaetha answered the head Fable Avenue matriarch. "And thank you, again, Maman Anansi."

Maman Anansi's projection bid Lillian and her family farewell. Papa Solomon informed his sister that he and Satchel "Old Goon" requested an audience with her, and they would meet her in Queens later in the day. Maman Anansi permitted their presence, saying she would be waiting. Then she bowed her head to the remaining, gathered conjurer folk as her casted spirit faded from the ceremony.

Madame Jeliya called back her familiars. The large felines turned away from keeping Jabo Judson at bay and hurried back to their mistress. The lionesses leapt at Madame Jeliya, and she absorbed the big cats into her person without flinching. Reverend Pouvwa noted to himself that he would never get used to witnessing ghostly big cat spirits leap back into their caster.

The conjure party emerged from outside of time as they whispered an incant in unison. Even Reverend Pouvwa assisted in the invocation that brought the mystical coterie out of the blue. Their step back into time didn't go unnoticed. Armand Gideon witnessed their wink into existence as he rode up to the uncanny scene occurring between the visible and invisible realms at the crossroads. He'd been driving long, and he'd lost trust in his eyes. He rationalized that perhaps the group of people were always there, crossing the road, instead of appearing out of nowhere from the middle of the cross section.

Armand's eyelids flickered, and more sights appeared. Two houses, similar in build and across the street from one another, formed out of air like blurry images focused sharp. Despite this phenomenon, the only thing Armand continued questioning was his fatigue. He slowed his car at the curb and cut the engine. A familiar face walked up to his vehicle. It was his grandmother, Savannah Forrester. He opened the door, unbuckled his safety belt, and slipped free from the driver's seat. His body slid through the slightly ajar door as if he was air itself. "Nana Forrester!" he exclaimed in a hushed voice so as not to disturb the afternoon calm.

Armand Gideon's entrance to the day had not gone undetected. The world might have spun in Lillian's eyes—her head intoxicated by ritual and incant mixed with the step back into time—but instinct rotated her sight toward the car that pulled up at the side of the crossroads, resting now at the house formerly owned by Gaston Fable. Familiarity honed Armand's car into focus, developing a distinct memory in her head. Reddish-brown Coupé with shaded windows parked up on the lawn. She'd seen that before. But there was no old mailman who ejected from the driver's side.

No. There instead she saw a handsome young man, close in age to her. His skin tone echoed the chestnut color of his car. But instead of the dull rust caking his vehicle, this man wore his color as if the Earth's rich soil swallowed the sun and the celestial body's brilliance remained undenied through its earthen burial. He was lean but muscular, appearing like a djinn conjured from smoke, or perhaps the serpentine smoke itself. His hair was a short burst of wool. Its growth was new, and even a new phenomenon to him. She could decipher by his movements he hadn't worn a crown of such nature; but Lillian could sense he liked it. His hair was as attractive as him, but she decided it needed a fresh twist to even it out. His triangular face was patched with a light sprinkle of hair around his chin and lip.

Her forehead tingled with otherworldly insight, still heightened from ritual. She extracted the young man's name. Armand Gideon, grandson to Savannah Forrester who was there to greet him. She came around his car and the two of them embraced. "Thank you, for all this, Nana Forrester," he said to her, his voice like a sigh. "I feel safe now."

"You are very safe here, my grandson," Savannah replied, patting his back.

Armand's eyelids lifted. They drifted over his grandmother's shoulder and spied again the gathering of people who were now on the lawn of the identical house across the street. "Who're them, Nana Forrester?" he asked her, eyesight centered on the young and beautiful Lillian Ghedemere among the pack of Elders.

The women separated from the men in the unit and strolled in the direction of Armand's arrival. Armand considered their approach an answer to his question, as Savannah hadn't immediately answer him, preoccupied with her fixation on his car. She disengaged from her embrace and sauntered over to Armand's haggard ride. Worn and beaten. Rusted and scarred. Those were the best ways to describe the vehicle. Savannah reached out a wide-fingered hand toward the barely living transport. She swept her palm over the exterior, a curious look on her face.

Armand was ready to comment, but before he could make a full turn toward Savannah, Lady Arachne and Simaetha Ghedemere drew closer to him. Lillian walked between them; and they flanked her like strong and mighty pillars. Behind her, as if in tow as guard, was Madame Jeliya. Armand felt compelled to give his full attention to them like a soldier in the presence of eminent royalty.

Savannah witnessed Armand's attentive posture. There was something watchful in his pose, defensive and distrusting. Savannah retracted her hand from the car and aimed it at her grandson. "Come on, there, Armand-sweetie," she spoke through a smile, words laced with incant to soothe whatever tension there was rising in him. "Them women ain't nothing to be afraid of. I do know them."

Armand's heart skipped at the words his grandmother addressed to him. He thought for a moment, and then his look of narrow-eyed wonder bloomed into a soft and relaxed expression. He cast his own charm over his shoulder. "Oh, I'm not afraid, Nana Forrester. Far from it, I must say." He turned his attention back to the four conjure women who encircled him. Armand admired their cultural garments that accented their beauty, whether at its youth, at center, or mature as the pillars that flanked her. "Well, I'll be paid in full by circumstance. Four beautiful women," he pointed out. "Five, counting you Nana Forrester. All here to greet me on this dusty way of a road. It's like something out of a mythology." He settled against the grille of his car, folding his arms. He remarked, "Hell, I shoulda beat a bad man a long time ago. God knows I've come across a few in my twenty-some-odd years." The four women smiled in unison. "All this beauty is an extra incentive. I'm just grateful my car got me this far." He tapped on it with a fist.

Lady Arachne inspected the dilapidated vehicle. Her eyes rose to meet Savannah's, and she remarked, "It does seem like a...*blessing*...doesn't it?" Savannah returned a stern gaze that lasted for a moment, setting Lady Arachne to stand straight and tighten her lip. The Fable Avenue matriarch returned an inquisitive eye to her friend. "Well, Savannah," Lady Arachne stuttered, "aren't you going to introduce us to your handsome grandson?" With her last two words she nudged Lillian on the arm. The young woman beamed a look that echoed Savannah's stern scrutiny, but the newly crowned Crossroads Queen fixed her face from her fleeting frown.

Savannah strolled to Armand's side, taking her grandson arm-in-arm. "Armand, these are friends of mine." She aimed a flat hand at each woman as she introduced them. "This is Lena Franklin." Her hand moved to the center and named, "Lillian Eledas-Ghedemere." She moved her hand to point behind Lillian and identify, "Thelema Heathwicke-Peters." At the end of the line, Savannah identified and titled, "Simaetha Ghedemere, Lillian's mother." Then she introduced her grandson. "This is my grandson, Armand Gideon, from my eldest child, Keiiah."

The conjure women greeted Armand in unison with the simple word of 'Hello' and a synchronized bow of their heads. Smiles decorated their lovely faces. Armand did much the same, trying not to make it too obvious that his eye lingered the most on Lillian's glow. There was such a unique air with her poise and presence. Her hair was a garden of tight, spherical coils that were arranged in careful rhythm. There was order in her. A balance that even crossed over to her peculiar skin color, near symmetrical down her body. One half of her was lighter than the other. She had one foot in the radiance of the dawn and the other in midnight's mysterious shadow. It was within that resolve where her two shades became a cohesive beauty, and Armand had a difficult time keeping his attention discreet. There then came a distraction, as Lady Arachne stepped forward and questioned, "Have you traveled long, Armand?"

He flinched, his vision no longer tunneled and focused on Lillian. "About five hours—six," he answered attentively. "I've lost track. I know I've been up since four this morning. Got on the road around six-thirty. I'm coming from Atlanta. Didn't have much to pack. Left a lot behind. Nana Forrester said she got some business people that'll handle my affairs, any loose ends." He looked at his grandmother and commented, "I'm a little confused as to how you got way down here, Nana Forrester." He looked over at the house and asked, "You live here now?"

Savannah went silent, ducking her head to dodge the question. She kept her eyes up enough, but Armand had a natural instinct about his grandmother, sensing something in her hesitation. Concern glistened in the conjure women's eyes as they spied her tied by tongue and irresolute. She told Armand, "Park your car all the way up on the lawn. Let's go inside and talk."

"Yes, ma'am," he answered. He stood up straight. Savannah removed her arm from around his and allowed Armand to walk away. He opened the door, got in, and started the engine. Savannah moved away from the car, slipping back into the conjure women's circle.

Lady Arachne whispered as they watched Armand back the car up, "That piece of junk car shouldn't be purring like it is. Hell, it shouldn't even growl angrily. He got that thing all the way from California to Atlanta to here?"

Simaetha and Lillian put eyes on one another before eyeing Savannah with a curious look.

"I know," Savannah rejoined with a snap to her voice. She exhaled, watching her grandson steer his rickety car onto the lawn. "There's a blessing there. A prayer cast before his journey, and he has no idea." Delight and vexation contended for expression, twisting Savannah's stomach into a knot. She untangled the emotional crumple by exhaling and shaking her head. "That damn daughter of mine!" she hissed.

Savannah separated from the conjure women's troupe, stepping in the direction of her grandson's parked car as he cut the engines and slid free. Savannah turned toward the women and summoned a sweet-toned farewell and a respectful bow of her head. "Lady Arachne, I'll speak on these matters with you later. Simaetha, it was a pleasure seeing you again." For Lillian, Savannah stepped forward and gave her a warm embrace. "My deepest felicitations, Miss Voodoo Lily." She hugged her tighter and expressed, "*Kaabọ ile,* Crossroads Queen."

"Thank you, Miss Forrester," Lillian said in return. Her eyes opened for a moment while embraced by Savannah. Without conscious thought, her regard fell over Armand as he leaned coolly against his beat-up wreck. She and Savannah opened their embrace in unison.

Savannah stepped away. Before she made a full turn, she said to Lillian, "Now go and do something about that head, girl. I know it's spinnin'."

Lillian chuckled. "Only partially used to this ritual," she remarked. "It's still not as bad as the first time, but I could use a drink—if not just to celebrate."

The women fell in line as they returned to Lillian's new estate. Savannah approached her grandson. She aimed her hand at the house and said, "C'mon, young man. Let's go inside and have us a talk."

"Yes, ma'am," he uttered in a gentle tone.

The house was different now. Armand wasn't aware of its preternatural change, but he was intrigued that its exterior was a mirror image of the house across the street. The quaint, two-story, center-hall Colonial home created a storybook ambiance to the crossroads', old-time, golden environment. Armand felt he'd stepped into a sepia photograph of the early twentieth century. An otherworldly calm came over him as he walked up to the house, viewing it while strolling up to the front door, which was a sight unto itself. Heavy and carved from wood, it was rendered with ornate designs of African symbols that were foreign to him. The sturdy, rectangular structure wore its whittled spiritual emblems as if it was presenting a famed mythology, like hieroglyphs. The door was inset within an archway. An old-style lantern hung over the door, dangling from the top of the curved structure. Over the entrance was an iron balcony, accessible by a doorway from one of the four bedrooms.

Armand believed his tired eyes failed him again. He could've sworn the door opened on its own, and after he'd noticed his grandmother mumble a set of unintelligible words. He yawned and rubbed his eyes with his thumb and pointer finger. He followed his grandmother into the house, and once inside, he turned halfway to close the door when he heard the click of its lock as it snapped in place. Armand wondered if the house was wired for some kind of Wi-Fi commands, regardless of having not seen his grandmother operate a smartphone or give command to any particular device.

He stepped into a quaint dining area off the right of the entrance hall. Victorian furniture decorated the room, from chairs to table covered with cloth to a dresser drawer topped with an old-style lamp, vases, a fancy half-full bottle of whiskey, and a tray with teacups and teapot. Under the window that was framed with curtains, there was situated a small, rectangular table with much the same items. A glass cupboard, again with the same items, was in the corner of the room.

Two types of drink rested on the dining room table. One was a glass of ice water stirred with lemon juice. The other was a glass half-full with whiskey. A pack of cigarettes rested next to the glass of liquor. Adjacent to that was a crystal ashtray. "Now, a little stop off here for a dram and some lemon water," Savannah said as she took a seat. She spoke as if sighing from a weight lifted from her, or perhaps, placed on her.

Armand took a seat. His eyes went from the whiskey to his grandmother. A sly grin dawned on his countenance. "Who gets the whiskey, Nana Forrester?"

Savannah answered her grandson, "The one closest to the grave, young man."

"I'm of age," Armand protested in a polite tone. "Over age, even."

But Savannah insisted, "You still a young gun to me, boy, and I'ma need you sober for this."

Armand's bright smile turned to a sunset, a stone-faced shadow masking his face. He didn't reach for the lemon water. Savannah didn't go for the whiskey. The drinks remained where they were. Armand cleared his throat and mentioned, "I know what was happening outside." He made a quick point with his finger over his shoulder and said, "That ritual and all." Savannah narrowed her eyes on Armand. He shrugged his shoulder. "Mom told me about your community." Then he added, sounding more like a question, "…Your…African…spiritual community…" He expressed a short burst of nervous laughter then swallowed the outburst and commented, "My eyes were playing tricks on me, Nana Forrester. Just tired, I guess. Long drive from this morning, like I said earlier." He lifted his head to tell his grandmother, "You and your friends seem to just walk out of nowhere. I never saw them in the middle of the road, crossing it." He looked at the glass of lemon water. He needed a drink. Anything. But he didn't reach for it.

Savannah's eyes remained narrowed on her grandson. She recalled the words in his letter to her and said, "You got a haunt on you, boy. You got something on your heart. It's what we call, in my community, an *inawo*." She saw his intuitive, inquisitive look. "It's a debt you need to pay to yourself, an expense to clean your soul. We also call it an *ẹru:* a burden, weight. Slave."

Armand's eyes moved from the lemon water to the whiskey. "Mom talks about how you speak," he replied to her. "The things you say," he added.

Savannah reminded him, "Well, you wrote your letter to me. Your mother doesn't even know you're here." She tapped on the table. "And here you are, boy. You've stepped foot into my domain, understand."

Armand's head dropped again. "I'm sorry, Nana Forrester," he apologized. "I'm not trying to offend you." He heard a clock ticking. The sound came from another room. It ticked, moment after moment, as if it was counting the interval of silence between he and Savannah.

Her face fixed. Her tone changed when she finally spoke, sounding desperate to a situation Armand wasn't privy to. "It's hard being a person of conjure, for all in my community. You can't do everything you like even though you have the power to bring much of anything you like into existence, anything you want—*desire*—straight to you. That power doesn't always guarantee change or happiness." Savannah's words trailed away. Water bubbled at the base of her eyes, and she looked away from her grandson.

"Nana Forrester, I apologize again," Armand told her in an attempt to draw her back and dry her eyes. "I got in trouble. I did a bad thing. I hurt somebody." He spoke quick, trying to reel her away from sinking into tears. "And you're right," he said. "I have this anger in me."

She turned her head to face him. "You need a cleansing, boy." She wiped the tears cupped at the bottom of her eyes. "But you need to see some things first."

Armand questioned, "What things?" He finally reached out for the lemon water.

The tall glass moved away from his hand. It lifted into the air, and Armand's wide eyes followed its levitation. He spied that the whiskey glass was also hovering above the table, bobbing as if buoyed in water. The glassware orbited around one another like heavenly bodies. The whiskey glass broke rotation and moved toward Armand. He reached out and closed his grip around it. Savannah brought the lemon water to her hand. She admitted before taking a long sip of the lemon water on ice, "Come to rethink my words, you gonna need that drink more than me."

Armand didn't take an immediate drink. He wanted to reverse time and witness the glasses' mystical lifts and rotation above the table. He surprised himself that his hand wasn't trembling when he eventually knocked back the whiskey in one gulp. He set the empty glass down in hopes he'd see the magic performed again. Instead, he came to a revelation, expressing, "My eyes aren't that tired, are they, Nana Forrester?"

Savannah rested her glass on the table, keeping her grip around it. "No," she answered her grandson. "There's a place called *akoko ita*. Those are Yoruba words meaning, 'outside of time'. That young woman, Lillian, she was being blessed to oversee her new duties as the Crossroads Queen. She's been through a long ceremony giving her spiritual sovereignty over this domain. She has the responsibility of helping travelers seek their proper path. Through her father, she is a rightful inheritor. Family cousins guarded it before her. Two old men and their wives. The Fable brothers. They passed decades ago. Place been on lockdown until about a year ago."

Armand's inquiry sounded ironically like an answer, "No selling the soul to the Devil, is there?"

Savannah shook her head. "No," she confirmed. "That's white folk talk, blowin' our mythology out of its proportions."

"We outside of time now?"

"Yes," she affirmed with a nod to her head. "People coming down these roads only see open land."

"And the gas station?" Armand added.

"No. That's outside of time too. Not sure how. That don't belong to proper conjure folk. In order to blend independent of time, lot of conjure folk blood had to be spilled, sacrificed. There's a hexed, anathematic-world. That place over there, it carries that fog. That's a bad omen of a place." She gave Armand a stern look. Her eyes were more than piercing. Armand felt as if his grandmother's gaze had become a brand, perceiving a searing imprint on him, marked as she narrated, "Since the dawn of existence, conjure folk have come to a crossroads somewhere on this Earth. You are doing so now." She let her grandson know. Then she warned, tapping on her heart, "There are crossroads and conflicts here." She pointed to the window and continued, "And there are crossroads and conflicts out there." She retracted her arm and nodded her head. Armand discerned knowledge and understanding floated behind his grandmother's eyes as she reflected. "The conjure community I'm a part of resides in Brooklyn on a street named Fable Avenue."

Armand expressed his perplexity. "So, do you live here in Mississippi, or do you live in New York? Mount Vernon or Brooklyn?"

"I live in Mount Vernon," Savannah answered. "As do two of the women I introduced you to." Then Savannah added for clarity, "Not the mother and daughter."

"Are you all down here for her ceremony…?"

Savannah stayed silent, though she shook her head. She took another swig of her lemon water. "The conjure folk of Fable Avenue are in conflict with some folk that been spreading hexes and curses for around six thousand years." She thought for a moment and then said, "Shit! Let's speak the truth here. The whole conjure world been in conflict with these folks." Then she listed, words slipping through tightened teeth, "Murderers. Kidnappers. Robbers. Enslavers." Another breath. She revealed, "Your cousin, Fey, is at the center of that conflict." Savannah looked away from Armand when she disclosed, "This same conflict took her mother and father long ago when she was six." Her eyes drifted back to him to gauge his reaction.

Armand rotated his empty glass. "Cousin Fey isn't studying art abroad, is she?" Savannah's face went dour. She confirmed 'no' with a shake of her head. "Does Mom know about all this?"

Savannah bobbed her head in the affirmative. She commented, "She don't care for it, but she got her knowledge. She know how to impart a blessing." Savannah gave an example by stating, "That raggedy-ass car of yours ain't get all the way from California to here on luck. There's a blessing spread on that vehicular vagrant you drivin'." She reached for the pack of cigarettes and pulled one free. She raised the end to her lips and spoke a low incant to set it to low flame and smoke. She blew on it, and then she proceeded to take a puff.

Armand smiled at the simple sorcery his grandmother performed. His gaze drifted out the window and spied his car on the front lawn. Though shaded by the curtains he could see the broke-down ride as if the silky, drapery weren't even obstructing his view. His car seemed more of a wreck than he'd ever paid to mind. He agreed with his grandmother. In all earthly scenarios the car should've stopped running a few blocks up the street from his house back in California. But here he was, clear across the United States, pushed by a rusted bucket of bolts that drove as if it was its first day off the lot. It was like riding on a cloud, he recalled. The entire ride itself. Anywhere he'd gone in his car around Atlanta, including the drive to the crossroads. It was a smooth journey. Looking raggedy kept thieves away. It didn't even put-put or hiccup exhaust. And he had his mother to thank for that.

It figures, he thought to himself while rolling his eyes. He believed it was all too in character for his mother to cast an overprotective aegis around him, segregating him from this rightful, mystical heritage of his. "Conflict within and without, huh, Nana Forrester?" he grunted sitting back in his chair. A feeling bloomed in him. He'd felt it before, concerning school. The feeling showed itself only twice in his life. It occurred on his first day of high school. It echoed on his first day of college. His gaze remained fixed on the window. His sight dwindled away the obstructing curtains, and he saw clear across the street to the identical house.

There she was standing in the open doorway with a cool and alluring lean in her stance, arms folded. Lillian Eledas-Ghedemere. She surveyed all that she was now crowned to govern. He watched her for a moment. Every now and then the silky obstruction came back into view, taking him away from his efforts through imagination to erase the curtain's presence.

He was compelled to ask his grandmother, "If I got a guide with me, I should be alright, right? Someone who assists travelers?"

Savannah didn't answer her grandson right away. Her silence pulled him from his immersion in the scenery outside and across the street. He put his eyes back on his grandmother. She was smoking, physically present but elsewhere. She had a fixed look aimed at the corner of the room.

"Nana Forrester," Armand called to her in a respectful voice.

Savannah exhaled and tapped ashes into the crystal ashtray. His voice brought her back to her surroundings. It wasn't just his call that made her recover, but also his question to her about a guide. She grinned and glanced at the window. She spotted Lillian across the street, looked at her grandson, and nodded her head. She told him, "Yes, indeed, grandson." She took a drag of her cigarette and let loose the smoke away from Armand's person. "You be careful," she warned him. "The guide you seek ain't like any guide you've had before." She gave him an eye, an overall look with pursed lips. "Best to get to know the company you keep and keep it in the culture."

"Yes, Nana Forrester," Armand yielded.

Savannah rested her cigarette down and told him, "You said some things in your letter to me. Some specific wordings. It makes me think you need some real guidance, nothing to joke about, take lightly, or try and get a date with a pretty, young conjure woman." Savannah pulled Armand's letter from her pocket, and she witnessed her grandson's body and facial features melt from a humble posture to a defensive one. He looked down, away from her. His eyes darted back and forth as if contemplating a means of escape from the next aspects of the conversation. She read, "*Sinister sorcery stirred hallucinations. I often find myself surrounded by a harem of horrors, and these ghosts wrap their hands around my neck, hold me down. Cool currents cascade through me.*" She skipped ahead, reciting, "*Something spoke to me, poking at me first, and then I heard the interviewer's voice saying other words that were really on his or her mind. It was like the pin of a grenade being pulled, and anger exploded in my throat, tightening it. I clenched my fists, Nana.*" She folded the letter back and placed it beside the astray. Armand was still looking at the floor. His eyes continued their wild behavior until she said to him, "I'm worried about you, young man."

Armand straightened. Alert and focused. He replied, "Oh, there's no need for worry, Nana Forrester. I feel better."

"By hurting somebody," Savannah affixed. She picked up her cigarette and smoked a few puffs. Armand regarded her words in silence. Savannah's exhales of smoke sounded to him like sighs of disappointment. He wished she'd speak. She did, and her audible words were far more comforting to him. "You hear other people's thoughts. You speak about knowing the moves of the boy you fought before he made them. I'm sure before he even knew them his damn self." Again, she rested her cigarette in a groove carved into the crystal ashtray.

Armand had a question. His lips didn't form it into sound, but his eyes sculpted it into a visual sentiment. He rubbed his hands together, fist into palm, rolling them into one another over and over. He made a quick glance at his grandmother's cigarette as it burned in the ashtray. He wanted to reach for it, take a hit and relax himself with its flavor and potency. But he stayed his hand and didn't ask for permission. He was respectful of his grandmother's territory; and he left it for her to take up and smoke again.

Savannah placed two fingers around her cigarette and lifted it to her lips. Puff. Exhale. Up to the ceiling. Then she addressed her grandson, "You have an *ogbon inu*." She defined soon after, "Intuition. Instinct." Cigarette. Finished. Put out. "All this means, Armand, is that you got the foundations of conjure in you. Your mother is my daughter." She aimed a finger and a quick eye toward the window. "She put her knowledge into practice. Her blessing got you here, despite her back turned to me and all this rich culture. Shit, your daddy half from Africa—straight from the continent with your grandfather. And the other half, from the Islands. He was raised strict Christian, but he got the blood of Africa and ritual in him." She pointed to Armand and summarized, "You and your siblings are the culmination of that black mix. You're at your first of many internal crossroads. Which direction will you step in?"

"I want to learn, Nana Forrester," Armand spoke up.

And so, Grandmamma Forrester nodded her approval. She told her grandson, "I know you got eyes on a specific guide, but you gon' have more than one." She went to lift her cigarette and scoffed when she saw she'd already finished it, its scrunched-up body flattened and bleeding its tobacco in the ashtray. "Shit!" she cursed, acting as if she didn't have an entire pack to take from. Calming, Savannah pulled free and lit another cigarette. Blowing smoke, she said, "I can't show you all the conjure world's history. We go to the beginning of time, legends and such. What I would like to show you is the history of Fable Avenue. It's locked inside the harmonies of an incanted jazz album. Now, if you can recall the woman I named for you as Thelema Heathwicke-Peters—"

"Yes, Nana Forrester," Armand acknowledged.

Savannah nodded her head and said, "Good." She concluded, "Well, her title within our community is *Madame Jeliya, Second Matriarch*. She's gonna take you through all that history in her sanctum on Fable Avenue. Rest up for now. You can take that trip-in-dream tonight. You gonna see some things, my grandson."

Perplexity buckled Armand's countenance. "Tonight? But you said, *'in her sanctum on Fable Avenue'*," he reminded, believing he was correcting his grandmother. "Fable Avenue's in Brooklyn, right? New York. Or, do you mean across the street?"

Savannah stood, cigarette in the grip of her fingers. "In a sense," she said. "More like down the street. Follow me, boy."

Armand was up and by his grandmother's side. He followed her on the short walk back to the front door. She turned the lock four times and traced with the tip of her fingers the letters *A-V-E* on the door. Armand caught a flicker of light scurry about the house as if the sun changed positions. He looked over his shoulder in reaction, but Savannah opening the door drew his attention to the new outdoors.

The majestic, old-time scenery of the crossroads was gone. In its place was a long stretch of street in Brooklyn fortified by mighty giants called brownstones that stood side-by-side, varied within the color spectrum of oranges, browns and reds. Trees were in full bloom on each block. Leaves in green, branches out and stretching toward the sunlight. The street was well gardened, and the flowers resonated with a curious luminescence that the conjure folk of the area made sure people with regular eyes only considered was the sun shining off the colorful petals. But Armand's eyes were not regular. Not anymore. He was attuned to the rightful magic of his culture.

The sight wasn't immediate. There was a small entryway tiled with African symbols. Another set of doors were stationed there too. Savannah opened one door and stepped out into the same day in another part of the world. Armand followed his grandmother. He buckled with each step, balance lost to him as he was consumed by disbelief. He put his palm on the doors to keep from falling. He was dizzy, as if he'd been spun around on a high-velocity ride at an amusement park. His eyes were wide, holding an expressive, child-like wonder in their broad study of this newly developed environment. He blinked to steady the world and put it in focus.

"Holy! Shit!" Armand exclaimed as he stepped out of the house that now held a brownstone's façade. Savannah smacked him on the back of the head for cursing. Armand flinched with the impact of his grandmother's flat palm. Head still whirling from the change in environment, Armand stumbled and caught himself on the railing at the top of the brownstone steps. He rubbed the back of his head as he stood straight again. "Sorry, Nana Forrester. I'm just not used to this. This is every day to you. For me it's— *'holy shit'!"* Savannah slapped him again! Her forceful tap against his head had more bite to it this time around. Armand buckled, snickering while he stood straight again and made attempts to apologize. But the high-adrenaline shock had now subsided, calmed into acceptance. He was here. New York. Brooklyn.

Fable Avenue.

Armand's upright posture fixed still as his faculties adjusted to the change and his balance was restored. It was like hopping to another world with a new atmosphere. His body needed to acclimate, and the adjustment felt like a slow process. In some regards, the experience was exactly that. His head went side to side as he looked down both ends of the street. He turned around when he reached the bottom of the stairs and looked up to his grandmother. He asked her, "I just want to take a walk, Nana Forrester. From end to end. Will that be okay?"

"Yes," Savannah permitted, a proud grin growing on her face. It widened as she watched her grandson commence his stroll down Fable Avenue. She reached into her pocket and removed her smartphone. She unlocked it and scrolled through her contacts to find Madame Jeliya. She needed to give her a call and schedule Armand's time later tonight. But her search stopped at her daughter's name. Keiiah Gideon. Her thumb hovered over the selection for a moment. She lifted her head and looked for Armand down the street, measuring his distance. It would be some time before he returned.

It was close to ten o'clock over in California. Her daughter would be up.

Savannah tapped on her name and selected her mobile number.

Three rings. Her daughter answered. "Ma…?" she replied. "Is everything okay?" Her voice was soft, but heavy with anticipation.

"Everything's fine, K," Savannah assured her daughter. "I'm fine." Then she just came out and said it. "Armand's here with me."

"Why is that boy in New York?"

"He was having a hard time finding a job in Atlanta," she told her daughter. There was no reply on the other end. Savannah took another look down the street. Armand was far away. She chided, "You know I'm lying, K."

"That old conjure woman instinct," Keiiah riposted. "Now, please tell me what my son is doing in New York?"

Savannah snapped, "I lied purposely, little girl. I said what I said because I wanted to see if I could feel an instinct coming from you." She began pacing on the brownstone landing. "That boy's car is in terrible condition but runs as if it's fresh out the factory."

Keiiah was quick to reply, "My ears weren't always closed, Ma. I learned to speak my Christian prayers like Daddy told me; and I was able to twiddle my fingers to their syllables and do some conjure, too." Her voice relaxed when she articulated, "Henry wanted me to show him more. I used to show him when we first dated. He knows about the conjure world. His family on both sides, y'know."

"I was just saying to your son," Savannah told her, voice just as unruffled now in the conversation. "His daddy all half-African and half-Caribbean."

"Yeah," Keiiah said in a low and sweet tone. "Some of his family that practice conjure, it's for religious purposes—take the ease off their spirit. But he got some that can *really* perform conjure. They got some incant in them. He tells me about them. Of course, they don't mix with the dominant Christian folk of his family. It always interested him, but he didn't want to be outcasted or considered *'of the Devil'* in his immediate family. We stopped talking about all of that when Emeline died. I don't like that world. You keep my boy safe from it, if he got to be there."

Savannah peeked down the street. Armand was lost down the way, far gone.

"He got into a little trouble in Atlanta, K," Savannah confessed to her daughter, who sucked her teeth and sighed in reaction. Savannah didn't need an arcane instinct to know her daughter rolled her eyes too. "He was getting frustrated that he wasn't finding a job," she continued. "Armand was on his way to his umpteenth interview. He came across a rough boy, a thug. They got into it in the streets. Armand took his frustration out on him and put him in the hospital. The young man was actually on his way to score some drugs of some kind. He was there with someone else. A woman. An older woman. She ran off, and was so into her next fix, she went on to their dealer. She didn't have all the money. Perhaps the man Armand hurt was the talker. She was found shot. Police see the whole thing as a deal gone wrong, though the woman was nowhere near where the fight took place when she was killed."

"But that boy could talk," Keiiah said to her mother. "He could say what all exactly happened to him."

"No, he won't," Savannah assured.

Keiiah understood, deciphering the tone in her mother's voice. Instead, she asked, "He's safe, yes?"

"He will be," Savannah replied. "And we'll find him a good job."

"Thank you, Ma," Keiiah answered.

"Now you be careful if you gon' continue dabbling in conjure and incant, child," Savannah warned. "Especially any foolish rituals you find in books. Them folks don't know what they talkin' about."

"Ma, relax!" Keiiah retorted. "I was listening growing up. I was. I even listened to the stories about white men in hoods armed with needles. I don't need that at my front door. I don't want it at my front door; and I don't want my children involved in any way. You want me safe? I know how you feel, because I want my children safe. Show Armand the world if you need to, but give him a warning. No twists in his hair to tune him into conjure. No dome to absorb or give off any kind of hoodoo. Keep him groomed and tamed."

Savannah growled, "Girl, what is this nonsense you speakin'? Your son is connected to conjure by biological lineage resting deep in his DNA that extends back to the beginning of time, not no damn hairstyle. These are some of the terrible ways of thinking that gave me such a hard time with you. The path you chose to walk had nothing to do with your father, or any kind of remembrance or honor of him in death. And you understand that I allowed you to walk independently of the world, waiting for you in the conjure culture."

"Not without some kind of scolding!" Keiiah hissed, interrupting her mother's rant.

Savannah ground her teeth against one another so hard she believed they would crack. When she spoke, the air that shaped her voice barely slithered under her tightly pressed jaw. "Girl, you think I returned to this culture—*our* culture, all of our culture—and I don't just mean myself and my children's. But you believe I returned to this culture with a finger-against-finger tappin' scheme to push your father's spirit aside once he passed. Like I found some kind of freedom. I loved—*and still love*—your father! I will always honor that man. But it was my *dishonor* of my power that killed him. You know my family's history. So, don't you dare!"

Both women took a breath. Their barely audible exhalations pacified their ire enough to return the conversation to civility. Long enough for Keiiah to express in an unruffled tone, "My son needs your help, Ma. For the sake of necessity, I won't put up a fight. Which is why I'll allow him to remain in New York."

Savannah broke into her daughter's words. Her tone was kind, but still resonated with parental authority and wisdom. "I would take my grandson in regardless. I love him; and he needs help right now."

"Thank you, Ma," Keiiah replied in a sincere and kind voice. "I just ask that you cast some kind of conjuration, some kind of charm, that will curb his curiosity. I know you don't agree with the way I raised my children. I taught them about the world. I taught them that an unjust and dominant system would persecute them on the grounds of being black. But I refused to teach them how special they were. They cannot know. Armand has a natural curiosity to explore, to know the truth. I saw it when he would get out of his crib at an early age. His youthful curiosity to investigate when we told him there was nothing sweet to eat in the house. He'd find it." Both women fizzed with a gentle chuckle that effervesced with reminiscence. "I knew he'd be the most challenging to keep this from. We've had our fights, too. I've kept him well-groomed, an absurd belief or not. I just don't want any needles showing up at his door, or men in hoods with him in their sights."

Savannah looked down the street. Armand could not be found, too far gone in the distance. She guessed he was nearing the furthermost part of

Fable Avenue from that end. He would be heading back soon, but it would still take some time before she'd get a glimpse of his image walking back her way. There was still the other end for him to survey.

"He's here, K. He'll be safe from the potential trouble he came across in Atlanta."

"Don't let him know we talked, Ma," Keiiah mandated in a soft voice to help ensure her request.

"I won't, K. He'll reach out to you on his own time."

"Thank you."

"Okay, then, girl. You get back to your life. If it's long before he reaches out, I'll call and give you an update."

"Thank you, Mamma…"

"You are welcome," Savannah replied to her daughter.

"All right," Keiiah stated, marking the end of their talk.

"All right," Savannah repeated.

"Okay," Keiiah added.

Savannah echoed, "Okay."

"Bye, Ma."

"Bye."

Savannah ended the call on her phone. She took another look down the street. Armand wasn't there. Perhaps he stopped at the Fable Avenue bakery, she considered, and found something sweet to eat. She returned to her intended task for the time being, scrolling through her contacts and pulling up Madame Jeliya. She called, and her instinct buzzed that the Fable Avenue matriarch had left her phone at home while she journeyed to the crossroads. Savannah considered an alternative. Lady Arachne had her phone with her. She hung up and looked for the other matriarch's number to relay the message. It was then that both women came from the brownstone across the street. Savannah's face burst with surprise. She locked her phone and pocketed the device. The matriarchs spotted Savannah and called her over. Savannah descended the stairs, walked through the gates, and traveled across the street.

"Where is your grandson?" Madame Jeliya asked with a wide smile.

Savannah answered, "Finding something sweet to eat."

16

The night's shade looked very different. The stars' glow was brighter. Their configurations held more meaning. The moon, half in glow, was only a supporting player in the sky, but its performance was no less memorable. The distance of these celestial participants didn't seem so far anymore. Armand Gideon hadn't left Earth, but he was in a whole new world. Everything was with fresh eyes, especially possibility and potential. Purpose overall.

He rested on the hood of his reliable-by-incant raggedy and rusted car as it lay parked on the lawn back at the crossroads. His legs were crossed, and he enjoyed a cigarette. Stargazing and puffing at two o'clock in the morning, he saw nothing but the stars and the moon and the silhouette of the identical structures across the street from one another. Nothing strolled through. No cars. No people. It was the perfect environment for reflection, and he needed that.

He also thought he needed another hit of whiskey from the cabinet after being inundated by dream and jazz that unfolded Fable Avenue's history. Two shots didn't slow the spinning whirl of all he learned, or the effects from the method in which he mentally digested the past. Armand was actually surprised when the liquor centered his thoughts and crystalized the bygone era of Fable Avenue's origins. Armand was at a loss of breath for it all, let alone words. So, alone he decided to be at this late hour—or early hour, such as it was in factuality. He looked to the stars and found himself washed with their cosmic calm. He was bathing up there in the heavenly waters while remaining tethered to *terra firma*.

History's clarity didn't seem so immense while gazing up at the vast cosmos. His senses unruffled. Past events didn't dissolve, however. He could still hear a history that fixed itself to his recall. Deep down south there was a rebellion. It happened over a hundred years ago, but it played fresh in Armand's head. Oppression and bondage succumb to clever stratagem and a hail of bullets and blades. Armand's inconstant senses sharpened to bring clarity to a thought he'd carried since awakening from the soothing sounds of jazz that serenaded the history he dreamed. The stars' twinkle helped soothe the rush. History and destiny's collide no longer came with a sense of vertigo. Armand could now focus. He saw clear again, as if he'd returned down the dreaming path, an area liberated by bullets, blades, and blood. And the stars twinkled its name. The cosmos translated in breaths of dust clouds. There was a place.

Water Bug Hollow.

Armand loved its story. He respected all else concerning Fable Avenue, especially the jazz man who pulled the mystical street out of the blue with the power of his blessed horn. He bowed humbly to the past life of this man named Horatio Peters. A revolutionist too in a life long ago. In a former existence he'd led a rebellion on a plantation. It was a beautiful uprising that trickled down through the ages and multiple lifetimes. A fight that waged to this day, connecting all in the conjure world. The villains altered. At the forefront of the conflict, passed down from a 'red-haired harpy', there was her son as the new antagonist.

Stanley Fallows.

A dangerous man who'd connected most of the global conjure community's malefactors. He was the past and present; and he strived to be the future. To maintain the world's existing state of affairs of chaos seeping through economics, politics and society. Armand's grandmother had spoken so much on the happenings, as did the two matriarchs of Fable Avenue he'd met. He'd learned of the true fate of his cousin Fey Forrester. He shook hands with her sweetheart. A young man of nineteen years named Gordon Goodspeed. He had power. He possessed a spirit known as the Lilac Flame, and he displayed for Armand his magnificent black- and lilac-cosmic Dooley forms.

Armand last spotted Dooley high above Fable Avenue, disappearing into the newly darkened sky. And then there was the African dragon. A construct visible to the conjure eye only. An aegis for the street. A protector shaped in a mythical creature's design.

It was intense. All of it. But Water Bug Hollow had a different ring to its history and present day. Magic was produced there by accident. There was alchemy in turning a wicked plantation into a safe-haven for runaway slaves amid the American Civil War's brutal and bloody politics. The safe-haven transmuted into a flourishing hamlet, producing a black aristocracy of trade-by-hand and hard work, and an intellectual class that went out into a world to participate in the growing wonders of post-war freedom.

History carved its mark in Armand's head as he dreamed. He awoke rested and educated of its affairs. He dived into every book that would mention Water Bug Hollow as a town or plantation. Its founder, Curtis "The Water Bug" Hollow was the subject of searches he made online. He'd seen the history, but he wanted to know if its genuine impact was recorded. There were plenty of opinion pieces. Many were not in favor of Curtis and his exploits. He was regarded as an outlaw to most historians. No context given to Curtis' battle under cruel circumstances against terrible men and women that enslaved him and his family. Armand had seen, too many times, outlaws of the Old West turned into heroes by history's remembrance. *Ironic alchemy,* he called it. He saw it the same with Curtis Hollow, inverted and perverted instead. This made his head spin with anger, boiling, and at the surface.

His indignation swelled when he learned that all of Water Bug Hollow's alchemy had been undone. Like the distortion of Curtis' history, Water Bug Hollow's present had been unwrapped and stripped down to a slum. Opportunity for growth was dissolved. Resources were thieved. The cultural infrastructure that once pumped with a proud heart during its yesteryears had deteriorated. Gang violence supplanted civil law and rule.

Armand could feel Water Bug Hollow. Its past. Its present. He also became aware that a path to the region was just beyond the backdoor of the house he was staying in. Through the front door there was Brooklyn or the crossroads. The backdoor led only to Water Bug Hollow. Armand could hear commotion beyond the door, but he never opened the house to it. He stood inches away, staying his hand from turning the knob. Freedom and culture's ebb were beyond the door, shaking the window with an inharmonious cacophony.

He couldn't sleep. He tried a drink. It didn't help. A smoke and ogling the stars soothed him. So, here he was surrounded by the calm of the crossroads underneath the heavens.

A noise was made, stealing Armand away from the belief that he was the only one in observance of the celestial bodies. There came not an elongated creak, but a low waft of wind from the open and shut of the front door on the house across the street. Armand turned his head, exhaling a stream of smoke from his lips. He grinned as he observed a fresh heavenly body step out onto the newly affixed porch. The addition to the front of the house was an indicator that the residence's mystical transition was still in flux. Not to be outdone, its identical companion sprouted a front porch all the same.

The one divergent was the presence of the woman with the symmetrical inconsistency to her flesh. Half of her was shadowed in the night sky. Her other half was painted with the glow of the African sands as they reflected the bright sun's glimmering shine. She of two halves was all beautiful to Armand's eyes; and through the darkness cloaking the legendary crossroads, he could see her. Lillian Eledas-Ghedemere dressed in the fashion of a traveling fortune teller. The glow of the half-moon above cast enough light to give her center stage, the porch her rostrum.

Armand uncrossed his legs and turned, letting them dangle over the car's hood. He slipped down onto the grass and walked across the street. The quiet was once again pestered by sound, light as it was, the ruffle of his footsteps through grass and dirt. He stopped at the border of road and lawn on the other side of the street and greeted, "Hi, Miss…Ghedemere, right? Eledas-Ghedemere," he added in a hurry to avoid any offense. Lillian nodded, and Armand continued his approach. "It's a fine night," he remarked. He leaned against the porch's railing and propped up one foot on the first stair. He looked straight up and commented, "The stars are putting on one helluva show, Miss Eledas-Ghedemere." He returned his attention to Lillian. She was staring at him with her head cocked a little to the side. A peculiar look on her countenance as she peered at him. Armand wasn't distracted or offended by it. He figured he must've looked peculiar to get a peculiar look. He was an outsider to her, after all, talking strange. He took a puff of his cigarette, exhaled the smoke away from Lillian, and extended the tobacco stick to her. He wasn't offering it, however. "You know I tried to light this thing myself—without a match." He retracted his arm and brought the cigarette back to him, looking down at it. "I wanted to see if I could use an incant on it." Back to Lillian, he asked, "Did I say that right? You know, use the word 'incant' properly?"

Lillian chuckled. "Yes," she answered him.

Armand nodded, happy to be correct. "I'm new to this conjure world," he admitted as if it wasn't obvious. "I've been playing catch up over the last couple of hours. Haven't put anything into practice though. I did try, Miss Eledas-Ghedemere," he stated as he smoked. "I tried with this here cigarette. I guess I should keep trying. I know how to make it disappear though," he joked as he took a hard toke of the tobacco stick. Lillian giggled again. Armand wanted to say something else that would charm the young conjure woman. He liked hearing the sound of her bubbly laughter.

Instead, Lillian spoke. Her voice was like a soft, sultry jazz ballad. "You've been catching up on your conjure, Mister Gideon? Is that so?"

"Yes, Miss Eledas-Ghedemere," Armand acknowledged. "More so the history of," he clarified. He liked the fact that she addressed him in the formal. She was being polite. But he did long to hear his first name spoken through the sound of her voice. He prompted that along by telling her, "You can call me, 'Armand', Miss Eledas-Ghedemere."

She nodded with a grin and told him, "I will, if that is what you wish." Then she added, "Armand." The sound of his name from her lips didn't disappoint. Armand blushed a bit, unnoticed in the dark, but unable to escape being perceived by Lillian's heightened instinct. She pivoted coolly and stepped toward a rocking chair. Another cool turn, and she took a seat, crossing her legs. "You can address me as Voodoo Lily, or you can simply call me Lily."

Armand took a drag of his cigarette as he ascended the stairs. Again, he exhaled away from the conjure woman. He said to her, "That sure is true-to-interesting, Miss Voodoo Lily. How you come across that name? Initiating ceremony? Ritual of some kind?" he guessed.

Lillian shook her head. Her smile trembled against her face, doing her best not to blurt laughter from hearing Armand's conjectures. His naivete resonated as charm and appeal to her. "No, Armand," she responded. "I was teased for being a strange, little girl growing up. I was wide-eyed and curious about the world. I could sense everything about it. I stepped with caution all the time, observing how things around me would resonate with aura. Then, to add, I have these two melanin tones painting my body. An easy target for teasing children."

"I'm sorry to hear that, Miss Lily. I quite like the way nature shaded you."

"Thank you," she acknowledged his compliment. "I could've used your kindness when I was a little girl. In all honesty, my mother taught me how to embrace both that and the nickname the other school children labeled me with," she made clear. "I was much like you are now. My mother felt it was time to introduce me to my heritage, my culture, and my father—his magic and the story of his long life, his prominent conjure family." She raised an eyebrow and grinned as she jested, "I was instituted into conjure far younger than you. I was six. It was all told to me like a fairytale." She made a face as she looked away, adding, "A fairytale that included four hundred years of blood and enslavement, a dissecting of culture and knowledge of self, thousands of years of war and the collapse of civilizations." Then she stated, looking directly at Armand, "My mother handled the more traumatic details in steps." She rocked in the chair as she concluded, "I am Voodoo Lily; and I own that now."

Armand gestured a bow. "It's a pleasure to meet you, Miss Voodoo Lily," he pronounced. He took his last puff and exhale, and then he fumbled awkwardly with where he could discard the butt of the cigarette. Lillian recommended that Armand just toss the cigarette aside. He did as tasked, and Lillian uttered a low incant and transformed the cigarette into bright ash that danced in the air like fireflies, creating a splendid lightshow that lasted for a small moment. Armand appreciated the sight and its contrast against the darkness. Lillian treated the occurrence with little mind. She did like observing Armand's wide-eyed marvel at the preternatural visual.

"So, you come here to settle down, Armand, and make a name for yourself here?"

Armand folded his arms. "I got a name, Miss Voodoo Lily. The problem I've always had is that I'm tall. I come off a little lanky. People always think they can get over on me. Maybe it's something in the face too—looks naïve, I guess. I didn't get a name as slick as yours, but I did some research and plucked out the meaning of my given name." He stated proudly, "Armand—army man, soldier."

Lillian's ears perked up hearing Armand define his name.

"I discovered that in the fifth grade. That knowledge sure as shit did do me well in a playground tussle. I was outnumbered, except I had the might of my name on my side," he clarified. "I was always a curious boy. I was always dippin' into something, lookin' to see what was behind all things, meanings, y'know. My last name? Gideon? Well that means 'great warrior'. I learned that Gideon was a Biblical hero, a judge of the Old Testament who led the outnumbered Israelites against the Midianites—whoever-in-the-fuck they are. Either way, he defeated them, killed their kings. With the odds against him, he won. A sense of pride came to me with that knowledge." He unfolded his arms and palmed the railing he leaned against before stating, "If I'd ever snuck up on all this conjure culture, my name would be the first incant that I spoke. My full name. Armand Gideon. Soldier. Great warrior. And God help you if you tried to test that. I had the unlucky knack to constantly find myself in such situations."

Lillian baptized him with a soft expression and welcoming words. "You're home, Mister Armand Gideon. This is your family. It always has been."

He quipped, "I think I may need another smoke." Both he and Lillian chuckled. She told him she understood the height his senses probably were climbing. He noted, "I've walked from Mississippi to Brooklyn in less time it took me to drive from Atlanta to here. Hell, less time it took me to walk across this street. I've dreamed of history while soothed by the melodies of an enchanted, old jazz album. I know Fable Avenue now, enough anyway." Silence fell over the night and their conversation. It wasn't too awkward, and Lillian had instinct to know there was more Armand wished to say, so she provided him time to speak, saying nothing to fill quiet. "I found myself in another tussle, Miss Lillian. It was a bad one. I hurt this guy, putting all the frustration of not finding a job into every hit I delivered to him. I left him unconscious and bloody." He exhaled and adjusted his lean on the railing. "I'm not a violent man. I'll defend myself, sure. I've had to throughout my life, but this time was different. Him being a bit of a street thug doesn't excuse my actions. I don't like that it was another black man, either. That doesn't sit well with me. As I got older, those fights hurt the most, even if I never took a hit." He clear his throat, remembered, and expressed his memory, "The whole time, my senses were elevated. I thought I was just anxious, and I was. I wanted to prove I could come out east of home and find my place. Instead I found east of home was no different from home, and I found myself a fight. A bad one," he added with regret in his voice.

Armand's body became eclipsed by a gray shadow. She didn't view the dark overcast as a bad omen, though she did interpret its presence as an *inawo*, his burden. She turned her head away from him and produced a sly grin as she thought to herself. She blinked her eyes, and in that moment, determined a resolve. "I am Queen of the Crossroads, Mister Gideon. I rule these parts. I've been sworn in by rite and blood." She returned her gaze to Armand. Her smile faded, and her stare was stern. "You're my first traveler. I am here to assist you on your path." Lillian stood and took a confident step toward Armand. When she was inches from him, she cupped his left hand with both of hers. "Take my hand; I'll show you. Or, you show me. Tell me something about your journey here, Mister Gideon."

The calm accorded to him by the stars' flicker and flash dampened, and Armand found himself once again wrangling with a sense of vertigo. The conjure woman's simple touch was not so simple in effect. She held in the palm of her hand his very breath, snatched of his respire. Something keen and haunting echoed in him with his hand nestled within hers. Armand couldn't tell whether his heart raced or slowed, whether his breath dived too deep or pushed out too far. Or perhaps it was as still as the night coloring their surroundings. He focused, not wanting to take too long in giving Lillian an answer. He remembered the stars. Their twinkle. The breath of the cosmos. The high heavens speaking in their language the place he remembered.

Water Bug Hollow.

He asked Lillian, "You ever heard of the story of Curtis 'The Water Bug' Hollow?"

"I'm familiar," she answered him, taking has hand and laying his palm out flat. "The story of African slaves in an uprising is always uplifting."

"You been?"

"No."

Armand turned his head, gazing over his shoulder at the identical house across the street. "There's a path through there. The backdoor leads to Water Bug Hollow, Louisiana. Place is now part of Jakobiville, which I learned was built around it." He turned back to Lillian. "Curtis stood up to the Jakobi family, and now through policy and hex the governing body, descendants of slave owners, are taking stock in our inventory." He exhaled hard as if he still had the smoke of the cigarette within him. "Yeah, I could use a smoke," he remarked. Lillian remained silent, keeping his hand within hers and massaging it. Armand was convinced that his draw to the conjure woman had little to do with the effect her touch was having on him. There was spirit in her caress.

"Let's walk that path," Lillian proposed in a confident tone. "Let's go beyond the door."

Armand questioned, "Now?"

Lillian pointed out in a matter-of-fact laced voice, "We're here. We're awake." She let go of his hand and stepped away from him. "Or when you're ready, traveler."

Armand thought for a moment. Then he informed Lillian, "I want to find a grave. Nobody specific. Curtis passed away in Maryland. He's buried there." He spoke his plans to Lillian, saying "I want to find at least one soldier in that war and speak to him or her." He snapped his fingers and shook his head. "Miss Voodoo Lily, I'd like to take that journey now if you don't mind. I am here, and I am awake."

Lillian beamed. She stepped down the porch's stairs, and Armand fell in line behind her. He was by her side in a few strides, and across the street they journeyed. Lillian and Armand climbed the steps of the identical porch, and then drifted through the open, identical front door. It was dark inside, but Lillian's eyes adjusted to the night. Shadows held shape and substance. Silhouettes cast form and figure. It was all truly identical to the house across the street. Everything was decorated in kind, molded to her taste and fancy.

The only difference was the back of the house in terms of function. The discrepancy lay beyond the door. On the other side. The Fable Avenue community wasn't there as it was for the house across the street. There was no communal sanctuary for African conjure and mysticism. This door led to a more pitch and grim existence.

Lillian rested her walk, allowing Armand to lead. But he too stopped inches before the door and found himself at a familiar impasse. *Bad medicine*, he thought. Lillian could sense Armand's trembling emotions. She said in a quiet voice, "It ain't been the right kind of dark cast over Water Bug Hollow for a good long while. Let's open its eyes, show that right kind of dark it's been missing. Bring its people home." Still they didn't stir. "So, Armand, let's go on outside and have a looksee." He didn't say anything in return. He didn't move, but Armand heard her. Lillian's voice was like a command from a superior officer despite being hushed. "Go on, Armand," she continued in a kind voice, stepping closer to him. "See what sort of burdens haunt the area. What's there, we will bring to heel."

Then there was movement. Armand looked at the palm of his hands, and then he surprised himself. He put his hands on his hips and he turned to Lillian beaming a bright smile that scurried away the gentle dark. He turned back to the door and remarked, "Well, hell. Introduce us." Hand on the knob, he turned it and opened the door.

Armand and Lillian stepped outside. There was another porch. The landing was broken in its wood, chipped of its paint and finish. A mirror made of timber that reflected the area's splinter and decay. There before Lillian and Armand was Water Bug Hollow in all its degeneracy. Clamor agitated the night's calm. Quiet yielded to yelling. A string of shouted curses was the standard for conversation. Tension towered over the setting like powerlines, and it was that strain that served as the power current running the rural area's people.

Armand walked down the porch's steps, taking a few strides past the stairs. Lillian was right behind him, panning her surroundings. Armand stopped. Still. He observed what was in front of him. He saw a distorted view of the beautiful mythology that lay at the foundation to Water Bug Hollow. It grew up from the ground like weeds and shackled and choked the present-day residents. He'd seen poverty before, but there was a disconnect to the penury in front of him. It shimmered under the dull streetlamps flickering in the night. But there was a gossamer thread of faith running through.

Despondency's overcast hung loose.

Willowy as hope's thread appeared, Armand calculated the Gordian Knot's unravel point from the tight despair he saw. He wanted to get to know the tithes that bind, not cheat and cut it. He wanted to be intimate with the fabric of laws responsible for creating the disorder that danced around him, whether lethargic and panhandling in rags or loud with tumultuous threats of violence. Water Bug Hollow had been hobbled, made neglectful of its own heart. Despite the crippling, there still beat a pulse, and Water Bug Hollow's history clanged voluble in Armand's head.

Lillian approached his side. "Won't be a grave found this night," she stated. "Let's not disturb the ground with anything more than the skip of our feet. Let the underground soldiers know that a merry band of two gambol across this battlefield."

Armand's face burst with surprise. "I like the way you talk, Miss Voodoo Lily," he said looking at her with his exploded look of astonishment. They both chuckled, and when the soft laughter trickled away into the night, Armand again put his gaze on the dilapidated domicile. He nodded, knowing the conjure woman was right. "Yes, Miss Voodoo Lily, I concur," he accepted and obeyed. "I'll let them warriors sleep. Ain't my place to disturb them. I feel like I need an appointment anyhow," he said with a laugh.

He did not move, and Lillian considered his pause too long for her taste. Observation was good natured, but measures of movement were needed. She coaxed Armand to take a step with a single nudge to his ribs. Together he and she took that stride. One. Lillian initiated the second step, and Armand followed. Two. The sequence of steps continued until eight. Voodoo Lily spoke a set of nonsensical words. An old incant about folly and foolery in the company of cooked rabbits. Their feet dangled over the next step, and then the pair skipped with a spirited walk into Water Bug Hollow's misery.

17

Early morning beamed, and so did Gordon Goodspeed. His shit-eating grin grew wider on his face as he repeated, "You sold me out, sun!" He giggled, teasing his brother-in-all-but-blood. "It's cool," he continued. "Really. We're still friends." The sarcasm in his tone was substantial. It was all a joke, but Benny Jah winced as he felt a sting in his stomach that resonated out and pinched his heart. Gordon used his instinct to keep an eye on the sidewalk as he held his face, blooming with a taunting smile, close to Benny Jah's cheek.

"Gordon. Stop!" Neyeli said to him, half smile on her face. Her hair resonated between the colors of amber and pink.

Gordon retracted his close countenance and faced forward, hands in his pockets as the three of them walked down Fable Avenue. Benny carried a grocery bag filled with ritual items in his arms. Gordon assured his friend, "I am kidding though, Benny." But derision didn't subside. He added for good, fun measure, "Smooth look on your personal conjure. Hard to get a hold of you for real. Made yourself so light you've been dodging my calls, my presence, this eventual, verbal ass whuppin'. Problem is, you made y' bottom lip so heavy, you let everything slip out."

Benny couldn't hold back a burst of laughter. His cheeks expanded as he tried to keep the chortle bottled. But within the blink of a split second, the pressure parted his lips and escaped. "That's funny!" he remarked still attempting to hold his face and laughter in place. He pointed to Gordon while giving a smirk and a side eye, "You got that one, kid."

Neyeli's countenance bloomed as her hair settled to a bright violet. Tension resolved.

Gordon asked, "You do understand I'm only teasing?"

Benny sighed, "Yeah, but still… Cedron was able to pull that I knew about Fey, plus your plot to get her back. What happens when we meet up with Willie again? That whip of his? Needlemen?"

"Look, sun, you told my brother because he had heart and instinct to know I had a haunt on me. The yumboes' big mouths didn't help, either. Something was bothering me, and he wanted to know—for my sake. Besides, I got an instinct too."

"Yeah?" questioned Benny. "On what?"

All manner of jest unfastened itself from Gordon's demeanor. He was unsmiling when he stated, "I'm sure Stanley knows Fey was only banished. She's out of the way. It gives him time to do whatever the hell he's doing with the kids he's stolen."

Neyeli's emotions revised her hair into a robust bronze. Concern filled her eyes, and she set a hand on Gordon's shoulder. "I'll be over as soon as I can, Gordon," she affirmed. "It shouldn't take long for Benny and me to deal with the *inawo* haunting the Water Bug Hollow church. Lady Arachne will be there to supervise. Maybe you should return home and get some rest before your journey." She retracted her hand.

Gordon opened his mouth to respond, but Benny beat him to it. "On second thought," he started, "why don't you join us. You're pretty good in a fight. We could use you."

"Not in my state," Gordon answered back. "I'd be a battery for an *inawo* with the burden I got on me. I'm calm upfront," he noted smacking his chest. "You'd be in for a real challenge, even if my Dooley spirit could match 'em pound for pound. It'd be a good fight." He pointed in Neyeli's direction and stated, "Besides, Neyeli needs me calm. She working double duty today."

Neyeli reacted by reiterating, "We'll deal with your encumbrance as soon as we sweep the church clean of its haunt." Gordon thanked her. The trio trotted up to what was now the Eledas-Ghedemere residence, one of them. The former residence of the late crossroads guardian, Gaston Fable, was now referred to as the Hollow House in reference to its path to Water Bug Hollow. The brownstone across the street, owned by the late Jackson Fable, was monikered as Crossroads Way. The threesome stepped through the iron gate and climbed the stairs. Gordon rang the doorbell, and Lillian Eledas-Ghedemere answered. She bowed at the neck toward her visitors.

Lady Arachne walked up behind her and introduced, "Lillian, have you been acquainted? This is Gordon Goodspeed, the young man who holds the lilac flame."

Lillian reached for Gordon's hand. He accepted, and they shook. "Yes. We met last October when I visited during the Four Days of the Spirit Festival." She retracted her hand.

"Oh, yes, of course. How foolish of me to forget," Lady Arachne commented.

Lillian's eyes swept over the trio standing at the door. She assessed aloud, "Well, if I recall correctly, I've met all of you."

"Yes," Neyeli confirmed. Then she commended with a bow of the head, "Congratulations, Lillian, on completing your rites for Crossroads Guardian and Queen."

"Thank you, beautiful conjure woman," she accepted the verbal salute. "Neyeli correct? Benjamin?" she called to mind and spoke their names. Benny and Neyeli confirmed with a nod. "I'm glad to meet you all again," she addressed. "My first traveler spoke of meeting you, Gordon."

Gordon noticed a shadow saunter up behind Lillian and Lady Arachne. The silhouette slid off the figure like a loose skin and revealed Armand Gideon. "Gordon!" he said with a friendly smile and giving a wave. He came into the doorway and leaned against the side. "Your spirit gonna be a part of this cleansing party?" he asked folding his arms. "Myself and the new Queen of the Crossroads here will be sitting in on all this. To observe." His words stopped as he took notice of Benjamin "Benny Jah" Brickhouse and Neyeli Campbell. He spied the grocery bag in Benny's arms. "That there all the necessities to scrub the, uh, the *eranow*…" Everyone chuckled, but Armand wasn't too embarrassed. He looked at Lillian, his eyes asking for correction.

Lillian provided the accurate terms for Armand. "*Inawo or ẹru*," she stated warmly.

Armand said as an apology, "Performing a little vivisection on the language. Pardon me. Instead of remembering two words it looks like I combined them."

Lillian patted Armand's shoulder. "It's fine, Armand. Conjure is an exact science that hasn't been exact. It's broken among us descendants of slavery. More than one word to describe one thing. We're consolidating it little by little. It understands. We do right by it."

Armand considered the point. "I'm still learning it all, y'know. If you all have trouble keeping up, God help me."

Gordon gestured with the sign of the cross. "You have been absolved, my son."

Armand smirked at Gordon's playfulness. Benny dropped the bag of items into Gordon's arms. "I like this guy," he said referring to Armand. He put his hand out. "Benjamin Brickhouse," he introduced himself. "People call me Benny Jah. This my pretty little sweetheart, Neyeli Campbell. We'll be moving the broom in the church today, if not, we'll be the broom doin' the sweepin'." Armand shook Benny's hand and gave his name. His shake was firm with Benny, light and gentle with Neyeli.

Armand witnessed Neyeli's hair shift in color from violet to a swirling red and orange. "Well if that ain't a sight!" he declared.

Benny eyed the new radiance shimmering in Neyeli's locks. "We've done this a number of times, Neyeli-baby. This run shouldn't be too different."

"It still always unsettles me," Neyeli replied to Benny. "Forgive my mood change. My hair always gives me away. It's nothing to do with you, Armand."

"Let's stay on the move, please," Lady Arachne hissed. "Inside. Inside," she corralled. The troupe adhered to the matriarch's command. Gordon moved inside stepping between Lillian and Armand. Lady Arachne stepped aside, allowing Gordon to pass. Neyeli was behind him, and Benny Jah took drag.

"You're Fey Forrester's cousin? From Cali?" Benny queried.

"I am. And I am," Armand responded putting his hands in his pockets. "I'm also aware of her circumstances. My grandmother got me up to speed on what you're dealing with."

Gordon turned around, walking backwards toward the other end of the house. "Miss Forrester told you, huh? Surprise it wasn't the braided Jamaican you walkin' alongside. A lot comes from his big mouth. Look close at his lips, objects may appear bigger than they really are."

"You got jokes, sun," Benny shot back, making a face.

Gordon kept his smile. He made his pivot, turning around to walk in the proper direction. Light chuckles conjured by his witticism were at his back. Lady Arachne led them to the house's tail door. Water Bug Hollow, Louisiana was on the other side. Neyeli's hair turned jet black as she neared the door. Her gaze resonated with determination, and it was she that broke the silence. "You ready for this, Benny-baby?"

Benny grinned. His eyes moved to the left and spotted Lillian and Armand. "You two wanna see us kick some ass?"

Lady Arachne smacked the back of his head. "Mister Brickhouse!" she scolded. "Respect the spirits you're about to encounter."

Benny rubbed his head. "Yes, Lady Arachne…" he sulked.

Gordon handed the bag back to Benny. "Let's hope that's the hardest hit you take today." He turned to Neyeli, and his demeanor changed to something more sincere. "I'll see you later, sis. Jokes aside, you guys be safe." He gave her a warm hug, and she accepted. He patted Benny Jah on the shoulder and said to his friend, "Give 'em hell, sun." He turned, gave Armand a hard handshake, and granted Lillian a gentle, parting embrace. "Good to see you two again," he told them. They acknowledged the same. Gordon stepped back and popped from existence, leaving behind a cloud of lilac dust that dissipated into sparkling snaps.

Armand shook his head. "That just won't get old, will it?" he remarked. But awe and wonder were put aside when Lady Arachne opened the door to Water Bug Hollow. Armand went still, his eyes slimmed, and his beaming expression drained. He kept silent, though there were words in his head he wanted to express.

Lady Arachne led their procession. Neyeli was close behind the matriarch, getting her first glimpse at the jazz-fabled Water Bug Hollow. Uplifted from brutal plantation to thriving, bayou hamlet. She surveyed the dingy scenery and tried to overlay the past's brightness with the present-day shantytown. She didn't have that much conjure in the world. The best she could do was control her emotions, and ultimately, her hair color remained jet black, fueled by a strong determination to exorcise the field.

The band of conjurers continued their expedition to the church, traipsing through the murky area. Benny Jah was at Neyeli's side. Armand and Lillian were behind them. Neyeli continued observing. It did her good to see that while Water Bug Hollow's heart was visibly shabby, its veins pulsed with the spirit of working-class people. But there was a hex in place that kept progress at a standstill. The efforts of legitimate labor were encircled by the underclass of riffraff that were either huddled in gangs or creeped and crawled as single, low-level thugs that assailed from shadows. The ruffians were only gatekeepers to a bewitchment disguised as law.

An electric squeal halted the conjurers in their walk. A squad car rolled up beside them, slowed down. The window on the passenger side lowered and the cop interrogated, "You folk ain't from around here, are you?" The car stopped.

Lady Arachne answered, "We're heading to the church."

"Why?" the passenger-side cop asked. "It's not Sunday," he further noted.

Everyone fell silent, except Benny. "Is this guy fucking serious?" he whispered.

"Excuse me?" the cop asked. The doors opened. The lights flashed. Blue, red. A dizzying shimmer. Both officers ejected from the car. "Can you speak up, young man?" The driver-side cop came from around the car, and both men approached the conjure party.

While tension's rose, an instinct tingled up Lillian's spine. The sense guided her eyes to the squad car's trunk, and her vision focused.

Lady Arachne stepped forward, positioning herself in front of Benny Jah. "Officer, I don't understand what the matter is," she stated trying to manage the ire in her voice. "We're only heading to the church. You can't get more innocent than that."

He ignored her and demanded, "Will the young man who asked if I was 'fucking serious' please step up."

Benny Jah moved from around Lady Arachne and the two cops converged on him. Lady Arachne glowered at Benny's maneuver. An orange color bled into Neyeli's hair as Benny riposted with an irritated tone, "Will the cops who haven't identified the initial problem please do so."

The cop answered with an order. "Open the bag and let me see the contents."

"Give me probable cause or show me a warrant and maybe I'll do so," Benny replied.

Lady Arachne cleared her throat. She put a hand on Benny's shoulder and said to the officers, "While I disagree with the young man's tone, I do believe he has a point in both his statements. Please identify the cause for all this and we'll be happy to comply."

The cops looked at one another. The driver looked in the church's direction, which wasn't too far off in the distance. The passenger cop specified, "We've had reports that drugs are being pushed out of that church. Someone in there is using it as a cover for an illegal operation."

"I can assure you that's far from the truth," Lady Arachne objected in a polite tone.

"We'll be judges to that, ma'am," said the driver, finally speaking up. He looked at Benny and demanded, "Show us the contents of the bag now!"

Benny's answer was swift. "No," he said.

"Excuse me?" the officer questioned taking a step forward.

"Officers! Officers!" Armand sauntered forward, getting between Benny Jah and the police. "There is nothing in this bag but a few items to set the spirit of the church right," he explained. The policemen glared at his presence. "You're right. The both of you. Not in the specific manner of speaking, your suspicions and all—if you don't mind me saying. There's no trafficking going on in that old church, but there is an anathema choking the atmosphere of that holy sanctuary." The cops' scathing frowns were penetrated by a small intimation of perplexity. Armand clarified with another word, "Malediction, a haunt or so. Y'see the reverend currently handling the church's affairs, he's a good Christian man, but he has some ways about him—old ways and superstitions. Now, don't let his flock know, but he's asked this lovely Vodou Queen here to dispel some of that energy most foul. He wants to change some things—he intends to. This is how he starts. Now I don't mean to offend, but please don't try and be judges to a situation. You're not judges. You're officers. Just do your duty justly, and we'll comply. That's all we're asking. Speak respectfully and have respect given."

Armand could feel the tension loosen. The cops let out a slow exhale. Benny opened the bag and tipped it forward for the contents to be viewed, and the officers examined the bag's interior. The orange color receded from Neyeli's hair, an action undetected by the officers.

"What's happening here?" Reverend Pouvwa's voice cut into the silence as he sauntered into the uneasy affair.

Armand put out his hand to Reverend Pouvwa. He greeted with a smile, "Reverend Pouvwa, is it? Correct?" The reverend accepted Armand's hand and they shook. "My name's Armand Gideon. These fine officers of the law were a little nervous that some talk around town could be true. There's been some rumblings around the campfire that drugs are being peddled out of the church."

Reverend Pouvwa retracted his hand. He stood straight. His stance was authoritative, and the officer's shrunk in reaction to his posture. "I'm not going to tell you two gentlemen how offended I am by that notion. I'll spare you, I'll spare you the volume in those words. What I will inform you about is my previous job. I'm a former detective out of New Orleans. *Look. It. Up.* The name is Mathieu Pouvwa, if you got any doubt. Trust me. I'm a of a son bitch, and I'm the son of the badge. The latter makes us brothers. But I'm the older, wiser brother. The one with important friends. And, I'm going to talk to those friends of mine back at my prior place of employment because they have connections into Jakobiville's police force." His look was stern. The finger he pointed was filled with jurisdiction and power. With his collar he had God on his side. With his company, and in the palm of his hands, he had conjure and incant. With his past, he had the authoritative advantage. "You disturb my holy grounds again with erroneous accusations, and we'll have another thing in common. The three of us will be *former* employees of a police force. Is that understood?"

It wasn't immediate. It wasn't exactly polite in tone. The two police officers resonated with a grumble, a sulking scowl made audible. "Yes, Reverend," they groused in unison.

"*Detective* Reverend," Reverend Pouvwa insisted through tightly clenched teeth.

The cops said together, "*Detective* Rev—"

"I was kidding," Reverend Pouvwa interrupted them. The others around him controlled their smiles. "Just Reverend," he rephrased, this time serious. "Now take your fallacious suspicions, and your presence, and see your way off this holy ground."

The cops scowled. The driver of the two looked up the road and noted the distance between the church and the gathered conjure party. They turned and slipped back into their squad car. No squeal peeped out of the car's siren. The squad car's lights shut off. The engine started, and the cops drove away.

Reverend Pouvwa stated, "Forgive me, Lady Arachne."

The matriarch replied, "You're not the one that needs to beg for my forgiveness." She turned away from Reverend Pouvwa and made a face at Benny Jah. Neyeli had the same look aimed at him.

Reverend Pouvwa clarified, "I was just going to rudely ask about a possible incant to trick their heads, turn them away."

Benny Jah interrupted Lady Arachne's reply to the reverend. "I'm sorry, Lady Arachne. They got the better of me." He turned to Armand and expressed, "Yo, Armand. Thanks for that back there. You got that situation calm, on a better track than I was putting it on." He extended his apology to his sweetheart Neyeli. "I just couldn't think straight. Their presence. Their questions. The arrogance of their authority."

Armand's demeanor changed as he listened to Benny Jah's words.

"I felt the same," Armand admitted. "I fought against the feeling, though. Wouldn't've been the best if both of us were acting up in their eyes." He summed up the possible situation by saying, "Two black men being uppity? We'd be in the back of the squad car right now."

"Or worse!" Lady Arachne hissed, her eyes still bent on Benny Jah.

Benny tried to sink away from the matriarch's stare and the shame he felt. He began questioning his instincts. That's when Lillian's voice emerged from the space of silence. "Pricked!" she said as if amending the word to Lady Arachne's previous statement. All eyes fell on her. She addressed Lady Arachne when she explained, "I had a quick instinct. My eyes went to their trunk. I sensed needles. Hexed."

Lady Arachne's expression was stern and pensive. She looked up the street where the squad car departed. "Someone knows we're here," she remarked in a low voice. Her eyes went to Lillian. "Take this information back to your father and Papa Solomon as soon as we're done with our duties at the church. No need to separate. Let's stay within our numbers."

"Yes, Lady Arachne," Lillian abided.

The matriarch turned to Reverend Pouvwa and dictated, "Reverend, please lead the way." He bowed at the neck, made a pivot, and started walking to the church. Every one followed. Lady Arachne was at his side. "Thank you for handling that situation back there, Reverend," she said to him. "Some tension had been dispelled before you arrived, but your authority was needed."

"I'm glad I could assist," he replied. "It felt good to make myself useful. I've been around here like an awkward adolescent. It's time I came into my own."

"Well, I'm very proud of you, Mathieu," she emphasized in a mother's tone of voice. She looked at the reverend and felt something different toward him.

Reverend Pouvwa felt good to hear the matriarch's sentiment.

Neyeli had her arm entwined with Benny's. Her conjure pulsed from her to him, and his emotions pacified. He apologized again, and Neyeli assured he didn't have to. "Let's get ourselves centered. We have ritual and banishment to attend to."

"That's right, Neyeli-baby. Let's get back on the clock."

Armand stepped up next to Benny Jah and relieved him of the bag in his hands. He lost a step, surprised by the bag's weightlessness. "I was expecting this to be a little heavier." Then weight settled into to the cradle of his arms. "What-in-the-strange-fellow?" he questioned.

Benny said over his shoulder, "That's my fault, or rather, my conjure—controlling weight and wind." Then he perked up. "Doesn't sound like much, but it's worth what I make it; and I've meditated and made some modifications. I'm that dude you want on your side, sun. You'll find your inner conjure in time."

Lillian noted, "Armand is scheduled for a stitching ceremony." She beamed at the newcomer to the conjure community. He held a half smile, having heard of such rituals performed.

"That's gonna leave you out of commission for a few days," Benny gave a heads up.

Armand replied with worry in his voice, "I've heard."

"You get to know yourself, though," Benny continued. "You get to see your burden, *inawo*." He nodded his head in the direction of the church they approached. "It shouldn't be like the fight we're about to wrap ourselves up in, but you'll get to know yourself personally and in a tough way."

Neyeli gave Benny a look. She turned to Armand and said as they approached the church's front door, "He's not majoring in life coaching."

"No," Benny retorted. "I'm majoring in business. That's what I'm about, and that's what I'm giving. Besides, California over here looks tough. He'll wrestle and tame that burden."

Reverend Pouvwa opened the church's front doors. The quaint and simple interior, draped in shadows, gave the impression of a yawning maw. The conjure party shepherded in the day's gray illumination. The dull, translucence still managed to color the darkness by exposing the interior. The pews waded in a stream of shadow, peeking from a dark cloud. Reverend Pouvwa spoke Psalms, Chapter 119, verse 105. *"Thy word is a lamp unto my feet, and a light unto my path."* His voice was a low whisper. He focused, and the Holy words became an incant. Bright flames popped into existence on the candles' wicks. He voiced another chapter and verse. From Exodus 14:21, only paraphrased. *"Then Moses stretched out his hand over the sea…and the waters were divided."* Curtains parted. Stained-glass windows were revealed. All manner of shadow dispersed. Reverend Pouvwa turned to Lady Arachne and said in a boyish tone, "Your lessons paid off. I've been practicing." She put a hand on his arm and beamed a proud smile. "I still feel a way about using Bible verses to create fire," he admitted.

Lady Arachne snickered, *"Chile, please!* Them bully cops out there represent the flames of Hell, not no Holy scripture-conjured flame. However," she stated before speaking an incant in a low, silky voice. The bright flames dimmed in both light and potency. A careful touch should the *inawo* get out of hand. "Let's mute the flames' vibrant passion, shall we? Just in case." She smiled at the reverend and said, "Take no offense. Your display was perfect."

Reverend Pouvwa bowed at the neck. "I'm far from offended, Lady Arachne. Thank you. I'm a little impressed with myself that I didn't burn the place down. Those disastrous attempts—humorous in hindsight—are fortunately in the past."

Armand and Lillian took a seat in the back left pew. Both had their legs crossed like aristocrats waiting to be entertained. Armand's eyes swept the church. He saw Benny place the bag of ritual items at the pulpit. He and Neyeli shook Reverend Pouvwa's hand while Lady Arachne made formal introductions.

Lillian whispered to Armand, "This is only my second *inawo* banishing." Armand turned and gave her a surprised look, prejudiced that she'd seen plenty. "My grand uncle was an old man burdened by the accidental death of his sister. She was sixteen when it happened. He was in his early twenties, and he blamed himself. I've never been quite sure as to why, but he held onto that moment even though he was able to communicate with his sister a few times. In his older age, the burden was scratching at him more than ever. The *inawo* was culled from his spirit and banished. He passed away in peace a year later, but he seemed so much happier for that short time." She told Armand, "A burden can really hold someone back, even someone with conjure."

Armand considered the point as he observed the ritual taking place at the front of the pulpit. Lillian stole discreet glances at him from the sides of her eyes. His hungry gaze swallowed the sacrament's unfolding. The bag lay open on a wide purple fabric that Neyeli laid out. Reverend Pouvwa placed the church's collection plate beside the bag. Benny Jah removed the contents for the hallowed liturgy. The first item he pulled was a helix-shaped, ebony scepter with a skull for a handle. He set the scepter above the plate. Next, he removed a bottle of white rum that was infused with African bird pepper. It was handed to Lady Arachne along with a cigar and an empty wooden bowl. A quick incant lit the cigar, and Lady Arachne put the smoking item across the bowl's rim. She opened the bottle of African bird pepper-infused white rum and poured it into the empty bowl, lacing the cigar with its contents as well. The last component to the ritual was a bowl wrapped in cling film to keep its contents from spilling. Benny undid the wrapping and set the bowl on the bronze plate. Inside was food consisting of fried plantains, black goat and rooster meat with coconut shavings and pistachios strewn over the mix. Benny planted a spoon into the bowl as if he was placing a birthday candle in a cake. Then he stepped away from the ritual items. Reverend Pouvwa followed him, standing at his side.

Lady Arachne whispered into Neyeli's ears. The young woman nodded. She turned to Lillian and proposed, "Would you like to join us in the opening prayer-song?"

Lillian's face erupted with surprise. "I would be delighted!" she answered. She stood and joined Neyeli and Lady Arachne in a hurry. Armand was happy for her, though he felt her emptiness when she left the pew.

The three women held hands. Lillian and Neyeli harmonized in a soft hum, and Lady Arachne sang a French-Creole ballad that spoke of calling a spirit for assistance in clearing an area of its hauntings and burdens. Lillian and Neyeli's harmonized hum melted into a silky call and response to Lady Arachne's singing. The young women's voices washed back to their initial harmony. Lady Arachne crooned the second verse. The chorus was repeated with Lillian and Neyeli's haunting repetition. Lady Arachne caroled on about violent deaths and spirits unrested, and for those spirits to rise and be put at ease. The chorus followed, and then the song came to an end. Neyeli gave Lillian a hug. Lady Arachne thanked her, and she returned to her seat.

Armand said nothing. His eyes were concentrated on Lillian for the song's entirety, but he decided to save his compliment for later. It would seem that within the moment, both he and Lillian were fixed on the ceremony's continuance.

Lady Arachne called Reverend Pouvwa to her. She bent down, picked up the bowl of food, and presented it to the reverend just as he stepped up to her. "Eat," she instructed.

The reverend did as tasked, taking a single scoop of the contents and scarfing it down. The taste was a swivel of savory and sweet. Spice pinched his tongue, and the honeyed flavor coated his senses soon after. He took three more scoops and greedily ingested the portions. He set the bowl down in a manner not like his own, exaggerated in movement. The overplayed movement continued when he wiped his mouth with his sleeve.

Lady Arachne bent down and took up the lit cigar and bottle of white rum. "That took no time, did it Nibo-Granmoun?" she commented. "Shit, you almost all-the-way-here. Don't seem like I need to blow your smoke." She took a hard drag from the cigar and then exhaled the smoke into Reverend Pouvwa's face. The smolder swirled around the holy man, making a globe of thick fog around his head. Then it converted into worm-thin strands that seeped into Reverend Pouvwa's ears and nose.

He shook his head with his eyes closed as if he was attempting to settle a dizzy sensation. He looked at Lady Arachne. Manners exaggerated, he inspected the conjure woman up and down. "The hell you got me here for, you sweet, sticky thang?"

"There are spirits unsettled here, Nibo-Granmoun," she told the possession.

"Ain't no children of mine!" he protested, nose in the air.

"They aren't young, no," she admitted. "But they are disquiet. They infect this hallowed ground—"

"Don't blaspheme me!" the spirit argued. "This place? Ain't no damn holy ground. Ain't no such thing. The consecrated soil was covered up. The dances don't take place here no mo', woman! Red-haired harpy made sure. You know that." He closed his eyes and remembered. "Oh, how I loved dancin' with them folk 'round that fire on that celebration. I invisible introduced myself to them. I remember them days." He scowled and said, "And I remember the backs that turned on it." His hips swayed in an effeminate manner as he walked around Lady Arachne. His hand rested on his hip just the same. "Where you been, Miss Sassy Spider? My other self ain't see you with Miss Maman Anansi in the morning with them kids."

"I have my duties," she explained. "And I need the assistance of the first person to die by violence, patron to those who die by unnatural causes."

He grinned. Then his eyes drifted down and spied the white rum in her hand. "Ooooooh, sweet pussy——cat! Look. What. You holdin'." He raised his eyes back to her. "Now, you sho' is tryin' to seduce me, you sweet, lickin' stick. Just like that time out in D'trah't. You naughty thing. Made me and that horse-nigga I poh-sessed-with-zest feel so good. Me ridin' him. You ridin' the both of us. Then us ridin' you! One of the best funerals I ever attended."

Lady Arachne didn't have time to reminisce. "You want this?" she teased, holding up the liquor, shaking the bottle as a means of seduction.

His eyes wandered back to his intoxicating, fiery liquid desire. *"C'mon and give me a drink!"* he sang in a deep, soulful fashion. Lady Arachne smiled and handed the bottle to him. He undid the cap and drank and drank and drank and drank. Half gone. He handed it back to Lady Arachne while smacking his lips. "Now let me have something to suck on, brown and thick," he articulated with a wide, toothy grin. Lady Arachne handed him the cigar. He smoked and blew. "You got this coated with that liquor brew." He reached down and swiped the scepter. Then he pranced to the podium. He let out a loud rooster's crow. It was time to really keep awake the unrested spirits. He calmed his holler and said, "Please turn to the Book of the Horn, Chapter Ten; Verse Two-Eighteen." He tapped the scepter's skull handle against the podium in rhythm with his words. It was hypnotic.

Lillian's ears translated the tapping and words into a lullaby. Armand heard thunderous, slow booms of a pumping heart. Benny's ears picked up something similar, but it sounded more like war drums pounding on the two and four. Lady Arachne just heard the tap, tap, tapping.

"I'm here to tell you about the killing of two men!" he hollered. "The year was nineteen hundred and thirty-three! Revenge boiled in a man. He was a ma-yuh-sician—piano man. He was a drinker, womanizer, gun-toting gambler. And *he* was the righteous one! Then there was the law provider. The law abider. The preacher. So. Filled. With. Sin. Took advantage of young girls. Yes, he did. He was an instrument to control the people. He kept them from their true history. He did the bidding of the wrong people—people unalike in nature. He did the bidding of people who were always, with nature, at war. Spiritually infantile and unable to mature. It all came together on a night that had been long smothered of traditional celebration. The people celebrated freedom; and that was taken away from them. The people celebrated culture; and that was taken from them.

"Not only did the preacher—their law provider—keep history and tradition from these people, but he took advantage of a girl only fifteen years in age. On that night, he forced himself on her after she'd given her blessing as a beautiful singer to a packed crowd in this here church. The gambler was this girl's guardian. He discovered what had happened, and that's when the killing began! The guns went *BOOM!* He killed the preacher. The area's police killed him. And their spirits have been restless ever since. Hexed ritual upon hexed ritual has only stirred the unease, pulled its strings. It ain't left. It ain't right. It's expanded and caught the people of Water Bug Hollow that live here now." He lifted his hand and shouted, "I blame you!"

The cross cracked.

A large cloud of murky afterlife seeped through the fracture and split in two directions. The dark, funneling winds configured into lanky exaggerated shapes of the men their despair represented. The candles' flames were extinguished of their brilliance, and a shadow fell over the church's interior. It seemed to even hold back the light penetrating the stained-glass windows.

Neyeli's coiled locks rippled into writhing snakes. The heads hissed and made quick flaps of their long tongues. She pulled two free. They straightened into short lances. The locks they'd possessed returned to normal, save the new color resonating from the follicles. The tails sharpened to a point. The mouths remained open. She tossed one to Benny, and he caught it, charging forward at the smoky, residual burden of Reverend-Mayor Lionel Ladon. The living strain, dressed in the rags of a once fine, tailored suit, had its back to the assailing Benny Jah. It turned its torso to face him and its elongated, smoldering face opened its mouth and screeched, welcoming the fight. Benny lightened his weight through conjure and soared up for an aerial attack.

The lingering, troubled inawo-Quincy, shaped in snaking haze and wearing the shredded digs of the former jazz pianist, launched into the air to meet Benny Jah. One smoky hand wrapped around Benny's wrist. The other hazy hand seized the young conjure soldier's neck. Both weightless, but inawo-Quincy took Benny by surprise. The murky specter added weight to its form and pushed Benny to the ground. The impact did little to affect the conjure-warrior, light as he was through his power. But the attack took him off guard, and consequence of the assault returned Benny to his normal weight as his back lay against the church floor. Inawo-Quincy took Benny by the collar and bawled a high-pitched resonance. The sound reverberated in Benny's ear and pinned him in place.

Footwear thudded heavy against the creaking, wood floor. Inawo-Quincy looked up. Neyeli was sprinting in his direction, snake weapon up and ready for a single, melee-ending strike. Inawo-Lionel hissed a deafening shriek that filled the church mere moments before leaping forward and torpedoing into Neyeli's body. The conjure woman slammed against the wall behind her. Her weapon dropped from her hand.

Inawo-Lionel landed a few steps in front of inawo-Quincy as he straddled and restrained Benny Jah. The two burdens volleyed shrills at one another. Inawo-Lionel entangled his fingers, balling his hands together. He swung his arms like a golf club. His interlaced hands, balled together, slammed into inawo-Quincy's chin. The ẹru lost his grip on Benny Jah and was lifted into the air with the impact. He crashed hard against the floor, landing a few inches from Lady Arachne. The conjure woman stepped away, swift but cautious, taking advantage of the moment as inawo-Quincy recovered from the attack. She ascended the stage and joined the possessed Reverend Pouvwa at his side.

Benny attempted to flip his body up onto his feet, but inawo-Lionel grabbed his shirt first and tossed him into the pews. The action was swift and violent, but Benny Jah remained conscious enough to lighten his weight. He bounced like a loose balloon, grabbed a pew, and flipped into a crouched position on the back of the long bench, regaining composure. He shook his head and blinked. He caught a glimpse of Neyeli jumping to her feet, weapon in hand, making a strike against inawo-Lionel. She swiped at him, but the lanky construct dodged. A thrust at him made him take a step back. Inawo-Lionel's body curved, stomach in, chest bent forward. He caught her arm, grabbed her neck, and heaved her to the back of the church.

Benny propelled himself at Neyeli's tossed body. His conjure pushed him forward, light and fast. He wrapped his body around hers and lightened their weights. They bounced against a stained-glass window without bruise or crack. Feet against the ground, they turned to face the inawo who were now engaged in fisticuffs against one another.

The possessed Reverend Pouvwa commented in a voice not his, "They still got fight with each other! Brother against brother. The millstones treating Water Bug Hollow, and its people, as grain in the grind." He closed his eyes and shouted, "This ain't our doing! But this *is* our responsibility!"

Armand listened to what was preached. He said in a low voice, "The instruments. Not the cause."

The inawo hurled fists at one another, and then they stopped and turned. Their black eyes, condensed spheres of swirling smoke, focused on Armand. They walked toward him, ghosting through pews, screeching in his direction. Their sharp shrills penetrated Armand's chest and escalated his heartrate. His awareness swelled, and the fight that existed within the phantom burdens gushed through him. He felt the rush of anger, a heightened sense of bedlam. The peak of an argument. Before the yelling, the gunshots, and the adrenaline rush of fear and the accomplishment of hurting someone, killing them. The release. The liberation of wrath and rage.

Armand grinned. He stood and climbed over the pew in front of him. Lillian got to her feet and reached for him. "Armand, don't..."

He said over his shoulder, "It's okay, Miss Voodoo Lily. I think I can tame these two." At the inawo he declared, "You boys got a fight for me?"

"Armand!" Lillian pleaded. "They want to bite you, get strength from the burden you carry!"

Armand put out his forearm, taunting the encroaching inawo. "My burden is I'm looking for a good fight. It's here in Water Bug Hollow. I feel a necessity to relieve this area of its burdens. They want to bite me, they'll only taste themselves. And cannibalism is bad for your health." He teased the inawo, "I dare you. C'mon. I'll get closer if you want." He scaled the next set of pews.

Benny calculated a charge at the inawo. The phantoms were distracted, but they'd put up a fight if alerted to his move. Benny said to Neyeli, "I still feel guilty about what I did to Cedron." He gave her a knowing look, a plea in his eyes. "It's a burden," he told her.

Neyeli sighed. She knew Benny's plan. They'd executed it before, and she so hated the desperate move, performed numerous times to her disliking. Always last-ditch. Reluctant, Neyeli put a hand on Benny's shoulder and used her conjure to increase the guilt within him. The inawo stopped. They turned with haste, hollering their banshee-like cry at him. They didn't amble in their steps. They raced.

Neyeli plotted a bold gambit. She stepped in front of Benny and made an attack at inawo-Quincy, attempting to stab him. He caught her wrist. Just as she'd planned. Before he could toss her aside, Neyeli put her hand against the smoke of his chest. Her conjure tapped into the apparition's consciousness, and his actions halted.

Inawo-Lionel continued forward, possessed of determination to bite and feed off Benny's hefty burden. But while Benny was indeed chained to his guilt, the use of his conjure granted him physical weightlessness to evade any offense made against him. He had to concentrate harder, however. His guilt-ridden mind seeped a sense of dizziness into him.

Armand watched still connected to the fight and rage. He balled his fists. His eyes bent on the actions in front of him. His teeth clenched, grinding against one another.

Neyeli communed with inawo-Quincy in the same moment. Revenge and rage were at his surface. Beneath the bitter recrimination was a duty to bring peace, to end the fight. Neyeli agreed. She spoke to the inawo through her conjure. Sounds of magic and mathematics conversed. *Take my instrument,* she said to the foggy wraith. It loosened its grip on her. She offered the straightened snake to the inawo, and it took it up in its waving-smoky fingers. Neyeli stepped aside, and inawo-Quincy dashed into the confrontation with Benny and inawo-Lionel.

Benny's steps, though light, were graceless. The world spun, and the headache he suffered was forcing his eyelids shut. He saw inawo-Lionel's charge even as his vision turned upside down. He planted himself firm, though there was little space to move before backing up into the wall. Inawo-Lionel grabbed Benny's arm and went in for the bite. Its mouth hung wide, and it remained that way as the creature froze. It attempted to cry its deafening shriek, but the noise was cut short and swallowed. Inawo-Quincy made its strike, stabbing inawo-Lionel through the back.

The world continued tumbling around and around for Benny. He wanted to throw up, but he controlled the urge. He focused on inawo-Lionel as its hazy frame reshaped into a faint specter of the broad-shouldered Reverend Lionel Ladon of long ago. Changed. Specter-Ladon turned and walked through inawo-Quincy. He made his way to the aisle, and walked to the pulpit. He dropped to his knees and put his hands together. He said in an echoing voice, "I do not ask for forgiveness. I ask for proper judgement. I will run from it no longer." A red glow outlined him. It grew and covered him whole. The gleam constricted on itself and then blinked away. Red smoke lingered behind, shimmering before dwindling away.

Benny's eyes moved from the apparition's vanishing to inawo-Quincy standing in front of him. "Thank you…" he told the inawo, consciousness waning. He had little strength in him, but enough. He jammed his weapon into the haunt's chest. Benny's feet gave out. He dropped to a sitting position on the floor, and his stomach turned, bubbling inside. He put a hand over his mouth and controlled the muscles in his stomach so as not to lose its contents. He closed his eyes as the snake weapon turned into a bright light before funneling into the inawo's chest. Specter-Quincy appeared. His clothes were redressed anew. He walked to the organ at the front of the church, and he started playing a soft and sweet gospel melody that provided a melodic benediction to the spiritual ceremony.

Lillian came from around the last pew and entered the two rows up where Armand stood. He was looking down, catching his breath with long, relaxed inhales and exhales. She put a hand on his shoulder and asked if he was okay. "Just a little embarrassed about how I acted."

Lillian assured, "You did well for someone who, just a few days ago, didn't know any of this existed." She got close to his face and joked, "I was a tad curious myself to see what would happen should they bite you. Now, that says what about me?" She tapped a finger against his chin to raise his face and spirit. Armand felt better, and he showed it through a boyish grin and a wink at the young Crossroads Queen.

Neyeli rushed to Benny. She palmed his shoulders and used her power to alleviate the burden weighing on him. His body felt light, and his conjure had nothing to do with it. He exhaled. Euphoria discharged through his bloodstream, but all of his burden was not consumed. He needed rest. His growing headache was far from subsiding, and it hurt to lift his head. He moved his eyes, though, and looking at Neyeli stabilized the world's spin. It was even a better remedy for his headache than her conjure.

"You okay there?" she asked Benny trying to meet his eyes.

"Nothing some rest and a blessing can't handle."

Neyeli patted him on the knee. "I'm a little drained too. Some of that burden got to me when I spoke with it." She looked over her shoulder and spotted Lillian. "Gordon might have to have another guide into the *mirak*."

Lady Arachne spoke incants into the air. Her words were silent, but Nibo-possessed Reverend Pouvwa finalized his sermon while continuing his raps against the podium with the scepter. "We are at rest!" he stated. "Let this peace forever surround us, sheath us with love. Let its brawn protect us. Let its acute vision watch over us. Wherever we are, let it be there. We are at rest. Let all be well." One. Two. Three raps. Quincy's spirit faded. A few more chords played on the organ, and then the music vanished with him.

Nibo-Reverend jumped from the pulpit. He bent down and snatched up the bowl and ate the remaining contents. He knocked the spoon to the floor and ate with his hands. When the food was no more, he turned his voracious appetite to the last of the white rum. He twisted the cap and tossed the bottom half of the liquor down his gullet.

Lady Arachne turned and faced him. "Come," she said. "Follow me." She made her way to the back. Nibo-Reverend followed. She told the others over her shoulder, "I'll be back. I need to put him to bed. Reverend Pouvwa will need an incant to recover from this."

"Yes, Lady Arachne," Neyeli spoke for them all.

Nibo-Reverend smiled broad. "You gon' ride me to sleep, sweet pussy—cat?"

Lady Arachne protested through a light chuckle, "Nibo-Granmoun, desires for this handsome reverend have been put aside."

"Same thing was said in eighty-three when it came to that Yoruba conjure man you met in Paris. Remember how that turned out?"

They disappeared through a door leading to a hallway.

Neyeli continued attending to Benny.

Armand caught his breath. He looked around the church, and he saw a change. There was a ripple in reality. The church's colors brightened. The shadows receded, yielding to the day's light that was now bright through the windows. The candles extinguished by the *inawo* entrance flickered with flame again. Unseen was the shaky façade's and foundation's reconstruction to a sturdy structure and base. Cracks in the walls healed. The three conjure folk and single initiate felt the change their eyes didn't witness.

Armand excused himself and went outside. He was welcomed to a brighter Water Bug Hollow. The fog had thinned, but its slight ebb only brought the dysfunction into focus. Armand didn't mind. Restless spirits could be raised and made docile. He nodded his head thinking at the notion. Focused, an instinct scratched his forehead. He paused for a moment. Something flashed in the distance. There coruscating in the reach was a beacon of spirit only his eyes, now flowering with conjure, could see.

Lillian walked up next to him. He turned to her and declared, "I know where the bones can be found." Lillian was delighted to hear Armand speak in such a way. He pointed to where he'd seen the swirling glimmer, and she gazed in the direction. There it was. A brief moment. A flash beckoning to come closer. "Can you lead me there?" he asked her in a humble voice.

"Yes," Lillian answered. "Follow your guide, traveler." She winked at him. Her eyes surveyed Water Bug Hollow and noted the fog had loosened some of its grip.

Enough.

Everyone saw something, but all sight was not with eyes. At first.

At the center of Jakobiville was a tall, tall, tall building. Inside, there were gestures of politics for the mundane and pedestrian. There were also politics for the occult and the greater mystery.

A glass of brandy was held close to Mayor Sampson Jakobi's lips when a sensation scratched the back of his neck. Tailor-suited in gray with a black tie and white shirt, the broad-shouldered, brawny mayor nearly spilled his drink by way of his reaction. No drop spilled, but he cursed to himself with teeth clenched. The scrape against his neck was coarse and unforgiving. Discomfort set in with no signs of easing. He put his glass down as the sting reverberated up his neck to the back left of his head, tightening his sinuses, and numbing the left side of his face.

He turned and looked out the high-rise window. He saw the day change too, but the brightness was dull to him. It was muted like the celebratory music coming from across the hall commemorating the pass of legislature agreed to on both sides of the political aisle. His bold features twisted. He turned his back and decided not to recognize the feeling and the change in the day. He seized his drink and knocked it back in one gulp.

Now he understood the sensation that drew him to have a private drink away from the party across the hall. "That nigger-conjure work ain't no good!" he said in his Cajun drawl. "It won't last," he told himself. He cursed and poured another drink. Tossed back. One gulp. Someone knocked on the door. "It's open," he said, finishing a third.

An older man stepped in. He was a burst of happiness and festivity. He too had a drink in his hand. He also wore a party hat and carried a toy whistle. "Mayor Jakobi! Everybody's looking for you. Whatchu doin' in here? Why you look so sour? It's a party!"

Sampson fixed his face and smiled. "You right, Perry. You right."

"Then come 'round that desk and get back in here. Your wife's lookin' for you. Your sons too! C'mon, now. You too young to look so dour. C'mon, boy! Don't let an old man like me out-party you!"

Sampson laughed. He was fifty-two in age, but that was still young against Perry's seventy-eight years. The biting ache that had been gnashing at his neck released a little bit of its teeth. He turned his back to the window. The change in the day behind him, he listened to the old man named Perry and returned to the party.

Conjure disregarded. Old black magic, to this strapping mayor, be damned.

18

Simaetha Ghedemere beamed brighter than the sun, and her daughter Lillian was the guiding light behind her luminous smile. The radiance of motherly pride cast Lillian in a spotlight. She was conducting a ritual at the moment, kneeling down next to Gordon Goodspeed as he rested in a plush chair. Mother and daughter, Madame Jeliya and the spirit of Gordon's mother, Althea Goodspeed, were all gathered in Gordon's *sanctum sanctorum*. From what was imparted to Simaetha, the area she now stood in was once a dank basement. By way of spirits conjured from some place beyond, the musty cellar inside the Goodspeed residence was magically refurnished to the bright, holy haven that surrounded her now.

Simaetha oversaw her daughter's inaugurating rites that crowned her Queen of the Mississippi crossroads. In such a short time, she was assisting in matters of great importance to the global conjure community. Simaetha considered her stay on Fable Avenue a welcomed blessing. It was a breather from politics, though the Fable Avenue community was often the center of conjure affairs regardless of location. No one was judging her here, she noted. No one was giving her an eye because of her daughter's father. Nor were there whispers of nepotism that focused on her daughter's rightful inheritance to the Clarksdale, Mississippi crossroads. Simaetha had reservations about her daughter becoming crossroads queen at first. When there was disdain from other conjure folk in her community, she reversed her convictions. Satchel had rightful claim. He made his argument among his family and *nasyon*. He gifted the area to his daughter. The mothers from Satchel's other children didn't like his decision, but Lillian's half-brothers and half-sisters were either considered too old, not as well versed and equipped in conjure, or they simply weren't as interested as Lillian. They were a part of the conjure community, but it was just tradition and routine with them, not the true magic of ancestry and the power to shift reality through ritual, incant, or a personal conjure.

Lillian was like a master in the craft, and Simaetha observed now her daughter as she soothed Gordon Goodspeed, the young man blessed with the renowned Lilac Flame. One of Fable Avenue's own was intended to guide him into the *mirak*. Her name was Neyeli, if Simaetha could correctly recall. She and her sweetheart assisted in exorcising angry burdens at the church in Water Bug Hollow. Neyeli was nursing her sweetheart back to fine fettle, and she too needed quality rest. Wrestling with *inawo* was no easy feat, and they took on two. Simaetha was greatly impressed, but she was also grateful for their being winded by the ordeal. Her daughter could step in and prove her prowess and merit. Fable Avenue's conjure culture would be a beacon for her and her daughter, Simaetha trusted. A stamp of approval for the other conjure communities to perceive.

Gordon was not quite de-stressed, but Lillian imparted a strong incant through the palms of her hands that effected the restless lilac spirit inside him. She also engaged in light banter, telling Gordon, "In the conjure circles I dwell in, we refer to you as *The Living Iboju Boy*' and your sweetheart, Fey, as *The Living Nkisi Girl*'."

Gordon couldn't help but smile at the sentiment, hearing that he was being referred to as a classic comic book character among the conjure communities. He considered the acknowledgment fitting. Since being imbued with the lilac spirit, he'd looked to comic books for inspiration on experimenting with his cosmic, conjure power. He couldn't perceive a more fitting title, at least not one that made him smile as wide. To be a part of something that brought such a childhood rush to him. It made the experience seem whimsical, even when he reflected on the darker constituents.

Gordon's childhood heroes were a part of something called *The Lwaverse*. Artists and writers from the conjure community created the wondrous comic book world of *akọni*, a Yoruba phrase that translated in English as 'heroes' or 'brave'. Gordon believed the conjure community brought it all to reality. To be as the illustrated champions was an honor not just to his memories of plunging in between colorful page after colorful page when he was a child, but to his culture now as a young man.

There was an effect that accompanied the information, beyond Gordon's chuckle. His tight anxiety loosened, and the incant that coated Lillian's hands seeped into Gordon's skin like an anesthetic. He became lightheaded, and there came an ebullience dancing in his head. It gathered at the back of his brain and funneled down his spine, exhausting restless energy that kept him tense.

Lillian smiled up at Armand. His ears echoed the names she used to describe Gordon Goodspeed and his cousin Fey Forrester. He added to the conversation, "Yeah! That's the comic book I grew up on. Black-owned comic book company. Love all the other characters and titles they've created. Haven't collected in years, but they stay with me."

"Conjure folk upstate built the 1120 Comic Company," Gordon informed. His voice sounded tired as the effect further set in. "Company was established August, nineteen-eighty-six," he dated. "First comic, *Iboju Boy and Nkisi Girl* was based on Elisheba Bloomscale and Lapen Jack…" He finished what he needed to say, but his words sounded as if he'd run out of breath as sleep was induced.

"My sister got a trade paperback of old *Iboju Boy and Nkisi Girl* issues," Armand relayed reminiscing about that Christmas. "I was hooked that day. My mother thought it was nonsense." He went to say more, but the silence that possessed the room clogged his throat. He noticed that Gordon had drifted off to sleep, and Lillian had gone with him. She was still, head down with her eyes closed, hand-in-hand with Gordon.

Madame Jeliya rearranged the items on Gordon's altar, plucking and placing them like pieces on a chessboard. She lit two incense sticks and blew an incant on them as they burned. She inhaled the smoke, walked to Lilian and Gordon, and blew the vapor over them.

Their sleeping bodies inhaled the hazy, incense cloud. The dream came immediately to them, born from smoke and cosmic matter summoned by the mind. It was not the usual dream. It was the *mirak*, and like so many visits to the reverie, the formless voice of lucid dream condensed to become the crossroads. Lillian held Gordon's hand. Her eyes panned the surreal scenery. The color of the sky, at dawn, bled into clouds that dripped into raindrops that never hit the ground. The rain evaporated into air, absorbed by the color of the dawning sky, repeating the phenomenon. Eventually the day steadied as sunny. The clouds disappeared along with the rain, and the surreal phenomenon never occurred again.

But there still lingered some oddities.

A large mouse with webs in its eyes devoured a plastic model of a science fiction spaceship. A dead fox lay next to it, scratched up and nibbled on. Newspaper articles were carried by a gentle wind like autumn leaves. A translucent image of Water Bug Hollow sat at the upper-left quadrant of the crossroads. Two, strong brownstones rested across the way in the upper-right quadrant. Flowers surrounded the mighty buildings.

Lillian's eyes happened to spy Gordon. He was suited in his skin-tight, cosmic outfit. His Chokwe-like African mask covered his face. She knew the name of this form. *Dooley.* Her eyes were drawn to the mask. Its gravity fastened her attention as she traced its contours like an artist to their subject before rendering.

Dooley too so was affixed. His eyes didn't focus on the phantasmagorical happenings around them but on the man seated behind a desk at the crossroad's center. It was his English professor from last year. Professor James Brede. He was there with an eerie grin running across his face. His sweeping hair draped a single curl down his forehead. A bottle of red wine lay on the desk at his left. A filled wine glass was situated next to it. Dooley wondered why the professor's presence was called to his voyage into the *mirak*.

Lillian let go of Dooley's hand and said to him, "Forward, Dooley. Speak with that man there. He's important to you, no?"

Dooley turned to the Crossroads Queen and said, "That's my college Literature professor. Professor James Brede." Dooley became pensive.

Lillian continued examining the mask. She was lost deep in its features before Dooley snapped her from her stare by saying, "It's a mystery. All of this. There's something deeper." He turned his head and focused on Professor Brede at the desk. "It's my conscience…? I think…?" Dooley pondered. He faced Lillian again. "Professor Brede taught me a lot about seeing beneath the surface of stories, to recognize and interpret a deeper meaning to a tale, convert a hidden message into something tangible and coherent." He tied his assumptions together and surmised, "Perhaps my mind is producing him as a way to conduct a session to go deeper and find the memory I need." Then he quipped, "I should've brought my school notebook." Lillian chuckled at his witticism. Dooley didn't revel in his humor. Jest came to an abrupt halt when a jarring thought punctured his mind. "Waitaminute!" he said in a low voice. His head turned again. "He and his wife were the last to see Fey alive, before she was hexed and performed a banishment on herself."

Fey's voice then played in his head. *"The Bredes are either needlemen or perhaps they were dolled in some way—*kontwòl'd. *Don't interrogate them again. If they were dolled, you could be putting them in danger."*

Dooley's eyes met Professor Brede's. His smile shifted in a manner so slight only Dooley's preternatural instinct could detect its new, sinister sentiment. Dooley answered Fey's faint voice, "And if they're night doctors, then I'm putting myself in danger." He paused for a moment. Lillian stared at him. Her instinct perceived Fey's voice, but couldn't decipher it. She knew Dooley was responding to the disembodied sound. So, she only observed. Dooley expressed, "But the two of them are pieces to this puzzle. I can get inside their mind. I can go visit Mister Brede. It would look less suspicious. I could be catching up on old times with him while probing his mind for memories. I'll be ready for whatever I find—consequences and all, whatever they might be." His words were more than replies. They were a memory. Something he'd already said.

Dooley flinched as if waking from a dream. He turned his entire body forward and stepped toward the middle of the intersection. His mask dissolved into smoke, seeping into his skin with each approaching step toward his college professor.

Gordon took a seat. Professor Brede just watched him. His smile lost its subtle, sinister sheen. The professor took a sip of wine and offered a glass. Gordon declined, and Professor Brede said in an apologetic tone, "No bread, I'm afraid. If I had it, I wouldn't share, anyway." He looked to Water Bug Hollow's tumbledown disorder and commented, "Slum left." He turned his head to the brownstones surrounded by bright flowers. "Flowers right." He looked back at Gordon. "I will not share my bread," he reiterated. "I will take the bread from everyone. There will be no feast." He inspected Gordon closely. Gordon did not move. "I always liked your eyes, Mister Goodspeed,"

Professor Brede noted. "Those lilac gems let me know what you really are." Gordon remained silent. His focus was on Professor Brede's face. It appeared translucent and detached from his head. The effect was understated, but a close inspection, aided by otherworldly vision, brought about the abnormal visual.

Gordon again heard Fey as he became engrossed with the unnatural sight of Professor Brede's crystalline and unfastened countenance. *"The villains that surround us in shadow wear masks made of flesh and blood."* A leather tool-roll fitted with needles appeared on the table. Gordon and Professor Brede looked down at them. They looked up at one another. Gordon noticed a crack on Professor Brede's cheek that ran to his chin.

"These needles are empty," Professor Brede exclaimed. Then he made a face. "My apologies, that's not entirely truthful," he admitted. "The tips are laced with a hex, naturally, but the needles' bodies are void of any essence. The essence of a conjurer from your community. These needles are special; they are specific for use, made in particular for conjure women. The strongest willed are the most fun to experiment on. We inject doubt and take confidence. Then we sit back and watch the results mutate into disease." He seemed proud of himself, but his pride was muted in his tone. "Do you know my first kill, Mister Goodspeed?" he asked. "I turned a conjure woman against her son. I visited her every day to watch her deterioration progress. She began to hate her own conjure, become afraid of it. She turned on her power, and she turned on her son. Then I pricked *him*, and he shivered—as they say—like a shittin' dog. He was an addict in withdrawal, but you see, Mister Goodspeed, nothing was withdrawn. It was inserted. A solution. It drove him mad, but it drove him to act, especially when I pricked him again. He felt so ashamed, but he did it. He killed his mother. I would never do such a thing. Not me. I'd never kill my mother." Professor Brede shook his head. "Manipulating your sweet, precious Fey's mother was the same way. Fey too. Their backs were scarred, and the two of you fought. Her pride defended the crime lashed against her." Cracks snaked up and across his face. A piece fell away, but there was something behind it. Revelation in another face.

Gordon watched. He knew. He watched. He waited.

Professor Brede snickered. He took another sip of wine. "It's so easy with you people. I swear to God." He rolled his eyes and coughed a bit as he laughed. He steadied his mannerisms to keep from choking on the wine as he swallowed. "You are so desperate for peace that you don't see the obvious." A few cracks in his face met with other cracks, and another glass-like chunk dropped off. "You refuse to see the cruelty beneath my smile, Mister Goodspeed. No different than the others in your conjure community when they took me in decades ago." Professor Brede appeared visibly vexed.

"I pranced around your neighborhood for so long because your people, for all their magic, wanted so bad to believe I wasn't my mother or father's son." A wedge of his forehead gave way, falling and clanking against the table. "You all negotiated around my existence and it got your precious Fey's family killed. Fey too."

"Ease up, there, Willie." Gordon heard Professor Brede's voice say. It wasn't coming from the man sitting opposite him. The voice came from his right. He turned his head and saw a ghostly image of Fey Forrester, subdued and on her knees. There were others surrounding her, their images just as transparent as hers.

Standing directly at Fey's side was a woman of ill-defined familiarity to Gordon. Her height was a little under six-feet tall. She had an olive tone to her skin, and her raven-hued hair draped in wavy curls that framed her dark-eyed, round face. She wore a choker inset with large, flat, grey stones flecked with red blotches. Gordon's recollection of the woman remained blurred, but a substantial clue appeared to him when he spied the man standing behind Fey. Gordon knew him. All too well. He was an older man with a dark-grey, Dutch-style beard. He wore a wide-brim straw hat, winter colonial wear with a two-tailed frock coat covering his heavy frame. His right hand held a whip, curled in his grip. Its brown color was blanched and speckled with faint, red splotches. This man's name was Willie. He'd been dubbed *Willie the Lich* by the conjure community.

Gordon knew the woman. Her name was Lucretia. He became acquainted with her when he'd walked through time and seen Fable Avenue's early days. Lucretia Tolvaj-Fallows. She was Stanley Fallow's wife, and she was known to snatch the personal conjures away from conjure men and conjure women. She magnified Cedron Goodspeed's conjure by impressing another conjure man's power on him. It intensified Cedron's anger, driving him to fight Gordon and Benny.

That was a helluva day, Gordon recalled.

The mistress of the field was here. The overseer was here.

Where was the plantation master?

There he stepped into existence, appearing as ghostly as the others, standing in front of Fey Forrester and dressed in a sky-blue suit with a white-collar shirt and black tie and to-the-nines in his guise as Professor James Brede. A glass of red wine was in one hand. A smile was on his face as he looked down at Fey. He flicked the black curl dangling at his forehead, and his physiognomy bled away.

Olive skin turned pale. His locks curled, their color emptied. Jet-black hair faded into a strawberry-blonde wash. There was Stanley Fallows. There too manifested a memory of Gordon and Fey conversing in another time, in other bodies. She told him something, and he remembered what happened. He turned back to Professor Brede at the desk. His face was riddled with cracks. The fractured pieces broke away as if made of brittle porcelain. The mask had now fallen, and the prime malefactor's face had been revealed.

Gordon remained silent.

Stanley said to him, "I don't negotiate, Mister Goodspeed. I take." He sipped his wine. "When I sleep, other's do my good work for me," he told Gordon. "When your people sleep, they rest and lose time. You're all so easy, and despite all of your conjure, your people are so damned tired. We laughed together as student and professor. But while we drank together, I always noted that we sipped from different cups. In my sips, I wondered what it would be like to slit your throat. You drank, laughed, and believed we were at peace. Equals." Stanley shook his head. "You always had an instinct about Professor Brede, Gordon," he continued. "The trick of my mask was nothing special. It wasn't hard to gaze beyond its façade. You just liked to feel at ease. I have to ask: Why, Mister Goodspeed? Why would you let your heart guide you when I as your enemy have you in a constant state of war? I have proven to be evil time and time again. I'm descended from hate, birthed from it. My very inception was a declaration against you." He waited for an answer. Gordon said nothing, and so Stanley said with a voice possessed of venom, "I've seen governments put international threats on hold to make sure your people never reach the height of spirit you all possess. Earthly, mundane affairs are distractions, and the world falls for them every time. Grand conspiracies mean nothing. Assassination plots, rigged elections, political corruption—that's all a ruse. Knowledge of your existence is the real target. I have seen terrible world incidents that have nothing to do with you be framed around your existence. All to control the narrative of you jungle spirits—keep most of your kind unaware and afraid." He jabbed a finger at Gordon and spat, "Don't you ever try and negotiate with my existence, Mister Goodspeed. This is the final warning." He sat back. "I'm not as strong as you, I'll admit. But I know ways to kill you. I know how to subjugate you, control that spirit of yours, and get you to do my bidding. So, with that knowledge, what reason do I need to be more powerful than you? I have Miss Forrester's essence. I'll have yours."

Gordon's eyes made a slow descend away from Stanley Fallows. He peered at the needles on display in front of him. They locked onto the siphoning instruments, and then as he contemplated, his eyes went to and fro. Pendulum swing. Thought was in rhythm with sight. Then his eyes stopped their sway. He raised his vision to spotlight Stanley Fallows. "We're going to kill you, Stanley."

Stanley shook a finger at Gordon. "I expect nothing less than violence. That's the way a savage spirit thinks, isn't it?" He shook his head and snickered while looking away. "Kill me?" He leaned forward in a forceful demeanor and scoffed, "Does all your self-righteous magic come down to that? Is that how you intend to fix the world, Gordon? Is that all you have for me?"

Gordon nodded. "Perhaps, Stanley. Maybe so. I accept that. We conjure folk have germinated unique magics all with the purpose of killing you. We have to kill you, Stanley. You said so yourself. Anything else would be negotiating with your existence."

Stanley's face became webbed with perplexity. "Existence, Mister Goodspeed?" he questioned. "I said 'presence'."

Gordon shook his head. "No, you didn't, Stanley," he disagreed. "You said *existence*—negotiating with your *existence*."

Stanley was dismissive of Gordon's factual claims. "The savage mind hears what it wants to hear," he voiced. He tapped his temple and snarled, "It hears what it needs to justify its irrational behavior." He pointed to Gordon. "You're the cruel one, Mister Goodspeed."

Gordon again nodded in a calm manner. He didn't disagree. "You're right, Stanley. I have been cruel. We conjure folk have been extremely cruel and neglectful. Letting you live has allowed so many to be hurt, nature and time included. That all stops. It's going to stop, and you're going to die. You're going to die like your mother, Sarinda, and all the influence you and she have brought will go with you."

Stanley clawed the table. His brow furrowed, and he snapped, "You'll have one chance to kill me, Mister Goodspeed. *One chance!* You better take it." He calmed, sitting back with a smile on his face. "I have a Grand Wish too, a Grand Conjure to summon through a Grand Ritual."

Gordon's countenance contorted, muddling into an untidy expression. "Yeah, but you need our blood to achieve it." Gordon was unimpressed, and his tone resonated loud with his lack of respect. "Any magic you create—that you wield—it's from our soul, Stanley." Gordon shook his head. "You're right. We've negotiated with your existence, and we bargained with our magic and culture." He stood, rolling his eyes and huffing. His mask seeped from his skin as shadow and smoke, solidifying to surround his face. "I'm going to find you now; and I'm going to hurt you." Dooley turned and walked away.

"I'll have monsters sent to your doorstep, Mister Goodspeed. They will hurt you. I'll get what I need from you to make myself whole. I've already pricked your precious Fey of her essence." Stanley's eyes wandered to where his other self stood over Fey Forrester. Dooley paused in his walk. He turned and faced the scene. He saw Stanley signal a needleman. The night doctor stepped forward, bent down, and plunged his syringe into Fey's arm, taking spirit and blood. *"You jungle conjurers have a grand conjure and wish to make,"* the other Stanley stated. *"So, do I. I too have a grand conjure and wish to bring about."* A cobalt-blue light, along with Fey's blood, filled the syringe's vial.

Dooley then heard a piece of dialogue from he and Fey's conversation that had taken place in a time long ago. *"Stanley took from me too… He had a needleman take from me…"*

The memory was now his. Unlocked, and for him to keep. Dooley looked away from the scene and replied over his shoulder, "Send your monsters, Stanley. I need to work off some steam, some savagery." He treaded heavily toward Lillian. She reached out her hand to accept his, but as he approached, she then lifted her palm and placed it against his chest.

"Gordon, you can't wake like this. Leave these emotions here," she urged.

"I can't sleep forever, Miss Ghedemere," he told her, voice as determined as the strides he made to rejoin her presence.

"A breath first, Dooley-spirit. Exhale, and I will wake you."

Dooley straightened. His body loosened, and as he released an unwinding breath, his entire cosmic suit seeped into his flesh. Out of the shadow reshaped the clothes he'd been wearing earlier in the day. Gordon looked relaxed, but Lillian was doubtful. "I can't stop you, Gordon," she made aware. "But I will warn you: *be careful*. There are children's lives to consider." She took her hand away from his chest, and Gordon put his hand in hers.

They awoke. Gordon jumped up from his chair. Althea noted the look in his shimmering eyes. His volcanic temperament passed through her and resonated like rays of the sun. His fiery constitution permeated Madame Jeliya and kept her attention locked on Gordon as he sprang to life. Lillian stood and leapt back, steering clear of Gordon as his cosmic suit folded over him as shadow and brume. From murky, conjured air to a solid, skin-tight outfit. His mask followed next, enclosing his face. His body burst into lilac spirit with such a force it made the occupants of the consecrated basement flinch, even his mother's ghostly frame.

"I know who that sonavabitch is!" Dooley barked. "And I know where the dragon nests! I'm gonna blind him. I'm gonna *blind* him!"

"Wait, Gordon!" his mother called out. "It's too dangerous!"

He was gone. Up through the ceiling, taking his lilac brilliance with him.

Althea stomped her feet and cursed!

Madame Jeliya said to comfort her, "I'm sorry, Althea. I'm sure he'll be fine. He won't be foolish enough to put the abducted children in danger." Her eyes drifted to Lillian who was now in Armand's embrace. Lillian looked up at Madame Jeliya, and their gazes fastened to one another, sharing the same uncertain look.

Baiting Hollow. Dooley's streaking, comet-like form arced downward toward an empty lot. Perplexity set in as he drew closer. He believed he should've seen a circular driveway that provided a path to a Spanish-styled, country manor. He landed in a blinding burst that dissipated his lilac flame and cosmic suit, which superimposed the earthly garments he wore. He landed in what should've been the manor's backyard, directly over where Fey had been accosted and punctured by hexed needle.

Gordon grated his teeth and growled, "Where are you?" He repeated, louder and angrier, *"Where are you?"* He took a step and snapped, "Answer me, *motherfucker!"* His lilac, spherical, third eye blazed bright against his forehead as he panned the area with his physical eyes. No one was around. He focused his instinct, pushing it wild, allowing it to scatter through the open area. His heightened awareness achieved a find hidden in a murky, hexed anathematic-world draping Gordon's objective from reality and his reach. He didn't need to turn around to observe his instinct outlining the contours of the Fallows-Brede manor.

Something without eyes was staring at him. Invisible to time, and only observed through Gordon's heightened instinct. It stood behind a sliding glass door in one of the manor's illustrious rooms decorated with art from cultures around the world. It was a peculiar figure. Tall and thin, wearing a black three-piece suit with a white formal-dress shirt, and a black bowtie. White butler gloves were on its hands. Its human neck was not visible, as where its head should have been there was instead a large, diamond-shaped and wooden-framed clock.

This peculiarity was summoned through a gruesome ritual called *Züle.* It was conducted by Stanley and Lucretia Fallows. Husband and wife followed, step-by-step, a resettling cantrip from Lucretia's malignant covenant from Eastern Europe. A worthy needleman named Artie Carlson was selected, and he was provided a burlap sack over his head while laying down on a ceremonial table. Holes were cut out for him to see, or more important, for Lucretia Fallows—with aid from her skeptic stone bejeweled choker—to inject a hexed needle deep into the center of his eyes. Then she sang an off-key *gyászének,* or dirge, while Artie expressed his distress in a torrent of bellows and guttural screams. Skeptic stone shavings were sprinkled over his punctured eyes. The dust held within it pieces to a *csalás,* a gonif spirit conjured by Stanley's malefic powers. Artie was reshaped, and would forever be this clock-headed monster called Lazy Crow. This was his well-deserved 'Bag Head' promotion.

The hands on his face whirled around in a hypnotic procedure. It was this activity that kept the Fallows-Brede residence in the unseen, hexed anathematic-world. Stepping up behind the clock-headed monster was the lord of the manor himself.

It was curious, as Stanley staggered weak to the clock monster's side to get a better glimpse of Gordon Goodspeed. Lucretia rushed to him, giving assistance. Stanley was different now. His hair flowed long passed his shoulders, thin and graying. A beard masked his face. While his hair was straggly, his beard was groomed to a perfect, triangular point. He was cloaked in a red robe that had stained into its fabric colorful, concentric circles, which were the essence of the Fable Avenue conjure children his needleman pricked and abducted.

Stanley was bare of his shirt and shoes with black linen pants on his legs. His chest was marked with red, angry-looking sores. He coughed hard into his hand and blood spattered against his palm. He rested the same hand on Lazy Crow's shoulder for balance.

Gordon felt the eyes on him. The spherical, lilac ball blazed bright against his forehead. He stepped backwards several paces. He stopped, and he turned his head to look over his shoulder. A quote from one of his favorite video games came to him. It was a simple set of words he felt compelled to utter over his shoulder at the invisible set of prying eyes. "I know you're there," he snarled in an accurate portrayal of the character's guttural, pompous voice. He turned around and walked to where the sliding glass door would've been. He was still, looking but only seeing through instinct and higher sense. There was presence. Stanley just stared at him. The crackling, electric hiss of Gordon's spherical ball of lilac energy was the only sound buzzing through the summer day. "Fey's alive," he confessed. "She never died," he expounded. "But then again, you knew that. Nice trick you pulled, you sonava bitch. All of 'em."

Stanley inspected Gordon. Up and down he looked, viewing the young man with his true eyes and not a mask. He said to Lucretia, "I didn't see him. I didn't see him coming, and he's here." To the clock monster, he directed, "Keep us invisible. Let him leave. Pursue him then." The hour and minute hands on Lazy Crow's face continued rotating.

"I know you and your wife disguise yourselves as James and Jaquelyn Brede," Gordon informed. "Change your faces, and look for other methods of employment, if you even need them. We're gonna keep watch on the university. So, if you show up, we'll kill you on sight. We don't need you alive to find the children." He took a moment before adding, "And you need them alive. So, I'm not worried."

Stanley remarked in a whisper, "Don't be naïve, Mister Goodspeed. I'm not beyond killing children. I'm not. My father used to kill children in front of their parents. He'd make some fight one another to the death or make their mothers choke them from life as a punishment. He even took them to bed for sport. Girl or boy, it didn't matter to him." He nodded his head. "Yes, I have those memories. I'm descended from those moments because I *am* my father, Mister Goodspeed. I'm not just his son. My mask of flesh honors his face. I'm him, and I'll kill to remind you that I'm not beyond killing your jungle, conjure kin indiscriminate of age."

Help! Gordon heard a man's voice shriek. The sound came with static and an unnatural rise and lowering in volume. *Emma! Fey!* the voice cried, sounding as if sinking into a hollow place.

Gordon turned around. His instinct's invisible tendrils uncoiled from the house and came together, pointing at the ground far away from him, but not quite near the shore. His cosmic suit formed around him, from shadow to solid, skin-tight fabric, and he ran to where his instinct was aimed. He stood on the spot, and he focused his instinct. His heightened sense emitted a pulse that bounced against a buried object and relayed back to him a message of what was entombed below him. Gordon's mask surrounded his face, and he dropped to his knees.

Dooley put his face close to the ground. He whispered, "Mister Banneker…?"

The voice screeched again, *Help! Emma! Fey!*

The sound reverberated like a frosty, explosive snap. Its din became visible in a flash of brilliance that blinded Dooley. He flinched and fell back, rolling around and shaking off the effect. Sight restored, Dooley crawled back to the area of Lewis Banneker's burial. He dug his fingers into the soil and scooped out a sizable amount of earth.

Dooley retracted his cosmic suit. His mask remained. He filled his pockets with the dirt he spooned into his hand, and he recalled his cosmic outfit around him again. He gave a concluding glance to the empty lot. He didn't bother reaching out with his instinct to feel its presence beyond the physical world. His body burst into lilac spirit and soared up into the air to arc back to Fable Avenue.

Stanley watched him leave, and when Dooley was no longer even a small glimmering spectacle in the sky, he vomited on the floor and glass. Lucretia bent down as she saw her husband drop to his knees. He panted, "We'll give them their children back. Not for free," he assured. "Mister Goodspeed's essence will run in my veins. I'll be complete. My robe will be complete. I won't be sick anymore." He looked up at his wife and smiled through his fatigue. "And we will have our grand wish."

Dooley's lilac streak soared in from above, ghosting through the ceiling. The occupants of the Goodspeed basement jumped. At the moment, only Althea and Madame Jeliya remained. Gordon appeared in his regular clothes out of a lilac puff of glittering smoke. Althea and Madame Jeliya's stern stares were like stakes pounded into his feet, keeping him in place. His head dropped.

"Conjure damn you, boy!" Althea growled. She floated to him, fists balled. "The trouble you could've placed yourself in!" she shouted. "The potential danger you could put our community's missing children in!" She slapped Gordon across the face with hand and spirit. "I was not ready to cross, to be torn from my family! And I am not ready to have my son's spirit at my side. Or worse: not on this realm—somewhere else. Like your sweetheart, like her mother, her father! And with you gone, who brings them back, Gordon? Who brings *you* back?"

Gordon recovered from his mother's strike, and he did nothing else, save drop his head. Althea's slap stung. An apparition's ethereal wallop was a cut deeper than anything physical could resemble. There was the true essence of emotion embedded into the aggressive touch. Gordon stayed silent, face pulsing from the sharpness of the hit.

Madame Jeliya presented her words in a calmer tone when she reminded, "We are at war, Gordon."

"Yes," he answered in a sincere and polite, apologetic voice. "My actions were reckless. I know that. Saying 'sorry' doesn't make it right. That's what hurts. I can't make it right." Gordon closed his eyes to swallow the swell building within them. Down to the lump in his throat, he consumed his indignation. He focused on the news he needed to bring. "I think we can conjure a voice that holds some insight into Stanley's plans."

Althea was too angry to care, bent eyes choking Gordon.

"Whose voice?" asked Madame Jeliya.

"Fey's father," Gordon answered. "Mister Banneker. I heard him."

Althea's anger dissipated enough to ask her son with a strong curiosity, "How? Did you. Hear him?"

His mother's strike resonated on his cheek. It branded him with shame for his disobedience and kept him silent when he proceeded to speak on the matter. He had to fight against his mother's chastisement that appeared stronger than Willie the Lich's cursed whip. Gordon's lip trembled when he confessed to his mother and Madame Jeliya, "I went to where he was buried. Our enemies buried him. They live there. It's their property, and it's in Baiting Hollow in Riverhead."

The expression in Althea and Madame Jeliya's eyes shifted into curiosity. "Then the Bredes are needlemen?" Madame Jeliya concluded. "Your professors?"

Gordon shook his head. "No," he replied. "The Bredes are masks made of flesh and blood. Under those masks are Stanley and Lucretia Fallows. Our enemies," he emphasized. "They kept their eyes on us at the vantage point of the university. Most of us have gone there. It makes sense." He looked at his mother and uttered, "Mom, I'm sorry…"

Althea didn't say anything, and her expression was blank when she nodded her head.

Gordon remembered the soil. "I have the earth he's buried in. I took it," he reported. "I, uh…" He looked at his altar, and then around the room for a jar. He disappeared for a brief moment, returning with a mason jar in his hand. He unscrewed the lid and dug into his pockets, ladling out the burial soil. Speckles of dirt peppered the plush floor, but Gordon managed to hand-shovel most of the contents from pocket to jar. He screwed the top on and presented the jar to Madame Jeliya.

The matriarch accepted it. "Althea, we'll need your presence to help with the ritual to conjure what we can. Not all of Lewis will be here. It will be faint." Then she asked Gordon, "What did he say when you heard his voice?"

"He was calling for help," Gordon answered. "He was calling for Fey and her mother."

Madame Jeliya nodded. "I'm glad Savannah isn't here, but I'll let her know—my way." The matriarch looked at son and mother. "I'll report this to Papa Solomon who will take the information to Maman Anansi. Is there any more to your report, Gordon?"

"Yes," he said, nodding his head. "My walk in the *mirak*. I remembered my conversation with Fey. I saw Stanley Fallows. He said he'll have monsters for me. He needs my essence to complete his wish. He revealed himself to Fey before…" His voice trailed away. Then he disclosed, "That's why I went…where I went. But the house wasn't at the lot. It was invisible, outside of time."

"No," Madame Jeliya objected to make a correction to Gordon's words. "It's hidden under what we call the *Coward's Veil*."

"The anathematic-world," Althea concluded. She said to her son, "These are war terms, Gordon. You'll hear more."

Madame Jeliya expounded, "Hexers twisted form of being outside of time. It takes great focus for them to pull it off. It can be detrimental on their physical and mental being. They might be using the children. Lucretia would know the means. I'm sure it's what has that yokel at the crossroads able to fade in and out of time. I don't like to think the amount of blood-sacrifices and hex magic used to pull off such a feat." She cradled the jar and made her way to the stairs. She stopped just before the first stair and turned to Gordon. She asked, "You're going to use yourself as bait, aren't you?"

Gordon kept his eyes on his mother when he answered, "Yes…" He had a determined tone, but he knew his mother's feelings on the matter. But she'd said it, partially anyway. War terms. She would hear more. "I'll get the children back. Me and Cedron's Gypsy Moon Misfits."

Althea rolled her eyes and shook her head. Then she faded.

Madame Jeliya ascended the stairs and left the basement. Gordon took a seat on his chair. He dropped his head and started shaking. His mother's strike set in, melting into sentiment and sinking into his physical fibers. He felt it. It scratched and stung. It coupled with the lingering, concussive sentiments of Fey's loss, drifting through time. His time step and the vertigo that would expand and contract at times, spinning him into headache and dizziness. They returned.

It made him think. He waited on a blessed watch like a fiend waiting for a fix. And in the meantime, he was a failed hero, unable to help the abducted children of the conjure community and mend families experiencing the loss. He might've made things worse for them.

His mother's otherworldly, aggressive frustration settled into him, and he pondered his uselessness. He believed he could fly into the sun and survive the furious heat of its core. He could perhaps absorb the fiery, celestial body and throw the solar system into chaos and destroy the worlds that rotated in its gravity. Gordon considered this a terrible realization of power beyond measure. And still he felt so helpless and useless.

All of that is going to change, thought Gordon as his eyes swelled with tears. "No masks, Stanley. It's you and me. Face-to-face."

19

Lillian spun and spun, whirling in jubilation for a deed well done. Armand observed her dance as he sat in the dining room, chair with its back to the table, facing the front hallway of the Hollow House residence. He smoked and watched her twirl.

Lillian stopped her spin. She faced Armand, but her countenance was aimed to the ceiling, bright with a smile. "Oh, the things we've seen!" she exclaimed to him. "I'm tingling with history in me." She hugged herself and expressed, "It's touching me; and I'm touching it." Her eyes closed, and she swayed her hips to a rhythm only her instinct could decipher from the air. It mixed with her joy, and she became euphoric.

Armand took a puff. He grinned and commented, "I admit: I'm jealous."

Lillian loosened her self-embrace, though her arms remained around her person. She looked at Armand and replied through her smile, "You don't have to be, Mister Gideon." She stepped into the dining room, exhaling. "I stepped into the *mirak*. I guided a young man on his path." She cocked her head to the side. Her joyfulness shifted into a soft, heartfelt expression. "I did this as the new Crossroads Queen. I provided guidance to the Lilac Flame." She made a face and added, "Reckless as he was with what he'd learned." She put her hands on her hips and let loose a long breath. "But he's returned, and he's remorseful—as he should be." Then she put her hands together, fingers intertwined. Her bright smile returned and she expressed, "I've never felt so much a part of conjure, a part of this culture." She spun again, the bell of her dress expanding with the rotation. "So much *maji* I performed. So much *idan!*"

Armand didn't recognize the words used, but his modest instinct could decrypt the words meant 'magic' in another language. A quiet voice in his head said, *Creole* and *Yoruba*, respective of the words Lillian uttered. He took another drag of his cigarette, and then he practiced what little incant he could muster. He tapped the ashes off the end and made them dissipate into thin air, so as not to litter the ground with his habit.

Lillian concluded her spin. Her vision continued revolving, stimulated by both her physical, graceful pivots and her intoxicating exultation. She didn't even employ an incant to settle her senses. Turning her head to the door that lead to the Louisiana region called Water Bug Hollow sobered her with reality. Lillian sighed. She looked at Armand and posed what should've been a rhetorical question. "Why do so many of us choose not to feel this way, to know the *maji* and *idan*?" Lillian put her gaze back on the door, attempting to stare through it. She presented a theory. "Because they don't understand they're naked."

"Oh," Armand uttered, intrigued.

She elucidated, "I don't mean naturally naked. I mean they've been stripped to their chains. The only clothes they wear are chains. In this take, the emperor has his clothes. It's the citizens that are nude and unaware." She took a seat next to Armand and touched his arm. "Let's find those bones!" Lillian declared.

Armand grinned and said to her, "Yes, Miss Voodoo Lily." He finished his cigarette and held the remainder of its body upright in his fingers. He concentrated a thought first. Focused. Eyes on the cigarette. He opened his fingers and it hovered in the air. He whispered an incant taught to him, and the cigarette detonated like a small firecracker. Armand moved his hand away, flicking his wrist as the aftershock of the small, violent burst stung his ring and middle finger. *"Shit!"* Armand cursed before indulging in a light chuckle.

Lillian reached for his hand, suggesting, "Let me heal that with a light incant."

Armand shook his head, objecting, "No, Miss Voodoo Lily. Let me feel this pain. I need a reminder on how I began at this. Clumsy and amateurish." He instead rubbed his own hand, continuing a series of curses.

Lillian got to her feet and proposed another suggestion. "Join me at the crossroads." She reached out her hand to Armand. He accepted, giving her his non-wounded appendage. He raised up from his seat with Lillian, and then she and he made their way to the door. Lillian skipped in her steps through the hallway, forcing Armand to join in on the gleeful hop. Outside. Lillian let go of Armand's hand and ran forward. He walked coolly to the crossroads as Lillian hurried in her pace. His hands were in his pockets, and his walk was careful as he descended the porch steps. Lillian resumed her spin at the middle of the crossroads. She slowed when Armand joined her, and the two danced close at a reserved pace.

Lillian put her head against Armand's chest, and they embraced as they rotated. They closed their eyes and Armand commented, "We could get run over. Or, are we outside of time?"

"No. We're in time. We could get run over," she joked in a matter-of-fact tone. "We shouldn't need an incant or personal conjure to hear a car coming, though."

"True."

So, they danced. Close. Slow.

Lillian remarked, "I think of Elisheba Bloomscale and Lapen Jack, and I feel this sense of responsibility." She exhaled. "It's not overwhelming," she assured. "It's exciting. I don't feel bound with duty. I feel free with function and purpose."

Armand concentrated on the names Lillian threw out. His grandmother spoke of so many key figures that were at the foundation of the conjure community. Gordon made a mentioned before passing to sleep. Armand repeated the names Elisheba Bloomscale and Lapen Jack in his head until he recalled their importance. It turned out, they were *the* importance. It popped into his head in single words or phrases. A puzzle of memory snapped together to give the whole picture. *Former slaves. American. Husband and wife. Elisheba Bloomscale.* Couldn't forget a name like that. *As for Lapen Jack, he came from a family bound by pacts and rituals.* Armand considered all of this for a brief moment.

Lillian peered up at the tall, California kid while they danced. She could see his mind at work. "Your Nana Forrester spoke to you about Elisheba Bloomscale and her husband Lapen Jack?"

"Day one, lesson one," he stalled with a smile and nervous laugh. Then it came to him. "I know. I do. Former slaves...? Husband and wife. Gunslingers too. My grandmother said he wore an African mask when they traveled, guns on his side, duster coat, and a top hat. She had an nkisi doll strapped to her hip. Some say it held a balance like Justice, Ma'at." He thought for a moment. "That's where the comic book came from..." His eyes were on the past, and Lillian gazed at him with a proud smile. Armand pulled himself out of memory, blinking wildly. He looked at Lillian and continued, "They attempted to document all this—all the spiritual aspects brought over from Africa, the similarities. The original intent, meanings... Yes?" he questioned aloud. Lillian nodded. Armand recalled more. "They came to these crossroads, presented their collected knowledge to its guardians. They declared the restored spiritual path Oju...Oju...Ojulee..." His memory faltered, and his speech struggled. The heat of embarrassment flushed his cheeks.

Lillian assisted, *"Ojulowo Atijo Oluwa."*

Armand nodded. He looked around, remembering his grandmother giving him the words. "Yes," he expressed, slightly annoyed at himself. "Oju..." He tried again, but he still struggled.

Lillian chuckled. She stopped their dance and began a lesson. Carefully, she pronounced for Armand to follow, "Oju-lo-wo."

"Ojulo*wu*," he attempted to repeat, getting the last vowel incorrect.

"No, Armand-sweetie, *Ojulowo*," she corrected, emphasizing, "*Woh, woh.* Not *woo.*" Then she told him, "Don't feel bad. I used to do the same thing."

"Yeah, but when you were six," he remarked.

Lillian retorted in a teacher's voice, "Everyone is six in the beginning, Mister Gideon, even prodigies."

Armand considered the point. With that, he took a breath and made a successful attempt upon exhalation when he stated, "Ojulo*wo*."

Lillian's face lit up. "Yes! Say it again so you have it."

Armand waited for her to say the word, prompting his repeat. But Lillian stayed her voice, and it created an awkward moment of silence. Armand understood that she trusted him to speak the word instead of parroting her sound. "Ojulowo," he said, restating it a few times until his confidence was solid.

Lillian moved to the next word. "Atijo," she continued.

"Atijo," he recited.

"Oluwa," she finished.

"Oluwa," he concluded.

"Now, all together: *Ojulowo Atijo Oluwa*."

"Ojulowo Atijo Oluwa," he replicated with perfect annunciation. He tried to gain extra points by defining the words. "Three words from the Yoruba language. Authentic-old-lords, or original ancient lords. Also, can be expressed as *Ojulowo Atijo ẹmi*, the authentic original *spirits*. It encompasses all known African spiritual paths from Ifá to the ancient Kemetic understandings." He pointed past Lilian and included, "People on Fable Avenue recognize the name, but they call their conjure philosophy *ọpọlọpọ-ẹya*." Lillian chuckled. Armand smirked and ended, "Yoruba for *many* and *parts*, or *multi-tribe*. Some say, 'bootleg'. I can remember that tongue-twister but not the main thing."

Despite Armand's self-deprecating sentiment, Lillian was impressed. She renewed their dance and tapped on Armand's chest. "You're still on your path. Don't be discouraged." She relaxed back in his embrace. "I'm on a path too," she declared in a soft yet determined voice. "Elisheba and Lapen Jack," she said the names, thinking on the time period when they existed. "Their efforts brought them to so many other crossroads. They visited them all; all over the world with different black guardians. Most have been closed off, extinguished by bad people with needles. I govern this one, and it feels exciting to be standing on history." She spoke with a sense of achievement. She didn't fear the responsibility, though its magnitude and gravity were immense, close to overwhelming. Regardless, Lillian Eledas-Ghedemere embraced it with a sense of pride.

They danced and danced. No cars disrupted them. Jabo Judson watched, but they weren't aware of the yokel's scowl, and they wouldn't have cared. His was not the only set of curious eyes spying on them.

Savannah Forrester focused on Armand and Lillian with a fixed stare. She sipped a cup of tea and watched. Her thoughts were jangled as she attempted to seam together sequences for Armand and Lillian. She liked their coupling. Lillian was a capable enough guide for him, Savannah believed, even as a fledgling crossroads queen.

Simaetha walked up behind Savannah. Much the same was on her mind, resonating louder in her head as her eyes fell upon the sight of her daughter slow dancing in Savannah's grandson's arms. "Are we not being intrusive and overprotective?" Simaetha questioned in a teasing tone.

Savannah looked down at her teacup, finally separating her eyes from the tender dance. She asked the mask-maker, "Do you think they have, or will, behold one another?"

"I would hope so," Simaetha exclaimed. "I like your grandson. He's a good man."

"He's angry inside," Savannah told her. "Terribly angry."

Simaetha nodded, accepting Savannah's words. "Of course, he is," she replied in a cautious tone. She proposed a theory, remarking, "All this time he had a power in him and no way to express it. He probably glowed with an aura, walked with a swagger, that got him shunned. And he had no idea why." She saw Savannah's head sway back and forth as the issues stated were considered. "It's been a long time since I've seen wonder such as his fill the wide-eyed expression and mind of a catechumen of our kind." She stepped to Savannah's side. "I don't tire of seeing that expression on a black face, curious eyes turned to rainbows of awe at the sight of our *maji* in practice. Your grandson is eager to know, learn of his heritage." A light rain made its appearance. Savannah and Simaetha watched Armand and Lillian only revel in it, continuing their slow, revolving dance. "Their beholding, I'd say, will be organic more because of circumstance, not just a spark of recognition between one another's inner Ixu and Gira." She looked over her shoulder at Lady Arachne. The matriarch was seated at the table, flipping around her tarot cards, engrossed in the spread she was pulling up. Simaetha brought her out of the engagement when she taunted, "I guess we should ask the Queen of Passion, as she holds dominion over all men she gazes on."

Savannah turned around to witness Lady Arachne send an unsmiling gaze in Simaetha's direction. The women standing at the window chuckled at Lady Arachne's reaction. The prophetess went back to dealing with her insightful reading.

"Oh, do have some fun, Lena," Simaetha pleaded as she walked to the table and took a seat next to Lady Arachne. "Tell us about the fun you're having with the reverend."

Lady Arachne looked up from her cards. She still didn't smile, but she held no glower either. Her expression was soft and sincere. Leaning back in her chair, she said, "I saw our young, good reverend in a new light, and it was nothing I, as the arachnid, could wrap my eight legs around."

Simaetha made a face and quipped, "Bored already?"

Lady Arachne smirked and waved the comment down with her hand. "Chil' please," she told Simaetha. "I saw him as a man—growing."

Simaetha raised an eyebrow. "And you wanted nothing to do with his...*growth?*"

"No, and I'm surprised," Lady Arachne admitted. "He carried himself with authority the other day against those white cops who'd harassed us—them boys with needles as well as guns." She looked at her cards and nodded her head. "I've been teaching him, and it was in that moment I saw... a *son* come into his own." She took a moment, and then she concluded, "He's frightened of his power, his conjure. After tomorrow's stitching, he shouldn't be. That will be the last time I hold his hand. Then he'll be the responsibility of an *okunrin-oluko*. He'll walk his Ixu path to master conjure and incant." She flipped a card. It was the Six of Pentacles. "Bored? No. Respectful...for once." She chuckled. "Let him walk on his own. He's grown up." There was more, and she was prompted to confess when she spotted the eyebrow-raised expression on Simaetha's face. It made Lady Arachne laugh harder, as well as admit, "I had a good, heartfelt talk with my matriarch-sister, Madame Jeliya. Since then, I've felt a release like never before. My passion has been calmed a bit." Simaetha's eyebrow rose higher, much to Lady Arachne's surprise. The matriarch chuckled again, and she answered the silent question. "There still is an insatiable Gira in me, if you're worried my fire has been extinguished. That's just who I am, who'll I'll always be, even at rest. Because if there's one thing I love and accept inside me—"

"It's a good, stiff man," Simaetha finished.

Savannah almost choked on her tea, the liquid caught in her windpipe when by reflex she chuckled, and her throat clenched.

"It's *myself,*" Lady Arachne corrected. Now her eyebrow was raised, and Simaetha's returned to standard, resting level.

Her final words on the matter settled Simaetha, and her sister-in-web nodded her head with approval. Lady Arachne looked over at Savannah. She noticed the rain had become heavier, and because of it, Savannah turned all the way from the window. Armand and Lillian had dashed back into the house across the street. "Your grandson is stitched tomorrow, too," Lady Arachne observed. "You'll assist?"

"As you've asked for back in April," Savannah replied.

"Maman Anansi and her husband will be there to do the heavy lifting," Lady Arachne informed. She asked Simaetha, "Will Lillian be assisting?"

"Yes, but very little," Simaetha answered. "Stitching is far different than going into the *mirak*. I would like her to assist with Reverend Pouvwa's stitching. She'll be with her father and Papa Solomon. Less emotions if she's not handling this young man I'm sure she has feelings for." She looked at Savannah and apologized. "I'm sorry. Your grandson has a name. He's not just 'young man'. *Armand.*"

"That's no problem here," Savannah assured. "When he need a good talkin' to and his ass whipped, that's what I call him. Take that name away from his behind."

Simaetha let out a hoot at Savannah's words. Lady Arachne remarked, "Wait! Wait! Wait, now! I think it would be sweet. Lillian could be the Auset to his Ausar, stitching his fourteen pieces back together. A black woman putting a black man back together—and beholding one another's Ixu and Gira in the process. Ain't no kind of conjure or incant more powerful than that, *chile*"

Savannah grinned and sipped the remainder of her tea. Simaetha addressed the women in the room, "It's just the politics of it all. I moved to New Orleans to get away from the conjure folk in Saint Louis. They had resentment for Lillian. They believed she got everything because who her father is." She leaned back in her chair and folded her arms. "Conjure folk can be 'niggas' too."

"Who you talkin' to?" Savannah put forward.

Simaetha disclosed, "I thought the conjure community in New Orleans would be a rich, revival of our ideology."

Lady Arachne rolled her eyes and scoffed, "You found out they got 'niggas' down there, too. New Orleans folk think they so high and mighty about all this. From the Vodou they practice to hoodoo or the Ojulowo-conjure. Girl, I hate to say it: *Nigga please!*"

"Satchel warned me it'd be worse," Savannah imparted. "He was right, but he was also trying to keep his daughter close. It's obvious Lillian is his favorite, and that didn't help matters. But she worked for her place. Favoritism had nothing to do with it. She worked hard. Many of Satchel's other sons and daughters weren't as interested, despite their mothers' insistence to put their names forward. I didn't have to do anything to make Lillian pursue her birthright. I still left. Lillian split her time. Despite any problems we faced in New Orleans among the community, it was easier to stay to ourselves." She took a moment before saying, "I like Fable Avenue. It's not my new home, but two of my three new houses lead to it. I consider you all allies."

"*Three* houses?" Lady Arachne questioned.

"I'll at least be a baroness in Water Bug Hollow," Simaetha said, speaking on the matter to reclaim the significant territory. "I don't need a grand title. I don't need to be titled O-Jewel Queen, but I will have a *non nòb.*"

Lady Arachne flipped the next card. The Empress reversed came up. She inquired, "Satchel as O-Jewel King or Papa, why not be O-Jewel Queen or sole matriarch?"

"Welcome to politics, Matriarch Arachne," Simaetha chuckled. "*You* will hold that position," she next revealed. Lady Arachne attempted, with little success, to keep the surprise from her face. "It will be an excellent bridge to fasten Fable Avenue, the center of the Northeast Ojulowo conjure community, to the Water Bug Hollow *nasyon*. All the communities look to Fable Avenue, and they appreciate you here."

Lady Arachne insisted, "We still answer to the Gwuinee. We respect the hierarchy."

Savannah set her cup down on the table. "Why the politics at all? The communities collectively study to carry out the ritual for the Grand Conjure or Wish. We have the lilac spirit, and though the cobalt-blue flame has been banished, we will conjure her again."

Simaetha made clear. "I know it's petty of me. My apologies," she stated. "It's the discomfort I've been accustomed to. I don't ask for much. Baroness. No more of a title than that. I just want my place, and no one to bother me in it."

"Sister, don't worry," Lady Arachne comforted. "No one has crooked eyes on you here. You're safe." She placed a gentle hand on Simaetha's arm, and Simaetha thanked Lady Arachne in a tender voice. "Only eyes here are the ones this woman's grandson has for your daughter." The women chuckled. Lady Arachne sat back. "Queen *and* matriarch?" she questioned. "I'd be more of a representative. That would only make sense." She pondered, and then she asked Simaetha, "Have you spoken to Maman Anansi about this?"

"Yes. Satchel spoke with her," Simaetha notified. "Papa Solomon took him to Queens. Maman Anansi was supposed to talk to you tomorrow after the stitching ceremony," Simaetha notified. "It was supposed to be a surprise." She took a moment before suggesting, "Please, matriarch, play the part, even if her instinct figures it out."

"I will," Lady Arachne guaranteed. "My concern is actually with another matriarch, of sorts," she said looking up at Savannah. "Your daughter. Armand's mother."

Savannah made a face at the matriarch. "My pride is not what you think, Lena," Savannah disclosed. "I'm *proud* of Keiiah," she revealed further. "She knows her culture, but I admit my own stubbornness within my family's personal politics. Armand will be stitched. He will know conjure despite his mother's protests. He's under our protection, and he needs to know the entirety of what he's witnessing." She walked around the table and took a seat. "I know you don't care for my beliefs, the curse of my family, Lena—"

"No, but I respect your conviction," Lady Arachne interjected.

"Thank you," Savannah expressed. "I can't take a risk with that knowledge. Armand knows his heritage. He knows there's conjure inside of him. I don't want that *idan* to turn on him, consume him, and strengthen his *inawo*. I want him to embrace it, put his arms around it and dance with it like he does our guest's daughter." She paused to smile at Simaetha before concluding, "I will deal with my daughter's outrage. Those clouds have gathered, and that storm is on *my* horizon."

20

So sat Maman Anansi in an elegant, wooden chair of excellent craft and design. Her throne was situated next to Armand as he sat on the edge of a bed.

Regal in her presence. She was a thousand tomes speaking on a thousand epochs molded into black-rendered flesh that reflected the solemn grace of the midnight sky. Wisdom and age defined her beauty. Atop her head rested a coiled crown of wool flush with the color of ash and cinder. She wore an off-the-shoulder gown that was the color of the ocean. Black, laced gloves encased her hands. A lighted cigar was tucked between two fingers, smoldering with heat and wafting smoke.

Upstairs in a bedroom inside the Hollow House. This is where Armand's stitching ceremony would take place. Seated on the bed, he was bare of shirt and shoes, and he held his hands together. His undressed torso and arms were decorated with white paint, wide brush strokes that drew up ancient symbols and concentric spirals and shapes. Armand's face was painted as well.

His leg jiggled with nerves. Spying this prompted Maman Anansi to take a drag of her cigar. She laid a hand on his fidgeting leg, blew her smoke into the air, and merely thought an incant that relaxed him. Then she sang an ancient song. *"Praise His perfect black. Reconstructed from His deconstruction by Her glorious act—fourteen pieces: His sun, His moon, and the twelve signs of the Zodiac. Take his energy—that inner-G—let it spiral up your back..."*

Armand felt his body become light and unwind.

Maman Anansi crossed her legs. "Hello, Armand Gideon," she greeted. He nodded in response, respectful not to speak. "I am Maman Anansi," she introduced. "I'll help conduct a ritual on you, your stitching." She then informed him, "You will dream when this is performed; you will have an experience within that dream. I can't tell you what that experience will be. The happenings dreamed are different for all people." Armand nodded a second time, acknowledging the grand matriarch's words. "When this is finished, you will be connected to your Ixu, have access to your personal conjure, wield tremendous power. You will learn the rituals to control it. You will have an altar, a guide—an *ọkunrin-olukọ*, a male teacher. He might be someone from the community. He might appear as a *Lespri Bondye*, a good spirit. An ancestor you're connected to by blood or purpose." She paused, seeing a question in Armand's eyes. "Inquire, Mister Gideon. You have a question. Speak it."

Another nod. He sat up straight and asked, "Will I see an in-in-*inawo?*"

Maman Anansi smoked. She grinned, and exhaled a cloud from the side of her mouth. Breath complete. Her smirk widened. "I've heard about you, Mister Gideon. You have lineage among the Fable Avenue conjure folk. Your grandmother. She'll be assisting today." She rested her arms, crossed, on her knees. "If you have a burden, one that can condense into the monsters called ẹru or *inawo*, you'll at least experience it." Another question formed in Armand's eyes, and Maman Anansi answered, "It might not manifest in your initial stitching. It might come across in the sickness you might contract— and you're bound to contract a sickness. We'll look after you."

"I don't mean to interrupt, Maman Anansi," Armand cut in. "My grandmother has done rituals on me. Nightly. She and Madame Jeliya."

"You'll still be bedridden," Maman Anansi warned.

Armand's eyes dropped for a moment. He thought about the experience that awaited him. The things he'd heard about it. He'd hoped the rituals performed on him staved off enough of its cruelty. He still acquiesced to Maman Anansi's heeding. "I'm aware," he voiced.

"We'll look after you," the Grand Matriarch reiterated.

The door opened by way of Maman Anansi's otherworldly doing. Savannah Forrester and Lillian Eledas-Ghedemere walked in on cue. The sight of Lillian was like a sedative to Armand. His anxiety's tight knots loosened, and most of his concern exhaled and escaped through his pores. Armand held himself upright. Savannah and Lillian filled the empty seats on either side of Maman Anansi. Savannah clapped in rhythm, and Lillian closed her eyes and spoke an inaudible incant. The assortment of symbols drawn up on his body warmed against his skin. Armand perceived the painted sigils to move, becoming animated in a slithering spin around his torso and arms. He glimpsed down, and saw that was indeed the situation.

Maman Anansi extinguished her cigar into a flickering flame. She put out her hands, palms up. "Rest your hands in mine," she directed. "Palms up," she added. Armand did as the Grand Matriarch instructed. "Close your eyes," she further ordered, and Armand complied with Maman Anansi's command. "Tip-toe into your birth month. Let it be an open field of lush greenery. Regardless of season, let it see new life."

The black behind Armand's eyes developed into the very picture dictated to him. The dream began. He was dressed the same, and the symbols sketched on his body moved with vibrant life. It was his birthday. It was November Eighth. It was calm, but it was uncanny. The field brimmed bright as if the sun was on full display, but the sky was a dark covering above. A cosmos absent of stars and moon and the casting luminescence of distant planets.

He took a seat in the field, legs crossed. He looked up and marveled at the sight, and that's when Maman Anansi's voice made a soft rumble through the cosmos' rolling blackness. *"Can you see the constellation that rules your birth month?"* she asked in a soothing voice. *"How does it approach you? Does it walk or crawl or dip and rise with weight trying to achieve balance?"*

A scorpion crawled through the grass, parting the emerald blades with its forward pincers and swift, tapping legs. It crept up to Armand. The critter straightened its narrow, segmented tail back and away from him.

"Look at it," Maman Anansi's voice descended from the clouds. *"Focus, and turn it into its constellation. Put it back into the sky. Make it a body of stars, and extinguish it from the Heavens."*

Her task seemed impossible to Armand, but he liked a challenge. He stared stern at the passive, predatory arachnid and imagined the accurate cluster of stars overlaying the scorpion's hard, rigid frame. Imagination was more than just figment. The small, celestial representatives were genuine in construct, and their heat burned the arachnid, melting its body. The dissolved fluid became a wide puddle in the soil, but soon phased into a gas that evaporated into the miniature constellation left behind. The small stars swirled into one, and their acute fire drained into Armand's focused eyes. His pupils then glowed with the weight of the Scorpius star coupling, and the fire spread to the remainder of his eyes. Armand experienced no pain, and he only had an instinct to tilt his head back. The light drained from his eyes, and the black sky was suddenly populated with the celestial scorpion's star configuration.

"All that," came Maman Anansi's voice, *"just to douse the glister of their anatomy. Can you do that, Mister Gideon? Can you make the true animal sacrifice?"*

He looked down. A ceremonial machete was in his hands, and he used it to stab the area where the scorpion originally lay. The ground swirled with smoke, and the constellation overhead disappeared. The midnight sky pulsed like a heart. Hand claps played alongside rhythmic drums. Armand's heart connected to the cosmic beat. Smoke billowed into the empyrean blackness. Puffed and puffed, it covered the sky and braided together and became clouds. A gentle rain anointed him.

Maman Anansi announced, *"You are now a flume, receptive of conjure's water that will flow through you."*

His hands filled again with objects. Armand gripped a bottle of rum in his right hand. His left hand fanned three tarot cards. The Four of Cups. The Five of Cups. The Seven of Cups. *No Six, no sequence,* Armand thought. *Interesting.*

"Drink and mist the seven directions," Maman Anansi mandated.

Armand stood. He knocked back a large mouthful of rum. He sprayed a mist of the rum forward. He sprayed a mist of rum to his left and right. He turned and misted the direction behind him. Up. Down. And then he swallowed. The rum consumed, spiraling down his throat like hourglass sands, the bottle dissipated from his grasp. He returned to his cross-legged, seated position, and he held his cards close to his chest.

Armand closed his eyes and exhaled. He lay his back against the ground, cards balanced atop him. He felt something trace the lines in the palms of his hands. A finger? A feather? He didn't know. Then there was a stinging sensation in his palm as if a needlepoint had been pricked through his flesh. A tug. He felt string threaded through the lines in his palms. It all came together and replicated. The prick, the tug, and the threading produced a tightening in his hands. By reflex, he snatched the cards off his chest and crumpled them. They burned into ash in the palm of his right hand. He closed his eyes and slept within the moment of a blink, and felt rested in that second.

The rain trickled away. The billowing clouds retracted and dispersed.

Armand sat up. The taut sensation in his palms slackened, but there still remained a pulsing as if his heart lay in both his hands. It was now night. The environment matched the sky, but he was no longer in the grassy field. It was a forest. A campfire danced in front of him, and shadows twirled on all sides, pirouetting against the trees.

His instinct heard the whisper of footsteps before the quiet sound rippled through the air. A second peal resonating in his head apprised him that what approached brought no danger. It was another man around the same age as him. He was dressed in a pair of dark-brown linen pants, baggy in their nature. A light-brown button shirt was worn around his person. The collar was up, and the shirt was unbuttoned at the cuffs and down the middle. His chest was exposed, displaying the same painted markings as Armand. His symbols were stationary. Armand's had settled, too. A medallion hung around the man's neck. His fingers were decorated with rings that were in the shape of veves and Adinkra symbols. The rings had been fashioned from gold, silver, and copper. The man held a lighted cigarette in between the fingers of his right hand. His feet were wrapped in sandals, and his face was covered by a red and brown, wooden Nigerian mask.

He dropped a globular-bodied bottle of rum at Armand's side. "Let's have some rum infused with gunpowder!" he declared. He sat across from Armand on a thick log. He lifted his cigarette to the small, rectangular opening parting the lips on the mask. He took a drag and blew out the smoke.

Armand picked up and uncorked the bottle. He knocked back a large gulp. He swallowed without spraying mist, and watched as the masked man set down a large lockbox and then take another drag. "Look at the stars, Armand Gideon." He pointed up and repeated, "Look."

Armand tilted his head back, cautious in his movement. His eyes remained on the masked man until his instinct tingled him an assurance of good welfare. There were a few more stars in the black sky than the morning had shown. They spelled I-X-U, and Armand spoke the word aloud. "*Ik-soo!*" he said. "*Ik-soo,*" he pronounced again. He looked back at the masked man, grin on his face.

"That's how it's pronounced," the masked man remarked in a congratulating tone. "We got folk that practice the power and lessons of *Macumba, Umbanda,* and *Quimbanda.* Them folk talk about *Exu.* E-X-U. This is the same, but different. Pronounced different. The I-X-U spelling is very significant." He expounded, "It's I," he pointed at himself, "and you," he aimed a finger at Armand and concluded, "with the crossroads between us. That's the 'x'." He tapped on his heart. "The Ixu is said to be the masculine half of the cosmos, the god-man at the beginning of time." He pointed up again and said, "Right there."

Armand took another peek at the sky.

The masked man added, "His consort is Gira." He asked, "You heard of Gira, man?" He puffed his cigarette. Smoke. Blown. He took up speaking when Armand shook his head, no. "She's the feminine spirit of female wisdom, motherhood, sexuality, beauty and desire." Behind his mask, his eyebrow cocked, and a smirk came to his face. "She's the beginning. She's black as Ixu and said to be a beautiful, *insatiable* woman." His grin brightened under the mask. "Always wanted to meet her," he declared. He spread his arms out and sang, *"She's the feminine half of the universe, the goddess-woman at the beginning of time."*

He smoked again.

Armand drank. He swallowed and requested, "Say no more!" And he insisted for good measure, "Especially if you're going to sing, 'cause you can't." Both laughed. Armand got up, head back, face aimed at the sky. "It's all coming to me now. I'm remembering." He pointed high and recited the tale. "She and Ixu were coiled together in sexual embrace," he began. "That was the universe before this one. But then Gira climaxed, and she gave birth to all we see while they remained unseen." He could see it all in the black-mirror sky. "Ixu at that moment became a driving force of the universe, animating the heavens and creating movement, stimulating change in the forward motion. Gira became the cosmic adhesive. Her motherly embrace ensured that nothing spun out of its course and destiny. Dark energy. Dark Matter," he titled as he watched the Heavens fill with the story he recounted and become populated with the missing elements of stars, moons, and planets.

The masked man tossed his cigarette into the fire. He got up and joined Armand at his side. He asked for the rum with no words just his hand out. Armand understood the gesture and passed the bottle to his new friend. He was curious anyway on how he'd drink the contents. It was a peculiar sight, but the masked man managed, slipping the rum between the slit that parted the mouth in the mask. Not a drop was spilled, and so all was earned.

"What's your name?" Armand inquired taking the bottle back.

"No name," he answered. "Just *Oluṣọ*, a guardian spirit. I do, for some reason, keep feeling a name, though. Daniel Nathan Adams. I feel like it's still just a designation. I've crossed paths and spoken with other Oluṣọ. Same thing with them. Just real odd," he said while giving a pensive stare at the ground. "I've met female Oluṣọ, and they've expressed hearing Dahnay Nancy Adams." He nodded his head from side-to-side and then concluded on the subject, "At least we all part of the same family."

Armand didn't think much on the issue, though he entertained a listen. He was mostly into his long swallows of gunpowder rum. "Guardian spirit, huh? I thought you'd be my Ixu," was all he said pertaining to the Oluṣọ's words.

"No. You are you, and we are together."

Armand accepted the Oluṣọ's statement with a nod, but he still had a question. He peered down at the wooden lockbox and asked, "Okay, Mister I Got No Name but a Title, what's in the box?"

The Oluṣọ turned. He patted Armand on the shoulder as he revealed, "That, Mister Armand Gideon, is your burden." He rose, slipped into the shadows, and disappeared. But his voice remained in an effort to affix his final statement with just one word. *"Inawo."*

Armand went still. Nothing around him moved, save the fire's measured gesticulation. Even the casted shadows were motionless. It went quiet, too. The flailing flames were hushed of their whipping snap. Noise and hurried movement only existed within Armand as he stared at the lockbox. His thoughts were speeding images, seemingly in contest with his heart for swiftness and sound. Rapid and reverberant heart and mind resulted in Armand perceiving, in his peripheral, the fire shift in a manner where he would've insisted to any that protested that its shape and gesture was that of a beckoning finger.

He looked at the fire. There was no discernable shape. Just flames. He looked away, and from the corner of his eye, the beckoning, fiery finger returned. Armand decided to sneak up on the visual with his eyes, but every movement of his sight toward the configuration, the flames returned to normal. So, he ignored the phenomenon.

Eyes on the lockbox. Armand reasoned with his trepidation that held him in place. A creature constructed of smoke and tempestuous ills was contained there in the lockbox. It could slither free, once the chest was opened, and condense into a monstrous depiction of his troubles. The only thing that stepped him forward was a childhood notion to challenge both fate and risk and spit in their faces.

Armand triple-dog-dared himself to move, and so he did.

His steps brought him to the lockbox. He stood over it, staring down at the ornate coffer containing his burden. He knelt on one knee and took up the case. It was lighter than he expected, considering the weight of his burdens were compacted inside. He set it down and unfastened the lock. The click disrupted the quiet. Armand opened the chest, and a sunset-colored light glowed dull through the crack. Lifting the lid all the way up made the light retract into its source. A large and rusted, slave shackle lay inside the box. Armand perceived each link in the chain as an ill that haunted him. He could translate the metal loops jointed together. Looking at the shackle made his head throb, his sinuses tighten, and a pressure build behind his right eye that resonated to the right side of his forehead.

Armand ignored the intense stress filling half his face, and he reached for the rusted chain. The pain amplified and paired with a pulsating hum. The murmur bubbled in his mind and filled his ears, making his head heavy. Something burst in his nose, and blood dribbled free. None of this occurrence inspired Armand to stay his hand from action. It roused him to snatch the chain, and holding the shackle caused the compression in his head to balloon. Armand gnashed his teeth. His lips trembled as they parted, fighting against the tightness. He closed his eyes, pressing his lids shut in an effort to keep his head from what he believed would be an inevitable explosion.

He pressed the chain against his forehead, and tears streamed down his face. He felt it all. His upper and lower teeth separated, and Armand screamed. In a show of strength, Armand stood, spun about, and tossed the chain into the shadow of the woods. With separation and distance between he and the chain, the compression in his head dampened. He opened his eyes and saw a light burst from inside the night's shaded veil.

The fire beside him diminished, and the land he stood over raised. A burst of air was heard and up he went like a geyser. Armand balanced himself against the rise, arms out with his body swaying around to keep upright. Looking down, he witnessed the bright light widen like a menacing maw and swallow the forest he resided in. The small patch of earth, now a pillar of compacted soil, expanded on either side and behind him. It became the edge of a treacherous cliff, and like a fool, Armand allowed one leg to dangle over its side. He put his arms out, his head back to the sky. He smiled.

And then he dropped. All the way down.

Hitting the light was like hitting liquid. But it wasn't water. It was a trifle thicker, and its luminosity burned. Armand's liquefied burden tossed him around. He didn't know whether it was organic waves or in truth a moving, living thing sentient enough to attack him. His instinct on the quandary directed Armand to the latter.

He flailed about, attempting to dodge waves with less than favorable results. He soaked up the burn, kicking to glide up through the thick, liquid anatomy. His open eyes were unblurred and unfazed by the burning wet surroundings. Internal waves and concussive funnels battered him, knocking him about and keeping him from ascending through the liquid beast's belly. So, he remained floating. Waiting. Palms open and out. Another pipe of whirling liquid spun in his direction. Closer and closer until it was close enough. Armand spoke an incant. His words in the invisible language were muddled with haphazard syllables, but that was his aim.

The consequence of Armand's actions manufactured a combustible pressure that was erratic and disproportionate. The thick, liquid pool collapsed. Armand slapped a muddy surface. Land had either been regurgitated from the detonated pool, or the earth Armand dived from descended and took its previous place below. Either way, the trees had been stripped of their leaves, and the soil drenched. Armand ran his fingers through the mud and pressed his face against the wet soil. The sting of the pool lifted. His headache was gone, and he breathed real air. He hadn't been holding his breath surrounded by the pool of ill omen, and breathing inside the liquid felt like swallowing while having a sore throat. It scratched and burned his nostrils, too. Drawing a real breath felt like sipping sweet wine, and it made his head spin just the same until enough breaths straightened the world.

Armand cleared his throat. He raised on his hands, arms extended, body up. He surveyed the night environment. He heard a haunting wail behind him and turned his head to confront it. The shadows and shades that formed the night slipped from their fixed positions like curtains stripped from where they hung. Sunlight was exposed, and the day was all around him. But the shadows weren't dispelled. They configured together and fabricated the horrific shape of a mammoth-sized scorpion. Armand got to his feet and faced the beast.

Made of twilight's near-dark and murk, there was still form and substance to the colossal creature. It swung a single pincer and hit Armand, lifting him off the ground. The impact was hard and jarring, but Armand celebrated the swat. He soared through the air, and it felt like days before he landed. When he did, the collision was rougher than the swing that brought him there. He tumbled, rolling until his mind didn't. Armand regained clarity and took advantage of his momentum, springing himself onto his feet. He stood, ready for a fight.

The scorpion of pitch and mist was already upon him, and its pincers and tail were cast down to crush or skewer him. Quick and quick and quick was its stabbing and pounding. Armand was swifter, evading every strike made at him. Mud spattered in all directions. Armand jumped back. He observed spherical bodies of light configure in zodiacal formation within the shadowy arachnid's body. The scorpion turned to face him, its legs wriggling its body into position, clattering against the wet ground.

Armand noted another curiosity. Three, distinct objects floated in the sunless void of the scorpion's massive pincers and under its stinger. They were skulls as large as his balled fists, and they were expertly crafted from otherworldly material. Perhaps they were never there before. The articles cast light that he would've earlier noticed. Though, Armand admitted, he was quite busy dodging pincer and stinger attacks, or sailing through the air when hit. But now his sight spied these three curios that his instinct determined were his personal *objet d'art*.

The ones enfolded in the pincers glowed red and green. The third, inhumed in the venom bulb, was black in color with a dark-purple shine humming from its core. All three had a shimmer of gold light surrounding them. Armand first believed he would pull the stars from the giant scorpion. Now he wanted these trinkets, and he had a plan to secure them.

He made a move forward, and the scorpion attacked as desired. It hurled its right pincer down on Armand. He moved away from the attack, and the massive claw crashed into the ground, splashing Armand with mud. He hopped onto the appendage and plunged his hand into its murky frame. Though the creature was made up of the pool's liquid, it felt like sludge putting his arm through it. But Armand was determined. He extended his arm until his open hand gripped his crimson-colored prize. His reward in his clutches, he pulled back with a proud grin on his countenance.

Armand couldn't savor the moment too long. The scorpion attacked with his other pincer, a linear strike at Armand perched on him. Armand lifted in the air, tossed the red skull aside, and touched down on the second claw just as it finished its attempted swing at him. Armand repeated the same action, jamming an open hand into the creature's pincer and snatching the emerald skull buried there. Celebration was again short-lived. Another strike at Armand, quicker and from the shaded, giant critter's tail.

Armand's instinct gave him clairvoyance to move away from the stinger's jab. The poisonous needle missed him, but the heft of the venom gland knocked against him and caused his dodge to turn into a clumsy flop to the ground. Like a seasoned ballplayer, he held tight to the green skull, even when the scorpion struck again.

Armand rolled. The stinger speared the muddy floor, but wasn't lodged there long. Up, and another strike. Armand rolled once more, and it wasn't only seconds before a lunge was attempted again. Armand rotated away from being impaled. He sprung up on his feet after completing the turn, leapt away as both pincer and stinger came down on him, and scooped up the scarlet skull he'd earlier tossed.

The scorpion skittered in Armand's direction. Armand sprang to his feet and ran, both skulls in his possession. He put the charging arachnid at his back. But two legs didn't compare to eight, and the scorpion gained on him. He jumped forward when the stinger was thrust toward him. It missed, and he was thankful. It slowed the scorpion down, and gave him a chance to scurry forward, gaining ground between he and the creature.

The skulls he held melted into light that seeped into his palm lines. Up his arms they drained. The colors went to his chest and erased the ceremonial lines drawn on his body, taking shape as lighted, skull tattoos on his pectorals. Their imprint on his chest produced an instinct. He paused in his sprint and right in front of him came down the scorpion's tail. Armand dropped to his knees and reached inside the venom sack, through the gelatinous, black fog. The sable skull in his grip, Armand pulled his hands back, placed the skull against his chest, and let the cranial trinket dissolve into light and seep into his skin to become a rendering between the other two skulls.

The tail lifted. Armand sprang forward, but a striking pincer smacked his ankle and knocked him from the air to the ground. He plopped against the mucky earth and rolled over on his back. Armand saw the scorpion crawl into position to have another stab with his stinger. Armand didn't move. He waited, eyes focused on the organic needle attached to the end of the creature's tail. It struck. He reached up and closed his hands, catching the stinger in his clasp. His tattoos radiated their respective colors, gold aura brimming bright around them. He bared teeth. His strength held, even as the large, black smoky beast pressed harder to break through his clutch. He sunk into the marsh. Then he had a thought, but not an instinct. *Conquer,* he assessed, *by embracing it.*

Armand let the stinger go, and the pointed appendage punctured the black skull tattoo centered on his chest. He hollered! His scream transitioned into a laugh that turned back into a thunderous cry. The sound he created altered between agony and exuberant relief. His body wriggled up and down like waves of water. His eyes rolled into the back of his head and he missed the moment when the scorpion's pincers burned along with its body. The tail twisted. Armand's exhale returned him to agony and kept him there until the tattoos on his body rose out of his chest and formed solid. The black skull's rise eased the scorpion's stinger loose from his torso with no puncture wound left behind.

The tail shrank and transmuted into a necklace of earth-colored beads that were thick and barrel shaped. The beads looped through the skulls, and the completed necklace snapped at a link enclosed around Armand's neck. The painted symbols he wore earlier seeped back into his skin.

Armand turned over, raised up using his hands, and then lifted himself to his feet. Muddy and exhausted, he bent back and roared. The trees of the forest sprouted from the ground. The mud dried, and vegetation littered the soil's surface once again. The night returned, and so did the campfire. The masked Olúṣọ walked out of the shadows with a new cigarette between his fingers. He past Armand and sat in the same place on the same log. Smoking.

Armand turned, walked over to him, and sat cross-legged. He and the Olúṣọ stared quietly at one another until the Olúṣọ rotated his head and spotted the lockbox. It was open and now empty. He returned his attention to Armand and said, "Yeah…" Then he went back to smoking.

Armand closed his eyes and woke up lying in bed. Everything felt heavy, and the room spun. Worse, it was blurry as he swam to the surface of consciousness from a deep slumber. His mouth was a place of sticky tar and heat, and when he swallowed he took the foul climate to his stomach. He became nauseous. His stomach pumped as if ready to cast up something rotten, but Armand was able to settle his insides.

He breathed. The blur in his eyes faded, and his vision sharpened. Lillian was there reading a book. This made Armand happy, and it relaxed him, though the rest of his malady persisted. He hiccupped and a burning liquid bubbled in his throat. His nausea flared, and he grit his teeth while baring them. His stomach boiled and growled in his attempt to keep its contents down. His body almost bent into a complete fetal position, but then it straightened as his stomach settled again.

"Armand," Lillian called to him as she leaned forward, taking a cup resting on a side table. She placed the open book on her lap, and she used both hands to help Armand take a sip of the incanted, herbal drink. He was reluctant at first, and then Lillian coaxed him by saying, "It will settle your stomach, mostly."

That was motivation enough. His limbs felt heavy, as if the muscles had been strained. He embraced Lillian's help with the cup, but made things easier for her by scooting up into a partial, sitting up position. From there, Lillian tipped the drink between his parted lips. He swallowed, and the relief for his stomach was immediate. Everything on him continued throbbing, and his limbs remained heavy. He was conscious of his physical being until the next elements of the drink soaked into his bloodstream.

Armand slumped back into the bed and went to sleep.

It was dark with no images. Calm. A much-appreciated peace.

21

Cedron tended the stove in the kitchen of the Brickhouse family's Harlem brownstone. He'd put together a fine feast fit for a conjured spirit. He knew his way around a kitchen, and he prided himself on it. The cooking area was his hub, and his legs hurried about as he gathered seasonings and whipped together a series of delectable treats. His steps were whimsical like a dance. Music played throughout the Brickhouse residence. Cedron spun. His conjure-coated legs gamboled with rhythm. He faced the ritual's repast and reveled in his culinary craftsmanship. There was cooked corn covered in banana leaves and chopped okra, onion, and dried shrimp.

A pair of arms looped around his waist.

Cedron smiled. "I don't usually let people into the kitchen while I'm cooking," he told Leah Peters as she rested her head against his back. She squeezed him tighter.

"That smells divine, Cedron-baby," Leah complimented in her low, smoky voice. "You better've made some extra for the folk 'bout to conjure up this spirit."

"What's my motto, Leah-baby?" he asked her, speaking over his shoulder.

Leah chuckled. She unbound him from her embrace. He turned to her and she looked up at him reciting, *"We can all eat."*

He turned to pick up a spoon. Remaining contorted, Cedron unwrapped a bundle of rice from a banana leaf, scooped up a spoonful, and also placed the remaining ingredients atop the rice. He rotated back around to face Leah, holding a hand under the spoon as he guided it into her open mouth.

Leah's eyes bloomed wide as the flavors burst on her tongue. She savored the bite, chewing slowly and relishing in the tang and heat of the spices and texture of the dried shrimp and okra mixing with the rice and onions. She swallowed, and she hated that the sample's moment had passed. She peeked behind Cedron, a bright, trickster grin on her round face. Cedron moved his mighty frame to hide the food from her view. "Slow up, Leah-baby, before you bring the wrath of a conjured spirit on us. We eat when the spirit is satisfied."

Leah gave Cedron a peck on the cheek. "You stepped up your culinary game!" she said as he leaned into her kiss. She maneuvered her arm around him and snatched up a small, torn section of a banana leaf that held the cooked ingredients. She giggled as she attempted to back up. Cedron put his arm around her and held her in place. She used her fingers to scoop up the food and triumphantly drop it into her mouth. She chewed, again savoring the taste, and also the victory of seizing another bite. "I got a thick frame, babe, but I'm swift," she told him.

"You swift all right," Cedron chided in a playful manner. "Swift to bring the wrath of a spirit on us."

"Spirit gon' be fine," she told him, putting a second scoop of food near Cedron's mouth. He opened, and she placed the food on his tongue. He enjoyed the flavor of his ritual tribute. "Well, damn. I put my foot in this. My mamma taught me right."

"Now you know why I had to resort to thievery," Leah remarked. She put the empty banana leaf down and let Cedron lick the taste from her fingers. She asked, "How you doing?"

"I'm doing fine," he said backing her up and initiating a slow dance.

"Your legs ain't tired, or your body keeping your conjure going?"

"Oh, I don't tire from this," he replied to her with a devilish grin on his face. "I got at this with that athlete's instinct." Leah gave him a look, and he gave her one in return. Cedron assured her, "I ain't pushin' myself beyond a limit. I conserve. You never know when the grown folks gonna give the Misfits a call to arms." Cedron paused for a moment. He thought and admitted, "I'm getting a little impatient on that end. I know they got something coming down our way."

Leah responded, "Me too. I want in."

Cedron's eyebrows went up. "You want in? On the frontlines?"

"Yeah, Cedron-baby!" Leah answered. "I lace my voice with incant to help teach the babies in my classes. I get 'em young. But I have a fire in me that's stirred to a point where it possesses my spine and I sprout wings. Thick as my frame may be, my wings of fire can lift me to the sky. I want to put my fire to good use, and reduce to ash men and women who bare needles. Them devils have our children!" Cedron felt the heat on her spine, prompting him to move the palm of his hands from Leah's back to her hips. She swiveled around in his arms and faced the front room. The heat running along Leah's spine diminished so as not to burn Cedron and disturb his concentration that kept his conjure wrapped around his legs and waist. She spied Neyeli and Benny Jah in the front room, putting together the other elements of the ritual. "Besides, why should the kids get all the fun? Exorcising *inawo*," she specified.

Benny remarked, "It's not all fun." He was still sluggish from his contest with the two inawo haunting the church in Water Bug Hollow. It didn't stop him from engaging in his conjure, using his ability to lighten the weight of a heavy, ornate, glass-top coffee table. He lifted the furniture piece with ease and set it aside to make a clear area for Neyeli to place down a circular cloth with red, black, and green stripes. The fabric spread out roughly one meter in diameter. He continued, "I hope this armor piece can rest me easy once I slip it on mah hand."

Cedron said to Benny, "Ain't feelin' up to snuff, sun? You got me fooled. You don't look so bad from where I'm standin'. You look strong enough to pull the iron teeth out of an *Asanbosam*."

Benny chuckled at Cedron's remark. He turned and Neyeli handed him the gauntlet, which she'd wrapped at the forearm and wrist with a marine-blue cloth. Benny set it down on the wider cloth on the floor, pulled out a vial of sacred dirt, and sprinkled it on the gauntlet's palm. Neyeli laid red snakeskin over the gauntlet's wrist.

"Let's get a good bowl of some of that conjure food," Benny voiced.

Cedron opened his embrace around Leah. She stepped away from him, and he turned and started preparing a bowl.

Leah asked, "How's that new boy? Miss Forrester's grandson?"

Cedron chimed in. "He just got stitched up, right?" he queried Benny and Neyeli.

Benny nodded, giving an audible answer as he put three necklaces made up of chunky, red and white beads around his neck. "Yeah. He's stitched. I think he's still recovering," he briefed.

"He still locked to that Ghedemere chick?" Cedron followed up.

Leah made a face. She turned to Cedron and scoffed, "Why she got a be a 'chick'?"

"I know, right?" Neyeli interjected, locks shifting between light red and bright orange. "Why not *Queen of the Crossroads*, which she was just consecrated and crowned."

Cedron rolled his eyes. "Because that's far too long," he riposted. "Can someone answer the question?"

"Yeah. They still connected," Benny said before attitudes could become more twisted. He joked, "The Eight Ball says, 'outlook is good'."

Neyeli's hair softened to pink and sky blue. She covered her mouth as she chuckled, stimulated by Benny's wit.

Still incensed over Cedron's choice of word for addressing Lillian Ghedemere, Leah pounded a closed fist against his chest. It did nothing to his massive frame, but he buckled to play along. Leah snapped at him, "And her name is *Lillian!*"

Cedron laughed. "Shit, I know her name. Damn!" he responded, straightening up. He turned and resumed plating. "She visited last October at the Four Days of the Spirit Festival. I met her then," he noted. He said over his shoulder, "You remember the festival? Where you was in town from Chicago and didn't say nothin' to a brutha until, like, the last day?" He turned around and hiked his shoulders, saying to Benny, "Which is such a chick move, right."

Leah laid into Cedron with a flurry of strikes against his chest. Benny laughed aloud while Neyeli bit her lip to keep her guffaws subdued. Cedron put his forearms up as guards against Leah's playful assault. She suppressed her smile as she warned Cedron through clenched teeth, "Don't you make me wrap my fire wings around you!" She hit him one last time. "Make this spirit we conjure whup yo' ass."

Leah turned. Cedron embraced her from behind before she could take another step. He kissed her in repetition on the cheek. "Leah-baby, you know I'm just playin'," he pleaded in a playful tone.

Leah rolled her eyes, a slight grin brewing on her visage. Her body loosened, taking on Cedron's weight and letting his arms hold her tighter. "Don't make me use my conjure voice. Have you all laid out and docile," she warned him.

Cedron nuzzled his nose against her cheek. He looked up at Benny and asked about Dajon. "Speaking of outlooks-is-good, what's good with y' little brother and that Melinda girl he still hangin' with?"

Benny's face contorted. His eyebrows lifted and he rolled his eyes. "Man, get the food ready!" he stated as he placed a ceremonial machete next to the gauntlet. "We all set here."

Cedron summoned a wide, shit-eating grin on his face. "Man, that's your little brother! He gettin' his. Why you so odd about it, sun? You big brother. Guide him, or at least root for him on the sidelines." His voice was loud in Leah's ear.

Neyeli giggled. Her hair turned navy blue. She said to Cedron, "It's so cute."

Benny still said nothing. Cedron stared at him, but Benny remained tightlipped on his end. There was no gain, and Cedron didn't want to delay the ritual any longer. He opened his arms and let Leah go after giving her a kiss. He slapped her bottom as she stepped out of his embrace, and she tossed a feigned look of disdain over her shoulder in reaction. Cedron smiled back her. He winked, and then he returned to preparing the plate with nothing more to distract him. He handed the contents to Leah who delivered the plate to the parlor area. She bent down and rested it with the other ritual elements on the cloth near the gauntlet.

Cedron washed his hands and joined everyone in the front room after lighting a cigar. They stood in square formation, at four corners around the circular cloth. Cedron handed the lit cigar to Neyeli after taking a puff. The empath took up the thick cigar between her fingers. She took a long drag and bent down. She exhaled the smoke over the ritual's items as Cedron and Leah hummed a spiritual, clapped twice and hit their chest once. They repeated the rhythm as Benny spoke, "Slayer of Enemies, High of Feather and Strong of Arm. Come forward African Lords of Hammer and Anvil, Lance and Chariot."

Humming. Clapping. Pound. Smoke covered the items. Neyeli rested the cigar on the plate of food. She stood and joined Cedron and Leah in hum, clap and beat. Benny joined too. All four in harmony. The fingers on the gauntlet trembled to their cadence. The metal scratched against itself, moving on its hinges where the fingers bent. A metallic crunch accompanied the sudden close of the fingers as the appendages on the metal glove balled into a tight fist.

The gauntlet's action signaled an end to the conjure folks' haunting hum, clap, and pound. The four remained still. The metal hand opened slow and with a chilling creak. The smoke that hung like a fog swirled together and over the open palm. The dirt sprinkled onto the hand turned to cinders. They purred in their iridescence. Their glow dimmed as they raised into the air and joined the transmuting, swirling smoke.

A ghostly figure alchemized out of the amalgamated smoke and cinders. He hovered over the open palm like a holographic projection. He wore a beige burnouse with gold trim. The hood was lowered revealing his clean-shaven, ovate face. He looked to be no more than thirty years old. He possessed a coil of tight, black curls that came together to create the shape of a dome. His skin was earth brown. A puffy, maroon-colored shirt was around his torso. Dark turquoise pants just as baggy and puffy covered his legs. Sandals were on his feet. Rings adorned every finger, save his middle and thumbs. Around his neck he wore a leather-cord necklace with a peculiar pendant attached to it. It was made up of two curved pieces made from silver that held between them a sphere made of gold.

He raised his legs and folded them, floating in the air as his cloak continued to dangle. He closed his eyes and dropped his head. A smile was on his face. His lips parted and he started laughing, throwing his head back, face to the ceiling. The four conjurers gave one another inquisitive glances. The conjured spirit projected quick peeps at them. He trapped his guffaws behind a smile that burned bright with relief.

"He's dead, isn't he?" he asked in an Afro-Arabic language. He saw the blank stares, and he managed to decipher it wasn't the lack of clarification pertaining to his inquiry. He made a quick observation of his surroundings. The spirit was aware of time and circumstance, though his instincts made him speak his native tongue. He was far from his own era, and far away from the land of his chief dialect. He asked again in English, "He's dead, isn't he?" The blank stares remained, and the conjured spirit sensed the hesitation was because of a lack of understanding on who he might've been referring to. So, the Moorish spirit explained, "There was a man of British Isle descent that wore the remaining piece to the Suit of Nines. A red-haired witch assisted him in accessing the magics blessed inside the gauntlet."

"Brice Cadogan," Benny spoke up. He pointed to himself and Cedron. "We tussled with him."

Cedron concluded, "Yeah, he got his."

The conjured Moor exhaled and expressed, "Thank you." He put his hands on his knees. "My wife said she could sense a lilac spirit. Has someone conjured that cosmic entity inside them?"

"Yes," Neyeli answered. Her hair altered in color to a deep purple. "The same who dispensed the man who manipulated the gauntlet. His brother," she nodded toward Cedron.

The Moor looked satisfied. "Ah! A triumph." Then he further inquired, "A cobalt-blue cosmic flame also?"

Neyeli again answered, "Yes. The lilac and the cobalt-blue spirits are sweethearts."

The Moor nodded. His face was muted with expression, but there was a sense of uncertainty behind his eyes. He told his audience, "That's good to hear, their love. But, their presence is a bit sad, too. Apparently, we're still in need of such devices, trying to correct the world." He took a moment to reflect. Then he stood up with flair and bowed in a regal technique. "Where are my manners. Good day, black conjurers. My name is Safwan Atiq, Second Wyvern and wielder of the Suit of Nines. I have a remarkable tale should you wish to hear it."

Cedron was proud of how things went with their conjure, connecting history with the present. He stood a little taller, saying, "Man, shit like this make you teary-eyed. I ain't gon' lie."

"My goodness!" Safwan exclaimed. "A pirate in a giant's frame!" he illustrated with his words. "And what is your name, *alqursan*? So far, I know you as Brother to the Lilac Flame."

"Cedron Goodspeed," he replied.

The Moor declared, "My instinct gives no false counsel. You command marauders, don't you, *alqursan*?"

Cedron smirked. "Do I wear it that well?" he quipped behind his haughty grin.

"Like a second skin, *alqursan*," spoke Safwan. "I know your kind very well. My best skirmishes were with men like you. My best allies, too. Good men, and great friends." He turned to Leah and proclaimed, "And for every devil there is an angel." He leaned close to her, saying, "Beautiful, black mu-rah, I see your wings of fire even when you do not ignite and spread them. What melodic syllables croon your name?"

"Leah," she answered with a flush of red in her dark skin. "Leah Peters."

"Your voice!" Safwan said as if feeling a pleasurable embrace. "I hear the incants that lace it. Powerful. I know how you keep this towering pirate tame in your presence."

Cedron passed looks between the winsome Safwan and his blushing sweetheart. He commented to the Moorish spirit, "You're a charmer."

"That's part of my story, Commander Goodspeed," he riposted with subtle, strategic syntax.

It worked. Cedron's eyebrows lifted. He regarded aloud, "Commander…? Huh! I like the sound of that."

With Cedron distracted, Safwan turned his attention to Benny Jah. "The soldier, loyalist. Light on your feet," he described. Then he queried, "Answer me this, a-Sir: Does my instinct fail me when it reveals you as the possessor of the Suit of Nines' remaining armor piece?"

"Nah," answered Benny. "Your instinct ain't fail you. It'll be on my arm, and I'll do it justice." He tapped on his chest and introduced himself. "Benjamin Brickhouse."

"I trust you will, a-Sir Benjamin," said Safwan in a sincere voice. "The gauntlet is a gateway to all the righteous spirits that wielded the Suit of Nines. Call upon our guidance if you need us." Then he turned to Neyeli. Her hair transmuted in colors, settling on a yellowish orange. "Absolutely remarkable! You hold the spectrum of emotion in the tightness of your locks, lovely mu-rah *iimbath*." His gaze and smile went from Neyeli to Benny and back to Neyeli. "You're together, courting…?" Benny and Neyeli answered with a nod of their heads. "There's so much conjure in this age. Have the three moons returned?"

"We not there yet," Cedron responded.

Safwan sighed, "So, there is still much for the lilac and cobalt-blue spirits to do in this time." His emotions didn't hang for long. His spirits were up and back in good light. "Work equates to adventure."

"Well, we sure on one," remarked Cedron.

Another instinct punctured Safwan's mental senses. It was melancholy, but the African Moor refused to let it buckle his posture. "I do sense the haunts of burden here. Very powerful." He turned his attention to Neyeli. "You can commune and exorcise them."

"Yes," she answered. "I have less experience on the communing part," she admitted. "But Benny and I have cleansed a number of people and places of their haunts."

Safwan raised his legs again and folded them. He returned his hands to his knees and directed in a gentle manner, "Sit, sit. Let us rest and tell tales of our day." The Moor's body descended closer to the floor. His burnoose ghosted through the ritual area and the floor as he came down. The young Fable Avenue conjurers took seat around him, their folded legs partially resting on the edge of the ritual cloth. "Conjure was quiet in my day," began the Moor. "Very mute. Everything about ancient aspects of the world was myth splintered into more myth dissected into legend. Conjure existed only as whispers. Story or practice wasn't even used to entertain children. The blacks of the world were fractured by politics.

"Performing conjure was seen as the Devil's work, and there was much improper use of it. The unethical practice of conjure is the reason the African Moors were sent into Europe," he explicated. "The Gothic King Roderick and the Christian Count Julian were a part of the lore. Julian's daughter was not in the Gothic King's court to learn. She was there to steal secrets on conjure pilfered from Africa. The true text of *The Sorcerer's Treasure*. Many attribute the work to the African Berber Bishop, Saint Cyprian. He had a hand in compiling the massive volume, but he was not the author of the arcane knowledge. Some speculate that Julian truly wanted another tome said to be possessed by King Roderick." Safwan paused for effect, and then he revealed, "The Book of Needles." Another stop in speech. He observed the eyes on him, reading them like cast divination stones. The young men and women who'd conjured his spirit understood what he spoke of on the surface, but the whole story eluded their learning. "That book was a text on a substance called wroch-blood, pulled from the *iyokù*, or residue, a miasmic matter left behind by irresponsible sorcery. Many conjurers were hired by European armies. They were like weapons. But without proper schools or *ásars* much had been misguided with conjure. Only possessions, monsters, and madness were born. Those politics had been at work for centuries.

"The dispute between the Gothic King and the Christian Count was reason enough for Africa's wandering warriors to unite and deal with the corrupt use of conjure in Europe and its study to be restricted to its original wielders." Safwan took a moment to reflect. His voice turned apologetic when he stated, "There were conjure scholars of my day that speculated it was all a ruse to bring the Africans into a crumbling Europe, reignite its dying flame. A lot of the wandering warriors that made up the Moorish army were indeed descended from the Kemetic Djedhi Khepri, the Wisdom Keepers of long ago. I don't entertain those ideas. There's no reason. As it stands, Julian's daughter was caught, and a terrible sentence was made upon her by the Gothic King. She was accosted. Word was sent to her father, and the Moors were called upon.

"The young General, Tarik Aben Ziyad, led the campaign on the orders of a man named Musa. He was given strict order to resolve the conflict, take all written works concerning conjure and return them to their home. That was not done. Conquest inebriated him with pride. The young General pressed through Spain taking city after city, town after town, establishing Moorish rule. It's said, on the orders of Musa, *'that bastard Tarik'* was whipped for three days straight. No written works were recovered, and the African Moor was now responsible for Spain.

"The positive was that conjure was more in use in al-Andalusia—responsible conjure. We could conduct campaigns to exorcise improper use." Safwan expounded, "What appeared to be unsuccessful attempts by the Moors to conquer other areas of Europe were very successful campaigns to destroy corrupt conjure practice. It was there that we learned the wrochblood residue, the *iyokù*, was put to use. It anointed the tips of sharpened instruments. Needles."

Leah and Cedron exchanged baffled expressions. Safwan noticed this. It was Benny that expressed their perplexity. "That's an earlier use of needles and accounts of needlemen soldiers than we've always been taught."

Safwan further described, "They formed their first, unified lodge after the fall of the Templars in thirteen thirty-three. There were more individualized, wicked practices beforehand. In my time. Small units of Needle Knights."

"Is that why the Suit of Nines was forged?" asked Leah.

"Yes," Safwan answered with renewed spirit. "My cousin's family fashioned the armor. An uncle on my mother's side. Al-Shakush Tanin. It was the year eleven ninety-five. My uncle created the suit. His wife blessed it. It took all her conjure to do it. Nine days of ritual. My cousin Maymun was to wear it, wield its power. He was the first born. He was strong and able-bodied, but his aspirations were not on conjure or incant. He desired to be a banker, an aristocrat." Safwan stopped his story and chuckled. "Such a delight to know that when the bearer of the suit slipped on its armor the appearance would change. Cape. Cowl. Sneaky burnouse with hood up. That was not how my cousin was garbed. No. The Suit of Nines gave him the fanciful dress of his desired occupation. So, he was a money man by day, handling the riches for many wealthy clients, investing in business and prosperous financial ventures. When needed, he donned the blessed Suit of Nines, and challenged armies looking to impede upon Moorish progress, or hunt down spies looking to seize scrolls or tomes dedicated to conjure." Safwan spoke with pride, but it wasn't exclusive to his cousin's exploits, but also what became a family trade. He noted as an assurance, "He did have the sense of mind to put on a bandit's mask and head scarf. He was the Wyvern for many years."

"The Wyvern?" Benny Jah blurted. "The suit could turn you into a monster?"

Safwan grinned at him. He winked and nodded his head. "Oh, no, a-Sir," he hastily addressed Benny's concern. "That is the moniker for all who wear the Suit of Nines—save the bastard who misused its blessing for so long. I can't imagine how much residue that *ghurayb* produced with his ill intentions." He shook his head, wiping away the thought of Brice Cadogan. "That aside," he said to Benny. "*You* will be the Wyvern. There is only one piece remaining, and you will wear it and continue the legacy. Even more important, you will assist the lilac and cobalt-blue spirits with putting the three moons back in the sky. You all will!"

Benny considered the responsibility. He'd procured it by wager. His eyes fell on the gauntlet, and the spirit he needed to recover from his last skirmish with the inawo was replenished. Cedron asked the conjured Moor, "Where are the other pieces?"

Benny listened with new ears when Safwan explained, "Destroyed, sadly. They had to be. Even this piece was considered gone. I was a spirit when the hunt for the Suit of Nines commenced." Benny gave his attention to Safwan. His focus was different from his friends' around him. He was like a student in class. He couldn't help but smile when Safwan explained, "My cousin's excursions with the Suit of Nines were fruitful, but he longed for another life. My uncle understood. Maymun and I were close. He knew my want for the life he lived. I asked him to recount his adventures every chance I had. I loved the tales. I imagined myself to be a part of them. I wanted to be an adventurer. He trained me. He gave me a job as cover, but being Second Wyvern was my true occupation. I did it well. The legend spread.

"I, under the mantel had cape and cowl, hooded burnouse, and African mask," Safwan narrated. "The feel of its power. Agile. Artistic with martial abilities. Enhancing ritual, conjure, and incant. Impervious to weapon attacks and some magics. I felt so alive, like the Wyvern was who I truly was." His excitement waned, and he sighed, "But you get old. You settle down. You pass on the responsibility." His eyes looked beyond the company that conjured him and saw the past. His life. "My daughter inherited my spirit of adventure, much to my wife's chagrin. She was Wyvern-Three, and she made this father of hers so proud. My grandson was next. I passed away before he handed the duty off to a close cousin. My spirit was so ingrained into the Suit that I could assist the wearer from beyond. When my wife passed, my spirit receded from the armor. It was my choice. Now, that we were on the same plane of existence, I decided to be with her spirit.

"My last peek into the Suit's affairs was when a descendant, in the year thirteen-hundred-six, was swindled out of the suit by her fiancé who sold it to a Templar knight attempting to gain the upper hand in France's persecution of his Order. My descendant killed her fiancé and went after the Suit. She was a powerful conjure woman on her own. She then tracked down the Suit and the man who'd purchased it. She found only a story. The Templar who'd bought the armor had been killed by his own, as they did not want to draw anymore ire with the Church for having such a relic. It was locked away for safe keeping. My descendant, using her natural conjure abilities, snuck into the Templar facility that housed the Suit of Nines. The Templars were alerted, and they had needles among them. She destroyed all but one aspect of the armor piece before being overcome by Templars. That piece, of course, projects my spirit as we now converse."

All eyes fell to the gauntlet with its palm open and sacred ground scattered over it.

The front door opened, and the attention was broken. Everyone turned to the door. Safwan did too. There was thirteen-year-old Dajon Brickhouse with his regular-folk friend named Noah Boone, a young man he'd defended from two bullies in the early months of autumn the previous year. The conjured Moor's otherworldly instinct recognized Dajon's conjure, and he could sense that Noah's conjure was buried dormant and not part of a family that studied such ancestral powers.

Dajon's instinct observed the scene he'd walked into. He took a quick glance at his friend whose features were wide with awe. Dajon's lip curled into a snarl. He looked back at the Moorish spirit cast by ritual and rolled his eyes and clenched his teeth. There was a quick breath, and then he said to his brother, "Benny, why you all got to hold your science experiment now?" Dajon turned to his friend and nudged him in the ribs. "It's cool, right? It's a hologram." He grabbed him by the arm and pulled him, getting a look at Safwan's spirit from another angle. Dajon bent his eyes at the hovering specter. The Moor took that as cue, and he shifted his form, flattening into a one-dimensional projection. Dajon pointed. "See? It's flat from this angle. It's all an illusion." Noah nodded, pressing his glasses against his face that remained suspended in surprise. His eyes peered down to observe the beam casting the projection. He saw the instruments displayed for the ritual laid out on the cloth. The gauntlet. The machete. The food. He saw nothing electrical. Dajon noticed his friend's gaze and put his finger under his chin, lifting his vision back up to the floating spirit. "Nah, kid," he prompted. "This angle."

Noah stared. "Wow…" he was able to expire.

Dajon agreed, playing it cool and saying, "Cool, yeah." Then he joked, "Still not as good as the graphics on this fighting game I'ma whup you on."

Noah's face changed into a disbelieving appearance, coupled with a grin. The projection was no longer a priority. "Lead the way, chump!" he barked at Dajon. "You don't have your cute little cheerleader here to swoon at your side."

Benny's younger brother held a grin too. Noah took it as a call to the video game wild, a pride that Noah had accepted the challenge thrown at him. But Dajon's smile was buried in the pride of drawing Noah's attention away from the ritual conducted in the front room. He waved Noah toward the stairs as he stepped in their direction. "C'mon then," he baited as the conjured Moor and the young incators around him watched in silenced.

Dajon and Noah trotted up the stairs. Noah did take one last glance at the projection. His eyes widened at his final glimpse, and there was a sensation that pumped inside him beside his heart. The impression caused his peek to linger. Dajon said something to him, and his attention was taken away, concentrating on throwing playful insults up at his friend as they ascended the stairs to Dajon's room.

The Moor's spirit fleshed out to a three-dimensional apparition. The conjurers turned their heads to him, no longer observing Dajon and his friend's departure. They heard the door close upstairs, Dajon and Noah lighting up the video game console to engage in virtual fisticuffs. Safwan's eyes focused on Benny Jah. He directed, "Nimble and loyal soldier, please stand." Benny did as tasked. Safwan knelt on one knee, bobbing in the air. "There was never any ceremonial or systematic passing of the Suit of Nines. The parent would take his or her child, who'd reached the correct age, to the wardrobe and reveal a secret passage of sorts behind it. Nothing fancy," Safwan explained. "Just another compartment to hold the Suit," he said. "I followed my cousin on horseback to his father's ironworks den. Your ritual, from what my spirit deciphers, was dealing with its malevolent wielder." He listed the second circumstance that was more of a direct result in Benny Jah receiving the gauntlet and title of the Wyvern, "Then, a friendly wager with a friend procured you this blessed artifact." Safwan stood and announced, "Benjamin Brickhouse, by way of fight and wager, I declare you heir to the legacy of the Suit of Nines."

Safwan removed his pendant from around his neck. He dropped the jewelry piece into the gauntlet's palm. It didn't faze through. In fact, there was a surprising clank when the phantom item landed against the palm. It dissolved quickly after.

Safwan bowed with the entirety of his upper body, one arm out, and the other tucked against his torso. Standing straight, he spoke his final words. "Put your mind at rest. You will then be able to commune with all that have worn the Suit." Safwan breathed deep, and he exhaled hard. "Ah! This has been refreshing. I thank you for conjuring me. The wonderful aroma, your words, and this configuration made my summons easy." He said directly to Benny Jah, "This power is now your responsibility. Wield it proper. Good day, a-Sir." Safwan wrapped himself within his cloak and vanished without leaving behind glittering particles or whooshing sounds signaling departure.

Benny planted himself on his knees and leaned forward. He removed the wrapped snakeskin and cloths encasing the armor piece. He proudly lifted the gauntlet and slid it on his arm. His fingers slipped into their corresponding compartments on the metal glove. A cooling current wound its way up his wrist. A magical operation then took place as the gauntlet molded to fit Benny Jah's arm, diminishing its heft but retaining its intricate design. The frosted air turned warm, and a soft glow emitted from the silver gauntlet for a moment, and then it disappeared.

Benny opened and closed the glove, acclimating to its weight on his person. He made a tight fist, closed his eyes, and imagined a thought. Benny felt the absence immediately, and he opened his eyes to behold the gauntlet had faded from his arm. He balled his fingers again without curtaining his eyes. He projected a thought, and there came upon him the magical armor piece. Safwan's necklace and pendant materialized around Benny's neck at the same moment the glove reappeared. Benny touched the dangling charm, lifting it to eye view. He let it go when Cedron jumped to his feet and charged him, vaulting over the ritual cloth with one step. He wrapped his large arms around Benny and lifted him. "Own that shit, sun! You got that!" he congratulated. "The Wyvern, kid! You ancient! You power!"

Cedron bounced Benny up and down a few times and then set him back on his feet. Leah was there to congratulate him, standing. She leaned forward and kissed his cheek. "*Idunnu*, Wyvern-Benny Jah," she complimented with a warm smile.

"Thank you, Leah," Benny replied. But then Neyeli put her hand on his arm and turned him to face her. Benny dissolved the gauntlet and put his hand against her cheek to caress her. He said to her in patois, moving his lips closer to hers, "*Criss ting, a fi mi.*" Neyeli giggled, and then she and Benny put their mouths together and kissed one another with deep affection.

Leah put her arms around Cedron, and she laid her head against his body. Cedron put an arm around her, and they watched Benny and Neyeli find conversation in the kiss they shared. Neyeli pulled away. Her face was glimmering with her smile. She tapped her forehead against Benny's. She suggested, "I know Safwan's spirit is probably well disciplined, but we should still give him a proper sending."

Leah slapped Cedron on the stomach. "That means we can eat my man's good food too. I'll get the rum." She let go of Cedron.

Neyeli stepped away from Benny Jah. "Let me help you get the rest of the food," she said following Leah into the kitchen. "We can still just eat around the cloth after we give prayer to the Moor."

Cedron watched the two women make their way to the kitchen. He stepped away from the edge of the cloth, bent down, and said to Benny while holding up two fingers, "You on two details. Got it? The Elders come for us to get them kids back, is one. The other, is anything Gordon asks for. Back him up."

"I'm on it, King," Benny responded.

Cedron patted Benny on the shoulder. "Good. You look good, soldier." He threw his thumb over his shoulder and said, "Let's eat."

Upstairs. Dajon and Noah came to a truce before coming to computer-generated blows. They instead resolved to take part in a game of sword and sorcery, side-by-side in a cooperative effort to banish evil through wizardry and staving off the wickedness' attempts to rise from the depths. Both chose their most powerful characters that focused on a shaman's conjure build. Noah downloaded his saved character from the console's server.

The two friends quested and looted gold, magical items and trinkets, trading weapons and curiosities while gaining experience and power. They roleplayed, sharing the details of their avatars. Dajon was a fallen, cosmic being who longed to be reunited with his cosmic queen, who he named *Ayika*. Noah was quite the opposite. His shaman studied the old ways, but was far from a righteous man. He desired wine, women, and gold, but had a far more vulgar way to express this through his early, teenage tongue.

The downstairs ritual, and its produced summons, was behind them, at least for Noah, who was under the belief that it was all a high-tech science experiment. Dajon's eyes were locked to the screen, fingers sailing across the controller, mashing buttons and aiding his ally. But his mind was on the ceremony below, wondering if the conjured spirit had been sent back to the unseen land, or the *ai ri ilẹ*.

Dajon's fixed attention splintered for a moment. The curtain in his room flittered as if greeted by a breeze. Neither the air conditioner in his room blew, nor was his window open for a gentle wind to crawl through. Dajon's instinct murmured, and he stole a speedy peep in the window's direction. A young man stood there. Behind the curtain. Dajon recognized him, and Noah would have too if he had the eyes to see him. It was Sean Commons, the seventeen-year-old hoodlum who bullied Noah, and who'd been hexed by Willie the Lich's cursed whip to shoot Dajon and put him in the hospital. It was this incident that dwindled Dajon's protective, dragon-shaped aegis over the Fable Avenue street, allowing night doctors to enter and take the area outside of time. A strike that led to the kidnapping of six children, and the stolen essences of five other conjure folk.

Dajon made a face. He tossed a nod at the window and remarked, "Melinda was standing right there when I first woke up. First day home from the hospital."

Noah turned his head. He looked in the window's direction. "That must've been a helluva greeting, pretty face like that." He returned his attention to the game.

Dajon was satisfied. Noah couldn't see Sean. He hit pause on the game.

"Hey…!" Noah protested.

Dajon lifted his hand. "Relax," he told his friend. "Let's really get in character. You're a womanizer. Let's get you a harem." Noah's expression contorted, perplexed by Dajon's statements. "I got some real nice magazines down in the basement. Nudie pics! I can probably snag one or two and get them by the guards downstairs. My brother and his friend wouldn't usually mind, but they with their sweethearts, y'know. Magazine's called *Gira Girls*. Old school. Kind of artsy. Black pinup models from the fifties and sixties. There're a few modern issues too. A few. The women all cultured out, so their costumes fit this fantasy environment."

Noah revised his face, now illuminated with glee. A devious smile snaked across his countenance. He looked back to the paused videogame. "I got it!" he blurted. "Our characters use a magical caravan to get around. It hovers by use of a magic stone. It can cast a shield too. My women stay in there."

Dajon bobbed his head. "Bet!" he concurred. "Okay. You stay here." He looked at Sean's spirit. "I'll be in the basement," he disclosed. His voice was stern.

Sean's spirit faded, ghosting away to the basement level.

Dajon got up. He told Noah he'd return shortly with three issues, and through the door he went. Downstairs. Dajon came across Benny and the others seated around the cloth. Benny noted, "The spirit's gone. You and your friend want something to eat? We can clean the area so he ain't weirded out."

Dajon hurried up to his brother. "We got a haunt," he reported. "Upstairs. My room."

Benny asked in a calm manner while chewing, "Your friend able to see this haunt?"

Dajon shook his head. "He can't see him. I made sure," he announced without detail. "I'm surprised, too. Noah and I got connection to him. It's Sean Commons."

Cedron blurted with a mouth full of food, "That nigga who shot you?" He took a moment to eye Leah and Neyeli, missing Dajon's affirmative nod. "So, I can call dudes 'niggas' but I can't call a woman a 'chick'?" Neither woman said anything, continuing to indulge in their food. "That's some chick-nigga shit right there." Leah forcefully nudged Cedron in the ribs. Cedron chuckled. He said back to Dajon, "Him, though, right?"

"Yeah," Dajon proclaimed. "I made it sound like I was talking to Noah, but I told him I was going to the basement." He grinned. His eyes couldn't help but drift between Leah and Neyeli. "Sorry, I promised him a look at some *Gira Girl* issues." He was surprised when the two smiled at him and expressed how they thought it was adorable he and his friend were 'growing up'. "Oh…" Dajon responded.

Benny swallowed, wiped his hands on a napkin, and then got up. "Let's go check this haunt out. See what he want with you, *li'l bredda*." They headed to the basement. Benny put his left arm around Dajon, conjuring his gauntlet on the other.

Dajon's face lit up. "Oh, it's yours now! You got it, Benny!"

Benny's face was slathered with a proud smile. "Yep, *li'l bredda*. I got it," he told Dajon. "Let's talk up a haunt and get you some magazines." He leaned close and said into his little brother's ear, "I won't tell Melinda."

Cedron overheard Benny. "That's how you teach baby boy," he remarked. He looked at Neyeli and Leah and asked, "Or is that instructin' him on a bad habit for his…'sweetheart'?"

Leah scowled. "Nigga, shut up and let these chicks eat they food."

"For real! Right?" Neyeli groaned.

Cedron rolled his eyes and dived back into the meal.

In the basement. Sean Common's specter radiated from the after realm. He wore the clothes he had on the day he died, not the day of his burial. He watched as the lights turned on and Dajon and Benny made their way down the stairs. The Brickhouse brothers ambled up to him. Dajon glared at him and asked, "You think you here to finish the job? We experts in this banishing life."

Benny pulled on the back of Dajon's collar. "Slow down there, conjure-thug. Have an instinct a bit. He ain't here to harm." He put a stern set of eyes on Sean and showed off his gauntlet-covered arm. "But make a misstep," Benny began his warning, "and I'll use my arm to deal with you."

Sean spied the gauntlet. Its power tapped against his flickering form. While he didn't have a heart, there was a rhythm and pulse to his spirit. It raced no different than a heart would had he come in contact with a dangerous situation.

"I deserve that," he stuttered. His voice resonated with such dejection and remorse that it fluxed through Benny and Dajon's instincts. Subtle tremors coursed through them, and they became attentive to Sean's presence. "From either of you," he continued. "I deserve that." He put his hands in his pockets and turned away. "I visit them," he said, his voice evoking the sounds of confession. "All of them. People I've hurt—in one way or another. People I bullied, like y' mans upstairs. People I sold drugs to and got they life off track. Family I disappointed." He thought for a moment before saying, "Shit, family that disappointed me…" Then he continued his list. "I've haunted dudes I partnered with, got then them time with my schemes. My kids. They crazy mothers. Everybody I can remember; and where I am now, I can remember them all." He faced Benny and Dajon. "I visit graves too. It's come to that with some people. I didn't put them their directly, but I started them on that road." He pointed at Dajon, his hand shaking. "But you? I'm sorry the most. It could be you here." He sheathed his hand back into his pocket. "From what I've found out, you'd understand all this more than me."

Dajon's voice was low when he responded. It even rattled. "That why you here? Give your last sentiments? Apologize?"

Sean shook his head. "No. Making my rounds on people, giving my last sentiments—as you say—that's to pass the time." He stopped in his talk. His body shook as he glowed. His face crumbled into a quivering display of anger. He pointed again, saying, "You—anybody in your family—had the right to put me here after what I did." His eyes darted back and forth between Dajon and Benny. "But not her! Not that lawyer bi—" He stayed his words before finishing his statement. He corrected by naming, "Stephanie Dumas."

Benny knew. Few didn't, and Dajon was one of them. Not even Stephanie's father was aware of the deed his daughter executed. He believed all the matriarchs had knowledge, at least by now. Lady Arachne was the hold out. Papa Solomon was aware. He confided in Gordon who then confided in Benny. That was one secret Benny could keep. He didn't tell Dajon or even their mother or father. The story that made the rounds was the hexed scars Sean received from Willie's whip overwhelmed him, and he died in his jail cell.

"What's Stephanie have to do with this?" Dajon asked.

Benny looked at his little brother. Sean looked at Benny. Then his eyes met Dajon's. He revealed, "She killed me, and she was cruel about it."

Dajon looked up at his brother. Benny nodded, affirming the truth.

"She's been avoiding my spirit," Sean continued, his voice rattling with rage. "And I have to talk to her, because we got some things to talk about. You two are gonna help me. I've hurt you and your family, and I'm sorry for that. But you're gonna help me with this."

At her house in Queens, Stephanie Dumas enjoyed a cup of ice tea while working from home.

22

Albert Ford Banneker had the wrong address, but he was grateful for his mistake when he knocked on the door and Lady Arachne's beautiful, slender frame flickered free. His arrival was perhaps a little strategic. He didn't say anything at first when she opened the door. He just stared at her with a wide-open smile that was surrounded by a thick and coiled, gray beard. Upon seeing her approach, Albert removed his gray, short-brim fedora.

It would've all been awkward had Lady Arachne not responded much the same. She was frozen in Albert's presence. Her smile was wide, and open mouthed, but her eyes inspected him with a curious scrutiny. She was surprised at his presence on her doorstep. She knew him, but he hadn't been on Fable Avenue in decades. His average height was still supported by a brawny, workman's frame. The beard was all the hair he now possessed on his head. The dome of his empty scalp, touched by the sun's light, shined with all the brown of his skin.

Lady Arachne spoke first, questioning Albert's appearance. "Albert...?" she said. "Al Banneker? Is that you?" She noticed a decorative lock box in one hand.

Albert shook his head, open-mouth smile still caked on his face. He took a moment to answer, "Yes. Yes, ma'am. It's me, Lena." He looked up and inspected the brownstone. "This ain't the Goodspeed residence by chance?" He looked back at her and lifted the decorative lock box in his hand. "I got something to deliver to the youngest boy in the family." He thought for a moment. "Boy's name is, uh, uh, Gordon," he added.

Lady Arachne made a face, deducing Albert's underlying motivation. "Albert! You know good-and-damn-well this ain't the Goodspeed residence!" She waved a finger up the street and told him, "They up the road." She looked over his shoulder and spotted his forest green, mid-size 1970s car. "You drove all the way from Maryland?"

"Yes, I did!" he proclaimed in a proud voice, chest out. "I crafted something for the boy. I heard he can time step. He need to keep his bearings straight."

Lady Arachne leaned against the door. She went into her pocket and pulled out a clove cigarette. She put it in her mouth and used an incant to light it. She took a puff and exhaled. "Y'all some-timin' conjure-folk get the news late down in Baltimore. The boy got the lilac flame in him. Your grandniece, Fey, she got the cobalt-blue spirit. Them two are sweethearts. Right now, we got us a war with a hex-man and his ilk. That Fallows boy we let walk among us. He went bad like his mamma.

"Us 'some-time' folk tried to warn y'all," Albert reminded, pointing at Lady Arachne, making a face. "Warned my nephew too."

"Yeah, yeah. I heeded them exhortations. I warned folk too. Lewis was stubborn. Others sat comfortable just the same. So, we here now. Your grandniece been banished, floatin' all through a void. Gordon looking for her. I got him on assignment for some other things, too."

Albert's eyes swallowed Lady Arachne's entire frame, but his smile didn't reappear. His head in politics, he sucked his teeth and said, "Taking in that Fallows boy was no good, Lena—Miss Lady Arachne. Lewis all friendly with him, and shit!" He calmed himself and then focused on her clove cigarette. "Seems you all on Fable Avenue smoke what you want, regardless of the law, huh?"

Lady Arachne just took another drag. Exhale. Smoke filtered from nostrils and lips as she retorted, "We can do proper conjure, Albert. Gordon and your grandniece can turn to light and fly to the stars. We folk on Fable Avenue, and the conjure world over, can manipulate and summon arcane elements. *Chile,* we don't follow the law of physics, let alone man's law."

Both old-time conjurers shared a laugh.

A beat. Albert requested, "You care to join me on a short drive up the street?"

Lady Arachne pursed her lips and playfully batted her eyes. She twisted her upper body, and posed. "Why Mister Banneker, are you asking me out on a date?"

Albert made a face. He shook his head and denied the allegations. "What kind of date is that, Lena?" He put his hat back atop his head in an effort to dig into his pocket and pull out his smartphone. He unlocked it and looked at the screen. His voice was still in defense of himself when he said, "I just need help finding four-twenty-one Fable Ave—"

Lady Arachne extended her arm and smacked Albert on the shoulder. "Man! From your instinct to technology, you know how to find that place."

Albert chuckled to himself. He pocketed his phone after putting it to rest. "Woman! You gon' get in the car? I came all the way from Baltimore—"

"To deliver a package!" Lady Arachne cut into his words. "*I* just happen to be here. Don't you stand there and try and sweet-talk me. Shit!" She stepped outside. Albert backed away and watched Lady Arachne as she spoke an incant that closed and locked her doors. "Let's go," she said.

Albert tugged on the brim of his hat. "Yes, ma'am." He turned and stepped down the stairs. Lady Arachne raised an eyebrow at Albert as she followed in tow. His car was facing the wrong direction parked on her side. Lady Arachne shook her head. Albert walked around to the passenger's door and opened it, holding it open for Lady Arachne to slip inside. She thanked him, took one last drag of her cigarette, and then tossed it into the air. She blew an incant in its direction, causing the rolled, puffing stick to turn to ash.

Albert liked what he saw, the display of Lady Arachne's power. He again pulled on his hat's brim and called her 'ma'am'. Before he shut the door, he handed Lady Arachne the lock box, and she accepted it, resting it on her lap. She strapped the seatbelt around her as Albert jumped into the driver's side and did the same. He started the car, and while checking his mirrors for a moment to pull onto the road, his eyes fell on Lady Arachne. Up and down went his vision, and then it rested on her countenance.

Lady Arachne possessed half a smile, but her eyes bent on Albert. "Whatchu looking at, old man?"

"Oh, Miss Franklin, ma'am, I see so little of real conjure women that know their power," he explained. "I like to take this opportunity to delight in the moment."

Lady Arachne flapped her lips. "Drive on down the road!" she scolded in a lighthearted manner.

Albert pulled out of his parking.

Up the street. Gordon saw all of the goings-on between Lady Arachne and Albert Ford Banneker. Eyes closed. He tapped his fingers against the recliner's arm in step with the tingle against his neck. It sounded like rain against a roof. The ringing tone of his instinct buzzed with a blues guitar's twang. Tapping feet followed the slam of a car door. Outside. Gordon saw it all in his head. Two pair of feet clap, clap, clapping against the street, the sidewalk, and up to the Goodspeed brownstone's front door. He knew the reason Albert and Lady Arachne approached his abode. That is to say, he was expecting it all. At this hour. On this day.

Gordon's power often drained him, but at this moment, it sapped his patience.

The doorbell rang, and with its trembling din came the ceasing of his instinct's buzz and the tapping of his fingers. Time caught up with his impatience, but even still, Gordon decided to play it cool. He took a moment and let the doorbell ring again. His eyes opened, and he stood. His body blinked from existence with a simple thought. He appeared on the outer foyer between the two doors. He unlocked both set of doors with a simple thought, and he opened the outermost set. "Albert Banneker," Gordon said.

"That's right," Albert answered with a kind smile. "Decided to come up on business." He put his eyes on Lady Arachne, and his child-crush grin grew wider. "The long drive had its pay off, in sorts." Then he said looking at Gordon, "Wanted to see the young man that got the lilac brew in him." Albert inspected him. "Sweetheart to my grandniece who got the cobalt-blue spirit." His smile washed away, and he shook his head as melancholy filled his eyes. "I know there's hope, but it's just a shame where things stand." He lifted the decorative box, returned to him by Lady Arachne when they stepped out of his car.

Gordon accepted the package. "Thank you, sir," he said with a voice full of gratitude. He unsnapped the hinge keeping the ornate box closed, and then he opened it to discover a circular timepiece handcrafted from gold infused with copper to give it a radiant, rosy hue. It was inset within a piece of foam, cut to the watch's shape in the center, covered by a black cloth. Attached to the mystical device was a chain matching in color. Gordon backed away from the door. "Please, come in. I insist," he told Albert and Lady Arachne. He turned and drifted through the door, his body intangible for a brief moment. "I'll be in the basement," he informed before popping from existence.

Albert flinched. "You don't see them type of tricks in our conjure *nasyon*," he commented. "I can make an incanted charm or trinket. Not much more than that. Even our patriarchs and matriarchs can't do much more than a little flick of the finger or tongue, make you a little warmer or colder, comfortable with the temperature. Not much more without a real, strong ritual behind the blessing."

"We all play our part, Albert," Lady Arachne comforted.

Albert winked at her. "Yes, we do, lovely lady." He held out a hand, allowing Lady Arachne to pass through the doors first. She thanked him with a youthful smile on her face, and then she took lead. Albert manually locked the doors after entering the brownstone. He followed Lady Arachne through the house, down into the cellar to Gordon's *sanctum sanctorum*. Albert's eyes were wide, swallowing the brightness, the style, and everything about the space that reminded him of the seventies. "This is that *cosmic* conjure funk!" he said.

Lady Arachne beamed at him. "Is there any other kind of funk?" she said with her eyes slimmed in seduction.

"You know funk cover all them elements and directions now, Lena," Albert replied.

Lady Arachne made a face, bobbing her head left and right, acknowledging the sentiment.

They continued with their muted, coquettish banter while Gordon's attention was ensnared by the mystical craftsmanship. He held Albert's artistry in both his palm and broad-eyed gaze. Gordon found no numbers around the face of the clock when he opened to its features. In their place, twenty-four African symbols from a variety of spiritual sources. Veve symbols. Adinkra scripts and *patim pemba*, or *firmas*, from Palo Mayombe. And Kemetic hieroglyphs. The symbols were not random in choice. Each symbol used was from the specific African spiritualism needed to assist a spirit in its travel through time.

Gordon also noted the curiosity of there being no hands on the clock. Instead, an obelisk skillfully cut from sapphire popped from the center of the face when the cover was clicked open. It was needle sharp, and Gordon considered Albert's expertise was as much of his conjure as was giving the mystical item its blessing.

Gordon looked up. Albert was instructing Lady Arachne on old-school dance moves. The slender matriarch proved she still had grace, and executed Albert's directions step-for-step and slide-for-slide. Gordon made small noises, half-formed words, trying to cut into the old timers' fun.

"Ex… Excuse… Excuse me, Mister Banneker…"

Lady Arachne and Albert slowed their giddy and groovy momentum. Their final spin landed Lady Arachne in Albert's embrace. Her toothy smile trembled for a moment before dwindling away. She cleared her throat, but didn't attempt to leave Albert's hold. She braced herself, a palm against his shoulder.

Albert turned away from Lady Arachne and addressed Gordon. "How can I help you, young man?" he asked in a kind voice.

"How's this work?" Gordon inquired.

Albert moved his arms from around Lady Arachne. She fixed herself and stepped aside as Albert walked over to Gordon. He took up the timepiece and told Gordon, "You just strap this onto your belt. You can close it, and you can tuck it into your pocket." He handed the watch back to Gordon. "Only one person I know time-stepped. That was my son. I helped in the ritual. He wanted to see his mother and I, our family, together. Happy one last time, before he saw us divorce and go our separate ways. A picture just wasn't gon' do." His voice trailed away.

Lady Arachne viewed Albert through a sorrowful lens.

"I'm sorry," Gordon apologized.

Albert couldn't lose his jolly smile for long. "No need, young man," he said in a boisterous tone. "It's in the past."

Gordon's gaze returned to the preternatural watch in his hand. "Yes, it is," he remarked. He lifted his head, eyes on Lady Arachne. "My mother will watch over me. You two don't have to stay around—unless a ritual is needed."

Althea appeared, as if on cue. Albert tugged at the brim of his hat while addressing the specter. "Ma'am!". In the middle of she and Albert exchanging pleasant greetings, Althea noticed Lady Arachne's smitten demeanor while in the elder gentleman's proximity. The apparition noted to herself that not even the matriarch's young playthings earned such language from her body, subtle as it was.

Albert addressed Gordon, "No ritual needed. That item there has its blessing. Something powerful," he stressed.

Gordon nodded at Albert. Althea said to Lady Arachne, "You can show Mister Banneker around, Lady Arachne. You can take him to the crossroads, Water Bug Hollow, the entirety of our street. I'm sure it's changed since the last time he was here."

Lady Arachne did her best to cover a vexed expression aimed at Althea. Her eyes moved to Albert, and her annoyance with the specter melted into a warm smile directed at the curio-maker. She strolled up to him and took his arm around both of hers. "Come on, Albert. Let me show you some landmarks."

Albert made the turn with Lady Arachne, heading back to the stairs and saying their goodbyes to Gordon. At the first step, Albert remembered something. He moved his arm from Lady Arachne's embrace and trotted back to Gordon with a single finger raised. "One thing, young man," he started. "My community down in Baltimore, we not tanks when it comes to conjure, but we have knowledge." He tapped his head. "We know things." He looked over his shoulder at Lady Arachne and remarked, "Sometimes those things don't get taken into consideration." Then he returned his attention to Gordon. "From my immediate family to the conjure folk in Baltimore, nobody thought taking in Stanley Fallows was a good idea. I wasn't happy when my nephew, your sweetheart's father, got close to him." He waved off the sentiment. "But that's all in the past, right?" Gordon nodded. "But there are some things you need to worry about in the present." He held up a hand, fingers spread apart. "Five things. There's always at least five of them. Some legends go as high as seven. Monsters. Sinister things. Nothing specific. It's just been a thing. The lilac-flame and the cobalt-blue spirit have always faced five deadly haunts, sometimes six. Conjured against them by great foes, a father or mother of lies."

Stanley told him as much when they met in the *mirak*, but now Gordon had a notion that focused on being warned far earlier. Gordon paused in motion for a brief moment. His features locked for a slender moment as he thought back to his first reading with Lady Arachne concerning his spirit. She'd pulled the Five of Wands, which warned of strife, clashing. Gordon believed at the time it was an internal context, an unease between he, his brother Cedron, and his best friend Benny. Now with the disclosure of haunts cast against he and Fey, his perception was altered.

Albert interrupted Gordon's thought. The visiting conjure man pointed at him and advised, "Keep your spirit up. Keep those with some good kick and power in their conjure close." Gordon considered what the old man said to him. He thought about Mister Banneker's final words on the matter. Unease with his brother didn't come to mind. That had been resolved, with a knockdown, dragged-out fight no less. No, his brother's crew came to mind. Gordon focused on the irony drawing the Five of Wands in that initial reading. Whom he believed to be the source of the conflict the card foretold would turn out to be his allies. To be fair, they were his allies all along.

How could he have thought so differently?

Fey's yumboes flew into the basement, shooting through the ceiling as beams of light, and then condensing into their physical forms. Albert stepped back. He shook his head. "Those from my grandniece?" he asked with pride filling his features. "I know her mother could conjure one of them things. I met that little sprite a couple of times."

"Yes, sir," Gordon answered. "Those are Fey's—and her mother's. Yumboes."

"Oh, yeah," Albert said staring at the diminutive, winged creatures. "Yeah, I've heard that vernacular. It's a Senegalese word."

Gordon responded in the affirmative as he showed his mother the timepiece. Althea marveled at the device's design. "You are a remarkable artisan, Mister Banneker," she complimented the curio-maker. "I can also feel you're very skilled at giving a blessing. There's much power in this item. Thank you for crafting the watch for my son."

"My pleasure," he replied. "Thank you for the compliments, ma'am, but I didn't bless the watch alone. I had help from my community's matriarch and patriarch. We only have two; a husband and wife," he detailed. "They're strong with blessings."

Fey's yumboes surrounded Albert. Gordon introduced them, calling off their names. Gordon also suggested, "Why don't you four go with Mister Banneker and Lady Arachne."

Silver landed on Albert's shoulder and whispered something in his ear. He replied to her, "I remember you too, little Silver." She zipped away, landed on Spook's jeweled console, and whispered into the black mirror. Gordon observed Spook's screen light up with script for a response. *It's okay. I'll be busy,* the face of his black mirror read.

Silver nodded, kissing the screen and zipping back to her sisters.

"Come on," Lady Arachne waved Albert and the yumboes toward the stairs. "We'll be one, big, happy family. Come on." She looked at Althea and called the spirit's name to get her attention.

Althea nodded, acknowledging the matriarch. "Yes, Lady Arachne. Gordon will be fine under my supervision. I'll send a signal should there be an emergency. You, Papa Solomon, and Madame Jeliya."

"I'll keep my instinct open for any distress call," Lady Arachne assured. Then she said to Albert and the yumboes, voice like a drill sergeant snapping orders, "Come on, now! Let's go on a sight-seein' tour."

Albert chuckled. He turned and walked to Lady Arachne with the yumboes buzzing around him. He followed the matriarch up the stairs and out of the brownstone. They walked down the street, leaving Albert's car parked outside the Goodspeed residence.

Gordon strapped the pocket watch's chain to his belt, as instructed by Mister Banneker. He slipped the magical gadget into his pocket, and then he picked up Spook, setting down in its place the lockbox he received the mystical timepiece in. He sat on his plush seat, pushed back, and the chair reclined. Althea sailed up to his side. She cast a soft smile at her son as he relaxed in his chair, placing The Judgement card atop Spook's console. The ancient device closed. Gordon put his arms around the mechanism and lay back.

"Gordon," Althea said to him. Gordon looked up at her. "You are so brave," she commended in a sweet tone.

Sleep pulled at his eyes. He managed a smile through the drowsy onset. "I have good parents…" he uttered before falling fast to sleep.

Althea's delighted smile widened. She closed her eyes and thought of a prayer to help guide her son. She recited it in her head. Her eyes were pulled open by the sudden brilliance that cocooned Gordon's body. A blistering radiance concealed him, and Althea knew his spirit had been cast through time. She only hoped that wherever he settled, he would be hand-in-hand with the other half of the brave, heroic equation.

Fey Forrester.

Space ∞ Time
"This familiar seems quite familiar."

Sleep didn't possess him, and history didn't reveal itself to him. Instead, Gordon possessed history, revealed through slumber's cloudy door. He was in the past. His spirit filled the body of a Moorish man lying flat on a bed in deep meditation. His arms were at his sides, palms flat against the mattress. Just moments before he came to consciousness, a lilac glow surrounding the man whose body he inhabited, and it operated as a doorway for Gordon's ethereal build to walk through. The radiant gleam disappeared in a snap that only Gordon could hear. Even as the light vanished, his eyes remained closed to darkness.

And so, the first thing Gordon did was open his eyes. A white ceiling stared back at him. Gordon procured the room's composition without moving his eyes or angling his head. His instinct rendered for him a complete picture of the room. The image blurred and started waving as a slight sense of vertigo set into his head. He was able to shake it off, and considered his spirit anchoring itself, using the mystical might of the blessed pocket watch to keep him steady in this new time period. His instinct first revealed to him three intricately designed, brass-framed mirrors mounted on separate walls. One mirror hung over a mantel and fireplace. The second mirror hung over a desk. The third covered the height of the wall it was mounted on, positioned at the left of the ornate doors that led into the hallway.

At the center of the room was a medium-sized, ovate table with curved wooden legs and a marble top. Resting on the table was a bottle of wine and two glasses. Next to the bottle and glasses was a tray of treats. On one side of the table was a plush couch flanked by two, wooden chairs. A wide rug, brimming with patterns colored in reds and blues, lay underneath the furniture. Gordon could sense that every object in the room was cut to an exact, rounded degree. There was nothing that was half an inch or more, all manner of shape was precise to an accurate size. Shapes were whole in their numbered measurement in a very conscious manner, close to obsessive-compulsive. Or ritual.

It was morning. The day was gray, but the white walls were washed in the natural light that made its way through both clouds and curtains. Nothing in the room compelled Gordon to stir. Nothing inanimate, at least. But then his instinct tingled and buzzed with severity. Within that moment, Gordon thought himself having possessed a man bruised by violent battery, placed in an infirmary for recovery.

Gordon relaxed. His instinct retracted and so did its potent vibration. Drawing back his sense brought its reason for such blistering recoil into focus. Fey was next to him. Asleep, and enjoying a much-needed rest from tumbling aimless through a void that was often black. At times it swirled with all the images history had to offer, as she streamed into vortexes that would lead her drifting soul to points in time.

Gordon used his instinct again, feeling Fey through an otherworldly sense so as to be spiritually close to her. He felt Fey was calm, at a blissful repose. Her outline and every curve that he missed and longed for developed like a photograph from his mind to his bubbling third-eye. Then he turned his head, and he saw her in the flesh of her flesh. Her hair was in short twists, the faint maroon dye no longer softly brushed into the follicles. Perhaps the erasure of the colorant was a result of her banishment or sailing through the void and time. Her spirit had shed the corporeal intrusions. Magic resonated beneath her dark-brown flesh as a shadowy, cobalt-blue aura.

Darkness made her bright, and Gordon seeing her with his two physical eyes was like recalling a warm childhood memory. His heart pinched in its pump, a split moment of a hard pressure of love through his veins. He reached out and touched her soft skin, caressing up her arm to the curve of her shoulder.

She woke, but her eyes remained closed. Her mouth stretched into a smile. Gordon's touch was as warm as the comforter draped over her. She had instinct too, and she used it just the same, seeing him even with her eyes closed and not facing him. She curled up as his body formed around hers, becoming another sheet to keep her tucked in comfort. Gordon put his arm around her, and she relaxed. There was no more falling. There was no more drifting. She was grounded, anchored with the man she loved and greatly missed.

"Gordon," she said. Her voice sounded like a song to him, and he held her tighter. Eyes remaining shut, Fey informed, "It's the year sixteen-sixty-three. We're in a countryside village named Étude in France." She turned around in his arms, facing him with a bright smile. Her large, beautiful eyes opened and swallowed him whole. They flapped like butterfly wings as she moved close and kissed him deep. They fed and drank from one another's lips, tasting flavors they had not savored in months. "Do you remember?" Fey asked, taking pause from Gordon's lips as his found her neck in substitution of the absence. "We were together long, long ago."

"Yes," he answered her. "I remember, Fey." They refrained from kissing, taking a moment to trace one another with their eyes. Disbelief peeked from behind their expressions, but exuberance remained tightly fastened to their countenances.

Fey moved first, looking down at her person. "Are we us?" she asked. "I just feel myself. I see me?" She looked back at Gordon. She touched gently the side of his face. Again, her eyes went up and down. "I see you," she commented as if breathing a sigh of relief. "Do you see me?"

Gordon ran his fingers along her cheek. "Of course, I do, Fey-baby." He watched her shut her eyes, relaxed in his presence. Gordon pulled her close. A moment before, Fey moved into Gordon's deeper embrace by instinct. He put his lips close to hers and said in a hush, "France, huh? I'd love to kiss you on the steps of Versailles."

Fey giggled. "I don't believe that's possible, Gordon-baby. I think we're at the beginning of its build, and it was in phases." She rubbed her nose against his. "I appreciate the offer," she told him. Gordon kissed her, and she fell into the abyss of his lips, equaled to the drift she had through time. He was both her anchor to remain grounded and her feather to fly. Within Gordon's kiss, Fey tasted the worth of missing him to this moment. A few pecks to the lips and sides of the mouth closed the passionate session. "The two of us together, Gordon, is inevitable." She caught her breath and asked, "Did you sleep to fall into history?"

"Yes," Gordon answered. "I'm using a device to keep myself stable. Your father's uncle built it."

"My father…?" she expressed, face quivering with a kaleidoscope of emotions.

Gordon noticed, but he didn't want to lose the moment defined by reunion and happiness. "Albert Banneker," he named. "He's from a small conjure community in—"

"Maryland," Fey interrupted with an even voice. "I know them," she said. "I've *heard* of them. Their *nasyon*," she clarified. "Their work in conjure is small, but it's very useful. Conjure is stretched thin where they are. They're busy keeping communities of regular folk together in Baltimore." She was silent, thinking. Gordon said nothing. He just observed her proximity to him, and he didn't want it all to slip away. He dived through a dream into this time period, and he didn't want to rise and wake without Fey at his side. She spoke again, saying, "They considered my father a fool for helping Stanley Fallows." She sighed. "Perhaps he was," she added.

Gordon kissed Fey on the forehead to ease her tension. Then he remembered communing with her father's spirit buried in the ground at Stanley Fallows' estate. He opened his mouth to reveal the information, but Fey was up and out of the bed, running to the full-length mirror hanging on the wall near the door. Gordon held the information on his tongue, swallowing it as he took a breath. He also held back the arrival of her cousin, Armand, to the conjure community, as well as his Stitching Rites that brought out his personal conjure.

Fey, at the moment, observed what should've been her reflection, but she faced a mirror image that was not her own. She swayed back and forth, cloaked in a pink, silk nightgown. The image cast back to her was that of an African-Moorish woman in her mid-thirties. She was voluptuous but sculpted with an athletic frame. Her hair hung in thick, long locks, and her flesh was darker than Fey's. A cobalt-blue, spherical ball burst onto Fey's forehead. The image in the mirror didn't reflect the same phenomenon. With her insight conjured, she dived into the memories of the woman she possessed. Fey was respectful not to pry into any intimate affairs. Fey only filed through to find the woman's name. *Efra al-Kaadi.*

Fey smiled at the mirror, and Efra's reflection smiled in unison. Both women's lips moved, but only Fey's voice was heard. "Hello, Efra," she said to the unalike mirror image. She chuckled.

Gordon walked up behind her clothed in beige pants and a matching silk shirt with its buttons open to expose his chest. He occupied the body of a man that was far different in appearance than him. He too was African-Moorish. He was tall, broad and muscular. His skin was dark-brown, and his face was clean of hair. Atop his head was a low, tightly curled cut. Gordon pointed at the image. The brawny Moor pointed back at him.

"Well, that's not me," he quipped.

"But it is," said Fey in a whimsical manner, staring at Gordon's dissimilar reflection. Her eyes were fixed on his muscular form and imposing, authoritative presence. It pulled at her, though affixed to the mirror's reflective glass.

Gordon opened his shirt wider, and so in concurrence did the physically stalwart man in the mirror. Gordon palmed the sides of his waist. "Get your fill, Fey-Baby. Go on and look," he teased. Then he raised an eyebrow and looked at Fey through the side of his eyes. "You already are."

Fey made a face, and she slapped the back of her hand against Gordon's bare stomach. He remained firm, and she returned her hand to his muscular abdominal area, massaging his stomach and chest. Her eyes paid close attention to the mirror. "Oh!"

"Hey!" Gordon snapped. "That's me you're feeling."

"Not in the mirror," Fey said in a mumbled tone that sounded like a carnal purr. She retracted her hand, giggling at Gordon. "I take precaution exercising too much of my spirit in this woman, but I'm still able to conjure my third eye. I discovered her name. She is Efra al-Kaadi. Who are you, Gordon-baby?"

Conjuring his lilac, spherical third eye took more concentration than usual for Gordon. His body was somewhere else, or more appropriately, some*time* else. Conjure-tech brought him into history, anchoring his spirit to the past as it possessed another. Conducting his abilities through this Moorish man involved a high-level of his will; though Gordon sensed he occupied someone strong within his own conjure. Bringing out his third eye was no longer like taking a simple breath. He experienced this earlier when he used his senses to gain knowledge of the room around him, though there were different factors at play. The man he possessed was in a meditative state, and Gordon believed any vertigo he felt was his own spirit keeping balance in this time. Now he was up and moving, and he noticed clearly the difficulty in which to execute his power.

Gordon was able to achieve his focus. He dived into his host's memories and pulled his name, skipping over any intimate affairs. "Abim al-Kaadi," Gordon uttered. "We're husband and wife." Fey's expression brightened. She questioned aloud what the two would be doing in the French town. She used her instinct to decipher the area. Gordon admired the ease in which Fey was able to use her abilities. He adjudged it came with her experience of drifting through time as a spirit, tunneling into people's bodies of varying eras. He observed her, relieved to be in her presence despite the circumstance. Then his eye became distracted, and her voice dampened to Gordon's ear. He watched Fey's divergent reflection echo her movements. A light snapped in his eyes as revelation dawned on him. He flinched because of it, and he peered at the woman in the mirror duplicating Fey's gestures.

Gordon saw something. He looked at the muscular Moorish man staring back at him, and he believed there was something more to reveal than the man's name. Gordon brushed against something familiar in this man, Abim. The flourish of light crackled before him again like a lash of lightning crossing the skies. For a moment, his mind conjured a layer of thick, white paint over the faces of the Moorish man and woman. It was for only an instant that he saw both beauty and terror wrapped in a cosmetic mix applied to their faces. That stunted moment was a lifetime to Gordon, seeing the skulls drawn up on their countenances.

He blinked, and the masks were gone. The moment remained fixed in Gordon's head, and he on its meaning. The astonishing disclosure locked Gordon's jaw in place, and like Medusa, it turned him stiff as stone. His body was still, eyes fastened on the reflections he and Fey cast in the mirror.

Fey inspected the room. She panned their immediate surroundings, but she stretched her senses using her third eye to cull the full knowledge of their whereabouts into focus. "There's a superstition about this small village," she announced. "Strange practices happen here. It's a town dedicated to study, and it's been named for it." She looked down at her arms, holding them out, palms up. She looked in the mirror at the differing image shown back at her. "What are we doing here?" She shivered from the cold that slithered through her spine. "I sense needles here," she exhaled in a low voice. "Tips tainted with hex." She turned and asked Gordon, "Does your search for The Lovers card continue?"

Gordon didn't answer Fey. He was still transfixed on the familiarity staring back at him in the mirror, dressed in the flesh of a Moorish man and woman. His right arm trembled as he raised it to point at the reflections. His differing image did the same back at him. "Fey…" he managed to speak. "I think I know who we've…"

There came heavy knocking against the door. "Monsieur al-Kaadi," a young, male voice penetrated through the thick, wooden door. "Madame al-Kaadi," he continued. *"Nous sommes là pour vous préparer. Pouvons-nous entrer?"*

Gordon and Fey's higher senses translated the French language. Fey turned to Gordon and whispered, "Servants."

"Here to prepare us," Gordon reviewed. He thought for a moment, and then he said to Fey, "Probably a bath and a nice pampering." He stepped back a few paces and eyed the door. It was locked from the inside.

The young man spoke again, *"Nous nous excusons pour toute intrusion, mais les plus hauts, les plus grands et les moins nombreux sont sur le chemin de votre réunion."*

Fey and Gordon looked at one another. Their expressions matched, skewed in perplexity. "The highest, the biggest, and the least are en route?" Gordon questioned in a low voice.

"Probably titles," Fey concluded. "More like, the Higher, the Greater, and the Lesser. I've been hearing so many languages lately, I can get a clearer sense of meaning faster than usual. Plus," she added, "you're doing a lot with your spirit to stay tethered in time." She panned the room in a slow move up and around, as if she was searching for evidence in a crime scene. "There is something about this place. I've never heard of an Étude, France."

"You said it's a place dedicated to study, Fey-baby," Gordon reminded her. "Shrouded in superstition. My guess is that we're meeting with the heads of the secret society that run this place."

Fey's perplexed expression was invaded by annoyance. She hissed, "As spies or traitors to conjure folk?"

"Spies," Gordon answered her. "I'm sure of it."

"How?"

"Monsieur!" the voice called. "Madame!"

Gordon used an incant to unlock the door. *"Entrez, s'il vous plaît,"* he permitted.

The door opened. Two servants walked through. One servant was a young man, and the other a young woman. Both were in their early twenties and of mixed heritage between African and European. They made a polite bow toward Fey and Gordon.

"How long before our meeting begins?" asked Gordon in French. A faint form of dizziness set in as he used his power to speak the language.

"Stewart Bloodworth, the Higher, Hening Courbé, the Greater, and Lord Percy Weyer, the Lesser will arrive within two hours," the male servant answered. "It's enough time to bathe and primp the both of you." A pleasant smile spread across his desert-colored face, and he introduced himself. "My name is Petite Le Garçon." He made another bow.

The young woman spoke up, announcing through a similar bright smile, "My name is Elsa L'enfant." She turned to Fey and told her, "I will be serving you, Madame."

"Thank you, both," Fey replied, returning a happy expression. "Could you excuse my husband and me for just a moment? You can wait outside the door. We won't be long."

"Yes, madam," both servants replied. They bowed, and then they exited the room.

Gordon stumbled a bit. He stepped back and caught himself on the chair positioned in front of the desk. He breathed and regained his stance. "Son-of-a-bitch! A little winded..." he remarked. "I was searching Abim's memories while you were talking. We're meeting with high-ranking members in The Order of the Fifth Science. Aristocrats with secrets, at the end of the day," Gordon defined. "This Stewart Bloodworth, the Higher, Hening Courbé, the Greater, and Lord Percy Weyer, the Lesser aren't the leaders, but they got pull."

"What are we doing here?" Fey inquired.

Gordon pulled the chair out and sat down. "We're here to appraise conjure items," he answered. "Authenticate them. We're spies; and we're also thieves here to steal a few things." He closed his eyes and rubbed them as a lightheaded feeling filled him. "Goodness!" he exclaimed.

"Gordon, are you okay?"

"Just a little wonky," he assured Fey. He pressed his eyelids together. Then he opened his eyes after shaking his head. "A bag of jewels, that's one item," Gordon named. "A black mirror is the second. Third item is a book. I know what they're for," he concluded, looking up at Fey and hoping she would recall the familiarity of the materials he listed.

She didn't. Instead, Fey responded, "No Tarot cards?"

Gordon raised his shoulders and shook his head. He told her, "It's possible they're part of the items, but I know what we're here to lift." He looked at her with a curious expression and asked, "Don't those items sound familiar?" Her expression was blank as she searched a fractured set of memories. Gordon assisted her splintered recollection by stating, "The book is the *Nigrum Nigrius Nigro*."

Fey's instinct buzzed as it lassoed what should've been an easy memory for her to recall. But it was down deep, awakened by Gordon naming the book. The remembrance widened her eyes and dropped her lower jaw. "Those are the occult curios that helped build your kam-ptah!" It was all coming to her in a rush. "You told me two people came through a portal and built the…the…" she struggled again. Before Gordon could assist, she recalled the words. "Alchemical chamber!" she blurted. She gasped deep, and though she covered her mouth, the volume of her voice remained substantial. "Ohmigod! Spook! We're taking the parts that created Spook!" Then she realized a thing, of which Gordon was already aware. She looked in the mirror. Efra's eyes looked back at her. "But they were made of light!" she exclaimed, her voice now hushed. "You said their bodies were made of light!" She looked down and inspected herself, searching for something, but not quite sure as to what. Eyes on Gordon, she spoke, "I thought they were some kind of cosmic beings." Her thoughts drifted away from the subject matter. Another memory dawned, and Gordon could see it behind her eyes. She dropped to her knees in front of him and reached out to embrace him with a tight hug. "Gordon-baby!" she blurted. "We used to travel to the stars as spirits. We danced with cosmic entities."

Gordon tightened his embrace around Fey. "Yes," he told her, kissing her on the forehead. "We did."

She sighed, "I have to get back. I can't drift forever."

Gordon pressed another kiss on her. "That's what this is about," he assured her. "We're going to bring you home." He loosened his arms from around her. His eyes watched Abim and Efra reflect their actions in the mirror. "I could've sworn I told you about the time I saw them underneath their lighted flesh—their true selves. It was kind of funny, a bit. They were naked. I saw her, and he saw me staring…at her." Fey stepped back and slapped Gordon hard on his arm. He chuckled. "Yeah, he had a face on him that wanted to do much the same." He rubbed his arm where Fey struck him. He stood and walked around her, stepping back in front of the mirror to observe Abim. "He's got a name now," he stated. He put his attention on Fey-Efra as she walked up next to him. "Her too," he added.

Fey eyed the door with a severe stare. "We should be attended to. We've taken long enough. We have people to entertain." She sucked her teeth and shook her head while looking at Gordon. She scoffed in a low voice, "Petit Le Garçon!" She questioned in the same tone, translating, *"Little the Boy?* That's the name he was given? *Little the Boy?"* she repeated. "And her, no different," Fey scoffed. "She has a name, at least. Elsa. But Elsa L'enfant?" she shook her head, eyes closed. *"Elsa the Child!"* expressed Fey, disgusted by it all. "I have so much to say."

"Well, we're in those days," Gordon reminded her, though she was far from needing to be aware. "Mulatto servants born of rape and slavery, demeaned in name. A reminder they are looked at no different than their full-blooded African brothers and sisters."

"Times have changed?" Fey commented with a sardonic expression. Satirical in her remark, but neither she nor Gordon laughed. Instead, they both sighed and shook their heads. "There's a difference between being in these times, experiencing it firsthand, rather than reading a history book," Fey remarked further. "And global, African slavery is in full force at the moment—undeniable." She pulled a childhood memory of her grandmother's attitude changing toward a befriended white family. They were close, and the young couple wanted her grandmother so much to be godmother to their children. But Fey's grandmother discovered, by eavesdropping on what sounded like an innocent conversation, that the family desired a black woman to rear their children. A mammy, of sorts. Her grandmother disconnected herself from them. Fey pushed the memory aside, focused on the present, experiencing the past. "Open the door, Gordon."

Gordon made a gesture with thought, and the knobs turned. "Please, come in," he ordered the two servants.

Petit and Elsa stepped inside. Petit spoke, "Monsieur Abim, please, with me." He held out a hand to Gordon, and Gordon stepped up to him, walking past him as Petit tucked his arm back to his side and left the room behind Gordon.

Elsa made a bend of her knee and a bow to her head. Fey managed half a smile at the mulatto servant's curtsey. "Madame Efra," Elsa called with her hand out ready to usher Fey to her bath, perfuming, and dressing. They left the luxurious guestroom.

The residence was palatial, and Fey didn't expected anything less. The bedroom she woke up in was a marvelous display of design and *accoutre*. She was first taken to a small bathroom where she was allowed a private moment for relief. From there, she was escorted to the cleaning bath. The room was just as illustrious as the bedroom. Three more servant girls waited for her. They were European in heritage. Their eyes pored over her. She stripped without shame, and she saw the women's stare expand wider than their initial gaze. They saw Efra al-Kaadi. They saw her blackness and cosmic-reflecting beauty. Fey hoped she wasn't being too exploitive in the proud way she stepped into the bath. She knew she was on display, as herself or Efra. She relaxed her pose and slipped into the warm water. The women appeared to argue over who would begin her wash. Fey noticed Elsa at the door. The servant girl was blushing.

On the other end of the small manor, Gordon paid little attention to the details that surrounded him as he was guided through the halls. He was too busy remaining focused, keeping himself tethered in time. Much was in the manner as the guestroom. All shapes of furniture and decorations were exact, and there were very few items that didn't have a true shape of square, circle or rectangle. His first stop too was a toilet room. The bath he was guided to was situated in a room just as fanciful and decorative as the one where Fey had been brought.

Gordon's attention was on the three French servant girls that immediately scrambled to wash him once he was undressed and dipped into the water. Their hands appeared to be more exploratory rather than washing his body. He felt the press of their fingers into his flesh, their careful examination of his physical presence, or rather, Abim's. When his manhood was fondled, to a soft chorus of blushing chuckles from the women, Gordon tensed up, cleared his throat, and addressed them in a firm voice, "Just the cleaning, ladies. Thank you." He did manage a smile and a wink, but nothing to invite further mishandling of his, or Abim's, person.

Petit presented to him mint leaves to chew and a small brush to wipe over his teeth. He was given a cup with warm water. Gordon took it, washed back the contents, and gargled on them. Petit put out a bowl, and Gordon spit into. He thanked Petit, and the servant bowed at the neck and stepped away.

Bathed. Gordon was dried, perfumed, and clothed in the elaborate robes of a Moorish conjure man. They were large for him, at first. And then some form of conjure magic molded the clothes to fit him. He wasn't aware if the shamanic attire were ones Abim brought or they were provided by the manor's hosts. Gordon didn't use his instinct to extract an answer. He was too distracted, affixed with a grin as his eyes passed over the wardrobe that dressed him, feeling as if he had become a venerable warrior in his favorite space saga.

Petit and another male servant led him back to a white room adorned with empty pedestals. There was a round, dark-colored wooden table in the middle. Six chairs were stationed around it. Again, there was an obsessive-compulsive attention to the detail of measurements and shapes, but Gordon's instinct overlooked the peculiarity.

Gordon took a seat. Petit informed him that his wife would be joining shortly. "Should I check in on Madame Efra?"

"No, Petit," Gordon answered. "That's fine. She'll be here when she's ready."

Petit bowed, and then he queried if Gordon was hungry. Gordon replied that he was, and Petit said he would fetch a plate of fruit and cheese. Gordon commented that would be wonderful. Petit again bowed; a satisfied smile on his face. Then he left the room with the other servant to fetch glasses, a bottle of wine, and treats from the kitchen.

Gordon sat alone. He looked around the room amazed to be sitting within history instead of simply dreaming of it. The thought dizzied him again. He relaxed, concentrated and righted himself stable. Petit returned to the room with all he'd promised, including the bottle of wine and glasses. Another male servant placed down a jug of water, which Gordon believed would be better suited for him than wine. His head was already easy to spin, and he was anxious about snatching the items as Abim, keeping focused if he needed to run or perhaps use conjure. He thanked Petit and the other male servant and the two dismissed themselves with a courteous bend of the neck and the curl of a pleasant smile.

Gordon didn't eat or pour himself a drink. He instead closed his eyes and journeyed through Abim's head to pluck out the plan for the heist. It appeared there would be a kidnapping. Fey would be taken, or rather, Efra. Allies would assist in her staged abduction, aided by an all-black, bat-winged sprite. This four-person team was now stowing themselves into position to act. The yumbo was a conjure, and Gordon wondered about it. Also, part of the plot, Abim was set to take a carefully placed bullet. The revelation struck Gordon with so much surprise that it veiled his viewing of the plan in a black shroud and pried his eyes open. He gasped in reaction to what he'd witnessed. The last thing he wanted was to be shot, even if just for show. He became dizzy, but he relaxed and fixed his vision and spirit's stability.

The doors opened. Gordon turned his head and observed Elsa lead his beloved Fey Forrester into the room. Fey was clothed in the elegant ruffles and wide-belled dress of the seventeenth century, French fashion. Gordon stood upon Fey's entrance, and he was compelled to bow his neck at her. Fey winked at him, sailing up to his presence. He bowed again and took her hand, pressing a gentle kiss against the back of it.

"You look absolutely beautiful," Gordon remarked standing straight. He stopped short of saying her name, remembering Elsa was not gazing on the same woman as his eyes beheld.

"Thank you," answered Fey in a soft, humble voice. She turned to Elsa and dismissed her. The young servant woman took her leave, shutting the door when she departed. Fey blurted to Gordon, "Efra can conjure a yumbo! I could feel it when I was washed. I asked for privacy after I dressed, and I pulled him from his realm to our world."

Gordon replied in a low voice, "Yeah. He's an accomplice."

Fey revealed in whisper, "To the heist? I know about the kidnapping," she further divulged. "Tsoro, the yumbo, informed me."

"Did he go through the details?" inquired Gordon with his eyes on the door and his mind on the thought of being shot to add authenticity. He didn't wait for Fey to answer. Gordon described in an anxious voice, "He's going to snatch the items for us. You're going to be kidnapped. I'm supposed to be shot—not looking forward to that." He took a breath, attempting to relax. "Hopefully, I can maintain footing in this time. The abductors are allies posing as villains."

She pondered for a moment, though her concern had nothing to do with Gordon's fate in the heist. She quipped aloud to herself, "This familiar seems quite familiar." She shook her head, pulling away from the inquisitive moment. She had an answer, at least an assumption. She first stated, "It was nice to talk to him." And then she surmised, "I'm sure it can be attributed to my longing to speak with my own conjured yumbo." Her eyes went to the floor and filled with reminiscence. Gordon saw happiness and melancholy intertwined in her gaze. She looked up at him, head back in the operation as if she and Gordon were a part of its plan from the beginning. "I know two of our allies' names, an African conjure man and woman. His name is Fashe. Her name is Kamanni." Fey grinned. She blinked her eyes in a slow manner. A small funnel of black smoke whirled from her shoulder, spinning until it condensed into a pint-sized, humanoid figure with a round head, pointed ears, and bat-like wings. The eight-inch-tall creature had gold eyes, black flesh, and facial features molded in the appearance of a West African phenotype. His hair was locked. Two tendrils dangled at either side of his forehead while the rest of his locks were pulled back into a short ponytail centered high at the back of his head.

Tsoro's feet touched Fey's shoulder. He and Gordon looked at one another. Both raised their eyebrows, moving their faces closer. Gordon too felt a familiarity with the creature in front of him. His physical appearance strengthened Gordon's otherworldly perception, first perceived when he encountered the vision of Fey's abduction as a thought, a plan in Abim's head. Fey remarked, "He can see us, Gordon. I startled him. I told him who I am, and that everything would be fine."

Tsoro retracted his face and turned to Fey. She pet him under his chin and he leaned into her touch, smiling, eyes closed like a grateful cat siding up to its owner.

Gordon remained pensive as he pieced together the feeling of being acquainted with this conjured yumbo named Tsoro. He was surprised at the conclusions. He didn't make a comment, though. Instead he took a seat and instructed Fey to do the same. "Tsoro," he called thereafter. "Hide behind one of the empty pedestals."

Fey added in a motherly manner, "You will know our signal, Tsoro. Our allies will be dressed as guards for the Fifth Order. You will appear once I attempt to unravel an enchantment on the mirror. That's what I've gathered from Elsa's memory." She leaned toward him and encouraged, "Be scary, little, curious yumbo. This will be your bright performance." She kissed the side of his face, her lips large in size against the petite creature's head.

Tsoro stood proud. He leapt into the air, flapped his wings, and spirited away behind a marble pedestal. There he remained still, wings folded behind him, hovering in the air and waiting for his moment to reveal himself.

Fey sat next to Gordon. She commented, "The yumbo is very well learned of our affairs, conjure and world history. He's a bit of a bookworm, knows ancient languages and all. I wanted to speak with him more. He made me forget about this whole affair." Gordon didn't react. Fey caught him staring at the ceiling, looking for something. "Gordon!" she snapped. "Did you hear me?"

"Yeah, sure. I did, really!" he protested, eyes remaining on the ceiling. He looked at Fey and said. "I'm just wondering if he's laughing at all this."

"Who?"

"Spook."

"What does Spook have to do with this?"

Gordon looked at the pedestal where Tsoro was hiding. He grinned, and then he turned his attention back to Fey. "Silver has always had an affection for Spook, if you can remember. Can you recall?" he asked Fey. He watched her as she searched her own mind, which she found more difficult than pulling from the woman she possessed. "She's very enamored," continued Gordon. "She's always sensed the yumbo spirit inside."

Fey's eyebrows rose. She pointed to the pedestal where Tsoro hid. "Him…?" she questioned, voice trailing away before the word was fully formed. "Tsoro? He did have a familiarity to him…"

Gordon looked back at the ceiling, wide grin plastered to his face. "Yeah, I think so."

There was a gentle knock against the door. Petit spoke, "Monsieur Abim. Madame Efra."

Gordon and Fey looked at one another. They nodded. Gordon responded, "Yes, Petit?"

The doors opened. Petit stepped inside and then sidled up to the open door and announced, "I present the High Honorable from the Order of the Fifth Science. Stewart Bloodworth, the Higher, Hening Courbé, the Greater, and Lord Percy Weyer, the Lesser of."

In they walked. Announced order.

There came Stewart Bloodworth, the Higher, a man with olive skin, a light, graying beard, and sharp features on his squared face. His hair was a low-cut, tangled mesh of curls. His expression rested at being unimpressed with the world around him, though his interests were high on the matter of conjure and old magic.

Hening Courbé, the Greater was a short man with a slim stature. He was balding at the top with gray strands intertwined with brown on the sides of his head. His face was a caricature of features with his rosy cheeks, button nose and beady eyes. A thin-lipped smile lined his face. He walked up to Stewart Bloodworth's left and remained there as both men planted themselves firm.

Lord Percy Weyer, the Lesser was the youngest of the three men, and it showed in his boyish face. He too had features much the same as

Hening, a caricature aspect to them as they rested on his long, oval face that was topped with blonde hair. His smile was toothy, and his wide-opened eyes made him look like a child anxious to tear open his presents on Christmas day.

All three men were dressed in the highest fashions reserved for politicians and businessmen. Gordon and Fey stood as the men entered the room. When they lined up with Stewart Bloodworth in the middle, Gordon stepped up to them, Fey in tow two steps behind him. He bowed quick and curt in his greeting with no manner of extending a hand. Gordon even played up a grandiloquent pose when returning to his stance. Fey's posture was firm, straight and strong, and she offered only a smile to her hosts.

Stewart Bloodworth remained distant. "No need to stand, our blackamoor guests," he addressed in French. "Please, have a seat and let us engage in philosophical pleasantries concerning magicks and spirit." He waved his hand toward the table and gave a second insistence for Gordon and Fey to have a seat.

There was no protest or prideful hesitance. Gordon and Fey returned to their seats. Stewart and the two other Fifth Science Order members sat across from them, Stewart between Percy and Hening. He addressed Petit to prepare plates consisting of the treats in front of them, to pour them wine, and place a goblet in front of the guests and the newly arrived lords of the house. Petit took to what he was tasked with, and there was silence throughout his preparation. As he worked, the Fifth Science Order's entourage entered the room. Many were guards, armored with ominous, masking helmets bearing horns and molded into a demon's face. Four carried items locked in black boxes. The items were placed on four of the pedestals, unlocked, and opened.

The entourage lined the front of the room. Petit took space up against the doors once he closed them. Everything in place and order, Stewart Bloodworth asked Gordon and Fey, "Have bâtard Petit and bâtard Elsa treated you well?"

Bastard? That's the official title for them? Fey kept her face firm and said nothing. Gordon sensed her frustration. He expressed to Stewart Bloodworth, "Their service has been commendable. Thank you for putting them on our watch and at this station."

Stewart tipped his head forward. "Yes," he said. "You blackamoors hold a value to the European world, specifically you and your wife, your knowledge. You will be proud Moriscos with new names. Your surname will be *Naipe*, and you will be baptized as Christians, and you will be celebrated. This will allow you to move about in our civilized societies. This will be the reward for your knowledge. We cannot thank you enough for coming forward and appraising the articles we've managed to procure." He put his hand out toward the pedestals where sat the items of interest. Then Stewart lifted his goblet of wine and made a toast, "To you blackamoors. We are humble to your knowledge. We Thank!"

"We thank!" echoed Hening Courbé and Percy Weyer in strong unison.

Gordon and Fey weren't quite sure if they needed to make a verbal reply. They instead lifted their glasses a little higher as a sign of accepting their hosts' gratitude, and then they lowered their cups to their lips and sipped. Gordon didn't ingest, afraid that the inebriating effects of the wine would loosen his possessing spirit's anchor within time and Abim's body. His stomach was empty, after all. He kept his lips pressed against the cup's rim, only miming a quick sip. He rested his cup on the table, and Fey did the same.

Gordon thought for a brief moment, and then he spoke. "There are so few authentic items of conjure that can be found. There are still so many secrets even to us who practice the rituals of true conjure."

Fey added, "My husband and I have decided to step away from these politics. We have chosen to see the world before it collapses." The three men raised curious eyebrows at Fey's choice of words, but they remained silent. Fey continued, "Our only peek into an ancient world of magic is by doing our best to authenticate any items that have been forged from its mysteries." She turned her head to the occupied pedestals. "What occult items of value have found their way into your hands?"

Stewart stood. "The same as we have discussed," he answered Fey. "No more than the four we've managed to acquire from excavating temples of worship that were established when your people ruled southern areas of Europe. Please, *fille noire*, see for yourself."

Fey got up from her seat. She turned to Gordon and waited for him to stand. He did, and both he and she made their way to the closest item. Hening Courbé the Greater scurried up behind them to provide exposition. The first item was a rectangular scrying mirror carved from obsidian and blessed by African conjurers to peer into the cloudy futures and pasts of clients come to have their fortunes read and their dreams interpreted.

But there was more to the powerful object, and Hening Courbé the Greater had the information at the ready. "This arcane novelty is more than the average scrying mirror blessed by you conjure people." Hening paused for a moment in his explanation to add an aside. He noted, "I don't believe in creatures of myth. From my studies, all fantastic beasts are nothing more than metaphor, symbols for quintessential properties."

Gordon acknowledged the sentiment, but amended, "That is true in most circumstances, Monsieur Courbé. However, this world is deep in its history and age. So many living things have passed through its epochs. There are gateways to other worlds that can be opened by strong, conjure folk.

From these worlds can be pulled familiars for companionship and other tasks."

Courbé the Greater pondered the information given to him with a contemplative hum, a squint of his eyes, and a look away. His vision then reset to Gordon. He perked up and stated, "Perhaps that is the reason for the information that accompanies this piece. It can, supposedly, house otherworldly creatures—spirits perhaps—that can inhabit the strange glass and be consulted. I'm not sure it would be of any use to us in the Order, but I'm happy it is among our collection." He ushered Gordon and Fey to the next item on display. Inside the box was a set of sparkling jewels. "Our Intelligence has gathered that these jewels were somehow shaped around a small sigils made of differing metals—arcane symbols imbedded with magical properties. Some have guessed it is to print incantations like an Italian *Scrittura Tattile*, a machine to impress letters onto paper. This would be simple buttons instead of long rods to make the impressions."

Gordon and Fey peered at the jewels. Both pondered the many times they'd pressed those gems as keys into the ancient *kam-ptah* device, foraging for information. They also remembered the times the keys glowed with life when the spirit Gordon nicknamed 'Spook,' brought forth information needed to piece together and solve occult puzzles and mysteries. There was history all coming together with the aid of a time-stepping device. Tsoro the winged yumbo. The items before their eyes. The African Moorish man and woman Gordon and Fey possessed. They thought about how all of these pieces would come together and mean so much to their lives. They shared a look and sent a thought to one another. Then they followed Hening Courbé to the next item.

"A book," he briefed in a simple word. "An old book," he expounded. "Perhaps that's the way it's supposed to look. It could be a fake," he suggested. With a smile he added, "But that's what you're here to appraise, the conjure value of these items. Correct?"

"Yes, yes, of course," Gordon assured.

"It's blank, but we know there is some value. Our Lesser, Percy Weyer—who excavated these items—his team was able to decipher an old text that spoke of this work called the *Nigrum Nigrius Nigro*. Supposedly this book holds a treasure trove of conjure secrets from epochs ago. It's all written in an invisible language that only conjure folk can read. And even more endearing, the book allows this invisible language to be read when the time is right and the eyes are pure. A beautiful sentiment, is it not? There is so much poetry in conjure."

Fey coupled Courbé the Greater's sentiment with the encroaching memory of composing with Gordon the living epic called *In 13 Pieces*. While her recollection of the rhythmic piece was uneven, there still was a concrete emotion that traveled through her recall.

Hening Courbé the Greater paced to the final artifact. It was a deck of Tarot cards. Gordon and Fey were drawn to the sketched and eccentric conjure tools in such a manner where it felt more as if they lifted and floated to the cards rather than walked. Their heartrate increased with the proximity to the cards. A choir of reverberation sang within them, and both Gordon and Fey could feel their displacement in time and space. Something made them aware of the bodies they possessed, and they felt separate from time and existence around them.

The distortion intensified as they stood over the cards. There was nothing truly magical within the operation at hand. It wasn't the cards or anything associated with conjure. The inexplicable twist and warp of reality was caused by the conscious sense of being in the presence of historical objects they had become familiar with in their own time. That was the source of the displacement, coupled with being in the proximity of the answer that could put everything right.

Fey had more balance than Gordon, but her head too wobbled with the inebriating effects. Both took a moment to speak an inaudible incant to center their capabilities. The simple wording reversed their effects, and Fey and Gordon were once again anchored to their surroundings.

Fey took up the cards in a careful hold as if she was lifting a newborn. She shuffled them, pushing each card aside desperate to pluck free The Lovers card. She sifted through the deck twice, and the card was nowhere to be found. Her eyes lifted to Gordon, wide with worry and surprise. "It's not here!" she said to him. Fey turned her attention to Hening Courbé and snapped, "This deck is incomplete! It's missing The Lover's card."

Courbé the Greater stiffened for a moment. His body then started trembling, as did his Fifth Order brothers. All three influencers became firm with unease. Hening Courbé took a step back. He put a hand on his chest and beamed a quivering smile. He stuttered, "M-m-m-most b-b-b-b-beautiful and most gracious Madame Efra, I plead to you, your mercy. I thought it was already understood that your associate had taken The Lovers card. He said it was already discussed…"

"Our associate…?" Gordon queried while keeping puzzlement from his features.

"Y-y-yes," Hening Courbé answered. "Ratamutum," he named.

Gordon and Fey's instincts translated the foreign word. It was an amalgam of two words from the Hausa language. Hang. Man. Fey looked down at her hands. The last card she shuffled was the very name of the mysterious man who had intercepted their prize. The Hanged Man.

"He is assisting slavers with the card's reverse power," Hening Courbé continued. "The Great Alchemy is taking place. Ratamutum is as dedicated to putting the people of Africa through their gross transition. Tribes and nations are already being turned against one another for the benefit of the Great Alchemy."

Fey's heart dropped, and tears shuffled to the edge of her eyes. She turned away so as not to be seen. Her head lowered, and from the view of the Fifth Order it appeared she was closely inspecting the cards in her hand. Gordon sensed Fey's sorrow. He joined her side and watched her as she extracted three cards and lay them on an empty pedestal. She pulled the reverse Two of Cups, the reverse for the Five of Wands, and the reverse for the Seven of Swords. The drawing's meaning distracted Fey from her melancholy, though true interpretation was buckled and misshaped with her lack of experience with Tarot. Her focus, at the moment, though sharper than Gordon's, had its obstacles to pull a clear translation. But something was coming through, and Gordon noticed her concentration on the three cards in front of her.

Gordon leaned close to Fey's ear and asked, "What do you see?"

"Distract them," Fey replied in a curt whisper. "I haven't received a clear message."

Gordon nodded his head, accepting his orders. He held out his hand and asked for the remaining cards. Fey passed them into his hand while keeping her eyes locked onto the cards in front of her. Gordon pivoted with an imposing authority that made Hening Courbé flinch. Gordon requested a quill and ink, and Stewart Bloodworth the Higher barked the orders at Petit Le Garçon, to which the servant executed with haste.

Petit placed a silver bottle of ink and a feathered quill on the empty pedestal next to the cards' wooden box. Gordon thanked Petit, and the mulatto servant stepped aside. "Take your place at the door," Hening Courbé scoffed at him. Petit walked away and posted up next to the door.

Gordon pulled The Moon card. He rested the remaining deck inside the wooden box and placed the card between the box and the silver ink bottle. He dipped the quill into ink and scribed Erzulie's veve symbol on the back of it. His instinct bloomed for him an extrasensory perception of an occurrence playing out in a time period centuries forward. Lady Arachne, third matriarch to the Fable Avenue conjure community tingled with an otherworldly sensation that compelled her to take up The Moon card. She turned it over and watched as ink faded up onto it in the form of the veve Erzulie symbol etched by Gordon's shaky artistry hundreds of years in the past. Next his penmanship appeared as he scribed in a dark, rich ink the phrase *Love Will Find U* in his time period. It materialized as time-worn and faded in hers. Lady Arachne's instinct revealed to her the origin of the handwriting and drawn symbol. Gordon's higher discernment permitted him access to the matriarch's reaction as she showed the card to Albert Ford

Banneker, Fey's great uncle, as they stood in her divining sanctuary.

Gordon beamed a proud smile. He looked up at Hening Courbé the Greater and proclaimed, "Authentic!" The three members of the Fifth Order exhaled audible relief. Gordon shook his finger, telling Hening Courbé, "Ah, the deck is incomplete, but it is true. Its power continues to resonate even as it sits fragmented by the loss of one card. We can rejoice there is knowledge on the card's whereabouts."

Stewart Bloodworth the Higher sprang from his seat as he heard Gordon appraise the validity of one of the objects in their possession. "And the others…?" he asked, setting a careful tone of authority in his voice. He made steps toward Gordon with his eyes locked onto him. Percy Weyer the Lesser joined Stewart Bloodworth's side as he passed.

Gordon turned to Fey. He saw that she was locked in a staring contest with the three cards in front of her. The cards' revelation was still attempting to dawn in front of her eyes. She could only hear and see in short bursts of static sounds and imagery. It was chaotic. The brief moments of clarity projected into her consciousness revealed Abim and Efra murdered by clandestine figures determined to steer conjure onto a blind path of bondage. The small morsels of precognition accorded by the cards left a searing sensation to Fey's physical vision. She looked away, conscious to maintain a calm expression in front of her hosts.

Fey straightened herself, presenting a lovely smile as she turned and faced the Fifth Order members. She gave her attention to Gordon when she realized he was looking at her. She reviewed the dialogue she'd missed while in trance. Her divine senses relayed the words and tones to her in a playback. "Abim," she called Gordon. "Let us review the others items." They stepped in unison to the bag holding the jewels, cut and blessed for fit into an ancient device.

Gordon lifted the bag and scooped out the jewels, laying them on the pedestal. He put a severe expression as he feigned deep contemplation, furrowing his brow and putting his face closer to the sparkling items. He straightened. Fey took his place doing the same thing. She mustered enough telepathic strength to send a warning to Gordon. **They're going to kill us," she sent to him through magical thought. **I saw it, or rather, read it. Nothing set in stone. The cards gave me a warning. Let's be on guard and move the heist along.**

Fey's voice in his head loosened the anchor his spirit clung to for the purpose of remaining stable in history, and within possession of Abim's body. Gordon didn't respond. He used his spirit to balance himself and keep the room from spinning. Centered. Gordon replied aloud, "Let us remain careful then." His words, taken by the Fifth Order's members, were different from what he meant. To play further into his role as occult appraiser, Gordon lifted one gem, holding it close to his eyes while facing the three Order members. "It is indeed a button for an archaic machine. Its power will draw out forgotten languages and mold words into powerful incantations." Gordon concentrated. He was hesitant, knowing the incant he was set to perform would sap him. He braced himself for the drain. Focused. Gordon made the gem glow bright with conjure. The Fifth Order members, and their guards, became a choir of humble awes. Gordon extinguished the incandescence and returned the gem to the bag in a nonchalant manner, though dizziness took time to dispel from his head.

Fey reported, "The book is genuine too."

Gordon nodded and announced, "That just leaves the mirror."

Both pivoted. Their backs were to the three Fifth Order aristocrats. Fey lifted the mirror in a slow and dramatic fashion. She turned to face the Order members, and the proud smile she beamed melted quickly into surprise as she revealed, "This is a fake!" Her words were a lie, and they were effective. The Fifth Order members shook with shock, and audible gasps were heard even from the guards. Stewart Bloodworth the Higher crept closer to her with careful steps as if he was approaching a wild, bucking horse. His palms were raised, and he crouched low and cautious as he neared Fey-Efra.

He stuttered as he spoke, "I don't mean to doubt you, Madame Efra…" His words trailed away, he straightened his posture and calmed, though anxiety remained as a haunting on his face. "I just ask for clarity on what makes this object inauthentic."

Fey held the mirror in her hand. She gazed at it, feigning a pensive stare. "Perhaps I was too quick to conclude," she said to Stewart Bloodworth. She returned the mirror to the pedestal. Pivoting back to face the Higher, Fey relayed, "No different than the glow you witnessed when my husband—" Fey paused. She looked at Gordon and smiled at him. Gordon's lips made a subtle move up into a sly grin. Only Fey's heightened sense observed his movement. To her, it might as well have been a full-blown, toothy smile. She sensed he wanted to wink at her, but he made no such attempt at the gesture. A red-hot flush to her flesh did its best to come through her dark skin. She dropped her head and coughed a nervous laugh. Raising her head, composing herself, she continued, "—my husband…made the gems glow bright. There is an instant feeling, a connection to the blessing inside a sacred object. The feel of its conjure," she summed up. She aimed her hand at the obsidian scrying mirror. "I felt nothing from this mirror. Nothing," she reiterated.

Percy Weyer the Lesser stepped up to Stewart Bloodworth's side and said in a desperate manner, "But you said you were quick to make judgment. There is something more to say, correct?"

"Yes," Fey replied. "I initially felt an emptiness that left the tips of my fingers feeling hollow. But that, in and of itself, is a sign." She spoke with effect when she informed the Fifth Order members, "Something is blocking my capabilities to sense conjure." Her tone was like that of a detective giving a slow, dramatic reveal to a culprit that left behind identifying pieces in scattered clues. "This scrying instrument has an enchanted lock on it. I can conclude the mirror's authenticity, but like all locks, I would need either key or combination to open—" Fey lost her words, and her expression blended into fright and curiosity as the black mirror's surface glowed with a faint purple florescence.

The Fifth Order members' eyes were transfixed. Their hearts pulsed in sync with the glow's hum resonating on the mirror's face. Fey backed away. Gordon did the same, eyes just as fastened to the mirror's pulsing incandescence. Guards moved their hands to the handles of holstered or belt-clipped weapons. The last gesture before everything was unmoving. While the room's attendants remained still, the stirring energy burst into a glittering, lilac-colored cloud. Streaks of electricity snaked through the billowing smoke with a loud crackle and pop. Motion resumed. The Fifth Order members ducked and took cover. The guards unsheathed their weapons. Gordon and Fey ducked away from the flare's flash.

The cloud whisked away to reveal Tsoro's diminutive, bat-winged presence. The yumbo flapped its wings, hovering over the scrying mirror for a moment before scurrying about the room in wild zips and dives at the occupants. Confusion erupted next. The Fifth Order members ducked lower, taking moments to look up and observe the untamed creature of myth zipping through the chamber. Guards aimed their weapons. Those with pistols tried to follow the quick whooshes and barrels around the room. Those with blades kept the tips of their steel extended, following the yumbo's erratic flight pattern.

One guard reacted. There was another pop and flash from an unclipped pistol. The armed sentry's target was not the intrusive, airborne imp. His shot was aimed at the youngest Fifth Order member, Percy Weyer the Lesser. The hard, metal pellet struck aristocrat at the side of his neck, deflected up through his jaw, and smashed several of his front teeth as it continued out of his mouth and lodged into a wall.

Percy wrapped his hands around his neck as blood gurgled out of the gaping wound and poured from his mouth. He squeezed his throat and pressed his lips together as an overflow of blood gushed up and out, spilling through pressed lips, and dripped down his chin. His finger's tightness did nothing to clot the flow of blood. It seeped through and stained his collar and shirt. He dropped to his knees, clinging to the life that gushed from his wounds in a violent, red wave. Inhaling resulted in an exhaled cough. The reaction intertwined with spurts of blood from his mouth that slapped the floor.

Gordon turned his head. His eyes fell upon the killing, watching Percy attempt to conserve his breaths to keep from spitting up blood or choking on it as it filled his throat. He heard Stewart Bloodworth scream, and looked over to witness the Fifth Order member reach back over his shoulder where a dagger was lodged. A third guard wrapped an arm around Fey's neck, a pistol to her head. Gordon pivoted to strike, an instinctive move to catch Fey's assailant unaware.

There was another pop of a pistol. Gordon spun around, but not by choice. A force drilled itself through his arm and twirled his body about as if a large monstrosity took control of him and whirled him like a topspin toy. The attack was a crude reminder of the larger play in a game of theft and retrieval. Gordon fell on his arm.

He bled.

Abim bled.

Gordon's mind connected his possessing soul to the nerves in Abim's body, and he experienced a sensation of what felt like his arm doubling in size, tightening and exploding with fire. A hole had been introduced by a pellet through his appendage at the bicep.

Gordon shook. He heard yelling. It was all unintelligible. The room contorted and blurred, and a lilac brilliance bubbled at the edges of his vision. He rolled onto his stomach, but the relief of pressure on his arm didn't relieve the pain. An electric shock detonated within his wounded arm. Gordon gritted his teeth. He rolled onto his back and exhaled, left hand reaching over to comfort the wound on his right arm. His hand trembled before resting against the bullet hole in his bicep. Around him the screams increased into a vertigo-inducing bluster.

There was a sensation against Gordon's chest. He felt an invisible hand press against him, and then reach through his torso. It clutched his soul possessing Abim, and it yanked at Gordon in an attempt to tear him from the Moor's body. Gordon gathered all his senses and braced himself against the tug and wrenching of his control on Abim. He writhed, both in spirit and physically, curling up less from the gunshot's pain and more from his wrestling with keeping moored in time and physical control on Abim's body.

Gordon's back arched as he resisted being taken from time. He rolled over, and he witnessed through blurred vision all the chaos melt into a frenzied cluster. The sight in his left eye sharpened long enough for him to see Percy Weyer the Lesser dead in a pool of blood, hand remaining clutched around his throat, the grip now loose and the blood free to flow, spreading onto the floor as a macabre, surrendering flag. An attacker disguised as a guard had an arm wrapped around Stewart Bloodworth the Higher. Another shouted terms of capture that Hening Courbé the Greater listened closely to. A third was pulling Fey from the room. She reached out for him, crying his real name, telling him not to leave. Gordon put his hand on the bleeding wound. He exhaled, and a thought came to him as his vision strained and turned murky.

This is staged, thought Gordon. Only the Fifth Order members and their guards were unaware of the play they participated in. Fey was aware. So why then was she so concerned with Gordon's wound and the attack made upon her. Why was she screaming his real name?

Gordon's answer presented itself as his shrouded vision shifted from a foggy gray to a blanketing lilac. Strands of electricity snaked across it like a storm cloud. Gordon realized in that moment he'd lost his struggle with the sensation grabbing at his spirit. A luminescent, lilac cocoon wrapped around him. The brilliance was warm and comforting, allowing Gordon to acquiesce to its embrace and spirit him away.

The effulgence could only be seen by Fey's eyes. Gordon was now gone, regardless of how she attempted to cast her voice like a rod to reel him back to time and physical possession. Gordon was no longer a participant in events. He was a detached, omnipresent observer, witnessing history in dream.

Abim groaned, teeth grinding against one another. His hand tightened around his wound. It was more than a scratch, but it was all for show. He exhaled, feeling as if his limbs had a tingling return to blood flow. His head effervesced with clarity as if he'd woken from a dream, though memory filled him with all that his body participated in and most of his words spoken. He welcomed the disorder aggregated around him. He heard his wife yelling a name. *"Gordon!"* He knew not who this was, and he felt a change in tone to his wife's voice. There were similarities, but there rang a subtle timbre foreign to him. Abim looked up, and while guards scrambled to the side of the remaining Fifth Order members, staring down weapons and a Moorish maiden's capture, he saw Fey wrapped in the arms of a brigand holding a pistol to her head.

Abim blinked, and the façade of Fey Forrester washed away, replaced by the familiar face and frame of his wife Efra. She was playing her part, working against her captors with arms out, calling to him. She was now pleading, very real. Tears drained from her eyes, and she repeated, *"No! No! No! Come back!"* Her delirium played exceptional, a performance well-received by all who witnessed it. But Abim sensed something more. There was not much to his part besides allowing his wife's capture by allies who feigned as cutpurses for occult objects.

Abim balanced on one knee. He screamed back, "Efra! I will find you!" He jumped up and charged forward. He allowed Hening Courbé to hold him back. He used little strength, but he still presented a challenge for Hening Courbé to keep in place. Abim found this amusing, but remained locked within his expression of distress. He stepped back and hollered, turning away from his wife being whisked from the room.

The bandits were gone, their allied yumbo carrying the occult items with them. The remaining guards counted their dead. Their captain looked at Stewart Bloodworth and Hening Courbé for a set of orders while Petite Le Garçon took advantage of the settled happenings to call upon a nurse to attend to the wounded.

Abim took his hand away from his injury. He spoke an incant. His voice rumbled like the sound of an earthquake, a purposeful gesture to gain the attention of those who surrounded him. His flesh mended, and as muscle and the fibers of his skin regenerated, it pushed out the hard, cylindrical, metal pellet lodged into his arm. Blood ceased its flow from the once-opened wound, coursing through his body as if no detour had been ripped into him. The red stain on Abim's sleeve, and the tear in the fabric, were the only evidence of an attack upon him.

Abim's onlookers were frozen with surprise. Their faces were shaped by awe at Abim's otherworldly power. This was the effect he wanted to have. He strode past them with no obstruction or protest as he made his way out of the room. "Plot your maneuvers if you must. I have no time to waste. My wife is with these fools." His voice's reverberation shook the men around him from their fastened state.

Hening Courbé made a step in Abim's direction, pleading with the Moor to stay and plot with them. "A man of your talent and strength! Your power in conjure!" he shouted. "There's a reason they attacked you first. No harm can come to your wife. They need her alive." But Abim ignored the Fifth Order member's pleas, and Stewart Bloodworth grabbed Abim by the arm to hold him back, but the nobleman occultist was too weak from his injury.

When it came to the Order member's wound, a nurse, brought by Petite Le Garçon, cared for the injury. There were no mystical, ancient words spoken in an otherworldly harmony, just the raw sting of medical needle and stitch. Stewart was stalled. "You may leave," he permitted through gritted teeth. "There's no force like raw force. Let them fight." He called on the guard captain and said, "Four men to escort the Moor into battle. No, five!" he corrected.

"They can follow," Abim growled, all in act. "But they won't keep up."

Abim left the room, out into the hall. He was proud of the wild flashes of lights and puffs of smoke that had been metaphorically drummed up to dazzle unsuspecting marks, and overjoyed at his own acting and the theater he'd put on display. Mirrors were to cast reflections opposite from their nature. His guise was a suitable, reversed echo. The ruse had been put in motion, but there were still tricks to be played. Five of the Fifth Order's guards followed him into the hall and through the manor. They kept their distance and their hands on their sheathed weapons. Abim continued forward, happy to have witnesses at his back. The greatest trick to pull was centered on his extravagant and glorious demise.

Abim hurried his steps, shuffling quicker until he was in a ripened sprint toward the exit. The guards matched his pace, but were still far behind. They saw Abim barge through the doors, and as wooden masses swung back to a hard close, they heard an immediate scream. Their charge increased in speed, and like Abim before them, the guards pushed through the doors, their force doing damage to the hinges and locks.

Abim was on his knees, a thrown knife centered in his chest. He gasped, turning his body and raising his arm to one of the guards that surrounded him. The guard held onto Abim as the Moor struggled to catch his breath. It appeared blood was filling his lungs as his heart pumped its final sighs of life through his system. Ahead of them was the carriage carrying the bandits and the stolen arcane items. Leaning out of the carriage's open doorway was a young conjure man named Fashe. A crafty smile glowed on his face as he shouted to the guards, "Pursue us, if you like, but you will only follow this traitorous naggar-Moor to death's eternal abyss!"

An inaudible incant passed through his devious smile. Then he twiddled his fingers and snapped them. Abim's body ignited in a horrific whirl of fire. The guards backed away as the flames swallowed the Moor like an open mouth. They'd never seen a death more frightful. The Moor screamed, his eyes possessed wide with horror. Angry flames consumed him in an instant, his body transmuted to smoldering ash and into a simple memory that floated away in the breeze.

The act of conjure manipulated all that witnessed its brilliance to freeze in movement. These five guards had seen displays of magnificence in a single sitting, more than most in a lifetime. But circumstance didn't permit the guards to take witness of the trick's entire performance. The gag played out as Fashe's crafty smile shifted to a snarl, and he ducked back into the carriage, closing its doors. An empty space next to him was suddenly filled with whirling ash and smokeless flames that rendered into Abim's complete, physical manifestation in the unbruised flesh. His face exploded with laughter and happiness. He clapped, and then celebrated by gifting Fashe an enormous hug.

Their mission was accomplished.

Free from Abim's embrace, Fashe exhaled and leaned against the door. His conjure had been propelled to its farthest boundary. His eyelids wavered as he struggled to keep them open for the party's debriefing. He was happy to initiate the conversation by asking the woman sitting opposite him if they were being pursued. Her name was Kamanni, and she answered, "No, *a-sihir-rajul*." She exhaled and almost passed to sleep. Her attempts to keep herself awake appeared to be a cumbersome task. "I…created an illusion of us traveling in a different direction." She added, concerning their brothers and sisters-in-arms, "Haji and the others have a head start. We'll meet them at the rendezvous."

Abim nodded. He leaned forward and patted Kamanni on the knee. "Get rest, sister-warrior. You and Fashe have exhausted yourselves."

Kamanni didn't argue, but she stayed her rest for a moment. She turned to Fey-Efra and apologized. "For my roughness," she clarified.

Fey-Efra assured the conjure woman that it was all show, and it needed to be sold. Kamanni accepted Fey-Efra's words. Then she rested her body at an angle, closed her eyes, and went to sleep. Abim sat back and turned to advise Fashe to do the same, but the Moorish conjure man already had his eyes closed and his breath in a slow rhythm at rest. Abim addressed his wife. His words were delayed as his eyes caught a glimpse of Fey's presence dressed in his wife's fashionable garments. It was only for a mere second, but he'd seen her, and she was familiar. A second time had the image of the short-haired black woman appeared, earlier shouting at him when she'd been taken by Kamanni. Just the same, the image lasted for only the blink of Abim's eyes, becoming a questionable moment. There he saw his wife Efra, and his conscious self was satisfied.

Abim paid no attention. So much illusion had been put on display like flashing lights. He believed they left an effect to his vision. He reached out and put his hand on his wife's knee. She smiled at him, adjusting the box holding the arcane items recovered from The Fifth Order.

Abim inquired, "Your winged pet?"

"Retracted to his realm," Fey-Efra answered him. "My body his portal."

"And you, most importantly, Efra? Are you fine?" Abim's voice was possessed with concern. He referenced Kamanni's words. "You did seem real in your performance. Are you well? Did the charge frighten you?"

Fey-Efra told Abim, "I was genuine. I imagined you taken from me. I was taken from you. I imagined it was all real. How would I act should I lose you…Abim?"

Abim was quick to reply. "Or, someone named 'Gordon'," he commented with half a smile and his eyes conflicted between the expressions of relief and concern.

Fey-Efra turned her head and looked out the window. "Perhaps you misheard me, love," she advocated. "So much chaos, so much going on," she expounded. Abim pulled his hand back. He became pensive. Fey-Efra looked at him with a quick turn of her head. "I'm sorry, Abim. Did I offend you?"

Abim chuckled. "No. No, Efra-love," he responded. "I'm thinking about the chaos—the disarrangement we can't see, that wasn't present." He thought of a single word, a title. He spoke it into existence in a low, deep voice that carried heavy weight. "Ratamutum," Abim thundered.

"The man who has our love," Fey-Efra added. She returned her gaze to the window and watched the world go by. A cobalt-blue brilliance sprang out of Fey. It enswathed her spirit, and like a mouth, inhaled her essence. There was no pair of eyes the luminous aura was cast against. It didn't disturb Kamanni or Fashe's sleep. Abim didn't throw his hands over his eyes and attempt to dodge the brilliance that flooded the cabin. It was invisible to all but Fey as it swallowed her spirit and carried her to a funnel that she passed through, a void where she continued an aimless spin through all space and time.

Efra blinked her eyes as if coming from a dream. Her memory stitched together the action of the last few hours. She peered down at her lap and examined the box she held tightly. "We have a mystery, yes," she told Abim. "But we now have what we need to connect our time to another. We've tossed the bones and read the shells for our world's future. We can create the chamber for the lilac flame and cobalt-blue spirits, bringing them knowledge that will be lost over the coming centuries. That is enough."

Abim nodded, but he couldn't help but express disappointment through a sigh. "The Tarot is incomplete," he said. "We can't give the Eterijah an incomplete deck."

"You think this is the last of our adventures, Abim-love?" Efra asked her husband while beaming a sly look.

"No," he chuckled. "I wish it could be," he added, not sure if there was more truth in his words than intended. He started laughing at the notion.

Efra scolded, "You'll wake our conjure brother and sister!"

Abim looked at Kamanni and Fashe. Both were locked in their unconscious state. "No, I won't," he corrected his wife, shaking his head and amplifying his laughter. "They're getting the sleep I wish we could enjoy." But he simmered his guffaws, first placing a hand over his mouth, and then simply swallowing his voluminous humor. He took a few breaths before commenting aloud, "We should have a complete deck for tribute…" He shook his head in a short, frustrated manner. "Maybe the Eterijah will hear our humble pleas."

"That deck is a wondrous find, even if missing one card," Efra brought up. "A lot of focus went into crafting those cards. Incanted ink made from rare flowers, conjure artists, the ashes of the original, Kemetic deck. A lot of focus was put together to see the many paths and flows of possibility within time and chance, bring about a wanted outcome. It should be worth *something* to the Eterijah."

And so it was Abim accepted his fate for ongoing adventure. "To Africa then," he declared, doing his best to shovel enthusiasm into his voice. He raised an eyebrow and continued, "To Azur-Fah and its kingdoms of the Cosmic Clock." Abim shook a finger and calculated, "Perhaps our mysterious Ratamutum will pursue us, and we will unmask another traitorous conjurer, take from him the card we seek."

Efra agreed. Both she and Abim stared out the window and wondered. Their next path of adventure rested on their minds for only a short while before their thoughts drifted to far more important ideals.

Returning home and embracing their two boys, Ithun and Seizan.

Bright. Lilac flash.

23

Gordon emerged from sleep with a jump and holler. The lilac brilliance surrounding his body broke into bright strands of energy that retracted into his eyes, mouth, and the sphere glowing at the center of his forehead. His mother's specter floated in front of him with Fey's yumboes flanking her. Lady Arachne was there too, holding tight to The Moon card in her right hand. Albert Ford Banneker stood next to her.

Everyone had an expression on their face, though Lady Arachne's and Albert Banneker's features were loosening after the overbearing glow reduced in intensity. Albert had curiosity scrawled on his face. Lady Arachne was anxious from visage to posture. Althea had sorrow watering her eyes. The yumboes seemed frightened. But as Gordon's violent recovery from his trip through time by dream came to a restful calm, their expressions dripped into relief.

Gordon put his hand on his chest. His heart bellowed thunder inside him. He took several deep breaths in an attempt to steady himself. His eyesight perceived the world as a running oil painting viewed through a window running with raindrops. He blinked and used his power to dock his visual faculties into a coherent portrait of reality. Using his spirit's power to straighten his perception sapped his strength, but the world around him sharpened into its actuality, and he managed not to pass out. Another breath. Gordon lifted Spook off his lap. Silver and the other yumboes swooped in and took up the conjure-tech with their tiny hands, and flew it to rest atop the alchemical chamber. Gordon swallowed. He rubbed a hand through the coiled twists of his locked hair. He observed everyone looking at him for a moment, and he inhaled again. He was now calm and relaxed.

His eyes fell on the mystical timepiece clamped to him, now dangling from the chain, loose from his pocket. He lifted it with an open palm, moving his hand up and down repeatedly as if judging its weight. "I was there," he said, looking up at the people around him. The yumboes returned to hovering around Althea, save Silver who sat next to Spook. The ancient mechanism's black-mirror face was now upright with The Judgement card resting on its bejeweled console. Gordon eyed Spook. He thought of the pieces making it up, the jewels and mirror. The past and them unconnected. Now they were intact, fastened to another mystical object to make up the entirety of the body. There was also the spirit of the sprite making it all function.

Albert shook his head. It was slow and deliberate as if he was contemplating something profound. But there was more pride in his gesture's intentions, and he made it known when he stated, "I'm glad my device was able to work for you."

Gordon looked away from the people. His eyes were wide as he recalled his journey and experience through time. "Bet your ass it worked…"

"Gordon!" Althea scolded her son. Her tone was stern, but there was a crack in the severe expression on her face. The fracture was not in her eyes, focused and hawk-like as they were. It was curled on her lips as a smile, grateful to see her son's mental and spiritual faculties intact. Regardless, she believed he still had his manners to mind. Gordon apologized, and Althea responded to his apology by stating, "Don't make me come from the other side to beat your behind?" He chuckled, and her smile grew wider. "Again!" she reiterated, drawing humor from a somber moment that was a few days past.

Albert hesitated to cut in to mother and son's reunion, but he said, "I'm just grateful there was enough blessing in the watch to send your spirit back, ground you there in time."

Gordon thanked Albert, as Lady Arachne stepped forward and bent to one knee in front of him. She presented The Moon card. The writing he'd inked onto the back of the card centuries in the past was fresh as if he'd written the words moments ago. Lady Arachne explained without prompt of inquiry, "I pulled the ink back to the surface. I couldn't quite read it when it first appeared. I could sense your history-hopping had something to do with this. I hurried back here."

Gordon's eyes were fixed on the writing. All he could think was that he'd just held this card in his hands. He'd just written these words and the Erzulie symbol on its back. These were actions that spanned only minutes ago, but centuries past. "Fey was there, too," Gordon announced in a soft voice. "We possessed the bodies of two Moors, a husband and wife. They could perform conjure. They met with members of a European occult order. The Order of the Fifth Science," he clarified. "We were in a hidden village in France, appraising objects that had conjure value." He elucidated on one item only, informing Lady Arachne, "Your deck of Tarot cards was there."

The matriarch's face perked up. "Oh! So, this Fifth Science Order could still possess the card?" She concluded aloud, "Perhaps buried where this obscure, French village was, or perhaps still stands."

Gordon shook his head. "No," he told her. "Someone has it," he continued in an apologetic tone. "A conjure man named Ratamutum. The Hanged Man. He's using it—" Gordon paused. He considered the tense of his words. He corrected, "He…*used*…it…" His eyes went slim as he contemplated, trying to make sense of time and space. "Jeez! What tense do I use?" he asked himself. "I guess he 'used' it—the card. It's already happened. It's in the past."

Lady Arachne put a hand on Gordon's knee. She asked, "What was it used for?"

His expression changed. Disappointment and sorrow collided on his face. He sat back and exhaled a heavy sigh. "He used The Lovers' reversed abilities to assist slavers in turning African tribal nations and urban nations against one another." Gordon's melancholy became contagious. Everyone had something to say, but no one said anything. Gordon broke the silence. "The ideals of the Pious Wars weren't lost to its long-ago time, Lady Arachne. They followed conjure folk and influenced the Terrible Occurrence, slavery. One of the Fifth Order members referred to the time of slavery as the Great Alchemy," Gordon revealed. "He said this Ratamutum person was dedicated in assisting Europe in the slave trade they created, but he had different reasons. He believes putting the people of Africa through a 'gross transition' was for the better."

"Gross, indeed," Lady Arachne commented with a huff. "Apparently, jive-ass, butter-biscuit eatin', house-nigga coons existed then, too."

Gordon assured her, "I'll find The Lovers card. I got this close. We'll discover its location here in our time. The deck went from these benevolent, conjure folk to The Line we stole it from. Somehow. Some way. The Lovers card is somewhere."

Lady Arachne nodded, Gordon's words making only a minor impression. She stood and sighed, "Stay enthusiastic, Gordon. I believe you'll find the card. I do. I'm just worn down a bit. The card was separated from the deck all these centuries ago. Now I'm understandin' it was for the most diabolical of purposes. I can only hope it still exists. I couldn't sense its properties when I was recreating the deck. It's possible the terrible, perverted use of its reversed power might've caused it to consume itself, burn up."

The thought sobered Gordon. He could only respond by saying, "I'll continue my search."

"Thank you, Gordon," she replied. "Conduct your search for my missing Lovers." Her voice was appreciative and sincere. She concluded with a bow at the neck, "I trust you will bring the companions to me."

Gordon was not the only one in the room that could sense Lady Arachne's distress, anxious to recover the missing card of her powerful deck. Gordon attempted to put the Fable Avenue matriarch at ease by reminding her of his stake in the pursuit. "I don't mean to be disrespectful or argumentative, Lady Arachne," he stated first, "but I too am invested in finding The Lovers card. For my own interest," he amended.

"Absolutely, Gordon," Lady Arachne replied. "And your interest extends to all the conjure communities." She put a hand on her chest. "I'm anxious," Lady Arachne admitted. "Please understand that I'm in no way upset with you. We're dealing with so much these days." She took a much-needed breath. "The card still exists. It *must*. It *has* to. Its sibling cards have called out to it in readings. Disregard my slip into pessimism. I trust your endeavor will yield success."

"Yes, Lady Arachne," Gordon said with conviction. He handed The Moon back to her, and the matriarch accepted the card's return. She thanked Gordon and returned to Albert's side.

The old man walked up next to Gordon and bent down as Lady Arachne did before him. "Can I hold it, Mister Goodspeed?" Then he re-titled Gordon with the moniker, "Mister Baron Lilac?"

Gordon grinned, handing over the watch, unclipping it from his person. "Baron Lilac," he repeated. "I like that."

Albert held his artistry in his hand. He spied the device with pride, and he remarked, "It took a lot of power to bless this. Put old folk like myself to sleep. No young juice went into this." He winked and displayed a wide, toothy grin. "I like my craftsmanship, indeed, Baron Lilac. More than that, I appreciate the elder-folk that put their blessing in this thing to make it work." He gave the mystical pocket watch back to Gordon. "Glad we're all playing our part."

"I appreciate the heads up on the deadly haunts," he stated as a matter-of-fact. "I'll keep my instinct up. Any more information on what I can expect?"

Albert stood and patted Gordon on the shoulder. "A fight, Baron Lilac!" he stated with what Gordon felt was too much enthusiasm. He put his hands in his pockets and said to Gordon, "Our folk ain't got much information. We got a little, maybe even the missing pieces needed by the bigger *nasyons, nachons*. If you haven't learned it here on Fable Avenue or with the Gwuinee, you better scour the hundreds of smaller Ojulowo conjure folk 'round the world. Africans brothers and sisters can be real secretive, though."

Gordon nodded, pondering the effects of the Terrible Occurrence, how it fractured information and even swallowed it whole from existence. He was grateful for the rituals still in use or created from strong conjure folk. To some degree, he already received a warning from a reading with Lady Arachne when he was first possessed with the lilac spirit. He misread the cards presented to him, the Five of Wands. Perhaps if Lady Arachne had the ancient cards she now possessed, a better understanding would've guided his flowering, otherworldly instinct. Lady Arachne only saw conflict, nothing specific. Her job was not to interpret, but to guide Gordon's blooming, higher instinct along the path to develop the unseen future into a foreseeable destiny.

Gordon considered a third option: two meanings in one card draw. Most likely, that was the correct path of understanding. At least, for his pride, that's what he told himself.

"I'm sorry, sir," Gordon apologized to Albert. "I take all our nasyons seriously."

Albert batted Gordon's words away with a swipe of his hand. "No need for an apology, young man. I wasn't being defensive. I was being matter-of-fact."

"Yessir," Gordon replied. He rubbed his eyes and then wiped his hands on his thighs. "I'm going back in, but I need some space." He looked at Althea. "Ma, you can go be with Pop. I'll keep the yumboes here." Then he reiterated, "I just need a moment."

Althea's eyes hinted a puzzled look. It exhaled from her countenance as fast as it came. She sensed something about her son, but she didn't pry. He would be in good hands; and she would be alerted should anything go awry. She gave Gordon a simple nod, but it was Lady Arachne who spoke. "We'll leave you be, Gordon," she said. Then she turned to Silver and gave the order, "Watch him close. Alert his mother first should something happen. I won't be too far. Albert and I will be at the crossroads."

Silver saluted with a swift dip of her head.

Althea faded, beaming a fragile, parting smile at her son. Lady Arachne and Albert dismissed themselves and made their way up the stairs. Gordon used his ears to listen for their footsteps leading to the front door, and the lock of the door once they'd made their exit. He used his instinct to provide him a real-time view of their departure. Albert and Lady Arachne, were at the moment, walking through the brownstone's front gate.

Gordon opened his eyes. He requested that Jade, Zee, and Em return to their realm and grant he, Spook, and Silver privacy. The three yumboes didn't feel slighted. They puffed away in colorful clouds of whirling smoke as Gordon spoke the incant to return them to the sketchbook. Gordon put his eyes on Spook. He stood and walked over to the alchemical chamber where the arcane device rested, Silver standing next to it. Gordon grinned, squatting down in front of Spook's screen. Before he could speak, Spook's black mirror lit up with ancient characters translated for Gordon by way of his instinct. *I'm starting to remember that particular event in history…going a little smoother, however, Mister Goodspeed.*

"The outcome was all the same, correct?" asked Gordon, surprised that his words trembled and broke up his confident tone. Then he amended his statement by adding to it Spook's proper name. "Tsoro…?" He chuckled a bit and said, "I think I had an instinct about you when I named you 'Spook'."

Silver's features burst with delight, and she danced in place hearing Spook's name spoken aloud. Her wings flapped, and she lifted into the still tapping her feet as if planted firmly on a solid surface.

My memory comes back a little more every day since activated through this device, the ancient script read along the black mirror. *I was conjured in that time by Efra al-Kaadi, but I could possibly be older. Silver helps. Talking to her.* There was a pause in the script. Spook was thinking, and Gordon could sense it. He waited patiently for the device to speak again. The words eventually appeared. *I think it best that we keep this a secret. For the sake of the space-time continuum.*

Gordon started to snicker, and then he considered Spook's warning anything but humorous. He asked Spook, "Are you serious?" to which the device replied, *I'm afraid I'm quite serious, Mister Goodspeed.* Gordon straightened. He saluted with a quick nod toward the conjure-tech. Silver stopped her flutter and dance and settled back atop the alchemical chamber next to Spook. She sat cross-legged and looked up at Gordon. He asked her, "Do Zee, Em, and Jade know, too?"

Silver answered, "Not the whole story. They do know it's a yumbo-spirit that possesses the mechanism."

Gordon tipped his head to either side while looking up at the ceiling. "Seems to be enough of the story." Then he clapped his hands together in a tight, fisted grip. He said to Spook, "Close up, Tsoro-Spook. We headin' back into that time-connecting dream." He looked down at the mystical watch dangling from the chain clipped to his belt. He reeled it up and cupped it in his hand. "If I see Fey, that's a bonus. But we gotta find that Lovers card." As he put the watch in his pocket, he caught a glimpse of ancient text scrolling across Spook's obsidian screen. The words read, *Perhaps, if you see Miss Forrester, you will aid one another in the capture of the Hanged Man, Ratamutum.* Gordon pondered the possibility, and he liked it. He faced Spook and responded, "Yeah. We can force the card from him, depending on who we possess. Then bury the card somewhere I can find it in this time. That's a lot to hope on, but I'll keep it in mind." He ordered Spook again to close up, and the device shut with The Judgement card inside.

Gordon picked Spook up and walked back to his chair. He reclined within its comforting embrace and held Spook tight against his chest, arms crossed. The effect was quick. History called to him, and he was pulled into the dreaming to view it.

Silver sat atop the alchemical chamber with her wings folded and legs crossed, now dangling over the edge of the capsule. Her palms were planted firmly on the edge, and she watched Gordon drift peacefully into slumber. She noted that no brilliant, lilac glow cloaked him while he slept, and she looked disappointed because of it.

Love. Blasphemy.

"…the ebbing, subtle tides of conjure."

History developed out of a dissipating, lilac mist that sparkled with a hint of cobalt blue.

Eyes were wide spying the festive setting of a glorious dining area resting within a quaint cottage that was tucked away in a dense forest in Europe. A finely carved, rectangular table played host to an ambrosial feast that warmed the air with its savory scents. A plump bird was the centerpiece, roasted crisp and seasoned to enhance the brown in its cooking and the natural juices marinating the skin on the surface and meat beneath. Freshly baked bread billowed in a basket. Bowls of chopped and spiced vegetables both cooked and raw were spread out among the feast. Roasted leg of lamb with rosemary was another delectable delight served alongside the main meat.

Tani Duhu didn't need conjure to prepare the meal, though she was just as adept at manipulating the subtle quintessence woven loose in the atmosphere. There was never a temptation to sprinkle the spice of incant in any of her tender, culinary expeditions. She was too proud, and justifiably confident that her grandfather's skill and knowledge was passed to her. That confidence dotted her fingertips, touched the cuisines she prepared, and spread across the tongues of any in attendance to her flavorful craft.

Tani was fire condensed into physical flesh, tall and svelte but still with curves and definition to her shape. She had sunset-colored flesh and hair as fiery as a celestial star. She was dressed in the elegant gown and robes of a conjure woman. Bangles decorated her arms, large looped earrings dangled, almost touching her shoulders. Necklaces wrapped tight on her neck, fanning out in size like golden waves of sound made visual. She appeared as more of a queen than table setter, and Tani believed she was nothing less than noble. But as wife, as mother, as provider, she needed no fancy-jeweled diadem.

So, she moved with the grace of a dancing flame as she set the table, humming a soulful tune plucked out of Africa from time immemorial. She set down jugs of wine for adults. Pitchers of juice for the children. The last remnants of conjure folk she called family were in attendance to the meal. They waited patiently, standing against the wall around the dining room. Her husband was there, and she liked his eyes on her. It didn't make her nervous or blush. It inspired her to perform. From conjure to fine dining. This band of conjure folk, branded outlaws in a dangerous new world order, playfully named themselves the Merrymakers. Two families. Four friends. Allies. A small tribe together.

This was family, present to enjoy Tani's meal. Duty would call to them when the meal was finished. A year of disappearance and forage, and then to re-emerge and convene with answers to secure the future. Her closest friends, Abim and Efra al-Kaadi had already done so much. Not only had they secured conjure items of great import, but they made a bold journey to an invisible kingdom, permitting the use of a device known as The Winding Staircase. Use was close to forbidden, but the charm of the husband and wife conjure couple swayed all the kings and queens of the twelve houses, and their guardian Eterijah to permit use, allowing Abim and Efra to journey through time and assist a boy possessed with one half of the lilac and cobalt blue spirits of re-creation.

A deck of mystical cards spoke destiny to Efra and Abim. They followed the instructions the cards laid out. The same set of Tarot guided Tani and her husband upon a path. Though the deck was incomplete, one card missing, it remained strong in its ability to divine and forecast. Tani's personal expedition into preparing the exceptional meal was an attempt to recreate the missing love in a savory taste and sustenance. With the meal now ready to serve, Tani understood this night's dining to be destined.

On time. As she prepared. Four others joined the party. Three men and one woman. Fashe. Haji. Kamanni. Feechi. Filing through the front door, they each expressed their sentiments on being famished, and how the meal was tempting to just dive into.

"You are all so patient," Tani said to her conjure family, now extended. "This meal is now ready," she announced as she stood straight and beamed with pride. She stepped back and allowed her waiting party to take their seats.

Everyone stepped forward, ready to take their place at the table. Their eyes were locked on the food, but their words were aimed at Tani for creating such a feast. Her husband, Akuram Duhu, walked up to one of the two chairs placed at table's end. The seats were designated for him and his brother-in-conjure, Abim al-Kaadi. Tani would occupy the seat at her husband's right, and their seven-year old son, Been ah Kibir, would be next to her. Tani had a small family. One husband. One child. But her love was vast, and she was so proud to have them.

Akuram kissed his wife on the cheek and praised, "The mark of your culinary genius is conjure unto itself, my love." Tani leaned into her husband's affectionate gesture. She accepted his words with eyes closed, a humble hand on her chest, and bow of her head. She mouthed her gratitude but never made it audible. She turned as her husband took his seat, and she ushered their bushy-headed son into his chair. The young boy thanked his mother, and Tani again stepped aside, waiting for the remaining people of her extended conjure family to take seat.

Abim al-Kaadi sat in the second chair situated at the head of the table. Both he and Aƙuram were the embodiment of leadership, though their physical presences couldn't be more opposite. Aƙuram was strapping, but not as robust as Abim. His leaner physique gave off the appearance that he was tall, but in truth, he was a few inches shorter than Abim. Long, thick dreadlocks flowed down from the top of his round head. Their only physical similarities rested in their proud, pitch color. While Abim sat comfortably in his conjure robes, Aƙuram was dressed in a billowing collar shirt made from silk and buttoned to its top. A black vest was worn over the shirt. Around his legs were a pair of black pants. On his feet, boots the same color. His belt was adorned with blessed trinkets.

Efra al-Kaadi sat two seats down from her husband, on his left. Their two children, Ithun and Seizan, sat between them. Seizan was adjacent to his father. Ithun sat at his mother's right. The boys were close in age to Tani and Aƙuram's son Been ah Kibir, which made them all good friends. Seizan was the oldest, age ten. He and Ithun were separated by three years.

Ithun favored his mother's soft features, handsome as a young prince could be, and always armed with a sly smile. Seizan inherited his father's austere disposition, and as he would eventually march into adolescence, time would etch the chiseled, rough-hewn features worn by his father.

Ithun broadcasted a cunning grin as he surveyed the feast. Something knocked against his leg, taking him out of his crafty concentration. He raised his head swiftly and spied Been ah Kibir casting a crooked smirk in his direction. He felt another strike scrape his shin. Been ah Kibir giggled. Ithun's smile dimmed. His temperament turned as hot as the meal in front of him, and he attempted to strike back. He sank into the chair, doing his best to extend his leg and return a blow to his rascally friend. He connected, and his artful grin returned to him, tossed at his long-time friend.

Ithun's retaliation was met with another barrage of kicks from Been ah Kibir, coupled with salvos of mischievous laughter. Ithun's comeback grin waivered, and he chanced another volley of punts in return. One thrust out with his leg grazed his brother's calf. Seizan flinched! His face screwed into a scowl, and he elbowed his younger brother in the ribs as he howled, "Hey!"

Ithun reacted to his brother's attack. "Ow!" he said grabbing his side.

"Hey!" Abim's thunderous voice rippled through his children and stiffened them straight to attention. "Behave. Now!" he warned.

Efra masked herself with a look of concern that casted a shadow over her sons' antics. She loved her two boys, and in these dark times she celebrated their innocent, childish hijinks. But the false face of severity she wore was as effective as their father's stern growl at them.

Tani put her hands on Been ah Kibir's shoulders. She leaned close to his ear and scolded, "Sit still, Kibir! You can play after dinner." Then she straightened. Been ah Kibir adjusted himself in his chair. He beamed a subtle smile at Ithun. Their scrimmage was far from over. Ithun matched his friend's muted grin, and made a slight nod of his head.

Aƙuram called, "Son!" Been ah Kibir was attentive to his father's hail. Aƙuram shook his head at him, and no more was needed to be said. But the father had something extra for his only child. He pitched an indistinct, proud smirk at Been ah Kibir and the wink of an eye.

Tani noticed her husband's gesture. She reached over and slapped his shoulder. *"Aƙuram!"* she reprimanded her husband. "The boy has his manners to mind."

Aƙuram chuckled at his wife, and tensions started to unwind. "Let the boys be boys, Tani-darling."

Tani disagreed and said, "After dinner. For now, they sit still." But she too had nothing but a large heart for her son, and she delighted in the carefree and cheer conjured at such a bleak moment. Even with this thought, she didn't approve of the roughhousing around the table. She took her seat, and as she did, jugs of wine and juice were passed to fill the occupants' cups.

Aƙuram knocked on the table three times. Everyone granted their attention to him. He raised a wooden cup of red wine and turned to Abim and Efra. "Welcome home," he saluted. "Again," he appended. Abim and Efra nodded at him. Aƙuram set his cup on the table. He continued his words, "Your efforts in this struggle will not go unnoticed. We trade time away from our children, but we convene to celebrate what we find. Abim and Efra on your recovery of stolen and misused conjure items. My wife and I on our pilgrimages inside Africa to study with the best minds that can still employ the old magic, tap into—what is now—the ebbing, subtle tides of conjure." To the remaining guests, Aƙuram addressed, "Fashe, Kamanni, bless you for your support. You push your conjure, and you assist in guarding us or aiding in high-risk operations." Both Fashe and Kamanni knocked on the table three times to acknowledge Aƙuram's words. Then he turned to the last two adults, Haji and Feechi. Aƙuram called them by name, and then he said, "Your research and reconnaissance has helped us connect to the hidden conjure world of our times, to our brothers, sisters, and small tribal factions that have preserved the old ways, beyond worship and into practice. Your value is immeasurable." Then to the children he declared, "You three are the bravest of all. You stand strong and patient while we chase shadows. We as your parents know you are in good hands, though we struggle with being absent from the greatest magic we've ever conjured: You three."

The boys bared toothy smiles, proud and attempting to live up to the words by sitting up straight, chests out. Aƙuram lifted his cup again, finalized his speech by stamping it with a loud, single word that was extracted from a long-ago time in Africa. It was divine and declarative. Then Aƙuram proclaimed the feast to begin.

The mothers assisted their sons. The other attendance dived in to fill their plates. A small, sneaky bite from Aƙuram pulled from him a compliment to his wife. His preview of the meal was as divine as the word he used to finish his speech. Tani beamed a seductive at her husband, and she winked too. Abim nudged him from the side and reminded Aƙuram to wait for the blessing before digging in. Aƙuram lifted his hands and backed away from his food, chuckling at his good friend's playful chiding.

Light conversation accompanied the preparation of plates. The boys teased one another, and their rough play with kicks under the table resumed, even with Seizan jumping into the fray. Their assaults continued until they were again scolded into separation. Abim led the blessing, and the conjure folk dived into their feast shortly after. Little was said when the meal began, and when there were words, most of them were bestowed onto Tani for the food's flavor.

Conversation eventually blossomed, and an hour into the talk, drink, and eat, Tani whispered something to her husband, and he shook his head rapidly acknowledging her sentiments. She rose from the table and glided into the kitchen. Aƙuram swept a knowing gaze over the feast and its attendance. Tani returned, a silver tray in hand, with an intricate and shiny metal dome atop it. She set it in front of her husband and whisked away to the kitchen.

The room turned silent. Everyone moved their eyes to the ornate dome and plate. The children anticipated desert. The adults, filled with drink had only a faint, fuzzy tingle funneling through their higher instinct. Abim patted Aƙuram on the back and again paid another compliment to Tani's culinary skills. "The sweet pie," Abim stated, "is what I have been waiting for. I love savory, but I crave the sweet pie or pastry."

Tani returned, another domed plate in her possession. She positioned it in front of Abim, stepped back, and lifted the dome off the first plate. There was no sweet pie revealed. A metal implement lay across the plate. An arrow made of iron. A sculpted man with his arms crossed sat at the tail. At the front end, extending off a triangular, wing-like pattern was a sharp tip.

The metal object's reveal partially dispelled the cloud of inebriation. Abim stared at it for a moment with a perplexity written on his countenance. He cleared his throat, attempting to shape his voice into words. But it was Aƙuram that spoke, which answered a few questions Abim had on the tip of mind and tongue.

"This is a replica of the first instrument that carried wroch-blood on its tip," Aƙuram detailed. "It's what inspires the weapons used against us by the Lodge of Needles. A small, tribal faction known as the Ifo possessed it. They gifted it to me and Tani when we visited them years prior." He turned to Abim and said, "This is what history looked like. This was politics crafted to deadly pin-point precision."

Abim looked at his friend for a split moment. Now on his face hung surprise. He blinked a few times, and then he aimed his gaze back at the reproduced weapon. Aƙuram pointed at the needle and named it, "It's called a *zenduzo*. The East African word, *sindano*, appears to descend from this word. Needle," he translated into their Afro-Arabic language. He sat back and sighed. "Time has shifted, hasn't it? And it has so much energy." He made a half-hearted attempt at a joke, saying, "It runs, and I can't keep up with it." Then he resumed his somber tone. "I don't fight it anymore. I never have." He sighed again. "All our sacrifice, and still these old ways of ours turn to dust. We're old with incant and conjure, my friends. Old lessons have been segmented and scattered everywhere, no different than the entirety of our black collective." He balled a fist, shook it. "We've connected to other conjure folk, but like so many of the other lost nations—enslaved or gone poor—we fight over the meanings to our ancient magic, rituals, and all. We've chosen personal value and egos and the inability to respect one another over the harmony of the original intent to our ancient writings."

Abim put his hand on his friend's back. "Brother, we still strive for completion. It gets hard. I know," he consoled.

Aƙuram snarled, "What are we really doing, Abim? How are we fighting? We should be flowing with time's shift. Let alchemy occur."

"A *Great* Alchemy…?" Abim questioned, eyebrow raised.

Aƙuram ignored his friend. He shook his head, drowned in his gloomy thoughts. "Let's start over. Amenhotep the Fourth did this. Akhenaton. People continuously believe he brought in monotheism. We know that's a fallacy because we were never speaking about gods in our mythologies; a simpleton's view of history. He was starting over. His deity, Aton, was a focal point. It was the sun. It was symbolic of a new day. Dawn. It was the cosmos. It was creation at the beginning. In time, like the points of the sun and our universe, it would've stretched out to encompass the old lessons as proper study went back into them—*proper* understanding of the ancient ways. His circle was the embrace. *Jeerah* and *Eksuh*." He looked up at the ceiling. "The stars were fixed for us to follow." He put his eyes on Abim. "Like stubborn children we've rebelled against what has been perceived as their tyranny. We've created rituals to sacrifice the celestial animals of the night so that we would no longer feel their influence. We've done so much, save one thing: accept our fate."

"My friend," Abim pleaded. "We come from the study of a woman's words spoken long ago. Even the stars aren't fixed. They have their time and movement. Prophecy is but a suggestion. Trust me, my friend. We have got to keep faith. We cannot let this crush us. Your speech…is dangerous."

Aƙuram sat silent. He let his wife's actions articulated for him. Tani stretched out her hand and lifted the dome from the second plate. Abim spied the revealed object out of his peripheral view. It's preserved bright colors flashed as if a burst of light detonated beside him. His head turned, slow like the hand counting the seconds on a clock. His neck locked into place, head aimed at the plate, eyes fastened to its presence. It was The Lovers card. Beautiful in its illustration's design. An African couple walked naked hand-in-hand. Beneath them was a winding path. A scene made of smoke swiveled out of their backs, most likely from an energy wrapped around their spines. The smoke filled the firmament above. Planets, stars, and moons came into existence. It was understood that the black cosmos was an extension of themselves. Out of this black couple came all that existed.

Abim's alcohol-induced perception evaporated, turned clearheaded. A distressing notion acted as a barrier, damming overjoyed sentiments that wanted to discharge through a physical expression of raised, clenched fists, shaking as he shouted with triumphant glee. Abim had been in search of The Lovers card for two years. His quest began when he'd procured the other cards of the deck, taken from a European order studying the science of African conjure, old magic. But all manner of exultation was contained, forced to shrink upon itself as Abim recalled his mark informing him the card was in wicked use by a mysterious man named *Ratamutum*. So, it was of no question to Abim as to how his friend was able to procure the incanted, prescient card.

Little surprise flickered within Abim as his higher instinct deduced the ineluctable facts that cloaked his long-time friend. Abim didn't resist revelation's tide. He didn't wrestle with the mystery's unshrouding. He was cut by it, hurt; but he embraced the truth no different than the dark of night accepting its dispersal by the faint hum of the early sunrise.

Abim's understanding was the border of the moment before and the moment after. What came next was swift action by Aƙuram, though Tani's movement was executed an instant before her husband's. All else seemed to move in a slowed motion as Tani raised her hand, twiddled her fingers, and spoke an inaudible incant. A black film covered the children's eyes. Their mouths started to drop, fear settling in as they lost sight.

Aƙuram snatched the metal weapon from the plate and slammed it through Abim's chest. The Moorish conjure man spit blood onto his food, and a few splotches spattered on Aƙuram's hand. The offending friend stood and clutched a fist in Efra's direction. A black and red beam bound her hands at her wrists. Aƙuram let go of the ancient needle and balled his fist behind Abim's head. A black and red beam constricted around his neck. Aƙuram drew his arm back in a quick manner, as if he was tugging on a chain. Abim jerked, slamming into the back of the chair.

Kamanni revealed a dagger and lodged it into Fashe's neck. The conjure man died instantly from his wounds and smacked face-first into his plate of food. Blood pooled out from his wound.

Robed mercenaries kicked open the door and stormed inside, crossbows up.

Haji and Feechi were killed with arrows to the throat and forehead.

Aƙuram and Abim winced in unison, but different purposes motivated their resonances. Abim gasped and screeched for air. Aƙuram whined and choked on angry tears. He put his lips close to his dying friend's ear and growled, "In your infinite wisdom, brother, you stepped through time and assisted the future. Do you know what this means?" Abim listened, but sound was having less meaning to his ears. Sight was blurred, and he did his best to keep his eyes on his wife and children. Mouth open. Tongue out and twitching. His eyelids flapped with the last exhales of his life. "It means the Great Alchemy *must* occur!"

Aƙuram's conjured noose tensed taut around Abim's neck. The tightening caved in muscle and bone that sounded like a string of thick, wooden sticks splitting. Abim's face froze. His eyelids raised and fixed. Eyes swelled and almost ejected from his skull. His tongue went limp, and then his body slumped like autumn leaves into a pile on the table in front of him.

Aƙuram opened his fist. His fingers trembled with trauma. His nose ran, and his eyes trickled tears. He stared at his friend's lifeless body. His conjured bind now dissipated from Abim's neck. Aƙuram's teeth chattered. He heard words scratching at his ears. It was Efra. She cursed him! Her children, blinded and spared of the sight of their father's murdered, lifeless body, clung to her tight. They cried. They hollered. Aƙuram's son, Been ah Kibir continued asking his mother why he couldn't see anything. He asked, "Why are Seizan and Ithun crying?"

Tani didn't answer her son. She simply held him, arms around his shoulders.

Aƙuram used an incant to tranquilize the tension shaking him.

Stewart Bloodworth, the Higher entered the dwelling as the robed bowmen encircled the dining table. In his hands was a bronze scepter crowned with a rock the size of a child's fist, and perfectly shaped as a globe. It was gray in color with red speckles arranged in an unsystematic pattern embedded in its surface. The spotted stone had a dampening effect on conjure and those that could wield it. Stewart Bloodworth, the Higher paid a steep price to be blessed for a small window of time to manipulate its power. He brandished the scepter and its stone around the room.

An invisible weight blanketed the conjure folk occupying the residence. The otherworldly binds wrapped around Efra's forearms dissipated, and the murk crowding the children's eyes dissolved. Efra cloaked her arms around Seizan and Ithun, holding them close and burying their faces into her torso. She looked at her husband's lifeless body, cautious not to share the gruesome scene with her children through a thought, though the red-spattered rock's influence was greater than her will.

Stewart Bloodworth and Aƙuram met eye-to-eye. The Fifth Order aristocrat shifted his gaze to a crossbowman and nodded. The robed soldier aimed and fired an arrow into Kamanni's skull. The conjure woman's head fell back, dangling over the chair. Aƙuram flinched with the make of the kill. An indignant expression filled his countenance, aimed at Stewart Bloodworth, the Higher. "We had a deal!" he snarled through clenched teeth.

A bowman draped a black hood was draped over Aƙuram's head. Stewart removed a one-shot pistol from his belt and aimed. He fired, and the cylindrical bullet broke through fabric and flesh, lodged into Aƙuram's heart, and killed him.

Seizan turned his head and witnessed Aƙuram's death. Viewing the callous kill put the young boy's eyes on his father's lifeless body. He broke free from his mother's embrace and dropped from his chair to his knees. He grabbed his father and tugged at his sleeves. *"Come back, Pa-pa! Come back to life!"* His words meant nothing to the dead. His brother Ithun spied their dead father through an open eye that was not smothered by his mother's tight clasp. He swallowed the loss, but he remained calm. He put his arms around his mother, squeezing as tight as she held him. His heart raced, and he was terrified.

Been ah Kibir stared in disbelief at his father's murder. He shuddered twice. Once as the bullet was fired into his father's chest. The second time came when Aƙuram's body slumped dead to the floor. The image of his father before being hooded was preserved in his sight. His father standing tall. On his feet. Been ah Kabir's mother embraced him tighter. She said to her son, "This is change, Been ah. This is alchemy. And we will all be better for it." Horror was branded on the seven-year-old boy's face. It burned into his eyes, pushed deeper into his mind. Forever. There.

Stewart Bloodworth, the Higher signaled three soldiers with a toss of his fingers. The men swarmed around Efra and Ithun, shouting at them. *"Come with us!"*

Seizan heard his mother and brother in distress and turned his head to face them. He attempted a jump in their direction, but a robed soldier caught him by the collar and held him back. Seizan wrestled with the hold, his feet scraping the floor. He outstretched his arms, reaching for his mother and brother who too struggled with the grapple of armed, robed soldiers. In no more than a flutter of the eye, it appeared Ithun crawled from one side of his mother to the other, defying the strength of one man and stretching his arm out farther to extend his hand to Seizan.

Heartbeat. Accelerated. Mind at its seat to overlook the soul and fasten itself to the cosmos. Palms out, lines glowing to connect to the ebbing, subtle tides of conjure. The young children defied the unseen and weighty veil of the scepter's stone's effects. The light streaking across the lines in Ithun's hands swelled, close to contact with the growing lines in his brother's palms.

"The Good God damn the strength of these savage, jungle warlocks!" cursed the robed soldier pinning back Seizan.

Closer. Their palms. Then, in no more than a flutter of the eye the three guards holding Ithun and Efra toppled onto one another as mother and child disappeared into the ethers. Seizan's face burst wide with surprise and horror at the sudden absence. The use of conjure against the suffocating effects of the scepter's stone caused a distortion in the atmosphere that sent a sharp change in pressure directed at the scepter's holder. Stewart Bloodworth, the Higher, lifted off his feet from the impact and slammed into the wall next to the door.

"The Good God damn you, jungle demon!" Seizan's captor yelled at him as he pushed the young boy into the wall. Seizan bounced and stumbled back toward the soldier with little control of his faculties. The soldier removed the crossbow strapped to his shoulder and smashed the butt of it across Seizan's face. The boy collapsed. His body sprawled out, hand landing on Aḱuram's body. The bright, green glow slithering across the palm of Seizan's hands seeped into Aḱuram. A spark flashed but was unnoticed. Other soldiers surrounded Seizan's unconscious body. They aimed their crossbows down at him and waited for movement. There was none. Seizan was still, face bloodied, broken, and bubbled with purple bruises from the single strike.

Stewart Bloodworth jumped to his feet and swung the scepter at Tani, holding it with both hands. Before his attack collided with her, Tani whispered the words, "This. Is. Alchemy…" She closed her eyes. The scepter's stone crown struck Tani in the temple, and her body crumpled to the ground. Been ah Kibir remained pinned in place and expression. He didn't feel his mother's grip loosen from around him. He stared at nothing. He didn't see the soldiers crowding around his father's lifeless body and Seizan's unconscious figure.

Been ah Kibir continued seeing his father standing, unhooded and staring at him. The vision remained locked even as he was bound and tossed into the dark corner.

Stewart Bloodworth collected The Lovers card and the ancient needle. He called three soldiers to his side. To their captain, he ordered the two boys be shipped to the New World. He gifted Tani to the captain and the remaining men, and then he left. Not too soon after, the captain ordered three of his soldiers to take Seizan's body to the slave stables. "Tell them we'll have another coming." The captain approached Been ah Kibir, knelt down, and slapped him across the face. "I've noticed how slow this one is. He might not be worth much. The other one is a fighter. He'll make a good worker. Young too," he noted. He stood and addressed the soldiers holding Seizan. "Hurry back. They'll be food enough to dig from. And you'll have your turn with the jungle woman's body. Go. Go, now." The men rushed through the door to attend to his commands. The captain ordered the table cleared of food, taken to the kitchen. "Put the jungle witch on the table. Open her legs and mouth. Everyone will have their time with her." The captain turned. He kicked Been ah Kibir in the gut. He knelt down quick to catch the boy's body. He held him up by the neck. "This is what happens, jungle boy, when your kind try and use their greater powers." He threw a closed fist into the child's face, caving in his cheek bone. Been ah Kibir's lower lip split and he spit blood. "Do you understand, neggar boy? Huh?"

He was propped up against the wall to watch.

The vision of his father upright and alive at the head of the table dissolved into the present. The whipping flames of the fireplace pulled on shadows like puppeteers working a marionette. The blaze never tugged the shade away from Been ah Kibir's corner, and the boy remained draped in shadow.

The scrumptious meal laid out on the table was substituted by his mother's limp body. An arm hung over one side. Her legs dangled over the long end. Her clothes were torn away, and he watched waves of men crawl feverishly over his mother like fire ants from a broken hill. His attention was half-conscious, but more of reality locked into place as he witnessed his mother's translucent spirit rise from the pile of men that desecrated her once-living, corporeal frame.

The men did not have eyes to see, and so her appearance transpired unshared by Been ah Kibir's vision. The men were distracted by the flesh, as it were. Tani's body expiring from life had gone unnoticed.

Her spirit glided over to her son who was now shaking with fear as his mother's afterlife approached. Been ah Kibir's mouth opened with the intent to holler, but Tani's naked spirit landed in front of her son and bent down. "Hush," she said in an eerie croon of her voice. "Hush…" she prompted again. When her otherworldly voice resonated in her son's ears, he calmed. Been ah Kibir paid no attention to the men engaged with his mother's physical frame. Her spirit said to him, "Have no worries for my body, my sweet boy. Those men cannot harm my soul, my spirit. My flesh is no longer my definition. This terrible happening has transformed me. This is alchemy. This is the change that must occur for us to rid the world of the cursed words made flesh." Tani smiled. "You will change too, my wonderful boy. Been ah Kibir. You will change." She tapped him on the nose, and he felt a warm liquid-like sensation press against him. "Your father changed. He was strong at birth under the name Aƙuram Duhu. That is a strong name, is it not?" she asked her son.

A calm now on his face. Eyes focused on his mother's specter, the boy nodded.

"Yes, it is," his mother acknowledged. "But your father and I were taken in by a beautiful nation called the Ifo of Africa. Your father and I were transformed in name. He became Ratamutum. Strong. Forever and always."

His name spoken. The body twitched, grunting to life. Ratamutum palmed the floor and lifted to his feet. Been ah Kibir spied his father, but Tani moved his attention back to her. She spoke, soft and with promise of transformation into conjure and all its grand power returned to the world.

Ratamutum walked up to the men violating his wife's once-living body. He balled a fist and conjured several black and red loops around the necks of the captain and soldiers waiting their turn. He pulled back, and the summoned ropes woven by the fabric of conjure tightened. Their necks popped, and their lives were extinguished in an instant. The other soldiers fumbled over one another as the killing of their captain and fellow soldiers were noticed.

Pants at their ankles, weapons out of reach, Ratamutum killed the remaining men with his binding black and red beams. He tossed the men left and right, slamming them into walls with the use of his conjure, beams fastened tight-to-death around their necks. The room became a whirlwind of bodies, and then the tornado settled with soldiers strewn out around the room, necks broken, bodies bloody.

Ratamutum approached his phantom-wife and son. Been ah Kibir turned his attention to the hooded, undead figure now standing next to Tani. She straightened her posture, and both parents stared down at their child. Tani was smiling. Been ah Kibir gazed at Ratamutum's sheathed head and saw his father's face behind the hood. The hanged man extended a hand down to his son, Been ah Kibir's bindings burned away without case of pain, and he accepted his father's hand, which felt warm. He was hauled to his feet, and then his mother's spirit said, "Come, Been ah. To the kitchen. Let us finish your meal as your father waits here for the bad men." Been ah Kibir followed his mother as Ratamutum sat at the table. He turned his head to

Abim, who was now on the floor. His dead friend.

Ratamutum stared at his wife's ravaged corpse lying on the table. The hood didn't shield him from the terrible sight. He took comfort in his wife's voice speaking to his son, nurturing. She was transmuted. Alive, and more in conjure than all could imagine. Soon he heard the rattling whispers of three Fifth Order soldiers ambling to the door. They laughed as they described dropping off the 'neggar' boy. The door opened, and the three men walked inside. Their perceptions didn't first perceive the actuality of the scenario. Then came the absence of their fellow soldiers and captain cavorting with the conjure woman. Sharpening into awareness was the grisly scene of snap-necked soldiers littered around the dining area. The two flanking soldiers only noticed Ratamutum when he throttled them to death with his invoked binds. Their necks sounded like shattering glass and acted as an alarm to the final soldier. His eyes exploded with surprise, and he pivoted to turn.

Two steps out the door was not far enough for the soldier to escape. A black and red bind circled around his neck. A robust force yanked him back into the cabin, through the air, over Ratamutum. The soldier's body crashed against the wall, continuing to choke on the bind squeezing life from him. Ratamutum stood. He walked over to the soldier, looking down at him as the soldier clawed at his neck, his fingers ghosting through the conjured bind. Ratamutum closed his fist harder. The bind constricted, and the hanged man wrenched his arm up. The soldier buckled as his neck was crushed, and then his body settled dead against the floor.

The bind disappeared.

Tani and Been ah Kibir, with his belly full, returned to the dining room. Ratamutum joined their side. He held his son's left hand as Tani let go and walked over to her body. She kissed its forehead and it burned to ash in a brilliant display. Tani breathed in and inhaled every particle of her embers. She returned to her husband and son and held Been ah Kibir's right hand. The family traipsed over the Fifth Order soldiers' dead bodies and walked out of the quaint cottage. Been ah Kibir walked hand-in-hand with his dead father and ghostly mother. He never got tired, and he thought it interesting when the walk continued over a long stretch of water without them falling in. Soon they came upon the shores of North Africa, but still his feet didn't tire from the walk. On they continued. Walking and walking.

Their journey ended in the sea of sand at the camp of a nomadic tribal nation of conjurers called the Ifo. It was night, and fires burned bright. A troupe of men wearing long robes and wide-brim hats made of straw encircled them. They carried spears and wore coverings on the lower half of their faces. They escorted father, son, and mother into the nation.

Little Been ah Kibir consumed the beauty resonant within the aura of the fires and shadows flickering off the housing in the encampment. The people, masked with cloth or a beautiful arrangement of colors painting the face, were like pillars that extended to the heavens. They stood with confidence, anchored in knowledge and power. Men and women were clothed in colorful trousers and skirts, cloaked in robes or long flowing blouses. The sword or the spear was the weapon of choice. For the higher-minded members of the nation, there was conjure.

Been ah Kibir and his family were led into the chief's residence. Selotes Bilísi greeted them with open arms as they filed into his home. He wore a gray robe with beige trousers and a long, black billowing shirt. Sandals were on his feet. He was old. He was very old, but conjure and will preserved him. His flesh was like reddened copper, polished and without blemish. His face was aged by wisdom, rectangular in shape. His long locks were gray like storm clouds, but the bushy hair that lined the sides of his face and covered his chin was red like hot metal.

Selotes Bilísi stopped short of the family presented to him and clapped his hands together. "Great praise to the transmutation!" he shouted surveying the beautiful frame of Tani's glowing, pellucid presence. "The beauty you have become." He turned his hands into fists when his eyes fell on Ratamutum. He observed the bullet wound tunneled into his heart, the bloodstain. "The rise," he stated. "The defiance in alchemy." Then he knelt in front of Been ah Kibir and said, "Your flesh and your spirit will be renamed, young boy. Your father is Ratamutum. Your mother is Duhu Firistess. They are no more, and yet they are much more." He tapped on Been ah Kibir's chest. "And you, little boy, you will be much more too."

Been ah Kibir's body shivered with a subtle tremor. His face brightened, and he waited for the moment of before to pass to now, and then be new forever after.

Selotes Bilísi tapped on the boy's chest again. Three times. Selotes Bilísi told the boy, "A powerful conjure man you will become. You will lead sentiment. You will alchemize feeling, passion. All the acts of transgression and misdeeds will be for you to usher and command. Henceforth you will forever be known as Ariq Haunts."

Ratamutum and Duhu Firistess bent to one knee and humbled their heads.

Selotes Bilísi rose and said to Ariq Haunts, "Welcome to our palace with invisible walls. The foundation of our castle is wherever our feet may touch. This is Domdaniel, young Ariq Haunts. This is Sudozion."

Lilac rain dripped onto the scene like tears. The rain became heavier, and time was swallowed up by a pale, violet fog that glimmered with a subtle whisper of cobalt blue. The scene closed to the eyes of an aimless spirit and a pair of focused eyes dreaming of the past.

24

Eyes opened. The room was blurred by moisture clouding Gordon's vision. He sat up in his chair, Spook in his arms. He sniffed, rose from the chair, and returned Spook next to Silver atop the alchemical chamber. Silver noticed Gordon's eyes, the melancholy articulated on his face. She said nothing, but her face replicated Gordon's countenance.

Gordon sat on the floor cross-legged and wiped his eyes. Spook opened. Across its black-mirror face scrolled the ancient text, *Shall we remain silent on the matter, Mister Goodspeed? Taste the gravity of choice as the space-time continuum's collapse sweats its flavor on the tips of our tongues. Swallow and bury it.* Silver read the words and her sadness thickened. She put her hand on the back of the raised mirror and rubbed it gently.

Gordon didn't answer Spook. He barely saw the words materialize on the screen. His head was distracted by the lingering scenes of the history he dreamed. He didn't jump back into Abim's body. He couldn't prevent the betrayal, the murder. And though he could sense Fey's spirit observing the history as she funneled through time and space, she too was helpless to avert the slaughter and enslavement.

History was immutable.

Gordon looked up at Spook as he remembered the significance the family held for the encased yumbo. Efra was his door to the world. Spook knew the family, but he was unaware of their gruesome fate, having been brought to the current time to assist *the Lilac Flame.*

Gordon then recalled an important fact to the history. "She's alive!" he declared to the yumbo possessing the arcane conjure-technology. Silver had little knowledge of what he referenced, but her face brightened. "Efra's alive, Spook!" He got up and returned to his chair. He leaned forward and rubbed his eyes. "Her son manifested conjure, despite the presence of that stone." He put his hands down and whispered to himself, "Sarinda Fallow's people use that stone…" He remarked putting his eyes back on Spook and Silver, "There's still a lot of history to view. We finally saw The Lovers card. That bastard Stewart Bloodworth took it." He was up again. In two strides he was standing over Spook and Silver. "Spook," he called. "I want you to pull up as much information on the Fifth Order as you can. They have a faction still operating, we might have a whereabouts for the card." Spook didn't respond. Silver looked up at Gordon with sorrow drooping her large eyes. Gordon acknowledged with a nod. He asked Spook, "Does your spirit have tears?"

Of course, Spook replied in the ancient text. *I'm happy that Efra is alive, in a sense. A son is with her. Ithun. Seizan, he… The deception. The betrayal by a brother-like friend. I knew them all. The adventures. The smiles. The fun to reconnect culture. I remember, but now duplicity hangs over it all like a pall. Being brought here a part of the scales tipping for the shroud to fall and reveal hidden intentions.*

The brightness in Gordon's face dimmed. He sighed, "Oh, Spook…"

Silver leaned her head against the obsidian mirror. *I don't blame you, Mister Goodspeed,* replied Spook. *I had a job to do. I have a job to do. I'll find you that information on the Fifth Order. Until then, let me hide as I cry.* Silver moved away from Spook's mystical, sable screen, off his console. The black mirror lowered and closed against the jeweled keys and The Judgment card. Silver felt cold with the loss of Spook up against her.

Gordon shifted his sight from Spook to the Alchemical Chamber. He thought about the capsule's construction and the ideals of the two that assembled it. *Was there a conflict of interest knowing the future?* He pondered on Fey, her actions and consequences. He backed up a few paces, pivoted, and surveyed the wall. A step forward, he put his hand on the concrete. He expressed a quick prayer, hoping it would glide through time and shield mother and son. Efra and Ithun. He backed away and took a seat on a stool. He continued facing the wall, and Silver flew to him and perched on his shoulder. Gordon continued watching the wall. He knew many conjure men and women fought back against the powers of slavery and needle factions looking to negate the African conjure culture.

Gordon hypothesized. *Efra. Ihthun.* He considered the notion that it might've been better to request Spook to sift through time for any strange tales concerning folk heroes using their ability to disappear into shadow to battle slave factions. Gordon reflected on one such folk hero. Supposedly, he was trained by his mother, too. His name was *Kuto.* His enemies called him *El Negro Lobo.* The Black Wolf. "If I could go back, reach back. I would become the Black Wolf. Maybe that was Fey and I. Perhaps, we meet in time again to fight back."

He removed the timepiece from his pocket and examined it. Then he observed the wall, making a wish that when he next dreamed of history, he would reunite with Fey and step through space and time to become legends in the past.

$\mathcal{P}$erhaps it was a perfect day, or night, as it were. It was hot, and the humidity painted droplets of sweat on the brows of the people wandering the streets in Water Bug Hollow. Despite that, Armand Gideon believed this night was ideal as he stood at the entrance of the area's only church, feet planted firmly on the top step leading to the door. His body faced Water Bug Hollow's main streets with his head cocked back, gazing up at the billowy overcast that shined with a cool, silky white glow as the moon fought to have its presence known. The clouds also blotted out the twinkle and shine of the heavenly bodies behind it. But like all curtains to a grand stage it could not keep the stars veiled for long.

Armand spotted a vulnerable area where the clouds had been parted and the stars performed in a proud manner to show off their light. He didn't see the clouds as too intrusive. He fabricated the notion in his head that the fog possessing the area lifted back up into the sky, at least most of it. But there still lingered a sliver of nature's breath surrounding the church. It thickened within the remainder of Water Bug Hollow, its body winding like a ghostly python through the streets and hovering inside alleys to shade illicit goings-on. But the fog did nothing to keep concealed a beacon of spirit that faded in and out, illuminating the airy murk even when some of its light receded. Armand had seen it before, days earlier. He could hear its hum even with a great distance between him and the pulsing light. As a result of the stitching ritual, the hum turned into distinct sounds, a voice speaking. It wasn't a hollow echo, or an eerie moan that resonated from the *ignis fatuus*. It was a distinct voice, comical in nature.

"Bring yo'se'f o'her!" it would say—*demanded*—if truth be told. Its sounds stuttered through a scratching static attempting to reach out from its realm to the Earthly physical. Armand stalked the throbbing, phantom sconce for the last few days, all in one place. He kept an eye on it as much as it beckoned for him. He was in his usual stance, puffing on a cigarette, staring out and listening to the same old lines of directional dialogue. It always spoke more once the light believed it had his attention. *"C'mon o'her, boy! Let y' woman do a rich-ale. Le's getta talkin'. Letcha woman know I'ma solja. Letcha woman know I'ma solja..."* And then he would repeat his words again. *"Bring yo'se'f o'her..."*

The red, black, and green skulls on Armand's necklace glowed bright in unison with the distant, hovering flare. Armand liked looking at the musical lightshow against his chest, watching the rhythms mix. The spirit's voice, and his skulls' light, pulsed. He wished he was a musician to see if there was a relevance to the measure and meter of the kindled palpitations. He desired to play along, but he was content with his conjure, the fulgent skulls, riding the irradiated flow.

The church doors opened behind him. The newly crowned Crossroads Queen, Lillian Eledas-Ghedemere, walked out and stepped up next to him. She was dolled up in her gypsy style, and in her hands was a miniature, iron pot. Inside the pot was an assortment of dwarfed versions of conjure tools used to bring forth the spirit of weapon wielders. These instruments were also crafted from iron. There pocketed within the maw of the iron pot were four glimmering railroad nails, a machete made to only eight inches, a pint-sized anvil, a diminutive hammer, a small shovel, and an arrow only six inches in length. Stuffed among them were two non-iron objects. One was a green and black cloth, and the other was a green and black wax candle.

Lillian gave a small raise to the miniature cauldron, holding it by its handle. She remarked, "All the necessities, Armand. Let's go have a talk with this soldier." She tipped her head in the beacon's direction.

Armand acknowledged Lillian's sentiment. He asked in a cordial tone, "Would you like for me to carry those, Miss Voodoo Lily?" He puffed his smoke and blew the excess away from Lillian. She handed the ceremonial pot to Armand and thanked him for the thoughtful gesture. He accepted and stepped down the stairs. Lillian followed. Her eyes traced Armand's frame, and she noted his clothes. Simple jeans and black shoes, but wore a white collared shirt. The collar was pointed up, and the two buttons under his neck were unfastened. His cuffs were unbuttoned as well, rolled and pushed back below his elbow. Around the white shirt he wore an opened, black vest with purple pinstripes. It was adorned with pockets to hold incanted curios or baubles, but remained empty at the moment. He was all conjured out to the nines, as was the saying from conjure folk.

In two quick steps, Lillian passed Armand, taking lead in the walk toward the shimmering beacon that only their attuned eyes could discern. They journeyed through streets layered with fog and thick with the tension of frustrated citizens bogged down by life's hustle, spinning in the hamster's wheel of indigence. Armand consumed his surrounding with wide eyes, and the visual meal made him nauseous. His physical frame was not the only part of him having a hard time digesting the scenery. His conjure did little to settle his stomach from the scene. He attempted to fast from the malnutrition caused by the destitution. But there was collation every time he looked out to commune with the beacon. Smoking didn't help, but he indulged.

Seeing was necessary. He had to swallow it. He had to taste it and let the putrescence that Water Bug Hollow had become sit in him, from mind to soul. Armand considered it worse than most cities because he knew there was conjure and culture buried beneath the dilapidated surface. He waded through Water Bug Hollow's impressive history from brutal plantation to black, residential area started and maintained by ex-slaves who participated in a triumphant uprising against their plantation masters. Perhaps all impoverished areas echoed Water Bug Hollow's story in one way or another. Armand had only just received an ancestral polish on his eyes to see conjure in the world. Should he step into other areas populated by downtrodden African-Americans—or the global African diaspora for that matter—he would probably spy the same happenings of buried magic acting as fumes to keep a moth-eaten, societal fabric tattered and mangy.

Lillian sensed the throbbing conflict in Armand. She slowed her steps to walk parallel to him. She observed Armand's stoic face. On the microscopic level there battled the emotions of disgust and melancholy hiding behind a mask of indifference. Her heightened instinct burrowed beneath his mask and perceived his true feelings.

"Armand-baby," she called him. "Water Bug Hollow is no different than your car." He turned to her with a surprised expression on his face. He'd been so lost in his thoughts, and so concentrated on keeping his face straight, he'd forgotten that another person was accompanying him on this trek. Lillian thought for a moment. "A hex stirs and perverts a hidden beauty rather than a blessing kindling a misshaped exterior."

Armand recovered from his initial surprise. He shook his head in agreement. "Yeah," he spoke up. "My mom has conjure." When he uttered the words there was a soft smile of pride on his face, and in his features, there resided a look of longing. "She snapped her fingers, Miss Voodoo Lily, and she made sure my car could putt-putt its way from California to Atlanta." He raised his cigarette to his lips. "That's an ugly car, ain't it?"

Lillian chuckled. She spoke a silent incant and burned his cigarette from existence.

Armand sucked on air. He made a face when no smoke swirled through his pursed lips. He checked his fingers, and his eyes barely saw the trailing ashes of the disintegrated cigarette. "Oh, come on, Miss Voodoo Lily!" he protested. "I need a polluted breath to calm my senses."

Lillian knocked her shoulder and arm against Armand. "Embrace those rising tides tingling your head and heart, Armand-baby. You're about to need every ounce of conjure kindling inside you. We have a spirit to talk to."

The blistering beacon waned in its shine, dwindling only to a flash of feelings that tickled Lillian and Armand's conjure senses. It was completely faded from anything resembling a light by the time their walk concluded at an alley on John Arthur Avenue. Up the road, on Washington Street, was the beat up remains of a building that once was a plantation house. After Curtis 'The Water Bug" Hollow's war changed the landscape into a free town for black people, it became a dining spot by day and an afterhours juke joint by night. It also provided rooms for townspeople and activities of ill repute. At present, it was the headquarters for one of the areas roughest street gangs called The Four In Hand Crew.

Night blossomed, and the building once known as Eve's Hallow leaked from its doorways the wild thugs and bullies of Water Bug Hollow's dregs. Mean mugs and snarls guarded the door. Cursing cutthroats swarmed around its exterior and bled into the streets. Their activity shaded by fog and shadow the farther they journeyed from their hub. Armand kept his eye on them, his heart racing to break sound. He wasn't scared of confrontation with the loud, local ruffians. There was just always something about the close proximity to the tension of balled fists, the potential for hurt and anger to explode into physical altercation. Something in him fed on it, and its psychoactive nutrients charged his internal motors. Perhaps it was Armand's personal closeness to an explosive expression, ready to rain riots on those who abused their authority to intimidate people of so-called lesser standing into subjugation.

Lillian's instinct deciphered Armand's locked stare. He was still from head to toe. Reflected in his eyes were the seedy activities blooming up the street. "In the alley, Armand-baby," she prompted him.

Armand turned to her, blinked his eyes, and came to. The tension in him released through a soft exhale. He nodded his head, agreed aloud, and then proceeded into the alley. Their higher senses perceived no one but them occupied the narrow passage space. Close to the center of the area was where they set their ritual in place. Lillian reached out her hand, mouthed an incant, and called the cloth stuffed into the small cauldron to her. The fabric swirled out of the iron pot, unfolded straight, and then settled on the craggily alley floor. Armand placed the cauldron down on the cloth.

Together he and Lillian placed the four railroad nails at the cardinal points of the iron pot. The pint-sized anvil was placed in the northwest quadrant of the spread. The small shovel lay at the southeast. The six-inch arrow rested in the southwest, its tip aimed in the same direction. The diminutive hammer was laid in the northeast. The machete-shaped dagger was arranged across the top of the iron pot, from one side of the rim to the other. The ritualistic weapon was off center to make room for the green and black candle.

Lillian spoke a flame into existence. It fluttered on the wick in shapes, morphing into the various tools laid out around the small, iron pot. She stood up and asked Armand if he was ready. "Be warned, Armand-baby, the spirit we call out of the ground is a soldier. He fought in the Water Bug Hollow freedom war. He's gon' be fiery. *Petwo.*"

Armand responded, "I'm *petwo* too, Miss Voodoo Lily!" He spread his arms out and inquired, "I mean, ain't we all got some fire in us?"

Lillian made a face and rolled her eyes. She let him know, "There is a stark contrast between having fire and being fire, Mister Gideon."

"Well, let's see what fire got to offer," he responded with a wink.

There was no need for debate. There was ritual work to do. Lillian closed her eyes and placed her hands on her chest, fingers interlocked. She recited, *"On this rock – we build a House of Trees – forest green and black in night – three days in of seven's sight! We conjure you – Warrior Gu – Ogu – Ogun! Under this night's clouded moon – we lay train track nails – into earth to create invisible rails for you to sail and be rebirthed into our physical world! We need your breeze to help defeat the fog and regrow the trees!"* The vibration of Lillian's words undulated into the darkness. The candle's flame brightened and increased in size, but nothing else stirred from ground or shadow when Lillian ceased her words.

Armand went to speak, but Lillian raised a finger to silence him.

"H'w 'bout'ch'all th'r?" a scruffy voice crawled from the darkness.

Armand looked to his left. A man walked up to them from farther down the alley. He wore a wide-brim straw hat, tattered blue pants, and a short-sleeve green shirt stained with dirt and marked with burns. He looked more old-man farmer than soldier. He had an oval head with patches of hair forming around his upper lip and chin. A pipe was in his mouth, and he smoked on something that wasn't earthly.

He asked, "Y'all call me out?"

Lillian faced him. "Yes, good soldier," she answered in a polite voice. "We did. We saw your beacon. Its light sounded like your voice."

"Was my voice, Missy!" he snapped. "I felt burden lift. I felt an ease I ain't felt 'round here in a long time. I could see again." The man walked to the alley entrance. He observed the knavery and mischief possessing the Water Bug Hollow streets. "The hell goin' on heah?" he questioned, eyes monitoring the rascality playing out from corner to corner. Armand and Lillian stepped up behind him. He turned to Lillian and asked, "Today August the twe'f? This don' look like a fest? Feels like that curse. Ol' reh'head, white w'man came prancin' in here, foolin' folk with her talk—all the devil's charm in her pretty smile."

Armand named, "Sarinda Fallows."

The man faced him, aimed a finger, and said, "Yeah—wicked w'man. *Wick-ed!* She honored the devil we put in the ground. Fog came slow, but it came. Blinded me and sum otha speeree. We were *sòldas.* Kept eye on Hallah Bug, even after the war. There was se'n uv us." He held out his hand to Armand. "Name's Haw's Jawj," he introduced himself.

Armand shook Horace Georg's hand. "Hello, Mister Horace Georg. Name's Armand. Armand Gideon." He held a hand out to Lillian and acquainted, "This is Miss Lillian Eledas-Ghedemere, called Voodoo Lily, current Queen of the Mississippi Crossroads."

Horace Georg's brooding decorum livened. He faced Lillian at attention, a soldier ready to serve. He bowed at the waist, arms pressed flush to his side. "Ma'am!" he addressed, standing straight. "Haw's Jawj! Helluva fighter with a bayonet," Horace advertised. He relaxed. "I got many of them crocodiles. Shot 'em or stab'em dead." He again faced the rough, choleric etiquette sweeping into the streets and blending with the fog. "Curse still lingers," Horace commented. He looked at Lillian and asked, "You two he'p lift the curse 'round my way?"

"No, Mister Georg," Lillian answered. "We're representatives of a conjure community, or *nasyon*, that assisted in cleaning up the hexes that plagued Water Bug Hollow church. We intend to clear the remaining hexes."

"Cahnja folk?" Horace contemplated aloud. "Yeah, we had awr blessin' in us. Curtis did. No real magi'. A rich'ale uv prayer to…to what'n'eva's out there. We had a sense of fight, a speeree hungry for freedom, change things. We embraced that." He smiled as he reminisced about the days of battle and bloodshed to secure Water Bug Hollow's free-state future. "We killed them crocodiles and got our freedom. Good and dead, we kill 'em jokers." He looked at Armand and Lillian, wide smile still on his face. "We didn' wait for no guv'ment war boys to come through. We *was* a blessin' for this area. Magi' and rich'ale sometimes got two feet, a rifle, and a de'term'nation to be free. Tha's us. Man, woman, and child." Then he made note, "I could read and write. I could," he emphasized. "Wasn' whut I's heah to do. I's heah to slay crocodiles, bring peace to the area. We'd los' watchal got now. That true, Afri' magi' got caught up in the brushfire of them harsh years of slavery—mos' uv us, anyway, cut off from that culcha. But we had awr magi', awr kinda cahnja." His smile faded as he continued observing the wild scene in front of him. There was laughter, but it was coated with a thick layer of anger, tension ready to burst and hurt someone. It wasn't carefree or attuned to the moment of freedom. It was a cloak worn over frustration and hostility. "I don' like what I see here. It don' feel free."

Armand and Lillian remained silent, allowing the spirit named Horace Georg to feel out the area, sweeping it with an expression of hurt and disgust watering in his eyes and scowled up on his face. Armand's instinct buzzed. It formed into a thought and transfigured into words on his tongue. The silence was broken then as Armand asked, "You said you're a part of seven soldiers buried in the soil, which is part of your haunting and protective work?"

Horace didn't look away from the street dealings, but he answered in an enthusiastic tone. "Oh, yeah, young man!" he perked up. "White folk di'n set one foot 'nside Watah Bug Hallah. Sho' luh to talk deviltry 'bout us, though. We was buried on the property to protect the area." He beamed at Lillian and added, "We had there then a blessin' made over us. Folk called in from Mar'lan' did the magi'." He shook his head, crossed his arms, and put his attention back on the people of the night. "That red-haired harpy brought in the fog. Had that blood rock. Foul mouth with curses and hexes all in it. He'pt her traipse in. Fog got thick over time. First thickenin' came with the church built, 'specially with the dis'greem'nt 'tween two men—a reverend and a piano man. Angah lingahed 'bout. Them two men killed one 'nutha. Reverend forced himse'f on a young girl. Was, uh, like, uh, devil's sacrifice, stren'thnen the devil already buried here." He thought for a moment and then amended, "Y'all put end to that fog. Put them two fellas to rest." He took the pipe from his mouth and continued, "The Jakobi fog came up afta them fellas kill' one another. Awr protection was pushed down. Hol' land choked when them bones of Patricia Gale Freda were scattahed." His eyes looked on, but he was seeing something else now, a tragedy near twenty-five years old. "Them bones not all dugged down togethah. Them devils made her Aw'saw. Split her up like him, they did."

Lillian and Armand turned their whole body to the risen spirit.

"My father mentioned that name to me!" Lillian exclaimed. "They killed her…" It wasn't a question. She knew the answer. Her instinct deciphered the knowledge that exuded from Horace's spirit as if she was reading tossed bones or shells. Hexers didn't just dig her up, perform a ritual on her bones, and scatter them. They'd killed her. Lillian saw a shadow of the past form in her head as if it was a memory. The scene was blurry, but there stood black-suited men wearing surgical face coverings surrounding a man wearing a plague mask. The hazy recall transmuted into moments spanning no quicker than seconds. The men rained down a frantic assault on Patricia Gale Freda, horrific in all ways. She'd already been accosted by them sexually. Now, they stabbed her with hexed needles, shouting curses and slurs at her. Their voices were muffled, but Lillian's instincts deciphered the sounds. The blurry scene faded away before Patricia's grisly dismemberment occurred. Lillian clenched her teeth, and anger made her body rattle.

Horace shook his head. "Did more than that, Miss Voodoo Lily," he interjected. Not aware of her higher sight having peered into the past, Horace explained, "Split that woman's 'lection. Split her votes," he noted. "Didn' make candidate. Them boys got they folk to help get a weaker opponent as the runner. She was supposed to be guh'nah queen 'round these parts. She had 'nishative to keep the devil's town from swallowing the Hallah. E'en wit'aut bein' guh'nah-queen, she had plans to uplift Curtisland. But them needle boys wasn' havin' that. They had plans for Curtisland too. Good ol' boy plans—plans they been wan'nuh put out. So, they went to work on her, limb from limb—scattered her bones and put curse on 'em." His eyes panned the area and he revealed, "Them bones buried in six places 'round these parts. A pile of her bones." He peered into the white, murky cloud that hung through the streets. Horace made mention, "Fog got to be the way it is now after that. Thick. Smotherin'."

"Where are her bones, good soldier?" Lillian inquired with a strong urgency in her voice.

Horace faced Lillian, countenance bright with enthusiasm. "Oh, Miss Voodoo Lily!" he exclaimed. "You and your hunter here gon' track them bones down, dig 'em up? Give them a blessin' to move on. Reconstruct her spirit." He nodded his approval. "That sho'nuff gon' sweep away this fog. Let us ol' blind *sòldas* see again." His face went somber, eyes back on the timeworn Eve's Hallow. "First bones buried there. Sho' is. That's why I don't feel freedom there no more."

"And the other bones, Soldier Georg?" asked Lillian. Her voice was humble but determined.

Horace's eyes grew as big as silver dollars. "The other bones, Miss Voodoo Lily?" he said with a growling chuckle. "Aintchu you guessed? That's where all these boys setup shop—them rough boys, gangs. Curse live hardest where these self-hateful folk roam." Lillian and Armand stepped out onto the sidewalk. They were drawn to the former house of soul and jazz once called Eve's Hallow, but they took no step forward when it was in full view. Horace walked up behind them and continued talking. "You got Wash'ton Av'nue. Ja'n Adams Drive. Jef'son Street. B'nj'min Franklin Street. Ham'ton B'l'vaad. Mad'son Drive. All a buryin' spot."

Lillian pivoted toward Horace Georg and thanked him, calling him a good soldier once again. She said to Armand, "We have to report this to my mother and father and the Fable Avenue Elders."

Armand confirmed with a head nod. He and Lillian started their pace away from Horace Georg when the spirit called, "Hol' up, young man! Hol' up and come back 'round here."

Armand paused from taking the next step forward. He turned around, facing Horace Georg's specter. The old soldier placed his pipe back in his mouth. Armand said in a respectful tone, "Yes, Sir?"

Horace puffed on herbal magic, and smoke billowed from his pipe. He waved Armand closer, and Armand obeyed the spirit. "You want me to teach you how to be a *sòlda*, don' you?"

"Yes, Sir…" Armand repeated.

"You know I can't do that, don' you?"

Armand nodded his head. "Yes… Sir…"

Lillian moved her head to the side, and she witnessed Armand beam a subtle smile. She looked at Horace Georg and noticed the soldier react to Armand's gesture. The spirit took his pipe out his mouth and jabbed the mouthpiece toward Armand. He asked, "And you already know why, don' you?"

Armand said for the fourth time, "Yes, Sir!" But, Armand didn't just repeat the words; he continued and presented an answer. "Because as a great soldier, I'm truly a hunter, a tracker in that role," he relayed with proud conviction.

Horace Georg looked at Armand with a raised eyebrow. "Yeah… Yeah, you are. You come back and see me, young man. I got a story for you. An Afri' story," he clarified. "Mwindo Epic," he named. "Also, gon' teach you some Liar's Dice. We don't play for sport. Never did. No, we play for souls, you heah? We play for souls."

"I'm sure, good soldier," said Armand, bowing at the waist. "I will return," he assured Horace Georg, standing straight.

Horace walked back to the alley. "Keep them rich'ale items down there," he requested. "I like to step in and out of this world at will. Them folk ain' gon' disturb it."

Lillian promised, "We'll leave the items, good soldier."

Horace thanked her, and then he watched as Lillian and Armand walked away. When the color of their frames turned to shadows and blended with the fog, he faded back to his side of existence. Up the street, Armand and Lillian's small and measured steps hurried into a sprint. Their hands locked together. They wanted to defy the fog and all the pain it brought, and so they laughed at it. Revolution was infectious, and Lillian and Armand's giddiness carried them up the stairs and through the church doors with a thunderous opening. The pulpit was empty, though controlled flames of conjure danced on the end of candle wicks.

Armand and Lillian composed themselves. Lillian's instinct reached out. A portrait of the small council room in the back was drawn up in her head. The room hosted her mother and father, Reverend Pouvwa, and the Fable Avenue Elders. Papa Solomon stood against a wall, hands in his pockets, fedora domed over his head. Next to him was Benny Jah. There also was Neyeli Campbell. There too was the Lilac Flame himself, Mister Gordon Goodspeed. He was on the other side of the room, resting against the wall with his arms folded. The vision dripped away, and Lillian grabbed Armand's hand again and led him down the aisle. She said in an excited manner, "They're still in the back! Come on!" They rushed through the door leading to a narrow hallway as fast as spirits. Their sprint slowed and came to a halt outside of a door left partially open by a mere crack. Armand smacked up against Lillian's back, forcing her into the wall. She braced herself with her hands, and the two of them laughed loud enough to stir the curiosity of the room's occupants. Though, with high instincts blooming in the conjure folk in the room, no one had to guess who lay in the hallway on the other side of the door.

Simaetha jumped to her feet, happy to see her daughter. She wore a long-flowing, purple gown that shimmered with gold glitter. Atop her head was a yellow papier mache crown. She twiddled her fingers and mouthed an incant that opened the door wide, revealing her daughter and her sweetheart, Armand, straightening their posture.

Lillian put a curious eye on her mother, mostly spying the make-shift crown resting atop her braided hair. "Momma!" she exclaimed. "What is that silly thing doing on your head?"

Simaetha embraced her daughter, bubbling with delight. She stepped away from her hug and said, "I have accepted—" she turned to Maman Anansi who was seated at the head of the long table, "—with Maman Anansi's blessing—" she faced her daughter and concluded, "—the title of O-Jewel Queen of Water Bug Hollow. I will be at your father's side, as he will be O-Jewel Governor." She tossed an eye roll at Satchel "Old Goon" and remarked, "Your father has an aversion to the use of 'king' as a title."

Satchel "Old Goon" bounced up from his seat. "You're one to speak, Simaetha-baby!"

"Well, I got over myself and accepted my title as 'queen'," she rejoined. "Lady Arachne will be Matriarch-Ambassador for Fable Avenue. This will be a most wonderful union." She looked at Lillian and explained as she adjusted the papier mache crown, "This silly thing, Lillian, is just us Elder-folk having a bit of fun. I proclaimed there should be a ritual besides Maman Anansi knocking a cane on the floor and a fist on the table."

"I came prepared," Maman Anansi spoke up. "I made that crown before I arrived."

The Elders laughed. The younger generation had half-hearted smiles on their faces as they rolled their eyes. That's when Armand noticed the metal armor piece fastened to Benny Jah's arm. He also spotted two items on the table. An African mask and a six-inch, wooden doll of an African woman, twirling in a dance, sword in one hand and a quarterstaff in the other. The items would come into play, but Simaetha's questioned, "You have something?" Her eyes went up and down, scrutinizing the eagerness twitching on their faces. She deduced, "Information?"

Lillian and Armand's features pivoted to stern. Armand put his hands on his belt in front of him. His legs were spread, and he leaned his upper body to the right. His eyes went slender in contemplation, but he didn't speak. He turned to Lillian and let the Crossroads Queen notify the room of what they'd discovered. Lillian looked at her father and told him, "Papa, Armand and I came across some disturbing news about Patricia Gale Freda. We followed the beacon Armand spotted, and we conjured an old soldier from the Plantation War. A man named Horace Georg. He and six other soldiers are buried here in Water Bug Hollow. Rituals were done over their graves so their spirits would protect the area. Folks versed in conjure, from Maryland, came to do the blessing. But Miss Fallows honored the devil buried on the grounds, Elias Jakobi, the slave owner taken down. His residue produced the fog, and, little-by-little, it grew."

The story caused a reaction in the other conjure folk in the room. Their upper bodies extended forward, hanging on Lillian's words. They'd heard much of the story, but not its causes and effects, and Lillian had yet to bring the story to its biggest revelation.

"There was an election held in the early nineties that would decide the fate of Water Bug Hollow, as Jakobiville grew from a small area itself— springing forth in the fifties to now," Lillian continued. "The descendants of the slave owner Elias Jakobi regained power, down to the very mayor that commands the political forces residing over this Louisiana region. They've been a political dynasty, ruling since the sixties. Patricia Gale Freda wanted to keep Water Bug Hollow independent, as the fighting spirit that freed it. This didn't work, but Miss Freda never had a chance. The fog encroached and became thicker." She looked at Satchel "Old Goon" and said, "Papa, you told me that when conjure soldiers were sent in to assist, night doctors took them out quick, something vicious."

Satchel "Old Goon" nodded. His eyes were on his daughter, but his vision recollected those days of war. "Yes, Lily," he said. "We sent conjure folk from all *nasyons* to keep ritual and prayer surrounding Water Bug Hollow. Hex was too thick by then. We wasn't rollin' with the power we got now that the Lilac Flame and Cobalt-Blue Spirit are among us. She ran for office without real protection."

"They set her up, Mister Eledas," Armand spoke up. "Set her up real good. First, politically. They railroaded her political intentions. Some from her own party in on it, too. I'm sure we'll find needles at the end of that clandestine act. Doesn't matter. Party names mean nothing. All loyal to the needle," Armand remarked. "And defeating her wasn't enough. Those bullies snatched her up, raped and beat her, and then they dismembered her." Looks of disgust discharged on all the faces in the room. Armand tightened his teeth. He couldn't finish his sentiment.

Lillian concluded, "They put a hex on her dismembered body. They celebrated and buried her cursed bones in six strategic places in Water Bug Hollow. Each burial ground rests directly where the Water Bug Hollow gangs assemble."

Simaetha removed the paper mache crown from her head. She crumpled it, and her face did the same, wrinkling into a dour mien. She first looked at Papa Solomon, but then her gaze rested on Fable Avenue's Grand

Dame, Maman Anansi. The matriarch simply presented a nod at the newly elected-blessed O-Jewel Queen. Simaetha stepped back to the table. She lifted the African mask that was carved from her artistry, and the wooden doll gifted to her long ago by a friend of her father. She returned to Armand and Lillian and presented the items. The African mask was given to Armand. Simaetha handed the wooden doll to her daughter.

Joy sprang up on Lillian's face as she clutched the doll her mother conferred on her. *"Dans-Dans!"* Lillian exclaimed. She gripped the doll and held it up as if she'd won a prestigious award. "I left her at home! I'm so glad you brought her for me, Mamma." She threw her arms around Simaetha and declared, "I'll need her for my new altar at the crossroads." Stepping back from her embrace, she said, "I…I wanted her to keep a blessing of protection from afar, but I'm so happy she's here." Lillian twirled.

Simaetha peered at Armand wiping his hand over the mask granted to him. She went to speak, but Armand looked up from tracing the mask with his fingers and interrupted the O-Jewel Queen's words. "Miss Ghede—" he stopped and corrected Simaetha's title, *"O-Jewel Queen* Ghedemere…this is the very mask a man in my dream wore. The dream from my stitching ritual," he clarified.

"I know, Armand," she replied. "Maman Anansi and Madame Jeliya helped me reconstruct your dream." She assured him, "I didn't pry. I only saw quick images. I saw the man in the mask, and I crafted that item for you. It's been blessed." She looked at her daughter and Armand. "In your hands, you each hold a lethal weapon crafted into ornate culture, and refined by conjure." Simaetha revealed, "You're deputies now. We need you to be our eight legs and deliver venom to our enemies in Water Bug Hollow, so sayeth a sister of the House of Weebu."

Satchel "Old Goon" said to Maman Anansi, "Two members of the Gwuinee family will be flying into New York once we remove the hexes and procure Water Bug Hollow. One of them is a cousin by marriage. His name is Terrence. He's from that Tzidkiyahu family. The other is a woman by the name of Naamah Mbu. Her father's from an old line going straight back to Africa." Satchel "Old Goon" aimed a finger, waving it between Lillian and Armand. "I'd like a full recovery of Patricia's bones quick as a deer's dodge."

Lillian agreed, telling her father, "Yes, Papa. We will carry out you and Mamma's orders."

Armand nodded, still in a gunslinger's posture, one hand on the front of his belt, the other dangling at his side with African mask in hand.

Simaetha suggested to her daughter, "You should keep the nkisi clipped to your hip at all times. She will give you strength."

"Yes, Mamma," Lillian answered her mother. She noticed Armand's reaction to the word 'nkisi' to describe the intricately carved, six-inch doll in her hand. He held up the mask and grinned. She knew what he was thinking, no higher instinct needed. She leaned into him with a wide, mischievous grin. "Oh, Mister Gideon, it seems like you've stepped into the role of one of your childhood heroes from that beloved comic book *Iboju Boy and Nkisi Girl*." She pointed at the African mask in his hands and held up the nkisi doll in hers. "Your mask, my Iboju Boy, and this here nkisi doll," she elucidated. Her face lost its grin, and she warned, "But, we're not playin' pretend. There are people who'll fight us to the death; and we'll be tested to defend ourselves."

Armand traced the mask with his eyes. He winked at Lillian and said, "That's fine, Miss Voodoo Lily. I got plans for these bullies."

Gordon bounced off the wall. He conjured his Chokwe-like African mask around his face. "That's right, kid," Dooley spoke up. He burst into a cloud of cosmic dust that burned into lilac sparkles, and he re-formed directly in front of Armand. The mask dissolved, revealing Gordon's natural face. "We all got masks to wear, sun," he teased. He aimed his head at Benny and joked, "That's the other Nkisi Girl, considering he got that armored trinket on his arm."

Benny stayed against the wall. Through the quiet laugher bubbling through the room, even from his sweetheart, Neyeli Campbell, Benny retorted, "Let's head up a game of Ogun Tarot, kid. See who got what."

Gordon went into his pocket and removed his phone, pretending to answer it. "Hold on! Hold on, sun!" he shouted back at Benny, raising his hand at him "It's Cedron. He says he's coming over to knock you out again, and I gotta save y' hide." Gordon chuckled, looking back at Armand. He explained, "My brother got a little messed in the head from a villain of ours. Knocked Benny out cold. I came through, saved him."

Armand laughed back. Neyeli comforted Benny who was rolling his eyes. Armand said to the Jamaican born youngster, "I like that shine on your arm, Benny Jah."

Benny snapped, "Captain Conjure over there sure gonna get a feel for the shine if he keeps mouthin' off."

"You boys behave!" Maman Anansi warned in a playful tone, though there was a subdued severity in her words. She looked at the others in the room and announced, "We can adjourn this meeting. I have to get back to Queens. It's late."

The gathering broke into smaller groups as they filtered out of the room. Benny and Gordon pushed one another around playfully, Neyeli there to see things didn't go too far. Lillian was enveloped by her parents, and while she was caught in the middle of them, Armand slipped outside for some time alone with his mask. He thanked Simaetha for the curiosity he received as he walked by her and Lillian. The Crossroads Queen allowed Armand to have time for himself. Stitching rituals, personal conjures, summoned spirits and young men possessed with cosmic entities, and that wasn't the half of what he'd experienced. He needed a quick breath.

Papa Solomon took a seat next to his sister and put his hand on her arm, keeping her from standing. "We're ready for a strike," he informed her. "Martin and Macario have been tailing Wyatt Jakobi, and they are about to make a bust on him."

Maman Anansi whispered in return, "I'll prepare the house for interrogation. I'll let Stephanie know. The absence of our children has gone on far too long. I want to give their parents some assurance that we're doing all we can to get them home safe. They've been more than patient, above and beyond the word. But I want my next update to them to be one that says they can see their children again." Papa Solomon agreed. He promised his sister that he would soon have positive news for her to relay.

Lady Arachne stood in the corner of the room, resting between Albert Banneker and Reverend Mathieu Pouvwa. She leaned toward the reverend and whispered something to him. He nodded his head, approving of a suggestion made, and he hurried outside to find Armand. He wasn't the first to surround the young man. Benny Jah and Neyeli Campbell were there with him. Gordon Goodspeed too.

The reverend waited at the door, listening to the youth. He admired their talk, and he let them continue on without his 'grown up' interruption. He liked seeing the youth from this angle. It was far different from when he was a detective.

Benny being teased moved into needling comments made toward Armand. They were congratulating him on earning his conjure and surviving the stitching ritual. "Man, you look like a guy who'd just lost his virginity." He put an armored arm around Armand as best he could, considering their height difference. "How you feel, kid?"

Armand leaned on the railing, falling easily out of Benny's attempted embrace. "Well, sir—Benny," he began. "It *was* much like losing my virginity, if I must say. Shit! I was nervous—wondering if I could perform." Neyeli, Benny, and Gordon chuckled. "But when it was all said and done, I embraced it. I went along for the ride, and it was a helluva ride. Took all my energy out. And if I can remember right about my actual virginity loss, the same it had in common, I slept very well for a long time—all that energy out of me." The group erupted in laughter again. Benny elbowed Armand's ribs. "Careful with that heavy thing!" said Armand through a chuckle.

"Right?" replied Benny. "Hey, we're gonna hit a conjure club in Harlem." He turned to Gordon and remarked, "Unless you're goin' home to be the sulking hero." He made an exaggerated sad face and asked, "Or do you have homework to do, traveling through time in dream?"

Gordon tilted his head back and pointed up at the clouds. "Right through there, sun. That's where I'ma take you. I'll take you up there like I did our friend Bryce Cadogan." Benny made a face. Gordon smacked him on the chest. "He called yesterday. He said he wants his gauntlet back," he ribbed.

Benny flapped his lips. "Please!" he huffed. "I took this back for the Moors who made it."

Addressing Benny's question to him, Armand declined joining them at the club. "I got homework of my own," he stated. The skulls on his necklace resonated brightly in their colors, humming in and out with rhythm. "I got a conversation to finish with the spirit we saw tonight. I got a story and a game to learn." Armand's demeanor morphed into a far more earnest vein. "I learned about this place. In dream, in books. Them boys out there making ruckus in the streets, making this place unsafe?" he phrased. He shook his head and said, "Those unfortunate souls ain't the scum that got a foothold on Water Bug Hollow."

"No, not at all," Benny agreed. "Those bastards live in high rises wearing suits, buying and selling corporations, passing off hexes as diabolical laws with only one thing in mind."

Neyeli took up, "The destruction of this sacred land by needle and curse."

Gordon warned, "Step cautiously, though. These cats out here ain't the real villains, but they ain't friendly either."

"Yeah, I know that," Armand concurred. "I've seen their fangs. They're almost as dangerous as them needles you all go on about."

"Don't you worry, sun," Gordon spoke. "You got allies. We'll take the raincheck, but we'll see you another night, Armand. Be careful out there." Armand assured Gordon he'd be okay, that he knew his conjure. "Have Lillian conjure up Dinclinsin through Ogun Tarot. I'm sure she know how. Help you put that new conjure to a test or two, kid." Then he turned to Benny and gave him a few soft pounds against his chest. "Race you to the Harlem club!" He tapped a final time and then popped away in a cloud of lilac-glittering dust. Benny showed his annoyance by pursing his lips and rolling his eyes. Before he could say anything, Gordon popped back into existence. "I'm sorry, man. Let me make this easy for you. Give you a fighting chance." His cosmic suit folded over his clothes, mask and all. He lifted into the air quick as a flash, body bursting into the spirit of the lilac flame. Dooley disappeared through the clouds, a soft glowing streak pulsing among the gray billows above, crossing over the Louisiana sky.

Benny huffed, "Sometimes he's just a smug prick."

Neyeli patted Benny on the shoulder. "Let him have his moment. He's happy. He's spent time with Fey."

"He spent time with Fey?" Armand blurted, his gaze taken away from Dooley's flight.

"Her spirit," Neyeli clarified. "Through space and time." She looked at Benny. "Let's see if we can give him a good fight. He's probably just getting to the crossroads." The two took off. They got to the crossroads house, entered and raced through. Outside, on the porch, Neyeli and Benny looked up to confirm her suspicions. Dooley's comet-like streak was just crossing over. Benny pulled Neyeli back into the house. He shut the door and initiated the knocking ritual. He opened the door. They were on Fable Avenue. They charged outside and down the brownstone's doorsteps. Neyeli made a pivot to rush down the street to Benny's family van. He grabbed her by the arm and stopped her. She looked down at his steel grip latched around her bicep. It felt like his flesh rather than the metal that fashioned the gauntlet. Blessings with incants were wonderful in that sense.

Benny smirked. He said to Neyeli, "Hold on. Let the van stay there." Benny put his ability to control gravity to use. He elevated his personal conjure with the blessings unlocked within the consecrated armor piece. He pulled Neyeli close, holding her tight. She put her arms around him, and she could feel her weight lighten. Their physical forms turned translucent, and a whipping wind whirled up around them. Their bodies faded, transfiguring into coils of air that funneled and lifted up into the sky. Dooley would beat them to Harlem by a long, long stretch, but he would be impressed with how his friend Benny pushed his conjure ability.

Back on the church steps in Water Bug Hollow, Armand stood by himself. A single finger was poked through the mouth on the African mask, and he twirled it like a gunslinger would a revolver. Reverend Pouvwa made his presence known, and Armand halted the spin of his mask. He heard the Reverend say, "You young ones give this former detective some hope. Bright spirits knowing their potential wasn't always what I saw out of the youth." He walked out of the door and onto the steps.

"Hello, Reverend Pouvwa," Armand welcomed.

"Hi there, Armand," the reverend replied. He conjured a pear into his hand and presented it to the young man. "Here. Have this."

Armand accepted the delectable gift. "Why, thank you, Reverend," he acknowledged. "Gifts all around for me tonight." He took a bite. The sweet juices splashed against his tongue, and the fruit's skin and flesh were chewed and swallowed. Armand was filled with a revitalizing sensation, as if waking from a well-needed sleep. "Ain't that something, Reverend?"

Reverend Pouvwa leaned against the opposite railing. He folded his arms and said, "I thought you could use that. Maman Anansi, with Madame Jeliya's assistance, deciphered that the fruit has healing qualities. I hear you don't have an altar and ritual as of yet to help regenerate the vitality your conjure can take from you when used. There's always the fruit."

Armand took another bite and swallow. "I thank you, again, Reverend," he restated with the same polite tone.

Reverend Pouvwa placed his hands in his pockets. He crossed his legs at the feet as he continued leaning on the railing. "You're very much welcomed, young man." He stayed silent, observing Armand as he ate, turned, and looked off into the distance at the Water Bug Hollow area. His eyes were in the direction he'd come from. He'd hope to see the spirit of soldier Horace Georg walk out of the shadows.

"Mister Eledas did a ritual of sorts with shells—or bones," Reverend Pouvwa attempted to recall. His face twisted in frustration. "He did something I'm not too familiar with," he uttered low, saying it mostly to himself. "I feel like you and I are much the same, Mister Gideon. In that manner."

Armand turned and faced Reverend Pouvwa. "I suppose you're right, Reverend. You are right in that regard. We're just strangers in all this strangeness, but there's still something familiar about it. It ain't like somethin' out of a dream, recalled after waking up."

"It's like coming home for the first time in a long time," Reverend Pouvwa finished.

"Yep, yep," Armand agreed. "Indeed, Reverend." They shared a chuckle. "That stitching ritual, huh? I was up against a giant scorpion." He palmed the middle skull on his necklace, lifting the decorative piece altogether. "Culled these things out of it. I fought it, took it down, of sorts. You?"

"I was a farmer," the reverend answered with a proud smile. "I was tending to crops, trying to keep rodents and an army of insects off them, making sure they grew. It was like spinning plates. Some kind of video game, or something. It just got faster and faster, all manner of pests just coming in. I got it though. I got the hang of it, tending to the garden and fending off the troubles."

"Yeah, yeah. Had to, right?" Then Armand remembered the reverend's initial statement. "You said something about a ritual? Done by Mister Old Goon?"

Reverend Pouvwa shook his head. "Oh, yes. I got some information for you. Mister Eledas did some figurin' through a ritual, and he'd got some instructions for you, concerning my fruit. Lady Arachne reminded me to tell you. Mister Eledas said you should bury the seeds of the fruit in gangland territory. Let them grow something healthy. Be healing and nurturing."

Armand nodded his head in agreement. He looked over his shoulder into the fog gripping Water Bug Hollow. "I'll drop some of them magic seeds right where Patricia's bones are buried." He faced the reverend and smiled. "That sound good, Reverend Jack?" he called him.

Reverend Pouvwa bounced off the railing. He patted Armand on the shoulder. "That'd do just fine, Mister Gideon."

The door opened. There was Miss Voodoo Lily. Armand looked at her and beamed. "There she is. The Queen of the Crossroads," he announced. He put a sly eye on the reverend and remarked, "We three represent a blended family, of sorts."

"Of sorts, Armand-baby," Lillian replied. "Reverend, how are you?"

"I'm fine, Miss Lily. I was just discussing the healing qualities of my fruit to Mister Gideon here," he summarized. "I'm carrying orders from the Elders to bury the seeds out there where the fog is dense in Water Bug Hollow."

Armand walked down the stairs to give Lillian room to step out of the church. She passed through the door, complimenting Reverend Pouvwa's idea. Armand chimed, "I figure we could dig up them hexed bones of Miss Patricia Gale Freda, and we could drop the seeds from the good Reverend's fruit into the soil. Bury that in their stead."

Lillian put her hands on her hips. The right hand covered the blessed doll carved from wood clipped on her belt. "That sounds like an excellent idea, Armand-baby. Let some healing start growing up out the ground."

"Yes, ma'am," Armand stated with a wink up to Lillian.

The reverend dismissed himself, and an uneasy silence fell between Armand and Lillian. She reminded him, "I have an instinct, Armand-baby. I can walk the pathways of your mind and get to know your thoughts."

Armand chuckled mechanically at the notion. He looked down at his mask and flipped it around in his hands. "I know, Lily-baby." He looked in the direction where Horace Georg's beacon, like a beating heart made of light, once hummed in and out of existence. "I need to have a bit more of a conversation with Mister Horace Georg," he announced. He looked up at her and added, "It needs to happen tonight. And it needs to be private, if you don't mind."

"Not at all, Armand-baby. You just be careful walking back there."

"I will, Miss Voodoo Lily," he assured her. Then a thought came to him. "Hey, who's Dinclinsin? And what's he got to do with something called Ogun's Tarot? Gordon mentioned something about all that."

"Ogun's Tarot is a simulation, of sorts," Lillian answered. "Conjure folk used to go into this realm and test their conjure and incants. A whole scenario would configure around them. Some called this place *digi-glas*, meaning mirror-mirror. A world that reflects ours, but isn't real." She sat down on the steps. "We're talking hundreds of years before slavery, practiced by African nations attempting to defend their lands. Now, in the last twenty years or so, folk step into this realm to see who can overcome a tough scenario using incant, now personal conjures. Works something good as our magic regains strength. In the days of slavery, well-practiced conjure folk who'd been enslaved, they couldn't go into the world, but they could bring the world to it. They manifested it through what was feared the most. A white colonial slave owner or overseer with a very cruel temperament."

"That's Dinclinsin?"

"That's Dinclinsin," she repeated in the form of an answer. "He's not really white. He just comes from the *digi-glas* world as a representation of fear and anything that will test you, put your conjure to the test. The enslaved Africans called him to this world as something that reflected those qualities to them." There was a beat, and then Lillian asked, "You want to be tested, Armand-baby?"

"I got enough tests, Miss Voodoo Lily. I think I just got some questions is all."

"Okay," she respected. "When you're ready." She stood and walked down the stairs. "I'll be at the house when you're finished with Soldier Georg." She kissed his cheek and reiterated, "Be careful."

He nodded his head as assurance. Lillian remained at the stairs, waiting for her parents and the other Elders to come from the church. Armand disappeared into the fog. He retraced his steps back to the alley where they conjured Horace Georg. Halfway there, he strapped the mask to his face. Horace Georg was already waiting for him, leaning against the left wall of the alleyway. "I c'n see you through that there mask!" he commented as Armand approached. "Them skulls gotchu in anutha realm. You walk here and there. C'mon in heah, boy. I got things set up."

Armand followed Horace Georg into the alley. Two worn, wooden seats were situated across from one another. A small table with a square top was between them, and it was just as worn as the chairs. Atop the table were two wooden cups filled with dice, five in each. Horace took a seat. Armand sat across from him.

"Y'see, Mwindo, he fought with his father," Horace Georg explained. "His father started servin' the dark lord who was a ter'ah on the land. His father was a great war'r, a righ'chus war'r before he pledged his allegiance to the dark lord. Story really begins with him. I'll get to all that. They fought with spears made from rays of the sun. Spec'tac'lah fight! But the dark lord had Mwindo's father's soul, see. So, Mwindo played a game of Liar's Dice with the dark lord for his father's soul. That's what he did!" Horace Georg peered at Armand, his stern gaze dissolving the mask shielding Armand's face. "I tol' you, boy. We don't play for sport 'round here." He shook his head. "No. Never did. We play for souls, y' heah?"

Armand nodded. "Yes, sir. We play for souls."

26

The world put on the cap of day and brightened away the stars, foggy as it was. Soon again it wore night's shade swathed with clear, black skies. The sun was gone but left behind its heat. No one considered it a generous or kind act. The portly fog billowing throughout the Water Bug Hollow area carried the humidity like an oblivious gift-giver. The stars stood still in the heavens, peering down on the story below. Their light focused on Water Bug Hollow's streets, where stumbled a pair of sweethearts inebriated by one another's affection, trampling over each other and rumbling with laughter as if possessed by wild spirits. Hand-in-hand, she was the Queen of the Mississippi Crossroads, holding a small basket of pears on her arm. He was simply Armand Gideon, a young man from California newly inducted into a life of wondrous conjure. Their brightness parted the fog crowding the streets; at least it seemed so in their heads. Their sorcery-laced lips were opened in carefree cackling, putting fear in the hexed fog.

Bent eyes were fixed on them, gleaming with disdain as they peered through the shadows or the thick, airy haze. Nature didn't seem to bother these two. No sweat drowned their features or stained their clothes. They didn't look as if they needed to take a break from their laughter and joy to deal with reality.

Lillian and Armand were aware of the attention their antics received. To them, their carrying on in the street was a web spun to capture attention like flies. They straightened their demeanor when they arrived at the former nightspot called Eve's Hallow. A few chuckles were expressed, but then both Armand and Lillian took a breath and calmed. They could feel the scoffs in the narrowed eyes that scrutinized their appearance. Lillian's gypsy attire. Armand's offbeat garb of white, collared shirt, black vest, black pants and black boots with a draping necklace decorated with three large skulls colored red, black, and green. There was also the question of why he had a shovel slung over his shoulder, balancing it even as he dipped forward and back, hooting with laughter.

"This is it, huh?" spoke Armand as he straightened his posture. His wide-eyed gaze fell over the old Eve's Hallow structure.

"It sure is, Armand-baby," Lillian replied with a glistening smile and a fixation as bright as Armand's. "This is—or was—Eve's Hallow. It was the jumpin'est spot in all of Louisiana way, way, way, *way* back in the day."

There gathered on the porch was a crowd of ruffians, varying in size but each muscled up with ego, rage, and a gun tucked under their shirts. Armand put his eyes on them. One-by-one. "Curious," he noted. He let go of Lillian's hand and spun around. She ducked. The head and part of the wooden body of the shovel swung over her head. Armand stopped after a complete circle was made. He dropped the shovel and swung his arms wild. By way of a mouthed incant he summoned into his possession a small, wooden table folded up and tucked under one arm and a set of wooden chairs, folded up and tucked under the other. He set up the scene, spun again, and in his hand appeared an African mask. He scooped up the discarded shovel and leaned it against one chair. Lillian set the table with the basket of pears. She uncovered the fruit and revealed two other items in the basket. These were two wooden mugs that were filled with five dice in each. With their eyes firmly on Armand's sleight-of-hand, they were unaware of how Lillian had quickly come into possession of the objects she placed atop the table. The gang members inched closer toward the newcomers to their hood, stepping away from Eve's Hallow's porch.

Armand sat down. Lillian stood next to him. He crossed his legs, strapped his African mask against his face, and ordered, "Gentleman, I request the presence of Ramiel Bishop, chief of your outfit." He removed a cigarette, lit it, and started smoking through the mask.

The gang members didn't know how to react. They shared perplexed looks as their eyes went from Armand to Lillian and back again and again. Disbelief was also sprinkled into their features, widening, growing with every passing moment. A seventeen-year-old, young and bold, yelled back at Armand, "Fuck you think you are, nigga? Who you to tell us what to do? We only listen to the chief!"

Armand smoked his cigarette. Inhale. Breath out. Snaking smoke. He quoted, "Theirs not to reason why. Theirs but to do and die…"

An older man named Sticks took out the gun tucked in the back of his pants. "You sayin' someone gon' die tonight?"

Armand spread his arms wide. "My apologies, sir," he said as if making a grand announcement. All the world of Water Bug Hollow heard him. "It's poetry, quoting Alfred Lord Tennyson. But please, holster your ego. The lady here prefers Kipling." Armand took another drag, coolly releasing the smoke through the open portal of the mask's circular mouth. "Let me Clue you in: *The female of the species is more deadly than the male.*" The armed man looked at Lillian. She lobbed a sly smirk back to him. She put her hands on her hips, right hand partly folded over the six-inch, wooden doll clipped to her belt. Sticks holstered his weapon. He leaned toward the seventeen-year-old boy and whispered something into his ear. The young man rushed into the former nightspot.

The remaining thugs stared at the two conjure folk.

Lillian and Armand stared back at them.

Chief Ramiel Bishop stepped out of the doors. "Whatchu mean he's some kind of magician?" he was heard saying through a snarl. His dark eyes squinted in observation. He must've been disturbed while having dinner, as he was chewing and swallowing the last of what he'd put into his mouth. He was sharp in appearance, not clothed in the jeans and tanktops of his soldiers. He was dressed in a long suit jacket, colored black. His pants and shoes were the same. A brown collar shirt was underneath, and a wide maroon tie draped down from his neck. A handkerchief, identical in color to his tie, was tucked neatly into his suit jacket's left breast pocket. He had brown skin, a low haircut and thick eyebrows.

Armand trumpeted, "My man, Mister Bishop!"

To which Ramiel answered, "I know you, nigga?"

"Not yet," Armand answered behind the mask.

A moment of silence. An inspection of sorts. The two gazed at one another. Armand awaited a move from Ramiel. The chief examined the peculiarity of the African masked man and the black gypsy queen standing by his side.

"So, you two got names? You seem to know mine."

"Who doesn't, Mister Bishop," Armand replied.

"*Chief* Ramiel," the gang leader corrected.

"Yes, sir, Chief Ramiel," Armand amended. "My name is Armand Gideon. There's nothing special about me." He pointed to Lillian. "Now, this beautiful woman next to me? She's the special one. Her name is Lillian Eledas-Ghedemere—"

"Is that supposed to mean something to me, nigga?" grumbled Chief Ramiel.

With a louder voice, Armand emphasized, "Called Voodoo Lily, Queen of the Mississippi Crossroads."

Chief Ramiel stepped to the table, looking down at the masked Armand. He addressed Lillian when he asked, "That's where y'all from?"

"Where we're from, Chief Ramiel, is of no importance," Lillian answered him in a regal voice, the sound of which was deep, warm, and soothing to Chief Ramiel's ears. He moved his eyes to her, his stance now loose rather than rigid as he was before. "If you must know, I hail between New Orleans and Saint Louis, the latter being more of my home. My herald here is from California, with New York in his blood as well." She looked down at the masked Armand and playfully scolded, "Which defines why he has such a flare for the dramatic. He's Hollywood and Broadway all in one," she joked. Armand took a puff of his cigarette. The smoke trailed coolly out of the mouth of the African mask, funneling up into a tornado-like whirl. Then it dissipated. Lillian put her hands on Armand's shoulders. She observed that Chief Ramiel had a curious smile and eye that coasted between her and Armand. Lillian announced, "Your base of operation was once Water Bug Hollow's famous dive."

"I know my local history, Miss Voodoo Lily," Chief Ramiel countered. "It was called Eve's Hallow. What I'm looking for is a point to, what you call, the dramatics your herald—and you—are putting on." His eyes moved to Armand, as it was the masked smoker that answered him.

"What we're looking for is buried on these grounds, Chief Ramiel," Armand proclaimed. "We wish to excavate, but not without your permission. Sort of," he added.

Chief Ramiel's eyes went from Armand to Lillian. "Sort of…?" he questioned.

Armand removed his mask and set it down on the table. He finished his cigarette and said, "We play! A game of liar's dice," he suggested pointing at the wooden cups holding dice. "We play for souls, Chief Ramiel. You do have one of those, don't you? And you do know how to play, correct?"

Chief Ramiel laughed. He looked back at his soldiers. His guffaws acted as a signal for them to join in, and they laughed with him. He pulled out the chair and took a seat, pushing himself flush up to the table. "Goddamn!" he cursed. "I'm in. Shit, yeah! Let's play for souls. I know how to play, boy," he assured. He slapped his hands on the table. Then he reached for the basket. "You mind?"

"Not at all," said Armand. "In fact, I insist. Share."

Chief Ramiel plucked a pear out of the basket. He handed it back to his soldiers. Sticks came and took it from him. "I'm a just and fair chief, Mister Gideon. I always share my profits and gifts as best I can, when I can." He bit into the fruit. He made an approving face, surprised by the flavor's intensity. "This is some good shit, Mister Armand Gideon." He looked at Lillian and joked, "Miss Lena Horne Voodoo of the Crossroads." Lillian just smiled. "Sticks!" he called. "Everybody! Eat up." He bit into his pear again, chewed and savored the flavor, and then he swallowed. He wiped his mouth and put down a few stipulations for the game's outcome. "I win: I get this sweet thing for the night. We head out to the River Boat Casino. One called *Saturday's*. We have some fun." He pointed at Armand. "You get buried with whatever you need to dig up." Chief Ramiel tapped on his chest in three places, triangulated. "Three in your chest—" He tapped on his forehead. "One in the head," he snarled. "That sound 'bout right, Mister Gideon?"

Armand and Lillian looked at one another. Lillian nodded her head. Armand replied to Chief Ramiel, "It sounds terribly misogynistic and fatalistically violent." Then he smiled. "I wouldn't have it any other way— coming from you, Chief Ramiel. The lady and I agree to those terms." He took up a cup, and raised it as if toasting. "Let's play."

Chief Ramiel stood for a brief moment to remove his coat. He draped it over the back of the chair, and then returned to his seat. He held a cup, shuffling it about, hand over the top. "Why Liar's Dice?" he asked. "We pirates?"

Armand shook his head. "No, no, no, Chief Ramiel. We're conjure folk—Miss Voodoo Lily and I. We know stories, and there's this one from Africa where a great warrior fought for his father's soul playing a game of Liar's Dice. They might've thrown shells in the original telling, but it's all the same." He slammed his cup onto the table, Chief Ramiel doing the same. "This is your territory, Chief Ramiel. Your hood. I, sir, invite you to bid first."

The chief checked his dice. He tipped the cup back, keeping the five dice out of view from Armand. He made his bid, a guess at how many dice had fallen on a particular number. "Three ones," he asserted.

Armand made the game fair. No instincts used. He checked his dice. He had no ones showing among his five fumble and roll. He tapped against the top of his cup, a gesture challenging the bid. He lifted his cup first and showed no dice displaying one. Chief Ramiel lifted his cup. He had two ones, banking on Armand having rolled at least a single pip. He cursed, lifted one die, and tossed it aside.

"You're a just chief, Chief Ramiel," Armand noted. "Your gang, The Four In Hand Crew, is very democratic, I hear. You give people a voice, a vote. A tradition, of sorts." They shook cups again, slammed them against the table. It was Armand's bid. He checked his dice. He had three fours. He feigned a tell, though he was plotting. But his facial contortions cast an expression of doubt. He called out his own number of dice to stay safe. "Th-th-three fours," he stammered. Chief Ramiel tapped against the wooden cup. He lifted and revealed he had no fours. Armand showed he had exactly three. "Spot on, Chief," he quipped.

Chief Ramiel lost another die.

The two men shuffled their dice in their cups. "Helps business along," Chief Ramiel remarked, continuing their conversation on his democratic gang. "Voting, and the like," he said. They slammed down their cups. Chief Ramiel checked his dice. "Three threes," he bid. "And, yes. It's a tradition, Mister Gideon, being just and fair in my family."

"A nation, you might call it, Chief Ramiel," voiced Lillian.

The chief looked up at the Crossroads Queen. There was something new and peculiar about her. She had in her hand a lacquered, espresso-stained wooden box that he didn't believe was there before. Odd symbols were carved around its base. He started to reply to her comment when Armand uttered, "Spot on." Chief Ramiel focused on Armand who lifted his cup. He had had no threes. Chief Ramiel had three. "Okay, Mister Chief Ramiel. We have ourselves a game." He winked and ribbed, "But I'm still up one."

Further bids were made after shakes and slams. Liars were called out. Dice were lost or retained. Rattles and pounds, and it all came down to Armand keeping two dice and Chief Ramiel relieved of all of his. Armand didn't gloat. There was no arrogant smirk cast or clapping in self-applause. It was as if he'd lost the contest. He was silent, and Chief Ramiel was in wait for something to happen. What did occur surprised the gang leader. Lillian set the lockbox in front of him, as if it was a prize for second place. Along with this, Armand stood, and Lillian sat in his stead.

"Go on, Chief Ramiel Bishop," she said in a soft, pleasant voice, the kind an encouraging mother would present to her child. "Open it."

Chief Ramiel tried to hold his smile. Keeping it half fixed on his face, he turned his body around to look at his soldiers. Their hands moved near the guns tucked into their pants. The chief nodded and turned forward. "Did I win or lose?" he attempted to joke.

But Lillian was serious when she answered, "That depends on how you react to what you see." She held her hand facing up and pointed at the lockbox. "Open it," she urged again.

Curiosity won the day. Chief Ramiel put both hands on the lockbox. He ran his fingers over its gleaming surface until he touched the latch and flipped it open. He lifted the lid and peered inside. It was empty in the eyes of his soldiers who leaned forward attempting to get a better look. But Chief Ramiel saw something. His eyes were adjusted to see the miniature construct of a rusted shackle and chain. The sight held the chief still, eyes fixed even as the chain turned to dust and ash, and then transfigured into a storm cloud. The billowing shifted from gray to dark with flashes and streaks of lightning illuminating behind its murk or across its tenebrous surface. The storm clouds also collected in Chief Ramiel's pupils, adjusting his sight to see behind the rippling overcast. Yesterday bled into days further back in history, and time that happened before was visually recalled.

The chief became agitated at the sight of dull clouds producing scenes that burdened him, offered answers to the questions of gang life and family relations. *How was the Four In Hand Crew really formed?* He squirmed in his chair, and he breathed deep to settle his unease. But there cast before him was his father, Upton "Up" Bishop, and a close friend named Gregory Salinger, called *The Salamander.* He was quick, and he could get into places. Upton used him to crawl into the seedier dives for contacts to help progress their own activities. Chief Ramiel saw them sitting in an interrogation room with government agents who were strong-arming them to jam up a civil rights activist named Clifford Davies. Clifford was a young man who believed he had lineage to Curtis "The Water Bug" Hollow. He wanted better for the neighborhood that had become overrun with gang violence. Chief Ramiel actually smiled when he witnessed a scene of the activist, his father, and his

Uncle Stephon just hanging out on the street, talking on how to clean things up for the better. Salamander Greg was there with them.

So was this revealed when the clouds parted.

"I'm callin' the heads 'mkuu' *or* 'kiongozi'. *They mean* 'chief' *and* 'leader' *in Swahili. Whaddy'all think?"* Clifford leaned against a building. He wore a brown flat cap and a tan jacket over a white, collar shirt that was tucked into black slacks. He had a small, round head that was spotted with small patches of hair around the sides of his dark-brown face and chin.

Upton Bishop thought about what he'd heard Clifford say. He was tall and heavyset, a belly pushing out his red, short-sleeved, collar shirt. He had on jeans and workman boots. At the moment, he rubbed his bald head while grinning. *"I actually like what you sayin', little Cliff. I do. I think it could work. I mean, Stephon just got out the pen. You steerin' my brother right with all the righteous talk. But, now they got Salamander here jammed up. We talk big, and we say the charges were trumped up."* He made a face, scowling as he admitted, *"They were real. But that's what the Chess Players do. We sell weed. It's harmless. We ain't into what them other jokers into. We run some numbers. To me it's all harmless. We ain't pimps. We ain't crack dealers. We don't run guns."* Those words were only true for the moment. It was interesting to observe. Ramiel guessed he was looking at a time before his birth in the spring of 1989. He knew what was being discussed. A change in climate for Water Bug Hollow, which many of its residents had seen go through a socio-economic decline since the fifties. Ramiel didn't care for those politics. He didn't have time. Water Bug Hollow became a whirlwind, and he wasn't about to get caught in its heavy bluster.

He did like seeing his father, a man he hadn't seen in ten years. Being a kingpin caught up to Upton. He was big-time leading the Four In Hand Crew. Numbers. Weed. Harder things eventually came in by way of his successor. Cocaine to the rich white boys. Crack-cocaine to the same group, plus Water Bug Hollow's downtrodden population. A major in drugs and gambling. A minor in gunrunning.

Ramiel ran things fair and balanced between his father's ways and in the ways of his father's successor.

That was Salamander Greg, who believed he did most of the work under Chief Upton, and he probably did. The footwork, that is. But Chief Upton was the brains to keep things hushed, under the radar. He was the charisma. And if need be, the muscle. Salamander thought otherwise, and he had Upton gunned down in the streets. It was broad daylight. A point was made, and Chief Gregory took control using the ruse of a rival gang having killed Chief Upton.

Chief Ramiel knew better. But he allowed The Salamander to bring him along, under his wing. He let the empire build. When the time was right,

Ramiel became chief by similar means. Burying The Salamander in honor of his father.

His eyes precipitated. Chief Ramiel didn't just see his father in the storm clouds, he saw himself there. Different clothes, not as tall or bulge-bellied. But he saw himself. He wanted to tell his father he'd been made chief. He put The Salamander to rest and the Four In Hand Crew was still a strong force in Water Bug Hollow. *Neighborhood politics be damned*, he thought to himself.

"Of course, it's all harmless, Up," Chief Ramiel's uncle said in a frustrated voice. *"That's why they got you roped up. Salamander jammed up. Me once locked up. But we know our history now. We know how they want to keep the Hollow hollow. This sacred ground."*

Salamander Greg didn't participate in the conversation in any productive way. He was fidgety, constantly baring his teeth in annoyance and looking around. Chief Ramiel also noticed Salamander Greg rubbing his left forearm persistently, and he knew why. Addiction.

The clouds came again, swelling into bulbous grays and blacks until they developed into another scene. Upton and Salamander Greg sat in a gray, concrete room that was filled with cigarette smoke. The smoke came from the two men sitting across the table from them. Both men were on the late forties side of middle age. The man on the right was average height, with a light-brown wash to his flat-pressed hair. He had glasses and a thick goatee. The other man was stocky with well-defined, angular facial features. A thick Cajun accent accompanied his words. Both men smoked like chimneys, clouding the room.

Upton spoke first. He chuckled nervously as he said to the two smoking gentlemen, *"Guy's harmless. He thinks he's an actual descendant of Curtis 'The Water Bug' Hollow. He just wants to make a difference in the neighborhood. Can you blame him? Things have gotten out of control. He got a simple job at the Arlington Johnson Law Office. He works nights as a proofreader."*

The man with the goatee adjusted his glasses and replied, *"Mister Bishop, the Water Bug Hollow area has become a breeding ground for gang activity. While that concerns us, there is a greater concern for a man like Clifford Davies to stoke the flames of militant activity by trying to go against our tide."*

Upton remarked, *"I think a guy like Clifford Davies can do better for this area than you or any law enforcement agency—"*

"Mister Bishop! Mister Bishop!" the man in glasses interrupted. *"Your opinion doesn't mean anything to your friend's case. A case, I reiterate, that can go two ways. We can drop all charges against Mister Salinger if you—perhaps your brother— and Mister Salinger here can steer more information from your mutual friend—any concrete information on Mister Davies' intentions."*

Upton scowled. *"With all due respect, Agent Morris, my brother is clean. You can't threaten him with anything he's already served time for. And Salamander here ain't done nothin'…big."*

"He carried drugs across state lines, which is why I and Agent Thane are here," Agent Morris reminded. *"He had on him two stolen firearms, and he stopped off to sell to minors. And it all connects to you, Mister Bishop. Putting this on you, and your activity, brings me to the second way this scenario can proceed. You and Mister Salinger behind bars,"* he warned.

Upton gave Gregory a harsh look. Gregory just kept his head down, rubbing his forearm persistently. The agents blew smoke, and dark clouds bloomed back into existence, rolling until a new scene opened up. Stephon Bishop sat in Clifford Davies' car. Clifford was in the driver's seat. It was early morning, and both men appeared as if coming out of sleep's fog. Stephon remarked that Upton was waiting for them in the apartment building across the street. Both men got out, and two black men wearing long t-shirts, ski-masks, and baggy jeans ran up on them, guns up and shooting. Bullets tore up their clothes and their upper bodies. They danced a violent jig, and their wounds spat blood in streams and bursts of red that turned into the storm clouds where days bled into one another, and time was forgotten among the fog. Lillian shut the box. Chief Ramiel blinked. He looked up at her as she sat back in her chair. A stunned expression was mounted on his face. He stammered on unintelligible sounds, attempting to make them into words.

Lillian spoke while Chief Ramiel continued his vocal troubles. "Your father was supposed to die there too," she revealed. "Shot by the same suspects that were never detained. Chief Gregory found them later. Your father shot them while they were bound to chairs and gagged."

Chief Ramiel finally had words. "The fuck did you just do?" he demanded. He also had more questions, but his latest utterance was the best he could do at the moment. His men drew their guns, one asking *What they got on you, Chief?'* But Chief Ramiel raised his hand behind him, waving his soldiers to holster their firearms. Neither Lillian nor Armand flinched at the sight of the drawn weapons. "Sheath them hatchets and spears, tribesmen!" he ordered, voice shaking. He brought his arm back, placing both hands on the table. "That moment sobered my father up to reality," he said clutching a fist. "Chief Gregory too. At that time, he knew how to whittle his way into things, connections. But he was a little knuckleheaded. Shit, Path always was. He had an addiction. My uncle and Clifford's murders put that aside. My father got what gangs were around here in order, united the four. That's what we are. *We* that outcome," he insisted. "*We* the Four In Hand Crew!" he spoke the name with pride. "I know my father had to Godfather some niggas. Just like in number One. He set a meeting with them. Few, if any, showed up." He tapped his finger on the table and said, "Now, I got my problems with the chief who came before me. I buried them with him. But I know his actions weren't his own."

Lillian blurted with a surprise look on her face, *"You do?"*

Chief Ramiel shook his head. "Yeah, I do. I know. He had an addiction. He got his ass beat for it. First, it was by my father's hands. My father couldn't have that going on in his crew. I gotta keep niggas straight myself." Chief Ramiel paused for effect. He pointed at Lillian and said, "Then it was this situation. I saw him rubbin' his arm. He was puttin' needles to his shit." He tapped against his forearm and added, "H."

Lillian and Armand looked at one another. Their gazes lingered, and it frustrated Chief Ramiel more.

"What?" the chief demanded.

They looked at him. Lillian said, "Those needles weren't filled with heroin, Chief Ramiel. They were filled with an arcane residue called 'hex'," she revealed. "A curse."

Chief Ramiel's face scrunched into further confusion when he asked, "With *what?*"

Lillian didn't answer his question. She instead told Chief Ramiel, "Chief Gregory was easy to get to. He was always wanting more for himself, and the two men calling themselves Agent Morris and Agent Thane knew that. They were surveilling him for some time. Your father, too," she added. "They stuck him with needles and changed his behavior to their suggestion. These men were more than government agents. They were a part of a network of terrible men called Needlemen or Night Doctors. They have plagued the conjure world for centuries."

Chief Ramiel's eyes went back and forth between Lillian and Armand. They narrowed in contemplation. "You don't practice the deviltry superstitious folk talk about, do you? You all for real with spirit, something higher." Lillian and Armand didn't answer, but Chief Ramiel had a natural instinct to know he was correct. "Whatchu lookin' for in my backyard?" he asked.

"Needlemen did a number on this area here," Armand responded. "The Queen and I have been tasked to undo all this fog. There are bones buried on your premises."

Chief Ramiel questioned, "Clifford Davies?"

"No," Lillian told the chief. "The bones belong to a woman named Patricia Gale Freda." She asked the chief, "Does your knowledge of local history know to whom I refer when I use that name?"

"Aspiring politician," Chief Ramiel spoke up. "She was an activist, or somethin'. She was the same as Clifford Davies." He took a moment and contemplated. Then he asked, "Them Night Doctors got to her, huh?"

"They got to all of Water Bug Hollow, Chief Ramiel," noted Lillian. "The other gangs have their burdens, too. My herald and I have plans for them, but since you're the strongest and most reasonable, we've come to you first."

"Whatchu need?" he asked them. He tossed a nod of his head over his shoulders and attached, "Besides them bones…"

Armand took up the shovel, slinging it back over his shoulder. "First, your permission to excavate those bones. Next, we need to resurrect Eve's Hallow into the jumpin'est spot in all of Louisiana—perhaps the States themselves." He tugged at the middle skull on his chain. A ghostly essence of the physical object was drawn out of the black skull. It turned solid in Armand's hands, glowing with a dark, purple hue.

Chief Ramiel and his soldiers fixed their gazes on it. Armand let it go, and it hovered over to the chief. The skull's face locked eyes with Chief Ramiel, a bright glow emitting from the sockets. The light was much like the clouds that swirled inside the lockbox. But instead of the realm of history, possibility was flashed into his vision. Eve's Hallow stood tall, doors stretched out, opened like welcoming arms. The interior lights flickered in rhythm to the musical waves, and people danced and raved with shots of rum. Legal gambling rolled with dice, flashed with cards put on display for a win against the house or another player. Numbered-wheels spun around and around like the dancing folk. The dance floor was a roulette wheel for a metal, cylindrical ball ready to stomp on the thirty-one black. Or the twenty-four black. People danced with their burdens, they didn't smoke or snort fog to run away from them. Water Bug Hollow's resurrection started here.

The lights in the hovering skull's eyes dimmed, and the skull blew away as dust. The particles trailed back into the black skull resting on Armand's chain.

Chief Ramiel took out a cigarette. He reached for his custom zippo lighter and pulled it from his pocket. It was pearl white with a picture of a man in a suit and fedora engraved into the face. Before the lighter was put to use, Lillian mouthed an incant and lit the end of the cigarette for the chief. He chuckled and pocketed his lighter. He took a drag, leaned back and crossed his legs. "Boys!" he called his soldiers to attention. "You go on and lead the Crossroads Queen and her herald, Mister Armand Gideon, to the yard out back."

Sticks answered, "Yes, Chief."

Armand planted the pointed-head end of the shovel against the ground. "You still get your prize, Chief Ramiel. You, sir, get to escort this beautiful woman on a night out. You have a casino-building-and-running business to learn about." He lifted the shovel and aimed it at the gang leader. "But don't you go and get any fresh ideas now. I trust you to be on your best behavior. I trust you'll be a gentleman. You treat this woman right—this *Queen*. I'm quite fond of her and all the conjure gypsy funk she's dressed in." He slung the shovel back over his shoulder and finalized his warning. "And if you value your own life, and the use of all your faculties, you won't disrespect her. She'll do more than burn the end of your cigarette."

Chief Ramiel smoked. "Ain't no harm gon' come to her, my man."

Lillian stood. She walked over to Chief Ramiel and presented her hand. He accepted, and she assisted in lifting him to his feet. They stared into one another's eyes. Armand said to the crew boss, "I cast you into the abyss, Chief Ramiel. I toss you into a void constructed of pathways and choices all laid out for you by the Crossroads Queen herself. This lovely woman has given you more than one choice. Turn your instincts into a scale, weigh the options, and choose wisely. If you turn your back on the history and the original traditions of this area, then I will become its violent embodiment to remind you who you truly are. Either way, in the end, you'll serve us; and you will have real purpose."

Lillian beamed a lovely smile. She pivoted and looped her arm. Chief Ramiel put out his cigarette and picked up the remainder of his pear. He slid his arm into her loop, and the two walked down the street together. Armand and the gang members were left looking at one another.

Armand lifted a finger and said, "Blink not once—" he then lifted a second finger and continued, "—blink not twice, but three times." The soldiers did as Armand tasked, and on the third blink of their eyes the table, chairs, and all gaming instruments disappeared. Armand stepped in the area where the rickety furniture had been. He clasped the African mask to his face, his eyes adjusting to unseen forces, such as the spirit of Horace Georg carting the folded table and chairs away. The mugs of dice were back in the basket, which was balanced on his head. The once-living soldier grumbled about going from servant to warrior to servant again. Armand chuckled behind his mask at the absurd occurrence. But he gave his attention to the Four In Hand soldiers and said with one arm spread wide, "Lead the way."

Gang member Sticks motioned for Armand to follow. "This way," he said in a gruff voice. He told the others to keep guard over the antics in the streets. He put a man named Paul Grey in charge of the small crew hanging outside.

Armand walked behind Sticks. The two went through a gate to enter a long alley that opened up to a spacious area covered with mounds of dirt and tall blades of grass. Armand aimed the head of the shovel outward, and then he swept the shovel's pointed head around. It became like a diving rod or the needle on a compass trying to find its magnetic north. It moved independent of Armand's hand, trembling like a tuning fork. He held the shovel carefully as it located the correct direction of Patricia Gale Freda's buried bones. Armand pranced merrily over to the burial site, the shovel trembling in his hand. He raised the tool and slammed the pointed, metal head into the ground. The earth split with the shovel's penetration, exhaling a sigh.

Armand snarled, "Patricia, let loose your angry spirit."

Elsewhere, Lillian Eledas-Ghedemere and Chief Ramiel stepped into a scene of jingling coins and slot machines singing in high-pitched chimes. Lillian and Chief Ramiel waded through the gaming floor. Their presence parted the room's bustling activity, men and women on their way to sit in ritual at the idol of their god of chance and high-stakes. A magician floated from patron to patron, especially the tables, entertaining with tricks and silly jokes. The patrons gave him minimal attention, wanting to get into their game or not have their ritual be interrupted.

Chief Ramiel surveyed the room. He felt he could actually hear the flapping flips of dealers shuffling cards. It was all a feeling of euphoric déjà vu to Chief Ramiel. He remarked, "I was always attracted to dice, cards, and games of luck. My father put me onto it, Miss Voodoo Lily. Dice first—craps, of course. I learned Liars Dice too. I like the cards, the faces, the jokers, the aces. They all look like they got some meaning. Overall, between cards and dice, I like the numbers, the mathematics, and the probability to change life with a roll or a flip."

Lillian nodded politely. She guided Chief Ramiel into a gaming room hosting tables for roulette. They stood at a table and watched as people made bets, cheered for their luck or shook their heads in shame at their loss. Lillian and Chief Ramiel observed. People did well and people lost. The magician entered the room, telling jokes and flouncing around with simple magic tricks. There were times where he relaxed his audience, but everyone was patient with him until he left their table. Through the room he traveled until he came to the roulette table Chief Ramiel and Lillian observed. One man with stacks of chips called him over, wanting to be entertained by both his wins and the entirety of the casino's atmosphere. But the magician was drawn to the chief and queen, and he wowed them, and any on-lookers in observance, with sleight-of-hand integrated with clever storytelling that corresponded to his tricks.

Chief Ramiel was amazed at the magician's spin on age-old simple card tricks, guessing his marks' cards. The magician dazzled with shuffles of his deck, new picks of cards, and separations of the fifty-two's stack. The chief was a mark, too. The trick came together seamlessly to show the chief's card was somehow tucked into his back pocket. Chief Ramiel's smile and laughter loosened him. He applauded the magician, and the man who'd called him over won another round at roulette. The magician's presence was considered good luck.

Chief Ramiel turned to Lillian and stated in a jovial tone, "A remarkable trick. Things like that get me every time. I love magic."

Lillian barely beamed. She swiped the deck of cards from the magician in a manner the best of thieves would congratulate. "That's not magic, Chief Ramiel," she said holding the deck of cards in the palm of her hand. "This is magic." The stack of fifty-two playing cards burned with a red and yellow glow before decomposing into dust that funneled up into a single, black line. The dust's stream arced to Lillian's opposite hand, which was also facing palm up. The black dust gathered together and reformed into its original state as a deck of cards.

The magician looked stunned.

The other patrons paid no attention as the winnings and loses continued at the table.

Lillian returned the deck to the magician, and he stumbled away. The crossroads queen chuckled. She told Chief Ramiel, "What you saw that so-called magician do was a trick. The look on his face!" she laughed harder. The gang leader attempted to be jovial, but even for all he'd seen, that was startling. "Conjure is real magic. That magician will never be the same, but it's time the world knows as well. Perhaps his frightened experience will be another herald of mine." She patted Chief Ramiel on his shoulder, swiping off small pieces of lint and string that somehow found their way onto his person. "We had so much fun at the casino last night, Chief Ramiel."

"Last night…?" he questioned.

Lillian answered him by saying, "Close your eyes, Ramiel Bishop." Her voice was sweet, and the chief followed her suggestion without question. Eyelids closed, and the appearance of the casino's interior dropped like a curtain closing on an act. Revealed was one of the backrooms in the Water Bug Hollow church. The roulette table morphed into a cot. The patrons disappeared. A few remained, their images changed and revealed to be Lillian's mother, Savannah Forrester, and Lady Arachne. The three women were in attendance to perform the stitching ritual on the gang leader.

Chief Ramiel's body swayed. It looked as if he was going to collapse forward, but instead he took a step, and then he took another. He did eventually drop, but that was when he was over the cot, crumpling safely atop the mattress. Lady Arachne and Savannah Forrester straightened the chief on his back. Simaetha approached her daughter and said, "The sun's peeking up, Lillian. You've had a hard night. Your sweetheart should be returning from his venture with the bones procured. Go meet him. Bring Patricia's bones to Madame Jeliya. She's waiting on Fable Avenue." Simaetha could tell her daughter heard her, listening closely, but her eyes were on Lady Arachne and Savannah Forrester conducting the stitching ritual on Chief Ramiel. Simaetha guided her daughter's eyes back to her with the raise of a single finger. "He's still a bad man, Lillian. The stitching ritual will not be easy for him. He will suffer, and he will most likely walk hand-in-hand with the burden, the *inawo*, of all the pain he's brought to people." She looked over her shoulder at the ceremonial rites being conducted on the gang leader. Both she and Lillian knew Chief Ramiel would barely survive the incident. Simaetha faced her daughter and said, "Oh, he's a charming ruffian, but he's still hurt a lot of people. He will always know it, especially when he sleeps." She kissed her daughter on the forehead. "Now go. Find your sweetheart."

Lillian stepped back and saluted her mother with a head bow. "Yes, Mamma," she said before pivoting and returning to the outside.

The day was faint with its breath. A few stars had taken their bow off the night's stage as a series of blues painted the sky. Light was dawning. Chief Ramiel was finding his way into dream, or nightmare was probably best to describe. Lillian was finding her way back to Armand, moving down the street into the fog. Her head felt as if it too was filled with the cloudiness that hung around Water Bug Hollow. She wiped her eyes, exhausted by lack of sleep and the extreme use of conjure and incant. She stumbled a bit, losing footing. But she remained upright, keeping her balance.

A small burst of vitality enlivened her when she spotted Armand walking her way, looking just as weary. Her warrior-herald had scavenged Eve's Hallow's backyard. The shovel was again slung over his shoulder with a sack filled with brittle bones hanging from the tool's neck. His blessed African mask was strapped to his hip. He smoked while he walked toward her. His handsome face, as well as his clothes, was blotted with dust and soil.

Both Lillian and Armand quickened their steps, and Armand managed to display a victorious grin at the sight of the Crossroads Queen. Cigarette smoke curled from his lips in bulbous waves. He was triumphant in his endeavor, proud to successfully serve the community that awakened a purpose in him. He debriefed Lillian, "I have secured the partial remains of Patricia Gale Freda, my Queen. It felt like freeing her from a prison. I could hear something faint as I got closer and closer to the bones. They buried Miss Patricia Gale Freda's bones thirteen feet down—all muddy and wet." He then remarked, "I'm a virgin to all this, Miss Voodoo Lily, but even I can make a positive guess that was a ritualistic choice. I gave a ritual back. I planted the reverend's seeds."

"Indeed, Armand-baby!" said the young conjure queen before congratulating him on his acquirement. "We've been tasked to deliver the bones to Madame Jeliya on Fable Avenue. Come," she said making a quick, aristocratic pivot. Armand sided up next to her, walking in step. "Are you tired?" she asked him as they crossed the street.

"Hell, yeah!" Armand replied rubbing his eyes with thumb and finger. "There's work to be done, though, Miss Voodoo Lily. We have to give a tribute to Curtis Hollow. He made this place for a reason. It was a place for folk to rest their burdens, break their chains." He nodded his head. "And I want all of the antagonists and intimidators to be brought to concession with the weight of the burdens they've brought to others."

Lillian considered Armand's words. She felt compelled to ask, "Is that justice to you?"

"It's settling what needs settling. All debts," he stressed. Then he listed, "Property, financial and spiritual—mostly spiritual. They've crushed the diamond of history, this place's history, and they created coal. I still find it valuable, but we've gone backwards."

It was another point for Lillian to consider, and she took it in to contemplate. "I want to build a place my mother and father can rest in, retire. My father is very old. I know his nickname gives it away," she chuckled. Armand gave her an admiring glance. Lillian continued, "But he can be so damn nomadic. Constant travel!" she remarked. "He's spry. Incants and conjures keep him going, but I see he likes putting his feet up, setting down the politics. My mother is much the same. She travels, blessing objects. She's a nurse, popping in on a hospital in New Orleans and Saint Louis. She helps the administrations, truly, a medical consultant. But she's like my father too. She needs to exhale a bit. Now she's queen." There was a beat directed at mulling over her words. "I want to give them a home," she concluded.

They came upon the crossroads house, entered and made their way to the door to Fable Avenue. Lillian carried out the knocking ritual and opened the door. Before them was Fable Avenue. Lillian took lead down the stairs. Armand followed. The Crossroads Queen spoke a silent incant and locked the doors. The queen and herald walked to the Peters residence. She climbed up the stairs and rang the doorbell. Madame Jeliya answered and ushered Lillian and Armand into her home. Armand unstrapped the sack from the shovel and left the dirty instrument outside. He handed the matriarch the sack of bones, and both he and Lillian were thanked for procuring them.

Madame Jeliya escorted the couple to her sanctuary below. It smelled of burned meat, and a cloud of smoke hung in the air along with the odor. A bulky and dark-brown-skinned man was there. Intimidating, hunched because of his massive frame extending up to the ceiling, he sat in a circle of unlit, blood-red candles. Drawn inside the circle was a symbol of a grave marked with a large cross and two coffins on either side. Next to him was a bottle of purple-colored wine and a bottle of rum. A fork and spoon lay atop one another next to a bowl of burned chicken, from where the smoke and odor emanated.

He was dressed in an undertaker's outfit. The sleeves of his tail-coat, as well as the sleeves of his white, collar shirt, had been torn off. Thin strands of fabric draped over his broad shoulders and dangled down his muscular arms. Atop his head was a wide-brimmed hat that shared the same color as the rest of his clothes. He had on no socks, and wore a gun belt around his waist. One holster was angled in front of him, tucked inside was a short-barreled Schofield revolver. Two other holsters, dipping low, hung at his sides. Both holsters carried black-handled, double-action revolvers. The belt was also a host to a series of ritual daggers. Four daggers were in the front. Eight were in the back. On their handles were miniature human skulls made from ivory and painted blood-red, black, or purple.

His face was painted up as a skull, and between his snarl-curled lips he puffed on a cigar. Madame Jeliya handed him the sack of bones, calling him by his rank and title. "Baron," she said.

He took the bag from the Fable Avenue conjure woman. His response was immediate. "A woman died really bad by really bad, bad, bad, bad people. Not my kind of bad men, Miss Lovely Jeliya." He put his eyes on Lillian and Armand. "Some folk, I like they criminal ways. Not these bastards. I hope they get there's." He looked at Armand and removed the cigar from his mouth. "You gon' help me?" he asked sneering. "Yeah, you gon' help me, boy. You got that *kòlè*, you got that *dife*. We gon' set them sinners ablaze to hear them scream, yes? We'll turn them into pigs and eat them." Then he snickered, "Well, *I'll* eat them. Y'all don't grind on the pig 'round here. But, hey, I'm a *kriminèl*."

He was intimidating, but Armand was intrigued by his presence. An instinct deciphered that he was a conjured spirit, one dedicated to swift and violent justice, criminality, and death. None of this was surprising or new to Lillian. She'd seen this 'Baron' before. He even smiled at her, though it appeared more as a snarl. He growled when he greeted her as the new crossroads queen, saying 'hello'. She welcomed his attention and responded by replying in a sweet tone, "Hello, Baron Odaran."

He opened the sack and looked inside. "Her bones," he said to no one in particular. "They shake. They dance and produce fog." Baron Odaran closed the pouch and pounded on it until the bones were dust. Then he went into his pocket and pulled out a cigar wrap. He unfolded it on the floor and poured the ashes of bones inside. He rolled it properly and lit the end with an incant. He removed his other cigar and tossed it into the air where it burned into nothing. He smoked the new cigar in one long drag and exhaled a column of smoke that formed, in a faint moment, into a woman stretching out in desperation.

She cried in a voice that faded in and out, *"I was so wrong…"*

Madame Jeliya felt Patricia Gale Freda's terrible story. "We will make it right, *bèl fanm*." She said a blessing as the smoke as dissipated, putting the pieces of the freed spirit to rest. The matriarch knew there was plenty of spirit remaining restless. But an effect did occur. The fog surrounding the area of Eve's Hallow burned away just as the first rays of sun rushed over the horizon. The trees reached up higher with their branches, stretching out as if to pull the sun to them. The willows arched free of burden. They did not weep. They bowed humbly in observance to the small town's history that rebirthed at the root, and coursed strong through their branches and leaves.

A dome was forming, and Water Bug Hollow's family trees regained strength.

27

Wyatt Jakobi liked what he heard crooning from the horn player's trumpet. It lifted his spirits from the workday he just ended. The day was partly cloudy, and both sunshine and horn fought against the cumulus, ashen bloom. Not every note was perfect, a few were strained, but it was still soothing. Silk. Hot melted butter. That's what he compared the slow and soft, jazzy number to as the music caught his ear the instant he stepped out of his place of employment, the Howard Phillips Psychiatric Institution in Hammonton, New Jersey. His eyes followed the notes as if they floated in the air in front of him. All instinctive warning and understanding on the possible dangers of horn playing—in his other lines of employment—were wiped completely away. He was entranced.

His did see something. Perhaps animated waves of music did prance up and down, skipping on the air from across the street, leading back to the bell of the horn they were assembled from.

Visual musical notes in existence or not, his eyes—at the very least—followed the sweet sound to its origin. And there across the street stood a tall and dark-skinned, middle-aged man blowing jazz through his horn. A fedora hat calling for donations was propped up on its crown. The horn player was more than mesmerizing. The song was a distraction from common sense. Wyatt dug into his pocket and removed a five-dollar bill from his wallet, fumbling as if the notes themselves became threatening, demanding the money at gunpoint. Once he was euphoniously strong-armed into giving up his cash, Wyatt stepped into the road, compelled to deliver his tender to the horn player.

A car soared passed Wyatt at rocket speed, it's bulk almost killing him. Wyatt backed up onto the sidewalk. The driver sounded the horn, and the cacophony broke through the trumpet's golden-sweet hums, as did the driver's guttural cursing shouted out the window. Wyatt blinked. The music was now gone from his ears. He pivoted, making his way to the train that would take him into New York City. He shuffled quick, his head inundated with a memory, warnings of siren-like, melodic jazz playing seductively in the ear. But there it came again, muting the growling grind of cars. The horn's pleasant harmony stopped Wyatt. He turned and faced the horn player. Two hard notes were hooted, and Wyatt again stood at attention. A tingle coursed through him, electric and cool. He felt as if someone had stripped him naked, and odder still, it seemed air currents passed through him as if he wasn't made of anything somatic.

Wyatt stepped into the street again. Cars raced as if on a track. No one honked or shouted curses at him. They didn't see him, and he didn't care about them. It was all about the music's silky sounds. The wind cut through his body, and the cars filling the streets at dizzying speeds did the same. The material world was not a solid, physical matter to Wyatt. He was not within its time, and so he crossed the street without harm from a speeding, monstrous vehicle flattening him against the pavement.

Wyatt dropped his five dollars into the horn player's hat. The man thank him with a polite, old-time tone to his voice, which Wyatt considered peculiar since man's lips never left the trumpet, and the music never ceased. But it had been a long day for Wyatt, and he also considered that he was just tired. This wasn't his only job, and he felt as if he'd been putting in double-shifts on both ends.

The notion of rest was wrestled from his head when he realized movement around him appeared to drag as if someone hit slow-motion on a video player. The dashing cars crawled to a near halt. People walking in the street dragged out their footsteps, movement of lips while talking into a phone, or some other fiddling, personal matter crept at a slug's pace

The horn player continued moving at an ordinary pace, save perhaps his fingers racing across the instrument's valves. Another person stepped along at a normal pace. It was a tall and brawny, gruff-faced, black man wearing business attire and a gray, medium-length trench coat that framed his broad shoulders. His eyes were fixed on Wyatt. His face brewed with determination, and Wyatt trembled with trepidation. But his mind was at odds with itself. The jazz that played behind him pacified his senses to ignore his primary tendency of flight from what he determined was a danger, an imposing black man walking up on him.

Wyatt struggled to speed up when he witnessed the black man reach inside his coat's interior pocket. Wyatt stiffened. The black man pulled out a wallet and flipped it open to display what looked like an official badge. It wasn't, though it was a medallion. A brass compass with a needle's twitch that was as mesmerizing to behold as the horn player's music was to hear.

"Wyatt Jakobi?" the compass carrier said with authority. "My name is Martin Kimball, private investigator. You're being detained under the suspicion of conspiracy against the conjure community of New York."

Wyatt didn't pretend to not know what the man was talking about. His understanding of the happenings around him filled his head. He wanted to curse as loud and with as much vigor as the driver who'd almost run him over. His harsh words would've been for the black man in front of him, the community he'd come from—its culture—but most of all, Wyatt wanted to curse his own ego for being taken off-guard.

He couldn't if he tried.

The jazz serenading him, now coupled with the private investigator's voice laced with the power of suggestion, made him wholly passive. The last thought Wyatt had before giving in concerned his pride as a needleman, being strong-willed, able to resist a conjure man or conjure woman's silky bewitchments. He often bragged about it. Now, here he was ensnared in a charm, having completely overlooked his understandings of what he called their 'jungle mysticism.' He would kick himself if his faculties and thoughts could work in tandem to carry out a self-proposed action. Instead, he was putting his hands behind his back, locked by an invisible pair of handcuffs.

A gray sedan drove up. Wilson Barnes was in the driver's seat. Martin's investigating partner, Macario Montez, sat on the passenger side. The trunk opened, and Martin Kimball directed Wyatt to get in. The private investigator's voice mingled with the soft notes that swirled in Wyatt's ears, and Wyatt felt an undeniable need to listen. He ducked into the trunk, and Martin closed it on top of him. The private detective turned and watched Papa Solomon finish his playing. The old man bent down and swiped his hat from the sidewalk, removed the five dollars, and plonked his hat atop his head. Both men slipped into the back seat from opposite sides of the car. They'd entered not just the car but the middle of a deep, philosophical debate going on between Wilson and Macario.

"Sun, no! It's not a contest!" Wilson insisted.

Macario gave him an incredulous look and responded, "So, you're saying toffee apples beat candied apples? That's ridiculous, man!"

Wilson shook his head, huffing. "No!" he blurted. "I'm saying it's a trap. They're both poison."

Papa Solomon and Martin looked at one another and exchanged perplexed looks. Papa Solomon dropped his head into his hand and rubbed his finger and thumb across his eyebrows.

Macario huffed back, "Oh, Christ, Wilson! This ain't what I need. More of your self-righteous-ass, healthy ways to eat." Then he pointed to the cigarette in Wilson's lips. "And you smoke, so what's the point."

Wilson took a drag. "And I drink," he admitted. "But nah!" he said waving his hand. "It ain't that. What I'm saying is they're both traps. You either breaking your teeth on one or you're scratching out your gums with the other."

"Wouldn't you scratch out your gums with both? I mean the bits of candy…"

Wilson disagreed and said, "You too busy screaming on the teeth you broke up."

Macario laughed, and Papa Solomon raised his head. "We've procured what's really important. Ease us into time, Wilson. And please get us to Queens so we can interrogate this punk."

Martin looked away, eyes out the window. He started chuckling.

Wilson put the car in drive and moved into the road. He concentrated and maneuvered into traffic, being careful. Before he used any mysticism to flow alongside the normal world with proper, chronometric-dimensional movement, he inquired to Papa Solomon, "Would it be best to keep outside the physical, Papa Solomon?" He peered at the patriarch in the rear-view mirror and explained, "I mean, it's after five o'clock. An attempt into the City from Jersey gon' give us heavy traffic."

The patriarch considered the point. He also had another to make. "I'm a little winded from usin' the horn. You can pull this off by yourself?"

"I got his back, Papa Solomon," Macario assured.

Papa Solomon approved, telling Martin to assist. He then sat back, his family horn in his lap, and commenced to get rest. Wilson and Macario concentrated on keeping the car outside of time, ghosting through traffic's inactivity.

Once they past the barrier of traffic into the New York City, they eased into physical time. Wilson pulled into Maman Anansi's house in Queens a little after dusk. The Grand Matriarch stood in wait on her porch draped in one of her signature, regal outfits. Her daughter, lawyer Stephanie Dumas, stood next to her in business attire. Wilson parked. Martin was the first to pop his door and step out. His face remained stern and professional, but his insides were bright and smiling as he spotted Stephanie standing in a glow cast down on her from the porchlight. Papa Solomon and the others emerged from the car simultaneously. The trunk was opened moments before, and Martin stepped back to open it.

Papa Solomon slipped Wilson the five-dollar bill before walking up to his older sister and declaring their part of the mission accomplished. Blessed him with praise, and then all eyes were on the activity going on behind Wilson's car. The three men were hidden from view, the trunk up and acting as cover. Macario and Wilson flanked the private investigator as he made the incanted suggestion for Wyatt Jakobi to get out of the trunk. All three men watched close, though Jakobi was submissive, making no attempts at any defiant moves.

Wilson took a peek around the trunk. He eyed Stephanie and whispered to Martin and Macario, "Stephanie looking good. She know what she doin' in them clothes."

Martin's lip curled. He grabbed one of Wyatt Jakobi's arms and dragged the man from behind the car. He snapped at Wilson, "Show some respect, black conjure man." Wilson snickered and shook his head. He rolled his eyes, shut his car's trunk, and fell in line behind Martin. Macario was in tow. Martin brought Wyatt to the Grand Matriarch. "Maman Anansi," he stated her title, a slight bow to his head. Wilson and Macario did the same.

Martin added a courtesy greeting to Stephanie. "Miss Dumas," he said, paying the same head-bowing respect toward her.

Stephanie beamed at Martin in return. "Detective," she replied.

Wilson rolled his eyes again. An artful expression appeared on Maman Anansi's countenance. She jested, "Law and Order, the Balance and the Sword, all coming together." Then the Grand Matriarch turned in a swift motion. *"Follow!"* she commanded the party. Everyone fell in line behind her. Maman Anansi guided her guests to a quaint room off the dining area. Small and intimate, there was a single, wooden chair set within a semi-circle of plush, white chairs. Maman Anansi's husband, Andre Alec Dumas sat and enjoyed a glass of bourbon. He lifted the glass as a salute when the others entered.

The Grand Matriarch and Stephanie stepped aside, permitting Martin entrance. He spoke an incant and Wyatt was able to separate his wrists. He ordered the needleman to sit. Wyatt obeyed, sitting up straight and attentive, hands on his knees.

Martin moved away from him, and Maman Anansi approached. She asked the spellbound man, "You know who I am?"

Wyatt looked up at her. His expression was blank, and he said nothing.

Maman Anansi opened her hand, palm up. Soft, green strands of light coiled out of her palm like blades of grass from the earth. They twisted into one another and formed a small, glowing knife. The matriarch gripped the ethereal blade and jammed it into the top of Wyatt's head. She replied to her own question, "I'm your conscience, little man!" A low hum resonated from the glowing, embedded dagger. It trembled as its tenor vibrated, and its otherworldly effect made Wyatt more suggestable. And as violent as Maman Anansi's incision was, Wyatt sustained no physical pain or damage. A preternatural truth serum flowed through his brain. His body was numb and his mind was an open vault. Maman Anansi turned to her daughter and said, "Your witness." Then she respectfully moved away.

Stephanie stepped up to Wyatt. She put her hands in her pockets. "Your name and age?" she asked.

"Wyatt Waltham Jakobi," Wyatt answered. He added, "Forty-four years old."

"Place of employment?"

He replied, "Howard Phillips Psychiatric Institution in Hammonton, New Jersey."

"What's your salary?"

There was no hesitation, or emotional tone, when Wyatt responded, "Forty-three thousand, two hundred and eleven dollars a year."

Stephanie inquired, "Is this your only job?"

"No."

"Please state your second area of employment?"

"I deliver needles and other occult paraphernalia to men and women who are called Night Doctors, also called Needlemen."

"Do you work for Stanley Fallows?"

"No," he stated. He continued in a monotone, matter-of-fact way, "My services are contracted out to Stanley Fallows by way of my family down South. I'm a small chain in a fragile truce between my brother Sampson Jakobi and the Fallows family."

Stephanie looked over at her uncle, who'd taken a seat. He met her eye and presented a quick nod of his head. She continued her interrogation. "Are you aware of Stanley Fallows kidnapping six children from an African-American conjure community in Brooklyn, New York?"

"Yes."

"Do you know the whereabouts of these children?"

Only a few seconds passed between question and answer, but the room felt as if time had been fastened still between the interval of inquiry and reply. "Yes. They've been moved around, but I know their current location. They are kept at a warehouse in New Rochelle. It's referred to as The Garden."

Exhale. Everything was summed up in Maman Anansi's vocal sentiment. "Ah! Progress!" she stated with a raised eyebrow.

Stephanie had more questions.

"Have the children been harmed?"

Time again elongated, but the answer came, disturbing as it was.

"The children have been changed," Wyatt informed.

Stephanie couldn't decipher whether anger or fear made her tremble, though she remained professional and collected. Her interior faculties raced, from heart to mind. Even the otherworldly abilities she possessed vibrated with a heightened sense. The other community members in the room were much the same. She saw her mother's face bend into a hard, cold stare at Wyatt. Her wrath collected like the energy she could manipulate into kinetic, concussive force or psychic conjure shaped into throwing knives.

Stephanie inquired, "How have the children been changed?"

"Mistress Lucretia transfigured them into potted flowers," he revealed. "Their skin was hardening, becoming immune to the needles. A curious thing. So, Mistress Lucretia used her hex to transform them. Their petals regrow, and their essence is better handled when applied to Master Fallows' garment as a dye." Wyatt perked up. He was happy to express, "He's making a cloak! It's far easier than injecting himself with their essences. Direct flow into his bloodstream nearly killed him. He's still very sick. My brother hopes he dies, but he doubts he will. He already has a blood condition, so there's hope."

"So, the truce is indeed fragile," noted Macario.

Martin interjected, "Yes, but they still know how to come together against us."

Putting the interrogation back on track, Stephanie asked, "Can you give the address of this warehouse?"

"Fifteen-Thirty-Two Lockwood Avenue. It also houses needles. It acts as a pharmaceutical facility. It's mostly empty, though. No offices. The children are kept in an area under hexed grow lights that keep their petals sprouting right after they're plucked."

Stephanie looked at her mother. Maman Anansi made a face hinting at her admiration for Lucretia. She expressed to Papa Solomon, "What's that saying you picked up from Lena? Always give your enemy a compliment." She shook her head positively at the notion. "Lucretia Fallows..." she said the name thinking of the woman's enchantment. "She is a witch through and through. I hate to give that bitch credit." She looked at her brother and said, "But, I have too, correct."

Alex finished his bourbon and commented, "I hate to go against Lena's words—Vencil, you hold them close as an ideology." He looked back at his wife. "Don't give this *bon-marché kopi* that much credit. This woman ain't no *bèl sòsyè* like you, Cal-T. Or any good Afra-conjure woman."

Maman Anansi's agreed with her husband's words. "Let's prove that true, husband. Let's get up, knock her on her ass." She stepped up and declared to Papa Solomon, "We'll be able to reverse the transfiguration and cleanse the children's minds. It'll be a long and hard process, but we'll be successful. We'll use all-out conjure."

Papa Solomon put forward, "Cedron and his band will make a strike against this 'Garden' site. Quick, too. Don't know how long Stanley's had them children configured like that. Ain't good for the mind. I'll send the Misfits in for a midnight hit, use the dark as cover. Procure the children." He said to his sister, "I'll need you and Thelema to hold a ritual to keep them protected. I'll dispatch Gordon with them. The Garden won't be a light target. We'll need as much firepower as can be conjured to bring back the children."

Maman Anansi agreed with her brother's strategy.

Papa Solomon peered at Wyatt with a curious and long, stern gaze. "Speaking of Thelema, Cal, we'll keep this catch a while longer. I want to draw out more of his story. Thel work on this boy good, especially if he's under your influence. He's only an errand boy, but I'm sure this fool has been tasked with many errands. There could be more Gardens out there, ones growing needles and other weed-like hexes meant to choke us."

Everyone in the room digested the patriarch's words.

Then, the doorbell rang.

Maman Anansi's face brightened. She said in a perky tone, "Oh! Company! How unexpected—even for us with higher senses. Let me get that." First, she turned to Wyatt and removed the conjured throwing knife from his crown. His head fell forward, eyes closed, but he remained in the chair without toppling over. "Let's permit this fool some sleep," she insisted. Maman Anansi dissipated her conjure and traveled to the front door. She opened it and found Benjamin Brickhouse standing alone on her porch.

"Benjamin!" Maman Anansi addressed him with surprise swashed on her face. "What brings you out here from Harlem?" She looked around. There was no car in the driveway, and she sensed he used his conjure to travel here on air, coupled with the use of the armor piece he'd won in a wager. "And at this house…"

Benny hesitated before telling her, "We have a bit of a problem, Maman Anansi."

Her instinct deciphered Benny's thoughts. He had news, and that news stretched the features on the Grand Matriarch's face. Worry and surprise flushed and withered on her countenance as Benny's information was revealed to her in thought. She asked, "When did Sean Commons' spirit make itself known?"

"A while back," Benny answered through a sigh. "I wanted to tell you at the church in Water Bug Hollow, but there was never a private moment. Thought I could isolate you here."

"Do you know what's happening at the moment? Inside?" specified Maman Anansi.

Benny backed away. He covered his mouth with his clenched, armored fist. "Oh! My bad, Maman Anansi. You and Uncle Andre tryna spark some romance—"

Maman Anansi cast a raised-eyebrow at Benny. "Mister Brickhouse, there is an interrogation of a needleman happening. We've found the children's location." She motioned for Benny to enter. He walked inside, and Maman Anansi closed the door. "Second things first: Tell Cedron that you Gypsy Misfits are needed. Have him contact Papa Solomon. And first—" Then Maman Anansi called loud, *"Stephanie!"*

Her daughter cropped up from around the corner. She saw Benny, and before she addressed her mother, she questioned his appearance by simply saying his name. "Benny…?"

Maman Anansi spoke before Benny could say anything, or her daughter could use instinct to decrypt the situation. "Upstairs!" she said with a voice flush with severity. "Your brother's room!" she punctuated.

Stephanie went stiff. She spoke in defense, "Mamma, I-I-I…I can't go into…"

"Don't argue!" said the Grand Matriarch. "This ain't no courtroom and your conjure ain't got that much power to persuade me. *Upstairs! Now!*" Stephanie turned around. She took a moment to concentrate her instincts, but her mother's mind was surrounded by a thick aegis that extended to Benny as well. All she heard in her head was the electric hiss of her instinct scraping up against her mother's strong, hard, and stubborn mental shields. Maman Anansi grumbled behind her, "You'll know what this about when we get upstairs."

"Yes, Mamma…"

No higher sense needed. Stephanie knew. Benny's presence and her mother's call to attendance could only add up to something that had been haunting her in brief sightings. She stepped into her brother's room and turned on the lights. It was clean, not necessarily how he used to keep it. Empty, but oddly so filled with life in snapshots. Interests from movies to sports posters. Album covers placed everywhere. Guitar and keyboards. A desk with an old computer, video games situated next to it. What made it feel like an icebox among all the memorable warmth was his absence. Even when his spirit visited by will or conjured for light conversation, the potential for all he could've been was still diminished. Stephanie's family was luckier than most. They had a connection to an ancient magic that was fastened to the two forces that created the universe and all the nooks tucked into the cosmos that not even light could touch. So, enjoying conversation with kith and kin under proper ritual or through a simple thought was not a strange notion, especially now that the lilac flame and cobalt-blue spirit had re-entered the world. But Stephanie was too hurt by her brother's loss to ever enjoy his presence.

She sat at his desk. Benny took a seat at the foot of the bed. Stephanie suppressed the reflex to reprimand him for sitting there. That was her brother's place. Her mother's hard stare also put her words on pause. She was a child again, and she was in trouble with her mother.

"I don't need to put no knowing-knife in your head, do I girl?"

Stephanie made a face. "No! Mamma. No… Why?"

Maman Anansi thawed. "Because I want to know what you were thinking, or how you could *not* be thinking. You know why Mister Brickhouse is here?"

Stephanie answered her mother, "I can guess, Mamma. That boy's spirit came to him. Sean Commons." Then she confessed, "I've seen him too. Passing glimpses of his specter looking at me. He's there long enough for me to notice and know he's angry for what I did."

"He's restless, sis." Her brother's voice was heard before his spirit manifested, standing next to his bed. "You need to talk to him. Make amends. He could become an *inawo*—your *inawo*, sis. That gets dangerous for you, and it gets ugly within its resolution." Enock urged again, "Make amends. He not the guy that killed me. That dude got justice."

Stephanie looked at her brother. For all of his spectral presence, she only saw a candle with its wick no longer aflame. Her eyes welled with tears for him. She sniffed them back and wiped her face. She told her brother, "For you. I'll talk to him for you."

Enock walked over to his sister and squatted in front of her. Stephanie looked away from him, as he used all the power in his spirit to make solid a single finger to draw her eyes back to him. "Do this for *you*, sis. I'm already resting in peace. I'm good…" He smirked and added, "There's even a couple honnies I got on the other side."

Stephanie said nothing, but she nodded affirmatively to his suggestion.

Enock stood. Maman Anansi beamed at him. He faded, but didn't leave the earthly plain. He materialized downstairs, standing in front of Martin Kimball. Alec perked up with his son's entrance. "That's my boy!" he cheered. "On visit from the otha side!"

Enock gave a quick acknowledgment to his father. "Hey, Pop-Pop. How you good, old man?"

"Drinkin' an' kissin' yo' mamma good in this retirement!" he answered his son.

Enock grinned. "You keep good, Pop-Pop. Keep good." He turned to Martin and said in a stern voice, "You. Like. My sister. She. Likes. You." Every word was emphasized with great importance. "Yo! Look out for her. She going through something."

Martin said nothing, but he made a promise in his head. Enock could hear it.

The spirit nodded at the private detective, and then he faded away.

Wilson commented, "Black as you is, sun, you do be her *white* knight."

Martin gave Wilson a look.

Wilson chuckled, and so did Macario.

Martin managed to smile.

28

oft shoes stepped.

Silent.

Gordon strolled down Lockwood Avenue in New Rochelle. It was close to midnight. A small, dark cloud concealed the moon's bright and prying, pale eye. The moon was far from full, but its curiosity was clear enough. The billowing, airy inkblot veiling the moon was the consequence of conjure performed by wise-women matriarchs residing in a sacred sanctuary in the Brooklyn borough. The stars spied him, but nothing else. No manner of creature, be it human, animal, or some summoned swine. But something lay in wait, casting odious, frothy shadows of their own, dubious projection.

Gordon took advantage of the night and all its shades, slipping in stealth through the veils of pitch. He stepped up to the corner of the street, peering across at the warehouse that was his destination. Rusted-brown brick peeked out behind the black of night. The structure's posture was foreboding. It was mighty like a giant's clutched fist, daring any mortal to penetrate its fortitude. Not only did it appear impenetrable, but the building being draped in the night's shades cast a spine-piercing chill to the average man or woman.

But Gordon wasn't average. He possessed a cosmic power named the *lilac flame*. It made him feel safe, but it didn't stop his human instinct to hesitate at the sight of the warehouse stronghold. Clutching at the spirit within him wasn't what bolstered his poise. He thought of the children detained inside. That's when Gordon looked up and noticed conjure cast in stealth. While it didn't resonate a frequency that could be detected by villains with attuned ears, Gordon's shimmering, pale-violet eyes spied the conjure at play. A whirl of winding wind that looked like a quick, drafted sketch of lines rotating against the starry sky. It traveled straight, and then angled up the side of the warehouse. Gordon blinked, and his eyesight zoomed in, bringing the edge of the building closer to his view. He saw the sketches of wind materialize into the silhouette of his childhood friend, Benny Jah. While his hoody-wearing frame was shrouded in shadow, even with the moon covered by clouds, Gordon could make out the gleam of the shiny metal piece that cloaked his arm and intensified his conjure. Also stepping out of Benny's conjured airy, intangible state was Benny's sweetheart, Neyeli Kimball.

Gordon grinned. He blinked again and his eyesight retracted back to normal. Then Gordon disappeared, popping from existence. His physical form recombined atop the warehouse, standing next to Neyeli with his hands in his pockets.

"We beat you!" Benny whispered at him.

Gordon snickered, "I'll give you somethin' to beat."

"Boys…" Neyeli chimed in.

Gordon and Benny settled their playful machismo. Then all three tossed hardened stares at the rooftop entrance. Gordon spoke first. "They've had these kids buried and potted in this place since…" he shook his head and finished, "for far too long." He looked at his two friends and stated, "We go in there with minimal conjure play. We sneak right, using the information from our bastard-needleman informant, and we bring 'em home."

"Yeah," Benny Jah said with his eyes on the door. "Yeah, we get 'em home. That's what we gotta do." He looked at Neyeli. She looked at him, lifting her eyebrows, projecting her opinion without a word spoken.

She turned to Gordon and asked, "We go in there and have ourselves a look-see. Let's find out how minimal is 'minimal conjure play?" She shook her head and put her eyes back on the door. "We're in for a fight, aren't we?"

"Yeah, Gordon," Benny took up. "I sense a trap."

"Of course, it's a trap!" Gordon hissed at his two friends. "We dealin' with Stanley Fallows. He see it comin' before it comes—and he lookin' to get my blood and essence. And here I am." He walked forward, pivoting to look at his friends as he made steps backwards toward the rooftop doors. He spread his arms as wide as his smile and suggested, "So, let's spring his trap." Gordon added a shadow to the night, but it didn't slide to and fro with the little light that existed. It seeped from his skin and dissolved the clothes he wore. In the blink of an eye he was wearing a black, skintight outfit sewn from cosmic cloth. The same ethereal substance wrapped about his face and solidified into what looked like an African, male Chokwe mask. "Let's give this place some spirit," he suggested.

Dooley popped away, leaving behind black lines of energy that emitted a soft, lilac glow on their edges, whisking about in atom-formation. Benny Jah put his arms around Neyeli and used the power of his armor piece to transform both of them into gossamer, black, sketches of air that ghosted through the rooftop door and formed back into Benny and Neyeli on the other side. They flanked Dooley. He jumped onto a railing and looked over. All the way down. He whispered to his friends, "Stick to my brother's plan. I'm the draw out. You'll know if I'm in trouble." Then he dived, head first.

Halfway down, Dooley's physical form changed into multiple black streaks. He materialized solid toward the end of his descent, flipped, and landed soft on his feet. He stepped toward the door in front of him ready to change into ether and dissolve through the physical barrier. His instinct buzzed around his neck like a noose's tight embrace on a swaying, hanged man. He wheezed, and a thought occurred to him. Dooley again phased out of the physical realm, and the asphyxiated effect dispersed. His instinct rang again, this time hissing atop his crown. Dooley turned his torso, fists balled and ready for action, looking about. His cosmic-imbued eyesight peered through the darkness and spied a billowing, white fog filling the room and spinning into a cloud that shifted into a physical form.

Its name was now Grave-Clothes. It was once an esteemed needleman named Mathew Quinn. Another who'd been recast, put into the mold of this hazy configuration by Stanley and Lucretia Fallows through the nightmarish ritual called the *Züle*. Now he was a Bag Head, one of the five nightmares convoked to hold court against the lilac and cobalt-blue flames.

Grave-Clothes' physique floated off the ground. It dripped fog, and was swathed in a cloudy wrapping, mummified and cocooned in murk from the unseen, and hexed, anathematic world. Grave-Clothes still supported the crinkled bag over his head, now drained of its brown, leathery color to a bleached contrast.

The blanched specter dived down, arms outstretched, reaching for Dooley. The cosmic spirit dodged, leaping backward and ghosting through the door. Grave-Clothes followed, and Dooley was ready for him. He threw a punch and connected, channeling an extra force of cosmic power in his fist. Grave-Clothes tumbled to the floor. His impact shook him from the shadow realm into the physical. He recovered, though now with a stumble in his step.

Dooley remained in his intangible state. He used the power of his spherical, lilac-colored eye to survey his dark surroundings. It was a warehouse no different than any other. There were three levels in a wide-open space connected by wall-hugging, narrow walkways and bridges. Dooley kept his physical eyes on Grave-Clothes. The monster was now on his feet. He rushed forward, phased from reality, and lunged at Dooley.

Dooley transmuted into a solid state, and Grave-Clothes incorporeal body passed through him. While no physical effect occurred, the haunt's ghost through Dooley's body caused Dooley to slump to one knee. His face contorted behind his mask and he thought to himself, *That drained me of a few vitality bars*. He turned his head, looking over his shoulder to spot Grave-Clothes coming around for another attack. Dooley got to his feet, ready to shift into another plane to throw fisticuffs with the cursed specter. He put himself in stance when an invisible garrote wreathed his neck. Dooley jerked, making a quick decision to form into the ethers again. He regained composure, linked his hands together and threw them into Grave-Clothes' back. Another cosmic surge writhed itself through the immaterial being, knocking him to the ground and back into the physical.

The power also shook through Dooley, heightening his senses. His instinct exploded and he looked across the wide-open room to see a woman wearing a blood-red pants suit with a black, gothic, cowl that draped over her head and spread wide across her shoulders. Her fingertips were pressed against one another in a triangular formation, pointed down. Blood-red strands of electricity writhed around her. Her name was Adamina Red, but only at Lucretia Fallows' rebirth of her. She was born Alyssa Hand in Savannah, Georgia. At the age of twenty she was initiated into a small, but notorious, sect of hexers denominated as The Curse Words. Her specialty was forging and anointing needles, and when she was called up by Lucretia Fallows to serve in a company designated as The Blood Curses, her heart raced and she hastened to New York. She arrived and underwent the painful, surgical ritual that would draw out her hex. Now here she was. No longer forging needles. Adamina believed she was the needle, the hexed tip that could turn and twist conjure into a noose, strangling a conjure man or conjure woman with their own power.

Dooley deciphered this woman was at the epicenter of the hex that throttled him when he was turned solid. He calculated a precarious tactic, and executed it in haste. Dooley solidified and burst into his lilac form. With no hesitancy or doubt, the cosmic spirit catapulted forward as a glimmering, lilac streak. His body pierced the red-blood, electric aegis whirling around her. His harpoon strike bore through Adamina Red's abdomen. Her body doubled over as Dooley's lancet configuration passed through her and tunneled out the other side. The dazzling, lilac javelin restructured into Dooley's black, cosmic-suited appearance. Electric, lilac strands wriggled off him and dissipated into smoke.

Dooley knew her now. *Alyssa Hand, called Adamina Red. Known affiliations: The Curse Words and The Blood Curses, aka The Blood Cursers.* The latter was his current entanglement. He snatched from her mind the number of rogue's in the gallery. There were five. As promised in old-man Banneker's prophetic warning. Dooley only counted two, and he was already breathing heavy from wrangling with them. But there was more to his strike against Adamina Red than just knocking the walking blood curse to her knees, where she now wheezed and stumbled in recovery. He'd sent out a shockwave to his allies. All the information he'd learned. They were now caught up on current events. There was a rogue's gallery in wait. And so too waited Dooley as his brother Cedron plotted and his crew, the Gypsy Moon Misfits, scurried into position to assist. Even Benny Jah and Neyeli remained unmoving behind the door leading to the staircase. Their stillness was from wait, anticipating the other Blood Curses' seep from the shadows. Neyeli's hair burned maroon, excited for the battle.

Dooley's spherical, lilac eye burned bright. The large room became illuminated in its shine, and the other Blood Curses were stripped of the shadows that concealed them.

The first Dooley spotted couldn't be missed. The creature named Tine was a large, icy-blue-skinned mass of bubbling muscle and might. As if his size and strength weren't intimidating enough, the behemoth—once a simple man named Kenneth Zupan who worked in marketing for a company based in Knoxville—was covered in the pointed ends of hexed needles all over his arms and hands. Dooley snapped a mental picture of the beast as it ducked its head walking under the first set of walkways mounted high above. Dooley sent Tine's image directly to his brother's mind. A sly whisper accompanied the visual. *You get the pretty one, Cee.*

On Dooley's immediate left was a woman who took the name Ole Higue. A partial shadow continued cloaking her in the far corner of the warehouse. She stepped out of it, hissing like a snake as she walked closer to Dooley on the tips of her toes. She wore white pants with brown boots. A cream-colored blouse covered her top, and over that was a tan vest. She was pale with brown hair and light-brown eyes. Her skin was covered in wrinkles, but they were not natural. Ole Higue was once a thirty-year-old woman named Selene Swansong, a computer specialist from Westchester County. Dooley knew this history, as pulled from Adamina Red. Selene the Ole Higue was now vampiric, or rather *soucouyant*, in nature, but her victims had little to worry about when it came to her teeth. They were no sharper than the average human, perhaps duller. But the two, black talons on each hand that were once her fingers, inherited the cast of intimidation.

The four converged. The fifth Blood Curser attempted to play off his reveal as if Dooley's light had not shooed away his shaded cover. Lazy Crow stood on the first walkway. His eyeless and squared clock face peered at Dooley over Tine's shoulder. His hands were in an embrace behind his back. The clock hands on his visage moved hypnotically, casting a mysterious power that amplified his allies' abilities.

Dooley looked back at Lazy Crow and addressed him by his birth name. "Oh, c'mon, Artie," he taunted. "C'mon down here and join the rest of us." He pondered for a moment and then said aloud, "Something familiar about you, clock-boy. Like we've met before, or something. You been watchin' me from afar? Perhaps when I showed up at the Fallows' place?"

Lazy Crow lifted off the ground, keeping his stance. He floated over Tine's shoulder and hovered near a recovering Adamina Red. "Mister. Good. Speed," he said, his voice an icy whisper in Dooley's ears. The rhythm of his speech was like the tick of a clock. *Appropriate and on the nose*, thought Dooley. "You. Have. Something. For. Us. Mister. Good. Speed."

"Just like folk," Dooley groaned out loud but to himself. "Always thinkin' what's mine is theirs and actin' like they ain't stole somethin'." He sensed Ole Higue creeping closer, her sharp talons fanned out and ready to strike at Dooley to extract blood and essence. Dooley snarled under his mask.

He snapped, "You want a piece of me? You can have it. Where're the children?" But he didn't allow Lazy Crow or any other Blood Curser to answer. The cosmic spirit burst into a lilac fire, and then thinned into a stream that zipped up into the spherical third eye resting on his forehead. He pounced, tearing straight at Ole Higue, his thin, comet form piercing through her chest and coming out the other side.

Ole Higue screamed, but didn't lose her footing. She turned and took a swipe at Dooley as he shifted solid in his black, cosmic form. Dooley dodged with a simple but swift step back. Ole Higue made another attempt, thrusting her talons down on Dooley. He again evaded her strike, but the force of a train slammed into his side, covering his whole body. Tine took a few steps forward and threw a heavy punch, hitting Dooley while he was distracted by Ole Higue's attacks.

The garrison of needles lining his fingers didn't puncture Dooley's cosmic outfit or skin, but they added an extra wallop to the giant's strike. Dooley slammed into the wall, cracking the concrete structure. While the force would've killed an average human, Dooley simply had the wind knocked out of him, which didn't make matters any better. He became disoriented. The room lost the light of his glow for a moment, and then it became like a rave's strobe lighting.

Lazy Crow ticked, "The. Children. Mister. Good. Speed. Will. Stay. Firmly. Planted. With. Us."

Dooley curled his lip beneath his mask, frustrated and writhing in pain. But he absorbed the shock of Tine's attack, and he anchored his spinning vision by using the power of his lilac eye. The scenery around him slowed long enough to calculate where his enemies stood. He again burst into slender flame and zipped like a slung pebble. He landed between Tine's eyes, crashing against icy-blue flesh. The gargantuan lifted his head and hollered! The sound rattled the warehouse's steel pillars. Cosmic, conjure energy coursed through Tine's body like a searing fire. A bright glow emanated from his flesh, charged with Dooley's lilac, cosmic power.

Ricocheting, Dooley again crashed against Ole Higue's chest, lifting her off her feet and knocking her against the exit door. Dooley's frantic, pinball assault next crossed Adamina Red's jaw as she attempted to use her power to turn his cosmic conjure against him and slow him down. Grave-Clothes was missed, hanging back from the frenzied assault. Dooley's rebound raced toward Lazy Crow. The floating, clock-headed monster didn't flinch. He bobbed in the air, eyeless face targeting Dooley's comet-like approach closing in. The hands on his clock face rotated counter-clockwise, and a wave of anathematic hex rippled toward Dooley, slowing his approach, and bringing it to a grinding halt.

Dooley reverted to his black, cosmic-suited form. He floated in the air a few meters away from Lazy Crow. His body contorted as if there was an invisible hand wrapping its fingers around him. He fought against the pressure, and then a concussive force hammered him back to the ground. His body rolled when it smacked against the concrete floor, but Dooley remained coherent even as his body took the blows from the anathematic power and crash. He managed to flip himself up onto his feet in time to witness a recovered Tine tossing another powerful punch at him.

Dooley assumed a defensive stance. His lilac eye glowed brighter than before, and as Dooley balled his fists, a wide beam of lilac conjure issued forth and acted as an aegis when colliding against Tine's robust fist.

Dooley continued channeling all the cosmic power he could summon to keep Tine's fist from connecting to him. The stubborn titan fought against the conjure energy keeping him from his target. He screamed, attempting to increase his adrenaline to carve through Dooley's projected spirit.

Lazy Crow pivoted his entire body as he floated, face aimed at Tine. He considered assisting his fellow Blood Curser by amplifying his strength or decreasing Dooley's. But he felt a presence. He turned and spied Ole Higue approaching the black, cosmic spirit. Her talons ready to strike and extract Dooley's lilac essence. If he had lips, Lazy Crow would smile. He was pleased to see that, with Dooley distracted, Ole Higue could seize the opportunity. And so, she crept closer.

Lazy Crow descended next to Adamina Red and lowered her outstretched hands glowing with blood-red energy. "No. Let. This. Happen." He turned to her and expounded, "Disturb. The. Scene. And. He. May. Escape. The. Pricking."

Adamina Red nodded.

Lazy Crow turned his head to check on Grave-Clothes, and when he spotted him, he saw there was trouble. Benny Jah, his body intangible and wading in the anathematic realm, tussled with the foggy-cloaked phantom.

If he had lips, Lazy Crow would curl them in frustration.

The hands on his clock face tick-tocked, and his senses heightened. He realized, looking at Dooley, that this wasn't the Blood Curses' trap to ensnare the lilac spirit, using the Fable Avenue children as bait. This was these jungle conjurers' trap to rescue them, using the lilac spirit as bait!

A beam of energy lassoed around Adamina Red's neck. It hissed! Adamina Red was able to observe the energy around her neck was only half the cord that wrangled her. The other half extended in front of her as an orange-glowing snake's head snapping its fangs at her. Neyeli Kimball stood behind the Blood Curser, puppeteering the snake-lariat.

Face curled up in a vexed expression, Adamina Red wheezed, "You think me frightened, jungle witch?" She dug her fingers into the constricting conjure, and she burned it with her hex. The glowing and living rope unwound from her neck. It gyrated, fell to the ground, and then slithered in a hurry toward Neyeli, ready to attack. But the young conjure woman called the incandescent serpent to her hand, recharging it to her faction.

Lazy Crow was too distracted to assist Adamina Red. The clock-headed monster witnessed Dooley execute an impressive maneuver. The cosmic spirit grabbed Ole Higue by the wrists and pulled her in front of him. Then he cut his wide, lilac beam and blinked away, leaving Ole Higue in the path of Tine's massive fist. Barrier removed, Tine's fist propelled forward, connected with a devastating force against Ole Higue, and broke through the concrete wall, into a hallway leading to the exit.

The building shook with the impact, and Tine retracted his fist while hollering. Ole Higue lay unconscious, sleeping through the intense pain of her bloody and broken body. Tine scoffed, curling his lip and huffing like a mad bull. He turned his attention to Dooley, who'd reemerged from his disappearance in front of Lazy Crow. Tine charged, but was too late to save Lazy Crow from a heavy strike from Dooley's lilac eye that knocked him across the warehouse. Tine powered another punch, cocking back his fist. But before he could launch a strike in Dooley's back, he found himself overrun by figures conjured from shadows, on command to attack by Tap.

Dooley sensed the cavalry had arrived. Cedron, his body fully onyx with gold, circuit patterns running around it, jumped onto Tine's back, doing his best to put the behemoth in a headlock. Tine bucked! Cedron held tight. The giant grabbed the shadow beings crawling on him, tossing them around the warehouse.

Tine's shadow flinging, with Cedron draped around his neck, became less random and more directed to the area where Raymundo Shaw rushed in slinging his energized light arrows at Tine. The diabolical mass absorbed the projectiles, and while Raymond's power did little to injure the giant, the magic missles' impact delivered a distracting force. Tine dealt with the nuisance by grappling several shadow figures scaling him and hurling them at Raymond. The archer ducked away, rolling on the ground.

Lazy Crow recovered from Dooley's thunderous strike against him, sitting up on his elbows and crawling backward to raise up against the wall. Dooley zipped at him to deliver a salvo of pugilistic artillery. But the clock-faced monster released a vibratory wave of anathematic hex that slowed the cosmic spirit down to a crawl. The ripples of anathematic residue transformed into an invisible hand that caught Dooley in its clutches. Dooley struggled against the grip Lazy Crow transmitted in his direction. An attempt to shift intangible had little results, as Lazy Crow was able to slow down Dooley's power.

Wall crept. Risen to feet. "You. Possess. Un. Limited. Cosmic. Power. Mister. Good. Speed. But. You. Are. Not. All. Power. Full." Lazy Crow increased the gravity on his anathematic wave, curling Dooley into a fetal position. The Blood Curser reached into his pocket and removed a hexed syringe. If he had lips, he would've smirked. "What. Reward. Awaits. Me. When. I. Present. Your. Essence. To. Master. Fallows."

Dooley cursed as he continued wrestling with the invisible anathematic hand keeping him in place. He reached out with his senses and saw that everyone had their own struggles afoot. Benny Jah continued his fisticuffs with Grave-Clothes. Neyeli battled with Adamina Red for supremacy of her own menagerie of conjured snakes. Cedron, Tap's shadow beings, and Raymond were locked in confrontation with the giant.

Lazy Crow inched closer, and as he did, an old saying popped into Dooley's head. It was something his grandfather would tell him. *Always wait twenty seconds.* He'd counted only up to three when a wide, spinning, fire discus collided with Lazy Crow and knocked him aside. Dooley landed on foot and knee and caught his breath. He glanced to his right to see Leah, bent forward. A large pair of fiery, angelic wings retracted into her spine. Dooley thanked her through telepathy, and then he stood, rushed over to the syringe Lazy Crow dropped, and crushed it with his foot.

Pilfering occurred high above. Or rescue, as it were. Tap, and his shadowed love interest named Aloka, looted the garden of the six, potted, beautiful flowers that were the kidnapped, transfigured Fable Avenue children. The room acted as a greenhouse, built with tinted mirrors instead of translucent glass and glowing with dull, yellow lights transmitting hex. With Dooley and the Gypsy Moon Misfits distracting the Fallows monsters, Tap and Aloka entered the room and gathered up the six potted flowers. Tap stepped back, three pots in one grip, one in the second. The dull lights beat down on them. Its hexed beams were slow to effect at first, as they seeped into their heads, causing a terrible ache. Tap ultimately vomited from the hex's influence.

Aloka started fading. A few of her fingers lost their rigidity, effecting her grip. She dropped to one knee, managing to set down the potted plants in her possession. Tap remained on his feet, though wobbling. He turned around. One step at a time, he made his way to the door. He struggled against invisible chains while his feet felt mired in thick, hardening concrete. His vision blurred, and his head experienced a crushing pressure. He gritted his teeth, straining against the nausea brought on by the lights' dull, yellow glow.

Tap fell to his knees. He put the potted flowers down and then fell forward. He struck his palms rhythmically against the floor. On a fifth and sixth hit, two shadows sprang up. "Y-y-y-you…ain't…g-g-got m-m-m-much…t-t-t-time…"

The shadows leapt up high, their bodies shimmering in and out of existence as Tap started succumbing more and more to the glowing hex cast off by the lights. Aloka joined her brothers. She vaulted high up, smashing the lights. She and her brothers' timing had to be precise, as their dark bodies washed in and out of somatic form.

The shadows in the rumble below also suffered from the same fate. Dooley and the Gypsy Moon Misfits continued keeping the Blood Cursers at bay. Most took the giant, with even Leah getting into the fray, projecting her spinning feathers from her fiery wings. Dooley, Neyeli and Benny Jah tag teamed Adamina Red, Lazy Crow, and Grave-Clothes. The clock-faced monster attempted to nullify his adversaries with his baneful curses, but when one was slowed, another was there to take place and give fight. Lazy Crow defended himself with skill and hex, but a piercing sensation disturbed the ticking on his clock, and his senses heightened to another inconvenience. He had a moment to aim his face up. High, high above. He sensed another set of shadows and conjure creeping about to steal the children.

If he had a mouth, he'd bare teeth in dissatisfaction.

Up. On a high level of the warehouse. Vitality flooded Tap's body as his shadows smashed out the lights. He coughed and wheezed as he jumped up to his feet. Aloka and the other two shadow beings collected the potted flowers, each taking two. Tap told his shaded sweetheart, "Imp-p-p-ressive. B-b-b-but, I-I-I th-th-th-think you coulda used the-the l-l-l-light switch…"

Aloka's facial features were dark, buried in the midnight pitch of her shadowy flesh. But Tap noticed a sardonic expression beam from her black depths.

Below. All the way down. Lazy Crow discharged a wave of hex that repelled his enemies away from him. The same effect buffed Tine's strength when it collided with the enormous beast. Lazy Crow projected a command into Tine's head. *"Get. The. Robbers!"* His whispering, tick-tock voice boomed like a cannon in Tine's mind. *"They. Have. The. Children!"*

Tine swiped his arms around. Leah and Cedron ducked away. Raymond dived to his left. A few shadows were knocked aside, but a set managed to dodge the monster's arms and balled fists.

Tine reached up. He clawed into the concrete, his fingers breaking through the solid structure. He climbed, hauling himself up just two floors under Tap, Aloka, and the other shadows. His mountainous physique broke through bridges and catwalks as he ascended.

Tap looked over the side of the railing, keeping his balance as the building shook from Tine's ascent. He looked back at Aloka and her two shadow brothers. "Go!" he shouted. The shadows hurried away, traveling to a set of stairs. It would've been an easy escape without the potted plants in their hands. They could shift through a wall, but the physical objects in their hands could not make the intangible travel with them.

Tap clapped his hands. He stomped his feet. Another shadow emerged. Another and another and another and another until a second squadron was summoned. Like ants on a wasp foe, the shadows spilled over the edge and scrambled down toward the scaling giant.

The shadows on the ground floor raced upward after the mammoth. Dooley zipped into the engagement, a streaking, lilac projectile. Raymond shot a salvo of lighted arrows up at Tine. Leah launched a series of fiery-feathered discuses up at the monster while Cedron slammed a powerful fist into the wall to shake the building and throw the foul creature off balance.

Tap moved aside, racing to catch up with Aloka. Tine's hand slammed into the structure where Tap had been standing just moments before. The beast paused in its climb. Conjure projectiles crashed against him. Shadow beings crawled over him. Dooley slammed into his back, attempting to send cosmic shockwaves through Tine. The mammoth gnashed his teeth and absorbed the discomfort, shaking it off as if it was nothing. His prowess amplified by Lazy Crow's buffering.

The lilac flame and the other conjure folk were distracted. Somewhat. Two were still entangled with Grave-Clothes. Lazy Crow turned his attention to the match and saw his ally holding his own. Adamina Red raised her hands to assist her fellow Blood Curser.

"No!" hissed Lazy Crow. He turned his head to her. "We. Leave!" He faced Grave-Clothes. *To. Master. Fallows!* Back to Adamina Red. "Assist. Now."

Adamina aimed her right palm at Benny Jah. Her left was directed toward Neyeli. Blood-red, energy writhed around her hands. She projected her power at the two, young conjurers. Benny solidified from the anathematic realm, coughing as his conjure dampened to keep him safe from the abhorrent dominion. His heaviness increased, and he dropped to the floor with a thud and clank as if made of metal. Rusted chains wrapped around him. Adamina's casted power caught Neyeli off guard. Rusted chains formed around her wrist and attached to the floor, holding her in place.

Free from the fight, Grave-Clothes' ghostly figure floated in a hurry toward Lazy Crow and Adamina Red. His murky cloud absorbed them and levitated toward Ole Higue. He took her unconscious body into his smoke, and then he disappeared with his allies.

Adamina Red's rusted chains dissolved into dust. Benny regained his natural weight. He and Neyeli caught their breaths, but only for a quick moment. They joined Raymond and Leah's side and looked up at their target.

Above.

Tine was overrun by shadows, bombarded by conjure hurled by Raymond and Leah. Neyeli joined in the attack, flinging orange-glowing, snake-like javelins up at the shadow-covered Tine.

"Be careful!" Leah said to Neyeli. "Cedron's also on that thing's back!"

And he was. He took up his former position of holding onto the creature's thick neck, clinging tight as Tine climbed and bucked. Cedron also shared space with the shadows that wriggled over the humongous beast.

Tap and his other shadows ducked into the stairwell and hurried up to the roof. Edmundo Shaw was there waiting. He waved Tap and the shadows to him, yelling, "Grab on to me!" Tine broke through the roof, screaming! Edmundo backed up. His eyes went wide as he witnessed the monstrous behemoth smash through from below. "That's big…!"

Tap wrapped his arms around Edmundo. "Sh-sh-shadows ca-ca-can m-m-make the jump! J-j-just g-go!"

Edmundo turned and vaulted into the air, arcing over the street. Aloka and her shadow brothers followed, flower-children in their hands.

Tine on the roof, the shadows vanished from him, their master too far to stay conjured. But he was still adorned with a human trinket around his neck. Tine paid the ornament no mind. He spotted Edmundo's line of trajectory and was ready to follow when Cedron swung down to drape from his neck like a medallion. He used his strength to bend the giant down. Cedron's feet touched the roof. He swung a heavy fist across Tine's chin.

"It's just you and me!" Cedron growled, swinging another fist across Tine's face.

Tine backed up. He locked his hands together and hammered them down at Cedron. The onyx-skinned warrior dodged left. Tine's fist-made cudgel slammed against the roof, cracking the structure. Continuing the motion, Tine swung his locked-hand mace in the direction Cedron dived. Cedron leapt away, Tine's vicious strike just missing him.

Lazy Crow's expansion of Tine's power had dampened, but the difference was between being hit by a car or a train. Neither suited Cedron, though he wasn't aware of Tine's power-level at the moment. He just continued dodging.

Then he realized. He was being corralled back to the crater from where Tine had risen. Cedron rolled, springing to his feet. He turned and faced Tine, the edge of the opening at his heels. Cedron looked up and up and up at Tine. The monster towered over him, stepping closer.

The opponents grinned at one another.

Cedron noticed a twinkle against the night that outshined all the stars in the sky. He asked Tine, "You know my favorite color?" The ogre's grin turned into a snarl. "Lilac," Cedron answered.

Dooley's comet form pierced through Tine's back. A lilac flame surrounded the giant. He arched and screamed, fists balled. Dooley came from his cosmic form on the other side of the crater, skidding like an ice-skater. He and Cedron observed Tine stumble. Cedron ran around to the beast's side.

"Bruh!" he shouted at Dooley, making a fist with one hand, keeping the other outstretched and opened.

Dooley detonated into his lilac configuration. He streaked toward his brother's opened hand. His energy seeped into his brother's palm, running along his golden circuitry until he came to his clenched fist. Cedron jumped up and struck Tine hard with his clenched hand. He connected on the cheek, diffusing his own conjure and Dooley's cosmic, lilac energy through Tine's body, knocking the giant unconscious.

Tine dropped through the crater in the roof. Falling, falling, and falling. Leah and Benny Jah ran one way. Neyeli and Raymond scattered in another direction. Tine crashed! His impact leaving a vast crater in the floor.

Dooley swirled off his brother's fist. He took shape out of his blazing, lilac persona. The cosmic energy seeped into itself and funneled away, leaving behind Dooley standing next to his brother in black, cosmic-suited form. He elbowed Cedron and said, "I heard you, man. That was sweet. Poignant, even. Your favorite color…"

Cedron pushed his little brother away. "Please!" he scoffed. "My colors is black and gold, sun."

"I know what I heard," Dooley replied, lifting his shoulders.

"Right…"

Then came a distraction. Both felt the humidity scatter. Clouds gathered, and it started snowing in June. Cedron and Dooley looked at one another. Both beamed guilty expressions, Dooley behind his mask. Their use of conjure had disrupted the weather.

Again.

Cedron remarked, "It'll pass. It'll pass. It's just a light…snow…in June…" He hoped it would pass, anyway. "Not like New York ain't ever seen it before."

Dooley expounded, "Upstate? Maybe. Early June? Sure. But, this is definitely summer."

Below. There came a returning player to the skirmish. The wraith Grave-Clothes seeped into the wide-open arena. His foggy figure increased in volume, and he swept over Tine's unconscious body. He took the giant into his form and realm, and then he spirited away.

It was quiet. The scattered heroes shuffled from the shadows and gathered around the empty crater in the floor. Dooley landed softly in the cracked and depressed floor. Cedron dropped next to him. Tiny snowflakes came with them. Benny Jah looked up through the massive hole in the roof. Neyeli held out her hand and questioned, "Is this snow?"

"It'll pass!" Cedron replied with a forceful voice.

Dooley's mask retracted. "Wilson's up the street with the van," Gordon announced. "The kids are secured."

"Yeah," Cedron concurred. "Now the real work begins. Gettin' them back to human."

Gordon told his brother, "I'ma take the sky back home. You guys get to Harlem by van. Stay sneaking."

Cedron made a face. "Just come with us to the van. There's a basket of that reverend's fruit. Take a pear or apple. Revive," he suggested in a tone that did more than hint he was giving an order.

"I'll head home," Gordon objected politely. "Use my altar."

Cedron shook his head in reluctant agreement. "Okay, but you rest up!" Cedron demanded holding up a stern finger at his brother. "Mom and Pop told me to watch out for you. Cosmic as you might be, you need rest. Kneel at your altar. Give thanks and recharge."

Gordon nodded, agreeing. He and Cedron embraced hands, and Cedron pulled him in for a hug. Gordon exchanged the same goodbye with Benny Jah and the others. Then he called his cosmic mask around his face, burst into a lilac blaze, and took to the sky high enough to simply be a long, streaking, shooting star.

Cedron and his Gypsy Moon Misfits filed out of the warehouse and up the street. The matriarchs' power, concentrated all the way from Brooklyn, kept them cloaked. Humidity returned to the summer air. There was now a light drizzle, and Cedron felt vindicated and relieved.

They found Wilson in the van. Edmundo was in the passenger's seat with Tap and Aloka in the back. Tap's other two shadows had been dissolved. Aloka opened the side door. Leah and Cedron stepped inside, careful of the potted flowers. Raymond followed. Benny Jah and Neyeli remained outside the van.

"We'll take the skies too," Benny reported. "Meet you in Harlem."

"Sure thing, Jah," Cedron replied. "Be safe. See you soon. We eat this fruit and revive."

Benny closed the van's side door. He used the Gauntlet of Nines to alter into air. He scooped up Neyeli and brought her physical form into his ethereal state. Up he swirled, ascending into the sky and riding to Harlem as wind with a strong current of his own.

Dooley was already home, landing on the roof of the Goodspeed brownstone. The lilac blaze cooled and washed away. He disappeared from the roof, coming into being in the magically refurnished basement. Dooley snapped into existence in front of his altar. Silver and the yumboes swarmed around him, happy to have him home. His mask dissolved, and Gordon smiled at the luminescent imps. They were bright, and their chirping and dance livened the atmosphere more than the magical lights that held the basement aglow. But, he was exhausted, and he cursed himself for not taking some fruit. Gordon looked down at his altar. He didn't have time for a ritual.

"Hey Silver, Spook…everybody else," he called. "I'm worn out…" he confessed. "Had a helluva time. Met a few new friends. Rogues, good-honest villains. It snowed!" he exclaimed. Then he shook his finger and stated, "Story for another time." He spied the yumboes and expressed, "You winged-folk would've had some fun, stinging up the summoned vermin. There was even a giant," he exhaled. The yumboes looked at one another with intrigued looks. Gordon's body trembled. "Spook!" he hailed. "Open up the chamber. I'm going into the dream," he added walking away from his altar and taking up the mystical pocket watch lying on the ancient device's jeweled console. "Say your goodnight to Tsoro, Silver," he proposed while strapping the occult watch to his cosmic suit. "Just in case…" he said under his breath.

Silver whizzed over to Spook and landed on his console. She sang a heartfelt goodnight to the yumbo spirit that possessed the obsidian mirror. Spook returned the reply with a series of characters across the black mirror's face. The other yumboes delivered The Judgment card, laying it across the keyboard made up of gems. Silver hovered away, and Spook closed.

Gordon took up the otherworldly technology and slipped inside the chamber.

He held Spook close to him. He thought of history, and hoped to meet his sweetheart, Fey Forrester in another time.

The Alchemical Chamber closed tight.

Gordon drifted to the past.

Way of Love

"It's what I have to believe, Ithun!"

Waves of lilac light dissolved into sparkling dust, dwindling into the psyche of a twenty-four-year-old man cloaked in all black. His thoughts turned into stars that shimmered against the night background. Their twinkle was one of the few things in existence aware of his presence, watching him as he perched on a lower rampart that lead to a mighty bastion. The stars peered through the black cosmos and spied the shadow that veiled the young man, and they anticipated his next move.

Cloaked in heavy shade, he was draped in a black cape and cowl, black tunic and gloves, and black pants and boots while perched on the wall of a slave port in West Africa controlled by the Portuguese. Like an attuned cat, and the ogling celestial bodies above, the young man's eyes could pierce the night. The sun might as well have been blazing at high noon to him. While colors were in icy-blues and greens, like an inversed photograph, shapes and movement were there. A small source of light was all that was needed. The sconces that lined the enormous, fortress-like slave port were enough illumination for Ithun al-Kaadi.

Whether under the cover of night or out in the open within the day's brilliant bloom, he'd seen so much in his life. His eyes even swallowed sights unseen by the average person, as he was born into a world of conjure magic. His family practiced a mystical art called *al-kirawo*, which connected its practitioner to the divine within them and brought out latent abilities to control the four visible elements and other subtle forces. Through whispered speech, the wave of a hand, or concentration of the eyes, the four elements of earth, water, fire, and air were at a conjurer's command. It was not an easy feat, especially in this modern epoch where the stars were unforgiving in configuration, and their placement and shift cutoff a practitioner from tapping into the ever-flowing waves of immense energy given off by the universe. Study. Ritual. All had to be rigorous.

There was also a bit of lottery about it all.

Could a person perform conjure? Perhaps. All one needed to do was study, study, study. Perform a heartfelt ritual, and cut the strings from the stars they were aligned with to receive the cosmic energy being held back. Perhaps a person's cosmic spirit would rise. And it could be passed on. Conjure folk were very prejudicial in these times as to who they would marry and create a lineage. Conjure's candle flickered a dull flame, but traditionalists wanted to keep the fire dancing. Crude thinking permeated the measures of maintaining conjure, sparking small squabbles that turned violent in protecting the honor of conjure. One issue shaped Ithun al-Kaadi's life at an early age. Such an issue was that some conjure folk believed the terrible atrocity of enslavement, committed by the European against the African, was a necessary evil to create a change so profound and traumatic, that it would resurrect the spirit through its horror. The African slave trade.

This sentiment killed Ithun al-Kaadi's father, murdered by his closest friend. A man Ithun referred to as Uncle Aƙuram. It was a bloody mess of an affair. It was betrayal to secret forces that were controlling not only the African slave trade, but driving a hunt for conjure folk seeking out ancient relics and tomes of knowledge to keep their history and culture intact.

Aƙuram, the betrayer, was himself a casualty of the bloody mess. Once he as a tool was no longer useful, he was broken by his masters. His wife and son were snatched away to slavery, so believed Ithun. The same fate awaited he and his mother and brother. Ithun's brother, Seizan, was seized by slavers and taken to the New World. The frenzy of capture and slaughter stirred Ithun's conjure to manifest in that moment. He disappeared into the ethers with his mother who had been holding onto him. His brother remained in a slaver's grip, and Ithun never reached him.

The instant forever haunted Ithun. Not even his imagination would extend his reach to his brother's hand, so near in touch. Study of his power is what gave Ithun release. Perhaps he could blink to the other side of the world, coming within proximity of his brother because of memory and lineage link. His theory included the notion of finding his brother through willpower fused with his conjure to blink away. He thought about it often.

It could be said that Ithun al-Kaadi had a journal stored in his head. His thoughts were always running, always observing, and always defining the situations he was in. Even now, or especially now, as he faced the formidable task of infiltrating the well-fortified stronghold that was the *Sobre a Gangue Slave Port*. Ithun narrowed his eyes, focusing on the mighty composition that seemed more fortress than it did a holding grounds for captured Africans, blackamoors of differing tribal nations and kingdoms. But this was the precaution for those that wore the cosmos on their flesh and in their lineage. Each captured man, woman, and child had the potential to manifest conjure. So, conjure had to be used against them as hex. Clandestine, occult arts that slavers, and their maleficent benefactors, were well practiced in. A trail of hex was what led Ithun al-Kaadi here, accompanied by his mother, who also hid in shadow dressed in the same fashion as he.

Efra al-Kaadi was several shadows behind him. She, like the stars above, waited for her son to make a move. Among her many abilities was the skill to tiptoe with the silence of a soft wind, but it was Ithun's magic that could disconnect them from sight and swallow them into ether, traveling to another point. He was tasked with blinking them past guards, or within reach to tussle with them quick and swift, and then up atop one of the massive towers.

Ithun scoped the slave port. The flames dancing on sconces were like beckoning fingers, daring for he and his mother to draw closer. The fortress-port was decorated with artillery, mounted or held by militia units that were a part of a garrison of a thousand men.

There's nothing to fear, Ithun told himself. *Your actions have become whispers possessed with fright among this kind. They fear you.*

Whispers indeed sailed low from lips to ear, speaking of the disappearing duo, often referred to as *The Night Ghosts* or *Los Negro Lobos*. A mythos had been shaped around Ithun and Efra's activity. Thankful Africans prayed to their gods and goddesses for Ithun and his mother Efra to appear. Where they could, they did. They liberated many who had been sentenced to servitude across the great waters. Ithun let it be known that he was called *Kuto*. Efra referred to herself as *Weka*. Thus, citizens snatched into bondage invoked *Kuto* and *Weka*. The man and the woman that lived in the air and emerged from the breeze.

Tonight, was not a night for liberation, however. It was possible that liberation would coincide with the night's true objective, but it was not what drew mother and son to the ominous slave port.

The air was humid, sluggish in movement and oppressive in presence. There was no relieving breeze. Ithun and Efra felt nothing while shrouded in an incant. Efra saw her son take a few steps forward. She matched his action, stretching her power to devour sound, snatching up the taps of their footsteps. He in turn did the same with his conjure, reaching back and enfolding his mother in the ethers and carrying them forward to a small unit of three guarding soldiers. Their appearance was both a surprise to the trio of troops and a climax to the observing stars' anticipation.

Mother and son's presence resulted in the quake and shiver with fear. Sword, musket and pistols were useless. Out of nothing came a fight. Efra popped behind one man and made short work of him. She grabbed his face and slammed it into the wall as hard as she could. His face broken and bruised; blood and ripped flesh festooned his countenance. Ithun burst from a light cloud of black smoke and wrapped his hands and legs around the back of a second guard. He used all his weight to cause the man to drop. In the fall, Ithun palmed the back of the man's head and echoed his mother's attack on her target. The man crashed face first onto the rocky ground. His face would never be same, shattered in structure and bubbling in bloody bruises.

Ithun sprang up. On his feet quick, assisted by his conjure. He stood in front of the last man. He put a tough grip on the man's musket and vanished. He appeared behind the man and slammed the butt of the weapon into the back of the soldier's head. Swift and easy, the man dropped into a deep slumber.

Ithun and Efra scurried like cats. Up the wall they scaled. Ithun used his conjure to pop them out of existence, latching onto an area of the wall that jutted out. Then, in a *poof!* He and his mother were gone from sight, leaving behind a cloud of black smoke. They would reappear farther up the craggily facade. Not always a guarantee that enough of a protruding edge would be where they'd end up. But Ithun pushed his conjure, lifting he and his mother over the fortress walls, materializing out of a sable cloud.

Mother and son raced down the new level. Efra took lead, an otherworldly sensation tugging at her. She continued lacing their feet with incant to soften their steps. Guards in their path were dealt with in few moves. Brutal bluntness of fist or foot rendered them motionless. Ithun's use of conjure to dodge or quicken his steps surprised and stunned his opposition. Men were dropped, and mother and son moved on. They stowed away into the slave castle, integrating with the shadows filling the hallways.

Mother al-Kaadi followed her heightened perceptions. Her head became possessed with throbbing waves, and they increased as she and Ithun drew closer to the slave warden's office. A turn down the hall brought Efra and Ithun face-to-face with a squad of thirteen guards. Efra, off balance by the pulsing feeling thundering in her head, crouched away from the mob. The guards aimed their muskets on sight of the duo. Efra moved behind a corner leading into the new passage. Ithun dissolved from sight. The hail of cylindrical bullets struck the wall behind him, kicking up debris. The musket's smoke was blinding, filling the soldiers' forward sight.

Ithun was behind them. He clunked heads together, burst away, and came into existence to kick or swing a fist into soldiers. He confiscated one-shot pistols in his blink, tossing them aside. He re-emerged from ether to strike with heavy jab or kick. The guards' numbers dwindled. Mamma al-Kaadi jumped into the fray and assisted her son. Focused, and pushing the thumping in her head aside, Efra fell three guards while Ithun knocked out two more.

No talk. All action. The hallway was littered with unconscious bodies.

Mother and son stood outside the closed, wooden door leading to the slave warden's office.

An uncanny power resonated behind the door. Love. Reversed. There also echoed two powerful emotions. There was an intense, selfish inclination to possess power, wealth, resources and the control over human lives. A breeze swirled into Ithun and Efra's higher sense carrying a name. *Chamti.* With it, his definition. *Cupidity.* An accountant who pocketed every other coin he counted from his wealthy clients who were none-the-wiser.

But while he had ambition, his partner in this crime had none. Slow, reluctant, he sat yawning with a heavy breath projected to smother the air and turn any zestful man or woman lethargic. The wind communicated his name too. *Okod*, the idle king. *Idleness.* Once a tavern owner. His real name no longer mattered. His depravity made him fit for the role. He'd lure his patrons to sleep, poisoning their meals. Be it man or woman, he'd take advantage of them, and then he'd slit their throats. All while they slept.

Their powers permeated through the door. Ithun and Efra could feel them, but were far from influenced by their presence or hexing magic.

Ithun kicked the door open. He and Efra walked inside.

Chamti and Okod stood as still as statues. Two European men. Their pale skin could have been mistaken for white marble. The otherworldly blight that coursed through their bloodstream sapped what little color the two men had. Okod was far shorter than Chamti, and he was rotund from belly to facial features. He also wore glasses. He was bare of hair while Chamti sported straight, bright locks fashioned into a platinum ponytail. Both men were now gray of eyes. They were donned in white, ruffled, long-sleeve shirts covered by a brown frock coat. Black breeches with white stockings and black shoes covered legs and feet.

A pale-green luminescence surrounded their bodies as they flanked a desk where sat the slave warden, Collin Cantrip. He was a conduit for a grim ritual, held in a trance by the two men on either side of him. His fingertips were planted on the desk, the palms of his hands arched. Between his hands was a Tarot card positioned in the reversed state from his point-of-view. It was The Lover's card. Etched on its face was a divine scene of a naked black man and a naked black woman walking hand-in-hand on a winding path. Smoke swiveled out of their backs, wrapped around their spines. It filled the firmament above. Planets, stars, and moons came into existence. It was understood that the black cosmos was an extension of themselves. Out of this black couple came all that existed. A small banner floated over their heads. The word *EKSUH* written in an ancient language. Above the woman's head was written *JEERAH*. A banner was also beneath them, centered with ancient characters that read *The Valley Of.*

All three men chanted something unintelligible. A hex laced their mumbled speech. The effects turned love counterclockwise. Okod and Chamti acted as conducting rods for Collin Cantrip's abominable curse to spread the anathematic currents that inspired dispute and conflict among the men and women of Africa. The foundation of tribal nation or urban center kingdom fractured, and minute affronts would then inflate to sanguinary disputes. The nations overseeing the slave trade and Africa's dismantling would profit from the conflict. Favor and arm one side. Weaken and enslave the other. Return for standing tribe or kingdom. Break the potential for a conjure man or conjure woman to rise among them. The triumvirate power cell had been radiating their abhorrent hex for the ghost spell to ossify a stranglehold throughout the parent continent.

Okod's emotional power quelled the already captured inhabitants chained away in the lower levels of the slave stronghold. The three men didn't stir from their occult craft, anchored in reciting foul curses and emanating hate, greed, and lethargy.

Miles upon miles upon miles away there walked a brother to Chamti and Okod. The revolting, cursed clouds they summoned washed over him. He was dressed in the garb of a mercenary of his time, this man named Kerst. He was brawny with a pointed, triangular beard, and he too was drained of color. A long, pencil-thin mustache sprouted above his upper lip, pointing left and right. He swung his sword with one hand, musket resting over his shoulder with the other. *"Yfel swipian dôð hwiða mid mîn hilting!"* he cried. *"Dôð weder hrôpan ðunrian! Wægn swegl screpan wið lîgetung! Na durkusa ga mai zunubi kirkirar! Hâlettan Ariq Haunts!"* Where his feet stepped, wrath followed trembling the earth with quakes. The ill that possessed him moved him like a marionette. He dragged a cloud of disdain and agitation, and he brought fury to the already volatile storm.

At the slave stronghold. Ithun stared at the malefic, trifold alliance. His keen, preternatural sense deciphered the happening in proper context. He wondered how much of their spider's web influenced the diabolical trade of African bodies. He wanted to run a trial on an assumption. Could he blink a thought from his mind and make it emerge into theirs, probing for the answer on his brother's whereabouts, or perhaps find the intricate pathways of knowledge encrypted in their brains to pinpoint the location of those in the slave trail who did possess such details.

Efra had no such ambition, but she didn't possess the same conjure as her son, which encouraged his passion. She'd lost her firstborn son and husband. A coffin locked them in yesterday, and she acquiesced to the verity that neither could be exhumed from time. She claimed Ithun, and she held tight to him.

Efra put one foot forward. She was cautious. Her conjure swept the noise from under her feet as it pressed soft against the floor. The hexing triad didn't acknowledge her presence or movement. They continued their dire hex on the lands of Africa. Okod looked straight ahead. Chamti looked straight ahead. Collin Cantrip had his eyes fixed on The Lover's card, and so did Efra. She finished her approach, standing over the table. Her eyes lifted and spied each man. None of the three moved in opposition to her. She knelt down. Her eyes became level with The Lover's card. She closed her eyes and focused.

Ithun watched his mother, but also prepared for a possible strike from any of the three men.

Efra opened her eyes the moment her mind stumbled upon a specific detail concerning the present situation. She straightened, reached down, and pulled The Lover's card off the table.

The slave warden ceased his rambling. His eyes twitched. His lips trembled, and his mouth opened. His tongue wiggled free as if a tight grip was made around his neck, and he started gagging. His throat ballooned and then popped. Blood gurgled out of his mouth and spilled onto the table. A yellow substance gushed from his eyes, mixed with blood and tears. It dripped down his face and spilled onto the table. His nostrils did the same. His body convulsed as if possessed by an angry spirit, and his palms touched the table. A pool of blood collected under his hands.

Collin Cantrip stuttered on a murmur as his body continued jerking, undulating out of his control. The sound he made was equivalent to a cat hacking on a ball of fur. There looked to be no end to the blood and yellow pus that drained from him.

The movement broke Chamti and Okod's still monotony. Their eyes spotted Ithun, and they grinned at him. "Hello, Kuto!" Chamti said, brightening up. "Our master sends his regards. Ariq Haunts," Chamti named. "The Grand Trickster! Son of Ratamutum and Tani-Duhu Firistess!" It was these names and titles that moved Ithun from being simply curious to fully attentive. "So many ploys are at play here," Chamti said through an eerie smile. His head didn't move, but his eyes looked down at Collin Cantrip. The slave warden continued discharging a waterfall of pus and blood from every opening on his face. His ears now leaked. Chamti's grey eyes peered at Efra. He told her, "You've lit the fuse. The hex has detonated. Thank you!"

Collin Cantrip drained and collapsed onto the table, wading in the shallow puddle of his own fluids. Ithun stepped forward, fists tightened. Okod rolled his eyes. "No harm," he said. "Not by you." He looked around the room. "You can have this castle for now. The slaves are yours. A gift from Master Ariq Haunts." Okod and Chamti vanished, swallowed up by the expansion of their pale-green auras. Their light disappeared, leaving behind the burning sconces that cast the room in an orange hum.

Efra stepped back. Ithun put his hand on his mother's shoulder, and he folded space and time to transport them to a staircase they'd earlier passed. They traveled to the lower level of the slave citadel. Only shadows and flickers cast from sconces roamed the arched hallways, but mother and son raced with cautious tread. The remaining guards and soldiers roaming the stronghold were behind in their search for the duo that leveled their compatriots. A few dropped their muskets and pistols and scattered from the slave port in terror. Some kept weapons in hand incase they'd come across the night ghosts that left their fellow sentries sleeping in a pile.

Ithun and Efra did have a small skirmish against a squad of seven guards on their way to the slave hold. The encounter developed no different than the other confrontations. Ithun blinked around the men, leaving them bewildered and dizzy. One hard punch or kick sent them to the floor and slumber. Efra took advantage of her son's mystifying ability. When a soldier twisted or contorted in an attempt to predict Ithun's reappearance, the toss of fists would lay them flat and unconscious. The guards were managed, felled, and mother and son continued into the lower levels.

In the slave halls. There were moans haunting the corridors. The weight of Okod's inertia hex no longer hung over the captives like a pall. The scraping of chains accompanied the dirge. Ithun rushed to the first door and looked through the small, barred window. He put his hands on the bars and then flashed away, taking the entire door with him. He appeared just two paces back from the room. He dropped the door. Its tumultuous, echoing crash on the floor silenced the captured Africans' lament, and the rattle of their chains.

Ithun stepped over the door and then into the holding cell filled with men, women and children.

A man leaned forward. His eyes adjusted to the dimly lit area. He saw the blurry silhouette, and the outline of cape and cowl agreed with rumor and legend. "Kuto!" he shouted.

Efra joined her son's side. She too was recognized. "Weka!" another pointed out.

Mother and son went to freeing their fellow Africans, but freedom wasn't the end goal. The guards were gone. The unconscious were locked up and stripped of their clothes and weapons. The sailors among the captured took to the vessels at the docks with a mission to strike slave ships heading to the Americas. The hunters and explorers in company pledged to return the citizens to their rightful nation or kingdom, making use of the horses, camels, and horse-drawn carts outside for transportation. A few warriors went with them. Another handful of fighters accompanied the sailors. But the bulk of the servicemen remained to take the slave port, turning it into a rebels' fortress.

Efra spoke with two sailors, a husband and wife. His name was Ekow and she was Dzifa. She retained their services as seafarers whenever called upon. Ekow and Dzifa bowed at the neck toward Efra. For freeing him and his wife, Ekow pledged his service whenever needed.

Mother and son then disappeared.

Efra had The Lovers card. Act one of her plans was achieved.

Ithun had done his duty in service to his mother. Now, he had a brother to search for across the great water. Both would discuss their ambitions at another time.

Lilac shade scrubbed the scene clean from existence. A long way from their operation. Many mornings later. A little before noon in a city north of the skirmish. Ithun al-Kaadi strolled through the market finishing an errand for his mother. A bag of produce and meats were in his hands. He donned a smile, but there was a weight on his mind and shoulders. Weeks ago, he'd heard something while engaging in combat with two bizarre entities. They answered to a person with familiar parentage. Someone he believed dead. Ithun concluded that if this person lived, perhaps his brother would be alive as well. Perhaps his brother survived the long and dreadful journey across the great waters, shackled and cramped tight with other African bodies. Perhaps he survived the New World air, polluted by the foul stench of burning flesh, screams, and the mix of sweat and blood.

This thought was on his mind as he scooped up and paid for items his mother asked him to obtain. The thought persisted as he made small talk with shop owners and when he bumped into familiar faces crowding the marketplace. This thought accompanied him home. With the prizes from his mother's list secured, Ithun returned to his place of residence, a quaint, two-bedroom apartment he shared with his mother. Efra sat at the kitchen table enjoying a glass of water made ice-cold through an incant. The acquired Lovers card rested in front of her on the table. "Put the food away," she tasked her son.

Efra was a partner in beating up slavers and procuring objects of conjure, but she was still mom. By reflex of this understanding, Ithun rolled his eyes. Efra spied her son's gesture. "Young man!" she scolded in a gentle voice. "There's no reason to give your mother that face."

"Yes, ma-ma," Ithun replied to her. "I apologize." He continued with his extended chore, storing the produce separate from the meats in two different chests that were situated next to a third chest that housed drinks of all kinds. Ithun shut the lid of the chest and tapped three times, reciting an incant that filled the cases with cool temperatures.

"Ithun," Efra called. "Sit for a moment." Ithun obeyed his mother, taking a seat across from her at the table. She told him, "I'm not blind, Ithun." She ran her fingertip along the rim of her goblet, creating an awkward silence. Then she spoke, "I don't want to see you become blind."

"Ma-ma…?" he questioned, not understanding the meaning behind her words.

Efra looked directly at her son and expressed, "He's gone, Ithun. It hurts, but he's gone." Ithun turned his head away from his mother, huffing. "My son is gone, Ithun. My husband is dead. Your brother and your father," she stressed, upset at his reaction. "I don't want to lose you to a daydream. I don't want you haunted by monsters."

Ithun looked at his mother and said in a sharp tone, "I can handle any manifested burden, ma-ma."

"Can you?" she fired back at her son. She swallowed her frustration, leaning across the table. "I know how much it hurts for you to blink away. Not physically. It hurts your heart. Your conjure is a reminder of the first time your ability came to you and saved us from a terrible fate. You and I, but not your brother." She reached for Ithun's wrist, but he pulled back and crossed his arms, still looking away from his mother. Efra sat back, taking a breath.

When Ithun needed to speak, he faced his mother, leaned his body forward, arms remaining crossed. "Did you not hear that created creature speak all those nights ago? He said his master was the son of Ratamutum and Tani-Duhu Firistess." He leaned even closer, crossed arms resting on the table. "*Ratamutum!*" he underscored. "That name, ma-ma! *Son of Tani*, ma-ma?" He shook his head, sitting back against the chair. "They taunted me. Sent me a message. So, it's no coincidence."

Efra lifted her shoulders. She too crossed her arms. "And so, what?" she asked. "Your friend Been ah Kibir lives. He carries on his father's work by assisting in this so-called, Great Alchemy. That's proof your brother is alive somewhere digging ditches with no salary, chained to others to keep fields tilled and clean? Huh?" her voice elevated. Ithun slumped back, eyes falling away from the increasing distress on his mother's face. She had more to say. "Or—by *Eksuh-Jeerah*—who knows what else is being done to his body?"

Ithun mustered enough courage to fire back, "Perhaps!"

"No, Ithun! No!" Efra shouted back at her son, bursting into tears. "No! He died, Ithun! He died fighting back! Your father was taken by surprise—taken by betrayal. But your brother fought back!"

Ithun's face twisted. He asked his mother, "And how do you know this?"

Efra uncrossed her arms. Her elbows hit her knees, and her head dropped into her hands. She wiped them away and sniffed back tears. Efra told her son, "It's what I have to believe, Ithun!"

He accepted his mother's answer, attempting to fix the glower scrunching his face. He pointed to The Lovers card and questioned with sincerity, "Then what's this for, ma-ma? What'd we risk our lives for?"

Efra wished she had wine to sip on, get lost in its inebriating flavor. Her eyes spotted the ancient card expressing the love of two cosmic beings from the beginning of time. She thought of her husband. "Your father and I…" Thought and tears interrupted her speech. She choked on memories, hiccupped on days gone. Efra cleared her throat, took a breath, and started again. "Your father and I posed as supporters of the Great Alchemy. We were called to a tucked away village in France to appraise conjure items. We were invited by a secret order. They've since been gobbled up by other orders." Efra crossed her legs. Her breathing returned to normal. Ithun watched his mother recall yesteryear. He thought he'd see a smile as she spoke of a mission she'd gone on with his father, but no such gesture rose on her horizon to brighten her face. She looked away from him, out the window. Beyond the opening in the wall was not the city streets and people walking by. It was the past in her view. "They gave us lodging. We slept, meditated the next morning." Now came brightness on Efra's countenance. Ithun in turn smiled back at his mother simply because she was smiling at all. Efra looked at Ithun and told her son, "It was like out of a dream. Things felt light, as if we were not a part of reality. Your father felt it. I felt it. We always talked about it."

As was usual when Efra thought of this particular event, she could feel the sensation again. The story detached her from the physical world. She floated and felt free, and even close to her deceased husband.

"Perhaps, we were intoxicated by the moment," she rationalized. "Or maybe our conjure connected to the objects we were there to appraise. My memory of the moment goes in and out. It's like raising your head above water and dipping it back in, all in a rapid motion."

Ithun was now calm because his mother was calm. "Okay, ma-ma," he said to his mother.

"The plot was perfect, and we secured what we needed," Efra continued. "The peculiar thing of it all, was that this item was not among the rest of the Tarot deck." She paused. Her eyes slowly drifted back to her son. "That's when we learned of Ratamutum, the name and man. How he was using this item to reverse the sentiments among the peoples of Africa, turn us against one another, assisting the European in escalating tensions over spiritual philosophies or a land dispute. He being our closest ally, we never guessed it was him. No instinct. We were blind. While your father and I had other plans with what we secured that day, we vowed to acquire The Lovers card to bring love back to the people of Africa, unite us against the European and Arab slave traders." She looked at the lone Tarot card.

Ithun thought about the few conversations his young ears picked up between his mother and father. He asked, "Ma-ma, did you and pa-pa…step through time…?"

It took a moment, but Efra answered, "…Yes. Your father and I aided the future. It was both a daring and arrogant act. Foolish, really. We journeyed outside of time to the fabled Azur-Fah and convinced the Maiden kingdom to not only allow us entrance, but to sanction use of the Winding Staircase."

Excitement burst on Ithun's face. He blurted, "You've journeyed outside of time and into Azur-Fah?"

Melancholy laced Efra's smile laced as she remembered the adventure with her husband. "Yes, my boy. Through a grueling ritual we made a Star Path appear. We discovered the Maiden realm was where the Winding Staircase resided. We traveled through four of Azur-Fah's twelve realms of Constellation to get to the Maiden realm. The prince consort and the Maiden Neggura, or queen, listened to our reasoning and granted us a right to enter and stand before the Winding Staircase. It took convincing, but it was done. Their Eterijah—"

Not meaning to be rude, Ithun again cut into his mother's recount and blurted, "You met a cosmic-curator…a star-steward?"

"Yes, I did, son," Efra responded. "And she spoke to the eleven other Eterijah. Those eleven were furious at what she'd done, giving us access. No tribute either? *How dare she!*" Efra scrunched her face, and then she sighed. She proceeded, "So, she was banished, exiled to serve as a matron, guarding over the men and women taken into bondage across the Great Water. Many higher spirits have gone there since the Great Disaster's beginning. Understanding conjure assists in communicating with them. I've heard we've become clever in our bondage, creating new ways of conjure." Efra took a sip of her cool water. "She returned, however," she stated. "Eterijah Iyansan," she named. "There must always be twelve Eterijah, and her seat would've been vacant. Ritual designated the Maiden kingdom's second daughter, Princess Qkumo-Ṣẹda to takeover duties. Iyansan was allowed to return to train her. The princess was, at the time, very young. She must be twenty-four now, perhaps, I guess. Time works different outside of it. She could be twelve. She could be hundreds of years old and look as if she were in her teen years." Efra turned solemn. "As to her transgression, Eterijah Iyansan realigned the stars for us, a great undertaking, even for a powerful Eterijah Iyansan. I remember her holding Second Princess Qkumo-Ṣẹda's hand when executing the task, showing the little girl how powerful she would become. The Winding Staircase twisted into a helix. Your father and I walked up. We went somewhere else. A space between time and place. We studied to come to a future moment where it would be safe to assist a descendant of the first people in bringing about the Grand Ritual and Wish. We came to a glowing doorway and stepped through. We went in naked. We didn't have to. We just wanted to have the feeling over our bodies. Freedom. Eterijah Iyansan gave us a glow…" Her voice trailed away. She skipped details and took up by saying, "We assisted a boy, a young man. He'd gained a cosmic spirit. One of two that are a part of very old legends. We supplied him with the *Nigrum Nigrius Nigro*. We built for him an alchemical chamber, supplied by the Maiden realm. I also gave him Tsoro who possessed a black mirror connected to a *kam-ptah*."

"Oh! Really!" Ithun said, perked up. "I was so hurt when I learned the little aziza had to go. So, that's what his 'duty' was, then."

Efra made a half smile. Too much of yesteryear weighed her down. "Yes…" She tapped against The Lovers card. "There are other allies concealed within a mantle of invisibility. We need to take this to them, have it appraised for tribute."

Ithun's face contorted. "Appraised? Isn't this authentic?" he questioned. "We saw its use…"

Efra interrupted, "This is real, Ithun. I would like to know if it's *enough*. Enough for tribute. Eterijah Iyansan might be gone now. I'm not sure if Second Princess Qkumo-Ṣẹda, in her duties as reining Eterijah, would extend such kindness as her predecessor. I'm hoping Eterijah Iyansan hasn't fulfilled her duties. Should the princess be of age—twenty-four—she should be beginning her rituals to take on her Eterijah responsibilities. We might still have time." Ithun still didn't understand, and he remained quiet, hoping his mother would elucidate. Efra shook her head and exhaled another sigh. "I'm old, Ithun," she stated shaking her head. She smiled and said, "Oh, don't count me too far out, young man. Your mother here still has her elegance and beauty, but her conjure and incants are frail. I don't have the vitality to execute the taxing ritual to summon the Star Path—not even with your youth to assist. I was barely cognizant coming out of pinpointing this card's power in use." She lifted a finger. "But," she stated, ready to reveal an understanding, "Azur-Fah, like so many divine kingdoms, are shallow. They will permit admission with tribute and a *partial* ritual. One I could perform and feel less taxed when executed." Then she joked, "As Above So Below, yes. There are always negotiations."

Ithun chuckled at his mother's humor.

Efra asserted a theory, stating, "I think the card will do."

Ithun understood. Then he realized how far he'd been pulled into his mother's story. His upper body had been leaning far forward, forearms on his knees. He sat back, straightening up in the chair. He thought for a moment, and then he affirmed, "I'll help, ma-ma."

Efra thanked her son. "Things have become complicated, Ithun." She gave her son a stern look. "Make no mistake, my precious child. We are not the reason for this atrocity. The so-called Great Alchemy is a Great Disaster. Do not look at the African fools that aid this enslavement as the ones perpetrating it. Some of our people are greatly misguided. They are making excuses for it. But it is those of the European nations that are carrying this act out. They have found an ally in the tawny Arab, but it begins with them. It has always been their wish to dismantle and control the original people and our magic." Efra rubbed her forehead and moaned. She remembered aloud, "It wasn't too long ago that a queen of a tribal nation called for my services—our services. She needed a blessing. Even now she puts up a great resistance against foreign intrusion. She has her magic, but calling for assistance is not buried in pride." To Ithun's surprise, his mother declared, "I refused to help her. I learned she started negotiating to bring peace. That's all fine, but she was giving up her people in these negotiations. It was to show her power over her people and their loyalty to her, so I've heard. Politics have stalled her fighting spirit. Politics have tranquilized her rebellious heart. This dismantling has confused us all." Efra shook her head, disappointment weighing her down.

Another surprise came.

Efra promised her son, "If we gain a way to Azur-Fah, we will travel with Eterijah Iyansan across the Great Water, and we will locate and liberate your brother should she spy him with her keen, divine eyes. We will. I promise. *If* Seizan still lives," she stressed.

Ithun said nothing. He shook his head in an accepting manner, and then his face trembled, looking for an expression to fit the moment. Ithun only planted a palm on the table and lifted himself to his feet. He stared at his mother and nodded with a firm posture like a soldier ready for duty. Efra blinked, and her son was gone from the room. He was several blocks up the street in an alley. He needed a walk. Ithun's disappearance left behind a cloud of black smoke and dust. Efra watched the residuum dissipate. She palmed the table with both hands, exhaled, and meditated to regain equanimity.

A cobalt-blue beam surrounded her body. It emanated from within, flowing over her like an oil spill. Her physical form was whisked away underneath, and when the glimmer lifted another was in its place.

Fey Forrester's sailing spirit found a familiar residence. Her fall from space and time left her faint and out of breath. She remained still and gained composure. Her head went left, right. Then she looked up as her heightened senses perceived slumbering eyes in another time watching over her. She looked around the room again. There was no one there but her. No meditating body for a second spirit to possess. Fey closed her eyes, focused, and raced through the memory of the woman she possessed.

Fey's journey recalled a heist, and she and the woman's memories intersected. There was a trip through time. Fey's trip. She met her sweetheart, Gordon Goodspeed. Her last sight of him was through a moment of carefully crafted chaos. She next witnessed a bloody betrayal that left, crestfallen, the woman her spirit again inhabited. Fey darted through stored history to see Efra training her surviving son in the use of his unique conjure, stitching together an outfit for use on dangerous missions. Efra joined her son, keeping close eye on him as they attacked slave ports and freed captured Africans. Names were bestowed on the dark avengers. A reputation gained. Their latest incursion was pulled up for Fey to observe. She lost concentration when Efra's view spotted a desired conjure item.

Fey opened her eyes. Again, she needed to catch her breath.

It was then that her eyes brought into focus the sought-after item. She stared at it for a time. "Oh, my God!" she expressed in a hushed voice. Her hand shook as she lifted it and reached out for the much-desired Lovers card. She held it close to her face and inspected its beautiful, bright etching. Her mouth hung open in awe the entire time. A rumbling of thunder, and a small quake of her surroundings, broke her focus. Fey knew the two phenomena were not natural and only existed to her senses. The pair of napping eyes that observed her were attached to a person expressing frustration at what he was witnessing, how he couldn't be there to hold her, kiss her. Fey considered whom else could have been seated with her. Instinct told her it would've been Efra's grown son. Fey remarked, "I don't think it would've been appropriate for us to kiss the way we wanted to, Gordon."

She sensed her witticism soothed the tension in her sweetheart as he dreamed of her in time.

Fey plucked her precise whereabouts from Efra's memory. "I have something else for you, Gordon," she said staring at The Lovers card in her hand. "I know a lot can happen in three hundred and thirty-some-odd years. But I'm in a place called Bitaqa, Mauritania." She paused. "I don't know how long I have. I'll bury this here. You find it."

The matter was settled. It was a good plan.

But a lilac fog covered the scene moments before a cobalt-blue beam coursed over Fey's body, hurrying her spirit back to an aimless fall through time and space.

Her desired, self-assigned mission unaccomplished.

Gordon emerged from sleep. Eyes wide. Heart racing. A little less than an hour had passed. The chamber opened, but Gordon used his power to pop away. He came into existence sitting on his recliner, Spook in hand. He rested the device on his lap and opened it. "Spook, give me information on Bitaqa, Mauritania."

It wasn't long before characters appeared on the black mirror's face. *Bitaqa, Mauritania: A town with a population of less than five hundred people at the time of its fall by Arab-Muslim forces in the year 1703.* Gordon scanned other facts, but noted only one more. *Sacked and abandoned in the same year, its remains dwindled, and would later be referred to as the City That Became One With The Sands.* Gordon exhaled a heavy sigh. He didn't believe he'd find anything there. He'd make the flight after rest, but he would discover Fey had jumped time before completing her task. He huffed and palmed his mouth. He moved his hand away from his face and leaned back in his chair.

Gordon turned his head and stared at the wall. A doorway once glowed there, and he hoped it would do the same again, even at the pain of his eyes.

Anxiety set in. Its ally was exhaustion. Both hit Gordon like a freight train, or Tine's hefty fist. He hadn't truly rested. It could be argued that he indulged in a double-feature action flick and emotion-draining family drama. His own love story too, separated by time and space from his sweetheart Fey Forrester. A reunion was teased, but he couldn't interact. He grumbled something indistinct, followed by cursing again. *"Goddamnit!"* He bit down hard on his frustration.

Gordon closed his eyes for a moment and calmed. He remarked, "Always wait twenty seconds." There was more to spy in history through slumber, but not now. Gordon needed real sleep. He got up, set Spook down on the Alchemical Chamber, and then he knelt at his altar. He performed a ritual, spoke an orison, and felt the hand of sleep wrap around his body. He lay on his back by his own accord, and then he disappeared from the basement. He popped into existence in his bedroom upstairs, tucked comfortably under the covers.

Silver emerged from the ethers in the basement. She flew over to Spook and perched on the Alchemical Chamber's edge. The yumbo and the obsidian looking glass stared at the wall where once glowed a door through time.

Rumors were afoot of a haunting in the Water Bug Hollow cemetery, hanging thick like the lingering fog that nestled in between the headstones. Circulating whispers of locals glimpsing specters and strange, glowing presences throughout the area were not uncommon to Water Bug Hollow's present or past. Sturdy as the air was humid, there travelled murmurs. Such was the current tale floating around the age-old settlement.

It had been reported that a man and woman, appearing no older than in their twenties, were seated at a table playing a game consisting of dice and cups, cackling and drinking rum, fog curled around them. The young man was black, and it was said that he was human looking, for the most part. The woman was said to be crafted from onyx and gold. Both would stare at any who would approach them and ask if they wanted to join the game. On approach, especially if aggressive in movement, the man and woman and their cups and dice would disappear. The table and chairs would stay behind until touched by a human. Cats were known to hop atop a chair or table and lay comfortable. Stray dogs would wander and swivel through the table's legs, and settle underneath the wooden furniture. But table and chairs would dwindle and become as the fog if any mortal man or woman lay hand, foot, or bottom upon them.

The stories persisted, and gang boss Nicholas Lamar's interest was piqued when news of the haunting reached his ears. Night dawned, and Gang Boss Lamar braved the darkness and its potential dangers of rival gang members. His strong backbone was as fortified as the armored car he was escorted in, strapping as the armed men he sat between. His car drove through the mixing fog and heat. It coasted southward down a dubious trade route that his soldiers secured in a war against the Hamilton Boulevard Loud Mouths.

The car pulled up to the graveyard's front entrance and stopped. An old black fellow named Grady Gerhart waited outside the gate holding a lantern. He was dressed in all black, from frock coat to pants to shoes. Even his gloves and buttoned-up collar shirt were as pitch as the night. He barely stirred when the car drove up, its lights piercing through the fog and announcing the vehicle's arrival. Gang Boss Lamar's armed guards ejected first, and Groundskeeper Grady straightened himself in their presence, as best as his old, hunched back would allow. One of the men slipped him a roll of bills, and upon accepting the money, Gang Boss Lamar stepped out of the car and approached him.

Groundskeeper Grady looked up at Boss Lamar. "They're here!" the old man expressed in a low but excited voice. "I've seen them. Sho' I did. They real as you and me. They over on Lot L-Two." He turned slightly and pointed with eyes and finger. Then his sight swayed back to Lamar. "Right at yo' li'l brother's grave."

"Lead the way, old man!" Boss Lamar snapped, his patience as thin as he.

Grady first looked to either soldier. Then he lifted his lamp, bringing illumination to fog and the night. The light blurred, trapped in the low-hanging, dense cloud. Its presence added a bewilderment to the darkness and did nothing to push away nature's heavy and muggy exhalation. Grady turned and removed keys from his pocket. He fiddled with the chain until he found the appropriate key for the gate. Boss Lamar's impatience kept his eyes on Groundskeeper Grady. He observed the old man fidget with the bundle of keys and was impressed when he was able to sort out the gate key straightaway.

Grady unlocked the gate and allowed the men entrance. Boss Lamar walked into the cemetery and stopped. He looked at Groundskeeper Grady and repeated his initial order, "Lead the way, old man."

The groundskeeper shoved his keys back into his pocket. He scurried over to Boss Lamar and then passed him, leading the men through the thick fog that smothered the graveyard. A dome of light surrounded them as the area of fog was touched by the illuminated lantern. The dense mist thinned as the pack wound through the cemetery and advanced toward Boss Lamar's family grounds where lay his father and younger brother. The haze hanging over the area seemed to originate from the cigarettes smoked by the young man and woman who sat across from one another at a wooden, makeshift table. They laughed and puffed. A fruit basket and two wooden cups were positioned on the table between them.

The young man was dressed in black pants and shoes. An untucked, white, collar shirt and a black vest covered his top. While he was adorned with five necklaces, four were simple and beaded, the fifth outshined them all. Literally. Adorned with three fist-sized skulls, red, black, and green in color, the necklace was a statement piece, and each skull glowed bright with their respective colors through the darkness and fog. An African mask was clipped to his belt, dangling as he sat on the chair.

The woman had on a full-length, pleated skirt. Orange and red in color, it was complimented by a black tunic that was spotted with red dots across its otherwise pitch fabric. Her skin was interesting, a symmetrical blend of onyx and gold. She took a drag from her cigarette, taking in the otherworldly, shifting and slithering fog. She turned and exhaled her smoke at Boss Lamar and his soldiers. The light in Grady's hands dimmed to something tolerable to the eyes. Boss Lamar pushed his cheek out with his tongue and raised an eyebrow. He stepped up to the young man and woman and said, "Oh, you ain't gunna up and disappear?"

"No," the woman said through a smile. "We've been waiting for you, Mister Nicholas Lamar." Then she corrected herself by adding his street title. She amended, "*Boss* Nicholas Lamar." She reached out her hand, and she was too pretty for Boss Lamar not to accept. "My name is Lillian Eledas-Ghedemere. I've come all the way from Mississippi to speak with you. Clarksdale, Mississippi to be precise," Lillian informed taking her hand back. She turned her eyes on the man seated across from her and introduced him. "This handsome gentleman is my consort and sentry. Mister Armand Gideon," she named him.

"It's been days, Nicky El," Armand said up to Boss Lamar. "Days. Yes, it has. We've been haunting these grounds just waiting for word to light that curiosity of yours," he briefed.

Boss Lamar had to admit to himself, he liked the sound of being called 'Nicky El'. But these two were playing games and carrying on over his brother's grave. He shook his head, though the movement was slight, as he was contemplating his next words. "Took some time for this to come to light on my end," he responded, looking back and forth between Armand and Lillian. "First of all, it was the talk of two spirits in the graveyard—" he let loose a smile that broke a little of the tension, and the presence of fog too, so it appeared. He shook his smile away like a flame shaken from a match. He returned his demeanor to austere. "But, that's all superstitious folks in the Hollow. Grain a salt type of things."

"Indeed," Armand returned. Then he quoted, "If you believe in thangs you don't understand, right?"

Boss Lamar perked up again. "Yeah!" he blurted. "But, the story of you all wouldn't quite go away. Rollin' off some fool's tongue e'r night—sometimes a group of fools, all in agreement that the graveyard got a haunting." He put his hands in his pockets and started pacing around the table. "Strange too," he remarked, scratching his head. "It all felt like I was supposed to hear 'bout you two—seems that's the case, after all. So, I got to work, and I know some people who know some people who know some people who like to shake down some folk for information." He stopped on the other side of his brother's headstone, using the grave marker as a buffer between him and the table. He concluded, "And they shook up a buzz 'bout two flies in the buttermilk that fit your description—" His eyes panned Armand, and he interjected, "—A brotha with an African mask—" he looked at Lillian and said, "—And some gypsy-voodoo, Earthy chick with a game of dice and a basket of fruit. Folk I got as spies say you up there talkin' to that no-good Chief Ramiel." He made a face, closing his left eye while cocking his face to the side. "The Ram and I…we got an unease about us. Clashing politics," he stressed. He fixed his face, waiting for a reply. But he asked, "You scopin' packs? The two of you? It don't really help you desecrating my brother's grave." He looked to the headstone beside his brother's and said, "I'ma go 'head and say, you disrespectin' my deedee too. Just all defiant about his resting spot and his son's."

Armand looked at Lillian.

Lillian looked at Armand.

She smoked and exhaled while nodding at him.

He extinguished his cigarette.

Armand turned his head to Boss Lamar and said to the gang leader, "My man, Nicky-El!" Boss Lamar caught himself chuckling at the name bestowed on him. Then Armand resumed, "I have something for you. It belonged to your brother, who wanted you to have it when you were ready to see it. Your temperament wouldn't allow it, though. I think you're ready now." He pointed to a rectangular, wooden lockbox on the table that Boss Lamar wasn't quite sure was there before.

Boss Lamar hesitated, intrigued. He eyed his soldiers. Their hands hovered to swing back and draw their weapons. He made a subtle nod of his head. Even through dark and fog, his men caught the signal. Lillian and Armand made no movement, but they sensed the gang leader's motion for his goons to stay their hands. Boss Lamar remained behind the headstone. He took out a cigarette, lit it, and started smoking. "My brother's death was a big deal 'round these parts."

"We're aware, Boss Lamar," Lillian spoke in a soft, sincere voice.

Boss Lamar took a drag. He exhaled and choked on his memories. He cleared his throat and told Lillian and Armand, "You touchin' on a dangerous subject. I ain't a soft man, but this is sensitive."

Armand moved his eyes to Lillian. She nodded and stood, stepping away from the table, disappearing into fog and night. Armand addressed Boss Lamar, "There's nothing soft about expressing pain in loss. It takes courage. I wish we could've met under different circumstances, but Water Bug Hollow has gone through a change—artificial in its design. I need your help to bring it back to what it once was, Nicky-El. Where your crew hangs—that two-story house on Hamilton Boulevard—there's something I need to dig up in your backyard."

Boss Lamar interjected, "Some kind of evidence against you there?"

"Not me, Nicky-El," Armand said with a shake of his head. "No, no, no. The evidence buried there shines a light on the cause of Water Bug Hollow's change and turn, especially the instruments and tools used to gun down your brother. Officer Norman Ross."

"Ain't a name you should be sayin' 'round me," Boss Lamar warned. "That bastard got a badge that protects him from the justice he needed to see when he murdered. Killed. Gunned my brother down."

Armand nodded out of respect. He aimed an open hand at the empty seat across from him and suggested, "Best me in a game of Liars Dice, Nicky-El, and I guarantee you the justice you seek against Officer Norman Ross." He added, "I mean no disrespect by repeating the villain's name aloud. Please, let us sit and tell sad tales of the death of kings."

Boss Lamar tossed his cigarette aside, walked to the empty chair, and sat down. He reached for a wooden cup in front of him, placed the palm of his hand over the top, and started shaking. The corners of the dice knocked around and rattled against the sides of the wooden cup and smacked Boss Lamar's open hand. He revealed, "Learned how to play from a videogame. It was a side activity. You could stop in a bar, have yourself a go at it. Take a rest from the pursuit of family and redemption."

Armand replied, "I learned through a myth. The power of story, huh? That's what we play for. Family and redemption."

Boss Lamar slammed the wooden cup on the table.

Armand did the same.

"What's that buried in my backyard?" asked the gang leader.

Armand responded, "The truth?"

Boss Lamar looked at the ground, his brother's burial site. He looked at his father's grave too. Then he said to Armand, "I think I'm owed—you desecrating my family resting grounds by playing games on their graves, and all. Even still, someone wanting to shovel up your backyard does draw some curiosity." Then he checked his dice. He called out a number. No dispute was made. Dice were revealed, and Armand lost.

He tossed a die to Boss Lamar. "You earned it," he remarked.

"And the buried evidence?"

"Bones?" answered Armand, shuffling his dice.

Boss Lamar's face twisted, looking disgusted. "Bones?" he questioned. "Human?"

Armand smacked his cup against the table. Boss Lamar shuffled and did the same. Armand said, "Very much so, and there's more. The bones belonged to an angel, metaphorically speaking. They belong to a woman who had Water Bug Hollow's best interests at heart. A ritualistic killing was made of her, violent beyond violent. Old days violent. Slave days. The shaking of her accosted spirit from her bones has shrouded Water Bug Hollow in this here, haunting fog," he pointed out. Armand made a bid. Boss Lamar didn't challenge, and Armand lost again. He scooped up a die, stretched his arm across the table with a little lean over in his stance, bottom up from the seat. He smacked the six-sided chance piece in front of Boss Lamar and sat back in place.

Another two rounds were done in silence, and Armand grinned

when he evened the playing field.

Boss Lamar questioned, "If I win, you still go digging around on my property…?"

Armand's grin never faltered. He shook his cup and described, "You ever see the animated classic Transformers, The Movie? From the eighties. Not that CGI shit. Man, that's a wild film. There's a scene with these malevolent rulers on a planet. They were part robotic, part organic. They each had five faces," he stressed. "The faces were mounted on this oval structure, and it would turn like a merry-go-round. One face would talk to you, it would spin, then another took up the conversation or finished a phrase. Well, they judged people in a trial. The defendant would step up, one face would ask, *'Guilty or innocent?'*. Then another face would slide into view, and it would say, *'Innocent!'.* " Armand slammed his cup down on the table. Boss Lamar mirrored the action. Armand then concluded, "And even when judged innocent, the people on trial would be fed to sharks." He chuckled. "I saw this strange thing about eighteen, nineteen years ago, or so. I was five or six. I always wondered: What the hell kind of judgment would they receive if they were guilty?" He made his bid and added, "Never understood that scene until I was a little more grown up."

Boss Lamar just nodded his head. He called liar on Armand's bid. Dice were revealed. Armand lost with Boss Lamar correctly calling his bluff. The gang leader gained another die. Armand never again recovered in the game. He lost all his dice, but he took defeat with a humble expression on his face. As promised, he handed over the wooden lockbox, sliding it from his side of the table to Boss Lamar's.

The gang leader squinted his eyes, trying to peer through the deceptive darkness. He could've sworn that Armand's fingers never touched the box. They were close, mere millimeters away, but no contact. He looked at his soldiers and Groundskeeper Grady for any reassurance. They said nothing, eerily still as statues.

Boss Lamar didn't linger on the trickster shadows, the glow of Groundskeeper Grady's radiant lamp, or his flickering eyesight. He brought the wooden box closer to him, unhooked its hinge, and opened the lid. Inside, his eyes spied a miniature construct of a rusted shackle and chain. He blinked, and the corroded manacle crumbled into a pile of dust, which shifted into a dark-gray cloud. Boss Lamar's lips moved to form a question. He tried to bend his neck to look up at Armand and question the happening going on in front of him. But his neck locked in place, and his lips only quivered. Lillian stepped out of the shadows behind him, positioning herself just to the left of his chair. Boss Lamar didn't stir. His eyes remained locked onto a mournful scene that was more symbolic than historical.

Nicholas Lamar gazed on an image of himself sitting atop his younger brother's headstone, perched like an angel watching over the grave. His brother, alive and well, rested with his back against the marker, legs stretched out, and his hands on his chest, tapping lightly every-so-often. He was preserved at the age of his death, set to enter his senior year of college. Twenty-two years old was when Officer Norman Ross shot him twice for an attempted assault and public threats to life on a police officer.

"He got the best of me," Gerald Lamar said to his brother. "He taunted me about you, me being in college. He made a joke of me striving to be a lawyer—talked about your drug and blood money was what paid for college." Gerald snickered. "Like my scholarship had nothing to do with it. I threw that back in his face. That was strike one. He got me aggressive now. All he doing is building a justification to carry out his orders to gun me down, y'know. System orders. I kept swingin' the bat at all his pitches. I told him I wasn't gonna defend you from your street mess. Nah! I was goin' after real criminals like him. Bad guy cops. I told him I was gonna break the code of silence in the police force." He laughed a little, thinking about it. "Ruffled his feathers." Then he thought. "Is it *rustled* his feathers or *ruffled* his feathers? You'd think I'd know," he reflected. "All that education and this newfound ability to tap into knowledge while on the other side." He didn't say much more on the matter, and he continued on when he noticed his big brother Nicholas didn't respond. He didn't even chuckle at the think-about. Gerald continued, "Yeah, I told him that I'd find something. I told him his badge wouldn't be able to protect him." Then he noted with a dramatic flair, *"Strike two!* I was gettin' loud, uppity in this good ol' boy-in-blue's shaded eyes. He told me to calm down. I said I'd do him one better, said I'd walk away. I turned my back a little too hard. He didn't like that. Foul tip. Another at bat. He walked up to me, grabbed my arm. I was infected now. Angry, as a nigger shouldn't be—even when they should be.

"I took my arm away from him. I told him I know my rights, and I'm studying my rights." He shook his head. The rage in his throat now in his voice. "I was a nigger now—outright, that is. Always a nigger in his eyes. Officer Ross was free to do what he wanted to do. So, he gave my buttons one last push so that he could act with the power of his badge backing him up." Then Gerald concluded his tragic tale. "He shouted I was resisting, tried to grab me up again. Then came strike three, a fatal swing that knocked me out this game called life. I threw my hands up, stepping away so he couldn't grab me! I was hostile to him. My arms going up, anything could've been in my hands—so his word would say. Two in the chest. First one hit my heart. The second wasn't even necessary."

The course of events flashed in the tears Nicholas Lamar tried to blink away. He saw everything his brother described.

Gerald's voice relaxed. "I played right into his hands…"

He looked over his shoulder as he lay perched on the head stone. Seated at the table, he stared fixedly through watering eyes at his brother. His perched doppelganger mouthed as he said aloud, "You ain't got to apologize for another man's evil, little brother…"

Gerald responded to his brother in an indifferent tone, "True…" Then he said with a little more heart, "Folk be wasting time on that shit." Then he assured his brother, "This is real, y'know. Us talking. Dad's here. He want action out of you. He want justice. I'm a little nervous telling you that, cuz I know, when Dad gives order, you willing and able."

Nicholas lifted his eyes and spotted Armand on the other side of the table. The gang leader's face was a mess of streaks running from his eyes and nose. He sniffed and asked, "This real…?"

Lillian put a hand on Nicholas' shoulder. He flinched, jolted by her presence and touch. "Yes, Nicholas. That is your brother talking to you from the other side. No tricks," she stressed. "We don't deal in tricks."

"And we don't suffer bullies," said Armand fastening his African mask to his face. "On your call, Nicky-El," he proclaimed in a strong voice. "Officer Norman Ross: guilty or innocent?" he queried.

Gerald looked up at his brother, from lockbox into reality. An eyebrow was raised on his otherwise relaxed countenance, anticipating his brother's answer.

Nicholas sat back. He straightened, and he answered, "Whatever it takes to feed that motherfucker to the sharks."

Armand motioned to the fruit basket. "Have some fruit," he suggested.

Nicholas reached for a cluster of strawberries and a peach and started eating. Calm cooled him as he bit into the peach and swallowed its sweet nectar. The juices swiveled around his tongue and funneled down his throat, a bright sensation coating his senses. He devoured the fruit he pulled from the basket, and he felt replenished from burden's fatigue. His brother asked him, "You feel good, big brother?" Nicholas nodded his head, and Gerald added instructions, "Good. Just listen, now. Listen to Brother Armand and Sister Voodoo Lily."

Nicholas looked at his brother. Gerald's eyes were now closed, resting in peace. He raised his head and spotted Armand leaning toward him, over the table. Armand informed, "I got instinct, Nicky-El. I got a higher instinct." He tapped his forehead. Then he continued, "My instinct gives me insight, and it allowed me to know you before we met. But most of all, I know him. Mister Norman Ross," he named. "Officer, that is. I know he still has his job. Therefore, most importantly, I know his schedule. He was at the casino on this night with a co-worker. She's also the woman he's having an affair with while his wife and kids are at home thinking he's on patrol."

Nicholas remained still. His jaw was tight, teeth crunching against one another.

Armand continued, "Yes, Nicky-El. It's time we seek out the injustices against us, have a real moment with them. We've been so afraid up to this point to do so."

Impatient with the night, Nicholas made the motion to stand.

Armand flagged Nicholas, waving at him to keep a seat. "No," he told the gang leader. "Mister Norman Ross isn't at the casino any more. He's at his co-worker's house. *We* will confront him there—you and I. Dismiss your soldiers and the groundskeeper."

Nicholas turned to his two guards and ordered for them to return to the car, Groundskeeper Grady to escort them. No one hesitated on his command. Light shifted, and with the three bodies, sunk into the fog. Nicholas placed his attention back on Armand, waiting for what would come next.

The Crossroads Queen instructed, "Nicholas, open your palm."

Nicholas did as tasked.

Voodoo Lily proctored, "Think and think about the burden that binds you. Think and think about how you would cut it free."

Nicholas eyed his palm. He concentrated, and strings of bright, yellow light extended up from his open hand and took shape. It was a hatchet, an African Songye, ceremonial axe. The instrument had a glowing blade shaped like a fan with points at the end. Its bronze-coated, wooden handle was like that of a club or baton, with either end carved out to create an intricate, African mask. Nicholas gripped the weapon with a strong hold.

Voodoo Lily expressed to him, "That conjure is temporary, Nicholas. You still need a stitching to bind you to it. You'll keep it long enough, I'm sure."

Nicholas stared at his conjure, blade ablaze and writhing with a holy incant. His brother opened and aimed an interested, single eye at him. And even though a glowing, wide grin stretched across his face, Gerald sighed. His eye closed, and his grin retracted. The lid to the box closed.

Voodoo Lily stepped back. Armand rose from his chair. He waved Nicholas to stand, and the gang leader followed the gesture's order. He walked with Armand through the graveyard, toward the cemetery's entrance. Armand said to Nicholas, "Remember, Officer Norman Ross likes to smoke when his girlfriend goes to bed." He put his arm around Nicholas. "This isn't just business, Nicky-El. This is personal." He shook Nicky-El with the arm slung around him. "Nicky-El, you're about to be the envy of every Negro in the world."

Behind them, Voodoo Lily vanished, taking the table and the items on top with her.

The fog filled in her absence.

Nicky-El and Armand stepped out of the graveyard gates. The gang leader gave a curious side-eyed glance at Armand and raised a finger to point at his glowing necklace. "What you representin' with that necklace and African mask? Who you claim?" Armand didn't answer him, and Boss Lamar became impatient. It all added up to the night, how it became tedious as if mired in mud. Minutes were stretched, and Nicky-El had no tolerance. He had justice to seek and deliver, an atonement to make. He gripped his conjure tight. It glowed brighter, seemingly dispersing the fog. He decided to ask Armand another question. "We walk?"

Armand lit up another cigarette. He took a puff through the cut out on the African mask's mouth. He exhaled and added to the murk in the air. He didn't answer, he just walked up the street. Nicky-El followed. Armand hummed an old tune from the late sixties. His harmony brought a smile to Nicky-El. He had more questions, and so he asked, "What I got in my hand here? How you explain that? Me talkin' to my brother, and all?" Armand didn't answer. "You had such a talkative air when we was playin' games, but you all quiet now."

Armand took a quick puff and exhale of his cigarette. He pivoted and became a roadblock to Nicky-El's walk. Nicky-El stopped as abruptly as he was deterred. The African mask stared into him, close. Face to face. Armand wore a grave expression under his mask that seemed to manipulate the facial expression on the mask itself. He told Nicky-El, "We're going to pull off a magician's trick like none before." He pointed to the gang leader and stressed in a low hiss, "We're going to make disappear the vile cop that gunned your brother down in cold blood. This is a transition, Nicky-El. Don't you see the fog we're trying to clear?" He let Nicky-El ponder on the notion for a moment before continuing. "Do you know how much lifeblood our actions are investing in sweeping this haze from Water Bug Hollow?" He asked, then provided the answer. "Our entire life's blood we're paying. And with no disrespect, it's not just your brother's justice we're seizing. It's a territory of spirits wandering aimless as haunts, black brothers and sisters who aren't aware they've died—incapable of passing to Ginen, the cosmic, unseen realm. The Valley of Ixu-Gira, as I have learned." He stepped through Nicky-El like a ghost. Armand said over his shoulder to Nicky-El, "Do you know where we stand in history? My mistress is the guardian of such a place."

Nicky-El turned to Armand. His spin was stuttered as his speech when he replied, "Yes… Y-y-y-yessir…"

The masked Armand turned and faced him. He put his cigarette in his mask's mouth and ghosted through Nicky-El again. He traipsed back through the fog and up the street. Nicky-El followed. Something occurred, and it wasn't Armand's conjure at play. It was the Crossroads Queen's.

Armand exhaled smoke, and he said over his shoulder, "Why do I have more tears in my eyes than you? Can you not comprehend the gravity, the enormity of this hour?" It was Nicky-El's time to remain silent and provide no answer to the question given to him. "You have another hand," Armand spoke. "You'll make conjure there too when you're stitched and bound."

Time yielded to Nicky-El now that his inner restiveness was at ease. Distance appeared to fold and warp, wrapping in on itself and shortening the steps between here and there. The Crossroads Queen was unseen, but her power of conjure was at work with the twist and distortion of time and space. Roads were shortened to their destination, her conjure assured.

Armand and Nicky-El were in a suburb of Jakobiville, standing across the street from a quaint house owned by Patrolwoman Kim Dougherty. She was sound asleep in her bed with central air blowing a cool breeze throughout the house and countering the mugginess outside.

She'd shared her bed with a co-worker just hours earlier. He'd risen since then to have a smoke outside, leaving her alone for a moment with her long blonde hair sprawled out between his pillow and hers. It was late. He didn't bother to put on pants. Officer Norman Ross indulged in a cigarette while standing on the porch of his mistress' house in his white boxer shorts and a t-shirt. Flip-flops were on his feet. He smoked and contributed to the fog. Through the haze, Nicky-El could see Officer Norman Ross as if no fog shrouded his image. The kindle of the ashes on his cigarette acted as a beacon, its vibrancy humming brighter and softer as the chiseled cop puffed.

Nicky-El closed his eyes and heard his brother's voice recount the story of his murder. His teeth ground as he listened to his brother blame himself for his unjustified murder at the hands of a police officer. Nicky-El opened his eyes. The fog didn't affect his vision. It disappeared from off-duty officer Norman Ross. The curtain lifted as if to give Nicky-El the respect to lock onto his target and take aim.

He gripped hard the handle of his hatchet. He walked forward, out of the fog. Norman Ross puffed, exhaled, and then he noticed Nicky-El step into the street. He squinted, attempting to make clear the sleep in his eyes, the smoke burning his throat, lungs and vision, and the fog creeping away from the figure walking up to him. Nothing much came into view. The only thing clear was in the eyes of Nicky-El, seeing a man protected by a corrupt system of justice and irony.

Nicky-El tossed his hatchet. The throw was swift and quick, and more so, it was accurate. The glowing blade dug into Norman's forehead without splitting flesh or drawing blood. The effect was still the same. Officer Norman Ross' vision went black. His jaw dropped, mouth agape and bleeding smoke that swirled up into the fog. His eyes widened, freezing within the moment on how he was caught off guard. His arms dropped, and his fingers unlocked from around the cigarette. The visual was cartoonish, a live-action interpretation of an animated character scared white. Officer Norman Ross' body stiffened for a moment. It leaned back at an angle, and then it crumpled against the porch.

The hatchet's wraith blade injected into Norman Ross' mind the burden he and his squad brought to the innocent people of Water Bug Hollow. Even the guilty that had been treated unjust.

A headache thundered inside Nicky-El's head. The cerebral tremor shook him with such grief that he dropped to his knees. He almost toppled onto the street. His palms hit the road catching him. He started breathing hard, and the pain only increased. He tried to speak, but his words rolled into gasping heaves. His throat constricted, and his heavy breathes weakened to a desperate, guttural wheeze.

Armand bent down next to Nicky-El. He smoked through his mask.

He told Nicky-El, "What you feel right now, Nicky-El, is the irony in all this." He raised his head to take a peek at the cop sprawled out on the porch. "You, and this cop here, have a lot in common. You're both plagues on Water Bug Hollow," Armand revealed as he tapped ashes onto the street. "You're both cogs in the same oppressive machine. It just took something extreme for you to realize that. You've made mothers and fathers and brothers and sisters weep, too." Armand pointed to Norman's collapsed body. "That sonava bitch consciously upholds a system's prime directive to spread fog in Water Bug Hollow." He looked at Nicky-El as the gang boss choked and shivered in an attempt to shake away his massive headache. "So, do you, Nicky-El," he said through clenched teeth and mask. "You assist it. You're its slave." Armand stood up. He kept his gaze on the wheezing gang leader. "Today, Nicky-El, we remove your duty as an *inawo*, burden and haunt on Water Bug Hollow. Today we exercise you of the fog."

Nicky-El's vision blurred. The creeping fog had nothing to do with the impairment. The loss of air and smothering headache were at excessive play. But there was something clear. A car sped toward him and Armand. But as if it was made of the fog itself, or perhaps him and Armand were composed of its gossamer stitch, the car traveled through them. Even at the late hour, people roamed the streets. Few in number, but enough. No one noticed him and Armand or Officer Norman Ross laid out in his underwear and t-shirt.

There were pairs of feet that approached them. A tingling sensation occurred on the back of Nicky-El's neck, resonating down his spine and up into his brain. Nicky-El looked up, still heaving, reaching for as much air as his constricted neck would allow. His eyes jiggled as he kept them from rolling back into his head. The world was a kaleidoscope of imagery, but his vision assembled the pieces that made up the two people in front of him. Their image was coherent and cohesive. It was the spirits of his younger brother Gerald Lamar and their father, Cassiel Lamar. His imposing presence made it seem as if the fog was running from him. It should've been a happy moment for the father, seeing both his sons together. But Nicholas had added too much burden to the already dense murk in Water Bug Hollow. Cassiel too. He looked at Gerald. His smile came to him.

Cassiel knelt down in front of his gasping son.

"You got to do better, Nicky-El," said Patriarch Lamar. "Use my strength, son. I need to be a part of settin' things right, too. I was a part of that disagreeable generation, became violent with one another when the Elders were all railroaded and locked up. Use your brother's heart. Let this man here—" he pointed up to Armand. "—and the Crossroads Queen guide you right. You delivered vengeance. You got the justice we need. Now make things right."

Nicholas' voice pricked through his tightened throat. A squeak was first heard, a humble heave of air. In and out, Nicholas breathed heavy and hard, puncturing through the narrow passage and widening it. He exhaled, "I. Will. Do. Better. Dad… I will…I'll do right by the living, and I'll honor the dead…" Breath came to him, and he breathed deep.

Cassiel shook his head. He looked at his youngest son who told him, "We're good here, Dad. Nick's got this. He do."

They faded. Nicky-El wobbled to his feet. He took a moment to allow the world and his legs to cease their turn or tremble. Armand tossed an arm around Nicky-El. He took a final drag of his cigarette and then tossed it into the fog. He slapped Nicky-El's chest and said, "Now that wasn't too hard, was it?"

Trauma remained in Nicky-El's throat. He savored every breath, heavy as the humid air made them. He wiped his brow, and he and Armand stared at Norman Ross' lifeless body. The burden was too much for the officer, and he succumbed to an aneurism. Nicky-El's conjured hatchet dissolved from Norman's forehead and reassembled in the gang leader's hand. A sense of calm filmed him, and he could truly breathe again.

Nicky-El, focused on Officer Norman Ross' wide-eyed corpse, informed Armand, "You can dig up all you need. I just want his bones to stain the news cycle. Let it all out."

Armand nodded, agreeing to the terms. "He'll be remembered as a hateful prick," he replied. "Let his corrupt bones be an offering and exorcising all at the same time. The finding of his half-naked body on the footsteps of his mistress' house will edit his narrative. All manner of him being a loving family man will be erased, and the corruption will flow from there." He spied the doorbell and added, "No cameras will pick up our spirit, if there be any. The corrupt prick died of a brain aneurism." He turned his head toward Nicky-El and winked through the mask, a cock of his head made, and then he said, "Darling? We need a little crossroad-side assistance."

Miss Voodoo Lily heard her sweetheart's call from across time and space, her nkisi doll resonating with the color of his voice projected by his mask. She folded the two elements, and spirited Armand and Nicky-El and from the suburban home.

Voodoo Lily and Armand's dig occurred the following night.

Fruit was planted, and another set of Patricia Gale Freda's bones were unearthed and taken to the Fable Avenue Elders and Voodoo Lily's parents. A ritual was performed by the matriarchs, and the fog receded a little more from Water Bug Hollow.

Nicky-El was presented to Maman Anansi and Madame Jeliya and stitched to his conjure.

He would rather have returned to choking near to death, as his stitching ritual was a painful, terrifying experience filled with nightmares and burden.

As deserved.

31

A new night with old fog covered Water Bug Hollow. The muggy brume thickened in the areas it still possessed, doubling down, stubborn for its trimming and thinning in other regions. It was a night where the air was stuffy. Its bloated heat made a gulp of its invisible element seem like a gulp from the ocean. Taking a breath wasn't simply filling the lungs. It was an intake of troubled waters, and Water Bug Hollow did so have its murk of burden.

Armand Gideon and Crossroads Queen Lillian Eledas-Ghedemere, called Voodoo Lily, on principle would not negotiate with the weighty fog. They came from a spiritual culture that believed the people of Water Bug Hollow deserved wards. The Crossroads Queen had paved a new path, a new course away from a dubious destiny forged by people unalike in nature. Armand was her first traveler down the path, and now he was a guide for it. His first destination was to her, and hand-in-hand, as if they were the divine couple displayed on the sixth card of the Tarot set, they were bonded in duty and heart.

So, it was night. The thick air and fog didn't bother them. Duty motivated them. Love of people and culture and each other bound them. Here the two sweethearts took it upon themselves to trespass into the dangerous territory that marked the seat of a brutal street gang called The Five Elements. Voodoo Lily was tucked in the shadows watching Armand toil away at digging up the dead in the adjoining area of a rundown building. His face was splotched with dirt and dust and a thick layer of sweat, which also soaked through his open vest and unbuttoned tunic. It wasn't the humid air that bothered him, it was the lather of good, hard work and duty that came through his skin.

The three lights of his skull pendants dangling from his necklace provided him sight, physical and otherwise. The dark was no bother, and his trinket would've made for a relief to cool his working body, but Armand appreciated the sweating.

There was a third person in attendance, but he remained silent and as translucent as air. His name was Alphonse Latif. He was familiar with the area. Not just Water Bug Hollow, but the specific region he, Voodoo Lily and Armand now occupied. He once ruled the now dilapidated region. The Five Elements were far different then. The people told tales of him. Alphonse was referred to as The Wiseman, and he had the neighborhood on a more prosperous and self-sustaining trajectory. But, he was killed in the late nineties, and everything collapsed without him.

Alphonse's spirit was pulled from the ethers after consulting with specter Dinclinsin—a phantom that wore many terrible faces to test who ever summoned it. So, here invisible was Alphonse Latif, answering the call, conjured by ritual.

Bugs sang their bayou songs, but that was mostly all that disturbed the night air. The sound of Armand's shovel cutting into the earth, the hushed tear of grass and root and the soft whoosh of wind as Armand tossed the gathered pile in back of him. The quiet made it easy to hear Darrien Hicks' whispered chatter with three of his fellow street soldiers. He discussed business, and though his voice was low, there was a forceful gruff in his words. Business wasn't suffering, but there came a threat in the streets that could definitely dampen life and earnings. Two rivals had brokered a peace and strengthened their numbers, and this didn't make Darrien Hicks happy at all.

"Lamar and Bishop linking up squads and businesses," he grumbled to his armed associates. "Keep an eye out and your heaters gripped," he further warned. "I ain't get an invite yet. I take that personally. I do. Makes me a li'l nervous. My mind wanders as to whether or not I'm long for this life. I got some territory crucial to own, business too." His soldiers stopped hard. Their eyes cast a wide-eyed stare on the single person digging deep into their backyard. Darrien Hicks put pause in his step and peered at Armand shoveling away at his lawn. His face contorted into an offended expression. "Do I know you, nigga?" he growled.

Armand dug up a few more piles of dirt before ceasing his excavation. He jammed the shovel's head into the ground and leaned on it, taking a breath. "You've felt my influence, Mister Hicks. I'm here to give you a proposition."

Darrien's eyes scanned Armand. His vexed look twisted into an even angrier face. "On what business?" he demanded.

"Surprises, Mister Hicks," Armand answered swiftly, a sly smile penned on his visage. "That's all, my friend, surprises."

Darrien's soldiers drew their guns and aimed at Armand.

"We'll finish digging," Darrien noted in a calmer tone. "I know what kind of daisy we'll plant there. We got a whole garden of bodies."

"I'm sure you do, Mister Hicks," Armand replied unfazed by the firearms aimed in his direction. He pointed to his sizable dig and stated, "But the body buried here wasn't of your placing, and I have interest in its bones— not in being buried with them, which I take it you're implying."

Darrien snickered at Armand. He ordered his soldiers to lower their guns, and they obeyed their boss. "Some kind of evidence bein' planted on me, huh? If I ain't got nothing to do with bones buried there, then what's your interest?"

"The bones do concern you, Mister Hicks," Voodoo Lily's voice galloped from the shadows in a cadence as cool as her walk emerging from them. A cloud impeding the moon's shine scurried away, allowing its strong beam to extend down and hold the Crossroads Queen in spotlight. Darrien turned, startled by Voodoo Lily's entrance. His soldiers raised their guns at her. "You see, Mister, Hicks, your castle's foundation—like so many fortresses built for war—is a strong, strong, *strong* stack of bones."

Darrien's curiosity dwindled into impatience. He scowled at Voodoo Lily and scoffed, "You watch where you step, girl! You don't walk up from no hidin' spot 'round me." He turned back to Armand to address him. A stern finger pointed, but Darrien froze before reprimanding him. The fright holding him in place melted a bit, and he quivered with uncertainty. Armand put on a new face. Literally. He fastened his African mask to his countenance. Its hollow, black eyes stared at Darrien with a haunting glare. The uncanny visual was more off putting by the circular mouth on the triangular face-covering.

Armand said through the mask, "I know you, Brother Hicks." His voice sounded like shards of ice and glass shattering into pieces. His voice returned to normal when he next spoke, but there was a deep echo to its timbre. "I invite you to my cabin where we can negotiate the terms of our dig on your property. Maybe a game of liars dice with cigarettes and wine, maybe fruit. My cabin is tucked away in the bayou surrounded by the children of Sebek. Inside that cabin you'll find me and my portrait. Its colors will spring into existence out of the sheer curiosity of seeing life being birthed on canvas. How's that conjure sound?"

Voodoo Lily noted, "I, Brother Hicks, will be its painter."

Darrien's uneasy shiver ceased. He was absolute zero. No movement.

"Boss man, your call…" said one of his soldiers.

Voodoo Lily waved her hand. Black streaks of conjure undulated around the soldiers' guns. The weapons were erased and substituted with snakes that turned and bit the street soldiers' arms. They didn't scream. They barely reacted. The venom was immediate in paralyzing them. They slumped to the earth floor. The snakes slithered away and disappeared into the fog.

Darrien's short, stocky frame regained mobility. He looked at Voodoo Lily. He looked at Armand. They didn't move, but Darrien felt as if they were two walls coming in on him. That's when he noticed a peculiarity adjacent to Armand. There was movement. The area next to Armand warped and twisted as if being viewed through rippling water or distorted glass. It became clear, a translucent figure shifting from shadow and then to the physical flesh. And there he was. Alphonse Latif materialized out of the blue next to Armand. He was as stocky as Darrien, but with a fuller face, prominent cheeks and a thick mustache. He carried his authority through his heaviness, and Darrien stood straighter in his presence. He knew immediately who he was, and Armand enjoyed the look on the gang leader's face as reality bent to a new understanding.

That's when Armand reconsidered his offer for a game. Not all gang bosses were meant to have equal treatment with a polite introduction and a proposition for a game of chance called liar's dice. Some were too far gone, all the way through bone, blood, and flesh. Men like that could only be dealt with one way, according to Armand Gideon.

Directly.

Armand commented, "You've turned your back on history and tradition. You've murdered children to send messages to rival leaders." He shook his head in disgust. "I change my mind," he growled. "You're not worthy of liars dice. You're simply a liar."

Alphonse Latif had something to add, "These young folk gave me some insight to you, my man. They showed me you've been poked with too many needles and a whip's been scratched across your back. You like too many folk in Water Bug Hollow. You allowin' your scars to hurt other people 'steada learnin' how to heal those scars and pass that knowledge on."

Voodoo Lily again swiped her hand across the air. Once more came the black, brush-stroke-like energy over the dig at Armand's feet. The pit deepened, and the pile of dirt behind Armand rose with additional dirt.

Armand observed the hole made deeper. He looked at Voodoo Lily through the mask and scolded, "All this time I've been puttin' my back into it, Lily-baby, and you coulda been using conjure to dig up these bones!"

Voodoo Lily beamed a grin that gave light to the moon. She raised an eyebrow and retorted in a seductive voice, "I like seeing you put your back into it, Armand-baby."

Armand's face, behind the mask, looked like the expression on the African mask itself—eyes wide, mouth opened in surprise. He chuckled and said to Darrien, "That's a woman there, big boss." He turned to Alphonse Latif. "Am I right?" The spirit allowed a crack in his stern expression. A slight smile curled on his face, but he kept hard eyes on Darrien Hicks. Armand returned his spooky-mask gaze back to the gang boss and told him, "It's time for bed!" To Voodoo Lily, he addressed, "Darling…"

The Crossroads Queen waved her hand again. Her black, space-fold conjure whipped around Darrien Hicks. It whisked away his will to fight back and removed his desire to scream in terror. The conjure work then swapped the gang leader for the unearthed bag of bones. Darrien Hicks now lay in the deep grave and the sack of bones rested where he once stood. Armand bent down and aimed the mask's hollow, black stare at the gang leader. He reached for the red, glowing skull looped onto his necklace, placed his fingers gently on its surface, and then pulled them away.

A ghostly variant of the red skull rested in the palm of Armand's hand. He set his hand inside the open grave. His fingers opened like flower petals in bloom, and the shimmering, see-through skull descended over Darrien Hick's face. There its lighted shape lost form, appearing to melt and spread out over the gang leader's countenance. Darrien now wore a mask much like Armand, though his was made of red light.

Armand did the same with the green skull on his necklace, dropping a shadowy replica of the green-glowing skull into the opened earth. The light spread wide and encased Darrien in a shimmering casket. "Reflect, Mister Hicks, on all the burden you've placed on Water Bug Hollow—the corruption that assisted in rotting the foundation of a once-proud hamlet." Armand rose. He dug into his pockets and pulled out a handful of seeds. He dropped them in the grave and remarked, "Something good will grow from this."

Voodoo Lily twiddled her fingers. The pile of dirt filled in the opened earth. Darrien Hicks rested inside, safe to breathe through conjured light. All he would see and feel was the weight of consequences his reign of terror brought to Water Bug Hollow. Deep in the Earth, Darrien Hicks' ability to scream was restored. Thirteen feet below, the gang leader shouted at the top of his lungs as heart and mind were penetrated with the horrible images of his street deeds and orders carried out.

Voodoo Lily stepped to Armand's side, taking up the bag of bones as she neared it. She handed the bones to Armand. She addressed Alphonse Latif when she inquired, "You can handle things from here?"

"Yes, Madame Crossroads," he replied like a soldier reporting for duty.

"My father and Horace George's ritual will keep you in place, walking among us?"

"Yes," he assured in the same manner. He pointed to Darien's unconscious street soldiers. "I'll start with them," he told Voodoo Lily. He glided on the earth floor, hovering inches off the ground as he moved to the three young men, arms crossed. "You two can go and be about the good work," he said to Voodoo Lily and Armand as his feet touched the ground.

"Yessir!" Armand said with a nod.

The Crossroads Queen and her herald turned and walked into the fog. There was a *whooshing* sound as Voodoo Lily ignited her time-and space-fold conjure and spirited them away back to the Water Bug Hollow church. Rituals were conducted on the bones by Voodoo Lily's mother and father, and the Fable Avenue Elders. Spirits were summoned, and the haunt of a woman's screams were hushed into a calm slumber. Another fraction of her anguish had been tempered, but there still persisted a restlessness that fueled the area's turmoil.

The fog yielded to ritual, and with the affliction residing in bones soothed to a relieving sigh, the stubborn fog retracted its murk even further. Its thick, dawdling vapor had its tail between its legs. It licked its wounds, regaining its composure, still ready for battle.

32

Sometimes the crossroads sweethearts liked to rest. This late morning Lillian Eledas-Ghedemere and Armand Gideon were very relaxed and at ease. They puffed on *fascinare cannabis*—bewitched marijuana—entertaining two, Fable Avenue guests.

Blowing smoke with them was Benjamin Brickhouse and Neyeli Campbell. Armand and Benny chose a strain of smoke called *Captain Kujo's Fire*. The women indulged in *Queen Nani's Storm*. The strains were different, but their destination for the clouds was the same. Neyeli's hair shifted from sky blue to hazy purple, over and over.

There was one problem, however. It was a minor detail the four of them overlooked as they sat in the living room of one of the crossroad houses. This wasn't exactly a day of rest, and time was ticking away as they joked and laughed and smoked and enjoyed one another's company.

Armand jumped onto the couch, barefoot but wearing blue jeans, an opened brown collar shirt, and his incanted African mask clipped to his hip. His red, black, and green skull necklace glowed with a soft hum as he took a puff and spread his arms while exhaling. His head fell back and he hollered. Neyeli and Benny giggled. Lillian sat, legs crossed, in an old-style chair. She smoked, felt good, and smiled up at her hunter-warrior and herald. She hadn't seen him so loose and happy while not on a mission in the midst of duty, or in heated passion with her. She smoked, and she felt good seeing him so unfastened.

But Armand was celebrating his work. He was Washington crossing the Delaware. The couch was his boat. He exclaimed, "Them gang boys been in deep hoodoo since Miss Voodoo Lily of the Crossroads done gave me orders!" Benny and Neyeli chuckled harder. "They seein' that hoodoo justice right here." He jumped down, posterior slamming against the couch cushions as he landed in a seated position. "An endless supply of cosmic conjure against what? A bunch of misguided fools with hand signals?" He aimed his refer stick at Lillian and noted, "When this beautiful conjure woman rearranges her fingers, she bends and folds time and space like laundry."

Lillian remarked, "I don't do laundry."

Benny chortled. He puffed again and blew smoke.

"Shit, conjure queen," Armand drawled with smoke fogging his head. "You sure as hell takin' out Water Bug Hollow's dirty laundry. You cleanin' the place up." Then the smoke took over as he repeated, "Up, up. Up! Up. Up. Up!"

Benny looked over at Lillian and said, "He's right about that, Miss

Eledas-Ghedemere. All them ups."

Lillian replied in a collected manner, relaxed by her smoke, "It started with the two of you clearing out the church. I give my thanks. That break in Water Bug Hollow's hexed fog is what we needed—" then she winked at Armand as she concluded, "—to take out the laundry."

Armand beamed. His head dropped, head full of billowy incant and haze.

Neyeli raised her refer smoke, making a toast. "We accept your appreciation, Miss Voodoo Lily!" she stated. "If there's anything more we can lend…"

"Your presence," Lillian spoke, cutting into Neyeli's words. "Members of the Gwuinee family will be here after the reconquest of Water Bug Hollow. My father wants Eve's Hallow resurrected when the fog is clear. He wants conjure and soul blaring from that old juke joint. It's going to be a grand opening. Please come! All the Fable Avenue Elders will be there. It will be an event, an amazing spectacle." She rose, slow and dramatic. She rotated her shoulders and swiveled her hips as smoky incant and hazy conjure filled her head and lightened the weight of her body. She felt as if she didn't stop rising, hovering above the floor. She stepped forward, graceful like a dancer. Her left leg extended long. Her right leg bent to support her weight. "There will be a dance!" she declared. She jumped up and twirled in the air, landing perfectly on her feet. "It will be the beginning of the March of the Burdened as they make a long journey to the crossroads for healing."

A thought occurred to the Crossroads Queen. She blinked and used an incant to clear her head of the smoke. She looked at Armand, a wide, bewildered look blazoned on her face. Her eyes dropped as she remembered this wasn't a day of complete rest.

"Shit! The crossroads!" she blurted. She blinked, and she blinked again. "Ah!" she shouted. She looked at Benny and Neyeli, stepping over to the coffee table. She bent down and smashed out in the ashtray the remaining refer stick she'd been puffing on. Her eyes remained on Neyeli and Benny Jah. "We're taking part in banishing that damn yokel at the crossroads."

Everyone burst into sobriety, muttering incants to clear their heads. Armand was the least effected, still being new to casting a curative incant. But he was able to gain balance and composure. His head remained light, and the euphoric feeling clung to him with a soft grip. His head lifted and dropped as he struggled to put his socks and shoes on. "God—d-d-damnit!" he cursed.

An instinct tingled against Lillian's forehead. She turned and looked down the hallway. The doorbell rang! She straightened her posture and hurried to answer it. At the door, she fixed herself. Regal in stance. She cleared her throat and took a breath. She opened the door. On the other side was Brooklyn, New York. Fable Avenue, where the house's façade was that of a lovely brownstone. She stepped through the foyer and opened the entrance doors.

There was her father, Satchel "Old Goon". Beside him was Fable Avenue's sole patriarch, Papa Solomon. The conjure Elder held in his hand a mystical trumpet, a wondrous artifact that had been passed down through lifetimes. Lillian beamed as she spotted the rugged, street conjure man named Wilson standing behind her father and Papa Solomon. Neyeli's rugged and handsome uncle, Private Detective Martin Campbell, was next to him. The last man she wasn't too familiar with. She'd seen him before on occasion, definitely on her visit to Fable Avenue last Halloween. He was cinnamon colored, of average height and stocky build. Though it was summer he wore a long, thick overcoat. Gloves with the fingertips cut from them were on his hands and an old, broad-brimmed topper hat rested on his head. His real name escaped Lillian, but she remembered that Fable Avenue residents referred to him as Top Hat.

"Ah!" Lillian proclaimed with a shining, cheerful expression. Her eyes fell to her father when she said, "My eternal father—" She looked up at the other people gathered at her door and finalized, "And the cleanup crew."

Satchel "Old Goon" chuckled at his daughter's words. Papa Solomon beamed. Satchel looked at him and remarked, "Now that sounds like a conjure and soul group I'd like to listen to." He turned to his daughter and gave her a hug. "My Crossroads Queen! My daughter! How you doin', baby girl?"

"I'm fine, Papa," she replied bending down to embrace the very short man. Her eyes opened and panned the remaining guests. "You're here for the banishment? All of you?"

"We know this yokel dude ain't goin' quietly," Wilson remarked.

Lillian stepped away from her father, and she took position at the door, back against it. She invited the men in, and they sauntered inside with a slow and methodical determination. Lillian could see the men were focused. Then she heard her father sniff the air, and her heart skipped. She maintained her composure. He looked back at her with a scowl on his face. "Whatchu kids been puffin' on?"

"Paaapuuuh!" the Crossroads Queen whined. "We're okay. We've cleared our heads."

"Lillian! I need you focused today!" he chided as he walked back up to her.

The other men passed. Lillian closed the door. "I'm balanced, Papa," she insisted. "I am. There will be no escape for this pesky yokel today." Then she confessed to her dwarfish father, "It actually slipped my mind, today's duty—the banishment. We're gathered here, but we thought it was tomorrow morning. Armand and I have just been hard at our own work with Water Bug Hollow. Benny Jah and Neyeli have been fighting haunts and villains with the Lilac Flame. We were looking for some come down…"

Satchel remarked, "Come down with some get high?" A knowing eyebrow rose. But then Satchel "Old Goon" nodded his head. "I understand," he told his daughter. "Just make sure you all together. Rest comes tomorrow, I suppose—if you ain't got a thing planned."

"No, Papa…" she replied. "There's a bigger plan for our final marks. We need to go over some things with Reverend Pouvwa."

Satchel "Old Goon" again made a nod with his head. He turned to join the others in the front room. Then he made a quick pivot. Lillian almost slammed into her father. She stopped abruptly to avoid the collision. "You got any more on you, cuz—"

"Papa!" she chided playfully.

Satchel grinned and chuckled. "I'm just playin'. I don't fool with that stuff no more…all the time…as much…" Lillian made jest by slapping her father's shoulder. "What? I don't. I don't." Father and daughter joined the others. Satchel spotted Armand seated on the couch. He approached him, swinging his fists to playfight. Armand flinched. "You lookin' a little loopy-headed, boy. That smoke got you?" Armand confessed with a sleepy shake of his head. Satchel "Old Goon" patted his arm. "You still got some growin' up to do. That smoke ain't like other smoke. It's got power in it! Yes, it do, what it be!" He cocked his head to the side an inspected Armand. "No help. You got to learn how to incant that off by yourself."

Armand attempted another incant. More of the fog in his head dissolved. "I can still see clear," he stated. "You need me, Mister Old Goon? You got me right here!" he assured.

Satchel replied, "Good. Gather me up some materials, walk off what numbness you still got smoggin' up your head."

Armand got up and took a moment to catch his balance. He looked at Satchel "Old Goon" and addressed, "Yessir…?"

The old, old man told him, "Okay, now, I need a shovel, a bottle of rum, and a cigar." He pointed to Top Hat and said, "That child over there said he'd give up his stovepipe hat for the ritual. Need to bless the spade."

Top Hat heard Old Goon refer to him as a child. He considered the thought, even as a man in his late thirties, he was just a youngster for a man claiming to be over one-hundred and twenty years old. So, he let it slide.

Armand focused more on the latter part of Old Man Satchel's words. Influenced by the lingering *fascinare cannabis*, Armand quipped, "All us spades need a blessing."

Old Man Satchel hollered up a hard guffaw. He said to his daughter, "Lillian, I like this one!"

The Crossroads Queen replied to her father with her eyes locked onto Armand, "I do too, Papa…"

Armand ambled up to Lillian, wide grin on his face. "Why you soundin' all sheepish, *iyaafin?*"

The word used meant 'lady' in Yoruba, and Lillian was impressed with Armand's use, conjuring it up through instinct. But she didn't fall into his hawk-like gaze and wide and haughty, Cheshire grin. She mirrored his expression, mocking it more than borrowing the features for the same use. She slapped him on the arm and huffed through her smile, "Go and get my father the tools he asked for, Negro."

Armand bowed in an overdramatic fashion, "As you wish, Miss Voodoo Lily." He raised straight and set about his task.

Papa Solomon wasn't as cheerful, casting a glower at Neyeli and Benny Jah. "You two sobered up?"

"Yes…Papa Solomon…" they said together in an apologetic tone.

Papa Solomon huffed, "I don't mind you all puffin' on the silly smoke, it's just we got a hard banishment to perform."

Neyeli's hair blushed gold and pink. She explained in a sincere tone, "We really did believe it was tomorrow, Papa Solomon. We did. And we're clear-headed now."

Top Hat and Wilson snickered behind Papa Solomon. The Fable Avenue patriarch turned, aimed the bell of his horn at the two, and scolded, "Don't encourage 'em!" Top Hat and Wilson fixed their faces. Papa Solomon walked around Benny and Neyeli and started a conversation with Satchel "Old Goon".

Wilson and Top Hat resumed their teasing chuckle, and Benny made a playful attack on the two men because of it. "I'll swipe the air out of your lungs," Benny threatened.

Wilson pushed Benny into Top Hat's grip. "You ain't even got your glove on, kid!" he growled, throwing punches inches from Benny's stomach as he lay locked into Top Hat's hold.

"Don't take but a thought to put it on, but with you two shitheads, I don't need it!" Benny fired back.

While the playground antics continued, Martin stepped up to Neyeli and gave her a hug. She hugged him back. He warned her while embraced, "You stay clean, little niece. I'm a cop, but Papa Solomon is *the* cop!"

Neyeli flapped her lips. "Oh, please! He know he blow ritual smoke from time to time."

"I don't know," Martin responded as their embrace ended. "Him and his sister stay pretty clean. A cigar and dragon spit every-now-and-then, I know. Some rum…" He patted Neyeli on the shoulder and changed he subject. "How you been, young lady?"

"I'm fine. Your brother—my father—is fine."

"He didn't call the police on me, did he?"

"What? Why?"

"Beat him so bad at Samedi's Tarot the other day, I'm sure it was some kind of crime."

Neyeli rolled her eyes. Again, she flapped her lips. "Oh, please! You two. If it ain't that, it's pool."

Wilson tugged at Martin's suit jacket, getting his attention. "I think your brother's cool. It's Cedron that wants another round."

Martin scoffed, "Next time I give King a tribute for a job, I'll pay him in increments of his pride back."

Top Hat buckled with the comment. Air sputtered from his nose as he covered his mouth in an attempt to hold back laughter. Wilson threw his hands up and made a face. "Oh-kay!" he exclaimed. "That deads that conversation."

Martin grinned. He turned back to Neyeli and the sly smirk melted into a concerned expression. "I need your help, Neyeli," he said bending down toward her and in a low voice. "Not me, really. I mean, yes, me, but…"

Neyeli couldn't hold back her instinct, though it didn't take a higher sense to see Martin struggling. Her hair turned pitch in color as she put her hand on his arm. She used her conjure to soothe him. "I know, Uncle Martin. It's Stephanie, correct? Benny told me."

Martin felt better. He nodded his head for a long moment before finally expressing, "Yeah…" It was more an exhale of air than an intelligible word, but Neyeli understood.

Neyeli told her uncle, "Let me know when you, she, and her haunt are ready. We can alleviate this burden for her and the haunt. It won't all be in one session, but she'll feel better with each one before we can separate them."

Armand returned to the room with a shovel hung from a strap resting on his shoulder. He had in his hand an unopened bottle of rum and a cigar. His ears perked up, catching most of what Neyeli had spoken, and using an instinct to decipher the rest. He said nothing on the matter, but noted it. He looked at Satchel "Old Goon" and removed the shovel from his shoulder and handed him all three items. Satchel "Old Goon" accepted the ritual tools and thanked him. The old, old man called for his daughter. *"Lill-lay!"* he shouted. *"Lill-lay!"*

Lillian glided into the room through a hall that led to the backdoor. "Yes, Papa?"

He held up the items and said, "Give permission, Crossroads Queen."

Lillian stepped aside and waved her hand down the hall. "The crossroads are through here, Papa." Everyone fell in line behind Satchel "Old Goon" and Papa Solomon. Lillian walked in tow after everyone passed.

Satchel "Old Goon" opened the backdoor and walked out onto a front porch that overlooked the dusty Clarksdale, Mississippi crossroads. The conjure party shuffled and spread out onto the porch, greeted by a warm, humid wind that filtered through a hazy day.

Satchel "Old Goon" dug into his pockets and presented everyone with a short piece of thread blessed to keep them safe. He turned and then continued down the stairs and out into the street. He observed the gas station in front of him. It was translucent, not at all within the physical plane. The eyes of the conjure folk were the only ones that could see it as it hung in the murk of the anathematic world.

Papa Solomon walked to the front of the porch and turned, facing the others who created a half crescent around him. He looked over his shoulder. He spotted Satchel "Old Goon" lay down the shovel and then twist the cap off the bottle of rum. He pocketed the cap and stuffed the cigar down into the bottleneck. He spoke an incant over the cigar and a flame burned at the end, twisting into a soft burn. Smoke swiveled up, carrying the cigar's thick aroma mixed with a sweet waft of rum. Satchel "Old Goon" set the bottle down on the shovel's rusted, metal scoop.

A fleet of cars sped down the road, their roaring engines alerting Satchel "Old Goon".

Lillian lifted a hand, beginning to concentrate and fold space and time around her father to move him from their path. Papa Solomon put a hand on her arm, lifted his horn to his lips and played quick a succession of notes that pulled Satchel "Old Goon" and their party outside of time. A car horn blared, but went silent as Satchel "Old Goon" faded from the physical realm. The car continued on, ghosting through the old, old man.

Satchel "Old Goon" stood straight. He turned and furrowed his brow at Papa Solomon. "The hell you take us outside of time for? The ritual ain't done yet!"

"To keep your old, black ass from bein' road kill!" Papa Solomon yelled back. "Next time have a little patience and don't go runnin' out into the street like a child!"

Satchel "Old Goon" boasted, "Actin' like a child is what's kept me so young and spry!"

Papa Solomon huffed at the old, old man's words. He looked up and spied Jabo Judson emerge from the now clear and solid gas station. The scrawny, stringy-haired yokel posted up against one of the pumps, arms crossed. He started chuckling as he watched the conjure folk in front of him. The day's mugginess cooled with the spread of anathematic smog infecting the atmosphere. Jabo Judson cackled at Satchel "Old Goon" and said,

"Master Fallows said y'all'd come. He can see y'all's movement. Take him a li'l longer now. He a li'l sick tryin' to adjust to your jungle blood in his veins." He turned his head and spit on the ground. "I've been in wait for you all, I have." He looked up at Papa Solomon and beamed a snaggletooth smile.

Papa Solomon turned his back to Jabo Judson and addressed the small conjure party. "I'll slow time down. Keep that idiot still. Wilson, you amplify my effect."

"Bet!" the rugged conjure man acknowledged, throwing a fist into the palm of his hand.

"Martin, Neyeli, you two make the arrest and cleansing," Papa Solomon continued. "Neyeli, you wield the shovel, bury it inside the station's floor. Martin, you give the banishment on the halfwit, make sure Captain Yokel goes down with his ship." His eyes spotted Benny Jah, Top Hat, and Armand. "This idiot seems confident. He might have some backup in there. Now my half-assed playin' can slow the action, assisted by Wilson. But you three lead the tussle with whatever comes charging out with needles in their hands." He addressed Lillian, "You ain't just sittin' this out, Madame Crossroads. Benny and Neyeli have some intel on some heavy hitters. They show up, you confuse space and time, and join in that skirmish."

Lillian nodded.

"Stovepipe!" Satchel "Old Goon" called Top Hat. "Bring that silk hat down here so we can complete this here ritual."

Top Hat looked at Papa Solomon after rolling his eyes. He said to Lillian, "I'm lettin' y' old man slide a lot."

"Thank you," Lillian replied.

Top Hat stepped down off the porch and hurried to the street. He removed his top hat, and from his coat he took out a pair of glasses that had only one lens fastened to the frame. He presented the accessories to the old, old man. Satchel "Old Goon" accepted the hat and placed it next to the shovel. He put the glasses on the brim.

"Rum and cigar been burnin' right," he remarked. "Now's the time." He unclipped a pouch hanging on his belt. He opened it and tossed roasted peanuts that had been sprinkled with ground coffee beans. He showered the altar. The prominent smoke billowing from the cigar thickened and broke into two distinct clouds, one purple and the other white.

Jabo Judson's eyes widened as he gazed on the spectacle. His jovial expression dissolved, choking his squeaky guffaws. Concerned shaped his eyebrows and he started spouting, "No! No! No! No! No!" Jabo Judson bounced off the station's pump and ran around maniacally.

Satchel "Old Goon" spied Jabo Judson's antics. He told the yokel, "I come from an old-line conjure *nasyon*. There's a warrant out for you. Your time's come."

Jabo Judson stopped his frantic pacing. He aimed his wide-eyed and open-mouthed expression at Satchel "Old Goon" and Top Hat. He repeated, "No! No! No! No! No!" He shook a finger at them and then paced again.

Top Hat crossed his arms. "We're gonna bury you," he declared.

Jabo Judson paused his disordered steps. He bit his thumb and flicked it at Old Man Satchel and Top Hat. The two men looked at one another and chuckled. Jabo Judson dropped to his knees, bent forward and licked the ground. Top Hat and Satchel "Old Goon" were reviled by the act, making faces as they observed the yokel lapping up the dust and dirt on the ground.

Jabo Judson straightened up on his knees. He licked the same thumb he flicked at the conjure men and then wiped it across the ground. He spit on the trail his thumb left behind, and then he stood and swiped a line with his leg.

Air shifted and became combative between the benign world outside of time and the anathematic fog invading the atmosphere. Thunder rolled a low, intimidating growl, harkening the arrival of a descending fog that swept around Jabo Judson. A chill further intruded the atmosphere. The fog moved to Jabo's left, undulating like a slithering snake. Out of its turbid form there manifested six figures. Four were men wearing long white coats over brown suits. Surgical masks draped their faces, and in their hands, they held syringes. Two were dressed similar and also holding the needle-tipped weapons. Their faces were covered by seventeenth-century-styled plague masks. A wide-brimmed hat rested atop all of the night doctors' heads.

Another manifestation occurred. The butler-attired, clock-headed monster called Lazy Crow. His arrival sent a chill down the spines of the conjure folk, including Neyeli and Benny Jah who'd tumbled with him before. The unnerving sense amplified when out of the fog formed the ghostly, floating figure swathed in a cloak of mist. Grave-Clothes. Neyeli's hair reacted. Its color whirled into the shade of maroon, where it would remain for the fight's duration.

Papa Solomon raised his horn and played a soft tune to induce an incant that would sedate their adversaries' movements. Wilson put a hand on Papa Solomon's shoulder and concentrated to expand the patriarch's power. Lazy Crow's clock went tick, tick, tick. Tock. Papa Solomon's fingers shook and faltered on the valves. Wilson's arm trembled. Both men felt Lazy Crow's hex pushed up against their power and hold their conjure at bay.

Lillian raised her hand and attempted to fold time and space to disrupt Lazy Crow's curse. The hands on his clock-face struggled to tick, and he trembled from both frustration and Voodoo Lily opposing his hex. Papa Solomon regained some momentum in his fingers, and he started playing again. Wilson returned to amplifying the patriarch's power, but even with

Lazy Crow battling against Voodoo Lily, the clock-monster's spread of chrono-delirium had its effect against he and Papa Solomon's effort.

Grave-Clothes transfigured into a blotch of haze and charged the Crossroads Queen. Benny Jah lunged at the incoming fog, shouting, "We've danced before, haven't we!" Gauntlet called to his arm, Benny lightened his body's weight until he was as intangible as the advancing misty haze. Sharing the same ethereal plane, Benny Jah clutched the overcast, humanoid, cloaked figure. He grappled with Grave-Clothes in mid-air and rolled onto the ground. They tumbled, and when straight, Benny Jah had the misty monster pinned.

Grave-Clothes reacted, snarling under the murky wraps that covered his face. A length of fog unraveled from the Blood Curser and wrapped around Benny's neck, constricting and pulling back. Benny was too determined to be fazed. He bared his teeth and slammed an armored fist into Grave-Clothes' face and stomach as he straddled him.

The needlemen, while not at full speed, managed to whittle into the confrontation. Armand strapped on his African mask, jumped the porch's railing and rushed to challenge the night doctors. Neyeli pulled two, glowing snakes from her locks. They straightened in her grip, shifting in appearance to Zulu Iklwa short spears. She followed Armand into battle.

Armand tossed ghostly forms of the glowing skulls dangling from his necklace. He hit two needlemen and knocked them back before they could stab the Old Goon or Top Hat. The night doctors tumbled to the ground, flipped, and recovered on their knees.

A plague-masked needleman made Neyeli his target, swiping his syringes down on her. Instinct allowed her to forecast the needleman's stabs and swings and block accordingly. His strikes were like hiccups, and his image moved like a motion film missing frames. The needleman was caught between the effects of Papa Solomon's power and Lazy Crow, while also struggling with Voodoo Lily, fighting against it. The needleman's spastic and irregular movements made for a frenzied fight. A second, surgical-masked needleman attacked from the side. Martin tackled him to the ground, slammed a palm on his chest and shouted, *"Duro!"* The needleman froze, becoming immobile with Martin's arresting conjure locked into his body.

Neyeli kicked the needleman she sparred with in the stomach, pushing him into the path of one of Armand's skulls. The projectile crashed against the needleman's head, knocking him out.

Benny Jah maneuvered from Grave-Clothes' hold by putting form back into his body, allowing the foggy cloth choking him to ghost through his person. Grave-Clothes shifted solid and drove a fist up into Benny Jah's chin. The foggy figure disappeared, blinking away from under Benny Jah's body to continue its sail toward Voodoo Lily. Benny again lightened his weight and pursued him.

Two needlemen subdued. Four remained standing. Though they were impaired by half an incant wrestling with their bodies' momentum, they possessed a dark drive to defend Jabo Judson's service station bastion. They calculated gauged that their inconsistent movements, jammed up by a fight between incant and hex, could be used to their advantage. Needles out. They readied for a fight, but an ominous creature blocked their path.

A transformation achieved by the conjure man Top Hat. He remained humanoid in figure, but his skin was darker than night itself. From his head grew a long and thick pair of antlers with multiple, sharp prongs. His body was broad with the muscular legs of a goat, hooves like an ungulate animal. His long, winter's coat enlarged with his size. When he roared, his mouth shaped and extended like a wolf's snout. He dashed at the remaining needlemen, bowled one over and impaled another on his prongs. He shook his head as if the night doctor weighed no more than a rag, and he flung him to the dusty road, stomach bleeding out. Wild and untamed, he batted around the remaining needlemen, and left them the same.

The ferocious Top Hat, like a feral bull ready to charge, scrapped the dust road with one hoof. He howled and stormed ahead, slamming a shoulder into Lazy Crow. The Blood Curser was lifted off his feet and hurled through the gas station's glass door.

Jabo Judson surveyed the situation and calculated a loss. He turned and ran into the gas station, jumping over the downed and disoriented Lazy Crow whose hands on his clock-face were spinning rapid and out of control. Though he appeared dazed, the clock hands' rapid movement was an attempt at regaining his balance and a sense of the world around him. Jabo Judson didn't assist the Blood Curser. He continued running, making his way to the back of the gas station.

Satchel "Old Goon" pointed to the shovel and yelled to Martin and Neyeli. "This is ready!"

The private detective dashed in the old, old man's direction, Neyeli close behind him. Martin scooped up the shovel, tossed the bottle of rum to Old Man Satchel, and then pitched the shovel to Neyeli. Her glowing Iklwa-snakes were unsummoned, and she caught the pass. Then she and her uncle bounded after Jabo Judson.

Lazy Crow's clock hands slowed as he recovered. He got up and called, "Grave. Clothes. Let. Us. Depart."

The misty-clothed Blood Curser zipped toward Lazy Crow, abandoning his fight. He transmuted into a large puff of smoke that covered the clock-faced monster and then vanished, taking with him the chilling anathematic world's infection.

Top Hat reverted back to his common form. He took up his hat and put it on his head. He looked at Satchel "Old Goon" and inquired, "Should we follow?" He nodded toward the gas station.

"No. They'll be fine," answered the old, old man.

The interior had its irritation. A back door led to a maze of long hallways with doors that led into longer hallways. The various rooms bent and twisted, dipped and rose, and niece and uncle used the full extent of their instincts to keep up with Jabo Judson who was dashing through halls and ducking into random doorways. One pass through a door had them spy Jabo Judson's exit from the hallway, four doors down. Martin raced in the yokel's direction, opened the door, and caught up to Jabo Judson before he could shut the next door leading to another hall. The private detective grabbed the yokel by his arm and forced him back through the door. Jabo attempted to fight back, but against the might of Martin's muscle, it was useless.

It took only a single punch to knock Jabo Judson off balance. Martin had more for the yokel. He grabbed him by the collar and slammed him against the wall. A hit to the chest while screaming, *"Duro!"* made Jabo docile until Martin commanded, "Walk!" Jabo obeyed. Martin twisted one of Jabo's arms behind his back. He grabbed his neck and led him back down the hall. Neyeli let her uncle pass. She followed close behind as Martin, pushed Jabo Judson along. "Lead!" Martin ordered Jabo. The yokel's legs walked the correct hallways and doors to guide uncle and niece to the front of the gas station.

Martin let go of Jabo. The yokel stood still, Martin's conjure keeping him in place. The private detective walked in front of Jabo Judson and spoke, "I banish you, unalike and created creature. By the power of Ixu and Gira, I banish you. By all that was created by the First two, I banish you. By the sun, the moon, and the stars, and the cosmic black body that holds them together, I banish you. The earth will swallow you. The air will leave you. The water will clean your stain on this realm. Fire will burn you from existence. By all that is natural, I banish you."

Martin turned to Neyeli and nodded.

She aimed the shovel's sharp and rusted spade down and slammed it through the floor.

The tile split and cracked as if it was as soft as the most fertile soil. The shovel's head dug deep into the floor's unnatural make, and the building started shaking. Neyeli and Martin made a quick escape. They joined their conjure party on the porch and watched the gas station collapse in on itself and funnel into the earth like an uncanny animation. The needlemen lying on the road were dragged into the ground with it. Wind and thunder and lightning accompanied the preternatural gas station's consumption into the earth like a magnificent, orchestral soundtrack. Papa Solomon played a triumphant tune through the horn and brought the party back into time.

The day was humid and hazy, but it was clear and cool to them. Lillian's heightened senses could feel the entirety of the crossroads' mysticism.

Papa Solomon turned and walked inside the house, ready for a swig of something strong. His body shivered from the use of power. He appealed for the rum Satchel "Old Goon" was holding. The old, old man passed the bottle to the Fable Avenue patriarch. Papa Solomon removed the extinguished cigar corked in the neck. He knocked back a long shot and exhaled a heavy breath. He turned to Benny Jah and Neyeli and asked, "That was them, huh? Those two special lookin' monsters, right? Blood Cursers?"

Neyeli nodded in the affirmative. Her hair swirled in a gradient of violets and light blue as she relaxed.

Benny Jah answered aloud, "Yes, Papa Solomon."

"Ain't so damn tough," he snarled taking another heavy swig of rum. Then he continued on inside the house, now behind Martin and Wilson. Neyeli, Top Hat and Benny Jah followed. Lillian remained on the porch with her father and Armand flanking her. Her eyes focused on the blessed shovel planted into the ground where the gas station once stood.

Satchel "Old Goon" put his arm around his daughter and said, "It's all yours now, Crossroads Queen."

Lillian grinned at her father. "Always was, Papa," she told him. "We just had some squatters." She made a face with her quip.

Satchel "Old Goon" chuckled at his daughter's witticism. He took his arm from around her and walked inside the house. His parting words were, "I guess we could *all* go for some smoke, now." And he laughed and laughed as he passed through the door. "These Fable Avenue folk sure know how to throw a banishing party."

Armand, mask now fastened to his hip, embraced Lillian around her waist. He turned her around and started dancing with her, swaying back and forth in place. "And next we reclaim the Hollow that Curtis built. We're so close," he said looking deep into her eyes. "War is a marathon, not a sprint. Ain't that about right, Crossroads Queen?"

Lillian blushed a little. She remarked in a sultry voice, "You know, for a man who was illiterate in conjure just weeks back, you sure know how to put a spell on a girl as versed in it as me."

Armand grinned, "I still take my time with you, *iyaafin*. You are a marathon, Miss Voodoo Lily, not a sprint." Then he kissed the Crossroads Queen deep on the lips.

She put her arms around her warrior-herald, and they indulged in one another's tastes.

33

Excited? It seemed too weak a word for what Gordon was feeling. He paced back and forth in his sanctuary, taking moments to shadow box imagined opponents. Spook and Silver observed him. He looked as if he would jump and click his heels at any minute, but he only continued the shadow fight. He threw an upper cut and quipped, "Got 'em! Maybe on the ropes!" he swung up another. The cosmic, lilac force that radiated Gordon electrified, more than usual, every molecule and atom that made up his person.

Glorious news rang throughout the conjure community, even amid an outbreak of skirmishes against clandestine outfits of needlemen. The Elders concluded the assailments by the hexing horde felt desperate, heightened by a sense of panic. They were brutal and ferocious, and managed to frighten some conjure communities into submission. Few conjure folk knew more than incants, and rarer still was the manifestation of a personal conjure.

Gordon blinked, dodging a jab from an imaginary opponent. He solidified out of lilac dust and black strands of cosmic energy. He took a step back, and then he threw a straight punch. "Take that witcha!" he snarled. His Chokwe-like mask formed out of shadow, covering his face. He made a pivot as another invisible adversary pounced. He taunted, "Iboju-Boy Dooley ready to kick a little ass!" He jumped up and executed a fancy kick, came down and pitched another straight-on punch. Dooley imagined the new opponent was a little more formidable. He was able to dodge his kick and knock away his punch. Iboju-Boy Dooley vanished, ending up behind his foe. His imagination allowed this breed of dog to have a little more bite in him—a hex exactly.

He thought as he fought, thinking of the recent triumphs the conjure folk had claimed against Stanley Fallows and what appeared to be his inexhaustible regiment of needlemen. Dooley was a part of those victories. Children who'd been kidnapped months prior were rescued, though they'd been transfigured into flowers as an easier means to drain their conjure essence from the colorful petals they sprouted. Efforts had been successful in restoring the children to human form. However, they remained in a deep slumber, recovering and cared for by Fable Avenue's apothecary, Miss Lavette Ross. The children had been carefully moved to the top floor of her brownstone. It would be a long time before they would fully recuperate.

Iboju-Boy Dooley used a series of blinks to confuse the unseen villains. He then initiated a set of kicks, flips and punches that knocked his opponents down.

Victory!

His mask transmuted to shadow and receded into his skin. Gordon took a seat to think while catching his breath. Ancient text scrawled across Spook's screen. It read: *Not sure what happened, but I think he won.* Silver scanned the words and chuckled. The diminutive, winged sprite's giggle caused Gordon to look up and read what was on Spook's screen. "There's still more to fight," he remarked.

Then he recalled the excursion to rescue the Fable Avenue children. The harrowing ordeal brought to light a cast of villains named the *Blood Cursers*. These were needlemen and women with their own set of specific hexes to engage conjure folk. Gordon received warning that the rogues' gallery was destined to appear and battle his cosmic spirit. The Lilac Flame and the Cobalt-Blue spirit were often set upon by a troupe of anathematic characters where- and whenever they manifested in conjure folk history. Gordon, teamed with his brother's crew—the Gypsy Moon Misfits— scrapped with the five-person squad. They were tough, and they were determined to keep Gordon and the Gypsy Moon Misfits from recovering the abducted children.

But keeping the transfigured children was not these villains' only aim. Stanley Fallows had stolen the elemental essences of certain conjure folk, including Gordon's brother and Fable Avenue matriarch Madame Jeliya. Fey Forrester was also pilfered of a sizeable amount of her cobalt-blue spirit. Stanley was attempting to map cosmic DNA with the objective to graft it to himself and lock reality in place, degenerating beyond redemption and eliminating all conjure. That was his desire and wish, and he was constructing a grand ritual to bring it to fruition. There was one outstanding essence he had yet to procure.

Gordon's.

The cosmic, Lilac Flame had yet to be pricked and pulled from Gordon's body, and Gordon meant to keep it that way. Stanley Fallows' plan wasn't whole, and Gordon took pride in that.

But Gordon's cosmic spirit sparked with the news that a small conjure team won a crucial victory against a blockade that haunted the crossroads. It was a haunt in the form of a simple 1950s-era gas station, and it was run by a snaggle-toothed, oily- and stringy-haired, lanky man named Jabo Judson. He looked dumb and unassuming, but he knew ritual work to summon an army of needlemen at will. Jabo Judson kept a lazy eye on the crossroads for Stanley Fallows with his tricks at the ready. That was no more, as both his good eye and his lazy eye were permanently blinded and closed in banishment. Gordon heard from his friend Benny Jah that the Blood Cursers named Lazy Crow and Grave-Clothes showed up for the rumble. Their presence made little difference. The yokel and his establishment were forever banished and buried.

Victories were plentiful, and the conjure folk against their enemies were merciless.

There were still two outstanding objectives, and their fulfillment rested on Gordon's shoulders. He could feel the presence of their weight as he thought of them, a burden that needed no *inawo* to manifest into a smoky, monstrous apparition to get his heart racing. Gordon was tasked to find two precious articles lost to time. One was an ancient tarot card. Specifically, it was The Lovers card. It was a powerful item, ancient in craft and pictorial design. Fable Avenue's third matriarch, Lady Arachne, sought to restore The Lovers card to the rest of its set, which she possessed. Once her deck was unabridged, she would have the ability to peer into possibility and pull out the prophetic path paved for the global conjure community. Gordon had a theory on the whereabouts of the card. His conjecture was as far-fetched as it was far out. But things were always trippy among conjure folk. A heavy, metaphysical and psychedelic postulation would be nothing new among a people who could perform magic by tapping into the subtle, dark quintessence that made up the cosmos.

Gordon was still in thought. He leaned his body forward, resting his lips against the tips of his fingers while his hands were clasped together. Silver mimicked Gordon's posture in an attempt to intercept his thoughts, but it was Lady Arachne that received Gordon's thinking. He broadcasted his sentiments on The Lovers card.

Lady Arachne, he called to her through telepathy. **Pardon my intrusion, but I have word on The Lovers card.**

Gordon! Lady Arachne buzzed back at him. It was just his name that she responded with, but the timbre in her voice was light and sweet, and she seemed distracted. Gordon even perceived a giggle from her as her words entered his head. He didn't pry, and Gordon liked hearing the grave tone usually filing Lady Arachne's voice dissipated. **Have you located my desire, little lilac spirit?** It was the word 'desire' that guided Gordon's instincts. He couldn't help but accurately interpret the light, airy facet to Lady Arachne's voice that resonated a satisfied, passionate release. An occurrence that transpired an hour earlier. Gordon stayed his instincts, curbing its nature to ferret about.

Gordon answered her, **No, Lady Arachne. My apologies for misleading you. I have information—a theory. There are figures in history converging on The Lovers card. It seems to be a focal point, bringing them into one another's stories. I believe each story holds a clue to the card's whereabouts. It's been in France. It's been in a small, Moorish taifa. It's been in North Africa. I feel such a strong connection to the card when I view it in dream. I might be pulled into history to retrieve it. Fey and I, together. I'll bring her and the card here.**

Lady Arachne responded, **Interesting, Gordon. I wish I could see your dreams and witness these magnificent characters dancing in history that have you coming to this wild conclusion.**

Gordon could feel the smile stretching across Lady Arachne's face. He could also sense that it had nothing to do with the information he relayed. She projected the smile wide and bright, and the gesture brought a picture into focus. Gordon observed Lady Arachne as she was in the moment, seated at her vanity in her master bedroom. She was clothed in a silk nightgown with nothing underneath. This revelation caused the image to blur on Gordon's side of the vision.

The matriarch's image sharpened again. She was doing up her dreadlocks in a bun. There was a lightness about her, and then Gordon discovered why. Albert Banneker appeared over her shoulder, his reflection in the vanity mirror. He was exiting the bathroom, naked up top and recently dried. A towel was wrapped around his waist, and Gordon was grateful for that.

Gordon opened his eyes, breaking his concentration on the vision but remaining interlocked with Lady Arachne, mind-to-mind. He continued conversation to keep things from shifting awkward, much like the moment they shared when viewing the cobalt-blue flame passionately uttered through prophecy. **I'll, uh, press on in the search, Lady Arachne. I've come close before. I saw Fey again. She tried to bury the card in time so that I could fetch it in the present day. It seems she was pulled from time before she had a chance.**

You'll find it, Gordon. I believe in you.

She was talking, but not really to Gordon. Her lips and voice were going through the motions as she coursed with uplifting emotion. She smiled again. A picture developed in Gordon's head. Gordon could see Albert Banneker rubbing the Fable Avenue matriarch's shoulders.

A calm washed over Gordon, a spillover from Lady Arachne's bubbling emotion.

Gordon mirrored the matriarch's smile. He sat back in his chair and exhaled. Silver gave him a curious look, eyebrow raised. **I'll find the card, Lady Arachne.**

A god's speed, Mister Goodspeed... her words rang radiant and content. This time, Gordon was positive on where her feelings were emanating. **Mister Banneker says to be careful should you run into your gallery of rogues again, Gordon. They have been quite a nuisance, I've heard."

Yes, Lady Arachne, Gordon replied. Then he disconnected from her mind and her emotions that spilled into him. He stretched and stood. Exhaling, he looked at Silver and said, "Sorry, Miss Silver. I have business with your boyfriend."

Silver chuckled. She looked at Spook's screen and blew a kiss. A single word appeared on his black screen. It translated to 'received'. Silver's wings fluttered at such a speed to where they disappeared from the normal eye. She hovered up and sang in her language that she would observe while Gordon slept. He thanked her and stepped up to the chamber as it opened. He scooped Spook up and closed the ancient device. He slipped into the chamber, resting on his back as the massive capsule closed him in.

Spook against his chest, Gordon crossed his arms around the archaic mechanism and closed his eyes. The primeval computer analyzed The Judgment card tucked between its closed screen and console. The bejeweled panel lit up. The metaphysical evaluation scanned a new time, finding a new story in history. A heavy feeling pulled at Gordon's chest, and his breathing eased. The same feeling anchored his eyes shut. Calm and darkness filled his senses until sleep recreated history as a dream.

Be No Death

"I make family of you all…"

Victus always reminisced on his birth name when he buried a fellow slave, and a lilac fog spelled his name in quick clouds that dispersed before showing off the clear day. He believed the knowledge of his full name, before the life of distressed servitude in the Americas, kept him alive. The young African man he'd lowered into the ground hadn't known his true name. The slave masters of Swymmer Plantation called him 'Kip,' and their word was final. Kip in return, and in private with the other African slaves, referred to the plantation as the Devil's Den. They all agreed, and their word was final.

Kip had been purchased as a child fifteen years ago. Now he was dead at the age of twenty-three, asphyxiated by the sun's severe stranglehold, a tendril wrapped around his neck like a hanged-man's noose.

Wicked slave masters made the sun an angry adversary in the New World. It had become a barbarous, multitentacled monster that clung hard to its victim's while it transferred all its infernal heat to every inch of the hardworking body—and the Africans brought to this new land had their bodies worked hard in open fields and in every corner where the most laborious work could be doled out.

The sun was easily mistaken for a loyal pet, the way it followed a person and bonded close to his or her flesh. Victus believed that when an African slave died in the field, his or her true, spiritual relationship with the sun was restored.

Kip looked at peace, as best he could, with the sun on his dark face. The sun was made a villain, but there was still nothing more nefarious than the slave master's or overseer's ferocity. It was they, after all, that altered the sun's disposition. Nature had become angry at the African.

Kip's smooth and sable skin radiated like a black pearl with sun now in harmony with him in death. The celestial light also shined a spotlight on his vandalized face, more so than when he was alive. Kip's left cheek had been cut off, exposing his teeth. His lower lip was missing just the same. A piece of his nose had been disfigured too. He sustained these wounds three years ago after hesitating on killing another African slave that was alleged to have stolen food. He became an example in a long line of examples for disobedience to the slave master's word. Kip longed for death in those first few days of being given his injuries by the overseer on orders of the slave master. He remained alive, a grotesque, walking illustration to remind the African slaves on the plantation of the consequences for insubordination against any command.

People usually felt the whip, but worse could occur when the slave master felt necessary. Victus received the whip a few times simply for not having heard a given order, not reacting fast enough. When he was young, he questioned the logic of a command. He was beaten severely—a fist fight where he couldn't retaliate. He was thirteen, two years after arriving in the American colonies for work under terrible thralldom. He'd seen slaves' fingers or toes cut off, one or perhaps two appendages at a time. Victus himself had the tip of his right middle finger and the tip of his pinky snipped. He was fifteen, and it was to show young, African slave boys and girls the dangers of disobedience. Victus hadn't done anything wrong. He was just the one pulled from the older boys to be an example. He was hit with a full fist from the man who maimed him because he cried and screamed when the marring occurred. Victus was happy to hear the man died three days later. But his brutishness was substituted for another. Overseers had different names and faces, but their brutality was consistent, passed down like a previous family heirloom.

Victus had seen an African woman's ear severed as a punishment dispensed by the plantation mistress, who also ordered the tip of her tongue cut off too. Victus was unaware of the African woman's crime, but he knew the retribution. He'd witnessed tongues cut out from slaves many times, not just that one incident. The maiming of an African slave was usually harsh, but not too enfeebling. An African slave still needed to work.

Kip's marring was doubly cruel because he was never permitted to cover up. Kip was a good, young man. He was a hard worker. He just refused to kill another African slave, and he paid the price for it. But he was never remorseful. He was changed, for sure. A cloud had come over him, but he never admitted regret.

Perhaps the sun spared him, thought Victus as he made Kip's face whole again by giving him earth as a mask and blanket. Then Victus tossed in more of the earth's body to become the walls of Kip's final resting house, covering him completely with all the dirt he'd dug up for his grave.

He thought a silent prayer to bless the burial.

Victus' inaudible incant secreted from mind to brow, produced as sweat. It dripped like rain and watered the earth's soil at the spot of inhumation. It soaked into the terra firma and spiraled deep, deep down until it reached the disfigured and tranquil face of the slave called Kip. It stretched and replaced sinew, mixed with earth, and filled in what was missing from Kip's countenance. It made the young, African man whole again. His chest moved up and down as his nostrils breathed in the earth. If that wasn't remarkable enough, he didn't choke. Life was there and life was also absent. It was not yet Kip's time to rise. He was a planted seed.

Victus remembered his name, antithetically, but he was incognizant of the conjure that manifested in him. He was Seizan al-Kaadi, life-giver to the dead. He never knew that, though he was aware that he was descended from a long line of conjure folk. He didn't remember much of his childhood. His name was all that he preserved. He could recall he had a brother, and he was abandoned by him and their mother. Their father was murdered, betrayed by a good friend. It was chaos.

Seizan was seized, and now he spent his time in a New World burying the dead and working the fields in a faraway land where the sun had become an angry adversary. And the slave masters of Swymmer Plantation called him 'Victus.'

Their word was final.

With his burial duties finished, Victus stretched his stature of average height to the heavens. He looked like an extension of the night sky invading the day with his willowy frame, shovel still in hand. His dark skin and bald head welcomed the sun, making peace with the heavenly body turned damnable monster. He believed his slender frame permitted him steady agility for slipping from the sun's unabridged clutches, though he was at the moment drenched in the sun's effects from his labor.

His face was clean-shaven, hardened and aged through a strenuous life of restless servitude. Brown, tattered slacks covered his legs. Shoes just as shabby clothed his feet. His tunic was on the ground behind him, revealing the numerous, keloid scars he received from the multitentacled monster of the whip. There was an assortment of monsters in this New World, and they were all controlled by the overseers or the plantation masters.

A British man picked up Victus' tunic and handed it to him. His name was David Duckinfield, and he and Victus were the same age. He wore much of the same type of clothing, though his threads weren't as threadbare. He wore a tan vest around his shirt. A flintlock, one-shot pistol was clipped to his hip.

David was an indentured laborer. He'd come to the Americas eight years prior looking for his own way, another way than what his homeland had to offer. He was educated in business, and he decided to put his craftiness to use in the New World. Swymmer Plantation is where he found himself, and he didn't find things much different. His belief was never discouraged. David was determined to make something of himself in the Americas. He was under a five-year contract for work on the Swymmer Plantation, and he put himself in a favorable position as the overseer's assistant. David was kind, and he and Victus were good friends.

David had a face that reminded Victus of an owl, from eyes to nose. But he had a friendly demeanor that offset the otherwise severe stare he could present. David was taller than Victus with an average build. While the sun was turned cruel toward the African slave, it was even more grave to David. His face was reddened, and he was never without a wide-brim hat atop his round head, pushed down on his brown mass of hair to keep him safe. This was not quite so different from the other Europeans on the plantation.

"He's probably better off down there," David said to Victus. He held a half smile when he spoke, but his concern seeped through the expression in his eyes. "That's more pain than any man could bear," David continued. "Kip was a good man. He was an efficient worker."

Victus took the shirt from David and thanked him. He didn't acknowledge David's thoughts on Kip with anything more than a head nod. David liked observing Victus' movement. The slave was like a force of nature in motion. Every gesticulation was an intriguing, shadowy dance. David's fascination with the slave couldn't keep his already uneasy smile from melting away. He thought another subject would do, and he attempted a go at the new matter.

"Master Helyar wants a word with me," he told Victus. "He said it would be good. Overseer Barclay tells me he's impressed with my work. He predicts I will have an early end to my tenure in servitude, perhaps a promotion for my good standing. Overseer Barclay says he'd like to see me on his company, which would mean a good thing for you and the other neggar slaves. I can be a buffer for his cruelty. And you can help me keep the other neggars in line with whatever they are tasked. You can be their reason— a representation for any lack of intelligence. Help them avoid Overseer Barclay's violence." He shook his finger in a stern manner at Victus, happy expression on his face.

Victus raised an eyebrow at David's sentiments, but he still didn't address them with words. He put on his shirt, leaving it unbuttoned. His actions were forceful, putting his arms through the sleeves. He was offended by David's use of the word 'neggar'. It was a twisted form of a more ancient and African locution that connoted 'king' or 'queen' and 'god' or 'goddess'. Here it was under an abusive tongue, even one as gentle as David's. Victus reminded David on several occasions not to speak a bastardized pronunciation of such a sacred word, but it always seemed to be in David's nature to forget.

The British man pointed to Victus' shovel and noted, "It could make you worth more than just a gravedigger."

It was here that Victus spoke. "I find burying the dead a noble task," he uttered. His voice was like the echo of thunder, rich and as deep as the vast cosmos. He stepped toward David and patted him on the shoulder. "It puts a suffering man or woman at peace." Then he walked past him. He turned and spread his arms. "It returns their relationship with nature to a harmonious state." He propped the shovel across his shoulder.

David beamed a genuine smile. "That's a touching view, Victus. I need that from you, but I need it for the living."

Victus traded smiles with David, though under different means and definitions. The African slave twirled around. He spread his arms again and expressed, "The living? We're all dead in this wasteland. What land is left where no dead are buried on this plantation?" He turned back to David and resumed his stance with shovel over shoulder. David had now lost his smile, thawed into a stern expression. "The affairs of this land stretch far beyond this plantation. This is what the pale presence has made the so-called New World. They have come up like a snake in Paradise."

David's eyes narrowed. He turned his head, and then he shook it. "No!" he disagreed with a firm voice. "No, Victus, that's where you're wrong. It's a harsh land; and harsh men preside over it with discordant edict." He tapped a finger against his chest. "But that's where good men like me come in. We change things. The fate of your people is with good men like me."

Victus gave David a curious look. He walked toward him, head cocked. "I'm a literate and cultured *neggur*." He put a finger to his lips and made a noise in jest to signal silence from David. "Don't let Master Helyar or Overseer Barclay become conscious of this." He pointed to himself. "I've read your Bible. There's prophecy in it that there will be three-hundred years of slavery for a righteous and chosen people. Held captive in a stranger's land."

David's expression furrowed as perplexity colonized his features. "Victus that's the story of the Jews in Egypt. That's not a prophecy," he corrected his friend. "That's happened. It's history."

Victus shook his head, undeterred in his belief. "No, Good Man Duckinfield," he told him in a whisper while shaking a finger in his face. "There were never slaves in Egypt. So, taught my father to me, if fading memory serves this slave correctly. Where I come from, that is a prophecy that at this date, is unfolding as we speak. That is part of the Great Argument among original people conscious of the First Two. I can remember one word from the yelling that killed my father and made my mother and brother abandon me. Alchemy."

David stared at Victus. His puzzled appearance burst into skittish chuckles. "Alchemy?" he questioned. He looked away for a moment to fix his face, but his laughter couldn't be contained. He addressed Victus, "You're cultured only in claptrap, absurdities." His chuckled didn't cease. He stepped aside, patting Victus on the shoulder. "Alchemy!" he huffed through his chortling. "Where did you learn such a word, African?"

Victus didn't answer David. He stared at him with a grim gaze.

"Mister Duckinfield!" a heavy voice called. "Mister Duckinfield!" the voice repeated. David and Victus reacted. They looked up and spotted the captain of the overseers approaching, Overseer Barclay Begbie. "Come here, young man," he said in a pleasant tone, though still yelling from afar. "Leave that boy where he is. I bring good news." Overseer Barclay finished his approach. He was barely understood, but all the people of the plantation were accustomed to his unique inflection. It was part garbled East Londoner transitioning into something uniquely American. It was a wonder how that was, considering the bulk of his life was spent on London streets, a rough lot indeed.

Barclay Begbie was a walking whirlwind of fiery emotion. A middle-aged man with wild black hair that was usually topped with a black, wide-brim hat, such as it was now. He was clean of beard with a face that looked as if it was chiseled from stone. He had an ominous face scored with wide, gleaming eyes, an angular, beaky nose and a scowl for every African slave. He walked hunched over, wearing a medium-length, black jacket. Always dressed in black pants that tapered a little below the knee, white stockings raised the remaining way, and black shoes on his feet. He was half-way a gentleman in this regard of appearance, but no one considered him civil. The two-shot pistol and whip at his hip were too often in use to mistake him for anything well-mannered.

"Leave the neggar to his duties," Barclay said again. He waved David closer. "Come, come. Master Helyar wants his word with you. Come!" he stressed.

David turned to Victus and ordered him, "Don't move from here, Victus." Then he said as if Victus was hard of hearing or couldn't understand Barclay, "Master Helyar wants a word with me. It sounds like good news. I'll return shortly." He patted Victus on the shoulder and walked away with Overseer Barclay.

Victus turned his back to their departure. He planted his shovel into the ground, dropped his head, and sighed. A breath. Head up. Eyes opened. He saw too many unmarked graves. It was a consistent song sung on the Swymmer plantation, and its choir was ever increasing. He spotted the sun high in the sky. A thick, black cloud stretched across its face. It was the only pollutant on an otherwise clear day. Victus had a vision at that moment, and the sun joined the cloud in color and pitch. He grinned and looked over his shoulder at the two-story, plantation house.

Victus surveyed his environment. The other African slaves and European laborers moved through their day like blood through veins. Grim life channeled through the plantation. Panning his surroundings was to see if anyone was close to hear him. From a distance, it would be believed that Victus was giving a final prayer to the buried, but he was speaking to something greater. He returned his gaze to the blackened sun and the thick, dark cloud streaking across it.

"I remember you, First Two," he expressed. "I remember a few of my lessons. The violence of whips and shouts and slurs drown my past and float my present, but I remember you, First Two." He sighed, and then he asked in a sputtering voice, "Do you forgive my family for abandoning me to this fate?" He rolled his eyes and bounced his head about as he contemplated. "I know," he expressed. "I know that question should be addressed to myself, and I've answered it." He paused before saying, "It's not a simple answer, because I still wish a judgment on them." He kept his eyes from watering. "I don't have magic in me," he expressed. "The art of conjure has shifted or died in transition. But I still have prayer. I still have thought. And I've felt the hurt in my brother's heart. I've felt the hurt in my mother's heart. She has abandoned me in thinking me dead. So, I forgive them, but I want their burden to haunt and hang over them forever." He snarled, twisting his tight grip on his shovel. "They will walk with chains. They will know my forgiveness under that weight. Suffering to the fool and trickster that spread deceit. The alchemy produced has been a loss of magic. Only misery and monsters grow in this land. So, for them, I will infect the sky as your omen now possesses the sun and the day. Burden will rain on brother and mother for not interfering with these devils' ordained, malicious deeds against the original people. I then will turn my attention to the Devil's nations, and I will leave their lands in flames." His eyes saw the fiery picture of his revenge, and his anger climaxed to a violent boil that saw no action outside of his vision. He sighed. The plantation's image came into view, and he observed other African slaves and European laborers moving through their day like blood through veins. It appeared to be the same sentence for both. The plantation was alive for as far as the eyes could see.

Victus pulled his shovel up from the ground and slammed it back into the soil. The instrument's metal head glowed a pale purple for a moment before striking back into the earth. It was an occurrence overlooked by Victus, his eyes on the plodding, African slaves toiling about the grounds. He didn't even feel the ripple through the earth cast by the brief moment conjure was on display, glowing from the shovel's head.

Victus grit his teeth and cursed. The plantation was where he was, where he'd be.

Business was in order in the master's house. The front door led directly to the kitchen where Master Helyar Swymmer sat with his two sons, Godwin and Crispin. Godwin was the eldest. He'd turned twenty-six a few weeks prior. Crispin was twenty-three. Both were educated, and their faces favored the soft features of their mother. Godwin was the plantation's negotiator, and he knew law better than any lawyer. In the New World, laws were forever in flux, but Godwin kept a steady eye on legislative affairs for his father. Crispin was the accountant. There was not a penny squandered under his supervision, and he kept his father well-informed of the best deals and the lowest costs. In circumstance where a large expense was unavoidable, it always paid off under his advice. The Swymmer plantation worked in lumber and shipping. Together with his brother, Crispin was able to give the Swymmer family a head start in crop development. Other plantations were maturing land for settlement, but the Swymmer plantation was making waves in cultivating cotton, tobacco, sugar and rice. Crispin was an expert in steering his father's business ahead of other plantations' dealings.

Both men advised their father that it was time to rely on the African slaves for laborious work, and to make compensated employees out of the indentured European men and their families. Helyar Swymmer agreed with the notion, and it was on that idea where Good Man David Duckinfield was brought in for review and opportunity.

David strolled into the plantation house directly behind Overseer Barclay. They entered through a side door that led into the kitchen and dining area. He spotted his Master Helyar seated at the dining table and flanked by his two sons. A feast of eggs, sausage made with ground rabbit meat, heated grains, and fresh fruit were in front of them. Hot coffee and red wine were also served. It smelled wonderful. An elderly, African woman assisted the mistress of the house, Cwenhild Swymmer. The manor mistress pointed and made commands for the African woman to carry out in setting the table.

"Welcome, David," Helyar greeted in a booming, excited voice. "Have a seat here at the table. I insist." David complied. He reached out to each of the Swymmer men and shook their hands, starting of course with his Master Helyar. He smiled and addressed all three men with due respect, and he gave his head an affirmative nod. He propped himself in an empty seat and waited for his Master Helyar's next words. It was Overseer Barclay that Master Helyar spoke to next, telling him, "Grab a plate and a drink, Mister Barclay. You can go on into the front room and have a seat there while we discuss business with Mister Duckinfield." He looked at his sons and lifted a stern finger. "No one touches the food until Mister Barclay has his plate, you hear."

"Yes, Sir," spoke Helyar's sons.

Overseer Barclay stepped up. The African slave woman handed him a plate and he snatched it from her. "Thank you, Master Swymmer," he expressed. Then he gave himself a modest amount of the prepared food. He didn't linger once his plate was made. and he did as was requested, stowing into the front room to have a seat and eat. No one moved until he was gone, and David didn't find the moment awkward in its silence. There was a certain civility about it. Overseer Barclay was gone, and business was conducted. To a degree, however. The first order Helyar announced was for everyone to dig in, and David and Helyar's two sons were happy to carry out the command.

His wife and her slave were dismissed from the room. Before leaving, Cwenhild leaned over and whispered something to her husband. It was a private matter, but David's ears couldn't help but make out a familiar word through the room's silence. It was the name of a slave he knew, an older man named Wallace. The matter seemed to concern him.

Helyar nodded his head at his wife's whispered message. David noticed Helyar's features bend with concern. Old man Swymmer looked at his wife and said, "Yes, yes, my dear. I'll have Barclay look into it after the meeting. Thank you. Now, be on your way." They exchanged kisses on the cheek, and David thought for a moment on how his Master Helyar could be warm and kind.

Cwenhild hastened away. She had a bite to eat prepared for her upstairs where she retired. Her slave went with her.

Food on plate, and drink in their glasses, business was finally underway. "You plan to marry, Mister Duckinfield?" Helyar inquired to David.

"In time, yes, Master Helyar," David answered, his voice cracking a bit from chewing food and nerves. He swallowed and concluded, "I have no woman on my arm at the moment, but I intend to. Marriage is something I look forward to."

Helyar responded with a raised eyebrow, "You…you thinking about having children?"

Food was in David's mouth. He chewed quickly and wiped his lips with a cloth napkin. "Most definitely, Master Helyar. That is my plan," he assured before taking a sip of his drink. "I wish to have a wife, children—a family, yes. That's why I work now as I do. I want to be a part of a strong business, help with managing." He strived for his own business, but decided to keep his greater ambitions to himself.

"Have children," advised Helyar. "My boys have been the best partners in business that I could hope for." Then he specified, "That *any* businessman could hope for." He scooped up more of his meal and ate. Then he leaned back in his chair after a sip of coffee. He looked out of the window at his slave and labor force. He thought of something, nodded his head, and looked back to David. "My boys have seen the future, and they say it will be. Economic fortunetellers for me, they are," he joked. Godwin and Crispin smiled. David chuckled as he chewed. "They've kept me ahead of the curve for business. The house looks modest, but I tell you that will change, again— like my vocal cadence has undergone change." Helyar had lost his old-world accent, but the guttural tone that made his words sound like rocks being pulverized remained. He cleared his throat before continuing. "They brought you to my attention, beyond just your duties of being a laborer." He took another hit of his coffee. He set the cup down and pointed at David, "You know your way around a stock of slaves. You can manage a good-sized herd." He looked at Godwin and then to David. He inquired, "You ever been to the Province of New Jersey, up north?"

"Yes, Master Helyar," David answered. "I came through Massachusetts, down into New York. I passed through the New Jersey Province on my travels here. My debt came through all my travels—the debt you claimed for my service."

Helyar bobbed his head, thinking. "I'm doing business with a family up there called the Wolverhamptons," Helyar told David. "Good people." He put his arm around his son Godwin. "My boy here is set to marry their eldest daughter." He shook his son with pride and then let him go.

David reacted. "Congratulations!" he said to Godwin.

"Thank you," Godwin responded, a natural blush flushing his face.

Helyar continued, "They run slave pens, slave inns in the Providence of New Jersey. They hold the neggars until they're ready to be sold at auction or shipped to other pens or inns. Business is increasing for the Wolverhampton family as the African finds its Biblical purpose. I'm a Bible man, and I know. This has all been understood since the days of Noah. This moment right here, the African's servitude, that is. They're a people fulfilling a curse, you know. Ham and Canaan and all that." He paused. David pondered the words spoken to him. Then Helyar resumed, "There's some disputes going on up north between West Jersey and East Jersey. Now, I don't care about the politics but it's hurting my business partner, Mister Clyde Wolverhampton. In turn, it hurts me."

"Of course," David said, a little anxious.

"I have a lot of business with other businesses," Helyar laughed, and David forced a laugh with him. The plantation master quieted himself and returned to a sterner demeanor. David fixed his face as well. "There's a settlement-plantation not too far from here. I've bought in with enough money to claim the greater share of it. The plantation was run by Master Reilly Lewis." He winked at his son and noted, "Crispin here, he is newly engaged to their middle daughter." David congratulated him. Helyar stated, "The plantation is to help cultivate the land, bring in settlements. They have slaves and a lot of land. So, I'm redeveloping their structure. We're going to create an inn, pens for imported African slaves—specifically for Wolverhampton to bring down here, keep his livestock out of conflict and his business still thriving. He wants to also expand and create actual inns, a lodging service for people." Helyar shook his head. "I don't need that part of his business. I want to be a part of building and waking up this New World, not helping it sleep."

"Of course, Master Helyar," said David, still waiting to hear his role in the business.

Then Helyar came to the very piece of information David anticipated. "Your contract with me will be terminated from this day forward—"

David brightened up. "Oh, thank you, Master Helyar! Thank you!"

Helyar pointed at him and enforced, "But you'll still work for me." He straightened himself. "You want to know how you'll earn a wage, Mister Duckinfield?"

"Yes," David answered without hesitation, gaiety still illuminating his face.

"I want you to assist my son Crispin in moving the Wolverhampton livestock to the new inns and pens built from the former Lewis plantation," Helyar informed. "You'll then assist Master Reilly in maintaining the African livestock. My eldest, Godwin, is looking into the structure of breeding camps. This will help on lost cargo coming from over the water. And, if you keep enough of the females with child, the length of the journey would almost have you ready for a new production line."

David's smile faltered with what he'd heard. It flickered like a flame in a fast-moving wind, but he held it steady and bright.

Helyar carried on, disclosing, "I also want you to head your area of the operation with your own stock of slaves."

David blurted, "I would like Victus in my stock." He then considered his talk was out of turn. He humbled his posture and stated, "If…that's a possibility. He and I are close mates."

Helyar nodded his head in contemplation. "That might be seen as a problem," he responded after a moment. He looked outside, and with his eyes on his slave force he said to David, "We don't want him believing that he has an equal status as you, Mister Duckinfield."

David insisted, "He won't, Master Helyar. I can assure you."

"You can assure me?" Helyar questioned, eyes back on David.

"Yes, Master Helyar," David exhorted. "Victus is very aware of the plantation's scale of command and order. He respects it, and he knows his place. I can assure you—as stated—that he will know me as his field boss and you as his master."

Helyar lifted an eyebrow. Godwin looked at his father and interjected, "I think it would be best, father." Helyar looked at his son, eyebrow still arched. Godwin nodded toward David and said, "Mister Duckinfield here already has a working tie with Victus. No need to have him break in another from the stock. With Victus, he could have other slaves fall in line quicker."

Helyar pondered again, eyes to the ceiling. He agreed, but he had a final decision to propose. "You can have Victus. No more from the stock I have around here. You can pull from whomever you bring from

Wolverhampton's inns. That sound fair? I was just trying to keep close to my stock as much as possible." He pointed at David and proclaimed, "Victus is yours."

"Thank you, Master Helyar," David spoke in a respectful tone.

"I will still be his master when you're in my manor," Helyar reminded. David agreed. Helyar addressed his son Godwin, "Draft up a statement ending this young gentleman's contract." He looked at David and told him, "When he has your papers in draft, we'll have your signature. We'll move forward with business that'll bring us into the future. Let's drink!" They lifted and clanked glasses and gave a praise to Master Helyar and his plantation. They drank! Helyar put his glass down and told David, "Mister Duckinfield, you are neither indentured in my employ, nor are you a neggar. You will, from this day, refer to me as 'Boss'. You will denote me as 'Master' of the Helyar Plantation when representing me in business. Obviously, you'll shorten it to Boss Helyar so as not to drive our partners insane with too much title." Everyone at the table laughed, as did Helyar. He relaxed his guffaws and concluded, "For the remainder of the time here, call me 'Sir'—just 'Sir'."

"Yes…Sir," David acknowledge.

"Let's enjoy the food," Helyar said. Everyone at the table returned to their breakfast. Little was discussed in the way of business. When anything was mentioned it was from Helyar's lips. He ended the meal saying, "This isn't much a kingdom yet, but we're getting there. I want a large manor built here—something I can pass to my eldest. This is the second house built on this ground. Too many ghosts had me flatten the old one. I had the money. I wanted something larger, and larger still. I also aspire to have a large manor built at the former Lewis plantation. Crispin will inherit that house. But we'll also have quarters built on this land. It'll all be marvelous." He finished the last bites of his breakfast and took a sip of wine. He looked outside and stated, "That land out there, for miles and miles, will be a city of plantations. I want most to be stamped with the Swymmer seal. If not mine, business partners I've bought into."

"It's a good dream," said David, keeping his smile.

Helyar nodded his head in agreement. Then he flashed a two-fingered signal at his eldest son. "Go on now, Godwin, and draw up the papers for Mister Duckinfield." Godwin stood and scurried away to see about his father's orders. Helyar told David, "You are hereby, in an unofficial manner, free from servitude with no pay. Everything will be official when you sign your new papers that will bind you to a job with a good wage. It'll be some time before the papers are in order. Go about your day until then, Mister Duckinfield. Inform your acquired African slave that he is now in your care. Get him up to speed on the new order of things."

David exhaled through his smile. He reached across the table, holding out his hand. "Thank you, Sir!" he pronounced. Helyar's lips stretched into a warm smile. He accepted David's hand and gave him a firm shake. He cupped his other hand over and shook again. "I will not disappoint you, Sir," David told him. "You won't regret your decision to bring me aboard."

Helyar let go of David. "I'll have Barclay come and get you when the papers are ready." Then he reiterated, "Give it a day, Mister Duckinfield. Talk to your new slave, tell him the new order going forward. Then rest. Also, let your slave know they'll probably be a burying soon."

"Oh…" said David, unable to contain worry in his face or voice.

Helyar nodded his head, eyes closed. He waved the ordeal aside. "Yes, yes. My wife's told me of a neggar that's gone lame. A neggar named Wallace. We'll inspect him over. He might have to be put down because of age. Not much use coming from him, if it's bad."

"Yes… Of course, Sir," David uttered with a faltering voice and expression. He stood, feeling the need to escape his situation. But Helyar called him to attention, and he straightened. "Yes, Sir!" he answered.

Helyar pointed to the gun on David's hip. "Let's give you a more up-to-date instrument," he said to David. Looking at his son Crispin, he instructed him, "Go into the gun cupboard and take out the two-shot pistol."

"Yes, father," Crispin responded. He got up and saw to his father's command, returning shortly with a two-shot pistol for David. He handed it to the newly promoted plantation man. "Already packed with powder and cylinders. Just cock and fire if needed."

"Hopefully, that won't be necessary," David responded, accepting the weapon. He substituted it with the one on his hip and handed the older, one-shot pistol to Crispin. The younger Swymmer boy set it on the table. David expressed his thanks again, and then he left the house after a polite dismissal from Helyar.

David rushed back to Victus, finding the African slave standing where he'd left him. He approached his side. Observing Victus' profile, he saw the young man had his eyes closed and was in deep contemplation. David's expression sank. "Victus," he called him. "Victus, I have news you need to hear." Victus opened his eyes and aimed them at David. "…You're now…under my command."

Victus chuckled. He turned and leaned coolly against his impaled shovel, hand on his hip. "Your command?" his deep voice boomed. "Are we in an army, David?"

David chuckled at Victus. "No. Of course not," he replied. "Don't be silly, Victus." He lost his smile, attempting to come up with words to soften the actuality. He put his hand on Victus' shoulder and told him, "My indentured servitude has been absolved. Your Master Helyar has put you under my authority. We will make a change in his business. We will!" he insisted. David took his hand off Victus' shoulder. He stepped away and stood tall. "I own you now," he stated. Then he put his arms up in defense. "I don't say that under the same definition as your Master Helyar would speak it—and you *will* have to continue addressing him as Master Helyar."

"And you, David?"

"You can call me 'Master' as well," he told Victus. "Or you can call me Boss Duckinfield," he suggested. "The larger picture, Victus, is that with me in my position, cruelty will first stop toward you. Then I will make my move on being overseer. I've felt Overseer Barclay's wickedness as well, don't forget that. I have a few lashes from his whip as scars. I know your plight, and the plight of the other African slaves. I'm an ally." He put a stern finger in Victus' face, and a grim expression formed on his countenance. "Don't forget that," he gave notice. "And I can't have you being uppity either. My position rests on my control of you and a herd of other slaves gifted to me. Is that understood?"

Victus felt the only ally near him was the sun itself. Its monstrous heat dissolved into a comforting cloak that nurtured the furnace of anger residing in him. Incongruous to his rage, it calmed him for the time, because it was not time.

"Yes, *Boss* Duckinfield," yielded Victus.

David made a face and shook his head. "Doesn't sound right, does it?" he questioned. "Perhaps it would be best for you to call me Master— Master Duckinfield."

"*Mister Duckinfield!*" they heard Barclay shout from afar. David and Victus watched the overseer's familiar approach.

David smiled. "Are my working papers in order already?" he asked with a new and bright confidence in his stance. "I thought I'd earned the day."

Barclay went straight to business, putting aside David's words. "Master Helyar needs you to oversee a situation," he informed him. "There's a slave. He's an old man. He broke his leg falling from a ladder a few weeks back."

"Yes," David recognized. "The slave named Wallace. I'd heard he'd been injured—at least reminded of it."

"He's not healing well," notified Barclay. "Mistress Cwenhild brought the doctor over two days ago. He propped up the leg. He said give it time, see how it heals. It hasn't."

Perplexity invaded David's face. It was a subtle wave of incertitude, as he managed to keep his face straight. He asked in a faltering voice, "It's only been two days? Wh-wh-what does this all have to do with me?"

Barclay looked annoyed. He put a hand on his hip and pointed to

Victus. "Master Helyar got you in charge of a stock now, dammit!" he huffed. "It ain't much, boy. It's only five neggars, but you got a charge! You need to know how to handle your stock. Get your pistol out. Master Helyar wants you to put the old slave down. He's no good." He turned around and walked away. "Come on! Bring your new neggar with you!"

David looked over at Victus with fright washed over him. Victus peered at his shovel and said in a somber tone, "I'll need it later, I suppose."

"Keep your voice soft!" David scoffed at him. "Let me handle this." Then he raised his voice to say, "Come, Victus!" David stomped away, hurried steps, catching up to Overseer Barclay. Victus was close behind him. They went to one of the eleven slave cabins on the plantation. Wallace was inside resting on a cot made of hay. A young, blonde laborer in his early twenties named Tiberius Goodall watched over Wallace who was coming from sleep, moaning because of the pain in his deformed, injured leg.

Barclay walked to Wallace's side, shooing Tiberius away. The laborer moved. Wallace peered down at the old, African slave and then over at David. "He hasn't walked in weeks. He's attempted to, but he screams when he puts his left foot on the ground." David didn't acknowledge Barclay's words. His eyes remained fixed on Wallace as the slave writhed and moaned, coming from a deep rest. "Look!" Barclay snapped, pulling up Wallace's left pant leg in a rough way. Wallace's leg was bloated and misshapen. The bone, in an attempt to heal, contorted its structure, tearing into muscle and nerve. It was slung between two boards that were beginning to warp with the leg's distorted and swollen shape.

Victus' head dropped. He sighed. He ground his teeth together as he postulated a probable outline of events. Wallace had a terrible fall, and because of his age and being African, the best of care was kept from him. No one but his wife and fourteen-year-old son rushed to his aid, and even her screams were ignored. The other African slaves couldn't help. Victus' eyes bent on David as he thought on the likelihood that no European laborer felt the need to give aid.

David winced. He huffed and put his hands on his hips. "Let's give him another week," he proposed. "The doctor propped his leg. Let's give him a fair amount of time to heal."

Barclay disagreed. He barked at David, "He groans through the night, man. He's in pain, and nothing's going to fix that."

Like a rise of dawn, Wallace's screams became brighter and brighter, filling the slave cabin. His eyes opened wide and he grabbed David's arm. "I'm not afraid of death. I just know I got fight in me, young man."

Barclay slapped Wallace. "You address him as Master Duckinfield," he growled. He aimed a stern finger at David. "And you!" he snarled. "You have an order from your boss, Master Helyar."

David looked at Barclay. Then he looked at Wallace. He didn't dare turn and make a glance at Victus. Wallace held a groan for as long as he could, and then he shouted, expelling the pulsing and burning pain coursing through him. He was sweating now. He looked at David and shook his head. He struggled to speak, "I'm a man with family. Only good Master Helyar ever did by me was allow me a wife. I've got a boy—fourteen."

"Only good?" growled Overseer Barclay.

David said, "Let me handle this." He turned to Tiberius and inquired, "Are you familiar with his woman and child?" Tiberius nodded. "Fetch them now to see him off." Tiberius gave another nod and sped away from the cabin. Victus' face burst with disbelief. David finally looked at him and said, "Assist Overseer Barclay with bringing Wallace outside. We can bury him behind the cabin. His family will always be able to give prayers to him."

Victus didn't move. His face and body were frozen in astonishment. He heard the murmur of David's voice ordering him again in a sharper tone. It echoed as if Victus was coming from a dream, and he wasn't aware if the voice was part of the dream or the waking reality. David got into his face and snarled his name.

"Victus!" he hissed. "Now!"

But still Victus didn't move, even when Barclay stepped up to David's side. The overseer's hand hovered over his whip. David saw Overseer Barclay at the ready to make use of the weapon. He interfered by allowing the violence to come from his own hand. He took a step forward and smacked Victus across the face with his backhand.

"Victus!" David shouted through tight teeth. "Assist Overseer Barclay! Now!"

Victus recovered, huffing to exhale his anger. "Yes, David," he said in a low voice.

David got in his face and asked, "Did we not have a discussion beforehand? Hmm? What did we decide?"

Victus understood what David was pressing. He amended his words, saying, "Yes, *Master* Duckinfield…"

David collected himself, taking a breath. He told Victus, "Better." Then he whispered into the African slave's ear, "We will talk later."

Victus didn't reply. He walked up to Wallace. The older, African slave had calmed his moans, but the pain continued bubbling and boiling inside his buckled and crooked, swollen leg. He was relaxed, but his forehead remained laced with a rosary of sweat. Victus assisted Overseer Barclay with standing Wallace up and helping him off the bed. They followed David out of the cabin, Wallace hopping on his good leg while propped up between them. His moans made a return through soft muffles.

Victus whispered to him in an Afro-Moorish language, *"I will see you buried; and I will see them buried too."* But Wallace's attention was on the pain increasing in his leg. Coupled with having forgotten the language he was born with, he had no knowledge of the language Victus was using. Wallace like so many other African slaves didn't know his birth name. Victus repeated, *"I will see you buried; and I will see them buried too."*

Wallace heard him speak the words, a lull in pain and wailing allowing his ears to focus. He chuckled at Victus, "You give me prayer, young gravedigger? I'll be your duty today." He choked and coughed on his light laughter.

Tiberius returned. Wallace's wife Dinah and his fourteen-year-old son Simon were with him. Dinah was younger than Wallace, aged thirty-one. She stared at her husband being dragged. She didn't move her eyes away from him even as David walked up to her and put his hands on her shoulders. "Your name is Dinah, correct? Yes?" he asked. "You're Wallace's woman? This is his son Simon, yes?" Dinah didn't answer. David filled in the silence with exposition. "We've worked together on occasion. My name is David Duckinfield. You can address me as Master Duckinfield. I've labored with your husband before. I don't believe we've had an introduction, and it pains me to have it be in this situation."

She hesitated to take her eyes off Wallace as she watched Overseer Barclay push Victus away from her husband and force Wallace to his knees. Wallace shrieked, bending his warp, distended leg at the knee. Barclay pressed the palm of his hand against Wallace's shoulder and ordered him to be quiet. Wallace did mute his bellows, an insufferable task as it was, gritting his teeth and showing the pain contorting the features on his face. But his resolve to hush and swallow his agony came at the sight of his son. Wallace dropped his head for a moment, exhaling.

David insisted, "Dinah, I need you to answer me."

Dinah glanced at David for a moment, and then her eyes returned to her husband. "Yes," she answered him. She started breathing harder. Her heartbeat quickened. She asked David, "Is Wallace okay?"

"His leg won't heal properly," David addressed her concern.

Dinah's eyes locked onto David as she inquired, "And you have to take it?"

David shook his head. "That won't solve the greater problem, Dinah" he informed her. "He's lame, and that makes him no good to Master Helyar."

"Are you going to send him away?" Dinah asked in a low, faltering voice, sounding as if she was swallowing her words.

Victus folded his arms and waited.

David listed, "He's old, badly hurt, and no labor can come from him." He hesitated before saying, "He has to be put down, I'm afraid, Dinah."

Dinah swallowed a large breath of air before covering her mouth. Life was sucked out of her, and she teared up. David's grip on her arms was the only thing that kept her from dropping to the ground.

"Dinah," David called. "Dinah," he said again as the woman's knees gave way. He needed all his strength to keep her upright. He turned his attention to Simon and ordered, "Take your mother, boy. Keep her on her feet."

Simon stared at his father. Wallace nodded to him. Simon nodded in return. Then the boy saw to David's command. He held his mother, and in her son's arms, Dinah found the strength to hold herself upright. David backed away and then pivoted toward Wallace. He removed his two-shot pistol and thumbed back one of the hammers.

Victus' stoicism dissolved. He took a step toward David and grabbed his arm. "David!" he called him. "This is cruel. Don't let them see this."

David stopped his walk. His face broke into a look of surprise, eyes aimed at Victus' grip on his arm. His sight shifted to Overseer Barclay, and David became self-conscious. Anger wrapped around his neck and choked him. He swung the muzzles of the pistol across Victus' face, catching the African slave near the eye. Victus' fingers loosened from David's arm, and he stumbled back. David took the moment to knock Victus with the butt of the gun, toppling Victus to the ground.

Victus instinctively used his palms to lessen the blow of his fall. A soft, green glow slithered across his hands and seeped into the soil. A spark flashed but was unnoticed. Victus considered it the shock of the blows he took and hitting the ground. The flow of conjure wriggling into the soil latched onto the perished bones of a slave girl long ago buried. It used the dirt to mend once decayed life back into flowing blood and sturdy bones. The same sorcery rendered earth into flesh around the bones, and root tangled into locked and coiled hair. Clay and soil transfigured into the woman's beautiful pitch, and her organs beat with new life. She breathed in the earth. Each breath pulled the soil into her, and the dirt provided clothes for her to wear. Beige trousers and brown boots were fitted to her legs and feet. A white, ruffled blouse and a black, silk vest covered her upper body. Wrapped around her head, gathering the coils of her long, African braids, was a red bandana. Her eyes remained closed. She hummed, and Victus heard her low, harmonic tune.

"Master Duckinfield!" David demanded, gun aimed. Victus looked up at him, and David pointed the gun in another direction. David kicked Victus in the face and African slave ended up on his back. David looked back at Barclay and lifted a finger for the overseer to remain still. He kept his finger

raised as he made his way back to Wallace and knelt down. "I'm not cruel!" he told the old, African man. "I give you a last moment with your woman and son. Take it now!"

Wallace peered at David with a look of disgust. He turned his gaze to Dinah and Simon. Dinah was on her knees, and Simon had his arms around his mother as she sobbed uncontrollably. Wallace said to Simon, "Let your mother weep, but don't you weep. With my last breath, you breathe deep and inhale my spirit and my strength. You be strong, son. If I don't cry, you don't cry!"

Victus rolled back and forth on the ground. The world was blurry to him, and his ears picked up the faint sounds of a soulful hum that changed into a smooth and silky, crooning voice. A buried woman sang beneath him, *"Who – who – who brings the earth to me? And who – who – who brings the air to breathe? And who – who – who – who lights the fire in my soul? And who – who – who – brings the water for us to grow? Gardner! Gardner! Gardner of the night! In the palm of your hand, you can breathe us life. Gardner! Gardner! Gardner of the night. In the black of your hand, you give off light! Breath to death! Light to night! Here I rise from an eternal rest and bring peace to plight!"*

David aimed the gun at Wallace's head. Barclay stepped back. "Look at me!" Wallace shouted to his son. "Look at me, Simon. Know this world. Look at me!"

His wife and son kept their eyes on him. David pulled the trigger and killed Wallace with a single shot to the head. Neither his wife nor son flinched. Wallace fell over dead, eyes closed. The shot was clean, broken through his skull and halfway into his head. David fired his second round and delivered an additional clean shot, ensuring death.

David returned his gun to his waist. He directed Tiberius, "Escort them back to the grounds. Let them resume their duties." Tiberius acknowledged his orders with a nod, and then he snapped his fingers and ordered Dinah to her feet. David sauntered up to them and aided Tiberius in getting Dinah and Simon to return to their labors. Dinah proved to be as fixed as stone, eyes fastened to her husband's lifeless body, praying for his eyes to open and him to beam a smile at her.

Simon stepped in front of his mother and said, "Ma-ma, let's go."

Dinah closed her eyes and looked away. She exhaled the last sight of her husband, and followed Tiberius away from the gruesome grounds. David watched mother and child walk away, and when they were far in the distance, he turned his attention to Overseer Barclay. He stepped up to him, unclipped his pistol, and presented the firearm. "Have this reloaded for me," he ordered Barclay. "Return it to me in haste. Victus will bury the body."

Barclay took the weapon. "I'll have this loaded and returned with speed, Mister Duckinfield," he assured. "I'll inform Master Barclay the situation has been managed. You did good, Mister Duckinfield."

"Thank you, Barclay."

The overseer made a pivot and sped away to his tasks.

David turned and spotted Victus still on the ground, laying on his side. He walked in front of his view and squatted down. "I can't have you disrespect me, Victus," he cautioned with a stern voice. He looked in the direction of Barclay's departure. It was a brief moment. He saw nothing but the plantation house. Then he looked down on Victus and stated, "Change cannot occur unless things appear to be the same. You have to respect the authority over you that I've been granted. Cruelty will not fade overnight. And if for the sake of change, if I have to display cruelty, I will."

Victus heard David, but it was the singing that had his attention. It was soft and deep, and as comforting as his mother's voice when she would carol an ancient hymn. It paused for a moment and spoke to him, but it never lost its silky resonance. *"Listen to him,"* she said. *"Us seeds can't grow if the gardener's not around to till."*

Victus blinked. He saw David looking down on him. "Let me plant another seed for the macabre garden," he said to him.

David rose. Victus raised a hand to him for support, but David just looked down on him. He said to Victus, "Bury him behind the cabin. It will be a private burial ground for his woman and son." Victus got to his feet. David waved for him to follow. "Come, Victus," he called. "Let's take the body there."

Victus sighed. He followed David to Wallace's body and lifted the slumped carcass from under the shoulders. David took the legs, but the two of them didn't carry the body together. David aided Victus by helping him prop Wallace's body over his shoulder. Then David led the way to the back of the cabin while Victus hauled Wallace's dead body.

David led Victus to a spot and pointed. "Here," he stated. "This is a good place." Victus set the body down gently. "I'll retrieve your shovel, Victus. Don't move."

He left. Victus looked at Wallace's body. Two holes were in his head, and blood and war were plentiful on his face, but he looked at peace. Victus reiterated in his original tongue, *"I will see you buried; and I will see them buried too."*

He heard David call his name, and Victus turned to him and received his shovel. "When Wallace is in the ground, inform his woman and child of his burial's location. Mark it for them, if you like. They can hold a mourning service before they retire for the night. Once that's finished, you're free to retire for the day. Check with me beforehand. Let me see your work. If Master Helyar has more orders for you, I'll seek you out." He gave Victus a friendly tap on the shoulder. "I'll be in my quarters until then." Victus said nothing. He watched David as the Englishman put his eyes on Wallace and then back to him. "Give him a good burial, as I know you can. Bless him as I know you will. Good day, Victus." Then David was gone.

Victus first removed his shirt and tossed it aside. Then he dug his shovel into the earth, and he began his burial duty. There was no retiring for the day, as hollowing out Wallace's resting place lasted until dusk. Victus met the sunrise with digging a grave. He now bid it farewell as he finished another. Dinah and Simon returned to their cabin, but Tiberius didn't permit them to visit the burying, an order carried out through David's word.

Finished. Victus dragged Wallace's body to the edge and lowered him into the grave. Victus created an angle on the side he used to lower Wallace, allowing for the body to slide into place at the bottom. Victus sat with his legs dangling in the open ground. *"I knew men and women who could speak ancient phrases and lift objects off the ground,"* he told Wallace's corpse in his native tongue. *"I was three years shy of beginning training in such arts,"* he explained. He lifted his hands into view and said looking at his palms, *"My hands know nothing of conjure."* He stood and smiled. *"So, I'm made to be clever."* He took up his shovel and started returning the pile of soil back to its place, blanketing Wallace in his final resting place. *"Sleep well,"* he told Wallace. *"Become earth and let life spring from the dissolve of your bones and flesh."*

Wallace was buried. Victus found two, twelve-inch sticks and made an 'x' formation, marking the grave. He stood and shut his eyes, sticking his shovel into the soil. His palms glowed green, and the energy turned invisible as it used the shovel as a conduit. When it reappeared, it was a pale purple glow resonating for a moment on the shove's end. Its resonance seeped into the ground while Victus pressed his forehead to the tip of the shovel's handle end. He thought of a prayer, and its words went from mind to shovel to the ground where it touched the fatal punctures in Wallace's head. Conjure occurred, and the natural elements around the body cobbled the flesh back together. That was not all that happened by conjure's touch. Inside the body, magic had touched every area of the deceased man. Wallace's chest moved up and down as he breathed beneath the soil.

Victus loosened his grip on the shovel and walked away from the tool. He swiped his shirt from the ground and covered himself. Then he retracted his shovel from the soil and made his way to the front of the slave cabin. He opened the door and the moon's cool beam jumped over his shoulder and dashed inside, permitting sight into the darkness. His eyes scanned the slaves nestled close together on beds of hay and grass. Dinah and Simon were already sitting up, holding one another and waiting for Victus to enter.

"Lady Dinah," Victus addressed her. "Your husband rests. Come. You and Simon have been permitted to say your love to him." Neither Dinah nor Simon hesitated in standing. They continued holding one another as they got to their feet and walked to the cabin entrance. Victus bowed at the neck as they passed. He followed them behind the shack, the cabin door closing as he stepped away. Victus kept his distance at the corner of the cabin, keeping his eyes on Dinah and Simon as they stood at the grave's makeshift marker. He could hear Dinah sobbing, and then he heard her singing a passionate dirge. Her voice was low, but it didn't go undetected by the plantation masters. David was sent to attend to the situation.

He emerged from the shadows like a ghost, coming from the direction of the plantation manor. A frown populated his face. "Victus!" he hissed. All of his chastisement was echoed in the tone of his voice. "Victus!" he spat again as he drew closer. "What is this howling? It's scaring people!" He pointed at Dinah who hadn't noticed David's entrance as she was lost in song. David walked away from Victus, not hearing his answer. "Dinah!" he snapped at her. "Stop that! Now!" Simon pulled on his mother's arm and dragged her from her mournful harmony. He brought David to his mother's attention, and she quieted her song. David returned his scowl to Victus. "What is the manner of this?" he again demanded.

"She was mourning," Victus answered, controlling the ire stirring in him. "You gave permission. I relayed that permission and she—"

"Only should it still be daylight, Victus!" David interjected. "And I said for you to come to me once the burial was complete—for me to review your labor." He turned and ordered Dinah and Simon in a calmer voice, "Come! The both of you. To your beds. You can mourn your man in the afternoon when the first half of your day's labors are finished." He waved them forward and aimed a finger at the cabin. "Go! Save your prayers for then." Dinah and Simon, arms around one another, made their way back to the cabin. David confronted Victus. "Retire, Victus. None of this carelessness anymore." Victus didn't reply. His silence was how he complied. "I'm in there going over a journey we will take to the Providence of New Jersey. That won't happen for a long while. There are pens being built to haul more neggars for work. We'll be escorting livestock out of a conflict in the providence and down here. The pens are being built on a plantation five miles east of here. Your Master Helyar claims the greater investment in that plantation. The livestock will be brought there." He took a breath. "Get rest, Victus. You'll shadow me tomorrow. Your duties will be simple. No one will be buried." David put his hands on his hips and asked, "I don't need to escort you to your cabin, do I?"

"No," Victus answered.

David shook his head, acknowledging Victus' words. "I'll see you in the morning then. Have a good rest." He looked at the grave and nodded his head again. "Fine work, Victus." He walked back to the plantation manor.

Victus watched David disappear into the darkness. He had a thought, and it focused on song and harmony. He thought of Dinah and the voice he heard earlier. He put the two together and postulated with very little confidence backing his thoughts. So, he decided to make an inquiry. He made his way to the front of the cabin and snuck inside. He ducked and slithered through the darkness, finding Dinah up with her back against the wall. Simon was already asleep next to her. Tears watered her face, and her lips trembled. Victus joined her side. She turned to him and warned, "You'll be next in the ground, gravedigger, if you're caught in the wrong cabin."

Victus turned his head and smiled at Dinah. "Then I would be free, Lady Dinah."

"Is my husband free?"

"Perhaps yes, perhaps no," replied the gravedigger.

Dinah's tears stopped as Victus responded in his enigmatic manner. It halted her emotions. "Why do you speak in riddles?" she asked Victus, her voice still cracking in rhythm with her melancholy.

"Your husband is free, I'm sure," Victus began. "Your voice binds him here. You harmonize your pain with such beauty. I heard you at his grave. I heard you singing earlier this day over his body."

Dinah peered at Victus through the darkness. Her features were jumbled in perplexity. "I sobbed when he was killed. I didn't sing, gravedigger."

Victus didn't explain himself further. He had his answer, and his confidence stood on a strong and sturdy foundation. Victus told Dinah, "Shed your tears tonight. Sing tomorrow for all of us slaves to hear. Send your husband's spirit on." Victus didn't wait for a reply. He stood. Dinah said nothing. She followed his motion up, lifting her head and eyes as she witnessed his outline stand in the dark. Then Victus hurried from the cabin and was gone.

He returned to the spot where Wallace was killed. He looked over his shoulder. His eyes culled shapes and shadows from the dark. Buildings stood silent. Windows flickered with little light inside the plantation manor. Victus discerned he was alone. He looked down and reconsidered the notion. He knelt and asked the ground, palm against the soil and grass, "Has the sun's heat made me crazy? Or does the Earth sing?"

The night became still. Then a reply resonated through the green. "Can you find my brother-by-half, gardener? His name is Denis." a woman's voice asked from beneath the soil. "He's buried behind the devil's cabin."

Victus peered over his shoulder at the plantation manor. It hadn't been a small cabin since long before he arrived. Helyar always bragged about how he expanded house and family and business. Victus sat with his legs crossed. "Why does the Earth speak to me and give me commands?"

"I am not the Earth, gardener," the woman replied. "I'm simply buried within it. I'm like so many of Africa's children nestled in the plantation graveyard. Curious you don't seem to ask how this is all possible."

Victus grinned. "I believe in stranger things," he quipped.

"Then you will not jump with fright to know magic from your hands put life back into my rotted bones."

Victus didn't jump, but he opened his hand and peered at the lines. He did flinch as a streak of conjure, like a small current of lightning, wriggled through his palm lines, buzzing as it traveled. He closed his hand in an attempt to catch the light. It snapped from existence, and Victus could feel its energy leave his palm. He opened it again. Nothing was there but flesh and palm lines. He shook his hand. Nothing. The voice below chuckled at him.

"Your power will resume in time, Father-Number-Three," she said in a soft voice.

Victus questioned, peering at the ground, "Father-Number-Three?"

"Father-Number-One created us all with Mother-Number-One," she answered. "Ixitu and Gurah. That's what my people called them."

Victus nodded. His smile returned. "Ah! The First Two," he acknowledged. "Eksuh and Jeerah we say among my folk."

"Yes!" the woman blurted. "Father-Number-Two put life in Mother-Number-Two, but wicked men drowned him. Mother-Number-Two was defiled by Devil Helyar, and brother-by-half was birthed. Devil Cwenhild had her burned, ashes scattered. She let the child live until eighteen. Brother-by-half was so fiery. He had vex as a conjure in his heart. He hated his father. He hated his father's blood. We plotted murder, but other Africans were too scared. I died when he died, brother-by-half. He was eighteen. I was twenty-nine and beautiful. There was once a handsome African man who tried to defend me. He was unsexed, and he didn't live too long after that. He watched the men defile me as he bled out and died."

Victus heard what he believed was sobbing. He sighed. His eyes closed and he imagined the pain buried in the soil. All the buried bodies together. He said in his language, *"I will raise you all, and we will bury them."*

She knew what he said. All language was decipherable to her now. "I breathe soil. Soon I will breathe air. I will rise from this grave and above the plantation. I will build and captain a ship made of the heaven's firmament, silver, and mystical mist." There came a pause in the woman's voice. Victus panned the area. No overseer was roaming the grounds. "Father-Number-Three, will you find my brother-by-half and raise an army from the ground? I want to burn the wicked plantation and take us all back to Africa on a boat carved by conjure."

"Father-Number-Three?" Victus contemplated aloud. "You'd be the first child I raised, but not the first child I sired. There are nine or ten children from my line—that survived birth, that is. Two were put down by their mothers, given mercy of death rather than the pain of a slave's life. Two struggled to breathe." Victus remembered and fell silent. Then he said, "I was around your brother's age when I was used to breed. Helyar—" and it made Victus feel defiant to use Helyar's name without attaching 'Master' to it. "—has always been attempting to breed slaves rather than purchase through auction." He stood, eyes locked on the ground. "I will find your brother and assemble his pieces. Then I will raise all of you. Those I've buried and those that have nurtured the earth before my time. I make family of you all."

"Meet me in the night, gardener," she replied. "A little talk to plot our course—where I am plotted on this course. You will find that this growing rose has toxin-tipped thorns, and she wishes to scratch the devils that put her here."

Victus then considered he didn't know the woman's name. He introduced himself first. He bowed politely and revealed, "My name is Seizan al-Kaadi. They call me Victus Gravedigger." He straightened his posture and inquired, "What is your name, Captain-of-a-ship-yet-built?"

"*Ah!*" she exclaimed. "You have knowledge of your name and language!" She sighed and expressed, "Oh, how I dream of Africa. I believe the land will sing my name when I reach its shores."

"It's become a violent place," Victus noted. "Kingdoms and nations are at war with one another. They capture and sell their own to the European, and we are dragged here to this fate. They side with the enslaver to rid them of rival clans, petty grievances escalated."

"Violence?" the woman questioned. "You speak to a woman buried. My life slaved and abused by European men. I was accosted and killed by whites. My eyes saw others live that life when my torment was in an interlude. My brother-by-half's throat was slit by his white father, and our mother was burned to death at the white mistress' command." She let Victus ponder that thought. He did so with his eyes closed and anger grinding his teeth. Then she carried on, saying to him, "Seizan al-Kaadi, called Victus Gravedigger. Yes, it's true. There are stories of Africans selling Africans into this Hadean bondage. But, we must ask ourselves, and never lose sight of: *Who are we selling one another to? Who has created this market and desire for our dark flesh? Who continues to profit while we attack one another? Who has set we as a people on each other?* Growing up around this chaos has given me proper perception to the devils that ignite the world on fire. You know the effects, not the cause. You've known the tools, the instruments, turned against one another in a rush to assist the devil in tilling the lands for war." Victus nodded his head, agreeing. He opened his eyes and stared at the ground. The plantation manor behind him, its outlines coming through the darkness of night. Its windows flickered with dull light from candles. The woman declared, "I reject the slave master's name given to me. My mother had a name for me. She screamed it as she burned from Lady-Devil Cwenhild's fire put upon her." There was a slight pause before she unveiled her name. "Vae," she told him. "My name is Vae, Victus."

He knew her now, and he fell in love with a sense of duty to her. He bowed again. "I will find your brother-by-half and raise him," he promised. "You will have your ship, Captain Vae." He looked over his shoulder, glimpsing the plantation manor. He thought aloud, "Let me not tempt a grim fate. The conjure in my hands wouldn't serve me dead as it does the buried folk."

"We plot a strategy at this plot tomorrow, gardener," Vae said up to Victus.

"I'll return," he vowed. "Same time." It was hard for him to separate from the buried woman, but his strength was draining, and sleep was crawling over him. He walked away, bidding Vae a goodnight. She did the same to him.

Victus carried his shovel with him. He had the tool slung across his shoulders with his arms folded over it. He thought about his conjure, how it functioned. He pondered how many more seeds stirred beneath the soil, waiting to rise up as weeds and choke the lives out of the lords of the plantation, especially its chief lord. It was while he reflected on the notion that he heard his name. *"Victus!"* a voice expressed through the darkness.

He flinched, startled by the voice. His first assessment was that it was either David or a plantation laborer ready to scold him and inform Barclay or Helyar that he was roaming the grounds beyond his hours. Despite the chilling swathe of trepidation, Victus swung his shovel off his shoulders into a warrior's grip. He pivoted and aimed the tool like a spear but found himself staring into darkness surrounded by only the night itself. He looked down at his hands, fingers clasped tight to the shovel. He blinked and started shaking. He questioned his sanity, wondering what sort of sequence of events would've transpired had it actually been a European laborer of the plantation, or David or Overseer Barclay. Here he was, at the ready for a fight rather than compliant.

"Victus!" the voice snapped again.

His hands blurred, and the ground came into focus. Victus realized where he stood. He bent a knee and put a palm against the earth. "Kip?" he inquired in a whisper. He put his face close to the earth and asked, "Do you breathe soil, brother?"

"I breathe the Earth, indeed," Kip said up to him. "You've made my face whole and put conjure in me, Victus. I know things. My parents had no time to gift me a name, but I'll return to Africa and find title there. The wind will sing in my parents' voice, and I'll know who I am."

"You know who you are," Victus said to the buried man.

Kip replied, "That's true, Victus! I've come to know a lot about myself in the few moments I spent being a meal for death. I know I possess a conjure. I will aid you with it, Brother Victus. I'll be a soldier in the army you raise, but it's through my conjure that we buried will rise from the earth. I will turn the land to marsh, and we buried folk will climb from the soft soil and march as monsters against the plantation's owners. We will be the ship's company captained by Lady Vae, and we will return to Africa."

Victus lifted a single eyebrow. He beamed and exhaled relief. "So, you've been listening?"

Kip responded, "We've all been listening. We await your call, General Victus. And we are eager to serve on Captain Lady Vae's vessel home."

Victus nodded. He stood tall and proud, extended toward the pitch sky. He kept his shovel in hand and bid Kip a goodnight. The buried man sent a farewell up through the earth, and Victus returned to his cabin. He found a place to sleep among the slaves. His shovel was propped up next to him. He stared in its direction, through the dark. *They gave me an instrument. They will regret that.* He spoke in his native tongue, mumbling to himself. *"I will dig their graves next, and I will bury them with it. They will not rise from their violent passing. When they die, they die."*

"Be quiet!" hissed a male African slave from the dark.

"I fight for you," Victus told the man in a language not understood by the recipient. He said nothing more and went to sleep.

Slumber had the potential to be calming, but it was disturbed by the sharp tone of someone speaking his name. "Victus!"

He didn't know what to believe before opening his eyes. Victus wondered if another buried African's voice reached up through the ground to get his attention. He opened his eyes and observed the cabin's floor before discerning the black, boot tips in his view. He processed the tone beyond the cutting use of his name. He recognized the accent and timbre and knew instantly before looking up the voice belonged to David Duckinfield. Victus got to his feet immediately.

"Wash up, Victus," David said, voice still in a sharp, stern tone. "You missed your wash last night, and you still have the stench of work on you. Get into your washed clothes and meet me at the manor." He snatched the shovel and shook it in front of Victus' face. "This should've been returned to the shed, Victus!" he chided. "If you were caught with a tool, you could be charged with having a weapon. Stop being careless, especially with all I have on the line!" He waved him off. "Now go! Wash up. I'll be waiting at the manor."

Victus attended to his tasks. He hurried in departing from David, gathering first his second pair of clothes. There was a sense of urgency to clean, and he found himself the first bondsman at the warm tub in a wash cabin not too far from his. He stripped and washed himself from head to toe and dressed when finished. A few more African slaves entered and did the same. Victus left his dirtied clothes with an African woman named Clarice. She informed Victus his clothes would be washed and he could retrieve them at the end of his daily labors.

Victus' eyes spotted the tool shed as he walked to the plantation manor. He thought of his shovel and put his hands together as if in prayer. He closed his eyes for a moment as he paced to the master residence. He had no practice in his conjure. Victus longed for his shovel, but he speculated that he didn't need the instrument for a conduit to reach the buried bodies below. Finishing his approach to the plantation house, he considered how the residence was expanded. Would Vae's brother, Denis, rest within its foundation, he thought to himself. Victus also wondered if his conjure could reach his buried body within the floors.

He glanced over his shoulder at the tool shed. African slave and European laborer percolated through its small doors. Victus reconsidered his notion of requiring the shovel for the task of reviving Denis. He left it up to something higher to guide his conjure. Perhaps the conjure itself. The power in his hands knew when to be at work, even without his knowledge. Victus spotted Wallace's burial, and he guessed the executed, African slave might be stirring now just the same. If this were true, thought Victus, then he could indeed trust his conjure. Victus groaned. He wanted to speak with Wallace and see if the older, African man would reply.

Victus tucked the notion of revived buried men and women away as he walked up to David. He straightened, and David addressed him, "Victus! You look sharp. We're a little late, but it's good to see you presentable." He got close and whispered, "Just stand next to where I sit. You'll shadow me for the day. Perform any task I give you. Be at the ready."

Victus nodded.

David smiled. "Good, old friend." He put up his finger in Victus' face. He said as a stern reminder, "The work we do here will bring change. Let's not forget that." He lowered his finger and stated, "Perhaps it will give us peace of mind. A good worker like Wallace would want that. Let's go." He turned swiftly and Victus followed him into the house's side entrance.

They passed through the kitchen and into a hall that broke off into separate rooms. Victus noted the front door at the end of the hall. A set of stairs leading up to the second floor lay at the door's left from Victus' perspective. Helyar's office was located three doors down. Overseer Barclay stood outside. "He's been waiting," he notified with severity.

Victus didn't look at the overseer directly, and Barclay made no fuss over the absence of gesture. The meeting was important, not conduct. Not for the moment. Victus scurried inside behind David. Helyar stood in his office, gazing out his window. He and his sons were dressed in their finest clothes. Victus considered they almost looked civil. Helyar spun around and brightened with a smile. David apologized for being late, but Helyar dismissed the expression with a wave of his hand and a laugh. "That's no matter," Helyar noted. He aimed a hand at a chair and instructed David to have a seat. David followed the order, and Victus propped up next to him. David crossed his legs, waiting for Helyar to speak or sit or both.

The plantation master remained standing, as did his sons.

Two more men joined them, walking in from the hall. Their presence alerted David and Victus. They turned and observed the men's entrance. David and Victus knew them as indentured laborers. Port Hawkins was one man. People called him 'Portly' as a nickname, owing to his size. He never seemed to mind, being good-natured about it. The other was named Francis James, a man with a strapping build, square face, and always a clean cut of hair. Their attire was fanciful, no longer swathed in the sweaty rags of labor. Helyar greeted them with a handshake and an invite to sit. They pulled up chairs next to Victus and sat down. Victus smiled and greeted them with a nod, covering his surprise to seeing them attend the meeting.

Helyar pointed at the window. "Do you see what's out there, gentleman?" The question was rhetorical, but all three men aimed their gaze through the window and narrowed their eyes, hoping to find the approving answer. "Right there, where we now have the outhouse for piss and shit, is the plot where the old house stood. That's yesterday. That's the past." He faced the men and jabbed his finger at the floor. "This is what will be." He swiped a finger at David, Port, and Francis. "You three are the beginning of a new branch." He then addressed David. "These two men, Francis and Port, they will be your soldiers. All three of you will have your share of slaves, a stock in the Swymmer company. David will command the lot. I will be the Boss and Master." His eyes focused on David. "You up to lead?"

"Yes, Sir," David answered.

Victus' ears lost the conversation's sound. Helyar had more to say, and he discussed in detail the jobs for Francis and Port alongside David. Victus' eyes drifted to the window. It was more than just a simple glance or a reflex brought on by boredom. He separated from the situation. Helyar informed Francis and Port that their servitude would be terminated, and their debt to him exonerated, should they complete the task of herding African livestock from the Providence of New Jersey down to a plantation a few miles from Swymmer's. David rose and was invited to sign a new contract to become a paid employee in Helyar's business. There were cheers and wine poured and glasses clanked in celebration.

Victus heard none of it. He was stone-faced and blind to the business transaction. His vision, aimed out of the window, pulled the near-empty lot closer to him. He could feel his palms becoming hot, pulsing as if he held a beating heart in each hand. The phenomenon wasn't enough to distract him from the faint call emanating from the ground outside, but he was conscious of the thumps in his palms. He tightened his fist to suppress any faint light from what might've arose from his hand or slithered as conjure energy across his palms. Helyar and David, and the other slave drivers, didn't take notice. They were in as much loss of what they were doing as Victus was in staring at the outside. He'd discovered the burial site of Vae's brother-by-half, and Victus was disgusted as he became aware on how it was being desecrated. He witnessed several African slaves, escorted by an overseer, heading to the outhouse to relieve themselves over the burial site.

Victus looked away. Seeing the room was no better. His eyes bent on the celebratory sight of David commemorating his inclusion to the Devil's Den. Two more indentured laborers were on the verge of being a part of the legitimate workforce. Victus surmised there would be more. He watched them drink and make small talk while comfortably seated. There was no rest for his eyes. The debasement of a buried man was either in focus, or it was a room full of devils delighting in dishonor. Overseer Barclay had been invited inside to join the party, an additional sight that disgusted Victus. The most offensive visual, however, was David sitting with a proud expression, legs crossed in fancy. A glass of red wine in his hand. Victus believed he could smell the wine's aroma as he stood behind David and observed the slave drivers' merriment. It was sweet, but it was also metallic like iron. That was when Victus heard the clanging of a heavy hammer against an anvil.

The gravedigger felt different, reshaped in body and motivation. He said to himself, *I am the Day. I am the month of May. I am the Toy.* He repeated this incant with his eyes closed and for an extended time. Helyar took notice. Victus' demeanor, with his eyes closed and lips moving, mumbling something low, cut the slave master's talk short.

"David," he called. He pointed at Victus and asked, "Is there something wrong with him?"

David looked up and over his shoulder. There was Victus acting peculiar. The others took notice. Everyone wore a scowl, save David. He attempted to hide an embarrassed expression, but his face flushed red. He stood, fumbling with his glass of wine. "Victus!" he snapped.

Victus' name was like a whip. It slapped him across his back and chest, and it sounded like a high-pitched, irritating howl. His lips ceased their movement, and his eyes opened straightaway. He saw everyone looking at him, and he found the confused and uncomfortable looks on their faces amusing. Victus showed no signs of reveling in his slave masters' unease toward his behavior. He grinned and laughed on the inside.

Victus thought of a plan, and he played his part as slave to further its execution. "I apologize, Master Duckinfield. Forgive my mumblings in prayer. I haven't had a meal since yesterday morning. My bowels stir to movement for meals yet to be eliminated. I feel dizzy."

David patted Victus on the shoulder. "You had us running late, Victus. Let this be a lesson on managing your time, rising early to serve. You can't stand at my side if you're lightheaded without your grains." David looked down at Victus' pants and then returned his eyes to his. "And we can't have you soiling yourself," he announced. He faced Helyar, bowed at the neck, and requested leave in a humble voice. "Victus isn't at full strength. He toiled yesterday with burial, and he assisted me in putting Wallace down."

Helyar nodded, acknowledging David's sentiments. "You don't worry, David," the plantation boss assured. "We're about done here. Take Portly and Francis with you. Get them familiar with your command. Take the neggar to dine on what's left of the grain and water."

"Thank you, Sir," responded David. He reached over and shook Helyar's hand.

Helyar allocated work as formal dismissals for all in attendance. His sons were given command to return to their paperwork and scrutinize law and monetary issues with the business. Barclay was ordered to the field, directing his flock of overseers against the slaves and laborers. David was tasked with mapping a safe route to herd the slave stock from New Jersey.

Helyar declared to David, "Listen here. You'll need to coordinate with Master Reilly at his plantation. Make that journey in two days. That should be ample time to put together a route, have my sons review it, and also hammer out a plan to move the livestock to the new plantation inns we're building." He put a stiff finger in David's face and urged, "No boats. No commission of any water vessel. I have seen too often slaves transported off the coast result in mutiny. No. The African is ignorant of this land. It frightens them. They understand there are dangers out there. Keep the livestock on terrain. We have carts, cages and guns to keep them in line. It will be an ordeal, but it will be safer for business."

"Absolutely, Sir," David agreed with guarantee in his tone. "I will plot a course today, and I will present it to Godwin and Crispin by sundown." David could see Helyar was impressed. David beamed, and then he stood straight. "Francis, Port," he rounded up. "With me." He turned and said sharply, "Victus! Come. Let's deal with you." David hurried from the room. Victus followed. Francis and Port said departing words and then caught up in a dash. They flanked David, edging Victus to the back. "There you are, gentlemen," David welcomed. "We've had brushes on this plantation, us three. Slight nods and smiles as we endured our tough labors," David described. "And those labors have paid off, sort to speak. Now we will have prosperity. Do any of you gentlemen have a true fancy for business?"

"Yes, Boss Duckinfield!" Francis and Port answered together.

David waved off the formality. "Please, gentlemen. My name is David. Please, use it, and not sparingly. We are in business together." Then he noted, "There is a hierarchy for the time, but we are all in this together. There are ways we must carry ourselves, gentlemen. Take my posture, for example—my posture in the meeting we just came from. Now, I recognize— as should we all—that Helyar is our master, even still. He's our boss. He is the Man of the Manor, and I would do nothing to defy that, nor would I ever attempt to go against it. I have respect." He paused for a moment, appearing careful to craft his words.

Victus spied David's careful contemplation. He wondered if David was truly thinking of his next words, or was he playing up the role of the deep thinker.

David continued, "My respect aside, that does not mean I have to appear any less important. I believe my robust pose gives strength to our boss, Helyar. I sit tall, even when leaning and relaxed." He stopped walking. Francis and Port came to a halt too. Victus stopped short, almost running into the three men. The brief, clumsy moment pulled hard glares from Francis and Port to him. David put his hand on Victus' shoulder. "My importance also comes through ownership. I have property." He patted Victus' shoulder. "Victus gives me importance."

Victus grit his teeth and swallowed his anger. He wondered if his conjure could take life as well as give it. He listened to David chuckle a bit before making a pivot toward Francis and Port.

David carried on, "Is that not ironic gentlemen? In the hierarchy, Victus is lesser, but he gives me importance so that I can be greater." He shook his finger and resumed walking. Francis and Port followed. Victus took his time, but didn't want to be too assuming. "When you have your stock, you must carry yourself the same way. Ease the cruelty the overseers dole out. We're not savages. We must be stern. Yes. We set the chain of order, but we must not be brutal. Lashing out at the African slaves can be bad for business. It makes it appear that we don't have control over our property." They neared the dining shed, and Victus hoped there would be food left to eat. He stopped when the men in front of him stopped. David added, "Pick a good slave among the stock we receive. Let them be at your side at all times." He looked at Victus and said, "Inside, Victus. Have your meal. Have water to calm your hunger pains."

Victus bowed his head at David. He entertained David, calling him 'master' and saying 'thank you'. Before he stepped into the dining shed, David ordered Port to supervise him inside. The stout man kept in pace with

Victus as they entered.

The dining shed was not empty. A few slaves remained eating. The pot was no longer hot, but there were a few grains left for Victus to eat. He wasn't even hungry. He got a pile of warm grains on a plate and a wooden cup of water. He took a bite and made a face upon swallowing. The grains were tasteless. Victus thought to himself that no African could have cooked the bland food he ate. He consumed his meal with haste, and he downed his warm water in the same fashion.

"You have to shit?" asked Port.

Victus nodded. He stood and put his hand on his belly. "The food slowed my stomach pain, but I still need to have a movement."

"Come on," said Port. "Let's get you to the outhouse."

Victus followed Port from the dining shed, leaving his plate and drink on the table. They regrouped with David and Francis who seemed to be engaged in pleasant conversation. David turned to Port, and with excitement on his face, he instructed, "Port, come with me! I've heard from Francis that you have an eye for map reading, and you're quite familiar with trails leading north. I'll need that eye to review the maps to find a route."

"Yes!" Port reacted, his face bursting in delight. "I've always liked observing the land around me. It was no different when I made my way here." He tapped his head. "I remember names and passages."

"Find us the cheapest and safest route from the untamed people of this land," David made the obvious recommendation. Port agreed. David directed Francis, "Please, deal with Victus. Meet us at the laborer house. We'll have to treat this journey like a military expedition, because of the wild men out there. There was an attack on the stores in town just a week ago. Retaliation for negotiations they were disagreeable with."

Francis voiced, "Yeah. I heard the news. It spread fast. Some of us worried it would come here."

"Your military experience will help with that," David noted. He crossed his arms and narrowed his eyes. "I heard you were supposed to be an overseer, Mister James."

"Yes," Francis admitted. There was a bit of a correction on the statement, and Francis amended by informing, "But not for the neggars. It was supposed to be for the laborers."

"Ah, I see. Well, put your skills to use. Get Victus to the outhouse, and then meet Port and I at the laborers' manor for planning."

"Yes, *Mister* Duckinfield—" Francis grinned. "Let me at least show some courtesy to your title and status. It's the military man in me."

"Yes. Thank you, Francis."

The former laborers separated, and Victus found himself under Francis' supervision. They didn't exchange any words as they made their way to the outhouse. Conversation would've been awkward, as Victus found himself becoming distracted as they drew closer to the outdoor lavatory. The palms of his hands throbbed and snapped with prickling sensations. Victus feigned a clumsy maneuver as he approached the outhouse's shed. He tripped over his feet and fell on the ground. It was a convincing display, causing Francis to flinch at the sudden, perceived loss of balance. Not much needed to be done for a laborer to believe an African could be so clumsy, and Victus used that to his advantage. He braced the fall with his palms against the ground, and when they touched the soil, he felt a jolt of conjure leave his body. The exertion added to the effect of Victus' simulated stumble, as his body convulsed for a moment on impact.

"Are you sick?" Francis questioned.

Victus didn't answer immediately. He concentrated on the connection he shared with his conjure as it flowed through the earth and reconfigured Denis' decayed body. Victus felt his heart beating. He could hear Denis breathing. Soil filled his nostrils and acted as oxygen. The natural earth filled his lungs and gave him breath to speak. His voice echoed through the ground, its sound only audible to Victus.

"The filth vandalizing my resting place doesn't bother me," uttered Denis. "It's the most honest the plantation can be. It's all a shit house."

Victus couldn't help but chuckle. He said in his native tongue, *"You will breathe clean air soon enough."*

"And I will pollute it with the smell of blood and liquor," Denis responded.

Victus got up and came face-to-face with Francis who held perplexity on his face. "Are you sick?" he asked again.

Victus answered, "No. Still recovering from having nothing to eat for a long time."

"What's your name?" he asked, eyes still narrowed on Victus.

Victus returned an equally peculiar glare at Francis before telling him, "Victus…"

"Hurry yourself, Victus. Don't make me late. I have important matters."

Victus complied with a nod. He rushed into the outhouse and stood there for several minutes before emerging. Francis signaled for him to follow, and the two of them made their way to the laborer house.

It wasn't a mansion, but it still had its charm. There were mostly rooms where the indentured servants slept. But it had a kitchen and dining area. There was also a recreational room for mingling and winding down after the day. Another room was a small office, wherein Victus and Francis found Port and David. They were huddled around a table with fierce gazes studying a map. Francis announced his entrance, and David looked up. His face was awash with a stern expression. His voice was pleasant when he welcomed Francis into the room, inviting him to take part in the planning. But, tone and countenance changed when he dismissed Victus to the corner.

Victus obeyed, and he had no problem setting himself off from the three men. Standing never became an issue for the four hours he endured, as he watched David and his small band sit and contemplate from pacing or being upright. Victus spent most of the time attempting to stretch his conjure and communicate by thought with the revived Africans he restored to life. He discovered that his conjure didn't extend into that discipline, at least not at the moment. He witnessed the sun become an ally, believing the celestial body hastened its journey across the sky to reach midday. He hoped it would hurry to night just the same. Night would bring about conversation with Vae, and he could inform her that Denis breathed again.

Victus was allowed a midday meal. David escorted him to the dining hall. Francis and Port continued reviewing the maps, mulling over a fine-tuned plan to present to Crispin Swymmer. He wasn't hungry, but he appreciated sitting. Walking out of the laborer house proved his extended length of time standing in the corner did indeed take its toll. His legs ached as if he were an old man, and he had no time to rest as David hurried him to the dining shed. He was eager to sit once he had his meal, and David left him to dine with the other African slaves. It wasn't long before the newly-promoted laborer returned with Wallace's wife and teenage boy. Also standing there was a blonde, heavy-bearded overseer with glasses named Groy Landon, another freed and promoted indentured laborer. Victus greeted mother and son's presence with a soft smile.

David instructed him, "When you've finished your meal, Victus, please supervise the mourning for Wallace's woman and his child. Dinah would like for you to say a prayer. Groy here will keep watch over you three." He turned to Groy and directed, "See that Wallace's woman and child return to their duties. Bring Victus back to me in the laborer house."

"Yes, Mister Duckinfield," Groy assured.

David said no more. He walked away, returning to his meeting with Francis and Port in a hurry. Victus didn't want to linger on his meal. He finished in a hurry to give Dinah and Simon their time to mourn, as it was later than permission earlier granted. He ate and stood. Groy signaled to Victus and Dinah to follow. The overseer asked Dinah, "Your man is buried behind your shack, correct?"

"Yes," she answered in a humble voice.

"Shame he had to be put down," Groy continued. "I worked with him a few times. He was a good workhorse. I had the same fall. Leg broke too," he informed. "It was fortunate that someone was around. People were alerted, and I was rushed to Doctor Clemson a few towns up. I'm grateful I healed."

No one responded to Groy's words. The only voice to make a sound came from the ground, and it was audible only to Victus. *"You hear me now,"* Wallace said from his grave. His words were formed in Victus' native language. *"Why doesn't my beautiful wife hear me too?"*

Victus, Dinah and Simon ceased their steps at the grave's makeshift marker. Victus put his head down and closed his eyes. Looking to be in prayer, he answered in his language, *"We don't attempt to understand conjure at this hour, Brother Wallace, but you will rise, and your family will hear you speak."*

Groy screwed up his eyes at Victus, curious that the African slave spoke his native tongue so well. He considered that Victus had been a part of the plantation long enough, and he hadn't stirred any trouble. He still believed he would bring this to Overseer Barclay's attention.

There was an instinct in Victus, a buzzing tremor that tingled at the base of his spine to the crown of his head. Groy's suspicions filled his thoughts. He looked over at Groy with a hard stare, making the overseer flinch. Victus relaxed. He turned to Dinah and addressed her with an apology. "I'm sorry, Lady Dinah," he said to her. "I remember only a few words and blessings in my African language. Some expressive words here and there," he was prompted by instinct to explain. "We might not come from the same Africa, but please allow me to bless your husband's body."

Dinah beamed a sweet smile that was infected with sadness. The viral melancholy put a blight in the brightness of her eyes. Tears welled up as a symptom. "That is why, Victus, I wanted you today," Dinah confessed to him. "I know nothing of an African language. I wanted someone with a tongue laced in Africa to bless my husband." She tried to smile as she detailed, "You could say 'clouds' or 'cats run too fast to catch'. Anything. Just let it be words from our homeland."

Victus nodded. He and Dinah and Simon bowed their heads again, eyes closed. Groy observed. He reminded, "You all need to make this fast. We can't be behind in labors, now."

No one acknowledged Groy, directly. Victus said to Wallace, *"When you rise, Brother Wallace, please break that man's legs in a horrible, horrible, horrible way."*

"By your command, it will be done, Gardner-General Victus," the buried man responded with pleasure. He then had a request for Victus. *"Tell my wife, I will hold her under African stars. Tell my son, the brave endure. They are promises I always gave."*

"And ones you will keep," Victus replied. *"We're getting out of here. All of us!"* Victus added as he finished, "Amen…" He looked at Groy and grinned. He considered that what he did next would get him flogged or worse, but he couldn't resist. He said to Dinah and Simon, speaking in an exaggerated

manner in an attempt to rile Groy, "The African spirits have spoken! They have sent a message in your husband's voice! He says, Lady Dinah, that he will hold you under African stars. And to you, young Simon, he says the brave endure." Victus nodded his head, again exaggerating and playing up his shamanic hijinks in front of Groy. "Yes, young Simon. Endure." His face contorted into an inflated, stony-faced glower.

Dinah held back laughter, but it was not to keep the overseer from being offended. It was because, while Victus was clearly acting as a fool, he had just spoken words that had only been expressed by her husband. Pondering this more and more, her face shaped into an expression of wonder. Simon did the same, though he smiled bright to hear words his father always spoke to him.

Victus placed the palms of his hands against Dinah's head. There was a pulse, a quick surge of conjure that emitted not light, but still produced a profound effect. Dinah flinched, a wide expression of surprise bursting on her face as if a mild shock had scratched her. She knew! She had knowledge, and Victus told her in his language, *"We're going to kill every last one of them and go home."* She understood his words! *"Keep Simon away from the violence,"* he urged. She nodded her head in compliance. Victus stepped away from the mourning woman—who now was not quite so sure she was a widow. He walked over to Groy and pronounced, "The spirits talk of you as well, Overseer Groy. They say—" and he spoke in his native, African tongue, *"The risen dead are going to hurt you so bad you will scream with such intensity that the stars will come together and form a second sun to push away the night as they celebrate your suffering, you fucking, horrible bastard."* He smiled at Groy and told him, "Which translates into, 'Your job be blessed.'"

Groy kept his suspicious gaze. "That's all fine," the overseer snapped. "Now let's get the woman and the boy back to their labors. You, to the laborer house."

"Indeed," Victus smiled with a quick bow of his neck.

The three African slaves all fell in line behind Groy. Dinah yearned to speak more with Victus. He knew things, and she wanted to know them too. She had an instinct, but it flickered only enough for her to trust Victus. Dinah felt a pain in her stomach when she was forced to separate from Victus. Mother and son were returned to their individual duties first, and then Victus was brought to the laborer house. He resumed his position in the corner as Groy and David made light pleasantries before the overseer was dismissed. Hours passed, and Victus felt his conjure soothing any aches that would stir in his legs. He watched the sun bleed many colors from the horizon as it set, and then the sky redressed in darker shades.

David and Francis and Port sat. They were drained of mental and physical energy. Victus listened as David commented, "I thought this would be easier. I did. I really did." Francis and Port laughed. "I think the route we've created is cost effective and the safest. It's a mix-match of other routes leading to non-safe points, veering from them, and connecting with safer paths."

"The old man has his superstitions about coastal travel," Francis noted. "I understand. It's a good test for us, David." Francis laughed. "I guess we're casual now, Boss. You're David to me." Both men shared a chuckle.

"I'm not a seaman myself, anyway," Port chimed in to the initial subject matter. "I like the land. I have my superstitions as well."

Not too long after their chatter, David adjourned the meeting. There still remained the task of handing their work over to Godwin and Crispin. David decided that Victus' presence wasn't needed, and the three men walked Victus to his cabin. The African slaves were preparing a deep-seasoned meal. Groy and two other overseers supervised the meal's preparation. Groy's eyes shifted in suspicion when Victus was brought to the African slave dinner, but Victus paid him no attention. Groy noted to David that Victus knew prayers to spirits.

"He can recite them in his native language," Groy reported. "He could sick bad devils on us. The African women were known to speak curses that could raise the devil inside their men to kill."

David laughed the notion off. "Victus is a good workhorse, Groy. He has caused no trouble," he explained. "He has too big of a heart to hurt anyone. He detests violence. I've seen it firsthand. He can't stand cruelty, and neither can I. Besides, his superstitions are simple and silly. Just keep watch, Groy."

The overseer nodded, but felt the need to add, "I've still put our captain on notice."

David issued a severe warning, "Well, if Barclay sees it fit for punishment, have him come to me before anything is done to my property. There will be hell to pay otherwise. I have demons to unleash too, if needed, Overseer Groy."

Groy backed down and returned his gaze to the festive Africans. David walked away with Port and Francis. The aromatic scents of cooked meat and spices permeated Groy's nostrils and twisted his stomach. He commented to another overseer, "Smells overcooked. I like a little blood in my meat."

Victus enjoyed the meal. Gifted, leftover meat was flash-fried to an outer-layer crisp. Spices added an extra bite to its flavor, and it was topped with rice and vegetables. This was a far cry from the grains he had earlier, and on scent, it bubbled Victus' stomach and watered his mouth. The overseers were offered a plate, but they declined.

Victus noticed movement to his right. He turned and witnessed

Dinah take a seat next to him. They sat in front of the fire, seated on a thick log. Victus smiled at her, but she didn't return the gesture. Her face, beautiful and black, flickered with shadow and the reflection of flame. She looked at Victus and asked, "What else did my husband say?"

Victus bobbed his head. He answered in his African tongue, *"We talked. He didn't have time to say much except what he told me to tell you."*

Dinah looked down at her plate of food and told Victus, "I don't need to question how this has happened, I just trust you. You touched me, and I can now understand your African speech."

"Good," he replied. *"I need you to listen and trust these next set of words. Tomorrow night, this plantation will burn. Woe unto the European laborer or master who resides on this land. Keep everyone in your cabin inside. Go to the other cabins. You will have an escort. Keep everyone in the other slave cabins inside. There will be an uprising in more ways than one. Justice's fire will consume the evils of this plantation. A plague of vengeance will climb from the depths, and it will run amok."* He added, *"So let it be written, so let it be done."*

An instinct tingled Victus' brain. He ate to be inconspicuous, but he knew Overseer Groy's eyes were bent on him. Groy turned to a fellow overseer and remarked, "The gravedigger cuddles close to the new widow, doesn't he?"

"She doesn't feel safe," the other guessed. "She needs a new bear to guard her, a bull rather. That gravedigger's got muscle, but he's a little slender, no." Groy and the other overseers laughed at the sentiment. Simon saw his mother close to Victus as well, and he didn't like the proximity.

The overseers continued watching the festive Africans. One of the overseers named Baen found himself surrounded by his young son and daughter. They rushed over to him and asked if they could throw rocks at the 'black-skinned people'. Baen's wife stepped up beside him and explained it would be okay before they went to sleep. Baen chose a ten-year-old African girl and a sixteen-year-old African boy. Groy suggested a third, and he singled out Victus.

Dinah gasped, overhearing the conversation. Victus told her, *"Make no scene, Lady Dinah."* He finished his food and set his plate down. Groy walked over and lifted Victus up by the arm. He brought him over to stand beside the ten-year-old African girl and African teenage boy. Then Baen's two, young children pelted them with rocks they'd gathered, laughing as they did so. Victus and the other two suffered minor cuts and bruises from the rocks thrown at them, and it carried on for several minutes. The activity was only stopped by Overseer Barclay's arrival, as he announced curfew had begun. Victus first made sure the ten-year-old African girl and sixteen-year-old African boy were brought back to the care of their guardians. He wiped blood from his forehead and cheeks. There was also a cut on his neck, but everything was minor in detail. He felt it lucky the overseer's children were very young in age. His instinct revealed to him their ages were six and seven. They didn't have the strength for larger rocks.

The African slaves were given time to clear the area, extinguish the fire and gather the plates and wooden utensils, which were returned to the dining cabin. The overseers kept a close watch on the African slaves' activities, and after a supervised wash, and when all was tidied up, they separated the African slaves into four groups and shuffled them off to their appropriate cabins for the night. Victus didn't sleep. He rested, but he continued using his instinct to confirm that the other African slaves drifted into a deep slumber. When no one would stir from a sound, Victus slipped from his bed and moved through the darkness toward the door. His higher sense perceived no presence near the cabin. He walked out into a clear night. The stars were outshone by the appearance of a bright, full moon. Victus ducked into a shadow that rested at the cabin's edge. There he waited.

By a higher conjure or luck, a thick, black cloud was molded together, and it scurried in front of the moon, hindering its spotlight on the area below. Victus praised the elements for conjuring the cloud, quieting the visibility of his activity. He remained cautious as he moved about the plantation grounds, keeping low and in the darkest, shadowy areas. He'd become more adept with his instincts, using the mystical faculty to examine the estate for patrolling overseers, pistol and whip-bearing watchmen. His journey came to an end at Vae's resting grounds He used his instinct and felt no one's presence. He put his face close to the earth and whispered into the soil, "I found your brother, Captain Vae. He's buried where slaves and laborers relieve themselves. I find this a vile desecration of his hallowed ground."

"Ah!" Vae spoke up to him in a pleasant voice. "The Gardener-General returns!" she announced. Her voice turned angry. "I'm sure that cruel mistress, who veils herself with a smile and false humility, commissioned that undertaking." Then she shrugged off the offense. "That is no matter, Gardener-General. Tomorrow night, we rise and we raze. They will find themselves on the other side of your blessing."

"More indentured laborers have been freed," Victus informed the buried woman. "They join the ranks of slave holder, overseer, and wicked contributors to a twisted system. Their children and wives are disgustingly no different." He felt more scars on himself, received from hurled rocks. Then he revealed, "In two days, they will journey to another plantation to prepare a slave center."

Vae's laugher bubbled up from beneath the soil. She said to Victus, "They plan on leaving in two days? They'll be leaving all right!" Victus heard her exhale and then say, "Thank you for locating my brother-by-half. He has unfinished business with his father. We will all unearth tomorrow night and burn this place to the ground."

Victus panned the area, his gaze remaining long on the plantation manor. He also cast his instinct, and its pulse detected no immediate danger in the vicinity. When he concluded that he was safe, concealed in shadow, out of view of any patrol, he returned his eyes to the ground. "Tomorrow, Captain Vae," he reiterated. "When the sun sets, we will all rise for war and entertain the stars."

"I will see you then, Gardener-General. Rest well."

Victus kissed his palm and placed it on the ground. He heard Vae exhale a gratifying breath. He beamed softly, and then he crept back through the shadows. His path led him back to the burial place for the African slave named Kip. He stopped over the grave and said to the buried man, "Look alive, my friend."

"Is that supposed to be a joke, Gardener-General?" he quipped in return.

Victus broke into a short, muffled laugh. He panned his vision, quickly getting a firm readout of his surroundings visually and intuitively with his instincts. He still sensed no danger. "Add luck to conjure," he commented in a low voice. Then he addressed Kip, informing the buried man, "At this hour tomorrow, I will come to you. My request will be to turn the land to marsh so the buried-returned can climb free. Are you ready for such a conjure task?"

"I will lessen the entire land," Kip assured. "My conjure will be on full display, and it will be a wonder to behold. We will rise."

Victus put a palm to the earth. "Rest, Kip," he advised. "You have a great task to perform tomorrow. The world will see you again and know the great conjure man that you are."

"Goodnight, Gardener-General."

"Goodnight, soldier."

Victus parted from Kip's grave. He stayed low and scurried back to his cabin, slipping inside and back into bed without notice. He relaxed with his eyes closed, worried and excited about the following night's war. He wasn't a warrior, and what he knew of war came from fractured memories of his mother and father saying the world itself had turned into nothing but war. But he never witnessed anything until that fateful night where he saw betrayal and it led to blood spilled. What put Victus' mind at ease was thinking on what he would be doing during the day. He would be in a corner, standing in place, validating David's newfound status as a businessman.

It was boring to think about, and it put him to sleep.

The next day brought nothing but familiarity, and it was as dull as the thoughts that put Victus in slumber. It was hot that day, and the sun's extreme heat stretched into every area of the field and the house. There was barely escape from its treacherous inferno, but Victus found himself wrapped in shade, and feeling guilty while standing in the shadowed corner of the plantation manor's office. It was close to noon, and he'd been on his feet for three hours. This time he'd bathed and his belly was full. He thought on the moment he traversed the grounds following David and his small crew to the plantation manor. He passed Kip's grave and the buried man said, *"Good day, Gardener-General! The plantation will fall!"* It made Victus smile. When he passed Vae's burial spot she said the same up to him. *"Good day, Gardener-General! The plantation will fall!"* And so, did too Wallace echo the same sentiment when Victus passed his resting area. *"Good day, Gardener-General! The plantation will fall!"*

Victus reveled in that recent memory, especially now as he watched African slaves toiling in the fields, whipped by the sun's sweltering tendrils. The corner he resided in dampened the sun's harsh heat and smothered its light. He still perspired, but a restless wish for the night was partly to blame for the beads of moisture crowning his brow. He watched as Helyar's two sons reviewed David, Francis, and Port's strategy for travel to the Providence of New Jersey and return with a stock of slaves.

Godwin sat and looked over the details. Crispin stood over him, bending down to inspect maps and notes scribbled into journals to put the plan in focus. David, Francis, and Port sat watching the men. Like Victus, their sweat was not an issue entirely brought on by the heat. The review fared well, however. There were a number of critiques given to some of the pathways and trails that were mapped out. The Swymmer brothers noted a few that had become hostile in recent weeks. It was information neither David, Francis nor Port would've been privy too, as at the time they were indentured, and not acquainted with recent information. The Swymmer brothers and David's crew then revised the coming and going, there and back again. It took another hour, and Victus watched as the men paced and plotted and finally reconstructed new routes for travel.

"It still has to go through the king of the manor," Godwin joked with a celebratory glass of wine in his hand. He winked and took a sip.

The other men in the room had their glasses. David nodded at Godwin's sentiment. He replied, "We will revise and revise again until we get it right. But I believe, Master Godwin, with the combined knowledge in this room we have devised a plan your father can be proud of. We can't plan too long. We need rest before leaving to have it looked over by Master Lewis."

Crispin chimed in, saying, "Our father is anxious to herd the livestock down to the new pens, but he is patient." He looked at his brother and added, "We'll send a man ahead once we've arrived and start moving the stock down through the trails. He'll have a message to assure father we've completed half of our journey, and we'll be coming home."

"Yes," Godwin agreed, taking another sip.

The men continued drinking. They made friendly chat, and then convened for a midday meal. The Swymmer brothers promised to present their father with the constructed plans for travel. "We should have word by tonight," Godwin pledged. "We will have a dinner and talk it over."

David stood and shook both Godwin and Crispin's hands. "Yes, indeed!" he exclaimed. "We're almost there. This is so exciting!"

With the meeting adjourned, Victus was escorted to the slaves' dining cabin where he spent the remainder of the day. He was put on cleaning duty, from the dining cabins to the slave cabins to the labor house. It passed the time, keeping Victus focused on the moment and not allowing his thoughts to wander into the night's activity. The sun withdrew its heat, even as it remained in the sky. It had become an ally again, and Victus perceived the heavenly body as scurrying across the sky to quicken the day and bring out the night.

Dinner time arrived. The meal took place outside of Dinah and Simon's cabin. A vegetable and rice soup was made, and the African slaves traded stories filled with wonder and adventure. There was song, but they were not allowed to dance. Victus was able to find Dinah, and again they ate their meal together, close to Wallace's grave. "Does he speak?" Dinah asked.

"Tell her I will see her later tonight," Wallace spoke up through the earth. "We will be hand-in-hand to watch the plantation burn."

Victus told her in his language, "He does speak. He said he will hold your hand tonight. You will watch the plantation burn."

"How amorous," Dinah remarked. She sipped the stock that remained in her bowl.

Victus' vision sifted through the crowd. Groy was watching him close. Victus finished his meal while keeping an eye on the overseers' placement around the African slaves enjoying their meal. Dinah put her bowl to her lips and knocked back the remainder of her broth. Wallace's laughter bubbled up from the ground. "She always loved her soup! Too liquid for me. I needed a hearty meal of meat. The plantation always skimped on heart."

Victus relayed Wallace's sentiments to Dinah. She burst into an exuberant laugh that caught the attention of most of the people gathered, especially the overseers. Victus was only concerned with Groy's eyes. He put out his bowl, signaling Dinah to place hers within it. She did as cued, and then the two of them ambled over to the pile of finished bowls and stacked theirs with the others.

A thought then occurred to Victus, and he returned to the spot near Wallace's grave. Dinah followed, and when they stood close to Wallace's burial, Victus took Dinah's hand. An electric snap transferred from his palm to Dinah's, and she flinched for a moment, but she didn't let go of Victus's hand. An instinct caused her to grip it harder.

Victus said in his African language, *"Wallace, speak."*

"Dinah, love…"

She heard the voice. It rattled her heartbeat and stirred her thoughts like a sudden wake from a long rest. She gasped and tears came to her. Victus turned and smiled at her. He whispered to Dinah, *"Say nothing. Be careful how you stir."*

She attempted to regain composure.

"Dinah, I will rise tonight," Wallace told her. "You and I will—"

His voice disappeared from her attention. She suddenly felt a loss from her hand, fingers forced open and loose from Victus' hold. She lost her balance, stumbling to her side, away from Victus. She rolled on the ground, and after her tumble was able to regain a stable stance. She heard a voice shout, *"You will not replace my father!"*

Dinah looked up and observed Simon attacking Victus. The gravedigger grabbed the teenager at his wrists and held him back. "No!" Dinah exhaled, brushing herself off.

"You buried him! You use the Devil's tricks to speak my father's wise words!" Simon yelled at Victus. "Now you want my mother!"

The overseers laughed at the ordeal, joking with one another if they should intervene. The other African slaves went silent, watching the awkward occurrence. The use of the phrase 'Devil's tricks' caught Groy's attention, and he became suspicious under his amusement.

Dinah charged her son and wrapped her arms around his waist. "No, Simon!" she pleaded. "The gravedigger does not wish to have me!"

Simon continued struggling against Victus' strength. Both cast bent expressions at one another, baring teeth in their grapple against the other. Victus inched his grip to Simon's hand. He told the stubborn teenager, "Listen, boy. Listen close!" He put his palm against Simon's, and the pulse of electric conjure transferred. Simon shuddered, almost losing his footing, and only keeping upright by the hold around his waist from his mother.

"Simon! Boy! Stop this!"

The teenage boy heard the voice. His eyes widened in disbelief, and his mind tried desperately to hear the sound as Victus, but it was too distinct to be the gravedigger's voice. Simon attempted to rewind time and see Victus' lips moving, but they were still, arched up as he bared teeth at him. Simon relaxed as he determined the impossible was the only answer. He relaxed his wrestle with Victus, but his breath was rapid as his expression widened.

"Just listen!" Victus hissed at him in a low voice. "Say nothing, or you risk destroying *everything!*"

"Simon!" Wallace called his son. "This is divine conjure at work.

This is not a devil's trick. You hear me, son? This is old magic from Africa. It resides in the gravedigger's palms, and it has brought life back to me. Ease yourself, my son. Relax." Simon complied. Victus smiled at him. Simon sniffed back tears, and then he threw an arm around Victus and held him close, one hand still embracing the gravedigger's hand. Dinah let her son go and sighed relief. She stood and thanked Victus.

The gravedigger let Simon's hand go. He walked away from the teenage boy's embrace and announced to the crowd, "A misunderstanding! I presided over his father's burial. I blessed the grave, and I heard his father's voice!"

Victus continued addressing the crowd, purposefully loud. Dinah turned her son to face her and told him, "I need your help tonight, my son. We will see your father tonight. There will be terrible things that go on tonight. The three of us will keep anything from happening to the other Africans." She hugged him, and he hugged her in return.

Victus finished his rousing explanation of blessing the ground where Africans lay buried, and he dispersed the uncomfortable silence that fell over the other African slaves. They rejoiced and finished their meal in song.

"Thank you," he heard Wallace say from below.

"Thank you," he heard Dinah's voice behind him.

Victus turned and smiled. He looked at Simon and remarked, "I understand, young Simon." The teenage boy nodded at him. That was the only exchange between them. Victus then took Dinah and Simon by the hand and walked to Wallace's burial. Wallace spoke to his wife and son. They listened until Overseer Barclay butted into the African supper and announced curfew.

Victus let go of Dinah and Simon, and the three of them split up for duty. Victus reminded Dinah before they parted, telling her in his language, *"I will visit your cabin. I will be with your husband."* She acknowledged with a nod of her head, and then Victus went his separate way from mother and son. The Africans cleaned their space, split into their respective groups, and were hustled back to their specific cabins.

Victus waited until his instinct buzzed that everyone was asleep. He got up and made no sound as he crept to the door. His instinct felt the overseers on the prowl, and he deduced the pattern in their patrols. Victus slipped from his cabin. Shadow embraced him when he opened the door. The moon lessened its light, and it used a dark cloud as a veil to hide behind. The star's stepped back on the night's stage and dimmed to allow darkness to act as the headliner in the nightly drama. Thankful for the black, blacker than black itself cover of night, Victus made a stealthy, but hastened journey to the toolshed. Everything from conjure to blood pulsed in him as he drew nearer to the tool keep. He could feel the shovel. He called to it with his conjure, and it called to him with the heartbeat of the earthly elements that crafted it.

A dispirited feeling infected Victus when he found the door's handle equipped with an iron-lock. He cursed under his breath and panned the area with eyes and instinct. He saw nothing, but his instincts focused on the eroded wood making up the shed's frame and door. He tugged the handle, and the iron lock broke through the decayed wood. Noise was made, but Victus wasn't worried. He opened the door, dropped the handle and lock on the ground, and walked inside. He seized his shovel, left the shed, and shut the door. His instinct felt no one approaching. He ducked down and sneaked through the night.

Victus had a sense when he neared Kip's rest. He didn't stop to see. His higher perception made sense of his feelings. His actions at the shed were being investigated by two roving guards, attracted by the noise. Their lanterns swept the area and tunneled through the night. Victus didn't leave a clear path for them to follow, and his instinct notified him the watchmen were reporting the disturbance to their superior. Victus continued on with no concern. He rested his crouched walk at Kip's burial.

"Brother Kip, I call you to duty," Victus said to the buried man. He then commanded, "Soften the ground for Captain Vae and Brother Wallace to rise."

Kip stirred to action. His conjure emanated from his buried body and made marsh of the terrain around Vae and Wallace's graves. With the ground turned mush and malleable, Vae and Wallace reached up through the softened soil and undressed themselves of their terra firma garments.

"They have risen, Gardener-General," Kip announced.

"Thank you, Brother Kip. Remain seeded. I will return and call upon you to ease the entirety of this yard's rigid surface." Then he quipped while tapping on the soil, "Stay put."

Kip said nothing, but he grinned. Victus moved on. He was squat, movement through the darkness like a crab. But he became upright when he beheld the feminine-shaped shadow standing tall on a disturbed and opened area of the ground. Victus kept on his feet, feeling the ground become impressionable as he made his way to her.

Vae was clothed for fortune-telling and seafaring. She spun in the night with skin covered in its pitch. She smiled bright at the moon, and all the heavenly bodies renewed their light to get a glimpse of her. Victus didn't mind the spotlight, and his instinct concentrated on the woman in front of him. The ink of his flesh heated and produced a sizzling blush on sight of her physical presence. Vae turned to him and cast a bright smile through the night.

"Gardner-General!" she called. "It is a nice night to live."

Victus inched closer to Vae, entranced by her beauty and the sound of her once disembodied voice now cascading from her lips. He was honest in his speech. Perhaps too honest when he stuttered, "My…my body hasn't reacted to a woman in a long…" He blushed, embarrassed, and he shied away from finishing his sentiment. Enough words were spoken for Vae to understand the gist of his speech.

She embraced Victus, and he put his arms around her. "I need a sharp instrument, Gardener-General," she told him. "I want to cut weeds and engage in ritual."

Victus nodded his head.

"What are you two doing up?" a voice questioned. Victus turned. Groy was there. It appeared that Vae's presence had rattled his instincts and diverted his higher danger sense. His lantern's light washed them in a bright, humming glow. Groy's features twisted as his gaze fell on Vae. "Who are you, girly?" he said through his glower.

Victus loosened his embrace and stepped out of Vae's. "The spirits spoke to me, Groy," he told the overseer. "They came through my hands; and I laid these hands on the ground and brought forth life long ago killed, dead." Groy went to unclip his single-shot pistol, but someone from behind grabbed his arm and roped it behind him while also covering his mouth. The lantern fell and cracked, but its flame wasn't extinguished by the impact. Victus continued, "One other soul I've put life back into is the man holding you." Victus addressed the man grappling Groy. "Wallace," he called. "Do you remember your first order of business when you rose from the earth?"

Wallace tossed Groy to the ground. The overseer attempted to balance himself, but he found the earth soft and penetrable. Wallace's hard fist slammed into Groy's cheek and the single punch rattled the overseer. His vision flipped and blurred, and before it could center and focus, another hard fist hit him again. His cheek bone cracked inward, and he felt the heavy knuckles of the undead African bury deeper into the side of his face. The weighty hit pushed sharp fragments of broken bone into muscle and nerve. Groy's arms gave out, but he didn't fall unconscious.

Wallace squatted over Groy and sat on the overseer's back. He bent his leg up at the knee and looked at Victus for command. "Make a wooden leg out him," the gravedigger said. "Wallace, break!" Wallace twisted Groy's leg and foot, several snaps occurring. Groy screamed loud enough to draw the stars brighter in his vision as his head jerked up and his eyes widened to the heavens. "Again!" said Victus. Another hard contort of Groy's appendage, and the overseer's shriek increased. Victus called for another break, and it was done. "Break one more time," he ordered. "Again!" *Break!* "Again!" *Break!* Groy passed out. Victus nodded. He knew an alarm was sounded. He told Wallace, "Take his pistol. Get to your family."

Wallace complied and fled into the night.

Vae picked up the lantern. She and Victus shared an instinct, and soon the forecast from their higher senses emerged from the darkness. It was on their left, a pair of throbbing lights pulsing from lanterns. Vae and Victus faced the encroaching illumination as two guards approached with their pistols raised. The watchmen's feet sunk into boggy earth and they lost their balance. Vae took advantage of their slip. She raised the lantern in her hand and blew into it. The flame danced wild, but its waver didn't flush it from existence. Vae's revived spirit manipulated the flame, reshaping it into a large hand that reached out and twiddled its fingers at the lanterns gripped by the watchmen. Their lanterns burst, and the fierce fire consumed both men. Their screams were smothered, as the mystical flame filled their throats and liquefied their airways. The giant, blazing hand retracted into Vae's lantern. The fire took a feminine shape that Vae's instinct knew was the spirit of her mother. The resurrected African woman beamed.

The two plantation guards toppled over. They tossed and turned and the otherworldly conflagration surrounding their bodies burned brighter and hotter, crushing them in a searing death. Vae and Victus turned away from the blaze and made their way to the plantation manor.

Groy's screams had already alerted the people at the labor house. The overseers' residence was emptied, and the inhabitants were armed and ready. The male members of the Swymmers family were gathered on the front porch. David was with them, and they all had pistols in their hands. Their eyes peered into the darkness to see, but little was discerned. The light from Vae's lantern cast bright, pulsating wavelets that bent the shadowed cloak of night around she and Victus. It distorted the onlooker's perception of the area surrounding the two African rebels, making the night appear as disturbed waves of water on the sea. Cwenhild Swymmer watched from a master bedroom window. The African slave woman named May-May peered over the plantation mistress' shoulder. Both women were wide-eyed and anxious.

There came a burst of lilac conjure, bubbling up around the spade on Victus' shovel. It twirled around in the air like a windmill, and when it pointed to the ground after a number of spins, it was slammed into the earth. There was a pulse only felt by Victus. It resonated throughout the plantation's many acres, splitting into crooked strands of light, and gathering up the remains of buried African slaves to reassemble. Their bodies were made whole from fragments of bone and earth. Flesh was restored and command was awaited.

The Swymmer men and David looked on. They remained still and perplexed at what little they could see. Victus' voice penetrated the darkness. He yelled, "Kip! To marsh make the entirety of this land!" There came a soft, crackling sound like the stir of thick and sloppy porridge. It heightened in volume, and its tone changed to sound like snapping root. Bodies emerged from the earth within the darkness. Areas of the land sank inward, and out of the depths crawled bodies long dead.

David and the Swymmer men strained their eyes to pierce the night's pitch, attempting to use the few lantern posts stationed around the manor to get a glimpse of the goings-on within the darkness. The light from Vae's lantern continued warping the night and keeping the activities of the rising resurrected in shadowed aegis. Not even the people filing out of the labor house could see the resurrected Africans growing from the earth and surrounding them, but they could hear the pulpy earth shifting, and movement closing in on them.

Vae sent a silent thought, communicating with her mother's flickering image by projection of an extra sense. The lantern eased its magic, and the night brightened with the moon's renewed brilliance. A horde of Africans long passed crowded the plantation. Kip was the last to rise, taking up a position behind Vae and Victus. With each step, the land congealed, returning to firmness.

Wallace and Dinah and Simon sneaked through the night, going from cabin to cabin and using voices laced with incant to soothe the anxiety in the enslaved Africans.

Outside. Helyar Swymmer panned the stretch of African man, woman, and child that his eyes could perceive. Much of the gathered mass faded into silhouette, but the plantation master discerned their presence. The astonishing sight alone was not the cause of his facial features widening in the horror he attempted to suppress. Among the congregation was a familiar face. It wasn't Vae, as her lantern's spiritual light masked her face. It was a child conceived by force, eighteen years grown into a young, angry man.

Round head. Light-brown skin with a drop of a reddish hue flush in his flesh. Short, tightly curled hair. Denis was a murdered young man long ago, interrupted in his attempt to kill his father. Here he was. A sin returned to haunt with a vexed judgment.

Helyar fired his pistol at Denis. He had to take a shot, and so he did. The cylindrical projectile tore through Denis' throat, the same killing region that felled him decades earlier. Denis stumbled with the impact, and he dropped to his knees. He winced for a moment, and everyone looked at him. He dug his fingers into the ground and scooped up a patch of soil, applying the dirt to his bloodless wound. The fatal injury mended back together as he wiped the gathered ground across his neck. Denis stood. Healed. He coughed up the flintlock projectile and spit it into his hand.

"I bleed for no man!" Denis hollered. "I am reborn, and I have a new father." He pointed at Helyar and declared, "You are no longer blood, but I will spill yours for the terrible acts you violently forced on my unwilling mother!"

Helyar fired his second shot! It landed in the same place, through the throat. Denis went to his knee and restored his flesh with a patch of earth again. He spit the second projectile in his hand.

Victus walked up into a lighted view. "David!" he hollered. "I tell you now, you have been deceived. Denounce the wicked company you keep and restore your good morals. I promise you will not suffer a terrible, terrible, agonizing, painful death."

David didn't move. It took time before he turned his head to Helyar. The plantation master whispered to him, "I don't know the deviltry at work. I can't explain the iniquity that stands before this house of god, my manor. I do know some superstitious boys who prick dead Africans with needles, but I don't care for their occult ways. I bless you, David. I do. I bless you as another son come unto me. Go with God, David. Walk toward these black devils and broker peace for us all."

David nodded, standing taller with the anointment of Helyar's blessing. He looked at Victus, clipped his pistol to his hip, and walked down the stairs to approach the African man. Victus said as David ended his steps toward him, "Be careful in your speech, David. I warn that you speak with heart. Be a friend. You were once a forward voice that now speaks backwards." He held out his hand. "Be as a friend to me, David. Show peace and give me your weapon."

David hesitated for a moment. He examined Victus and saw a stoic look in his eyes, an expression of acceptance. David gave him his pistol, and Victus looked at Vae. "Retrieve his wife and child," he told her.

David appeared perplexed, face twisted. "Victus," he said. "I have no wife or child."

Victus cocked the gun and placed the muzzle at David's head. "I pity you, then. No one to watch or mourn." He fired both rounds, and the hard, cylindrical pellet propelled from the double-shot flintlock broke through flesh, bone, and brain. David's head burst, and he died instantly with no pain to suffer. As promised. His body collapsed, knees giving way, sprawled out onto the ground with pieces of his head missing. Blood and brains oozed onto the plantation yard.

Victus and Helyar locked eyes.

Helyar scowled at him. "He was your friend, neggar-devil!" he shouted.

Victus lifted his shovel from the ground. The lilac haze continued glowing around the metal head. "He became your legacy!" Victus fired back. "Your heirs!" He aimed his shovel at the manor. "My family!" he yelled to the assembled, life-renewed Africans. "There's liquor in the cabinets! And there's blood in every room!"

The risen Africans leapt to war! A few did so literally as they lunged high into the air, crashing through labor house and plantation manor windows. The undead keeping on the ground didn't walk. They ran! Plantation master and slave-legacy holder were attacked. Heads were slammed into walls. Bones were broken. Necks were snapped. Jaws were ripped from their joints! And bodies were pummeled. There were flashes of brilliance and clarity in the remaining moments of their lives. Their attackers were beautiful shadows, angelic in nature. The slave-legacy holders cried for forgiveness. They shouted for mercy; and they wondered, in their last moments, who the devil could truly be.

Denis watched Helyar and his two sons retreat into the manor. He turned and looked at Vae and Victus. Vae took her brother's side. "We have business," she said to him. He nodded, agreeing. Victus watched as they made their way inside. He panned the plantation, reaching out with his instinct to appraise the revolution around him. The risen were killing every potential of legacy for the plantation, and he was at ease.

Living, African slaves in the manor hid in closets or covered themselves in shadow. May-May found herself empowered by the revolution. She wrapped her arms around slave Mistress Cwenhild's neck. The plantation mistress squealed and fought back. She bent her body against the older, African woman's strength, twisting to and fro in an attempt to wrestle from her grip. The women toppled to the ground. May-May smacked her head against the wooden bedframe and opened her arms. Cwenhild jumped to her feet and kicked the African woman in the stomach. May-May buckled, but the reaction allowed her to reach forward and catch Cwenhild by the ankle. She yanked her off her feet. The slave mistress hit the ground with a hard thud, bruising her arm.

She'd fallen near the dresser. Underneath was a lockbox, and she pulled it out quickly, fidgeting with its latch to open it. May-May inched up, back against the bedframe. Her old bones ached, but she rallied enough strength to turn her body and brace her arms around the bedframe, attempting to stand.

Cwenhild opened the box. A loaded, two-shot pistol rested inside. She snatched it and cocked back one hammer, turning her body around to aim at May-May. The African woman was almost on her feet, and Cwenhild was ready to shoot. The plantation mistress fired, but May-May jumped away. The projectile punctured and split into the bedframe. May-May slammed against the ground. She recovered and scurried toward the closest door. She burrowed inside, but then cursed as she realized her mistake within the darkness. She had fled into a small closet large enough for her to sit and huddle herself knees to chin. A place where she was forced to sleep on some occasions. She turned with her last bit of strength and closed the door, holding the handles tight to keep Cwenhild out and at bay.

"I'll burn you alive in there, you ungrateful, black witch!" Cwenhild hissed. "You been waiting to take my blood, haven't you!" May-May continued gripping the doors' handles tight. "I'll show you cruelty. I will!" Chains clanked. A lock clamped. "I'll set you on fire!" Cwenhild assured again. "You won't be the first black witch I burned to ashes!"

May-May's eyes watered. She slumped down, knees bent close to her face. She put her arms around them and listened as Mistress Cwenhild breathed rapid, wild. May-May didn't mind death, and she accepted it. She thought about her arms wrapped tight around Miss Cwenhild's neck, remembering the moment. She smiled. "I fought you, Miss Cwenhild," she said in a low voice. "It felt good…"

"Now, you know better!" said a third voice. It was young, feminine and not aimed at her but addressing Mistress Cwenhild. There was a shot fired, but May-May heard no body fall against the floor. The young, feminine voice repeated, "Now, you know better…"

Something heavy was tossed and hit the wall. The object's thud caused May-May to flinch in the darkness. Mistress Cwenhild shouted obscenities, and the young, feminine voice cackled until it became a low, animalistic growl. It was like that of a lioness, and what May-May heard next was like the sound of a pounce and strike. Bones snapped like twigs, and flesh was torn from the body with a slow, tortuous sound. The only noise louder was Mistress Cwenhild's voluminous, ear-scratching screams. May-May sweat. Her lower lip trembled, and then she heard another peculiar clamor. It was a guttural whoosh, like that of a massive fire bursting into existence. Mistress Cwenhild's deafening shrieks escalated, swelling into an unbearable last breath that rattled May-May's senses. The door that shielded her from the horror shook wildly, its jangling chain thwacking the doors.

May-May sat conflicted, wanting to cover her ears from Mistress Cwenhild's agonizing shrieks but also revel in them. She let her ears listen until she could take no more, but as she lifted her hands, Mistress Cwenhild's cries ceased, leaving behind a silence that blocked out the clamor happening within the mansion below and outside on the grounds of the plantation.

A young woman humming interrupted the quiet, and the clamor of mutiny rose up behind it like a supporting choir. May-May's old body stopped shaking, soothed by the thrum resonating just outside the closet where she sat, locked inside. The next musical cue was the note of a lock clicking from its hatch. Then came the clatter of a chain loosened. The door opened, and a lantern's light washed over May-May for a bright, brief moment until its resonating brilliance retracted and reshaped into the diminutive, fiery body of a woman dancing over a candle.

May-May looked up at Vae standing over her, reaching out a hand. "Beautiful elder one," Vae addressed her. "Take my hand. I'm here to help." May-May accepted, and she was assisted to her feet by Vae's gentle pull.

The first thing the old, African woman noticed was the massacre. Little light was provided by the feminine-shaped flame dancing within the lantern, but still May-May could see. The walls were plastered in blood and viscera. The room was painted in slaughter with severed limbs and torso burning to a crisp inside wagging flames. May-May swept her eyes around the room where Mistress Cwenhild occupied every space, ripped asunder. Her survey ended on Vae who's clothes were slathered in blood.

Vae told May-May, "I hated that woman. My mother did as well."

May-May nodded. "I hated her, too," she replied. She looked at the fiery woman glowing as the lantern's flame. "I remember you! Looks like we all got our licks on her tonight." No more was said, and all was understood.

The women left the room.

Downstairs. Denis found Helyar, but Crispin and Godwin defended their father. They fired their flintlocks at the risen young man. One shot missed. Three projectiles pierced Denis in the shoulder, the head, and in the heart, but he didn't fall. He opened his hand and a bone-handled dagger formed out of air. Crispin charged him, a last desperate attempt to save his father and land. Denis gouged his blade deep into Crispin's neck. A heavy stream of blood spurt from Crispin's wound when Denis dislodged the weapon. Blood spray coated ceiling, furniture and walls. Denis pushed Crispin aside to die, and the young slaveholder wrapped his fingers around the deep cut to hold the last of his liquid life inside.

Helyar cursed, eyes on his dying son. He looked at Denis and shouted, "You're the Devil's instrument! You're a cursed man!" Then he ducked into the darkness as Godwin rushed Denis, a feeble effort engaging the resurrected, young man.

Denis dodged two swings from Godwin's fist. Punches aimed at Denis' face only swiped air. A shot at his stomach produced the same result. Denis jammed his knife through Godwin's wrist and taunted, "If your attempt was to damage air, you'd make a fine warrior!" He grabbed the back of his neck, bent him over, and used his grip as a brace to pull his blade free. Godwin buckled and blood gushed from his wound. He wrapped his hand around his wrist to keep the injury from becoming a fatal pour. Denis brought the knife down into Godwin's back and left it there. Godwin smacked the ground, squirming in a slow flail as he bled out.

Helyar emerged from a shadow. A scowl on his face. He looked at his dying sons and then at Denis. "Is this what you returned for, boy? You trying to finish that plot drummed up by your righteous indignation and that black witch of a half-sister of yours?" He stepped toward Denis with a confident stride. He put his arms out and proclaimed, "Won't make a lick of a difference, my boy. Killing me won't do a thing for this world—revenge never does. Your heart won't be the same." He stopped his walk. "You see, Jesus said—"

Denis slammed his fist into Helyar's nose. He felt cartilage crunch and shatter. Buried anger rose in his swing and shattered Helyar's facial structure. A second swing across the plantation owner's face was hard enough to turn his cheek bone into dust. "Your sons were the Devil's instruments!" Denis shouted. "You are the Devil's agent!" Two more hits and Helyar's legs gave out. He toppled to the floor, damage cast on him by Denis' pugilistic bombardment. From skull to jaw, there wasn't an intact bone that made up his facial structure. Denis went to his knees, straddling Helyar's body. He pummeled the slaveowner with a fury of balled, heavy fists to the head. Flesh burst open and bone crumbled under the battery. Denis swung and hit and swung and hit and swung and hit until he'd beaten Helyar Swymmer clear to death.

He caught his breath and stood. Vae was there with her lantern in hand. "Not even our mother's fiery power wants to touch that odious man," she commented.

Denis exhaled. His eyes fell on his bloodied hands. "I feel so much better having killed him." He teared up. "I am this devil's son. Am I to inherit this devil's ways?"

"I've never known a devil to resurrect from death," Vae told her brother-by-half. "Never heard of a devil freeing people from bondage. Even in the Bible, a book held so precious, I've known God to do a good deal of killing." She put her arms around her brother and assured him, "You are not of the devil, my brother. Africa will cleanse you and rename you, and you will be born again, once again."

Denis nodded his head. A smile dawned on his face. Vae beamed back at him. He took another deep breath, and then he left the house with his sister. They joined Victus as he watched resurrected Africans tie up overseer Barclay to a thick tree. The bound man struggled, but there was no squirming out of the hold the Africans tied him in. Victus walked over to Barclay, shovel slung over his shoulder. When he neared the overseer, he put a hand on his shoulder and discharged conjure from his palm. "Everyone will have a take at you tonight, overseer," Victus told him. "You will not perish from your wounds until sunrise." Victus backed away, and with an acute, authoritative voice, he said, "You will feel every blow, every strike, and every lash made on your person, Barclay. You will suffer as we have suffered." He cocked his head and sighed. "This isn't vengeance. We're not so petty. This is simply judgment."

Victus walked away. Risen Africans surrounded the bound Barclay, waiting their turn to have a strike and a cut at him. The overseer's screams were immediate.

The living African slaves, now freed, followed Wallace, Dinah, and Simon out to the Swymmer plantation's liberated fields. Victus addressed them by saying, "You are all family; and we do not wrestle against flesh and blood." He looked toward the night sky, and then he put his eyes on his hands. Victus made a fist and said, "We are the cosmic powers that *preside* over *true* darkness and all its beautiful secrets—children and women and men of cosmic color."

Victus regrouped with the risen Africans. Living and resurrected mingled to know one another, reunite with killed loved ones. Vae and Victus stowed away until a feast was advised. Vae dictated the menu. It had to be precise, for the meal was a ritual to a water spirit.

And so did the resurrected and the liberated prepare a precise meal to feast on. They had to drink water and champagne from the pantry and naval wine. Coffee with sugar and cream were partaken as well. Melon and boiled cornmeal served with riced cooked in coconut milk, mixed with lima beans. Fried bananas were cooked first as an appetizer, and it was good to feast. Roosters and ducks were rustled up and made for the larger meal. Goats were painted with indigo symbols before they were slaughtered with song and prayer, cooked with spices. Vae sang a song to the King of the Sea, and the freed and resurrected Africans sang along, though they'd never heard the song before. They shared an instinct, and it blessed them with the lyrics Vae crooned.

Victus watched Vae carol on while leaning against his shovel. He beamed as he observed her beautiful dark face lit up by the bonfire's luminescence. The children brought sea shells and turquoise beads and other jewelry scavenged from the plantation manor. Vae continued singing as she was gifted presents. The women danced and turned fishhooks into earrings, and Vae called upon the element of silver and the cosmic haze and the dark firmament above to craft a vessel to carry them all back to Africa.

There was song. There was dance. There was judgment upon Barclay the overseer. There was good eating, and it was all a ritual. Vae's ship was created in honor of her recognition to the King of the Sea. It would manifest at noon when the plantation survivors made an exodus to the coast. At that time, Barclay succumbed to his numerous wounds when the sun's rays rose over the horizon. Vae used her mother's fiery spirit to set the body ablaze with such conjure intensity that he was reduced to small fragments that were barely ash. The tree he was bound to was unscathed. The ropes, too.

A long trail of African folk filed away from the plantation. Kip used all his power to change the land to a marsh so morass that it swallowed everything resting on it. The plantation manor, all the slave cabins, the labor house, and the dead that littered the fields descended beneath the earth. Forever covered. The ground was then made solid again. "I hate to give the Earth a stomachache," commented Kip.

The walk was long, but nothing hindered their journey. Spirits danced around them and kept them invisible, outside of time. They arrived at the coast at noon, and a large warship emerged from the sea and Vae dropped to her knees and spread her arms wide, head back and a smile up to heaven. The others did the same, Victus next to her. She shouted, "Goue! Agoueh! Agive! Give us this vessel *Immamou!* Heaven is not our destination. The terrestrial Africa is where we desire to go. We do not seek Guinee at this time, nor will we sail through the seven gates. There is much to be done. There is much dirt to cleanse from us! Bless us, *Agwe!* Be as an underwater torch to heat the water and burn our pursuers. Watch like a greedy dog with your red eyes, *Agwe!* And touch any vessel that makes war with us with the power of the sun's rays. Let them sink, *Agwe!* Let them be taken by those thrown overboard, *Agwe!* We thank you for this offering."

The blessing ended. Gratitude was spoken in many African tongues, as instinct now guided the people to remember their languages. And the resurrected men, and the living men newly freed, along with the resurrected women, and the living women newly freed, and the children of either house, boarded the ship and found comfort on a floating home.

Vae shouted her commands, and her crew fell in line. She captained the vessel to Africa with Victus at her side. The Gardener-General looked to the horizon and thought of his mother and brother. There was still hurt in him, but much was soothed by his newfound conjure and its use in the destruction of the Swymmer Plantation.

The day was clear, but a dreaming eye in another time focused on what could not be seen. There came clouds that covered the sky. They were lilac, and there was nothing ominous about their intrusion as they covered everything in the scene, but it didn't end there. It transitioned to time passed and water traversed across the great Atlantic Ocean. Shimmering, lilac clouds dissolved in rhythm to their sparkle and revealed a bright dawn. Vae stood at the helm of the magnificent watercraft called *Immamou*, a borrowed vessel from an otherworldly fleet belonging to a spirit deemed The King of the Sea. Waves were plentiful, but they were petite and friendly. Their scurry quickened the warship's travel along the water, and while the ocean's swell lifted and lowered the craft, its rhythms were very soothing.

Africa's coast did not appear on the horizon, but its ancient magic was represented by a colossal phenomenon that was only viewed by the newly blessed eyes of Vae's crew. All gathered topside to observe the appearance of a wide island that was otherwise outside of time. Victus stood next to Vae with one hand on his hip and the other balancing the shovel slung over his shoulder. An otherworldly tremble sprang from the root of his spine to the top of his head. From there it traveled free and hurtled across the distance from the waters between the *Immamou* and the island outside of time. His instinct transmitted to him a familial awareness. He closed his eyes and he saw a woman's silhouette against the darkness. Eyes opened, he blurted, *"Mother!"*

Vae reacted, hearing Victus speak. He dashed toward the front of the ship, wriggling through the assembled masses. When the people noticed Victus, they parted and let him through. The waves seemed to share Victus' eager temperament. The tides lifted and moved the vessel closer to the island at an increased speed. Victus maneuvered his way to the forward-most part of the ship, almost climbing the bowsprit. He remained sturdy on the ship, both hands on the handle of the shovel as he used it for balance. The closer the *Immamou* sailed toward the island, the more Victus' eyes strained in desperation to see his instinct's premonition manifest in the physical, waiting on the island's shore.

Vae steered the ship aground, and everyone braced themselves as the large craft made a sudden stop, confronted with dry and immovable land. Victus didn't lose balance, nor did his vision stumble from its focus. No woman was there to greet the ship. Standing at the ship's moored prow was a brown-skinned man with a single and thick, slate-colored dreadlock atop his head. He was dressed in royal robes. Dangling from his belt was not a royal scepter but a hammer-pick. He was surrounded by guardsmen drawn up in loose, black clothes with their faces wrapped in black cloths with only their eyes to be seen. They drew their swords as Victus inched his way closer to the boat's edge, but the royal man signaled with a wave for his soldiers to sheath their weapons. They obeyed.

Victus swept his eyes across the landscape. There was a beautiful seaside town that served as the immediate backdrop beyond the royal man and his guards. Lush fauna intertwined with residential and commercial structures. Victus could see a magnificent, alabaster palace laying at the island's center. Majestic, yes. But there wasn't one point of interest for him within the remarkable visual. What he longed to see wasn't there, and so he questioned his instinct, dropping his head. Vae and the assembled Africans marveled at the sight where Victus did not.

"You travel on a sacred vessel," the royal man spoke up to Victus, who lifted his head and looked at him attentive. "I can trust you because of this. So, I welcome you to my kingdom. My name is King Ziko Yswil."

Victus didn't say anything, but he didn't have to. Vae stepped to his side and acknowledged the king by calling his name. "King Ziko!" she said down to him. "I would bend a knee in your presence if I had the space."

King Ziko waved away the sentiment and remarked, "No need, sable maiden."

"*Captain!*" she corrected with a smile.

"No need, *Captain,*" the king amended.

Vae exhaled. She examined the king in front of her and felt the entirety of his long life. "Forgive me, King Ziko," she told him, beaming an admiring smile down on him. "I know you don't mean to cause offense. I can sense your long life has seen many great women."

"Oh, it has," King Ziko said with a nod. "I'm married to one."

There was a beat before Vae replied, "I'm sure." She took another moment before responding. "I was merely presenting my rank. I am captain of this ship. Captain Vae." She turned to Victus and introduced him. "This man at my side is named—"

"*Seizan!*" a woman cried.

Eyes up! He saw her, and there she was. Efra al-Kaadi. His mother.

Victus closed his eyes tight, as tears welled up in them. He ground his teeth and looked away. Hurt gripped his heart, and anger clogged his throat. She said his name again, and he sniffed away his sorrow, opened his eyes, and looked at his mother. She was clothed in a billowing, yellow dress with an orange sash around her waist and a headwrap the same color. Victus blurted, "*Ma-ma!*" His tears were unstoppable, and he slumped to his knees, dropping his shovel. The tool fell from the ship and lodged into the sandy beach below.

Efra too was overcome with tears. Her body trembled, and her legs buckled. King Ziko caught her and said into her ear, "This young man is your other son?" Efra nodded her head. King Ziko took a breath and returned a stern gaze to Victus, who had regained balance. "I know your brother, Good Man Seizan," he said up to him. Victus stood tall. His face was wide with anticipation and still streaming with tears. "He assists my sons and daughter on an important mission."

Victus balled his hands into fists. "What mission?" he inquired.

"Wickedness and sin corrupt the stars," relayed King Ziko. "Your brother and my sons and daughter journey now to bring love to the cosmic Eterijah and restore the Maiden kingdom. They could use your help." He looked at Vae and requested, "Have you warriors among your crew?"

Vae and Victus looked at one another. She grinned, but he appeared uncertain.

Victus looked at his mother, and he thought about his brother. The hurt was still there, soothed only little by reunion.

Lilac fog flooded the scene.

34

wake! In a start!

Fast!

Eyes opened. Wide. Heart racing.

The dream ended.

History faded, and all that remained was the darkness encapsulating Gordon Goodspeed inside the Alchemical Chamber. Gordon's first instinct was to be frustrated. The archaic capsule opened and he hopped out with Spook tucked under his arm. The chamber closed, and Gordon leaned against it, setting the sentient device atop the closed chamber. Its face lifted from the console. The yumbo Silver flew up into the air and landed on the ancient mainframe's bejeweled console.

Gordon put his brightly-glowing, lilac eyes on the wall to his right. "Nothing!" he hissed. "Didn't learn shit!" He shook his head and crossed his arms, burying himself deep in his thoughts. The lack of information on The Lovers card's whereabouts was not what nettled him. Silver could see his real distress. She understood Gordon's impulse to sulk, but she considered that he needed to express his thoughts aloud to alleviate stress. She asked if he'd seen Fey, her musical voice and language soothing his bubbling emotions. Gordon exhaled as he shook his head. "No, Silver…" he answered the winged sprite. He confessed, "That's the real problem, to be honest." Gordon's admission wasn't much of a surprise to the otherworldly creature. Silver comforted Gordon by admitting she missed Fey. Gordon agreed. "Yeah. I guess I'm a little selfish on that note. I've been with her twice. Seen her three times. It's reassuring that she's okay. I'm sure if anything was wrong, my spirit would know."

Gordon's thoughts turned to Victus-Seizan, focused chiefly on his reunion with his mother, Efra, and his mixed emotions. He reflected on Fey again, thinking on her reckless decision to go after Stanley Fallows by herself. Gordon uttered, "It was a gutsy move. I can admire that." It didn't curb his annoyance that she didn't include him. "We'll always have Paris," he quoted. He turned his head and spotted Silver out of the corner of his eye. He went to speak, but was interrupted by his mother's voice.

"Gordon!" she called.

The sound didn't come from inside his mind. It resonated in the room, echoing in a loud, ghostly fashion. Gordon sprang up from leaning against the alchemical chamber. He looked around the room and responded, "Ma…?"

"I'm with Maman Anansi and Madame Jeliya," she said. *"We're in Madame*

Jeliya's sanctuary. Come at once," she summoned.

Gordon popped from existence, leaving Silver and Spook behind. The scenery around Gordon dissolved from his perspective and reshaped in an instant as he came into existence inside Madame Jeliya's wondrous sanctum. Head Matriarch Maman Anansi was there dressed in a white gown and headwrap. Madame Jeliya stood next to her in a long-flowing, pink skirt with a black vest and white and ruffled, sleeveless blouse. Her lions rested in different corners of the room. Gordon's mother appeared behind him. "You look tired," she observed.

Her presence made him flinch, pivoting toward his mother in the same motion. He took a breath and answered, "I haven't gotten real sleep, Ma. Even my instincts are a little off. I didn't sense you there." But then a feeling came into focus. Gordon turned from his mother as if a strong, invisible grip pulled at him. He spun coolly, and his twirl ended on a perfect view, spotting the mason jar filled with the dirt he'd gathered at the location of Mister Banneker's burial site. A ghostly image flickered in and out of existence quicker than a blink. There and then gone, but Gordon's heightened memory recorded what he'd witnessed. The man was of average height with brown skin and a clean-shaven face. He wore a sky-blue suit, and Gordon recognized the man as Mister Forrester himself, Fey's father.

Maman Anansi and Madame Jeliya were smiling at Gordon, though their lips wavered noticeably.

He pointed at the jar. "I saw that!" he exclaimed. He stepped forward, finger still aimed. "He was there… You did it…!"

Lewis Banneker appeared again, his image as blue as his suit and translucent. He snapped away like bad reception, squiggling and zig-zagging from existence. "We're trapped…" his voice filled the room, echoing in a desperate tone. "We serve him…"

Gordon's eyes went to Maman Anansi and Madame Jeliya. A dour expression took over their faces. Then again appeared Fey's father, image wriggling, snapping steady for only a moment before distorting again. He spoke, but his words were out of synch with his lips' movements. "Distress…!" he said, voice filled with an eerie static. "We're trapped… Ana… Anathematic sphere… Spirits… Banished… Emma! She's turned… GWO… Endless… Pl—" He snapped out of existence, and Gordon looked at the two matriarchs. His face was full of questions.

His mother glided passed him and stood at Maman Anansi's side. The head matriarch said, "It's only an echo. Lewis was always clever. I'm sure he mustered all his strength to leave it through whatever pain he was put through before Stanley and his henchmen finished torturing him." Her voice cracked with anger as the scene of sadistic needling performed on Lewis Banneker flashed in her head for a brief moment. A memory plucked from the Lewis' faint echo. "He's looking for his wife and daughter," Maman Anansi continued after a brief pause to gain her composure. "He and Emma's spirits appear to be banished to the mythological place called the Endless Planes." Gordon recalled the childhood lessons. It was a realm where *inawo* and anathematic fog churned together and became giants called GWO. That was one aspect. It was a house with many mansions, and paradise could also be found. Maman Anansi said, "He has mentioned few words. We can make that much sense, putting them together."

"We've heard more," Madame Jeliya took up. Gordon faced her. "Lewis' spirit wants his conjure back that Stanley pilfered from him."

Gordon shook his head, confused. He looked away and tried to put all the pieces together, but he didn't come up with a clear picture. His instinct was faltering. "I need real sleep," he said under his breath. He raised his head and said to his mother, "I saw him with Emma. His spirit and her spirit took Fey, thirteen aspects of her spirit. It was a part of Stanley's ritual to banish her." Then he recalled Lewis' desperate words. "They serve him…" He exhaled and nodded his head. "Up to speed."

"Stanley was responsible for their deaths, Gordon," Althea told her son. Then the specter opened the palm of her hand. There was a flicker of spiritual energy that formed into a machete. The conjuring made Gordon flinch. He saw his mother standing firm, tight grip on the sharp melee instrument. "The Endless Planes are a beautiful but frightening place," she spoke in a determined voice. "Spirits are warned about its many mansions, doorways to other planes of existence. The monsters there, such as GWO. I can find him, but I'll need assistance. The ordeal will need an ambitious ritual." Her voice calmed when she listed, "Reverend Pouvwa, the Crossroads Queen, Top Hat, and Maman Anansi would be needed." Then she revealed to Gordon, "They will remain physical and concentrating, but you Gordon, you will be at my side in this other world. Your lilac spirit will give a boost to my own power on that side."

"And Fey!" Gordon blurted.

"Miss Forrester?" Althea questioned.

Gordon lifted his shoulders. "They're her parents, Ma," he made clear. "She should be there."

Althea opened her hand. The machete dissolved away. She beamed. "I see your point," she said with a nod.

"We'll cut Stanley's eyes out," Maman Anansi declared. "That will be a priority once we have Miss Forrester returned to us." She asked Gordon, "How has your dreaming been going? Did we wake you? Your mother had been calling you for some time."

"No, Maman Anansi," answered Gordon. "I was just coming out of the dream. There are forces mounting in history, coming together. It's all centered around the sixteen-hundreds and the slave trade. There are conjure folk fighting it, but ancient politics and views from the Pious Wars puppet their movement, divide friends and family. I've heard names of a pantheon of deities in Africa, the Eterijah—"

"How beautiful, Gordon!" Madame Jeliya exclaimed. "Have any of them made an appearance? The Eterijah? A few became the Orisha and assisted the Africans in escaping their enslavement. Such power!"

"I heard of one specifically. Eterijah Iyansan…" He turned to Maman Anansi. She beamed, proudly. There was not a person in the room that didn't know Iyansan as the Oya spirit that would be born into flesh as her great grandmother, Theresa Amat. "I also saw one of the invisible islands," he mentioned. "It was governed by the Alchemist with the Hammer and his wife, Oris Del. My last dream ended there. I'll report what I've seen to Lady Arachne."

His features faltered, and all three women could see the exhaustion in Gordon's face. Maman Anansi said to him, "You are correct, Gordon. You need *real* sleep."

Gordon nodded, and then he yawned. "I'll do my altar ritual," he assured. "Will be good to just sleep. No drama," he joked. The matriarchs and his mother simply beamed at his humor. It was more serious than Gordon was letting on, and they knew that, even without the use of a higher instinct. Gordon popped away.

Althea exhaled.

Maman Anansi said to her, "I'm afraid he won't have his real sleep until Fey is back in his arms."

Althea responded to the head matriarch, "My thoughts exactly, Maman Anansi."

35

Miller Mitchell didn't have a good feeling about the assembly he attended. There were too few cool heads and too many guns. He sat at a long, rectangular table between two men he'd often been at war with for control over illicit activity in Water Bug Hollow. They had a shaky ceasefire for the time being, but recent activities stirred tension. As if sensing there was a bubble coming to a heated boil, a religious activist in the area reached out to the three gang bosses. So, it was this neutral territory where they met. A church. The only church in Water Bug Hollow, and it was headed by the very person that corralled Miller Mitchell and the two other men under one roof. The only thing peaceful about the meeting thus far was the silence.

Tam 'Cutter' Hall was on Miller's left. A young and light-brown skinned man with cornrows. He ran the Hundred-Dollar Block on Benjamin Franklin Street. Coleman Parker was on his right. He was a heavy-set man with a large head, always wearing sunglasses, even now, indoors. Miller knew that behind those shades Coleman's eyes were gliding all over the room, taking guesses at what circumstances were truly behind their gathering. Coleman liked to dress like an old-school hip-hop emcee. He had on a red tracksuit, Kango hat, and he was adorned with gold necklaces. He ran the Bastard Buck Wilds on Madison Drive, and they lived up to their name.

Each brought a set of three, armed guards. The bosses were also armed.

Peace had a slim window of opportunity, and the unease in the room moved Miller to speak. "What is this, y'all?" he asked either leader on each side of him. "Why we here? I mean, is this a hit or a bust?" He aimed an open hand at the door. "Some pious nigga wanna call us all together. Nah." With the same hand, he tapped his fingers on the table hard. "C'mon, now. Darien's gone missing. That's one of the roughest niggas this hood has ever seen. His crew seems dismantled. So, I repeat: Is this a hit or a bust? I wanna know who called this meeting."

His question was answered in both action and voice. The door opened. Two familiar faces walked in, though four men walked through the door. Recognized was Chief Ramiel Bishop, boss of the Four In Hand Crew. Boss Nicholas Lamar, head of the Hamilton Boulevard Loud Mouths, was the second identifiable man. Chief Ramiel held a rectangular, wooden lockbox in his hand. Boss Lamar had one as well. The third man also carried a wooden lockbox. He was older than Chief Ramiel and Boss Lamar. He had long braids and a go-t, was a little taller than average, and looked very capable of holding his own physically. He was an imposing, dark, brown-skinned man wearing a denim jacket, jeans and workman boots. His presence took the air out of the room, dropping the mouths of the three men sitting. Coleman removed his glasses to get a better look. There was something familiar about him.

Their entrance was unexpected, and both the sitting gang leaders and their guards became alert. But it was the last man to enter that caught their attention most of all. He was the one that spoke.

This young man was tall and lean with short, wild-haired, dressed to the gypsy nines. His black pants belled out at the base. His tunic did the same at the end of the sleeves. Around his loose garment was an unbuttoned, black vest, and there were two curiosities that adorned him. The first was a necklace ornamented with three skulls the size of a balled fist. They resonated with an eerie glow, shimmering with an aura of their colors. Red. Black. Green. The second object he possessed was an African mask clipped to his side, dangling like a gunslinger's six shooter.

"I called the meeting," was what he said to them. He walked in, and he sat down at the head of the table. Ramiel and Lamar sat across from the other bosses. The older man dressed in denim and workman boots sat between them. All eyes were on the man at the table's head. He introduced himself, "My name is Armand Gideon. I'm a Cali boy with a little New York in me." He chuckled. It was sinister. No one smiled. They stared. Armand stopped his small laughter and put an eye on the men who'd already been seated and waiting in the room. Armand stated their names as he aimed his finger at them. He started in the middle. "We're all in the same boat, so there's no harm in me revealing some details. Miller Mitchell, boss of the Chain Gang Crew. Formed in the mid-seventies by a group of black men who'd turned their lives around in prison. They learned Arabic, Swahili, and studied an African spiritual science. The Chain Gang's original purpose was to assist men when they got out of prison. Just ten years later, the original nine heads were either dead or railroaded back to prison. Crack came. New leaders seized on the cheap, viable business opportunity, and Water Bug Hollow started its decline into madness." Next, he called out Tam 'Cutter' Hall. "Active boss of the Hundred-Dollar Block crew." Tam sat back and straightened his shoulders. "Same kind of scenario with your group, though the Hundred-Dollar Block came up in the early eighties, if my research has served correctly—and it has. The Hundred-Dollar Block was supposed to be about creating business and stimulating positive cashflow in Water Bug Hollow. Same scenario took place. Railroaded or dead leaders resulted in illicit business and negative cashflow, not just in money running out of Water Bug Hollow, but also having a hexed currency. Dirty money," he emphasized. Armand pushed his cheek out with his tongue. "Huh…" he said, thinking. Then he pointed to the final man. "Coleman Parker!" he hollered with a

smile. "I like them chains!" He slapped the table with an open hand. "The Bastard Buck Wilds! Quite a sensation, ain't they! Formed out of the illegitimate sons of former gang leaders and captains from a long-dead crew known as the Royals. The leftovers from a bygone era. Formed your own crew to show 'em how it's done." Armand snickered. "You all know my associates here. We have Ramiel Bishop and Nicholas Lamar. In the middle is a man named Alphonse Latif, former leader of The Five Elements gang."

Miller, Tam, and Coleman didn't know what to do with their eyes. They looked at Alphonse, and then they jiggled with fright at Armand. Back and forth, trembling as did their arms and lips. Miller did his best to speak. He shook his head and protested, "No, no, no, no! You talkin' 'bout some nigga been dead for a good minute. Everybody done heard 'bout that dude."

Armand stared at Miller for a moment. Then he looked at the other two. "Anyone else wish to deny it?" No one said a word, and even Miller sat back, slumping in his chair. "Very well," Armand expressed in a cool manner. His eyes shifted to Ramiel, Nicholas, and Alphonse. He nodded his head. The three men slid their lockboxes across the table. The other three bosses put out their hand at the same moment and caught the wooden gifts. They stared at them, and their silence lasted for some time.

Coleman looked up at the men across the table, and then he put his attention on Armand. "What's this for?"

"Open them," Armand instructed. Coleman, Tam, and Miller exchanged looks. "Trust me," he beamed while placing a hand across his three, glowing skulls. The gesture produced conjure, lowering the apprehension in the three gang bosses and their armed guards.

Miller Mitchell, Tam Hall, and Coleman Parker looked at the boxes in front of them. All three men unhooked the latches and opened the wooden cases with visible trepidation. The trembling fear was reshaped into wide-eyed confusion when they found inside their boxes a single skull. Miller's skull was the color black that resonated with a dull pitch and deep purple color. Tam received a red skull in his box, and it too hummed with a dim emanation of its color throbbing from its frame. Coleman stared at his green skull as its drab, lighted atmosphere pulsed with a low brilliance. Tam and Miller were as locked with their eyes on their skulls as Coleman. The three gangster heads didn't move.

The auras pulsating from the grim objects coalesced into red, black, and green smoke that filled the three gang bosses' eyes, seeping into socket and sclera and pupil. Their lower jaws dropped and trembled as the harm they'd committed against the Water Bug Hollow community, along with their personal burdens, overwhelmed them with loud audio and horrific visions. Hard drug use was flashed to them in bright, flickering colors accompanied by screeching sounds mixed with terrible screams from the souls of ruined lives.

Armand told them, "Before your eyes, the three of you gaze upon a lifetime of burdens." He stood. He walked to the door, opened it, and permitted Reverend Pouvwa entrance. The holy conjure man entered in all black with his white, theological collar. He walked around the table, opened his hand, and conjured a delicious and distinct, consecrated fruit for Tam, Miller, and Coleman. He blossomed from the palm of his hand a bright-red apple, and he set it down in front of Tam. A delicious, plump plum was flowered out of conjure and placed before Miller. He summoned a lustrous, green pear and presented it to Coleman. Armand continued, "If you denounce my offer to join me to bring peace to Water Bug Hollow, I will have you buried as I did Mister Hicks. I'll see to that in my own Court of Burdens." Armand observed the bosses closely as the smoky haze swiveling up from the skulls filled their eyes. "You will own the burdens now, and they will own you until your debt is fully paid." He returned to his seat. "Here me, Mister Mitchell, Mister Hall," he said to the two gang bosses. They didn't look up, but they were attentive to Armand's words. "My mistress and I have summoned the spirits of two founding members of your gangs. These men are from a time when the aim within your crews was far more favorable, charitable to Water Bug Hollow. They will be your mentors. A stitching ceremony will hem their spirits to you two, and you will learn from them." He looked at Coleman and addressed, "Your gang of bastards will be advised by all three spirits we've summoned—that includes Mister Latif in our presence." There was a silent agreement among the entranced three gang bosses, and Armand's heightened instinct could feel their acceptance to his terms. "Eat the fruit presented, gentlemen, and swallow your strains."

The three did as they were tasked. They bit into their respective fruits, teeth puncturing the soft and succulent flesh, sweetened by the gush of natural juices. They swallowed, relaxed, and the incanted fruit made them submit to conjure's power. They exhaled, calmed of the anxiety the life of the streets had injected into them. Ramiel and Nicholas knew there was more suffering to come to the three bosses sitting opposite them. It wasn't going to be easy.

Armand and Reverend Pouvwa looked at one another. Reverend Pouvwa nodded his head. Armand did the same, and then the reverend made his exit, attending to additional dealings in another room. It was in that other room where Reverend Pouvwa joined Simaetha Ghedemere and Voodoo Lily. Mother and daughter. Also present was a group of young men and women whose lives were afflicted by the terrible politics of the streets. Gang violence. Their offenses on the street were minor, if they existed at all. In no way were they the cause of any of the more brutal deluge in Water Bug Hollow, but they were greatly affected by it.

The youngest, Andrew Badgerson, was seventeen with a father in jail for a violent robbery that led to murder. His mother was on and off drugs, but stable enough to work. Life and addiction got the better of her, however, and her stability wavered. She overdosed one night. Simaetha was her nurse at the hospital, having transferred from a New Orleans medical center to one in Jakobiville. Voodoo Lily and Armand went to claim her son, and Andrew was brought into the fold before he made his way to his mother's dealer to take out his frustrations.

The oldest of the group, Elodie Ellison, was twenty-two. She had been raised by her grandparents since the age of fifteen when her mother and father were killed at a stoplight and robbed. The streets were ready to ensnare her as college and a low-paying, bartending job burned her out. No sleep. Long hours between both responsibilities. She was close to selling anything from her body to drugs. The bar she tended had one of the gangs as a silent partner, but by the time she decided to make her transition into what could make her more money, the gang had been taken over by a new crew in town that had only two members. A man and a woman. Their description was odd. She heard the man wore an African mask. The woman was a conjure queen. It was they whom Elodie spoke to, and now she was here.

Between Andrew and Elodie's ages were the remaining two in the room.

Myèl Claire, eighteen, was a runaway from a violent foster home. She had been living on the streets for six years, surviving by becoming a very audacious thief. She knew where every cache of stolen jewelry was hidden, and she pilfered it when she needed something. Her exploits took her into dark areas of buildings owned by the neighborhood's most violent gangs. She stole enough not to be noticed, but jewelry was hard since people had their favorite pieces.

John Morgan was nineteen, and he was in love with Myèl Claire. He'd helped her escape from the foster home, and the two of them made their life on their own. He was being raised by his grandparents until they both passed from old age. His brother, a gang member, was murdered when he was thirteen, but he knew some secrets. The biggest secret was people he could trust as fences for stolen goods. Even stolen drugs, which paid more. The risk to sneak and take a drug stash was high, and high was a prerequisite for engaging in something so dangerous and stupid. But they pulled it off and made one hell of a sale. The payoff was bountiful, and John joked they should perform a *Medieval Monday*, to which Myèl asked what that was. John told her, *"When history or a legend manifests itself in your time. Let's be Robin Hoods. Let's give back. Let's got donate some of what we got to the church."*

It wasn't like they didn't have the money to spare. Reverend Mathieu Pouvwa was there to greet them, and after a few words, John determined he was a cop. *"Ex-cop,"* corrected the reverend. *"Detective, actually. Ex-detective."* It was after that correction that Reverend Pouvwa gauged there was only one reason a person would be so keen on observing any cop mannerisms. He didn't even use an instinct other than the ones he'd nurtured as a detective. The reverend moved John and Myèl to confess, and now they found themselves among this breakfast club crew.

They sat on fancy pillows situated on the floor. Simaetha and Voodoo Lily sat in front of them on wooden chairs, legs crossed. A bag of trinkets rested next to Simaetha. The scene mirrored a classroom setting for young children. Simaetha peered over her shoulder as Reverend Pouvwa entered the room. "Ah! Reverend!" she exclaimed. "Come. Join us." She returned her gaze to the youth and said, "I was just telling these younglings about going from the misfits of today to the saviors of tomorrow." Simaetha smiled at each of them. Then she looked at her daughter and signaled. Voodoo Lily stood. "Reverend," Simaetha called. "Your fruit, please."

The holy conjure man opened his hands and summoned four peaches. He presented them to Voodoo Lily. She took one and called, "John Morgan." The young man got to his feet and walked up to Voodoo Lily. She gifted him the luscious peach and instructed him to not yet eat. Next, she called Myèl Claire to stand next to him. She gave her a peach, called Elodie Ellison, and did the same for the twenty-two-year-old bartender.

Andrew Badgerson was last to receive his peach. He got to his feet, excited, even expressing how he felt there to have been a change in Water Bug Hollow's vibe. He took his peach and said while staring at the sacred fruit, "I'm still angry, though." He looked up and put his eyes on Voodoo Lily and Simaetha Ghedemere. "Always have been, I guess. Things don't much have a chance here in the Hollow. Seems like folk don't care."

"We care," Simaetha assured. She rose, carrying with her the bag at her feet, and took her daughter's side.

Voodoo Lily held Andrew in her gaze, melancholy filling her eyes. She looked at the young man, but she directed her words to all four of them. "Eat this fruit, let the juices cleanse you of burden, and enjoy the conjure you receive." They bit into the peaches. The sweet flavor coated their tongues immediately, tingling their sense of taste. The juices were refreshing, and an instinct snapped inside their heads. They could feel the fruit's liquid turn to light inside their bodies. They ate their peaches down to the pit, and Voodoo Lily collected the remains inside a clay pot for use later in the four's stitching ritual. Voodoo Lily returned to her seat. She watched her mother reach into the bag and remove a hand-crafted, African mask that had a small bell attached to its chin.

Simaetha presented the item to John Morgan and announced, "Behold! Gizo! Your conjure name." John held the mask with both hands, entranced at the hollow-eyed face staring back at him. To Myèl, Simaetha handed her a finely-crafted, six-inch, metal carving of a woman holding a beehive above her head. A metal ball was placed inside the beehive, ready to jingle when given a shake. "Myèl," she said in a pleasant voice. "Your birth name already buzzes and stings with your conjure's intent."

Andrew received an African mask that was just as intricately crafted as John Morgan's, but it was round instead of triangular in design. A small, bronze bell was fastened to its chin. To Andrew she bestowed the name 'Black Arum' and he reveled in both the mask and the moniker.

Elodie Ellison was the last. A six-inch, metal carving of a woman holding up an African teapot was given to her. A metal ball jumbled around in the teapot, and Elodie held the item still so as not to rattle it. She too had a conjure name selected for her. Simaetha announced her as *Sandife*, and Elodie found it to be a pretty name. The bald, brown-skin woman thanked Simaetha. Her gratitude wasn't just for the gift, but for all that had been done for her.

Voodoo Lily rejoined her mother's side. The four had seen conjure performed, but it was always dazzling to behold again. Simaetha said to them, "Biloko-Iboju Boys. Biloko-Nkisi Girls. You have a grudge to settle in the concrete jungle. Your lives are no more. You will be as spirits when called on. There is more to your transformation. You will be stitched to your conjure and spirit. Let us go to the crossroads."

Time and space folded around Voodoo Lily, Simaetha, and the Biloko Four. They disappeared, and Reverend Pouvwa stood alone in his church. He turned to leave, but stepped back when the door opened and Armand walked inside. "Voodoo Lily took them to the crossroads," the reverend told Armand. "Your soldiers are being prepped, Brother Iboju. Their stitching ritual is underway."

Armand exhaled. He took a seat and admitted, "I'm anxious, Reverend."

The pious man sat next to Armand. He conjured a peeled starfruit and suggested for Armand to have it. "Settle yourself," said the former detective. "You've been playing too cool, kid."

"I've been thinking about the next move," he confessed to the reverend. He took a bite, and the flesh of the fruit and its juices calmed him when swallowed. Armand pondered that Voodoo Lily was able to decipher the path Water Bug Hollow had been placed on by the Jakobi family. "The next part of the fight ain't ours, Reverend. Not mine, anyway. It's the Biloko Bunch—those kids." He chuckled and added, "Who I ain't much older than." The reverend gave a light laugh too. Armand continued eating. He chewed, resting his forearms on his lap, leaning forward. He remarked, "Being a trickster ain't my style. I like the head-on fight, y'know. Like what Gordon and his brother's crew get into. I liked being at the crossroads and using my power like a fist, hurting the bad guys physically. I liked watching that gas station-outpost thing go into the ground forever, swallow my enemies."

"Wish I could've been there," Reverend Pouvwa stated. "Though, not sure what I would've added. Maybe throw fruits and vegetables at the opposing team." He and Armand burst into laughter.

"That would've been a sight, huh?" Armand observed. He slapped his knee and stomped his foot. His laughter lasted for a good while before draining his guffaws into another, long sigh. He sat back and patted his chest. His mood returned to grim, so he had another bite of the incanted starfruit. He felt better. It was good conjure medicine, but it didn't take his mind off a future tasks. He raised an eyebrow and stated, "We got the rest of them bones to dig up, Reverend. Your fruit's seed to plant. Put bones to ritual. That'll disperse the remaining fog hauntin' Water Bug Hollow. Then we got some spirits to consult. See what's next on the to-do list for this place."

Reverend Pouvwa patted Armand's knee with a fist. "We're new at this game, Brother Iboju," he said to Armand. "We're doing all right."

Armand grinned at his new moniker. He shared the name of one of his favorite comic book heroes. "Brother Iboju?" he remarked. "Ain't that somethin', preacher? How many Spider-Man fans can say they grew up and became Spider-Man?"

Reverend Pouvwa pondered the point and then answered, "Oh, they'll say Spider-Man or whatever hero made them become their own hero."

Armand looked around the room. His eyes landed on the reverend. "No offense to the holy house we sit in, but fuck that. I wanted to be one of the Iboju Boys."

Reverend Pouvwa and Brother Iboju became volcanoes erupting with laughter.

36

Not a lot of tools were needed for ritual. Water Bug Hollow was empty of fog and despair, and in honor of that victory, some spirits just walked the streets. Horace Georg was one such spirit. He liked to remain seated outside the alley watching people stroll by in the sunny day. Digging up Patricia Gale Freda's hexed bones didn't hold back the humidity. It was still hot, but Horace Georg couldn't feel that. He could bask in the bright day, even if it remained somewhat hazy. Nature was going to be what nature was going to be, especially when it came to summer in the deep south. Despite that, the sky was bright and blue, and the sun spread its tendrils as it beamed proud in the sky. Horace Georg smoked his otherworldly tobacco in his otherworldly pipe, legs crossed and leaned back in his chair.

Then someone had the nerve to disturb the close-to-perfect day. It was a voice shouting, *"Old man!"* And it came from one of the few people that could see him sitting at the alleyway. Horace Georg frowned, and the person owning the voice laughed teasingly as he walked up to him. It was Horace Georg's student, Armand Gideon. The young conjure man was decked out in his Ojulowo-gypsy fashion, walking with a kick in his step.

"Boy!" Horace Georg scoffed, puffing on his pipe. "You all loud! Cut into my good day!" Armand continued laughing. Next to him was the Crossroads Queen. She was clothed in a blue dress with a brown sash. Her hair's thick, Bantu twists were as wide as the sun or any multi-pointed star. Her flesh glowed bright, even on its darker half. "H'w you, Miss Voodoo Li'l?" he asked while beaming.

"I'm well, thank you," she replied.

Armand came between Voodoo Lily and Horace Georg. "I don't get to be happy, old man?" he said with a smirk. "Ain't you proud of your protégé?"

Horace Georg returned the haughty smile. He took his pipe out of his mouth and nodded his head. "I guess I am," he said sitting up straight and proud. He threw a thumb over his shoulder and said, "Seats back th'r, ifin' you wan' sit."

Armand walked into the alley to retrieve the chairs for he and Voodoo Lily. Horace Georg noticed Voodoo Lily had been holding two Tarot cards in her hand. One was a colorful drawing of the Orisha Ogun. He was a strapping, bare-chested black man with a large, steel mallet in one hand and a sword in the other. On his back was a beautifully crafted shield. He was bald with a gold band around his head that was bedecked with jewels. He wore a black and red, kilt-like cloth around his waist and sandals on his feet.

Behind him was a cauldron filled with his tools resting next to an anvil. The second was a classic Tarot card, the Five of Wands, hosting an image of five boys fighting with wooden rods. Depending on the read, they could either be mocking a fight or engaged in a real altercation.

Horace Georg lifted a curious eyebrow at the cards held by the Crossroads Queen. He puffed on his pipe and exhaled. "O'ly two ca'ds t' see Dinclinsin?" he inquired.

"Yes, good spirit," she answered. "My conjure will handle most of the pathway into the *digi-glas*."

Horace Georg puffed again. Nodding his head over and over, he stated, "Yeah. That's right. Crossroads Queen." Armand returned with the chairs. He planted them next to the elderly spirit, and he and Voodoo Lily sat down. "So, you ready?" the old revolutionary asked the two seated next to him. Voodoo Lily answered with action, placing the two cards at her feet. She sat back and looked at Armand, and he looked at her. The two then put their eyes on the elderly spirit. "Go, 'head. Make him angry," he said while puffing on his pipe.

"I'll go first," said Armand. Then he proclaimed, "Mademoiselle Charlotte is a fussy, ill-tempered, brat!"

Voodoo Lily added, "She ugly, lazy, and disrespectful! She ain't got nothin' on Ezili Freda Dahomey. Now that's a woman with class!" An unearthly quake rattled beneath them. The heavy tremors could only be felt by the old spirit and the two conjure folk present. Voodoo Lily used her crossroads conjure to rearrange time and space. The world was wiped away in a flailing, black blob that resembled an octopus, and in a bright snap of light, the three were transported to what looked like an open, grassy field in the deep south.

Dinclinsin appeared, and he stomped his way in their direction. He was a burly man who wore a reflective, domed mask over his face, and he had on a pair of beige, nineteenth century slacks, a white, ruffled tunic and a blue frockcoat. He held tightly to a curled-up bullwhip, and he shook it at Armand and Voodoo Lily when he finished his approach. "You dare speak ill of my mistress?"

Armand shook his head and lifted his shoulders. "I ain't the one fuckin' her, homie," he commented.

Voodoo Lily rolled her eyes. "We need this Lwa's help, Brother Iboju," she reprimanded. "Try not to upset him." A sly smile came to her, noting the humor of it all.

Dinclinsin snarled, "What is it you seek this time, the two of you? Another gang member revealed?" He squatted, putting his reflective face close to Armand's. The young conjure man observed his countenance's warped image staring back at him. It stretched oblong and in odd directions against Dinclinsin's domed, mirror mask. "See something you fear?" asked the Lwa in a taunting tone.

"Yes," Armand answered, peering at his distorted face in the reflective mask. "I'm just too exhausted to care anymore."

Dinclinsin huffed and stood straight. He stomped his foot out of frustration. He turned his domed, reflective mask to Voodoo Lily. "And you?" he asked.

"We're not here to fight," she made clear. "No scrimmage is necessary. We ask for you to assume the form of guilty men and guilty women that are a part of a web." Dinclinsin cocked his head to the side, looking at Voodoo Lily with a curious, masked eye. She expounded, "There's a triad of sin that hangs over Water Bug Hollow. I've discerned this using my pathway conjure; and I've seen their paths but not their faces."

Dinclinsin turned his reflective gaze to Armand. The young conjure man lifted his shoulders again. "I'd rather punch a person straight in the jaw, but I guess I'll settle for exposing and humiliating the opposition," he said. "I request, in a humble voice, please reveal the faces of tyranny, Sir Dinclinsin, so that we may expose them to the world."

Dinclinsin didn't answer Armand. Instead, he looked at Horace Georg who sat smoking his pipe with a stoic look on his face. The old spirit just raised his eyebrow and shrugged. Dinclinsin huffed back at the aged haunt, which was their only exchange. Then the cantankerous Lwa returned his gaze to Voodoo Lily and Armand. The mirror mask ceased reflecting the images in front of it. The distorted images warped and bled into one another, swirling into the face of a young man, twenty years old, who had tired eyes. His head was framed in long, straight brown hair, and there was no more than a stubble on his face. Dinclinsin named him. "Dalton Jakobi," he grumbled. "The mayor's son. He stabbed a woman multiple times and killed her baby too. He wrote on the wall, in his victims' blood, *conjure should belong to the devil and I am the devil it should belong to'*. His mother and father were proud at the blood sacrifice initiation."

Though familiar with the terrible transgression, Voodoo Lily and Armand's faces twisted in disgust.

"Dalton Jakobi was acquitted of all charges," Dinclinsin continued. The revelation angered Armand, but he remained still in his chair. "His team of lawyers shifted guilt to a drug addict named Sawyer Boothe. You see, needles are not just for conjure folk. Sawyer is kept sedated with hex. You can choose to snag him from his confinement in a Jakobiville ward, or you can find Dalton Jakobi's morbid, proud confession. He's jotted his pride down in a journal. The guilty ones will always have their confessions at the ready. Find his."

The young man's face melted away, leaving behind a blob that pulsed and rotated until it reshaped into a pleasant-faced woman in her mid-forties. She had dirty-blonde hair that was styled in a curly pompadour.

"Carleigh Fran," Dinclinsin announced. "Editor-In-Chief for Jakobiville's largest and most influential paper. She's being railroaded by a man named Ashton Long. He has a recording of her in a meeting. It's related to Dalton Jakobi and more."

Voodoo Lily bit down hard on her own teeth. "I can already guess what she's saying on that recording," she scoffed, folding her arms.

Carleigh's countenance remolded until the face of a cleanshaven, middle-aged white man appeared against the glass. He had a slender head, squared at the brow and chin. His skin wrinkled like old leather, and he had small, beady eyes that gleamed with malice and suspicion. Thin, brown hair covered his head, silver strands sparse throughout.

"Judge Felton Hoyt," Dinclinsin growled. "He's a needleman in the employ of Mayor Sampson Jakobi, and he's a loyal soldier in the courtroom. Judge Felton is outwardly critical of the mayor, but in private, they are good friends. He presided over his son's trial—not in public view—assisting in manufacturing the verdict from behind the scenes. There is more to him, I sense. Expose the judge, and you will weaken the Jakobi hex."

Armand's face twisted perplexed. "I've been told that needlemen are often quiet, right? Even with initiations," he observed. He looked at Voodoo Lily and then to Dinclinsin. "Something's always bothered me about Mayor Sampson's son. Why make noise loud enough to hold a trial, especially when you have such a prominent, political name?" His gaze continued to dart back and forth between Voodoo Lily and the summoned Lwa. His instinct buzzed, and Armand found his answer. "That's sick," he scowled.

Voodoo Lily sighed, agreeing. They were surrounded by macabre, she thought to herself, but she said nothing. There was silence all around. Then Dinclinsin addressed Armand, saying to the young man, "Yes. You understand, boy. It *is* sick."

Armand reached into his vest's interior pocket and withdrew a small bottle of rum. He extended the drink to Dinclinsin. The Lwa snatched the offering from Armand and put it in the pocket of his frock coat.

"We thank you, Dinclinsin," said Voodoo Lily. "We will seek out and expose these guilty devils. Our Biloko will recover the confessions. We'll bring them back for more scrimmages, Sir Dinclinsin. They have real scenarios to prepare for."

Armand became distant, lost in thought. He wished he could be on the frontlines of the expedition. Voodoo Lily sat back and used her power to bring them out of Dinclinsin's realm, returning all three to the alley's entrance. She looked over at Armand, he was frozen in silence.

Horace Georg removed his pipe from his mouth and pointed at

Armand and Voodoo Lily. "Y' c'n lea' them seats th'r," he said. "I know yual got w'rk t' do."

Armand flinched, coming out of his cogitated state. He said to Horace Georg, "Thank you again, warrior-spirit. Enjoy your day; and I apologize for the interruption."

Horace Georg smiled and waved his pipe at Armand. "Stay loud and proud of your fightin', hunter-soldier," he advised with a wink. He told Voodoo Lily to take care, and she replied with a sincere salutation. Then the powerful Crossroads Queen used her pathway conjure to spirit them away. Horace Georg sat back and delighted in the bright day. He remained seated and smoking even when the sun set and the stars and moon came out to play.

Voodoo Lily and Armand wasted no time with their orders to the *Biloko Bunch Four*.

Act one of a three-part play commenced.

Three nights later. There was no fog, and there was very little haze. Out of nowhere came two humanoid, naked shadows. They sprang from a rippling fold of time and space. Interesting in appearance, there were tree leaves sprouting from their arms and legs. One was feminine in shape with a sporty figure to her frame. It was the bald and beautiful Elodie Ellison, now transfigured to her eloko mien. She was *Sandife*, a name anointed on her in a ceremony where she received a stitching to her inner conjure. In her hand was an nkisi doll, which made her an nkisi girl. Creeping swiftly through the night by her side was Andrew Badgerson. He was also transformed, sprouting leaves from his arms and legs, naked without shame. He was *The Black Arum*, a masked eloko, an iboju boy.

Black Arum sprouted thick, vine-like shadows from his body, bridging buildings together for he and Sandife to scurry across. It was only a fraction of his plant-based conjure abilities. He was a dangerous flower, but he hoped things were quiet tonight for the raid at hand. He'd practiced his power through Ogun Tarot, but it had only been for a few days. The scenario he now found himself in with Sandife was given a test run through the illusionary realm called the *digi-glas*. Things didn't go too well. There was constant fighting. A group of men and women called needlemen were everywhere, impossible to move around them, even in silence. Detection was all the time, without fail, which led to failure. Practice, practice, practice. For days, and even hours earlier from now. Black Arum had little rest between run throughs and the real thing, and here he was.

This was real now, but he felt confident. He had needles of his own to give if necessary. He worked out a strategy of attack with Sandife. They had one practice to perfect it, and they did. But again, this was the real thing, and they had little rest between now and the last run through.

Judge Felton Hoyt was the target, but neither the Jakobiville courthouse nor his suburban mansion were the night's mark. Their destination was a luxury apartment building where a guy resided. The judge's guy, because everyone had a guy, and Judge Felton Hoyt's guy was named Graham Higgs. He was a fixer and a needleman captain. It was said he slept with a hexed syringe in the drawer next to him and one tucked under his pillow. He himself had been injected with hex and anathema for the purpose of magnifying an already imposing frame. He was over six feet in height, bald atop his head but decorated with a thick beard the color of ash and smoke. Sandife and Black Arum imagined he would be alert, even when sleep at this late, late hour near early morning. Graham was aware that hexing fog had been dispelled, and benevolent conjure was afoot.

They crossed a bridge of vines straight onto the rooftop of Graham Higgs' apartment complex and straight into a roaming party of three needlemen. The scuffle was a success on the part of the virgin conjure folk, though clumsy in execution and filled with luck as it was. It was more a reflex of fright than a strategic strike on Black Arum's part. He stiffened in the air, limbs out as his body issued a swarm of black, slender needles. Sandife's heart skipped, and she perceived Black Arum's strike to be a part of the maneuver they'd practiced. She jumped forward, leaping past Black Arum as she pursed her lips, posing them as if to whistle. She blew, exhaling a slender, yellow flame that puffed into a fiery cloud blessing Black Arum's needles. His needle swarm transfigured from physical and poisonous magic missiles to a psychic assault.

The salvo of needles found their targets, all three needlemen. The attack was so strong it almost left them permanently comatose. There was enough mental capacity left in them to obey Sandife's commands, but she first had to recover from the intense feedback ringing through her head as she felt the men's minds drain of independent thoughts, memories, and terrible deeds. Sandife sat down on the roof, back against the ledge. Black Arum sat next to her. He had a smile on his face, easily seen as his lips poked through an area of the mask missing its wooden flesh. He looked at the woman and said in a low voice, "It worked!"

Sandife attempted to match his sly grin as she caught her breath. Her lips curled only halfway. She looked up at the three needlemen who were now standing and staring down at them. They waited for her command, eerie glares piercing as half of their faces were covered by surgical masks. Sandife couldn't look away, almost consumed by their presence as their thoughts continued lingering in her head. Sandfie's heart raced as a fright she'd not experienced since childhood crept into her. Boogeymen. Monsters under the bed and closet. Night doctors that would take her away. Old tales from kinfolk talking about the Ku Klux Klan and the descendants of hatred. She looked upon them now, and she could feel the enormity of detestation for her and her newfound conjure.

Black Arum's instincts intercepted Sandife's trepidation, and he put a comforting hand on her shoulder. "We got control of this thing, beautiful woman," he assured her. "We got em." He made a gesture with eyes and head up at the needlemen standing before them.

Sandife turned her head and beamed a full, warm smile at Black Arum. "We do," she acknowledged. The needlemen's thoughts slipped away like water funneling down a drain. Sandife's breath returned and she stood to address her converted soldiers. "Lead us to Mister Higgs," she commanded. When she spoke, shimmering puffs of her cosmic fire emitted from her lips as if she was elegantly blowing smoke from a cigarette.

The needlemen turned. "This way, Madame Sandife," one spoke. All three made a hard pivot, and they led Black Arum and Sandife to a door into the apartment building. They went down several flights of stairs. The three needlemen said in a monotoned unison as they traveled lower and lower into the building, *This door is locked, but the devil doesn't live there...*" Both Black Arum and Sandife's instincts buzzed when the phrase was spoken. Beyond the doors were luxury apartments accessed only by elevator and special fire exits. Down they traveled, and farther still. Sandife wondered how high the building was, or if any hex was being used to confuse reality. She'd heard of such things, but her instinct never presented an alarming buzz.

Farther down. The needlemen stopped at a door and said together, *"This door is locked. The devil slumbers here."* They turned and looked at Black Arum and Sandife. *"Luxury complex,"* their voices echoed. *"Luxury-floor eleven."* They collapsed after speaking, breathing but dead of mind.

Black Arum and Sandife looked at one another. They jumped to the railing and dived below, landing on the next level's rail and nosediving to the next. They appeared as cat's dashing through an alleyway, careening through the twisting staircase's narrow passage. They used newfound higher aspects of their instincts to decipher the correct floor to land on. It was floor thirty. The last floor before the ascent into master, luxury-floor apartments, routing the floor numbers back to one. A special cardkey would be needed before making an ascent up. The thought occurred to Black Arum and Sandife.

"We could go through the window," Black Arum suggested.

Sandife shook her head. "Too much noise," she whispered.

Black Arum had another idea. He opened the door leading into the hallway on the thirtieth floor. He scurried to the corner and pressed his back against the wall, concentrating with his eyes closed and teeth gnashing against one another. Shadowy vines slithered against the walls and stretched toward any mechanical, peeping eye monitoring the scene. The cameras were covered in shadow, and Black Arum and Sandife dashed to the elevator and pushed a button for it to rise. They looked left and right. They figured no one should've appeared from their homes at this time of night, but caution wasn't something they were going to brush aside. They could only imagine what people would think seeing naked beings with black, alien-like eyes and leaves growing out of their earth-brown skin.

The elevator opened. No one was inside, and Black Arum and Sandife were grateful. Black Arum manipulated shadowy vines to smother the eyesight of the camera inside. The door closed, and Black Arum created new shadow vines that snaked through the solid-steel elevator and wrapped around the elevator's mechanics, taking control. Black Arum nodded. "Going up!" he quipped, triumphant. The elevator ascended, and Black Arum's instinct intertwined with his shaded flora, causing the lift to stop at the correct, master floor. The door opened, and both Sandife and Black Arum slipped into the darkness of the grand and luxurious front room.

Graham Higgs' master suite was a palace condensed into a large, open-concept apartment. The spacious living area was filled with ornate columns, plush seating, and beautifully rendered paintings. All the place was missing was elaborate tapestries hanging from its walls with flaming sconces on either side. There was an intricately embroidered, red and gold runner that stretched from the elevator doors to the luxurious front room. Black Arum and Sandife stepped light-of-foot onto the runner, slipping between two, magnificent pillars.

Their instincts droned like an irritating mosquito close to their ears, specifically their left ears. Black Arum turned his head where his instinct directed him. A syringe came down on him, gripped by a needleman. The attack was quick, striking from the dark, but Black Arum's senses could see his assailant as if all the lights in the palatial apartment complex were on and shining to their fullest. Another blessing was that Black Arum's instincts appeared to slow down time, energizing his reaction. Black Arum caught the needleman's forearm, and upon tightening his grip, time returned to speed. His next instinct was to slam a fist twice across his attacker's cheek. While Black Arum's punches were hard and knocked the needleman off balance, resolve mixed with hex kept the man on his feet.

The needleman, stepped back, taking himself out of Black Arum's grip. He gained stance and made a riposte, swiping his syringe at Black Arum's midsection. The masked eloko's instinct only slowed the assault against him by a little. He managed to jump back, arcing his body and tucking in his stomach. The needle's tip only cut air, barely missing his abdomen. Instinct took over from there, and Black Arum felt as if he was a puppet connected to strings. He jumped, swung and threw kicks that landed, barreling his opponent back. He dodged and countered, feeling a little disembodied. He hadn't been in fights since middle school, and he managed to avoid them in the rough arena of high school. But instinct bestowed him with moves he'd only seen pulled off in martial arts movies and video games. The needleman wasn't fazed, which was dazzling. He blocked and parried, and every hit landed on him wasn't a finishing blow. Hex kept him strong.

With instinct maneuvering Black Arum's movements, a realization of offensive power dampened. Sandife fared much the same against her needlewoman opponent who assailed her with syringes in the clutches of either hand. Both women moved with a dancer's finesse, crouched low and pouncing high like cats. Never had Sandife moved like this, stretching limbs in either direction for extended reach with kicks and punches. Her body never felt more limber, even at the height of her days in track and field. But her skilled adversary matched her move-to-move in blocking, and the hits Sandife landed seemed to only antagonize the needlewoman further.

The apartment's lights shined bright, temporarily blinding all in fray. Six more needlemen and Graham Higgs joined the fight. Sandife found herself overwhelmed, and the scenario of failure conjured up by the *digi-glas* trials looked inevitable. Until eloko conjure woman and eloko conjure man remembered the unique powers they possessed.

Black Arum continued sparring with his initial needleman along with a second needleman and a needlewoman. He managed to spiral around their efforts to encircle him, but at every turn he saw an assaulting opponent. Every twist away from one enemy turned into a close-call endeavor with another. Then it occurred to Black Arum there was more to conjure than simply a higher instinct. He sprouted a series of shadow vines from his person, wrapping his attackers in his twisted and shaded verdure. The needleman and needlewoman were subdued arms, legs, and mouths wrapped up in cosmic vines. His final attacker, pouncing from behind, was filled with a swarm of needles issued from Black Arum's upper back and shoulders. The needleman crashed to the floor as the needles liquified and filled his bloodstream, causing a pain so immense he simply passed out before he could even scream.

A hard punch across the face from Graham Higgs hindered any celebration. Before Black Arum could recover, the needleman-fixer was slamming his body into him like a raging bull. The blow tossed Black Arum across the room and into one of the pillars near the elevator. He smacked against the floor, limbs spread out. He curled up, groaning. Graham Higgs made his approach, two needles out, thumbs on the plungers.

Sandife was surrounded. Her instinct calculated Black Arum's circumstances, motivating her to recall her personal conjure as a part of her arsenal. A needleman lunged at her! Sandife dodged his leap with ease. The engagement setup her gambit as he recovered and jumped in front of her. Sandife's other two opponents flanked him, and with them lined up as they encroached, Sandife inhaled and conjured the psychic fire from her lungs.

She blew out and spewed a dazzling ball of flames that set all three syringe-wielder's heads ablaze.

Nothing physical was smoldered, but their independent thoughts went up in cinders. She pointed her finger and gave command to attack Graham Higgs. Heads still ablaze, her converts turned and rushed the burly needleman, tackling him before he could stab Black Arum with hex from his syringes.

Graham Higgs' might was impressive. He tossed the defected needlemen aside as if they weighed nothing, but conjured needles foreign to him stung his body, and a psychic fire cooled the hex amplifying his strength. He dropped to the floor. Pride stung more than Black Arum's needles. It fueled him to make effort to jump back into a fight. Balancing himself on his forearms, he attempted to stand. While on one knee, he saw the shadows of Sandife and Black Arum cast over him. He looked up at them with contempt.

Sandife snarled, "We expected your trial to be more difficult. It's disappointing to see you take a knee so easily."

"This isn't a forfeit, little missy," Graham told her, trying to regain strength.

"It might as well be," she said, taking a deep breath and breathing psychic fire into his face. He didn't scream. His autonomy was quickly burned away, and when the flames diminished, his posture was indeed submissive. "Now, give us everything you have on Judge Felton Hoyt."

Graham Higgs didn't fight back. There was no resistance. He yielded, "Yes, Madame Sandife…"

Act one was concluded. A vault was opened, and numerous notes and thumb drives were uncovered by Sandife and Black Arum. The spoils of war were secured. They returned to where their night began, and a doorway manipulating time and space consumed them. The Water Bug Hollow church was where their adventure ended.

Act two opened up on a Bayou setting. The atmosphere was different from the Jakobiville skyline. Here, there hung a thick atmosphere of moisture in the night air. It was otherworldly, but it wasn't unnatural. The epicenter of mugginess came from the preternatural ripple where sprang forth two eloko spirits creeping between the tree branches. Their silhouettes pranced between the shadows, sprinting along tree limbs masked by the thick, dangling Spanish moss.

John and Myèl were no strangers to the felonious game of sneak and snatch. Now as lithesome spirits, their furtive schemes and skills were virtuous. They whisked their way through the trees with graceful movements that blended in with the faint sway of branches.

Spanish moss was not the only mask worn. John Morgan was equipped with the African mask carved and blessed by Madame Simaetha.

He was now *Gizo*, the eloko spirit. Bald and with earth-brown skin, leaves sprouting from his limbs. His sweetheart, Myèl was the same, though she wore no mask. Her nkisi doll dangled from a wrap of leaves around her waist that acted as a sash. She didn't mind the absence of her braids or the golden luster to her naturally amber skin tone. Her eloko form was freeing.

They were both as naked as nature. Free and out in the open, the air didn't bother them, whether cool or heavy with humidity. They played with their acrobatics as they drew closer to their destination. Flips and twists into the air, backwards and onto branches extending from trees in front of them. Gizo and Myèl giggled as if the difficulties of their task were not just a few yards ahead. They darted into the thick of a moss-covered tree, peering down at the illicit affair below.

Only two were gathered in the name of duplicity, and a tithe was being paid.

Myèl and Gizo's eyes were as one, and they spied Carleigh Fran dressed-to-cliché in a tan overcoat wrapped around her frame, collar up no less. She approached her contact, a man named Ashton Long. He was of average height and build with brown hair and a cleanshaven face, dressed in jeans and a cheap, worn sports jacket. He had his hands in his pockets, and he looked jittery.

"Bad time to quit smoking, hey?" Carleigh joked, her mid-western accent coming through. "I should be the one nervous," she commented, leaning close to Ashton and putting her face close to his. "You got *me* jammed up. I'm at your command, little whelp."

"I'm not trying to be a bad guy, Carleigh," Ashton said, stuttering on his words as if he suffered from a chill. He sniffed and said, "I just need assurance that I'm in at your paper, seated in a good position, making good money—which includes the money you have for me tonight."

"You're in," Carleigh assured in a cool manner.

Ashton relaxed, if only by a little. He said to Carleigh, "I wasn't getting anywhere over at the Jakobiville Inquiry. Berger doesn't know how to run a press. I was putting out quality stories. I was keeping his paper in print."

"People did buy just to read your stuff," Carleigh yielded with a smile. "Shit, you could put digital publishing in danger. You're that good, Ashton. I had my eye on you, ready to poach. When we had our meeting in my office, I thought I had something. It begs the question: Why not move on from the paper? Do something big in a place like New York or Chicago."

"This is closer to home," Ashton answered with a sharp tone. "I'm a small-town boy," he told Carleigh as he looked around, head moving, eyes darting. "I decided to put my information to good use, make something out of it. Not giving it to Berger is a 'fuck you' to him."

Carleigh kept her grin, watching Ashton fidget.

He put his gaze back on Carleigh and asked her, "You have the money with you?"

"I do," she replied. She stayed silent for a moment, and then she asked, "Who's the leak?"

Ashton made a face, shrugging his shoulders. "Look, I can't hand over that information," he said in an apologetic voice. "I can give you a copy of the recording as proof. You've heard it already, but…"

Carleigh understood. "Politics is a strange game, Ashton. A dangerous one too," she emphasized. "I run a newspaper that keeps things in balance. I'd like to know who has a guilty conscious about that. It's a tight and loyal ship. Or, so I assume." Ashton said nothing. "I know the meeting you have recorded. I remember the people in that room. The suspects are few, but I know they're not—"

"I bugged your office," Ashton admitted. "Everyone had their suspicions of your paper, its favorable leaning toward the mayor. I wanted the story at first. I thought I was just going to hear about his son's troubles. There was so much more said. I liked what I heard, but not in a journalistic way. I decided I wanted in, the security of it all."

Carleigh beamed at Ashton, admiring him. "I have your money," she said. She reached into her trench coat pocket, and then she made an attack. It was swift. No human eye could've caught the motion. A quick swing, drawing out a syringe that she sank into Ashton's unprotected neck. She thumbed the plunger, and filled Ashton's body with hex, putting him to sleep. He slumped against the bayou's muddy surface, and out of the darkness stepped three, masked needlemen.

Carleigh knelt down and checked Ashton's vitals. The needlemen surrounded her, waiting for command. "He's alive," she informed them. "Take him home. Erase all evidence he has on that meeting. Take as long as you want. This hex will keep him asleep until he's not. When he wakes, he won't remember any of this, and his ambitions will take him up to Chicago. Damn shame," she cursed, pushing her hands into his pockets. "He is one helluva reporter."

"You could make him one of us," a needleman suggested.

"Nah," Carleigh disagreed. She pulled out the thumb drive and held it close to her face, eyes locked to it. "He doesn't have the stomach for the bigger picture, and he's too squeamish for a blood sacrifice." She looked up at the needleman who addressed her, telling him, "I admire the fact he stooped to this level."

Carleigh turned backed to the thumb drive held between thumb and finger. It was then that something made of glass smacked her hand. It was spherical, and broke on impact. From the burst came a puff of white smoke and a network of fine, sticky thread like that of a spider's webbing. The thumb drive slipped from her hold, and Carleigh found her hand bound to her face by a gooey fixative.

"Behold!" Myèl announced as she dived to the swampy ground. "The Spheres of Influence!" The needleman readied themselves, syringes gripped like daggers. Myèl summoned two glass spheres in the palm of her hands and slammed them to the ground. They broke, even against the marshy floor, and great swarms of golden-glowing bees buzzed free. Most attacked the needlemen, who took off running from the conjured, insectoid will-o'-the-wisp. Two golden bees zipped away from the swarm and snatched the thumb drive from the ground, delivering the gadget to Myèl.

Gizo tracked the fleeing needlemen from above, dashing through the trees on all fours. The whirling and buzzing bees hastened behind the surgical-masked men only to run them away. Gizo dived down, conjuring and tossing glass spheres at the escaping needlemen. The spheres broke, and puffs of gray smoke and webbing wrapped around their bodies. They slammed against the ground, heavily cocooned in Gizo's Anansi webbing. The bees made a sharp turn and redirected their flight back to Myèl. Gizo jumped up into the trees and used the branches as pathways, returning to Myèl. He dropped down next to her, witnessing her bees shimmering away into the ethers.

Seven bees remained behind. Four stung Ashton on the back of his neck. The puncture was curative, but it would've hurt had he been conscious, especially added to the burning sensation that coursed through his body, dissolving the infectious hex needled into him earlier.

Carleigh received painful pricks from the remaining three bees. Her hand, webbed to her face, muffled her cries. Her screaming was for only a moment before falling unconscious. Ashton woke when Carleigh lay sprawled out on her back. He rose, a feeling of euphoria easing any anxiety in him. The bees dissolved away, and he glimpsed a second of their existence. He smiled and exclaimed in a child-like manner, *"Will 'o' the wisps! Wooo!"* Then they were gone, and Myèl and Gizo stood on either side of him. He looked at one. He looked at the other. "Who're you groovy kids? You like freaks or something…?" He looked them up and down. They were naked.

"We're Bayou spirits, Mister Long," Myèl answered.

"You like being naked at night?" he asked.

"It's freeing," Myèl replied. "We'd like to ask you for all the recordings you have of Miss Fran and that infamous meeting of hers."

"Oh, sure," he told Myèl in a cooperative tone. "You guys gonna expose her?" he inquired. "She said some bad things about Water Bug Hollow, what the paper does to keep a narrative over it. I mean, it can be a rough place, but they purposefully keep it bad in their press. She said they report crimes different when they come from the Hollow. You should hear it. She gives examples about how they frame a story of a kid in Jakobiville who murders someone against how they report a murder in Water Bug Hollow. Any crime, really," he added. "The biggest one is how they helped steer the public to believe Mayor Sampson's kid was innocent of that heinous crime. He did it! Yes, he did. Won't ever catch him, though. That boy ain't right, killin' that woman and her child and all…"

"We can imagine," said Gizo.

"No, you can't. It's different when you hear it. It's sinister. It's like listening to witches and warlocks devising a spell to cast."

Myèl and Gizo looked at one another.

"Come on," Ashton signaled. "Let's go to my cat."

"Your cat?" questioned Gizo.

"My car!" Ashton corrected. "Did I say 'cat'? Didn't mean to. Car. Car. It's just up the way." He inspected Gizo close. "That's a funky mask, bro… So weird…" He perked up and asked, "Can I tell people about this?"

"You won't remember it," Myèl stated matter-of-factly. "None of this. Your recordings, your blackmail."

"Blackmail?" Ashton flinched. He turned, ready to walk away. He noticed Carleigh's body on the ground. "Oh, shit! Is that Miss Fran? What the hell is on her face? Can she breathe?"

"She'll be fine," Gizo assured. "She tried to silence you. We were here to help."

Ashton became excited. "Oh! Like superheroes? Wow!"

"We came for the recordings, Ashton," Myèl said, breaking into Ashton's wide-eyed delight. "Please take us to the other copies."

Ashton relaxed. "Yeah. Yeah. To my car. Not my cat. Right this way…"

He continued talking and talking, asking questions, and running his mouth from the Bayou to his apartment. He was apologetic after a few questions, saying to Myèl and Gizo, "Sorry for the questions. That's kind of my job as a journalist…" Myèl and Gizo secured the other copies of the recording, and Ashton drifted to sleep. Gizo carried him to bed, and then the two spirits whisked away into the night, fleeing through Ashton's window. They returned to the area where they'd mystically entered the bayou. The same fold of space and time occurred, and they stepped inside, instantly taken to the Church of Water Bug Hollow.

Myèl and Gizo were content with their latest sneak and snatch, and Gizo exclaimed, "What a wonderful *Medieval Monday* we've performed!"

Ashton would remember nothing in the morning.

With broken pride, Carleigh woke frustrated and nervous about her failure. The needlemen shared the same anxious sentiment.

37

Mayor Sampson Jakobi sat still at his desk in his study. The sun, shaded by dark curtains, was prevented from making an entrance. He didn't want any light to shine. He needed to be invisible to the world, including any celestial body observing from above. His insides vibrated with anxiety. His heart attempted to out-pace his internal, nervous tremors as his eyes locked onto the phone resting in front of him. He'd placed a call, and it was reaching out and ringing on the other end. It felt like an eternity between each digital pulse. The person on the other end was taking his time picking up. In that time, the internal, skittish rattle Mayor Jakobi experienced infected his leg, and it started bouncing under the desk. It continued until Stanley Fallows answered the phone.

"Good morning, Mayor," Stanley greeted, speaker booming crisp with his voice. He sounded sluggish as if he'd come from sleep.

Sampson's mouth trembled when he asked, "Did I wake you, Stanley?"

"No, Mister Mayor," Stanley assured. "I'm recovering from a consistent regiment of rituals being performed on me. How are things on your end?"

A laptop was opened on his desk. A morning paper was there too. His eyes observed the headlines. Both digital and print media were ablaze with articles exposing corruption in Jakobiville. Each word felt like citizens holding pitchforks and torches, calling for the head of Mayor Sampson Jakobi, though he wasn't named specifically.

"You haven't heard?" the Mayor inquired. "The news hasn't stayed local. There's a bit of a wildfire here. It's gone national with every rookie and seasoned-veteran journalist willing to fan the flames, keep the blaze strong."

"No," responded Stanley. "I haven't seen, but I know. What's our problem, Sampson?" Stanley inquired. "Because I'm sure it will become *our* problem. My faculty to spy on fate's web is faint because I'm preparing for the time my mother gave me, Mayor Sampson. But I can pluck the tone of your voice and feel the silk, cosmic strands of fate vibrating in a frequency that tells me trouble has swathed your triumvirate. Judge. Narrative manipulator. Son."

The rising annoyance in Stanley's voice was what Sampson needed to make him sit straight and even oust his jittery nerves. "It's already *our* problem, Stanley—before the headlines," he snapped with an ugly, twisted expression on his face. "Look, they got Felton jammed up something good. The evidence is notes, a journal. Meetings were taped. It doesn't look good for him."

Stanley was silent for a moment. Then he chimed in, "I'm looking at an article now. All this sounds serious." Then Stanley listed, "Fixing cases along community demographics, which in turn, fixes them along other demographics. Offenders in Water Bug Hollow seeing harsher sentences than—" Stanley chuckled a bit, a devil's snicker. "—more wealthy areas of Jakobiville," he finished. He scanned more and then responded, "His nickname 'The Noose' spoken of. It says here that in a recording he declared a state of insurrection on outsiders, working on creating what felt like modern-day sundown towns. He appeared so squeaky clean too. No, it doesn't look good for him."

Sampson sighed. "Water Bug Hollow is at the center of all this, and therefore, so am I."

"Look at what we have here," Stanley teased as he came across another intriguing story with Jakobiville and Water Bug Hollow in focus. "Miss Carleigh Fran. Tsk, tsk, tsk," Stanley continued poking fun. But this story upset him, as it was another victory for conjure folk dispelling hexes in Water Bug Hollow. "How could she have been so stupid, Sampson? A recording? The hexes she put into print and digital—controlling the narrative of Water Bug Hollow…" his voice trailed away, and Sampson could sense Stanley's weakened, ritual-worn state was overtaking him. He listened close as Stanley caught his breath. The mayor's eyebrow raised, and he wondered if the beast had gone too far in seeking a cure to the conjure folk equation. "Water Bug Hollow is a kingdom my mother dedicated a great stock of her prowess in keeping sterile. She resurrected your struggling, limping bloodline, Sampson, and rested in your family's hands the keys to oversee that kingdom. Do you understand that? Keys. *Not* a crown. The diadem is reserved for me, as are many heavy things—*responsibilities*—weighing on my head and shoulders." Stanley sighed. "My mother had Curly. Look what I got." He again released a heavy exhale. "My lineage gives me right over the Kolonists. That's why those pricks do their best to keep me at arm's length. Well, I won't seek their approval anymore. Sometimes a new party needs to be created. A family, perhaps."

Sampson guessed Stanley was looking for an explosive, delighted response. The mayor remained silent, taking a drink. Then he said, "I have my concerns."

"Why?" Stanley hissed back. "That time and age my mother gave me is almost upon us. The Kolonists will slink as cowards with what I'm going to achieve. I will create Wonderland in all its humdrum."

"It's not that, Stanley," Sampson said, worry in his voice. "Felton helped with trafficking. He had notes on what we were doing. Them jungle conjure folk we experimented on, drugged and pimped out to The Line, The

Cancer Kings, and the Kolonists Kings. The little boys and little girls. The men and the women. Every name. The burning to ash and smoking them, seasoning our food with them. Those jungle spirits got a hold of it. That's absent from every article I've read, but I can understand. I'm sure they want to handle that personally." He cleared his throat. "Also, my son's case," he continued. "Carleigh spoke on that in the recording. What was handed over, the recording the press received, it was edited. There's no mention of my son." He paused, but he wasn't finished. Stanley could sense that, and so he didn't interject. "Dalton had visitors two nights ago. Same night as Carleigh and Higgs. This was all very coordinated. The description of his visitors was quite different from the very unique jungle spirits that Carleigh and Higgs tussled with."

"Unique?" Stanley question. "What's unique, Sampson? Describe it for me."

Sampson couldn't quite believe it himself, as he recalled in his head the eloko descriptions, even with all the phenomenon he'd been exposed to in his life. "Carleigh and Higgs said they were like living trees," Sampson reported. "Carleigh didn't see much. It was night. She said they were more like shadowy extensions of the bayou trees. The needlemen with her corroborate Higgs' experience. It was Graham who told me, though. Heard they had leaves growing from them. They were bald, naked. Skin wasn't like bark. I asked. But it had this smooth, brown look to it. Graham fought them. He almost had the upper hand, but, you know these jungle folk."

"Your son?" Stanley inquired.

"These two were human enough," he told Stanley. "Sounds like rumors I've heard recently. When the fog disappeared. One had an African mask. A man." He took time to note, "Seems like the male-folk like wearing such things. The jungle trees had the same for the men. He said the female was seated in a chair. A shadow veiled her face. It was late at night. His apartment."

It sounded like steel being bent in the jaws of a mechanical monster. The noise came on so sudden that it made Dalton Jakobi lift his body from the desk, having dozed off while engaged in work for his father. Even a curse had its blessing, and what ran in Dalton Jakobi's veins gave him insight in deciphering the discordance's origin, and that its cause was an otherworldly conjuring. He opened his drawer and grabbed his hex-tipped syringe. He stood and made cautious steps out of his office and to his apartment's front room.

Something strange stared back at him when he entered. Three somethings, to be exact. The first was simply the scene itself. Then there were the two components that made up the peculiarity. First, a tall and lean, wild-haired black man dressed in black pants that belled out at the base, a white tunic, and a black vest. Dalton didn't know what was more curious about him. His style of clothes? Perhaps. There was also the African mask covering his face. That should have been the apex of the intrigue that adorned him. But there was also the matter of his necklace. It was a macabre bauble decorated with three skulls, each the size of a balled fist. There was a preternatural glow to them, an eerie shimmer of their three colors. Red. Black. Green.

The second oddity was a woman seated in a strangely carved, wooden chair. Dalton guessed it was her throne. Crowned heads with African features and knotted hair were carved at the ends of the arms and on either side of the back of the chair. She was regal in her presence. Her face was cloaked in a shadow, even when Dalton flipped on the lights, taking heedful steps into the room.

She spoke, "We believe you have a confession to make, Dalton."

The man next to her struck! A quick grab of the black skull off its chain. A translucent copy occupied his hand, but the physical and glowing black skull remained fastened to the chain running through it. He tossed it with a simple flick of his hand, and it traveled quicker than Dalton could react. It crashed against his face, feeling like a warm, moist towel wrapping around his head. The impact knocked him back, and he stumbled for a moment. When he recovered, he realized that his syringe had been dropped, but it didn't matter at that point. Dalton Jakobi wasn't in a position to fight back.

"We need your journal, Dalton," the woman said to him in a kind tone. "There is something terrible confessed in that demonic tome you keep."

Dalton obliged. He went to his room and retrieved his journal for the conjure woman. It was on the nightstand next to his bed, not even hidden. He presented it to her, and she accepted his offering. She thumbed through it until she came across the entry she needed. The day I killed that woman and her child is so sacred to me. I have a needle now. I have a purpose. *That's all she cared to read. She told Dalton, "We'll be back for you, Dalton, and when we return, your father's power won't be able to protect you."*

Then they were gone, leaving Dalton with a clear memory of everything that transpired. He lived to tell the tale, and he never went to sleep that night.

"You wanted to boast some kind of power, Sampson," Stanley growled at him. "You *insisted* that your son's blood ritual be very public. You *insisted* he be caught. You *insisted* to show the world that no one could touch you or your family. Was that to show the Kolonists you had what it takes to be King of Kings? You're owned by the Fallows estate. *I* insist you *never* forget that. Your pride put you in this position, Sampson. I can forgive your brother, Wyatt's, idiocy for being caught and giving up the location of my garden where my precious flowers were kept. I attempted to bend that setback to my fortunes, drawing out the Lilac Flame. As such, if I can keep the conjure folk of Fable Avenue distracted from my greater purpose, or under the belief that being absent of all the blood I need hinders my progress, well that's fine. I have plans for another attempt at the missing essence. It's more than my pride at stake. And, as long as they're distracted, I can further my good work."

Sampson's eyes scratched the face of his cell phone. He gnashed his teeth and wished that Stanley felt his grating expression scraping and cutting deep along his back. Sampson wished his malefactor death in that moment. Then he reconsidered quickly. That would leave him vulnerable. There would be a short-term profit in the eyes of the Kolonist Kings. He didn't have the might to deal with the conjure folk, and Stanley's work could grant him eternal life.

"I'm sending Willie down to help you with your problems," Stanley notified. "Your needles are spread too thin in law enforcement, not strong enough in other areas. It would only cause more of a stir." There was a pause. Stanley waited for an answer. Sampson was too stubborn to give one. Stanley filled the silent void by iterating, "Be very careful, Mister Mayor. The strength of the fist that's ready to rise is like nothing our myths have prepared us for. You were tasked to keep an area in fog. That fog has been lifted by a very conscious, conjure community. Once they feed the foggy-headed people, they'll indoctrinate them. That is a danger."

"I'm aware, Stanley," the mayor assured with an annoyed tone in his voice.

"Are you? Then answer me this one question. Who are the most powerful practitioners in the conjure community, Mister Mayor?" The mayor didn't answer. He knew whatever he said would probably be wrong. Stanley noted, "I'll take your silence as ignorance—an ironically smart move on your part, Sampson." Then he informed the mayor, "Don't be fooled. The most powerful practitioners in this conjure community are the electricians, the plumbers, and the carpenters. It's the tradesmen who can pass on their knowledge and help a community thrive. Most importantly, they can separate themselves from their dependence on your political power—financially and socially. So, I say again. Beware. The fog has lifted."

Lesson learned, and point taken.

"Yes, Stanley…" Sampson conceded.

"Mister Mayor, good day."

The conversation was over. Sampson closed his phone and did nothing more except drink until the weight on him felt light. His wife entered. Harper Jakobi. She was still in her nightgown, and she was a shimmer of brightness in Sampson's mood. "Why are you in here all in the dark?" she made a fuss, going behind his desk and opening the shades wide. The room was flooded with the new day's light. Sampson winced with the sun's bright intrusion. Harper took a seat opposite her husband. She saw the phone on the desk and asked, "You spoke to that son of a bitch?"

Sampson looked at his wife. The liquor swimming in his head gave him the strength to smile, and Harper observed the drunken, sleepy look in his eyes. "I did," he answered her through his inebriated grin. "And he is a son of a bitch, my dear." He played mechanically with his now empty glass, twirling it slowly. His eyes focused on the glass. "He don't understand, Harper!" he huffed, making a face. "He just don't!" He looked up at his wife and said to her, "His mamma resurrected our family, our legacy, because she didn't really believe in her son. He was a dimwit. He was all into music and all about himself. He ain't changed worth-a-damn-hell on his pride!"

Harper looked at her husband, eyes never wavering. She believed in him, so she believed in what he was saying.

"He needs you, Sampson," Harper told him. "He needs your help because you are so important in all this. Don't worry about these setbacks. Jakobiville needs you, too. No one's calling for your head, Mayor Jakobi. They want answers to the new problems you are so capable of dealing with."

Mayor Sampson's smile widened. "I suppose so, my darling."

Harper asked, "Do you need to let off some steam, Mister Mayor?"

"Of course," he responded, smile becoming more devilish.

"Should I wear the red wig and let you call me 'Sarinda'?"

"Of course," he responded, devilish grin at its full length.

38

July. Middle of the month. It should've been hotter in Water Bug Hollow but incants made it otherwise. The night was too special for there to be any discomfort. The thick, hexed fog that kept the area at boiling tensions had been fully dispersed. Gordon Goodspeed, shouldered tightly between his brother Cedron and best friend Benjamin Brickhouse, was part of a dense crowd packed in front of the reconstructed juke joint named Eve's Hallow. They stood at the foot of a stage positioned at the fore of the gaming establishment's entrance.

They waited. The festivities were moments away from a soft opening on a Thursday night. Gordon pondered on how the barrelhouse wore many faces, some very similar. It was first erected as an oppressive, governing seat, an ominous yet palatial plantation mansion that loomed wide and tall over the enslaved African descendants that tilled the fields and were the helping hands inside the manor. The enslaved harvested a healthy income for the Jakobi family.

It then became a fortress of sorts. A bastion for strategy against an army of enslaved Africans staging an uprising. It failed in this manner, and the Jakobi patriarchs and matriarchs and their children were killed. A deed that was looked upon by the enslaved African descendants as a 'deed that must be done'. The road paved in blood was manufactured by a long war that paralleled the civil strife plaguing the American nation, stirred with similar politics. Much like the country, time of enlightenment and reconstruction followed.

The new era saw the mansion become a benevolent place for directives that guide the region into a bustling hamlet named Water Bug Hollow. It would be a place for the African-American survivors of the plantation war, and a sanctuary for former slaves to start a new life in the final days, and in the aftermath of, the American Civil War.

Raucous celebrations occurred yearly, honoring the last battle in the plantation war. The manor became the legendary jumping spot denominated as Eve's Hallow. It nurtured boisterous jazz, served succulent dishes of soul food, and housed refer and tobacco smoke-filled backrooms where gambling and whoring took place. Sharp dressed, wide-brimmed, fedora-wearing pugilists and gun-toting fortune hunters prowled the grounds on the hunt for a monetary score with a dice roll or a winning card hand. The much sought-after score included a hit on a puff of smoke, or long-lashed, eye-batting woman with a short-tail skirt and a sway of her hourglass figure. Anything pretty was also packing, a gun tucked away in a fancy purse, clipped high on the thigh or low at the ankle.

A conjure had come to Water Bug Hollow, and so did walk in a hex, sporting blood-red hair and wearing a tight-fitting dress over a voluptuous frame. Her wickedness sought to shut down any potential Water Bug Hollow had of regaining a conscious understanding of ancient conjure. Stealing birthrights wasn't her only aim. Outlying cousins of the Jakobi clan acted as buried secrets ready to be cultivated weeds, returning close to a century later as a chokehold for the descendants of the rebellious Africans that dared to fight and kill their enslavers. The red-headed tregetour, using the crafty tricks she juggled, made sure to steer the neo-Jakobi bloodline into Water Bug Hollow's path. They would become the political dynasty that ruled over Water Bug Hollow, incorporating it into the larger municipality of Jakobiville.

Gordon stared up at the newly designed gambling den and pondered more on the post-war glory days. *What times!* he thought to himself. While there was no consciousness of conjure to defend Water Bug Hollow from the red-headed harpy's tricks, magic was present to protect. It was within those renown days that a remarkable jazz songstress named Theresa Amat, called Mama Indigo, fortuned a telling with her last breath after she gave birth to a daughter that would continue her chanteuse lineage. That fortune told inked his destiny decades before he was born. She said, *"Dooley is a lilac flame, fluttering and flickering and shooting up into the sky where I see three moons reside. Red. Black. Green. There are golden halos surrounding them and they beam a kiss. Ah, procure this grand conjure and wish."*

Gordon looked up at the starry sky. He heard their harmonics and thought of his sweetheart Fey Forrester. Theresa Amat didn't speak of the cobalt-blue spirit that Fey would transfigure into, though Gordon certainly learned later what manner of activity articulated Fey's role into the world. An O-Jewel Queen, at the peak of ecstasy, would holler Fey's augury. She and her husband frolicked drunk and naked and together, much like Gordon desired when it came to his sweetheart-lost-to-time.

Soon, he considered as he put his eyes on the present-day O-Jewel king and queen.

Armand Gideon and Lilian Eledas-Ghedemere, hand-in-hand, stepped out onto Eve's Hallow's center balcony. They peered down at the gathered conjure folk, an assembled flock from around the world, representatives from other communities. Also gathered were Water Bug Hollow natives, many of them unaware of conjure or the rituals done to relieve hex and gang violence. The effects were felt, and a heavy sigh was exhaled over the last few weeks. Everyone anticipated the re-opening of Eve's Hallow. Police and news coverage were in attendance. With recent news of exposed corruption on both the media and within the law, many were suspicious of their presence.

Voodoo Lily, dressed like a royal fortune teller, greeted the large audience with a pleasant, bright smile. "Hello, Water Bug Hollow," she addressed. "And welcome to the grand re-opening of a magnificent landmark!" Her voice was loud, clear, and it soothed the onlookers. Behind Gordon stood Voodoo Lily's father, Satchel "Old Goon" Eledas. Next to the old, old, man was Voodoo Lily's mother, Simaetha Ghedemere. Gordon didn't have to turn around to know the pair wore a proud-parental smile for their daughter. He could feel it against his neck, but that was probably instinct.

Next to the delighted parents were people associated with Satchel "Old Goon". They were from the Gwuinee family, the second-oldest community of conjure folk. They were the law, and they held edict over conjure affairs in the Americas and the Caribbean. Their presence among the other conjure communities was as nerve-wracking as the police and the media. They could be strict about the performance of conjure among normal folk, even with Fable Avenue.

Their visit was always in pairs, a man and a woman. The man, an older gentleman in his late forties, was named Terrence Tzidkiyahu. The 'T' in his surname was silent. He was tall with dark-brown skin and a thick mustache hogging all the space between his lip and nose. He'd flown in four days prior with the woman next to him, and there was never a time when he wasn't always decked out in white slacks, white shoes, and a wide-brimmed hat the same color. A red, collar shirt with a black tie were the two items of clothing that went off the color script. Terrence's family had their hands in every legal and illegal game hall owned by conjure folk. The Tzidkiyahu family claimed to be direct descendants of the *Zé Pilintra* spirit and energy, and so dressed appropriately. It was said their founding patriarch was formed through the roll of the dice and the turn of a royal straight flush—spades, no less. No hearts, all *malandros*.

Terrence had his metaphorical sights set on two things. First, there was his family's percentage of Eve's Hallow. Second, he fancied a game with Water Bug Hollow's converted gang leaders. Cedron wanted in on the sport, a hunt for a precious item of Terrence's choosing. But Terrence's recreation was for initiates to conjure, and therefore Cedron had no place in it.

Next to Terrence was Naamah Mbu, a woman in her mid-thirties whom many considered the gavel for the judges among the Gwuinee folk. While most of the Gwuinee had ties to conjure sects in the Caribbean, Naamah's father was a bridge to Africa. He was connected to a conjure faction that worked diligently to study all manner of spiritual phrase written and uttered to decipher any blessing or hex locked in its syllables. Papa

Solomon and the matriarchs often butted heads with her family. With the emergence of he and Fey as lilac flame and cobalt-blue spirit, Fable Avenue had leverage to see undisclosed, decoded sacred scripts. Lady Arachne believed Fable Avenue could do without them. She had faith in her ancient cards to find much-sought answers.

Armand spoke, recounting the history of Water Bug Hollow, amending to it the area's decline into drugs and gang violence. He declared the reconstruction of Eve's Hallow was an event that marked a new day.

"The neighborhood's love for itself shows this can be done without political interference, requested or otherwise. *We* reduced the problems marring this sacred area—this *historic* region!" he proclaimed. "*We* uncovered the buried and hexed bones of innocents slain. *We* gave blessing to the burdens injected into the marrow, and we scattered the fog straining the downtrodden existence in Water Bug Hollow." Armand shook his head and articulated, "We are a *nasyon!* We are *nachon!* Nothing can sully this moment. Not the bias narratives of the media in attendance—" the crowd roared with a triumphant *hurrah*. "—Or the presence of men in badges equipped with needles."

The citizens of Water Bug Hollow were aware that Armand was addressing the police overseeing the celebration, but the mention of needles was lost on them. Conjure folk found the statement too bold, but it did draw applause from many among them. Savannah Forrester remained arms folded, however, a single eyebrow arched. Her face bent in scowl as she watched her grandson make his statement. Her ire mingled with the unshakable discomfort of knowing this would be a big story. It would reach her daughter's eyes and ears, and she would have some explaining to do when it came to her son's direction.

Savannah exhaled a soft sigh thinking of it all.

At the same moment. Gordon looked over his shoulder to see Terrence and Naamah's reactions to Armand's words. There was nothing to decipher from their expressions, and he didn't use any instinct to pry. The two just watched stoned faced like judges not wanting to appear too emotionally involved. It was all business, so it seemed.

Gordon put his eyes on Satchel "Old Goon". The old, old man was doing the same as him, peering in Terrence and Naamah's direction to glimpse a response from the Gwuinee representatives. He held an awkward smile, waiting patiently. But Terrence and Naamah never looked at him. He stared for a long time, too.

Nothing.

Gordon put his eyes back on Armand just as he shouted in a declarative rhythm, "This is Water Bug Hollow!"

"Hollow! Hollow!" repeated a collective of unseen persons.

There was a percussive resonance that followed the chorus, and Armand announced again, "This is Water Bug Hollow!"

"*Hollow! Hollow!*" the ensemble led the refrain.

Another heavy drumbeat filled the air like a cannon round set off. Eve's Hallow's doors swung open, and a mob of people rushed from the entrance to the stage. The first explosive march was of a battalion of barefoot men dressed in white hoodies and baggy jeans. Hoods up, their faces were veiled under masks fashioned from cloth and decorated with a sketched image of the crossroads. They jumped into a stage-stomping, African dance that rattled the platform. They flipped and spun and performed gyrating acrobatics with sharp grace.

Gordon's eyes flickered with a bright, lilac pulse. He saw something. There were faint, ghostly figures that moved in synch with the dancing men. The tall, wiry shadows were unmistakable in their smoky frames. *Inawo.* They acted as marionettists, controlling the movements of the men they danced behind. The second wave of performers were the same. Women clothed in full-length flower skirts and ruffled shirts, veiled the same as the men were masked. Each one, barefoot and light on their feet with *inawo* coordinating their movements. In rhythm with their burdens.

They chanted, "*This is Water Bug Hollow! Hollow! Hollow! This is Water Bug Hollow! Hollow! Hollow!*"

Gordon looked around. He considered not everyone deciphered what his eyes could see. The citizens of Water Bug Hollow were definitely blind to the otherworldly happenings involved in the dance. The choreography was beautiful to them and nothing more. He wondered if the conjure folk whose eyes were attuned even believed what they were seeing was real. If they had instinct, they should, Gordon thought.

He looked at Benny-Jah. His friend nodded, a concerned look on his face. Neyeli leaned her head forward, eyes in Gordon's direction. She saw it too.

"*This is Water Bug Hollow! Hollow! Hollow! This is Water Bug Hollow! Hollow! Hollow!*"

The rallying chant and drums startled Gordon. He stood straight, eyes on the stage.

"*This is Water Bug Hollow! Hollow! Hollow! This is Water Bug Hollow! Hollow! Hollow!*"

The *danse macabre* carried on in a flurry of impressive gambols, twists and leaps.

"*This is Water Bug Hollow! Hollow! Hollow! This is Water Bug Hollow! Hollow! Hollow!*"

The composed sequence was impressive. A calm occurred in both the audience and dancers. The chance of tumble or clumsy fall diminished as movements turned tranquil. The performers locked hands and danced a graceful and haunting waltz. With the sudden fresh form of dance occupying the stage, there came a new chant spoken in a very quiet whisper.

"Ixu! Gira! Ixu! Gira! Ixu! Gira!"

Gone were the drums. A soft flute in their place. Somewhere in the crowd, Dajon Brickhouse drew upon his musical instinct to place a violin within the muted mix. It would sound wonderful, thought the young boy while also thinking of his sweetheart, Melinda Clarke. He wished she were able to witness the magnificence in person.

There came a susurrated reprise of the Water Bug Hollow chant. The men separated from the women, skipping off the stage and through the entrance with the exaggerated movements of sneaking thieves. The women followed, twirling and twirling, the bell of their gowns blooming wide in their spin like blooming flowers. Conjure dwindled the stage into the ethers, and there was a collective awe from the Water Bug Hollow citizens left in wonder on how the phenomenon occurred. The conjure folk simply grinned, even the two Gwuinee representatives stirred with a partial curve up in their lips.

Voodoo Lily and Armand stepped out of the entrance, and Voodoo Lily shouted, "Whatchall waitin' for? Get in here and throw some dice, coin, and card!" Despite the crowd's size, the people filed into the magnificent gambling house with a cordial ease. Armand and Voodoo Lily posted up on either side of the door.

The crowd loosened, and Gordon allowed for his brother and Leah to walk ahead of him. Neyeli was behind him. "Did you see that?" she asked in an anxious voice, her dreadlocks shifting to a muted green tone. "I have mixed feelings about that."

"Yeah," was all Gordon mustered as they inched closer to the casino entrance.

Benny chimed in, "There was something tranquil about it, though, Neyeli-baby. Took me off guard at first. I mean, we out here slaying those things, but I felt so relaxed. Seemed odd to be so at ease in the presence of so much burden."

"I felt that too," Neyeli responded. "That's what disturbed me the most."

Satchel "Old Goon", walking close to Gordon, had a brighter conversation with Naamah than expected. A brilliant smile echoed through the veil of Miss Mbu's long, braided hair. "Your daughter knows how to open a business," she commended. "Tamed *inawo* stringing their retainers in dance," she contemplated aloud, pride in full glow as she pondered the sentiment. "Creative. Not ethical, but creative."

Satchel "Old Goon" explained in a matter-of-fact timbre, "Papa Solomon insisted on a flag to raise, and he didn't want it to be a white one.

This is war, and he's definitely a wartime patriarch. That dance opening was a skull and crossbones."

"What good is a flag if folk without the sight of conjure can't see it for its full potential?" questioned Terrence, hands in his pockets.

"You saw it," Simaetha interposed with a raised eyebrow.

Satchel "Old Goon" chuckled at her quip. He looked at Terrence and said, "Cousin, your family will receive twenty percent from Eve's Hallow's take. Enjoy that." He addressed Naamah, telling her, "We can tame black folk's burdens, Miss Mbu. Conjure has come a long way thanks to the proximity of Fable Avenue with the crossroads and Water Bug Hollow. I do have to admit, them Fable brothers played their part in history."

Terrence tipped his hat, and that was the extent of the conversation.

Gordon considered himself corrected on how the dancing *inawo* went over in the eyes of the Gwuinee folk. All seemed well, and Papa Solomon appeared to have given his blessing to showcase something so bold and with grit.

At the door. Armand greeted them with shimmering delight. His arms were held out wide and he embraced Cedron and Gordon with brotherly hugs. He planted a gentle kiss on Leah's cheek and joked with her, "Congratulations on getting these two conjure thugs into some respectable clothes." Leah burst into laughter. Both Gordon and Cedron were in a style of clothing that matched Armand's attire, though Cedron had each finger covered in silver rings. Gordon was bare of adorning jewelry. Armand turned his attention to Neyeli and pressed a respectable kiss against her cheek. He continued his witticisms, using Benny as the brunt of his joke. "I know you did your best, sister." Benny was in blue jeans, workman boots, and a white hoodie. Neyeli's hair resonated violet as she chuckled at Armand's sentiment.

Neyeli turned to Benny. "He is who he is, and I love him for it," she noted.

"No glove tonight, Benny Jah?" inquired Armand.

Benny lifted his arm, absent without his armored gauntlet. "It's at my call if I need it, but I still feel naked," he remarked.

Cedron tapped Voodoo Lily on the shoulder and said, "How you doing, beautiful Crossroads Queen? I have a request to make."

"Oh!" Voodoo Lily was caught by surprise. "And what is that Brother Cedron?"

Cedron pointed to Terrence and stated, "I need you to tell your pop's cousin the Gypsy Moon Misfits are up for any game he got for a challenge—" he aimed a thumb at Armand and huffed, "No need to waste time on the new heads."

Everyone ruptured with a heavy breath of *"Oh!"* and a bend in their back.

Armand rolled his eyes. "I accept the challenge—at least a card game!" he responded. He lifted two fingers and said to Cedron, "I got two crews—seven if you breakdown the Wild Hollow Mafia! That's against your what? One?"

"You'll need 'em!" teased Cedron, shit-eating grin burning across his face. "We got somethin' for y' bunch of biloko and Wild Hollow Mafia—though I'm really feelin' that name."

Armand said while making a gesture with his thumb and finger, "You know, I was this close to calling them The Jungle Bunnies, for irony's sake."

Leah covered the laugh attempting to escape from her mouth. Heavy guffaws were drawn out of Gordon, Cedron, and Benny Jah. Neyeli shook her head, half a smile on her face.

Voodoo Lily rolled her eyes. Her regal manner melted away, and she said in a sharp tone, "No, he wasn't! I wouldn't let him!"

The gathered group moved aside as Gizo and Black Arum, sprouting their African-masked, biloko appearance, posted up on either side of the door. Cedron threw them a look. "Impressive!" he remarked. Many others were in deep reverence at their appearance, the Water Bug Hollow citizens passing it off as magnificent costume work and breathtaking makeup effects. Their usually exposed genitalia and buttocks were covered by leaves appearing as undergarments.

Gordon, Neyeli, and Benny-Jah remained outside with Armand and Voodoo Lily. Cedron and Leah continued on, entering into the festivities. Voodoo Lily hugged her mother and father tight when they neared. She saluted Naamah and Terrence with a polite and regal nod of the head. They bowed at the neck in the Crossroads Queen's presence, placing a hand over their heart that doubled as both a congratulatory and welcoming gesture.

Gordon was interested in Voodoo Lily's response when Naamah repeated her sentiment on the *inawo* dance. "I was speaking to your father on the riveting dance sequence. Tamed *inawo*. Intriguing..." the Gwuinee representative stated.

Voodoo Lily, returning to her royal demeanor, elucidated, "It's not an easy feat, even with the power of the crossroads at my disposal. It's fitting. People have either overcome their burdens or live with them. They are no longer haunted by them. They live and dance in harmony with their troubles. Because of this, they cause no trouble either." Gordon and Neyeli remained straight-faced, but Voodoo Lily could sense their unease. She addressed Neyeli, "My sister, it's a far more peaceful state of living than how they previously walked in life, causing strife to themselves or others. It's also far more merciful than the prison system would be. This is true rehabilitation."

Neyeli accepted the answer, but she was still visibly uncomfortable with the affair, and her new shade of hair gave her away. Papa Solomon and the matriarchs entered the assembly, saluted with praise for their presence. Savannah Forrester was with them. She glided by everyone and stepped to her grandson. "Come with me for a moment," she requested, keeping her disapproval absent in her voice.

"Yes, Nana," Armand responded. The two walked away to a private area where Savannah would warn Armand of the dangers in his speech.

Voodoo Lily petitioned for Gordon, Benny-Jah, and Neyeli to follow her inside.

Eve's Hallow was a world beyond. Its interior reflected the mythologies and legends that shaped the *Ojulowo Atijo Oluwa* spiritual system combined with the vintage appearance of the early, juke joint appeal. It all looked as if it was blossomed straight from the original creation. There were lithe men and women prancing around dressed in black, full-body suits that glittered with the heavens. Their appearance reminded Gordon of his shadowy, 'Dooley' form or the cosmic spirits he visited.

Women dressed as flappers served drinks and took orders while patrons gambled on the wide and magnificent gambling floor. There was a bar where Elodie Ellison served up drinks. Myèl Claire was on the stage, gowned in the fashion of the early days of jazz, belting out a sensual tune and backed up by a band. The area was awe-inspiring, and Gordon's lilac eyes swept the scene. He felt as if the cosmic realms he'd journeyed to above the Earth, made a home in Eve's Hallow's interior.

"There are secret games here," Voodoo Lily enlightened. Her voice was a swift whisper, as if her words were a warning. "Please, follow."

Gordon, Neyeli, and Benny-Jah found it hard to unfasten their eyes from the main floor's liveliness, but they accompanied Voodoo Lily to a smoke-filled backroom. It was a step outside of time, and there were gambling tables everywhere. Men and women sat across from their burdens. The game at hand was Liar's Dice. There was no money in play. There was an instinct about what was happening. Voodoo Lily confirmed when she explained, "Here is where the men and women of Water Bug Hollow indulge in a game of Liars Dice with their ethereal haunts to absolve their debt from them. There are tragedies here, played out with a win or a loss."

The Fable Avenue trio panned the room.

It appeared peaceful enough, but there was a price to the game. Losing caused intense stress. Winning resulted into a journey through a nightmare of weighted troubles until the person's burden burned itself out. It was a form of justice from an ancient epoch of conjure. There were rituals that existed in modern times, practiced on remote Caribbean islands and areas of Africa. They were considered dangerous, as participants would not often survive the engagement with their *inawo*. The playing of Liars Dice gave it some levity, until the nightmares kicked in.

Outside. Savannah Forrester spoke in a warmer tone than she'd intended. She first swallowed a large breath, holding it in and allowing it to fester into an angry cloud. But when she'd taken Armand aside, she'd seen the conjure man he'd become. Savannah exhaled and warned her grandson, "You have to be careful." There was still a chiding tone, but the knowledge of his involvement in dispersing the hex fogging Water Bug Hollow lessened her displeasure. "Those cameras tonight are managed by a relentless group of people looking to control Water Bug Hollow—and you exposed that. They are looking for retribution. Make no mistake. Be careful when you taunt them." Armand looked away. He dropped his head and sighed. "I know you have no tolerance for bullies, but these aren't the type that back down with a hit. These bastards knuckle up." Savannah heard her words. She scoffed, "Look at me, here! I sound just like your mother, so worried!" Armand looked up for a moment and rolled his eyes. He huffed, and Savannah told him, "Don't you lose sleep. I'll handle y' mamma. Been handlin' her since she came from me." She paused before saying, "An historic place is reopened. The local news got this, but it will spread. She'll see it. Your speech, too. I'll handle her." She put a hand on her grandson's cheek. "Go enjoy the night. You earned it, Armand. Stay close to that sweetheart of yours. She'll keep you out of trouble."

Grandmother and grandson shared an uneasy chuckle.

Armand said to Savannah, "Thank you, Nana. If anyone in the community was offended by my choice of words, let them know I apologize…" He thought about his words. "…Mostly…" he grinned. Savannah smacked her grandson upside the head. He laughed, and the two of them entered Eve's Hallow's high-spirited festivities.

Armand spotted Voodoo Lily emerging from the side gambling dens. Gordon and his friends were in tow. He walked up to them, and Gordon pounded his shoulder. "There he is!" he greeted Armand's return. "This guy right here! I swear! Ready to start a war with his mouth."

Benny joined in by saying, "I know, right! A mouthful on the rise."

Armand shied away from Gordon and Benny's words. He tossed a thumb over his shoulder and said, "My grandmother already roped me up on my…enthusiastic speech."

"I'll bet she did!" Gordon exclaimed. "You got things done, though, kid. It's a helluva sight." He swept his arm around the room. "All of this."

"It's not easy to haunt a block," Neyeli voiced. "Let alone dispersing hex and fog." She looked at Voodoo Lily and Armand and told them, "Congratulations to the both of you."

Voodoo Lily responded, "Water Bug Hollow is a consecrated land, blessed by Curtis Hollow's war against its oppressors. We tapped into that spirit. I know my man here did." She gave Armand a momentary, wanting look. Gordon noticed it, and he longed for the same look beamed at him by his beloved Fey Forrester. It'd been too long since he'd seen it. "There's a fog hanging over the entire world," Voodoo Lily asserted. Gordon heard her words, but he was looking away, thinking of his sweetheart. Voodoo Lily's voice was lost to him. He was pulled from his thoughts when Voodoo Lily expressed, "You and your dearest Fey Forrester bear the responsibility of dissipating it, Gordon."

He acknowledged with a nod. Neyeli put her eyes on Gordon, and her dreadlocks turned purple with sky-blue tips. Gordon chuckled and pointed at Armand, "But this one here!" Then he paraphrased, astonishment in his tone, *"We've uncovered buried and hexed bones? Gave blessing to the burdens injected into their marrow?* Seriously, sun?" Armand hid a sheepish grin. Gordon put his hands in his pockets, continuing to tease Armand by paraphrasing his speech. *"Bias narratives of the media in attendance? Presence of men in badges equipped with needles?"* He added for good measure. "I heard, 'kiss my ass'. That's what you said. I heard it!"

They laughed. Neyeli scratched the back of her neck, ducking her head low as she uttered, "Let's see what the press says in the papers tomorrow." She again addressed both Armand and Voodoo Lily when she said, "You basically declared a second independence for Water Bug Hollow."

It was a sentiment hard to ignore, but the young conjure men and conjure women did their best, filtering into the sea of game and music. Not yet twenty-one, Gordon, Neyeli, and Benny Jah could be on the gaming floor, but could not participate. It was still a wondrous experience to simply flow through the activities. And the music was a slam. People danced with their significant others or executed an erratic or elegant waltz with their troubles. Gordon saw everything, watching on while leaning against a wall. So many were paired. He saw his father and the spirit of his mother, she now concentrated into the physical realm. His brother Cedron enjoyed the company of his sweetheart Leah Peters. His brother-in-all-but-blood, Benny Jah was pressed up close to, whom Gordon considered his sister-in-all-but-blood, Neyeli. The king and queen of the revelry, Armand Gideon and Voodoo Lily danced tightly against one another. Even the Old Goon and Simaetha were paired up, the culturally genuine O-Jewel king and O-Jewel queen of the area. Papa Solomon danced with Madame Jeliya. Maman Anansi with Uncle Andre. Never alone, Lady Arachne was held by Albert Banneker.

The young, jazz songstress belted out a tune with lyrics declaring that she always got her dearest love, sooner or later.

The pairs swayed to the tune.

A hand folded over Gordon's shoulder. He turned and spotted Savannah Forrester standing next to him, a warm smile on her face. "I miss her too, Gordon. But she'll be back. We'll conjure that power." She took his hand and petitioned, "In the meantime, come dance with me. A friendly trot and turn." Gordon didn't protest. He walked out onto the dance floor with 'Nana' Forrester and maneuvered into a polite, slow dance.

Dajon took Gordon's place on the wall, observing the dance floor and all its pairs. He thought of his girlfriend, Melinda Clarke. He considered how much she'd love being among the conjure folk community. He'd told her so much about it as he assisted in nurturing her conjure ability. He also listened close to the music, and he considered where a violin's sound would accent the harmonics. He'd do an excellent solo, substituting for the singer's voice and crooning the song's lyrics through a sweet melody.

The night went on. There were winners and losers who gambled against their burdens or earned an impressive sum of coin. Eve's Hallow was open for business even as the sun came up and made its rounds in the sky. Print and digital media made the announcement. Armand's bold sentiments were echoed in every reporting narrative.

Indeed, Water Bug Hollow was in the midst of a second independence. Somewhere, in a luxurious study, a ruling devil slammed his fist against the morning paper resting on his desk.

39

After love, there was a beautiful sleep. Tight and close, there was more than each other that wrapped around Armand Gideon and Voodoo Lily as they lay naked in bed at one of the crossroads houses. In the master bedroom, they were cloaked with peace of mind as warm and as fluffy as the comforter that cocooned them. Water Bug Hollow was a functioning settlement again with Eve's Hallow as its first pillar of economic stability. The gambling den was also a second pillar for spiritual strength and catharsis. The Church of Water Bug Hollow, led by conjure man Reverend Mathieu Pouvwa, was its first champion of divine muscle and purgation.

Armand and Voodoo Lily's easy rest wasn't just an effect of a wild night debuting Eve's Hallow's resurrection, or the enlivened lovemaking that followed. Solace was achieved through the Gwuinee representatives' approval for the gamble and dance with burdens, and the unending heap of praise for securing Water Bug Hollow from the hexed fog that mired it in violent distress and befuddling, narcotic delirium. Exposing corruption in the judicial and fourth estate arenas governing greater Jakobiville was too a welcomed morsel.

So, the sweethearts roistered with the public until the evening was dead, and they made animated love in private until the remainder of the night was through. They rested, and it was far from the seventh day because Water Bug Hollow wasn't built or restored to life in a single day. Either way, sleep had never been so well deserved.

Outside their house, on the Fable Avenue side of the façade, a car pulled up and parked. Stephanie Dumas stepped out, taking a deep breath as she stared up at the mystical residence. She closed her car door and walked through the iron gate as if slipping discreetly through a secret passage. Her journey up to the front door was slow, pacing carefully as if each step was a loose board of wood ready to give way.

Stephanie made it to the door. She looked left. She looked right. She looked behind her. People shuffled through the streets heading to the subway or getting into their car to go off and blend in with normal folk at jobs. No one she knew saw her. She rang the doorbell and waited, forced to ring it twice more before Voodoo Lily answered the door in a long-flowing, light-blue silk robe. She examined Stephanie as her memory recalled who the woman was. "Miss Dumas? Correct? You're Maman Anansi's daughter? Stephanie…?"

Stephanie's countenance lit up with a bright smile. "Yes!" she replied. She cleared her throat as her smile wobbled. She noticed Armand walk up behind Voodoo Lily. He wore white sleep pants and a loose, long-sleeve tunic. "I'm sorry," she apologized. "I didn't mean to disturb the whole household. I've come with a request concerning a burden and your games played in the back of Eve's Hallow."

"Oh! Of course!" Voodoo Lily blurted. "Come in. Come in," she insisted, waving Stephanie inside while stepping back and making room. Stephanie walked through the doors and into the house. She noted there was no resemblance to a brownstone within its interior. Voodoo Lily closed the door. She and Armand flanked Stephanie, who reacted by making quick steps to the front room, heels clanking against the wooden floor. Armand and Voodoo Lily glanced at one another and then hastily pursued Stephanie to keep up. "Is there something we can help you with, Miss Dumas?" inquired the crossroads queen.

Stephanie's eyes surveyed the high-quality décor accenting the room. It was country-living and Victorian mashed together in an impressive approach she didn't believe could be pulled off in design. Eyes still sweeping the room, Stephanie expressed, "I have a haunt on me. A burden, of sorts." She twirled around to face Voodoo Lily and Armand. "I seek a private game to dissipate this loitering spirit." She requested, "May I sit?"

"Yes, please," Voodoo Lily responded in a polite tone.

Stephanie rested on a chair. She exhaled. Voodoo Lily sat opposite her, legs crossed. Armand remained standing behind the chair, arms on the back. Stephanie observed the both of them. She breathed out and straightened her mien. "First, let me congratulate you on a remarkable opening. Pretty big for a soft opening. The ambiance. The dancing. I could see the *inawo* in the dance number." Armand and Voodoo Lily expressed their gratitude. Stephanie was able to measure a certain anxiousness in the couple's tone. They were eager to hear more of her troubles. Maman Anansi's daughter continued, "The interior was so beautiful. I saw, and heard about, *all* the games." Stephanie went silent. She cleared her throat and fiddled with her hands. She returned to the true nature of her visit. "What I have on me isn't exactly an *inawo*. It's a haunt. Someone who passed into spirit clings to me."

Armand shook his head. "I don't believe that would be a problem," he pointed out. He looked at Voodoo Lily and asked for assurance, "Would it?"

Voodoo Lily replied up to Armand, "Not the way the games are set up." She remarked to Stephanie, "A burden is a burden." She sat back and probed, "Could you give some insight about this haunt?"

Stephanie nodded. She described in a hesitant voice, "He was a young, street thug I had to put down. Another black youth wasted. The deed on my hands." She sounded remorseful. Armand and Voodoo Lily shared another quick glance. Eyes on Stephanie, she continued, "His name was Sean Commons—*is*, as he remains with us—with me, anyway. He made an offense against Fable Avenue. He shot and almost killed a young boy named Dajon—"

"Brickhouse?" Armand finished. "Benny's brother!"

"Yes," Stephanie confirmed with urgency in her voice.

The crossroads queen and her consort shared another brief look. "We heard the young boy had been shot earlier this year. February," Voodoo Lily proclaimed with a rattled expression. "It's what led to the battle outside of time on Fable Avenue against all the needleman, correct?" Stephanie nodded her head, yes. "Armand's cousin, Fey Forrester, she was a casualty of sorts. Banished." Stephanie nodded again, confirming. "Benny's brother, Dajon, he's not traumatized in any way, is he?" Before Stephanie could answer, Voodoo Lily stated, "He was enjoying himself at the festivities last night. He seemed a little alone, but he mingled with the children his age in the arcade section. He wasn't standoffish." Voodoo Lily put a hand on her chest.

Stephanie assured, "Dajon is his sprightly self. He's fine," the lawyer assured. "Most of his friends are regular folk from his block in Harlem. Sean Commons was having run-ins with Dajon, bullying Dajon's friends. Dajon was actually able to hold his own in a fight with the young man, no conjure needed. Sean Commons retaliated. He had an accomplice too, in both cases. I interrogated him and discovered he had been deeply hexed. A soldier in Stanley Fallows army got to him. A man named Willie the Lich."

Voodoo Lily noted, "I've heard the name. I felt a presence that resonated with its syllables when I guided Gordon Goodspeed into the *mirak* to reconstruct his memory."

Stephanie leaned forward, fingers interlaced in a tight lock. She focused her words and revealed, "Mister Commons was the trigger man. I felt his kind of scars were not redeemable. Too much to fix. Willie's whip sidelined the Lilac Flame." She addressed Armand, "Your Aunt Emma and cousin Fey suffered terrible wounds from him. Neither recovered, and we've lost both of them. Madame Jeliya was a victim too when the street was attacked. She was able to recover." She saw Armand stiffen and become stern. Then Stephanie continued, "For Mister Commons, recovery for a person resonating with no knowledge of conjure—" she dropped her head, concluding, "I had no choice."

Voodoo Lily shook her head, eyes welling with sympathy. "No, no, no, Miss Dumas. This *is* a burden!" she affirmed. Then she looked up at Armand and tasked, "Set a gaming table for Miss Dumas, Armand-baby, immediately." Voodoo Lily asked Stephanie, "I'm sure you can make the time now?"

Stephanie unlocked her hands and sat back. "Yes. I can," she answered.

Armand dismissed himself to shower and jump into clothes for the day. Voodoo Lily briefed, "Is there a token from this Sean Commons? A bauble to summon his haunt?"

Stephanie opened her hand. "I took his life with a hex conjured from my palm," she described. "I hold here what I took from him." She stared at her opened hand as the paths in her palm bubbled with a soft, bronze shimmer. Threadlike spirals of light raised from her hand and coagulated a few inches above her palm. The gentle sounds of water rushing mixed with a vibrating hum until it shifted into a resonance that mimicked the crumpling of paper. The coruscating threads brightened, turned gold. A white-hot brilliance configured them into a solid-gold signet ring that dropped into Stephanie's palm. The lawyer clasped her fingers around it, holding it for a time. Then she maneuvered her fingers into a pedestal of sorts, straightening them to hoist the jewelry piece atop their tips. She inspected the face of the signet ring. Sean Commons' profile was etched there. Stephanie leaned forward and presented the gold-crafted bijoux to Voodoo Lily.

The crossroads queen waved her hand. "No, no, Miss Dumas. That's yours. Armand will take you to the gaming room and walk you through the ritual. You will engage Mister Commons in a playoff. Your win should exorcise you of this haunt. He will dance until he is ready to cross."

Stephanie palmed the signet ring. "Thank you, Miss Lily." She sat back and exhaled. Small talk was made concerning the scrimmage on Fable Avenue that took place outside of time, where the needlemen abducted children, stole essences. Stephanie confirmed the more specific details.

"Benny's little brother is a brave young boy," Voodoo Lily expressed thinking of the shooting.

Stephanie replied, "He is. He had us worried, but he pulled through."

"Yes…" she said. Armand entered. He was dressed and ready for the day. Voodoo Lily stated before he once again posted up behind her chair, "Miss Dumas has a token." Her words were a signal for Armand to escort Stephanie to Eve's Hallow.

He stopped mid-stride and turned to Stephanie. "Miss Dumas," he expressed in a gentlemanly tone. He bent down and presented two open hands, assisting Stephanie to her feet. "Through the back, across the crossroads, and through the house on the other side of the street," he said with a smile.

Stephanie beamed in return. "Please, good conjure man, lead the way."

Armand did as tasked, leading Stephanie Dumas along a path that traversed from Brooklyn, New York, Clarksdale, Mississippi, to Water Bug

Hollow, Louisiana. Voodoo Lily followed them to the door and watched their journey from the porch.

It wasn't long before Stephanie Dumas found herself seated at a gambling table in a private room at the Eve's Hallow casino and jazz lounge. The most impressive part of her voyage wasn't the trek through three different states in less than five minutes. It was the myriad of greetings Armand received when they entered Eve's Hallow. Former gang members, men and women, turned employees addressing him as 'boss' and saluting with a gesture of some sort.

In the room. Where it happened. Stephanie sat opposite an unoccupied chair. Two, wooden cups filled with dice lay on the table in front of her. Between the cups was a miniature, silver-colored cauldron fashioned from iron. "Your token, Miss Dumas," Armand requested. Stephanie dropped the signet ring into Armand's hand. He removed a small piece of vellum stationary. He crumpled the paper around the signet ring, placed it into the cauldron, and set it ablaze with a focused incant.

A black and amber flame leapt from the dwarven pot. Paper and ring were reduced to whirling smoke that spiraled out of the cauldron and floated over the chair seated opposite Stephanie. The smoke expanded and congealed into Sean Commons' translucent spirit. He sat still with a visibly nervous expression muddling his countenance. He and Stephanie stared at one another. "This is familiar territory for us, Mister Commons," stated Stephanie. "Peering at one another from across a table. I think the outcome for this encounter will give the both of us peace."

Sean moved his eyes around the dark room. He then returned his gaze to Stephanie and asked in a trembling voice, "Where's ya moms? Missus…Anansi—*er*—whatever? Where that pretty, little light-skin chick with the freaky, changin' hair?" He looked up at Armand. He inspected the young conjure man up and down. His eyes focused on his three-skull necklace and their glow. "He not that detective dude…"

"No," Stephanie answered. "He's not. He's the facilitator for this game. His name is Armand Gideon. He's a good man; and he can be trusted. I hope you can award me a little trust as well."

"*Bitch, you murdered me!*" Sean hissed with a voice that sounded like a wicked frost sailing through an ice tunnel. "You took me out. Popped me like this was the streets! You a pretender! You ain't justice! Fuck you talk about trust?"

"Because neither of us are rested over this," Stephanie countered in a calm voice. "You hover aimless. I'm haunted. This game provides the both of us with a solution."

Sean simmered. "Win or lose?" he asked.

Armand turned his head toward Stephanie and stated, "Declare your wager, Miss Dumas."

Sean questioned, "Why she get to decide the bet?"

"You're the burden, Mister Commons," Stephanie presented as a matter-of-fact.

Sean's face contorted. "*I'm* the burden?"

Armand admitted with a stoic expression on his face, "She's right you know."

Sean rolled his eyes and sneered. He scoffed at Stephanie, "What's the wager?"

The lawyer indulged the street spirit, "Should you win, Mister Commons, I will know your burden for the remainder of my life, though you would get to cross over in peace. I will carry with me the pain I've caused you, your family members who mourned, and all the personal burden you carry, including your criminal life." Stephanie paused for a moment, and then she finished the terms for the game. "If I win, I'm free of your haunt and you cross, but not without understanding the harm you've brought to others and yourself, and even those who mourned you." The terms were set. Stephanie added, "One sitting. No best of three or four games. One siting," she repeated.

Armand moved his gaze to Sean Commons. The young man's countenance was as still as deep water. It took a moment, but he responded, "I'll take that bet..." He peered up at Armand. "Let's do the game!"

Armand's face was frozen stern now. He asked, "You know how to play Liar's Dice, Mister Commons?"

Sean locked eyes with Stephanie. His voice stammered, and he sounded as if he had no choice but to utter the words when he replied, "I know how to play..."

Armand needed to hear nothing else. "Take up your cups—" he began, and Sean and Stephanie carried out his order. "Hand over your cups and rattle your dice." The two participants performed the actions requested by Armand. "*Slam down!*" the moderator hissed.

Stephanie and Sean slammed their cups open-side down against the table.

The game was in play. Armand left the room. Round and round, and round after round, bids and bluffs were made. Lies were called out or sneaked through, and dice were lost. No one cheered a win or scoffed at a dead die. Sean wasn't even reluctant when he tossed his final die to the center of the table, joining his other four. Despite his scowl, Sean appeared calm, possessed of a certain *amor fati*. He considered, in the final moments overlooking his loss, the game was necessary. A ghostly, cloth mask wrapped around his face, sewn together from a preternatural non-existence. A picture of the crossroads was etched on its front. Sean's head dropped back and he inhaled a deep breath before his person transfigured into a multi-colored puff of whirling smoke. Gone from the private gaming room, he was banished to perform a whimsical dance routine, joining a large cast of physical and non-physical beings out front at Eve's Hallow. A production conjured up at the top and bottom of every hour.

Stephanie felt the weight exorcised from her spirit. She closed her eyes and took a deep breath. "Thank you," she said to no one in particular. She opened her eyes.

Armand slipped back into the room and positioned himself behind Stephanie's chair. "Congratulations, Miss Dumas," he greeted. "There's a new dancer in the ballet. Would you like to see?" Stephanie kept her eyes fixed on the dice in the middle of the table as she nodded, yes. "Please, Miss Dumas. Right this way," Armand directed.

Stephanie got up and felt light as air. Standing straight, a smile curled across her face, and she stretched as if she'd woken from a revitalizing slumber. She giggled, and became embarrassed of her emotional display. She composed herself, but Armand assured her it was okay to feel relief. Then he escorted Stephanie to Eve's Hallow's entrance. Stephanie's lightness increased. There was zero gravity to her, an idealistic weightlessness that persisted within her as she observed the number performed in front of her. She didn't know which dancer was Sean Commons, and she didn't care at this point. He was no longer her burden. He was now offered up to the dance.

Beautiful as it appeared, the frolicking movements weren't as playful as they seemed. Behind the graceful moves were an agony of lifetimes felt physically and spiritually. Each participant had a timed term for their choreography. Until then, their screams resonated from outside of time, heard only by the dancer who poured out the abhorrent wail.

Stephanie observed the magnificent caper. Street dances mixed with tango, ballet and waltz-styled maneuvers performed in an elegant, free-form gambol. She didn't recognize Sean Commons from the other prancing contributors. She felt relief in that, deciding to not use her higher instinct to find him in the crowd. She gave respect, watching the dance in its entirety.

A few dancers faded. Others puffed away in bursts of smoke. Their disappearances were in rhythm to an unheard music, the same way they danced. Normal and regular folk considered the display an act of special effects. It was special, thought Stephanie. And it was effective. There was applause from the sparse crowd, gathered at this early hour on their way to work. Stephanie decided to take the production's end as a cue for her to return to Fable Avenue. She expressed her gratitude to Armand before leaving. "Thank you," she told him. "The game has absolved me completely from Mister Commons' haunt." She gave him a tight hug. "Thank you, so much…" she sighed in relief.

"You're most welcome, Miss Dumas," Armand replied as they stepped away from their cordial embrace. "Would you like for me to escort you back?"

"No, thank you, Mister Gideon," Stephanie politely declined. "See to your duties here. I know my way to the house and back to the crossroads."

Armand gave Stephanie a respectful bow of the neck. "Good day, Miss Dumas," he told her. Raising his head, he stated, "The house will be unlocked for you. Safe travels. I'm delighted we were able to exorcise your burden."

Stephanie thanked Armand again before making her way back to the crossroads. Through the mystical dwelling and across the street she travelled. Voodoo Lily greeted her on the steps. "I've felt your victory over your haunt, Miss Dumas," she hailed. "Rejoice."

Stephanie hurried up the porch stairs and hugged Voodoo Lily. "I give thanks to you, Crossroads Queen," she said through a sigh of relief. "You and your consort's game have given me a true catharsis." She stepped away from the embrace and exhaled again.

"What will you do with the remainder of your day?" asked Voodoo Lily.

"Oh, Miss Lily," Stephanie beamed. "I'm free now! Every movement seems so unanchored. I could stand still and just float to the moon." The two women shared laughter at Stephanie's joy. Stephanie's eyes watered with joy. She wiped and sniffed the tears away. "But, I'm going to pamper myself with a strapping, conjure man who knows how to summon up something lovely from the kitchen to the bedroom!"

Voodoo Lily winked and beamed a sly grin. "I know that's right!" she said with an approving shake of her head, laughter continuing.

Stephanie composed herself and promised, "Then I'm going to sleep, and I'm going to sleep well."

Voodoo Lily led her through the house to Fable Avenue. Stephanie departed with kind words, skipping down the brownstone steps, through the waist-high gate, and to her car. She started the vehicle and took out her phone. She called, and Martin Campbell answered.

"Hey, Stephanie-baby," he said with his gruff voice. "You good this morning?"

"I'm more than that, Mister Campbell," she replied. "I took the day off to relax with a ritual, and I've never felt clearer and without."

"Without what?" Martin inquired.

"Just without, Martin-baby," Stephanie addressed.

"I guess…" responded the private investigator.

Stephanie put on her seatbelt. She continued, "Well, what I can't do *without*, is a nice cooked meal from an amazing chef. Dinner. Tonight. It's what this queen calls for."

Martin chuckled. "Amazing chef?" he questioned. "Keep stroking a brother's ego, Stephanie-baby. The queen will have her meal." There was a moment of silence. Stephanie put Martin on speaker and set her phone inside a grip on the dashboard. She pulled onto the road and made her way to Queens. "To be honest," Martin's voice popped up. "I'm just fumbling around with paperwork here. I could swing by your place now."

Stephanie shook her head. "You stay put, Mister Campbell," she directed, feeling the weightless sensation taking over her body. "This queen gave specific instructions, and they're for you to arrive tonight. Dinner." She stopped the car behind a line of vehicles halted by a red light. Stephanie laid back in her seat. "The day is for me, Martin-baby. You're on tonight's schedule."

Martin commented, "I work better at night, anyway."

The light turned green. Stephanie moved the car forward. "You certainly do, Mister Campbell," she told him. "Tonight, Martin-baby. I'll eat anything you make."

"I'll chef to impress, Miss Steph," he rhymed.

Stephanie rolled her eyes and snickered, "Okay! Slow down now, there! Stick to cookin', Conjure Emcee."

"Enjoy your day, Stephanie-baby," Martin said, simmering his devilish chuckle. "I'll see you tonight. Take care."

"Take care." Stephanie ended the call and drove into a day where burdens were scattered to the wind. The day was hers and hers alone.

She decided against visiting her brother's grave, telling herself that her gamble probably allowed his spirit to be at peace. She would honor that. She played with the idea of visiting Sean Commons' resting grounds, but she questioned why and moved on. Stephanie enjoyed the partly cloudy day with a walk through the park. She sat on a bench and observed the people running through, children and parents with a day off like her. Smiles were everywhere, and she even played naughty conjure tricks by peeking in on the thoughts of lovers passing by. It made her think of Martin and the night's meal.

Home. Stephanie was too excited to rest. It was for the better, as she found out. Her house was a mess, and she didn't want Martin to see it this way. For a brief, humorous moment, she considered having Martin arrive and put him to work on straightening her place. But that would slow down his duties as the night's chef. And so, Stephanie dived into the task of straightening her house for company presentation. She showered afterward, primped, and slipped into a sleeveless, full-length, dark-gray dress.

The sun scurried away, and the sliver of moonlight shined like a beacon to lead the procession of stars into the night sky. Clouds moved in, and a light rain began. It wasn't long before it was a downpour, and thunder and lightning filled the night sky. Stephanie was worried that Marin would cancel, as he hadn't phoned saying he was on his way, and the rain was heavy.

There was relief when the doorbell rang, but before answering, Stephanie ran a marathon focused on a last-minute room inspection. Guilt needled her, leaving Martin out on her front porch as the rain came down.

Eyes to every room, she found all as pristine for presentation. She fixed herself, relaxed her breathing, and then she answered the door. A bright, seductive smile put Martin in a spotlight. He stood on the other side, grinning at Stephanie's while cradling a bag of ingredients in his right arm. His jacket and fedora dripped from the rain. It was nothing a quick incant couldn't cure when he walked through the door.

"Good evening, Mister Campbell," she greeted. "Please, come in."

Martin stepped inside and rested a kiss on Stephanie's lips. "You look stunning," he whispered into her ear, making her giggle.

Stephanie thanked him. She muttered an incant before Martin had the chance. His clothes dried. He expressed his gratitude, but found out her politeness was a gambit to distract him. Her real play was the bottle of red wine peeking over the top of the bag. She snatched the bottle and spun away from Martin like a whimsical thief. Light on her toes with no shoes on her feet, she skipped down the hall, boasting of her grab. Stephanie said over her shoulder, "Commence the meal, Martin-baby. I'll be waiting in the dining room."

Martin chuckled at Stephanie's antics. "You better stay there!" he huffed playfully. "Don't invade my kitchen trying to sample what ain't fully prepared." He removed his jacket and fedora, hanging the items in hall closet. "You know it's rude to have your guest hang his own jacket *and* cook dinner!"

"Chivalry is man's job!" she teased, scampering off to the dining room. "Now get in that kitchen, Mister Man, where you belong!"

The table had already been set with wine glasses and a bottle opener, which Stephanie used to pop the cork. She poured a glass, set the bottle down, and scooped up the drink. Martin asked her what had gotten into her. She sipped her wine, walked to the kitchen, and leaned against the entryway. "The sessions with my mother, you, and your niece. They've worked. I was reluctant at first, but now…I don't feel anchored by…the haunt anymore. I decided to take a day for myself. Me. No responsibilities. I'm feeling good…" she took a heavy gulp of wine. She switched her lean from shoulder to her back. "I'm glad you like me in this dress, Martin-baby, but this is for me. This a freedom dress. Glad that I am."

Martin kept his back to her as he removed ingredients from the bag and started the oven. He shrugged and said, "You make me feel underdressed." He was in jeans, a tucked in collar shirt, and shoes.

Stephanie snickered, "This from a man who wears a suit and tie every day to work." She drank her wine and scrutinized his physique as he worked her kitchen.

"Those cheap suits I got?" he retorted.

"Shit! Cheap they not. I know where you shop. Miss Roberts can conjure up a stitching, keepin' up her family's tradition."

Martin laughed, "Yeah, well, Miss Roberts gives me a discount."

"On tailor-made?" blurted Stephanie, almost choking on a swallow of wine.

Martin turned. A wide grin on his face. "The perks of being the area mystic detective," he told her. "Incanted to be bulletproof too. No extra cost."

Stephanie made a face, one eyebrow raised. "Them some perks, all right," she huffed. "The perks of bein' a tall and dark, strapping oak black man. She like you comin' back in her store—that's what that is."

Martin turned around again. He aimed a wooden spoon at her. "Are you in my kitchen?" he questioned. He stepped up to Stephanie and shooed her away with light raps against her thigh with the spoon. Stephanie attempted a dodge, but only lifted her leg and took the soft, playful spankings. She turned away and he smacked her on the bottom. "It's my kitchen, long as I'm cookin', Miss Dumas!"

Stephanie laughed, chased away to the dining room. Martin retreated back to the stove. She had more swallows of wine. "You look good dressed down a little, Martin-baby," she called out as she took a seat. "You got your freedom dress on too. Be free, brother."

"I'm not quite sure this is a dress—and you wouldn't catch me in one," he replied.

"Negro, you know what I mean. Stop bein' so macho."

Martin and Stephanie laughed together from separate rooms.

She sat and relaxed, drinking a little at a time and reveling in the aroma of cooked food filling her house. She abstained from using her instinct to decipher what Martin had in store for her, and she reflected on how that would be the only thing she would abstain from on this night. A *'tall and dark, strapping oak'* was in her kitchen, and she was going to climb up its dark body and perch herself on a long, thick branch.

Stephanie grinned at the thought, and she abstained from drinking no longer. She drank and she thought. Abstaining be damned.

Then dinner was served. An aromatic plate of food was placed in front of her. Her eyes swept the contents. Spicy shrimp curled up with tortellini shells, sun-dried tomatoes, and spinach leaves smothered in a creamy mozzarella sauce. Scent and presentation bubbled moisture on Stephanie's tongue, and she was all too eager to seize the fork presented to her. She was still kind enough to thank her chef, but she was quick to sample the flavorful meal. Her sampling was unique, taking an individual ingredient and appraising its isolated taste. Then, she tried a scoop of everything on her fork. She felt her spirit jump with each, savory bite. Her eyes rolled back into her head and she moaned as she chewed and swallowed.

A quick of sip of wine, and a wipe of the mouth. Stephanie regained her composure. "This. Is. Wonderful! Martin-baby." She looked up at him and commented further, "I feel like I'm stealing something. Really! A meal like this should be paid for. I *know* your family lost money when you stopped workin' at the restaurant."

Martin chuckled. "Thank you, Stephanie-baby. Let me get my plate and join you."

"Please…"

Martin went to the kitchen and prepared a plate. He returned and Stephanie poured a glass of wine for him. "There you go, Martin-baby." The aromas of a scintillating meal mixed with good drink and conversation. The air whirled with laughter, and affection permeated the house. The storm outside added to the ambience. Distance shrank between Stephanie and Martin, and closeness was intertwined with undressed dance and frolic. Stephanie climbed her mighty oak and, unanchored by burden, she reached a passionate climax that rattled the walls with her freedom cry. Her spirited release was an epic trilogy that put her fast to sleep.

In dream.

Stephanie stood in her evening dress, which was not dark gray and starry but cream-colored silk. She was surrounded by darkness. It was calm until she heard the fierce beat of African drums. The volume was low at first. Then it lifted and lifted and lifted loud until it became unbearable. With every strike it felt as if a force knocked against her and drew the wind from her breath. Something screamed at her, and she flinched. She turned, feeling a presence. And there he was. A Water Bug Hollow dancer jumped from the shadows and pranced around her with heavy stomps, arms lifted above his masked head. A mouth and wide-open eyes were painted on its face. He hollered at her, *"Together!"*

Stephanie turned and turned, following his feral movements. She shivered with an exaggerated fright; and her fear held her in place as the dancer's cloth mask dissolved and revealed Sean Commons' countenance. His hooded sweatshirt faded too, and he continued dancing wild and chaotic, hands reaching for the heavens. He hopped close to Stephanie, and she cowered at his movement. He leapt back and danced his random dance, stomping and hollering.

Ink stained his arms, crisscrossing in a pattern that resembled chains. The tattoo burned and bubbled, keloid and tore as metal chains emerged from his arms in a bloody burst. The changes extended and wrapped around Stephanie's wrists. Sean Commons danced and screamed, and something in the dark laughed and laughed and laughed at Stephanie.

"The young serpent will dance with the older serpent…" a chilly, disembodied voice prophesized. *"Despite what was promised her, assisted by contest, burden will have not yet ceased. Too indulged in hubris, victory will betray her. Under burden, a haunting will remain, and the two shall dance…and the two shall dance…"*

The ballet of possession commenced, and Stephanie Dumas danced in sync with Sean Commons as his chains fastened the two of them together. Stephanie screamed as he screamed, and her movements followed her out of the dream. She didn't wake from the performance. She leapt from her bed and twirled with grace. Then she screamed and stomped!

Martin woke with a start, breathing heavy and feeling the rapid-fire salvo of heartbeats in his chest. He used an incant to calm his senses and center the room's spin. Silhouettes in the dark stretched and swirled, but Martin's use of incant worked to adapt his eyesight to straighten the shapes and outlines. Stephanie's fitful dance cast conjure that continued the spinning of Martin's senses. He closed his eyes and used his instinct to reach for one of his socks on the floor. He tied the garment around his eyes, knotting it in the back of his head. Eyes fastened shut, Martin used his higher perception to navigate the darkness and observe Stephanie as she spun and spun and stomped and stomped, screaming and hollering.

Martin reached out with his hand, kindling his conjure to restrain. Stephanie resisted. Her flailing rhythms cast an aegis around her, and she continued dancing wild and naked. She twirled to her knees, cowered to the corner of the room and screamed, *"You!"* She pointed at Martin. *"You are my burden!"*

Martin sighed, "Stephanie-baby…" He attempted to use his instinct to discern the cause of Stephanie's unsettling behavior. His mystic awareness perceived an entity in the room. It was behind him, and Martin twisted around. The shimmering specter of Stephanie's brother, Enock, was there. Martin realized that it was him to whom she was pointing and yelling. She shrieked as his glow brightened.

Enock shook his head, hands in his hoody's pocket. He removed one hand and shook it at Martin. "The fuck I tell you, nigga? I said, 'help my sister'!"

Martin bared his teeth. *"What?"* he snarled, taking a step toward Enock. "I have been! We *all* have been! Your sister is a grown-ass woman!"

He pulled the comforter from the bed and wrapped it around Stephanie as she shivered in fright, bottom lip trembling. "Go get your mother!" Martin shouted at Enock. "Go!"

Enock sighed and faded.

Martin continued holding Stephanie, surrounding her with the blanket. He focused and used his conjure to quell her feverish shakes. Her trembling slowed, but it never stopped.

40

Sleeping in her beauty, like a princess in a fairytale, Stephanie Dumas was on display in one of the private viewing rooms at the Peters funeral home. The sun was up, but the day was far from bright. The early hours were dark and rough, and the somber tenor carried into the sun's rise.

The chamber was locked off to outsiders. Two viewings were scheduled for the day, but their service was late in the afternoon and in the evening. There was time to sort out conjure affairs *sub rosa*. Maman Anansi stood at her daughter's resting body. The leading matriarch was stone-faced. Eyes locked on Stephanie whose only signs of life were the subtle movements of her breath raising and lowering her abdomen and chest, hands on her belly. Stephanie's eyes trembled from behind the lids at such a quick rate they appeared still. She was clothed in her dark-gray dress. No shoes. Califia's ancient and otherworldly veil, by which the design of her dress was inspired, was wrapped around her forehead.

Martin sat at one of the pews. His hands were together, resting on the back of the pew in front of him, head down. He was tired, but he couldn't leave and possibly get well-meaning sleep. Madame Jeliya and Stephanie's father, communally referred to as Uncle Andre, stood in the doorway. "Thank you, again, Thelema," he told her. "She's finally at a good, calm rest."

"It was a fight," Madame Jeliya commented, eyes on Stephanie and the altar created around her.

Andre insisted in a polite tone, "You can give me the list of family names for the day's viewings. I'll keep things in order while you and Cal watch over Stephanie."

"That's kind of you, Andre," Madame Jeliya said facing him. "I'll stay by my sister's side and make sure Stephanie finds her way back." She sighed. "Vencil is at the Water Bug Hollow church now. He's not aware of the reasons on how this all went down. I didn't tell him what we pulled from Stephanie's memory when we last spoke. I just told him we were able to stabilize her spirit. I didn't want it to taint his meeting with Satchel and the Gwuinee."

"I understand," Andre noted.

Madame Jeliya exhaled a heavy breath again. "I hope the revelation doesn't blemish what we have going with the Eledas family," she expressed. "Or the Gwuinee, considering the connection."

"Your husband is quite the diplomat, Thelema," Andre affirmed. "This all comes down to a naïve, young man fresh into conjure and a young woman who's a neophyte to her duties as a crossroads queen. Stephanie used a good amount of focus to veil her intentions. She's a lawyer. She got that conjure on her tongue."

"Indeed," Madame Jeliya commented.

Andre spied Martin and stated, "Some negotiatin' gon' have to take place for that young man's dancing spirit. A proper amends need to be made, not no simple game."

Madame Jeliya repeated, "Indeed."

Andre patted her shoulder and made his way toward Martin. Madame Jeliya walked up to Maman Anansi's side as Andre took a seat next to Martin and uttered, "My little girl is smart. She ran game to get to that game."

Martin lifted his head and sat back. He sighed, and Andre could see all the weight of the circumstances in his eyes, and that was before exhaustion stepped in to add a solemn color to them.

Andre continued, "Go get some rest, son. Our girl's stable now; and she's in good hands with these two. C'mon. I'll drive you home in your car."

Martin nodded. His body swaying heavy with lethargy. He spoke with as much heaviness in his voice. "We have to get that boy's spirit back," Martin reasoned.

Andre agreed. "I was just telling Madame Jeliya the same." Then he warned, "Make no move until Papa Solomon gives the order. You hear?"

Martin assured, "I won't, Uncle Andre. I won't." Though, he let it be known, "When I do have a warrant, I'll also have my niece and her sweetheart at my side."

"That's fine, but no arrests except the boy's spirit," Andre notified. "The crossroads queen and her consort ain't guilty of nothin'. They got played."

"Yeah..." was all Martin said.

Andre got up and motioned for Martin to do the same. Martin complied and followed behind Uncle Andre who approached his wife and placed a tender kiss on the back of her neck. Maman Anansi turned and embraced her husband. She told Andre, "We'll move her to the house tonight after business has been conducted. Her spirit is distant but calmer."

"Good," replied Andre. "I'm gonna take Martin home so he can get some rest, or at least lay down. I'll be back to assist with the duties while you keep an eye on our girl."

"Yes..." Maman Anansi concurred.

Andre gave a parting hug to Madame Jeliya once her embrace with Martin ended. In the same moment, Maman Anansi assured the conjure community's private investigator, "You don't worry, Martin. We'll have this all straight, and our dear Stephanie will be without the haunt of her burden."

"I'll do all in my power, Maman Anansi," Martin vowed with a tight hug on the Grand Matriarch. He let go and stepped away. "Would it be okay if I stop by the house when you bring her?"

"Absolutely, Martin," Maman Anansi permitted. "We might need you to help secure her in the van for transport."

"I'll be on call," he pledged.

With a final look and silent orison to Stephanie's resting body, Andre and Martin left the viewing chamber. Maman Anansi lifted her face to heaven and exhaled, eyes closed. She huffed a hard grunt and dropped on a pew with a heavy thud. She made a fist with both hands and shook them. Madame Jeliya watched the Grande Matriarch with sympathy wide in her eyes.

Maman Anansi slammed a closed fist atop the pew in front of her. "Damnit!" she hissed, looking off to her left. *"Damnit!"* she repeated. Another huff, and she sat back with tears in her eyes. "You teach your children to make the best decisions…" She shook her head. "Still they do things like this!" Maman Anansi shook her head. The other matriarch said nothing. She turned back to Stephanie's sleeping body and thought of her two children, Oliver and Leah. She blinked while in thought, and a piercing flash of light wiped Madame Jeliya's vision clean. The sight of Stephanie at rest on the altar vanished. A horrific happening bled into the matriarch's perception, and Madame Jeliya saw a maddening arrangement of events running concurrent to her own.

Oliver Peters' upper body turned. He spied Miss Lavette Ross leaning on her arm in the nursery doorway, catching her breath. He sneered and faced her. Tremors shook his body while sweat moistened his wide, pear-shaped face. His countenance convulsed, shifting between fear, regret, and desperation. Behind him thrashed the children recovered from Stanley's capture. Their bodies convulsed under the bed covers. Regaining her balance against the door, the apothecary's eyes swept the children as they lay afflicted with a hex punctured into their necks, suffering violent, involuntary contortions. She looked at Oliver's hand holding the needle that spiked the children's spirits with imprecation. She readied herself for another fight should he make charge and attempt to plunge anathema into her.

Nyami the dragon peered through the rectangular, brownstone window. The large eye on the conjure construct blinked, closely inspecting the standoff between the conjure man and the conjure woman. A green puff of its breath, exhaled from its nostrils, floated by as it grunted its frustration.

Oliver continued trembling, tears running alongside his perspiration. He lifted the syringe, prepared to strike in appearance. In his head was the delirium directive steering him to attack Miss Ross. Oliver struggled against his injected, maledicted protocol. He turned the needle's tip to his neck, his hand choppy in its rotation as if fighting against the grapple from an invisible foe. His arm bent much the same, tipping the point of the needle against the vein in his neck that bulged with the stress of his actions.

Miss Ross reached out and shouted, "Oliver, no!"

Madame Jeliya slumped to the floor, reached up toward the ceiling, and echoed, "Oliver, no!"

He screamed in short, successive bursts, pushing the hexed-laced needle through his vein and deeper. He thumbed the plunger, administering the curse of a confined nightmare shared with the children shuddering in their beds behind him. Oliver collapsed and Nyami the dragon roared!

Maman Anansi jumped up from the pew and dashed toward her sister-in-conjure. She knelt down and consoled Madame Jeliya, arms around her as the second matriarch calmed her hysteria. "Hold your story together, sister!" Maman Anansi comforted, releasing a soothing incant. She rubbed Madame Jeliya's head, holding her tight.

She shivered, head turning toward Maman Anansi. "My baby! she blurted. "He's hurt the children! Oliver hurt the children!"

"*MOM!*" Oliver's voice tunneled through her head.

Madame Jeliya gasped and flinched!

The world around her disappeared again, and history revealed itself.

Oliver Peters ended another exhausting shift. He stepped out into the city as the sun was just casting the buildings in a golden sheet of light. Pedestrian traffic was beginning to flow along the sidewalks, and Oliver merged with it. He rubbed his eyes, but couldn't seem to get rid of the haze that infected his vision, not even with an incant.

Something whispered in a sing-song pattern, "You. Are. Sleepy. You. Are. Sleepy…" The voice spoke like a clock or metronome's tick-tock. Oliver looked over his shoulder, hearing the lullaby sung directly into his ear. His face curled in frustration, feeling the proximity of someone invading his personal space mixed with his state of fatigue. But there was nothing to see. All he observed were the streets filling with people and fog.

A woman bumped into him. She whispered something. Seductive. Direct into his ear. "Too lazy to crow for days, huh, Mister Peters?" She was a brown-haired, doe-eyed woman with a soft beauty on her peach-colored face.

Oliver stopped to question the woman. She turned around and joined the flow of traffic away from him. The morning haze widened, and Oliver blinked away confusion and weariness long enough to resume his walk up the block. A foggy cloaked phantom rushed him. Its presence blurred the already hazy day. Barreling toward him, it hissed, "In the blood cursed moon!" The wraith passed through him, and Oliver recoiled. No one around reacted to his movements, and instinct suggested to Oliver that he was in an unsafe place for conjure folk. He was not in time. He was not outside of time. He felt the crisp grip of the anathematic realm.

The first voice chuckled and sang, "Run. Quickly." Oliver looked around. He readied his conjure, primed to pirate any hex cast at him and rebound it back to its source. "Hide. Little. Coon." Oliver sprinted away. "We. Hexers. Are. Out. To. Get. You," the slow, eerie, and rhythmic voice teased.

A sharp pain spread across Oliver's back. The epicenter of the piercing discomfort was at his shoulder blade. He winced and turned. The whispering woman was there, a grin on her now hooded face and shimmers of blood-red electric strands whirling around her fingers.

Oliver reached over his shoulder to feel the syringe lodged in his back. Flickers of darkness bombarded his vision. His legs buckled, but he did his best to fight against the pull into unconsciousness. He stumbled, turning around. An oddity stood before him. It was a man with a diamond-shaped clock for a face. He recalled talks by Gordon and Cedron of such a creature. The clock-faced monster stabbed Oliver in the chest with a hexed needle and finished his creepy, old-school children's rhyme, "In. The. Blood. Cursed. Moon…"

Black. Time passed. No alarm clock, but something alarming woke Oliver Peters. A rough voice snarling, "I'm gunna whip you until you know what love is, boy!" A violent crack of air echoed, and a deep lash split the flesh on Oliver's naked back. His eyes opened in shock! A wide stream of searing heat bled warm blood and frosty pain across Oliver's back. His body stiffened! Hands above his head, bound by chains extending to the ceiling. He was somewhere in the middle of nowhere, stripped of his clothes. A large and cold, empty, green-walled room kept the day's summer heat at bay. There was no air conditioning chilling the room. The presence of four villains iced the atmosphere and dampened any comfort. Oliver didn't believe cold could get into him anymore than it was. Then his flesh was split by a hexed whip, and cold seeped into him with the purpose of imbuing the pain tearing at his nerves.

Oliver bit down hard on nothing, teeth gnashing against one another as he attempted to recover from the shock of Willie the Lich's two lashes. Lazy Crow, the clock-headed monster, stood at a distance on Oliver's right side. The smoggy phantom, Grave Clothes, hovered at a distance on Oliver's left. Adamina Red stood in front of him, close enough to kiss. She watched Oliver with a child-like curiosity, a strange sympathetic expression widening her already large eyes as Willie smothered his back with lash after bloody lash. She moved her face close to his, inspecting him as pain congealed shock in expression after every cut from Willie's accursed whip.

There was a pause in Willie's attacks. Adamina Red walked around Oliver's dangling body as he fought to stay on his feet, slipping when the pain buckled his legs. His back dripped, and his feet slid on collected pools of blood. Adamina raised her right hand, fingers sparking with blood-red strands of energy. She pressed against Oliver's bleeding, split flesh. His teeth drew away from one another as his mouth opened, and he screamed!

The events occurring at the start of the new day ran from Madame Jeliya's eyes as tears. The viewing room's environment faded back into view as she wept. She leaned into Maman Anansi's tranquil embrace and sobbed, "What have they done to my baby?"

There was more to the story, and young Dajon Brickhouse was the audience to the missing act. Having slept at his friend Noah's place overnight, he made a quick return home after having breakfast there. He noticed Lady Arachne's car parked at the sidewalk and wondered what the matriarch was doing at his house. He recalled past, sneaky deeds and speculated with a roll of his eyes which one he'd been caught in. The most recent was a quick coin dump and pull of a slot lever several nights ago at Eve's Hallow's opening. *It was only once!* Dajon whined to himself. *No one saw.* Then he considered and thought, *Well, someone clearly saw if that's what I'm busted for.*

He slowed his steps up the stairs in an attempt to savor the moment between freedom and being grounded or worse. Slow lift. Right leg. Foot planted on the first step, and a dragon's screech ran through his head from ear to ear. Dajon paused, startled by the sound of his conjured construct's wail. It came again, and he looked over his shoulder as a reflex. The other side of the street wasn't in view. Harlem brownstones dwindled away in drips of white light. Nyami's next cry shifted from sound to sight.

The words smelled foul. A terrible odor that burned as it rested inside the dragon's nasal cavity. Oliver Peters' speech was its origin. He spoke and sounded like himself, but his words throbbed with a heavy, anathematic miasma that caused the dragon construct to grunt and huff a puff of smoke from its nostrils. "I'm here to check on the children—for my Mom," Nyami heard Oliver say to Miss Lavette Ross at the parlor entrance to her brownstone. Close to his proximity, Miss Ross' nose, while not as acute as the dragon construct, smelled the odor of deceit filter through Oliver's hexed lips and tongue. A smell from sound raised Miss Ross' instincts. It was such an off-putting tone.

Harlem's décor configured out of light and concurrent events became a memory for Dajon to ponder. He turned around and rushed up the stairs and through the front door. "Mom! Pop!" he called as he entered the house, tossing off his backpack. "Mom! Pop!" he shouted again. His instinct directed him to the family room. Mister and Missus Brickhouse were there seated with Lady Arachne. Dajon had forgotten about her car parked outside. He stood straight when he entered the room, and he presented a bow of his neck toward the Fable Avenue matriarch. "Lady Arachne," Dajon greeted.

"Dajon," she uttered his name with a slight, knowing smile on her face.

Dajon deciphered Lady Arachne's countenance. Her presence caused him to remember his initial reaction to seeing her car on the curb. "Am I in trouble?" he questioned with his eyes wide and panning from his mother to his father to community matriarch. He searched their faces attempting to decrypt how this gathering concerned him.

All three adults were amused by Dajon's antics. Lady Arachne assured, "No, Dajon. You're not in any trouble."

"Okay…" Dajon blurted. "Good. I was in the arcade most of the night at the casino…"

Mister and Missus Brickhouse found Dajon's words peculiar. "Is there a reason you need to stress that, young man?" Missus Brickhouse questioned with a raised eyebrow.

"Answer y' mother, son," Mister Brickhouse insisted.

His father's voice was calm but possessed an air of fatherly, authoritative threat. Dajon always admired how his father was able to do that. It was because of that respect for his father that Dajon confessed, "One pull of a lever. One pull. On a coin-operated slot. I didn't win anything!"

Lady Arachne made a face, but quickly veiled her disappointment. Her eyes spotted Mister and Missus Brickhouse and waited.

"Dajon!" his mother scolded with the simple use of his name, which was another feat Dajon admired from his parents. All manner of chastisement with the utterance of just his name. "You could get into serious trouble if you're caught. You could put Eve's Hallow at risk!"

Dajon dropped his head. "I'm sorry…"

Mister Brickhouse chimed in, saying, "It took a lot of conjure work to square away all the legal elements and papers to reopen that landmark. If bad guys can't put a needle to it, son, they'll find a law to do it. Don't do that again. It was only once. Make sure it stays that way. Hopefully no cameras caught that!"

"Yes, sir…" Dajon questioned to himself why he opened his 'big mouth'. But he was in the clear. He lifted his head and inquired, "Miss Arachne, there's still some kind of matter, yes?"

"Yes, young man," she started. "I've known for some time now that you've been assisting Miss Melinda Clarke with conjure. I've been meaning to speak on this to your mother and father."

Dajon looked at his parents first. His eyes returned to Lady Arachne. He opened his mouth to speak, but only unintelligible bursts of air escaped as he struggled to find words. He didn't know whether to defend himself or simply explain. His expression froze, and he was still.

Mister Brickhouse stated, "We know you mean well, son. Whatever it is she can do, it's probably overwhelming to her since her parents know nothing of conjure, *Ojulowo* or *ọpọlọpọ-eya*. We know your heart's in the right place..."

Lady Arachne looked at Mister Brickhouse. "I still say her parents must be informed," she directed. "I know how this sounds—and maybe it sounds the way it sounds because, well, that's the way it sounds."

"Lady Arachne...?" inquired Mister Brickhouse.

The matriarch paused for a moment. "Chilton," she addressed Mister Brickhouse by his name, "perhaps it would be best for you to speak to the girl's father." Lady Arachne looked at Missus Brickhouse and stated, "...The girl's mother... She's just—"

"Very far outside the conjure culture," Missus Brickhouse stated with a slight chuckle. "I understand, Lady Arachne. Maybe we'd be surprised. She might be a descendant of the Evocare family."

Lady Arachne rolled her eyes. "I doubt that, *chil'*."

Missus Brickhouse turned to Dajon, and said to her son, "I'm sorry, honey. We're not trying to be mean toward your friend's mother..." Dajon didn't react. His expression remained frozen, but his body shuddered with subtle tremors. Missus Brickhouse's bright countenance melted into concern.

At the same moment, Chilton affirmed to Lady Arachne, "I'll have a talk with Melinda's father as soon as possible."

"Thank you," replied the matriarch.

Missus Brickhouse transitioned from chair to her knees, moving in a graceful motion with her arms out toward her son. She embraced him as her instinct perceived trouble trembling him. "Baby...?" Her voice burst as an extrasensory warning that pulled Chilton and Lady Arachne's attention to Dajon's shivering fit.

Chilton joined his wife's side. "Son...?" he said, feeling the weight of concern.

Lady Arachne stood up and reached out with her power to screen Dajon's mind.

Nyami uncoiled her long neck from around her resting body and lifted it up and over the brownstones she nested behind. Her neck snaked down the block, spotting Oliver's interaction with Miss Ross, squawking and snarling as it drew closer. Its body followed, crawling over the brownstones as its neck extended to its farthest reach. Cars rushed through the spectral beast. It was invisible to normal folk driving or walking through Fable Avenue's block, but conjure folk were baffled and became tense about the protective aegis' crawl through the streets.

Oliver heard the dragon. He could see the construct's approach from the corner of his eye, but he gave it no attention. The ghostly creature couldn't be missed. But the hex possessing Oliver alerted him to Nyami's intent to protect the area from a threat.

Him.

Miss Ross noticed too, and she said something to Oliver. The words she used were obstructing, hindering his progress to enter. Oliver heard a clock ticking. It sounded like a voice, streaming through his blood and echoing up to his head. His lips curled as the dragon moved closer, baring teeth. He raised his hand, opened his palm, and summoned a twisted configuration of his personal conjure. Thought and desire was culled from Miss Ross' mind, copied and deformed, and resubmitted into her head to grow as distress and nightmare.

The apothecary buckled and slumped to her knees. Her eyes were wide as dread filled her vision. She saw mistakes in her head. Her concoctions' formulae rancid and toxic. Conjure folk vomited before slamming to the ground, writhing in their final moments with violent pains as her potions dissolved their stomachs. Flesh burned, blistered and decayed as her lotions opened wounds and created new ones. Children died in their sleep with the contents of her medicines coursing through their blood, having turned septic and foul.

The nightmare possessed Miss Ross, and she sobbed while pleading for forgiveness. Oliver stepped passed her and journeyed upstairs to the nursery where the children lay asleep. He entered their room and removed a syringe that was filled with a nightmare. Each child's neck was pricked, and their body was infected with a shared torment in their sleep. The children's bodies thrashed about as the nightmare took effect. A terrible hex ticking away at their lives.

Below. On the steps. Nyami opened her maw and bathed Miss Ross in a fiery panacea. The nightmare burned away, but the dragon was careful. Too much fire could burn a person away with their hex. Miss Ross collapsed. She was drained of her nightmare, but also near empty of vitality. She caught her breath, stumbling as she used her entryway to regain her stance. Up! She turned and ascended the stairs with as much vigor as she could muster. She was bent down, using her hand on the stair in front of her to hoist herself along, body dragging against the railing.

Nyami raised her head and peeked inside the nursery. She spied Oliver Peters rotate his upper body and spot Miss Ross leaning on her arm in the nursery doorway, catching her breath. He sneered and faced her. Tremors shook his body while sweat moistened his wide, pear-shaped face. Good remained in Oliver, and it struggled against the possessing hex that governed his actions. Tears and determination populated his face as he turned the needle on himself, resisting the commands of the hex inside him, and impaling the needle down into *his neck. Miss Ross cried out, "Oliver, no!" Oliver's deed was already done by then, and Nyami understood the good in Oliver's intentions. He was going into the nightmare he'd injected into the children. He was going to keep them safe and together, and his last, frantic cry was to alert his mother—community matriarch, Madame Jeliya.*

The children shook with unruly, violent flails. Oliver too, his body on the floor. They needed soothing. They needed music, and so Nyami had an alert to shout as well. The boy who conjured her into existence with soft violin play. She tilted her head to the sky and roared a distress call!

Unseen history, recounted as a memory, washed away from Dajon's sight. His parents surrounded him, kneeling down. Lady Arachne stood over him. He was shivering. "N-N-N-Nyami…" he said. "I heard her. There's trouble on the street. Oliver…"

Missus Brickhouse caressed her son's face. She looked up at Lady Arachne. Before the matriarch could utter a word, Dajon blurted at her, "I think Madame Jeliya is gonna reach out and talk to you…"

Sister! the voice streamed through Lady Arachne's thoughts. **There's trouble on the street. My son has done something terrible! I sensed you at the Brickhouse residence. Is Dajon there? His construct sent a call!**

Lady Arachne informed Dajon, "You're correct, young man. Madame Jeliya has just reached out." She turned away and replied, **Dajon saw trouble. He heard his construct. I'll find Gordon to bring you and Dajon to Fable Avenue in a blink.**

I'm at the funeral home with Maman Anansi, Madame Jeliya informed. **Something terrible occurred with Stephanie! We have her on an altar here.**

Lady Arachne made a face and huffed. She dropped her face into her palm. **My goodness! Let me work on my end, sister. I'll send Gordon to you.**

Thank you…

Lady Arachne lifted her head. She groaned and put her hands on her hips. Then she reached out with her mind. **Gordon!**

41

Benny made a face and retorted to Gordon, "Change of scenery, my ass! *Cedron* wanted a change of scenery with Leah so you here in Harlem."

Gordon chuckled, shoving a spoonful of cereal into his mouth. He chewed and swallowed before answering, "Whatever, my dude. It all works out."

Gordon! Lady Arachne's voice tunneled through his mind.

He sat up straight, eyes wide. Benny reacted to Gordon's sudden movement by pausing his own. "Yo, sun, you okay?"

Gordon raised a hand. "It's Lady Arachne," he briefed. "She just reached out."

Benny rested his spoon into his bowl of cereal. "She supposed to be across the street talking with my parents? Everything cool?"

Gordon didn't answer Benny. He replied to the Fable Avenue matriarch as he stood from his chair, **Lady Arachne! Is everything okay?**

Lady Arachne inquired, **Where are you, Gordon?** Then she relayed, **Madame Jeliya needs your help. Something's happened on Fable Avenue.**

Gordon's expressions shifted in various ways defining concern. Benny did his best to decipher each facial transition. He waited, anxious for Gordon's mental conversation to end and for any information, especially concerning his family.

Gordon communicated to Lady Arachne that he was across the street. The matriarch responded, **I'm sending Dajon to you. Take him to the funeral home and find Madame Jeliya. Go to Miss Ross' brownstone. There's a problem with the children.**

Sure. I can pop right into the nursery, Gordon stated.

Good. I'll let her know you're bringing Madame Jeliya and Dajon.

Lady Arachne's cerebral presence drifted away. The doorbell rang, and Gordon left the kitchen to answer the door. His black, cosmic outfit crawled from his flesh as a shadow and then solidified over him with each step he made. He remained unmasked. "It's Dajon!" he said over his shoulder to Benny, crossing through the front room.

Benny jumped up from his chair and followed Gordon. "What's going on?"

Gordon answered the door. Dajon was standing there with violin case strapped across his back. Benny was relieved his brother appeared unharmed, but now he was further confused. Gordon waved Dajon inside, saying, "Come on in, kid!" Dajon stepped inside and Gordon closed the door. He turned to Benny and instructed him, "Go upstairs and tell my Pops that

I'm heading over to Fable Avenue. Something's wrong with the kids we rescued."

Dajon blurted, "Oliver's all hexed up! He needled the kids, stuck himself. It's a mess!"

Benny's facial features contorted. "Shit!" he cursed.

"They need soothing, I'm guessin'," Gordon calculated, eyeing Dajon strapped with his violin.

"Nyami's doin' the guessin'. I'm ready to play," Dajon noted.

Gordon told Benny, "I'm heading to Madame Jeliya at the funeral home. I'ma take her to the Avenue too."

"Walk good," Benny advised. "I'll tell ya Pops, now." He turned to ascend the stairs.

Gordon called, "Hey!" Benny stopped and faced him. "Armor y' arm up. Meet me there with Neyeli. I'm sure we'll need her too."

"Sure thing!" replied Benny, and then he returned to task.

Gordon advised as Benny climbed the stairs, "Fly! Don't walk or ride!" Then he grabbed Dajon's arm and the two blinked away. The environment rearranged itself around them like the shifts of a magic, colored cube. New colors came together, and they were standing in the viewing room in front of Stephanie's altar. Gordon and Dajon's eyes locked onto her sleeping body. Current circumstances on Fable Avenue were wiped from focus as Stephanie's eerie stillness kept them in place. Madame Jeliya and Maman Anansi rose from a pew and stepped up behind Gordon and Dajon. Gordon sensed their approach, and their advance broke him from his stillness. He let go of Dajon's arm and spun around. His face was a slideshow of questions.

Maman Anansi addressed his concerns with a simple statement. "It's been a dark start to the day, Gordon. My daughter is fine for now. Please escort Madame Jeliya to Fable Avenue. See to those events. I have everything under control here."

Madame Jeliya reached her hand out to Gordon. Her face was stained with the evidence of having been recently sobbing. She was together now with a sense of duty in her eyes. Gordon took her hand. He reached back to Dajon, putting his other hand on his shoulder. The boy hadn't moved since Stephanie's slumbering body entered his sight. Things didn't get better for his vision when Gordon popped them from existence and into Miss Ross' nursery. The children flailed and screamed! Oliver was on the floor doing the same. The imagery choked Dajon and cemented him in place.

Madame Jeliya knelt down over her son as he thrashed a spastic dance while trapped in the nightmare. She held out her hands, speaking incants to tranquilize her son's body. His shaking persisted, and Madame Jeliya's instinct stayed her ability to probe into his mind. She felt the caution.

It was a palpable sense, warning her that an extrasensory intrusion could collapse his mental faculties and funnel him into a permanent state of terror-induced reverie. She also detected the cursed scars on his back.

"Dajon!" Madame Jeliya called the young boy. "Dajon! I need you to start playing. Focus and project, young man." No music, at least not quick enough for Madame Jeliya as she watched her son gripped with nightmare and shakes. She called again, "Dajon!" But the boy didn't respond. He was too stunned and frozen, deeply distressed at the chaotic scene of children screaming and in a flailing fit.

Gordon spoke, "Madame Jeliya! We got more trouble."

He was at the window, peering down at Miss Ross attempting to simmer a gathered crowd consisting of the children's parents. Perched in the street was the construct Nyami. Madame Jeliya jumped up and rushed to the window. She looked down and observed Miss Ross contending with the anxious parents. "Shit!" the Elder cursed. "I'm sure they sense their children's distress." She stepped away from the window, turned, and rushed from the room. "I'll handle this. I'll be right back. Dajon! You get that violin playing, young man!"

No movement from the kid. Gordon attended to him. He rotated Dajon around to be face-to-face. Gordon told him, "Hey! Kid. You're at bat. We need you to start—" Dajon turned his head. His eyes drifted to the erratic children. He looked at Oliver on the floor. Gordon waved his hand in Dajon's face. Dajon looked back at him, face shaking. "Just relax, kid. Just breathe. I'll be right back. Okay?" Dajon nodded. Gordon closed his eyes, reached out, and focused. He located Papa Solomon's presence at the Water Bug Hollow church. He blinked away, coming into existence inside the church's conference room. He appeared in front of the closed door. The room's occupants jumped at his appearance. "My apologies," Gordon expressed. Papa Solomon was there with Satchel "Old Goon", Simaetha Ghedemere, their daughter Lilian, Terrence Tzidkiyahu, and Naamah Mbu. "There's an urgent matter happening on Fable Avenue." Papa Solomon's expression turned perplexed. Gordon informed, "I think Oliver got jumped by needlemen. Stanley's goons. He's hexed, out of control. They got him to needle the kids."

Papa Solomon stood straight and blurted, "My son!"

"They look possessed, trapped in fits," Gordon continued. "Oliver turned the needle on himself after the deed was done. You need to come with me."

Papa Solomon hurried to Gordon. He told the others, "Stay at the ready should I call for any assistance."

Everyone stood, concern dripping on their faces. Naamah affirmed, "With all our conjure, Papa Solomon. Travel well!"

Papa Solomon nodded at her. He put his hand in Gordon's, and he was taken from the room transported into existence on Fable Avenue. He was taken aback at the reality of being in his study, telling Gordon, "I assumed we'd be in Miss Ross' nursery."

"Nyami reached out to Dajon," Gordon noted. "She believes his music can soothe the fits Oliver and the children are suffering from."

"You need me to assist with the horn?" Papa Solomon inquired, patience slipping away with each word.

"Dajon's in shock, Papa Solomon," Gordon made clear. "It's an intense scene for the kid. Something needs to soothe *him*."

Papa Solomon took up his birthright. The horn never felt so light in his hands. "Deliver me to bedlam, Gordon," he ordered.

Gordon responded, "Yessir!" He put a hand around the Fable Avenue patriarch's wrist and took him into the chaos.

Papa Solomon understood immediately. Seeing his son writhing on the floor and screaming was a terrible sight. The children crying out in terror, shaking. He was as immovable, possessed with shock, as Dajon. Gordon went to the window and looked down. Madame Jeliya and Miss Ross were still confronting the frenzied parents. Gordon heard the screaming going on behind him. He saw the parents in hysterics in front of him. Madame Jeliya and Miss Ross shouted them down. In thrashes. In flails. Pandemonium possessed the avenue.

Then came music. Light jazz. Soft notes from a mystical trumpet muted the mayhem. Low at first, and then there was a heightened harmony. Gordon turned away from the window. He spotted Dajon. Apprehension and trauma melted off the young boy. He closed his eyes and opened his hands. He spoke an incant and the violin case strapped to his back unlocked and opened. His instrument and bow floated to his palms. In a graceful motion, he tucked his violin in place and started playing in symmetry with Papa Solomon. Music filled the room, a melodic blend of classical and jazz that dampened the spastic dance gyrating Oliver and the children. Dajon and Papa Solomon played and played and played and played until a relaxed posture endured in both the children and Oliver without the assistance of the soothing sounds.

Dajon opened his hands. His violin and bow retreated to the case on his back with the use of an incant. The case closed and locked by will of the same power. Gordon walked over to Dajon and patted him on the shoulder. "You did it, kid," he congratulated.

Dajon dropped his head. A dispirited look colonized his face. "Yeah…" he murmured. He turned and left the room, shuffling through the gathered persons crowding the doorway. Madame Jeliya, Miss Ross, and the parents were there. Miss Ross entered first after Dajon passed and headed downstairs. She knelt down next to Oliver's body and wiped the palm of her hand above his face. She spoke an incant, conducting a mystic examination.

"Miss Ross…?" said Papa Solomon.

She took a moment, finishing her extrasensory analysis. "The body is physically at rest, but his mind is ensnared in a nightmare. Soul trying to hold it together. I'm sure the children are the same. I won't probe any further. It could do harm. Only got what I could because of him being a little more at ease." She stood and tasked Gordon, "Can you lift him and bring him to the room across the hall? Rest him on any of the beds there."

"Yes, Miss Ross," replied Gordon, quickly attending to his duty. He scooped Oliver's stocky frame into his arms, cradling him. Gordon's elevated strength allowed him to lift Oliver with ease, but it was still an ordeal to keep the dangling limbs from tipping him off balance.

Madame Jeliya slipped into the room, and the parents moved aside as Gordon made his exit. "Be careful, Gordon," Madame Jeliya alerted. "He has…" she started sobbing. Papa Solomon took his wife's side and embraced her. "He has…hexed scars on his back. Whippings…" she let out before falling into a complete sob. Papa Solomon held her tighter.

Everyone was aware of the undertone from Madame Jeliya's warning. The terrible Willie the Lich had a hand in Oliver's grim turn. Gordon took his time crossing the hall, but he managed to make it into the room across the way and rest Oliver down on a bed.

Miss Ross permitted the parents to see their children after giving them a quick, mental exam. "What happens now?" asked Miss Alicia, mother to one of the older children, a sixteen-year-old girl named Michelle.

Papa Solomon answered, "We're going to extract them from the nightmare. I'm going to assemble my sister, Mister Goodspeed across the hall, and a few others. We'll find them. We'll bring their minds back to their bodies."

Mister Tierney, father to the unconscious, fourteen-year-old Douglas Tierney, railed, "A nightmare hold can be permanent. There can't be much time before that effect takes place."

"Permanent or *worse!*" Papa Solomon amended, force in his voice. "My wife and I have a son suffering just the same," he soothed Madame Jeliya as he embraced her, free hand up and down her back. "My son's ailments might be recent, and not as much of an addition as what your child has already been through—your *children* have already been through—but I have a determination to bring resolve as well." He took a moment, catching his breath. Mister Tierney too loosened his demeanor. Then Papa Solomon said in a more relaxed tone, "We'll make that prognosis, and we'll act in haste. I know it's been a long road. Your next actions will be very difficult, but you need to say your peace with your children and return home. Miss Ross will notify you of any developments."

There was reluctance, but there was also realization that nothing else could be done except follow their patriarch's orders. The parents surrounded their children and gave them prayers. Madame Jeliya slipped from Papa Solomon's embrace and left the room. Gordon was outside listening. She walked by him, went downstairs, and left the house. Gordon looked at Papa Solomon. Fable Avenue's patriarch at first kept his eyes on his wife's departure. Dismay dulled his expression when she took the stairs to exit the house. Then his eyes trailed up and met Gordon's stare. He exhaled and looked away.

The parents shuffled out of the room. Mister Tierney stopped and presented a sincere apology to Papa Solomon. "That's fine, Stephen. Thank you," Papa Solomon replied. "Look, I know this hasn't been easy on you all—"

"We're grateful, Papa Solomon," Stephen assured. "We're just tired."

"I know. Again, it'll be hard, but get your rest."

Stephen nodded, and then he left the room.

Papa Solomon looked at the children. Miss Ross attended to them. "Keep close to them, Miss Ross," he told her. "Send if there's any trouble."

Miss Ross stood straight and faced him. "Things should remain in order. Your horn and the boy's violin smothered their shakes." She beamed. "That gives me hope for exorcising them from the nightmare."

Papa Solomon nodded. He left the room, making his way to the stairs. Gordon remained leaning on the rail, arms crossed. "Keep close," Papa Solomon told him.

"Yessir," Gordon responded.

Papa Solomon left the house. Dajon was sitting on the front steps, head down. The community patriarch stepped down a few stairs, turned, and faced the young boy. "You did well in there, Dajon. You played well." The boy raised his head and gave a mechanical nod. He was in his moment, and Papa Solomon allowed his catharsis to run its course. "It's okay to reflect on any errors you made, but don't let it bring you down. Be proud of yourself, brave boy. You did well," he reiterated. He turned and walked home.

The dragon construct lowered its face to be at eye level with Dajon. It grunted. Dajon understood the noise it made. "I'm okay," he huffed, arms crossed and looking down. Like Papa Solomon, Nyami let Dajon have his moment. The dragon made its way back to its nest down the street and behind the brownstones. It squawked much the same sentiment as Papa Solomon's departing words. Dajon exhaled, and he thought about how well he played. A subtle grin broke through.

Down the street. Inside Madame Jeliya's sanctum. Fable Avenue's second matriarch prepared a third glass of rum and tonic for herself, which was more rum than tonic. Papa Solomon walked in. She sensed his presence and said over her shoulder as he entered from the stairs, "Children! *My* child!" she hissed. "In my damn house!" She turned and faced her husband. "This whole damn street is my house!" she declared. Then she tapped her chest and growled, "I know we're looking for the *primary* solution and, and, and, and some goddamned, grand ritual to right the world, but until that happens, my husband, people have to *die!* We need to make blood moves! These sickly men must die, and their insipid, consort cunts as well." She took a big sip, spilling a little of her drink as her hand shook with anxiety. She wiped her lips with the whole of her sleeve. "Should offspring come of their union, have no mercy on them, for they have shown no mercy upon my child; the children of conjure!" She made a swift pivot, walking to her chair and taking a seat. She crossed her legs, eyes bent and running with thoughts of retaliation behind them. Papa Solomon remained silent as he walked up to her. Madame Jeliya's lionesses were curled up on either side of her chair. The large, male lion, glowing with a blue incandescence, rested in a corner of the room. She lifted her drink at her husband and pronounced, "Blood moves, you hear me! There must be war!" She took a sip, swallowed and said while looking away, "The fight must be taken straight to these devils. These *grèf* who cause me grief." Her free hand stroked the lioness at her left. She looked at her husband and contended, "*You!* Are a wartime chief. *I* demand war. *You!* Make that happen." She nodded and took another swig of her drink. "I've heard them stories, Mister Peters. You've twisted and contorted the bones of people who've been off-code with conjure. People of our community close to selling us out or acting in despicable ways against their own kind. I've heard the tales of Papa Solomon. Yes, I have!" Madame Jeliya shook her head. "And the shit I heard you done did to men and women armed with needles chilled my blood and ignited the hottest passion between my thighs *all* at the same time." She took a moment before saying, "I want *that* nigger right now. I *need* that nigger right now, because war is required. By Ixu and Gira, *you* are the *pretos velhos* sent from the cosmos to make war, but *I* am the voice that calls for it. Right. Now!"

Papa Solomon took the drink from his wife. She caressed both her lionesses as he told her, "I hurt needlemen something bad." He took a sip of the drink. It was good and strong, inspiring as a drink of spirits should be. "Ironically, I worked alongside the man who commands them now."

"Well, he walked away and chose the losing side," Madame Jeliya snapped. "His mother's foul people. *Grèf!* That bastard sonava bitch!" She shook her head and exhaled. "Things I've heard you do to protect this community, Mister Peters, made me so hot I conceived children without one touch from you."

Papa Solomon chuckled, "That's a slight exaggeration." He took another sip of her drink. "And you weren't supposed to hear about those things I've done."

"Perhaps," she replied in a kittenish manner. "On both accounts, Mister Peters. Perhaps."

He handed the drink back to her. "We'll deal with getting our children from the nightmare. That's first. I'll follow protocol after that," he informed. "I've been promised a go ahead for war. We have our children, despite circumstances. The Old Goon has Water Bug Hollow. The next step is war. Blood moves. I'll talk to the Gwuinee folk we got here. Follow their rules, make it official. But, with or without their consent, there will be war." A beat. A grin. "You act like you didn't become my equal with how you pulled information from that Wyatt Jakobi's brain." He looked at her lions and remarked, "My sister just put a holy knife in his head."

Madame Jeliya eyed her husband. She was silent but talking loud with her stare.

He knew what she was saying, and so he replied to her, "As you wish."

She sipped.

She swallowed.

She was satisfied.

ajon listened as his older brother Benny reminded him, "You beat down bullies older than you, sticking up for people. You took a bullet, kid, and you woke up from that! You've conjured a dragon that protects the block. You're strong, sun!" Benny nudged Dajon as they sat on the couch in the Goodspeed's Brooklyn brownstone. "You're a Brickhouse," he told him. Dajon smiled. Benny added, "And I ain't talkin' about how the women we got eyes on are built."

Dajon gave his brother a curious eye. "Neyeli's as slim as they come," he expressed, arms still folded.

Benny shook his head. "Nah, kid," he said through a grin. "That's called 'slim-thick'."

"What?"

Benny waved the notion away. "Nothin'," he asserted. "Look, that just brings me to another point. You guiding a young girl through something that's scary on its own. She comin' into her conjure. Mom and Pops told me. You're a hero, kid. Trust me. Don't let this freeze up take that away from you. We all have that time. Gordon even told me he saw the heroes of long ago. Pious Wars shit. Know what he said? He said they was just human. Regular people with extraordinary abilities and still scared to death. But they fought. They'd freeze too, but they eventually thawed and moved. We all got that freeze moment."

Dajon looked up at his older brother and inquired, "When was yours?"

"I've froze up plenty of times. I got age on you, young one." Then Benny brought up and relayed, "Cedron did knock me on my ass. Knocked me clear out."

"True. But you still met the challenge."

Benny disagreed with a head shake. "Nah, kid," the older Brickhouse brother told the younger. "I *arrived* at the challenge. The challenge met me. Clocked y' brother right on this pretty face. I was out! Besides, my freeze up was simply never being able to tell Cedron the truth."

"That you helped put a bullet in him…?" asked Dajon. "I'da knocked you on your ass too."

Benny made a face, but a smile eventually came through. He chuckled, nodding his head from side-to-side, thinking. Then he commented, "Let's put into context: He was hexed."

"His strength wasn't!" Dajon retorted.

Benny rolled his eyes, smile in place. His head dropped. "Yeah, it kinda was."

Dajon remembered. "Oh! Yeah. Missus Fallows meddling. Still, though."

Benny raised a hand. "Still, though, you get my point is my point." He put his arm around his younger brother and shook him. "You're good, kid. *You're a good kid.* You're a hero very much depended on in these Street Fables."

Dajon relented and felt better. "Yeah…" he exhaled.

Benny palmed the top of his brother's hair and shook. He questioned, "You ready to do some more playing?"

"Yeah," Dajon answered.

Benny urged his brother, "Let's get up. They're setting the ritual now."

"Maman Anansi is here?"

"She should be," Benny replied. "Gordon blinked away to check on her, bring her here. They're moving Stephanie's body." His face contorted, perplexed. "You know anything about that? What's going on there?"

Dajon shook his head. "No. I saw it. Put me in a shock before I was brought to Miss Ross'. Maybe Sean's spirit attacked her. He was haunting her."

"Yeah. I guess." Then he uttered, "Just another day in the culture…"

Gordon popped into existence wearing his cosmic suit. No mask. He looked at the Brickhouse brothers. "We ready?" he asked, hands on his hips. "I just got Maman Anansi to Miss Ross' place."

"All good," reported Benny. "You mind if we walk there?"

Gordon shook his head. "Not at all. Saves me some strength for what's coming."

"Cool. Thanks." Benny elbowed Dajon before standing up. "Come on, little brother. Let's go."

Dajon leaned forward and opened his violin case. He retrieved his instrument and the bow, and then he got up. Gordon nodded his head and said, "I'll meet you there." Without moving, Gordon blinked from existence. He popped into being in the nursery where rested the six children trapped in the nightmare.

Gordon heard Miss Ross describe to Maman Anansi, "Nyami healed me, but the construct stressed its fire might drive Oliver and the children insane. Its fire left me fatigued, even as it restored me. I could barely get up the stairs."

"You did fine, Love," Maman Anansi assured. "You did. From my experience, dragons always know best," she jested.

The apothecary ignored the attempt at humor. She suggested, "Perhaps I could concoct a salve that could be rubbed onto them, put on their lips. Something that could cleanse the hex and the nightmare. All of this just sounds so elaborate, Maman Anansi. I don't mean to be contrary, just cautious."

The Grand Matriarch looked up and spotted Gordon's presence. "Ah! Gordon. Where is Dajon?"

"On his way," he answered. "He's feeling better and up to the task. Benny and him decided to walk, is all," he explained. "They'll be here soon."

"Good," Maman Anansi replied. "We'll be in the other room. Miss Ross and Madame Jeliya will be stationed here. Madame Jeliya will be up soon with Miss Campbell as well. Come on." She turned and said to Miss Ross, "This will exhaust all of us. It's going to push our conjure to the limit. We unfortunately don't have the luxury of time to create the proper serum or salve."

"Maman Anansi, I've considered the formula from what I already have at the ready!" Miss Ross pleaded. "I can put something together."

"Recalculate those recipes for after we disperse this nightmare from Oliver and the children," Maman Anansi ordered through a pleasant smile. "They'll need something to stabilize them and give them strength." She put a hand on Miss Ross' shoulder. "I understand your concern. I'm not being dismissive. As taxing as this endeavor will be, Love, it's certain. Now isn't the time for theoretical formula."

Miss Ross took a breath. "Yes, Maman Anansi," she said.

Maman Anansi told her, "But, I suggest you keep those formula for later use. So, we ain't got to be engulfed in a task like this again."

Miss Ross repeated, "Yes, Maman Anansi."

The head matriarch and Gordon left the room. Miss Ross took a seat, watching over the children. In the hall, at the top of the stairs, Maman Anansi and Gordon spotted Madame Jeliya with Dajon, Benny and Neyeli in tow. The small troupe entered through the front door. "Sister!" Maman Anansi called. "Miss Ross is in the room with the children. Can you assist there?"

Madame Jeliya led the climb up the stairs. "Yes," she replied reaching the top. She gave Maman Anansi a hug. "How's Stephanie?"

"She's fine," the lead matriarch reported. "She's still at rest, but she's at the house. Martin's with her. Gordon was kind enough to bring her there. It was a gentle pop and blink. Andre is covering for you at the funeral home. Community folk are helping, too."

Madame Jeliya nodded, thankful. She peered into either room. "Let's give this problem a resolve."

"Yes," agreed Maman Anansi.

Madame Jeliya turned to Neyeli and prepped, "You have your conjure in order. You will open and guide this story. You are strong, *etidyan*."

Neyeli took a breath. "Yes, Madame Jeliya. I'm ready." She looked at Maman Anansi.

The chief matriarch assured, "I will be a battery for you, Miss Campbell. When you need, you draw as much power as you need."

Neyeli shook her head. She turned and looked at Benny. He said, "You'll be fine, Neyeli-baby." She took his hand and walked with Benny into the room where Oliver was at rest. Dajon followed. Gordon stayed behind with the matriarchs.

Maman Anansi noted to Madame Jeliya, "The proper symbols have been sketched onto drawing boards and placed under the children's beds. Oliver's too. Two more boards have been placed on either side of his bed. Leah insisted on etching the symbols."

"Where is my baby girl?" asked Madame Jeliya.

"She's in the room with Oliver," she looked at Gordon and noted, "Cedron's there, too."

Madame Jeliya slipped by Maman Anansi and stated, "Let me see her real quick." She called her daughter as she hurried into the room, "Leah!"

Leah Peters ran into her mother's arms, and the two embraced tight. "I know you all will get him back," she said to her mother. "All of them!"

"We will, baby. We will," Madame Jeliya assured her daughter. "Those aren't just empty, optimistic words."

Papa Solomon joined the embrace.

It was an endearing moment for the Peters family, and it pained Maman Anansi to announce, "Cedron, Leah, Benny, you three will have to wait outside. I'm sorry, but we can't have you here." She said to Gordon and Cedron's father, "Maximillian, you as well." He was there by Althea Goodspeed's side. She was staying, her spirit assisting with travel into the nightmare.

The Peters family tightened their embrace, and then they exhaled and let go. "I've done my duty," stated Leah. "Bring 'em back," she said with watery eyes.

Madame Jeliya mouthed the words, *we will*.

Cedron patted Gordon on the shoulder. "Get 'em, kid."

"Conjure kin goin' in," replied Gordon.

Benny pounded Dajon's chest. He pointed and told his brother, "You got this…"

"I do," the little brother replied, pride glowing in his voice.

Benny gave a nod and a wink to Neyeli. She responded with a beautiful, beaming smile and a wink of her own. Maximillian kissed his wife's hands. "Dance," was all he said to her. She nodded her head at him in return.

He left the room with Cedron, Leah, and Benny. Madame Jeliya was close behind. She saw the small party exit the brownstone as she passed the stairs and walked into the room with the children. She took a seat next to Miss Ross. The two women smiled at one another with a sense of duty brightening the expression in their eyes.

In the room across the hall, four chairs were positioned in a half-moon configuration around Oliver's bed. Top Hat was on one end. Gordon sat next to him. Neyeli was to his right. Maman Anansi next to her. Seated and ready. Papa Solomon and Dajon Brickhouse stood behind them. Lips on trumpet. Violin rested on shoulder, chin tucked to instrument. Papa Solomon played, concentrating hard to let the spirit of his father and grandfather move his desperate fingers. Dajon strummed soft chords. Maman Anansi reached for Neyeli's hand, and the young woman put her hand in the palm of the matriarch's. They concentrated with their eyes closed. Neyeli's hair turned a cool, icy blue.

Gordon's mask configured over his face. He put his head down and concentrated. Top Hat did the same. Althea levitated over the bed and crossed her legs. She put her arms out to the side and opened her hands. She summoned two machetes, closed her eyes, and crossed the two blades at her chest.

The three travelers were pulled to sleep. Maman Anansi passed her energy to Neyeli, and the young conjure woman created a supernatural bridge for the slumbering dream trotters to voyage into the shared nightmare.

Calm. Serene. Quiet.

Not what was expected when they entered the nightmare.

They stood in an alleyway. Dooley in a fighter's stance, at the ready with his fists balled, body bent forward like a cat looking to strike. His spherical, lilac eye ablaze with cosmic, conjure energy. Althea, machetes in hand. Top Hat transformed, large and with sharp, extended antlers. Behind them was an empty city. It was a late autumn day. Red bled into a blue sky, and purple domed the heavens. Odd and grotesque imagery filled the emptiness at a slow pace.

The first image was of a young, limping Asian man. His head had been caved in with a blunt object, and his eye was dangling from its socket. He mumbled gibberish. Dooley, Althea, and Top Hat turned to see him lurch into the street. Another gruesome sight wobbled into view. A tall and burly, red-haired man with an arrow in his eye stumbled up next to the Asian man. The other half of his face had also been bashed in, but when he spoke, he was articulate. He repeated, "I died two ways…"

A brawny, middle-aged man strolled up. He had a thick mustache and slick black hair, gray on its sides. He wore a black, military-grade armored chest plate. His pauldrons were oversized and multicolored. He carried a large gun, the sight of which made Dooley, Althea, and Top Hat's fighting stances tremble with heightened expectancy. A cigar was crunched between his teeth and he chuckled. "Their deaths are my doing in another life…" he said merrily. "A whole 'nuther universe!" he added.

A thick herd of people flooded the streets. All directions. A handsome, blonde man with a dapper appearance, black suit and tie, was at the head of one pack. Hands in his pockets, he sauntered at the head of the massive parade and delighted in a blended British, Mid-Western American accent, "I make dreams within dreams within dreams. Inside the inside, and deeper inside. All the way down."

"Back up!" said Althea. "Into the alley!"

The three of them had power, but they couldn't fight them all. Top Hat took lead down the alley. Althea was in tow, a machete raised at the incoming crowd and her eyes locked onto them as she drifted backwards. She saw a change occur. The dapper British man remolded into a large, grey-flamed, fiery *inawo*. "Gaboon! Gaboon!" it shouted as it scraped the ground with its elongated, pointed fingers. The pavement sparked when the creature scratched against it. "Gaboon! Gaboon!" it continued hollering.

The population behind the *inawo* shifted, too. Their faces lost their flesh, stripped to the bone. Surgical masks covered their countenances, and their skull-exposed heads donned crowns of fire. They screeched, *"Good. Speed. Good. Speed!"* as they walked lamely into the alley, armed with hexed syringes.

Moving deeper into the alley, Top Hat spotted Oliver on the ground. He was writhing in pain, holding his stomach. His face appeared to be covered in bruises, and his shirt and jeans were torn with animal-like scratches in them. "Oliver!" Top Hat called, increasing his speed toward the wounded conjure man. "Oliver!" he called again.

Oliver rolled back and forth in an attempt to mitigate the pain slithering through him. He groaned when he heard his name. It was the best he could muster for a reply. Dooley and Top Hat knelt down next to him. Althea remained standing, keeping an eye on the encroaching, demonic night doctors and the oversized, fiery *inawo* leading them. Their pace was slow and ominous.

Oliver winced. He opened his eyes and spotted Dooley. His face contorted with a disapproving expression. Dooley had seen an expression like that before. It usually draped over Cedron's face when he was disappointed in him. "Why did you come here?" Oliver groaned as he slowed his body's roll back and forth. When Dooley stumbled on an answer, Oliver grumbled, "They're looking for you…"

Dooley made an incredulous look behind his mask. "They can't snag my essence through a dream," he objected. He looked up at his mother and asked, "Can they?"

"We won't take any chances," Althea replied. "You've battled men before on a dream plane. Bruises remained when you woke up." Gordon agreed with his mother's reminder. She then addressed Oliver, inquiring, "Oliver, honey, are you okay?"

"No," he said, erupting into a coughing fit. "Went in for a fight against that big one. The *inawo*-looking thing. I call him *'Gaboon'* 'cause he keeps screamin' it. Bootlegged his form. Went toe-to-toe. Scratched me up something good. I got his scars on my front, Willie's on my back."

"I'll gut him and cut him in half!" Althea promised. "Can you stand?"

He looked at Dooley and Top Hat, hands still wrapped around his stomach. "Get me up. I can limp something good." Dooley and Top Hat helped him to his feet. "Miss Althea, the Gaboon swallowed three children."

"What?" everyone questioned at the same time.

"He's got three children in him," Oliver briefed, hopping on his feet while maintaining balance between Dooley and Top Hat. "The others are hiding below. I got them there. Came back up to fight, stall."

"Get y'self scratched up," Top Hat added with a grimace inspecting Oliver's scrapes and bruises marking up his face.

Oliver reiterated, "Like I said, 'stall'."

"Despite my mother's ominous warning, you ain't got bruises in the wakey-wakey world," Dooley assured.

"Good. I'm still pretty…" Oliver quipped.

Top Hat grumbled, "Wouldn't go that far…"

Althea chided, breaking into their banter, "Boys!"

Dooley looked over his shoulder, "Ma? They gaining on us?"

Their heads back in the matter, Althea alerted, "Still a crawl, but they're coming!" She walked backwards, machetes aimed at the needle-armed devils draining into the alleyway.

"Around the corner," winced Oliver, hopping as Dooley and Top Hat held him up. "Under an RV. Open manhole."

The fiendish night doctors and the Gaboon overwhelmed the entrance. Dooley and Top Hat looked behind them and noticed a second wave pouring into the second entryway. The needlemen scraped their needle tips along the brick and hissed, "Good! Speed! Good! Speed!"

"Shit!" Dooley cursed.

Althea reproved, "Gordon!"

Dooley simply answered, "Ma! Look!"

Althea peaked over her shoulder. She cursed, "Shit!"

"I'll plow through them!" Top Hat huffed, scrapping a hoof on the ground, ready for a charge.

Althea looked up at the top of the buildings. "Gordon," she called her son.

"Ma?" he replied.

"Can you take them up in a blink? I can levitate."

"Yes, Ma," he affirmed. Then Dooley was gone in a snap. Althea soared upwards, keeping her eyes on the ground and watching the night doctors inundate the alley from either end. The two groups blended into one, and then they followed the Gaboon. Up. The fiery creature placed his feet against the side of the building and pursued. Althea's eyes widened as she witnessed the hideous villains scale the side. They chanted her last name, more a call to snatch her son's essence with their needles. The Gaboon scrapped the building's wall and hissed, "Gaboon! Gaboon!" Althea's lip curled, she bared teeth and cursed the nightmare. She looked away, facing upward, and continued her ascent.

Dooley turned his head in time to spy his mother raise over the ledge behind them. "Place Oliver on the ground," she ordered, floating swiftly in their direction. He and Top Hat quickly executed his mother's orders. They rested their battered friend against the building's ledge. Althea dissipated her machetes and knelt down in front of Oliver. "We don't have much time," she announced. "Those monsters are walking up the side of the building."

"I can buy us time," said Dooley. "It's me they're after."

Althea looked over her shoulder at her cosmic-suited son. "Not too far," she advised. "Just jump across to the other building. Let them see you."

"Sure thing, Ma," Dooley replied. He turned and darted to the edge of the building and looked down to observe the wave of horrid night doctors led by the Gaboon doing as his mother described, walking up the side of the building. He stared across. The building opposite the one he stood on was far taller. He climbed the ledge and leapt into the air, zooming up. The Gaboon screamed and leapt across, running up and chasing Dooley. A deluge of night doctors followed while a steady stream still pursued the others.

Still got a few coming your way, Ma! warned Dooley.

Althea looked up at Top Hat and ordered, "Watch my back. Gordon got some of them away. There's still a steady rise heading up."

Top Hat nodded. "Yes, Miss Althea," he acknowledged before turning around and taking a defensive stance. In wait and at the ready.

Althea addressed Oliver, "You were scarred by Willie the Lich, correct?"

"Yes…" he answered in pain.

"The scars you have now are not real. They're amplified by his lashings, and they're using the anathematic elements that create this nightmare. I want you to concentrate and reach out to Neyeli and Maman Anansi. They brought us here. She will show you that you're not scarred in reality, not with these scars. Connect with your physical form. See that *these* scars you wear do not exist."

Oliver blurted, "Willie's lashes…?"

"The effects will remain with you," Althea told him. "When we fight—and we *will* fight—you'll have to be very careful if wounded. This will happen all over again. Perhaps worse." She took a quick breath and then relayed, "You've been very brave, Oliver. You fought against Willie's lacerations to follow the children into the nightmare and keep them safe."

"Some got taken…" he interjected with a groan. "This…whole damn thing is my fault…"

"Hush that, Mister Peters. I was caught off guard once and needled too. It took my life. I'm still here, though—with your tattoo-artistic assistance, no less. So, I'm here for you, and I'm here for those children." Then Althea vowed with a counter to Oliver's first statement, "We're gettin' them back. It's why we're here. We're conjure folk, ain't we?" Oliver nodded at Althea's sentiment.

Over her shoulder, night doctors scaled the ledge. Top Hat charged into battle, head down and antlers pointed to strike. His stampede crashed into the demonic crowd, impaling three and knocking others back over the ledge. He lifted his head, shook, and threw off the skewered villains, tossing them away. More scrambled onto the roof, and Top Hat engaged as they surrounded him, swiping their needles in his direction. He dodged, punched, and used his enormous horns to keep the needlemen at bay. He called upon ancestors and hollered an animalistic cry! A robust shockwave pulsed from his body, propelling a regiment of night doctors, and tossing them over the building's side.

Concurrently, Oliver relaxed his heavy breathing and closed his eyes. Althea again urged him to concentrate, and he did. His focus opened a bright hole in the darkness behind his eyes. He heard his father's sweet horn mixing with Dajon's soft violin sounds. The music relaxed him, sharpened his focus. He heard Althea reach out to Neyeli, and he felt a hand take his, pulling him through the hole in the darkness. He saw the room. His father and Dajon playing behind Top Hat, Dooley, Neyeli and Maman Anansi as they sat, heads down and in full participation of the ritual. Althea Goodspeed floated above his resting body.

There were no scars. Not the ones he was given in the dream. The sight was therapeutic, and the lacerations and bruises he received nightmare-side mended into pristine flesh.

He opened his eyes. The roof was compromised. He got to his feet and recalled the Gaboon's essence, bootlegging the creatures long, thin, fiery fingers, fending off oncoming night doctors. He ducked and dodged the swipes made at him with needles or fists. Behind him, Althea ran her machetes down the front of one attacking night doctor, made a graceful turn, and gutted another. Each night doctor she fell, the mother specter-shouted at them *"You! Killed! Me!"* It was a mantra that thundered over and over as her blades severed flaming heads and disemboweled her enemies.

Dooley swooped in, making an immediate dive away from the building he'd been ascending. The Gaboon jumped after him, but even with a long leap and its velocity, the creature couldn't catch Dooley's speeding arc away from the building. The fire-headed night doctors storming the side fell back. Some dropped to their dooms, slamming against the hard pavement and bloodying the streets with a spattered mess. The other drones turned and ran down, jumping across to the other building at one point, running up its side. A third batch were able to execute a successful leap from the side of the building to the roof of the other, raining down and joining in the fray against Althea Goodspeed, Top Hat, and Oliver Peters.

There was Dooley, a black beacon streaking into the center of the three allies as their enemies impinged on the area. "Gaboon! Gaboon!" the Gaboon hollered as it pushed its way through the flame-headed night doctors.

"Ma!" Dooley called. "Take flight. I'm taking these two!" Dooley gripped the back of Oliver and Top Hat's shirts and blinked away. Althea lifted into the air, missing swipes from incoming needlemen.

Althea levitated away from the building, and the Gaboon and night doctors followed her over the building's edge. Some ran down the side. Others mindlessly barreled over to their long-drop deaths. Althea circled around the structure, searching for her son and Oliver and Top Hat. She floated through alleys and watched the streets flow with night doctors. They swiped at her, but to no avail.

Gordon? she sent.

Ma! We're on the RV, down the alley we popped into, around the corner.

Althea floated ahead, following her son's directions. Taking the corner, she found Dooley, Top Hat, and Oliver on the roof of the RV. It was surrounded by night doctors. Some attempted to scale the hood and spring an attack. Dooley kept them at bay with his concussive, cosmic beam while Oliver used a new bootlegged ability taken from Dooley's cosmic ray. He threw punches that extended lilac-colored energy from his fists. It was in the shape of a large, clenched hand, and it smacked into the hood-scaling night doctors, knocking them into other advancing needlemen. Top Hat reverted back to human form, kicking at the night doctors' flaming heads as they attempted to come up through the vehicle's hatch.

Althea glided forward, she ghosted through the front of the van, finding a moment where the night doctors were held at bay. She took by surprise the needlemen who'd invaded the vehicle, slashing and gutting them with quick and effective strikes. More stormed the motor home, and Althea spirited up through the roof. Her son and Oliver were in front of her. Top Hat was behind her. The vehicle shook, tipping back and forth. Althea levitated a few inches from the roof to keep balance. She asked, "Oliver, is there another way into the underground?"

Oliver continued throwing fists at the night doctors as he answered, "Not that I know of, Miss Althea."

"I think I have an idea, Ma," Dooley said over his shoulder. He lifted from the roof and zoomed forward in flight, just out of reach from the needlemen. Most of the crowd followed him. Even the Gaboon, who was once again pushing its way through the villainous crowd, changed directions to pursue the cosmic-suited champion.

The vehicle settled, though there was a sizeable number of stragglers to contend with. Althea was ready to fight them, tight grip on her machetes. Oliver's fists were aglow, and Top Hat resumed his animalistic appearance. They were prepared to engage the remaining needlemen until Dooley returned, flying close to the street. The onslaught of night doctors was behind him, the Gaboon at the lead. Their gait was hurried, but Dooley was far ahead of them. He slowed his flight nearing the front of the recreational vehicle to a literal crawl. He scurried across the ground, keeping low and creeping underneath the large transport.

He discovered the manhole and slipped inside. He landed on a floor made of steel, making a quick inspection of his surroundings before popping back to his mother and friends. "Ma, ghost down and down," he tasked. He grabbed Oliver and Top Hat by the arm and disappeared in a burst of glittering, lilac dust. Althea slipped through the roof, quickly past the needlemen crowding the RV's interior, and into the steel tunnels below the street.

"Good work, Gordon," Althea complimented her son. She turned to Oliver. "Lead us to the children."

The Gaboon's screech got their attentions. Heads up and facing the above world, they heard his crawl toward the manhole, ready to invade. "This way!" Oliver shouted. They turned their heads to him and followed.

The Gaboon jumped down, shrieking his name. Its steely squawk echoed through the cold, metal tunnel. Its unnatural tone scratched at their ears and left a feeling of fingers or spiny legs crawling across their bodies, even Althea's ethereal form cringed. Behind the Gaboon charged an army of needlemen. Syringes up. They yelled, "Good! Speed! Good! Speed!" They caught up with the large, fiery *inawo*, and pursued Dooley and the others through the tunnel.

Oliver stopped his sprint at a hatch in the floor. He grabbed ahold of the large, gold loop attached to it, attempting to lift. He struggled, and Top Hat assisted. "Thanks," said Oliver as they opened the flap together. "Not easy…" He looked at Althea and stated while catching his breath, "Two more down." They heard the Gaboon screeching and the night doctors' chanting behind them, emanating from the darkness. "We just have to stay ahead of them." Althea ghosted through the floor. Dooley and Oliver jumped down. Top Hat returned to human form to fit through.

It was the same cold, steel and sterile setting. Oliver led them in the opposite direction as the Gaboon followed them down into the new level. The mindless night doctors fell through, and from the shadows of the new area sauntered another regiment of needlemen. The mass of syringe-wielding, fire-headed fiends grew in size. Shrieks and chants echoed down the steel tunnel, catching up with Althea and the boys, gnawing and crawling over their senses.

They followed Oliver down the left-hand path when they came to a cross section. There was another hatch. This had a silver handle. Top Hat transformed and used his strength to open it.

Down. Cold steel. Sterile. A narrower tunnel.

The Gaboon and army of night doctors trailed. A new unit merged with them just the same.

"*Gaboon! Gaboon!*"

"*Good! Speed! Good! Speed!*"

Oliver at the lead. Icy voices scraping at their ears and scurrying up their spines.

The final latch. An onyx, looped handle. Top Hat's strength put to use. Opened, and down they went into a tapered tunnel. Walls and ceiling were so close it was disorienting.

"*Gaboon! Gaboon!*"

"*Good! Speed! Good! Speed!*"

Scrape! Scrape!

The sinister voices skittered behind them. Ahead, the children were huddled in darkness. Althea sailed over and knelt down in front of them. Katrina Williams. Leandra Shire. Douglas Tierney. They shivered, scared and close together. "Children, we're here to guide you out of this nightmare," Althea assured.

"*Gaboon! Gaboon!*"

"*Good! Speed! Good! Speed!*"

Scrape! Scrape!

Leandra Shire screamed hearing the Gaboon and needlemen's approach. Althea calmed her, but the slither of disquieting sounds continued hissing in echo. Icy vocals. Needlepoints scrapping. A fiery creature screeching its name. The tunnel became a chamber of sharp, piercing sound.

Dooley suggested to Top Hat, "They come any closer, put your head down, and you ram right through those bastards!"

"Gordon!" his mother hissed at his language. She turned back to the children and addressed, "Close your eyes. Focus. I'm going to reach out to Neyeli Campbell. You all know her? She's part of the community." The children nodded, affirmative. "She's being assisted by Maman Anansi. She's going to guide you out, back to the physical. Okay?" The children again nodded in the affirmative. "Good. Close your eyes. Focus. Ease your breathing."

"Gaboon! Gaboon!"

"Good! Speed! Good! Speed!"

Scrape! Scrape!

Down the narrow tunnel. Wriggling over the senses like a tongue savoring taste.

Leandra opened her eyes. Her breathing erratic. She looked over Althea's shoulders, past Dooley, Oliver, and Top Hat. She peered into the nothing where sprouted the voices of the Gaboon and needlemen. Shrieking. Chanting. Needle's scraping. The fiery-headed night doctors were washed of their flames. Dark. Anticipation. Unknown and fear.

Althea broke through the distraction. "Leandra!" she hollered. "Pay them no attention. Those villains are getting bottlenecked in the tunnel. They're numbers in this narrow space is a disadvantage, okay. They can't get to you. Just look at me." The young girl did as she was told. "Close your eyes," Althea said in a softer tone. "You'll hear music. You will be fine, young lady."

Leandra nodded her head. She relaxed her breathing and closed her eyes.

Music. A sweet horn playing jazz accompanied by a soft violin. Their sound fought back against the swarming dissonance. The children calmed. They heard Althea reach out to Neyeli and Maman Anansi. The two women's presence was felt, and their spirits found a path out of the nightmare, back to their physical bodies.

Althea opened her eyes. The children faded away. Gone from the nightmare. She turned her head and notified, "They're out. Safe. But that *inawo* still has the other children in its belly."

Dooley's spherical, third eye brightened. "Let's perform some surgery!" he declared. He burst into his lilac form and dashed forward, shifting into a streak of blazing light. His cosmic wildfire, javelin shape pierced the Gaboon. In him, but not through him.

Dooley's lilac-auraed assegai crashed into what felt like a hard wall. The impact forced him back to his black, cosmic-suited form. He hit the ground and rolled a few feet. He huffed, wind knocked out of him.

"Mister Dooley…?" he heard a young kid's voice question. He looked up. It was the ten-year-old boy named Keith Quad, the youngest child taken. Christine Pryce and Michelle Alicia stood on either side of the boy.

Dooley got up. His instinct buzzed, and he warned the three kids, "Get behind me! Get behind me! Against the wall!" The children did as tasked. Dooley backed up, shielding them as the Gaboon's sharp, slender fingers pierced the darkness. The creature stabbed at its own stomach, reaching in to collect Dooley's essence. The Gaboon's grasp was inches away from Dooley's abdomen. It stabbed and stabbed and stabbed at itself to find the cosmic spirit and extract his lilac essence.

Dooley had other plans.

He waited and calculated, timing the sudden, self-impaling actions from the Gaboon. He counted. Then he acted, grabbing at the fingers and drawing them in closer, bending them away from his abdomen. With a tight grip on three, slender fingers from each of the Gaboon's hands, Dooley stretched out his arms, causing the Gaboon to tear open a large, gaping hole in its belly.

"Run!" Dooley shouted at the children while struggling to fight against the *inawo*'s spastic arm movements attempting to wriggle out of his grasp. Christine, Keith, and Michelle darted past Dooley and leapt out of the *inawo*'s belly. Althea waved the children to her, and when they arrived, she turned them away from the battle. She talked them through the procedure that would wake them up and escape the nightmare. The children were compliant. Focused. Eyes closed. They heard the music. Listened to Althea's voice, and felt Neyeli's and Maman Anansi's presence. They walked the path and woke from the nightmare into their own bodies.

Madame Jeliya nursed their minds using strong incants to ease them. Miss Ross rubbed an ointment on their foreheads, assisting Madame Jeliya's power. A few of the children were given nursing bowls to vomit in as their bodies once again adjusted to the physical realm.

In the nightmare. Dooley cast himself from the *inawo*, launching through in his lilac-spear form. He shifted solid next to his mother, and she called for Top Hat and Oliver to come back her way. The Gaboon was on his knees, crying out as his stomach wound closed over. The night doctors slithered past him, their numbers fighting against the restricted space of the narrow tunnel. Their skull-faced heads were once again aglow.

But it was over. Althea and the boys secured the children. The nightmare had no power and no hold. They focused on Neyeli and Maman Anansi's presence. They heard the music and calmed. They walked the path and disappeared from sight.

The nightmare imploded, ceasing to exist.

Papa Solomon and Dajon continued playing, soothing.

Dooley's mask retracted, turning to a shadow, absorbed into his flesh. Gordon breathed heavy as he awoke in the physical realm. Top Hat came to and sighed relief, tapping a fist on Gordon's shoulder. Papa Solomon and Dajon stopped their music as everyone stirred awake.

Neyeli bent forward, face in the palm of her hands. Maman Anansi rubbed her back and complimented, "You did wonderful, Madame Mood Ring." Neyeli chuckled. She peeked up at Maman Anansi behind the curtain of her fingers. "It's not an official name," the Elder proclaimed with a sweet smile, face coming from sleep.

Althea disappeared. She found her husband on the parlor floor of their brownstone. She focused physical, wrapped her arms around him tight, face streaming with tears. "We got them!" she said. "We brought them home! Everyone's okay!"

Benny, Leah, and Cedron were there too. They stood. Leah made her way out and up the street. Benny followed. Cedron remained behind for a moment, staring at his parent's embrace. "I'ma leave you two be," he said, a grateful smile dawning on his face. "I'ma be down the way at Miss Ross'." Then he was gone.

Where Oliver rested. Papa Solomon stood over his son as Oliver's sleepy expression beamed up at him. "You did good, son," Papa Solomon told him.

"After gettin' caught out there," he stated. "I guess I made up for it."

"Don't you worry about that," Papa Solomon urged.

Madame Jeliya entered. She knelt down beside her son and stroked his forehead. Leah came up next to her, tears of joy on her face.

Benny congratulated his brother, shaking him and giving Dajon a tight hug. "You feel good, kid?"

"Yeah. Much better."

Benny turned to Neyeli. He walked away from Dajon and sat down next to her, rubbing her back. "You all right there, Neyeli-baby?"

She nodded, yes. "Eyes closed, but I wasn't sleeping. I need a long rest."

Cedron said to Gordon, "Let's head to Harlem. Let Ma and Pops have the house for the night."

Gordon agreed.

Papa Solomon heard the proposal. He said to the Goodspeed brothers, "Not too far. We have some talking to do with the Gwuinee folk over in Water Bug Hollow. I want you two in that meeting. It'll be in a day or two. Get rest, but stay alert."

"Yes, Papa Solomon," Cedron and Gordon answered.

Papa Solomon looked at his son in the bed. "How you feel?"

"Okay, I guess," he informed his father.

"You still got Willie's scars," Papa Solomon noted. He addressed Gordon and tasked, "When he's ready, you get him into your chamber."

"Yes, Papa Solomon," Gordon assured.

The patriarch looked at his sister and said to her, "One problem down."

Maman Anansi replied to her brother, "Ninety-eight to go."

Papa Solomon shook his head. "Yep," he stated. "And every last one of them are a bitch."

43

In the backroom of Water Bug Hollow's church. The table was full. Set with topics to dine on. Papa Solomon sat at one end, a chef ready to serve a hard meal to swallow. Maman Anansi was seated to his left. The head matriarch of the Fable Avenue and New York conjure community stepped back from her position of power to allow her brother to take lead as a wartime chief. The Goodspeed brothers were in attendance, seated next to Maman Anansi. Cedron, suited in black pants and shoes with a black vest covering a collar-shirt that had the first few buttons loosened. He wore necklaces dangling with theurgical symbols spanning various, African cultures. Black and gold rings were on select fingers. Gordon wore his black, cosmic suit. No mask.

Satchel 'Old Goon' Eledas resided on Papa Solomon's right. The Crossroads Queen, his daughter, was next to him. Standing against the wall behind Miss Voodoo Lily, was her consort, Armand Gideon, the three skulls on his necklace aglow. Her mother, Simaetha Ghedemere, sat on her right. Seated opposite Papa Solomon, on the other end of the table, were the two Gwuinee representatives. Terrence Tzidkiyahu, wearing his signature white suit. Naamah Mbu, dressed in all business and ready to listen and give her judgment. The church's guardian, Reverend Mathieu Pouvwa, stood at the door.

Naamah inquired in a polite voice how Papa Solomon and Maman Anansi's children were doing. Papa Solomon answered, "My son is fine. He's in need of rest, but he's up. He's about. Strong. His scars have been healed."

"Yes," Naamah said, perking up. "I heard you have an alchemical chamber in your possession. To hear legends manifested in our time stirs the heart," she noted before saying, "I'm so relieved to hear he's doing better. The children too, correct?" Papa Solomon presented a slight nod of his head, stoic expression on his face. Naamah turned to Maman Anansi and asked, "Your daughter?"

The head matriarch threw a quick, stern eye on Voodoo Lily and Armand before turning to Naamah and divulging, "She's still in a deep rest. Her spirit is stable. The situation is under control, as much as it can be. We have other matters to discuss." Her eyes went back to Armand and Voodoo Lily. Their faces were like stone, though underneath her expression, Voodoo Lily longed to articulate her distress and culpability over the situation. The chilly tone in Maman Anansi's voice, her insistence to move to other matters, made the young Crossroads Queen stay her words.

"I wish her well in her recovery," Naamah spoke carefully. "Papa Solomon, please…"

Fable Avenue's sole patriarch proclaimed, "There can't be part-time action against a full-time nemesis. Justice can only come through punishment. We've all felt the tip of needles in one way or another. Our people out there are so unaware of how deep this goes. We need direct war—" he saw Naamah and Terrence's faces contort, and he heard them sigh. Papa Solomon didn't let their actions deter his words. "—I consider myself a wartime chief. I will lead this war. I have intel on a prominent family. One stationed in law. They are craftsmen, needle forgers, curse anointers with hex. They are the largest suppliers of hexed needles. All the way up to the Kolonist Kings and notable members of The Line."

Naamah and Terrence made a quick glance at one another, disapproval mixed with regret in their eyes. Naamah countered, "Direct war is not an option. It can't be." No one stirred at the table, though Papa Solomon and the other Fable Avenue members felt coldly dismissed. "You mention prominent families, leading associates that are a part of clandestine elites known to us. Publicly, these are notable figures without blemish. They can't simply end up with stopped hearts in their cars or found dead in their homes. Even normal folk will become suspicious and see a pattern. No. Direct war is not plausible. More clever means, like those employed by Miss Voodoo Lily and Mister Armand Gideon here, should be applied to this situation."

Papa Solomon remained silent for a moment. Then he stated, "These people are immaculate. There's nothing on them. Besides, we would be going after their soldiers, burning their covenants. Our target would be Stanley Fallows and his family."

Terrence spoke, "He's very influential, Papa Solomon. He's not even the head of these clandestine elites, and he knows how to play chess with them."

"He's attempting to make it official," Papa Solomon interjected. "He's seeking head of the Kolonist Kings."

"Even worse!" Terrence parried. "We got needlemen in positions of high esteem around the country. The world, even. Fightin' them would put conjure folk in danger." He waved his hand around the room. "We all got somethin' on us. If the assassination wouldn't be a physical killing, it would be of our character. We just got Eve's Hallow rollin', and Old Goon here tellin' me we already got some jokers sniffin' around to see if all the papers are in order. You know them folk been sent by that bastard mayor."

"The mayor?" Papa Solomon blurted. "Come on, Terrence, we got the mayor by the balls!" He listed, touching a finger with each item, "We got his son's confession. *Written!*" He noted quick, "That sick son of a bitch!" He returned to his list. "We got evidence of covering up the crime, framing it around someone else, and we have the corruption in a local paper to lead public opinion. He’s already under pressure for things that have been exposed.”

“But ain’t nothin’ of his matters have been exposed,” Terrence threw back. “Why? Because we need to walk carefully.”

“For what reason?” Papa Solomon questioned.

Naamah answered, “Because there are other matters at play.”

“What matters?”

“Conjure folks’ lives!” the Gwuinee woman insisted. “We play our hand and there’s war. Brother Terrence mentioned Eve’s Hallow. Its papers will be put into question—”

Papa Solomon looked at Maman Anansi, face exploding with disbelief. He turned back and addressed Naamah, speaking over her, “Our incants cannot be penetrated even with their best curse.”

“We’ve seen them use laws to work around that!” Naamah reminded. “We have evidence of human trafficking. Their law enforcers experimenting on conjure men and women, children. What they’re doing takes us back to the days of plantation experimentations on our people. Drugged. Used for sex. Burned to ash and smoked to get high.” Tears bubbled in her eyes. “Children!”

Papa Solomon pleaded, “Expose this simply for the sex trafficking, something normal folk will understand.”

“Your son!” Naamah snapped, her words brimming with the African accent she picked up from her father. “A man I can only guess, coming from a powerful family such as yours—the Peters, godfathers and godmothers to Fable Avenue—on his square with conjure in full bloom in a way most conjure folk can’t conceive, and he was caught up. Look at the damage that was done.” Then she directed her next words at Gordon. “Your sweetheart!” she brought up. “The Cobalt-Blue Flame! The other half of the equation that will right the wrongs of this world—if all prophetic sayings and writings have been discerned correctly. Where is she?” Gordon’s eyes bent on Naamah. His teeth pressed hard against one another, and the lilac spirit burning inside him brightened with ire aimed at the woman in his sights. He stared and did nothing. “Banished!” Naamah blurted at him. She faced Papa Solomon. “A powerful instrument. *The* instrument!”

Papa Solomon nodded. He reset his face to calm, giving a look to Gordon, signaling with a nod to do the same. Gordon complied. The patriarch interlocked his fingers and rested his hands on the table. “With all due respect, Miss Mbu, let’s put some of your statements into context.” Papa Solomon adjusted himself in his seat. He leaned forward and stated, “Miss Forrester took matters into her own hands and—to say the least—got into some trouble. Her unfortunate actions were independent of the Fable Avenue conjure community.” He took a moment for his words to marinate and grow. Then he stated, “Let’s be perfectly clear. She’s banished. Problematic as it sounds, she can be re-summoned. We’re working on that.” He sat back in his chair. His hands remained interlocked on the table. “The strikes I have planned were calculated before the events of my son’s abduction and manipulation. This isn’t personal in that regards, but I won’t deny it’s a hell of a motivator.” Papa Solomon observed a slight grin bloom on Terrence’s face. “We need war. Stanley Fallows is in constant motion, and he—and people of his curse and hex—have constantly set our communities back because we were taking our time trying to figure out how much more evil he could get. His brood have stepped up their game. We all have horror stories. I understand the fear—”

Terrence contorted his face as he disagreed. “Hol’ up! Come on, Vencil!” he hissed. “You know that ain’t true. Conjure folk been *bidin’* time learning about putting this shit right. All this a rope-a-dope to get that one, good, heavy punch in. We still got to remain cautious.” He swiped his hand at the air. “And why bein’ cautious always got to be interpreted as fear by headstrong black folk?”

Heart sunk, Papa Solomon turned to Satchel “Old Goon” and remarked, “You told me their position on war changed.”

The old, old, man sighed as he fought against a guilty look. He disclosed to Papa Solomon, “Securing Water Bug Hollow was the goal.”

Papa Solomon questioned, “Yours or theirs?”

“I sit on the throne of Water Bug Hollow, but it’s *your* heritage,” Satchel “Old Goon” reminded. “You have access to gateways to the crossroads from Fable Avenue. Them roads is *my* heritage. My family—my *daughter*—takes the weight off your backs governing these two places because Fable Avenue has a responsibility with the Lilac Flame and the Cobalt Blue Spirit to conduct the Grand Ritual and bring about the Grand Wish.”

The two men stared at one another. The Old Goon’s left eye twitched, and he almost winked. Papa Solomon noticed, and he almost grinned.

Satchel “Old Goon” turned to Naamah and Terrence. He told them, “I got a nose for this kind of thing, and I smell trouble coming. War is inevitable. Stanley Fallows is a son of a bitch, but he’s united conjure folk in ways we ain’t been in a long, long, long time. Trust me on that. He gon’ unite the opposition. As we get closer and closer to what needs to be done, he’s gon’ come hard. We can’t wait. He won’t. Sure, he got the advantage not to wait, but he gon’ move soon and quick with plans he got.” There was a pause before he added, “I stand by Vencil Peters, Heir to the Horn, Sole Patriarch of Fable Avenue, co-Governor of Water Bug Hollow, called Papa Solomon, The Wartime Chief.”

Naamah was stoic. She considered things she'd heard, and the things she knew. "We have been arguing among one another since before people like Stanley were a physical spec on history's page," she reflected. "At first, an etch on a prophetic mural. That's when we became disagreeable, squabbling and wasting time. Tribalistic." She sighed again. "There's great work to do, righting mistakes that were made æons ago." Then she proclaimed, "Papa Solomon, should your soldiers come across any needleman, night doctor, or bag head, put them down. Should you discover information that would lead to clandestine covenants, bring upon them *imukuro, ipari*. Be as clever as Eshu when he runs as a rabbit."

Terrence grinned. "Yeah," he agreed. "Draw them out. Like the queen says, make it clever."

Naamah put an eye on Terrence, reacting to his description of her as 'queen'. "Why Terrence, don't you try and sweettalk me!" The people in the room were infected with relieving grins. Naamah addressed the Fable Avenue patriarch, "Step clever, Papa Solomon. Make your war, but step cunning and be full of tricks."

That's all Papa Solomon wanted to hear. He nodded in Naamah's direction. "Thank you, Miss Mbu."

Naamah adjourned the meeting. The people stood and hugged. There still remained a tight tension, but much was exhaled among the conjure folk.

Satchel "Old Goon" followed the Fable Avenue representatives into the hall as the others remained behind. Papa Solomon said to the old, diminutive man, "Thank you, in there. For real, Satchel. I was a little nervous on where you'd fall."

"I wasn't!" Satchel "Old Goon" snapped. "I was waiting for you to drag me into the conversation."

Papa Solomon rolled his eyes and flapped his lips. "Since when you ever wait to be dragged into a conversation, Negro?"

"Since I've known my place with Gwuinee folk," he replied all matter-of-fact. "Besides, Mayor Jakobi ain't gonna sit still on this. He's nervous. He ain't acted too heavy yet, but he will."

"Stanley probably has him holding still," Papa Solomon speculated.

"Don't doubt it, but I still gotta create a defense."

Papa Solomon assured the Old Goon, "You got proper soldiers. But if you need to borrow any of mine, just say the word."

Satchel "Old Goon" nodded in agreement. The two men shook hands and parted ways. Papa Solomon led the party back to the crossroads estate for the journey back to Fable Avenue. It wasn't even noon. The day had its haze, but it was organic, naturally summer in presence. The walk wasn't silent. Papa Solomon called Cedron to attention, telling him, "When

Oliver is better rested, see if he holds a metaphysical blueprint of his kidnappers. Let his bootleg conjure ability map out their familiarity. Get into *their* heads."

"Yeah, you got it, Papa Solomon," the crew leader said, accepting his mission. The older Goodspeed brother reminded, "Gordon got a readout on the Blood Cursers in our first scrap. Maybe he can work with Oliver to get that all sorted out." He looked at Gordon. He wasn't paying attention to the conversation, head down and looking at the ground as he walked with his arms crossed. "Gordon!" he called.

Gordon looked up. "Yeah…"

"You heard what's up?" asked Cedron in a forceful tone.

Gordon's instincts played back what was said around him. "Yeah. I'll work with Oliver on all that. See if we can't track these hell hounds down."

Maman Anansi put her hand on Gordon's shoulder, inducing a soothing incant that relaxed Gordon a bit. She sensed he'd been rattled by Naamah's statements concerning Fey Forrester. "Stay your course, for now, Gordon," she directed him. "Sleep and dream of history."

"Cedron!" Papa Solomon hailed for his attention. Cedron looked at the master conjure man. "*Papa's* Gypsy Moon Misfits."

Even Gordon had to grin at the suggestion. He looked at his brother and was surprised to see a smile on his face.

Cedron reacted with a chuckle, saying, "Okay, old man. You got that. For now…"

Papa Solomon put his arm around Cedron. "I know I do. I'm the chief!"

Gordon hurried his steps, taking lead among the group. He turned, walking backwards, and stated, "History ain't gonna dream itself. Let me stay the course." He popped away before anyone could react.

His sanctuary. The golden, otherworldly lights shined bright with the emergence of Gordon's presence. Shaded by privacy, Gordon balled his fists and threw a punch. "I can't believe that chick tried to throw Fey's actions in my face!" he snarled as he shook his fist. He turned. There was the alchemical chamber with Spook attached to it. The capsule opened. Spook folded, black-mirror face against its jeweled console. The Judgment card lay in between the screen and button gems. Gordon picked up his mystical watch from his recliner and fastened it to his hip. He climbed inside the chamber and lay flat.

The capsule closed, and Gordon shut his eyes. He connected with Spook, and the ancient device's magic lulled him to sleep.

Black.

Then fell seven drops of lilac dust followed by a steady stream. They collected and created a sandy sea. A gust of wind swept across the dreaming, and the lilac sands dissolved into history long ago.

Dense clusters of lilac static were wiped away by the immediate presence of a long-flowing, black cape swinging to its left as its wearer slipped around the corner of a dimly lit, long hallway. Otherworldly lights shined bright upon his entrance into the area. The luminescence emanated from behind glass displays carved into the onyx-marbled walls. The mystical lighting washed over the young man as he entered the hall. It could be seen that his cape, while black on its exterior, had an all-red interior.

He was short with a slender, athletic build and dark-brown skin. A handsome, chiseled face with a straight brow, high cheekbones and a defined jaw that narrowed to a point and was patched with low-cut facial shrubbery. A fiery puff of knotted twists burst from the top of his head. A light-brown, leather vest was all that clothed his upper body. He wore matching pants that belled out at his feet, which were covered by brown, leather shoes.

His name was once Been ah Kibir Duhu. That changed when he was seven years old. He was renamed Ariq Haunts, and his mother spent years reshaping his face to cope with loss and newfound responsibility. Forever masked, and now wearing the face of a much-admired folk hero named Iunes Kythe Glaive Del-Yswil, called The Miracle Maker, a bearer of greater luck for those who invoked him through ritual. Donning the trickster's face, Ariq Haunts masqueraded and made a name for himself as well. He was the Bringer of Bad Deeds. Cat met mouse, and their game of wits and opposing ideologies commenced. Their cantrips and maneuvers were often at the chagrin of their Elders.

Here, Ariq Haunts stood in the hall of his rival's castle, situated on an invisible island off the coast of West Africa.

Floating on display behind the glass windows were objects of magnificent conjure. The items had been collected and stored by the Del-Yswil family. Ariq Haunts didn't believe the artifacts were on display in any particular order, but he still considered that he walked a path that chronicled the history of adventurous exploits to seize and keep safe the powerful relics.

Eyes wide. Every item cast a distracting spell of awe over Ariq Haunts. The hall of treasures was not his destination, but it kept him moored in its port. The palace's library was his journey's end. Buried in the massive containment of books and scrolls was an eight-volume narrative titled *The Infinity Cycles*. It was a work created by the legendary penman, Haki Tagwaye. Ariq Haunts had an interest in volume six. It was titled *The Way to the Silver World, or The Many Manors of Constellation*. It contained a ritual to the realm of the Eterijah, powerful spirits that controlled fate and destiny by moving celestial bodies. Time was their expertise, and Ariq Haunts sought entrance to negotiate, even if by force, a fix to keep the people of Africa, the first people of the world, on a course that he believed would alchemize and strengthen them.

But Ariq Haunts' steady walk through the Del-Yswil Palace became mired in his admiration for the history in front of him. He viewed all the items as equals, but soon he became interested in a few specific trinkets. His sight was overwhelmed and fixed to rare and legendary articles both recognized through shared tales and new ones to his vision and knowledge. Wonder and esteem filled Ariq Haunts, and with each showcase he passed, there came an acute and persisting pull from the item on display. The awareness was so extreme that it started to feel like walls that wound and angled to create a maze. There were missing areas, places to slip through, and that's when Ariq Haunts realized that the items he grew interested in did not emit the same transcendental articulation as so many others on display. The absence of their pull allowed Ariq Haunts to find himself standing directly in front of a treasure that gave off no aura or invisible tug.

Ariq Haunts grinned. A thought occurred to him, and with its rise to his consciousness, the distraction and tow of the other items dispersed. He put his hands behind his back, one hand grabbing the opposite arm's wrist. He was now lucid, no longer seduced by the legends in front of him. Focused. He walked coolly through the hall with only fleeting peeks at the acquired trophies.

Replicas, he deduced. He chuckled at what he concluded was Iune's clever mind. "Ah!" he said aloud. "If I had been seeking these items, I'd be standing in the dim arena of the muted luck I bring to others." He shook his head. "So, this is how I make people feel when their luck sours." He decided to feel nothing, and he moved forward to his original pursuit. "Let me continue. Snatch and leave," he thought out loud. "Then I can get out of these terrible clothes." Ariq Haunts' notions drifted to an inquiry concerning the whereabouts of the authentic treasures he concluded were copies.

"Iune!" called a man's authoritative voice, interrupting Ariq Haunts' assessments.

Ariq Haunts spun around. The dispersed distraction was renewed in the presence of a man who was both legend and history standing upright and walking. King Ziko Yswil. Brown of skin with one, thick and long slate-colored dreadlock and golden-brown eyes. He stood dressed in royal robes. His mythical hammer-pick hanging at his hip. Average in height, muscle shaped with stories and conjure that scribed his long life into his flesh. He approached Ariq Haunts, a curious look on his aged face.

Ariq Haunts was once again entranced. A man who was epochs old stepped towards him. He looked no older than a man in his mid-fifties. A shaman and king fused into one powerful presence. Ariq Haunts wondered if the king's peculiar and scrutinizing expression was molded by his instinct, as it deciphered the person before him was not truly his son, Iune.

The masquerader reminisced on a moment when he was younger, when his mother's specter massaged his face. Her spirit felt like a warm gel on his countenance as she rubbed transition into his flesh. She asked him, *"Who do you admire most?"* and he answered, *"The great trickster, Iune Yswil!"* His mother vowed that over time sharing his face would allocate his wit to him as well. But she challenged young Ariq Haunts by inquiring, *"How will you outsmart him? The night lends its power of shadow to him for hide and sneak. The sun laces his lips so that his smile shines bright and charms and warms his marks to trust him."* Young Ariq Haunts pondered his mother's questions as his face took another shape. He had his answer. *"Then I will learn the night and seize the day!"* he proclaimed.

Remembering this was reflex, a natural tendency. Being in the presence of such a historical figure delayed Ariq Haunts' refined instinct. But he managed to beam a smile, and the hall of precious conjure items brightened and warmed a little more.

King Ziko Yswil approached the young man he believed was his son. Captivating as Ariq Haunts' smile was, an experienced instinct murmured with a faint drone from the base of the king's neck to the crown of his head. Ariq Haunts noticed the king's curious gaze that inspected his visage. He held tight to his smile, but he didn't rely on its potency to hoodwink King Ziko. He concentrated and reached out to one of his six acolytes, an assembled caucus of hollowed, hexed men and one woman that were now puppets to the serial, immoral acts they committed. His Six Others. The stout, European man named Okod received Ariq Haunts' mental transmission. He was a former innkeeper who drugged chosen stayers at his place of comfort. Lulled to sleep or lethargic by anesthesia, he would have intercourse with them, slit their throats, and watch them die.

Okod, Ariq Haunts called. His voice was deeper in composition in the mind, as if the universe itself spoke through with its soulful, cosmic-baritone harmonics. **A little inertia to slow down an instinct.** Okod reached out and lent his hex called *Idleness*, and Ariq Haunts became a conduit for its flow. His eyes brightened with a confident gleam, and Okod's aura resonated from them, slowing down the king's heightened intuition.

King Ziko relaxed his inquisitive expression. All that remained was his smile.

"Pa-pa!" announced Ariq Haunts with his arms out. They embraced, and the hug was long and comforting to false-faced trickster. He remembered his own father, a man that had been sapped of authentic life, reduced to a mindless, walking integument at the command of a chief shaman. His father barely recognized he or his mother, save when anger needed to be expressed. Then he was a man full of words and more. Muscle had even grown on him in his afterlife. A thewy executioner. But until the moment of action arose, he was a northern winter residing in Africa's heat. Ariq Haunts bared his teeth while still embracing King Ziko, locked onto thoughts of his father and what he'd become. He stepped back, fixed his face, and looked at the display. He commented, "I'm reveling in being a clever bastard."

King Ziko put his hands on his hips. "Clever, yes," he agreed. "But you are a man with both parents together in marriage. A bastard you are not."

Ariq Haunts kept his smile, but he pleaded with the king, "You know what I mean, Pa-pa." He thought for a moment and then said, "Perhaps I should call myself a son-of-a-bitch!"

King Ziko raised an eyebrow. "Should I report that to your mother?"

"Pa-pa!" Ariq Haunts protested again, belting out laughter.

King Ziko tapped Ariq Haunts on the shoulder and conceded, "I jest, Iune." He folded his arms and inquired, "Go on. Tell me. How are you a bastard son-of-a-bitch?"

Ariq Haunts' smile wavered. He dropped his head and revealed in a sincere voice, "I'm just proud of myself, Pa-pa." He pointed at the items that cast no power. "Replicas. The best place to hide them is not where they're supposed to be hidden." He looked at his father and grinned. "It puts no one in danger." Then he waited, hoping the king would take the bait.

King Ziko nodded his head. "No," the venerable man agreed. "The Mai Gadi tribes can handle any opposition."

Ariq Haunts jabbed a finger in King Ziko's shoulder. "Exactly, Pa-pa! Trouble finds the poor soul wherever they venture. The energy and ritual to find this invisible island would take a person strong in conjure."

King Ziko chuckled, "If they can get in, they deserve it."

"Right!" agreed Ariq Haunts, giving himself a mental pat on the back. "Slip past guards and traps, the same sentiment applies. But, should the poor soul negotiate through all of those politics, and manage to enter these halls, they'll find nothing but empty trinkets—if, of course, those are the items they seek. Informed of the items' true whereabouts, they have the Mai Gadi to contend with." Ariq Haunts was versed in the many tribal nations of the Mai Gadi people.

King Ziko grabbed the back of Ariq Haunts' neck and shook him. "You certainly are a clever bastard son-of-a-bitch, Iune Del-Yswil!"

Ariq Haunts grated his teeth behind tightly closed lips. He managed a smile, quivering as it was. "I. Sure. Am…" he expressed. He wanted to roll his eyes, but he stayed his movement.

"Do you know what I see, my son?" asked the father. He put his forehead against Ariq Haunts' and publicized, "I see your stories. Many are mine and your mothers, but I see your stories and handiwork. And I'm proud of you, Iune." He lifted his head and looked Ariq directly in his eyes. "I don't say it often, I know. You think I'm cold. Maybe I am. I've left behind the significance of a person's story in an attempt for you, and your sister, not to feel pressure to be made up of just stories. I see you've aligned yourself to duties, you're conjured as a protector and provider. I take it for granted, thinking you're just doing a job—regardless of the intelligence and flair in which you execute your work. But, I'm proud of you, Iune. I really am."

Ariq Haunts straightened, and King Ziko let go of him. The impersonator stared at the father and thought of asking him how his wife was doing, barren of her powers. Her serpent-lions bound outside of time, unable to be conjured. A trick that stimulated Ariq Haunts' pride. In his fixed gaze he also spied the slight sliver of an open window in time. A moment. He could strike, and he considered doing so. He thought of killing the king and having him bleed out in the hall, being found later by his wife and daughter and sons. That would be the ultimate trick, and Iune would know the burden of absence that Ariq Haunts journeyed with in life. Specter, barely-there mother. Husk father. The burden of responsibility to a greater alchemy. Villainized for belief.

Fixed in thought. Ariq Haunts stood still. King Ziko pivoted and walked away. "I'll leave you to admire your work," he told the young man he believed to be his son. The king disappeared around the corner, and Ariq Haunts peered at the glass cases. The authentic and the duplicate treasures. Together, appearing genuine.

Ariq Haunts inspected the replicas with great scrutiny. There was no trick here. These were indeed only sterile reproductions. He ran through all it took to find and penetrate the invisible island kingdom. He was clever in that regard. He bypassed ritual and tribute. His pride became a salve to remove the humility of observing a ruse he thought was better than any he could pull off. Even with fakes, Iune appeared to be the veritable one.

Ariq Haunts stood straight. He put his hands behind his back, one gripping the wrist of the opposite arm. He turned and walked away with a smile on his face. He remembered the times he caused chaos among African tribes and kingdoms, put them at war. He watched them perform ritual and invoke Iune to solve their problems. He watched from afar and learned. He did the same when he brought European slavers in to wreak havoc on African nations. He watched Iune Yswil and learned. He was still learning. But he would teach Iune a lesson soon enough.

He continued on to the library, and he spent hours searching for the eight-volume set of *The Infinity Cycles*. He called upon his votary named Chamti, the former accountant who swindled the richest families in Europe.

He channeled his *Cupidity* hex, used to locate what he coveted.

High atop a set of shelves, in an area called *The Grand Ninety*, he found the desired books he'd come to purloin. He needed to scale one of the ladders that maneuvered around the horde of stacked shelves. The climb up was a journey unto itself, dizzying in its height. The ladder shook as he ascended higher, and though his elevation made the ground appear as a dive into a treacherous pit, he was nowhere near the top.

Volume Six of the *Infinity Cycles* stared him in the face. Ariq Haunts reached out, careful to keep his balance. He pulled his hand back and thought. "No, no, no!" he chided himself under his breath. "The trick. Always the trick!" He again summoned power through Okod. He stared at the book until he was confident that any blessing it possessed was dampened to where he could remove it from the palace and not be detected. He snatched the book, and he reveled as the tome was in his hand. He made a careful descent to the ground, and he flipped through the pages, grinning with pride as he inspected the literature.

The ritual was here. He raised an eyebrow at one area of the rites needed to be performed. The river Niger. There were nine hidden entrances to Azur-Fah. One ritual. A taxing task. Entering the Silver World called for tribute. Ariq Haunts almost exploded with triumphant laughter, but he managed to smother any outburst. Quick wit now acted as a salve on the wound to his vanity he'd earlier received. He would seduce the gods and play into their pride.

He thought of Iune, and he thought of the trick. "I've learned your lesson, dear rival," he said in a hushed voice. "I've also learned my own lesson. Our storms continue on course for collision. Let it rain."

He left the library and stepped back into the Hall of Treasures. The mystical lights brightened in his presence, and then faded out with his absence. He turned the corner, and the red interior of his cape swung wide and filled a dreamer's sight. The blood-red image broke into lilac static that molded into a thick, furred coat worn around a youthful-looking man wearing the same face and build as Ariq Haunts.

This was Iune Del-Yswil, and he was clothed in the garments of his adversary. A furred coat, thick and heavy. Breeches fastened at the knee with buttons and at the waist with a drawstring. Stockings covered the lower half of his legs, hidden behind knee-high boots. A lace, ruff collar crowned over an open, royal-court doublet. No shirt. That didn't help with negotiating the African sun and heated sands while wearing what felt like an Atlas bear on his person. His clothes were physical illusions, but one he had to maintain through conjure. An incant alleviated any heat, and Iune trudged through the hilly, desert mounds until he came upon an area of Africa not yet swallowed up by sand. It was a luxuriant, dense forest, and deep inside was hidden a band of nomadic rogues steeped in diabolism.

Iune wasn't alone. He was accompanied by his chief friend. His only friend, to be true. His name was Olobiri. He was a few inches taller than Iune with a sturdy build. His youthful face was outlined with a light strand of hair tracing his jawline. His upper lip was clean shaven. Frozen on his countenance was a melancholy expression attached to the tragic happenings to his tribal nation. He was from the Anjonu tribe who had been enslaved and taken to parts of Europe and the Americas fourteen years ago. Olobiri was ten at the time, and he was saved by Iune and a young girl of his tribe that he favored in a curious, schoolboy-like manner. Her name was Shell, and she lent her conjure to him for protection while she was snatched by slavers. Olobiri could still remember the feeling of the protective conjure dampening. The power sighed as it dimmed. He always described it as the conjure becoming tainted by idleness. It forced Iune to save him over Shell, and it was a long time before the severe sadness in his face eased. Olobiri could smile now, if only on rare occasion.

Their trek down the final dome of sand, where the desert exhaled its granules into patches of tall, blades of swaying, wheat-colored grass was just as arduous as the miles that were footprinted behind them. Their off-balance tumble was less because of troublesome footing and more to do with the spirit of adventure. Iune was ages old, but his boyish face fixed him in his mid-twenties, which was Olobiri's true age.

And so, they toppled and rolled. Iune laughed. Olobiri grunted his excitement. Then the two sprang up into the tall grass, the border between desert and lush jungle. Iune leapt forward, charging on hands and feet like a cheetah in sprint. After a few, feline strides, he stood up and pressed his body against a tree. He looked over. Olobiri leaned on the tree next to his, arms folded and half a grin quivering on his face.

Iune skipped over to his friend and smacked him on the arm. "This is it!" he said. "We separate here. I'm on my own…"

Olobiri pointed and warned, "You be careful."

Iune peered into the forest. "Keep that conjure up. I should be fine under your protection." He looked at Olobiri and inquired with worry in his eyes, "You're rested, right?"

Olobiri cocked his head to the side and cast an offended expression at Iune. "I'm fine!" he snapped, taking a step back into the tall grass. The outer locks on either side of his head fused together and created a thick cone that turned to bone encased in keratinized skin, curving like horns on a ram. His remaining dreadlocks tightened against his scalp, down the back of his head, as cornrows. He turned and sat on the ground with his legs crossed. He closed his eyes and focused. A gold, spherical light emanated from his forehead. "They shouldn't suspect a thing. I got you covered." Then he sent through his mind, **A god's speed, Iune."

Iune felt the blanket of protective conjure drape over him. He saluted his friend and repeated with his voice, "A god's speed." Despite their salutation, Iune journeyed into the dense forest slow and heedful. The thick foliage blocked the sun and dimmed his sight. The heat remained, but its effects were dampened by the extreme shade the forest offered.

Iune fought against his instinct, which was to maneuver through the woodlands like a cat on the prowl, low on palms and soles. But he knew the posture would draw suspicion. Ariq Haunts never carried himself in such a manner. Iune remained upright, chest out as he followed his higher senses to an encampment erected by the Ifo people. It was a long travel, deep into the woods where he saw the large, green shell of leaves, globular and closed-packed to create huts for dwelling. Long, rectangular houses made of wood panels for walls and thick, tiers of leaves for roofs were scattered around the area along with squat and square houses molded from the same construct.

The village had its own presence, living within the living forest. It was a heartbeat that existed inside the body of flora and fauna. Its sense of life filled Iune as he watched the men and women flow to and fro to their destinations. Women were clothed in light cloths and wrappings from head to toe. Men the same, or with leather leggings and vests. Iune spied fishermen and women strolling with nets and baskets filled with acquired, aquatic hunts. Gardeners tended to the planting of seeds, the tilling of soil, and the season's harvest. Hunters carried game and weapons over their shoulder, hide for food and clothing. Children mingled with games of running and catch, or were shuffled into the larger house for schooling. Iune, considered the Ifo appeared stable for a wandering tribe, but this was just home for now. Movement would take place when the forest offered harsh weather that scattered game and made the soil barren.

Iune narrowed his eyes and focused his instincts to cull from the scene the deviltry the people had been known to create. His instinct discerned no immediate evil. His eyes saw no prompt deviltry undertaken. There was a sensation, motivated by knowledge. An invisible hand smothered his heartbeat, and air felt thick as his throat constricted. His brow sweat as he evaluated the information concerning the Ifo tribe. He'd dealt with some of its cohorts. They had a philosophy he believed was misguided. He didn't understand, and he would never fully comprehend their desperate actions.

Distracted by thought, something without living eyes spied Iune. Clothed heavy in a thick cloak and an executioner's hood that covered his face. No holes for eyes, but he had Iune in his sights. The ominous figure was soft in approaching despite its hefty, black boots. Iune didn't hear the evil called Ratamutum creep up behind him. There was no subtle heartbeat coming from Ratamutum for instinct or heightened sense of hearing to detect, and Iune was too engaged with the tribal goings-on in front of him. No warning was realized as the hanged man extended his right arm and balled his fist. Red and black strands of conjure surrounded Iune's neck and entwined into a noose. The trepidation that strangled Iune's senses before was now palpable, and Iune's concentration on .the Ifo village was broken with the feel of magic constricting his neck.

It was too late!

Ratamutum gestured with his arm as if tugging on a rope. Iune was yanked off his feet, the lithe trickster wrenched back with his arms and legs stretched out in front of him while airborne. His back slammed against Ratamutm's chest, and he bounced off, smacking face-first onto the forest floor. A quick incant brought Iune back to his senses and dulled the aches caused by collision. He rolled over and go to his hands and knees. Iune fought against the reflex to conjure from the ethers his signature weapons, a pair of sharp and indestructible gazelle horns with the bases carved into handles to wield as short lances, tipped with toxin from the remaining power of his mother's banished serpent lions. Calling them to his grip would expose his true identity. His attention was also diverted by his instinct's ability to decrypt an oddity regarding his attacker.

Iune's resistance to fight Ratamutum, and to decode the aura of curiosity surrounding the hanged man, was all caught up in a moment that passed as quick as a scurrying hare. By the time he'd become conscious of either thought, Ratamutum had smacked his midfoot against Iune's chest and launched the rogue back like a ball in sport.

Iune's arms and legs flailed as he careened through the air. The abrupt impact against a tree's thick body halted his flight, and once more, he found himself face down in the jungle's loose soil. He palmed the ground and lifted his body. Ratamutm's boot tip came into his view, and Iune decided it was best to catch his breath rather than dodge the anticipated kick up into his jaw. The hit flipped him up into a seated position, back against the tree he'd crashed into. He had bruises, but no blood was spilled.

Ratamutum reached down and grabbed Iune by the collar of his furred coat and raised him to his feet in a single pull. He propped Iune upright, balled his fist, and hit him in the chest with his right hand. He ran his left fist across Iune's cheek.

Now there was blood. Iune's lip. His nose. The second strike rattled and blurred his vision. More blood flowed, reddening his sight with an irritating sting. Ratamutum seized his collars again and shook him. "Tribes were freed! Ships sunk! The Grand Alchemy disturbed by the actions of a tramp and a bastard that stir hope in nations mired in complacency!" he chastised. "And you waste time playing hide and tricks." Ratamutum rubbed the fabric of his hood against Iune's face. Iune could feel the trembling anger in the undead man's features. His blurry vision spied the living corpse's loose shirt still stained with blood and torn with a hole where a projectile was fired into his heart. "We are the dissatisfied!" Ratamutum continued. "You wear that slimy, worm-ridden filth's face to loop backwards his fortunes." Ratamutum let go of Iune and backed up. Iune used an incant and heavy breathing to regain balance, but he left his scars to bleed. The Hanged Man grumbled, "We were all children once. I was a child once. Children play. *I* played, as a child. There's nothing wrong with that." He put his hands around Iune's neck and pinned him to the tree. His grip tightened, and he jabbed a finger into Iune's face, close to his right eye. "Except you're getting caught up in childish things." Then he growled, "The trick!" He scoffed, and Iune could tell he snarled the word through gritted teeth, lip bent up at one end.

Ratamutum let Iune go, and the trickster's feet hit the ground, causing him to realize that the hooded brute had lifted him in the air by his neck. Iune took deep gulps of air. He bent over, put his hands on his knees, and continued gasping. He peered up at the baleful, hooded figure. Wrath bent his eyes. The beating kept his face from contorting into a complete indignant expression. He thought for a moment about changing his mark, killing the hanged man in front of him. A quick stab with his gazelle-horn weapons, pierced through the heart. Iune could leave Ratamutum sprawled out and bleeding on the jungle floor. Ariq Haunts wouldn't know whether to thank him or seek revenge. Iune considered the idea that killing Ratamutum would leave his adversary confused. It would be the ultimate trick.

A glowing thing shined bright on Iune's right. Both he and Ratamutum turned their attention to the apparition of a naked woman who was tall and slender yet still defined with curves in her shape. Her spectral radiance was sunset in color. The fluffy twists in her hair whipped like a candle's flame resisting being extinguished by a gust of wind. It was Ariq Haunts' mother, Duhu Firistess. Her name was once Tani Duhu, but she changed with a terrible happening.

Duhu Firistess said to Iune, "Your father disciplines you because you prove to be a case in need of it." She sauntered up to Iune, her glow casting off streams of incandescence. "Chief Bilísi is the same, but he'd rather use harsh language. He would like to speak with you now. Come!"

Iune straightened. He took one last heavy swallow of air and used an incant to restore his vitality. Duhu Firistess turned in a sharp manner and floated away, gliding to the Ifo settlement. Iune followed, stepping past Ratamutum without acknowledgement, anger now misshaping his face. He quickened his steps and sidled up next to Duhu Firistess. Her bubble of light cast warmth and calmed Iune. She looked at him and said, "He's tough, your father. He's very, very tough. Lose his respect, and you gain his wrath. You test that notion too much." She breathed out, trying to keep her anger from rising. "I have a little more patience than him," she continued. "But even that wears thin, Ariq. I don't want to dismiss your past accomplishments, but please tell us what you're planning." Iune barely opened his mouth, though he wasn't quite sure what he was going to say. Duhu Firistess raised a hand, which made Iune flinch. She said in a terse tongue, "Keep your words, Ariq! Save them for the chief."

Iune's face retained a vexed look, but he fixed it before Duhu Firistess spotted his mien. They walked, and Iune thought. He knew little of Ariq Haunts' current schemes. His recent actions consisted of ransacking old libraries and temples with his band of Six Others and assisting slavers. As Ratamutum summarized while delivering his discipline, slave ships had been sunk, Africans were freed, and nations were inspired to fight back and realign from petty differences. The most substantial hint at Ariq Haunts' new game was a shaman that summoned Iune and informed him off a misdeed. The venerable, wise man was tricked into giving the ritual to gain access to Iune's invisible island. Then Ariq Haunts' footprints were filled in by sand, and his trail turned as cold as the desert at night.

Iune had his tricks, and he used them to trace the Ifo tribe's nomadic movements, finding them tucked away within the border of desert and jungle. Reconnaissance. A close eye, and wielding familiar garments to those close to Ariq Haunts, Iune plotted to gain information. It seemed there was none. He hadn't journeyed from his island since learning of Ariq Haunts' desire to gain access to his home. His sister motivated him to track and infiltrate the Ifo people. That was her blessing from their mother's dispelled serpent lions. The slither of their strength and wisdom on her tongue for diplomacy. Iune could persuade and charm, but that was for the trick. His sister could arbitrate. Law and order. Iune finally left the nest to venture out with Olobiri. Here he was.

He and Duhu Firistess walked into the encampment. Ratamutum was a few paces behind. Iune examined the goings-on, peering deep into the activities. There were no human sacrifices or drinking of blood. There were no wild and loud invocations for chaos. There was nothing but life living around its environment, making use of the fruits of its surroundings. Iune wanted to scoff and sneer. He considered the Ifo selfish against all other African nations.

Duhu Firistess stepped aside and stopped walking. Iune went to do the same, wanting to pose a question to the lighted woman, but Ratamutum's hand gripped the back of his neck and pushed him forward toward a long, rectangular house at the center of the village. Robed guards with spears and scabbarded short swords stood on either side of the entrance. They held their spears like planted flags, sharp ends facing the heavens. Their still stances shuddered with Ratamutum's appearance. They faced one another, stepped back, and bent to one knee. Their spears crossed above the door, and Ratamutum pushed Iune through the front entrance. He released his grip after sitting Iune down on a stool positioned in front of large leaves laid out in a square formation.

"Chief Bìlísì," Ratamutum growled, voice humble in the presence of the tribe's elder authority. "My desultory son." He bowed at the neck, and then he posted up in the corner.

A step. Heavy with sovereignty and supremacy, though clothed in light sandals. He might as well have been wearing dense boots. Age had no weight on him, but Iune could see volumes of experience molded and scripted in Chief Bìlísì's figure as the robed man walked out of the shadows. Old. Very old. He was built as if wrestling was his profession. He dwarfed the magnificence of Ratamutum. Copper-red in color. Polished, clean and solid. Thick and long, dark-grey dreadlocks contrasted against the red-hot puffs of hair that outlined his rectangular face and covered his chin. Chief Bìlísì was a conjure man spoken of in whispers, and Iune listened close. The trickster was in awe, even as a conjured legend himself.

The chief stood on the square and looked down at Iune. He inspected every angle of Iune's person, eyes dripping wonder that eventually narrowed and slowly molded his face into an expression of concern.

Iune speculated if Chief Bìlísì could see through his disguise, tunnel through Olobiri's ancillary buff and status effect. Chief Bìlísì bent down. His nose curled like an animal sniffing for familiarity. He stood straight and boomed, "What are your plans, Been ah Kibir?" Iune flinched, and Chief Bìlísì raised a finger. "You will have your consecrated, given name returned to you when you impress me to be worthy of it. Until then, boy, your human name is who you are."

Iune looked at Ratamutum, a quick glance to note his posture. *Arms crossed. Not at the ready. Relaxed,* he assessed. He returned his attention to Chief Bìlísì. *Soaked in his authority. Crowned in immodesty. Distracted with being chief,* Iune further appraised. He decided to keep the two men in place, playing into the interrogation. He sat up straight and proud, hands on his knees. "I keep my trick close," he told Chief Bìlísì. "I make no apologies, Grand Chief Bìlísì. What I have planned will further the Grand Alchemy's transmutation."

Chief Bìlísì raised an eyebrow. He cocked his ear toward Iune, and a look exposing his concentration appeared on his face. He played back Iune's words, the sounds of his voice. He was calculating timbre and spirit, and Iune realized within that moment he needed to make a true transition from artful trickster to lethal assassin.

He took his hands from his knees and put his palms up. Conjure was quick, but the brilliant flash of light that molded into Iune's gazelle-horn weapons seemed to stretch out between eternity and infinity. One came into solid shape. Right hand. Iune made a piercing strike at Chief Bilísi's abdomen.

Another day, with another opponent, Iune's mark would've been true and deadly.

Iune first felt the restraint keeping his arm in place. What followed was a tearing feeling in his shoulder as it locked against forward motion, resisting the sudden hold placed on his movement. An uncanny sequence of events next unfolded. Iune registered the red and black chains glowing around his wrist. Chief Bilísi stepped back, out of his square.

"Are you mad?" shouted Ratamutum still believing Iune was his son. He pulled at his power, and Iune's body was twisted around on the stool. His strike was now focused to the hanged man, and his grip opened by force, letting loose his gazelle-horn short lance. Time restructured its speed, racing quick as a blink, and moving Iune's weapon from his open hand straight through Ratamutum's heart that didn't beat.

A rusted, cylindrical projectile popped from Ratamutum's back as the gazelle-horn short lance broke through him. The hanged man stiffened. Time was slow again as the massive, hooded man dropped to his knees. Where his eyes and mouth lay behind the hood, bright puffs of orange smoke filtered through the worn fabric. Ratamutum collapsed faced down, and the gazelle-weapon broke farther through his chest. His conjured bindings around Iune's wrist burst from existence with the thud of his body against the floor.

Still. Disbelief. Both features frozen on Chief Bilísi and Iune's faces.

Iune thawed first, at least he believed he did. Chief Bilísi screamed and balled his fist. He didn't strike with a punch. He opened his grip and exposed the growth of his nails, long and pointed. The Ifo chief slashed down at Iune with all ten nails, his face wide with anger and the desire to smell a fresh kill.

Iune dodged! Chief Bilísi's strike smashed the empty stool, sending up wooden shrapnel. In Iune's dive away, the heavy, furred coat sailed off his person and dissolved into dust. Chief Bilísi's attack caused him to put his face deep into the coat's dissipation, and the mystical dust stung his eyes.

Iune's palms slammed against the floor, he rolled forward and launched himself into the air. On his feet, the graceful trickster turned and conjured his second gazelle-lance to his hand. Double grip on the handle, he braced himself in time to block the recovered chief's showering assault. The Ifo superior was blind with rage rather than the dust that previously stung his sight. Iune's swarm of well-timed parries fended off Chief Bilísi's horde of abrading assailments. The trickster was moved rearward with every hit against his weapon. He jumped back and dodged to his left, scurrying quick like a dashing cat. Chief Bilísi spun, following Iune's scuttle around him. He twisted, but didn't lose balance. The flaw in his movement came at holding his arms out wide, leaving his torso exposed. Iune leapt back to his feet, slashing a deep gash down and across Chief Bilísi's chest. A second swipe cut a horizon line on the chief's abdomen.

Chief Bilísi dropped to one knee, and his upper body tightened. He retracted his nails and clutched his chest as a sharp pain ran up his left arm. *"Ah!"* he snarled. "What venom have you struck me with, boy? *Ah!* You vexatious creature! *Guards!"* His head ached, and he felt the urge to vomit. The chief heaved, but nothing came up. He groaned, and Iune was ready to make the killing blow when the guards broke through the front door, spears at the ready. Iune backed away from Chief Bilísi. He opened his hand and his impaled gazelle-horn lance dematerialized from Ratamutum's dead body in a blinding light. The same light gathered at Iune's palm, configuring solid into his weapon. He held his weapons downward, making a hastened, swift move away from the guards' thrusts at him. The boots on his feet disappeared while he soared through the air. They left behind a cloud of trailing, black dust and exposed the curiosity of his bare feet. Sprouting at their midfoot was a single feather from an African, lilac-breasted roller, a blessing received long, long, long ago from a very grateful, tribal sorceress.

Iune's hurdle landed him at the head of Ratamutum's mortal remains. Iune dismissed his weapons on sight of Ratamutum's body. They turned into yellow strands of conjure and burrowed into the lines on his hands. His face dropped, eyes wide and watered with remorse. "No…" he exhaled in a low, stammering voice. The guards turned and charged him, spears out to stab. He heard their advance, but he became distracted when Duhu Firistess appeared on the other side of Ratamutum's body. Her sudden arrival halted the guards' approach.

The phantom witch gasped at the sight of her slain husband on the floor. Iune remained still, observing anger wash away the horror that muddied Duhu Firistess' radiant, ghostly visage. The glowing globule encasing her darkened, and she extended two, open palms toward Iune, projecting a torrent of conjure at him. Iune vaulted away! In the air, his eyes, coupled with instinct, found the cylindrical pellet that had been lodged in Ratamutum's heart. The pellet that killed the undead man decades ago. Iune scooped it up, holding tight in his grip.

Duhu Firistess projected another discharge of conjure. Iune sidestepped the fulmination, sailing through the door. Another blast grazed his leggings as he escaped. The fabric covering his legs deliquesced, melting away to a pair of pants that belled out at his feet, tailored from the hide of a gazelle. Iune pocketed the rusted, round bullet, and spirited away.

"Kill him!" Duhu Firistess screamed. "He is *not* my son!"

She backed away from the pursuit, attending to her chief. His body shook, and he slumped to the floor still holding his chest.

Guards poured from houses, even jumping over the structures or descending from the trees to give Iune pursuit. The nimble trickster removed the lace collar and doublet, letting the garments evaporate into the wind. His upper body was now clothed with his natural attire of an incanted vest made of rhino hide. Free from the weight, Iune was able to crouch down and sprint on all fours, cat-like and just as agile. Tribe folk shuffled away from the chaos as Iune dodged guards and hastened from the village.

The foliage provided shade, and Iune used conjure to duck into shadow and move swiftly ahead, losing the pursuing guards. He reached the edge of the jungle, feeling the soil's soft and wet texture shift into coarse grains of sand. There was no slowing down when he neared Olobiri. The horned, young man opened his eyes and drew back his focus. The gold, spherical light shining against his forehead disappeared, and as Iune passed, he darted alongside him. They raced up the desert mounds together like fleeing cats. No one pursued them, and it was hours before the two stopped their run.

Iune caught his breath on hands and knees. Olobiri sat on the sands doing the same. His horns reverted back to dangling dreadlocks as he gazed in the direction from where they had traveled. His instinct deciphered that they were not being trailed. Olobiri spotted Iune punching the ground, and he looked over at his brother-in-horn and saw him weeping.

Iune took a seat on the sands. His eyes, flooded with tears, peered in the distance. He covered his trembling mouth to keep the sounds of his sobs from escaping. He sniffed and wiped his cheeks before clutching the wild coils of his hair, gritting his teeth in frustration.

"Iune…?"

The trickster turned to Olobiri. "I killed his father!" he blurted. His words choked on another wave of tears. He cleared his throat and wiped his eyes. He aimed his hand in the distance and recounted, "I had a moment. There was no information to be gained. I was cornered by Chief Bilísi and Ratamutum." He cleared his throat again, standing and wiping the sands from his pants. He palmed his hips and shook his head. "I am always impressed when I see them. Magnificent beings. This time, I was face-to-face with all three of them. His mother, that beautiful phantom retaining her conjure power…" He recalled the image of the horror on her face when she saw her killed husband. "The Ifo, up close, they're such a paradox." He thought of his brief moments among the village and its wandering folk. He folded his arms and paced in a circle. "I made effort to take the chief," he continued. Then he shook his head, remembering the events. "Ratamutum stopped me. His move was fatal. My horn killed him…"

Olobiri jumped to his feet. "Iune! You took the Hanged Man?"

Iune tried to smile, but the gesture was lopsided and quivering. He shook his head to cover his facial dilemma. He chuckled a bit, but that too came out awkward. "I did wound Chief Bilísì." He turned away to save face. With Olobiri's back to him, Iune's expression broke into melancholy once again.

Olobiri lived for the adventure. Past the slaughter and enslavement of his people he found little motivation to rejoice. Every slick, sly trick and scheme produced such moments where his face exploded with victorious delight. The effect would last for a short timeframe—a day or two, perhaps three before the sorrow would creep back in. Often, he'd hope it would carry to the next time he and Iune were conjured to assist in luck and fortune. Here he stood marveling with a bright expression to the announcement that villains had been maimed and slain, but he sensed Iune's internal quandary.

Iune sat on the ground again, knees up and arms resting atop their bend. His head dropped and he sobbed. Olobiri joined him. He remained silent and waited for Iune to speak. The trickster exhaled, facing the sky. He sniffed back tears and looked at Olobiri, a smile shaking into existence. "You are my brother-in-horn," he told Olobiri. Then he eyed the horizon in front of him. "Ariq Haunts and I…? We are twins born through different wombs, and I just killed…" He shook his head. "Damnit! No!" He jumped to his feet. Olobiri flinched at Iune's spring. "I just put to death a villain! I scratched another with poison! I put him on his knees. Let the witch and whelp weep!" He stared into the distance with his hands on his hips, chest out, and legs apart. A stern expression was on his face, and he breathed hard until taking a very deep breath. He exhaled a grin and looked down at Olobiri. "Home," he suggested. "Let's rejoice with wine to get our heads swimming, and we'll share our exploits to impress the ladies." He shook a balled fist and declared, "My father is from a culture of braggarts. Let me make use of his blood in my veins, and show that I too live for the story of life!"

Olobiri got up. He wiped himself of sand. "Up, down, up, down. Sit. Stand."

Iune chuckled at his friend's words. He put a hand on Olobiri's shoulder and said, "Now we run. Let's be as quick as cats!"

Olobiri agreed, nodding his head. They crouched on palms and soles, and then darted off, kicking up sand as they went. The lifted trails of strand shimmered in the sunlight, turning from gold to lilac glints that brightened to a blinding gleam, masking the scene in a glowing, lilac curtain. It raised to reveal a starry night blocked by the tight foliage doming the jungle where the Ifo people were settled.

Ariq Haunts had returned home, and he was arrested on sight. He didn't channel the hexes from any of his Six Others to put up a resistance. News of his father's killing made him numb. The only thing he was grateful for was clothing himself in his familiar garments. Thick furred coat. Breeches and stockings. Knee-high boots. Lace, ruff collar. His royal-court doublet. No shirt.

So that he wouldn't call upon the use of his mischievous Six Others, he was tied up with incanted twine, dampening his powers and physical strength. A dense, conjured fog surrounded the lower half of Ariq Haunts' face. The mystical murk filled his mouth, leaving him unable to speak. He'd been secured to a bent, wooden cross that was brought to his mother's quarters. She floated and glowed while sweeping eyes and finger through the book confiscated when he was apprehended. *The Way to the Silver World, or The Many Manors of Constellation.*

Ariq Haunts observed his mother. Disenchantment possessed her eyes and incited the dismay that shook her head. Duhu Firistess raised her head to spy her son. He wept as he hung against the thick and contorted, wooden rood. She slammed the book shut and snapped at him, "No! You don't get to weep for your father!" She glided up to him, nose-to-nose. "I earned that right! Only. Me!" She backed away and shook the book at him. "You caused his killing." She lifted the book higher and said, "All for this! A book!" She smacked him across the face with the ancient tome. Ariq Haunts tightened, gritting his teeth and balling his fists. He recovered from the strike and hung his head. Duhu Firistess chided, "I act upon you as *he* would act upon you! Tough!" She pivoted, back to Ariq Haunts. She floated away, opening the book again and scrutinizing its contents. "What is this book anyway? What scheme and plot or trick justifies the sacrifice of your father and the mortal wounding of our Grand Chief?"

Ariq Haunts lifted his head and groaned a muffled answer.

Duhu Firistess faced her son in a swift turn. She chuckled. "You wish to speak?" Translucent tears watered her eyes. She sailed to him. "If my love for you, child, didn't equal your father's..." She waved her hand and the brume gagging Ariq Haunts dwindle away.

He breathed deep first. His tears salted his tongue, and he swallowed his sorrows. He didn't need the hex of his minion named Kerst to boil his blood and stir anger in him. He had his personal wrath, natural and from his heart. He glared at his mother and barked, "I've done the Great Work! Not even the Grand Chief can say that."

"*Your* Chief!" Duhu Firistess reminded, again shaking the book in Ariq Haunts' direction.

"I am my own chief, Ma-ma," he declared in an eerily calm voice. There was a gloaming to his pronouncement. Duhu Firistess tapered her eyes at him. He laughed, deep and dark. "You and Pa-pa and that foolish chief damn my tricks. You scoff at the games I play, but the contest between Iune and I has led to this moment. I am a griefer to the trickster." He beamed proud. "You want the Grand Alchemy to be fixed? So be it, Ma-ma. Your wish is my command. Pa-pa has transitioned, completely. Let him rest. He will be proud of me yet. Let him observe my machinations from the other side." His smile curved like the horns on a devil. "He's gained knowledge in death, so he already knows my schemes." He chuckled again. "Oh, and does he glower down on you, Ma-ma." Ariq Haunts' words straightened his mother's posture. She was attentive and doing her best to control the insulted look insisting to mold onto her face. "He curses you for filling my mouth with rancid flies and mist!"

Duhu Firistess' feet touched the floor, and she made slow steps toward her bound son. "Why are you so interested in legends…?"

Ariq Haunts shook his head at his mother, pride never faltering from his grin. "I've found the path to Azur-Fah. The Silver World, Ma-ma. It's in that book." Duhu Firistess looked at the tome in her hand and then back at her son, incredulity crawling on her face. Ariq Haunts kept his simper. "I will do it. I will. I will infect Azur-Fah and lock the stars in place. The Grand Alchemy will continue unabated. I will play into the Eterijah's egos, give them a magnificent tribute. My Six Others will possess them. We will take Azur-Fah and make fate out of destiny." Another deep chuckle emanated from Ariq Haunts, and he declared, "I will wield their sign of All Eternity, And Infinity. I will become the Time King."

He sounded insane to her, and she wore disbelief on her face like a second, radiant skin. "Why do you believe this when no mortal person, even with conjure, could wield such an item, if it existed."

Ariq Haunts nodded his head. "Because knowing doesn't require belief," he told his mother. "Why don't you *know* I can do it?"

Duhu Firistess didn't respond with words. She pondered her son's statements for a brief moment, and then she made a simple gesture with her fingers. Ariq Haunt's binds dissolved, and he dropped to the floor on his knees at his mother's feet. He rose. "Let me see him," he requested.

Duhu Firistess questioned, "Your father?"

"No," said Ariq Haunts rubbing the soreness in his wrists. "The chief. I will mourn at my father's body later."

Duhu Firistess walked past him. "Follow me."

Ariq Haunts walked in tow. He and his mother stepped from her long-house and walked to Chief Bilísi's residence. The guards pivoted, facing one another. They bent to one knee, and crossed spears above the door. Duhu Firistess stepped into the house. Ariq Haunts, close behind, moved forward to follow. The guards lowered their intersecting spears and blocked his entrance. Ariq Haunts lifted a single hand, ready to utter an incant and choke the life from the two sentries.

His mother saved their lives. "Permit him entrance!" she snapped at them, vexation in her voice.

Their spears raised, and Ariq Haunts walked inside.

His eyes, by instinct, were drawn to the area where his father was felled. He paused in step, mourned without tears for a brief time, and then continued to Chief Bilísi's bed. He knelt and cupped the chief's hand with both of his, examining his torso wrapped in medicine-soaked bandages to assist his deep, toxic wounds.

Chief Bilísi attempted to whittle his hand from Ariq Haunt's double grip, but he was too weak. His lack of strength rattled Ariq Haunts, and a piercing chill popped in his heart, iced his throat, and spiraled down his spine. The chief sneered at his presence, "What is he doing out of his binds, Tani-Duhu? His troublesome antics have left me wounded by that damnable trickster he so loves to play games with."

Duhu Firistess floated and glowed on the opposite side of the bed. She said to Chief Bilísi, "My son has a plot, my chief." She shoved the appropriated tome in the tribe master's view. "He prides himself on the knowledge of fairytales."

The wounded overlord found strength in anger, snatching the book and examined its cover. The words were ancient, and instinct barely translated the title. He grimaced and tossed the book aside. He looked at Ariq Haunts and derided, "A plot, no less, to fuel his ego than assist the Grand Alchemy." Ariq Haunts let go of Chief Bilísi's hand. "What dance have you created to impress the imp that's left me poisoned?"

Ariq Haunts addressed his chief, "This is how I'm going to save your life, because you're dying of a toxin with a strength greater than any healing incant or salve." He wiped a hand over the material dressing Chief Bilísi's wounds. "These medicinal bandages? They're prolonging the inevitable. Your death." He leaned closer to Chief Bilísi and revealed to him, "I've found the precise ritual to burrow into Azur-Fah, the Silver World. My Six Others, and myself, will infect the Eterijah. I will come bearing gifts, like the Danaans so feared by Virgil. Seven infections will be enough. I will find their treasured sign of All Eternity, And Infinity. While in their world and among their power I will be equipped to wield power, and I will fix the stars. The power All Eternity, And Infinity can heal you, old man. But we waste precious time on debate and insults."

Chief Bilísi grinned, and Ariq Haunts expected a barrel of laughter to erupt from their chief. Duhu Firistess and her son waited with wide eyes inundating with anticipation. Chief Bilísi lost his smile, and he grumbled, "Perhaps I misjudged you." He groaned, body beginning to ache with the toxin's sting. He turned his head to Duhu Firistess and smiled once more. "Genius," he proclaimed. "Bring my sword."

Duhu Firistess' bright phantasm puffed away in a burst of energy. Her apparition manifested at a table where there lay Chief Bilísi's sword. The weapon had a gold handle carved with a globe at the top, grip in the center, and an African face at the hilt. The blade was forged from black steel, and had an edge sharp enough to cut thoughts in half. Anyone who beheld the sword reconsidered their position opposite the bearer. Duhu Firistess' translucent form clutched the hilt and raised the sword off the table. She turned and floated next to her son.

"My chief," said the phantom woman as she presented the blade to him.

Chief Bílísì shook his head. "Ariq Haunts," he stated. "It's his. Give it to him."

Hesitant, but Duhu Firistess turned to her son and handed the blade to Ariq Haunts. He accepted the weapon and inspected its beauty. Chief Bílísì ordered, "Now, kill me."

Ariq Haunts questioned, "What? Is this a test or has the toxin blighted your brain?"

"Kill me with the blade!" the chief insisted. "Run it through my heart. Take what conjure I have left in me." He put his hand over his chest. "You'd never retrieve All Eternity, And Infinity in time. Preserve me. Add the sword and its magic to your tribute." He looked at Duhu Firistess and told her, "I loved you and Ratamutum as my children. Celibate as I had become when I took my spiritual path. You were as a daughter to me. Ratamutum, a son. This one here, boy turned man, a grandchild."

Duhu Firistess had no words.

Chief Bílísì addressed Ariq Haunts. "All Eternity, And Infinity has been lost to the ages," he remarked. His wounds burned, and he adjusted himself as best he could while lying in the bed. "You sneaked into the Del-Yswil kingdom, didn't you? The book is from there? Isn't it?" Ariq Haunts answered with a nod. "You've been reading, haven't you?" Ariq Haunts nodded again. Chief Bílísì closed his eyes and exhaled. "Immortality through alchemy. We will be such a greater people for all this. The evil brought to this world by Africa's intruders will transmute into resolve for us to finally bring balance to this problematic, physical world." He put his other hand on his chest. "Kill me. I know you will be a great chief to the Ifo. I know."

Ariq Haunts agreed. His movement was quick and threatening like a flash of lightning. He plunged the sword through Chief Bílísì's heart, and Duhu Firistess flinched at the action. The chief felt nothing, dying instantly. A grisly pageant of torn flesh and muscle, coupled with broken ribs and a punctured sternum, overlaid with puddling blood. The blade cut through the bed and broke into the wooden floor beneath the resting area. Ariq Haunts peered down at the gruesome sight. His chief slain. The display contrasted with the peaceful, resting look secured on Chief Bílísì's countenance.

Ariq Haunts exhaled, a supercilious sense coursing through him like the blood in his veins. His eyes bent as he studied the slain leader, and his lips curled into a subtle grin. His sight raised, and he noticed his mother easing her erratic breath and become calm. He always found her respire intriguing since her transition to spirit. Thinking of his curiosity prompted him to ask, "What do spirits breathe, Ma-ma?"

She looked at him with an odd expression. She went to speak, but her words remained on her tongue as magic occurred. The mystical weapon's black blade shimmered, and the light it produced draped over Chief Bilísi's corpse. The light retracted to the blade, taking the chief's body with it. The punctured sword through the bed was all that remained. Even the bloodstains vanished.

Ariq Haunts pulled the sword free. He held it close to his face and examined a newly fashioned design on either side of the unstained, black blade. A pint-sized, detailed hieroglyph of Chief Bilísi was etched into the middle of the blade's curve. A faint, turquoise glow outlined the sharp edge and vibrated with a whispered hum. A familiar sense tugged at Ariq Haunts, and his instinct communicated it was Chief Bilísi's spirit possessing the blade.

"Your father," Duhu Firistess uttered in a trembling voice, as she too reacted to the sword's purr and glow. "There is still conjure in his body. There's still a spirit. Put him to the sword. Add his soul to the blade's resonance."

Ariq Haunts agreed with his mother's orders. He pivoted toward the door and exited the house. Duhu Firistess followed her son. Outside. Activity was thin in the late hours of the Ifo village. A few stragglers walked the settlement. Guards were on patrol. No one interrupted mother and son's trek, not even to give their sympathy for Ratamutum's murder.

Duhu Firistess guided her son to the stone table situated under a conjure-made opening in the foliage. The moon's light extended down on Ratamutum's mortal remains. The phantom woman glided through the table and posted on the opposite side. She turned and watched Ariq Haunts approach. He stopped, and there he stood at his father's body. It was still and without life, but bubbling with conjure and a trapped soul. He examined his father from head to toe. Ratamutum remained hooded, and Ariq Haunts attempted to look beneath his father's veil. He blinked and looked away. "Immortality through alchemy…" he uttered, turning his gaze to the sword in his hand. He turned the sword downward, looked at his father, and then took a glance over his shoulder.

"No one will intrude," his mother assured.

Eyes on his father. He noticed the hands, oddly balled into a fist rather than relaxed and opened. Ariq Haunts raised the sword and violently brought it down through Ratamutum's chest. The black, preternatural blade impaled the body as well as the stone table it rested on. Magic transpired, and the blade cast a light that swallowed Ratamutum's body and was drawn back into the blade.

The sword lay upright in the stone. Ariq Haunts wrenched it free without struggle, and the table crumbled with the sword's absence. Ariq Haunts stepped back from the rubble to examine the blade. A hieroglyph lay underneath Chief Bilísi's right foot. It was his father, strong, hooded and raising a defiant fist. But his examination didn't last long, as his mother distracted him from the inspection. She held a somber, yet content look on her glowing face. Calm in her voice, she instructed, "Add my specter to the blade, Ariq."

He put the sword at his side and aimed a face contorted in disbelief toward his mother. "Ma-ma…?" he questioned.

Duhu Firistess floated by him, her ethereal body passing through the stone table's rubble. Ariq Haunts turned as his mother took a position behind him and knelt on one knee. "Strike me down!" she demanded.

Ariq Haunts protested, "Ma-ma! Please. Don't be so dramatic."

Duhu Firistess got to her feet, floating a few inches from the ground as she straightened. "Don't be such a coward, Ariq! Unite my nature with your father."

Ariq Haunts huffed and rolled his eyes, "Is this about dying!"

She slapped him. Her strike burning and stinging like no mortal weapon. "This is about *living!*" she hissed. "A passage to real life…" Then her voice calmed and she concluded, as Ariq Haunts recovered from her blow, "We can assist you no longer in this fettle." They went silent. Duhu Firistess broke the quiet first. "Transition. Alchemy. All Eternity, And Infinity. I know."

Ariq Haunts swung the blade fast. Both hands gripped the hilt. He cut through his mother's abdomen. Left to right. Her body bent, curving with the flourish. Her arms and legs stretched long as her specter remained attached to the weapon's sharp, soul-engulfing edge. Already spirit, Duhu Firistess simply seeped into the blade as Ariq Haunts was in swing. A hollow cry echoed faint through the woods, and when Ariq Haunts brought his sword around and out of action, the brightness that was his mother, Duhu Firistess, had been doused.

The moon's brilliance seemed dim to Ariq Haunts with the loss of his mother's luminescence to assist. He had to hold the blade closer to observe her stylized etch imprinted on the black blade. Her feminine figure, surrounded by a wriggled globule, was positioned under Chief Bilísi's left foot. There they were. The Ifo trinity engraved. Unified. Ariq Haunts conferred onto the sword a title. "The Sword of Union!" he expressed while marveling at the blade.

He left the area, walked to the village center, and jammed the Sword of Union into the ground. His mother, father, and his chief's spirit shimmered into existence. Ariq Haunts stood directly behind them. "Ifo! Gather!" shouted Chief Bìlísì's specter. "Come and see the transmutation, the grand change, ushered in by the wit and knowledge of your new chief! Ariq Haunts!"

Few among the Ifo that weren't guardsmen knew conjure or incant, but those who did called flame to their hand and walked to the village center, emitting light for others to follow. The flame casters raised their palms when they neared the specter triumvirate, and the rest of the Ifo people created a circle around the gleaming wraiths.

"We are a people without," the wraith of their chief proclaimed. "We are a people scattered, but change was inevitable. I took you in, and we transformed to a new tribe. We move. We wander. We are a people in inconstancy," announced Chief Bìlísì. "This is my final command to you. Behold your new chief, Ariq Haunts, and his henchmen the Six Others." Ariq Haunts' six acolytes didn't appear, but their presence was felt. "He will lead you to a final change." The former Ifo chief addressed Ariq Haunts over his shoulder, shouting, "Chief Ariq Haunts, Last of the Ifo Chiefs, command your people."

Ariq Haunts walked through the specters. The people bowed in his presence. The new chief called, "Yabu, crafter among us. Your chief calls upon your folk for a service." A slender man with a bushy, black beard and braided hair rose and stepped up to him. The new chief put a hand on his shoulder and said, "I need the talents of your sister, your brother, and you to fashion for me five wondrous trinkets." Then he listed, holding up his fingers as markers as he cataloged, "Three, splendid, gold chains. A wand crafted from azurite, wrapped in a copper cord, and topped with a sapphire gem. At last, a chest plate built from black steel and branded with the number nine at its center." Chief Ariq Haunts grinned. "Oddly specific, yes? But can it be done, grand crafter?"

Yabu beamed a pleasant smile in return. He tapped his forehead with his hand and stated, "By my forehead to my hand, it will be done."

"Thought to tangible. That's all I ask." His eyes remaining on Yabu, Chief Ariq Haunts directed the gathered Ifo, "Return to your rest, my people. My coronation is adjourned." The people rose and dispersed. The flame holders closed their hands and snuffed out their fire. The guards returned to their posts, and Chief Ariq Haunts dismissed Yabu. "Meet me in the morning," he told the crafter. Yabu assured his new chief he would be at the ready.

Alone with the ghosts of his former chief and parents, Chief Ariq Haunts lifted the sword from the ground and walked to the former Ifo Chief's long-house. The specters drained into the sword's blade upon removal from the soil. Chief Ariq Haunts retrieved the discarded tome, Volume Six of the *Infinity Cycles*. He rested his sword against the wall and sat on Chief Bilisi's bed. He uttered an incant and light blossomed in the longhouse's four corners. He re-read passages pertaining to long-lost treasures owned by the Eterijah, lost through either vanity or war. One caught his eye. It was a precious item much sought after by Azur-Fah, the Silver World. It was neither lost by way of war or pride. It seemed it was just a rumor. A mythology unto itself. His eyes narrowed on the cited treasure, reading its designation aloud, "The Immortal Created." He grinned, and then he looked at his sword. He reflected on his swindle and snapped his fingers as a thought occurred to him. "Six treasures, and I will present a proposal to find a seventh!" His haughty smile parted into a low chuckle. "Tick-tock, the cosmic clock must stop."

A billowing, bright lilac sheet turned the scene like a page in a book.

Sun high. At its zenith. Two men shuffled along in the desert. One was tall. The other was short. The tall man, a blackamoor with Portuguese blood was named Kioi. No surname, just Kioi. His rough, mahogany face was hidden in shade cast by the wide-brim, pointed hat atop his head. On his chin was a triangular blotch of hair shaped to a sharp point. A curled mustache ornamented his upper lip. From his thick eyebrows to his thinning mop of curly hair resting underneath his hat, there was an intrusion of gray in the pitch color. He was getting old. His face was pronounced with experience, but he had not yet gained his life's desire. A cosmic charter he called it, and as he would often ramble on about to his younger companion.

The short and stumpy man was named Jai Chilla. He was darker in tone and had a heart-shaped face that was speckled with hair from chin to jaw to upper lip. Both were dressed in billowy pants and sandals with straps that wrapped up their ankles. Loose tunics adorned their upper bodies. Both were decorated with jewels from rings to necklaces. A pistol and dagger were dangled at each of their sides with a sword sheathed at their hips. One offset description, Jai Chilla sheltered his short hair beneath a beige headwrap while Kioi covered himself with a green cape.

Jai Chilla listened close to Kioi, absorbing the words the old man preached.

"The people of Africa should declare their cosmic sovereignty!" sermonized Kioi. "Those nations that have been subjected to slavery have no cosmic charter to declare their heavenly sovereignty. They are enslaved because they believe slavery is real." He raised a finger and shook it while beaming a self-congratulatory look.

Jai Chilla reviewed what he'd heard, going over the words in his head. "So, slavery isn't real…?"

Kioi put fists to hips. He shook his head and drawled, "No! No! Not at all. It's ridiculous. Our Africans have become subjects to things not real because they do not have their Cosmic Charters. With a Cosmic Charter, those of the Heavens must recognize those of the Earth that declare cosmic sovereignty. Our African brothers and sisters are enslaved because of a belief in slavery itself!" He scoffed with a laugh. "Silly!" he said. "Slavery does not exist. We are indigenous not imported. You cannot import that which is already present. And are we not the original people? Are we not all present?" He huffed with a roll of his eyes. "It's not happening. There is no enslavement. The European tricks us."

Jai Chilla wondered, "Then what's happen to all the Africans said to be enslaved in the New World?"

Kioi put his arms around the shorter, younger man. "They are enslaved into the idea of being a slave. It is a deep trick."

"But they're not enslaved…?"

"No!" replied Kioi, again in a self-congratulating and victorious tone. "A hoax, so let me explain. Because slavery does not exist!" He took his arm from Jai Chilla. "It's not happening!" he insisted. "We must step out of this falsehood. We must declare our cosmic sovereignty under a Cosmic Charter. The European nations will recognize this, and they will cease their tricks. They must submit to this cosmic law. They must. …They have to…"

"I see…" uttered Jai Chilla making a face that said otherwise.

Kioi assured him, "You will fully understand in time, Jai Chilla. You will." His eyes caught a series of ruins in the distance. The remains of toppled towers and pillars sprang up from the desert sands, leaning and chipped away at varying sections. Kioi stopped his approach. He put a hand on Jai Chilla's chest for him to do the same. The two stood still, gazing at the ancient and half-buried, decayed city. Kioi's stare was more specific, studying the remains until he found a sunken temple with an entrance that was completely submerged. Besides its lean causing burial on one side, the sanctuary stood in a pristine state, standing out from the wrecked structures. "That's it!" Kioi exclaimed. He guffawed and jumped. "Son't of a bitch! That's it! The ritual worked. Our fortune is in there." He turned to Jai Chilla, who mirrored Kioi's excitement. "Come, young apprentice. Let us meet the Iune spirit."

Jai Chilla nodded his head, excitement wide on his face. He followed Kioi as the tall man took lead. Both were in full stride, sailing over the desert sands. They entered the ruins and slowed their pace. Kioi remained in the lead as Jai Chilla was close behind. They wasted no time stowing away into the temple as they neared the ruins. On closer approach, they observed the myriad of holes and chips in the building's facade. Sunlight was cast inside brightening the space. Walking proved cumbersome as the floor dipped, the building leaned on its angle, and was dusted with desert sands. They lost their footing a few times but never tumbled to the ground.

Kioi stopped. He put a hand on Jai Chilla's chest to keep him from moving forward. He'd heard a voice and cocked his ear to distinguish the chatter from the wind howling through passageways and holes in the structure. He turned to Jai Chilla and said, "It could be him to give us our fortune." His face brimmed with delight. "He might lead us to Constellation and have the Eterijah present us with a Cosmic Charter. We will have sovereignty!" He took a quiet and cautious step. "Come, my apprentice!" Jai Chilla nodded and followed. Kioi hurried, maintaining his balance through the incommodious interior.

Through a hallway. The voice grew louder as they drew closer. The language used was indecipherable, but Kioi and Jai Chilla pressed forward.

A feeling crawled through both of them that chilled their senses.

Kioi slowed his steps as he neared an opening into a small room. Each step closer to the entrance brought a heavy weight on his chest, and the icy feeling wriggling through him dropped even farther in temperature. The phenomenon was not just internal. Jai Chilla breathed, and he observed his breath condense in the air. Kioi didn't notice the chill. His eyes were too focused on the door. He could see into the room. Where all else in the temple was at a lean, the room was straight. Candles flickered, giving off a red light. The sun bore its way through the ceiling and brightened the space.

Kioi moved to one side of the entrance as Jai Chilla took post on the other. They peaked in and spied a young man clothed in a thick furred coat. Breeches and stockings. Knee-high boots. Lace, ruff collar. A royal-court doublet. He stood in front of six others. Five men. One woman. The seated six were without color to their flesh and of European descent. The pacing man addressed them in an old, European tongue. He paced, and he turned. Kioi could see his face when he made his pivots, and the older man's stomach felt as if he'd dropped from a great height. His heart beat quick, and his hands trembled. He looked at Jai Chilla and noted in whisper, "This is not our fortune. Damnit!" He huffed and grunted low, keeping from detection. "The muted luck we have," he continued. Jai Chilla watched him close, waiting for a cue. "We've stumbled upon the other face of Iune Yswil. Those are not the whimsical clothes of the trickster. Let us go. Quick but cautious."

They turned, cautious but not quick enough. Chief Ariq Haunts rushed through the door. His speed left a trailing blur, and he slammed into Kioi, knocking the rogue against the wall. He recovered and went for his sword, but Chief Ariq Haunts slapped his hand away and hit him with a heavy fist across his jaw. He didn't allow Kioi to fall back. He reached out and caught him by the neck and restrained him against the wall. Face close to Kioi, Chief Ariq Haunts bared his teeth and snarled in words Kioi could understand, "You want to interrupt my ritual? So, be it! I'll cut the heart and entrails from you, and I'll make you the sacrifice."

Jai Chilla roared and tackled Chief Ariq Haunts to the ground. Kioi swallowed deep and big, regaining breath and balance. He peered over at his apprentice and Chief Ariq Haunts' tussle. Jai Chilla was pinned down with Chief Ariq Haunts atop him. Punched twice, now being strangled. Kioi took up his pistol, thumbed back the single hammer, and pulled the trigger. The pop of the powder echoed through the hall, and the burst of smoke filled his vision. The cylindrical projectile ricocheted off Chief Ariq Haunts' thick, furred coat and lodged into the wall near Kioi. The rogue lunged forward, shoulders down, ramming Chief Ariq Haunts off his apprentice and against the wall.

Jai Chilla got up, wheezing and massaging his neck. "Run!" Kioi shouted, unsheathing his dagger. "Run!" he said again. Jai Chilla hastened his steps, and he was in full stride quick.

Kioi plunged his dagger down onto Chief Ariq Haunts shoulder. The heavy coat worn by misfortune's trickster broke the blade. Kioi retracted the broken dagger's jagged edge and ran it across Chief Ariq Haunt's face. A thick gash opened and spilled blood. The chief screamed! Kioi tossed his blade aside, stood, and darted away, catching up to Jai Chilla.

Chief Ariq Haunts clutched his bleeding face. An incant spoken, and his flesh mended. He let the blood remain. He snarled, opened his hands, and conjured the Sword of Union into his grip. He eyed the slender silhouettes of the rogues that intruded on his ritual. His vision narrowed, locking his aim. He swung his sword down as if making a chop, holding it out in the fleeing rascals' direction.

From the blade came the lighted specter of his father, Ratamutum. The phantom hanged man elongated, extending toward Kioi and Jai Chilla's escape path. The long beam, attached to the sword's blade, stretched and reached out attempting to snag the escaping men.

Kioi glanced over his shoulder and spotted the grappling ghost's approach. "Against the wall!" he shouted to Jai Chilla. Both men flattened up on either side of the hall. Ratamutum's spirit missed seizing them as he elongated past their presence. Kioi and Jai Chilla remained pressed and watched as Ratamutum's apparition retracted to the blade. The wraith snatched Kioi's cape and dragged him back with him. Jai Chilla jumped to action, catching Kioi by the boots and holding tight. Ratamutum's grip was strong, and Chief Ariq Haunts pulled the Sword of Union like a fisherman to reel his catch to him.

Jai Chilla grabbed his pistol and fired a shot down the hall. The projectile whizzed past Chief Ariq Haunts' head, and he flinched at the attack. Concentration lost, Ratamutum's grip opened, and the spirit was drawn back to the sword. Kioi and Jai Chilla stood and resumed running from the temple. Chief Ariq Haunts pursued. He swung his sword as he gave chase, and

Selotes Bilísi's spirit stretched free, tearing at the walls and bringing down the passageways Jai Chilla and Kioi escaped through. The two missed being crushed by inches, and they kept up their pace when they escaped to the outside.

The winding halls blocked by fallen structures and debris were no hindrance to Chief Ariq Haunts. He conjured his mother's spirit, and she wrapped her arms around him. Cloaked in her essence, Chief Ariq Haunts simply passed through any obstruction. He exited the temple and retracted his mother's spirit into the blade. He surveyed the area, looking for the escaping scoundrels. Spotting them, he gave chase beyond the ruins. He stopped at the summit of a sand dune and again chopped down in Kioi and Jai Chilla's direction.

Selotes Bilísi's massive spirit sprang from the sword's blade, arms out and nails extended from his fingers. The former Ifo chief screamed, face wide with rage and determination as his giant, translucent form slammed down on the sandy sea. High and wide, a vast wave of sand blotted out the sun and threatened to bury Kioi and Jai Chilla. It kept good on its promise, crashing down and entombing them under heaps of loose sand.

Chief Ariq Haunts watched and waited. It wasn't long before he witnessed Kioi and Jai Chilla dig themselves out of the reshaped area of the desert. They were only a little bruised and winded, and as they tunneled up to the surface, Chief Ariq Haunts ducked away from view. He grinned as he stepped away, uttering under his breath, "Bring him to me, you blockheaded, bumbling fools." He pivoted and returned to the temple. Holding the Sword of Union, he used his mother's spirit to assist him in walking through the passages blocked by fallen stones.

Jai Chilla's headwrap was loose, but remained on his head. Kioi fixed his hat and remarked, "Fortune still favors us, my apprentice." He peered in the direction of the ruins, catching his breath. "Let us head back to camp and make way to the city of Kadari. We'll rest there and enact a new ritual to invoke Oris Del, Iune's mother. This new personality of misfortune has become violent. We must notify her that her son has gone insane."

Kioi took lead. Jai Chilla followed. They walked long under the desert son, and they were grateful they returned to their camp. They indulged in provisions and sought shelter inside their tents. All the hours of rest were appreciated. They journeyed to Kadari on camel when the sun sank halfway into the horizon, collecting their provisions, taking up their tents, and rolling up their blankets.

Kadari was a walled city in Africa. Most of the African population was Mohammedan in faith, but there were many who practiced traditional, African forms of worship. There were African Christians and African Jews, and like the black Moors of Spain, there were places for everyone to worship in peace together. There were still illicit politics and talks with tawny Arabs to assist Europeans to enslave African tribal nations. Despite the affairs, it was sanctuary for Kioi and Jai Chilla. They paid a toll for entrance, and they found an inn soon after. Kioi was more familiar with the city than Jai Chilla. The young apprentice heard about the city's nightlife brimming with young women entertaining with dance and more salacious activities. Loud taverns with drunken men and women listening to poetry or thumping music. Watching Kioi setup an altar with figurines of Oris Del, offerings, and candles configured to her summoning, he understood there was no time for cavorting at this moment.

"It might take her days to appear or for a sign from her to come," Kioi told Jai Chilla as he lit candles and incense. "We will settle into the city, and we will know its happenings." He said the last part with a smile, and Jai Chilla gained trust that he would swim in the libidinous bustle the city had to offer. Jai Chilla moved aside as Kioi took a canteen of liquor and spit in the six sacred directions and then swallowed the rest. He said a prayer that took a moment, and then the ritual was done. He turned to Jai Chilla and said, "There is much activity in the city, but let us rest for now. I know you're eager, but you'll have your time to play soon."

The two prepared themselves for bed, hopping into separate cots, and then they went fast to sleep.

A sparkling, lilac wave moved across the scene. Night was substituted for morning, and it was days later in the city of Kadari. Three, cloaked figures walked through the walls surrounding the African city, stepping into time from somewhere else. Their faces were buried by shadow, a purposeful and preternatural occurrence. The one in front was clearly a woman, hour-glass in shape beneath her cape and cowl. Her beige, long- and belled-sleeved shirt stopped at her midriff. Her matching skirt trailed lengthy, lined with gold-colored embroidery, and covered her sandal-veiled feet, even as she walked. She was quite taller than the men that flanked her, but they walked with confidence in their stride. Her guards had no visible weapons, but their military step was shield enough to repel any thought of attacking. One sentry was barefoot, and on close inspection of his feet, a person would spy an oddity. A single feather from an African, lilac-breasted roller grew from either midfoot. Peculiar indeed, let alone traipsing barefoot through the streets or desert sands.

The three-person party came to an inn. They didn't go into the lobby, but instead proceeded to one of the rooms located along the long, horizontal building. The woman's two guards posted on either side of the room's door. She went inside, fazing through the door as if she was made of nothing but spirit and conjure. Perhaps she was.

The room was empty of persons. Light shined through windows and made a spotlight for a summoning altar constructed between the two beds. The woman sensed the ritual that guided her here. She sat on one of the beds and removed her hood. A fresh-faced woman appeared behind cowl and shadow. Long cornrows shaped her head and ran down her back, gathered in her hood. Her eyes held the weight of her authority, and her pouty lips were always at the ready for command or negotiation. There was melancholy to her stare, as she understood the gravity of the times she was summoned in. The confusion and the chaos, tearing apart ancient cultures and casting the first people into thralldom.

Zoya Yswil sat patient, watching the door with her hands on her lap.

Kioi and Jai Chilla approached from the other side. They slowed their walk when they noticed the hooded figures positioned on either side of their room's door. Jai Chilla dragged his feet. "Perhaps we should've gotten a room in the back and not one on the street, yes."

A warm wind swept over Kioi. The air was still, and so he discerned that it had not come from a passing gust. It was inviting like a gentle hand guiding him forward. He resumed a normal pace, and Jai Chilla walked in step.

"No," Kioi uttered in a low voice. "No, my apprentice. She's come. There's nothing to fear." His strides were now quick. Jai Chilla remained cautious, but kept up with Kioi. The tall man stopped at the door and looked at the sentries posted on either side. "This is my room," he stated. "I am entering."

"We will not stop you," the guard on the left spoke.

The one with bare feet proclaimed, "Your presence is most anticipated."

Kioi pushed his chest out and nodded his head. A proud smile ran across his face. He put balled fists to hips and voiced, "I am!" The guard with bare feet opened the door and then stepped aside. Kioi walked in with Jai Chilla in tow. Blue, ethereal lights illuminated the room. Kioi stopped his steps, and Jai Chilla knocked into him from behind. The short, squat man apologized, but Kioi was too distracted by Zoya Yswil's presence to be bothered by the collision or apology. He shuffled up to her, near his altar, and dropped to his knees. He clasped his hands together and bowed his head. He looked up and spotted Jai Chilla standing. "Humble yourself, my apprentice. You're in the presence of conjure royalty."

Jai Chilla expressed another apology and hurried as close to Kioi as he could without knocking over any part of the altar. He wasn't successful, as his knee toppled a few candles. Jai Chilla issued a third apology.

Kioi chided, "Hands together! Hands together!"

Jai Chilla did as tasked.

Kioi returned his attention to Zoya who had been waiting with a stoic look for the men's antics to settle. He said to her, "Mistress Zoya, I was expecting your mother. My ritual was for her. I'm… I'm honored just the same."

Zoya spoke, voice like a soft breeze coming from the ocean, "You got her attention. You have *my* presence."

"Yes, yes…" he agreed, head remaining down. "The message can be relayed just the same." He took a breath and then divulged, "Your brother has gone mad. Absolutely insane! Just a barrel of mad hyenas! He attacked us in the desert, luring us there under his persona of misfortune. The one with the gaudy clothes."

Zoya remained unmoved in expression. The door opened behind Kioi and Jai Chilla, but they remained in a humble position as Kioi continued his rant on Iune's behavior. His words blended into one another, recapping the encounter in the desert. Zoya's guards walked in and removed their hoods. Iune and Olobiri stepped up behind Kioi and Jai Chilla.

Zoya regarded her brother, and Kioi stole a moment to peak at the bureaucratic conjure woman. Kioi looked over his shoulder. He noticed Iune's attire under cape and cowl. He noted the garb and stated in a hushed voice, "Protective rhino-hide vest. Leggings cut from the pelt of a gazelle. No footwear—how could I have missed that! A feather from a lilac-breasted roller growing from the top of each foot…" He gasped, and then he turned his humble position toward Iune, Jai Chilla mimicking him. "Fortune smiles upon us yet, my apprentice!"

Both men stared at Iune as he addressed them, "I just want to know why you two, with your twisted 'science', your mentally deranged, and oft times, contradictory philosophy would ever believe I would assist you in whatever harebrained scheme you bumbling frauds have half-cooked and dared to serve up." He crossed his arms and said, "I'll. Wait."

Jai Chilla kept his face straight, cut by Iune's words.

Kioi blurted, "You know us, Prince Iune? I'm flattered!"

Iune and Olobiri gave one another a raised-eyebrow look. Iune said to Kioi, "I performed a ritual where I gathered knowledge on your antics, your misguided preaching and evangelizing buffoonery." He presented Kioi with an incredulous look. "Slavery not real?" He pointed at himself and remarked, "And you think *me* mad?"

Zoya rebuked, "Iune! These men have gone to great lengths and ritual to be in your presence. Show them respect, even if you disagree with their views."

Iune fixed his face, mostly. "My apologies, sister," he replied with a bow of his head. "It's just my pride. Ariq Haunts continues to elude me while wearing my face and branding me as a spirit of misadventure and misfortune." He returned his gaze to Kioi and Jai Chilla. "Fortune smiles on you? You have no idea." He walked to a desk and took a seat on an empty stool. "I've eavesdropped on your bizarre philosophy, yes. A plague upon your chatter and twitter!" He took a breath, anger in his chest and throat. He calmed at the second behest of his older sister.

Kioi didn't help when he remarked, "It's a complex understanding, Cosmic Charter and all. In closer observance, we've done this to ourselves. We're exchanging our fine robes for chains. The kings and queens of the first people have decided this. It is our time to be in a humble state."

Zoya rolled her eyes. She dropped her head in her hand and winced.

Kioi continued, "But we are tricked in our humbling to say there is slavery afoot. We seek our Cosmic Charter for sovereignty, and I call on your good fortune Iune, to guide us to it."

Iune raised his hand. "Please stop," he requested in as much of a respectful tone as he could. Iune was ages old and knew the evolution of language. He looked at Kioi, thought of Ariq Haunts, and sighed. "I always wondered why your rituals to me were the ones I heard the most," he stated while reflecting. "I've lost count on the ways I moved as quick as a shadow fleeing light to keep the fates from tearing your souls from your flesh. I kept your neck out of reach from the flying demon named Zmey. You remember your fight with the creature?"

"Yes!" Kioi spoke up. "What luck! That was you?"

Iune nodded with a look of indifference. "One of many instances where I've negotiated with providence to extend your breath. I've always been alerted to you—"

"What luck!" Kioi repeated.

Iune agreed, nodding with an abundance of disinterest on his face. "Indeed," he said with little enthusiasm. "Why, though?" he questioned. "Why would my spirit assist in getting you out of death's grip? Even the best people who've performed my ritual for assistance don't receive it." He crossed his arms. Finally, a sly grin brightened his face. "Fate has other plans," he declared. "Not for you, for me, and I must yield to them. I've been saving you for twenty years of your life, Kioi. Now, I seem to understand. You're my reward."

"For what?" Kioi asked. "And does this grant me a Cosmic Charter?"

Iune sighed. "Take me to where Ariq Haunts attacked you."

"Who?" Kioi questioned.

Iune leaned forward and made clear, "The man who wears my face. The one who assists misfortune. He intercepts rituals done for me and spreads poor luck. He is the one who attacked you. Ariq Haunts."

Kioi's face burst with surprise. "That wasn't a form of you? People have been under the belief that you've been giving setbacks in anger of misconducting your ritual." He humbled his head and stated, "My apologies, Prince Iune. I too was under the impression that you were becoming a jealous and angry spirit."

"I'm human like you," said Iune in a sincere voice. "I live outside of time on an invisible island. It's accorded me a long life and a proximity to conjure that blesses me a great deal. I celebrate the trick and the adventure, and I'm here for cunt and coin." He looked at his sister and voiced while chuckling, "I apologize for my vulgarity."

Zoya rolled her eyes and scoffed, "I can out-gamble you and drink you under the table." She wiped the back of one hand with the other and added, "And I like a long, black shaft between me." She put an eye on Iune, telling him, "I've had a lengthy, lingering life too, little brother. I can't be uptight about Ma-ma and Pa-pa's politics all the time."

Iune laughed harder as he noticed Olobiri's eyes go wide, staring at Zoya. Iune commented to her, "Careful how you speak. Olobiri is a moralist."

Zoya flapped her lips, pointing her thumb at their adopted brother. "Him? Making sure that *any* woman might be the right woman?" She inspected Olobiri from head to toe. "Up close and *very* personal."

Olobiri cleared his throat and stood straight, giving no comment.

Kioi and Jai Chilla's eyes darted back and forth between Iune and Zoya.

Brother and sister cackled for a long while. Zoya returned her expression to a solemn and authoritative appearance. Iune's sly grin remained, but only at half-mass. He called for Kioi and Jai Chilla's attention. "Take up your provisions. Unhitch your mounts. We walk through space and time with you leading the way. We'll leave at sundown. Take us to where Ariq Haunts attacked you. Then we'll talk about a Cosmic Charter."

Kioi jumped to his feet. "Right away, Prince Iune!" He made a quick bow at the neck. Then he turned to Jai Chilla and said, "Up, my apprentice. Up!" Jai Chilla stood. "Bow your head," Kioi instructed him. Jai Chilla did as directed. Then the two shuffled around, gathering their supplies for travel.

Zoya stood and walked over to her brother. "Ma-ma and Pa-pa have instructed me to follow along. Someone has to be mature. This isn't a game, Iune. These are troubling times. You and Ariq Haunts insist on making a contest of your ideologies, playing with the freedom, justice, and equality of a people and culture. I'm coming."

Iune hid his offense at his sister's words. He opened his arms and nodded his head. "Should my sister tag along and see what life is like beyond the invisible border, so be it." He got to his feet and grinned up at her. "It's far different than the less-than-upscale taverns on the island." He stepped away from her before adding, "Which Ma-ma and Pa-pa know you steal away to—e-e-even before I told them…to see the look on their faces, of course. Still didn't disappoint when I confirmed their suspicions!" Zoya cast a crooked look at her brother. He paced back to her, lips close to her ear. She did truly anticipate an apology from him, if still being playful and sardonic. Instead he told her in a very, very hushed whisper, "And before Pa-pa believes you're his chaste, little princess—" he looked over at Olobiri who was on his feet, straight and on guard, observing Kioi and Jai Chilla collecting their equipment. "—someone else would like to believe you're…" he cleared his throat before concluding, "…waiting on the right man…" He winked at his sister and then tossed his arms around Olobiri's shoulders while standing behind him. "You're a brother to me!" he told him. "But we're not really family." He shook him and whispered into his ear while putting an eye on his sister. "Take no offense," he insisted. "I mean that in a very *promising* way." He swept a hand across the room and pronounced, "Think of it! We could be in-laws and outlaws all at once. Defy space and time." He let go of Olobiri, slapped his shoulders, and then went outside.

Zoya masked her smile, but her eyes floated to Olobiri. His gaze slowly lifted toward hers.

Subtle smiles were never so prominent. Their glint radiated into a bright, lilac sheet that wiped the scene away and replaced it with another.

Twilight. The moon outbid the sun for dominance in the sky. A haze of light-blue resonated on the horizon, but stars twinkled and the moon ushered them in. A delicate wind brushed the sands, and out of its muted howl stepped into time a five-party unit led by Zoya Yswil. They manifested in front of the ruins where Kioi and Jai Chilla encountered Chief Ariq Haunts and his Six Others engaged in ritual. Both Kioi and Iune walked up to the ancient city remains, passing Zoya.

"Here…" pointed out Kioi. "It happened here," he further detailed. "I never experienced true conjure before, aside from rituals. It was a terrifying and marvelous display, aside from your friend trying to kill us. Exhilarating!"

Iune gave Kioi a curious look, but he didn't correct him on Chief Ariq Haunts' association to him. "Lead us in," he ordered.

Kioi nodded. "Yes. Right this way." He took lead, and the others followed him to the sunken, leaning temple. Inside. Blocked by fallen structure. "As I described, he attacked us with conjure from a cursed sword…or blessed, depending on how you want to view it."

"He probably believes it was blessed," Jai Chilla chimed in.

Kioi nodded his head in agreement and said, "Yes, my apprentice." He looked at Zoya and asked, "Can we walk through the collapse?"

Zoya shook her head, no. "Not in my state, right now," she informed. "Your ritual supplied enough power to call us, grant us walk here. I can rest, and we can wait for tomorrow."

Iune peered through the darkness using the minimal light shining through the opened areas of the temple. Olobiri turned his locks to horns. A bright, golden sphere swirling on his forehead provided luminosity. He and Iune spotted slender crawl spaces in the collapsed area. He jumped and hoisted himself up and through the space. Iune followed him into the slim section. The nimble two wriggled and slid through willowy cracks in the fallen debris without disturbing any additional issues. They exited, landing graceful on their feet inside a wide space. Iune sent to his sister, **We're through. We'll continue to investigate. Stay still.**

Good to hear, she replied. **I don't sense any threat in the area. We should be fine where we are.**

Yes. Ariq Haunts is long gone from this place. We'll investigate his ritual.

Olobiri swept the area with his eyes and conjure. The gold, spherical light on his forehead brightened as his instinct discerned the path to take. He proceeded forward with Iune behind him. Their steps were cautious and not hurried, despite their awareness that no danger was present in the immediate area. They walked quiet and careful, following Olobiri's instinct to the room where Chief Ariq Haunts conducted his ritual. Olobiri stood still as his conjure recreated the scene as it occurred.

Translucent images from a past occurrence appeared. Chief Ariq Haunts paced as his Six Others meditated. At one end of the room were six, large, opened chests. The Ifo Chief looked up and dashed away. His fight commencing with Kioi and Jai Chilla. The Six Others remained still as he engaged.

Chief Ariq Haunts returned and continued his ritual. He placed his unique sword in front of the soldier-turned-mercenary named Kerst, and then he made his way to the opened chests. He pulled trinkets from each, resting them at the feet of his Six Others. Okod, the murderous tavern owner, was gifted the azurite wand that was wrapped in a copper cord and topped with a large, jagged sapphire. A slender man named Mechlik received at his feet one of three gold chains Chief Ariq Haunts had to offer. Mechlik was a former cook whose curse inflicted upon people a voracious appetite, insatiable. Eating from his prepared plates provided no sustenance or fulfillment. His patrons craved more and more, and they ate until they died, and he fed off their misery.

"Body," Chief Ariq Haunts announced as he lay the gold chain in front of Mechlik. "Mind," he uttered, setting the second gold chain in front of a man named Idět. Naked with a dirty body and face, Idět was a young man who found it hard to own anything, always discontent and stirred to anger by someone else's possessions or qualities. Even now, his meditation was disturbed as he opened his eyes and peeked at the Six Others who had been presented with curios. He wondered to himself why he couldn't have been given the sword, or the wand, or the other gold chain that seemed to shimmer brighter than his. Idět's narrowed, green eye bent before he closed it and resumed his meditation. A sad lot, he only found relief when he injected others with his bitterness, and watched from afar as petty rivalries began, stirred to murder as people fought over trivial trinkets and mundane affairs. Chief Ariq Haunts moved on. The Ifo chief placed the third and final gold chain before the only woman in the Six Others. "Soul," said the chieftain.

Emiti was beautiful, alluring to all men, even those who desired other men. Women melted in her presence. She worked hard for her beauty, stolen from the essence of conjure women. Curly, raven hair was once blonde. One eye green. One eye blue. One from her mother, the other from her father. Her ivory flesh had been polished to a dark, olive tone. A residual effect from syphoning magic from conjure women whose beauty she pilfered before selling them into a sexual trade, sapped of mind and helpless against the men who purchased them for pleasure. Her sultry smile, on full lips, curved and slinked like her figure and walk.

Chamti, the erstwhile accountant and brother to Idět, was gifted the blackened steel-forged breastplate with the number nine seared into its center.

Iune and Olobiri's eyes never moved from the scene, swallowing every detail of Chief Ariq Haunts' ritual. They observed him sit cross-legged in front of his Six Others, assuming a meditative pose. All seven concentrated, and the ritual continued. The ceremonial rite peaked with a brilliant display of conjure. A white light shined over the Six Others' bodies, and their essences were drawn into the forged treasures in front of them. Chief Ariq Haunts stood and returned the treasures to the six chests. There came a faint echo from a detonation. The Ifo chief was not stirred by it, but the sharp clamor caused Iune and Olobiri to flinch, even if muted.

Chief Ariq Haunts turned around, and Iune and Olobiri turned to their right. A large hole was made leading outside. Translucent Ifo guards marched through, filling the room with their numbers. Chief Ariq Haunts commanded, "Take the chests to the caravan. We leave when the tribute is loaded, and we will walk the Star Path to Azur-Fah." The Ifo warriors and guards hurried to their task, grabbing up a chest two men at a time. They shuffled out, and Chief Ariq Haunts followed. Their shimmering, pellucid figures disappeared as they walked through the exploded wall.

The scene concluded. Iune reached out to his sister, **Ariq Haunts created tributes to give to the Eterijah. It's as suspected. He's looking for a way into Azur-Fah." He looked at the breach in the wall and said, "There's another exit. We're coming to you. Stay there.**

Yes, Zoya replied.

Iune and Olobiri exited through the man-made hole in the wall and returned to Zoya and the two rogues. Iune questioned Kioi, "How long has it been since your encounter with Ariq Haunts?"

"A few days," he answered. "Three."

"The close of today would make four," added Jai Chilla.

"Thank you, my apprentice."

"Shit!" Iune cursed. "He's far ahead of us, and we need to rest for the night."

Zoya agreed. "We'll pitch camp in these ruins. We leave at first light." It was agreed, and camp was set.

Lilac sands filled the scene, flowing downward through the funnel of a dreaming mind like an hourglass. Space shifted to an ethereal dominion, and time moved outside of earthly existence. The pale-purple sparkles dwindled into a bright sheet of sunlight that contrasted against a location positioned at night. A ritual performed, grand and taxing, opened a Star Path to an invisible realm. Chief Ariq Haunts stood in awe like the rest of the Ifo people he led. They stared and marveled at the border of Earth and another place.

Azur-Fah, the Silver World.

A world outside of time, bathed in the aura of conjure, and Chief Ariq Haunts marveled at all he saw while walking from the Star Path into the Silver World of Azur-Fah. He couldn't possibly see it all, but it was there, and it was a rainbow. The vast colors of the spectrum painted its way throughout the twelve realms seated on a single continent called Constellation. Ironic for a world known as 'silver'.

Both substantial and small bodies of water reflected the blue sky above with golden sparkles of the sun dancing merrily on the ripples and waves in the many lakes, streams, rivers and oceans. Where no city or town dwelled, emerald fields of grass, and honey-golden, arable meadows covered the lands. Rolling hills and mammoth mountains had their capes of snow or blooming pastures. Dense, clusters of forests spread into organic, complex networks and mazes within their interior.

There were four seasons, not all experienced equally throughout Constellation's twelve realms. There was snow in the Goat Hills and the Arrowed Hooves kingdoms most of the year. Rain, fog, and a gray ambience permeated through the Scales and Stinger realms.

Far away from Ariq Haunts and the Ifo people, here in the Maiden kingdom, it was late spring. Dawn stretched her brilliance across a magnificent city called Halitta, named after the kingdom's royal family. Every structure became suffused with the sun's morning rays.

At the center of the Maiden Kingdom's capital metropolis was a mighty palace made of silver. It was shaped for government and accented for war, if needed. Morning in the city gave birth to commutes, citizens darting through the streets on foot or taxied in a carriage drawn by creatures unknown to Earth. One such creature was the hytack, a horse-sized, bipedal seahorse-looking animal, with diminutive wings and furry legs shaped like that of a bird.

The growing traffic in the streets and on the sidewalk were not as frantic as the scurrying happening inside the silver palace. Pages and maids flourished with the first sign of light. Preparations were in order for a sacred ceremony held at the week's end, the passing of the Eterijah title from one generation to another. Eterijah Iyansan was relinquishing her status to the second princess of the Maiden kingdom, Qkumo-Ṣẹda Halitta. It was a bittersweet affair. The title had actually been stripped from Eterijah Iyansan by a unanimous vote from the other eleven Eterijah. Her crime was assisting in human affairs beyond protocol. It was an egregious issue in their eyes. Eterijah Iyansan had no regrets when ritual considered her successor. Princess Qkumo-Ṣẹda. A fitting inheritor now that she reached an appropriate age. A day in her life. Twenty-four years old. She was ready. Everyone from citizens to members of the royal court was excited.

Everyone except the princess herself.

In her room, seated at her vanity, and still dressed in her nightclothes, Princess Qkumo-Ṣẹda had her head down and rested in her folded arms. She groaned thinking of the week's end, the ceremony, and the responsibility she believed was being usurped from a noble woman and unjustly given to her. She'd dreaded the moment for twenty years. It was easy to get lost in childhood and school and other drama of growing up, but the inevitable had its moments of popping up in her head. Now, it was here, and it was front and center on her mind with nowhere in her head to be buried.

Eterjiah Iyansan felt the princess' distress. She glided through the upstairs hall on her way to Qkumo-Ṣẹda's quarters to console the royal woman. Seven armed guards, donning the royal army's robes, sashes, and wide-brimmed, conical fiber hats. They trailed behind her in rhythm and careful step to avoid marching on her pink, silk gown's long tail. The hall was lined with paintings, an army of golden statues, and the plush, royal carpet. A fleet of silk curtains, that broke the rays of the sun from absolute intrusion, covered the abundance of windows.

Eterijah Iyansan stopped at the princess' bedroom door. It was tall in height for her to gain entrance, as the Eterijah were considered giants for their lofty builds. Castles and houses, commercial and government buildings, were constructed to accommodate the Eterijahs' towering stature of no less than three meters. Eterijah Iyansan was six meters in vertical measurement, and Princess Qkumo-Ṣẹda, a young woman of average stature, could expect her height to stretch over the years after she gained experience in Eterijah power and title.

Each of Eterijah Iyansan's guards posted up beside a golden statue lining the hall as she gently knocked on the door. There was no sound from the other side, and so she called out in a soft, motherly voice, "Ṣẹda, are you ready for rehearsals?" There was no intelligible answer. She heard a low groan from the other side of the door, and it made Eterijah Iyansan beam. She considered that Qkumo-Ṣẹda had taken to one of her hopeful suitors. There were so many men clamoring for her attention, from adventurer to healer to royal counselors and advisors. The Eterijah, the princess' mother, and her oldest sister teasingly encouraged close exploration of all the prospective gentlemen.

That won't take my mind off this misfortune, the princess' voice played in the Eterijah's head. **I can't ignore the politics of what's happening, at least not anymore.**

"May I come in, Ṣẹda?" asked the Eterijah.

The princess sounded apologetic when she permitted, **Of course, Etti-Iyansan.**

The princess used her power without lifting her head. The door unlocked and opened, and Eterijah Iyansan made her way inside. The princess raised her head and faced the Eterijah as she took a seat on her bed. Qkumo-Ṣẹda's thick, wild spirals of hair that framed her ovate face, draped long past her shoulders and down her back. Mud-brown in color, when the light caught the gathered strands of her hair, a deep and rich shade of purple ran through her locks.

Qkumo-Ṣẹda addressed her mentor, **Everything seems…** Her telepathic disclosure paused, and she finished her words using her natural voice. "…So askew…"

"In what way?"

Princess Qkumo-Ṣẹda sighed. "I didn't earn this. The right to be Eterijah."

"You did," Eterijah Iyansan protested with as soft a voice as she could muster. She didn't want to scold the anxious princess. "It's come sooner than usual, yes." She chuckled before adding, "It's saved you eight thousand-seven hundred and sixty years of being under my tutelage." The effort paid off, and pulled a smile from Qkumo-Ṣẹda. The angelic woman said to her, "Every Eterijah chooses an apprentice. I conducted the same ritual to guide my choice; and I wasn't surprised at all when your name was spelled out in smoke. No one was. So, don't believe you're taking anything from me. I'm not being stripped of power. I'm passing it on to its rightful heir." She put a hand on her chest before stating, "I'm also taking responsibility for actions I committed against a code."

Qkumo-Ṣẹda nodded her head mechanically, eyes on the floor. "It's a stupid code," she remarked. "The first people suffer—our people inside of time. Besides, I was there. I barely remember, but I was there. I should be punished too."

"You were four, and what I did was wrong."

Qkumo-Ṣẹda smiled and eyed the ceiling for a moment. "Oh, the people inside of time used to look to the stars for guidance. There was ritual and dance, a call on our virtuous star alignments. Sometimes our times were in sync. Ojulowo allowed that. Us not so fast or slow, moving with them, just invisible to the naked eye. They sang or rhymed sweet summons to bring us to their aid. Buildings were erected based on the configurations in the stars we control! Stories were devised as maps to know the celestial realm, the turn of the Cosmic Clock." Then she huffed, "Someone came and needed our help! Was helping them so bad?" She faced Eterijah Iyansan with an abundance of happiness on her countenance. Eterijah Iyansan was relieved to see Qkumo-Ṣẹda merry and upbeat. She didn't bother to answer the princess' question, rhetorical in nature as it was. "My mother composed love letters to my father using the stars. She caught his attention with a bright twinkle. He looked up, and he deciphered her flickers and flashes, and he found a Star Path to walk and meet her. He thought Azur-Fah and Constellation was Pambunjila, the original world." Qkumo-Ṣẹda's delight faltered a bit, but she maintained her smile. "There're no three moons here. We share the same single moon of the world inside time. Even we've lost our power and direction. Few nations and tribes know us now, and terrible things are happening to them…" She became silent, reflective, and Eterijah Iyansan allowed her the moment, gazing at the princess through large and expressive, amber eyes. Qkumo-Ṣẹda brightened after her extended pause and stated, "My sister came along not too much later from my parents' union. My mother and father took her on many adventures. Ma-ma was not up to be neggura. Her sister was set to take the duty."

"And she didn't, and your mother took her place," the Eterijah noted.

Qkumo-Ṣẹda shook her finger, giving the Grand Maiden a sly eye and grin. "Not quite the same as what we got here, Etti-Iyansan. The queenship wasn't stripped from my aunt."

"No," the other replied. "But an exchange was made, and your mother accepted her new duties."

"My mother was trying to keep my father from being killed," the princess pointed out with a raised eyebrow. "Let's be honest. Taking the queenship and making him prince consort was a strategic move. She didn't want to experience nursing him back to health again, or worse, seeing him succumb in battle. He barely survived being struck by a hexed weapon." She sighed and said, "Of course, if it wasn't for that near-fatal confrontation, I wouldn't've been born. My mother took full advantage of my father when he returned to complete health—as it's often told." She chuckled, and so did Eterijah Iyansan.

There was a knock at the door. Qkumo-Ṣẹda's instincts buzzed, and she felt the presence of her sisters on the other side of the door. "Come in Tinta, Swey," she authorized. The door opened, and her two sisters shuffled through. There was a kick in their steps as they rushed over and crowded the princess. Both were still in their nightdresses, fresh from sleep.

Tinta was the oldest. She had brown skin and hair in arcing twists sprouting around her head. The ten-year-old Swey had tight, woolen locks draping from her head and in so much abundance they looked like they would throw the young child off balance.

Qkumo-Ṣẹda couldn't match the animated liveliness of her sisters, especially Tinta, who held her tight, shaking her with joy. She placed her cheek against Qkumo-Ṣẹda and squealed, "I am so proud of my sister!" Princess Ṣẹda feigned a smile, and Tinta noticed. "What's wrong?"

Eterijah-Iyansan answered, "She's nervous."

Tinta retracted her arms and stood straight. "That's to be expected," she reacted in a consoling tone. "So much will change for her. There's the transformation. There're the duties of leading the inauguration. The rites. Being inducted by the other eleven Eterijah. Banquets. The choosing of a consort. Council meetings. The discussion of affairs." She turned to Eterijah Iyansan and stated, "Dealing with the consequences of your transgressions— no offense, Etti-Iyansan. But even I fear there will always be an eyebrow raised at the Maiden kingdom, at least until the other Eterijah are replaced with their apprentices."

None of this made Qkumo-Ṣẹda feel better. She dropped her face into her hands, and Tinta saw the fault in her words. Eterijah Iyansan bent her eyes at the older princess. Qkumo-Ṣẹda commented, "That reminds me. I have to kill myself."

"The other Eterijah will not be a problem," Eterijah Iyansan insisted. Her voice darkened with each word, and her eyes narrowed even more on Tinta. The eldest sister cowered, an apologetic expression on her face. "They were delighted, and not surprised, that the winds scrawled her name as smoke in the air."

"Yes!" said Tinta, looking to redeem herself. "If there was ever a person born for conjure and the tinkering with star movement, it was you, Ṣẹda."

"There will be no trouble from the Eterijah," the Grand Maiden doubled down.

Qkumo-Ṣẹda raised her head and said, "I find trouble already."

"Such as?" the Eterijah questioned.

"In alphabetical order or from least to greatest?"

"Alphabetical order," Eterijah Iyansan played along.

No hesitation. Qkumo-Ṣẹda answered, "They're arrogant, banal, bullying, conniving, and controlling." She sat up and crossed her arms. "Shall I continue?"

The Grand Maiden pleaded, "Give them time to forget my offenses. You'll find strong allies there. They'll find you a relief more than anything."

Swey hugged Qkumo-Ṣẹda. "I won't let them bully you!" she declared.

Qkumo-Ṣẹda beamed a warm smile at the young girl. "Bless you, Swey. I know a strong, little conjure woman like you will give them the trembles!"

While Qkumo-Ṣẹda played with her younger sister, Tinta inquired to the Eterijah, "Forgive me, Etti-Iyansan. Was it so wrong aiding people inside time to travel past the troubles of the world and assist a structured conjure folk?"

The question found its way back into conversation. Eterijah Iyansan became stoic when she answered, "Apparently so." She exhaled a heavy sigh. "I don't believe I defied the stars. I believe I went along with what is so carefully written for us in the heavens. My only regret is that I didn't tell the two blacks our original name as a people. A name lost in the first of the Pious Wars, barely kept alive here. It's who we as blacks truly are. The Dulyfe—"

There came a succession of knocks. Urgent in their repetition.

The women's instincts deciphered the presence beyond the door, and Qkumo-Ṣẹda blossomed with elation. She got up from her chair and rushed the door, opening it with a jump for joy. On the other side was a lifelong friend. A lissome, dark-skinned and woolly-haired man with a boyish face, dressed in green leggings, vest, tunic, and shoes to match.

"Tyle!" the princess shouted throwing her arms around the man.

"Well! Oh! Yes! Indeed! It's me, and that's the truth." And the truth was something Tyle, the palace fool, could always detect, save from a powerful hex used against him. Not much else could shield him from validity or a person's intentions. "I don't mean to intrude, Princess." He spotted Tinta and Swey. "Princess-*es*. My apologies, Princess Tinta. Princess Swey. There is a matter." He looked at Eterijah Iyansan and notified, "A young man named Iune of Del-Yswil has walked a Star Path and come to Azur-Fah. He comes bearing tributes. Six in total, and one is for you, Etti-Iyansan." He bowed at the neck as he finished his briefing.

All eyes went to the tall and jet-black, mystical woman. She raised an eyebrow, showing her curiosity piqued. "Oh…!" was all she said as she recalled knowledge of a trickster named Iune. "Iune Del-Yswil? He's a trickster, if memory serves me correct. The last I've heard, he's using his skills freeing captives."

"He's a hero then!" exclaimed Qkumo-Ṣẹda.

"It's in the blood. His mother and father were champions of the Pious Wars."

Tinta made a face. "That's a long time ago," she commented. "That's when Constellation received its purpose to arrange and lock the stars."

"The order came from this trickster's grandmother and grandfather, on his mother's side." She made a side remark, "Powerful with conjure were they. Many thought they were Igzu and Geirah in the flesh. They had connections to the cosmos." She reflected for a moment and then stated, "His parents took residence outside of time, where he was born. Time works different for him, much the same as us," the Eterijah summarized. "His mother and father found purpose in confiscating dangerous artifacts. Items deemed too powerful, and feared to ignite another set of horrible and bloody battles. We don't have the luxury of fighting against one another. Not with the European's desire to enslave the first people of the world. But still we do." She stood and straightened herself. "Let me see his purpose. Tyle, lead the way, please."

Tyle nodded. "Yes, Grand Maiden," he said.

Eterijah Iyansan dictated, "Ladies, ready yourselves for a rehearsal for this week's ceremony. I will return and meet you in the ceremonial hall."

Tyle looked at Qkumo-Ṣẹda and told her, "I will return too, princess, and assist with the rehearsals." He hugged her, and then led the Eterijah Iyansan out of the room. Her seven guards fell in line, and then from the castle, they made a long trek to an open doorway to a conjured Star Path.

Chief Ariq Haunts waited with his tribe. Five of the Eterijah were present, and he spotted the sixth heading his way. The Grand Maiden approached bearing a pleasant smile.

"Iune Del-Yswil, correct?" she greeted.

Chief Ariq Haunts gestured with an exaggerated bow. "In your presence, Grand Maiden."

Tyle stopped and reacted to a tingle in his senses. His head cocked to one side and he observed the chief closely. A peculiarity surrounded the trickster. It was curious, and not quite suspicious at the moment, but an inkling was stirring in the palace fool that kept him alert.

"I bring tribute and a proposition," Chief Ariq Haunts addressed the gathered Eterijah.

"Why us, Iune of Del-Yswil?" asked the archer named Eterijah ọfa Kibiya. He sat, mounted on a mighty steed bred to hold an Eterijah of his build.

"I've read of your legends," the chief answered. "I have with me items that will provide restoration for your culture. They are not the authentic treasures lost. They are replicas with faint conjure to be as remembrances." He stepped back toward one of the six opened chests while still facing the Eterijah. He turned, removed the breastplate marked with the number nine, and held it up at the mounted Eterijah. "A piece of armor, a work of art in its replication. No different from the one lost to the Arrowed Hooves kingdom so long ago, save the authentic piece's powerful incant."

Eterijah ọfa Kibiya stared at the armor in disbelief. He motioned for his page to retrieve the item, and the errand-man hurried to his task. He brought back the chest plate and handed it to the Eterijah. The cosmic-curator dismounted to inspect the piece in his own hands. "Beautifully crafted," he expressed in a low tone. "Its resemblance is profound!" He looked at Chief Ariq Haunts and questioned, "Where did you come across this item?" He addressed the others before allowing the chief to answer, "This *could* be our kingdom's lost treasure!"

"How would you know?" asked Eterijah Ganda of the Carapace kingdom, rolling his eyes. "You've only known images projected from a crystal or paintings, you dolt!" he further insulted.

Eterijah ọfa Kibiya curled his lip and snarled, "Your kingdom and line always were jealous of this item. A shield for us and not you!"

"Have your chest piece!" Eterijah Ganda huffed. "It's our sword we seek to recover!"

"You act as if we stole it!" the Grand Archer defended.

A subtle smirk crept onto Chief Ariq Haunts' countenance. The gold chain holding Idĕt's essence glowed with a soft, green tone. A feeling fluttered through Tyle, and he sensed deceit.

"The item is not authentic, Eterijah," Chief Ariq Haunts reminded. "My apology for any duplicity. To answer your question, Grand Archer, the item was crafted to mimic the feel and look of your treasures that have inspired the imaginations of young and old alike. All of these items have roused the mind's eye."

Tyle's sense of deception receded with Chief Ariq Haunts' words, but he remained cautious of the trickster calling himself Iune Del-Yswil.

Chief Ariq Haunts announced, "And if it's a sword you desire, we have one crafted just as fine as the one lost to your kingdom, Good Aegis." He turned to the chests and picked up the Sword of Union and walked it to the Carapace kingdom's reigning Eterijah.

The Good Aegis inspected the weapon in his grip, admiring every angle and curve, its intricacies and design. Eyes locked on the blade, the sinister spirit within seeped through its handle and burrowed into the Eterijah's palm without detection, all of his faculties distracted. Kerst bled into Eterijah Ganda's person, possessed his arm and quickly spread through the body to take the mind and mute the soul before it could fight back. He blinked, and Kerst's presence owned the Eterijah's movements, memories, and voice. The Good Aegis' spirit was now encased in the sword.

"It's beautiful," said Eterijah Kerst, a sly and knowing grin on his face. He looked at Chief Ariq Haunts and winked. "Thank you," he nodded, and kept at bay the reflex to refer to the Ifo chief as 'master'.

Eterijah Dume Nag Ombe of the Cattleman kingdom had his doubts, and he expressed them through a thunderous voice. "These treasures sowed mistrust among us."

Chief Ariq Haunts soothed, "I understand your concerns, Mighty Bull. I assure you, these are but keepsakes. While there is conjure in them, they are only to reflect the heritage of what you've lost." He turned and scooped up one of the gold chains, presenting it to Eterijah Dume. "Has your realm not been removed of an incanted item? A gold chain that stored the strength of an army within it?" The Eterijah bent a knee to accept Chief Ariq Haunts' tribute. The chain grew in his hands to a size necessary to fit around the broad-statured Eterijah. He removed his horned helmet and slipped the Gold Chain of Body around his neck.

It might has well have been a noose. The unassuming, brawny Eterijah was choked out of the control of his body. It was a fleeting moment that came with a simple hiccup of air, and then Chamti's wolfish appetite consumed Eterijah Dume's soul case. He caressed the necklace, feeling the Eterijah's trapped essence inside the gold chain.

Eterijah Chamti stood and thanked Chief Ariq Haunts for his offering.

The Ifo chief bestowed the remaining treasures on the other Eterijah.

Eterijah Obule received the azurite wand. While indulging in the delight of the copper-wrapped baton that was topped with the large, jagged sapphire, the Eterijah of the realm of the Ram, was sapped of body, mind, and spirit. Apathy diminished his fiery passion, draining away into the blue wand he took a brief moment to admire. A new body taken, a soul laid to rest. Eterijah Okod enjoyed the trade.

Chamti demonstrated the strength of his cupidity. His acquisition of Eterijah Ọfa Kibiya's body was as swift as the Six Others' possession. The blackened-steel chest plate was strapped to him by servants, and the moment he stood to pose with his valued, mystical tribute, his body was no longer his. Eterijah Chamti gave a nod and wink to his chief, and the other put his sights on the remaining Eterijah.

"Ladies," Chief Ariq Haunts said through a wide smile. "Your tributes await, and with them a proposal." Gold chains were gifted to both of them. Chief Ariq Haunts stepped back and gestured with a genuflect posture. He stood straight and said, "I will find for you the Immortal Created."

Eterijah Iyansan chuckled at the trickster's confidence. Chief Ariq Haunts listened attentively to the Eterijah as she recounted, "There have been so many offers before you to do the same. There was a necessity at one time. It was rumored to have negated the sign of All Eternity, And Infinity, which fell into the hands of a sect of soldiers from the northern continent. The Grand Pair from our Lovers kingdom were conjured in an attempt to aid the Moors who ruled the southern area. Europe, you call it? The sign was turned into a terrible weapon against conjure folk. The Order of Needle Knights worked blood ritual after blood ritual to tame its power. Killing the Grand Pair of that era was a victory, spilling their blood and making a demonic offering with it. The knights used a negating stone to dampen the conjure, even in Eterijah.

"They bound the power of All Eternity, And Infinity to an earthly weapon. A spear, supposedly. It wounded the prince consort of my realm. He survived the stabbing, and still possessed a mighty vigor to destroy the weapon. He remembers very little after receiving the wound, but he recalls holding a small crystal in his hand. He swears it's what saved him, some power within it. He said there was a soft voice that spoke to him and kept him calm until his wife appeared, our kingdom's queen. We call her the ancient title of *neggura*. She nursed him back to health. That crystal has become sacred to the Maiden kingdom. It's been fastened to a necklace, and it will be gifted to my apprentice at a ceremony that will inaugurate her as the succeeding Eterijah of the Maiden kingdom." She looked at her fellow Eterijah and sighed. She kept her face, though her eyes stung with the presence of tears behind them. "There have been politics, and I've been asked to step down in my duties. I will join my husband and his other consort across the ocean to assist the enslaved who are able to remember the old ways and conjure our spirits. We as Orisha will provide strength." She said her words with conviction, standing tall. She put the necklace close, readying to place it over her head. Chief Ariq Haunts waited, still in motion for her to do it. She remarked first, "I hope there was no trouble in bringing these, or with the ritual. You live outside of time Iune Del-Yswil. We recognize that. There's no need for you to partake in rites and tributes to enter."

Chief Ariq Haunts held his face from shaping into a grimace. He locked his throat in place to keep from releasing his annoyance at the revelation. Then he remembered the trick, the Eterijah now under his control, and he took pride in his scheme. All the turmoil of ritual was worth it, and he wanted to brag to the mighty star keeper.

Eterijah Iyansan placed around her neck the gold chain offered as tribute, and while distracted with her emotions stirred from the mentioning of politics, Emiti seduced the Eterijah away from her power and into the Gold Chain of Soul. The spectral sentiment took a moment to admire the dark, dark flesh she now lived in.

Eterijah Iba Lansi, pillar of the Scales kingdom, slipped on her bright, glimmering necklace, and the bitter Idĕt held dominion over her flesh and mind, though he still resented that he couldn't possess her soul. The Gold Chain of Mind was now her prison.

Chief Ariq Haunts faced the Eterijah. They faced him. He grinned.

Tyle stood alone with a chill surrounding him. He shivered with the lies in the atmosphere, but he maintained his poise. He wanted to confide in Eterijah Iyansan alone, offer his warning, a foretoken.

Five of the Eterijah announced a return to their realms. Eterijah Emiti beamed a smile down on Chief Ariq Haunts and proposed, "Please, Iune Del-Yswil, I would be honored if you joined me in the Maiden kingdom." She examined memories and relayed, "Princess Qkumo-Ṣẹda is preparing for her ceremony. You can't attend the trial performance, or speak with the princess directly afterward, but you are invited to stay the week and be present at the true ceremony."

"It would be my pleasure, Eterijah Iyansan," the chief replied. He swept a hand at his tribe and guards. "My band will remain inside of time. We are one-hundred and twenty-four in number. No need to overwhelm your inns or palace rooms."

Eterijah Emiti waved Chief Ariq Haunts' worries away. "That would be no bother, but if your band feels more comfortable inside of time, I understand. However, we do have plenty of space at inns near the palace, and you personally can have a place inside the grand castle. The invitation to stay extends to your band."

"Thank you for the offer, Eterijah, but my people will remain inside of time." Chief Ariq Haunts approached his nation to have a final word.

Eterijah Emiti made a graceful pivot and walked away. Her guards fell in line, and Tyle walked close by her side. He looked over his shoulder and noted Chief Ariq Haunts being a good distance away, signaling to his folk. "Etti-Iyansan, my instincts are in disarray. I don't feel deceit, but there is something happening."

Eterijah Emiti had her answer for him. "You sense his trickster nature, Tyle," she explained. "I sense it too, but it's all in his spirit. There's no deception." She brushed the gifted necklace with her fingertips and stated further, "Even these replicas might be playing with your instincts. Everything around you is false."

Tyle hadn't considered these points, and being addressed in the makeup of Eterijah Iyansan, he felt comforted by the reasoning. They continued to the castle where inside Eterijah Emiti dismissed Tyle to check on Princess Qkumo-Ṣẹda, and to come and inform her when the royal family was gathered in the ceremonial hall. Tyle hurried to his task, and the Janus-faced Grand Maiden proceeded to her private chambers, following directions from the foraged memories plucked from the true Eterijah's mind. She permitted Chief Ariq Haunts entrance, and she ordered her seven guards to post outside. The door to the private quarters closed. It was a marvelous throne room fit for the towering Eterijah. Emiti took seat at her ceremonial chair. She crossed her legs and proclaimed, "We should have privacy for a moment, my chief. What is your command?"

Chief Ariq Haunts noticed Eterijah Emiti's ensconced demeanor, settled within the body she possessed and the throne she sat upon. He took a moment to marvel at his infiltration of Azur-Fah, and he grinned at the further actions in his agenda. "They will know Iune Del-Yswil as a thief," he sneered. "Search the Eterijah's knowledge. Pull for me the whereabouts of this necklace ornamented with the crystal. See if it will be needed at the rehearsal for this princess' rites."

"It's located in the queen's private chambers," Eterijah Emiti noted. She gave him directions that he committed to memory. "It sits on her vanity in a glass case. No guards are at her doors. All personnel will be shifted to the ceremonial hall for rehearsal."

"That will be no good," Chief Ariq Haunts considered. He put balled fists on his hips. Then he shook a finger and declared, "Ah! I know now. Request its use for the rehearsal. Send that fool Tyle to recover it."

Eterijah Emiti thought for a short time. "If this Eterijah's memory serves me correctly, it appears the prince consort would like it presented to his daughter at the ceremony without rehearsal," she informed. "A genuine gifting."

"Then I'll attack the queen on return to her chambers, and frame Iune as a master of misfortune, cast doubt and clouds over the royal family."

"And we can possibly use the power locked in the crystal," Eterijah Emiti affixed.

"In time. The play against Iune is recreational. All will know him as the trickster who failed the original people inside of time and locked them to a terrible fate. His story forever ruined. On our end, you will have him executed after I, dressed as him, create chaos that will slay the royal family. The Ifo warriors will take care of the whole bloody affair. I will best him yet!" He basked in pride of the thought, and then he said, "The rest is to plan. You sinister sentiments will conjure your hourglasses and flood Constellation with corruption. It will be off balance, and then mine to control. The remaining Eterijah will be lured our and assassinated. With the Maiden kingdom's royal family dead, I will tinker with the crystal attached to the necklace, unearth its secrets, and locate the Immortal Created. I'll wield its power, if the All Eternity, And Infinity is no longer. I will lock time in place, and destiny inside time will go undisturbed. The Grand Alchemy will be fulfilled."

"Yes, my chief."

Chief Ariq Haunts sat on the ground with his legs crossed. He dropped his face in his hands and sighed. "Then I can return to my natural face," he said to himself, thinking of his mother and father, and the former Ifo Chief, Selotes Bilísi. "Then my next caper begins…"

Eterijah Emiti sensed Tyle's approach and she stood up quick and rushed to the door. Chief Ariq Haunts lifted his head and got to his feet. Both composed themselves, raising the hex inside them to resonate confusion for the truth teller. Eterijah Emiti opened the door with the use of magic as Tyle finished his approached. "Come, Iune Del-Yswil," she ordered, walking past her guards and Tyle. "To the ceremonial hall."

"Oh!" uttered Tyle as the tall woman glided by him with their new guest. The Eterijah's guards fell in line, and Tyle hopped and skipped out of their way as they filed into place behind Eterijah Emiti. At the ceremonial hall, Chief Ariq Haunts was ordered to wait outside, and when the rehearsal was through, he was to turn his back to the royal family until they passed. There would be no reveal to strangers until the day of the inauguration rites.

Chief Ariq Haunts complied with a courteous bow, and then he watched as Eterijah Emiti, her armed entourage, and Tyle slipped through the doors. Alone. Chief Ariq Haunts was ready to enact his plan to create tumult. He slipped away. The halls were bright with new-day sunrays, but where Chief Ariq Haunts could find shadow, he dived into them and slipped into a vitreous state, appearing like glass, transparent with only a subtle frame to his form.

Palace guards were adjusting their patrols to the proximity of the royal family. With little shadows to hide in, Chief Ariq Haunts found the task of sneak-and-thieve cumbersome. He managed, and he congratulated himself with a fanciful pirouette when he reached the unguarded doors of the queen's personal chamber. He knew he had little time, and so he used his knowledge of incant to unlock the doors and slip through. Little conflict took place within Azur-Fah, and its people, especially the royal families, felt safe to leave locked doors without incant to sound alarm to alert intrusion.

Inside. Chief Ariq Haunts spotted his desired item. The necklace adorned with the small crystal floated above a gold, circular base by way of conjure while encased in a tubular-shaped glass. He approached, and at his first step toward the item, a low rumble swelled around him like a distant storm's first call. The room distorted with subtle waves that warped and bent Chief Ariq Haunts' vision. Surprise molded the expression on his face, and he stared at his body as if he'd become separated from it. He didn't feel outside of time or inside of time. Time was inside out and outside in. Time was everywhere.

A second step. Chief Ariq Haunts heard voices. The first belonged to Princess Qkumo-Ṣeda, as she playfully pleaded with her father to use the necklace in rehearsal. The next voice came from the prince consort himself, Raji Rah-Halitta. *"I want the presentation to be authentic,"* he pleaded with his daughter, suffering from a father's heartbreak at hearing his daughter whimper, even if she was only playing. *"No! I budge a lot for you girls, but I stand my ground on this issue. The passing of the necklace will be a genuine moment."* Princess Qkumo-Ṣeda moaned at her father teasingly, but the matter was settled. Chief Ariq Haunts couldn't see the happenings, but he guessed correctly the Prince Consort Raji Rah was giving his second daughter a consoling embrace.

A third step. The reality bending ripples retreated to the crystal, and time around Chief Ariq Haunts restructured, but it was later, and the knob on the door was turning. He sensed Neggura Halitta and a single guard. She sensed an intruder and opened the door wide, pointing and shouting, *"Burglar!"*

Her guard sprang into action, and so did Chief Ariq Haunts. He extended his arm, palm open, and used an incant to call the glass casing to him. Gripped, he turned in time to make an elegant dodge against the guard's downward swipe at him. The pitch-black man swung again, across. Chief Ariq Haunts ducked. Both swings were close, but the trickster's agility and youth fared better even against the seasoned warrior on guard. Chief Ariq Haunts observed the man attacking him. He was average height but brawny, bald with a grey-beard that was twisted into three, thick, beaded locks. Chief Ariq Haunts deduced, as he jumped away from a thrust to his midsection, that the attacking guard was none other than the prince consort himself.

He couldn't keep the game of slash and dodge going forever. The prince consort was too skilled and experienced not to eventually land a strike, and his frustration of missing was becoming a boiling point of inspiration. Chief Ariq Haunts siphoned power from the prince consort's vanity and ego. A few more sways and twists away from the blade's edge, and he danced around the sword strikes, eventually nearing the door. He turned and rushed to the room's exit. Neggura Halitta used conjure to immobilize the escaping thief, but Chief Ariq Haunts moved quicker than thought and the paralyzing beam soared beyond him, rushing past the armored prince consort, and absorbing into the queen's vanity without disturbance.

Chief Ariq Haunts smashed the glass casing against the queen's head, knocking her unconscious. The necklace fell among the shattered debris of glass laid out on the queen's slumped body. The baleful trickster turned and grinned at the prince consort before scurrying away, abandoning the necklace.

Prince Raji tossed his sword aside and rushed to his wife's aid, screaming for assistance. He used a telepathic wail to alert his daughters, and they hurried to their mother's quarters. On arrival, Princess Tinta embraced her youngest sister, turning her away, and shielding her from the horrific sight of their mother's limp body and bloodied face. Tyle was frozen in place, unable to look away.

Qkumo-Ṣẹda knelt down in front of her father as he held the queen up. She stirred, groaning and reaching for the blood streaming down her face.

"No, Ma-ma. Don't touch," she urged the queen. She moved her hand over her mother's wound and induced a soothing, healing conjure power over the queen's open scars. Seeping blood stopped. Near-escaping blood was dammed, and then flowed backwards as the lacerated skin mended back together. The throb pulsing in her head, and the radiating, deep hum, were muted by way of her daughter's power. The queen exhaled and put her arms around her husband. He held her tight.

Tinta let go of Swey and positioned the young girl in a manner where she could now see her mother, healed and renewed. "She's fine, Swey. A light tumble is all," Tinta comforted. The two of them walked over to their family, Tyle in tow.

"There was an intruder!" the king growled. "I've never seen him." He looked at Tyle and asked, frantic, "The man invited into our home, the one with the treasures, was he dressed in a heavy furred coat and odd clothing?"

"I had a doubt about him, but there was so much trickery around me," Tyle explained. "Forgeries and—"

"It was him!" Eterijah Emiti boomed. She stumbled around the corner, coming from down the hall. Her elegant gown was shredded in areas, its long tail torn to bits. A few cuts and bruises marked her face, smoking strands of mystical energy writhed off her body, and she was missing her newly gifted trinket. A fleet of guards not her own trailed her. "He's gone! My guards give him chase!" she shouted, out of breath and approaching closer. The guards took stance behind her, spears and swords aimed in the direction they'd come in, and keeping a distance from the royal family. "An agile little prick!" she snarled with a curled lip. She quickly noticed little Swey and amended for the queen and prince consort, "Forgive my language. I'm still reeling from our fight." She turned to Tyle and said, "My deepest apologies for not recognizing your suspicions."

"Should we alert the other Eterijah he gave gifts too?" asked Tyle noticing the necklace absent from the Eterijah.

"No," Eterijah Emiti answered in a sharp tone. "Patrols are on alert, but I fear he's made his way inside of time. Oddly enough, he took his necklace with him. I'll brief them once the ceremony is complete." She looked at the queen who was now on her feet, warrior-husband at her side. "Allow me a few days peace without being crowned in more controversy, your Majesty. I will stay on the matter. I'll have a close eye on the Star Path the trickster used to gain entrance." Neggura Halitta agreed. "If he attempts to leave, we'll find him. If he dares make a second entrance, we'll catch him there too."

"I can spare guards to join your outfit," Prince Raji recommended. "I'll make a pass every morning and night until the ceremony concludes." He gripped the necklace tight and said, "He won't dare make a move on this item when worn around Eterijah Qkumo-Ṣẹda."

The princess wondered the same. She commented, "I thought this Iune of Del-Yswil was supposed to be a champion of sorts."

Eterijah Emiti noted, "A villain now, seduced by the trick and the belief he has jurisdiction to possess any item his culture is convinced has too much power. He even offered to recover the Immortal Created."

"He almost had a clue," Prince Raji remarked. "You said his mother and father were heroes of the Pious Wars, Etti-Iyansan?"

"Yes, and I fear they might hold zealot tendencies now themselves," Eterijah Emiti opined.

"I want to hold court with them," Prince Raji declared. He looked at his second daughter and assured, "After the ceremonies. It can ease you into the politics you'll encounter. It would be your first tribunal."

Princess Qkumo-Ṣẹda hesitated to answer. She spoke quickly to make up for the time between silence and answering her father. "Yes. I have to come into these duties at some point. Why not jump right in?" Her voice shook a little, but she maintained a balance in her tone, never stumbling over her speech. She flashed a smile for a brief moment, felt it quivering, and relaxed her features while clearing her throat.

Neggura Halitta put her arms around her second daughter's shoulders. The queen had just been attacked, but she recovered, was healed, and felt the need to remain strong for the sake of her daughter's ceremony. She decided her sentiments needed a universal embracing. She said, "Let's please keep focus on the ceremony at the week's end. The rites of passage are supposed to be marked with jubilant festivities. Dance, song, and good food and drink. We're a little shaken, rattled like a child's toy, but we're still standing. If there wasn't a bit of excitement, it wouldn't be our family. Keep to the day's activities, but let's be vigilant." The queen looked at everyone around her and emphasized, "That's an order. Let's convene for midday meal, but let's not relax too much." She instructed her husband, "I want guards at Tinta's and Ṣẹda's rooms." She said to her youngest daughter, "Swey, you stay with me, little lady."

"Yes, Ma-ma," said the young girl as she took her mother's side.

"Let's stay on schedule today," the queen reiterated. "We're now to assemble in the dining hall for the midday meal." The queen gave her orders, and they were carried out.

Eterijah Emiti retreated to her private quarters for a cleanse and change of clothes. She didn't immediately settle in when she arrived. Instead, she took a seat on her throne and relaxed, cross-legged, and wearing a devilish grin. Hidden behind the large, ornate chair, was Chief Ariq Haunts deep in seated meditation on the floor. He wore the Gold Chain of Soul around his neck, drawing from the imprisoned essence of Eterijah Iyansan, and casting multiple illusions of himself darting through the city streets. The Eterijah's personal guards gave chase. They were confused, as there were numerous sightings and reports of him around the area.

He finished toying with the pursuing guards, and returned the mystical chain to Eterijah Emiti. She needed to focus with it before rejoining the royal family, so as to maintain control over the Eterijah's physical body without being consumed by its immense conjure.

She sat with the chain and recharged. Chief Ariq Haunts continued plotting.

A glistening, lilac line scrolled across the scene, wiping it away and replacing it with the affairs of Iune and Zoya Yswil stepping into existence with their small band. They'd come to the location where Chief Ariq Haunt's ritual took place days ago. Here they'd caught up with the end of his trail inside time. The chief was still far ahead of them in his schemes, and both Iune and Zoya were worried on how much damage misfortune's trickster had carried out under Iune's guise. Days or months might've occurred on the other side of time. The mystical realm could already be on fire. Zoya calmed concern when she deduced that should Ariq Haunts have already made a blaze of the twelve kingdoms, the stars would've reflected the chaos.

Outside of time to Azur-Fah was the band's next destination, through a Star Path to the Silver World. No great ritual was needed on their part, but there did come a straining exercise. Zoya negotiated a path's opening. She stood on the banks of the river Niger with her hands clasped together, fingers locked, eyes closed, and her head down. The undertaking demanded much of her mastery at being an intercessor between worlds. She focused, and to their surprise, transition occurred sooner than was expected. The river retracted from either end, bent to form a circle, and then whirled into an opening between the world within time and the world outside of time.

Iune and their company hurried to her side. The trickster said to his sister, eyes on the color-shifting hallway leading to Azur-Fah, "That seemed to go quick, yes…"

She looked at him and replied, "Negotiations barely took place. It's as if they're expecting us."

A foreboding chill iced Iune's senses.

Zoya perceived her brother's concern. She questioned, "Bad feeling?"

He countered, "About this? Not a good feeling, I'll tell you that. Ariq Haunts' tricks are at play." He took a breath and a step and added, "Let's proceed."

They moved through the spinning opening, which closed once they were inside and reformed into the waters of the river Niger. The band journeyed down the long, pyramidal-shaped hallway. Their features were covered in awe as bright as the changing colors on the walls, ceiling, and floor. Despite all the many things their eyes had seen, Iune and Zoya were encircled in wonder. Kioi and Jai Chilla were at a loss for words. They'd never before held a sight such as this. Brushes with conjure and stories that only the tongue and ears knew. Their eyes could only ever imagine until now. A journey to another realm. Olobiri was apathetic to the magnificent marvel, it was simply a path between here and there to him.

The hall ended, and the small party made their exit. Enter, Azur-Fah. The Silver World was dazzled in all the colors of the hallway they'd stepped from. Iune, Zoya, and Olobiri knew better, but still there was an instinct to look up in hopes to see three moons populating the sky. Red. Black. Green. Each having golden halos. There were no such heavenly bodies, but the pale-blue morning sky was still a wonder to behold, even with a few gray clouds smeared against it.

Kioi and Jai Chilla's reverence had come to an abrupt halt. Up was not the direction their sight was locked too. They faced forward and stared down the point of swords and spears. There too were aimed pistols or wide-muzzled, two-handed, thunder cannons locked with conjure and capable of expelling elemental properties.

Iune lowered his head from gazing at the sky above. His vision dropped, and as his sight ingested the scenery of the Maiden kingdom's main city in front of him, he noticed the army. More relevant, he noticed the two Maiden guard's in front of him, the tips of their extended blades resting menacingly under his chin and scratching against his neck.

Zoya and Olobiri flinched. It was Iune's turn to be indifferent, possessing an apathetic look on his face and a stillness to his body. He was a stone statue with a stoic expression as Prince Raji stepped forward and announced, "I am Prince Consort Raji Rah-Halitta! I do here by declare that under the authority of the Maiden kingdom, and in the name of my wife, her Royal Majesty, Neggura Halitta, that you, Iune Del-Yswil, are under arrest!"

Iune's eyes moved. Left. He viewed his sister and quipped, "I have a nagging suspicion he's been here." Attention on the prince consort. He lifted his arms. "You got me. I have been bested. I surrender. I cooperate. I have only one wish."

Prince Raji remained calm, but the bubble of anger was there, ready to burst and savage Iune to a bloody pulp. The swords at Iune's neck were lowered, and Prince Raji walked closer to him. The rage boiling the blood in his veins rose with each stride forward. "Granted," he growled in disbelief of himself. He was nose-to-nose with the trickster. "Within reason," he added.

"My sister represents me," Iune replied with his hands crossed to show surrender, allowing his hands to be bound.

Prince Raji stared at Iune. All of his anger compressed his features as he said nothing, vision tearing through Iune's eyes. He backed away, looking as if he was going to swing. He called over his shoulder at the guards who earlier had Iune at sword point, "Duke! Chuck! Arrest him!"

The two guards sheathed their swords and surrounded the trickster. They both spoke an incant to double-bind Iune's wrists. It caused for his arms to move from in front of him to behind him, an uncomfortable movement for Iune as incant manipulated his motion against his will. More guards swarmed. Hands gripped up and down Iune's arms and the back of his neck. Palms were situated all over his back, and he was hauled forward. Iune didn't resist, but the royal soldiers were rough in their handling of him. Olobiri watched, teeth grinding as he fought against his instincts to spring into battle and free his friend. He knew there was no place for that. He moved closer to Zoya's side.

Prince Raji commanded another set of soldiers to relieve Kioi and Jai Chilla of their weapons. The pair cooperated, and the same guards moved them along without binding.

Prince Raji crossed his arms and examined Zoya head-to-toe. Olobiri stiffened, far from fond at the inspection the prince consort gave to Zoya. He felt he was looking down at her as if she was a peasant to be spit on. The prince consort curled his lip and uttered, "You don't wear the robes of a justice counselor."

Zoya remained unflustered. "Clearly you all with a top-down view know the goings-on between my brother and a twin rival," she spelled out.

"No," said the prince consort in a sharp voice. "I've investigated and seen a worsening of your brother's trickster behavior. Ego twisting on itself, mangled into the disposition of an angry and jealous spirit. He's also contorted your kingdom's philosophy of confiscating items. He believes it's his right to take, and he had his sights on an item to be gifted to my daughter today at her inaugural ceremony. I witnessed this with my own eyes. I fought him. I saw him—" his voice came to an abrupt stop. Zoya jerked seeing the prince consort shudder with his eyes filling with moisture. Olobiri felt nothing looking at the man, even as Prince Raji covered his mouth, and took a deep breath. The armored and robed warrior wiped his sorrow away and returned to a state of authority and fury. "He attacked my wife!" He balled his fists and punched the air down at his side. He lifted the same fist and shook it in Zoya's face. "I'll blind him, I will!"

Olobiri continued fighting against his instinct to lunge at the prince consort. Zoya's head dropped. While she knew her brother was innocent, the compassion for the crimes committed against the royal family were a reflex. "My brother committed no crimes against the crown, Prince Raji. You have our word. There is an entity that wears my brother's face. His name is Ariq Haunts. He sneaked into your kingdom and did these terrible offenses. I'm sure that was days ago. We have been tracking him for four days inside of time to Azur-Fah."

Prince Raji was silent. Ire was chiseled on his face. His eyes were filled with retribution for what he witnessed happen against his wife, and the potential of an occurrence to take place again. He breathed heavy, slowly relaxing his demeanor. "My daughter… It's an important day for her. It's an important day for the Maiden kingdom." He exhaled and said, "We'll settle this. I have ways of finding the truth. Come with me." He gave a soldier's pivot and walked away. Zoya followed. Olobiri remained at her side like a loyal guard.

Jail was where Iune was taken. His bindings were never released, though his arms were repositioned to the front rather than behind his back. Prince Raji's soldiers were relieved, and Eterijah Emiti's personal guards filled the cell block. She entered, and Iune stood close to his cell's bars watching as she approached. The Eterijah's majestic presence peered down at Iune from her tall position. She straightened and flashed an ominous grin, knowing and victorious. A frost climbed his spine, and his instincts were rattled. He took a step back from the bars. He made a gracious bow and looked up at the colossal being.

"I throw myself at your mercy, Great Eterijah," he told her. "The nations of Africa that still remember the old ways of conjure sing glorious tales of Azur-Fah and its mighty Eterijah. I appeal to the kindness and pity caroled and crooned in the most splendid of lyrics. Certainly, they must be true."

She was unmoved, and her knowing grin remained, as well as the chill possessing Iune's backbone. One of the Eterijah's guards walked up to Iune's cell and lifted his head, moving up the wide brim of his pointed hat and revealing Chief Ariq Haunts. The Gold Chain of Soul glowed around his neck. His greater magic was a haughty, triumphant smile.

Iune grabbed the bars and attempted shaking them, only flailing himself about in anger. He stopped, pressed his face against the bars and growled, "You son-of-a-bitch! What have you done?"

Chief Ariq Haunts said nothing. He retained his smile, backed away, and headed toward the exit. The other guards and Eterijah Emiti fell in line.

"It's him!" Iune screamed. "He's here! Ariq Haunts *the Imposter! The Trickster with Less Than Half the Wits!*"

Chief Ariq Haunts stopped his movement. In his pause, he seethed while baring teeth, gripping tight the multi-bladed spear in his hand. It rattled like a baby's toy as anger coursed through him, shaking his hand. He stomped back to the cell and snapped, "My less-than-half-wits have you dead to rights!" He jabbed a finger at Iune, extending his arm through the bars. Iune backed up. "You will be remembered as a foul trickster, Iune Del-Yswil. They will hate you! They will no longer seek to conjure you! You will be a curse on lips and tongues, and children will be warned by their mothers, that if they misbehave, the malevolent Iune will get them!"

Iune backed up to the wall. He slumped down, sitting on the floor with his knees up. "But they'll never know you, Ariq Haunts—Chief of Folly and Fools."

The chief snickered, "For once, my pride doesn't get the best of me." He squatted, eye-level with Iune. "I will achieve the greatest alchemy for the people of Africa. I am its savior, cruel as my methods might be in assisting the European's thirst for our flesh and blood in bondage. The sons and daughters of Africa will know me in time. When they wield conjure again, return the world to Pambunjila, and see the three original moons in the sky, they will thank the great, African Chief, Ariq Haunts." He rose and proclaimed, "Now, if you'll excuse me, I have a royal family to slay while wearing your face. You will be charged by the folk inside of time for creating imbalance, but I will be recognized for restoring it. My alchemy of you continues." He walked away. In his strides he removed his hat to take off the Gold Chain of Soul. He tossed it into an empty cell and then exited the lockup. It clinked and clanked as it slid against the ground.

Iune jumped to his feet and hurried to the front of the cell. He shouted through his bars, "Is there no one else here that heard that?" Silence. Iune sighed, returned to the back of the cell, and sat down. He put his head against the wall and exhaled, "Paradises are so stupid."

Minutes passed. The door opened, and Prince Raji and Tyle walked through. Zoya, Olobiri, and the rogues Kioi and Jai Chilla followed behind them. Iune met them at the front of the cell. "He was here!" he asserted. "Ariq Haunts! He wears my face, Prince Raji—" he bowed his head and added, "Your Royal Majestic Highness of…however you're referred to…"

Prince Raji reached through the cell and grabbed Iune by the collar, slamming him against the bars. "You watch your tongue before it's cut out! Address me with respect!"

Zoya pleaded, "Your Majesty, my brother is a trickster. His natural reflex is to joke and toss around *bon mots*—"

Iune remarked, "Oh! She speaks French!"

Zoya gave Iune a severe look. She sighed and said to Prince Raji, "It was vexing growing up with him, trust me."

The prince consort opened his hands, letting Iune go. He pulled his arms back through the bars, and Iune remarked, "How do you even get those things through the narrow bars?"

Prince Raji shouted, "Tyle!"

The palace fool stepped to attention. "Yes, Sire!"

"Interrogate this trickster," the prince consort commanded.

Olobiri shook his head. He didn't like the proceedings. He believed his friend Iune when he reported that Chief Ariq Haunts had visited his cell. Olobiri wished a ritual had been conducted so that he could draw out its residuals and replay any of the happenings that occurred prior to their entering the cellblock.

"Yes, Sire!" responded Tyle. He walked up to the cell and asked, "Are you Iune Yswil, also called Iune Del-Yswil?"

Iune became earnest as he replied, "I am."

There was an immediate problem. Tyle felt nothing. His ability to identify truth was absent in him. It was gone without warning. He felt light, as if robbed of a thick, warm coat while traversing through a blizzard. He didn't make a show of it, considering the Eterijah's warning days earlier on how the trickster's powers might be interfering with his own. He thought the question might've been too easy, and so he inquired, "Did you assault Her Royal Majesty, Neggura Halitta, while attempting to steal a necklace? Did you engage in combat with the prince consort present?"

No jest and wholehearted. Iune answered, "No. I did not."

Nothing. The only sensation Tyle could feel was the rapid beat of his own heart. The emptiness concerned him. It wasn't just a matter of faint signals and muted buzzes with his instinct. There was nothing happening.

The prince consort turned to the palace fool and asked in an impatient tone, "Well…?"

Tyle stuttered on an answer.

"Well?" the prince consort repeated with more force in his voice.

"I don't know," Tyle responded. "The trickster's conjure negates my own. I feel nothing from him."

Prince Raji asked Iune, "What sort of demon are you?"

Iune became sincere when he relayed, "It's not me, Your Majesty. I swear. I have a rival, and he wears my face. His name is Ariq Haunts. He is part of a misguided tribal nation called the Ifo. They believe the tribulation befalling the people of Africa is part of a great, alchemical happening. They believe it will strengthen the people of Africa, and they assist European nations in enslaving the original people of the world. He was here! He has your Eterijah under a hex of sorts. His influence is magnified by—" Iune remembered the glowing, gold chain decorating Chief Ariq Haunts' neck. He'd seen it before, set down in front of the woman in his rival's crew called The Six Others. He remembered the Eterijah's smile. It was knowing, Iune thought, but it was more. It was seductive. It all started to make sense. "Your Eterijah is possessed by a terrible spirit! She's being controlled by—" A noise played in his memory. *A clink! A clank!* "There's a cursed object around here. He tossed it. I heard it. A gold chain with a haunting resonance." He looked at Tyle and said, "It's placement here might be twisting your instincts."

Prince Raji ordered Kioi and Olobiri, "Find this item—if it even exists!" He looked back at Iune and shook his fist. "No tricks, trickster!" he warned.

Iune didn't reply, inaction inspired by the stern look his sister shot him. He did, after all, have a sly and witty remark resting on the tip of his tongue.

Olobiri shifted his outer locks into curved horns. A gold, spherical light shined against his forehead, and it wasn't long before he pinpointed the chain's whereabouts in the corner of a cell close to the exit. "It's here!" he exclaimed, pointing into the prison chamber. "Looks like the one we saw Ariq Haunts use in his ritual."

Prince Raji raised an eyebrow out of suspicion. "You saw this demon performing a ritual and you did nothing?" he inquired, voice like a low roll of distant thunder.

"It was a clairvoyant recall," Olobiri snapped back at the prince consort.

Kioi peeked into the cell and confirmed, "There's something odd there. Looks to be a glowing necklace."

Prince Raji huffed. He removed a set of keys and unlocked Iune's cell. He grabbed the trickster and hauled him from the lockup. "Follow!" he commanded everyone. "Don't touch that jinxed object. Leave it be. Who knows what this trickster has planned."

Prince Raji dragged Iune to a suite far away from the jail cells. "Tyle!" he called again. "Make your cross-examination now," he commanded.

Tyle looked at Iune as the rascal humbled himself with his head down. The royal fool felt something. Sincerity resonated from the trickster. There were no foul elements like the ones he'd experienced when he'd first encountered Iune, or the possible second trickster that wore his face.

Tyle didn't need to ask for himself, but he needed for Prince Raji to bear witness. He recited, word-for-word, "Did you assault Her Royal Majesty, Neggura Halitta, while attempting to steal a necklace? Did you engage in combat with the prince consort present?"

Iune didn't change his answer. "No. I did not," he said. He did add an addendum to his statement, "There's a rival trickster named Ariq Haunts that has used deception to gain entrance to Azur-Fah. Your Eterijah is possessed by an immoral spirit. The warriors of his tribe have killed a set of guards and taken their clothes as he has taken my face. He's set to kill the royal family. He told me as much."

There was something, and Tyle's body trembled with revelation. He didn't simply feel validity coming from Iune, he saw the history between he and his rival. It concluded with their final encounter happening moments before they entered the cellblock. Tyle looked at the prince consort, concern washed over his face. "We are in terrible danger!" he warned. "He's telling the truth."

Iune exhaled relief.

Prince Raji's face became drenched in horror. "The breakfast banquet is starting. I'm supposed to gift my daughter with—" He placed his hand over his heart. *"My family!"*

"Your Majesty, continue on as if everything is normal," Zoya directed. "My brother and his friend here will handle everything. I'll accompany you to the ceremony as what we call a 'mock guest'."

Prince Raji concurred with a nod. He waved a hand and dispelled Iune's bindings. The trickster rubbed his wrists, grateful to be free. He thanked the prince consort and then requested Kioi and Jai Chilla be reinstated with their weapons. Prince Raji agreed. He made his way to the door with Zoya at his side. He turned and asked Iune, "Is there a need for a ritual to be done in your honor?"

Iune shook his head. "No, Your Majesty. A ritual would simply signal me to come, and I'm already here. There's no ritual I'm aware of that would strengthen my presence. Besides, my rival, Ariq Haunts, he might be alerted. We're very much aligned in that manner."

The prince consort understood. "A god's speed, trickster," he said. He informed Iune on the whereabouts of the ceremonial hall.

Iune saluted the prince consort with two-fingers. Prince Raji returned the gesture, and then he, Tyle, and Zoya departed to the banquet. The door closed. Iune lifted an eyebrow, a plan in mind. He turned to Olobiri and announced in a playful, exaggerated manner, "This has all given me a brilliant idea!"

The palace was flush with movement. The banquet hall was to capacity with nobles from the twelve lands of Constellation. The royal family sat at a long banquet table observing the guests guided in by stewards. Princess Qkumo-Ṣẹda was not seated with her family. She was in her bedroom attended to by courtiers as they assisted her in attire and cosmetics. Eterijah Emiti sat on the bed, overseeing the affair.

The prince consort knew there was deception about, but he

remained even-tempered. He smiled and waved at all his guests while delivering quick glances everywhere else. Tyle was the same as he stood against the wall behind the royal table. Prince Raji's soldiers were stationed strategically, but the prince consort was aware that a powerful trickster was at play. He believed his hopes lie in his worst nightmare. Another trickster. His trust didn't fall on Iune Del-Yswil. His confidence was in the wager he had on Tyle and his power to see truth. He turned around and beamed a smile at the palace fool. Tyle returned the gesture.

The doors to the hall opened, and in walked his second daughter, Princess Qkumo-Ṣẹda. The people stood in her honor. She was beautiful, even when veiled. She was dressed in a floor-length and sleeve-less, lilac and cobalt-blue, backless gown. A wide, dark-blue sash covered her waist. The zodiacal star sign of the Maiden was stitched into the fabric. An expansive, golden-brown headdress rested atop the princess' head. Her veil, swirling with the same colors as her gown, was attached to the ornamental head covering. A beaded collar, assembled from beautiful precious stones and gems, draped over her shoulders front and back. Two gold bangles lined each wrist. A golden arm bangle, fashioned in the shape of the Maiden symbol, wrapped around her triceps.

Eterijah Emiti followed behind, left of center. The Ifo warriors and Chief Ariq Haunts, disguised as the Maiden Eterijah's guardsmen, fell into formation behind the princess and Eterijah.

Worry dissolved from Prince Raji as he saw his daughter enter. He stood with his wife and two other daughters as Princess Qkumo-Ṣẹda entered. Aunts and uncles from the princess' maternal side of the family were also in attendance and seated at the table. Her father's people had been long, long gone inside of time.

Neggura Halitta and Prince Consort Raji came from around the table to meet the princess as she finished her walk up to her family. Princess Qkumo-Ṣẹda made a pivot and faced the audience. Eterijah Emiti and her guardsmen moved to the far-reaches of the illustrious auditorium. Neggura Halitta stepped up beside her daughter and announced to the spectators, "Duty is earned, and duty is often given. I didn't earn the title of Neggura of the Maiden Kingdom. It was passed to me by my sister. She had another calling. Closer to the spirit, is what she called it. She is now a beautiful and well-sought priestess. She trusted me with these duties to govern you all, to create my council, and bring order to our nation so that we can have order in all of Constellation's realms." She turned to her daughter and smiled. She put her gaze back to the audience and continued, "My daughter *earned* the right of Eterijah. She possesses the gift of aiding in rearranging the stars. Contention forced my daughter into early duty, but she is more than capable of taking the reins." She looked at Princess Qkumo-Ṣẹda again, beamed a smile, and concluded, "I am so proud of you!"

It wasn't proper to clap, and so everyone bowed at the neck.

The queen moved away, and Prince Raji stepped up in her place. He faced his daughter and said, "I'm not much for speeches." He unclipped the latches of the chain in his hand that was fastened with a jagged crystal dangling from it. He went underneath his daughter's veil and clipped it to her neck. "I survived a fatal wound because of this spirit condensed into crystal. It staved off death that day, and it allowed your mother to nurse me to health. You were the result of…celebration…" the princess blushed behind the veil as light laughter rumbled low through the crowd. Even the prince consort chuckled along. "I love my daughters, but this is your moment, Qkumo-Ṣẹda. Like your mother, I repeat, I am so proud of you." He hugged her against tradition in the affair, but the prince consort had his moment as he wished.

Again, there was no applause only respectful bows, and then Princess Qkumo-Ṣẹda joined her family at the banquet table, seated at the center between her mother and father. The Maiden kingdom's Eterijah would speak later at the ceremonial rites. It was now time to eat, or so the people believed.

Eterijah Emiti used a hex to lock the doors.

Chief Ariq Haunts flashed a hand signal.

Bows were raised. Arrows were flung. Their targets, the royal family.

There came a blur, two streaks of visible wind diving down from the balcony. The only thing faster was the wave of expelled conjure that slowed the arrows' momentum. The two factions of conjure almost tripped over one another. Iune and Olobiri's swift and indistinct shapes lunging from the upper tier were timed to snatch the arrows as the projectiles soared through the air in real time. The wave of conjure hampered that plan, and as their feet landed on the banquet table, time inched closer and closer to regaining its natural speed as the incant to quicken them drained.

The two sprang in opposite directions. Iune snatched three arrows as Olobiri swiped three more from the air. Time resumed for them. The disguised Ifo guards locked in another set of arrows, two per bow. They fired! Iune's heart skipped a beat, but barely had time to do that. Another pulse of conjure rippled through the room, and Iune caught a glimpse of the veiled princess with her hand partially extended. The arrows' flight slowed, and Iune and Olobiri tossed the arrows in their grips with keen precision. Knocking one arrow aside put it in the path of another and another, and soon the rippling effect toppled all of the arrows off their marks to rain harmless on the floor.

Iune and Olobiri jumped behind the banquet table and scurried under it. *"Lift!"* Iune hollered, and he an Olobiri flipped the heavy, wooden piece of furniture. *"Duck!"* Iune shouted a second order. The royal family took cover behind the barricade. The guests did the same with their smaller, round tables or chairs. Some sprawled out on the ground, covering their heads.

The queen stood, rose above the overturned table, and extended her hand to cast a crippling conjure wave. An arrow struck her hand, lodging halfway through. A second knocked her shoulder, and she fell back into Princess Tinta's arms. *"Ma-ma!"* cried all three daughters.

The prince consort drew his sword and jumped over the table. Iune followed, but where Prince Raji charged at any of the disguised, Ifo guards, Iune found his sister behind a table and joined her. "Go to the royal family! Find cover there!" he told her. Zoya agreed. They stood, and both of their instincts drew their attention over their shoulder.

An Ifo bowman pulled back to down the prince consort. Ready to aim, he was set to release his deadly strike when an arrow from above caught him in the neck, putting him down. His arrow was still propelled, but off its mark, clanking harmlessly against Prince Raji's breastplate clasped over his robes. The prince consort chose another Ifo to strike, and his slash was fatal, downing the disguised warrior.

A surge of palace guards descended from the interior balcony with Kioi and Jai Chilla among their ranks. Eterijah Emiti, huddled in a shadowy corner, reversed her hex on the doors. The tall, decorative entryways opened, and more of Chief Ariq Haunts Ifo warriors joined the conflict. Prince Raji's soldiers were well-trained, but the Ifo warriors' ferocity was fueled by their zealotic convictions, spurred to give a great fight. They had a mission, and their focus was as sharp as their weapons to complete it. Coupled with their own fighting skill, it made for a bloody and brutal match.

Guests shuffled through the fray to escape, but a few were struck down, meeting a gruesome end. Eterijah Emiti slipped away, her towering stature unnoticed as the fight pressed on. Her aim was to retrieve the Gold Chain of Soul and return to the banquet battle to assist, the imprisoned soul of the true Eterijah Iyansan at her command. She encountered a bloodstained mess in the hall. Palace soldiers' bodies were strewn throughout the area. Their slit or arrow-punctured throats muddied the pathway with their blood. Eterijah Emiti noted there was not an Ifo warrior among them, and their slaughter appeared swift and merciful.

Chaos was at her back, and in the middle of the frantic fray Iune was able to get Zoya behind the barricade. He surveyed what was in his line of vision, and his instinct noticed a peculiarity in the corner. There were grooves, and his higher sense buzzed when he observed a fancy sconce.

"Olobiri!" Iune called. His friend was quick to his side. "There's a secret passage. We'll join the battle and keep any of Ariq Haunts' warriors from the family. Zoya, take lead." He turned to Princess Tinta and inquired, "Is your mother okay?"

She spoke in haste, flinching every time an arrow thwacked against the thick, wooden table's surface. "She's fine. My auntie can heal her. Just help us get to the escape passage."

Iune nodded and answered respectfully, "Yes, Your Majesty."

Tyle crawled in between them. "Iune! I'll assist the royal family."

Princess Tinta's face contorted. Her eyes bent on the trickster. "Iune! *You're* the cause of this calamity! You need to be arrested!"

Iune rolled his eyes and snarled, "We were getting along so well. Will someone catch her up on the plot—preferably the one to *frame* me!"

Tyle waved his hands in the eldest princess' face. "No! No, m'lady. It's another trickster who wears his face that brings misfortune to our kingdom!"

Princess Tinta apologized. Iune accepted, and then he announced, "Royals, stay low and follow Tyle to safety. Most importantly, understand this: I, Iunes Kythe Glaive Del-Yswil am not the cause of this misfortune!" He stood, jumping onto the edge of the tipped table. Olobiri joined him, and as his friend took his side, Iune opened his hands and summoned his gazelle-horn lances. "But I most certainly will be the one to push it back!"

Whether he be innocent or guilty, Princess Qkumo-Ṣẹda couldn't help but smile up at the bold trickster. Iune tapped his finger against his tongue for good luck. A sly grin crawled onto his face, and then he and Olobiri leapt to battle. The royal family kept low. Arrows whizzed by their heads. Tyle scurried forward. He jumped up and pulled the sconce, opening the hidden passage. Arrows launched at them were slowed by the second princess' power, but Eterijah Emiti, who'd returned to the fray used the Gold Chain of Soul to dampen the powerful conjure woman's abilities.

Chief Ariq Haunts tackled Princess Qkumo-Ṣẹda. Her head hit the floor, and her headdress loosened. The attack left the princess' vision spinning. The Ifo chief straddled the princess as she lay on her stomach. He drew a dagger and lifted it to strike. "Your blood and your necklace!" he growled. Ready to stab the princess, his instinct started buzzing. Without a glance toward the guardsman thrusting his spear in his direction, he leapt off the princess to safety.

The princess crawled away a few paces, then she got up and staggered away. Ifo blocked her path to her family, and she pivoted, taking the winding stairs to the upper tier. Images doubled and stretched, and her balance was off, but the princess pressed on undeterred. Eterijah Emiti remained shadowed, using the Gold Chain of Soul to diminish the princess' power and confidence.

Chief Ariq Haunts pursued the royal conjure woman. He winded the staircase with six of his Ifo warriors behind him. Dizzy, but still in the fight, Princess Qkumo-Ṣẹda turned, raised her palm, and emitted a surge of conjure at her attackers. The chief and his horde braced themselves against a robust gale, planting feet firmly and leaning into its force. Her powers reduced, the princess' summoned squall was absent of vigor to topple her followers, but they were stalled in their pursuit.

In front of her, rising from the opposite staircase, was another unit of Ifo warriors. She turned to the banister and looked down on the horror and massacre below. Few Ifo warriors populated the floor with slain bodies. It was her father's guards and soldiers that littered the bloody, banquet room. Their defeat at the hands of a small band with a fiery, focused resolve. She spotted her father back-to-back with the trickster Iune Del-Yswil fending off the kingdom's novel adversaries.

The princess assessed her predicament. Chief Ariq Haunts and a crew of killers to her left. A second horde to her right. She, fixed in between with a whirling dizziness and a heavy weight on her person. She looked out and spotted a large, ornate and bulbous light fixture decorated with crystals. It was too far away for any mortal person to leap and catch, but she was far from being a mortal person. She climbed the railing and launched herself out. There was an immediate use of her powers, gathering a strong, conjured wind to propel her forward.

She landed against the hanging fixture with a tight grip and wondered straightaway what she'd gotten herself into. The light swung to and fro, wide and with the force of a bucking bull. The erratic movement swelled Princess Qkumo-Ṣẹda's already muzzy vision. She closed her eyes and attempted to use an incant to steady herself, but she felt a mental block from the full potential of her power.

Iune and Prince Raji spotted the princess' adversity. An Ifo warrior took advantage of the distraction and lifted his heavy sword to strike at the prince consort. Olobiri was faster than the would-be fatal swing. He impaled the warrior from behind with two daggers to the back. The Ifo dropped the large and heavy blade, but Olobiri's attack on him was not concluded. The lithe, deputy-trickster, dodged the weighty, fallen weapon and then brought down his daggers on either side of the Ifo's neck.

The prince consort was too preoccupied with his daughter's struggles to even notice the scuffle. He gasped as he watched her slip, barely holding the bottom of the chandelier. "There's something the matter!" he exclaimed under his breath.

Iune heard the prince consort. His eyes fell on the Ifo warriors on the balcony tossing their weapons at the princess. She managed to shimmy to the other side of the chandelier. She kicked her feet out and in, gaining momentum to have the fixture begin another swing.

"There's a trick at play," he said, looking around for any source influencing the circumstances. His instinct directed him to a shadowy corner. He narrowed his eyes and concentrated, and the Gold Chain of Soul's hazy aura became visible within the corner's dark veil. He stayed low and eluded oncoming Ifo warriors. The same attackers' movements pulled Prince Raji to his senses, and he raised his sword to defend against them. Olobiri and Jai Chilla came to his side as Kioi jumped to assist Iune, fending off storming Ifo soldiers.

With a clear view of the shaded corner, Iune hurled the horn-lance in his right hand. It disappeared into the darkness, and a cry was let out. The shadow dispersed, and Eterijah Emiti was revealed behind it. The horn-lance punctured her side, and Iune recalled it to his hands before she could grab at the weapon. She put her hand over the bleeding wound and mended her flesh with her power. The false Eterijah's concentration was broken, and Princess Qkumo-Ṣẹda jerked with the sudden fill of her conjure potential. The royal conjure woman let loose an ardent ripple of conjure that knocked everyone to the ground.

She let go and descended, but not without travail. Her loose headdress caught the chandelier and unraveled. By instinct, Princess Qkumo-Ṣẹda reached up and snatched the veil affixed to the headpiece, tearing it free from the rest of the fabric. Her descent was as whimsical as a feather. The princess' conjure slowed her fall, giving time for Iune to center himself under her descent and catch her in a cradle. Her veil covered her face as she landed soft and gentle in Iune's arms. He placed her on her feet and stepped back.

Princess Qkumo-Ṣẹda removed her covering, and her reveal had an effect on Iune without any use of conjure. Villains regained their stance, but Iune saw none of that. His eyes were fixed and his combat instincts were restrained.

A heavenly body. She had a carefully crafted hourglass figure burnished to a fine, brown-bronzed polish. She was naked of a shroud of hair, an appearance her ceremonial rites called for. Her head shaved bald a few days before the festival began. Curved eyebrows rested atop wide, brown eyes. One raised, inspecting Iune with a curious regard. Her bow-shaped lips curled into a knowing grin and then parted as she stated, "You're the great troublemaker, aren't you?"

It was reflex that guided Iune to correct her, but it wasn't quick enough. He froze before he could state he was a trickster by trade, as he spotted an Ifo warrior charging Princess Qkumo-Ṣẹda from behind. She was calm, and she never turned to face the danger racing at her with spear out ready to impale. Her heightened instincts appraised the incoming threat, and she extended her arm behind her, conjuring a controlling force that took hold of the spear from the Ifo warrior's grip. The weapon spun wild, smacking the

Ifo face's and crossing between his feet to trip him in his run. He slammed against the floor, head pounding hard enough to render him unconscious.

The attacks continued. Chief Ariq Haunts sailed from the balcony down toward Iune, spear aimed for the kill. Iune opened his palms and summoned his gazelle-horn lances ready for defense. He took stance and calculated his rival's descent, preparing for a swift block, but the princess had other plans. A shockwave of conjure pulsed from her, and the otherworldly discharge slowed the chief's dive.

Iune backed away, but Chief Ariq Haunts extended his spear. His stab at Iune sedated, and he hung in the air, suspended by the princess' power. He grinned at Iune, and then he aimed his haughty smirk at the princess. "Just as I intended!" he taunted before extending his foot in a real-time attack unaffected by the princess' conjure. The sole of his boot connected with her countenance, a swift kick that knocked the princess off her feet and to the floor, sliding until she hit an empty table, knocking it over.

Her nose was bloodied, and her vision was unsteady. Two Ifo took advantage of her delirium and ran at her with sword and spear. Princess Qkumo-Ṣẹda had sense enough to conjure an impenetrable, translucent aegis around her. Their weapons bounced off the blue, shimmering dome and knocked the warriors off balance. They fell forward, their bodies slamming against the protective cover and receiving a jolt of electric potency. They fell to the floor, clothes and flesh scorched. The shield dissipated as the princess' senses faltered.

Chief Ariq Haunts touched down, no longer under the princess' hold. He swung his spear at Iune, and the trickster blocked using his horn-lances. The chief assailed his adversary with a series of slashes with his weapon, throwing the spear about as if he was using a thin-bladed great sword. Iune backed up, blocking every swing and thrust made at him. The attacks challenged him to switch the hold on his horn-lances as Chief Ariq Haunts continued his furious rain.

The chief made a thrust that caused Iune to jump back. He repeated the same attack twice more, and when Iune had been reversed a good distance, he turned around and tossed the spear at the stunned princess. Iune unsummoned his weapons and hastened on feet and palms. He ran up Chief Ariq Haunts' back, launching himself off the Ifo chief's shoulders and straight to the spear. He was quick as the wind, caught the spear in midair, and moved it away from the princess' line. He crashed against the floor, and Chief Ariq Haunts grinned again.

"As intended," he sneered. He aimed a hand toward Eterijah Emiti, who was still nursing her wound. He called the Gold Chain of Soul from off her person and to his hand, placing it around his neck when it came into his grip. He reached out toward Iune and used the power trapped inside the gold chain to lift the trickster into the air. The spear Iune knocked away was also scooped up by Chief Ariq Haunts' power. The chief moved his arm to the right, and Iune and the spear were launched toward the back of the room.

Iune palmed the spear with both hands. He spread his legs wide and allowed the sharp end of the weapon to pass under his groin. The spear lodged into the wall, Iune perched atop it, maintaining balance as the body of the spear jiggled with the impact. He looked up, straightened his senses with an incant, and spied Chief Ariq Haunts snatch the princess by the neck with the use of conjure. He lifted her into the air, and pinned her to the wall.

He growled, "And now your highness, we will discuss the sparkly curiosity around your neck!" he closed his fist, and the necklace gifted to Princess Qkumo-Ṣẹda tightened and choked her. "Though, I have to admit, the discussion will be terribly one-sided!"

Iune scampered across the thin body of the embedded spear like a cat across a wire. He leapt, appendages extended to grapple Chief Ariq Haunts and wrestle him to the ground.

The Ifo chief was tackled, seized by Tyle!

Iune glided over their struggle, landing a few feet away. Ifo warriors stood over him. He leapt into battle, defending himself from their onslaught with horn-lances conjured to his hands.

Tyle shouted while holding Chief Ariq Haunts on the ground, "Princess! Run!"

The princess regained her faculties as her father came to her aid.

Tyle slammed a fist into Chief Ariq Haunts' back, releasing a surge of conjure through the mountebank's body. He buckled, but recovered quick enough to counter with his own power, launching Tyle off him. The chief stood and became surrounded by his horde.

Few palace soldiers remained, and those that did shouted a dedication to protect the royal father and daughter until they made their escape. They kept to their word, dying for their oath as Iune and his band fled with the princess, her father, and Tyle through the opened, secret passage. No pursuit was given, and Eterijah Emiti staggered up to her chief and inquired, "No chase?"

"Why? They'll be back," he said through a confident, deep-throated snicker. He looked up at her and ordered, "Get your rest. Heal from that wound. We have five other kingdoms to secure. We can still fix the stars by injecting this kingdom with a haunting infection."

An Ifo warrior came to Chief Ariq Haunts' side and reported, "We've captured surviving nobles attempting to flee. They've been placed in cells."

"Good. We have leverage."

His rival lived, and that stung. The clue to a powerful weapon escaped his grasp, but he was certain both would return in an attempt to reclaim the palace.

Iune joined his sister and the other royals at the end of a long chamber that led outside. The tunnel surfaced near a hidden stable. All for emergency, and this was one. They mounted camels and left behind the horses and the strange-looking hytack creatures. While waiting for her brother and the prince consort, Zoya convinced the queen and her daughters to come inside of time, promising them sanctuary with one of the thirteen Mai Gadi tribes. Those plans changed when they crossed back through to Africa. Prince Raji fell ill an hour into their journey. Keeled over on his horse, he moaned terribly until his sister-by-law galloped up to him and rested a healing hand on his back.

Neggura Halitta inquired, voice trembling, "Was he wounded?"

Though it pained him, the prince consort lifted his body and shook his head. "No. No, Qwirha," he assured her. "I feel a terrible weight. Something crushing."

The queen's sister, Priestess Chikondi, informed, "It's the effect of being inside of time." She said directly to Prince Raji, "You were born here, but you haven't felt the effects of these ticking hours in a long, long while, Your Majesty. Your old, terrible wound still has effect too."

Zoya overheard. "How long before time catches up with him?" she asked.

"He'll be fine, but he'll be in pain," the priestess diagnosed. "I can only give him so many doses of my curative touch to ease the pain. Time will eventually catch up."

"Then outside of time we'll take you," Zoya decided. She turned to her brother and ordered, "Set course for the coast. We journey home to Del-Yswil. Iune, take the lead. Jai Chilla, Kioi, in tow. We'll switch off leads as we go."

Iune barely heard his sister's command. He knew she said something to him, but her words were mangled as he remained under the spell of fixed concentration on Princess Qkumo-Ṣẹda, head now wrapped with a scarf to hide her ceremonial baldness. Olobiri listened, and he was aware of Iune's condition. It was motivation to beam a broad, meaningful smile. He galloped ahead of the pack, taking lead with Zoya. "Let him rest," he suggested. "He's got a lot on his mind. We'll trade off with Kioi and Jai Chilla for the time."

The party moved on. Inside of time. In Africa. Minutes became hours. The prince consort felt every ticking moment, and the group remained anxious about his condition. Priestess Chikondi administered an anesthetic conjure when necessary, but time was catching up as time went on. Prince Raji remained strong, keeping his pain muffled until soothing conjure was dispensed. The group was rattled, and Zoya preserved her strength to move them through the ethers to Africa's west coast. She focused, gathering her conjure for the grueling maneuver.

A battle was behind them. Time was encroaching, debilitating to the prince consort and slightly disorienting to those of Azur-Fah. Gradually the party eased, going with time.

Iune watched the princess as she observed the world around her, wide-eyed and child-like. It was rare that the trickster found his tongue in a knot, but here he was breaking his streak, and a villain was not the cause. In the sparse moments where Iune's gaze wasn't fixed on the princess, she took note of him, mainly his bare, single-feathered-decorated feet.

"Iune…" she whispered.

The trickster was lost in a sweet fantasy concerning the princess, but her voice punctured the daydream at the precise moment she uttered his name in his imagination. It wasn't so much in the same, breathy and excited tone he'd imagined.

"Trickster!" she hissed to get his attention.

Iune flinched. He looked at her. "Yes, Your Highness!" he responded.

"Your feet," she said pointing down at his appendages latched into the light-framed stirrups. "Do you not sport footwear because they might…" she hesitated, not wanting to offend or sound silly. But she used the word anyway. *"Pluck* your feathers…?"

Iune perked up with Princess Qkumo-Ṣẹda's interest in his peculiarity. "No, no, Your Highness. I have no need for shoes or boots or sandals. The feathers are a blessing I received from a priestess in a tribal nation."

Olobiri, eavesdropping on the conversation, added very low and deep under his breath, "I've been told it wasn't the only kind of blessing she gave him."

His comment went unheard, and Iune continued, "They give my feet protection. They also buff my quick maneuvers." Then he proudly proclaimed with his chest out, "Like my pants! Fashioned from the hide of a swift gazelle!" He slapped his hand against his vest and described, "A rhino's pelt! Keeps me strong, durable. Skin tough like my leather." He felt his father's culture front and center, and he embraced it. He told the princess, "Each item I wear is bound to me by a spiritual fabric, and they each hold a story of adventure on their acquisition!"

Olobiri listened. He turned to Zoya and said, "I had this morning, to break the fast, crisped bread." Zoya was confused. They all had fish and vegetables and lemon water with a stir of a small drop of honey. No bread was on their plates, at least she didn't remember anyone crisping bread before they trekked out on their mission, but Olobiri seemed to insist in his voice.

"I put butter on it," he continued. "But it was too much. You could say I was *laying it on too thick.*"

Zoya shielded her chuckle, and she did her best to shoot Olobiri a cutting look. Light laughter calmed, she pulled her mount closer to Olobiri and made a swift slap against his stomach. He welcomed the attention from her.

The princess heard Olobiri's comment, as meant. She too bubbled with light laughter. Iune blushed, losing his smile and putting his head down. He said to her, "I'm sorry, Your Majesty. I should be more sympathetic, considering where we just escaped. I promise we'll take back your kingdom. I swear my luck on it."

Princess Qkumo-Ṣẹda accepted the trickster's apology. "You'll add the reconquest to your long line of adventures, trickster." She attempted a teasing smile, but the tragedy of the loss of her kingdom was too recent.

Iune noted the somber look in the princess' eyes. He consoled, "It wasn't my intention to brag. I get it from my father's people, on his mother's side. Proud braggarts, they were. I take full blame, though, Your Highness."

"You can call me Ṣẹda, trickster. Everyone else does." She looked around, eyes swallowing the new world around her. "Besides, I'm not a princess here."

"You're royalty everywhere you walk, black woman," Iune noted.

Ṣẹda embraced the sentiment. It was something warm, and she found the world inside time cold. The fading sun provided little heat for her, but it was more than just a physical happening. The desert was truly sweltering, but she felt the plight and imbalance occurring here. She knew of the world inside time, but this was her first experience of its nature. A desert. In Africa, once called Alkebulan. This was where life and arts and science disciplines began. It was barren now, but very beautiful and with much to offer still in the way of resources. One such resource was human. The original man and woman. A resource taken by force. Ṣẹda felt their collective cries. Past. Present. Future. All dragged to a terrible fate in servitude.

Head up at the darkening sky. Ṣẹda looked desperately for three moons, but she only spied the pale, single satellite. Living her own life distracted Ṣẹda from the world's politics, but she had her history courses. Here she was in the middle of its most tragic story to date. She felt Africa's stress, and inside she wept along with it.

Tyle sensed Ṣẹda's grief. He sided his mount up next to hers, and he started to console her with a beautiful tune. *"Sweet baby,"* he crooned before telling her to stay her tears. His melody continued, and Iune watched, allowing the moment to have its peace.

Prince Raji shuffled his camel next to Iune's mount, coming in between the trickster and his daughter. It wasn't strategic, in the sense of being a concerned father. He'd had too much experience with attempts at steering his older daughters away from boys who didn't meet his approval.

"Let me apologize, trickster," the prince consort expressed his regret, swallowing the pain in his body.

"No need, Your Majesty," Iune replied. "I understand. You were concerned for your family. You were being a father, a parent, a husband. You saw your wife attacked, and the villain wore my face."

"You take it in stride."

Iune shrugged. "I'm used to the accusations by now."

Olobiri had an apology of his own to give, at least some explaining. He assured Zoya, "I was only teasing with Iune." He made his voice low again, whispering to her, "A nice change of tone from the sanguinary scene we left behind." He looked over his shoulder and surveyed the band of royals. He told Zoya, "The Ifo were relentless. I don't know what the hell we're doing."

She affirmed, "We're going to raise an army and return to cut at the new Ifo chief's pride."

Tyle continued singing, and everyone basked in his falsetto tones. Princess Qkumo-Ṣẹda looked up at the dawning, heavenly twinkles. The stars looked so very different to her inside of time, but they glistened and she felt at home gazing at them. She also missed home.

The stars continued gleaming, bursting into a lilac wash that ran up like a curtain on a new act in a play.

Dawn. Zoya and Olobiri led the others across an invisible bridge that connected the seen world with the unseen. The island was miles off the West African coast, but space and time bent once in the vicinity of the invisible bridge that was inscribed with incants dedicated to its ritual to bring it into existence. Stepping across the border of time in and out, Prince Raji's body regained its vitality.

On the other side stood King Ziko and Queen Oris. It could be said that time was very kind to Oris Del-Yswil, however she didn't much live within it. While she was definitely aged, and the time that did touch her tattooed her visage with lines of wisdom, her beauty was still timeless.

They were not alone. With them was a young man with an athletic build. He was dressed in a long, beige tunic, pants the same color, and a brown vest matching the color of his shoes. He looked around Olobiri's age. He was handsome, yet there was a rugged appearance in his countenance. Beside him was a woman dressed in a billowing, yellow dress with an orange sash around her waist and a headwrap the same color. While there was a lovely appeal to her, there also rested a tired, battle-worn sentiment.

Iune steered his mount to sprint ahead. He slowed when taking a position between his sister and Olobiri. He commented in gest, "Is everyone waiting to greet us everywhere we go?" He received no response, as Olobiri and Zoya wondered much the same. The young man and woman came into focus, and Iune lost sight of his parents, focusing primarily on the island's new guests. He hurried up to them, dismounting from the camel and going into a quick stride. Everyone was confused, except Olobiri.

Iune snatched the young man's hand and shook it wildly with both of his. "I know you!" he said to him. He looked at the woman and exclaimed just as excited, "And I know you, too!" Iune, still holding tight to the man's hand, turned and addressed the approaching band of wandering royals. The group stopped, and Iune let go of the man's hand. "Prince Consort Raji, Neggura Halitta, Daughters of the Maiden Neggura and Prince Consort—" he extended his hand toward his mother and father. He spoke with urgency as he introduced his parents. "I present my father, King Ziko Yswil and my mother, Queen Oris Del-Yswil. They've lived a long life. Old champions of an age gone by. They run the island. They gave birth to myself and my sister, hence 'parents'. Adopted my best of friends there, Olobiri!" He made the aside, "Tragic tale actually." He skipped over to his mother and father and stated, "This is the royal family from the Maiden Kingdom. We went to Azur-Fah. Lovely this time of year—minus the kingdom's collapse and capture. Ariq Haunts and his villainy now reign there. We have plans to rectify that." He made a face, but then perked up as he remembered an interesting fact. He shared it with his mother and father. "Oh! He's the new Ifo chief, Ariq Haunts is." He skipped back to the island's two guests. "But these two!" He turned to the mounted group and shouted with all his glee, "This is Kuto and Weka, and they—" he raised his arms and yelled triumphantly, "—kill slavers and free imprisoned Africans for a living!"

Ithun peered at Iune through a curious gaze. "The trickster Iune knows me…? I grew up on your storied exploits."

"*Know you?*" Iune swooned, grabbing Ithun's hand again and shaking rapidly. "*The Night Ghosts! El Negro Lobo! Kuto* and *Weka!*" He let go and slammed a fist into his other hand's open palm. "I have wished nothing more than to have our escapades crossover and—" He fell silent, and delight drained from his face. "What are you doing here? My apology for my animated spirit."

"It's his trickster nature," remarked Prince Raji.

"You know our son," Queen Oris noted.

"That I do," the prince consort replied. He looked over at Efra and acknowledged, "And like the trickster, I know you too, good woman."

"Yes, Prince Raji." She looked at Neggura Halitta and made a respectful bow of her neck. "Peace, Neggura."

Iune appeared vexed. "So that whole introduction was for nothing?

We all know each other?" His comment was ignored.

The prince consort's eyes moved to Ithun. "Your son?" he asked.

"Yes," Efra answered. "One of them. The other…"

The light banter could not prevent the change in the air, as somber reigned as king on Ithun and Efra's expressions. Efra displayed a card in her hand. Iune examined its face, noting the detail. A naked black man and a naked black woman walked with their hands embraced. The cosmos was above them, sprouting out of them. The names of those called *The First Two* were written in an ancient language on a banner above them. *EKSUH. JEERAH.* Scrawled on a second banner below them were the words *The Valley Of.*

"We were hoping to use this as tribute to gain entrance to Azur-Fah," said Efra. "We need to speak with Eterijah Iyansan."

"I am her heir apparent," announced Ṣẹda as she dismounted her camel. "She is indisposed," the princess informed. "Hexed, possessed by a wicked spirit that aided a foul trickster in taking our land."

The princess' presence brightened Efra's disposition. "Princess Qkumo-Ṣẹda!" she called out. "You've grown into such a lovely lady! You were so young the last time—"

Ṣẹda froze in response. A faint memory came to her. There were quick flashes of magnificent power on display. The woman in front of her was familiar. "I've only met you once, and so much of my life has been shaped around that encounter." Her eyes went up and down, inspecting Efra and pondering all the outcomes from that one experience.

Efra felt the need to apologize to the young princess. She knew the politics.

"Iune," Queen Oris called her son. He turned to his mother and gave her his attention. "This man Ithun knows Ariq Haunts. He grew up with him."

Shock exploded Iune's features. "I guess our stories have crossed longer ago, unsuspected."

"Yes," Ithun replied. "You speak of tragic tales, Iune. The footprints marking our journey here are deep with them. Time and space separate us, but so much holds it all together."

A lilac flash cut into the dreaming of history long ago.

44

Bright. Lilac sheet. Burned out to darkness. The dreamer awoke. The chamber opened, and it was time to leave the capsule. Gordon rose with Spook in his arms. His eyes moved instinctively toward the wall and glowed brighter with their lilac gleam. He saw the flickering images of his dream in the brightness his eyes radiated. It lasted for only a moment, and then faded into memory. Gordon hopped from the chamber, and it closed behind him. He set Spook down on the capsule's lid, took a seat on his plush chair, and exhaled long and hard with his eyes closed.

Relaxing his breathing, Gordon commented, "How can sleep feel so exhausting, Spook?"

The ancient device unfolded. Characters from a lost language lit up the face of its black mirror. Gordon opened his eyes and read them. *I do my part*, said the words. *I concentrate, I beam history into your sleep, but you feel it. You walk it.* You feel it. *It surrounds you, and you connect with all you see, and all the emotions that come with it. There's a lot that's happened, seen and unseen. Your spirit bears the burden.*

Gordon leaned forward. He breathed deep again and sighed just as hard. "Spook, I don't want you to feel unappreciated. You keep the dreamer in balance. That's me, most often. You harvest the residue of history from an object and shuffle the ethereal images into the opened mind of someone sleeping. Again, that's me, most often." He thought about the poetic narrative he and Fey Forrester composed. The black mirror inquired with a single word, *But…?* Gordon sat back, head tilted up to face the ceiling. "I miss sharing these moments with Fey."

Gordon's frustration stopped potential tears from flowing, making him more upset. Spook had a suggestion. He drafted a proposal on the screen. The ancient characters read, *This journey hasn't truly been your own. Maybe you can share a few of the historical stories instead of reporting them to Lady Arachne. It is her tarot card you pursue, after all.*

Gordon stared at Spook's advice and considered the idea. He smiled knowing the hypocrisy residing on the tip of his tongue, ready to be spoken. "Maybe once this history concludes," he counter-proposed. "It's a curious tale, Spook. I've heard of Eterijah, but I barely know anything on Azur-Fah. Seeing all this is crazy. There's so much more to the African past—to the black past as a whole. Even old lessons are new to me. Not to you, I'm sure." Spook wrote on his screen, *No.* Gordon stood and walked over to the device. "How come you never gave me some deeper history lessons, huh?" The old device answered, *You didn't ask.* Gordon rolled his eyes. He turned his back to Spook, saying, "Didn't. Ask. That's his answer. Wonderful. Marvelous." He paused and thought about the previous answer Spook had for his burden of viewing history in seclusion. The little machine was right. He bent his head forward, concentrated, and reached out to Fable Avenue's third matriarch. **Lady Arachne,** he broadcasted.

Speaking mind-to-detect-mind was different than speaking audibly through the mouth, the obvious aside. A person's heart was in their sending, and it was difficult to lie or have ulterior motives. Lady Arachne didn't just receive Gordon's mental call. She felt his honesty and sadness coupled together to create a heavy weight on him.

Gordon, the conjure woman replied. **Are you alright, lilac spirit?**

I'd like to share something with you, he answered her. **History in a dream, if you have the time. I've caught glimpses of The Lovers card, but now it's become a staple in the story. I would like for you to experience it too, the sight of it.**

Gordon's gesture warmed Lady Arachne's heart. She accepted. **I will be there shortly, Mister Goodspeed. Allow a lady time to dress.**

Their cerebral exchange ended. Gordon sat down and waited. He closed his eyes, and the lilac sphere of energy swirled into existence at the center of his forehead. An image developed from the blackness behind his eyes. It was the brownstone's exterior. Lady Arachne came into frame near an hour after he'd contacted her. Gordon opened the door and telepathically greeted the conjure woman, **Hello, Lady Arachne. I'm in the basement.** His sincerity brushed over her like a cool breeze. The door opened, and Lady Arachne was reminded of both the mysteries her life walked into, and the sundry of shrines and sanctuaries she stepped inside to learn of the unseen world and how her conjure connected to the black and beautiful void. The door closed and locked by way of Gordon's power after the matriarch entered.

He was masked and on his feet by the time Lady Arachne arrived in the basement. His Dooley presence startled Lady Arachne as black, ethereal smoke spiraled off his shoulders. The experience of seeing her first spirit at the age of five filled her. A most concrete, visual memory of the moment registered the complete spectrum of emotions that both chilled and warmed her. The spirit was a young boy too, older than her at the time, but younger than Gordon. Twelve, she recalled. His name was Martin Clyde. He'd returned to see how life had been since his death in 1922. He never said how he died, and Lady Arachne never pried when she came of age in conjure. She just liked to remember his youthful, black face. He looked around, talked a little, and he said, *"Interesting!"* Then he walked away, fading into the ethers.

Here was Dooley, and he had a story to share with her. Spook was in his hands with its black mirror faced up and The Judgment card laying at an angle across the device's bejeweled console. The ancient mechanism closed, and when its face rested against its precious-stoned keypad, the African Chokwe-like mask shifted into smoke and seeped into Gordon's flesh. He stood unmasked in his black, cosmic suit. There was no more smoke coming from his body. He handed Spook to Lady Arachne. She accepted and beamed, "Thank you, Gordon." She stepped back and asked, "Now, how does all this work? I've seen you and Miss Forrester simply lay flat holding the kham-ptah cross-armed against your chests. Is that all?"

"Yes, Lady Arachne," Gordon said to her in a humble manner. "You can recline in the chair or slip into the chamber." He aimed his hands at either suggested furnishing.

Lady Arachne viewed her options and chose the recliner. Gordon moved out of her path as she took a seat on the plush chair. She rested Spook in her lap and sat with an elegant posture, like a queen on her throne. "So, what will I see, Gordon? What history have you viewed so far?"

Gordon was ready to answer, summing up the history Lady Arachne would view. He wasn't sure where she'd be dropped in, or if she'd even see the story from the point-of-view he'd peered through. Perhaps the battle to take back Azur-Fah would've passed into history. It could possibly be the late seventeen-hundreds, and Lady Arachne's desire to find the lost Lovers would bring her focus to the definitive history that would locate their sketching's whereabouts. Gordon took a seat on a large and round, orange pillow. He folded his legs and looked up at Lady Arachne with a curious expression she likened to Martin Clyde's visiting spirit.

"Why was it so easy to turn black people against one another?" he asked.

His inquiry made Lady Arachne flinch just the same as his standing presence when she walked into the basement. He was no longer sending to her, but she felt the weight of every heavy syllable in the words constructing his question.

Lady Arachne didn't have a direct answer for Gordon, but she voiced an observation. "The *grèf*'s politics to trick us against one another continue to this day. It permeates our neighborhoods, makes us violent as opportunities to live are stripped away. It splits us into classes of religion, politics, and wealth—education or financial. The legendary Pious Wars are a reminder that we were arguing before our oppressors showed up. Arguing on the possibility of the terrible happenings that have occurred since those lost times." She took a breath to sigh. Then she continued, "There were those misguided Africans that were duped into assisting Europe in the dismantling of other African nations, or as you've reported, believed the terrible occurrence would stir something in us. Change us. A Grand Alchemy. Oh,

Gordon, the things we will embrace in an attempt to absolve us from responsibility of standing up and fighting back. Fear and ego are a terrible mixed drink, and we've had an unalike bartender keeping us drunk off the foul spirit to keep the world mundane. All so their dysfunctional rathskeller can exist." She sat back, queenly and divine in her poise. "Is that the history that's made up your dreams?"

Gordon nodded his head and affirmed. But he thought of Victus-Seizan's rebellion. He thought of glimpsing the world's original three moons. He thought of holding Fey in a time long ago. He recalled The Lovers card and its wondrous design. And he thought of Azur-Fah, the Silver World. "Yes," he told Lady Arachne. "But, I've seen really beautiful things too. I hope you see them as well, Lady Arachne." He stood, and with a trickster's triumphant grin, Gordon teased, "Now, it's time for bed, young lady."

Lady Arachne retorted, "Since you used the word 'young', I won't argue." She chuckled and reclined in the chair. She lifted Spook off her thighs and laid back with the primordial tech clasped on her chest, arms folded over.

Sleep was immediate, too quick for Lady Arachne to be surprised by the slumbering sensation taking her over. Darkness rippled, and then it became still until silk strands were spun across the sable void in an intricate network of fine threads that stitched history into existence.

The webbing first knitted an age accented by conjure and bloody, philosophical feuds. It didn't linger, but it lowered its view on a woman who was a major participant at the end of the sanguinary matters. Oris Del traveled across many lands infested with people hexed and misshapen by burden. Conjured serpent-lions provided her protection and sanctuary as she could slip inside their translucent, crystalline physiques for safety. She found a survivor hunkered down in a lecture dome at the center of a ravaged settlement. Ziko Yswil. He'd crafted a magnificent weapon, a hammer-pick laced with powerful alchemical properties to battle the wretched horde. Together they discovered other survivors, created a temporary kingdom, put together a motley crew of warriors, and teamed with factions from around the world to put an end to the long, calamitous schism.

A cosmic spider crawled across the scene, and a transition in time occurred.

Theft and betrayal next played in dream. It was seventeenth-century Europe where two, Moorish families resided. Allied conjure folk assisted in the heist of mystical items from a secret order. It wasn't long before the revelation of antagonistic viewpoints invaded a peaceful dinner. Family-close friends turned into mortal rivals. Rape. Murder. Enslavement. The discord between the families would continue even in the aftermath of that blood-soaked night.

Another crawl across time. Night. Two shadows scurried through the darkness rendering guards unconscious in quick scuffles. Son. Mother. They blinked in and out of existence across a well-fortified slave port. Hope for the captured sons and daughters of Africa resting deep in the stronghold's belly. An otherworldly encounter with the slave warden offered Lady Arachne, as the dreamer, a glimpse at a long-lost item she so very much desired. A strong emotion that was without sin and as potent as the elevated compassion illustrated on its face.

The dream shook as the matriarch's body convulsed, her mind attempting to reach out through time and seize the missing Lovers card. She had no mystical device to ground her, and she was almost shaken from the depths of history's dreamy retelling. A soft and gentle lilac hum eased her quiver, but her sight locked onto The Lovers card, and she saw history through its design.

Mother. Son. Love of child and parent. Love of Africa. Love of conjure and the world's first people. They brought freedom to those in chains, but it didn't release them from the shackles of burden. The man in the card's illustration turned to a young boy, and he was pulled away to the Americas. The dreaming conjure woman flinched as the card tore in half, flipped around with its two pieces and mended back together with a scene of the boy grown up. Shovel in hand. On a plantation in America. Conjure manifested, he drove that shovel's purple-glowing head into the ground, both hands on the tool. Up. From the depths. There rose the captured, accosted, and murdered African to make war with the devils of the plantation and burn it to the ground.

Victory.

Then flipped the card again. A new scene on its face.

Some stories begin with irony. Webbing dissolved through the parallel histories of two tricksters, rivals in righteousness and sin. Two sides, one coin. So close in conflict, they could be considered brothers or friends. The Fates' toss of their coin was always a means to find balance between them, with enough flips to one day hope their struggle against one another would land on its edge. Peace be obtained.

A philosophical ideology concerning the African slave trade was at the heart of their antagonism. The sinner considered it necessary, a terrible happening that would result in an illustrious alchemy inside an ancient people. The first people. The righteous one didn't hold to these ideals. Their contention folded over outside of time, where a pantheon of star-watching deities would fall victim to the misguided sinner's sly beguilements. Lady Arachne saw the Maiden kingdom fall, and the righteous trickster retreat with its royal family.

Back in time. Crossing the African sands. The trickster didn't concede defeat.

He would regroup and return to defy, what had become in his story, the tyrannous stars.

The face of The Lovers card returned to its glorious sketch.

Webs were spun over it, covering the entire scene.

Souls. Here. Now.

"I've been chosen to tell your story…"

Fresh, silver strands crisscrossed and formed a tangled trellis against a black, starry backdrop. The cosmic silk was spun over and over, connecting the stars until it filled the celestial setting's entirety. The lacework tightened and locked, turning thick and changing color like a leaf in autumn. Brown. Swirling. A tendril of sunlight reflected off the color and drew out a faint, hidden, deep and rich purple tone.

There she stood, barefoot and beautiful in her radiating brown skin. A silk nightgown, gifted by the island's royal family, clothed her graceful frame. Princess Qkumo-Ṣẹda balanced on a balcony railing high atop the Del-Yswil palace, situated outside of her guestroom. Her head was tilted up, facing the bright, morning sun as it rose over the watery horizon. Eyes closed and beaming a wide smile, she bathed in the sun's rays, hands behind her back and chest out. She absorbed the light, and used conjure to grow her hair, intertwined and twisted atop her head into tight, thick dreadlocks that were coiled together by ancient magic and the light cast by the sun. It tickled, but not in the same annoyance as might otherwise be experienced. It felt like breathing, exhaling.

The top of her head was now a garden of tight and thick woolly vines dangling past her shoulders, curled as her previous crown of hair. Ovate face framed in flocculent beauty.

Her footing was perfect. Still as a statue, but that didn't stop her friend Tyle from rushing through her room and onto the balcony with his hands out. "Princess!" he called. "Please, be careful. You could fall!"

Ṣẹda opened one eye, grin ablaze. "Oh, Tyle!" she snapped in a playful manner. She teased him further by extending one foot over the railing and taking a step out onto nothing. Ṣẹda didn't fall, remaining upright and in the air. She turned, levitating high above the far below ground. She addressed her friend collected and calm, "Don't be silly." Tyle huffed and crossed his arms. Ṣẹda chuckled at his antics. Then she tilted her head back and opened her arms out wide. "I'm letting the sun lock my hair!" she told him. The princess hugged herself and let the sun, mixed with incant she provided, conclude twisting and tightening her fluffy locks. Nature's grooming service assisted by magic. Finished. She paced back onto the railing and glided down on the terrace's surface. "I'd been waiting to get my ceremonial regrowth, but then…" Her voice turned somber. Reality set in. She was not a tenant at a bright and new luxurious castle for an extended period of recreation. She was a refugee. Her kingdom had fallen. Ṣẹda cleared her throat and attempted perking up. "It was lovely to take a day. Forget, if only for a little while." She barely held onto the merry spirit mustered in her voice.

Knocking rapped against the door before Tyle could speak. He twirled and faced the entrance into the extravagant guestroom. Ṣẹda peered over his shoulder, and both she and he spied the door. A second series of knocks tapped against it. Tyle again was interrupted from speaking. As he went to form words to reveal the person on the other side of the door, there came Iune Del-Yswil's voice, "Princess…" He stopped, remembering again she preferred being addressed common. "…Ṣẹda. We break fall—" Iune groaned. "Sorry… W-w-we break…fast soon."

Tyle finally got to put in a word. He turned his head to the princess and remarked, "So much rattle in his voice, he's like a baby's toy."

Ṣẹda slapped Tyle on the arm as she walked by him. "Stop that!" she chided. "He's a trickster, and he's doing his best to be polite. He's a nice young man, but making a game and amusement about all things is a reflex to him. He's trying." She shuffled into the room and traveled to the door. She heard Iune call for her again. "Yes, Iune. Thank you," she responded. "I'm not proper…er…*dressed* at the moment. I still need to take a bath." She bounced on her tip-toes and sported a wide smile, saying, "I was putting the finishing touches on my regrowth of hair." She turned, put her back against the door, hands behind her. "I used incant and sunrays to regrow and lock." She went silent and thought about her circumstances, and how things changed so quickly.

Iune said from the other side of the door, "I have attendants with me like yesterday. They're at the ready to fill your tub with water, temper it with the correct heat a-a-a-and even suds…"

Ṣẹda bubbled, "That sounds delightful, and much needed." She opened the door slightly and stepped aside. "Send them in." Three robed women wearing tall and angled headwraps passed through the door. Iune remained in the hall, back turned out of courtesy. Ṣẹda made a quick glance from around the door. He was still in his bedclothes, a long silk shirt and silk pants. His feet were bare as usual. She closed the door, and he remained outside.

Ṣẹda followed the women behind a dressing screen etched with the Del-Yswil heraldry, a hammer-pick with its head aglow, bubbling energy. Intertwined around its handle, and stretching in three directions, were creatures Ṣẹda considered to be very peculiar. The one extending to the left was red. The middle, aimed straight up, was black. The one extended to the right was green. They had the bodies of serpents and the heads of lions.

One woman stood at the head of the bathtub. The other two on either side. They sang an incant in harmony and water filled Ṣẹda's bath. A second mystical and sweet-sounding string of notations were crooned, and the water's temperature was warmed to a suitable degree. The women flowed into a final otherworldly hymn, and suds populated the top of the water. Ṣẹda warmed without having stepped foot into the heated water. Seeing conjure on display made her feel at home and less a refugee. She thanked the women, and they bowed to her with a polite dip of their heads. Then they gave the princess her privacy as she unclothed and slipped into the cozy waters to bathe.

Tyle remained on the balcony, gazing out to the breathtaking view the island's horizon had to offer. His head turned by instinct and spotted the three women standing in the middle of the room at the foot of the bed. They were giggling and staring at him. Tyle blushed and faced the rising sun again with a wide smile on his face.

Bathed and dried. Freshened and primped. Ṣẹda slipped into a new set of clothes gifted by the royal family. She clothed herself in a red and gold, frill-trimmed, skirt layered with three tiers. A white, long-sleeved shirt hung loose on her and dipped past her waist. Ṣẹda left her feet bare, but her neck was decorated with the crystal fastened to the gold chain her father gifted her at the inauguration. She sat patient as the three women slipped gold bands onto her newly tightened dreadlocks. She loved the accent of the jewels hugging her thick, brown and black coils of hair. She admired her reflection in a long mirror mounted on the wall in front of her as she placed large, looped earrings in her ear. Tyle complimented her look, especially the bands lining her dreadlocks. Finished, Ṣẹda jumped from her stool. With Tyle by her side, and led by the three women, she exited the room. Iune was there waiting, patient, back still turned to the room.

Ṣẹda walked up behind him and said in a teasing tone, "I'm decent, Iune." She continued moving forward.

Iune pivoted, but he didn't follow. He was stone at first, unmoving as his eyes moved up and down the newly, dreadlock-crowned princess. He could barely breathe at the sight. He choked on sounds coming from an agape mouth. Then he coughed, which stirred him to shake himself to motion, hurrying forward to match the small entourage's strides. Tyle fell in tow, and Iune and Ṣẹda were between he and the three palace maidens. There was quiet for quite some time. Iune snatched glances at the princess from the corner of his eye, observing her from hair to clothes and everything in between. Her newly formed dreadlocks changed her glow. Without them she was beautiful. With them she appeared so different, but so much in the same beauty. Iune made a quick turn of his head, facing the princess next to him. He had something to tell her, but he hesitated, unsure if diving into conversation on building an army was appropriate. The conflict stirred mostly because that wasn't his aim altogether. Iune had ulterior motives. He found himself looking at the princess for too long, and he needed to justify his stare. So, he spoke, "My sister has scheduled a journey to one of the local taverns. There is a group of rogues that will help the cause of taking your kingdom back."

Ṣẹda looked over at Iune. She couldn't help but smile at the trickster. "Thank you. I'm restless about the situation. I try not to think about—"

Iune interrupted, "Forgive me, Ṣẹda! I wasn't trying to make you think about the tragedy that's occurred, mire you in it."

"No, no, Iune!" Ṣẹda politely protested. "No. What I mean is the beauty of your island can make me forget why I'm here. It's so comforting. Outside of time. I feel at home. From my room I have the lovely sights of your island's simple villages and towns, or walking around on the streets, as your sister took me yesterday for shopping. The sea. The sand. The sun on the horizon. Then reality sets in, and I remember this isn't for leisure. My land is under strife. Inside of time, Africa is under strife too. I am them. They are me. We're connected. Inside of time. Outside of time. I'm an African woman all the time. Not sometime. Not on occasion." She spoke honestly when she said to Iune, "It does comfort me that there are people working for reconquest of my homeland."

Iune nodded his head and looked forward. There was an absence of life in his expression, and Ṣẹda deciphered he was nervous as well, very anxious. She faced forward too.

Neither Iune nor Ṣẹda could see the knowing grin on Tyle's face as his eyes went back and forth between trickster and princess, or the truth he could feel resonating from them both.

Ṣẹda decided to coax Iune into a more suitable disposition. She considered a trickster should never be in a sour mood, and so she had a play to put in motion. Before she spoke, her eyes spotted his bare feet decorated with a single lilac feather. Her eyes raised and looked at Iune. "Our fathers were sharing war stories last night," she detailed. "They probably went late into the night. I heard a few. I had to get sleep. They were smoking herb and drinking. Our mothers and sisters were chatting up their own storm. Your mother was a brave champion! She spoke of her grand conjures, but she never described them." Iune turned to her as they made their way down a flight of stairs.

"They were taken from her by Ariq-Haunts," Iune explained. "Serpent-lions. Magnificent creatures."

"Like those of your royal insignia?"

"Yes," Iune answered.

Then Ṣẹda positioned her play. "You have stories, Iune," said the princess. "What adventures have you been on? I heard of a Hall of Treasures documenting your exploits, trickster. What trophies have you procured?"

It was immediate. Iune perked up. He lifted a finger and corrected, "They are not trophies, princess! They are acquirements." His smile was corrected as well. It fixed, curled devious as memories blossomed in his brain. "Let us take a detour," he suggested. He told the three palace maidens leading them, "Through the Treasure Hall, please." There was no nod of their heads or look in his direction to express a facial or audible acknowledgement. The women simply made the necessary turns once down the flight of stairs, taking the trickster-prince and his royal guests to the requested chamber.

The hall lit up. Treasures on display. Their aura of conjure tugged on Ṣẹda and Tyle straightaway, pulling wide looks of wonder to the surface. Iune had a bright expression too, but it was stimulated with the stories he could tell for the items he secured. One caught his eye. A bracelet made of eight, large and lustrous tiger-eye beads. He waved Ṣẹda and Tyle to him. "This object right here has a tale," he said in an excited manner, pointing. "The Eight Eyes of The Tiger. Simple in its buff to give strength to its wearer. So, it attracted numerous brutes in wish to increase their physical prowess. One such man was named Yomelele. A very large, wandering, ogre-like man. I swear he had *nlawọ* blood in him. Never seen someone of such extraction— my parents have. But even in my inexperience with such an ethnicity, I'm sure this man shared some blood. He just didn't have the green skin or protruding tusks. But he sure did have the fight! He had no home, but he wanted to make a kingdom rightfully his. He did just that, stealing the bracelet and taking over a kingdom with it. An army of one. A few of the folk did a ritual, and I was called in. This ogre-man and I fought!"

"Oh, my!" expressed Tyle, hand on his chest.

Ṣẹda raised an eyebrow, intrigued.

Iune elaborated, "Not hand-to-hand. No. If I did that, I would've been checked straight into a graveyard. No. It was my speed against his amplified, brutish strength. I raced around him on all fours. He couldn't catch me, and that whipped him into a frenzy—as I planned. The people scattered, and I took the fight into the streets. He chased me! He was berserk! I jumped onto the Brute King's wrist, trying to wriggle the bracelet off his arm. The king slammed his mighty fist into a tower, and I scurried around to his back, dodging before I was crushed between his fist and the sturdy spire. I wrapped my arms around his thick neck. He bucked like a bull, screaming. A large shadow fell over us, and I looked up. The tower was falling, and I only had seconds to react. They were all I needed. I had confidence in my speed. I hastened to his wrist again and snatched the item off the king! The tower collapsed on us!"

"You were killed?" blurted Tyle, but promptly understood his blunder.

The palace maidens chuckled. Ṣẹda did the same. Iune was polite, but still quipped, "Well, not really. I am here to tell the tale, after all." Tyle blushed, especially as he made an eye at the giggling maidens. Iune's quip didn't help either. But the trickster continued, "No. I was able to shimmy the bracelet off his arm. You can see, it's large enough for me to wear as a necklace. I was impervious then. The tower toppled, crushed him, but I was left unscathed. The people were thrilled, even though there was substantial damage to their kingdom. The true king had an heir, and he took up his slain father's duties. I was a little disappointed."

"Why?" asked Ṣẹda.

"I *did* want to fight that ogre-of-a-man hand-to-hand, but with the bracelet's granted strength. I utilized the trinket's value by helping the people clean up the tower's rubble. I did so without a sweat or assistance." He moved down the hall a few more paces. Ṣẹda and Tyle followed. The maidens remained behind. Iune aimed a finger at a small display where floated a golden seal with mystical symbols etched into its face. A bright-red ruby sparkled at the center of the amulet. Iune began, "Some stories are sad. A man named Aalam Bankole. He conjured me, and I had to adhere to his wishes to bring him luck as he sneaked through a maze of traps guarding this item. He called the charm Elan's Endless Dance. The bauble apparently prolongs life, and he was attempting to outlive his children so they couldn't inherit his fortune. He didn't want to leave it to the state or make any charitable donation."

"Perhaps he should've learned an incant that dissolved his fortune on his death," Tyle proposed.

"Would've served him better," Iune agreed. "He instead went for this, and I had to appease according to ritual law. But he got drunk one night on our expedition, and he went off at the mouth when it came to his plans. I don't adhere to misfortune or misdeeds; and misuse of my summoning puts a person in mortal danger. There was no exception with Aalam. My bind to him from ritual was severed, and he would suffer the consequences with his life."

"Oh, my!" gasped Tyle.

Ṣẹda listened close to Iune's tale.

Iune took up, "He slept hard, intoxicated. I journeyed forward, outsmarting all the traps ahead, and I retrieved the amulet. When we woke the next day, I presented the charm to him. *What luck you bring!* he exclaimed to me. I told him he needed to be branded with the item. Over his heart. Truthfully, all he really had to do was wear it around his neck. His greed clouded his judgment, and I bet on that sentiment being strong enough to coax him into doing something tremendously stupid. He was opened to the deed, removing his shirt and baring his chest. So, I heated the amulet in our campfire after attaching it to the end of one of my horn-lances. I prodded him over his heart. He gritted his teeth as the heat melted his flesh. The smell was intense, and it almost knocked me out. I backed away and used an incant to cool and keloid the burn. The bewitched symbols were now on his chest, but in reverse. He clutched his heart as life was sapped from him, not extended. He died right in front of me."

"Clever," remarked Ṣẹda.

Anger and remorse twisted Iune's expression. "Cruel as well," he added, the boast gone from his voice. "I delivered his body to his son and daughter. His fortune was theirs. The idiot was so mad with his plans to outlive his children, he made no paperwork to keep them from their rightful inheritance. I've watched them since, and their descendants. That was two-hundred years ago, or so. I never told them the cruelty of their father. The fortune has served them well. I lost track of them in the last twenty years or so. The Sanqa nation," Iune named. "I hope they're okay—with all the trouble befalling Africa."

"They should be, Iune," Ṣẹda said to him. "I'd imagine they'd conjure you if trouble rose for their people."

Iune nodded. He led Ṣẹda and Tyle back to the three palace maidens. The women took lead and guided the party out of the hall. They retraced their steps to put them back on course to the dining hall for the day's first meal. Tyle again walked in tow, and Ṣẹda and Iune walked side-by-side ahead of him.

Iune felt invigorated by telling his tales, even if he'd ended on a doleful note. He looked at the princess and realized that's what she had planned when she inquired about his adventures. "Thank you," he expressed to her. "Your hair looks beautiful, and so do you, Your Majesty." His voice was strong with confidence, as if each syllable wore the Eight Eyes of The Tiger bracelet he'd just chatted about.

"Thank you, *Prince* Iune." Ṣẹda was sincere in her reply, but titling the trickster as a 'prince' carried a teasing tone. Iune didn't mind.

"I feel guilty," he said. "I look at you, Ṣẹda, and I forget about the tragedy that brought you here. I feel…joy at your sight and presence that you are here at all." Then he confessed, "I brought up the mention of my sister heading to the tavern because I was hoping you would join—Tyle too. It won't be all battle plans. Music. Drink. Dance!"

"I would like that, Iune," she told him, voice soft and sincere. Then she knocked her shoulder against the back of his shoulder. "I'll put you to work, trickster. You'll serve me even without a proper ritual done to justify your presence."

Iune grinned. He looked away for a moment, and then he said directly to the princess, "There's a sly line I could say, but I'd rather be a gentleman."

"Where's the adventure in that, trickster?" the princess cooed.

Iune considered Ṣẹda's point, and so he yielded by telling her, "I was going to say: Your alluring presence is ritual enough to summon me."

Ṣẹda rolled her eyes and laughed. "Oh, please! I'm not that easy."

"At being offended or impressed?" he asked.

"Both!" she answered. "Not at a silly line like that, at least." When their laughter cooled, Ṣẹda enlightened, "I've had adventures too, Iune Del-Yswil. Wild hunts with my father. We were saving creatures from poachers rather than hunting game. We rescued wildlife no longer roaming inside of time. Their pelts and blood have mystical properties, often sold to people inside time. The venom too." Her smile faded, and she thought of other happenings in her life. "Most of my stories have dire consequences." She told Iune of the time Etti-Iyansan assisted his hero, Ithun's, mother and father. Iune was aware, but he listened to Ṣẹda speak. Her air lightened, and even illuminated when she said, "I remember most a feeling of conjure as time in motion, expressing itself through Etti-Iyansan's power as she held my hand. It was like being in the heavens with the stars singing their shine to you."

They came to the dining hall, and Ṣẹda was crowded by her sisters and mother. Her female cousins and aunts joined in as well. Tyle, her father, uncles, and male cousins stood on the outside of the feminine circle surrounding Ṣẹda. Iune too moved aside. The swarm buzzed with admiration for her hair. Iune was swallowed up by Olobiri and Ithun's presence, Jai Chilla and Kioi, too. Iuen exchanged stories with the new troupe encircling him, but talk went quiet when they sat for the meal. Queen Halitta led a prayer as Ṣẹda and her sisters hummed in tune behind their mother's virtuous words.

The meal was remarkable, but it wasn't the reason for the sudden quiet. The silence made Ṣẹda recount the first day's meal. It was dinner, and filled with chatter. King Ziko and her father started their first round of exchanging boastful, adventurous stories.

This silence was uneasy.

Looking up and seeing Iune across the table, their eyes met and he winked, but the tension she felt didn't ease. Her instinct decrypted that her father was the center of the noiseless void. It increased the pressure Ṣẹda felt for both the need to speak and remain silent.

Speaking won the day. "Pa-pa," she said in a low voice. "You've said there's a hidden way into Azur-Fah, discovered as part of your travels. A tenth Star Path, correct?"

The prince consort continued eating. Everyone was consumed by his coldness. They kept to their meals, heads low.

Princess Tinta thought her father rude for ignoring Ṣẹda. She snapped, "Pa-pa! Ṣẹda asked a question. Ma-ma, make him answer!"

"Now look, young ladies!" scolded Prince Raji to his daughters. "It took a day, but it's settled in." Queen Halitta rubbed his back for comfort. He looked up, spotting King Ziko and Queen Oris. "I have no army here. No reason to aim my sword and shout a command. Men lay dying outside of time, in our kingdom. Our people's blood stain my hands, and I feel the weight on the breaking of Africa and the first people of the world. This Chief Ariq Haunts has neutered me."

"Pa-pa…!" pleaded Ṣẹda.

"He has!" the prince consort insisted. "I had a nightmare last night, a grotesque look at what has happened. There was so much noise, screaming. Men, women, and children gurgled on their blood. Forgive me if I don't mind sitting in shame and silence." The people at the table retreated to their meals, and the prince consort was overcome with the coldness of his own hostility. He sighed, "I apologize. Last night I smoked, I drank, and I forgot. My nightmares reminded me."

"We're all here together," said Queen Halitta. Her hand returned to her husband's back, rubbing and soothing him with a calming incant.

He looked at Ṣẹda and said, "I am so sorry. Yes. You're correct. There's a hidden path. A woman named Nanni Mayya Storii, an illegitimate daughter of a spirit named Aluvaiá. She can commune with the gates and open them from her position." He ate, chewed, and swallowed. There was conviction on his face as he pondered a strategy for action once inside. "But what will we do then?" His eyes were on Iune and Zoya. They had a promise to raise an army. He wanted, if not needed, to be assured—sold on the notion.

"We'll use simple mathematics, Your Majesty," said Zoya, all certainty in her voice. "The Ifo warriors are few. Strong, yes, but few. We'll battle them down to their numbers. We'll have the bigger army."

"They've poisoned six kingdoms," noted Prince Raji. "Surely the chief will have seduced more to his ranks, and perhaps culled the power of the bewitched Eterijah."

"The hidden path is your advantage, Prince Consort," said Queen Oris Del. "If there is a ruse to be played, my son will exploit it. Luck will be with you. If it's an army you need, my daughter will forge you one. She'll have warriors falling in line for you to command." She sat up straight and told Prince Raji, "I know how you feel—sterilized. Ariq Haunts stole my power from me." She reminisced, sadness in her eyes despite maintaining a smile on her face. "I could conjure serpent lions. Beautiful, crystalline beasts. I still try and reach out to them, feel them, and pull them back to our world. But like the world's three moons, they are gone." She raised her hand and displayed her palms. "As you can see, I have no lines in my hands. The miscreant filled in my flesh using a hexed crystal. My power was sapped, and my lovely beasts were taken from me."

King Ziko held his wife's hands. He said to Prince Raji, "I can gift you my hammer-pick, Prince Consort. My stories are behind me. I don't long for battle for new stories to boast. My daughter and son have inherited the braggart's tongue. Their footprints have enough ink, and their mouths filled with enough breath to speak even my wife and I's stories."

"Iune, anyway," Zoya joked regarding her father's words on a 'mouth full of breath'.

A wave of light laughter circled the table.

Iune saluted his sister for the quip with a repetitive, downward wave of his hand.

Prince Raji rejected King Ziko's offer. "Thank you, King Ziko for the gesture. It's tempting to wield a legendary weapon that you talk up so much, but my sword is all I'll need." He said to Zoya. "Within time or outside of time, it still ticks away. We can't wait forever. Where is this army?"

"Pa-Pa!" Ṣẹda reproved her father for his forcefulness.

Zoya waved her hand. "It's okay, Ṣẹda," she assured. "Prince Consort, I have close relations to rogues scattered about our island's taverns. I know tonight they'll gather at a dive called *Ole ọkan*. These rogues are also representatives to a unified African nation of tribes collectively called Mai Gadi. They can round up more soldiers as needed. They also have items of conjure, these tribes. Your kingdom will be secured, and all of Constellation will be cured of its seven poisons. Chief Ariq Haunts and his Six Others will fall."

Talk of war eased Prince Raji. He relaxed in his chair and resumed eating, actually tasting and enjoying the meal. Conversations started as a low murmur. By the meal's end, talk was a pulsating clamor. The dining table was abandoned by a few of the participants, but they didn't leave the room. Iune stood in a corner talking with Olobiri and Ithun, wooden goblets filled with wine in their hands. Iune explained to Ithun that he and Olobiri were brothers-in-horn, elucidating on Olobiri's ability to shift his hair into curved and hard outgrowths. He described his skill to conjure gazelle-horn short lances. Ithun interjected, "I know of your skills, Iune. I grew up listening to stories. From your vest to the feathers on your feet."

"Yes. All blessings from very grateful sorceresses," he confirmed. "Olobiri is also my sibling-in-trick. Zoya is blood, and she has a trick or two. She's swift in tongue, and her negotiation skills are unmatched. That's three members. With you, we'd be four."

Ithun inquired, "Are you asking me to join your pantheon of tricksters?"

Iune burst into excitement. "Yes!" he exclaimed. He knocked back a hard gulp of his drink. "Absolutely! We could get word out among the nations and states in Africa. We would be called the Clever Folk! Our exploits would go to Amexem, what they call the New World, the Americas. Adventure would await freeing captives and cutting down slaveowners."

Ithun was reminded of his brother Seizan. "That's where my mother and I seek to go."

Iune's face lit up. "Really?"

Ithun told the trickster, "My brother was taken into slavery."

Iune's bright expression dimmed. "I'm so sorry…"

Olobiri understood all too well.

Ithun's head dropped. He indulged in a swallow of wine. "That undertaking would be very personal for my mother and I. Personal and private." He looked up and saw Iune attempting to hide an expression of hurt brought on by his rejection. Ithun spotted Kioi and Jai Chilla across the room, standing against the wall and keeping to themselves. "You have recruits there."

Iune turned in the direction where Ithun aimed. He shook his head, disappointment and hesitation flooding his eyes. "No. No. No, I don't," he responded, making Olobiri chuckle. "I'd take Ariq Haunts before them—if he could be reformed, that is."

"Perhaps the tavern rogues your sister speaks of," Ithun tried again.

This time it was Olobiri's turn to scoff. His face screwed, and he huffed.

Ithun asked, "Did I say another wrong?"

"They can be rough," described Olobiri. "Too rough to be a trickster. They prefer a straight fight than sneaking around. Loud too."

"Strong has the makings of a trickster," Iune debated. He grinned and said to Ithun, "Don't let Olobiri's words fool you. There's one among these rogues named Hakim. He and my sister can often times be very close." Iune stepped back and beamed a teasing smirk at Olobiri. He divulged, "And Olobiri fancies my sister." He walked backwards, turned around, and made his way to Kioi and Jai Chilla. Halfway to where the two stood, Zoya snatched Iune's goblet of wine.

"Not too much to drink!" she upbraided her brother. "It's early. We're heading to the tavern soon. Let's be sober when we appeal for assistance."

Iune gave his sister a face, but he continued his strides toward Kioi and Jai Chilla instead of putting up a fight for his drink. Both men stepped off the wall they leaned against and stood up straight when Iune arrived. The trickster believed the two were going to salute, but they remained still as statues waiting for him to speak.

"You two are in your rights to take leave. There's nothing for you here," Iune told them. "There's no Cosmic Charter because there's no such thing as a Cosmic Charter, not as you believe." Iune wished he had his drink now. He even looked at his hand hoping his goblet of wine would manifest. He returned his gaze to Kioi and Jai Chilla and declared, "The atrocity you're trying to run away from is real. European nations are enslaving Africans and sending them across this ocean to their colonies in Amexem. Few can defend themselves with conjure. Its magic ebbs in these dark times. No paperwork is going to get you out of the responsibility of being on your two feet and making a stand against evil. We're all connected. No name change will save you. No believing this is only their story, those who've been captured, or somehow we're different and not them." He put his hands on his hips and noted, "There *is* a slight difference in us. We can be the conjured. We can be their spirit. Proper ritual performed will guide us to aid them." Kioi and Jai Chilla stared at Iune with a blank look in their eyes. He kicked the ground, looking down and searching for what more to say. Again, he addressed them, "There are those of us that are terribly misguided. They can be conjured from outside of time, like myself. Or they can be inside of time, whole nations of terrified Africans assisting evil men in enslaving their own people. It's not the majority of the horror story going on out there, but it is part of the reality we're facing. These are brothers and sisters we're fighting, which is why we'll make the kill swift for them. Then we'll be the conjured ready to assist the spirit of those fighting back, from here to Amexem. You're welcomed to join, my brothers."

Kioi and Jai Chilla looked at one another, and then at Iune. Kioi replied, "Iune Del-Yswil, it would be an honor if I could join you!" He put out his hand. Iune accepted, and they shook.

Jai Chilla extended a hand. "I'm with you, too!" he proclaimed. Iune shook his hand and informed them they would set out to the tavern to gather a few rogues for the coming battle. Both men said they would join, and Iune walked away. Jai Chilla said to Kioi, "Thank you, Kioi. I've seen so much of the world. Thank you for bringing it to me, putting it all in front of my eyes. All of this."

Kioi threw his arm around his short apprentice and pulled him close. "I accept your gratitude, good learner. Now it's time to get drunk and find bountiful women before we die in battle!"

"Die?" questioned Jai Chilla.

Kioi tapped Jai Chilla's shoulder with a balled fist. "Not just die! A fine, fitting death! Noble!" The words did nothing to put Jai Chilla's mind at ease. The two walked forward to join the circle of drink and conversation.

Later. A party of young upstarts headed out to the *Ole ọkan* roadhouse. Zoya led the band consisting of her brother, the trickster Iune, now clothed in his signature attire. His chief friend and brother-in-horn, Olobiri. The shadow-hider, Ithun al-Kaadi. The maladroit scoundrels, Kioi and his apprentice, Jai Chilla. Also, among their number was royalty from a mystical and cosmic realm. Second Princess to the Maiden Kingdom, Qkumo-Ṣẹda, heir apparent to the reigning Eterijah, star-steward, and her close friend, truth-seer and the palace fool, Tyle.

The last of the sun was on the horizon, sighing its final lighted breath. The beach held tight to its golden sparkle with the remaining rays, and the sky was painted with a gradient of purple to faint blue. A few stars twinkled bright, signaling gazers of the dawning, night sky. All were in full bloom by the time the party arrived at the tavern.

They were welcomed with cheers and raised cups, and Iune and Zoya introduced the newcomers along with the politics that brought them to the island. The rogues Zoya looked to recruit were there, and to Ṣẹda's surprise, they were few in number. Four men. There was Strong, a slim and bald man with light-brown skin. He was dressed in a tight, sleeveless shirt that had a multi-colored pattern around the shoulders and neck, black everywhere else. A brass diadem was around his head with a tall, white feather protruding from the front. He was clothed in green, baggy pants and sandals. He was a man of the world. A wanderer that found himself in adventure after adventure, and in doing so, studied the many hand-to-hand combat practices from cultures far and wide. A ritual to Iune before a voyage saved his life and brought him to Del-Yswil when a storm destroyed the vessel and killed all aboard. He was saved. Iune's luck.

Next was Hakim. A brawny, dark-skinned man with dreadlocks and a thick beard. He reminded Ṣẹda of her father from his stature to his clothes, and the intimidating sword strapped to his waist. He wore orange pants that were tucked into brown boots. He was covered with a matching shirt, yellow sash, and a white cape. His head was tucked into a turban that, like Strong's diadem, was decorated with a bird's feather.

Next was Aeshop, brown of skin, tall with a warrior's muscular frame. His robes were dark-blue and gold. A red headwrap covered his locks, though a few dangled loose. A sword and dagger were at his hip, a monkey rested on his shoulder, and a drink was in his hand. His sideburns grew down into thick blotches that lined his face, though his upper lip and chin were naked of hair.

Malik was the fourth man. His color was the same as Aeshop. His clothes were a green cape, lined with a yellow trim. White pants on his legs and a sash wrapped around his torso, leaving shoulders and half his chest exposed. On his head was a brimless, short, and rounded cap. He was a man of the spear, but his weapon was not on his person. These were men of action, impatient for the fight as they sat around in leisure.

Ṣẹda noted their scarce number, but she was quickly reminded on their connection to soldiers inside of time. She was happy to hear the men agreed to serve in armed conflict, eager for battle. They bowed graciously at her whenever she was present, addressing her as 'princess' or 'Royal Majesty'. They expressed their sympathies on hearing her kingdom's fate, but she could see awe behind their faces, a brightness that lay bare the admiration for beholding a woman from a realm of myth and legend. They were imposing, these formidable, African warriors. Ṣẹda didn't know their origins, but if someone told her they were physical electives deputized to carry the banner for thunder itself, she would believe the tale.

Hakim greeted Zoya with a kiss on her hand, commenting, "I hope we're at least friends at this gathering and when going into war, lovely woman."

Iune glanced at Olobiri. His friend was stone faced. Iune slid between his sister and the warrior. "You're a charmer," he answered as if Hakim was addressing him. He pointed to a table hosting a game of cards. "Don't we have a score to settle?"

Hakim turned and looked at the table. "We do," he grinned. He couldn't resist a good game, a formidable opponent, or a rematch. Iune represented all three.

The trickster peeked at Olobiri, catching his friend's eyes. Iune signaled with a hand gesture that he would keep Hakim busy. But that wasn't Olobiri's aim. He made a quick face and hand wave at Iune, an indication that everything was fine. Olobiri even joined in on the game with an ulterior motive to best the warrior in some form of combat. Iune set up each round for Olobiri to take the pot.

"It looks as if your luck has faltered against your brother-in-horn," Hakim teased after Olobiri's third win.

"Has it now?" retorted Iune with a knowing smile.

The band played raucous, mixing the elements of sporadic, Moorish music with heavy and intense tribal, African percussions. Dance ensued. Iune shared fancy footwork with Ṣẹda and Tyle. The room spun, and drink sloshed in the patrons' heads. Incants to keep balance were ignored, and liquid spirits were allowed to possess the brain.

Ṣẹda remained lucid, but not through any magic performed or innate tolerance. Her instinct continued guiding her eyesight to the door, looking beyond by means of a higher sense of sight. She saw the night. The beach. The horizon. The breeze that moved the ocean in trails invisible to normal folk. Finding a pause in the carousel, Ṣẹda made her exit from the spirit-house. Iune's eye caught her leave, and he followed.

Outside. Iune kept several paces behind Ṣẹda. She knew he was there, and she was aware he was giving her space to travel where her instinct was leading her. The beach. The ocean's water rushed inland, surrounding her sandal-laced feet. Ṣẹda cast a wave of conjure behind her that surrounded Iune, swirled into a fleck of mystical material, and then burrowed into his forehead. Iune felt the emotion attached to the projected conjure, and he was signaled by the princess' sorcery to approach. He walked up beside her.

"I can see their trajectories," she said to Iune, wide-eyed gaze peering out to the water. "I can see faint lines tracing the slave-trade routes." She looked up at the stars, and her face rippled sadness. "A configuration has been stolen from the sky."

The world disappeared around Ṣẹda. She saw a scene of Chief Ariq Haunts snatching the Piscean layout from the cosmos and handing it to an old and hunchbacked, European woman with stringy, gray hair and tattered clothes. Receiving the star alignment in her hand, she stood upright, de-aged, and her tattered clothes turned to expensive threads. The remaining stars in the sky spelled out her name. *Slikken.*

A bright and beautiful, picturesque day emerged in Ṣẹda's vision, as her eyes turned all black to peer into shadow and mystery. A tribal nation on the grassy plains of Africa bloomed with life. Good people attended to their daily work. Sincere and sneaky politics played their parts as both adhesive and corrosive, but still there was function. Neither completely good nor bad, an existence animated with polarities, and so lived life in this African village. Until evil came up from the ground and swallowed the villagers, commoner and royal chiefs alike.

It was horrific, Ṣẹda's vision. She flinched and gasped! Iune put his hands on her shoulders to comfort her. He called for her attention, but she couldn't hear him. She was locked into what her blackened eyes witnessed. A giant fish broke through the ground, screaming a spine-rattling squeal that undulated its eerie sound out and captured attention before its jaw swallowed the people whole. Up from the ground, oddly moving and gulping the people down into its belly before burrowing back underneath the land. The villagers ran, but it did them no good. Up again the fish came. It attacked, swallowed, and dived back into the earth again and again until all were consumed.

Ṣẹda coiled and tucked herself into Iune's embrace while now staring out to the water. Serenity again blossomed into existence before her eyes. An African kingdom. A walled city, mighty and proud and bustling with activity. Another terrifying rampage from a second monstrous, giant fish up from the depths, swallowing every African. All classes. Royal to Peasant. Artisan to politician. Men. Women. Children. Up. Swallow. Down. Repeat, until all that was left was an empty city in rubble and fire.

Underground. The two fish met and tunneled until they reached the west coast of Africa. Up. Above water. Bodies in their bellies incapacitated. Mouth open, and European slavers transferred the bodies from grotesque monsters to slave ships. Empty. The colossal and ravenous fish dived back into the water, tunneled through the earth, and went in search for more captives.

Ṣẹda's eyes returned to their customary, brown shade. For her sight, the night sky returned to its black and twinkle. The princess trembled in Iune's arms. "I have to kill them," she whispered to Iune.

"Princess…?"

"There are monsters that must be slain," she answered. "There's a familiarity in their pull to me. They are a misuse of the stars, and they now assist evil because of that misguided bastard, Chief Ariq Haunts." She moved out of Iune's embrace and peered out into the night. A frustrated look darkened her face and mood. "Damnit!" she cursed. The princess spun around and faced Iune. "I have the power to disappear in a blink like the hero you admire," she said to him. "I haven't mastered my ability, but I can feel it blossoming inside me. But I'd give anything to adopt your flair, Trickster-Prince." She turned her back to him again, looking out to the ocean. "I can feel them burrowing through Africa, looking for more to ensnare and take into bondage." She asked over her shoulder, "Will you help me stop them, Iune? Not in the morning. We must leave now. Inside of time. We probably won't find them until the sun comes up, but we must track them now."

Iune looked back at the tavern. Then he said to Ṣẹda, "Perhaps we should call our night now, return home, and get rest there. We can leave early—"

"I won't be able to sleep, Iune," the princess cut into his words. She kicked the ground and cursed again. "Shit!" She dropped her head into her hand. "I can feel it. I can feel the pain. The suffering. It comes from the people. It comes from the stars and their misuse." She looked at the tavern. "If I sneak out by myself, I'll get caught. With you, I'll have the cover of greater luck and darker shadows to steal about."

Iune grinned. "Well thought out," he congratulated Ṣẹda. "There's a bit of a trickster in your royal bones, Princess."

"Thank you, Iune," she accepted his words. "A bit, perhaps. But your helix is made completely of ruse and stratagem. With it, we can gain ground on these monsters."

Iune bowed his head. Tyle charged from the tavern behind him. "Princess!" the fool called. "Princess!" he said again, running past Iune and approaching Ṣẹda. "I felt it. Something horrible went through me, and it was attached to you. Are you okay?"

"I'm fine, Tyle. Thank you," she assured her friend. "I had a clairvoyance. I saw Ariq Haunts steal the Piscean alignment and grant it to a slave trader. She misemploys its power to conjure large fish to swallow kingdoms and nations whole. They return to her and fuel slave vessels with cargo. I can feel the terror of it all. Something must be done now. It can't wait."

Tyle noted the truth as he heard Ṣẹda speak. He then deciphered a broader aspect to the story. "Ariq Haunts' trick never entangled the Fisherman kingdom, but he has its alignment. His hex has infected all of Constellation."

"He's foolish enough to gift it to someone Iune and I will defeat. We'll snatch the alignment back, and we'll put the starts right!" Ṣẹda declared with great conviction.

Tyle heard her words, but it was a specific set of words that echoed in his head. "Just Iune and yourself?" he asked.

"I need you to stay with the group," Ṣẹda said to Tyle, hand on his shoulder. "I'll have a connection with you. I'll find you. Stay with Zoya. Go to the tribal nations they seek, round up the army, and I'll connect with you when you find Nanni Mayya Storii. We will stow into Constellation from her bridge outside of time, and retake our kingdom."

Tyle remarked, "You sound so confident, Princess."

Ṣẹda glanced over at Iune. She winked, gave a nod, and then told her friend, "We have luck and good fortune on our side."

Iune projected a telepathic message to his sister, requesting her presence with Olobiri and the other allies. She arrived with the entirety of their party, including the four, recruited rogues. He informed Zoya of his mission with Ṣẹda. Zoya understood. She instructed the allies to return to the Del-Yswil palace and get sleep.

"We'll catch up with the two of you…in time…" Zoya stated.

Iune asked Olobiri, "An escort mission and a wild monster hunt with a mystical princess, brother-friend? Sounds like an average day for us, yes."

Olobiri put his eyes on Zoya. Then he looked at Hakim. He told Iune, "I'll hang back."

Iune crossed his arms and gave Olobiri a curious eye. "Really?"

"Well, someone needs to be the surrogate 'Iune'," was his explanation, giving another look to Zoya and Hakim. "There won't be as many wisecracks, but I'll manage the position."

Iune grinned, making a quick glance at his sister and the warrior recruit. He leaned closed to Olobiri and said, "She prefers your dancing to his, brother-in-horn. They're also not standing near one another. Looks like a good sign."

"I have no idea what you're talking about," Olobiri insisted.

Iune smacked his friend on the shoulder. "*Ah!* You do have jokes!"

Ithun was also invited on the hunt, but he decided not to leave his mother's side until the true mission. There were affectionate embraces, well wishes and prayers. Malik gifted Ṣẹda with an ornate spear, telling the princess he would use its twin in battle. Ṣẹda accepted, and not to be outdone, Hakim granted her a dagger with sheath. Ṣẹda thanked the warrior and clipped it to her sash. It started a giving ceremony, as Aeshop and Strong provided provisions such as pillows and blankets and their camels for travel. Then the parties went their separate ways. Iune and Ṣẹda traversed the long, invisible bridge over water and inside time. Ṣẹda gave a silent prayer to the stars in the sky. She calculated their turn, and she noted their pattern behind the sun's light when the beasts attacked their cities. She forecasted the next target in the beasts' sights. A kingdom on the border of fertile soil, grass and barren sand. *Arewa ati Eranko.* They would kill one of the beastly fish there.

The webbing lattice crisscrossed over one another and appeared more like cuts into the visual history dreamed. A cosmic spider crawled, and a new scene emerged. It was a dream within a dream. A clairvoyance, in truth. Ṣẹda slept, and her mind, connected to home, peeked into Eterijah-Emiti's private quarters. The imposter sat in her chair attempting to meditate to keep hold of Eterijah Iyansan's body. She coughed up a fit, and the bark of her hacks caused her to drop her head. She started sweating.

Eterijah-Emiti cleared her throat and tried again to lose herself in a deep, transcendental focus. The Gold Chain of Soul glowed dim, and as Eterijah-Emiti settled into her concentration, the ghostly form of the true Eterijah Iyansan stood up, walked a few feet away from her chair, turned and faced the masquerader.

"How long can you keep the façade of being well, deceiver?" Eterijah Iyansan asked. Her physical body opened its eyes and glared at her. *"Do you think your malefactor is already aware of your predicament? You'll be dead soon, and I'll be free, back in my rightful, physical place."*

Her physical mirror grinned back at her. Said the pretender, *"Death doesn't frighten me. I'll be an hourglass with poisonous sands, and I will hex your time either way. Have your body back, Eterijah Iyansan. If your memory serves me correct, no one wants you here anyway."* She cackled loud and with an echo. The reverberating sound shattered the dream, and the clanking of the shards woke Ṣẹda from sleep.

It was morning. Deep in a rainforest. Ṣẹda lifted her well-rested head. The last scenes in her sleep didn't sap her renewed energy. The scene inspired fight in her. Iune was up, brimming with the same vigor as he roasted fish at the end of his gazelle-horn short lance. He looked at Ṣẹda and grinned as she rose to a sitting position on the blanket underneath her. "I thought fish would be an appropriate meal to break the fast. I found a river this morning. Caught a few." He felt the meat. It was done. He dropped it on a wooden plate with two other cooked fish.

"Where's the river, Iune?" Ṣẹda asked. "I need to wash."

Iune pointed with his horn-lance. "In that direction. Not too long. Don't worry about any company. I've already bathed." The princess shot him a wry smile and an eye. Iune stated, "I won't eat until you return."

Ṣẹda jumped up. She thanked Iune and was off to bathe. When she returned, they ate. The meat slipped off their fish bones with the pluck of their fingers. Among their meal of fish was a loaf of bread, berries, and two flasks of water. Part of the gifted provisions supplied by the recruited warriors.

Ṣẹda stirred up conversation by telling Iune, "The twisted spirit possessing Etti-Iyansan is dying, Iune."

Iune hummed in contemplation. "I assume the cosmic-curator's body and true spirit is too much to handle."

"You'd be assuming too much. And for once, you wouldn't be giving yourself credit," said the princess as she took a bite of her fish. Swallowing, she informed Iune, "The cut from your horn-lance wounded her. It pierced the body, but it's the foul and hexed spirit that feels the poison."

"I bring good fortune again," Iune complimented himself. His expression dropped as he looked at Ṣẹda. "My apology, Ṣẹda. I didn't mean for that to sound as pompous and vain as it did. It's just that…" his voice trailed away, and he turned his head from Ṣẹda. Frustrated, he looked back at her and stated, "I'm simply confident that I'll always win the day. My day is not over when it comes to Ariq Haunts. He's corrupted the fortunes I bring to people, stopped them. He's assisting evil men with tearing apart the first people of the world. The direct descendants of Ikzu and Gara, The First Two. He's misrepresenting the stars, their alignments, and the fortunes they tell." He straightened, chest out. "I smile and grin a lot. My wink and nod are not clandestine. They are but utilities in my arsenal. Trust me, they can frustrate the strongest of enemies. My smile blinds them, knocks them off balance, and steals their focus and confidence."

"Well, be careful, Iune," warned the princess. "Ariq Haunts and you are black tricksters at odds. European slavers gain regardless of who wins your games. Stopping your rival cuts them off from an advantage, but even I've seen that the stars are aligning to their malignancy. Their presence and strong determination fights to bring to heel the first people of Igzu and Geirah."

Iune thought for a moment, deep in contemplation. Then he looked at the princess and asked, "Is that how you pronounce Ikzu and Gara? Have I had it wrong all this time? My parents too?"

Ṣẹda laughed, "Let's not debate. It'll only distract us from the evils that plague us. I do wish the forgotten term for conjure, *Ojulowo Atijo Oluwa*, could be restored to the tongue. It sounds so fitting."

"Hmmm…" Iune contemplated. He was partially familiar with the term. It was a philosophy of conjure very ancient, even before his mother and father's time. A tribal nation he'd served with luck and good fortune preserved it, spoke in that manner, referring to conjure. The Pious Wars, of which his parents were champions, buried the term under politics, and it was lost to time. That brought Iune to think of Ṣẹda's first point, he responded, "Good point…" They drank from their flasks, clanking them together, and wishing it was a drink stronger than water. But they needed to keep their wits about them.

Ṣẹda glanced over at the spear leaning against a thick tree. Her sheathed dagger at its base. She looked at Iune and declared, "I want to be recruited into your Clever Folk pantheon! I heard you speak of it to that hero you admire."

"There's an opening," Iune replied with a bit of dejection in his voice. "It doesn't feel as if he'll be among the ranks." He pondered a thought, and then he said, "If I were as handsome as he, the charm I could resonate. The tricks that could be pulled. I wouldn't have to work so hard."

Ṣẹda rolled her eyes. "He's a handsome man, Iune, but I can sense the only woman he's been close to is his mother."

"Stop that!" Iune hissed. "He's talked of a few women he's been with."

"Very few, and if that. Trust me. I'm a woman who can sense such things."

Iune raised an eyebrow at the princess. "And how would you know of *such things*."

"I'm a twenty-four-year-old princess, Iune, not a celibate priestess. I have my experience."

"Oh…"

She tossed a smile and wink at the trickster and said, "Now *you* have experience. *Experiences.* Let me make that plural." She stated under her breath, "From what I can sense…"

Iune appeared rattled. He waved his hands. "Hey! You make me sound like a whore."

"I'm sorry, Iune. I was just—"

"I'm a slut not a whore," he corrected. "There's a difference."

Ṣẹda chuckled, "Such as?"

"The spelling."

They laughed.

Iune pointed out, "You see, Ṣẹda? You see how we can shut out the problems of the world and have ourselves a good guffaw?"

"Yes, Iune. But I don't want to forget. I want to use my wits to outsmart all the evil that tears apart the first people, vanquish it."

Iune liked Ṣẹda's talk. He wiped his hands and scurried away on palms and feet. Ṣẹda jumped to her feet as Iune, like a cat, following him to the base of the nearest and tallest tree. He raced up to the first branch, and Ṣẹda looked up at him while standing. He said down to her, "You want to be a part of the Clever Folk? Beat the leader." He looked up, then back to Ṣẹda, "To the top."

Ṣẹda made a face at the trickster. "Iune, this isn't fair."

He smirked, "It's not supposed to be. Find a clever way to beat me, even as I have the advantage." And with that, he was up the tree with a stunning display of acrobatics. Ṣẹda watched the nimble trickster scale the maze of branches, up, up, and up, choosing his path with both instinct and skill.

"That's not what I meant," Ṣẹda remarked.

Iune paused in his climb, nearly to the top. The princess' voice sounded close, in his ear. He looked up. There she was. Beautiful in her brown skin and bare feet, balanced on a branch like a graceful ballerina.

"Oh! So, that was a warning," he remarked.

"I want in," she bargained with the trickster, wearing the grin he'd lost on his face. "And I want a single feather growing from each foot." She walked out on the branch, hands behind her back.

Iune hoisted himself up onto the thick, tree bough with a fanciful swing and flip. He crawled behind her like a cat on a wire. "Do you even need the buff?" he questioned.

Ṣẹda spun and faced him. "You would do well to ally yourself with an Eterijah. That is what I'll be."

"Your council wouldn't allow it," Iune countered.

"I'll find a way to dissolve the council."

"A dictator then? How…insidious. You'll make it legal!"

Ṣẹda chuckled. "No. I'll find the Maiden kingdom's rightful treasure, the Immortal Created. An authentic piece. They will be in awe and bow. It's law."

"Perhaps *you're* the Immortal Created," the trickster proposed.

Ṣẹda giggled. "No," she disputed with a single word.

Iune stood. "Why is that funny?" he asked. "Your first name, *Qkumo*, in the Yoruba tongue means *she will not die*. Immortal!" insisted the trickster. "Your second name, Ṣẹda, means *created* in the same language. Your surname carries the same resonance."

Ṣẹda corrected, "My first name means *cut an ear of wheat*. My second name means, *from the star*. As in the Spica held by the Maiden constellation, the brightest star in her configuration."

"Oh…" said Iune sounding defeated. He sat on the branch and folded his arms. "Well, there's the issue of your destined height. When you gain power and title, you'll spring up. Won't be too sneaky then. Let's not forget the politics to consider. There's just too much of it to make you a member of the Clever Folk. I don't know. I mean—" and then Iune fell back, unhooked one leg from the branch, and held tight with his other foot lodged between the branch he dangled from and a second, thick branch growing directly above it, extended in another direction. "—could I depend on you if I was in a bind like this? You might be too busy with Azur-Fah and Eterijah politics to assist Olobiri and Zoya on a task to outsmart slavers." He waved his arms wild, feigning fear of dropping.

Ṣẹda loosened Iune's foot and he plummeted from the tree. The drop caught him by surprise, and feigning fright promptly turned into actual fear. It took a moment for his instincts to focus so that he might grab a branch, flip up, and climb his way back to the princess. He reached for a branch, quick as he could, but everything slowed. His descent was sedated by Ṣẹda's conjure, and he missed every branch making up the tree's labyrinth of limbs, steered without incident until he was gently set at the base of the tree.

A bright flash appeared next to him forming into Ṣẹda once its light popped away. Iune jumped to his feet. He put face and finger closer to the princess and inquired, "Ah! But can you fight?"

Ṣẹda put her hands on her hips. She walked around Iune and proclaimed, "I can conjure the sun's heat to scorch armies! I can toss wind and knock foes off balance! I can pull nine strands of lightning from the sky and make a flail to thrash my enemies!"

"Really? That last one? You can do that?"

Ṣẹda stopped in her pace. "I don't know. Maybe. I've seen Etti-Iyansan do it. I always wished to do the same, but it might be her personal conjure—among so many things she can do." Her eyes fell on the spear and dagger near the tree. "Iune," she called for the trickster, "let us kill an evil witch's beasts."

They gathered their provisions, mounted their rides, and raced from the jungle to fertile plains, close to the desert. They were too late. Arewa ati Eranko was sacked. All manner of man, woman, and child had been swallowed. Fire, rubble, and smoke were the new residents. Iune and Ṣẹda felt the sting of reality's cruel state of affairs for Africa.

Ṣẹda mourned, but she was undeterred. She calculated the stars' turn, and she saw another city in the line of Piscean path. She pleaded with Iune that they could not rest, and he agreed. They continued to a moderate-sized, African city named *Ukuzi Vikela*, an urban area constructed of mudbrick houses and buildings.

Slavery's politics heightened the mistrust of outsiders, forcing Ṣẹda and Iune to make an encampment outside its borders. They kept close watch on the city at night, falling asleep on the same resting blanket, in one another's arms.

Dawn. The blood-curdling shriek from the mammoth fish wrenched the princess and trickster from sleep. They leaped to battle. Ṣẹda snatched her spear and jumped to her mount, dashing forward, kicking up sand as she rode. Iune went to palm and foot, racing alongside Ṣẹda's camel. Both princess and trickster witnessed the enormous beast slam body and caudal fin into the city's structures. People scattered from interiors and through the streets, running. A few were swallowed up, which spurred Ṣẹda to action. She launched herself into the air, hands on her spear, surrounded by conjure that carried her high above the beast.

Iune jumped to Ṣẹda's abandoned mount, pulled the reins, and stopped the camel's charge. He sent to the animal, **Back to your friend at camp.** Then he jumped from the ride and resumed his cat-like scurry toward the city as the camel retreated.

Ṣẹda descended, spear aimed at the enormous fish's dorsal fin. Her weapon slammed a few feet below the upright appendage. She used all her conjure to hold tight as giant fish bucked unruly, squealing its echoing screech. Iune darted through the stampede in the streets, coming closer to Ṣẹda's aid. Nearing the flailing fish's back fin, Iune was smacked aside, carried long and projected toward the side of a building. Thinking quicker than his flight through the air, Iune conjured his gazelle-horn lances, and punctured their sharp points into the building's side. He jumped up and planted his feet on his horn-lances, standing tall and getting an overview of the scene.

Iune sprang upward, arcing high and with a trajectory close to where Ṣẹda hung tight with her spear. He extended his arms out, opened his palms, and conjured his horn-lances out of the wall they'd lodged in and into his hands. He slammed them deep into the colossal beast's side, joining Ṣẹda as the giant fish thrashed about from its wounds.

The princess loosened the conjure assisting her balance. Her fingers slipped, but she shifted focus to summon the vibrancy of the stars, channeling their potency into her spear. The weapon glowed, and the energy conducted from cosmos to Ṣẹda coursed through the beast. The giant fish screamed again, mouth wide and regurgitating the people it had swallowed. They were incapacitated, covered in muck, but alive. Ṣẹda refocused, recouped her balance, and tightened her fingers around the spear, resisting the beast's floundering.

He fish recovered, slithered like a snake through the streets, scattering citizens and breaking through structures.

"Ṣẹda!" Iune called. "Feet to fish. Jump off and stab it again." She looked at Iune, desperation on her face. He was ready. She was not. Much like with the bucking fish, she went along with the ride. Ṣẹda nodded, confirming. "On three!" yelled Iune. "One—" both trickster and princess planted their feet on the fish. "Two—" they braced themselves for launch. *"Three!"* They pushed off. Ṣẹda dislodged her spear. Iune leapt back, dislodging his impaled horn-lances impaled. Ṣẹda did the same with her spear. In air, he and she brought their weapons down on the fish for another assault. Their weapons stabbed the fiend, piercing deeper than their initial strikes.

The beast's holler wasn't filled with as much potency as before. Its light was fading, and Ṣẹda saw to it by injecting the purifying light of the stars into the dying monster. The administered, cosmic power seared the beast's insides. The fish's screams quieted. Its eyes closed, and then it fell onto its side.

"Hold tight!" said Iune.

Ṣẹda had another idea. She blinked away and popped into existence in midair behind Iune. She reached out and disappeared with Iune wrapped tightly in her arms. The colossal fish's dead body crashed into empty buildings, its weight pummeling the structures to ash.

Princess and trickster appeared on the street, catching their breath in one another's embrace. Iune had a quip. It was a good one, and on the tip of his tongue. He backed away, grinned and went to express his clever words when up from the depths came the second of the massive and mighty, Piscean beasts.

Ṣẹda's instinct divined that its belly was still filled from its morning meal. Like the people unconscious in the street, they were immobilized, but still living. She looked at Iune and the trickster concurred, "I sense it too!"

Iune charged on palms and feet. Ṣẹda blinked away, materializing atop the slain fish. She pulled her spear free and then used her conjure to catapult high into the air. Iune followed Ṣẹda's launch, gazelle-horn lances conjured to his hands and ready to assail the monster like its defeated sibling.

The fight wasn't going to be easy, as there stood the witch named Slikken riding the enormous fish's back, standing with perfect balance. She raised her arms and let loose a barrage of swirling hex that collided with Ṣẹda's stomach and knocked her out of the air, through a building window. The princess crashed into furniture and landed against plush cushions. Soft, but the wind had been taken from her. Her body throbbed with pain.

Iune was also bombarded by the witch's hex, casting him to the ground where he tumbled loose and off-balance. In his roll, he dissipated his horn-lances, palmed the ground, and flipped back to land on his feet. He dodged into an alley before the odd wriggle of the large fish crushed him. From the alley, he climbed to the top of a mudbrick building and chased the fish through the city, leaping from roof to roof.

Ṣẹda used an incant to regain her focus and an upright posture. She snatched up her spear and poked her head out of the window. She spotted the fish making an awkward change in direction. She deduced the creature wasn't here to feed, but to fight she and Iune for killing its other half.

Ṣẹda turned her head upward and spotted the roof. She popped from existence and emerged physical atop the building. She charged to the edge, jumped, and in midair, blinked away again. She manifested two buildings down, in midstride, repeating until she caught up with Iune.

The trickster was having a time scurrying away from the witch's hexed beams. She cackled, reveling in her newfound powers. Her excitement turned her wild. She sensed Ṣẹda and kept both trickster and princess at bay.

As long as no people were consumed, and the citizens ran to safety, Iune and Ṣẹda had no care on their engagement with Slikken. But it needed to come to an end. Iune sent to the princess, **Distraction! I'll go for the witch, you go for the fish!**

Iune stood straight. He tossed his horn-lances at the witch. She used her hex to deflect the projectiles hurtling toward her. Iune materialized his weapons back to his hands, dodging away from the hex spiraling in his direction. Ṣẹda blessed herself with an incant and pitched the spear like a javelin. A perfect throw! The spear struck the monster below its dorsal fin, and it trembled with the impact. The witch managed to stay on her feet, and Ṣẹda cursed under her breath, "Damnit!" The fight was quick with split-second decisions made to gain the upper hand. In her strike, Ṣẹda forgot to consecrate the spear with the power of the stars to further weaken the beast.

Slikken aimed an open palm at the princess and projected a salvo of hex. Ṣẹda disappeared, forming solid away from the hexed energy's path. She conjured a storm's heavy wind in her hand and cast it at the witch. Slikken surrounded herself with a domed aegis and deflected the princess' conjure attack. Ṣẹda blinked away, ending up on the fish's back a few feet from Slikken's aegis. The princess cast lightning from her fingers, but the conjured element simply bounced off Slikken's protective power, though it weakened the defense.

With the witch's attention diverted, Iune lunged off the building and toward the giant monster. Horn-lances in hand, Iune came down, goring the fish in its eye, slicing down through the soft, ocular tissue. The mammoth monster shrieked and bucked! Iune pulled his weapons free and stabbed the beast again under the eye socket, a sturdier penetration that kept him steady, hanging on as the giant fish flailed in pain.

Ṣẹda and Slikken dropped off opposite sides of the monster. Ṣẹda reached out and grabbed her spear, making a tight grip with both hands. Slikken crashed against the dusty street. Her protective aegis dissipated, she took the full impact of the fall. Her left arm and hip shattered, and she yelled in chorus with her giant beast.

With her hands around the spear, Ṣẹda called on the power of the stars to fill her palms. She channeled the energy into the weapon, administering it into the monster's body. The princess used an incant to give her strength enough to further sink the spear through the creature's scales.

Iune and Ṣẹda once again found themselves in a rodeo as the fish jumped and squirmed in agony. Poison and star fire tracking through its body. Mouth wide open, it regurgitated the population of an entire city, spilling out into the city streets. A wave of people covered in debilitating muck.

Princess and trickster were synched in their attacks. Both planted feet, pushed off, and transpierced the wounded, fiend. Ṣẹda seared the beast with the might of the stars, and Iune's gazelle-horn short lances fed a toxic burst of conjure through its body. The beast toppled dead. Ṣẹda blinked away with her spear. She snatched Iune on the other side, and then transported the two of them to a rooftop where they watched the enormous fish crash into several empty houses like its sibling before it.

The monsters' devastation was halted, and their bellies were emptied. The gigantic masses shifted into a bright light that swirled together and took to the heavens to become the benevolent, Piscean alignment. Iune spotted the wicked sorceress Slikken crawling through the street. She'd returned to her old crone appearance. Iune looked at Ṣẹda and instructed, "Take us down there. She has no hex in her now."

Ṣẹda reached out her hand, and Iune accepted. The princess blinked the two of them away from the rooftop and down on the street. The witch's injured crawl came to a stop at the sudden appearance of their feet. Iune aimed a horn-lance toward the slave trader. "I don't think so," he said down to her.

City guards surrounded the princess and the trickster. Citizens rushed them too. They came with praise, and the guards arrived with shackles for the old slave trader. The city's chief governor was escorted to the site, heaping admiration for Ṣẹda and Iune. "Good fortune has smiled upon us today!" he exclaimed. "Is there anything we can give you two blessed warriors for your trouble?"

Iune smirked, "This was no trouble—"

"It was a pleasure," Ṣẹda finished the trickster's statement. She addressed the governor, "I understand there's mistrust kindled among us by the slavers. Swallowed by these beasts were citizens from the Arewa ati Eranko nation. Let their numbers recover among you. Become allies."

"We've always maintained good trade and relations with their people," the chief governor notified. "This will be no stressful task to help them rebuild and recover. It will be a pleasure. We'll celebrate when they wake. The witch will be executed at our festivities. Will you stay?"

Ṣẹda said in an apologetic tone, "We cannot, Good Chief. There are other atrocities that need our attention."

"I understand," he said with a bow of his head. He said to Iune, "I know you, trickster." The chief governor wore a wide smile. He looked at Ṣẹda and asked, "But how do I address you, conjure woman?"

"This is Princess Qkumo-Ṣẹda Halitta," Iune answered. "Eterijah of the Maiden Kingdom."

The crowd gasped. Everyone took a knee and bowed their heads.

"Of great Azur-Fah!" the chief governor hailed. "The stories are true!"

Ṣẹda didn't feel comfortable with the entire citizenry on their knees with heads bowed to her. "Rise," she directed, and on command, the people stood. "A terrible thing is happening across Africa. Hold tight to your beliefs. Love one another. Our bond will be put to a monumental test." The people of the African urban center understood. They made a vow, comprehending the reality.

The trickster and the princess left the city. His weapons unsummoned. Her spear strapped to her back with a sheathed gifted to her by the chief governor. They made a slow, relaxing walk back to their encampment.

"I was hoping you'd introduce me as Ṣẹda, member of the Clever Folk," she said to Iune.

"I knew the reaction the longer title would invoke." He winked, teasingly. Then he asked, "Have you been choosing your words?"

"My words?"

"Yes!" responded Iune. "How the fish of the slave-trading witch was slain. It's one for the books, you know. You now have a story, an exploit. A tale that many will speak far and wide. That is the trickster's life. Collect stories for others to brag about over a mug of spirits."

Ṣẹda understood. "Ah! The Tale of the Eterijah Princess and Her Trickster Consort!" She wrapped both arms around one of his, and they walked forward together. "We will have plenty of stories. Killing the fish and jailing their witch. Reclaiming Constellation. We will inspire future generations so they may beguile the evil of the world. Our stories will have a trickster's life, yes. They will roam from African mouth to African mouth to all the blacks around this world. They will never tire of travel, and they will motivate the teller of their tales to put right any wrong in the world!" She put her head on Iune's shoulder.

"It seems you've found some words, Clever Folk initiate," Iune quipped.

"Initiate? Not yet," Ṣẹda countered. "Not until I have feathers on my feet, and I can walk across any terrain without footwear." They walked onward. Together.

A single, silk strand crossed the scene. Like rain, additional silk threads showered down, crisscrossing and forming a complex network through the visual plane. They burned bright until all but their light could be viewed. In a flash. Another day emerged.

A lone, mudbrick house stood on fertile ground. Conjure was expansive, and the house looked small on the outside. It housed two hundred and forty soldiers within its interior. Such was the domicile of Nanni Mayya Storii, guardian of hidden pathways. The door to her residence opened, and Princess Qkumo-Ṣẹda's companion, Tyle, stepped out into the brewing, new day.

The sun made its debut, barely peeking over the skyline. The shape of things close and far were still cast in silhouette. To the north, inching up over the horizon walked a feminine and masculine frame. Their approach pulled Tyle completely from sleep. His face brightened, as he anticipated shadow to slip from them and reveal Princess Qkumo-Ṣẹda and the trickster Iune. His instinct for truth reached out and divined the advancing figures were not as he wished. One was familiar. The woman. The man was not.

Before Tyle could use an instinct to decipher a small morsel pertaining to the man, a disturbing image followed over the horizon. An army was behind them, and Tyle could sense a few attributes to the incoming wave of men and women. Rough and rugged. Battle worn. It was an aura cast over the nearing army. There was a vibrancy of life and freedom, though some resonated with no life at all. His instinct for truth dropped in his head a single, macabre word. *Undead.*

"There's an army coming!" he yelled back into the mudbrick house. "Undead among them." He concentrated on the familiarity of the woman out front with the man. It was Efra al-Kaadi. "Ithun! It's your mother!"

Ithun charged from the house. Olobiri and Prince Consort Raji were behind him. Ithun amplified his instinct, and the higher senses reached out and touched his mother. He focused nothing on the people behind her. No concern for them. His instinct lightly brushed against the shadow of the young man next to her. He was familiar, but distant in memory. Ithun ran toward them, and his instinct deciphered his entirety.

Ithun's legs gave out, and he dropped to his knees, head down. His tears were instant, and while he couldn't complete his run, mother and brother could.

"Get up, Ithun," his mother requested.

Ithun's legs couldn't lift him, and he barely tilted his head up. His eyes streamed with tears. He attempted to address his mother, but his sight moved to his brother Seizan. His body dropped again, falling facedown at his brother's feet and weeping.

Anger expired in Seizan. He knelt down and consoled his brother. "I hear our childhood hero has admiration for you, Brother Ithun." The younger didn't respond. He continued with his tears. "They gave me a new name. Called me Victus. Took parts of my fingers. I was given dominion over the dead. Their burial. The slave masters would come to regret that move." He nodded his head. Ithun continued crying. "We killed every last one of them, burned their wretched plantation." Ithun gripped his older brother's clothes. "I came here with the intention to kill you and Ma-ma, because that's what the devil's den does to you. You're worked so hard you become confused. Even the sun is your enemy. You hate nature. You hate your own nature. It makes you angry at the wrong people."

Ithun lifted his head. His face was a mess of tears and anger. "That same poison infects an old friend. We saw the damage it did to our families. Papa killed. You..." His voice went away. He scattered the notion from his head. Seizan was here. His absence was no longer. Ithun said, "He calls himself Ariq Haunts now."

The brothers stood and embraced. Mother Efra's throat was clogged with tears. She kept them down and stood strong.

"Let's trade stories, younger brother," said Seizan to Ithun. "I've been to hell. So, I'm curious. What is this I hear about having to reconquer the heavens?"

Nanni Mayya Storii, a short and plump woman with long braids, a wide and chubby, child-like face, walked outside. She overlooked the new army and huffed, "Well, I'll make more room." She turned and went back into her house and used her conjure to expand her house.

Everyone but Tyle followed her inside. He remained, staring at the horizon. Nothing but the sky and sun were there.

Inside. Stories were shared. Seizan introduced Vae to his brother. He announced he and she would be consorts to one another, sinking slave ships with their phantom watercraft, *Immamou*. Kip, renamed Udaka by the winds of Africa, would be a deck officer.

A day passed. Then two. Another, and a fourth. Sun at its highest point. Tyle was on his hourly look outside when he saw the princess and the trickster cross over the horizon on mounts. He shouted, "They're here! They've arrived!"

Zoya emerged from the house along with Olobiri, the warrior Aeshop, and Prince Raji. Iune and Ṣẹda rode up to the house, slowing their mounts to a stop when they neared Tyle. Ṣẹda said to her father, "You're okay here?"

The prince consort tossed a thumb over his shoulder. "The interior is outside of time, as is a few paces around the house. I'm strong here."

Iune and Ṣẹda dismounted. Brother hugged his sister. Daughter embraced her father. Their secondary hugs went to Olobiri and Tyle, respectively. Ṣẹda noted, "We vanquished the monsters plaguing the lands. We sent them back to the stars. They're locked. Ariq Haunts cannot use them again. Not for a cycle at least."

"We'll take him long before then," Prince Raji noted. "We have an army. Your trickster's sister kept her word."

Olobiri informed Iune, "Ithun's brother arrived."

"From Amexem? He escaped bondage?"

"It's a terrible story, Iune," Zoya took up. "It has a wonderful end for him and others, but the plague of servitude is ongoing. There is no Grand Alchemy. That is certain. There is nothing but a terrible, terrible, brutal existence."

They went inside. Prince Raji walked his daughter to Nanni Mayya Storii. He said with a broad, joyful smile, "Nanni Mayya Storii, this is my daughter, Princess Qkumo-Ṣẹda. She left me a royal lady. She's returned a fierce warrior."

Ṣẹda looked at Iune and winked. She turned back to Nanni Mayya Storii and proudly proclaimed, "Yes! I killed the fish of the swallow-witch!"

The sorceress burst into shock, and she gasped on sight of the Prince Consort's second daughter and the crystal ornament dangling around her neck, which started glowing. It's resonance was in a language only the conjure woman understood. *"Inhloso yami isifikile!"* she whispered low and barely audible. Her eyes watered, and she dropped to the princess' feet, rubbing the ends of Ṣẹda's dress and kissing the fabric. She said over and over, *"Ukungafi kudaliwe! Ngakhethwa ukuthi ngilandise indaba yakho! Ukungafi kudaliwe! Ngakhethwa ukuthi ngilandise indaba yakho!"*

Ṣẹda remained still, though her posture made it seem as if she was ready to make several strides backwards, turn, and dash away. Prince Raji raised an eyebrow. Not much fuss was made over his arrival, Prince Consort to the Queen of the Maiden Kingdom. "What is all this?" he barked, though holding back a bit of bite in his voice.

Nanni Mayya Storii got to her feet and caught her breath. She reached out a hand toward Ṣẹda, and the princess received a warm, calm over her. Her pose rested at ease, and she leaned into the woman's touch.

But Nanni Mayya Storii didn't touch her. Her fingers came close to Ṣẹda's face, but they never caressed her.

"I can see you," said the guardian of hidden paths. "I've been chosen to tell your story!" She gushed with spontaneous jubilation, dancing with a hop back and forth on either foot, and a quick twirl around. She hugged Ṣẹda tight. *"I've been chosen!"* she hollered again.

Prince Raji's face bent on Nanni Mayya Storii's tightly clenched arms squeezing his daughter hard. Ṣẹda looked at her father, and with a nod, backed him down.

Nanni Mayya Storii opened her arms and gave a succession of bows toward the princess. She cupped both her hands under Ṣẹda's chin and said, "The Immortal Created is in my presence! *Kemmi Kem Wer!* Daughter of the First Two. Here in the flesh. Daughter of Ixu and Gira!"

The crystal attached to Ṣẹda's necklace shifted dark purple in color.

Prince Raji and Ṣẹda flinched.

Nanni Mayya Storii clapped her hands together and spun around. "Come!" she motioned, walking away. "Follow! You and your father only!"

Ṣẹda didn't move. She looked over at Iune.

Nanni Mayya Storii stopped and turned back to Ṣẹda.

The princess told the woman, "My consort must be present too."

"Your…consort…?" asked Nanni Mayya Storii, eyes narrowed on Ṣẹda.

Prince Raji had the same question written on his face as well, single eyebrow raised and aimed at both princess and trickster.

"He knew," said Ṣẹda. "He deciphered my name as *immortal created.*"

Prince Raji crossed his arms. "Did he?"

Iune thought it best to keep his eye on the plump woman and away from Prince Raji.

Ṣẹda snapped at her father, "Pa-pa!"

Nanni Mayya Storii chuckled, "Oh, no, no, no! Your name means *cut an ear of wheat from the star.*" She pointed at Iune and said with a flutter of her eye, "But that's good, trickster." She straightened and announced, "Well, he can come too. Come along then!" She turned and walked away with a kick in her step. Ṣẹda and Prince Raji followed. Iune walked with them after receiving a congratulatory slap on the shoulder from Olobiri.

Stepping into her sanctuary, Nanni Mayya Storii proclaimed, "Cosmic precious! She walks among us!" She turned around to see Ṣẹda, Prince Raji, and Iune gathered with her. The door was closed. "You have an army out there, but the imposter has the stars at his command. He's given residence to unalike spirits. Immoral wrongdoers. Their possession of just six Eterijah has thrown the stars out of balance." She said directly to Ṣẹda,

"You've seen the monsters created from the disparity."

"Yes, I have," replied the princess. She yearned to know more of being the fabled Immortal Created and what it meant. She was patient with the pathway guardian.

Nanni Mayya Storii addressed Prince Raji. "You didn't know?" she asked. "Your daughter is the cosmos in the flesh." She reached out a hand to Ṣẹda, not waiting for the prince consort to answer. "Your necklace, Cosmic Princess. Please. Give. I will show you."

Ṣẹda removed the necklace and handed it to Nanni Mayya Storii in haste. She felt compelled to ask, "I'm going to be an Eterijah, but what sets me apart from the others?"

Nanni Mayya Storii crushed the crystal in her palm. The conjure woman opened her hand and a cosmic aura burst from the shattered shard. The guardian said to Ṣẹda, "You are a woman of four parents. Two of flesh. Two of the beginnings. *The* beginning. You are a pathway unto yourself, Missy Immortal. The soul of a daughter of Ixu and Gira resides in you. Your name before was Kemmi Kem Wer." Nanni Mayya Storii tossed the cosmic globule up in the air. A burst of light was emitted from the galactic, gelatinous bubble, and a tale of Ṣẹda's beginnings was transmitted to their minds.

Nanni Mayya Storii dictated the narrative. The others witnessed the recount.

"Ixu and Gira had so many children. Kemmi Kem Wer was a curious daughter that was attracted to our world's celestial timetable. When she arrived, she controlled time and space here on Earth. They called her All Eternity, And Infinity." From the far side of the cosmos sailed a feminine figure. Her body almost invisible against the firmament, blending in with her celestial flesh and spiraling hair. She arrived through the atmosphere. "Kemmi Kem Wer was worshipped by the Moors, said to have been prophesized by Kemites and Nubians." There shown was a set of hieroglyphs overlaid with the cosmic spirits appearance in the kingdom of the Moors. Men and women fell to their knees. Then came a vision of blood spilled in sacrifice. "Pale knights with needles sought to control her power. They managed to subdue her—" Armies were slaughtered at her cosmic hand, but determination wrestled her to the ground and overcame the cosmic woman. "—using a negating stone and the blood of the Grand Pair from the Lovers kingdom in Constellation. A terrible kill, a cosmic blood offering. They used the Mephistophelean blood-ritual to trap her essence inside the sharp head of a spear, and they took to the world to conquer it, pushing back conjure.

"The spear tore conjure and soul from its victims' bodies, feasting. Your father was tasked to seek out and destroy the weapon. The spear of your destiny. Your mother's blessing gave him a defensive aegis."

A young Prince Raji battled against hordes of Needle Knights, coming across an ominous armored warrior wielding the spear. Their fight distorted nature, made the clouds and sun retreat. And the stars watched with great anticipation. The clash's crescendo came with a fatal strike against warrior Raji and his lionhearted riposte severing the spear at the head. In the same swift motion, he removed the head of the spear-wielding knight.

Prince Raji flinched as he relived the moment.

"The spear tip burst into light! The radiating glimmer burned the remaining enemies around your father and condensed into a small crystal. Kemmi Kem Wer's spirit bore herself inside Raji as a paradox, healing and drawing him closer to death in the same temporal distortion. Your mother and aunt slowed the incongruity fermenting inside him. Death. Life. The cycle. All Eternity, And Infinity."

There came a scene of Ṣẹda's mother and aunt treating warrior Raji with the use of powerful rituals, medicinal herbs not found inside time, and strong incants.

"Your mother nursed your father for more than three-hundred years accounted for inside time. That is what makes him suffer when dwelling within an Earthly duration. It kills him. He's still dying, it's just been slowed down. Outside of time, he'll be safe. Unless he's killed in battle, of course. Paradox's scar hasn't been completely healed."

The visual recollection dispersed, and Nanni Mayya Storii's sanctuary came back into view for all of them. Ṣẹda stepped closer to the conjure woman and said, "Where does me being Kemmi Kem Wer, the Immortal Created, fit into all this?"

The pudgy-faced woman bubbled with laughter. "Chil', what happened when your father regained strength?" She put her eyes on Prince Raji. "I imagine you and Neggura Halitta celebrated as two lovers do when being separated for so long—separated from intimacy." She said to Ṣẹda, "Your father put into your mother the spirit of Kemmi Kem Wer. Oh! I'm sure that was a powerful coupling." She burst into a hearty laugh. "Nine months later, as the story goes, Kemmi Kem Wer was reborn in the flesh."

A memory came to Ṣẹda. She as a four-year-old girl, holding Eterijah Iyansan's hand and marveling at the display of power the star-steward showcased, causing the Winding Staircase to move and shuffle Abim and Efra al-Kaadi through time. She could feel the course of energy rattling her young bones and rippling her flesh. These years later. At this moment. Ṣẹda understood. It wasn't the Eterijah's power exhibited. It was hers. Used as a key to turn the lock in time's door.

"She knew…" said Ṣẹda in a low breath as she examined the palm of her hands. "Etti-Iyansan! She knew!"

"You are time itself, Missy Immortal," Nanni Mayya Storii crowned. The princess turned and threw her arms around Iune. "Oh,

Trickster! I have a grand story to be shared!"

"So many titles you have!" quipped Iune.

"A story?" Nanni Mayya Storii questioned. "*I* was ordained to tell the story! And you? You don't just have a story You have a purpose." Ṣẹda opened her embrace from Iune and faced the conjure woman. The guardian waved her close. "Come, come! Lay your back flat on this high bed."

Ṣẹda removed sheath and spear and leaned the weapon against the corner. Then she skipped up to the raised bed in the center of the room, hopped up onto the soft bedding, and lay flat. Nanni Mayya Storii approached the end of the bed and peered down at Ṣẹda, placing her hands on either side of the princess' head. "I've trained all my life for this!" she said through a wide and open smile. "Boy my brothers and sisters will be jealous. We selfishly rooted for ourselves on this gamble. Caused no bad blood, though. We all look for purpose; and we didn't run away from the responsibility." She instructed Ṣẹda, "Close your eyes, Missy Immortal."

Ṣẹda shut her eyes. Nanni Mayya Storii did the same.

Iune and Prince Raji stood next to one another, observing the ritual.

The conjure woman touched her forehead to Ṣẹda's. "There's a spirit lost in time. She. A young woman. She spirals aimless through the void. She needs your help, Kemmi-Ṣẹda, to return home."

Ṣẹda's flesh turned midnight blue. A shimmering, cobalt-blue light glowed between the area where the two women's heads touched. It branched out and covered the princess' body. Swathed in light, electric strands swam around the bright luminescence. The gleam burst and dissipated from around Ṣẹda's body, leaving her a changed woman.

Gone were her thick, brown and black dreadlocks. Her hair was now a short, Afro bush of twists. Shorter in stature, but only by an inch or two. More voluptuous in shape. Her skin was darker, and her eyes were like the wings of a butterfly when she opened them. The young woman gasped, and Nanni Mayya Storii jumped back. The young woman sat up.

Iune observed her beauty. Prince Raji drew his sword.

"Where is my daughter?" the prince consort demanded. "Who are you?"

She couldn't speak the language. Not outright. Instinct guided her words to say in a language they could understand, "M-m-m-my name…is Fey…Forrester…" She surveyed her surroundings, eyes wide and swallowing the holy sanctuary she resided in. "Where am I? …*When* am I?"

Everyone stared at her.

Iune put his hand on Prince Raji's wrist and made him lower his weapon. The trickster had an instinct. He also had words, and so he remarked, "The original woman sure does only come in one flavor.

Beautiful…"

Other than those words, no one quite knew what to say.

A few moments passed. Fey looked at them. They looked at her. She used an incant to decipher her surroundings. The sixteen-eighties. Outside of time. The Parent Continent. Nanni Mayya Storii inquired, "You belong to the end times, don't you, dearie?"

Fey focused, concentrating on the words for an answer. It wasn't because she needed to search deep inside herself to find them. She knew who she was, and she knew where she was from. It was never more lucid than now in all her aimless, spirit wandering. Rude as it seemed, Fey's intent wasn't on answering the question posed to her. She focused on reaching across time for the young man she loved. She knew he must've been dreaming of this moment, looking for an invitation to send his spirit back and possess any of the male occupants in the room.

But, Fey felt nothing.

At least, she didn't feel what she desired most to touch. Him. Her Gordon-baby.

There in his place was another. The presence was familiar. A visual representation materialized in front of her. Thin, gossamer webbing. "Lady Arachne…?" she wondered aloud. "Maman Anansi…? No." She returned to her first instinct. "Lady Arachne. You see me." Fey smiled warmly, remembering everything of her life, even the hard times.

Nanni Mayya Storii took her by the hand and felt her story as Fey recalled her tale in her head. "A bad man banished you to the void," she sensed.

"Yes," Fey answered.

"He's got a treacherous wife and a harpy for a mother," continued Nanni Mayya Storii with a vexed growl in her voice. "We'll get you to the Winding Staircase and take your spirit to your proper time. The end times."

Tears soaked Fey's eyes, and then they streamed down her face. She looked at the people in the room and pleaded, "We're searching for The Lovers card. An ancient tarot card. It's needed in my time. Please…"

Nanni Mayya Storii wiped Fey's tears aside and told her, "I've seen the item you speak of. A woman in our ranks has it. There's some fighting to be done, little wander-spirit." The conjure woman instructed her, "I need you to lie back down." Fey reclined on the bed, lying flat on her back. Nanni Mayya Storii told her to close her eyes, and she did. Forehead to forehead. A cobalt-blue light radiated from between her and Nanni Mayya Storii's foreheads and then spread out to envelope her body. The light shimmered red and gold in an instant. Then it returned to cobalt-blue and whisked way, funneling into Ṣeda's bosom as her physical appearance re-emerged.

She raised up from the bed in a start, forcing Nanni Mayya Storii to move her head away and step back. "The cobalt-blue spirit named Fey Forrester resides in me! We need to take her home." She looked at Iune and her father. "Our past must connect to the end times and set her free. The lilac flame is there. His name is Gordon Goodspeed. There are conjure folk working to right the wrong, Iune." She said to her father, "Pa-pa, your command of an army has never been more in need. Ariq Haunts and his misguided Ifo must be defeated."

Iune assisted Ṣẹda off the bed.

"You need a Grand Pair to restore the Lovers realm," Nanni Mayya Storii advised. "The reigning Pair were slain. Their apprentices too. Ariq Haunts' army has grown, and his delusions continue to create a lack of harmony. Something needs to assist in exorcising the problematic duality gripping Azur-Fah in a stranglehold."

Prince Raji looked at Iune, "Your hero's brother." His eyes then fell on his daughter. "He and his beloved. Lovers. One undead. One alive. Duality in and of itself. He can raise the dead, and she sure as hell sounds like she can create it. She holds her mother's spirit in a lantern. In this desperate time, we must ordain them." Then he added to Ṣẹda, "You can't serve two kingdoms with you and your—" he looked at Iune and stated, "—prince consort."

Ṣẹda nodded. "By my cosmic right, I will ordain this man and woman as Eterijah of the Lovers realm." She turned to the trickster and asked, "Can you fight? We traveled long. We've come from a quarrel, used incant and conjure to race to our allies. I feel invigorated. How's your strength, Iune-darling?"

He grinned and answered, "Impatient for action."

Ṣẹda eyed her father. "Pa-pa?"

"My sword is ready. Thirsty." He sheathed his blade and put his arms around his daughter. "Your mother and sisters are not here, but they *are* here. You understand?"

"Yes, Pa-pa!" she answered.

The power quartet returned to the main room of the conjure-expanded house and assembled their army. Ṣẹda used newfound strength in her cosmic awareness to call out, "Seizan al-Kaadi! Vae! I need your presence at front."

Seizan, shovel in hand, and Vae with weapons at her hips and lantern in hand, stepped forward and stood side by side.

Ṣẹda addressed them, "This is not a conversation we're stepping into. This isn't a debate or argument. This is a fight against an injudicious man." She looked at Seizan. "You knew him long ago. He's different. We need to stop him. I've seen firsthand his misuse of the stars. Now he's put a void in duality. He has slain the reigning Grand Pair and their apprentices."

"I can resurrect them," Seizan stated as a stern matter-of-fact.

"No. They have become a part of their star alignment, adding to the shimmer," Ṣẹda corrected. "I need to ordain the two of you as the new Grand Pair of the Lovers kingdom. The new Eterijah. The two as one."

Seizan and Vae were stumped for words, though their mouths hung open as if there was something to say. They stared at one another for a long time before putting their eyes back on the princess. "We have a ship…" Vae proclaimed. "The Immamou. It was granted to us by an old god with a new name. We vowed to honor its use. Sink slave ships together. Rescue African captives."

"You will," Ṣẹda promised. "Ritual be done, and you Lovers will come to aid."

It wasn't as direct as Seizan and Vae had planned, but the only way the battle could progress, was if they accepted this new and strange title. Seizan had knowledge of Eterijah. Vae did not. She was willing to learn of its meaning by becoming the bearer of the label.

Seizan and Vae agreed.

Prince Raji declared the fight near. There would be no delay. Rest was over. The warriors raised their weapons and hollered! Nanni Mayya Storii waved her hands for the battle cry to cease. When there was no murmur, she instructed the large group to follow her to a room with an enormous mirror that would act as a portal to walk through.

Zoya remained behind. She wished Olobiri and Iune success, iterating that she would be providing a blessing. "I know you don't need it, Iune," she said to him, words faltering as she did her best to hold back tears. "Luck is on your side…" Then her tears streamed.

Iune kissed his sister on the forehead. "I can always use a blessing from my sister," he told her.

Her eyes drifted to Olobiri as he followed the army's march out of the room. "Return him to me," she commanded Iune. Then she folded her arms and huffed, "He wants me to wait on the right man? How typical! What about *his* exploits? Not really waiting on the right woman, is he?"

Iune looked over his shoulder at his friend's departure from the room. He said to Zoya, "Consider it practice. I hear from some women it's paying off." She gave him a look. Iune grinned. "I tell him the same thing about you." Zoya punched his arm. Iune rubbed the attack. "I'll be back just to repay you for that." They hugged again. It was difficult for them to let go, but the call for battle needed answering. Iune walked away from his sister and caught up with Olobiri. Tyle was also there. Iune expressed to the palace fool, "You can fight?"

Tyle showed off his staff. "I can. I can be clumsy in some arenas, but I'm quite capable in others." He slung the staff over his shoulder, marching forward with his chest out. He gave Iune a quick eye and said, "You don't believe me, do you, trickster?"

Iune knew he couldn't fight Tyle's instinct. "Just stay close to Olobiri and Kuto-Ithun. That's all."

Tyle huffed as he kept up his proud walk.

Iune decided to keep close to the palace fool. He considered Ṣẹda didn't need any protection, even as she returned the spear to Malik. She was a cosmic being in the flesh, and she could manipulate time and space. Her arsenal seemed capable enough, very sound. Olobiri was almost his equal in agility and fierce attack. Kuto-Ithun was a fighter blessed with a conjure to blink away in clouds of black dust. His mother could manipulate shadows and be a vicious combatant. There were warriors. There were soldiers. There were lithesome tricksters and cosmic souls. Then there was Tyle, the palace fool. Iune would stay at his side. Perhaps he'd be surprised by Tyle's skill.

The hidden path they took was through a tall and wide mirror with reflective glass that liquified to the touch, rippled and yielded to be passed through. March, march went the army. Prince Raji and his daughter Ṣẹda in the lead. Behind them were the newly ordained Lovers, Seizan and Vae. A garrison of three hundred and sixty soldiers separated the princess from her trickster, but they were in unison with a mind-to-detect-mind.

In Azur-Fah. The Maiden realm. The city of Halitta. Eterijah Emiti sat sickly in the private quarters of the cosmic-curator she possessed. The woman's towering body looked pristine with its dark skin. Flawless in shape, but the wicked spirit possessing her was maligned with poison, causing the body to buckle forward and tremble in its last moments. The specter of Eterijah Iyansan stood in front of her naked of flesh and clothes, shimmering with aura and beaming with a bright, cunning grin.

"I can wait," she told the woman possessing her physical frame. "Doesn't seem like much longer now." Eterijah Emiti attempted to lift her head, but she hadn't the strength. "Why don't you call him? Chief Ariq Haunts. Why not tell him you've been dying all this time?" She glided closer and knelt and sought to make eye contact, but the foul spirit moved her face away and started coughing. "He is such a seducer, the Ifo chief is. Perhaps he's the one that controls desire and heightens passion. You seem to be the one with so much pride at this moment."

Eterijah Emiti wheezed. Air gurgled in her throat as she tried to shout a curse at the goading cosmic-curator. Her throat clogged and tightened. She choked and then expired, body falling to the ground and passing through Eterijah Iyansan's ghostly form.

The star-steward returned to her body, but it wasn't a perfect transition. A heavy ache squeezed her as she repossessed her corporeal form. Her balance wasn't stable, and her limbs trembled. She opened her eyes, lids flapping from lack of strength and loss of faculty control. What she could see in her fleeting moments of sight was the room spinning. Every object produced a blurred, second image of itself. She rolled over and fell on her back, feeling inebriated. A leaden weight strained her neck and choked her as Emiti choked. It was the Gold Chain of Soul still resonating with the essence of Emiti's shadow. Its aura anchored the Eterijah's repossessed physical form, distorted her vision, and diminished her power.

Eterijah Iyansan struggled to lift her arms as she reached for the chain. Her nails scratched her neck, tearing her flesh and drawing blood as she attempted to dig under the links of the hexed object. She slipped her fingers between the links and used what little strength she could muster to lift the cursed object from her neck. Over her head and passed her hair. The chain glowed with its eerie hum on the floor.

Eterijah Iyansan breathed relief as she felt an immediate change. Gone was the weight, and her power and control over her faculties made a return. She felt a lingering presence in her private quarters. A faint shade of attendance. Something still haunted the room. Her eyes first spotted the Gold Chain of Soul. Despite its unnatural glow resonating with the residue of Emiti's foul spirit, Eterijah Iyansan's instinct comprehended the faint presence wasn't lurking within the hexed necklace.

She stood and looked around the room, following the intensity of the buzzing hum at the base of her neck rising to the crown of her head. It grew stronger as her sight and steps drew closer to the tall mirror on the wall. She touched the glass, and the images reflected rippled as if in clear water. A new buzz from her instinct, and she stepped back, waiting for the reveal.

Ṣẹda and the prince consort were the first through. Prince Raji paused, looking up at the Eterijah with a hand on the hilt of his curved blade. Ṣẹda didn't need Tyle to sense the truth. She could feel the Eterijah's benevolent spirit coming from the physical frame in front of her. Eterijah Iyansan knelt on one knee and embraced Ṣẹda as the princess ran toward her and threw her arms around her.

"Etti-Iyansan…?" the prince consort questioned.

It's her, Pa-pa! Ṣẹda sent, allowing for the probity to be felt from her mind to his mind. "It's her!" She hugged the tall Eterijah tighter. The women touched foreheads, and Ṣẹda telepathically transmitted her experiences, beginning with the attack on the inauguration and culminating with the revelation of her cosmic spirit. Eterijah Iyansan beamed.

So, you know, child, she remarked.

Yes, Etti-Iyansan. I know.

More of the army stepped through, and the benefit of the room's design to house the height and imposing presence of an Eterijah proved to have a second advantage as the warriors filled the area, though it was still very tight. Ṣẹda and the reigning Eterijah separated, and the cosmic-curator rose to her feet. Iune wiggled his way through the crowd of combatants and took a knee before the Eterijah. The towering woman peered down at the trickster, amused at his gesture.

"Rise," the Eterijah directed. Iune erected on command. "I thank you and your sister. It's been relayed to me that while your twin and rival is the cause of this misfortune, you and your family have played a significant role in keeping the Halitta royal kinfolk safe."

"Yes, Eterijah Iyansan," spoke Iune, formal and polite.

Iune's decorous demeanor further amused her. "You may call me Etti-Iyan—" She stopped her speech as she witnessed Iune, Ṣẹda, and the crowd before her peer past her with faces frozen in awe. Eterijah Iyansan spun around and observed the Gold Chain of Soul levitating off the ground, twisting and warping in its final moments before reshaping into a large, glowing hourglass. The sands spilled from top to bottom. Eterijah Iyansan stepped closer to the floating timepiece, lifting her palm to it, conducting a clairvoyant study. She felt Chief Ariq Haunts' plan, and its revelation made her snarl, "Clever…" She spun around and faced the army. "Let's take the palace!" She moved to the door, unlocking and opening it with an incant. She rushed into the hall, army behind her.

Ifo warriors populated the halls. Their numbers appeared multiplied, and in actual fact, they had. Chief Ariq Haunts possessed converts in his numbers, manipulated through the works of the Gold Chain of Mind. They were dressed in Ifo colors and his fallacious ideology.

The fight didn't start quiet or sneaky. There was a battle cry and a charge forward. Swords, arrows, and conjure plagued the air. It wasn't long before blood caked both walls and floors. The boxer named Strong struck with fierce melee strikes using foot and fist. Close in combat, he found himself swaying left and right, back and forth against blades and ranged weapons.

Iune scuttled on palm and foot, jumped to action, and called his gazelle-horn short lances out of the ethers. He didn't care to see blood, not from men and women he considered brothers and sisters—ill-judged as they might have been. After a few clanks against his opponents' weapons with his horn-lances, he found an opportunity to render the Ifo warriors baring down on him unconscious with a swift kick or hard, single punch.

Ithun and Efra handled the Ifo they encountered much the same. It was no trouble to dodge swipe or stab from a weapon aimed for Ithun, blinking away or ducking invisible into shadow. Jumping from the ethers and wrestling their foe to the ground and subduing them.

The Ifo didn't harbor the same concerns. Their hacks and slashes were fatal. Their assailment of arrows was not meant to wound. And what they cut, they killed. When the hall became slippery with blood, the fight shifted into different areas of the palace. Ifo warriors regrouped their numbers with other battalions, but the increase in count multiplied the fighting spirit in the prince consort and the warriors he led into battle. He matched the Ifo's ferocity, undisturbed by the outpour of blood and loss of life. His reclamation of the kingdom for family and cosmic right raised his prowess and determination.

Waves of trouble marched in regiments through the south, west, and east entrances of the palace. The remaining, malignant Eterijah paraded at the front of these inculcated armies. Meeting the brigade led by Eterijah Kerst, Chief Ariq Haunts relieved him of the Sword of Union and took lead.

Bloodshed streamed through the palace corridors, and the joining brigades of malignant Eterijah flowed into the tides of battle with their troops. Their numbers were plentiful but inconsequential to the clenched fist of Eterijah Iyansan's swarm. Shouting his commands, Prince Raji raised their spirits to raise their weapons. Iune's presence lifted their fortunes, as Ṣẹda and Eterijah Iyansan buffed incants and conjures, and Seizan raised their dead.

"Up from sleep and fight you mighty Blacks of Africa!" the former slave shouted.

Mai Gadi warriors sprang into battle with resuscitated breath. Life renewed, though their blood covered the floor, fresh vital fluid flowed through their veins. Wounds mended and limbs sprouted pristine.

Chief Ariq Haunts admired the gravedigger's alchemy, but it didn't favor him. He swung his sword, swiping the ground with the tip and oscillating up. Ratamutum's gargantuan spirit extended from the blade and slammed into Seizan. The gravedigger was taken off his feet and crushed against the wall. Iune leapt to Chief Ariq Haunts, and the tricksters clashed with weapons. Sword parried horn-lance strikes, conversely raining a storm of swipes and slashes that were only fended off by the duel-wielding trickster. Chief Ariq Haunts conjured his mother for assistance, and she struck at Iune like a bolt of lightning. Her specter impaled him like a lance and hobbled him back. He lost balance and toppled to the floor with his body emitting snaking streams of smoke.

Chief Ariq Haunts summoned again his mother's apparition. Her body stretched to deliver a fatal, flying sting to Iune as he struggled to regain his balance and shake off the pain. Duhu Firistess' ghostly form was intercepted by another, feminine wraith, one made of divine smoke and fire. Her presence reached back to a single, slender flame in a lantern held by Captain Lady Vae. Her mother wrestled with Duhu Firistess' spirit, keeping the wicked woman from executing Iune.

Sword and lantern clashed with spirit and fire. Chief Ariq Haunts growled and dug in his heels as he held his sword with both hands. Vae stood, lantern out, blowing into the flame to cast her mother free to put up a defense.

Iune looked up. The sight was impressive, a marvelous display between conjure folk, but it was a sickening display between kinfolk against one another. He dissipated his horn-lances and lunged at Chief Ariq Haunts, tackling him. Duhu Firistess' spirit retracted. The two tricksters rolled into the next battle-weary corridor. Iune grappled the chief's collar and screamed, "No!"

Chief Ariq Haunts struggled with the angry trickster atop him, doing little to fight back. He simply grinned up at him and spat, "I've seen the stars, Iune. I didn't even need to rearrange them. It hurt at first. I felt duped—for all my efforts and tricks to burrow my way into this invisible, African world." His lip curled. He raised his head off the ground and snarled, "We were right, my brother-in-trick! The destiny of the blackamoor has been locked."

Iune threw a tight fist into Chief Ariq Haunts' face. *"No!"* he repeated. "The stars have aligned to trial and tribulation, but they are devoid of your misguided ideal on alchemy!"

The Ifo chief put up no fight. He placed his concentration on reaching out to one of his Six Others. He was angry. Iune was angry, and the ruler of vexation came to assist, powered by the two tricksters' incensed emotions. Eterijah Kerst shouted and a flurry of dull-aura arrows sprang from his mouth. The ethereal projectiles riddled Iune, and while no visible punctures occurred, heat exploded inside him. Again, Iune was downed. He collapsed onto his side but remained conscious. Chief Ariq Haunts crawled away from him and stood, brandishing the Sword of Union.

Iune eyed Eterijah Kerst. Then he looked at Chief Ariq Haunts. He exhaled, "Your enslaver assists you now, brother, but they will make you tap dance and sing in their court as their little, rodent jester…"

In response, the chief put the point of his blade to Iune's neck. He poked and punctured the flesh, drawing a stream of blood. Chief Ariq Haunts stung Iune with the power of the iniquitous trinity possessing his sword. Iune buckled.

"Suffer the misfortune," hissed Chief Ariq Haunts.

Iune managed a sly grin through the shocks he received. "Savor the moment, chief. You'll never see it again…"

The Ifo chief flinched and froze for a moment. He bared his teeth and gripped the Sword of Union's hilt.

It was then that Kuto-Ithun popped into existence. He grabbed Iune by his rhino-skin vest and scowled up at his childhood friend. It was a brief moment whether calculated in or outside of time. Kuto-Ithun's gaze saw past the trickster's mask and recognized the boy he knew buried on the other side.

Chief Ariq Haunts identified the folk hero. A fleeting transaction between the two of them before Kuto-Ithun blinked away into nothing, taking Iune with him.

Trickster and shadow-jumper reappeared in the middle of another group engaging in combat. Iune leapt to his feet, horn-lances summoned. Kioi, Jai Chilla, and Tyle were among the allies. "Ah! Iune!" Tyle shouted, executing a fanciful twirl of his staff. "Join us three! We are Folly's Army, and we're bringing hell to these liars-in-flesh!" Tyle was in the fight and holding his ground, but Iune still considered the exchange of weapons and curses had to stop.

A roaring bellow of thunder tore through the halls, and Chief Ariq Haunts observed Eterijah Kerst hit by an explosive, cosmic force cast by Ṣẹda. He was lifted off his feet and hurled through a pillar. The column shattered on impact, crumbling into dust over the fraudulent Eterijah as the ceiling came down on top of him

Chief Ariq Haunts turned his attention to Ṣẹda. He readied his sword to cast the triad of shades at the cosmic princess. Eterijah Iyansan blocked his path, and he changed his mark to the star-steward. He lifted his sword and swiped the air in a wide curve. The ominous spirits of the former Ifo chief, Selotes Bilísì, Ratamutum, and Duhu Firistess jumped from the sword and rammed the Eterjiah. They crashed through a wall and into another chamber. Chief Ariq Haunts retracted his phantom menaces, looking around for Ṣẹda, his initial target. He spotted the princess rushing to Eterijah Iyansan's aid. Again, he readied his sword, but other actions stayed his weapon's conjure.

Eterijah Chamti, in the hulking body of Eterijah Dume, plowed through the palace wall on Ṣẹda's right. He charged with his head and shoulders low, adorned with a mighty, horned helmet. He swung his head up and to the left, slamming the side of his massive horn into Ṣẹda's stomach. The princess was taken off her feet, and her body sailed back, colliding into the wall behind her. Breath knocked out of her, and hard enough for her to lose focus. Neither incant nor conjure was at her disposal while the world spun and shook, vision doubling.

Eterijah Chamti turned his charge toward Eterijah Iyansan, who struggled in her attempt to stand, winded after Chief Ariq Haunts' attack on her. He rushed her, horns out, impaling the Eterijah! His lethal strike pinned her to the wall, and her body died immediately. Mouth wide open, Eterijah Iyansan exhaled her spirit. Naked. Black. Beautiful. Her specter seeped from its mortal shell, and she became something new.

Orisha.

She declared, *"I am Oya-Iyansan!"* and she reached for the heavens.

Outside, clouds gathered into a dark storm. A single braid of lightning funneled from the billowy, dark mass, through the castle, and into Oya-Iyansan's hands. It split into nine flails, and she cocked back the heavenly weapon and brought it down on the fraudulent Eterijah. The electric strands tore through his physical frame. The tendrils of lightnings' loud crack snapped the unsteady princess back into focus.

Ṣẹda summoned a vast, cosmic globule around both hands. Her flesh turned midnight blue, and her eyes radiated with the swirl of the cosmos. She aimed her hands at the false Eterijah and burned him to dust with her cosmic powers. The essence of the true Cattleman Eterijah flashed into existence for a moment, free from containment. In the same bright manner his spirit disappeared to the heavens to become one with his star alignment.

Chamti's hexed gold chain remained in the air. It buckled, warped, and reshaped into an hourglass. Sands at the top poured to the bottom. Oya-Iyansan and Ṣẹda paid it no mind. They exited the room and stepped back into the fight. Eterijah Kerst, recovered, and Chief Ariq Haunts were there to greet them. Oya-Iyansan used her flails against the Ifo chief. He let loose the triumvirate of wicked wraiths from his blade, and they shielded him from electric laceration. The trinity either caught the lashes in their grip or took the brunt of a wild whip. Oya-Iyansan pulled back and attempted another lashing with only the same outcome.

Ṣẹda engaged Eterijah Kerst. He grabbed the princess' wrists to keep her cosmic powers at bay, but touching her midnight-blue flesh burned his hands. He screamed, and his legs buckled. He went to his knees, and the princess eviscerated bone from flesh with a searing, pressure wave of cosmic conjure. Eterijah Ganda's spirit blinked into view, and then he was gone to the stars.

Chief Ariq Haunts' lost his grip on the Sword of Union as the weapon was ripped from his hands by an unseen force. The spirits vanished, and Oya-Iyansan had the Ifo chief clear in her sights. Chief Ariq Haunts dived away, and Oya-Iyansan's strikes missed him, barely clipping his heels. He hopped up, ran, and then slid on the floor, slipping into the fray between Ifo warriors and a regiment of the three-hundred and sixty brigade. The mystical sword he'd forged shifted into an hourglass. Its sands poured down.

The Orisha and cosmic princess observed the fight around them. Fires burned the halls. Blood painted the walls and stained the floors. Bodies piled up, and smoke congested the rooms.

"The gravedigger and his consort!" shouted Ṣẹda to Oya-Iyansan.

The Orisha didn't have time to react. Ṣẹda dashed away, reaching out with her instinct to locate Seizan. She was a blur as she glided through the battle, passing Olobiri and Hakim back-to-back as they fended off Ifo warriors.

The princess located the gravedigger and the matron-captain in the midst of battle. She sent a desperate call to him, and her body transmuted into cosmic conjure. Her celestial form possessed the head of his shovel, and Seizan slammed the spade end into the floor.

A wave of conjure passed through the palace and muted sound and slowed time to a halt. The fires cooled and the smoke dissolved. The dead were raised on either side of the fight. Life channeled backwards into them. Wounds mended and fractured bones were made whole. The false Eterijah burned into fiery ashes. Their hexed trinkets hung in the air to transfigure into hourglasses. Sands. Pouring. Down. In reaction, the virtuous Eterijah spirits were freed, swirling into cosmic quintessence that spiraled up to the heavens to reside within their celestial, star alignment.

Time rolled into proper movement, but the wicked didn't have time restored to them. Jailed in their own bodies. Still.

A dark cloud swirling with cosmic visuals appeared next to Iune. It revolved, spinning in place until the billowy mass transfigured into Ṣẹda. The trickster and princess observed the scene. Warriors with movement walked with cautious steps, their eyes fixed on their stationary enemies. A ticking clock was the only sound heard, until Iune asked, "Where is he?"

Ṣẹda had the answer, provided by instinct. "He's in the celestial map room," she informed Iune. She saw a brief image of Chief Ariq Haunts standing near a winding, golden staircase with sets of stairs holding the color pattern of red, black, and green. "He has movement unlike his Ifo people. He stands so still, you wouldn't know he's capable of shifting, as he gazes up at the Winding Staircase."

A small group formed and made their way to the fraudulent trickster.

He grinned when they entered, turning around in a sly manner. "At last," he said to them. "Don't think me defeated. My hourglasses lock everything into place. The Grand Alchemy will be."

Efra shook her head and chided him, "Abim and I saw firsthand how this so-called Grand Alchemy is a sham. You're marching your own people into a brutal system. A terrible network that will oversee the complete breaking of the first people. You have no idea."

Chief Ariq Haunts shook his finger at her. "No!" he riposted. "No, *you* have no idea! Look around you! Look at how alchemy has changed us! This fight! This bitter disagreement." He jabbed his finger toward Seizan. "You were there in that terrible system. You can now raise the dead. I've seen your story. Your consort's tragic end and reemergence into the world, up from the depths to slay the wicked. *That* is what I fight for. The Ifo do not move. Do they? Cocooned in stillness, and when time budges them again, they will be righteous." He put his hands on his hips and stepped close to Ṣẹda. "Oh, and I've seen your story too, princess. Your original, cosmic spirit, born of the First Two. The Immortal Created *and* the sign of All Eternity, And Infinity. Your soul has lived a life, hasn't it? All through alchemy, transformed through tragedy. Blood had to be spilled, and your spirit had to possess a dreadful weapon. It had to feast on conjure folk! It had to assist those unalike in our nature. Your father had to be brought to the brink of death, but in his restoration, you stand here now in the cosmic flesh." Another hard point of his finger, and the chief furthered his argument with Oya-Iyansan as his subject. "You died, Eterijah! And you stand before me now more powerful in spirit. You are an Orisha!"

The powerful woman countered, "My physical form was compromised when I decided to take on the duties of an Orisha fulltime. The council banished me. I was simply waiting for Ṣẹda to come of age and take my place."

Chief Ariq Haunts stepped back, eyes on the floor. He raised his head and said, "Well, my mother changed. She became spirit through terrible circumstances." Those very circumstances resonated as a bright memory the chief projected into the minds of everyone gathered. They watched as *waves of men crawled feverishly over his mother like fire ants from a broken hill.* Orisha to trickster froze with a face expressing horror. "Tragedy actualized her!" the chief continued. "It was the transformative ingredient in her alchemy!"

Ithun had enough. He grabbed Chief Ariq Haunts by his collar and shook him hard. "Your mother was *raped!*" he shouted, breaking the grotesque and miserable memory from being broadcast. His loud, reverberating voice rattled everyone in the room. He shook his broken friend again. "Do you hear me, Been ah? *Do you? I'll kill you if you don't!*" Efra went to calm her son, but Seizan held her back. "That…heinous crime…" he broke into tears before finishing, "…was done by evil, evil, *evil,* terrible men…" He pushed Ariq Haunts away. "You are no chief to me, Been ah! You led their kind here. You poisoned this spiritual abode. You've allowed this realm to be infected with their sands of time."

Ariq Haunts looked at everyone looking at him. "My life was high atop a mountain, my dear, old friends. That mountain shattered! The fall broke every bone in my body, but alchemy renewed me. Let the mountains fall, I say. I'll rise again. You can rise again. We will rise again, and we will be better for it. It's *you* who does not understand."

Iune sighed, "You confuse our disagreement with not understanding you."

Ariq Haunts shook his finger at Iune. He approached the trickster, snarling with his teeth bared like an angry animal. "You! You don't speak to me, foul trickster. I admired you through my youth *and* up to now. I *conversed* with your father! *You! Killed! Mine!*" He threw a hard gaze at Ithun and Seizan. "So much for our childhood hero…"

The memory stung Iune. The hurt of the game gone too far. An apology moistened the tip of his tongue, yet he said something entirely different. "Your father was already dead, Ariq," he told his rival, removing the pellet he took from Ratamutum and dropping it on the floor. "He was betrayed by the very people and nations you assist in enslaving us children of Great Ikzu and Great Gara. I put down a body that had long been extinguished of soul." Chief Ariq Haunts watched the rusted, cylindrical pellet bounce and roll, stopping at his foot.

Iune wasn't the only one with counterpoint. "Betrayal?" Seizan huffed. "You dare speak of all this, Been ah, as if betrayal doesn't start with the actions of your family? Your father killed our father! His best of friend. He allowed our family to be torn apart—*our* families, in the end of it all. We've never been the same."

Iune couldn't help but interject, "I'd like to note, for the record, that it was all a terrible accident—what I did to your father's remains."

Ariq Haunts beamed a sardonic smile. "It's all a joke to you, isn't it, trickster?" He turned and walked away. "I'm an optimist. I see the other side of tragedy. We'll be stronger for it. You're all fighting to protect the mundane. People out there barely know conjure. You talk of me turning *my* back?"

Ithun blinked away. He reformed in front of Ariq Haunts, blocking his path. "You call this mundane? Then why so many needles with wroch blood to neutralize conjure? Skeptic stones and weapons crafted from restrained, cosmic beings to kill conjure folk? Put us against one another, shuffle us through a system of horrific servitude? Why? Because we're so mundane?" He put his face close to Ariq Haunts. "I still see you Been ah Kibir."

Ariq Haunts walked around Ithun and stood in front of the Winding Staircase. He put his hands behind his back, one hand holding the opposite wrist. "For those that want to leave, go now. When the sands deplete, every invisible world—island or realm—will be locked outside of time. Your only access to inside of time will be if called by ritual. The invisible worlds too. Stay here, and that is all you'll be able to traverse." He further warned, "Destroying them will only hasten the outcome, and only the blow from a cosmic horn will allow access to the worlds outside time." He chuckled, "I chose a method to unlock my restraints with something that has only little odds of occurring."

Ṣẹda turned to Oya-Iyansan, concern splashed over her face.

The towering spirit knelt down on one knee and said to her, "I can't stay, cosmic woman. Even inside of time, a ritual must be used to call my spirit to aid, or give strength to the invoker."

Ṣẹda shifted to her cosmic form so that she could hug the ethereal Oya-Iyansan.

"I'll see you off to your mission," the Orisha said to the princess. "You have a spirit to deliver home, correct."

"Yes," responded Ṣẹda, stepping away from her long and tight embrace with the Orisha. She turned and addressed Iune. "Trickster, will you accompany me? I don't know what to expect traveling through time. I could use some good fortune."

"Yes, Ṣẹda. I'll be at your side," he assured.

"I'm sure we'll return, but, speak to your sister first. Let her know."

"Yes, Ṣẹda," repeated the trickster. He walked over to Ariq Haunts and observed the Winding Staircase with him. "Where is my mother's conjure?" he interrogated.

Ariq Haunts didn't answer right away. He presented a question of his own. "How will our games continue, trickster?" he looked at Iune and asked. "Are we at a stalemate?"

Iune turned to Ariq Haunts and stated, "I proposed an idea to your friend Ithun, forming a company called the Clever Folk. I declared an open invitation to you, should you be redeemed. I guess we're not fighting now."

Ariq Haunts smiled at Iune's offer. "I don't believe in your ideals, Iune," he told him. "I bring misfortune. Perhaps that would be the trick, yes. To bring misfortune to our foes." He shook his head. "I'm afraid I must decline. We will always be at odds until Pambunjila is restored."

Iune nodded, accepting the rejection.

Ariq Haunts revealed, "I've hidden your mother's conjure where the golden glow of the world's three moons reside. Restore them. Restore the world. Restore your mother's conjure."

"Iune!" someone called before the trickster could react to Ariq Haunt's disclosure. He turned. It was Prince Raji. "Your sister has journeyed from Nanni Mayya Storii's homestead. Your friend Olobiri and the warrior Hakim went to inform her that we've won the day."

Iune raced from the room and followed his instincts through the palace corridors until he found his sister. Zoya and Iune hugged tight. "We won…?" she questioned.

"It's not that easy…" he responded to her.

"It never is…"

They stood apart. Iune notified his sister, "I've been requested by the princess to follow her on an errand. We're stepping through time to deliver a lost spirit to her rightful era—a time long past what's happening here. She seems to be attached to those old legends of cosmic spirits, lilac and cobalt-blue. When I return, we'll celebrate from here to Del-Yswil island. It might be the only places we can travel to."

"What?"

Iune explained Ariq Haunts' hourglass trick. "We'll return. It will be bittersweet, but we'll raise glasses and—" he beamed a teasing smile at Zoya, "—wrap ourselves around multiple lovers."

Zoya chuckled. She noted, "Ma-ma and Pa-pa follow the path of balance. A coupling of two, restrictive. Perhaps I can be like the midnight sky, and have many stars gleam against my black body. I'll at least have two husbands to help me rule." She grinned, thinking of Olobiri and Hakim. "They'll learn to get along, behave at my order and command."

"I don't think we'll ever stop whoring, sister, and settle down," said Iune. It was then that Ṣẹda walked up behind him.

"Iune, we should go in haste," said the princess. "Not even I can hold this spirit for too long."

Iune spied his sister, one eyebrow raised on her visage and a knowing grin beaming. He lifted a finger and protested, "Shut up!" Then he said through a smirk, "…and I hope you're right, sister. I could follow our mother and father's marriage path."

Zoya returned to the map room with her brother and the princess.

Ṣẹda subdued Ariq Haunts, lassoing bands of conjure around him. Her father hauled him from the room and to the jail cells.

Everyone watched as Ṣẹda and Iune stood before the Winding Staircase hand-in-hand. The princess felt the stir of power inside her that could wind the staircase into motion.

"Wait!" Efra shouted. Ṣẹda turned and Efra ran up to her holding out The Lover's card. "Tell Gordon I said 'hello'. Take this to him. Perhaps they can use some love in their time."

Iune looked at the card. "Yes! The woman said this item was called for."

Ṣẹda accepted the card. "Thank you," she said. Her eyes looked over to Seizan. Vae joined his side. "We will reform the Eterijah council when I return. The fight in you will surrender to wisdom; and you will in time revive those dead in the mind." They nodded, accepting their new positions.

Ṣẹda and Iune faced the Winding Staircase again. The princess used her power with a single thought, and light flooded the room. The spectators turned away, but Iune and Ṣẹda saw the Winding Staircase begin to turn. It spun and spun and spun, until it formed into an ovate portal, floating against the bright light that filled the room.

The princess and the trickster walked forward, into the portal, and through time.

There was no fancy pattern of intersecting lines that veiled the scene. An immediate splotch of webbing overlay the brightness, until the two images became one and were siphoned into blackness.

45

Lady Arachne sat up. The dream was gone, but she anticipated its story continuing into her time. She stood, tossing Spook to the soft recliner as she got to her feet. "Gordon!" she called. "We're having—" Then she noticed Gordon was on his knees with his hands wrapped around himself. He rocked back and forth as if nervous or cold. She noticed his eyes growing many times their normal measurement, to the size of eggs. It was an uncanny and disturbing sight, as he shivered and stuttered through a guttural groan that sent a chill through the Fable Avenue matriarch. "…guests…" she finished.

Gordon couldn't hear her, too involved with his condition as his eyes burst with a bright, lilac illumination. Pale-violet strands snaked from his eyes, corkscrewing around one another and colliding against the wall. The energy gathered, stretching out to create an oval, lilac gateway against the cement panel. The pain wrenched Gordon's mouth wide open, and his gravely groans escalated into a fright-inducing shriek.

The lilac radiance, and the magnitude of his eyes, diminished. All returned to normal. A light, euphoric feeling swept through Gordon, and though he was sweating and feeling nauseous, a comfort blanketed him. He fell forward, supporting himself on one hand. He caught his breath, calming his gasps as he and Lady Arachne witnessed two figures step from the portal.

They were in shadow first, and then light revealed them.

Ṣẹda. Iune. Princess and trickster. A journey through time.

In the royal and cosmic woman's hand was Lady Arachne's desired article. The Lovers card. Her tarot deck would be complete.

Gordon got to his feet after shedding his cold sweat and nausea. "Ṣẹda," he greeted. "Iune." He walked over to them, and though he'd just stood, he bent a knee in their presence. "Princess. Trickster," he uttered in their language.

"Gordon…?" spoke Ṣẹda. "Good. Speed."

He looked up at her and nodded his head rapidly. "Yes," he responded. "I am Gordon Goodspeed."

"The Lilac Flame?" Ṣẹda questioned for assurance.

On bended knee, Gordon conjured the full facets of his cosmic suit, and then he surged with the luminosity of his lilac spirit. He returned to his partially suited phase. "Yes," he answered the princess.

"Rise, Gordon." He obeyed the cosmic princess. "I know Fey Forrester," she told him. "I'm here to bring her spirit to her rightful time. Beneath my somatic frame is a cosmic form. She is there."

Lady Arachne watched. Her body trembled as she used instinct to decipher as best she could the foreign and ancient words exchanged by Gordon and the princess. Her heart raced as the princess extended The Lovers card to him.

"Do you need this?" asked Ṣẹda. "Lady Efra al-Kaadi sends her regards."

Gordon aimed a hand at Lady Arachne and said, "This woman here has waited long for this item. Her name is Lady Arachne. She's one of the Elders in our conjure community. I've been searching history to locate the card. Now I understand. It was traveling to this moment in time. An instant to you; centuries to us."

"The Terrible Occurrence does not happen anymore?" the princess inquired.

"No," Gordon answered. "Slavery—black servitude—was abolished one hundred and fifty-five years ago now."

"That's not a long time…" remarked Ṣẹda.

"No. It's not, but you couldn't convince a lot of misguided people of that. Especially since its effect resonates deep. Things remained bad, even with the good we've fought hard to bring into existence. We've managed to create enough breathing room for us to function—change the laws that govern lands, and all. But there's so many problems—" Gordon stopped. "I don't want to depress you. This is such an uncanny and beautiful moment. …But we can be against one another. We kill each other. We're killed unjustly by people who police us. We can be very vicious toward one another." Iune's face twisted into a frustrated expression, tears welling in his eyes. "Not too many of us know our conjure, our magic. We run from our blackness, our history. There's a lot of self-hate and confusion. Some aid those who continue to oppress us." He accepted The Lovers card and told the princess, "We could use some love in our time. Tell Efra al-Kaadi I said, 'thank you'."

Gordon handed the card to Lady Arachne, and joy burst from her in streams of tears. She pressed the card to her chest and said to the princess and the trickster, "Thank…you…so much… Thank you!"

Ṣẹda and Iune presented a respectful bow of their heads to the matriarch, understanding her sentiment.

"This is the 'end time', yes?" asked Ṣẹda to Gordon. "When all will be corrected."

Gordon replied with a heavy determination in his voice, "Yes. We're close to bringing about the Grand Wish, conducting the Grand Ritual. The Lovers card will help."

"Ah!" Ṣẹda said through a smile. "And you'll also need your sweetheart, your Fey Forrester. The Cobalt-blue Flame."

Gordon's eyes welled with tears. "Yes," he responded. "I sure do need her."

Ṣẹda looked up, and she walked toward the stairs. "I feel a tug of power…" she expressed. "It comes from up these stairs…" She journeyed up. Gordon, Iune, and Lady Arachne trailed behind her.

Through the front room on the garden floor. The princess continued walking. Into the dining area. Out the door. She looked to her left, and her eyes turned black, swirling with the backdrop of the heavens. Her skin's color altered to midnight blue, and then she blinked away in a bright flash.

"She's been doing that more often since discovering she's the Immortal Created," quipped Iune. "I'm starting to get worried."

The humor of Iune's comment swerved past Gordon. He blinked in reaction to the remark, catching the fact the trickster revealed. "*She's* the Immortal Created?"

"Oh, yes. I guessed it. Despite what people want to believe, her name translates directly to it. Don't know how it was missed."

Gordon pondered the point. Then he grabbed Lady Arachne and Iune by the wrist and told them, "I know where she's going. Hold on." He popped from existence, emerging in the rear yard of Fey Forrester's family brownstone.

Ṣẹda stood at the base of Fey's silver effigy. She removed her clothes, and both Iune and Gordon stared. The trickster looked at Gordon and remarked, "They do tend to only come in one flavor, don't they? The original woman?"

Gordon answered, "Yeah… Beautiful…"

Iune grinned. He said to Gordon, "You're a trickster, aren't you?"

"Who with conjure isn't? You should meet my brother and his crew. We're also fierce warriors."

Iune retorted, "Who with conjure isn't?"

They fell silent, observing Ṣẹda as she touched her chest, just above her bosom, with the tips of her fingers from both hands. She reached into her skin. No blood was drawn. Nothing gruesome spilled. She peeled back her midnight-blue flesh and exposed the cosmic arena whirling behind her cosmic epidermis, opened wide as if separating the sides of a shirt unbuttoned at the middle. A broad and glimmering, cobalt-blue stream issued from the opened flesh and rained onto Fey's silver monument. Ṣẹda's body jerked with the kickback, as Fey's spirit gushed from the princess' cosmic interior. Ṣẹda stabled herself while floating off the ground, holding open her flesh as she expelled the cobalt-blue essence. The reverberation made Gordon, Iune, and Lady Arachne brace themselves. Iune and the matriarch shielded their eyes, but Gordon looked on, eyes unaffected by the intense blaze. This was Fey's spirit, and he'd so much longed for her presence here in their time.

The silver-sculpted shrine melted from top to bottom. Behind the silver coating was the luminous, cobalt-blue spirit. Fey Forrester had returned, but a determined instinct guided her. Rebirthed from the Immortal Created, the daughter of the First Two, she had purpose, and she took to the sky. She sounded a telepathic cry intercepted and translated by Gordon's mind. His mouth hung low, and he gasped with the knowledge of his duty.

He walked up beside Ṣẹda who mended her midnight-blue flesh back together, hiding the internal cosmos. Masked as Dooley, he turned and looked at the princess and Iune. "A change gon' come," he told them in English. They understood. "You might want to stick around for this."

"We'll stay as long as we can, Gordon," said Ṣẹda. "A disagreeable trickster named Ariq Haunts has played foul schemes. He's the patron saint of sabotage and misfortune. Don't worry of our stay. Go to your Fey Forrester. A god's speed," she blessed him.

Dooley winked behind his mask. "Actually, Miss Ṣẹda, it's pronounced: *Goodspeed!*"

"Oh!" expressed the princess.

Another wink from Dooley and he requested, "And tell Miss Efra that Tsoro is doing well!"

"Tsoro…?" the princess questioned.

Dooley didn't clarify. He launched into the air with those parting words, bursting into his cosmic, lilac design, and leaving a pale-purple streak behind him.

South. They traveled. Clarksdale, Mississippi. The crossroads. They were there in minutes.

Down from the sky, Fey dived as a blazing, cobalt-blue streak.

Up from the horizon came Dooley to meet her, a flaming lilac stripe.

They convened at the center of the crossroads, coming together at full speed. A wave of conjure echoed from their bodies as they wrapped their arms around one another and engaged in a deep, long-awaited kiss. They twirled around. Their streaks intertwining at the tip end, and up they flew to the heavens in a tight embrace.

Past the atmosphere. Into space.

Their entwined bodies became one. Lilac-cobalt-blue.

Up and up.

They penetrated the moon and exploded into a cosmic conjure that shook the solar system on code and on balance.

The pale moon ruptured, splitting with the impact.

A temporal distortion turned into a vacuum, and the shattered, pale moon collapsed inward. A white-hot cross burst from the center of the crumbling lunar mass, and out of the celestial chaos came the world's original three moons shimmering into existence.

Red. Black. Green.

A bright, bright, bright return. Even if naked of their golden halos, their presence was still magnificent to behold. Conjure kept nature in order. There was no sudden, heavy gust of wind because of a new gravitational paradigm. No plate in the Earth's crust shifted, and the seas waved only a gentle 'hello' at the return of the three moons in the sky. Their presence was not disturbing to the natural order of nature and Her atmosphere.

The only happening was all eyes to the sky. Wide and in awe. Everyone saw something. With their faces lifted to the heavens, everyone saw everything. The world had its three moons again.

Ṣẹda, Iune, and Lady Arachne were such people fixed in their reverence.

Moments before. A phone call was made.

California to Mount Vernon, New York.

Keiiah Gideon lunged into her anger as her mother, Savannah Forrester, answered her call. "What have you gotten my son into?" she demanded. "I saw the news! *National news!* His damn speech at that juke joint! You got him in that damn world of yours, don't you, Mamma? Don't you!"

Savannah exhaled. She believed herself ready for this moment. She closed her eyes to call the words to her tongue, and in the moment of shutting out the world, a bright flash penetrated the darkness behind her fastened eyelids. Savannah felt a strong tremor tunnel through her. She opened her eyes and peered out of her window. Her hand trembled, and she almost lost her grip on the phone. Her face was wide with shock and awe.

"Mamma!" Keiiah hollered.

Her breath raced alongside her heartbeats. She heard her daughter yell at her again through the phone, and while staring at the phenomenon in the sky, the words she searched for came to her.

"I didn't involve your son in my world, little woman," she told her daughter with the sweetest sincerity. "I… I made it easier to explain the world outside as it is now. I prepared him for what the world has just become."

"What?" Keiiah hissed.

"Look, my daughter. Look out your window at your culture in the sky…"

"Mama, what in the world are you—"

A sudden pause. Savannah heard a clunking sound over the receiver. She set her cellphone down and placed it on speaker, allowing her daughter time to recover from shock. Savannah stared outside until that time came, fixated on the three moons in the sky. Her phone buzzed a new call, and her son's name and picture flashed as his call came through. She didn't answer. She just kept gazing at the celestial miracle. Tears streamed down her face. Savannah perceived her granddaughter's rebirth too. Fey's yumboes flew into the room, led by Silver. Their faces were as bright with joy as their vibrant flesh. The moons had returned, and they could sense Fey's living presence in the heavens.

Savannah covered her mouth as her words trembled free. "Th-th-thank you…f-f-f-for talking to me…Africa…"

The yumboes nodded in agreement.

46

oments before. New events hadn't happened yet, and so the single, pale moon remained half seen in the afternoon sky. Martin Campbell stood at the front entrance of the Fable Avenue side of the crossroads house. He was flanked by his niece Neyeli. Her color-changing hair was jet-black in shade. On the other side of Martin was Neyeli's sweetheart, Benny Jah who was equipped with his medieval, metal gauntlet. The private detective rang the doorbell, and Crossroads Queen Voodoo Lily, answered the door. Her face was alight with an illuminated smile. She opened the door and invited her fellow conjure folk inside.

"I am so glad you've arrived!" she stated in a merry manner. "I bear fruit!" They walked in. Voodoo Lily shut the door using incant, and she locked it just the same. She led her guests to the front room and then spun around to face them. She opened one hand and put on display a newfound conjure ability. A black, gelatinous mass bubbled above her hand, warping and stretching until it came together, forming solid into a shiny, black apple with a black stem and gold leaf. Voodoo Lily put a hand against her chest as she stared wide-eyed and open-mouthed at the uncanny fruit. "Dark matter apples!" she exclaimed. "Oh! This makes me *otito Aje!* I am a Voodoo Lily tree, not a simple flower. I too come bearing fruit." She bit into the materialized, black apple. "And the juice! My goodness! This is delicious. Move over Reverend Pouvwa and eat your heart out!" she joked. Then in a sultry voice she proclaimed, "Oh, how Armand just loves to eat my delicious, tart fruit."

The display was a marvel. Benny Jah and Neyeli wanted to taste while showering the Crossroads Queen with flattering remarks of skill and conjure, but they remained unsmiling. Voodoo Lily then realized her guests' stony-faced expressions. Her instinct buzzed with a warning to the 'why' of their presence.

"So…what may I do for you three?" she asked. Her tone matched the severe expressions on their faces. "What brings you to my crossroads?"

Martin spoke, "Stephanie Dumas came to see you."

"Yes…" Voodoo Lily acknowledged.

"She played a game for her burden, correct?" he further interrogated.

Voodoo Lily felt boxed in. The detective's imposing and authoritative aura surrounded her. Voodoo Lily repeated her answer, "Yes…"

"Things have gone terribly wrong," he informed her. "She's been unconscious since that night. She's intertwined with the haunt. The game wasn't a proper exorcise. Is Armand around? We need to reclaim Sean Commons from the dance."

Voodoo Lily was still for a moment. "I am truly sorry to hear about Miss Dumas," she expressed her regret after a time. "I've made my efforts to speak with Maman Anansi, give her my sympathies. Offer anything I can. Those efforts have been ignored."

"We're here on Maman Anansi's behalf," said Martin. "Your assistance will be to offer up Sean Commons from the dance."

Voodoo Lily thought about Martin's request and replied to his demand, "I'm not sure what you want is entirely possible."

"It's gonna have to be," the detective pushed back.

Voodoo Lily fell silent again. She looked at Benny Jah and Neyeli sided up to the detective. She sighed, "We didn't know the consequences. We were under the impression it was fair."

Martin responded, "Well, I'm a cop at heart, Miss Voodoo Lily, and you know what we say about the law and ignorance. Conjure law's the same."

Voodoo Lily cocked her head. "Are you here to arrest us, officer?" Her voice was defiant.

"No," he told her. "My statement was made to show that I *will*, by any means, take back the haunt and have it reworked through the proper ritual. We are here on the authority of Maman Anansi."

Voodoo Lily turned and walked toward the opposite exit. Her guests followed. "I've made it clear that I'm not so sure what you want can happen, Mister Copper, but I'm sure you'll be willing to try." She stopped at the door and turned around. "I warn you, there are laws and rules for these games as well." The door unlocked and opened by way of her incant. "Please, speak with Armand."

"Do *not* give him a heads up, Miss Ghedemere," Martin warned.

She was honest in her response to the detective. "I can't promise you that, detective," she revealed. "Walk with haste is all I can advise." She moved aside and said, "I'll unlock the house on the other side of the street. You have my permission to pass through."

Benny Jah and Neyeli followed Martin outside to the fabled, Mississippi intersection. They crossed the street to the twin house. Up the porch stairs. They heard a click of the lock coming undone. The door opened, and they walked inside and through the residence to the other door leading to Water Bug Hollow, Louisiana.

They marched to Eve's Hallow, and as they stepped on the consecrated ground, everything around them dropped away to darkness. Outside of time.

The trio was still, braced for action. Out of the shade bubbled a chorus of eerie laughter. It echoed and surrounded them. Spherical lights attached to the end of canes lit up in rhythm as the laughter continued. Holding onto the lighted walking sticks were men and women dancing with their burdens. They spun, flipped, and twirled around the threesome in a stylized, well-choreographed dance.

The laughter ceased, and soft music played as the spirits and people waltzed on.

Armand Gideon walked out of the restored barrelhouse. He held out his arms wide and announced, "The dance is electric, is it not?"

Martin, Neyeli, and Benny Jah moved carefully around the pirouetting players and made their way to the entrance, confronting Armand.

The gaming house manager continued, announcing, "I know why you're here. I'm afraid results for all games are final. I can't let you interrupt the dance, take away from its flow. That would be dangerous."

Benny Jah spotted the members of the Biloko Bunch crawling alongside the building's façade. His gauntlet glowed with a white-hot glimmer. Neyeli took notice, and her hair shifted grey. The Biloko named Gizo asked, "Is everything alright, Mister Gideon?"

"We're fine here, Gizo," Armand responded with a sly grin, eyes locked on the three in front of him. Nicky-El stepped out and took his side.

"No need for a fight, kid," Martin stated as a warning. "We just need a soul that has no business being among that choreography."

Neyeli added, "I can sense where Mister Commons is among the dancers. We can make this quick."

Benny Jah clenched his fist. He said to Neyeli and Martin, "How 'bout you two go make that arrest. I'll handle the rookies." Armand's face couldn't contain his surprise from Benny Jah's comment. Benny grinned up at him as Martin and Neyeli filed back among the dancers to find Sean Commons' spirit. "Got ourselves a good, ol' fashion crossover, huh? A bit of a Civil War of sorts." He spotted Nicky-El conjure a glowing hatchet to his hand. "You read K-Fos?" Benny-Jah asked, eyes locked onto Nicky-El's hatchet.

Armand spotted Nicky-El's movements and shouted, "No!"

It was too late. It happened. The former gang leader raised and tossed his conjure at Benny. The young conjure man lightened his weight. He moved just in time, turning around as the hatchet neared him. He reached out with his gauntleted hand and snatched the mystical blade from the air. "You know y' mans Boom Star? Remember that alternate-future-timeline arc when he was repowered as Rebound?" He made a full turn and hurled the hatchet back at Nicky-El. The otherworldly weapon slammed into his chest. Nicky-El shuddered with the impact. His body went limp, and he crumpled to the ground useless. "He'll be fine. Just a mild case of the temporary paralysis."

The Biloko Bunch lunged at Benny. He became light as air and spirited away, leading them into open ground. Sandife attacked first, spewing a wide stream of psychic fire at Benny Jah. He rolled away before the mental heat left him in the same state as Nicky-El. Light and airy, Benny Jah floated with ease. He aimed his gauntlet to Sandife and increased the weight on her upper lip and jaw, shutting her mouth tight and putting an end to her fight.

Gizo and Myèl tossed their spheres of influence at the young, gauntlet-clad conjure man. Great swarms of bees and webs chased him down. Black Arum called his dark matter vines from the ground, and the cosmic tendrils reached out to grapple and restrain Benny Jah.

Benny dodged and kept ahead of Myèl's bees. He swerved and allowed the webbing conjured by Gizo to wrap and entangle a few of Black Arum's vines. He slowed and let the remaining vines draw closer. He turned and grabbed one, struggling with it. He lightened his body until he was air, and the other vines passed through him while his hands remained solid. He lowered the density of the vine in his hand, making it easy to manipulate. He grabbed another and did the same. He darted to Gizo and Myèl, wrapping them up in the vines. He increased their weight and density to bring them down. The vines were so heavy, not even Black Arum could manipulate them. He'd lost his control. He fired his needles, but Benny had a plan for them too. He became a ghost, and the projectiles passed through him.

But the bees still swarmed, and Benny Jah led them away. Around and around until he was able to guide them straight into Black Arum. Their psychic stings immobilized him, and Benny Jah was finished with the rookies.

Armand gave a sardonic clap as he stepped forward.

His movement was quick, and took Benny Jah by surprise when it occurred. Three skulls tossed, exploding in Benny's face. Blinded. Benny Jah used an incant to regain sight, but it was too late. Armand was there, fists aglow with the power of his three-skulled necklace. His punches were pulled, but not without their wallop. Benny Jah was dealt fist to face and fist to midsection. He buckled, stepped back, and swung with the might of his gauntlet.

Armand caught the fist. Benny's face burst with surprise.

"It's something, isn't it?" Armand noted. "Willpower," he expounded. "Have enough, and you can hold back the heavens and rearrange its chosen stars."

The darkness split. The conjure holding the area outside of time dissipated, and the day returned. There came a flash, and Benny Jah and Armand looked up and witnessed the moon disappear in a blinding flicker. Out of the sudden display of cosmic power came the emergence of three moons in the sky. Red. Black. Green. Their golden halos didn't shimmer, but that didn't stop the sight from being any less magnificent.

"Holy. Shit…" Benny Jah remarked.

The fighting friends stood still, bodies locked in the last moments of their struggle, eyes to the sky. A long time passed before Armand suggested, "How 'bout a truce, homie?"

"Yeah…how 'bout it, kid…?"

The rookie and the journeyman stared at the celestial phenomenon above them, faces wide with awe. Their grips on one another loosened. They stood side-by-side just looking up.

Benny Jah asked Armand, "So…what's your favorite story arc in *The Lwaverse* comics?"

It took a while, but Armand answered, "Curio Plim's descendants."

"The two brothers that carry his name, Curio and Plim? Or his great-great-great-great grandson Curio and his wife *Plima?*" Benny Jah asked for clarification.

"The ones who met the Barefoot Barons," Armand replied.

Benny Jah agreed. "Oh, yeah… That shit was fire, sun…"

East coast and west coast bumped fists and just kept looking up at the three moons in the sky that bound them by conjure and heritage.

47

Rewind. Time. Before the moons' rise. Harlem.

Chilton Brickhouse sat in the family room of the Clarke's brownstone. He nursed a glass of Uncle Nearest whiskey while seated across from Melinda Clarke's father, Berklee.

"My apologies," he told Mister Clarke. "It's really no alarm. I just want you to be aware of what's happening between my son, Dajon, and your daughter, Melinda."

Berklee responded after sipping a swig of his drink, "I know. I see them getting closer. They're that age. Melinda's mother was wary, especially after what happened last February. I had another opinion. I stated it. She and I talked it out. We're fine. I like Dajon."

Chilton was curious, so he asked, "How'd you come about that opinion?"

"Came at the hospital," Berklee answered. "Dajon's a good kid. He treats Melinda well. She likes him, as friends or otherwise. But, I saw so many people rallied around this boy for him to pull through. I saw you, your wife. That's family. Dajon seems to know that. A lot of family there. You all were praying too. That's important to me."

Chilton took a swallow. He hummed in contemplation, pensive on his next inquiry. "What about culture? Is that important to you as well?" Berklee went to answer, opening his mouth to speak. Chilton interposed, "…I ask because what you saw at the hospital was more than family. There were families bound by a culture."

"I've heard, to some degree," Berklee spoke. "Melinda talks a little on how you all convene over in Brooklyn. She says it feels like you people own all the blocks on Fable Avenue."

Chilton made a face. "We do," he expressed, glass close to his lip to take a drop.

Berklee nodded his head. "I like that. Black folks owning things, holding onto things, especially with all the gentrification that happens down in Brooklyn."

Chilton agreed with the sentiment. He thought of Berklee's words, and his eyes lifted and landed on a photo of he and his wife. He looked away, but Berklee saw the motion.

Mister Clarke cleared his throat and asked, "Is there a problem with Melinda being biracial?"

Quick to answer. "No. No. No. Not at all. I mean, somebody mad. Somebody always mad, right?"

"Right…"

Chilton leaned forward, arms on his thighs. "We live in Harlem. There's a lot of us kind of folk that live in Queens—all the boroughs, really. Upstate too. Whole state, to be honest. National." Chilton was rambling.

"I'm from the Bronx originally," Berklee noted. "That cool with you?"

"Yeah. I guess. I mostly grew up in Jamaica. Maybe you got a problem with me not bein' Foundational Black in America—as some folk call it."

"You good. I'm good."

The banter was nice, but Chilton didn't need any heightened instinct to tell Berklee needed a point to the talk. "Despite having folk scattered about New York, we call ourselves the Fable Avenue community."

Berklee narrowed his eyes, searching for a meaning. "Okay…"

"The Fable Avenue…*Conjure* community," Chilton amended.

"Oh… Okay."

Chilton sat up straight. "I know. You hear the word 'conjure' it…brings up notions of Satanism or misunderstood, New World Voodoo, or something. There's nothing Satanic about *Vodou* or what we practice. I can assure you."

"I'm open. You ain't making a human sacrifice or no shit like that?"

They both laughed.

"No. No. No," Chilton repeated through his chuckle. He simmered and explained, "We practice an eclectic system with roots in African spirituality."

Berklee joked, "My girl and your boy get married, she got to convert?"

Chilton's mantra resurfaced. "No. No. No." He bobbed his head from side-to-side before stating, "But…your daughter's been asking questions. Curious. My son—Dajon—he's been giving her answers. What it's all about, what we practice and do. I just thought you should be aware, and understand there's no offense—or if you believe Dajon is overstepping any bounds you have, religious or otherwise. I'll make him stop."

Berklee shook his head and adopted Chilton's catchphrase. "No. No. No. I'd rather these two kids be exploring that than bein' curious about…what their hormones are tellin' them at this age."

Chilton lifted his drink as a salute. "Hey!"

"Hey!" Berklee echoed, mirroring the lift of spirits.

Chilton relaxed and exhaled. It wasn't the whole story, but that would do for now. "I just didn't want you to be taken by surprise or upset."

Berklee chuckled and replied, "I'm a Christian, as best I can be. Different, but all the same, right?"

"Right… But…"

"Look, if myself and my wife allowed Melinda to keep hanging out with Dajon after he was shot, a set of little fairytales won't be a bother."

Chilton held his gaze a little longer on Berklee. Paused. His eyes lingered, bent on Melinda's father. Berklee finished his drink and didn't notice. Chilton decided to do the same. He knocked back his drink, but his eyes were fixed to Berklee Clarke. A hard swallow. He cleared his throat and rested his empty glass on the coffee table. "Good drink. Good talk. Thank you. Glad everything's been squared out." He stood and said, "Let me get going."

Berklee set his glass down too. He rose and shook Chilton's hand, who put a little more strength into his grip. "Fine grip, Jamaica." He patted his shoulder and walked Chilton to the door resisting the urge to rub his sore hand from the shake.

Door opened. Out onto the steps. A bright flash in the sky made both men flinch.

"That a plane crash? An explosion?" asked Berklee as he blinked the quick burst of light from his eyes. "Oh, shit! Not another nine-eleven!"

A heavy resonance rolled through the air. People ran from their houses and looked up while people already on the street halted their walk and angled their heads to the sky. Chilton and Berklee heard a collective gasp and rushed down the stairs, turned around and looked overhead.

Red. Black. Green.

Three. Massive. Moons.

Berklee's eyes were as large as the moons in the sky. He had no words. Chilton glanced over at him and offered, "You smoke?"

Berklee stammered, "If I didn't…I'd start. I can't believe what I'm seein'…"

Chilton pulled the open pack he had on him. "You got a light?" he asked.

Berklee finally took his eyes off the celestial occurrence in the afternoon sky. Chilton's voice was so calm despite the happening above, and the relaxed tone was just as curious to Mister Clarke. "No…" Berklee answered, eyes bent in perplexity.

But, Chilton already had an instinct for the answer. The inquiry was strategic. With Berklee's eyes on him, Chilton held the cigarette's front end to his lips and blew an incant across the top. A flame sparked and lit the tip. Berklee flinched. Chilton handed the cigarette to him. "It's not that impressive," he told Melinda's father. "It's a simple incant. It's not a personal conjure."

"A…personal…what now?" His hands and lips shook as he took a drag.

Chilton cocked his head back and basked in the glory of the three moons. "Your daughter? Melinda? What she can do is impressive. Dajon tells me she can manipulate darkness. She can configure the absence of light into cosmic globes that create light and vice versa. Dajon's been teaching her how to control her conjure. Her spiritual power."

"My daughter can what…?"

The cigarette fell from Berklee's lips and slipped through his fingers. Chilton used another incant to stop the cigarette from hitting the ground. An additional incant levitated it up to him. He clipped it between two fingers and politely asked Berklee, "Mind if I take a puff?" Berklee shook his head and Chilton took a smoke. He chuckled to himself as he exhaled, looking back up at the sky. "I don't know what they did, but they did it. I sure as hell never thought I'd ever see the three moons back in the sky. Legends crystalized into reality, my man."

"You never what…?" Berklee questioned.

Chilton waved his hand, brushing Berklee off. "Nothing," he told Melinda's father, passing the cigarette back to him. "Just fairytales."

They looked up together, staring at the wondrous miracle with two, very different manners of expression on their faces.

There hung the three moons as they looked down at the whole world. There was so much to observe from their vantage. One such happening was in a quaint, Long Island neighborhood called Baiting Hollow. The transpiring matters played out on both sides of the spectrum. Inside of time. Outside of time.

On one side of the coin was the visible world. There, a lone van pulled up to a circular driveway that connected to an empty lot where once stood a stately, Spanish-style house. The van's engines cut and out stepped its occupants.

Cedron Goodspeed. Edmundo and Raymond Shaw. Jamie Ryan, called Tap. A feminine shadow figure at his side. Leah Peters exited the van too. Her father as well. Vencil Peters, called Papa Solomon. He had on a black fedora, a leather jacket, jeans, workman boots, and a trumpet in his hand. Following behind Leah Peters was the large and ghostly glowing beast conjured by her mother. A lion named Mister Magistrate.

Papa Solomon stood at the forefront, and Cedron's crew, the Gypsy Moon Misfits, formed up around him. They stared at the empty lot because they knew the lot wasn't truly vacant.

The other side of the coin. An invisible world. It wasn't outside of time, as conjure folk knew. It was a hazy place forged by foul magic's hexed residue. The Anathematic World. Gaseous and poisonous. Only the hateful could remain in such a setting for long. And they were gathered there as a heinous horde of needle wielders and hexers to hear their master speak on the triple and multicolored, cosmic sign orbiting above.

He spoke to them. His Family Fallows.

Stanley appeared healthy. Color was restored to him. Muscle and definition to his physique too. His shoulder-length, strawberry-blonde hair didn't appear oily or stringy. It bounced with life, groomed by his beautiful wife Lucretia, shaped like a pharaoh's nemes. Cleanshaven, though he planned on regaining his thick go-t. He'd grown accustomed to the facial hair.

His wife placed around him a multi-colored robe that was dyed with the essence of conjure children. He walked out onto the raised deck overlooking the backyard, the beach, and a herd of needlemen and hexers. He wore no shirt. No shoes. Navy-blue pants covered his legs. The robe, through a sanguinary, binding ritual, provided him with the faculty to absorb the essences pigmenting the cloak. An intravenous form for supplying his body with pure conjure quintessence. Symbiotic with all of the conjure elements he'd stolen. Though, he still lusted and required a remaining, alchemical component to render him whole for his intended ritual. The consecrated fabric was missing a lilac colorant.

Stanley Fallows' wife stood behind him, at his left. Brooding and beautiful. The clock-faced monster, Lazy Crow, was directly next to him on his right, standing some feet away. His face tick, tick, ticking away. Lazy Crow's affiliated cabal, the Blood Cursers, were among the crowd below. Willie the Lich, too.

There was a sea of needle holders who were anxious to listen and take command.

Stanley looked down at the eyes looking up at him. They were wide with wonder. Unblinking. Fixed. Broadcasting loud the question: *What happens now?*

He looked up at the three moons in the sky and smiled. He didn't feel defeat. The army assembled before him was a fraction of what existed. They had numbers. They had control. From law to commerce to media. Final authority. Command. Dominance. All these secular ideals granted them jurisdiction over the physical world.

"This is right on time, my family," he addressed the people. His voice was thunder to them, a blanket of comfort in a changed world. "I might not have every color needed to dye my robe, but I command a lot of power in me now. Wonderland is here; and Wonderland is gone. There are fools around us. There are gods in the sky. But there is only us right here to set things straight. The world has been led out of darkness, and we see the demons and the devils let loose." He stood straight, knocking his fist against the railing. "My mother gave me an age and a time," he continued. "I have finally fulfilled both." He aimed a finger up. "Look at the reddest moon that infects the sky now. Know that it holds its color so that you may know the blood spilled in this next age. That time and age my mother gave me? It's here. We're here. Yesterday is over."

The Family Fallows gazed up. Papa Solomon and Cedron Goodspeed's crew kept their eye on them, though sight unseen. The celestial bodies peered on. The story they had been paying close attention to just walked into its final chapters. A miracle occurred among the stars, but wickedness had gathered like storm clouds and made its peace with war, and so came the story's uncertainty. The heavenly bodies couldn't help but beam bright, as scintillating as the reunited lovers glowing misty, cobalt-blue and lilac too. The lovers that held one another tight out in the endless planes of space, above a world with three moons.

End Act III

To all the pop culture referenced, tonally or directly, thank you. From Clue to the Breakfast Club, and everything in between.

Historical chapter titles inspired by the song "7" by Prince, from the album "☥" (1992).

MORE TITLES @

www.TwinGriffinBooks.com

www.ingramcontent.com/pod-product-compliance
Lightning Source LLC
Chambersburg PA
CBHW011934130726
47904CB00014B/2364